Doris Davidson is a retired primary school teacher who still lives in her native city of Aberdeen. She has been writing novels since 1984 and the first to be published was *The Brow of the Gallowgate* in 1990. Her married daughter now lives only twenty-five miles away but her son, an art teacher, also lives in Aberdeen, and he presented her with a grandson in 1987.

H. H. Lumsden.

D1146730

DORIS DAVIDSON

The Back of Beyond

The House of Lyall

Grafton

HarperCollins*Publishers*
77-85 Fulham Palace Road
Hammersmith, London w6 8jb

The HarperCollins website address is:
www.harpercollins.co.uk

This omnibus edition published in 2004
by HarperCollins*Publishers*

ISBN 0 007 71205 7

Typeset in Postscript Linotype Minion with
Bauer Bodoni display by
Palimpsest Book Production Limited,
Polmont, Stirlingshire

Printed and bound in Great Britain by
Mackays of Chatham plc, Chatham, Kent

The Back of Beyond

Like Rosie Jenkins in the story, I love my whole brood, each of them ever ready to help me with anything I need to know, or anywhere I want to go. So, my eternal thanks to Jimmy, Sheila and John, Alan, Bertha and Bill, and Debra.

Matthew, of course, deserves a special mention. At fourteen, most youngsters steer clear of elderly Grans, but he helps me in so many ways, not least by keeping my mind young, for which I am very grateful.

Then there is Susan Opie, my editor, whose patience must be stretched to breaking point with my persistence in sending her manuscripts which are far too long, and because I use too much of the Doric, a dialect which people outside Aberdeenshire find impossible to understand. At my age, however, I find it very difficult to change. Sorry, Susan! And thanks!

1929-1939

Chapter 1

❧

'You'll have to tell her the night, Ally – we're leaving first thing in the morning.'

Alistair Ritchie gave a rueful sigh. 'I suppose I will, Dougal, but I'm dreading it.'

'You should have let her see ages ago she was wasting her time.'

'I did try, but she's got it in her head I'm the only one for her, and nothing'll shift it.'

Dougal Finnie gave an exaggerated sigh. 'I'm right sorry for you. It must be terrible to be that irresistible to women.'

Annoyed by his pal's smirking sarcasm, Alistair burst out, 'You wouldna think it was funny if it was you.'

Having arrived outside the Finnies' house, Dougal turned in at the gate, still laughing, and Alistair swung his leg over the bar of his bicycle to continue on his way home from work, his mind going over what had led to the momentous step he was to take the following day. He had made the decision when he and Dougal were propped against the back wall of the kirkyard a week and a half ago – a secluded corner where they told each other things they wouldn't, couldn't, tell anyone else – and he'd been complaining as he so often did nowadays about Lexie Fraser pestering him. 'She's been after me since we were still at school, but it's got worse since . . .'

'Some lads wouldna mind that,' Dougal had grinned. 'She's a real bonnie lassie.'

'Oh, she's bonnie enough, but since her father walked out

on them, there's been something . . . off-putting about her, like she'd smother me wi' love if she got half a chance.' He paused, then said reflectively, 'That was a funny business, wasn't it? I'd have said Alec and Carrie Fraser were a real devoted couple, and I can hardly believe what folk's saying about him, and yet . . .'

Dougal screwed up his nose. 'My Mam says there's nae smoke withoot fire. Dinna forget Nancy Lawrie left just the day afore him, and she's never come back, either. They musta been meeting someplace else to keep it secret, but folk's nae daft.'

'I canna help feeling sorry for Lexie, for she doted on her father, but it looks like she's trying to get me to make up for what he did. Every time I go out a walk wi' her, she's all over me like a rash you've just got to scratch, and I'm feared I'll give in some night and do something I shouldna.'

The twinkle in Dougal's eyes had deepened at that. 'I'm surprised you havena done it already.'

'Have *you* done it wi' somebody?'

'Dozens o' times. You dinna ken what you're missing, Ally, I bet Lexie's hot stuff.'

'I wouldna mind trying it, but nae wi' her. I feel like running the other way every time she comes near me.' He had hesitated briefly, then added, 'To be fair, though, I think she just needs . . . somebody to . . . Her Mam canna be much company.'

After a moment's silence, Dougal had looked at his friend thoughtfully. 'How would you like to be rid o' her . . . for good?'

'I'm desperate to get rid o' her, for she clings to me like a blooming leech, but I draw the line at murder. You should ken me better than that, Dougal Finnie!'

'I didna say *get* rid o' her, you gowk! I said *be* rid o' her. You see, Ally, I'm sick fed up o' working for Bill Rettie in

4

the garage, aye clarted wi' oil and grease, and nae chance o' promotion. Any road, what he pays me hardly buys a packet o' fags, so I've made up my mind to go to London and look for a better job. What about coming wi' me?'

His first reaction, Alistair recalled, had been to say no. After two years of being delivery boy and general sweeper-up for the butcher in Bankside, the village four miles west of Forvit, he had recently been taken on as an apprentice to learn the trade. It would be a few years before he got a decent wage, but it was a steady job and he wasn't keen to give that up. On the other hand . . . he'd be well away from Lexie in London. 'When was you thinking on going?'

'As soon as you like. I could go to Aberdeen on Saturday and book our passages – the boat's a lot cheaper than the train. Are you on?'

'Um . . . um . . .' Deciding that the pros more than out-weighed the cons, Alistair had given a decisive nod. 'Aye, I'm on – if my dad'll stump up the money for my fare.'

His mother hadn't been too pleased about it, though. It wasn't the money, just the fact that he was going so far away from home. 'You're only new sixteen,' she had said, sadly, 'ower young to be on your own in a place the size o' London.'

'I'll nae be on my own, Mam, I'll be wi' Dougal.'

She had shaken her head at this. 'He's never been a good example to you, aye getting you in some kind o' mischief.'

His father had come to his defence here. 'Ach, Bella, leave the laddie be! It's time he was taking a bit o' responsibility for himsel', showed some independence . . . and Dougal'll keep him right.'

Alistair smiled at the memory of this contradictory state-ment. Dougal had always told him what to do, not that he was a bully. Far from it. He was the best friend a boy – or man, come to that – could ever have, though he was inclined to

5

jump first and think after. Anyway, his father had given him his fare money, and in the morning, his mother had pressed two pound notes into his hand to keep him, hopefully, till he found a job.

But he still had one thing to do before he left Forvit.

Alistair's steps were slow and reluctant as he went to meet Lexie Fraser for the last time. He dreaded the scene there was bound to be, and was afraid he might say something she could take the wrong way. If she thought for a minute that he felt something for her, she would spread it about that she was his girl, and if he *did* something he shouldn't, she might say he'd put her in the family way and he'd have to marry her. Aye, he'd have to watch his step tonight.

With Benview three miles from the village and the Frasers' house half a mile this side of it, they'd never walked in the woods between Forvit and Bankside like the other courting couples. Their trysting place was midway between their homes, where a footpath from the road led up to a tower which had been built as a look-out post during the Napoleonic Wars by the then Earl of Forvit. It was here that Alistair meant to break the news.

Although there was a track from his house diagonally up to the tower itself, he always went down to the road to meet her, and she was there first, as she always was. She hadn't heard him coming, and he wondered for the umpteenth time why he felt as he did about her. She *was* a bonnie lassie, fair-haired like himself but maybe about five feet two to his five ten, with rosy cheeks and blue eyes a shade lighter than his. She had a good figure for sixteen, her bust not too big nor yet too small, her middle nipped in by the belt of her navy trench coat, the one she had worn to school. She had once made him span her waist, and he'd nearly been able to make the

6

tips of his fingers meet. She thought her bottom was too big, but to his mind it wasn't all that bad . . . quite neat, really.

She turned at the sound of his footsteps and tucked her arm through his when they got on to the stony track. Her chattering didn't annoy him as much as it normally did – in fact, he was glad that she didn't expect him to do any of the talking – but when they came nearer to the tower his stomach started to churn at the prospect of what he had to do.

They sat down in the small niche she had recently begun referring to as 'our special place', and when she came to the end of a long, involved story about something that had happened in the general store which she helped her mother to run since her father left, he cleared his throat nervously. 'I've something to tell you, Lexie.' His heart sank at the way her eyes lit up, and what he had planned to say died on his lips.

'Go on,' she urged. 'Say it, Al . . . darling.'

It was far worse than he had imagined – she must think he was going to say he loved her – but it had to be done. 'I . . . that is, me and Dougal . . .' Her horrified expression made him race on. '. . . we're going to Aberdeen first thing in the morning.'

The renewed hope in her eyes told that she had jumped to the wrong conclusion. She must think he was taking his friend with him for advice on buying something for her, an engagement ring, maybe. 'I'm sorry, Lexie,' he said quietly, 'we've booked our passages on the London boat.'

'You're going to London?' she gasped. 'What for?'

'To look for decent jobs. We'll never make anything of ourselves here.'

'But Al . . . you and me . . . what about us?'

Her blue eyes had dimmed, practically brimming with tears, but he had to be brutal. 'I've tried telling you before, Lexie. There's no us, not the way you'd like. I'm sorry, but that's the way it is.'

7

'But, Al . . . I thought . . . you felt the same about me . . .'

'I've never felt that way about you, Lexie. I like you, but that's all.'

The tears flooded out now, and he sat uneasily silent while she sobbed, 'You do love me, Al, I know you do!'

He hated her calling him Al, it reminded him of that awful gangster Capone he'd read about, but he also hated to see her crying. 'Aw, Lexie,' he muttered, sliding his arm awkwardly round her shoulders, 'you'll find somebody else.'

'I don't want anybody else!' Turning to him, she laid her head against his chest. 'I love you! I've always loved you and I always will!' Her mood changed like quicksilver, and she looked up at him accusingly. 'You're just like my father, you're deserting me and all, and you don't care what happens to me.'

He was outraged by this. 'That's not fair! I never pretended to be anything more than a friend, and at least I've told you I'm going away. Any road, it's not up to me to look after you, that's your mother's responsibility, and your father'll likely come back once he's . . . Please try to understand, Lexie. I need to get away. I want to make something of my life, and even if I don't, I won't come back here. I don't like hurting you, Lexie, but that's the way it is.'

Her eyes were beseeching now, her words a mere whisper. 'You'll surely give me a goodbye kiss?'

Feeling a proper heel, he bent his head to her upturned mouth and was immediately engulfed in a suffocating embrace. Frantically, he tried to think how to extricate himself without physically hurting her, for her passionate kisses were making an unwanted desire start in him, a desire he had no wish to fulfil.

'Stop it!' he shouted, shoving her roughly away and scrambling to his feet. 'I know what you're trying to do, but it won't work! I've told you – I don't love you and I'm leaving wi' Dougal in the morning.'

She looked at him pathetically now. 'But . . . you'll come back to me?'

'If I come back, it'll only be for a visit, to see my mother and father. Now, get up and I'll see you home.'

'Damn you, Alistair Ritchie!' she shouted. 'You've just been amusing yourself wi' me and you're abandoning me like my father, and I never want to see you again! Go away and leave me alone!'

'I can't leave you up here by yourself in the dark. Come on, Lexie, be sensible.'

'Sensible?' Her voice had risen several tones. 'How can I be sensible when you've just said you don't love me any more? You led me on, and I'll never forgive you!'

'I didna lead you on, Lexie,' Alistair said, desperately, 'I never said I loved you . . . it was all in your mind. Come on now, stand up and I'll take you back.'

She got to her feet slowly, refusing the hand he held out although she stumbled over the stones in their path when they made their way down the hill. They had almost reached the road when she murmured, with a little hiccup, 'What would you think if I killed myself? That's what I feel like doing.'

Sure that this was an attempt at moral blackmail, he snapped, 'I'd say you were mad!'

'I *am* mad . . . mad about you,' she whispered, stopping to look at him with her blue eyes wide and pleading.

'You'll soon forget me. Look, Lexie, you're just making things worse. Even if I wasn't going away, there'd never be anything between us, not on my side, any road.' In an effort to coax her out of her self-inflicted misery, he took her hand. 'Give's a smile, Lexie. I don't want us to part on bad terms.'

'But you still want us to part?'

9

'It's best.'

'For you, maybe, not for me.' She yanked her hand out of his. 'But have it your own way, Alistair Ritchie! Go to London and do what you like!'

'I will, then, and you can see yourself home from here!' He turned and strode back towards the track that led to his house, seething at her for being difficult yet feeling guilty for hurting her. Not that he should feel guilty, for she had done all the chasing, made all the advances. Of course, once he realized what was in her mind, he should have let her know he wasn't interested, but she likely wouldn't have listened.

Having watched Alistair stamping out of sight, Lexie walked on down to the road. She *had* felt suicidal a few minutes ago, but not any longer; she needed a man to depend on more than ever. She had often heard that jobs weren't so easy to come by in London, and he'd be back in a few months with his tail between his legs.

Her mother looked up in surprise when she went into the house. 'You havena bidden long wi' Alistair the night.'

Lexie flung her coat on a chair. 'We'd a row! Him and Dougal Finnie's going away to London in the morning.'

'That's funny. Meg Finnie was in the shop yesterday and she said her Dougal was leaving, but she never said Alistair Ritchie was going wi' him.'

'Dougal had forced him. He wouldn't have wanted to go.'

Although Carrie Fraser's interest in other people had dimmed since her husband had walked out on her, her judgement of character was still as shrewd as ever. 'I aye thought he wasna as keen on you as you was on him,' she observed.

'He was so! Dougal had got round him ... like he's aye done.'

'If you'd had ony sense, Lexie, you'd have gone for Dougal. He's more spunk in him than Alistair, and he'll do well wherever he is. Besides, Joe Finnie's a lot better off than Willie Ritchie.'

'But it's Alistair I love, Mam, and I know he'll come back to me.'

'I wouldna count my chickens if I was you, lass.'

Carrie turned things over in her mind for some time after her daughter flounced off to bed. Something worried her about Lexie these days. Of course, her father going off without a word like that was enough to knock any girl off balance, but she should be getting over it a bit – it was three months now. He must have known how badly Lexie would take it, for she'd always been a daddy's girl – and she, his wife, could still hardly believe it. What bothered her was why? If only Alec had considered them before . . .

Carrie shook her greying head despairingly. There had been a rumour – she'd just heard snatches of whispers, for folk shut up when they realized she was listening – but Alec would never have . . . he hadn't been a demanding man, not even when they were first wed. He'd never have needed another woman, but that's what they were saying. Of course, Nancy Lawrie had gone away just the day before him and never come back, and her mother had said she'd no idea where she was. That was why folk were sure she'd been expecting his bairn and he'd left to be with her – what else would they think? But Alec would never have touched a young lassie. He was a decent man, and Nancy Lawrie wasn't much older than Lexie.

Her sorrow and sense of betrayal still too raw for her to cope with, Carrie heaved a shuddering sigh. She didn't think she'd ever get over it, so why should she expect Lexie to forget? Poor lass! Alistair Ritchie could have helped her, but maybe he could see there was something not right about her nowadays. It wasn't anything her mother could put a finger on, but she was definitely different, more serious ... over-serious, that was it ... intense. She was young, and should be enjoying herself more, but she had likely heard what they were saying, and all, though a true family man doesn't up tail and leave his wife and daughter without a word, no matter what sort of trouble he finds himself in. He buckles to and faces up to whatever it is, but ... fathering a bairn on a woman that wasn't his wife, a girl, really, twenty years younger than himself? In a place like Forvit, he'd have been the butt of the filthiest of crude jokes, and he wouldn't have liked that.

Running the general store and sub-post office, as well as being an elder in the kirk, he'd always held his head up, taken a pride in not going drinking with the other men, and especially not playing around with loose women, for there was a few of that kind about, even in this wee village. His interest lay in music. His father had taught him how to play their little harmonium, and he had played the pipe organ in the kirk since he was fifteen. He took the choir practice every Wednesday, the only night of the week he ever went out, and that was where he'd got friendly with Nancy Lawrie, for she was one of the sopranos.

But bad blood will out, though there had been no hint of it before! And Lexie was his daughter, so maybe there was something unnatural in her, as well? It wasn't noticeable, thank heaven, but the shock could have been enough to bring it to the surface – for just a wee while, please God! One good thing, she was coping all right in the shop, learning the postal work and all, and that could take her mind off things. And she'd find another lad. Of course she would!

*   *   *

Lying on top of the bedcovers, Lexie was angry at her mother for being so perceptive, but whatever she said or thought, the girl was certain that absence *would* make Alistair's heart grow fonder, and she was prepared to wait for months, even years, for him to come back to her. But suppose he kept his threat and didn't come near her when he came back to visit his mother and father? What then?

She contemplated this awful thought for some time, then decided that it would be up to her to seek him out and make him admit he loved her, as she was sure he did . . . deep down. He was the only man she'd ever want, and even if it took until they were middle-aged, till they were both grey-haired, she would get him in the end.

Chapter 2

❧

While the Aberdeen Steam Navigation Company's 'Lochnagar' was docked at Leith, the two youths stood at the rail to watch the activity involved in the taking aboard of some twenty or so new passengers and their baggage, a welcome break from the long hours of having only seagulls and water to look at, their faces spattered by the spray sent up as the ship's prow cleaved through the angry waves.

The lengthy interlude over and on their way once more, Alistair cast a sour glance at his friend, to whom he felt somewhat less than friendly at that precise moment. 'Could you nae have got a better place for us than right up at the sharp end?'

Dougal seemed rather put out. 'What did you expect for fifteen bob? A luxury cabin? Second class return was two pounds, but single was one pound, seven and six, meals included. I ken't my mother would gi'e me enough to feed the five thousand, so I said we wouldna need meals. I saved you twelve and a tanner, and that's the thanks I get.'

'Aye, well, but I thought I'd get to London dry.'

'Ach, stop your girnin'. Tell yoursel' Lexie Fraser's getting further and further awa' every minute. Does that nae cheer you up?'

They ate their second 'meal' now, rationing their pooled resources – a crusty loaf, a hunk of cheese and a pound of cold sausages from Alistair's mother, a large meat roll, a jar of her rhubarb chutney and six hard boiled eggs from

Dougal's. Meg Finnie had also packed into the small canvas bag a flagon of home-made ginger beer to wash down the dry fare. Not long after they had packed away their remaining food, the sun peeped uncertainly through the clouds, and the sky slowly came ablaze with light.

'This is more like it,' Alistair observed, as the heat penetrated his damp clothes.

'Aye, thank goodness,' Dougal muttered. 'Maybe you'll be happy now.'

At Newcastle, while the new passengers came up the gangway, Dougal invented some reasons for their making the journey. 'See that woman wi' the red hat? I bet she's a Russian spy going to London to report to her bosses, and that man wi' the mouser's a forger, wi' his attache case full o' counterfeit notes.'

Alistair had found a new worry. 'What if the boat sinks wi' the extra weight . . . ?'

'Ach, Ally,' Dougal exploded, 'would you stop imagining things?'

Anchors up and in motion again, they decided it was time to settle for the night. The covered-in sleeping area, roughly triangular, could only be described as steerage class, but no one else was there, so it was with relief that they unfolded the bedding and made up two of the six bunk beds.

Finding it difficult to get comfortable on the lumpy mattresses and pillows, Alistair suddenly sat bolt upright. 'Did you get some place for us to bide in London?'

'We'll easy find a place.' Dougal looked sheepish for not having thought of this.

When a stocky, middle-aged member of the crew looked in some time later to check on how many had taken advantage of this basic accommodation, they were still sitting brooding,

15

shoulders hunched, fair and dark heads bowed, blue eyes and brown staring dejectedly at the rough, grey blankets. A flat cap sitting at a rakish angle on his straggly white hair, the man regarded them speculatively. 'I hope you two aint expecting to find the streets of London paved with gold? All you Scotch laddies seem to think . . .'

'We're not as daft as that,' Dougal objected, offended by the implied slight.

'Just as well, then.' The man hesitated, then asked, 'Have you jobs to go to?'

Dougal's frown deepened to a scowl. 'Aye, we're all fixed up.'

The seaman walked away with disbelief written all over his weather-beaten face.

'Why did you tell him that?' Alistair wanted to know. 'It's a downright lie, and he didna believe you, any road.'

'He can believe what he likes. We'll easy find jobs, I can feel it in my bones.'

Alistair still wasn't convinced, but, giving his chum the benefit of the doubt, he kept quiet. Dougal had said he'd been thinking of going to London for a while, and he must have found out how the land lay as far as getting work was concerned. He would realize they couldn't live on nothing. Of course, the Finnies were well off. Joe, Dougal's father, had his own farm, and even if it wasn't the biggest in the Forvit area, it certainly wasn't the smallest, so he'd likely given Dougal a fiver at least, maybe even a tenner, to keep him going till he was earning for himself, whereas all *he'd* got was a measly two pounds, which wouldn't last long when they'd to pay for board and lodgings . . . if they ever found a place, that was.

But the Finnies' money and the Ritchies' lack of it wasn't the only difference between him and Dougal, he reflected. He was inclined to be a bit of a pessimist, whereas Dougal always found something bright about every situation, and managed to wriggle out of all the trouble he got them into with his mischievous ways.

In the morning, they made a breakfast of bread, cheese and chutney, washed down with the last of the ginger beer. The day passed uneventfully, eating when they felt the need of sustenance with only water to wash things down, taking a stroll now and then to save their legs stiffening up.

Thirty-five and a half hours after they had left Aberdeen, a movement of the other passengers told them they were nearing their destination, and they joined the line waiting to disembark, taking the opportunity to drink in the sights – the dirty buildings, the bustle of sea traffic as the boat made its way through the docks. At long last, however, they stepped shakily onto dry land, still feeling as if they were rising and falling with the tide.

'Which way do we go, then?' Alistair wanted to know, but Dougal's non-committal grimace made him burst out, 'You mean you havena found out anything aboot anything?'

'I thought . . . I thought . . .'

Seeing Dougal so obviously at a loss for words or action of any kind made Alistair more than a little frightened, as if a crutch he depended on had been taken away, but anger soon took over. 'How are we supposed to find a bed for the night, then? Or were you hoping somebody would throw a blanket over us if we lay down here?'

A heavy hand on Dougal's shoulder saved him from trying to justify himself, and he looked up into the kindly grey eyes of the seaman who had spoken to them the night before. 'I can tell by your miserable faces you're worrying about something. You said you had jobs, but it wasn't true, was it? And you've nowhere to live either, right?'

'That's about it,' Dougal muttered.

'If you wait till I get finished, I'll try to figure out something for you. I shouldn't be more than 'arf an hour, and there's plenty to see here in Limehouse.'

Trying to show that he was in no way daunted by their homeless predicament, Dougal pointed along the quay to where a few of their fellow passengers were standing. 'What are they waiting for? Are they taking another boat to somewhere else?'

'They'll be going upriver to the Houses of Parliament. Sightseers. Now, just stand there and don't wander off. I'll be back as soon as I can!'

Their waiting was lightened by the activity around them although Dougal seemed a bit preoccupied, and it didn't feel like half an hour to either of them before the seaman was with them again. He swung his seabag from his shoulder down to the ground, but before he had time to say anything, Dougal put forward the idea which had occurred to him. 'Look, we'll be OK. If you just tell us where to find the YMCA, we'll . . .'

The man's bellowing laugh stopped him. 'It don't allus do to be so independent. My trouble-and-strife's been speaking about taking in lodgers to make some extra cash, and you look like real decent boys, so why don't you come home with me? She was going to put a card in the grocer's window, but you could save her the bother, and I can guarantee she won't fleece you like some landladies.'

Alistair glanced at his pal then said firmly, 'We won't be able to pay her much . . . not till we find work.'

'My Ivy's a trusting soul. Me name's Len Crocker, by the way, and we've a two up, two down in Hackney. Oh, there's a bloke I want a word with. Hang on a minute.'

'That's a bit of luck,' Dougal smiled, when the stocky little man moved away.

'Aye, he seems real nice, but his wife mightna like us.'

'We can look for somewhere else, and the same goes if we dinna like her.'

Alistair pursed his mouth. 'You ken, Dougal, I'm having second thoughts about this.'

'We'll be fine. There's plenty of jobs in London if we look in the right places.'

'Maybe, but how'll we ken where the right places are?'

Dougal sighed and waved his hands airily. 'We'll find them.' He looked pensive for a moment, then added, 'I tell you this, if Ivy's anything like her man, we'll be in clover.'

'If she takes to us.'

'Ach, Ally, stop looking on the black side. If you turn up there wi' a sour face like that, she'll definitely nae take to you.'

Back with them, Len hoisted his seabag on to his shoulder again and boomed, 'Right, me hearties! Best foot forrard. Home James, and don't spare the horses, as they say.'

Each carrying a cardboard suitcase – containing two changes of underwear, shirts, flannels, jerseys, several pairs of hand-knitted socks, plus their Sunday suits and shoes and half a dozen well-laundered handkerchiefs – the boys had difficulty in keeping up with him as he strode out briskly to where they would get a bus to Hackney. Once seated in the double-decker, he kept up a running commentary on everything they passed, and in no time, it seemed, he said that this was where they got off. 'Just a step or two now,' he assured them, but they went through a veritable maze of identical streets before he announced, with some pride, 'This is it! Home sweet home and the fire black out.'

Alistair and Dougal exchanged alarmed glances, but his throaty chuckle let them know he was only joking. He opened the immaculately painted green door and shouted, 'I've brung two young gentlemen to see you, Ivy, love!'

They were ushered into a small sitting room and had only time to notice the brightly burning fire when a buxom woman with very blonde hair, probably in her forties, bustled in. Her slight frown vanished when she saw them. 'Well,' she simpered, 'this is a naice surprise. When you said young gentlemen, Len, I didn't expect them to be this young.' She shot her husband an enquiring look.

'That's not me usual welcome,' he grinned, grabbing her round the waist and planting a kiss on her full mouth before explaining, 'They're from Aberdeen, and they've nowhere to live, so I said you might . . .'

She jumped in quickly, addressing Alistair as she straightened her skirt. 'Ai suppose Ai *could* take you, if you're willing to share?'

At this point, Dougal thought it expedient to acquaint her with all the facts. 'We can't pay much till we're earning.'

'That's quate all right,' she smiled, not taking her eyes off Alistair, 'we can arrange all that later. Ai suppose Len told you Ai'm Ivy, so what's your name, dearie?'

'I'm Alistair Ritchie, and he's Dougal Finnie.' He felt most uncomfortable under her intense stare.

'Alistair?' she beamed, and, obviously finding the effort too much, she stopped trying to sound more refined than she was. 'I like that, so Scotch, but I expect you're hungry after coming all the way from Aberdeen. Five hundred miles anyway, isn't it? Show them up to the spare room, Len, love, and I'll rustle up something for them to eat.' She had turned briefly to her husband but directed her last words once more at Alistair. 'Just come down when you're ready, dearie.'

The upstairs room was large and airy, with a wide double bed, a wardrobe, a tallboy, a basket chair and a wooden-armed chair. Dougal grimaced. 'Nae exactly the best of hotels, is it, but it's clean, so I suppose it'll be OK.'

'There's just one bed,' Alistair pointed out. 'I've never had to share a bed before.'

'Neither have I, but ach, we'll manage. It's that big we'll have to look for each other in the mornings.'

The window, Alistair discovered when he went across to it, looked down on a small, well-tended garden at the rear of the house, a neat little patch of lawn surrounded by several flower beds which had the promise of being colourful in spring and summer. 'One of the Crockers must be keen on gardening,' he observed. 'Ivy, likely, for Len's job must take him away a lot.'

Coming up behind him, Dougal nudged his arm in a knowing way. 'She's taken a right fancy to you . . . dearie.'

'Oh, I hope no',' Alistair groaned. 'She's as old as my mother.'

'She could teach you a thing or two if you let her, you lucky devil.'

'Nae fears! I dinna want her near me, and I'm nae sure if we shoulda come here.'

'Like I said, if we dinna like it, we can look for somewhere else. Hurry up and put your things past, for my belly thinks my throat's cut.'

Agreeing that Dougal should have the top two drawers of the tallboy and Alistair the other two, they didn't take long to stow their few belongings away. Dougal was all set to go downstairs as soon as they put their empty cases on top of the wardrobe, but Alistair insisted that they should at least wash their hands before eating their meal. Luckily, Len had pointed out the doors to the lavatory and the separate bathroom, so they didn't have to ask, and some minutes later, hair slicked down with water, boyish faces shining, fingernails spotless, they went out on to the landing, where their appetites were whetted by the delicious smell wafting up from downstairs.

'Oh boy,' Dougal whispered, 'I'm going to enjoy this, whatever it is.'

They were rather taken aback by the huge amount on their plates as they sat down at the table, and they couldn't help noticing that, although they had a pork chop along with the sausages, eggs, beans, fried bread and chips, their host and hostess had not. Dougal opened his mouth to say something about this, but Alistair gave his shin a surreptitious kick under the table. It was obvious to him that the chops had been cooked for Ivy and Len's supper, and the sausages had probably been intended for their next day's dinner, but it would have been bad manners to draw attention to it.

Ivy took the opportunity now to find out more about them, her peroxided head nodding at Dougal's replies but her lipsticked mouth smiling at Alistair. She showed great surprise when she learned that Forvit village consisted of only about twenty houses, a general store which was also a sub-post office, and that butcher meat was bought from a van that came from Bankside, four and a half miles away, three times a week.

'Well!' she exclaimed. 'You're going to know a big difference here.'

'There's a kirk ... a church, of course,' Alistair volunteered, 'and a doctor, though the chemist's in Bankside, and all, and the garage.'

'Wot about a police station?' Len put in. 'There must be police in Forvit.'

Dougal grinned now. 'There's no crime, so ... no police. The nearest bobby's at the far end of Bankside.'

Len pursued the subject. 'Wot if 'e couldn't handle something that happened? A big robbery, say, or an assault, or ... a murder?'

Stumped, Dougal looked at Alistair then said, uncertainly, 'I suppose he'd have to get help ... from Huntly, that's ten mile away, and they'd likely send a squad from Aberdeen if it was a murder, but ... that's twenty mile the other way.'

Ivy gave an exaggerated shiver. 'Stop speaking about murder, you're giving me the collywobbles.'

Laughing, Len pushed back his chair with a satisfied sigh. 'I'll soon sort you out, love. I'm off to me Uncle Ned now, so don't be long. See you in the morning, boys.'

It was only a little after nine o'clock, and Ivy giggled at the surprise on the two young faces when she explained the rhyming slang. 'My Len loves his bed, though he likes it best when I'm in there with him.' She gave a lewd cackle and dug Alistair playfully in the ribs as she stood up to clear the table.

Embarrassed, he said, 'Dougal and me'll do the dishes for you if you want to go up ...'

She found this highly amusing. 'He can wait for it, the randy blighter.'

'We don't mind helping, honest.'

'Tell you what, then. If Dougal puts a few lumps of coal on the fire, and lays the cork mats in the left-hand drawer of the sideboard and the tablecloth, neatly folded, in the right-hand drawer, you can come and dry for me. How does that sound?'

'Suits me!' Dougal smirked wickedly, ignoring his friend's look of desperate appeal.

Trapped, Alistair helped to load the tray with dirty dishes, and carried it through to the small scullery where Ivy turned on one of the taps in the slightly chipped earthenware sink and left it running until steam billowed up from the enamelled basin nestling inside. Then she rolled up her sleeves, turned on the other tap and let the cold water run in until she could comfortably hold her hand in it.

Watching her, Alistair said, admiringly, 'You're lucky having a tap with hot water. My mother has to boil kettles on the range for everything.'

'She should get in a back-burner. That heats the tank, and in winter, when the fire's on all day, the water's still hot enough to wash next day's breakfast dishes, and once the fire's going proper, the water heats again to near boiling. In summer, of course, I don't light it at all, except on Mondays and Fridays, that's wash-day and bath night for Len and me, and I light the gas boiler for the dishes and washing faces and hands and so on.' She pointed vaguely in its direction, then picked up the bar of yellow soap sitting in a dish between the taps and swished it around in the water to get a lather.

'You're a good-looking boy,' she observed, as she wielded her dish mop. 'Do you have a steady girl back home?'

He shook his head, thankful that he could answer honestly. 'Not now.'

'I bet she didn't know the best ways to please a man, like I do.'

The colour raced up Alistair's neck. 'I wouldn't know about that . . . we never did . . .'

Ivy's smile broadened. 'Don't tell me you're a virgin, Al? I can't believe it.'

He wanted to throw the dish towel at her painted face and run out. She was being far too suggestive for his liking, and she was calling him Al, the hated name Lexie had used.

Patently enjoying his discomfiture, Ivy went on, 'I'd like to get you on your own, some time, to show you what I can do.' She fell silent, quite possibly picturing in her mind exactly what she would show him, and when she finished washing up, she squeezed past him to dry her hands on the roller towel fixed to the wall beside the pantry.

Her next move terrified him. He could feel her breasts pressing into his back, her pelvis rubbing against his back-side, but he endured the unwanted, and unsettling, contact until he had dried the last plate and could sidestep away from her. At a safe distance, he turned to look at her and was disconcerted to see her eyes going straight to his crotch.

'Yes, you'll do me,' she murmured seductively, 'and you won't be shy with me for long, I swear.'

'I'm not shy,' he protested, 'but I don't think . . .'

'No, dearie, you're right. We've plenty time ahead of us and we'd better leave it for now and get back to Dougal before he starts imagining things.'

He followed her into the sitting room where Dougal looked up from the well-worn, moquette-covered armchair where he was reading the newspaper. 'All done?' he leered.

Hoping that his pal hadn't heard anything, Alistair sat down on the other easy chair, avoiding the settee where their landlady had placed herself. She embarrassed him no further, however, but kept them laughing over the next hour with stories about her neighbours and the people she met when she went shopping.

At half past ten, she suddenly said, 'Oh my Gawd, look at the time.' She stood up and stretched her arms. 'You must've been wondering if I was ever going to shut up. Len says I forget to stop once I get started, but I'm sorry for keeping you up so late, I expect you're tired out. By the way, Al, dearie, make sure all the lights are off down here when you come up. Nightie night, both.'

'Good night,' they chorused, and when the door closed behind her, Dougal looked slyly at Alistair then burst out laughing. 'I told you she fancied you.'

'Stop being so daft!'

'The walls here are paper thin, so I heard what she was saying ben there. You're in for some good times with Ivy Dearie, Ally boy.'

'Not me!' Alistair snapped. 'If you want her, you can have her with pleasure.'

'It likely would be a pleasure, and all, for I'd say she's all set for a fling, but it's not me she wants, worse luck. Now, would you say she was out of the lavvy yet?'

The two boys spent most of the following day looking for work, and returned to Victoria Park at ten past five exhausted, ravenous, and very despondent. Luckily, Ivy had a huge hotpot waiting for them, and while they ate, Len regaled them with humorous anecdotes about his time in the Royal Navy during the war. Afterwards, Dougal volunteered to help with the dishes this time, but it was Len who replied, 'Thanks, it's my turn tonight, mate, and I could do with an 'and.'

Alistair's heart sank at the prospect of being left alone with Ivy, but she said nothing outrageous, probably because Len was within earshot. Nevertheless, he still felt really uncomfortable with her.

The dishwashers completed their task in record time, and the next two hours passed with the youths answering more questions about their homes and families. Both said they had a sister, but whereas Flora Finnie, six years older than Dougal, had gone to America the year before, Alice Ritchie, three years younger than Alistair, was still at school. The evening ended with them discussing the kind of jobs they had hoped to find, but after that day's fruitless search, were far less confident of ever finding now.

Ivy commiserated profusely with them over this, but Len said, as he got to his feet, 'Ne'er mind, boys, I put word about you round the pub at lunch time, so something's bound to turn up. Me mates are a good bunch.'

In bed, ten minutes later, Dougal observed, 'We're going to be all right here, Ally. Ivy's a great cook, and that's the main thing, isn't it?'

Convinced that he had nothing more to fear from her, that she had just been testing him before, Alistair agreed. 'I just wish we could be bringing in a wage, though. She mightn't feed us so well if we can't pay our way.'

As luck would have it, he was in the lavatory the following evening when one of Len's 'mates' came to say there was a job going in the factory where he worked as an electrician. 'They're looking for a youngster to train as a clerk in the Counting House,' he told Dougal, 'and when I said I knew of a couple of sixteen-year-old Scots boys looking for work, they said to tell one of you to call first thing tomorrow.'

'That's great!' Dougal exclaimed. 'I've never worked in an office, but I always got top marks for handwriting at school.'

'There you are then,' beamed Ivy, 'it's just the job for you.'

When he came back, Alistair was honestly pleased for his friend, but found himself wishing that his bowels hadn't needed emptying at the crucial time.

Sensing his disappointment, Ivy gave his head a motherly pat. 'Don't you fret, Al, dearie, your turn'll come.'

Having to report for work the next morning, Len was up well before dawn, and Dougal also left early to find the factory and make sure he wasn't late for his interview, leaving Alistair hurrying to get out in order not to be left on his own with Ivy. She, however, had other ideas. 'There's no rush, dearie,' she purred, her hand fixing on his sleeve as he tried to take his jacket down from the peg on the hallstand in the narrow hallway. 'It's time we got better acquainted, ain't it?'

'I have to go out,' he protested. 'If I don't find work, I'll not be able to pay anything for my board.' This wasn't strictly true, but she wasn't to know that.

Her plucked eyebrows lifted. 'Haven't you never heard of payment in kind?'

'No,' he answered, puzzled. 'What's that?'

'You see me all right and I'll see you all right, savvy?' She came closer and put her hands up his pullover. 'I'm going to be ever so lonely till Len comes home again.'

Comprehending now what she was up to, he said, hastily, 'No . . . Mrs Crocker . . .'

'You'll like it, Al, I promise you.' Her hands ran over his chest, but didn't stop there, and as they continued down, he burst out, 'No, no! I can't let you . . .'

'Yes, you can, you're a big boy now.' She made a grab at him and laughed with delight. 'Yes, Al, a big boy and getting bigger by the minute.'

He'd been praying that someone would come to the door, or that there would be some kind of interruption that would let him make his escape, but he could stand no more of her caressing. 'That's it!' he shouted, shoving her away and almost knocking her off her feet. 'I'm going to look for other digs, I can't stay here! You're man mad!'

Clearly gathering that she had gone too far, Ivy stepped back. 'OK, OK, dearie, I know when I'm beat. I thought you were the answer to this maiden's prayer . . . but it seems I made a mistake. I'm ever so sorry for trying it on with you.'

She pulled such a repentant face that he had to laugh. The only way he could see of dealing with a woman like this was to make fun of her. 'A maiden?' he gurgled. 'You? It must be twenty years since you were a maiden.'

He held his breath, but she wasn't at all put out. 'Cheeky beggar,' she grinned, 'but you're right. I'd the first bite at my cherry when I was twelve . . . that's twenty years ago almost to the day.' His patent disbelief made her give a loud screech of laughter. 'No fooling you, is there, Al? All right, I'll come clean – twenty-four years ago, for I was thirty-six last month . . . and that's the Gawd's honest truth.'

He felt a sudden rush of pity for her. At first sight, he had thought she was about forty, but looking at her in the cold light of this October morning he could see the crow's feet ound her eyes, the slackness of her mouth without its thick coating of lipstick, the dark roots of her bleached hair. She was fifty if she was a day, and she was likely trying to prove, to herself as much as to other people, that she wasn't past it. 'You're still an attractive woman, Mrs Crocker,' he smiled, wanting to soothe her, 'but I don't want to get involved with anybody. I want to concentrate on making a career for myself and then . . . well, I don't want to come between any man and his wife, so I'll look for a girl a bit nearer my own age. No offence intended,' he put in, quickly.

'None taken,' she assured him, although there was a touch of wistfulness in her faded blue eyes. 'I shouldn't have done what I did. I was playing a silly game and you were right to let me know how things stand. I can forget if you can, so what say we start all over? Before we leave it, though, I must tell you I admire you for the way you handled it, Al. Like a ruddy diplomat you were, and you'll make a damned good husband to some lucky gal one of these days.'

The tension having gone, he felt easy enough with her to say, 'Thank you for those kind words, Mrs Crocker.'

'Make it Ivy, for Gawd's sake, dearie, else you'll make me feel my age. Now, shall I make you another cuppa before you go job-hunting?'

'No thanks . . . Ivy, I'd best be moving.'

By three o'clock that afternoon, Alistair was wishing that he had accepted Ivy's offer of tea. His feet were throbbing from trudging through dozens of streets, each with a small scattering of shops to fulfil the needs of its denizens. In his anxiety for employment, he had even asked three butchers if they had a vacancy, though he'd have been better staying with Charlie Low in Bankside if he was going to stick to butchery, so it was just as well that there was nothing doing in any of them. He was so depressed that he was actually quite glad when it started to rain, and thankful that it was heavy enough to provide him with a good excuse for calling it a day.

Ivy tutted at his dripping clothes when he went in. 'I'm sorry I'm making such a mess of your clean floor,' he muttered, but she waved away his apology.

'It's not the floor I'm worried about,' she assured him, as she pulled off his jacket. 'You'll catch your death if you're not careful. Go up and change into something dry and I'll give you the good news when you come back.'

He couldn't for the life of him think what good news she could possibly give him, and pondered over it while he towelled his legs dry and draped his flannels over the hot tank in the cupboard at the top of the stairs. Presentable again, he ran down to hear what she had to say.

Ivy had the fire burning 'half up the lum', as his father would have said, and he stood with his back to the heat, his brows raised in question. 'You'll never believe this, Al,' she began, her voice trembling with excitement, her mascara'd eyes gleaming with satisfaction.

'Go on, then,' he said, impatiently, 'tell me.'

'I went shopping as soon as you left – I put my face on first, of course – and I got speaking to old Ma Beaton five doors down on the opposite side, and the nosy so-and-so asked me who the handsome young men were she'd seen going in and out of my house. Not a thing happens in this street without her knowing, 'cos she sits behind her net curtains all day and watches everything that goes on.'

Feeling rather let-down, Alistair muttered, 'Is that it?'

'No, it's a long story and I have to tell you everything so you'll understand.'

'I'm sorry, carry on. You were speaking to old Ma something . . . ?'

'Ma Beaton, and I told her you and your pal had come

30

from Scotland to look for jobs. I said Dougal was fixed up –
he came back at twelve to say he starts on Monday and then
went out again – but I said you were still looking and she
said to try Ikey Mo. He'd been telling her he was thinking of
taking a young boy on to help him. So I went and told him
about you, and you've to see him tomorrow about ten.'

'B ... but ...' stammered Alistair, 'who's Ikey Mo, and
what kind of shop is it?'

Ivy spluttered with laughter. 'That's not his real name. I
can't remember what it is, but Ma Beaton calls him Ikey Mo
because he's a Jew.'

'What kind of shop is it?'

'A pawnshop. I started going there when Len came out of
the Navy, for he was out of work for months and I used up
all our savings, but when he got a start on the North boat,
I didn't need to pawn no more stuff. I used to go to Uncle
– that's what most people call him – every week, and he's a
nice old bloke.' Noticing Alistair's deepening perplexity, she
said, 'Don't you know what a pawnshop is?'

After hearing what was entailed in the pawnbroking business, Alistair said, 'I'm sorry, Ivy, but I don't think I'm fitted
for that.'

Her face darkened. 'Ain't a pawnbroker good enough for
you?' she snapped. 'Is that all the thanks I get for going
out of my way to ask about it for you? You think it's
beneath you?'

He was quite shocked by her outburst; he had spoken
without thinking and hadn't meant to offend her. 'Oh,
please don't think that! I'm really grateful to you ... and
the old lady, but it's just ... I'm worried because I don't
know anything about ... what was it you called it? Pledging
things. I wouldn't know how much to give for them.'

'You'll soon learn,' Ivy smiled, her spirits restored. 'The
customers'll tell you if you don't offer enough, and Uncle'll

31

walk into you if you give too much.'

'That's what I'm worried about.'

E. D. Isaacson, as the sign under the three brass balls pro-
claimed the pawnbroker's name to be, was like no man
Alistair had ever seen before, and because he was busy attending to a tall, belligerent woman, the boy had a chance to study
him fully. He was shaped rather like a tadpole, his head big
in proportion to his short body and legs. His grizzled, curly
hair was quite thick, yet his crown was covered by a small
skull-cap, and his long nose protruded above a bushy moustache and rounded beard, reminding Alistair of a cow looking
over a dyke. Whatever his failings in appearance, however,
his attitude to his customer held all the patience of a saint.

Alistair was so fascinated by the unfamiliarity of the man's
physical make-up that he was unaware of the woman going
out, and was startled when the old man spoke to him. 'Sorry
to keep you waiting, my boy. What do you think of my little
emporium, hmm?'

Having paid no attention to his surroundings, Alistair took
a guilty glance round, but feeling it would be unwise to keep
his prospective boss waiting for an answer, he hardly took
anything in. 'It's very nice.'

'You think you could work here?' The old man's eyes held
an appealing twinkle now, despite the lines of fatigue above
and below them.

'I believe I could, but you'll have to learn me . . .'

'Not to worry, my boy. I shall teach you everything, but
what do I call you, hmm?'

'Oh, sorry, my name's Alistair Ritchie, Mr Isaacson.'

A deep menacing rumble came from the region of the man's
stomach. 'And who is this Mister Isaacson, may I ask?'

Alistair couldn't think what he had done to anger the man.

32

'It said . . . E. D. Isaacson on the sign,' he ventured, 'and I thought that was you.' He heaved a sigh of relief when the rumbling erupted into a series of full-blooded belly laughs.

'Nobody ever calls me Mr Isaacson,' the pawnbroker said, breathless after such unaccustomed mirth and taking a handkerchief from his waistcoat pocket to wipe his eyes. 'It's sometimes Ikey Mo because I'm a Jew, although they mean no disrespect. Some call me Edie, because of my initials, but I'm Uncle to most people.' After a brief pause, he added, 'My first name is Emanuel, if you would feel happier with that.'

Alistair gave it a few moments' careful thought. 'Ikey and Edie sound disrespectful to me, but Uncle doesn't feel right, either. I'd better make it Emanuel . . .'

'Shall I tell you what would give me even greater pleasure? My dear mother used to call me Manny, and no one has addressed me so since she passed away . . . over thirty years ago. Do you think you could manage that? And I shall call you Alistair, a fine Scottish name for a fine Scottish boy.'

'When do you want me to start . . . um . . . Manny?' He found it much easier to say than he had thought.

'The sooner the quicker, hmm? What do you say to . . . at this very moment, Alistair, or do you have to let your landlady know where you are?'

'Ivy knows where I am, and I'd love to start straight away.'

And thus began an unusual friendship, which deepened as the years went by and blossomed into as close a bond as any two men of different religions and generations could possibly share.

Chapter 3

❧

Alistair's uncertainties about his aptitude for the job were quickly banished by Manny's patient teaching. During slack spells, he learned how to repair clocks, large and small, and watches from the cheap to the expensive, not that many of those found their way into E.D. Isaacson's shop. Most customers wanted to pledge something, and after they went out, the pawnbroker explained why he had given what he did for the article brought in.

'Mrs Fry's husband has been unable to work since he injured his back last year,' he said, one morning. 'Sadly, she had just given birth to their fourth child at the time. They are all under school age, and she finds it extremely hard to manage on the paltry sum his employers dole out to him, less than twenty per cent of what he was earning before the accident. I suppose they are lucky, really, because his firm is one of the few who give anything at all in such cases.'

Another woman, middle-aged this time, had been widowed some months previously. 'Mrs Borland is slowly selling off all her possessions,' Manny observed mournfully, 'and goodness knows what she will do when everything is gone. She will most likely have to apply to the parish, and losing their independence is something all these women dread. It also means the loss of their self-respect.'

'So she'll never manage to redeem her things?' Alistair asked, wonderingly.

'I am afraid not, my boy. She knows that and I know that,

and I also know that they are worthless. Nothing will sell, but what can I do? I cannot let her starve, can I?'

Alistair's opinion of the elderly man rose with every day that passed, and he set out to absorb as much as he could of what he was being taught about human nature. He could not blame, any more than Manny could, the poor wives whose men drank most of their wages, or gambled them away, or refused to work at all, and admired them for struggling to keep their families fed and clad and, most importantly, together. On one occasion, however, he felt he had to comment on what seemed to him a betrayal of trust. 'The gent's watch that woman redeemed was real gold, wasn't it? How could a family as poor as that afford anything so expensive? And she didn't say anything when you let her get it back for less than you gave her for it in the first place. She's cheating you, Manny.'

'No, Alistair, never think that. All the women who come to me are as honest as the day is long. In this case, Mrs Parker's husband came from a well-to-do family, and was given the watch for his twenty-first birthday. His father, however, did not approve of the girl he wished to marry, and headstrong and deeply in love, young Parker left home in order to make her his wife. They now have three sons, and although he does not regret what he did, according to his wife, he still cherishes the watch, the one and only item of any value he possesses, and makes a point of wearing it to church every Sunday. You see, she has never told him that it languishes in my safe from Monday to Saturday each week. It is her way of proving that she can manage on what he gives her.'

'But she's living a lie,' Alistair burst out. 'She's not managing, or if she is, it's because you're helping her. She's cheating you as well as her husband.'

Manny shook his head. 'Oh, Alistair, how little you know of these people. They do the best they can with what little they have. I suppose you think Mrs Parker should *sell* the watch to me? If she did, her family could certainly live comfortably for a year or so, perhaps, but at what cost? The loss of her husband's respect, his love? Because she would never, ever, be able to buy it back for him. Can you understand that?'

The youth looked sheepish. 'Yes, I see what you mean. It must be terrible to have to live like that.'

Dougal Finnie was also having new experiences. At first, he felt as if he were caged, having to spend his entire days indoors at everyone's beck and call, but there were compensations. Apart from the cash office where he worked – they called it the Counting House – there was a despatch office and a general office, the staff of both including several girls . . . not ordinary girls, though. He had never seen such beauties, far outshining any of the girls he had known back in Forvit.

As he told Alistair one night in bed – where they exchanged stories of the events of their days – 'I'm going to be spoilt for choice, Ally, short ones, tall ones, slim, well-rounded, blonde, dark, redheads, they're all there! Would you like to make up a foursome one night? I could tell my one to bring a friend with her for you.'

Trying to imagine the kind of girls who would appeal to Dougal, Alistair said, 'No thanks, I'll find a girl of my own when I'm ready for it.'

'Och you, you're getting to be a right old stick-in-the-mud. Or are you waiting for Ivy Dearie to make another move?'

'Shut up!' Alistair grinned to show he didn't mind being teased now. Originally, he had felt cheated that nature had robbed him of the office job, but things had worked out quite well, for he was more than happy working with Emanuel D. Isaacson.

* * *

Alistair was exhausted when he finished on Christmas Eve, with dozens of mothers, and a few fathers, rushing in because they needed money, so he was glad when Manny said he was closing the following day. The Crockers' house was decorated in a manner neither of their boarders had seen before, with tinsel everywhere, holly, mistletoe (which allowed Ivy to kiss all of Len's mates who came in during the evening), and long strings of cards and paper chains stretching from wall to wall. Several cards came from Forvit to the two youths, who were deeply touched that so many people had remembered them and even felt a trifle homesick, although they pretended it was all a bore. There was no card from Lexie Fraser, however, and Alistair was relieved that Dougal didn't seem to notice his disappointment.

Ivy had provided a sumptuous meal, a whole turkey with all the trimmings, plum duff and brandy butter, mince pies, much more than they could eat, and when she was placing the covered half-empty dishes on the coolest shelf of her larder, she laughed, 'You'll be getting this left-overs for the rest of the week.' They did, and still enjoyed every bite.

No celebrations were held on Hogmanay or New Year's Day, much to the boys' surprise, especially Dougal, who had been accustomed to seeing the men of Forvit village well under the weather by midnight and continuing to bend their elbows until they dropped off to sleep where they were sitting, or ended up at the side of the road after going outside to be sick. Dougal had never understood what enjoyment they could have got from that. Alistair's father, though not exactly teetotal, only took a glass of malt whisky to see in the New Year, or on rare occasions, for medicinal purposes.

Over the following weeks, Dougal regaled his friend with tales about the girls he had chatted to in the cloakroom

– one toilet for both male and female staff – or taken for a short walk in the lunch break, or whose bottoms he had pinched in passing, all of which Alistair recounted to Manny the following day when business was over. At first, he had wondered if the pawnbroker might not be interested in such goings-on, but when the old man began to ask what Dougal had been up to the previous day, he knew that his employer was enjoying hearing about the youthful exploits and tried to inject as much humour into the telling of them as he could. One occurrence, however, was certainly not as amusing to Dougal as it was to Alistair and Manny.

They had been living in the Crockers' house for about four months and were in the middle of supper when Dougal said, with studied nonchalance, 'I'll have to get my skates on tonight. I'm meeting a girl at seven.'

A *frisson* of envy made Alistair's appetite vanish, and with it, seemingly, his power of speech, so it was Ivy who asked, 'What's her name?'

'Amy something. She works in the general office and she lives just two streets away from here, so I won't have to walk miles from seeing her home. How's that for good management?' He looked extremely pleased with himself.

'Very convenient,' she laughed.

When Dougal left the table to go and make ready for his tryst, Alistair followed him upstairs and stood in the open doorway of the bathroom while the other boy filled the basin with hot water then ran his hand over his chin. 'Um . . . do you think I should shave again? I did shave this morning, but look at me. That's the worst of having dark hair. You're lucky, being so fair. You don't really need to shave at all.'

Piqued because this was true, Alistair said nothing, and Dougal went on, 'I've been fancying Amy for days, and I met her in the corridor this morning and not a soul in sight, so I dived straight in and asked her out. I didn't think she'd come, because . . . oh, you should see her, Ally. She's a corker! Lovely blonde hair, natural, not peroxided like Ivy's, and a figure . . .' Unable to find words to adequately describe it, he sketched an exaggerated hour-glass shape with his hands. 'I'd better shave, I don't want to rough-up her soft skin.'

'When you meet her, couldn't you say something's cropped up and you'll have to make it another night?' Alistair asked plaintively. 'When Len's at home.'

'You don't need to be scared at being left on your own with Ivy.'

'I'm not scared, I just don't feel comfortable with her.'

Negotiating his safety razor round his nostrils, Dougal snorted loudly and waited until his downy whiskers were gone before lifting the towel from the rim of the bath and patting gently at his tender face. 'Shaving twice a day's a bugger!'

'You didn't need to shave again,' Alistair pointed out, sarcastically. 'I know I've only got to shave every third day, but that doesn't make me any less of a man than you.'

'No?' sneered Dougal as he made his way to their bedroom with his chum following at his heels. 'I bet I'll have more girlfriends than you, and be married first, *and* have a child first, and all. Not that I intend settling down for years. I'm going to hunt around till I find the right one.'

'We'll see,' Alistair said, darkly. 'If you go on the way you're doing, you'll end up having to marry some poor lassie before she drops your bairn. That's if her father hasn't got at you long before that.'

Still grinning, Dougal shook his head. 'Not me! I'm smarter than get caught like that. Look Ally, can you fasten this front stud for me? My fingers are all thumbs.'

When Dougal was finally satisfied with his appearance, Alistair picked up the Zane Gray he'd been reading and accompanied him downstairs, saying as Dougal went out, 'Think on me stuck here wi' Ivy when you're enjoying yourself wi' your Amy.'

He jumped guiltily when Ivy came through from the scullery, but she hadn't heard, and was regarding him apologetically. 'I'm sorry, Al, but I've to go out as well. When you were upstairs, Daisy Smith from down the street came in and asked if I'd sit with her mother to let her visit her older sister. Greta's on her own, and she fell and broke her hip, poor soul, and Daisy's going over to give her house a bit of a tidy. I'll be away for at least a couple of hours, maybe longer, but you'll be all right, won't you?'

'It'll give me a chance to finish this book. It's due back to Boots's library tomorrow.'

Alistair settled back in the most comfortable easy chair when she was gone, and was soon engrossed in *Riders of the Purple Sage*, a saga of the Wild West – so engrossed, in fact, that he did not hear the front door opening less than an hour later, and was startled when someone came into the room. 'Oh, thank God it's you, Dougal!' he gasped. 'I nearly had a heart attack. But why are you home so early? Did things not go right with you and Amy?'

'No they bloody didna! Her face was made up to the nines and she'd high heels and a tight jumper, and I thought she was sixteen, but she's just fourteen, would you believe?'

With others, they had to speak in English to be understood – although their broad vowels and guttural voices made it difficult – but when they were alone, they reverted to their native dialect, as Alistair did now. 'You didna . . . ? Nae wi' an underage quine?'

'She didna say how auld she was till I . . . I wouldna've touched her. I thought she'd give in once I got her going, you ken, but the silly bitch hadna a clue . . . about a bloody thing! God Almighty! She thought kissing would gi'e her a

40

bairn, and I'd a helluva job convincing her it wouldna, and then, when I'd been holding myself back and kissing her as tenderly as I could, I thought I'd chance going a wee bit further. She wasna ower keen on me touching her chest, but when I tried to lift her skirt, she went bloody berserk!'

Alistair had to let his laughter out now, and it burst forth like a blast from a volcano. 'It serves you right! You went out with the intention of seducing her.'

'No, I didna! Like I said, I thought I'd work on her till she wanted it and gave in without a murmur, but . . . she went mad, raving mad!'

'She'd been terrified. She was only fourteen, you said?'

'She didna tell me afore that! She was screaming blue murder,' – here he put on a high falsetto voice – '"Don't you dare touch me! I'm only fourteen and I'll tell my father you interfered with me."' His tone deepened again. 'Then she kneed me and ran off like the wind, and I was left in absolute agony.'

Alistair was laughing fit to burst. 'I wish I'd seen it! The great ladies' man weaving his spell and getting his nuts cracked.'

'It's nae funny, Ally, it was damned painful, I can tell you, still is.'

But his friend couldn't stop teasing. 'Tell Ivy when she comes back, and she'll kiss them better.' He doubled up at the idea of this, and tears ran down his cheeks.

He had unwittingly hit the right note. Dougal's outraged expression disappeared as he joined in Alistair's laughter. 'By God, that would be a sight for sore eyes, right enough!'

When they simmered down, he said, ruefully, 'I tell you one thing, Ally, after this, I'll ask how auld a lassie is afore I ask her oot.'

When Manny was told the next morning, he thought it was the funniest thing he had ever heard. 'What a card that friend of yours must be,' he gasped, holding his aching sides. 'I wish I could have been there.'

'That's what I said, and all,' giggled Alistair, 'but it hasn't taught him a lesson. If it had been me, now, I'd never want to go out with another girl, but he's different.'

Manny nodded. 'Yes, you are as different as chalk and cheese from what you say. He is such an extrovert with the opposite sex and you seem to be timid with all females. But I can tell that you have hidden depths, my boy. There is passion lurking inside you, and when you eventually meet the right girl, love will strike you with the impact of a sledgehammer. You were born to be a one-girl man, and you will derive more happiness from that one girl, Alistair, than Dougal will from a dozen of his kind.'

Thinking about this later, Alistair decided that if everybody saw him as Manny did, they would think he didn't have much go in him. One girl? What red-blooded male stuck to one girl? If Dougal asked him again to make up a foursome, he'd damn well jump at it. How would he ever recognize the right girl if he never met any?

After this fiasco, Dougal was noncommittal about the girls he went out with ... for at least three weeks. With his natural effervescence, he couldn't keep it up for long, so things returned to what they had been before Amy, and both Alistair and Manny, at second hand, were constantly diverted by his descriptions of what had happened on his dates.

'Fay's nice enough,' he said one night, 'if she'd just keep her trap shut. She's got a voice that would clip clouts. Like a blinking foghorn ... and she never stops.'

'I didna ken foghorns could clip clouts,' Alistair said, trying not to laugh.

Dougal tutted his exasperation. 'Ach, you ken fine what I mean.'

After another night out, he flopped down on the bed beside Alistair. 'God, Ally,' he sighed, 'it was like pulling teeth getting anything out of Ella. The only thing she was interested in was kissing.'

'That should've pleased you,' Alistair grunted. 'That's what you want, isn't it?'

'I'd like a breather sometimes.'

Dougal's first opinion of Gladys was 'Nae bad', something of a compliment coming from him, but after their second encounter he had changed his mind. 'Why do girls aye have to go and spoil things?' he asked bitterly when he came home. 'As soon as I get my hands above their knees, they carry on like I was sex mad.'

'So you are,' laughed Alistair. 'It's all you ever think about.'

'Oh, be fair! I dinna jump on them the minute I meet them. I build up to it.'

'Well, all I can say is – you're nae a very good builder.'

'D'you think so?'

Alistair gave a serious nod, then smiled expansively. 'I'm nae expert, but to my mind you should take things as they come. Warm them up, or whatever you want to call it, and when they're ready, they'll tell you.'

'Oh, aye!' Dougal was heavily sarcastic. 'They'll say, "Please Dougal, I'm ready for it now." For God's sake, Ally, ha'e some common sense.'

'I said I wasna an expert.'

This was the pattern for several weeks until, once again, Dougal seemed to draw a veil over his activities. 'I think he's had another setback,' Alistair told Manny one morning.

43

'He hasn't said a word about his nights out for . . . oh, it must be a month now. Something must have upset him. Something really bad.'

'He will not keep it from you for long, Alistair. I know you are worried about him, but he is a survivor. He will get over it, whatever it is.'

Studying Dougal closely each time he came home from presumably seeing a girl, Alistair thought that he didn't look at all downcast and came to the conclusion that he had got over it, as Manny had predicted. It was strange, though, that he didn't want to discuss it. Letting another two weeks pass to see if Dougal would confide in him, give him a name and all the lurid details, Alistair finally summoned up the courage to ask.

'You're awful quiet about things these days,' he observed, as Dougal was putting on his sports jacket. 'Did you come up against another Amy, or somebody like that?'

Dougal turned and looked him straight in the eyes. 'I've turned over a new leaf.'

Watching him fold his handkerchief and place it meticulously so that only a corner was peeping out of his breast pocket, it occurred to Alistair that his chum might be speaking the truth. 'I wondered why you were keeping quiet about your conquests, but that's the third night you've gone out this week, and you've made such a fuss about shaving, and brushing your hair with brilliantine, and taking ages to make up your mind what tie to wear. Have you met somebody special?'

Dougal made sure that his Woolworth's tiepin was straight before murmuring, rather bashfully, 'Aye, this one's special.'

'Come on, then, spit it out. What's her name?'

'Marjory Jenkins, but she likes to be called Marge. She'll be seventeen in September, and we've been seeing each other for a couple of months now.'

44

'So she's only sixteen? I thought you'd learned a lesson about dating them so young.'

'She'll soon be seventeen and I'm nae eighteen till October, so that's just about eleven month between us. That's nae such a difference, is it? Anyway, I couldna help myself, Ally. She's perfect! She's got darker hair than mine, nearly black, and curlier, her eyes are a deeper brown, and her mouth . . . it's a Cupid's bow, perfect for kissing.' Now that he'd started, Dougal couldn't stop detailing the girl's charms. 'She's a perfect figure, and all, though I haven't laid a finger on her.' He turned to look seriously at his chum. 'Honest, Ally, I havena touched her. Oh, I've kissed her, hundreds of times, but . . . well, I think I love her. No, I *do* love her, and I'm not going to do anything to upset her.'

Alistair was on the point of saying he'd got it bad when he realized that Dougal *had* got it bad, and it wasn't fair to tease him. Instead, he said, meaning every word, 'I hope it turns out OK for you this time.'

'Thanks, Ally, but I'll have to hurry. Mustn't keep her waiting.'

'Dougal's fallen for this one,' Alistair told Ivy when they were on their own. He had survived dozens of evenings with her by this time, and although she sometimes came out with suggestive remarks, she hadn't actually done anything he could object to and he could usually laugh off what she said. 'Her name's Marge Jenkins, and she's a bit young, to my idea. She's not seventeen till September.'

'So there's not even a year between them? My Len's four years older than me, and I was seventeen when he first asked me out.'

'According to what Dougal said, Marge isn't like you. I don't mean any disrespect, Ivy, but he says he hasn't tried anything with her, so I think she's a bit prim and proper.'

'Prim and proper?' Ivy threw back her head with a loud

burst of laughter. 'You're dead right there, Al! Nobody could ever have accused me of being prim or proper, and I wouldn't have thought a girl like that would appeal to Dougal, though they do say opposites attract, don't they?'

When Dougal came in, much later, Alistair said, 'Everything OK?' Not that he needed to ask. His friend's blissful expression said it all.

'Everything's perfect.'

Alistair let this pass, although 'perfect' was the only word Dougal seemed to be able to come up with as far as Marge was concerned. 'Does she work with you?'

'Oh, no, she works in her father's hotel in Guilford Street, off Russell Square.'

This meant nothing to Alistair, who knew very little of the rest of London. 'How did you meet her, then?'

'I'd to deliver an account to her father, by hand because it was overdue for payment. It was Marge who opened the door, and I was bowled over. Just like that. Any road, she took the account to her father and came back to say he was busy and could I wait? She was standing so near me I could've reached out and pulled her against me, but I didn't dare. Do you get that, Ally? I couldn't. Anyway, there we were, looking at each other, and I thought, you've got the chance, ask her out before her father comes and throws a spanner in the works. So I blurted out, in my best English, "Would you care to come out with me some evening?" And that was it.'

'She agreed?'

'Well, her young sister came in with a signed cheque – Mr Jenkins does all the cooking and he was in the middle of doing something he couldn't leave – and Marge told Peggy to go away, and then she said, "Tomorrow at seven? At the end of the street?" I've never felt like this about any other girl, Ally. Marge is definitely the one for me.'

'I can't understand why you didn't tell me before.'

'I thought you'd torment the life out o' me, love at first sight and that sort of thing.'

'I'd like to meet her sometime, to see what she's like.'

'To give your approval? That's OK. I'll ask her tomorrow to bring her sister with her on Saturday ... she's got two. The youngest's still at school, that's Peggy, Marge is the middle one, and I think she said the oldest, Gwen, was eighteen.'

'Maybe you'll fall for her instead,' Alistair teased.

'Never! But maybe you will.'

'Not me. I've other things to think about; I've no time for girls.'

This was perfectly true, for only that morning, Manny had given him something of a surprise. 'I have had this dream for years,' he had said while they were eating the sandwiches Ivy provided for her lodger and his boss. 'I want to put aside the pawnbroker business some day, and open a watchmaker's shop which will also offer new and antique jewellery for sale. Of course, my dream will have to wait until I can afford to get better premises, but it might be a good thing if I did a little scouting around to find some little items to start me off. Even if it could be years before I am in a position to open such a shop, I could be building up a stock for it. You are more or less confident about dealing with customers on your own, so I could start going round the markets. I am told that one can often pick up a good bargain from the stalls. What do you think, hmm?'

'You'd trust me?' Alistair gasped. 'You'd leave me here on my own?'

'Of course I trust you. Your face has been an open book to me since you first walked through that door ... honesty, willingness to please, a wish to justify your wages by working as well as you can. In any case, I have nothing worth stealing at the moment – except the gold wrist watch Mrs Parker still brings in every Monday. But please do not think that

I am taking advantage of you. I will increase your wages by five shillings because you will be in sole charge. I wish I could make it more, Alistair, but . . . perhaps some day soon, hmm?'

On Saturday evening, on the way to Guilford Street on the underground, Alistair's stomach was churning with anxiety at the thought of meeting Gwen Jenkins. If she was anything like Lexie Fraser had been, he'd be terrified of her, and if she was as prim and proper as her sister seemed to be, he wouldn't know what to say to her, and Dougal would be too taken up with Marge to pay any attention to him.

His heart sank when he saw them – one a short but beautiful brunette who must be Marge, and the other a tall, elegant, model-like redhead who looked as if she would wipe the floor with him if he stepped out of line. God, this was going to be an evening he'd never forget . . . but not for any of the right reasons.

Before Dougal could make the introductions, Marge said, 'Gwen was sorry she couldn't come. She fell downstairs this morning and sprained her ankle. This is Petra, an old school friend I ran into yesterday, and she agreed to step in.'

The redhead inclined her head stiffly to Dougal, but when Marge said, 'Petra, this is Alistair, your date,' she turned her heavily mascara'd eyes to him, then silently slid her arm through his. They walked to Hyde Park, and because there wasn't room to go four abreast on the pavements, they split up into couples, much to Alistair's embarrassment, although he consoled himself by thinking it would be different in the Park. It wasn't. Dougal and Marge were oblivious of anyone else, strolling hand-in-hand and looking into each other's eyes so often it amazed Alistair that they didn't bump into something . . . or somebody. With Petra – it had to be a fancy name – glued to his arm, he plodded on with a heavy heart.

They took the bus back, and about two stops before they were due to get off, Petra jumped up. 'This is my stop!' She made a dive for the stairs and had jumped off the moving vehicle before Alistair took in what was happening. He turned round to Dougal in dismay. 'She should have said . . . I didn't know . . . I thought we'd all get off together.'

Marge smiled. 'Petra was always a queer fish. That's why I never kept in touch.'

'She didn't enjoy herself, that's one thing sure.'

'Don't worry about it. Gwen'll be able to come next time.'

'I don't think we should arrange a next time,' he said, looking apologetic. 'I'm not a great one for making conversation or anything like that. I'm not like Dougal.'

'I felt awful,' he told Manny the following day, 'but Petra scared the pants off me.'

The pawnbroker gave what was almost a snigger. 'A rather inappropriate turn of phrase, don't you think?'

Alistair's spells on his own extended from mornings only in the first few weeks to whole days, at the end of which Manny would return happily exhausted to show his 'manager' his latest acquisitions. Before putting them in his safe, he would spread them out on his counter and discuss each item with Alistair, asking his evaluation first and then pointing out good points or flaws in the precious stones, and soon the newly-eighteen-year-old was surprising himself as much as Manny by the accuracy of his assessments. He was also showing quite a talent for repairing even the oldest of the timepieces.

A truly sheepish Dougal broke into his self-congratulatory ramblings one night some four months later. 'I've asked Marge to marry me.'

Alistair was stunned. During the evening of the foursome with the stuck-up Petra, he had gathered that Marge wasn't the prim and proper type he had imagined, but a lively girl full of fun, and every bit as lovely as Dougal had said. 'I didn't know you were as serious as that about her,' he murmured. 'Did she say yes?'

'She did that.'

'But you can't afford to keep a wife?'

'I've been saving as much as I could since I started going with her, it's near a year now, and I think I've enough to rent a cheap flat somewhere and furnish it.'

'How the mighty are fallen,' Alistair muttered, then shook his head. 'No, don't mind me. Marge is a real nice lass and I wish you both well. Congratulations.'

After his next meeting with Marge, Dougal was not quite so elated. 'She told her family she'd accepted my proposal and her father hit the roof. He said she was far too young to think about marriage, but he might agree to it when she's eighteen – that's near a year yet – as long as I ask him for his permission properly. I'll have to ask him for her hand like he was a Victorian father. Did you ever hear the like?'

'He's making sure his daughter doesn't marry some ne'er-do-well,' Alistair pointed out, 'and I've got to admire him for that.'

Dougal snorted. 'You would. Any road, he said he'd let her get engaged, though I didn't want to have to put money out on a ring. The trouble is, if I don't, he'll think I'm a stingy blighter.'

It was Manny who solved Dougal's financial problem. After hearing of it from Alistair, he said, joyfully, 'I picked up a beautiful ring at Balham market about a month ago, remember, and I only gave thirty shillings for it, as I recall.'

Alistair was about to remind him that he had paid five pounds for it and it was worth much more, when it dawned on him that this was Manny's way of helping Dougal. 'Will I tell him to come and have a look at it?'

'I do not wish to force him into anything, Alistair, so just make the suggestion.'

Manny arranged to keep the shop open for an extra hour the next day to give Dougal time to get there after work, and during his sojourn round the stalls and second-hand shops, he picked up another two rings which he thought might be suitable.

Scarcely able to believe his luck when he saw what Manny produced, Dougal gave all three rings his deepest consideration, although he returned several times to a delicate arrangement of two emeralds and one diamond. Neither Alistair nor Manny were at all surprised, therefore, when this was the ring he finally plumped for. 'I can't believe it's only thirty bob,' he told the pawnbroker as he handed over a crisp pound note and a ten-shilling note that needed careful handling to avoid being ripped along its many creases.

'It is fairly old,' Manny replied, without a blush, 'and if your lady friend does not like it, she can come and choose for herself.' After a pause, he added, gently, 'But perhaps you would rather she did not know where you bought it?'

'I don't think she'd mind, and thank you very much for everything, Mr Isaacson. You don't know how grateful I am.'

When he and Alistair returned to the privacy of their shared room, he took the worn leather box out of his pocket to admire his purchase. 'It's lucky your boss had this ring in stock. Look at it ... two emeralds and a diamond ... for thirty bob!' His jubilation changed abruptly to uncertainty. 'D'you think she'll object to getting a second-hand ring? Will she think it looks cheap? Will her Dad realize ... ?'

51

Alistair felt as if he were between two stools. Manny wouldn't want him to let Dougal know the real value of the ring, but he couldn't let his pal run away with the idea that it was worthless. 'It's not classed as second-hand, it's called an antique, and it's worth a lot more than thirty bob.'

Instead of soothing Dougal, this information made him scowl. 'So Manny pulled a fast one on me? Well, I'm not taking his charity, and you'd better give it back to him in the morning.'

'It wasn't meant as charity.' Alistair had to deny it. 'He buys things much cheaper in the markets because the stallholders don't know what they're worth, and even if they did, they wouldn't be able to sell them for that. You just landed lucky that Manny had got those three rings so cheap.'

'It was good of him to think of me, then,' Dougal admitted. 'I can see why you like him, Ally, he's a kind-hearted soul.'

'Have you heard from Alistair lately?'

It was a routine question, asked of Alice Ritchie almost every time her mother sent her to buy the groceries. 'Mam had a letter yesterday, and he says Dougal Finnie's got engaged, though it'll be another year before her father'll let them get wed.'

Lexie Fraser nodded pleasantly. She wanted desperately to find out if Alistair had a girlfriend, but she couldn't make it too obvious. 'Is there any word of them . . . ? It's been two years since they went away, and surely they'd get some holidays?'

'Well, I suppose Dougal's been saving his money seeing he's going to be taking a wife, and Alistair's happy enough to keep working. He says Manny, that's his boss, leaves him in full charge nowadays, and he's teaching him how to value jewellery and things like that. Besides, he's an old man, and I think Alistair feels responsible for him, in a way.'

'But he should get some time off . . . it's the law . . . all employees should get a week's holidays . . . every year.'

Guessing what Lexie really wanted to know, Alice took pity on her. 'They've good lodgings, that's one good thing. Ivy, that's their landlady, she torments Alistair it's time he got a ladyfriend and all, but he says he's not ready for that yet. He's happy the way he is.' She was glad she'd made a point of it; Lexie's relief was almost tangible.

'He hasn't got much spare cash, of course, with his lodgings to pay, and getting his washing done, and buying fags, he says he never has anything left at the end of the week. I'd better not waste any more time, though. Mam'll be wondering what I'm doing. I near forgot, how's your mother keeping?'

'She's not very great, but the doctor says there's nothing more he can do for her.'

'I'm sorry to hear that, Lexie. Tell her I was asking for her.'

'I'll do that, Alice. Cheerio just now, then.'

Lexie waited until Alice cycled off before turning the placard on the door to 'Closed', and putting the snib down. It was on one o'clock, and she knew her mother would be waiting for her dinner, though she just picked at it like a sparrow, but the girl still didn't hurry to attend to her like she usually did. Hearing about Dougal's engagement had unsettled her. Alistair had always copied his pal in everything he did, so it was a sure bet that he'd be looking for a girlfriend now.

If only he'd come back, even for a wee while, she'd do her utmost to make him see that she was the one for him, that he was the one for her. She had gone out with a few of the local lads since he'd been away, but she hadn't found one that could make her pain go away. She had loved her father so much, right up to that awful evening when he didn't come home from the choir practice. She could still hardly bear to think about it. Even when she woke in the night, she pushed it aside and dwelt only on Alistair, assuring herself that even if he had deserted her as well, *his* absence wouldn't last much longer.

When he came home, he would understand. He would sympathize, make it all right. He wouldn't be like the folk that said her father had put Nancy Lawrie in the family way then run off with her. It wasn't true! It couldn't be true, no matter what they said!

If she didn't have her mother to consider, she'd go to London to be with Alistair. His sister would give her the address of his lodgings . . . she could pretend she just wanted to drop him a friendly note, for old times' sake. But there *was* her mother to consider. She had gone steadily downhill since . . . The doctor was the only one who had done anything to help at that awful time, Doctor Birnie, that was. He had given them both sleeping pills as soon as he came, and had left a small supply to see them through the next few days as well. The police had been useless. They had sworn they were searching for her father, but as far as they were concerned he hadn't committed a crime, so they weren't really bothered.

Tam and Nettie Lawrie, Nancy's parents, had fared no better. It had been glaringly obvious that the police believed the two missing persons were together – though they'd disappeared on different days – and had likely been saying, 'Good luck to them.' Poor Nettie had been in such a state, Tam had given up his job and taken her to be beside her sister, but they'd never said where *she* bade.

They were lucky getting away from Forvit, Lexie reflected, for she was stuck here until her mother's illness took its final toll. The new doctor – he was still called new though he'd come well over a year ago – had only diagnosed the cancer last summer, and had told her, the daughter, that it was

54

too far gone to treat. Not that there was a treatment for cancer. It was just a case of not letting a soul know what she was suffering from – there were still folk that thought it was catching – and waiting for the end.

Yet, however long it took, however much she came to resent the responsibility and drudgery of caring for her, she would never deliberately cut her mother's life short, much as she might feel tempted to stop her pain. How could God let this happen? It was a crying shame, that's what it was. As if the woman hadn't gone through enough already, with the whole village saying her man had left her for a girl young enough to be his daughter.

Shaking her head at the morbidity of her thoughts, Lexie straightened her back and went through to the house.

Chapter 4

Marjory Jenkins had been waiting, somewhat impatiently it must be said, for her eighteenth birthday, on which day her father had more or less promised, with one provision, to agree to her marriage, but time was just crawling past. One month before her dream would come true, she decided to make sure that all would run smoothly.

'I was thinking,' she said to Dougal the following evening, 'you're having Alistair as groomsman, and I'm having Gwen as bridesmaid, and they've never met yet, so why don't we get them to come out with us some time soon?'

'You're sure your father's going to let us . . . ?'

'I'm positive . . . as long as you ask him for my hand in the approved way. He's a bit old-fashioned – says a suitor should show proper respect.'

Dougal expelled a silent breath through pursed lips. 'I'm not looking forward to this, you know. I'll likely make a right muck-up of it, but I'll do my best.'

'I know you will, my darling.'

The endearment, plus the radiance of her smile, made him take her in his arms to tell her how much he loved her – serious sweet talk did not come easily to him but it was well known that actions spoke louder than words – and her earlier suggestion that they should introduce her sister to his pal was forgotten until they were saying good night some time later. 'Bring Alistair with you on Saturday,' she murmured, 'and I'll bring Gwen. The hotel's never busy at weekends – most of the reps go home to their families and we've only a couple of tourists booked for bed and breakfast – so Mum's giving Peggy the chance to be on duty on her own, to fetch drinks and things like that.'

He had to gird his senses together to take in what she was saying. 'Oh . . . yes, yes. I'll bring Alistair with me, even if I've to lead him by the nose.'

She giggled at that. 'Is he really so shy?'

'Maybe not quite as bad as that, but he *is* shy with strangers, especially girls.'

'That's funny. Gwen's the same . . . with boys, I mean. She was let down badly a couple of years ago, and she's scared to trust anybody now. Did someone let Alistair down?'

'No, it wasn't that. This girl was making a pest of herself, that's what scared him off.'

'Oh gosh, I hope they're not awkward with each other. I don't want anything to spoil our wedding day.'

'Nothing will, they won't want to upset you. No matter how they feel about each other, they won't show it.'

'Dougal, I could slaughter you for this!' Alistair fumed as they made their way to the meeting point. 'It's going to be bad enough on your wedding day, if it ever comes off, without having a rehearsal.'

'It's not a rehearsal,' Dougal soothed. 'It's just for Marge. She wants to make sure everything'll be plain sailing. Any road, maybe you'll like Gwen.'

'Have you ever met her?'

'No, but she's Marge's sister so there can't be that much difference.'

Alistair had known several instances where sisters or brothers had entirely different personalities, but he deemed it best not to argue. He didn't want to worry Dougal, whose mind was bent on making things perfect for his perfect fiancée.

It turned out that, apart from their sylph-like figures, the sisters were almost exact opposites. While Marjory was a curly-headed brunette with a creamy skin, Gwendoline had straight blonde hair and a fair skin; Marge was outgoing and bubbly, effervescent as a shaken bottle of beer, whereas Gwen was quiet and reserved. Despite this, despite his own reservations about the meeting, after five minutes in her company Alistair was talking to her as if they had known each other for years. Her friendly manner, and genuine interest in what his work entailed, encouraged him to describe his customers, give little thumbnail sketches of their lives, marvelling all the while at the compassion she showed for the poor downtrodden women and their families.

'It's a shame,' she murmured, at one point. 'People shouldn't have to live like that.'

'They're used to it,' he assured her, 'to living from hand to mouth. It's likely what their own mothers had to do, it's the only way of life they know.' Noticing that her lovely blue eyes were moist, he felt angry at himself for upsetting her, and changed to describing some of the items Manny found in the street markets.

They had been walking for almost an hour before it dawned on him that he had been doing most of the talking. 'You'll be fed up listening to me. Tell me about the hotel,' he coaxed. 'You must have some strange characters coming there?'

'Some,' she smiled, 'but not many and not too strange – most of them have been coming to us for years. It's the lady tourists who . . . they've probably never been in a hotel before and treat us like slaves.' She gave an imitation of the kind of haughty women she had to deal with, which ended with them giggling together like children.

By the time they reached the point where Dougal and

Marge were waiting for them, Alistair knew that Gwen was the only girl for him. He would gladly have lain down on the ground and let her trample all over him if that was what she wanted. Not that she would, for she wasn't that kind of person.

As he bade Gwen a cordial, and rather reserved, good night at the corner of her street, Alistair wondered if he would ever have the courage to kiss her at all, never mind in the passionate way Dougal was kissing Marge.

'That went off all right,' Dougal observed when they were walking back along Russell Square. 'I didn't see any sparks flying.'

'Gwen's really easy to get on with.'

'Oh, aye? Would I be right in thinking you've fallen for her?'

'I didn't say that.'

'You don't have to. It's written all over your face.'

'I like her,' Alistair admitted, colouring.

'Maybe you two'll be walking down the aisle a few months after us.'

'I wouldn't mind if we were, but maybe Gwen doesn't feel the same way.'

Gwen *did* feel the same way, although he didn't find out until almost two weeks later. They had been going for walks together, but on this particular night, because it was raining quite heavily, they went to a small cinema which showed, in its hour-long continuous programme, a few cartoons, an educational short, plus a roundup of world news, and because it was quite late by the time they got there, the only seats available were doubles in the back row. Sitting this close to the girl of his dreams, it still took Alistair ten minutes to slide his arm round her, and another five to pull her towards him. Then without warning, she turned to face him, and her lips were only inches from his.

For the next hour and a half, he was conscious only of her, of the whispered words of love, of the kisses that made his heart race almost out of control. The strains of 'God Save the King', heralding the end of the show, brought them both to their senses – they had sat unwittingly through forty-five minutes of repeats – and they ran, hand in hand, as fast as their legs could carry them, so that Gwen could be home before the hotel doors were locked for the night. One last snatched kiss was all they had time for, but Alistair made his way back to Hackney happier than he had ever been in his entire life.

He could hardly credit it. He wasn't handsome, nor wealthy, nor particularly clever, he couldn't make jokes like Dougal, so how on earth would a girl – the most beautiful girl in the world – be attracted to him? What could she see in him to love, for she must love him before she let him kiss her like that. He couldn't believe his luck, and he'd save every penny he could – give up smoking, buy nothing that wasn't absolutely essential – so that he could make her his wife. But maybe she didn't love him? Alistair himself could not recognize it, but, even before the kissing, he and Gwen had blossomed in each other's company, lost the apprehension of the opposite sex which their previous experiences had engendered in them.

'Good God, Ally,' Dougal teased after tea one evening, while they jostled each other for space at the bathroom mirror, 'you've been out with Gwen three times this week.'

'You've been out with Marge four times,' Alistair objected.

'That's different – we're engaged and you only met Gwen about three weeks ago.'

'And I knew right away how I felt about her.'

'You'd better warn her not to say anything about you and her to her father till after our wedding. For any sake, don't rock the boat.'

That night, as soon as Alistair met her, Gwen said, 'Dad's laying on a special meal for Marge's eighteenth birthday next Saturday, and you're invited, too. He's closing the hotel for the day, so I think he's going to give his permission for her to get married . . . but only if Dougal asks him properly. How does he feel about it, do you know?'

'He's scared stiff, but no doubt he'll do it. Um . . .' Alistair stopped, his face colouring.

'Yes? What were you going to say?'

'I was wishing . . . but it's too soon.'

'Too soon for what?'

'If I said I . . . wanted to marry you some day, what would you say?'

'I'd say that's what I wanted, too.'

'But it'll take me years to save enough, so we'd better forget about being serious for a while yet, and not show Marge and Dougal we're jealous of them.'

Ivy Crocker couldn't help teasing Dougal when the boys set off for the 'special meal'. 'You're not going to the guillotine, you're only going to ask her father one simple question. You can surely manage that?'

'Oh, Ivy, I hope I can! I feel like my mouth's full of tongue.'

She turned to Alistair now. 'It'll be your turn next, Al.'

'Not for a long time.'

On the way to Guilford Street, he muttered, 'Ach, Dougal, I'm as bad as you. I'm dreading this, for I'll feel like a fish out of water. I don't know any of them.'

'You know Marge and Gwen, and I don't know any of the rest of them either. Don't back out now, Ally, boy, I need you there to give me some self-confidence. You see, I'm worried that he never asked to meet me before this, and I'm not sure

61

I can pluck up courage to say what he wants me to say, but if I don't, he'll think I'm a pretty poor fish.'

'You'll manage fine without me.'

'I won't! I'll dry up, I'll stammer and stutter and look a right fool.'

'That's nothing new,' Alistair teased. 'I suppose I'd better come, to please you, but don't expect me to say anything.'

'As long as you're there, that's all I want.'

When they arrived at Jenkins' Hotel, Marge took them downstairs to the kitchen where her father, a huge white apron draped round his vast body, was sitting at a long, well-scrubbed table putting the finishing touches to a mouthwatering trifle. He did not look up until the decoration was completed, which disconcerted Dougal but gave Alistair time to study the man. He was grossly fat, his backside overlapping the stool on which he was sitting by several inches all round, his flopping belly almost covering his knees. His neck bulged red from the top of his starched collar and although his cheeks had not yet become jowls, it was a sure bet they would eventually. Because his head was bent in concentration, it could be seen that his crown was sparsely covered, yet his grey-speckled dark hair was cropped close like a soldier's.

Both youths jumped when Mr Jenkins banged down his fork and barked, 'Which of you two Jocks is after my Marge?'

It was not an auspicious opening, but Dougal managed to answer with no trace of the nerves which had been consuming him all day. 'I'm Dougal Finnie, Mr Jenkins.'

The man's eyes swivelled round. 'So you must be Alistair Ritchie?'

'Yes, Mr Jenkins.'

The man gave a sudden roar of laughter and, as they stared at him in dismay, a woman's voice said, gently, but with a hint of amusement, 'Don't tease them, dear. I'm Rosie,

62

by the way, the girls' mother, and don't let Tiny scare you. It's just ... it's so long since anyone called him Mr Jenkins. He was twenty-five years in the army, ending up as sergeant/cook at Aldershot, and he put on so much weight tasting everything, somebody once called him Tiny in fun, and the name stuck.'

They couldn't help but laugh at the incongruity of the nickname, and it put them entirely at ease. 'I'm pleased to meet you ... Tiny,' Dougal said, holding out his hand.

'Ditto, my friend, but if my daughters have everything ready in the dining room, I think we should eat now. Business later,' he added, winking at Dougal, who looked at Marge and shrugged in resignation.

Whoever had taught Tiny his trade, Alistair thought as the meal was coming to an end, deserved a medal. The minestrone soup was delicious, the roast lamb was so succulent it almost melted in the mouth, the roast potatoes were crisped to a T, the other vegetables were just as he liked them, and the trifle ... he had never tasted anything like it! And eating was clearly a serious business in this household, very little conversation had been made. Mrs Jenkins, Rosie, was dwarfed by her husband. She was slight, but obviously wiry, because she had mentioned, while the soup was being served, that she did the actual running of the hotel.

'Tiny's just the chef,' she had laughed. 'I'm clerk, treasurer – though he signs the cheques – handyman ... the boss, in fact.'

Her husband had beamed at her, in no way put out at being relegated to the status of an employee. 'I'm boss in the kitchen, though. That's how I like it.'

Rosie's fair wavy hair had a suggestion of silver about it, yet it may have been as blonde as Gwen's when she was younger. It was drawn back off her face which was devoid of any make-up yet her cheeks were a pale shade of rose and her lips were red enough in their natural state. Her face was oval like Gwen's, and even if she looked delicate, Alistair decided, she must be a strong woman. He wondered, idly, if Gwen or Marge, or both, took after her. He had often heard it said that if you wanted to know what a girl would be like in twenty or thirty years, you only had to look at her mother. He liked Rosie, even on this short acquaintance, and he wouldn't mind if the girl he loved turned out exactly the same.

It dawned on him suddenly that there should have been a third sister, and almost as if she had read his mind, Rosie said, 'You'll have to excuse Peg. She objected to not being allowed to ask a boy to tea like her older sisters, and she's taking her dinner downstairs.'

'She'll get over it,' announced Tiny, wiping his mouth with his linen napkin and pushing back his chair, extra wide and clearly made especially for him. 'Now, Dougal,' he said, 'it's time for you and me to adjourn to the residents' sitting room to get our business done. Gwennie, you had better stay here with Alistair, and Marge and Peg'll help your mother to clear up and do the dishes.'

And before he knew where he was, Alistair was left alone with Gwen. 'I feel awful, you having to stay with me while your mother and sisters are slaving away downstairs,' he whispered. 'I could easily sit here and wait till you give them a hand.'

'You don't need to whisper, nobody'll hear us. Don't you like being alone with me?'

'I'd do anything to be alone with you . . . for ever.'

She smiled and whispered, shyly, 'Why don't you make the most of it, then?'

This made him pull her off her seat and on to his knee. It wasn't exactly comfortable, two of them on one dining-room chair, but they were making the most of it when Tiny poked his head round the door. 'So this is the way things are?' he exclaimed, giving a great guffaw of laughter at the guilty way the two young people sprang apart. 'I thought it might be, but I wasn't sure. I came to let you know that Dougal has said his piece and they're all gathered in our sitting room, but ... Alistair, I think you and I should have a little talk, too? Off you go, Gwennie, this won't take long.'

Wishing that the floor would open up and swallow him, the trembling, scarlet-faced Alistair was sure that the man would tear him apart for daring to kiss his eldest daughter so fervently. 'I'm very sorry, Mr Jenkins,' he began, the words quavering slightly, 'I shouldn't have ...'

'So you think I'm going to bawl you out? You look like a rookie in front of the ser'nt major. Good God, Alistair, I was young once myself, hard as it may be to believe. I took advantage of every opportunity I could to kiss a pretty girl, and, even if I say so myself, my Gwennie, like my other two daughters, is a very pretty girl. In fact, I'd go as far as say I'd have been disappointed in you if you hadn't kissed her, but there's kissing and there's kissing, if you see what I mean, and you were a bit too ... you're serious about her, aren't you?'

'Yes, I am, Mr Jenkins ...'

'Tiny, for goodness' sake! Mr Jenkins sounds like I'm a preacher.'

'I *am* serious about Gwen ... Tiny. I love her, and I mean to marry her some day, when I can afford to support a wife.'

'Is money the only reason you're holding back?'

'Of course it is. I'll have to find a house and furnish it ...'

Tiny pulled thoughtfully at his earlobe. 'I think we had better join the others. What I had planned to say to Dougal will apply equally to you, so listen carefully.'

Alistair followed him through to the back room, where a magenta-faced Dougal was standing holding Marge's hand, while Peggy and her mother, both smiling expectantly, were sitting on a long sofa with Gwen, who lifted her downcast head as the two men entered and eyed her father with some apprehension.

He let his eyes roam around them before plumping down on what was meant to be a two-seater couch but he filled it completely. 'I've just had a bit of a surprise,' he said, finally. 'I had prepared a little speech saying I was giving my blessing on a marriage between my daughter, Marjory, and Dougal Finnie, a young Scot . . .'

He was interrupted by the clamour of his family voicing their congratulations to the happy pair, and had the grace to wait until things were quiet again before he continued. 'I was going to say I was looking forward to having Dougal as a son-in-law and give him a few words of advice, but . . .' He looked round the assembly once again, stopping when he came to the nervous Alistair, who had taken up his stance beside Gwen, and letting out another of his deep belly laughs. 'I'm not a blinking cannibal, boy, so don't look as if I was ready to throw you in a pot.'

Rosie stepped in now. 'Get on with it, Tiny. It's not fair to keep them in suspense.'

'This is a moment I'm going to cherish all my life,' he told her, 'so let me proceed at my own pace.' First grinning reassuringly at Alistair, he directed his words at Dougal. 'The thing is, I cannot let Marge go. I need her here, because I would never get another girl to act as waitress-cum-chambermaid-cum-kitchenmaid as my three do. No one else would put up with me, the way I order them about, but as I always say, what's the good of keeping three dogs and barking yourself?'

Dougal was looking aghast. 'But Tiny, you said . . . you gave your permission . . .'

'And I meant it, every word, but . . . you can't take her away. You will move in here. As I see it, you'll be

66

sharing her room without having to pay a penny for rent, getting all your meals without having to stump up for board . . .'

'What's the catch?' Dougal's eyes had narrowed. 'There must be something.'

'You will do any odd jobs that need doing, decorating, moving furniture and any heavy lifting, but only in the evenings and weekends. I'm not expecting you to give up your job. And that's it!' Tiny turned to Alistair now. 'You heard what I said to Dougal, so is there something *you* want to ask me? Or would you rather do it in private?'

Gwen's hand-squeeze was enough for Alistair. 'We don't need to do it in private. I would be grateful if you would give your permission for me to marry Gwen, maybe next year some time?'

'Next year?' Tiny erupted. 'I'm giving you the chance to make it a double wedding! It'll save putting two lots of stress on my wife and be less of a financial strain on me. We'd have everything over in one go and the hotel would get back to normal.' Noticing Alistair's sudden pallor, he said, 'You're not getting cold feet are you?'

Rosie stood up at this point. 'Give the boy a chance to get his breath back. Come on, Peggy, help me to make some coffee.'

'No, Mrs Jenkins . . . Rosie,' Alistair corrected, because of her slight frown, 'don't bother. I don't need time to think. I love Gwen, and I think she loves me . . .'

The girl blushed to the roots of her hair but said, firmly, 'Yes, Mum, I do love him.'

'And if Tiny wants a double wedding,' Alistair went on, still addressing his future mother-in-law, 'I can't see any problem . . . if *you* don't object.'

'I'm delighted,' she beamed, 'but we'll need a few weeks to prepare everything.'

Tiny took over again. 'We'll ask the vicar how soon he can fit in the wedding . . .'

'The banns'll have to be called for three weeks running,' Rosie pointed out, 'and it's too late for tomorrow to be the first time, so it'll be next Sunday and the two after that.'

'So we'll make it in four weeks, boys. That'll give us enough time . . .' His wife's frantic signal made Tiny stop to amend this. 'Five weeks from today apparently, to please my dear Rosie. Does that suit you?'

It was Gwen who made the decision. 'That's perfect, Dad. Marge and I can choose our wedding gowns together, and there'll be time for alterations if they're needed.'

'The wedding breakfast will be here in the hotel, so nothing too fancy, eh?'

'Can I go with them and get my dress, as well?' queried Peggy. 'I'll be bridesmaid for both of them, won't I, and I'll have to look nice.'

Thinking that a new dress would save her youngest daughter taking umbrage again, her mother nodded.

'How many will I have to cater for?' Tiny wanted to know. 'Just family, isn't it?'

'And Dougal and Alistair's families, as well,' Rosie reminded him.

Neither of the young men commented on this until they were on their way back to Hackney. 'I don't know what my mother's going to say about this,' Alistair declared. 'I haven't even told her I've been seeing Gwen.'

Dougal pulled a face. 'She likely knows by now. I told my Mam in my last letter and she'll likely have told yours.'

'The wedding'll not come as such a surprise, then, thank goodness.'

Manny Isaacson was delighted by Alistair's news. 'I'm so

happy for you, my boy. I was rather selfish, you know, hoping that you would not be looking for another job with more pay so that you could afford to marry your Gwen, but this seems an ideal arrangement for everyone concerned. However, there is one thing you have not touched on. Are you not thinking of giving Gwen an engagement ring? She might feel envious of her sister . . .'

'Gwen's not the jealous kind.'

'Nevertheless, I think that she should have one, and nothing would give me greater pleasure than to . . .'

'No, Manny,' Alistair interrupted. 'I won't let you *give* me one, but maybe you're right. Maybe I *should* get her an engagement ring, but I want to pay for it myself.'

The older man lifted his shoulders and turned up his palms in the expressive manner Alistair had come to recognize as a Jewish gesture. 'I do not have much of a selection at the moment, but it should not take long to pick up something decent and reasonable.'

That very afternoon, Manny returned to the shop beaming as if he had lost a penny and found a pound. 'It was like a miracle, Alistair,' he told his assistant. 'You've heard me talking about young Bill Jackson? He took over his father's stall in the Portobello Road last year, if you remember. I was telling him I was looking for an engagement ring, not too expensive but not rubbish, you know? And he said he had the very thing. It seems the nephew of an old lady who had recently died was disposing of some of her belongings, and he said he didn't need the money, just wanted to be rid of them. Young Bill, a genuine man if ever there was one, gave him ten shillings for the lot, believing that what they held would be fit only for scrap. So you can imagine his amazement when he opened the second crate, to find a jewellery box with several pieces of jewellery in it, at least two of the rings, even to his inexperienced eyes, worth more than ten pounds, never mind ten shillings, as he put it.

'He had sought out the nephew to acquaint him of this fact, but all he said was, "Keep them, and count this your lucky day." So I asked Bill what he wanted for the two rings, and he let me take them on spec. Whichever one you pick, he said he'll be quite happy if you give him ten bob for it, which is what he paid for the whole lot, remember, and I can assure you, Alistair, that each is worth in the region of one hundred pounds.'

'But are you sure you're not spinning me this yarn to make me feel . . . ?'

'No, my boy, I am telling you the absolute truth, and if you are wondering why young Bill . . .' Manny paused with a chuckle. 'I call him young Bill because I knew his father, but he must be over fifty and a dyed-in-the wool romantic. That is why he is making this gesture, and to show how much he trusts my judgement of you, he said you can let your young lady choose for herself.'

Gwen happened to be on duty that evening, and so the excited Alistair took the rings to Guilford Street to let her have her pick. She exclaimed over both of them then said she couldn't allow him to buy her anything so expensive, and was dumbstruck when he told her the story behind them. 'Take the one you like best,' he urged. 'I'll never get a chance like this again.'

Shaking her head in awe, she tried each one on the third finger of her left hand in turn and admired it from all angles, saying, 'I can't make up my mind, Alistair. I thought the solitaire diamond at first, it catches the light so well, then I wanted to have the three smaller stones . . . what do you think?'

'I'd say the solitaire looks a bit big on your finger, your hands are so dainty, but it's for you to choose.'

'Take that one back to Manny then, and thank him for thinking about us, and ... oh, yes. Tell him to thank the other man, too ... I can hardly believe it, Alistair. I wasn't expecting to get an engagement ring, but I adore it.'

'I'm not taking it for ten shillings, of course. I'll give him thirty, like Dougal ...' He halted, appalled at giving away his friend's secret. 'Oh, I shouldn't have told you that, Gwen. Promise you won't let Marge know.'

'I promise, though I don't think she'd mind, any more than I do. We know you two don't get big wages, and thirty shillings is quite a lot.'

His heart aching with love for her, he had to kiss her for understanding.

'What's got into you the day, Lexie?' Her body getting frailer by the day, Carrie Fraser could still glare at her daughter. 'You've been snapping my head off ever since you came ben from the shop.'

The girl sat down at the side of her mother's bed. 'Bella Ritchie was saying her Alistair and Dougal Finnie's having a double wedding.'

Carrie frowned accusingly. 'You never said Alistair was going steady.'

'I didn't know, and neither did Bella till this morning.'

'Oh aye?' A knowing smile flitted across the invalid's pain-lined face. 'A sudden wedding, eh? A bairn on the road, likely.'

Lexie had been wrestling with this unwelcome thought ever since Alistair's mother had left the shop that afternoon, and she still refused to believe it. 'It's Dougal's girl's sister,' she muttered, miserably.

'What difference does that make?'

'Bella says the double wedding was their father's idea. He

doesn't want two upheavals in his hotel, so Alistair's been rushed into it.' Although this was not exactly what his mother had said, it was the only explanation the spurned girl could accept.

'Will·the Ritchies be going to London with the Finnies, to see the weddings?'

'Bella says they've been invited but they can't afford the train fare.'

'They could take the boat, like Alistair and Dougal.'

'She says she's terrified of water. The very idea of being on a boat makes her sick.'

Carrie nodded. 'That'll just be an excuse. She likely doesna want to go. If I'd a son, I wouldna like to see him getting led up the garden path by some painted London trollop that had trapped him into it.'

The final phrase comforted Lexie. Alistair *had* been trapped into it. He would never look at another girl unless she'd put herself out to catch him, and poor Al, he didn't like hurting folk. Still, it couldn't last. A marriage without love never did, and he'd come back to Forvit ready to fall into the arms of the girl he could trust, the girl he knew did love him, the girl who would never stop loving him.

Assuring herself of this, she suddenly felt much better. 'Ach, it's his life and he'll just have to get on with it, the same as I'll have to get on with mine. Do you fancy a cheese pudding for your supper?'

Carrie slept even less than normal that night. Lexie was taking Alistair's wedding far too calmly. She couldn't still think he'd come back to her? A marriage was for life, no matter how bad it was. This was proof that Alistair had meant it when he said he was going to settle in London and Lexie would just have to accept it. He wasn't the kind of man who would break the vows he'd have to make.

Alec had stood by his vows, Carrie told herself, until the memory of what he had done hit her again, then something occurred to her that hadn't entered her head before. Had Tom Birnie told him she would never get better of what ailed her? Had he not been able to bear the thought of her dying and him having to face life without her? Aye, that was it. That was why he had run away.

The mental and physical suffering she had endured since that terrible night had made her neurotic and overemotional, and the tears of relief that burst from her now verged on the hysterical, but in no time at all Lexie was there with her, cradling her like she was a bairn, shushing her and telling her not to worry.

'If you think I'll go to pieces because Alistair Ritchie's taking a wife, you're wrong, Mam! It was a shock at first, but I'm over it, and everything's going to be all right. Shut your eyes now and sleep, like a good lass.'

Lexie lay alongside her mother for the rest of the night, assuring herself, over and over again, that everything *would* be all right for her. Alistair was being pushed into a union he didn't want but he would soon realize who he really loved. He'd come back to her within a year or two, and he'd make up for all the time he'd been away.

Chapter 5

❧

'You are looking very sad today, Alistair.' Manny regarded his assistant shrewdly. 'Did you have a disagreement with your young lady last night?'

'It's nothing to do with Gwen. It's a letter I got from my mother this morning. She says they can't afford to come to our wedding.'

'Ah, that explains it! You have been so looking forward to seeing them, but do not forget that it is a long long way for them to come.'

'I know, but I thought . . .' He swallowed abruptly.

'How long is it since you left home?'

'It'll be three years come October.' Alistair knuckled his eyes as if to rid them of an irritation – an almost nineteen-year-old man dared not be seen to cry – then went on, 'But there it is . . . one of the hurdles life sometimes puts in our paths.'

'You are too young for such philosophy, my boy.' Manny felt so deeply for him that he could not concentrate on the market stalls that forenoon. He had intended to look for something unique as a wedding gift, but nothing he saw fitted the bill, and he gave up well before midday.

On his way back to his shop, however, a wonderful idea struck him. It would be a gift *par excellence*, a gift sure to please Alistair – and seeing him truly happy was certain to please his bride. But – and it was a but looming menacingly in the wings – would the boy accept it as it was meant, or would he consider it a hand-out? He was so touchy about that sort of thing.

When he entered his premises, the pawnbroker locked the door and turned the cardboard placard to 'CLOSED', saying, 'I want to talk to you without anyone interrupting us.'

Perplexed and apprehensive, Alistair followed him into the little back room – Manny's bedroom, living room and kitchen, the lavatory was in the tiny back yard – where they usually sat to have their lunch-time snack, always on the alert in case a customer walked into the shop, although there was no risk of that today.

Manny waited until a mug of tea was set in front of him. 'I have been doing some thinking, Alistair,' he began, 'and don't go jumping in bull-headed until I have finished what I have to say. Unhappiness is not a good companion, nor is it conducive to full attention to whatever work is in hand, and that applies to me as well as to you. I have been puzzling over what to give you as a wedding gift . . .'

'There's no need for you to give us anything!' Alistair butted in.

'There is perhaps no need, but it is something I want to do. When a young couple are setting up house, it is expected that relatives and friends will give bed linen, kitchen utensils, anything which would be of use in a home, but it is different in your case. You will be living in a hotel, with everything you need readily available to you, and so I have been looking for something, an antique perhaps, I was not sure what but I was sure that I would know it was right when I came across it. Sadly, I have seen nothing.'

'It doesn't matter, Manny,' Alistair muttered as the old man took a sip of tea. 'We don't need . . .'

'Let me finish,' his employer scolded. 'On the way back, it came to me – a gift without parallel! Return tickets to London for your parents and sister.'

Alistair shook his head angrily. 'No, I can't let you do that, Manny.'

'You are flinging my gift back in my face, hmm? I believe it to be the best I could possibly have thought of, and the milk has been spilt ...' He smiled at the young man's bewilderment. 'The tickets are already bought and the seats reserved. You see, hmm? Consider, also, how your Gwen would feel if none of your family comes to your wedding. She will not want a groom standing miserably by her side wishing that his mother was there. Furthermore, so that she will not feel left out, she can come to the shop and choose a necklace or something of the kind which will be my gift to her.'

Despite his advanced age, Alistair could no longer hold back the tears, but they were tears of happiness, of gratitude, of love for this old man who had been like a father to him since the very day they met.

The twenty-eighth day of September 1932 dawned as bright and warm as a day in the middle of July, and there was pandemonium in the Crocker household as four adults made themselves ready for the big occasion – Rosie Jenkins having decided that it would be nice to invite the grooms' landlady and her husband as guests. Alistair would have loved to ask Manny, too, but he could see that it would cause difficulties, because Dougal couldn't invite all the people who worked with him. With only one bathroom – there was a dividing wall between it and the lavatory, thankfully – Len said he'd do his ablutions in the scullery, as long as nobody came in and saw him washing his 'naughty bits'.

Ivy joked that she wouldn't mind who saw her 'naughty bits', which made them all laugh, although it gave Alistair cause to worry. He knew nothing of a woman's 'naughty bits' and maybe Gwen wasn't as innocent as he thought. Hadn't

Marge told Dougal ages ago that her sister had been let down by some bloke when she was younger? But she'd have told him, wouldn't she? She wasn't the kind to hide anything as serious as that. She was bound to know he would find out . . . on their wedding night. Tonight.

Ready first and waiting, a tight bundle of nerves, for Dougal to tie a satisfactory knot in his tie, Alistair's thoughts strayed to the previous evening, when they had met their families at King's Cross – the better-off Finnies had been quite happy to spend money on fares to see their son being married. The reunions had been very emotional after such a long separation, hugs and kisses (unusual for Scots) exchanged tearfully on the platform, and then they all piled into a large hackney carriage to be transported to Guilford Street, where Rosie had seen to making rooms ready for the important visitors.

The meeting of relatives and soon-to-be-in-laws had gone off very well, Alistair recalled, everyone taking to everyone else, and his mother had even found an opportunity to whisper that she was pleased he was marrying such a nice girl. 'She'll make you a good wife,' she had added, 'so you make sure you treat her right.' He would have married Gwen supposing the verdict had gone the other way, of course, but it was better that it was so favourable.

He was brought back to the present by Dougal's loud sigh of satisfaction. 'Thank the Lord, that's it straight now. You know this, Ally, I'm in a right old state! I don't know how you can look so calm.'

'Maybe I *look* calm,' Alistair mumbled, 'but I don't *feel* calm.'

The last five minutes, waiting for the cab which would convey them to the Register Office where the ceremony was to take place, seemed an eternity to both young men, but Ivy, looking very smart in a midnight blue grosgrain suit and matching straw hat, stopped nerves getting the better of them. 'I don't know what I'm going to do without you two handsome blokes,' she giggled. 'I'll have nobody to share my bed now when you're away, Len.'

Knowing his wife's propensity for exaggeration, he gave a hearty guffaw. 'They wouldn't have come anywhere near you, Ivy, and . . .' he pretended to scowl, 'if they had, I'd have knocked their ruddy blocks off.'

Ivy chuckled again. 'A girl can dream, can't she?'

The arrival of the taxi put an end to the conversation, and they were soon being borne as swiftly as possible through London's rush-hour traffic.

Breakfast was an embarrassing time in the hotel for at least four of the people round the table the following morning. As Dougal confided to Alistair on their way back from seeing their families off that evening, 'I didn't think it would bother me, but I felt awful sitting there with them all knowing what Marge and me had been up to. Oh boy, what a time we had, hardly a wink of sleep all night. How did you get on?'

'We were the same.' Alistair had no wish to discuss the rapturous hours he and Gwen had spent in their first taste of sexual intercourse, for he had discovered, to his infinite relief, that his bride was still a virgin.

'My Mam and Dad were really taken with Marge,' Dougal observed after a minute.

'Mine were taken with Gwen and all,' Alistair was happy to say. 'It's a pity we're so far away, though. I'd have liked to show her round the Forvit area.'

'I promised Mam I'd take Marge up for a holiday in the spring. We could all go together . . . oh no. The girls wouldn't get off at the same time, of course.'

'I couldn't afford it, any road. Gwen wants us to save

as much as we can, in case babies start coming ... you know ... ?'

'Oh, I see.' Dougal seemed taken aback at her planning for this at so early a stage.

'I might manage to take her away somewhere for a few days, though – Kent, maybe. I've heard it's lovely there.'

'Aye, that would be nice. Em ... Ally, how d'you think we'll get on in the hotel?'

'What d'you mean, get on?'

'Well, we're bound to feel like two goldfish in a bowl with everybody watching us. I did tell Tiny I wanted to buy our own wee house, not too far away so Marge could still work for him, but he wouldn't hear of it.'

'Ach, we'll get used to it.'

'We'll have no privacy, that's what I'll miss.'

Alistair grinned. 'We hadn't much privacy at Ivy's, either. She always liked to know everything we were doing.'

'Aye well, but that was different. I wasn't wanting to take you to bed every spare minute you had, like I'll be with Marge.'

'You knew what you were taking on, and you'll just have to put up with it.'

'How did the wedding go?'

'It was just perfect, Lexie.' Unaware that she was turning the screws on her listener's tortured heart, Bella Ritchie gave a full description of her visit to London, breaking off if another customer came in and carrying on again afterwards as if there had been no interruption. 'It was different, wi' two brides. I thought they'd be dressed the same, being sisters, but they're nothing like each other. Dougal's wife, Marge, she's the bouncy kind, full o' life, and she's dark-haired like him, though I'd say hers is even curlier. Gwen, now, that's

Alistair's wife, her hair's a lovely blonde, natural like yours, nae like some I saw doon there, and it shines pale gold in the electric light. Her face is thinner than her sister's and she's a lot quieter, but they're real nice lassies, though I didna understand half o' what they said, they spoke that quick. Mind you, they'd a job makin' my Willie oot, for he couldna think on the English for what he wanted to say.'

'But you managed to get on with . . . Gwen?'

'Nae bother! I couldna have wished for a better . . .' About to say 'a better daughter-in-law', Bella finally remembered how attached Lexie had been to Alistair before he went away and caught her runaway tongue. '. . . a better day,' she substituted, clumsily. 'Sun shining and an awful lot warmer than it is up here. And the Jenkinses is just like ony o' us. Nae side to them though they've got a fine big hotel. There's a younger sister, and all, Peggy her name is, and the three o' them work there, waitressing, cleaning the rooms and such like, good workers, they are.'

'Oh aye?' Lexie felt obliged to make some kind of comment.

'Rosie, their mother, she's a right nice soul, slim like them and quiet, but it's my opinion she rules the roost, though her man wouldna like folk to think that. He was the biggest surprise we got. You should have seen him, Lexie . . . a great fat mountain o' a man, and he does all the cooking sitting on a stool in the kitchen in the basement. The meal – the wedding breakfast they cried it though we didna sit doon till four o'clock – oh, I canna tell you how good it was. Willie said it was the kind o' soup he likes best, the kind you can stand your spoon up in, I canna tak' him nae place, then he said the fancy stuffing wi' the roasted turkey went round his heart like a hairy worm, and I coulda kicked him, but they seemed pleased aboot it.'

'They likely took it as a compliment.'

'Aye, and so it was meant . . . if they understood it.'

'Was it a kirk wedding?'

'No, no! It was in a Register Office, then back to the hotel in taxis. Mind, I'd've been happier if it had been a kirk wedding, but . . . ach, I suppose that's the English way o' doing it, and the registrar had us a' in tears at the gentle way he advised them to respect their vows, even Tiny, that's Alistair's father-in-law . . .'

'Tiny?' Lexie gave a brittle laugh. 'That's a funny name if he's so fat.'

'It was a nickname he got in the army. To get back to my story, Gwen being the oldest daughter, her and Alistair was wed first – she'll be nineteen next month the same as him. Dougal was best man and young Peggy, I think she's fifteen or sixteen, she was bridesmaid for her two sisters, and Dougal had Alistair for *his* best man.'

'What were the brides wearing?' The poor girl couldn't help but prolong the agony; she was so anxious to know as much as she could.

'Well, Marge was in a sky-blue crepe-di-Chine dress, fitted bodice wi' a gored skirt – I was surprised she'd chose blue when her eyes are so dark brown, but it really suited her. Gwen looked a picture in a deep pink two-piece, moygashel, I think it was, and Peggy had a plain cream . . . no, darker than cream, more biscuit – plain linen kind of frock wi' a Peter Pan collar. Rosie had on a navy costume wi' a velvet collar, very smart, wi' a white blouse and a white straw hat.'

'And was there any other guests . . . besides you three and the Finnies?'

'Mr and Mrs Crocker was there, them the boys lodged wi', nice woman Ivy is, and all, maybe a bit ower much to say, but she was friendly enough. That was the lot.'

'I'd have thought Alistair would've invited his boss. Alice said it was him that paid your fares.'

'The Jenkinses just wanted a quiet family do. But Mr Isaacson – Manny, he likes to be cried – he came to King's Cross to introduce himself when we were coming hame; he's a proper gentleman. He's the first Jew I ever met, and if they're a' like him, I dinna ken where folk get the idea they're oot to rob everybody. I tried to tell him how grateful I was to him for sending us the tickets, but he said he'd bought them as a wedding present for Alistair, because he'd been that disappointed we werena going. That's the kind of man he is, like I said, a real gentleman. And Rosie and Tiny wouldna tak' onything for letting us bide there for the two nights, so we've had a right treat and it didna cost us a brass farthing.'

Having exhausted her subject, Bella said, breathlessly, 'I'm forgetting to ask. How's your Mam just now?'

Lexie shook her head and gave a dismal sigh. 'She's not good. The doctor says it's just a matter of weeks.'

'Oh, I'm sorry, lass, and me raving on like that about the wedding. Can I do anything to help you, Lexie? Would you like me to come and sit wi' her sometimes?'

'Thanks, Bella, but her sister came up from Perth on Sunday for a fortnight. I doubt if she'd know you, anyway. She doesn't know me, sometimes. I think I'll need to get somebody into the shop when my Auntie Mina goes home, so I'll have more time to look after Mam.'

'Poor Carrie. Look, I could easy sit wi' her every day to let you keep working. Me and her aye got on fine.'

'It would be too much for you, Bella, walking three miles here and three miles back every day. Anyway, I don't think she'll last much longer, to be honest.'

Thus prepared, Bella was not surprised to hear, less than a week later, that Carrie Fraser had died in the night. It was better that she was at peace, especially for Lexie's sake. And she was glad on her own behalf, and all, Bella thought guiltily. She was so easily tired nowadays she doubted if she'd have had the energy to walk to the village to sit with the poor woman, never mind walk back.

When he arrived at work about two weeks after the wedding, Alistair's solemn face prompted Manny to say, 'Have you and Gwen had words?'

'No, no. I just learned that the girl I used to go with at home . . . her mother died.'

'Ah! And you have discovered that you still feel a little something for her?'

'I . . . I feel sorry for her, that's all. Carrie Fraser was a real nice woman, and Lexie's left on her own now.'

'You are having regrets, hmm?'

'I'll never regret marrying Gwen, but . . . ach, Lexie'll be free to find somebody else now. She was a nice enough girl, just a bit overpowering, if you know what I mean?'

'She was too pushy? She wanted you to make a full commitment?'

'That's right, and I wasn't ready for it. We were just sixteen.'

'And now, at the ripe old age of nineteen, you are a happily married man.' Manny threw back his head and laughed.

'I *am* happily married,' Alistair retorted, a little put out by his employer's amusement, 'and even if I'd never left Forvit, Lexie still wouldn't have got me to marry her. She was bad enough before, but after her father walked out, she was ten times worse.'

Manny's smile vanished. 'Her father walked out? It is not surprising, then, that the girl was a little unbalanced. Why did he go? He must have had a reason, poor man.' He shook his head mournfully.

'There was rumours he'd run away with a girl he'd put

83

in the family way, but the folk that knew him best found that hard to believe, for he was a good-living man – elder in the kirk, trained the choir, and he'd not long taken over the treasurer's job.'

Manny stroked his beard. 'Would he have been in financial difficulties?'

'There was no money missing. They got auditors in to make sure, but it was all in order, and so were his own accounts in the shop and the post office.'

'No outstanding debts?'

'Nothing! It's a complete mystery.' Alistair's sigh was long and slightly ragged. 'Now this! Poor Lexie, I hope it doesn't push her over the edge.'

Manny hastily changed the subject. 'How is *your* dear mother?'

'She's fine, as usual, running after Dad and Alice . . .'

'As she had run after you when you were at home, no doubt?'

Alistair grinned now. 'Aye, that's right.'

Having seen her Auntie Mina on to the bus for Aberdeen where she would catch the train to Perth, Lexie lay back in her chair. She should feel utterly exhausted after the stir of the funeral, but it was as if she were floating on air. She had no one to worry about except herself now that her mother's suffering was at an end. It would be a perfect situation if only Alistair Ritchie hadn't left. He would have married her now, and they would have lived happily ever after. But Alistair had gone to London, and he hadn't had time to tire of his bride, so it would be useless to give up everything to go down there after him.

Feeling a tear trickling down her cheek, Lexie wiped it away angrily with her forefinger. Why should she cry? She hadn't given up on him yet. Give it another year or two, and things could be different.

Tiny attacked the pastry violently with the rolling pin. 'I should have known!' he stormed. 'All the ruddy Jocks I ever knew were randy buggers! The trouble was, I thought it would be Dougal who'd strike home first, but it's my Gwennie that's been nobbled and it's only nine weeks since the bloody wedding. Surely Alistair could have waited a year or two before he filled her belly.'

'Calm yourself, Tiny,' cautioned Rosie. 'Do you want the girls to hear you?'

'I don't care who hears me.' Nevertheless, he did lower his voice. 'I can't run this place without Gwennie.'

'You managed with just two before Peggy left school.'

Tiny made a rude noise. 'Gwennie's worth Marge and Peg put together, as you know perfectly well.'

'Well, it's done now and you can't do a thing about it.' Thinking that it would be wise to issue a caution, Rosie continued, 'Don't say anything nasty to Alistair, or criticize him to Gwen. At least they waited till after the wedding to start their family.'

'Good God, Rosie! You don't think he'd been at her before they were married? I'll knock his teeth down his ruddy throat if he had!'

'For heaven's sake! I don't for one second think that, so take it easy! Your face is as red as a beetroot. You'll give yourself a heart attack if you're not careful.'

'Could you blame me?'

'Yes, I'd blame you! Gwen'll be able to work practically to the time of the birth, provided you don't make her do anything strenuous. And with four women in the place, there'll be no shortage of nurses for the little one when it's born.'

85

Her husband glared at her in exasperation. 'You're looking forward to this . . . to being a grandma, aren't you?'

'I certainly am.' Rosie gave a rapturous sigh. 'And when you're a grandpa, you'll feel exactly the same.'

His whole attitude changed now. 'I suppose so,' he grinned. 'I can see me in a year or so, dandling a little boy on my knee . . .'

'There's no room on your knee for anything except your fat stomach,' chuckled his wife. 'You'd better stop tasting everything a dozen times, so you'll lose some of that blubber and have room for your grandchild.'

Deeming this not worth a reply, Tiny contented himself by flinging a dish towel at her.

Chapter 6

In May 1933, when Alistair received the telegram saying that his mother had died, it was so unexpected it almost tore him apart. She had never given the slightest hint in her letters that she was ill, and he hadn't suspected a thing when she was in London for his wedding. It placed him in a proper quandary. His father and Alice would expect him to go home for the funeral, but how could he leave Gwen when she was so near her time?

'Mum says first babies are usually late,' she assured him, 'and you'll only be away for a few days. In any case, if it does come early, I've all my family to look after me.'

Everyone told him he should go, but it was Dougal who clinched it, observing with his usual candour, 'What could you do even supposing you *are* here when the labour starts? You'd likely panic, and put Gwen in a panic, and all. No, Ally, that kind of thing's best left to the women, they know what to do . . . well, Rosie does. She's had three.'

On arriving in Benview, Alistair was dismayed at the change in his father. His face was drawn, his back bowed, his eyes red-rimmed and dull. 'Is Dad all right?' he asked Alice, realizing as he spoke that she, too, was looking haggard.

'He's taking it bad,' she murmured, 'though we knew it was coming, for the doctor said the bout of flu we thought she was getting over had left her so weak she couldn't fight the infection she picked up. Even if you know something's inevitable, you can't believe it's really going to happen, and when it does, it comes as an awful shock ... like God's betrayed you. I know it sounds silly, but I'm sure Dad feels the same. And he's going to feel a lot worse after the funeral and he's left on his own.'

'Oh, my God, aye!' In the sorrow which had threatened to fell him, Alistair had given no thought to what would happen afterwards. 'Will he manage by himself?'

'He says he will.' There was a brief silence before she added, 'I said I'd forget about going to 'varsity, even if I've passed the prelims, but he wouldn't hear of it.'

'You can't do that, Alice. Mam and him wanted you to get some kind of degree, so you could have a professional career. They couldn't afford to put me through university, and in any case, it was you that was the clever one.'

'I'm not bothered about having a career. I'd rather stay at home and look after Dad. It's what I want to do, Alistair,' she said quickly as he opened his mouth to argue. 'I've no ambitions. I don't want to be a doctor or a solicitor or a teacher. I just want to get married and have a family ... maybe two boys and two girls, and keeping house for Dad would be good practice for me.'

'But you're not eighteen yet, Alice ...' The force of her glare stopped him telling her what a mistake she was making. It was her life to do with as she wanted. After all, hadn't he given up a steady job himself to go to London?

The ordeal of the funeral was only fractionally more harrowing than facing Lexie Fraser again. He had known she'd be there, of course – she'd always been friendly with his mother – and he had primed himself to treat her as if they'd never been anything more than school friends, but it wasn't so easy. Most of the people there believed that they had once been sweethearts if not lovers, and when he went over and shook hands with her, he could sense the knowing glances that were being exchanged behind his back. Worse still, he was so emotional anyway that his heart beat a little faster when she clung to his hand and regarded him with eyes moist with tears. Thankfully, she'd had to move away to let someone else voice their condolences and ask how he was getting on in London, and he was kept thus occupied until the minister arrived to say a prayer over the open coffin.

When the men returned from the interment in the kirkyard, Alice took her brother aside. 'Lexie's in an awful state,' she whispered. 'You'd better walk her home.'

He looked across to where Lexie was sitting forlornly in a corner, dabbing at her eyes with what looked like a sodden handkerchief, and was almost swamped by a surge of pity for her. It did flit across his mind that she could get a lift from the doctor, the one who had taken over after Doctor Birnie left, but it was really up to him to make sure she got home all right. He owed her that.

He was disconcerted by the way her face lit up when he made his offer, but once it was said, he couldn't take it back, and his father nodded gratefully as they went out.

'How's he keeping?' she asked as they set off on the three-mile walk.

'Not too good. They'd been married for nearly twenty-five years, you know, and he's going to miss her.'

'Aye, he's bound to. It's a long time.'

Their conversation, as they strolled along, revolved mainly around people they had both known, and he was thankful that she confined herself to answering his questions, and not asking him anything personal. It had to come, of course.

They were approaching the track to the tower when she looked askance at him. 'Do you remember when we used to go up there at nights?'

He didn't want to be reminded, but he couldn't tell her so. 'We'd some nice walks.'

'Nice walks? Oh, Al, you surely haven't forgotten how you used to kiss me?'

'I haven't forgotten,' he muttered. He hadn't thought about it while he'd been in London, but being with her again brought it back, the youthful, innocent kisses, given solely to find out what kissing a girl felt like, though if Lexie hadn't been so pushy, so forward, there was no saying what it might have led to. But she had spoiled it . . . and put him off girls for years.

'I never had another lad,' she said, coyly, 'not even when you took a wife.'

His wife was something he felt safe to talk about. 'I'd have liked you to meet Gwen. She was sorry she couldn't come up with me, but it was too far for her to travel. It's just a couple of weeks till our baby's due.'

'Your Mam said she was expecting.'

She stopped walking, abruptly, as if she had come to a sudden decision. 'Will you take me up to the tower again? Please, Al, just this one last time . . . for old times' sake?'

A coldness swept over him. 'I'd rather not, Lexie. I'm married now, and . . .'

'Being married shouldn't stop you from being friends with me. Come on, Al. I thought . . . you know I lost my mother, and all?'

'Yes, I know,' he replied stiffly, angry at her for taking advantage of the situation and annoyed at himself for forgetting that it was only a few months since Carrie's death.

'I need some . . . affection, Al . . . please? I don't want you to kiss me, or anything like that, just walk with me so I'll have that to remember. Or are you too high and mighty now you live in London and speak like you'd a plum in your mouth?'

There were tears in her eyes again, real tears, and he guessed that she was masking her vulnerability by being sarcastic. Poor Lexie. She was right. She had nobody now, and why shouldn't he take her up to the tower . . . for old times' sake? 'Come on then,' he said, albeit a trifle brusquely.

She walked decorously by his side, wanting to know more about his wife, about his in-laws, and he answered as best he could until she asked what they were going to call the baby. He and Gwen had not discussed the matter of names. 'If it's a boy, I'd like to call him Douglas,' he said, after a moment's consideration. 'That would be after Dougal, you see, for he's been a true friend to me all our lives. If it's a girl . . .' He paused, then shrugged. 'I haven't thought about that.'

'What about Alexandra?' she suggested, smiling.

'I don't think that'd be a good idea.'

'Why not? I've been a true friend to you, and all, more than a friend, and it would make me truly happy, Al.'

'No, Lexie, I can't. It wouldn't be fair to Gwen.'

'Haven't you told her about me?'

'There was nothing to tell, was there? It was all in your mind.'

'Oh, Al, how could you say a thing like that?' Bursting into a flood of tears, she whipped round and ran back down the hill.

He didn't chase her, but tried not to let too great a distance develop between them. He had to keep his eye on her in case she did anything silly, because she was obviously on the verge of some kind of breakdown.

It wasn't long until she slowed down to a walk and he caught up with her. 'I'm sorry, Lexie,' he said. 'I *have* always looked on you as a friend . . . just a friend, though, but Gwen might think there was more to it if I wanted to call our baby after you. Can you not understand that? How would you like it if you were married and your husband wanted to call your daughter after his old girlfriend?'

'So you still think of me as a girlfriend?'

Her voice was so low that he had to bend his head to hear. 'Well, we did go together for a good few months.' He knew he shouldn't have said it. He should have made it clear that he meant a girl friend, not a girlfriend. There was a world of difference, but now wasn't the time to be brutal.

They walked on in silence for some time, then Lexie murmured, 'I'm awful tired, Alistair. Would you mind if I took your arm?'

He did mind, but all he could do was shake his head, so she tucked her hand under his arm, hanging on as if she were totally exhausted, as quite possibly she was, he mused, compassion for her welling up in him again. His mother's funeral was bound to have distressed her by reminding her of her own mother's death, and she had nothing to look forward to when she went home except empty rooms. He had no idea how it happened, but when they reached the two-storeyed house at the rear of what had been her father's shop but which she had run for a few years now, his arm was round her waist, and she was saying, as she fitted her key into the lock, 'You'll come in for a cup of tea?'

The fire was set but not lit, and although the May evening was quite warm outside, there was a chill inside – no feeling of welcome. It was the first time he had ever been inside her home, but this room wasn't all that different from his mother's kitchen. There was an almost identical oak dresser with ornaments in its small pigeonholes, a few china plaques on the walls expressing various Victorian sentiments, several pot plants here and there, a fender round the fire with a padded stool at each end and a high-backed armchair at both sides of the hearth. There was one difference, though. Where the Ritchies had a neat tartan rug thrown over their worn couch, Carrie Fraser had used an old curtain, faded so much by the sun that it looked as if it were striped – a washed-out crimson and a pinkish white.

Flopping down on this, Lexie gave a sigh and stretched out her legs. 'Oh, Al, I'm sorry I forgot. It wasn't worth lighting the fire when I was going to be out all day, but once I put a match to it, the kettle'll not take long to boil.'

He pushed away the insidious thought that she *had* remembered that the fire wasn't lit and this was an excuse to keep him with her a little longer. She was so upset, it wasn't fair to doubt her. 'I'll light it.' He took a box of matches from his jacket pocket, struck one and held it to the paper in the grate. After blowing on it for a few seconds to make sure it was properly kindled, he turned to her again. 'Would you mind if I smoked?'

'I always loved the smell of your cigarettes,' she smiled, 'so sit down beside me and smoke as many as you want.'

Unwilling to upset her by sitting anywhere else, he edged down on the couch, lit one of his Gold Flakes and leaned back. He'd had a gruelling day himself and was glad of the rest. 'Never mind about making tea,' he told her in a minute. 'I'd better not stay, or Dad and Alice'll think I'm lost. I'll just finish this and get going.' He looked around for an ashtray but couldn't see one.

Lexie understood his predicament. 'Just put your ash in the begonia,' she told him. 'There's no rush for you to get home, is there? I'd be glad of a bit of company for a while, for I feel a bit lost.' She turned to him, appealing, 'Please, Al?'

Even in the dimness of the kitchen, he could see the anguish in her pale blue eyes. She wasn't shamming. She *was* lonely. She *did* need comfort. And he hadn't had any real comfort himself since he came back to Forvit. His father and sister were both too wrapped up in their own grief to worry about his. 'Come here,' he said, gruffly, putting his arms round her and pulling her close.

She wasn't pushy this time. She lay against him passively, the tears trickling down her cheeks until he could stand her misery no longer. 'Oh, Lexie,' he murmured, 'I know how you're feeling. It's a terrible thing to lose your mother, but we all have to go some time.' Realizing that this was unlikely to give any solace, he made up for his insensitivity by bending his head to kiss her.

On his way home on the train next day, he was beset with shame at what had happened. It had been his fault, not Lexie's, because even now he could remember how his body had responded to the arching of her back. With Gwen being so far on in her pregnancy, he hadn't touched her for weeks and Lexie's lips were so sweet, the old remembered smell of her so heady, that he'd been utterly lost.

He had unbuttoned her blouse, kissed away her faint murmur of protest and fondled her hungrily. Oh, the bitter shame of letting lust overrule sense. She hadn't encouraged him. On the other hand, she hadn't *dis*couraged him, either, and it hadn't been until he was a hair's-breadth away from the unthinkable that it seemed to dawn on her what he was doing and she started pounding at his chest. That was when his sanity had returned.

He had almost thrown her from him and, in spite of her flood of tears and bitter pleadings not to leave her like this, he *had* left her, and had run like a wild thing until a stitch in his side forced him to stop. He had leant against a tree to get his breath back and slowly slid down until he was sitting on the mossy grass at the roadside, where he had remained for well over an hour. It had taken him that long to get himself in a fit enough state to go home. His father wouldn't have noticed anything amiss if he was flushed to the gills and looked guilty as hell, but Alice would have spotted right away that something was up and demanded to know what had happened.

They were both in bed by the time he reached Benview, and, in the morning, he was able to answer his sister's query as to why he'd been so late in coming home the night before with a half-truth. 'Lexie asked me in for a cup of tea.' He had half expected her to torment him about taking so long to drink it, but she'd let it go, thank goodness.

Feeling his eyes weary – his guilt hadn't let him sleep much – he closed them for a moment, and the next thing he knew the train had arrived at King's Cross. He'd still been awake at Newcastle, but he must have dropped off and slept through the commotion of all the other stations they'd stopped at. The rest had done him good, though; he felt better now.

On the way to Guilford Street, he came to the conclusion that he had overreacted to what he had done to Lexie. He had maybe gone a wee bit further than he should have, but he'd thought it was what she wanted. It was her own fault, and she shouldn't have got in such a state, battering at him like he was trying to kill her, though it was just as well she had. If she hadn't stopped him . . . by God it didn't bear thinking about, and thank goodness there was no chance that Gwen would ever hear about it. Lexie would never belittle herself by telling anyone, for it had been a proper fiasco.

As he had done ever since he moved into the hotel, he entered by the area steps and, as soon as he went into the kitchen, Tiny said, with a touch of sarcasm, 'So Daddy's home at last?'

It was a second or two before Alistair understood. 'You mean Gwen's had the baby already? Is she all right? Is *it* all right? Is it a boy or a girl?'

Before his father-in-law could answer, Peggy walked in,

excitement making her more forthcoming than normal. 'Go up and see your daughter right this minute, Alistair. She's absolutely gorgeous.'

He took the stairs two at a time, passing Rosie without a word, his heart swelling with love for his wife when he burst into their room and saw her lying in bed looking as sweet as she always did, just a fraction paler, more fragile.

She held a finger to her lips. 'Don't make a noise, Alistair. She's asleep.'

He tiptoed across the room to kiss her. 'When was it? Was it bad? I wish I'd been here for you.'

'She was born yesterday and it wasn't too bad. Everything went as it should. Don't you want to look at her?'

Peggy hadn't exaggerated, he discovered. He had never seen such a beautiful infant before. No hair as such, of course, just a fuzz of fair down which suggested that she'd be blonde like Gwen and him, a teeny red, wrinkled face, minute hands perfectly formed and opening and closing as if searching for something to hold. She captivated him for ever by grabbing the finger he obliged with and opening her eyes. 'She looked at me,' he crowed, 'and her eyes are as blue as cornflowers.'

'All babies' eyes are blue for the first few weeks,' observed Rosie who came in at that moment with a tea tray in her hand.

'She's like a little doll,' he breathed.

'You won't think that for long,' laughed Gwen. 'Wait till you hear her bawling.'

Rosie grinned. 'She can definitely make herself heard, but you must be hungry, Alistair, and I kept some dinner for you.'

He tore himself away from his daughter to go down to the kitchen where they always had their meals, the dining room being kept for the guests, but he couldn't eat very much, he was so pleased with the tiny being he had created ... with a little help, of course. In less than half an hour, therefore, he was racing back to see her, and his heart contracted when he saw his wife with the infant in her arms. They made a perfect picture of Madonna and Child.

'Why don't you lay her down again?' Gwen asked, holding the small bundle out to him. 'I've just fed her and she's fast asleep.'

In holding his tiny daughter, even for the short time it took to put her back in her cot, Alistair experienced an emotion like no other he had ever felt. The sheer depth of it filled him with awe. It was as if he were looking down upon the innermost part of his being.

'How did things go in Forvit?' Gwen asked, as he straightened up. 'I'm sorry, I should have asked before, but ...'

'Don't worry about it, everything went off quite well. Dad's real down, as you'd imagine, but Alice says she wants to stay at home to look after him.'

'That's good. It'll stop you fretting about him.'

Sitting down on the edge of the bed, Alistair took her gently in his arms. 'I didn't think it would be possible to love you more than I did before, but ... now you've given me such a lovely daughter ...'

Her kiss stopped him, and all he could think of for some time was how lucky he was.

His wife drew away at last, stroking his cheek as she said, 'We'd better choose a name for our little one. Any ideas?'

'No, nothing. I'll leave it up to you, seeing she's a girl.'

'I'd like to give her a name to herself, not after relatives, and the midwife who attended me was really nice, so I asked her name and she said Chantal, her mother was French. It's spelled C-H-A-N-T-A-L. Unusual, but nice I think.'

After just a moment's thought, Alistair said, 'You know how folk shorten or change names, somebody might make it . . . Chanty.' He pronounced the ch as in cheese, not, as it should be, as in shell.

'What's wrong with that?'

He smiled apologetically. 'It's what folk in Forvit call a chamber pot.'

Gwen gave an embarrassed chuckle. 'That won't do, then. The only other one I thought of was one I saw in a magazine once. Leila. That couldn't be changed much?'

'I suppose somebody might say Lee, but it wouldn't matter, would it?'

'I'd prefer if they didn't, but it wouldn't be so bad. So that's settled, is it?'

'What's settled?' asked Dougal as he and Marge walked in. 'We did knock,' he added, as an afterthought.

'Your mother's name was Isabella, wasn't it?' Gwen asked then. 'So how does Leila Isabella . . . Rose strike you?'

Marge clapped her hands. 'That's great. Leila Isabella Rose. It has a ring to it.'

Dougal slapped his pal's back. 'I think we should go down and get Granddaddy to wet the baby's head with us, then we could go out for a wee stroll.'

'You've started something,' he began, when they left the hotel some twenty minutes later, Alistair having flatly refused to take more than one drink with Tiny. 'Marge has gone all broody on me.'

'Ach, your turn'll come, maybe it's better to wait, though I'm not sorry *we* didn't.'

'I'm forgetting to ask. Did the funeral go off all right? How's your father?'

'He took it bad, Dougal, but Alice is going to keep house for him.'

'That's good. Um . . . did you see Lexie Fraser?'

After an infinitesimal hesitation, Alistair nodded. 'Aye, she was there and Alice made me walk her home.'

The twinkle reappeared in Dougal's eyes. 'Did she try to get you to . . . ?'

'She didn't try anything, it was me.' He could have bitten his tongue out for the slip.

'*You* tried?' Dougal was shocked. 'But I thought you didn't even like her.'

'I never said I didn't like her, I was fed up with the way she was going on at me.'

'So she didn't go on at you this time, but you did what she's aye wanted? Good God Almighty, Ally, what were you thinking about? She'll tell the whole place . . .'

'She'll not tell anybody anything. You see, I didn't actually . . .'

'That wouldn't stop her from telling folk you did.'

'She's changed, Dougal. She's not as forward as she used to be, she wasn't forward at all. In fact, I was real sorry for her.'

'You'd a lucky escape, boy. Think what could have happened if you *had* done it.'

'I know, I know. It doesn't bear thinking about.'

'Did you get a chance to speak to my Mam or Dad?'

'Just for a minute or two. They were both looking well, I thought, and saying how pleased they were at seeing Marge at Easter.'

For the remainder of their short walk, Dougal asked after their old school friends and Alistair told him what he had learned about them, sometimes reminiscing about the exploits they and their 'chums' had got up to.

Lying beside his sleeping wife later, it occurred to Alistair that Dougal had always been the ringleader, and that he had always followed on, done what Dougal had done or told him to do. For once in his life, though, he had achieved something before Dougal managed it. He had made a daughter, the loveliest daughter any man could ever wish for. He had never knowingly felt jealous of Dougal at any time over all the years they'd been pals, yet it gave him a kick to feel that he was his own man at last.

'Congratulations, Alistair, my boy!'

Manny's welcoming words took his assistant aback. He had wanted to tell the good news himself. 'Do not look so surprised,' the old man laughed. 'I am not psychic. Your charming sister-in-law came to tell me about your daughter. Well done! But you will have to make a son before you have a gentleman's family. How is dear Gwen? I do not suppose that she is thinking, just yet, of having any more children?'

'I shouldn't think so, but she seems quite well. She said she didn't have too bad a time.'

'I believe that women usually play down what they suffer during childbirth. It is a time for the exclusion of men.'

'Did you never want children, Manny?'

'Anna and I both wanted babies, but it was not to be.' The pawnbroker averted his head for a moment, obviously to hide his sadness, but it wasn't long before he was smiling again. 'I was so pleased when Marge gave me the news that I closed the shop and went out in search of a gift for the little one. Wait and see what I found!'

He took a square wine-velvet-covered box from his safe and laid it on the counter. 'Open it, Alistair.'

Nestling amidst some pale pink cotton wool was a gold bangle which the new father removed reverently. 'Oh, Manny, you shouldn't have. I know you didn't pick this up in any of the markets. It's brand new, isn't it?'

'I have taught you too well, my boy. Yes, it is brand new, as befits a brand new baby, and when you have chosen a name for her, I will have it engraved inside. It is adjustable, and will fit her even when she is a grown woman.'

'Oh, Manny.' Alistair felt all choked up. 'The things you

think of . . . but you really shouldn't.'

'Let me know when you have chosen her name . . .'

'It's Leila. We chose it last night – Leila Isabella Rose, after the two grandmothers.'

Manny nodded his approval of this. 'Leila Isabella Rose. Yes, that rolls off the tongue very nicely. Now, when your dear wife is feeling up to it, tell her to bring little Leila Isabella Rose here to let me see her.'

It was on the point of Alistair's tongue to ask his employer to be godfather, and then he wondered how a Jew would fit into a Church of England ceremony. Come to that, he thought, how would a Church of Scotland man fit in? He knew nothing of the ways of the Episcopalian church. In any case, Gwen would likely want Marge to be godmother and Dougal to be godfather, so he had better not make any ripples by suggesting Manny.

When he went up to Gwen that night, his employer having made him swear to say nothing about the bangle, he was delighted when she said, 'I was thinking after you went to work. Manny's always been so good to us, we should ask him to the christening.'

'That's a lovely idea, my darling, and he wants to see her, as soon as you're fit to take her to the shop.'

'I'm supposed to stay in bed for ten days, so it'll be more than two weeks before I can walk as far as that. Marge could take her, though.'

'He wants to see you as well.'

'Say I'll come two weeks on Wednesday. That's not one of your busy days is it?'

'No, that'll be ideal.'

Damn Alice Ritchie, Lexie thought. She had been getting over the upset of Bella's funeral and what Alistair had done – or

101

more like it, not done – and his sister had stirred it up again. He'd become a father while he'd been in Forvit, maybe at the very time he'd been with her, kissing her, raising her hopes that he did want her, and she had spoiled it with her stupid fear. But now, even if he could tear himself away from his wife, he wouldn't want to leave his daughter. Not for a few years.

She was still prepared to wait, though. However long it took him to realize that she was the one he really loved, she would be here for him. From what Alice had said, he was having to do odd jobs in his father-in-law's hotel after he finished work for the Jew every day, and he would soon get fed up of that. And if the bairn, as most bairns do, kept them awake at nights, that would tell on him, as well. His body would rebel; he would start to get short-tempered with his wife and fall out with her ...

Yes, it would be worth while to wait ... like a cat at a mousehole, like a spider in its web. He was bound to fall into her trap ... not that she considered it a trap and nor would he by that time. His marriage would have fallen apart, his heart would be broken and she'd be there to pick up the pieces.

Chapter 7

❧

'You're useless, Dougal Finnie! D' you know that? Absolutely, bally useless!' Marge glared at her husband. 'Gwen's had her second and you haven't even managed to make one! We've been married for two years, for goodness' sake.'

'It could be your fault.' He felt obliged to make this quite clear.

'Not mine,' she sneered. 'Nobody in my family's ever had problems having a baby.'

'Nor in mine,' he snapped. 'I've a sister in America, and Mam had another son that died when he was three, so there was three of us, the same as you Jenkinses. One thing, you can't say I haven't tried, can you?'

She gave a tight little smile. 'No, I can't say that.' Capitulating suddenly, she sighed, 'I really do wish we could have a baby, Dougal. Don't you?'

'You know I do, my darling.'

As he made ready to go down to breakfast, however, he wasn't quite sure that he did want a baby, after all. They seemed to cause an awful upheaval in people's lives. Look at Alistair. He'd had precious little sleep for months after Leila was born, she'd been a fractious wee toot, and she'd just settled into a normal routine when the new one made its debut ... correction, his debut. Ally had never shown much sign of gumption let alone a powerful sexual drive, yet he'd put his wife up the bloody spout twice in little more than a year. He didn't need to be so cock-o'-the-walk because this one was a boy, though. He wasn't the only man on earth to make a son ... and by God, Dougal Finnie would give his eyeteeth to be in their brotherhood. But he'd better go downstairs before Marge came up again reading the riot act.

They were all seated round the table when he entered the kitchen, and Peggy was saying, 'Thank goodness it's over! I didn't get any sleep for the noise Gwen was making. I thought she was in the throes of death.'

Dougal couldn't resist teasing her. 'I didn't know dying people kicked up a noise.'

She tossed her head, then a loud knock on the door made her jump up. 'I'll go.'

'I wonder who that can be?' Rosie remarked. 'The post came half an hour ago.'

'It's a telegram,' Peggy announced as she came in again, 'for Alistair.'

Watching the blood drain from her son-in-law's face as he read it, Rosie asked, anxiously, 'Is it your father?'

Willie Ritchie's foot had been punctured some weeks ago by one of the tines of a harrow. He had tried to kick away a stone in its path but hadn't been quick enough to get out of the way himself. The resulting wound had never healed properly, but Alice's last note, saying that he was quite poorly, hadn't prepared her brother for this. 'He died yesterday,' Alistair moaned. 'Oh, God, I should have gone home to see him when she told me about it first.'

'You weren't to know this would happen.' Rosie was always on hand to soothe and comfort her small brood if anything untoward happened.

'I should have thought,' he persisted. 'The spikes would've been coated with earth and dung, and the poison must have gone right through him.' He turned to Dougal. 'The same as old Robbie Rankin, remember, Dougal? About five years ago?' Alistair looked at Rosie in anguish. 'I can't leave Gwen just now.'

'You have to go,' she said quietly. 'You can't miss your father's funeral. Gwen's got all of us to look after her, and your sister's got nobody.'

'She's got lots of friends, and I know you're worried about Gwen.'

Rosie looked away for a moment, then admitted, 'She's not too good. The doctor's coming back today, but I'll take care of her. There's no need for you to be here . . .'

'There's every need for me to be here,' he cried. 'Good God, Rosie, if anything happened to her and I was hundreds of miles away, I'd never forgive myself.'

She met his eyes now. 'Perhaps you're right.'

Dougal offered to send a telegram to Alice, and after carrying out that duty, he went to tell Manny Isaacson that Alistair would be off work that day. 'Gwen's quite ill,' he explained. 'It wasn't such an easy birth this time. The baby's OK, but . . .'

'Oh, that poor girl. I shall pray for her speedy recovery . . .'

'And another thing,' Dougal went on, 'Alistair got word this morning that his father had died, but he's not going to the funeral . . . because of Gwen, you understand?'

The old man was obviously shaken by this further bad news, and it was only when Dougal was leaving that he rallied enough to say, 'I am so very glad that the infant is all right. Is it a boy or a girl?'

'A boy.'

'The gentleman's family . . . but the two events to occur at the same time . . . it must be a truly traumatic time for Alistair. Please convey my heartfelt sympathy for him at the loss of his father, and tell him that I shall not expect him back to work until his dear wife's health has improved.'

*   *   *

Tiny having put on so much weight – he was over the twenty-stone limit of their household scales – Rosie asked Dougal if he would mind doing something for her.

'Anything,' he grinned. 'Your wish is my command, madame.'

'Cheeky!' she smiled back. 'It's for Alistair really. I should have thought of it before, but with all the worry ... You know the lumber room up on the top floor? There's an old bed-chair there. We bought it for Tiny's father when his wife was in hospital, though she was only in two weeks when she died and he went back to Swansea. That was the only time it was used. Sadly, he didn't last long himself, after that.'

'Alistair doesn't need a bed-chair,' Gwen protested weakly. 'He'll sleep with me.'

'He will not!' declared Rosie. 'You need all the rest you can get and so does he.'

But Gwen was adamant that he wouldn't disturb her, that she would prefer to feel him beside her if she woke in the night, and so the unwieldy old wooden bed-chair was left in state in the lumber room, to have further dust added to that which had already accumulated over the past fifteen years.

Despite his wife's protests, Alistair did spend a two-night vigil in a rickety basket chair by the bed, afraid to sleep, even for only a few minutes, in case she needed him. It was a full week before the doctor pronounced her out of danger and the whole household breathed a deep sigh of relief. Alistair, gaunt and hollow-eyed, cried, 'Thank God!' and bent to kiss her pale, sunken cheek before practically collapsing on to the bed at her side.

When Alistair saw his sister's writing on the envelope the following morning, he said, 'This is it! A telling-off for not going up for the funeral.' But it wasn't.

Dear Alistair,

It's a shame you couldn't get to the funeral, but I do understand and I hope Gwen's much better by now. A lot of folk turned up, for Dad was well liked, and most of them asked about you, especially Lexie Fraser. She and Meg McIntosh helped me with the funeral tea, I'd have been lost without them.

Dad has left me enough money to see me through the university, but I haven't made my mind up yet if I still want to go. I'm not really over things, for it was a bit sudden at the end. Oh, and I nearly forgot. He left the house between us but he told me he knew you wouldn't want to leave London, and I'm to stay here as long as I want. I hope that's all right with you.

You'll both be tickled pink it's a boy this time, though it's a pity Dad didn't know he had a grandson. Have you picked a name yet?

Give my love to Gwen, and kiss Leila and her baby brother for me. I hope I'll be able to see them some time soon.   Your loving sister, Alice.

'Who's Lexie Fraser?' Gwen wanted to know, after she read the letter.

'Just a girl Dougal and I went to school with.'

'She didn't ask about him, though?'

'I suppose . . . I suppose she knew me best.'

'In other words, she was the girlfriend you told me about. Don't blush, Alistair, I'm not angry or jealous. Was she the only one?'

'Yes, she was,' he muttered, thinking that it sounded even more damning than if he had confessed to a whole harem.

'Ah,' his wife said, thoughtfully, 'how long were you and she . . . ?'

'It wasn't the way you think. We were still at school when we started going out for walks and there was nothing in it, till ...' He halted, shaking his head. 'No, there never was anything in it, Gwen, darling, not on my side. She would have liked there to be, that was the trouble. I came to London with Dougal to get away from her.'

A delighted smile lit up Gwen's pale face. 'So I've Lexie Fraser to thank for having you as my husband?'

'I suppose you could put it like that. One thing's for sure. I would never have married her, whatever she thinks ... thought.'

'You believe she might still be hoping?'

'No, of course not. I hope you don't think ... I'd never look at another woman, ever!'

'I know that, my dear. I'm only teasing. But getting back to Alice's letter, we'll have to think of a name for our little man.'

'I used to think I'd like to call my son after Dougal,' Alistair began, but Gwen's last two words had given him a new idea. 'Back home, young mothers often spoke about a baby boy as 'my wee mannie' – it was an affectionate term, you know? – and though I know you wouldn't want to call him Emanuel, that's Manny's real name, his sign says E.D. Isaacson, so what if I ask him what the D stands for?'

The pawnbroker was so overwhelmed with emotion when he learned why he was asked his middle name that his assistant feared he might have a heart attack, but he didn't take long to pull himself more or less together. 'This is truly a great honour for me,' he murmured after a brief pause. 'No one has ever ...' He stopped again to regain his still wavering composure, filling the awkward moments by opening his safe and taking out a gold wrist watch. 'I bought this as soon as Dougal told me that your Gwen had given birth to a son, but I wish now that it had been something more suitable for an infant.'

Alistair, too, now had difficulty in remaining calm, and his voice trembled a little as he said, 'Manny, that watch is something he can cherish for the rest of his life. You couldn't have bought him anything more fitting . . . though you shouldn't have.'

The elderly man wiped a tear from the corner of his eye with his thumb. 'You do not understand. As you know, my Anna and I were not blessed with children, and it is so long since I lost her . . . I have had no one, except you. You are the son I never had, Alistair, your Gwen is my daughter-in-law and your children are my grandchildren. You have made my life complete, so please do not be angry with me for buying gifts.'

'I'm not angry, Manny, please don't think that. I just felt it wasn't right for you to spend your money on us when you had your mind set on buying bigger premises. You'll never get your antique shop at this rate.'

'Antique shop?' Manny snapped his fingers. 'Poof! What is a shop full of the most expensive antiques in the world compared with the happiness I feel at being able to do something for your two precious little cherubs.'

And so David (Manny's middle name) William (after Alistair's late father) Trevor (after Tiny) was christened, and Manny having declined to act as godfather because of the difference in religion, Alistair paid tribute to Ivy and Len Crocker by asking them to be godparents. Both vowed to take their duty seriously, but during the meal, Ivy had them all laughing by keeping up a teasing conversation with Tiny who gave as good as he got.

At four o'clock, when Rosie, Peggy and Marge were down-stairs in the kitchen tidying up, and Tiny, Dougal, Manny and Len were engaged in a discussion on politics, Gwen said, 'Shall I fetch the baby down, Ivy, so you can see him properly?'

'Ooh, yes please! I'd love to see both the little lambs.' She waited until the younger woman had left the room and then leaned over towards Alistair. 'You haven't half done well, Al, but I knew you had it in you, when you were lodging with me.' She covered her mouth momentarily to suppress a giggle. 'Oh, my Gawd! I nearly said when we were living together! Now that would have been something, wouldn't it?'

He could only respond in the same vein. 'Aye, it would that, though you were so randy you'd have exhausted me.' It was easy to laugh with her now. She couldn't help herself and she probably didn't mean half of what she said. 'I wouldn't have had enough stamina left to make any babies with Gwen.'

A wistfulness crept momentarily into her eyes, then, in a quick change of mood, she said, 'I'm really glad for you, Al, love. You deserve the best.'

'And I've got it,' he assured her, looking up as his family entered the room – his darling wife, looking radiant in a London tan woollen costume and carrying a bundle swaddled in a lacy shawl, with their beautiful daughter hanging on to her skirt. Leila was obviously newly awake, her eyes still hazy with sleep, but she soon perked up.

'She's so lovely,' cooed Ivy, who had seen her regularly since she was born. Diving into her handbag now, she extracted a small parcel which she handed to the little girl. 'I can't give your brother a present without giving you something, too, can I?'

The fifteen-month-old shook her head gravely and tore off the paper to see what was inside, then without saying anything she toddled into the hall and they could hear her feet slowly negotiating the stairs to the kitchen. 'It was only a rag doll,' Ivy said in concerned apology. 'Didn't she like it?'

'She loved it,' Gwen smiled. 'She's taken it down to let her Grandma see it.'

Ivy was reassured in a few moments when Rosie came in carrying the little girl, followed by Marge and Peggy, and for the next half hour or so, attention centred on Leila, who was adept at playing to an audience. Needing only little encouragement, she recited several nursery rhymes, missing some words and getting others wrong, sang 'Twinkle, Twinkle Little Star' – which came out as 'Tinka, tinka, icka tah' – three times and 'Umpy Dumpy satta wo', twice. To follow this, making it a mammoth production, she executed little dances her Auntie Peggy had taught her and then proved that the show was over by saying, as she climbed on to Rosie's knee, 'Aw done, Gamma.'

Baby David, as though aware that his sister was stealing the limelight although this should have been his day, slept through all her antics cradled against Ivy Crocker's ample bosom, and the party, as it had become, broke up just after five o'clock.

'Thank God that's all over!' said Marge, a little testily, after the guests had gone.

'Yes, it's been some day,' Tiny agreed.

Gwen looked keenly at her sister but said nothing until she and Alistair were in bed. 'I think Marge's jealous,' she told him. 'She's desperate for a baby.'

'So Dougal's been saying, but it's something you can't arrange to order.'

'I don't like to ask, but would he be . . . ?' She paused. 'Could he have lost interest in . . . that side of things?'

Alistair had to laugh at this. 'Not Dougal, I can assure you of that.'

1935 had just begun when Tiny collapsed. The hotel had been closed on Christmas Day, but he had prepared an impressive dinner for his extended family, and despite Rosie's warnings not to overdo it at his age – 'You're sixty-seven, for goodness' sake, and would be retired if you'd been working for a boss' – he wouldn't let anyone help him. He produced another feast for New Year's Day but the upset of him being rushed to hospital as they were about to sit down to the meal banished everyone's appetite.

He hovered on the brink of death for twenty-one hours, and just when his wife and daughters thought that having survived the heart attack for so long he would pull through, he slipped effortlessly away.

Both Alistair and Dougal had their work cut out trying to comfort the three sisters, but Rosie, who had lost her partner of thirty-five years, was the calmest of them all. She told her sons-in-law to register the death and contact the undertakers so that the funeral could be arranged, then she sat dry-eyed and holding herself as erect as she had always done, seemingly impervious to her husband's demise, or more probably, unable to take it in.

The birth of Alistair's second child had made Lexie Fraser take stock of her situation. There didn't seem to be any chance of him leaving his wife, not now they had two children, and it had begun to be very painful to think of him, excruciating even to try to picture him with his expanding family. Alice had shown her a studio portrait he'd sent of his wife cuddling an infant in a christening robe, Alistair standing behind her chair with a fair-haired little girl in his arms, which had haunted her waking hours and disrupted her nights for weeks.

The pain was easing a little, but something else had reared up in her mind, something she had pushed resolutely away over the years since her father's disappearance. At the time, having been so angry and upset by the lack of interest shown by the police, she had been unable to think of anything else, yet there had always been this feeling of ... She couldn't remember if it had been fear, or pain, or what, and she had filed it away during the years she'd had her mind on Alistair, but there was no one now to help her.

The doctor – Dr Birnie, it was, or Dr Tom as he'd affectionately been known – had done his best to comfort both her and her mother, but he had left Forvit a few months afterwards. He hadn't wanted to go, but his mother-in-law had had a slight heart attack, and his wife, the elder daughter – the younger had been working in America – had gone to Stirling to look after her. After a few days, she had told Dr Tom on the phone that she wanted them to move there permanently. He'd had to find a replacement before he could go, of course, and had been most apologetic to all his patients, more so, perhaps, to her mother and her, Lexie mused.

Because she was so young at the time he left, and hadn't yet recovered from the shock of losing her father and the stories that still circulated about him, she had fastened on Alistair with such intensity that she had scared him off, and she had blamed her heartache on his desertion of her. Just once, while she was struggling to cope with that agony, had a picture flashed through her mind.

It had been gone in an instant, and she hadn't been really sure if it was of something that had actually happened or if it had been a dream, a nightmarish dream. She didn't want to think about it. She had the feeling that it was something horrible, something so nasty it would change her life for ever, so it was probably a good thing that she couldn't recall exactly what had taken place, or when. She could remember the bobby being there, and the doctor giving her mother sleeping pills with the caution, 'They're

pretty potent, so wait until you are in bed before taking them.'

She had been given two, as well, and it was just as well
she'd heard that caution, because she must have gone out
like a light seconds after swallowing them.

Lexie gave a shivery sigh. She didn't like dwelling on that
awful time, it was too disturbing for her, so she turned
her mind once again to her present circumstances. She
desperately needed someone to depend on, to gather comfort
from, and with there being no chance of Alistair ever coming
back to her now, she had better look elsewhere. Most of the
boys she had been at school with were either married or
had found work in some of the big industrial cities in the
south. Only two were still bachelors and still living at home
– Gibby Mearns and Freddie McBain, neither particularly
good-looking, but both with steady jobs in Aberdeen. Gibby,
the postie's oldest son, drove a long-distance lorry for a large
haulage company, and Freddie worked in the office of one of
the shipyards.

Yes, one of them would be her best bet. She wasn't cut out
to be an old maid.

Chapter 8

❧

The hotel had been closed for exactly ten days when Rosie, matriarch now, the unrelieved black of her apparel emphasizing her pallor, called her family together.

'I want you to listen and weigh up everything carefully before you say anything,' she instructed them, looking at her three daughters in turn because it was from them that the inevitable arguments would come. 'I know your father only did the cooking . . .' She waved away what Marge was trying to say, and went on, '. . . but it was the meals he produced that brought people back, the kind of meals that only the top hotels could offer, and at half the price. That was why we'd a clientele of company reps and businessmen, and I can't hope to continue that. Your father was a Regimental Cook Sergeant when he married me, so he wouldn't let me do anything except serve, and even if I could probably manage to provide good plain fare, that's not what the hotel was famed for.'

The alarmed glance which passed between Gwen and Marge made her add, a little sadly, 'I see you can guess what's coming. I'm going to sell the hotel and buy a decent-sized house so we can still all be together.'

Marge could hold her concern at bay no longer. 'But, Mum, all you have to do is engage a good chef, and we'll all help you to carry on, Gwen and Peg and me. I know it won't be the same for you, but we'll manage, I'm sure we will.'

With a shake of her head, Rosie said, firmly, 'Just managing isn't enough. In any case, I couldn't afford even a mediocre chef, so it would fall to me, and if I'm tied up all day in the kitchen who'll keep account of things – what each guest is due, what we owe the tradesmen at the end of each month, order the provisions, make the guests feel at home? Who'll listen to their troubles, comfort them if their wives have been unfaithful, or left them, or died? That was a big part of what I did over the years.'

'We could do that,' persisted Marge, 'and you could show us how to do the rest.'

'I wouldn't have time, and there's something else to consider. You and Peggy will eventually have children, too, and a hotel isn't a place to bring up families . . .' She broke off, pausing long enough to compose herself, but such was the impact of what she had told them that none of them said a word.

After only a few seconds, she continued, 'What we get for it should buy a fairly big house with a garden for the little ones to play in.' She looked at her middle daughter again, waiting for further objections, but she had lapsed into silence, and Rosie hoped that she hadn't upset her by speaking about gardens for the little ones. She had thought that Marge and Dougal were purposely waiting a few years before they had children, but maybe they *had* been trying. Poor Marge! A change of home, and not having to work so hard every day, might do the trick.

Rosie felt better now. 'I think it would cheer us all up. A more modern house, with a good-sized garden, away from all the traffic and bustle. We'd need six bedrooms at least – one for Gwen and Alistair, one for Marge and Dougal, one for . . .'

'You don't have to worry about Marge and me, Rosie,' Dougal put in, as if he knew what she'd been thinking a moment or so earlier. 'I've enough laid by to put down a deposit for a nice wee place of our own. I've been thinking about it for a good while, but I didn't like to say anything in case you thought I wasn't happy here.'

'But don't you want us to stay together?' Rosie was bewildered now. She had never imagined that her attempt to keep the family round her would result in splitting it up.

'We don't need to be living in each other's pockets to be close,' Dougal persisted. 'We can still see you regularly, and you wouldn't have to buy such a big house.'

Alistair shot a silent question at Gwen and got a nodding reply. 'We were thinking of renting a place,' he told his mother-in-law, hesitantly, 'to be on our own, you know?'

This double blow left Rosie nonplussed, so it fell to Peggy to pour oil on the troubled waters. 'I think it's a good idea for us all to live our own lives. I used to get tired of you two bossing me about . . .' She gave a faint smile to show that she bore no grudge. 'Mum and I'll still be together and I can take a job somewhere to help out with expenses.'

Rosie heaved a sigh of resignation. 'I suppose . . . if that's what everybody wants?'

A sharp wail from upstairs made Alistair jump up. 'That'll be David, likely.' As he passed his mother-in-law to attend to his son, he gripped her shoulder reassuringly. 'It'll work out fine, Rosie. Dougal and I'll be masters in our own homes, and if you want us to do something for you at any time, you'll only have to let us know.'

'I feel awful,' Alistair admitted to Manny the following day after telling him what had transpired. 'Are we being selfish? Is Rosie right? Are we splitting up her family?'

As usual, Manny gave his manager's troubles his full consideration. 'It is difficult to say, my boy. From her point of view, you probably are, but you can prove it otherwise if you visit her frequently and issue an open invitation for her to visit you. From what I have seen of your mother-in-law, she is not an unreasonable woman, and she will realize that you and Dougal need to have time alone with your wives, and as long as you let her see her grandchildren as often as she wants, she should be satisfied. In any case, things may change. Tiny's death, coming when there was hope of him pulling through, was bound to have unsettled all of you, and when Rosie is able to think rationally, she may not want to give up the hotel at all.'

Alistair shook his head. 'No, her mind's definitely made up about that, and she's quite right, you know. I don't think it would be the same without Tiny in the kitchen and her at the helm, but you'd better not let Gwen or Marge know I've said that.'

The next three months were extremely busy for the Jenkins family, especially Rosie. She took to visiting estate agents with Peggy, asking to view any houses they had for sale, but found nothing that attracted her. They were all too small to her mind, although Peggy said they were big enough for the two of them.

It was Dougal who first found what he was looking for. 'One of the despatch clerks says his parents have booked one of the houses going up in Lee Green,' he told Alistair. 'It's a bit out, but I'm going to have a look at them on Sunday. Fancy coming?'

He hadn't wanted Rosie to know but Marge let it slip, and so the whole 'shebang of them', as Dougal put it, made the journey to SE 12. The neat semi-detached villas made a deep impression, each with a small patch in front for a garden, and a much larger piece at the rear. Going into the show house, completely fitted out so that prospective buyers would have a clearer picture of the possibilities, they discovered that the ground floor consisted of a square lounge at the front, a smaller living room behind it, and, alongside that, a scullery with a door into the 'garden'. Upstairs were two decent-sized bedrooms, and, reminding Dougal and Alistair of the Crockers' house in Hackney, a separate tiny lavatory and a narrow bathroom.

Most of the houses in the street were finished, some actually occupied already, but two still had to be painted and the surrounding ground levelled out. 'What d'you think?' Dougal asked Marge, her smile encouraging him to ask the Site Manager for more details.

'Not bad for under £500, eh?' he observed to his wife, as they all trooped along to Hither Green to catch the train back to Russell Square. 'I've got the deposit and I should manage the mortgage, so I put my name down provisionally, is that OK with you?'

She smiled her approval. 'Perfect. I loved the house.'

'The man said I'd better make up my mind quick, because there's only two left.'

The final outcome of the expedition, however, was something Dougal was none too happy about. When he went to the builder's office on the Tuesday to sign the contract, he asked if anyone had bought the last one.

'I was hoping I could persuade you to take it,' he confided to Alistair that evening, 'but I near fell in a heap when the girl said a Mrs Rose Jenkins had been in on Monday morning and settled for it. I ask you, Ally. I thought Marge might be able to conceive once she didn't have to worry about Rosie hearing us, for I think that's what's been wrong though she never said, and now! Speak about living in each other's pockets!'

Alistair couldn't help smiling. Gwen had kept at him to make the commitment, and she'd looked disappointed when he said Woodyates Road was too pricey for him, but Rosie, bless her, had let him off the hook. 'Has she bought the house you're joined on to?' he asked Dougal.

'No, that's one thing I'm thankful for.'

'So Marge'll know her mother can't hear what you get up to in bed, not with the width of two garage runs between your house and hers.'

Rather than put a millstone round his neck, Alistair finally settled on renting an old terraced house – furnished, if a little basically – in Bethnal Green, only a short bus run from Manny's shop. Like Dougal, he had been worrying about furniture, and had warned Gwen that she'd have to put up with second-hand for a while, so all that concerned them now was buying essential household items. Then Rosie told them that there was enough furniture, bed and table linen, dishes and cutlery in the hotel to equip all three houses and still leave enough for the new owners to start off with.

Now came a time of frantically begging for tea chests and crates to pack things in, the three young women making sure that everything was fairly divided and each item marked with its proper destination. Of course, with the amount of upheaval going on, it was not surprising that Leila and David were fretty, and Ivy's offer to keep them from the day before the removals until the day after was gratefully accepted. It certainly wasn't a time to have small children running around under everybody's feet disrupting things.

The more time Lexie Fraser spent with Ernie Gammie, the more she came to like him. He was thoughtful, asked no questions of her and, most important, he was courting her – the only way to describe it – in the good old-fashioned way. He hadn't kissed her until the fourth or fifth time he saw her home, and he hadn't tried anything else even yet, and they'd been keeping company for almost eight weeks now.

Remembering, how that had come about, she gave a satisfied little smile. Over the past six or so months, she had gone out with three other men before Ernie, but once was enough with each of them. As soon as they got her where nobody would see them, she'd had to fight them off, even Gibby Mearns, who had known her since she was five and should have known her better than try. Davie Lovie, the van driver who delivered newspapers to the shop, hadn't been quite so bad, but he hadn't asked her out a second time – probably because she wouldn't let him do what he wanted – and although Freddie McBain had waited until he took her home, he was as determined as the other two to get her flat on her back.

But Ernie wasn't like that. She had been surprised when he walked into the shop that day; and even more astonished when he asked her out; he'd never shown any interest in her before. 'Somebody told me you were married,' she'd replied, to let him know that she knew. It was why he had never entered into her plans.

'Cathy died two years ago.'

'Oh, Ernie, I'm sorry. I could kick myself for . . .'

'No, you were right to say it, and you're the first one I've . . .' He paused, uncertainly, then ended, 'I haven't looked at anyone else since I lost her.'

She learned on their first date that he had joined the Aberdeen Fire Service, that he and his late wife had had no children, and that he was still living in the house in King Street that he had rented when he got married. 'I've been thinking about emigrating,' he had told her, 'to get a new life somewhere different, but I can't make up my mind – especially now things are starting to look up for me again.'

This small compliment – she was sure it was a compliment – was all she had needed to accept his invitation to see a show in Aberdeen, and that had been the first of many truly enjoyable evenings, though it had always been the first house of the Tivoli or the early showing of a film so that they could get a bus back to Forvit.

On their first date, she had said, 'I'll easy manage home on the bus myself.'

He had taken her hand and squeezed it. 'No, I'll see you home. I wrote to my mother to say I'd need a bed there tonight – tomorrow's my day off.'

She was grateful that he had made this arrangement, his father's farm was only a mile and a half off the main road, so he didn't have far to go after he'd seen her inside. And it saved her from worrying whether or not she should ask him to stay over at her house.

She was certain she was doing the right thing at last, and she wished that she had known much earlier that he was free ... and how nice a man he had turned out to be. Take tonight, for instance. After meeting her at the bus terminus, he had suggested taking a tram to the Bridge of Don and walking along the prom. 'It's too fine a night to be sitting inside a picture house,' he had smiled, and then his expression had changed. 'That's if it's OK with you?' he had asked, anxiously.

'I'd love it,' she had told him, and so she had.

On their stroll, they had talked of this and that, and she'd been tempted to ask about his wife, what kind of woman she was, what she looked like, how she had died, but it was too early yet to be so openly inquisitive. If he felt like telling her, he probably would, though maybe he didn't like to mention what had caused her death. It could have been cancer, and that wasn't something people liked to speak about, though she wouldn't have minded – she'd had long enough experience of it with her mother. It was just another illness, an illness that couldn't be cured, and dying as a result of it was nothing for the family left behind to be ashamed of.

They sat down for a while on one of the benches over-looking the wide expanse of calm sea, dotted here and there with homecoming trawlers making their slow way into the harbour, but one much larger ship made Lexie ask, curiously, 'Why's that big one not moving?'

'It'll be sitting at anchor waiting for the pilot to come and lead it in,' Ernie told her. 'You see, there's all sorts of currents and things that captains from other places have to beware of.'

'Where would that one have come from?'

'It's definitely a foreigner because of the flag, but it's too far out for me to make out which country's it is.'

In another twenty minutes, they were treated to the spec-tacle of the tiny pilot boat shooting into sight from behind the harbour wall and then turning round to escort the visitor to its allocated berth. Having watched until both vessels were out of sight, Ernie said, 'I think we should make tracks again. We don't want to miss the last bus.'

They walked smartly along to the Bathing Station where they would catch a tram into town, and the air having grown a little colder, he put his arm around her waist as they waited. 'I've been thinking on buying a second-hand car,' he said. 'It would be a lot handier than having to depend on public transport like this. What d'you think?'

'It's not up to me. Can you afford it?'

'Just about, but we could go anywhere and stay out all night if we wanted, too.'

She had nearly said he could stay *inside* all night with her, but she still didn't feel free enough to let him do what he wanted ... if he wanted it. She would be better to wait to see what developed before making any rash commitments.

Alistair could see that Gwen wasn't happy in their new abode. Even after two months, she was missing her mother and her sisters. 'I didn't realize how much work the children were,' she wailed one evening, while she was washing out the clothes their offspring had been wearing that day. 'Mum or Marge or Peggy always saw to them if I was busy, but now I've got to do the cooking, the washing and ironing, make the beds and do all the cleaning, as well as look after the kids all day.'

Alistair pushed aside the thought that she was blaming him – she knew that they couldn't afford a mortgage like Dougal was paying – but he still felt a wave of indignation at the thought of her lack of effort. 'You've been blooming lucky, you know,' he said, brusquely. 'Not many young mothers have built-in nursemaids like you had at the hotel.'

Noticing her bottom lip trembling, he regretted his brutality. She was right – two infants must be an awful handful, and other mothers would have learned from looking after their first before a second came along, whereas Gwen had been thrown in at the deep end, so to speak. 'I'm sorry, darling. It must be terrible for you on your own all day, but I have to work. I can't leave Manny in the lurch, and we need the money.'

'I know it's not your fault, but I get so tired, and . . .'

'Come here,' he said, gruffly, reaching out and taking her in his arms. He hated to see her crying, especially when he looked at the situation from her side. He was blaming her for not making an effort, but he was just as bad. If he'd really wanted to, he could have bought the house Rosie was now occupying. Paying the mortgage would have been a struggle, but they would have managed, somehow. But . . . it was too late now. 'Let me finish the washing for you, sweetheart,' he murmured against her neck, 'and you can go to bed. An early night should help.'

Left on his own, he dutifully scrubbed, then rinsed, all the little garments and spread them out on the pulley hanging from the scullery ceiling – the weather was too dodgy in October to chance leaving them outside all night – before tackling the napkins which were soaking in a pail. That was when he felt true sympathy for his wife. Fancy having to do this every day, maybe more than once, he thought, screwing up his nose. Wee David wasn't a year old yet, but he smelt like a blinking adult.

Before going home the following night, he made a detour to see Ivy, to tell her how worried he was about his wife, and as he had hoped she would, his former landlady volunteered to have the 'little dears' for an afternoon every week. 'More than one, if she wants,' Ivy had grinned, 'for I could eat them, they're so adorable.'

'We're not so desperate you need to do that,' Alistair laughed, 'and you'd better not let Gwen know I've been talking to you. She's a bit touchy.'

Ivy gave his rear end a playful pat when he turned to leave. 'I'll be the soul of tact, you know me.'

She did more than have the children for an afternoon a week. Working round to it gradually, she got Gwen to admit how tired she always felt, and how much of a struggle it was to get to Lee Green on her own with an infant, a toddler and a bag bulging with nappies for David and a change of clothes for both in case of 'accidents'. This, Gwen explained tearfully, meant that she could only see her mother on Sundays, when Alistair was with her. Not letting the young woman suspect a thing, nor putting any pressure on her, Ivy arranged to accompany her there every Thursday and also to take the children off her hands for the whole of every Monday to let her get her weekly wash done and ironed, weather permitting.

'And so peace reigns once more in the Ritchie household?' Manny queried, amiably.

'Oh yes,' breathed Alistair. 'Gwen's much brighter, and Ivy's tickled pink at having the brats. It's a shame she never had any of her own, she'd have made a good mother.'

'That so often happens. My Anna was the same ... also your dear sister-in-law,' Manny added, in case his employee thought he was lingering on his own trouble.

'Dougal's awful disappointed that Marge hasn't fallen yet. He doesn't think she'll ever have any, and Rosie keeps asking when they'll hear the patter of tiny feet, so you can imagine tempers are a bit frayed there. As a matter of fact, he's speaking about joining the TA so he can have some peace. He says they train at weekends and have a week's camp in the summer, and he wants me to join, too, but ... I can't leave Gwen.'

'No, it is different for you,' Manny agreed. 'He can go off with a free mind, knowing that his wife's mother and sister are next door if anything happens, or if she merely wants company. Still, if you did want to go, I am sure Ivy would be only too happy ...'

'I couldn't ask her to do any more, she's been so good to us already. I don't suppose she'd mind, but I don't want to take advantage of her.'

'You are right, my boy.' Manny lifted his black homburg and settled it comfortably on his head. 'I may not come back until afternoon sometime,' he said, as he opened the door. 'Billy Ternent has asked me to have a look at some property he is thinking of buying.'

As he made his way to the bus stop, he pondered over what he had been told. He was always glad when Alistair confided in him; it took his mind off the worry which had been growing in his mind of late. No word had appeared in the newspapers, but it had begun to filter through by word of mouth that Adólf Hitler had been clearing the Jews out of Germany since he came to power, and so deep was his fixation against them, apparently, that there was every likelihood of him doing the same in Britain if he ever got the chance.

No! Manny scolded himself, he must stop fretting about something that may never happen, and think of a way to help poor little Gwen. It was only natural, never having been separated from them before, that she was missing her mother and sisters, as Alistair should have realized, but what could be done about it?

David had newly been bathed and changed when he filled his nappy, and Gwen felt quite irritated with him as she stripped him once again. 'You do it on purpose!' she ranted. 'It's the same every blinking day!'

'Blinking day?' queried little Leila, watching the operation with interest.

Her mother dropped the offensive articles into the pail she'd made ready. 'I meant it's a . . . bad day, darling.'

The little girl shook her head. 'See sun! You pwomised.'

'We *will* go out, when I get this brother of yours ready.'

'David bad, Mummy?'

Gwen could feel her throat tightening in self-pity, her eyes prickling. 'He can't help it, though, he's only a baby.' It had been different when Leila was a baby, she thought, miserably. At the least sign of discomfort from her daughter, either Peggy or Marge had hastened to comfort her, and change her if that was what was wrong. She looked at her tiny son now, her heart filling with love instead of the anger she had felt a moment before. Things were getting her down so much that she'd have to be careful not to lose her temper altogether and do him some harm. She'd read of mothers who killed their infants because they were so tired they couldn't cope with them.

She was throwing on her own coat – Leila having been

told to rock the pram if the baby started crying – when the doorbell rang. 'Manny!' she exclaimed anxiously, when she saw who it was. 'Has something happened to Alistair?'

'No, no, I am sorry to have alarmed you. I was on my way to one of the markets when I suddenly felt like coming to see you. But you were going out?'

'I take the children for a walk every morning and do the housework when they're having their afternoon nap, but it doesn't matter. I'm so glad to see you. Won't you come in for a cup of tea?'

'If you do not mind, may I accompany you on your outing? I was not looking forward to trailing round the stalls, but walking with a lovely young woman? That is something I have not done for many a long year.'

A flattered smile stole across Gwen's face. 'I think you would have been a one for the girls when you were young, but I'll be glad of your company.'

As they negotiated their way through the morning shoppers, Manny drew Gwen out to talk about herself, about her life at the hotel, and she described it so well that he could picture the three sisters making beds, helping in the kitchen, waiting at tables with a smile and a few words for each of the businessmen.

'You miss it, don't you?' he murmured.

'I shouldn't, when I'm kept busy with these two, but it's not the same. I think it's the adult company I miss.'

'Especially your mother and sisters, is that not so?'

'Yes,' she admitted, 'it's them I miss most. I miss having them to tell my troubles to, and I get so tired, sometimes, and I've nobody to speak to till Alistair comes home at nights. I do see Ivy Crocker twice a week, but she's more interested in the kids than me.'

During the past fifteen minutes, Manny had been turning an idea over in his mind, a suggestion which would benefit himself as much as Gwen, and her last words gave him the courage to voice it. 'I hope you do not think that what I am about to say is in any way improper, but I would consider it a privilege to be allowed to repeat this morning with you on a weekly basis. I, too, often feel the need of a confidante, someone with whom I can discuss my little worries . . . not that I have many since Alistair took over the running of the shop.'

'I'd love to have you with me once a week, Manny, but are you sure you want to? I hope it isn't because you're sorry for me?'

'No, I want to, I assure you. I am an old man now, and many of the people with whom I come in contact do not have much time for me, but you have been so friendly, I can talk to you and not feel I am being a nuisance.'

'I should hope so!' Gwen said. 'But I've been doing most of the talking today.'

'There will be other days, yes?'

'Yes, of course, and if it happens to be raining on any of the days you come to see me, we can have our chat inside. How does that sound?'

'Ideal, and shall we make it Wednesdays?'

When they returned to the house, he accepted her offer of a cheese sandwich and a cup of tea, and remained with her after the children had been settled upstairs for their nap. 'I suppose Alistair has told you that I used to have a dream . . . ?'

Gwen raised her eyebrows. 'Used to have? Oh, Manny, you haven't given up on having an antique shop, have you?'

He didn't answer for a moment, then said, softly, 'If I tell you, you must promise not to say anything to Alistair. I want it to be a surprise for him.'

'I won't tell him.'

'I am not really fit to be making a daily trek round the

stalls and second-hand shops, and I have also decided that I am too old to start out on a new venture, but I have not forgotten my dream. I have . . .' He stopped to consider the wisdom of going on and came to the conclusion that it was not fair to expect the young woman to keep such momentous information a secret from her husband. 'No, my dear, I shall leave it there. You will both have a pleasant surprise when the time comes.' He was relieved that she did not press him for details, yet he should have known she wouldn't. She was every bit as honourable as Alistair. They were a perfect match.

Gwen did tell her husband that Manny had called, and that he was making it a weekly occurrence, but she did not mention what else he had said, and although Alistair knew why the arrangement had been made, he said nothing about that, either.

For many months to come, therefore, Gwen's weeks were fairly social, what with seeing Ivy for about fifteen minutes every Monday morning and afternoon, when she collected the children for the day and brought them back, and all Thursdays, when they went to Lee Green. Then there were Sundays, when Alistair went with her to see her mother and sisters again as a family.

Wednesdays, of course, were for Manny, who gradually opened out and told her about his wife having to go out cleaning in the early days of their marriage until the pawnshop was making enough for them to live on, about his parents and his grandparents, who had originally come from Poland, about how honoured he felt to be accepted as part of her family, and she, in turn, told him about her father's army career, about her mother being in service at a farm on the outskirts of Aldershot, which is how she had met her husband.

On several occasions, when she was telling Alistair in bed

about her Wednesdays, she remarked that she felt closer to Manny Isaacson than she had ever felt to anyone else.

'Even me?' he asked, a little hurt.

She gave him an extra-special kiss. 'Even you. I love you as a wife's supposed to love her husband, but I love Manny like a favourite uncle.'

And so the Ritchies, the Finnies and the Jenkinses lived their rather ordinary lives oblivious of what was going on in Europe. Only Manny could see the threat of war looming ever and ever nearer, and he kept his fears to himself.

As did too many others.

Chapter 9

His mother's letter devastated Dougal. 'Why didn't she send a telegram?' he wailed to his wife. 'Fancy waiting till a week after the funeral before she tells me.'

Marge laid her hand gently on his bowed head. 'She knew you'd a mortgage to pay, so she probably thought you couldn't afford the fare to Scotland.'

'I'd have managed somehow. Oh, God, I wish she'd told me before ... I'd have liked to have seen him again before he died.'

'She says people at the funeral told her they thought he'd been looking tired and ill for months, and I think she's blaming herself for not noticing till it was too late.'

'She was aye too damn busy keeping her house so clean you could eat off the floor,' Dougal observed, sharply. 'It would have been the end of the world if anybody had seen a speck of dust on the dresser, and she didn't like when Dad told her there'd be houses when we're all dead and gone.'

He ranted on about his mother's obsession with having everything excessively clean and tidy, how his father had tried to make a 'clootie' rug one winter but his mother had gone mad about the fluff and bits of thread that blew about so he'd had to stop, and Marge let him get his angry frustration off his chest.

His mother's next letter just told him that she was managing fine, the one after that said she had got one of the men to throw out all the rubbish in the outhouses, the next one said she had asked the Salvation Army to collect his father's clothes. Then came the final blow. 'I've sold the farm and everything that goes with it,' she wrote, 'and I'm leaving for America tomorrow to be with Flora.'

'God Almighty!' Dougal exploded, making Marge jump. 'What's wrong with the woman? Tomorrow? It's today she's sailing! Has she taken leave of her senses?'

Marge felt a strong resentment against his mother for not only excluding him from his father's final hours but selling up and going off to live with her daughter in America without as much as a by-your-leave from her son. Marge had always had the suspicion that Meg Finnie was a woman who ruled the roost – though she had been very friendly when they went to Forvit for a week one spring – and this was proof, wasn't it? She might at least have asked Dougal what he thought about her giving up the farm and the house that had been his childhood home, not waited until everything was cut and dried. But knowing her husband as she did, Marge deemed it best not to mention that; it would do more harm than good.

'Your mother's bound to be lonely,' she murmured, tentatively, 'and we're too far away to help if she needs anything, or if anything goes wrong. She'll be better where your sister can keep an eye on her.'

Giving a sigh so prolonged that his wife thought it would never end, Dougal muttered, 'I suppose so. It's just . . . well, she's cut my last link with Forvit, and I wish I'd seen the house just one more time. I'm sure there must be odds and ends of mine still there.'

'They'd just be childish things, though?'

He managed a weak smile. 'Treasures at the time. Ach, don't mind me, Marge, I'm just being sentimental. You're quite right. Mam *will* be better with Flora, and it's her life, after all, though I know I'll never see her again, either.

133

I'll never be able to afford the fare to America. The east side would be bad enough, but Flora's man's a deputy sheriff in one of the counties in Oregon, that's right over on the west.'

'If she'd been sailing from Southampton, you could have met her at King's Cross and gone down there with her, but Greenock ... that's not far from Glasgow, is it?'

'Aye, it's on the Clyde. If she hadn't gone at it like there wasn't a minute to lose, I'd have tried to get up there to see her on to the boat and wish her *bon voyage*, but she'll be on the Atlantic by now, telling the captain the stewards aren't keeping the cabins clean. And I bet she'll not be seasick, for whatever kind of food they give her, it wouldn't dare to disagree with her.' Dragging his sleeve across his eyes, he got to his feet. 'If I don't go now, I'll be late for work ... and don't worry about me. The shock knocked me for six, but I'll get over it.'

That morning, Marge did not follow her routine of clearing up after her husband had gone, but kept sitting at the table thinking how heartless his mother was. It was the only word to describe Meg Finnie, though the woman herself wouldn't think so, and likely neither would Dougal once he simmered down. But, to have been blessed with a son and then shoot off to the other side of the world, actually emigrate, without a thought for him, what else was that but heartless? If she and Dougal ever had a son, she would never let him out of her sight. She would lavish all her love on him ... till the day she died.

She often dreamed in the night – not sleep-dreaming but wide-awake-dreaming, which was better because she could arrange things to suit herself – of having a little boy of her own, younger than Gwen's David but having the same happy-go-lucky temperament. In her mind, she called him Ritchie, as a compliment to Alistair whose son she was more or less appropriating in her imagination. They would each take after their own father, David was fair like Alistair, and Ritchie would be dark like Dougal. In her wide-awake-dreams David was living next door and the two boys would have fun and adventures together, and sometimes their parents would be up to high doh with worry because they were late in coming home from the Heath, or from school, or wherever they'd gone.

Her heart aching for her pretend son, Marge told herself not to be silly, and got to her feet. It would be six years in September since she and Dougal were married, and there was no likelihood of them having a son now . . . nor a daughter. There was work to be done before she popped next door to see that her mother was OK. It was a bit of a tie-up, really, but she didn't mind. Peggy had been heartbroken when the boy she was in love with dumped her for another girl nearly a year ago, and had moped about the house for weeks with a face as long as a fiddle, so they'd all been glad when she applied for a job with the Civil Service and was taken on as Clerical Assistant. The snag was that Lee Green was such a distance from the City and she hadn't time to come home in the middle of the day, so Marge had volunteered to give their mother something hot and substantial for lunch.

Of course, Rosie still insisted that she could manage to cook something for herself, that she didn't need to be coddled like a child, but she was inclined to do stupid things. Marge had been alarmed one day to find her standing on top of the coal bunker cleaning the kitchenette window. She had used a chair to get up there, but one slip and she would have fallen onto the cement slabs Dougal had laid along the back of the house.

'You could have broken your neck!' Marge had scolded, after helping the almost sixty-year-old down to terra firma. 'You're not as young as you used to be, you know.'

'You're only as old as you feel,' Rosie had grinned, 'and today I feel about twenty.'

Marge had shaken her head helplessly and ushered her inside. 'You could have asked me, if you were so desperate to have it done, or Dougal or Peggy could have done it at night, but no! You're so dashed independent!'

It had worried her, though, and now she always had this fear lurking at the back of her mind that her mother would kill herself with her acrobatics at her age. That was why she didn't like to leave her too long on her own.

In late September of 1938, although trenches had been dug in Hyde Park to erect air-raid shelters, buildings were being sandbagged as a protection against bombs and ARP posts were springing up everywhere, Londoners, like the rest of Great Britain, were going about their business as usual, confident that Chamberlain had smoothed things over. He'd come back from his talk with Hitler in Berlin with a smile on his face, hadn't he? He'd waved a piece of paper and promised everybody there would be peace in our time, so what was there to worry about? Them old farts in Whitehall would put the wind up Wellington himself, if he'd still been alive, with all their doom and gloom.

People like Dougal Finnie, however, who had been in the Territorial Army for some time now, kept their thoughts to themselves. It would only put the fear of death in their women folk to tell them that war was inevitable no matter what the Prime Minister said. They tried to hide their fears, reasoning that it would be a shame to spoil the beautiful weather they were enjoying, though they couldn't understand why the majority couldn't see for themselves what lay just round the corner.

*   *   *

'What does Dougal think of the situation?' Manny asked Alistair one morning. 'He should know what is going on.'

The younger man screwed up his nose. 'Well, he did say, on the q.t. mind, that they're being geared up for war, and if it does come, they'll be hauled in right away to help the regulars.'

Manny nodded wisely. 'Yes, I am afraid Britain is on an irreversible path. We were lulled into thinking that Hitler would abide by the promises he made, when those in power must know the kind of man he is. Being Chancellor, Fuhrer, has given him a false impression of his own importance, of his own abilities, of his fitness to rule the entire world, and, unfortunately, he does possess the power to sway the German people with his oratory – the ravings of a lunatic, if they could but see it.'

'Of course, being a Jew, he'd be against Hitler,' Alistair observed to Dougal in Lee Green the following Sunday, while they were relaxing in deck chairs in the Finnies' garden with a bottle of beer. Dougal had just come back from his TA training and Alistair had been for a walk over Blackheath with his children, who were now sprawled out in their grandmother's garden next door. 'He believes all the stories going around about what's happening to the Jews in Germany. I think it's a lot of scaremongering, myself. They wouldn't have had the Olympics in Berlin in 1936 if things like that were going on. All the spectators from other countries, never mind the athletes, would have seen if the Jews were being persecuted, wouldn't they? And don't tell me King Edward would have been so easily fooled, him and Mrs Simpson. She'd have noticed something, I bet.'

'People only see what they want to see, and hear what they

want to hear,' Dougal said, darkly. 'That's what's wrong with the world today.'

'So you think it's true? You honestly think there'll be war?'

'No doubt about it, and now's the time to start preparing yourself for it. There's word they're going to supply shelters for people's gardens, so take one if you're offered it.'

'The Jerries'd never bomb London, surely.'

'It's the first place they will bomb. If they manage to knock out the capital, the whole country would be theirs.'

'Has something upset you?' Gwen asked Alistair on their way home, but he couldn't tell her. He didn't want to alarm her unnecessarily, because he didn't honestly think there would ever be another war, no matter what Dougal, or anybody else, said.

Having been seeing Ernie Gammie once a week for around three years, more often when he was on holiday from the Fire Service, Lexie could hardly say she was satisfied with the way the romance was going. He was so . . . gentlemanly, that was the only word to describe him. He still kissed her as though he loved her, but the second a hint of passion crept in, he backed off, and he'd been shillyshallying for far too long. Tonight, however, she meant to ginger him up a bit. She took extra pains with her appearance, brushing her blonde hair until it shone and glinted like gold, and coaxing it into the new pageboy style that seemed to be all the rage, according to the magazines. She smoothed some Pond's Cream over her face and neck, added a touch of rouge to her cheeks and softened it by applying a lavish amount of Phul Nana powder. The last touch was a firm coating of Yvette Tangerine lipstick with a pat of powder over it to keep it on a bit longer. This last was probably a waste of time, she thought, for Ernie would kiss it off in five minutes. She did nothing to her eyes, they were lovely enough as they were . . . so he was always telling her. 'I could get lost in them,' he sometimes murmured, 'so big and so blue.'

Her pulse speeded up at the thought of the next few hours, and also the extra hours she was going to offer him. She could hardly bear to think about what might happen then – the willing sacrifice of her virginity to a man who had once been married and would know everything there was to know about making love. It would make up for all the bad things that had happened, for her father, for Alistair, for her mother.

The little tap at the door made her run to let her soon-to-be lover in and, if she thought his kiss was a little perfunctory, she put it down to his shyness at being asked to spend the evening in her house. If only he knew, she exulted, he would be spending the night there, as well – in her bed!

'Something smells good,' he remarked as he sat down on one of the armchairs.

'Thanks,' she grinned, 'I hope you enjoy it.'

'I'm sure I will.'

She couldn't help feeling that there was a lack of warmth in his manner towards her, but he seemed to be quite impressed with what she served him, nothing fancy but good homely fare, and it wasn't until they had cleared up and were back sitting at the fireside that he said, 'I'm afraid I've something to tell you. I'm being sent on a three-month course, then I'm being transferred to Birmingham.'

'For good?' she gasped. She hadn't expected anything like this.

'I might try for promotion in a few years and be posted somewhere else, but it'll depend on how well I do down there.'

He fell silent, obviously waiting for her to pass some comment, but what was she to say? She wouldn't demean herself by pleading with him not to go. He had never made any commitment to her, the love had probably been in her imagination, and it was his career he was speaking about, after all. She couldn't even ask him if there was any chance that he would come back to her. 'I wish you luck, Ernie,' she finally got out.

A small sigh of relief escaped him. 'Thanks, that means a lot to me. I've really enjoyed our times together, and if I'd been left in Aberdeen . . . who knows? But you're a lovely person, Lexie, you'll find somebody else.'

He didn't even kiss her goodbye when he left, but held out his hand for her to shake, and she went inside without waiting until his car drove off. Damn him! she thought. He had walked out on her! Like her father! Like Alistair! Well, she wouldn't get serious with any other man, even if he swore on a stack of bibles that he loved her.

Something she had once read came to her now. 'Love is to man a thing apart, 'tis woman's whole existence.' She probably hadn't got the words exactly right, but their meaning was as true now as it had been when the poet wrote them.

But she would get over Ernie Gammie! Just as she'd got over everyone else who had betrayed her!

Throughout the winter of 1938–39, more and more rumours circulated of unrest in Europe, newsreels in the cinemas showed Hitler's storm troopers marching into this country and that. And overnight, it seemed, grey bloated fish-shapes appeared in the skies over the large cities – barrage balloons to stop enemy aircraft getting through, and anchored to the ground by long cables – and still the British stoically ignored what they knew in their hearts was almost upon them.

*　　*　　*

Lexie Fraser was fed up – the only folk she ever saw were women buying groceries and odd things like shoe polish and laces, and old men collecting their pensions and getting their supply of XXX Bogey Roll for their stinking pipes. Nothing exciting ever happened.

She had expected to see Alistair Ritchie at his sister's wedding in May, but he hadn't come. Of course, Alice had made excuses for him, saying he'd a wife and two kids to support so he couldn't afford the fare, but he could have, if he'd wanted. Not that Alice had been upset about him not showing up; she'd been so soppy about Sam Guthrie, she wouldn't have noticed if there had been nobody there except the two of them. As it was, it had been a really quiet wedding, no big show, a handful of friends, a sandwich tea in the kitchen at Benview after the kirk service, and that was it.

Even the best man, one of Sam's workmates, hadn't been anything special. She'd offered to put him up for the night, and had made him walk to her house to try to sober him a bit, only because he hadn't been fit to drive back to Aberdeen. He'd been at the sorry-for-himself stage, bewailing the fact that no girl ever stuck to him for long, and she'd been sorely tempted to tell him to try washing himself with Lifebuoy to see if that would get rid of his b.o. And so, although Alice and Sam still teased her about her one-night-stand with what's-his-name, she was still a virgin, a finicky virgin who couldn't find a man to make her heart beat like Alistair had once done, and more recently though less strongly, Ernie Gammie.

Although she often told herself she should have nothing to do with men, she still felt a craving for male company, and after she had got over Ernie letting her down, she had begun to go to any dances that were held within ten miles of Forvit – there was always somebody with a car willing to give her a lift. She had hoped to meet a man who would at least take her out occasionally, but of those who *had* made a date with her, two could only speak about football, motor bikes and engines of any kind, and the rest had just one thing on their minds. They all knew that she lived on her own, and at first, she'd been thrilled when one of them tried it on – Pattie Morton from Bankside, for instance. He was really good-looking, and he'd taken her to the first house of the theatre in Aberdeen one Saturday, and when he took her home she had invited him in without thinking. She had expected him to kiss her so she wasn't upset by that, but she had ended up having to fight him off. She'd decided to refuse if he asked her out a second time, but he hadn't.

But Pattie had been a gentleman compared with Ed Ross. *He* had an old BSA motor bike, and she'd been quite thrilled to be sitting on the pillion with the wind whistling in her ears and whipping against her cheeks. It had been quite an exhilarating experience, but then he went and spoiled it by running off the road and into a wood. She'd hardly got herself seated on the ground when he was on top of her, and she'd a devil of a job to stop his hands – and worse – going where they shouldn't.

'No wonder you're still an old maid!' he had shouted at her as he jumped on his bike and roared off, leaving her to walk all the way home, like the ill-mannered lout he was.

So she'd been cautious after that, hadn't let any of them see her home. But some were just as bad inside a cinema or theatre, even at the bus terminus, or wherever they thought they would get away with it . . . but she always managed to stop them. Not a soul asked her out now, once the word had got round.

It did puzzle her sometimes, though. She couldn't understand why she got in such a panic about it, when she wanted to know what it was like, wanted to do it at least once so she would know what other women were speaking about, but the minute she heard the man's breathing quickening, her stomach started to churn with terror and her body went rigid, and if his hand strayed anywhere near the leg of her knickers, she went mad and fought like a tiger.

If only she had somebody to confide in, to help her to get at the root of her problem. Once upon a time, she would have had Alistair Ritchie, not that she could have spoken to him about anything like this, or if Doctor Tom had still been here, he'd have reasoned it out with her. Folk still spoke about how kind he'd been, how he'd listened to everything they had to say.

The shop bell tinkling, Lexie looked up to see Doodie Tough coming in, sidling in would be more like it, she thought, for the woman had a queer way of walking, though there was nothing wrong with her tongue. She could speak till the cows came home and never draw a breath, as the saying went.

'I'm nae needing much the day, Lexie,' Doodie began, 'jist a quarter o' back bacon . . . and cut it thin so it'll be enough for me and Dod and oor Georgie.'

'Right.'. Lexie lifted the bacon joint off its shelf, placed it in the slicing machine and reset the thickness gauge before she turned the handle. 'And how are you this morning?' She knew that asking would bring forth a whole catalogue of ailments, but it was out before she thought.

'I'm nae that good the day.' Doodie's face took on a more melancholy expression than normal. 'My varicose veins are gieing me gyp, my corns are yarking like the very devil wi' the damp weather, and I've come oot in a rash.'

'I'm sorry to hear that.' Lexie wrapped the sliced bacon in the greaseproof paper she had laid ready. 'Was it something you ate?'

'If it was, it come oot o' this shop!' Doodie did not dwell

on it, however, and carried on, 'What's mair, I broke ane o' my false teeth last night eating a caramel, and I thocht it was a nut and swallaed it.'

Hard pressed not to laugh, Lexie gave a sympathetic mumble, then said, 'Now, was there anything else, Doodie?'

'A box o' Swan Vestas. Dod likes them best to light his` pipe. I tried him wi' a twirl o' paper to use like a taper, you ken, but he wouldna even try it. He's set in his ways, my Dod, and getting worse every day, the thrawn auld bugger.'

She cackled loudly, and knowing that there were few couples in Forvit as close as the Toughs, Lexie laughed along with her while she handed over the matches and counted out the change from the half crown Doodie tendered.

Thankfully, the woman didn't linger, and Lexie was putting the bacon back in place when something niggled at her mind – set off by Doodie Tough's visit, but nothing that she had said today. Lexie had the feeling that it was something she had overheard when she was quite young, something quite important to her now, and she knew she wouldn't get any peace until she did remember.

Chapter 10

❧

The Prime Minister's broadcast was over by the time the Ritchies reached Lee Green on the first Sunday of September, but Alistair had no need to ask the outcome. Peggy looked shocked, Marge was sobbing because Dougal had been mobilized the day before, and Rosie was trying to comfort her. 'I keep telling you, dear, he won't be in any danger. The regulars'll bear the brunt of the fighting, though I can't really see Adolf tangling with the British Army, not when we beat them last time. It'll all be over in a few months.'

Understanding that his mother-in-law was warning him off the subject, Alistair did not voice any opinion, and the rest of the day passed in forced merriment.

Gwen, however, had sensed something in her husband that made her distinctly uneasy, but she waited until they were on their way home before she asked, 'I hope you're not thinking of joining up, Alistair?'

He couldn't meet her eyes. 'Yes I was, if you must know . . . but Manny depends on me, so I'll stay with him till I'm called up.'

Certain that married men with children wouldn't be conscripted, Gwen said no more. Pushing him to give up the idea of going into the forces might have the opposite effect.

War now a reality, the government was underlining its earlier advice that parents in all major cities should evacuate their children to protect them from air raids, and train loads of poor youngsters, with labels on and carrying square gas mask boxes, had already been whisked away from their tearful mothers.

Gwen couldn't bear the thought of six-year-old Leila and David, newly five, being taken away from her, and she certainly wouldn't go with them and leave Alistair on his own. 'I don't know what all the fuss is about, anyway,' she told him.

'They're expecting the Jerries to bomb London,' he explained.

'So they say,' she sneered, 'but Hitler's not that stupid.'

'Dougal said there's nothing surer.'

'And he's an authority on Hitler, is he?'

'Alistair says I'm not facing facts,' she told Manny when they were on their usual Wednesday morning walk, much shorter than it used to be on account of his failing legs, and without Leila and David except in the school holidays, 'but it's an awful decision to have to make – my children, or my husband? What are mothers supposed to do?'

'The government thinks that all those who live in big cities, and are free to do so, should go to some rural area away from the danger,' the old man answered unwillingly, because he didn't want to lose her company, but he considered that it would be best for her. 'It is only sensible, hmm? Getting out before the mayhem starts?'

'You feel sure we'll be bombed?'

'I would bet my life on it.'

He left Gwen feeling that she was between the devil and the deep blue sea. She couldn't trust her darlings to absolute strangers, as so many other mothers had done, and how could she leave Alistair in Bethnal Green where he might be killed? But there was no real fear of bombs! There couldn't be!

That evening saw the first serious quarrel the Ritchies had ever had, short but bitter.

Alistair set it off by saying he was going to write to Alice. 'She's got plenty of room to take you and the kids, so you'd better start packing.'

'I'm not going anywhere!' Gwen declared, eyes dangerously bright.

'Yes, you are! You're taking Leila and David to Forvit, and you're staying there till the war's over!'

'I can't see any need ... nothing's happening ...'

'Not yet, but it will, and a mother's first thought should be for her children,' Alistair said, brusquely.

'A wife's place is with her husband,' she snapped.

'This husband can look after himself.'

'This wife happens to *want* to be with her husband and children!'

'Don't be so damned thrawn, woman!'

'You won't change my mind by flinging your Scottish swear words at me!'

Their voices had been rising steadily, and now Alistair threw his arms up as he roared, 'I wasn't swearing! I said you were stubborn! And that's exactly what you are! A bloody stubborn woman, with no thought for anybody but her bloody self!'

'So what's that if it isn't swearing?' Gwen countered, but it was clear that she was on the verge of tears. 'I wasn't thinking of myself. I was thinking of you. I thought you'd want to have your children here where you could protect them.'

'I want them, and you, out of harm's way,' he said, but his voice was less harsh.

'I won't put them away, Alistair, and I can't leave you here on your own. I'd never sleep a wink wondering if you were all right.'

Stumped by her brimming eyes, Alistair caved in, and took her in his arms. 'I'm sorry for shouting at you, my darling.

I know how you must feel, and like you said, nothing's been happening anyway.'

'Nothing's going to happen! No air raids, no bombs! It was just a silly rumour. A lot of those children who were sent away have come back already. People just panicked, that's all it was.'

Not altogether convinced that she was right, Alistair nevertheless stopped arguing.

However hard she had tried, Lexie Fraser could not grasp the elusive shadow which had flashed too quickly through her mind all those months before, so she had been quite glad, in a funny sort of way, when Mr Chamberlain announced that Britain was at war with Germany. Most conversations in the shop were now centred on how Forvit would be affected, a few sons, or brothers, or boyfriends already having volunteered or been called away as Territorials, so she was quite pleased that her last customer one day was Alice Ritchie, Mrs Sam Guthrie now, of course. They had always been good friends, although there was a three-year gap in their ages.

'I'd a letter from Alistair yesterday.' Alice eyed the shopkeeper warily.

Years of practice had enabled Lexie to show no emotion at any mention of his name. 'What's he saying to it, then?' she asked, matter-of-factly.

'He wants Gwen to come up here with the kids till the war's finished, but she won't hear of it. He's scared London'll be bombed and he wants them to be somewhere safe, so I think they'd a big row. It beats me how she can bear to keep her bairns down there when they could be killed, and I could tell Alistair's not happy about it.'

Lexie didn't really feel up to discussing the problems

148

Alistair Ritchie was having with his wife – she had given up on him years ago – and was relieved when Alice changed the subject. 'I'm a bit worried about Sam,' she confided. 'He's speaking about joining up though I'm trying to talk him out of it.'

'He'll not be happy if you stop him.'

'He could surely wait till the baby's born?' Alice sounded quite tearful.

'You said last week he hadn't touched you since you told him you were expecting, but if he's away for months at a time, think what he'll be like when he's home on leave.'

'Aye,' murmured Alice, thoughtfully, 'there's something in that.' Then she burst out laughing. 'Ach, Lexie Fraser, you're an awful tease, and I still don't want him to go.'

Locking up and going through to the house to make her supper, Lexie mulled over what she had been told. She could understand Alistair's wife not wanting to come away up here, hundreds of miles from her husband, for God knows how long. Any wife would feel the same, and Alistair was being unreasonable to expect it. It was funny the way things turned out, though. At one time, she'd have jumped for joy at the idea that things weren't going smoothly for the Ritchies, that there was every chance of them splitting up, but not any longer. In any case, was there any truth in it?

With absolutely no warning, Lexie's musings were blown apart by what could only be likened to a bolt of lightning, a flash which set free something deep in her memory . . . but just a few words. She had been standing in the shadows just inside the door of the kirk, she could remember that, waiting for her mother to stop speaking to Bella Ritchie and catch up with her, when she'd heard a snippet of a conversation between three women who hadn't noticed her there.

'. . . and they're saying she was taking up wi' him for months afore . . .'

That was all she could remember, but it had definitely been Doodie Tough's sharp voice. The words had meant nothing to her at the time, but they aroused her curiosity now. Who had been taking up with who? For months before what?

Lexie's appetite had vanished and she got no sleep that night. Like all small villages, Forvit had always spawned gossip, true and imagined, and this titbit could have referred to anybody . . . even if they seemed unlikely culprits. The woman had obviously had some standing in the community because Doodie's cronies had been standing with their mouths agape and eyes glittering. Funny how things were coming back to her, though it wasn't them she was interested in. It was who was at the centre of the scandal.

Going over all the women who might have fitted the bill – and bearing in mind that she would have been too young at the time to recognize illicit goings-on as such – Lexie could only come up with three candidates – the minister's wife, the doctor's wife, the wife of the banker in Bankside. Two of them could be crossed out straight away, the first would have been too old, the second too fat even then, but Mrs Kincaid, the banker's wife, was a possibility. She was around fifty now, still quite attractive, dark hair shot with grey, always well-dressed and very friendly, spoke to everyone she met.

Had Mrs Kincaid been the scarlet woman? It didn't seem likely. Her husband was a really handsome man, dark eyes that twinkled at everybody, and a straight almost Roman nose. He was well over six feet tall, still as slim as he was when he was younger, still playing golf. No, Mrs Kincaid could be ruled out, as well.

There was nobody else. Her own mother, being the postmaster's wife, could have been classed as a 'somebody', of course, but she'd never gone out at nights and she would never have had a lover. She had been in poor health for as long as Lexie could remember, which was likely why folk had been so ready to believe ill of her father when he disappeared. She could almost hear them saying that Alec Fraser was a good man, a decent man, but ... a man who could turn his back on an ailing wife would be capable of anything, even going off with a lassie young enough to be his daughter.

Her stomach giving a jolting heave, Lexie's thoughts wavered. Had it been him and Nancy Lawrie that Doodie had been speaking about? '... she'd been taking up wi' him afore ...', but if it was her father and Nancy she'd have said, '... he'd been taking up wi' her afore ...', for it would have been his name that would have raised people's eyebrows.

Glancing at the little clock at her bedside, Lexie stretched out to flick off the alarm switch. She didn't need it today. She'd have to get up in twenty minutes anyway, and there was no risk of her falling asleep now. Who had the woman been? Young enough to be having an affair, important enough to have made the village tongues wag? Who?

A speck of excitement suddenly took wing inside her, growing in intensity until she felt suffocated by it. Why hadn't she remembered before? The present doctor had come after Tom Birnie went to join his wife in Stirling, which would have been quite late on in 1929, three months at least after her father had gone off – maybe six, because he'd had to get somebody to buy his practice before he could leave.

So! Lexie drew in a long, juddery breath of relief, and let it out slowly. It could be Margaret Birnie! She might have been seeing another man before she left to look after her mother. Doctor Tom was often out all evening, sometimes nearly all night – like he'd been with her mother and her, Lexie recalled – and she'd have had plenty opportunities. She'd been a really pretty woman, they had two cars, and she could easily have driven miles to meet her lover. That was it, thank goodness.

Flinging back the bedclothes, Lexie swung her feet to the floor. Why couldn't she remember what else Doodie had said that long-ago day?

1940–1945

Chapter 11

❧

Never had Marge Finnie sat by her wireless set for so long at a time. It was an effort for her to leave it long enough to prepare the meals she took next door to her mother but could only pick at herself. While Dougal had been home over New Year, he had told her proudly, 'Our mob's going to France as part of the BEF.'

'BEF?' she had asked. 'What's that?'

'British Expeditionary Force,' he had explained.

Out of all the people present at the time, only his young nephew had been impressed. The others had expressed their fears for him, but David, on the Ritchies' usual Sunday visit to Lee Green, had said, 'Gosh, Uncle Dougal, I bet you're excited.'

'I am a bit,' admitted Dougal, adding truthfully, 'but I'm not looking forward to it.'

'Why not? You'll be able to kill as many Jerries as you want, won't you?'

'That's enough, David,' Alistair reprimanded.

Marge had realized that he was trying to prevent the four women — her two sisters, her mother and herself — from realizing that it could also work the other way, but if *she* had tumbled to it, they probably had, too. She had worried herself night and day ever since, making herself ill at the idea of Dougal being wounded or, worse, killed — she could scarcely bear to think about that — but since France was on the brink of falling, a new fear had blasted its way into her mind. The Germans had the BEF in full retreat, according to the reports, and it seemed likely that every last one would be taken prisoner. The announcers, usually so cheerful during their reading of the news, gave no false hope, and neither did the newspapers. It was as if, Marge thought, everyone had given up.

But they couldn't give up! There were thousands of men's lives at stake, French as well as British. Surely there was some way of rescuing them? Couldn't they be lifted away by air? When she had mentioned this to Alistair last Sunday, though, he'd said, softly but firmly, 'Planes would be shot down before they got a chance to land, and in any case, I don't think we've enough aircraft to pick up even half the men involved.'

While she tried to prepare herself for bad news, she couldn't help wondering what her husband might be facing if he had been captured. He wasn't a coward, of course, and no matter what the Germans did to torture him, he wouldn't tell them anything. She wasn't strong like that, unfortunately. She doubted if she'd have the strength to go on with her life if anything happened to him.

If he was spared, she'd never go dancing with Petra again, although she had done nothing wrong. Some of the servicemen were clearly out for all the fun that was going, and anything else on offer, but it was mostly girls who were the predators, Petra being one of the worst. She dressed up to the nines, full war-paint on, and instead of her usual aloofness, she was so animated she wouldn't have been out of place in a Disney cartoon. There was no point in falling out with her for what she had said about Dougal, though; she wasn't worth it.

Marge was angry at herself now for doubting her husband even for one minute. He would *never* play around with other women. She trusted him. She would always trust him . . . for as long as she lived . . . if he came back to her.

Tears were slowly edging down her cheeks when she heard the back door opening and knowing it was her mother, she pulled out her hankie and hastily tried to wipe them away. 'Mum! It's not dinner time yet.'

Rosie, bothered with arthritis now, made her stiff way across the room. She didn't intend to let her daughter swamp herself in misery. 'We won't get any dinner at all if you can't tear yourself away from that thing! Anyway, I came to give you the latest news.'

Ashamed at being caught weeping, Marge said sharply, 'I've heard all the latest news. Why d'you think I'm sitting here?'

'I mean the latest *latest* news,' Rosie said airily, unfazed by her daughter's reception of her. 'Alf was telling me somebody in the grocer's knows somebody who's got a cousin with a boat on the Thames, and *he* told his cousin – the one with the boat told the one Alf knows – there's a whole lot of them there . . .'

'I know! Dougal used to take me to Windsor to see them. But what . . . ?'

'Just listen! They've all been asked to help to get the soldiers off the beaches.'

'But little boats like that could never . . .'

'Well, that's what Alf heard, and he seems to think it could work.'

'Alf's an old woman,' Marge sneered. 'He believes everything anybody tells him.'

'He's been a good neighbour to me,' Rosie pointed out. 'Since your Dougal went away, he's been keeping my grass cut, and he gives Peggy a hand to weed sometimes.'

'I know, but don't you think he's a bit . . . soft? In the head, I mean.'

'He's got all his marbles, and he's not a pansy, though some people think he is. It was his mother's fault he never had a girlfriend, you know – she kept him running after her till the

157

day she died – and he thinks he's too old now. But he can only be . . . what . . . in his late forties?'

'More like his fifties.' Marge couldn't keep her annoyance up any longer. 'Um . . . will I put on the kettle for a cuppa?'

'Yes, love, that'd be nice. And I'll have my dinner here, if that's all right with you? You won't miss anything, I'll listen to the wireless the time you're getting it ready.'

It was several hours before reports came across the airwaves that a great armada of boats of all shapes and sizes had started on the unenviable task of evacuating as many of the troops stranded on the Dunkirk beaches as they could.

'Now do you believe Alf?' Rosie was pleased that her neighbour had been vindicated.

'I'm sorry,' Marge muttered, 'but I've been so worried about Dougal I couldn't think straight, but I feel better now I know he'll be home soon.'

'You don't know for sure that he's at Dunkirk, though?' Rosie felt obliged to remind her daughter of this.

'I feel sure he is, Mum, but I suppose I'll just have to wait and see.' Marge was relieved that her mother left it there. She wasn't sure . . . of anything. For all she knew, Dougal could be lying dead somewhere. She strangled this thought before it suffocated her. He couldn't be dead. She'd have felt it in her bones, in her very heart, whereas all she felt was this uncertainty, as though she'd been caught up in a sort of limbo.

'Your sister-in-law must be very worried about Dougal,' Manny remarked on the second day of the evacuation.

'I thought she might be glad of some extra support, so when Gwen said she was going to see Marge, I told her to stay with her till they found out, one way or the other. David and Leila know to go to Mrs Wright next door when they come home from school. She took them in yesterday.'

'You should have told me, my boy. You could have closed the shop early. And you must go home in time for them coming out of school today, and for as long as dear Gwen is away. You do not want to impose on your neighbour, do you?'

'She doesn't mind. She loves the kids.'

Alistair would have liked to ask Manny if he was well enough. For some time now he had noticed how frail the old man was becoming, how grey and crepey his skin was, but he knew better than say anything. His employer did not take kindly to being reminded of the passage of time, but he shouldn't be living alone at his age. Manny was one of the old school, who considered nothing was wrong with them as long as they could stand on their own two feet. The weakness in his legs had stopped him from going round the markets, but it hadn't stopped him from being in the shop from just after nine each morning, though Alistair had told him he should take things easy.

He'd been wondering if he should sound Gwen about asking Manny to live with them, so that she could keep an eye on him, but he had better wait till this business at Dunkirk was over. He gave a shivering sigh.

Manny looked at him compassionately. 'You are also fearful for Dougal?'

'If anything happens to him,' Alistair muttered, 'it'll be like I've lost part of myself. We've been friends since the day we started school. We did everything together, we came to London together, we shared a bed, even married into the same family. If he doesn't come back, it'll tear the heart out of me – out of all of us.'

Manny nodded his understanding. 'I think you should be there when your children come out of school today. Go home now, pack a few things, and take them to Lee Green. It is better for all of you to be together in this worrying time. If it is bad news, you will help each other through it, show your sister-in-law that she is not alone in her grief. Oh dear, perhaps you think I am morbid, talking like that, but if we prepare ourselves for the worst it helps to ease the pain, and if the worst does not happen, so much the better.'

'You know, Manny, I think I *will* go to Lee Green today, that's if you don't mind?'

'I do not mind. In fact, I feel like going with you.'

'You're welcome to come . . .'

'No, no, my boy. Although I regard myself as one of your family, I am not truly a member. Tell dear Marge that I am praying for Dougal's safety, and do not come back until you know for sure what has happened. I can cope, I am not finished yet.'

By a strange quirk of fate, Leila was alone in Marge's house when the soldier walked in and, in spite of several days' growth of beard and the strain evident in his grey face, she recognized him immediately and flung herself at him. 'Uncle Dougal! It's you!'

Hoisting her up in his aching arms, he gave her a bear hug. 'Aye, my lamb, it's me! Where's everybody?'

'They're all in Grandma's. I didn't like seeing Auntie Marge crying, so I came here to read my comic for a while.'

He set her down gently. 'We can't let your Auntie Marge cry any longer, can we? We'll go and surprise her, eh?' Catching sight of himself in the mirror above the fire, he pulled a face. 'Maybe I'd better wash and shave first, eh?'

The little girl waited, excitement bubbling inside her at the thought of being the first to know he was safe. She would have liked to run and tell the others, but knew that it would spoil his surprise. It had been awful, watching Auntie Marge crying, and Grandma and Mum trying to comfort her though they were nearly in tears, too. She had wondered why they were so sad when they didn't know what was happening. They shouldn't have been so sure Uncle Dougal was dead. If she could remember that bit she'd read somewhere . . . what was it again? Where there's life, there's hope? No, that didn't fit. Where there's hope, there's life. That was it, and she had never lost hope. That was why Uncle Dougal had come home safe.

Grown-ups were funny – not ha-ha funny, just queer funny – and it hadn't been only the women. Dad had been gripping his mouth tightly, and he'd blown his nose a few times before she came out, like he was trying not to cry. She loved Uncle Dougal nearly as much as she loved her Dad, but *she* hadn't cried, though she might have, if he hadn't come back.

The adults proved to be more than funny when she and Uncle Dougal walked into her Grandma's house. Auntie Marge cried louder than ever when she saw her husband, and she didn't stop even though he held her close and patted her back and whispered things in her ear. Grandma was dabbing at her eyes, and Mum was wiping her cheeks. Worst of all, tears were running down her father's face, but he was gripping David's hand to stop him from jumping on Uncle Dougal's back, which he was likely to do, but it wouldn't be fair at this special time.

Leila gave a satisfied sigh. She'd never seen anything so romantic as the way her uncle and aunt were kissing each other now. It was as good as the pictures, better, because she *knew* them, was related to them. Wait till she told her chums at school!

Looking fondly down at her sleeping husband, Marge blessed Alistair Ritchie for his understanding of the situation. 'Come on, troops,' he had laughed to his children about half an hour after Dougal had made his surprise entrance. 'It's time we went home.'

Rosie was horrified at this. 'Wait till Peg gets in from work. She'll make something to eat. Or why don't you have a look in the pantry, Gwen, and see what there is?'

'Only if we let Marge take Dougal next door.' Alistair had stood his ground. 'Can't you see he's dead on his feet with exhaustion?'

'I *am* a bit tired,' Dougal had said, which was when his wife had fully realized the ordeal the evacuation must have been – he never ever admitted to being tired.

As they entered their own house, she had said, 'I'll run a bath, just the regulation five inches, of course.' He followed her upstairs and went into the bedroom to undress, but in the few minutes it had taken her to put in the plug, turn on the taps and fetch a large towel from the airing cupboard, Dougal had fallen asleep on top of the bed-clothes, still wearing the ill-fitting clothes he'd been given to replace his waterlogged uniform when the rescue boat landed at Dover.

That was about all he had told them, really. Maybe he would tell her more tomorrow, or maybe he would never tell her. Maybe he wouldn't want to be reminded of the long hours of waiting until he was picked up from the beach nor of the terrible things he must have seen. He looked so vulnerable lying spread-eagled across the bed that her heart swelled with love, and wishing that he had turned down the blankets before exhaustion overtook him, she covered him up as best she could without disturbing him. She would lie down on the settee in the living room for this one night, because she, too, had a lot of sleep to catch up on.

Bending down, she kissed her husband's cheek, scarcely able to believe that he had come home safely, then tiptoed out. She found an old eiderdown at the back of the cupboard at the top of the stairs – she'd meant to throw it out long ago but was glad now that she hadn't – and rolled it round her before she lay down. All the earlier worry and the later excitement, however, prevented her from falling asleep. It wasn't seven o'clock yet, she saw when she glanced at the clock. No wonder she couldn't drop off.

She hoped that none of her family would come in to see if Dougal was all right. What would they think when they found her in her nightclothes on the settee and she told them her husband was in bed upstairs? After a while, she heard soft voices bidding each other good night, and guessed that Alistair was taking his brood home. She listened in case Peggy might take it into her head to come and see Dougal, since she hadn't seen him yet, but nothing happened, and before long, Marge herself had fallen into a deep sleep.

'Poor devil!' Alistair commented, as they walked down Burnt Ash Road to the railway station. 'He's been through a helluva lot, by the look of him.'

'Language,' cautioned his wife. 'Little pitchers . . .'

'Sorry, dear, but it's awful, isn't it? It makes me want to get in there and fight the bl . . . blinking Jerries.'

Young David proved that little pitchers did indeed have big ears. 'Are they always blinking, Dad? What makes them blink?'

'No, no,' Alistair smiled, 'it's just an expression.'

'What does it mean, then?'

'It means they're bad. The awful Germans, or the nasty Germans. See?'

'Are you really going into the army like Uncle Dougal to fight the blinking Jerries?'

'No, he's not!' declared Gwen firmly. 'He's got a wife and two children to consider, not like Uncle Dougal.'

Seven now, Leila took it upon herself to pour oil on the troubled waters, although she probably didn't know that was what she was doing. 'Auntie Marge was really glad to see him, wasn't she?'

Her mother nodded. She, too, had been impressed, and a trifle jealous if the truth were known, by the tenderness of the kisses they had all witnessed earlier, but David said, scornfully, 'I didn't think soldiers would be as soppy as that.'

'When you fall in love with a girl,' Alistair laughed, 'you'll be just as soppy as him.'

'Why do you never kiss Mum, then? Don't you love her?'

His father's cheeks reddened, but he said, 'I've loved your Mum ever since I met her, but there were times when I didn't show it enough.'

'What times? Why?'

Gwen ruffled his curly head. 'You were one of the reasons, I think, and Leila. I was so busy attending to you two, I didn't have time to show Dad how much I loved him. He must have felt neglected.'

'When I get married,' Leila said, dreamily, 'I'll never neglect my husband. I'll tell him every day, every hour, every minute, how much I love him.'

'I think every minute would be too much of a good thing,' Alistair smiled.

David blew a loud raspberry. 'All this talk of love and kissing! Yeugh! It makes me want to puke.'

'David!' exclaimed his mother. 'I will not have you talking like that! Where did you hear that word, anyway?'

'One of the boys at school says it all the time.'

'If I hear you saying it again, you'll . . . you'll be sorry.'

'Puke, puke, puke,' the boy muttered under his breath, but, although they heard, they decided to ignore it.

As Alistair said, much later, 'Puke's not really so bad, is it? But we'll have to watch him. He picks up every damned thing he hears.'

'Remember that, then.' Gwen's eyes suddenly clouded. 'You're not really thinking of going into the army, are you?'

'Yes, I am. Dunkirk has set the country back. The army needs replacements for the men who were lost.'

'Please, Alistair, don't go. Look at what Marge's had to put up with these last few days. Do you want to put your children and me through the same agonies?'

After a pause, he mumbled, 'If it wasn't for you three, I'd have been off months ago.'

'But you still have us.'

'That won't stop me from being called up, you know. In fact, I'm surprised they haven't done it already. I registered with the over-twenties.'

'You'll soon be twenty-seven. Surely they'll have enough without taking you?'

Her eyes were so distressed that he pulled her into his arms, and, whether it was a result of the eventful day he'd had or not, he found himself wanting her more acutely than he had done for years.

'I bet Dougal and Marge will have been . . .' she whispered afterwards.

'I doubt it.' Alistair ran his fingers down her neck. 'I don't think Dougal's up to it yet, but once he comes to himself properly, then . . . !'

'I wonder if all the worry they've had will make a difference? I know they're both desperate for a baby, and this might have done the trick. What do you think?'

'I've no idea.' Alistair wished that she hadn't brought up this subject. With all the upheaval and uncertainty in the world, he hoped that he hadn't made his wife pregnant a few minutes ago. They had a big enough struggle to make ends meet as it was, what with the rent to pay, and gas and electricity. This old house was a killer in the winter, and coal was getting dearer and dearer as well as scarcer and scarcer. He couldn't expect Manny Isaacson to give him more wages; what the shop was taking in barely covered the old man's expenses as it was.

Afraid that Gwen would expect him to make love to her again, he gave her a quick kiss, said, 'Good night, dear,' and turned away. The only safe method of contraception was to keep well away from your wife in bed.

Chapter 12

❧

The Battle of Britain, as it came to be known, was over at last, the little Hurricanes and Spitfires had pluckily repelled the enemy's attempts to blow our airfields and all our aircraft to smithereens. Yet despite this unexpected and insulting defeat, Hitler was still set on beating the British into submission. The Luftwaffe's heavy bombers were sent in – the Dorniers, the Focke-Wulfs, and thus began the Blitzkrieg.

Civilians now found themselves in the front line. Not only the Home Guard, air-raid wardens, ambulance drivers, firemen, medical staff, munitions workers, but those merely going about their daily business. This was when the true meaning of war was brought home to the man (and woman) in the street. Being the capital, London took the brunt of the raids at first, night after night of bombs screaming down, night after night spent in the large shelters built by the councils, or in Anderson shelters provided for back gardens, or Morrison shelters intended for those confined to the house but who were often too afraid to make use of them in case they were trapped inside like mice.

There were some, of course, who relied instead on their own makeshift boltholes – under the stairs, in a narrow lobby, in the cellar, even just under a table – and those who made a point of 'not giving in to the murdering bastards', who did nothing when the howling of the alert sirens rent the air. As the days passed, and they saw the havoc that was being wrought, the devastation the bombers were wreaking, their bravado was replaced by rationality or, more likely, by the need for self-preservation.

Night after night, Alistair Ritchie had helped his wife to carry the food and blankets she had laid out ready to take with them to the council shelter just along the street, where they and their neighbours tried to take the children's minds off the bombs by playing games with them and singing songs. Neither of these methods were 100% effective, especially when the terrifying sounds of explosions came nearer and louder. At times like these, every single person shook with fear, youngsters sobbing and clutching their mothers, who prayed while they held them that it would end soon.

'I don't know what to do, Manny.' Alistair Ritchie shook his head viciously as if that would dispel the worries he had. 'It looks like Jerry's trying to bomb us into submission now, and Gwen still won't hear of going to Forvit with the kids.' He paused, then went on hesitantly, 'Could you have a word with her, please? She'd listen to you.'

Laying down the pocket watch, an heirloom, which he was repairing as a favour to an elderly neighbour, Manny removed the little magnifying glass from his eye and regarded his manager sadly. 'I am sorry, Alistair, but I could not take that upon myself. It is entirely up to you, but let me warn you, my boy. Women are fickle creatures, and if they feel that they are being forced into something, they will fight against it.' He picked up the magnifying glass, but before fitting it into his eye, he cleared his throat. 'Um . . . I take it that you . . . still love her, hmm? You do not have what they call the seven-year itch?'

'Oh, no! I've never stopped loving her!'

'And I know that she has never stopped loving you. That is good. There must always be love there for a marriage to

survive, but you must persuade her to change her mind . . .
and soon.' He replaced the glass, retrieved the watch and the
subject was closed.

'I hear your Sam's joined the Air Force,' Lexie remarked to
her friend.

Alice Guthrie sighed heavily. 'I couldn't talk him out of it
this time. He just went to Aberdeen and signed up, and he's
got to report at Padgate on Monday. He's just a big bairn
really, thinking he'll get to fly an aeroplane some day, though
I've kept telling him he hasn't got the brains to be a pilot.'

'He'll be a lot safer on the ground, at any rate. It's a wonder
to me your Alistair hasn't joined up. With Dougal Finnie just
getting away from Dunkirk by the skin of his teeth, I'd have
thought he'd be itching to do his bit and all.'

Alice's shrug was hardly worthy of the name. 'There was
no word of it in Gwen's last letter. She says he doesn't want
to leave Manny, but no doubt he'll be called up shortly.'

'Lizzie Wilkie was saying the first lot of troops are to be
arriving at Ardley before Christmas, so Hogmanay should be
a bit brighter than we thought.'

'For you, maybe, not for me. Even if Sam gets home, I'll
still be stuck in the house with wee Morag. He's always gone
out boozing with his pals about seven o'clock, and he comes
home too drunk to remember anything about seeing in the
New Year.'

'You'd started on the wrong foot with him,' Lexie laughed.
'You should have let him see on your wedding night it
was the end of him being a single man. But that's your
own business, and if there's any soldier-boys going about
the place, I'll tell you all about it if I manage to click
with one.'

'Well, thanks,' Alice said, heavily sarcastic, 'and have

me green with jealousy?' But she was laughing as she left the shop.

Lexie, however, wasn't laughing. Her last chance of, perhaps not going as far as getting a husband, at least getting some fun out of life, lay with the men who would be arriving at Ardley House some time in the near future. Rumour had it that there would be over two hundred, and there certainly had been dozens of large Nissen huts erected in the grounds, so she should have plenty to choose from. And, as Lizzie Wilkie had pointed out, there weren't that many girls left in Forvit now. A lot of the younger ones were in uniform themselves, branching away from their humdrum existences and going out to find adventure for themselves. She had considered following their lead, but it would have meant giving up the shop her father had worked so hard to establish . . .

Her father. He was the centre of so much of her thoughts. She had almost learned to accept that he had run away to be with Nancy Lawrie – not Margaret Birnie, that had been a daft idea – but another, far more distressing explanation had occurred to her the other night and she couldn't get it out of her head.

Maybe Nancy hadn't gone away at all! Maybe Alec Fraser had offered to pay for an abortion, but she had refused and threatened to tell the whole village if he didn't support her and the infant when it was born. Knowing that his life would be in ruins if she did, he might have lashed out in his anger and accidentally knocked her off her feet. She *could* have hit her head on a stone and when he tried to help her up, he had discovered that she was dead. He would have been aghast at what he had done, but his first thought would be to protect himself, to hide the body.

Lexie's troubled mind blotted out the actual disposal and picked up the story where it had crossed Alec's mind that one or more of the other choir members might have known about him and Nancy ... even about his indiscretion. His overruling instinct then would be to escape, to flee from the aftermath of his crime.

'A penny for them, Lexie. You was miles awa'.'

Startled, she looked up into the inquisitive eyes of Mattie Wilkie and forced a smile. 'Alice Ritchie was saying Sam's joined the Air Force, then we got speaking about the soldiers coming to Ardley, and I was just thinking ...'

A sly grin spread over the older woman's face. 'Was you hopin' to get a lad? My Lizzie's the same, but she's younger than you. You'd best pull your socks up if you're nae wantin' to be left on the shelf. Now, can I get a quarter o' tea and a half loaf, for I clean run oot and Joe'll be hame for his denner in ten minutes.'

Lexie was thankful that the woman was in a hurry, she usually hung about hoping to have a gossip with the next customer. She had an edge to her tongue though she meant nothing by it, yet she shouldn't have said that about being left on the shelf. She would have to find a lad soon, Lexie told herself, and not be too choosy. What was more, she'd have to put what she'd been thinking about her father completely out of her mind. It was just a lot of nonsense. He'd been a good-living man, and even if he *had* slipped with Nancy Lawrie, he'd have owned up to his responsibility and taken the consequences. In any case, what was the point of dwelling on it? It wouldn't change what had happened.

Alistair kept pressing Gwen to take their children away but, adamant that it would be giving in to the enemy, she still held out against it, until one Sunday morning in January 1941, when they emerged into the open air to find that the house behind theirs had been damaged. The bomb had actually fallen in the roadway, but the blast had practically sheared off the entire side yet left the gable of the next house intact.

Looking out at the pile of rubble and realizing what a narrow escape they'd had themselves, Gwen at last questioned if she had been doing the right thing. Leila and David were pale and haggard, jumping nervously at the slightest noise, and she was to blame by being so stubborn. It wasn't fair to keep them in London when most of their chums had been sent away again. Only a few stragglers were left, those with mothers as stupid as she was.

Not surprisingly, while they were preparing to make their usual Sunday visit to Lee Green, Alistair told her that he'd had enough. 'I'm writing to Alice tonight and that's final! And I don't want any nonsense from you about not going. I want the three of you out of London, and you'll stay away until I say you can come back. Do you understand what I'm saying?'

It was Rosie who wondered, when they told her what they were proposing, if Marge would also be welcome at Forvit. 'Your sister knows her, Alistair, so I'm sure she wouldn't object to taking Dougal's wife along with yours.'

Gwen put her finger on the one flaw in this arrangement. 'Who would look after you, then? Peg's out at work all day, and you can't manage by yourself.'

'If she left things for me to heat up, I'd manage perfectly well,' Rosie declared.

'If we ask Alf,' Peggy put in, colouring a little, 'I'm sure he'd look in now and then. He's got a dicky heart, and he feels bad about not being fit for any of the services or anything. Checking on Mum, he wouldn't feel so useless.'

Gwen did make a tentative effort to get her mother to go to Scotland with them, but Rosie wasn't having that. 'I'm not letting that cocky little German clown put me out of my home. When I leave, it'll be feet first!'

This didn't make her daughters feel any easier. As Gwen said to Alistair later, 'She should have years ahead of her yet, but if she stops in Lee Green . . .' Realizing that this was the argument he had used to her, she said, softly, 'OK, you'd better write to Alice.'

An answer came by return, saying that they were all welcome, for as long as was necessary. 'Sam's been trying to get somewhere for me and Morag to stay,' her letter went on. 'He's stationed at Turnhouse, and I've been worried about leaving Benview empty, but with Gwen and Marge here to look after it, I can go with an easy mind.'

'Alistair's wife and kids are coming here to get away from the raids,' Alice told Lexie when she went to cash her RAF allotment. 'They've hardly been out of the shelter for weeks and weeks, poor souls. He can't give up his job, of course, but Marge, that's Gwen's sister, she's coming with them. Well, I'd better get back, for I've things to get ready and they'll be here tomorrow forenoon.'

Nothing fazed Lexie for the rest of the day, not even the grumpiest of grumpy old folk who came in to collect their pensions and wanted to chat though there was a long queue waiting behind them. She was normally flagging more than an hour before closing time, but this wasn't a normal day, and she locked the shop door jauntily at six o'clock and walked through to the house with a spring in her step.

If Alistair's wife and kids were going to be staying at Benview for any length of time, she thought, as she lit the gas ring under the kettle, he would have to come to visit them at some point. It must be almost nine years since he was married, and the magic was bound to have worn off. It might be worth while to make friends with his bairns. The

173

way to a doting father's heart would surely lie through his children, wouldn't it?

Her mood changed suddenly. What the devil was she thinking of? Alistair Ritchie hadn't figured in her plans for a long time now ... and there was still the long-awaited arrival of the troops to look forward to.

'It's worked out fine,' Alistair told Manny after seeing his family off at King's Cross. 'Alice is glad they'll be in the house to keep it heated, and it's a big relief to me. Marge has rented out their house, and Rosie says I should give up ours and move in with her, but I don't want to upset Peg. I think there's something between her and Alf Pryor next door, and it'd be a shame if I spoiled it for her. She's never kept a boyfriend long before, and Alf's a really nice bloke though he must be nearly twenty years older than her.'

'If she loves him,' Manny observed, shrewdly, 'twenty years is a mere nothing. But what have you decided, Alistair?'

'I'm going to stay where I am. Lee Green's too far for me to travel every day.'

Manny made no comment, and Alistair wondered if the old man had realized why he hadn't volunteered for the forces as he'd spoken about after Dunkirk. When he'd had time to think, his affection for his employer had been stronger than his wish to have a go at the Germans. He couldn't leave poor Manny in the lurch.

Alice Guthrie was shocked when she beheld the little group trailing off the bus – two women and two children, all looking like ... oh, she couldn't find words to describe them. Rushing forward, she clasped the boy and girl to her breast. 'You poor wee lambs! Was it a terrible journey?' Letting them go, she took the bags they were carrying and led the way along the rough track to Benview. 'I hope you're not too tired; there's a good bit to walk,' she apologized. 'And I bet you'll all be ready for a cup of tea once we get in?'

Getting no response from any of them, and thinking how sunken their eyes had been and how they'd looked as if they didn't care what happened to them, she came to the conclusion that what they needed most was peace and quiet.

'Come upstairs and I'll show you where you'll be sleeping,' she said when they entered the house. 'I've taken Morag in with me so Leila can have her room. Gwen and Marge, you can have the other double bedroom, if you don't mind sharing, and David's in what we call the boxroom, but I've cleared it out and he should be quite comfy.'

She showed the girl and boy their rooms first, saying, 'Don't worry about anything. Just get undressed and into your beds, and I'll take up a tray with something to eat.'

'No,' Gwen said, wearily, as Alice ushered Marge and her along the landing. 'They won't want anything and neither do we . . . thanks. We had sandwiches with us on the train, and flasks of tea, so we're not hungry.'

After standing for a few minutes watching the two women unpacking some things until they found their nightdresses, Alice said, 'I'll leave you to it, then. The bathroom's next door to you. Sam had it put in over a year ago – another room we never used.'

Before going downstairs, she looked in at Leila and wasn't altogether surprised to find her already asleep as was David, when she peeped round his door. Poor wee devils, she thought, compassionately. It was going to take all four of them a good while to get over their terrible ordeal.

*   *   *

Even in the shelter with all the noise going on, Alistair slept better that night than he had done for some time, and guessed it was because he didn't have to worry about his family any more, just himself. He emerged into the daylight with a light heart. His house was still standing and there didn't seem to be any damage near them as far as he could see. He boiled the kettle to have a wash, then made himself some tea and toast. The house was so quiet, though. He missed the chatter of his children, his wife's constant urging at them to hurry up and get dressed.

On his way to work, he discovered that the bombers hadn't been all that far away the night before. Many of the buildings he passed had been damaged by blasts that had completely destroyed others, and as he went on, it became more difficult to get through. He was almost sick with apprehension when he neared the end of Manny's street, and his legs faltered when he rounded the corner and saw that the pawnshop was no longer there.

'A direct hit!' he was told by one of the gang of workers trying to clear the area.

'What about the . . . have you found the owner?' Alistair could barely get the words out, he was so upset.

The weary tin-hatted man eyed him sympathetically. 'The old man in the back room? Did you know him? I'm sorry, mate. He's dead, crushed under a pile of rubble. We wouldn't have known to look for him except a woman a few doors along came and told us he slept in there. Her place got a good shaking up, windows all out, doors blown off, yet she was all worried about him. Was he a friend of yours?'

'I worked for him . . . and he was the very best friend I ever had.' Alistair staggered a little now, the shock beginning to tell on him.

'Are you all right, mate?'

'I'm fine. It's just ... I wasn't expecting this ... I never thought ...'

'You'd better get off home, mate. There's nothing you can do here, and there's an awful lot like you this morning, with no work to go to.'

He drew the curtains when he went in – Manny wasn't there, of course, but he wanted to show some respect for the dead man – then sat down by the fire. It wasn't lit, but it seemed the only place to sit. He had to come to terms with what had happened before he could face anybody. Losing his job was a mere fleabite compared to losing Manny. The old man had been part of his life for so long, going on without him was unthinkable.

Alistair huddled into his chair for hours, numb with cold as well as shock, until at last the tears came, the welcome, warm tears which initiated a thawing in his innermost being. And only then, after allowing himself the luxury of rinsing out the awful, painful, gnawing grief – which didn't banish it altogether but made it slightly easier to bear – was he able to consider what he should do. Not that he had to ponder over this for long. Fate had decided for him, hadn't it?

His expression was grim when he went to Lee Green in the late afternoon. 'Oh, my Lord!' Rosie exclaimed, her cheeks blanching when she heard about Manny. 'That poor, dear old man ... all alone at the end.'

'Aye, Rosie, that's what's eating at me, and all. But I keep telling myself it had been quick and he wouldn't have suffered ... would he?' His eyes sought her reassurance.

'I shouldn't think so,' she comforted, 'but what are you going to do now? You don't have a job and ...'

'I've been to the recruiting centre,' he admitted, a little sheepishly, 'and I've signed on for the Artillery. They said it mightn't be long till I'm told where to report, and I'm not allowed to sublet our house, so I'm going to give it up altogether and come here till it's time to go . . . that's if your offer still stands?'

Rosie eyed him sadly. 'You're very welcome, dear, for as long as you want, but are you absolutely sure the army's what you want to do?'

'Absolutely certain! I'd have joined up before, but I didn't want to let Manny down.'

Rosie looked pensive now. 'Do you know if anything was left of Manny's shop, any jewellery or valuables of any kind?'

'Nothing, apparently, and if there had been, somebody would likely have taken them. There's a bit of looting going on, you know.'

She frowned her disapproval of this. 'That's awful! How can people take advantage of other people's misfortunes? What's the world coming to? The Germans trying to blast us all to Kingdom Come, and our bombers doing the same to them. It's the poor civilians that are suffering most.'

'It just came back to me,' Alistair said suddenly, 'when the war started, Manny made me take all his best pieces to the bank for safekeeping.'

'That's a blessing, then, but what will happen to them now? Will the bank claim them now he's dead?'

'I've no idea.'

'I think you should go and ask, Alistair . . . if it's still standing.'

'It's not really any of my business, though. Manny did once speak about a cousin or a second cousin, in Australia . . . somewhere just outside Melbourne, I think he said. It was his only relative, so he'd be the next of kin, wouldn't he?'

'Tell the bank manager about him, and maybe you should see his solicitors, as well. They'll need to know things like that, unless Manny had it in his will. Did he ever say anything about a will?'

'No, never, but he was always so well organized, he must have made one.'

Rosie seemed better pleased. 'Of course he would, but if he didn't put his cousin or whatever's address down, you could save them hunting all over Australia for him by letting them know he lives near Melbourne.'

Alistair thought it highly unlikely that Manny would not have given an address for his heir, but decided to go to see the solicitor the next morning anyway. Apart from pleasing Rosie, it would give him something to do, and they would have to be told that their client was dead.

Chapter 13

❧

To the bank manager – a short, thin balding man with sharp features – Manny Isaacson's death meant just another name to add to the rapidly increasing list of accounts he'd had to close lately, although he did express sorrow that the old man's life had been terminated so suddenly and so violently. 'Mr Isaacson did not leave a great deal,' he went on, after consulting his records

'Not in cash, perhaps,' Alistair agreed, 'but I deposited some jewellery on his behalf at the start of the war for safekeeping.'

The man looked at him apologetically. 'I can not release anything to you without proper authority.'

'I wasn't expecting you to hand anything over to me, but I wondered if he'd deposited his will with you at some time.'

'Ah.' The other man stroked his upper lip reflectively. 'I have been manager of this branch for less than six months, so I am not familiar with transactions made prior to that, but if you care to wait, I can find out.'

Alistair was puzzled by the peculiar, almost accusing, look the man had given him as he passed. Surely he didn't suspect him of trying to steal the jewellery? It was just as well that he *wasn't* the heir. How on earth could anybody get proper written authority from a dead man? He shouldn't have come. He should have gone straight to the solicitor and let him deal with it.

While he waited, with nothing else to occupy it, his mind

went back to Manny, the one and only real friend he'd made in London, apart from his in-laws, and that was different. Of course, there were Ivy and Len Crocker, but that was different, too. In any case, Len had retired some time ago, and they were now living in a small fishing village not far from Newcastle to be near Ivy's sister, who had married a Geordie during the last war. They still kept in touch, of course, sending birthday cards and gifts to his children on their birthdays, though Ivy was godmother only to David. The monthly letters she had sent to Gwen, though, had dwindled down to a hastily written note in a card at Christmas. That was how things went, he mused. Your friends change over the years; they move away and find other friends, and so do you. In any case, he'd never been one for having a lot of friends. Acquaintances, yes, but friends, no. He was slow at getting close to people, a result, probably, of being brought up in a house with no near neighbours.

He wondered now how Gwen and Marge would take to the isolation. He didn't think Gwen would mind. She was quiet, a home body, whereas Marge was . . . well, Marge was just Marge – a goer. She didn't like being stuck in the house. Her next-door neighbour on the other side from Rosie had told him once that he'd seen her going into a dancehall in Lewisham a few times. 'I don't suppose there's anything in it,' he had gone on. 'She likes a laugh does Marge, but I thought I'd better tell you, and I'll leave it up to you if you tell her mother or Dougal.'

He hadn't told anybody. Knowing Marge as he did, he was quite certain that there was nothing in it, that she had just wanted to break the monotony of being alone while Dougal was serving his country. She had been looking for some amusement . . . and she'd get precious little to amuse her in Forvit. It crossed his mind that maybe

Rosie had guessed what had been going on. Had that been why she'd been so adamant that Marge should leave with Gwen and the kids? It would be a shock to his sister-in-law's system, though. She'd never walked farther than she could help, and she'd be stuck in Benview from one week's end to the next, unless she used shanks's pony. No buses ran past Alice's house. The bus from Aberdeen to Strathdon did go through Forvit, but when the Ritchies wanted to go into the city, they'd had to walk, or bike, a full mile of rough track before they came to the turnpike and could get transport, and if they were just going to the village, it was three miles there and three miles back.

He and Alice had walked to school in the early days. He'd forgotten that in his anxiety to get his family away from London. He'd been nearly ten before his father bought bikes for them at a roup, a house clearance, but if they were still in the shed, they'd be rusted out of commission by this time, so Leila and David would have to hoof it. Well, it hadn't done him or Alice any harm, in fact, it had likely kept them in peak condition – neither of them had ever been off school through illness.

'Sorry to have kept you waiting so long, Mr Ritchie.' The manager bustled in again, taking Alistair's mind off the past. 'You were quite right, there was a significant amount of valuable items deposited in our vaults by you on behalf of Mr Isaacson, but I am afraid that I am not, without written authorization, at liberty to . . .'

'I don't want them,' Alistair put in, angry because of the thinly veiled hostility in the man's eyes. 'I had to be sure they were still here, and I also wanted to find out if he had deposited his will with you. You see, I know something of the whereabouts of his next of kin, which I thought would be of use to you, but if you don't have the will . . .' He stood up and said coldly, 'Good day, and I'm sorry to have troubled you.'

The man shot to his feet, all apologies. 'I am sorry, Mr Ritchie, I did not mean to be offensive, but you must understand that I have to be careful.'

'Yes,' Alistair sighed, rather regretting his own attitude, 'I can quite understand that.'

When he went outside, he took a few deep breaths to compose himself. The man had been right. It *was* his duty to protect what had been entrusted to his care, but he could have explained things in a less aggressive manner.

Arriving at the door of Brown, Smith and Baker, Solicitors, Alistair wondered if he should just give up and let things take their own course. It really wasn't up to him, but something was urging him on, almost as if he couldn't let go of Manny until he was sure everything that could be done was being done. Everything? That jolted him. What about the funeral? Somebody would have to arrange it. He opened the street door and went up the narrow stairs to talk to whichever of the Messrs Brown, Smith and Baker had dealt with Manny's affairs.

'I couldn't believe it!' Alistair told Peggy when she came home from work that evening, while Rosie, having already heard the good news, leaned back in her chair to watch her daughter's reaction to it. 'There I was, all set to tell him about Manny's next of kin in Australia, and he held out his hand and congratulated me.'

'I don't understand,' Peggy frowned.

'Manny left everything to me.'

'He couldn't have had much to leave? You've said yourself the shop wasn't doing as well as it used to, which was why he couldn't give you a pay rise, so . . . ?'

Rosie could contain herself no longer. 'He hasn't left much cash, but he'd a whole lot of jewellery deposited in the bank, and it's all Alistair's now.'

Peggy's chin dropped. 'Wow! How much, d'you reckon?'

'I don't know how much is in his bank account, but the jewellery must be worth a good few hundred, from what I remember of the things I put in.'

'You'd no idea he was going to leave it to you?' The question came from Alf Pryor, almost like one of the family now, giving Rosie a hot snack for lunch, and spending all afternoon preparing an evening meal for her and Peggy, who had soon persuaded him to dine with them when she came home from work. Having heard the tale along with Rosie, he'd had time to consider it from all angles.

'Not the faintest!' Alistair assured him.

'However much it is, I'm happy for you!' Alf exclaimed, a grin transforming his usually serious face. 'Will this make you change your mind about going into the army?'

'Oh no. I told Mr Brown I'd volunteered and would have to report soon, and he said I could sign all the necessary papers the first time I'm home on leave.' His eyes clouded. 'The funeral's been arranged – well, not only Manny's. Apparently the borough council takes that in hand for people with nobody to see to things. It'll just be one service . . .'

'Not in a mass grave?' exclaimed Rosie, horrified at the thought of it. 'Manny would hate that.'

'No, no, they get individual graves.'

'But they could be different religions. How do they deal with that?'

'Apparently they provide a vicar, a priest and a rabbi.' Alistair shook his head sadly. 'I wish I could have afforded to give him a proper funeral.'

'You can, though . . . can't you?' demanded Peggy. 'You'll have all the money from the jewellery when you sell it.'

'I did mention that, but Mr Brown thinks it would be best to leave it where it is, to let it appreciate in value. Besides, he's had dealings with Crawford, the bank manager, before and doesn't think much of him. It seems he's a bit sticky at releasing cash, and he'd likely be worse with jewellery. Mr Brown said I should accept that I won't benefit from my windfall, as he called it, for a few months, and he advised me to let the council funeral go ahead, and to be honest, I don't think Manny would have minded. He never liked a fuss.' Alistair looked helplessly round the other three. 'In any case, there's absolutely nothing I can do.'

'You won't need to touch your inheritance till after the war,' Rosie reminded him. 'You'll come back to Civvy Street a rich man.'

'Not exactly rich,' he pointed out, 'but a lot better off than I've ever been. I can still hardly believe it!'

'So you keep saying,' Rosie smiled, 'but there are times when what seems to be the blackest of situations turns out to have a silver lining – or in this case, gold and precious stones. If Manny had meant it to be a surprise, he's certainly succeeded.'

'I wish he'd given me a clue, though. I'd have liked him to know how grateful I am.'

'He'll know,' Rosie murmured, nodding sagely. 'He'd have known before he did it. He knew the kind of man you are, honest and reliable.' She turned to her neighbour now. 'I've been very lucky with my son-in-laws, you know, Alf – two really fine men.'

Alistair's cheeks flamed, and Peggy said, 'Oh, Mum, you've embarrassed him.'

It was she who was embarrassed next. Alf cleared his throat nervously, and said, perhaps more loudly than he meant, 'I agree with you there, Rosie, and I sincerely hope you won't be disappointed in your third . . .' He paused and looked imploringly at the elderly woman, then ended, 'Rosie, I'm asking your permission to marry Peg.'

There were three separate gasps before Peggy flung herself at him. 'Alf! Why didn't you . . . You never asked me. You didn't even give me a hint.'

Over her head, he looked at her mother. 'Rosie?'

'Yes, you have my permission.' She gave a gurgling laugh. 'I've expected this, you know, and I couldn't understand why it was taking you so long.'

'I've been meaning to ask you for . . . oh, years, but I could never get the words out. It was you speaking about your two sons-in-law that gave me the courage.'

She beckoned him over and kissed his cheek. 'I'm even luckier than I thought. I'll soon have three daughters married to three wonderful men.'

After congratulating the happy pair and toasting their future happiness with the sherry Rosie had kept hidden for this very occasion, Alistair said, 'I'd better get going.' He wasn't really in a celebratory mood and he didn't want to put a damper on things.

'You'll have something to eat before you go?'

'No thanks, Rosie. I want to get things organized at home. I'll have to pack all our personal belongings before I can give up the house, and clear out all the useless odds and ends we've collected since we moved in. What about the furniture though, and the rest of the stuff you gave us when we started out?'

Rosie took a moment to think, then said, 'They're yours, so it's up to you, but you'll need them after the war, won't you? Why don't you put them in store somewhere?'

'That'd be a bit expensive, though? The war could go on for years yet.'

Alf cleared his throat. 'If you don't think I'm being out

of order, you could move them into my garage. If there isn't room for everything, my cousin in Romford also has a garage standing empty. He gave up his car a few months ago and is thinking of renting it out. It wouldn't be nearly so expensive as paying for a proper store.'

'The very thing!' exclaimed Peggy.

'I can give you a hand to pack everything,' Alf offered. 'I can come over any day – not tonight, of course.'

Quite overcome by everything that was happening, Alistair was forced to swallow before he said, shakily, 'Thanks, Alf, I'll let you know. I'll have to get some tea chests or boxes of some kind first.'

On his way home, he concentrated his thoughts on Peggy and her future husband. They were a well-matched couple, both quiet and soberly dressed, and the age difference scarcely showed; despite his wiry hair being streaked with grey, Alf's face was unlined, his blue eyes bright and clear, his back straight for all he was six feet tall. He had an air of eternal youth about him, and Peggy had always looked older than her years, not going in for much make-up or fancy hairstyles. Of course, Alf wasn't as fit as he appeared to be, but, as Peggy often said, as long as he took things easy, he shouldn't do himself any harm.

When he went into his own home again, Alistair's spirits dropped. 'Home sweet home and the fire black out,' as Len Crocker had said on the day he and Dougal arrived in London. But that had been a joke. This was reality. There was no cheer in any of the rooms as he wandered through them, and he decided he'd be as well going to bed. He would make a cup of tea, then he'd fill a hot water bottle, and then oblivion . . . hopefully.

He filled the kettle, lit the gas ring then sat down at the kitchen table. And now, with nothing else to take up his attention, his thoughts turned to Manny again. Manny, his employer, his friend, his confidante, his mentor. But Manny had been more than all of those. He'd been like a father. In fact, Alistair decided, he'd been much closer to Manny than he'd ever been to his real father. There had been a bond between them, a steel-cabled bond which could never be broken, not even by German bombs.

How patiently he'd explained the business of pawnbroking to his raw helper, how well he'd schooled his apprentice on human nature, how much interest he'd shown in all the teenage boy had to say, sorting out his trivial troubles, never telling him what to do but guiding him towards the right solutions. Later, when he discussed world events, he hadn't shoved his opinions down an impressionable young man's throat, but had deftly let him come to his own conclusions and shown no disappointment if they were not in agreement with his own.

But Manny had also done what he could to help him materially. He had made it possible for both him and Dougal to give their future wives decent engagement rings. He had given Leila and David valuable christening gifts, gifts they would treasure for ever. He had been like one of the family, yet he never took advantage of it. He had never wanted to intrude, no matter how fervently Gwen or Rosie assured him that they would never look on him as an intruder. It seemed that he preferred his own company out of business hours − no, that wasn't right. It wasn't preference, it was reserve, an inborn reserve, that held him back from mixing freely with other people. That was why he'd been on his own when ... his life came to such an abrupt end.

This last thought was too much for Alistair. Laying his head on his arms on the table, he let the tears flood from him, tears that held guilt that he hadn't forced the old man to come and live with them, gratitude for all he had done for the Ritchies, but more than anything, deep sorrow at his passing. After God made Emanuel·David Isaacson, He had broken the mould. It was an old saying, a trite saying, but how true in Manny's case.

The piercing whistle of the boiling kettle broke into his troubled thoughts, and mopping his tears with a somewhat damp handkerchief, Alistair got to his feet, filled his hot water bottle and went to bed without bothering with tea. Two hours later, he was roused from a deep sleep by the banshee-howling of the sirens, but he didn't move. If the Jerries wanted to kill him, let them. He was far too tired to care.

Alice Guthrie looked up in alarm at her sister-in-law's loud gasp. 'What's wrong? Has your house been damaged?' She knew nothing could have happened to Alistair, because it was his writing on the envelope.

'No, it's Manny. He's been killed.'

'What?' cried both Alice and Marge.

They were still sitting at the kitchen table. The children had gone off to school on the old bicycles Alice had managed to summon up from families in the village, and all three women had been reading the letters they had just received from their husbands. 'His shop got a direct hit,' Gwen went on with a catch in her voice.

'We'll have to go down for the funeral,' Marge declared.

'Yes, you can leave the kids with me,' offered Alice.

There was a moment's silence as Gwen read more of the letter. 'It's too late. The funeral's past.'

'Why didn't Alistair tell us sooner? Why on earth did he wait so long?'

'He says he was too upset, and he didn't want us to go charging down there.'

'Just as well,' Marge muttered. 'We couldn't really have afforded the fares.'

Gwen's hand shot out suddenly to stop further remarks as she came to another item of news. 'Listen to this.'

In a few moments her listeners were demanding to see the letter for themselves and scanning the neat writing while they each held a side of the pages. 'My God!' exclaimed Marge at last. 'You lucky blighters!'

'He does say they won't get any of it till after the war,' Alice pointed out. 'Still, it must be nice to know there's a nest egg waiting at the end of the tunnel.'

'I don't know what to think,' wailed Gwen. 'I can hardly believe it, and will you please give me my letter back? I haven't finished reading it.'

Her head bent over it again, and Marge said, accusingly, to Alice, 'I can't understand your brother. He's been writing every day and this happened nearly a week ago and he never mentioned it.'

'Like he said, he didn't want you to go charging down there.'

'But he must have known we'd have wanted to go?'

'He hadn't wanted Gwen to see how upset he was.'

Marge nodded now. 'That's more like it. He must be absolutely devastated – he loved that old man ... we all did.' Both women jumped as Gwen let out another wail.

'Oh, no! I should have known he'd do that! But why couldn't he have waited?'

'What's wrong now?' Marge sounded testy.

'The day Manny was killed, Alistair volunteered for the army.'

'You knew it was only because of Manny he didn't go before.'

'Yes, but ... oh, Marge! He should have told me as soon as ...'

Marge shook her head sadly. 'Think how he must have felt, Gwennie – as if *his* life had come to an end, as well . . . his life as he'd known it, I mean. No Manny, no job . . .'

'No wife and kids, either,' Gwen said, bitterly, 'but he didn't care about us, did he?'

'Of course he did! He sent you away from London because he loved you and didn't want anything to happen to any of you.'

Alice, keeping out of it until now, said, rather sharply, 'You should be proud of him, Gwen. At least he didn't go to pieces at what had happened. He took a decision to do what he could to pay the Germans back for . . .'

'Yes, that's what it had been.' Gwen sounded quite relieved. 'It was a shock, that's all, after reading about Manny . . .'

'Not forgetting the windfall,' Marge reminded her. 'Are you sure he didn't have any more surprises up his sleeve?'

Her sister looked down at the letter again. 'No, he just says how pleased he was at Peg and Alf getting engaged, and we already knew that.'

They had been told in a letter from Peggy five days earlier, which had been the subject for much discussion at the time.

'I'm glad I had time to get over that,' Gwen said now. 'I had enough to take in today. Poor Manny! He used to come to see me once a week before his legs gave up.' She paused, her brows coming down in puzzlement. 'You know, I think he did try to give me a hint once that he was leaving everything to Alistair, but he didn't come right out with it and it didn't dawn on me what he was meaning.' Her face clearing, she went on, 'Alistair must have been heartbroken. He worshipped that old man, and he always said he'd have joined up long ago if it hadn't been for him. Yes, I can understand now why his first thought was to have a go at the Germans.'

She paused, then smiled. 'Anything interesting in any of your letters, girls?'

Marge shrugged. 'Nothing much in Dougal's, just how much he's missing me. He's bored stiff in Wales, and wishing he could get back into the fray, but I'm just thankful he's in a place where he's safe.' She turned to Alice. 'What's Sam saying?'

'I was waiting to tell you. He's been told he'll be at Turnhouse for the foreseeable future, so he's rented what had once been a farm worker's cottage on the outskirts of Edinburgh, not far from the drome. He's expecting us down the day after tomorrow, so after we go, you two can have a bedroom each, and . . .'

'That means . . .' Marge hesitated, then grinned wickedly. 'You know what I mean. Good show!'

'Did I hear you saying we could have a bedroom each?' Gwen inquired, returning her letter to its envelope. 'That's good. Alistair says he might manage a visit before he has to report at Catterick, and I was wondering where he would sleep.'

When the children came home, Gwen told them first, quietly and patiently, about Manny, and then, to save them dwelling on it too much, she gave them the good news. 'Daddy might be coming to see us soon, before he goes into the army.'

'Oh, great!' shouted David. 'I can't wait to see him in his uniform.'

'He won't be in uniform, not yet. Next time he comes, though.'

It was Marge who noticed the boy's hand slipping into his pocket occasionally, then transferring something to his mouth. 'What's that you're eating?' she demanded.

'Some sweets we got from the shop lady.'

'You shouldn't have been in the shop!' Gwen snapped.

'We weren't.' David was at his most indignant. 'She came out and gave them to us – a bag each. She said she used to know our Dad.'

Alice laughed. 'That's Lexie Fraser. She was . . . um . . . at school with your Dad and your Uncle Dougal.'

'You mustn't take sweets from her again, though,' Gwen warned. 'They're rationed.'

'She said she never eats her ration,' Leila defended her brother. 'She said she knew Dad really well when they were young.'

'And she winked,' David added.

Once again, it was Marge who picked up the underlying meaning to the seemingly open gift to two children, but she said nothing until she and Gwen were in bed. 'What did you make of that shop person?'

'Giving them sweets? It was good of her, but she shouldn't, they might come to expect it, and it's not good for their teeth.'

'That's not what I meant. David said she winked when she said she knew Alistair really well when they were young. She could have been a girlfriend.'

'She was. He did tell me, and it was long before he met me. Anyway, she could have been winking about the sweets. Maybe they weren't off her ration. Maybe she just helped herself from the jars, or boxes, or whatever.'

'I'd watch her, if I was you.'

'Don't be silly. She knew who they were and she was just being friendly with them.'

'Well, don't say I didn't warn you.'

Alice packed two suitcases and an old valise with her own and her small daughter's clothes. 'Sam says we don't need anything else,' she told Gwen and Marge while she waited –

the doctor had promised to take her to the railway station in Aberdeen. 'The house is fully furnished, even chamber pots under the beds. Just as well, for the lavatory's outside.' Giggling, she added, 'It'll be back to using a chanty in the middle of the night, or getting my bum frozen in a privy. I thought I'd seen the last of that.'

'Never mind,' consoled Marge, grinning, 'Sam'll soon heat it up again.'

Gwen ignored her sister's ribaldry. 'Are you sure you'll manage all that, Alice?'

'Sam's going to meet us at Waverley Station. Their camp isn't all that far out of Edinburgh. Here's the doctor, thank goodness. I was worried that he'd been called out and couldn't take us.'

A quick flurry of good wishes and they were gone.

'And that's us left on our own,' Marge declared, sitting down with a bump. 'We don't know a soul, we can't speak the lingo if the postman's anything to go by. I can hardly understand a word he says.'

Alistair arrived the next morning, and having travelled overnight after two days of intensive clearing out his rented house, he did not look at his best, but it didn't matter to Gwen who rushed at him as if she hadn't seen him for years not just two weeks.

'You won't want me hanging around,' announced Marge, 'so I think I'll get out Alice's bike and take a trip to the village shop. I'll get a loaf of bread, shall I, and we'll need some butter, so I'll need the ration books.'

Gwen made a face. 'It's a good thing you remembered, I'd have forgotten, but get some bacon as well, if you can.'

'Sorry, Marge,' laughed Alistair. 'I haven't had time to speak to you yet.'

'No, you've been too busy kissing your wife, but it's OK. I can take a hint.'

She hadn't been on a bicycle since she was a little girl living in army quarters in Aldershot, and she was quite wobbly until she got the hang of it again and set off along the track. Never having cycled more than the length of a short street before, she was amazed at how far a mile seemed to be . . . one rough, rutted mile before she reached the road, with another two miles to go.

She took more notice of her surroundings now than she had done when she was here with Dougal a few months after they were married. She had thought it was hardly fit to be called a village then, but she had supposed that there must be another few streets tucked in behind the houses fronting on to the main road. There didn't seem to be any hidden streets or lanes, nothing. Passing two low cottages on her left, with gardens given over to vegetables as at Benview, she was surprised that there was only a field of turnips or something to her right. After the second little dwelling, there was the opening which Dougal had told her led through to the Frasers' house, only Lexie would live there now, of course, and then the shop itself.

Curious about other habitation and/or amenities, she cycled on, past about six houses of varying styles and sizes and in different degrees of repair, but each with its fenced garden. Then came a much bigger house, with correspondingly bigger garden. Then she came to the Royal Hotel, where according to Dougal, all the local men took refuge from their wives when they were on the warpath. She had asked him to take her in, but he had explained that no 'nice' women went drinking in Forvit. It wouldn't worry her, Marge decided. She liked a drop of sherry now and then, but wouldn't be too upset if she never saw the stuff.

The next house had a Great Dane in residence, barking at

her until she was clear of his 'space'. Then she came to the church, not very imposing, but big enough, she supposed, for all the congregation it could have, with its graveyard at one side and the vicarage – or whatever the Scots called it – at the other. There was a long gap now, suggesting that two, or perhaps three, houses had been knocked down to make way for more modern housing, which would be a pity. The appeal of Forvit lay in its quaint old cottages and lack of any kind of symmetry.

And that was the end of it, a bridge over what was little more than a stream, and moorland from then on. In fact, the village could be described as an oasis set in the midst of miles of heath. Dismounting, she turned her cycle round and started back.

The last house on that side – the first coming this way – was a more up-to-date, three-storeyed building with a long walled garden. A brass plaque on the gate said, Dr Christopher Geddes, Surgery Hours 3–4, 6–7. Well, Marge thought, she knew where to find the doctor if any of them were ill.

Next came the little school, with its tarred playground at the side farthest from the doctor, followed by the Jubilee Hall, with 1897 engraved in the lintel stone, which, of course, was the date of Queen Victoria's jubilee year.

Proud of remembering this, and having come to the field of turnips once more, she came off the bicycle and wheeled it across the street, glad to have a break. Her legs were aching, her rear end was practically numb and she was frozen to the marrow . . . and she still had three miles to go before she reached 'home'.

She was glad to see two women in the shop. It gave her a chance to stand at the side of the open door for a few moments and have a good look at Lexie Fraser. She was actually quite a pretty woman, with rosy cheeks and hair that was as fair as Gwen's, eyes a lighter shade of blue, and roughly the same height. Marge could more or less understand what she was saying, but the other two women were speaking in a kind of rapid-fire gibberish. Marge did manage to make out a few words here and there, but it wasn't until Alice's name was mentioned that she took an interest and concentrated as hard as she could.

'Did you ken Alice Ritchie's awa' to Edinburgh to be wi' Sam?' the waiting customer observed. 'The doctor was to be takin' her an' Morag to Aberdeen.'

'Alistair's wife an' her sister'll be left to look after the place,' commented the one being served. 'Have you come across ony o' them yet, Lexie?'

'I've spoken to the bairns, Doodie, nice wee souls they are. The girl's real shy, but the boy's more friendly.'

'Weel, we're nae wantin' their kind here. Up fae London and likely lookin' doon their noses at us. What do you say, Aggie?'

Her friend nodded. 'No, Doodie, we'd enough o' English folk when yon minister and his wife was here ... I canna mind his name, but you'd have thocht he was God himsel', the wey he swaggered aboot, and as for his wife and her short skirties ... she was a stuck-up besom.'

'They werena Cockneys, o' coorse,' Doodie pointed out. 'It was ... Liverpool they belonged, and what a queer wey they spoke. Thank goodness he only bade five month.'

Aggie looked archly at Lexie now. 'You an' Alistair was affa close at one time, wasn't you? We a' thocht you an' him would get wed some day.'

Lexie's face darkened. 'And so we would, if Dougal Finnie hadn't dragged him away down to London with him.'

Marge's involuntary gasp at this made them aware of her presence, so she walked inside. Lexie obviously recognized her as Dougal's wife, but just as obviously had decided to brazen it out. 'I'll be with you in a jiffy, Mrs ... ?'

'Mrs Finnie,' Marge said icily. 'Mrs Dougal Finnie.'

The other two women whipped round, their faces colouring, then turned back to Lexie, who said, smoothly, 'That'll be four and sevenpence, Doodie, if you please.'

Doodie counted the money out on to the counter, four shillings, a sixpenny bit and a penny, then stood aside to let Aggie be served. The tension in the shop was almost tangible, and nothing more was said, so when the second transaction was over, the two women left the shop.

'I'm sorry about that, Mrs Finnie,' Lexie said then, 'but I didn't notice you there and in any case I didn't know who you were. Besides, I was only·speaking the truth. Alistair wouldn't have gone to London if it hadn't been for Dougal. You see, we were . . .' She gave her head a slight shake. 'But it's best to let bygones be bygones, isn't it? What can I get for you?'

The bread, butter and bacon paid for, the ration books duly marked, Lexie said, 'I don't think you should say anything to Alistair's wife. It was over between us long ago and there's no sense in upsetting her, is there?'

'There's nothing to tell anyway . . . is there?'

Lexie's red cheeks took on a slightly deeper hue. 'If you're asking if Alistair and me . . . were lovers, the answer's no.'

'He arrived just before I came out.' Marge watched for the reaction.

'Alistair's back?' Lexie gasped, her face aflame now.

'He'll only be here for a few days, so he wasn't wasting any time when I came out. I could see they weren't wanting me there.'

Marge hoped that this would stop the woman from trying to see him, but as she cycled back, she couldn't help feeling sorry for her.

'You don't know how much I've missed you, Gwen.'

'I missed you, too, darling, but it must have been worse for you, losing Manny . . .'

They were snuggled together on the old sofa Alistair remembered being told to keep his feet off when he was a child. He wanted to make love to her, but after almost ten years of marriage, it didn't seem proper to be so lustful, especially here . . . in the middle of the day.

'Yes, it was a terrible shock.' He was glad she had given him a lead into what he'd been turning over in his mind since the funeral. 'I'm damned glad you and the kids are away from it, so I can have an easy mind when I'm away. Better still, Mr Brown, that's Manny's solicitor, he's arranging for Crawford at the bank to sell one or two of the pieces of jewellery if he can, and add it to the account they opened for us with the two hundred Manny left. That'll let you draw a few pounds every week to help out, for the allowance you'll get from the army won't be very much.'

'I know how much Marge gets,' Gwen put in, 'and we'll easily manage between the two of us. I'm used to having to be careful with my spending.'

'Yes, but you can't expect Marge to pay half the expenses here when you've the two kids to feed as well. Anyway, it's done now and you don't have to touch it if you don't need to. It can lie in the bank till the war's over – God knows how long that'll be. Oh, I nearly forgot. Mr Brown drew up a proper will for me, so if anything happens to me, everything'll come to you.'

'Don't say things like that, darling. Nothing's going to happen to you!'

'We have to face facts, dear, and it's best to be prepared.' He stopped momentarily then rushed on, 'But I'll tell you this, if I do get killed, I'll murder the Jerry that did it.'

His grin was not enough to make his wife take this in the

light-hearted way it was meant. 'Don't be morbid, Alistair Ritchie!' she cried, tears gathering in her eyes. 'You have to make your mind up you won't be killed.'

'Oh, my sweet, I'm sorry for upsetting you. I was only joking, and it's time we got on to something else. Have you been to the village yet?'

'Not yet. Alice has done all the shopping since we came, but Marge and I will have to take turns now she's away, I suppose. She said we could use her bike, though I don't know when I last rode one.'

'It's something you never forget,' her husband consoled.

'Oh, I nearly forgot. Leila and David came home with sweets the other day. He said the shop lady gave them to him. She said she was an old friend of yours.'

'That's Lexie Fraser. I told you – she was at school with Dougal and me.'

'Nothing else?'

'What d'you . . .' The answer dawning, he chuckled loudly. 'Oh, I knocked around with her for a while, two fifteen-sixteen-year-olds playing at being grown up, you know.'

'Just playing at it? You weren't . . . you didn't . . . ?'

'We stopped at kissing, if that's what you mean. Just kids kissing, nothing in it.'

'You're sure that was all?'

'Look, Gwen, darling, I've only ever loved one girl in my whole life and that's you. I've never thought twice about any other girl, and I never will. You're my whole life, Gwendoline Ritchie, you and the kids.'

He pulled her to him and their kisses might have made him forget his reluctance to do anything on his mother's old sofa if Marge hadn't walked in.

'Oh, shit!' she laughed. 'I've come back too soon, have I? Couldn't you two have waited till bedtime?'

Flustered, Gwen sprang to her feet and smoothed her

clothes. 'Don't be silly, Marge. We haven't seen each other for weeks and we were . . . talking things over, that's all.'

'I believe you, thousands wouldn't.' Marge set the shopping bag down on the well-scrubbed table in the middle of the kitchen to unpack it. 'You know, I'm getting quite an expert on the bike again, if only my bum gets used to it.' Rubbing her rump wryly, she began to put away her purchases.

'Was it Lexie Fraser who served you?' Gwen tried to sound nonchalant, but she was desperate to hear something about this girl, woman now, who had once been part of Alistair's life.

'Yes, she was serving two middle-aged harpies when I went in, Aggie and Doodie, but she knew who I was. It wouldn't be difficult. We must be the only two strangers within miles of the place, and she had likely seen me when I was here with Dougal.'

'That would have been Aggie Mearns and Doodie Tough,' Alistair observed, his memory having successfully put faces to the familiar names. He glanced at the clock. 'Can I use that kettle to wash and shave, or was it for making tea?'

Both women burst out laughing at this. 'There's a bathroom upstairs,' his wife told him, 'with hot and cold running water. Alice's Sam had it put in.'

Alistair pulled a face. 'Shows how long it is since I've been here. OK, won't be long, but I have to get this stubble off before my wife complains of my sandpaper chin.'

When he went out, Marge eyed Gwen affectionately. 'He looks better than I thought he would, what with Manny's death, and going in the army. How does he feel about that, has he said?'

'I think he's quite looking forward to it.'

'No regrets? After all, he volunteered as a reflex action after Manny . . .'

'He wants to do his bit, for Manny's sake.'

'Well, I hope this damned war doesn't last long.' Marge pulled a face. 'The locals don't want to be friendly, they're anti-all-English.'

'Surely not.' Gwen was shocked at this. 'You'd been imagining things.'

'That's what they were saying, anyway, before they realized who I was, but I suppose we won't come much in contact with them, so it won't bother us.'

'Should we invite Lexie to come and see Alistair? They *are* old friends.'

'He'll be gone the day after tomorrow, and I'd have thought you'd want him all to yourself . . . no old ladyloves butting in.' Marge wasn't meaning to instil suspicion in her sister's mind. She was just being careful.

Chapter 14

❧

The first contingent of the Black Watch had not arrived at Ardley House until the 26 April, and for two full weeks not even one private had made an appearance in either Forvit or Bankside, and the female populations of both were beginning to wonder if their dreams of romance were to come to nothing. By the end of the third week, however, most of the young soldiers had made contact with one or more of the girls in all the villages within a ten-mile radius of their base, scouting around in jeeps and trucks, on motor cycles, even riding bicycles. Lexie Fraser, being in the shop-cum-post office, saw more of them than anyone else, but sadly found that the majority of them were much too young for her – or, to be more precise, *she* was much too old for *them*.

But salvation was at hand. Some of the local farmers decided to do their bit for the war effort by funding a 'get-together' to welcome the newcomers; what could be more patriotic than providing amusement for the fighting men? The Jubilee Hall in Forvit – built by the laird of the time to celebrate sixty years of Queen Victoria's reign – was filled to capacity during the entire evening.

The Royal Hotel had supplied the drinks, free for the first hour and half-price from then on, which resulted in such shenanigans as made the owners regret their generosity and vow never to repeat it. Both youths and girls being determined to find a suitable partner, there were several Paul Joneses played, and the bus the army laid on didn't come to take the boys back to camp until two a.m. This official introduction of soldiers to locals was a great success, at least one instance of true love being initiated, but mostly just brief encounters. Each side would need to get to know the other better before any commitments were made, temporary or otherwise.

Lexie Fraser had played the field of the NCOs, nearer her age, but when the dance ended, was no nearer to finding a life partner than when it began, but she had thoroughly enjoyed every minute.

'Wasn't it great?' she asked Lizzie Wilkie the next day. 'I really enjoyed myself.'

'Aye, you made a right exhibition o' yourself,' Lizzie said, caustically, 'but I suppose you was desperate. The men round here havena had much time for you lately.'

Ignoring the slur, Lexie gave a carefree laugh. 'You're just jealous, and you needn't worry. It looks like I was cut out to be an old maid, but, I tell you this, Lizzie, I'm going to get as much pleasure out of life as I can before I settle down with a cat at my feet and a bag of knitting on my lap.'

The other woman looked somewhat ashamed. 'Ach, Lexie, I didna mean what I said. You're right, I was jealous, but I'd like to see you finding somebody.'

'I'm not bothered, honestly.' She looked up as the shop bell tinkled and addressed her next words to the new customer. 'None of the wives round here are really happy, isn't that right, Gladys? Every one of you's forever complaining about your man.'

'That's different,' Gladys said, indignantly. 'We complain about them, but it doesn't mean we're nae happy wi' them. They can still make us . . . forget the bad things they get up to. Tak' my Chae now.'

'No, thank you very much,' Lexie giggled, while Lizzie spluttered with laughter.

'You can laugh a' you like,' Gladys declared firmly, not in the least put out, 'but even though he comes rolling in fu' on Saturday nichts, he still . . . he can . . .' She broke off, her cheeks pink. 'No, no, you single lassies dinna understand, but I wouldna change him, supposing the maist handsome man in the world walked in right this minute and offered me a thousand pounds to share his bed.'

'Fat chance of that,' Lexie muttered, doing her best to keep a straight face.

'Aye, well, you're right there, but you ken what I mean. I took my Chae for better or worse on oor wedding day, and I'm quite happy to thole the worse, for the better couldna be better, if you get my meaning?' She gave a lewd wink. 'Now if you're nae in a hurry, Lizzie, would you let Lexie serve me first? I just want a bit o' haddock for the supper. Is that fresh?' She pointed at a shimmering enamel tray under the glass counter.

'Fresh in from Peterhead this morning,' Lexie assured her.

'Gi'e me two, then, that biggest ane for Chae, and a littler ane for me.' While the fish were being wrapped, she fumbled in her purse, then laid down the exact money and left with a cheery, 'Ta-ta, then.'

Waiting until she went past the window, the two younger women gave vent to their laughter at last, holding on to the counter until they simmered down. 'Oh, my God,' Lizzie gasped, holding her aching sides. '"Tak' my Chae," she said, and I near fell ower when you said, "No, thank you very much." I dinna ken how you managed. Her Chae's got a big fat boozer's nose, and his face is mottled-purple, and his eyes look two ways for Sunday. It would turn my stomach if I found him lying in the bed aside me.'

'It's his great beer belly that sickens me,' Lexie gurgled, 'hanging over his breeks like that. And Gladys isn't what

205

you'd call slim, either, is she? I wonder how they manage to get near enough to ...? Their two bellies would be a big obstacle.' They looked at each other and dissolved into another fit of uncontrollable raucous laughter.

After a few moments, Lizzie managed to get out, 'I suppose his bandy legs help them to get closer. They're that bowed Sandy Coull's auld sow could run under them.'

It was perhaps fortunate for them that another customer walked in at that point, a passing motorist who, being an absolute stranger, had an instant sobering effect on them. Lizzie paid for the items Lexie had already set out for her, packed them in her shopping bag and walked out with a surprisingly dignified gait.

The monotony was getting to Marjory Finnie.

'I'm sick of this,' she moaned one morning after the children had set off for school. 'We've been up in this Godforsaken hole for months now, cut off from everything and everybody, and there's nothing to do except work in the blasted garden. I didn't mind having to do our wee patch at home after Dougal went away, but I never thought I'd have to tackle anything like this – it's like a bally field. Just look at my hands.' She held out the offending parts of her anatomy to let her sister see the reddened, chafed palms and callused fingers.

'Mine are the same,' Gwen told her, 'but think of the perks. We never have to buy any vegetables, all we have to do is pull them or dig them up when we need them.'

'I wish they got up by themselves,' Marge said ruefully. 'All this pulling and digging, and weeding and raking, I'd be as well in the Land Army, and I'd get paid for it.'

'You wouldn't pass the medical with your bad ear, and your asthma.'

'I haven't had one bout of asthma since I came up here – fresh country air's good for chest troubles – and being a wee bit deaf in one ear wouldn't be a handicap in the Land Army, now would it?'

'You can't go into the Land Army, Marge. I couldn't bear it here on my own.'

'It's not all sweetness and light under your bushel, then? You're as homesick as me.'

'Not really. It's just that . . . oh, I don't know. Alice is expecting us to keep her garden going the way she had it, and I haven't a clue how to plant things for next year.'

Marge's face became a study in horror. 'We won't still be here next year . . . will we?'

'I hope not, but Alistair says I've to keep the kids here till the war's over.'

'It's all right for him. It's where he was brought up, and I suppose he sees it through rose-coloured specs, but we've been accustomed to the stir of London, going round the markets on our days off, or off up west to window-shop. This isn't even a dead-and-alive hole . . . it's just dead. Only one street, one shop, if it can be classed as a shop, one church, one doctor according to what Alice said . . .'

'But it's much better for the children,' Gwen pointed out. 'They look much healthier already with all the good, fresh air and all the open space around us, nothing to see from our windows except hills . . .'

'That's what I'm complaining about,' Marge sighed. 'The Back of Bally Beyond, that's where we are, and I'm sick of it. Dougal wouldn't know if I went home . . . not until he has his next leave.'

'You can't leave me here on my own!' Gwen burst out. 'Please, Marge, don't go! I couldn't cope with looking after this place by myself! I wouldn't know where to start.'

'I was only joking, Gwennie.' Marge's smile, however,

was perhaps a little forced. 'Dougal would have a fit if I went back to Lee Green. But about this blasted garden . . . I suppose we could ask somebody? The postman seems quite nice.'

'What about asking Lexie Fraser in the shop if she knows of a young lad who might come and give us a hand? Do the heavy work.'

'I'm not asking her, Gwen – I just can't take to her. You'll have to do it.'

'You know I don't like asking people for anything . . . but all right. I'll ask her next week when it's my turn to do the shopping. Now, if you fetch the pail, I'll dig up the potatoes this time, to save your precious hands.'

They worked in silence, until the ringing of a bicycle bell made them straighten up. 'You're busy, I see,' observed the postman, a small wiry man, always cheery and ever ready for a chat, though the two Englishwomen hadn't jumped to his bait yet. 'A letter for you, Mrs Ritchie, but nothing for you today, Mrs Finnie, I'm afraid.'

As Gwen tore open the envelope, he remarked to Marge, 'I'm nae one to interfere, but tell your sister she'd be better to use a graip to lift the tatties, nae a spade.'

'A grape?' gasped Marge. 'What use would a grape be? And where would we get any up here?'

His rather sharp features were transformed by a wide smile at this. 'Nae a G-R-A-P-E, a G-R- . . . Ach, I'm nae sure how you spell it, G-R-A-I-P I suppose, and you'll mebbe ken it as a fork. That's what she should be usin'.'

The perplexity in Marge's eyes deepened. 'But a fork wouldn't make any impression on this earth, Mr . . . um . . . ? It's as heavy as blooming lead.'

He threw back his head and roared with laughter now. 'The name's Sandy Mearns, an' it's well seen you're nae a country lassie. A garden fork, that's what you need for this job, so you can dunt aff the earth afore you put the tatties in your bucket.'

'Dunt aff?' Marge looked more bewildered than ever.

'Eh . . .' The man searched for words she would understand. 'Knock off, before you put them in your pail. I'll show you.' Opening the gate he was leaning on, he walked up the path and round the corner of the house, to return in a few moments carrying the implement he was recommending, clearly having known which of the three outhouses held the garden tools. 'Watch, noo!' he ordered, sticking the fork into the ground behind and under the withered leaves of one of the plants, giving it two hefty thumps with the sole of his right boot, then levering it up again.

'This is the wey, look. Shoogle it aboot a bit, then gi'e't a dunt against your knee.' The bang on his knee dislodged most of the soil clinging to the potatoes, and as he transferred the vegetables to the pail, he said, triumphantly, 'D'ye see? It's nae near so hard work.' He handed the fork to Marge. 'You tak' the next shaw, noo.'

Her effort didn't produce as many potatoes as Sandy's, but she was quite pleased with what went into the pail. 'It's easy when you know how,' she exulted.

'Aye,' he grinned, 'I tell't you.' First giving his grimy hands a wipe down his trousers, he removed his cheesecutter and ran his fingers through his thinning mousy hair. Then he took the palm of his hand across his damp brow before putting the hat back on. 'I'd best be goin', though, or folk'll think there's nae post the day.'

Marge wondered how to show her gratitude. She had the distinct feeling that he'd be offended if she offered him money, and settled for asking if he would like a cup of tea.

'Thanks, Mrs Finnie, but I'm late as it is. Anither time, mebbe.'

'Right, well, thank you very much, Mr Mearns.'

'Sandy, for ony sake, an' it was nae bother. Cheeribye, noo, and I'm sure you'll get your man's letter the morn.'

'What was all that about?' asked Gwen, some minutes after the man had cycled off.

'Sandy was showing me the proper way to lift the spuds. Watch.'

Gwen was astonished at the way her sister unearthed another lot of potatoes, but only said, 'Sandy? For goodness' sake, Marge! You didn't ask his name, did you?'

'No, he told me.'

'You should have asked if he knew anybody who'd give us an hour or two's help now and again. That would have been more to the point.'

'I clean forgot, Gwen, I was so interested in what he was doing. But we can ask him tomorrow, or next time he comes. What's Alistair saying?'

'He says they've been kept at it, marching, drill, all sorts of things, but . . . the good news is, he has a few days leave after this initial training's finished, before he's posted. He'll be here next Friday.'

'I hope I get a letter from Dougal tomorrow. Wouldn't it be great if they could be here together?'

Alistair was amazed at how well the large garden was looking, almost as good as when his father had tended it, and deeply impressed by the potato pit installed by Barry Mearns – Sandy's thirteen-year-old son – but, on only his second day home, he said, 'If you don't mind, Gwen, I'll take Alice's bike and have a wee scoot round to see some of my old pals.'

'I don't mind,' she assured him. She couldn't get over how handsome he looked in uniform, and David had been ecstatic at having a Dad in the services.

'He might go to that Lexie person,' Marge remarked when Alistair had gone.

Gwen smiled happily. 'I hope he does. It'll be nice for him to see her again.'

After discovering that all his school friends had been called up or had gone into the forces voluntarily like himself, Alistair wished that he had spent his precious time with his wife. As he passed the shop on his way home, however, it crossed his mind that at least he could have a few words with Lexie. They'd been quite close at one time – too close for his own comfort on the day of his mother's funeral – and she couldn't still be angry at him for going to London.

Her face lit up with pleasure when he walked into the shop. 'Alistair! I didn't know you'd come home.'

So long used to Gwen's soft tones, he felt a brief stab of irritation at Lexie's rough country voice. She hadn't changed much physically, either – waist still as small, bust still as rounded. She wasn't so refined-looking as his wife, but prettier than he remembered. 'You're looking well,' he smiled, trying to rid his mind of what he had almost done the last time he was with her.

'You, and all.' She glanced at the large clock on the wall. 'It still wants five minutes to dinner time, but ach . . . nobody'll be in now, so I may as well shut.' She came round the counter, brushing past him as she went to lock the door. 'Come through to the house so we can speak without being interrupted.'

He followed her through. He wanted to hear all the gossip of the village and Lexie didn't disappoint him. She told him that Gerry Lovie had run away with Dod Prosser's wife about five years ago, 'Then Dod upped and off himself, God knows where to.'

'I was hoping to see Gerry Lovie,' Alistair said, sadly, 'and I did think it was funny his mother saying she didn't know where he was, but that explains it.'

'And remember Bunty Simmers? Well, her father threw her out for not telling him who put her in the family way. Jake Simmers was aye a narrow-minded, cantankerous brute, but his wife hasn't spoken to him since, and nobody's ever heard tell of Bunty.'

She went over as much as she could recall of the events that had enlivened the small community over the years; humorous, like the time Willie Kemp had been so drunk he'd fallen off his bike on his way home from the pub and landed in a bed of nettles; sad, like when Maggie Durward, Johnny Greig's wife, died in childbirth at the age of twenty-four; tragic, as when Freddy Findlay's four-year-old daughter fell in the mill race and drowned before anybody could get her out.

Alistair listened avidly, dredging his memory to put faces to the names, seeing the people concerned as they were when he had known them. Time flew past, but neither of them noticed until a loud rattling of the shop door handle shocked them out of the past.

'Oh God!' Alistair exclaimed, looking at his watch and jumping to his feet. 'I've been here over an hour and a half. Gwen'll be wondering where I am.'

Lexie got off her seat reluctantly. 'I should have opened half an hour ago, but that's the first person that's needed in. So . . . what the hell?'

He waited for her to go into the shop area first, and as she passed him, she said, 'If you don't want to be seen, you can wait there till whoever it is has gone away.'

'No, it doesn't matter. I left Alice's bike outside.'

Following her through, he waited until she unlocked the shop door and walked past the astonished customer with a smiling, 'Aye, aye, Gladdy.'

Jumping on the bicycle, he hoped that he hadn't laid the grounds for talk, it would be embarrassing for Lexie, but she could fend for herself, and they hadn't done anything wrong, anyway. His conscience was quite clear.

'Where on earth have you been?' Gwen greeted him, when he entered the house. 'We've had our dinner and yours is in the oven, but it'll be all dried out by this time.'

'I don't mind, I can eat anything after the muck we got in the mess. I'm sorry I'm late, though. I was all over the place trying to get hold of some of my old mates, but they're all away, so I went to the shop as a last resort, and ... well, Lexie was giving me all the gossip, what's been happening since I left.'

'I could do with a friend,' Gwen sighed. 'I feel isolated, so far from the village.'

Marge nodded her agreement to this. 'Why don't we go home, Gwennie? Back to Mum and Peg ... we could be there for the wedding.'

'No!' Alistair said, firmly. 'You can go back if you want, but my wife and kids are staying right here. God Almighty, have you forgotten what it's like in London?'

The children took possession of their father when they came home, and both Gwen and Marge were glad when he offered to take them out of the way for a while. He took the short cut through the wood to the tower, joining the path from the main road about three quarters of the way up the hill, and while they walked, he exaggerated some of his experiences in the Artillery for the benefit of his son, who hung on to every word. Leila was content to listen, though she kept a firm grasp of her father's hand.

When they reached the top, he made them look around them while he explained the various landmarks and named the mountains in the distance, Ben this and Ben that. 'So that's why the house is called Benview,' David exclaimed,

213

delighted at having made the connection. Then the two youngsters ran to have a closer inspection of the old ruin, and Alistair sat down, his mind turning to another time he'd been there – the night before he sailed to London, the night he had finished with Lexie. It struck him now how brutal he'd been, snapping their relationship as if it was nothing stronger than a matchstick. She'd been much more vulnerable at the time than a normal sixteen-year-old because of her father deserting her, and there was no doubt that he'd wounded her badly, for she had never taken a husband. Poor Lexie. She wasn't so pushy now, and he'd honestly enjoyed their talk. She had brought his youth back to him so vividly . . .

'Dad! What d'you call this?' David was holding a fluttering insect between his fingers. 'I say it's a daddy-longlegs and Leila says her teacher says they're called crane flies, or something like that.'

Alistair couldn't help laughing at the boy's earnestness. 'Well, son, we called that a daddy-longlegs when I was a boy, too, but maybe crane fly's its real name.'

'Miss Rettie says it is,' Leila said quietly, 'and she's always right.'

'OK, then, crane fly it must be,' her father chuckled.

'But me and Dad's still going to call them daddy-longlegses,' David insisted.

'Let it go now, son. We'd better get back before Mum and Auntie Marge send out a search party for us. I'll be in the bad books if I'm late again.'

'Who keeps the bad books?' David wanted know.

After making love to his wife for the first time in months, Dougal was in a state of happy contentment, smoking a cigarette to let a decent time pass before reaching for her again, when she upset his euphoria by whispering, 'I'm thinking of going home, Dougal.'

Irritated that her mind was on other things, he blew a smoke ring at the ceiling before snapping, 'Home? Back to Lee Green? Don't be daft, woman! They're still being bombed. Not every night, maybe, but too damned often. What brought this on? Have you and Gwen had a row?'

'Of course not! I'm bored out of my mind here, that's what. Nobody to speak to, no cinemas, no dance halls, nothing to do at nights except listen to the wireless . . .'

'At least you don't get any air raids,' Dougal growled. 'You're not going back, Marge, and that's final. I'd be out of my mind worrying about you.'

'Would you? Honestly? Oh, Dougal, so you still love me?'

'I'll never stop loving you, my darling.' His face showed his surprise that she had ever doubted it. 'You mean everything to me, always will, you should know that.'

'I know I've been silly, but I don't think I'd actually have left Gwen here on her own with the kids. It was just . . . oh, Dougal, I miss you so much, and I'll never stop loving you, either.'

Dougal ground out the stub in the ashtray. 'Thank God for that! When I was away from you, I did sometimes wonder.'

She felt like teasing him a little. 'There are some troops stationed not far away, apparently, but I've only ever seen one or two of them in the village when I'm shopping.' She kissed away his frown, and lay back again, adding, 'I'm not interested in anybody else, darling, and never will be. Don't ever forget that!'

'I'll try, Marge. I know you'd never cheat on me. It's just being so far away . . .'

'I wish you could have been here to see Alistair. Fancy missing him by one week.'

'Aye, I'd have liked to see him. But that's war! Come here, wench!'

She turned towards him eagerly. Ever since she had got his letter saying that he'd be home on Saturday, she, too, had been happily anticipating their first night together.

On Sunday, it was David who suggested that they all take a walk to the tower. 'Dad took me and Leila up there when we came home from school one day, remember, Mum?'

Gwen nodded, but made sure that she kept the children in front with her, to leave Marge with her husband.

It was a sunny day, warm for the end of October if rather windy, and David darted hither and thither looking for wild flowers or interesting insects, while eight-year-old Leila walked sedately by her mother's side, chattering about things that had happened at school.

Ambling some distance behind them, Marge broke a silence by saying, 'Is something bothering you, Dougal? You've hardly said a word since we came out.'

'I was thinking,' he said, slowly, quietly. 'It's watching young David, I suppose, but I can't help wishing . . . oh, Marge, I wish we could have made a son . . . or a daughter.'

Her heart swelled with a painful love. 'I know how you feel,' she murmured. 'I've felt exactly the same ever since Leila was born, and it's been worse since we came to Forvit and I see the two of them every day.'

Dougal brightened as something occurred to him. 'Maybe being in Forvit's the answer. A change of location could do the trick. Maybe I hit the bullseye last night? What d'you think?'

She blushed. 'Possibly, my dearest. You tried hard enough.'

Their laughter made Gwen turn round. 'Aren't you two going to share the joke?'

'Maybe . . . in a couple of months,' Marge grinned.

Chapter 15

❧

Even after months of longing to be with his wife, Dougal, like Alistair, was drawn to seeking out his old pals to talk over old times, and, like Alistair, found that they were all in the forces or had moved away from Forvit altogether. Unlike Alistair, however, he had made his search in the evening, and he was taken into most of the houses he called at to have a 'news' with his school friend's father.

Along with the chat, of course, he was offered a dram for good luck, or, from those who had long since run out of whisky and been unable to restock, a glass of port or even home-made rhubarb wine. He should have known the effect this mixing of drinks would have, but it wasn't until he came out into the fresh air after his sixth call, Sandy Mearns's house, that it hit him. His legs and feet had wills of their own, each going in a different direction, his eyes couldn't focus properly and somebody had set up a smiddy inside his head – the hammer hitting the anvil, clang, clang, clang, and no sign of it stopping. It wouldn't have been so bad if it had been a regular beat, and it was driving him out of his mind as he wove his way along the centre of the road.

Out of a conglomeration of confused thoughts, one kept coming to the surface – Marge would go absolutely mad if she saw him like this. In an effort to clear his head, he sat down on the cobbled pavement, wondering, as he did so, if he would be able to get up again, but telling himself he could worry about that when the time came. He had been sitting, back against a wall, for some time when the church clock began to strike, and even in his inebriated state, he knew he'd have to count the strokes.

Nine! That wasn't so late ... unless he'd missed one. But he couldn't go home until he'd sobered up a bit, and sitting here wouldn't help. He'd have to try to stand up. The hotel bar closed at half past and he didn't want every man in the place laughing at him.

Stretching his arm out behind him, he tried to brace himself against the wall, but it was hopeless, so he slid his hand along until he found something for his fingers to grip. After several attempts, he found himself leaning on a long window-sill with his nose against the glass ... looking into the shop. Lexie Fraser! She'd give him something to clear his head! Why hadn't he thought of her before?

Having wit enough to know the shop would be shut, he managed to get himself round to the house without serious mishap – his knuckles got skinned against the wall, but that was nothing. Pulling himself as erect as he could, he gave three loud raps on the door.

It was opened within seconds, and Lexie snapped, 'Dougal Finnie! What brings you knocking at my door at this time of night? The shop's closed and I'm not opening ...'

'I wanted a wee word with you, Lexie ... in private.'

'And what's so private you couldn't say it in the shop tomorrow?'

Although irritated by her sarcasm, he said, humbly, 'Can I come in ... pleazhe?'

'I never thought I'd hear *you* pleading to get into my house.'

'Shtop your daft nonshenshe!' he slurred, pushing past her.

She closed the door with exaggerated care, then followed

218

him inside, and stood in the middle of the kitchen floor with arms folded across her bosom. 'What a state you're in! Has your wife thrown you out?'

He looked ashamed now. 'She will, if I go home like this.'

'Oh, you want something to sober you up, is that it?'

'If you wouldn't mind, Lexie.'

Her voice softened at his hangdog expression. 'Right then. A strong cup of tea with no sugar or milk, that should do the trick. If it doesn't, we'll try a few more.'

He was on the third cup of revolting tarry liquid before he felt his head clearing, but his stomach had started to revolt.

'If you want to be sick,' Lexie said, seeing his face change colour, 'the lavatory's through there.'

Having got rid of everything he had eaten and drunk that day, he washed his face and hands, shuddering at the sight of himself in the mirror, and wondering what his hostess would say to him now. She'd laugh her head off, more than likely, because he'd never been very friendly towards her when they were young.

Lexie didn't laugh, however. She eyed him with some concern. 'I hope nothing's wrong, Dougal, to make you get as drunk as that?'

'Nothing's wrong,' he muttered, 'I've just been a silly fool.'

He told her what had happened, then added, 'I should have realized . . .'

'It's easy to say that afterwards,' she said, softly, 'but not when you're enjoying the company. Anyway, you'll know not to do that again.'

'I'll never do it again, that's one thing sure, and . . . thank you, Lexie, for helping me. Marge wouldn't have been pleased if she'd seen me like that.'

219

'I like your wife,' she smiled. 'I don't know her very well, of course, but I've got the feeling she doesn't like me very much.'

'Marge isn't like that . . .' he began, and then he remembered. 'She knows Alistair used to go with you, and she's scared you'll try to get him back.'

Lexie looked down at the fire, still with a little glow in it. 'I'll be honest with you, Dougal. At one time, I'd my mind set on getting him back, even when I knew he had a wife and two kids, but that was before I met them.' She lifted her eyes to meet his. 'I couldn't take him away from them now, suppose he wanted me to, which is the last thing he'd want. So tell your Marge, and her sister, to stop worrying. I still look on him as an old friend, but that's all.'

'You've never married, though.'

'I've never met a man I want to marry.'

'You will, one day. You're only twenty-seven. Time yet to find a husband.'

She stifled a yawn and laughed. 'I need my beauty sleep, though. I've to get up for the papers in the morning.'

He jumped to his feet, astonished to find that the sick, dizzy feeling had abated. 'I'm sorry, Lexie. I never thought . . . I shouldn't have bothered you.'

'I was glad to help, but don't get drunk again. Think of your wife.'

Continuing on his way home with a quicker and steadier step, Dougal couldn't help admiring her. She'd had her share of troubles, she'd been left to run that shop and post office single-handed, and, reading between the lines, Alistair hadn't been the only man to let her down, yet the years had definitely matured her outlook on life.

He was a bit rattled to find the ground floor of Benview in darkness when he arrived back, and Marge pounced as soon as he went up to their room. 'Where have you been,

Dougal? You said you were only going to see a few old pals, so I expected you back about half past eight, and it's after half past ten.'

Deciding that honesty was the best policy, he told her everything, but when he had finished, Marge regarded him icily. 'You're disgusting, and Lexie wound *you* round her little finger like she did with Alistair.'

'She got me more or less sober. Marge, you've got her all wrong. She's changed! She doesn't want Alistair back. If you'd been there, you'd know she really meant it.'

'Well, thank heaven for that. Are you coming to bed or not?'

He undressed as quickly as he could, but he was relieved when his wife just kissed him goodnight and turned her back. His constitution wasn't up to what he'd been doing for the past few nights.

At the beginning of December 1941, Marge spotted a poster in the shop and stopped on her way out to see what it said. 'What's a Hogmanay Do?' she asked in a minute.

'It's being put on by the men at Ardley,' Lexie told her. 'They'd one at Hallowe'en. A wee concert first, singing and would-be comedians and magicians and turns like that, all soldiers of course, and even if they weren't professionals, some of them were really good. Then, about nine o'clock, they treated all us civilians to a slap-up meal better than any of us had seen for a long, long time, and then the fun began.'

Marge was intrigued. She hadn't known that any kind of entertainment was ever on offer in this backwater of a place, but she did wonder what these country people classed as fun. 'What happened?'

'The dancing started! And the drinking, of course.' Lexie

regarded her with open curiosity now. 'Would you and your sister like to come? You'll have to put your names down for the bus. It picks up the Forvit folk outside the shop at half seven.'

Marge pulled a face. 'I'd love to come. I'm desperate for something to brighten my life, but I know for a fact that Gwen won't even consider it.'

'If she's worried about leaving the bairns, I'm sure I could . . .'

No longer harbouring any suspicions about the shopkeeper, Marge said, 'I'll tell her, but I still don't think she'll come. She's always been a home bird, not like me. I hate being stuck in the house night after night listening to the wireless with the wind howling down the chimney and my legs getting mottled with the fire.'

Lexie reached under the counter and produced a sheet of paper with quite a number of names on it already. 'I tell you what. I'll put you both down, just in case.'

Watching Marge's retreating back, Lexie couldn't get over the difference in the two sisters. Marge was such a friendly person and seemed to be full of fun, and Gwen was so quiet, so reserved. It was just as well they married the men they did. Dougal had always been go-ahead, the same type as Marge, and Alistair had always stayed in his shadow, much more quiet, more serious about everything. She was glad he'd found the right girl.

The entrance of a customer made Lexie look up with a welcoming smile, although Doodie Tough wasn't exactly one of her favourites, poking her long nose in where it wasn't wanted and spreading her gossip to the four winds. 'That was Dougal Finnie's wife, wasn't it?' Doodie asked.

Not wanting to encourage her, Lexie ignored the question. 'What can I do for you today, then, Doodie?'

'Is that the list for the bus at Hogmanay?' The woman swivelled the paper round so that she could read it. 'Oh, well, would you look at that?' she exclaimed, as Mattie Wilkie came in. 'The twa Cockneys are to be honourin' us wi' their presence at the Do. I just canna tak' to them, me.'

'Me either,' nodded her friend. 'There's something about them, you ken, like they look doon on us country fowk.'

Lexie tried to stop them. 'What was it you wanted, Doodie?'

'A plain loaf, a pound o' rice, a bag o' sugar, and ...' She broke off and delved into her shopping bag. 'See, I've wrote it doon.' She handed over a crumpled piece of paper and turned to her companion again. 'It's the posh wey they spik that annoys me – puttin' it on, of coorse, makin' oot they're better than us, though I can mind on Alistair Ritchie when he hadna a backside to his breeks.'

'Na, na, Doodie,' Mattie protested, 'Bella Ritchie wouldna have let him go aboot wi' his bare erse showin'. She'd have putten in a patch.'

'You ken fine what I meant!' Doodie did not like to be corrected. 'Will you be at the Do, Lexie?' she enquired now.

'I hope so. If it's anything like the last one, it should be a big success.'

'My Lizzie canna spik aboot naething else. If she doesna get a lad this time, she'll be right disappointed.'

'I thocht she got a lad last time,' Doodie put in. 'I mind on seein' her wi' a lang streak o' misery ...'

Mattie managed a wan smile. 'Oh, him? He ... tried it on wi' her, but she tell't him to get lost.'

'A lot o' the sodjers was like that, though,' Doodie remarked. 'You ken Mina Robbie at Milton o' Crombie? Well, her lassie's expectin', an' her father'll kill her when he finds oot.'

Mattie's eyes had clouded. 'There was a lot o' that went on in the last war, as weel. A gey puckle bairns come into the world withoot a father, poor things.'

'That'll be one pound, seven shillings and thruppence, Doodie!' Lexie said loudly, thumping a box of yellow soap, the last item, down on the counter.

'As much as that? Wait or I get my purse oot.' Her eyes were glittering with what could only be triumph as she tendered a pound note and a ten shilling note.

While Lexie counted out the change, she recalled having heard somewhere that Ricky, Mattie's twenty-five-year-old son, had been illegitimate. He had been born in 1916, then, so the father could have been a serviceman. But it was nobody else's business, she thought, turning to Mattie, who only wanted a *Press and Journal*. 'Jock likes to read it when he's takin' his denner,' she explained.

Lexie heaved a sigh of relief when the two women went out, tearing some other poor soul to pieces, probably. This was the one thing she didn't like about village life; there were always people ready to think the worst of everybody else. Not that she would care what any of them said about her, but she should maybe warn the two Londoners not to give the likes of Doodie Tough any chance to spread scandal about them.

Gwen wasn't sure about Marge going to the Hogmanay Do. 'What will people say?'

Her sister tossed her dark curly head. 'They can say anything they bally well want, but I'm not backing out now. It's only a concert, a meal and maybe an hour of dancing, for heaven's sake, and you know I'm bored stiff here. You can come and watch I don't step out of line. Lexie Fraser offered to sit with Leila and David to let us both go.'

Gwen shook her head. 'I never cared much for dancing, nor for meeting new people. Besides, we're both married women.'

'What's that got to do with it? It's not an orgy, just an evening's innocent fun.'

'But you said last night there'll be drinking as well as dancing,' Gwen reminded her. 'That's a lethal combination.'

'I won't be drinking much.'

'The men will, though, and a drunk man can overpower any woman. No, Marge, I don't think you should go, either.'

Marge looked at her sister now with a touch of anger in her eyes. 'I know you don't want to go, and you're older than me, but you can't boss me around like you did when we were kids. I'm going whatever you say.' Her expression softened. 'I don't mean to be nasty, but I've been pining for something to brighten my life, and this Do's just what I need. It'll set me up for months.'

Gwen gave a resigned sigh. 'How far's this Ardley Camp, anyway?'

'About ten miles, Lexie said.'

'For heaven's sake! How are you going to get there? You're not thinking of cycling as far as that, are you?'

'God no! I'd have corns on my bum for weeks if I did. They're laying on a bus, pick up point outside the shop. I'll leave the bike there, and I'll only take one drink so I'll be all right for coming home. Say it's OK . . . please, Gwennie?'

'I suppose . . . oh, just don't forget you've got a husband.'

Marge's spirits were effervescent now. 'It'll be great to get the feel of a dance floor beneath my feet again, and a man's arm round my waist.'

'But . . .' Gwen began, but her sister's ecstatic, yet determined, face stopped her from going on. Marge clearly didn't mean to let this opportunity slip through her fingers.

'Nobody's got coupons to buy anything new,' Lexie had told Marge when she asked what she should wear to the Do. 'Just a smart summer frock.'

'I've put on a bit of weight since we came up here,' Marge moaned to her sister on New Year's Eve, when she was putting the finishing touches to her make-up. 'I've had to wear this old dirndl dress, it's the only one I feel comfortable in.'

'You look nice, Auntie Marge.' Leila had been watching all the proceedings with interest. 'I wish I was old enough to go dancing.'

'Another few years and you will be. Gwen, are you sure this hairstyle suits me?' Marge poked her finger into the upswept roll of hair at her temple.

'Stop fussing,' Gwen ordered. 'It's perfect.'

David, who had been looking on with a jaundiced expression, suddenly observed, 'What a bloody fuss for a nicht oot!'

Gwen turned on him angrily. 'David! Who did you hear saying that word?'

He knew immediately which word she meant. 'The loons at school say it.'

She decided to let it go meantime and have a quiet word with him tomorrow about swearing and using the rough Scottish words he heard in the playground. Her mind was too taken up tonight with worrying about what the evening ahead held for her younger sister. Could Marge be trusted to behave like a married woman?

'Be careful now,' she warned, when they all went outside to see Marge off. 'Don't drink too much, and don't give any of the men any encouragement.'

226

'No, Miss.' Marge grinned cheekily as she tucked the skirt of her tweed coat – which she hadn't wanted to wear but had been too cold not to – round her knees to keep it clear of the oily chain. Then she flung up her left hand in a wave and laughed, 'Now, as I take off on my trusty steed . . .' She burst into song. 'Goodbye, Goodbye, I wish you all a last goodbye.'

It was a song they loved to hear on the wireless, but Gwen said, sharply, 'Don't say that, even in fun. You never know what could happen.'

With the light streaming out through the open door, they watched her until she disappeared round the bend in the track, her flowered headsquare flapping, then Leila took her mother's hand and drew her inside. 'Don't worry about Auntie Marge, Mum. She can look after herself.'

It was wearing on for three o'clock in the morning, however, before the wanderer returned, by which time Gwen was imagining all sorts of things – her sister running off with a man she had fallen instantly in love with, or so drunk that she was lying in a ditch somewhere between the village and Benview, or worse still, the bus skidding on the icy road and all the passengers either dead or seriously injured. She had got herself in such a state that she couldn't stay in bed, and was sitting in the kitchen by the dying fire when Marge came bouncing in.

'Where have you been?' Gwen burst out, anger taking over from anxiety. 'I've been out of my mind with worry.'

'Oh, Lord, Gwen, I'm sorry! Nobody told me it would go on till two, and I'd to wait for the camp bus to take us back. Actually, I landed quite lucky, because when Ken, the driver, saw me getting my bike from the side of the shop, he came off the bus and said, "Hop back in and I'll lift that thing aboard. There's no sense in you having to cycle when I can drop you right at your door." Of course, he couldn't take a bus up the track, so he didn't manage to take me right home, but it was a big help, just the same.'

'He wasn't ... he didn't ...?' Gwen couldn't quite put her fear into words.

'No, he didn't,' Marge laughed. 'He was too busy telling me about his wife and his two kids. Ho, hum!' She rolled her eyes expressively, then carried on, 'It was lovely, though, Gwennie. I really enjoyed myself. The concert wasn't as bad as I expected, the meal was pretty good, and I never missed a dance. Oh, and I only had one port and lemon to start me off, and a few glasses of pop. Iron-Brew they called it, quite nice.'

'I made a fresh pot of tea a minute ago. D'you want a cup?'

'If you like. But d'you know what I found out? Going there on the bus, I was sitting beside one of the girls – most of them were much younger than me – and she said there's going to be a dance laid on once a month in the church hall for servicemen. It's the first I heard of it, so that's something to look forward to.'

Marge broke off long enough to accept the cup she was handed and to take one quick mouthful before she was off again, but her sister was so tired that she hardly took in the descriptions of the piper who played in the New Year, of the Highland Fling two of the squaddies had danced, of the singer who had been with a touring band before he was called up and the applause for whose rendering of 'We'll Meet Again' had almost brought the roof down. 'And at the finish,' Marge went on, 'the padre stood up and said a prayer for all the loved ones who were absent, and all who were missing them. It was so moving, Gwennie, there was hardly a dry eye to be seen, and it made people more aware of what they were doing. I think even those who had intended having a little fling before they went home, or had planned an illicit assignation, thought better of it. So you see, there was absolutely nothing for you to worry about.'

Not a thing, her sister silently agreed, except what might develop at the monthly dances in the church hall. Regular doses of temptation could prove too much for Marge. She got to her feet wearily. 'I don't know about you, but if I don't get some sleep, I'll be like a walking zombie tomorrow.'

Chapter 16

❧

Nearing the end of March 1942, with Marge at her third dance in the church hall and the children asleep upstairs, Gwen Ritchie made a pot of tea and had just sat down to write to her husband when someone knocked at the door. With no near neighbours, this was so unusual that she wondered whether she should answer it or not, but whoever was out there would only have to turn the knob to get in, because she never locked up until her sister came home. Besides, she told herself sternly as she went to obey the summons, this place wasn't like London. There were no burglars or bad people in Forvit.

She was a little disconcerted to find a rather tall soldier on the doorstep. 'Sorry to bother you at this time of night,' he said apologetically, 'but I need some water.'

'Water?' she echoed, hoping that he wasn't ill ... but he looked the picture of health.

'The old bus is blowing off steam,' he told her. 'Somebody must have forgotten to check the radiator and it's overheating.'

An icy hand clutched at her stomach. There was no sign of any vehicle for as far as she could see, but of course, the track was too narrow for a bus, if that really was what he was driving. 'How ... how did you know there was a house up here?'

'Well, I gave a young lady a lift home on New Year's morning, and when she told me where to drop her off, she said she and her sister were living up the track in a house called Benview.'

Light dawned. 'Oh yes. I remember Marge telling me she'd got a lift with her bike. It was very kind of you.'

'I'm afraid I'm here to reap the benefit of my good deed.'

His engaging grin convinced her that there was nothing sinister on his mind, no evil intentions. 'What . . . um . . . ?'

'A jug of water's all I need . . . a big jug.'

'You'd better come in till I see what we've got. You'll have a cup of tea?'

'Thanks.' He sat down at the table and laid his forage cap on the floor beside him. 'As I recall,' he began, watching her fill the second cup which had been set out, 'your sister said you were evacuees from London.'

'Well, our husbands insisted that we take the kids away from the bombing.'

'How many kids do you have between you?' he asked, conversationally, curling his hands round the large cup she handed him.

'Marge has nearly given up hope of having any, but I've got two, a girl and a boy.'

'That's a coincidence,' he smiled, 'I've got a girl and a boy, as well. Pam'll be nine in five weeks, and David's ten past.'

'Gosh, that's another coincidence. My son's David, too, but they're the other way round – he'll be eight in August, and Leila's nine in May.'

'Well, I'll be damned. Oh, I beg your pardon, Mrs . . . em . . . Ken Partridge, by the way. At your service.' He gave her a smart salute.

'Gwen Ritchie.' Her face had coloured at talking so freely to a man she had just met, but he didn't feel like a stranger, somehow. 'My husband's in the Artillery.'

'I'm Ordnance Corps attached to the Black Watch.' His smile broadened. 'So now we're old friends, but I'll be in

231

trouble if I'm late. I've to take the boys back to camp, and some of them get a bit rowdy if they're kept waiting.'

'Don't forget the water,' she giggled, jumping to her feet and opening the door of the cupboard at the side of the fireplace. 'Will this old jug hold enough?'

'That's perfect, but let me fill it.' While they waited for the water level to rise to the brim of the ewer, he said, 'Will it be OK if I bring this back another time? It'll take me a while – it's quite a walk from the main road, isn't it?'

'A mile.' Gwen would have offered to walk with him and take the jug back herself, but she wasn't exactly dressed for a late-night hike. It crossed her mind, as she closed the door behind him, that it would be quite nice to see him again, but the thought made her feel guilty. She was a happily married woman, why on earth should she want to see Ken Partridge again?

Giving this due consideration, she decided that it wasn't for his good looks, anyway, though his cheeky grin was what had made her feel at ease with him. Nor was it the colour of his hair, for she had never liked red-headed men, she didn't know why, and his was the brightest ginger she'd ever seen. His eyes had been really nice, though – an unusual green, but soft and kind with an attractive twinkle – she'd felt like a young girl every time he looked directly at her. Not that she had fallen for him, nothing like that; maybe it was because he seemed a kind of kindred spirit, yet she'd only known him for, at the most, twenty minutes.

Before sitting down again, she took a good look at herself in the overmantel mirror, and was sure she could make out a glint of silver in her hair, not so blonde as it had once been, and her skin was rougher, with working outside so much. For all that, she looked fit and healthy. The open air life was doing her good. It hadn't done much good for her hands, though, she thought, studying them ruefully. Her nails were broken, her fingers and palms always ingrained with dirt, no matter how much she scrubbed them and smothered them in cold cream at nights. Still, she consoled herself, sitting down at the table again, at least the children were safe from air raids up here.

Her mother's letters didn't tell them much – she just said 'our friends still pay us calls', which obviously meant they were still being bombed – but Peggy wrote, in her less frequent scrawls, that some weeks they were in the shelter for nights on end, and hardly any houses in their street had escaped having windows blown out ... or in.

> There's been a few incendiaries, but we've escaped so far. Alf and I both signed up as fire watchers – not for the same nights, of course, because of Mum – so I'm on duty every fifth night with old Mr Hornby from No. 16, patrolling our little patch and making sure we don't miss any of the blasted things, though God knows what good I could do with only a 70-year-old dodderer to help me. But I'm being unkind. Cyril Hornby's dedicated to the job, pail and stirrup pump always at the ready. He sends regards to Marge and you.
>
> By the way, you might be interested to know that I've persuaded Alf not to wait until the war's over before we get married, (he might be past it by then, ha ha!).

'She's come out of her shell lately,' Marge had commented. 'She wouldn't have said anything like that before. Thirtieth April at Caxton Hall, no big fuss.' She sniffed. 'I wish we could see her, though.'

Remembering, Gwen heaved a prolonged sigh. Peggy had also told them not to feel bad about not being there, she knew they'd be thinking of her. She had no idea how they felt – their baby sister . . .

She sat up abruptly. For heaven's sake, she was getting as maudlin as if she'd been drinking! She'd have to pull herself together and finish writing to Alistair. Thank goodness she had something different to tell him tonight. Lifting the Swan fountain pen he had given her for Christmas some years before, she described the short interlude with Ken Partridge in as interesting a way as she could, telling all the facts yet studiously avoiding anything that might hint at how relaxed she had felt in his company. She didn't want to make her husband jealous of a man she may only see once more, and that only if he kept his promise to return the chipped willow-patterned ewer.

At five to twelve, she boiled the kettle for Marge coming in. The dances in the church hall did not go on until all hours like the Hogmanay Do at Ardley Camp. The Rev. James Lennox made sure that everyone had left the hall by 11.30, so that his beadle could sweep the floor and lock up while it was still Saturday, and so that he, himself, could be in bed at a decent time of night. Even in his student days, he had never been one to burn the midnight oil.

As she always did, Marge came bouncing in, stopping in her tracks when Gwen observed, with a touch of mischief in her eyes, 'I'd a visitor while you were out.'

'A visitor? At night?' Marge was astounded. 'Who was it? It wasn't a man, surely, and you here on your own? Or were the kids still up?'

'Give me a chance to tell you. It was Ken Partridge from the camp – the one who gave you a lift on New Year's morning, remember? All he wanted was a jug of water for the bus, and the kids were in bed asleep, and . . .'

'You didn't take him in, did you?'

234

'Of course I did. I gave him a cup of tea, as well, and he's coming back . . .'

'Oh, Gwen, no!' Marge wailed. 'After all the times you've lectured me about giving men the wrong idea, you invite back a . . .'

'I didn't invite him, he has to return the jug.' She explained the circumstances in as much detail as she could.

'Yes, yes, I understand,' Marge said, impatiently. 'From what I remember of him, he's quite a nice chap, really – missing his wife and kids something awful, and a bus would be far too wide to come up the track. I suppose he was on the level.'

'Of course he was! Why on earth should he walk all the way up here if he didn't have to?' Gwen paused, her eyes clouding. 'Unless it was you he wanted to see, and the water was just an excuse.'

'No, I don't think so. I'd say he was one hundred per cent genuine, but for goodness' sake, don't let any other strange men in. The village women would love to get their teeth into some juicy gossip about us, and if any of the men, soldiers or not, overheard them saying you were on your own here on the nights there's a dance in the church hall . . .'

'You're letting your imagination run away with you,' Gwen smiled. 'Now, drink that tea before it gets cold, and let's get to bed.'

Another horrifying thought had struck her sister, however. 'You weren't dressed like that when Ken Thingummy was here, were you?'

Looking down at Alistair's old flannel dressing gown, which she'd taken to using because it was so cold in Forvit in the winter nights, Gwen couldn't help laughing. 'Yes, I was, but I hadn't put my curlers in nor put on my cold cream, thank heaven, otherwise he'd have run a mile when I opened the door.'

Both young women doubled up with laughter at the thought of this, but later, before she fell asleep, it occurred to Gwen that Ken was a married man and would probably be used to seeing his wife similarly adorned ... unless her hair was naturally curly and her skin smoothly perfect, and she wore a flimsy negligee instead of a man's thick robe.

Quite late on Monday afternoon, when Gwen was inside because it was her turn to make the tea, Marge heard a vehicle coming up the track, and straightened up from weeding the winter cabbage patch. It was a few moments later before the jeep came into view, negotiating the stony surface slowly and carefully. 'Hi, there!' she greeted the tall sergeant who got out. 'So it *was* you?'

'It was me,' he laughed, 'and I've brought back the jug your sister so kindly lent me. Is she anywhere about? I'd like to thank her.'

'Inside,' Marge said, laying down the hoe and leading the way.

It was she who offered him a cup of tea, she who hogged the conversation, but quite often, Ken turned to include Gwen. He seemed to be enjoying himself, and looked up with a start and glanced at his watch when David burst in, Leila a little way behind him.

'Good grief! Look at the time! I've been here for over an hour.'

Nevertheless, he took time to introduce himself to the boy and girl before he made his way to the door, saying, as Marge saw him out, 'Good company doesn't half make the time fly past.'

She didn't stop to think. 'Well, look, Ken, you're welcome here any time. We'd be glad of some more of your good company.'

236

'Are you sure I won't be intruding on your privacy?'

'I'm sick to the back teeth of privacy,' she grinned.

David, who had also taken it upon himself to see this very first visitor off the premises, now put in his tuppenceworth. 'Auntie Marge, why can't he come to tea on Saturday, when me and Leila don't have school?'

'That's a good idea,' she smiled, thinking that the boy needed a man around, even for an occasional afternoon. 'That's if you can manage?' she added, turning to the sergeant.

'Yes, I'm not on duty this Saturday ... unless I'm on jankers for being late today.' Grinning, he turned to David again. 'Would you like a run in my jeep? Just a bit down the track.'

'Wouldn't I just?' The boy climbed aboard eagerly, and waved to his aunt as the vehicle rattled off.

She returned to the kitchen. 'I suppose you heard all that?'

Gwen nodded wryly. 'I certainly did, and you're the one who told me to be careful ...'

'Sshh!' warned her sister. 'Walls have ears, remember.'

Leila gave a most unfeminine snort. 'I know you mean me, but why are you telling Mum to be careful? Ken's a very nice man.'

'I was only joking,' Marge assured her.

After that first Saturday, when the two women joined and enjoyed the game of rounders in the afternoon, and sat with their new friend listening companionably to the wireless after the children were in bed, Ken Partridge became a regular visitor, but never again while Gwen was on her own. He gave most of his attention to David, showing him how to dribble a football, how to hold a cricket bat (a flat piece of wood) and judge the speed of an oncoming sponge ball – all the knowledge a father might pass on to his son, Gwen thought one day, but unfortunately Alistair had been in the army before the boy was old enough to take any interest in these skills.

When Ken learned that Alistair was arriving home on leave on the last Monday in May, he said, 'I'd better stay away till he's gone back.'

This put Gwen's mind at ease. She hadn't mentioned in any of her letters that Ken was visiting regularly, though she couldn't say why. There was nothing going on that her husband shouldn't know about.

Marge, however, said, 'There's no need. I'm sure Alistair would like to meet you.'

'I'd better not. I know how I'd feel if my wife produced a man who'd been visiting her while I wasn't there. I go on leave myself in the middle of June, so it'll be four weeks before I see you all again.'

After he left, on one of the bicycles made available at Ardley, Marge gave her sister an enquiring look. 'Haven't you told Alistair about Ken coming here?'

'I just told him about the first time,' Gwen said, a little on the defensive. 'It didn't seem fair . . . when he's so far away . . . I thought he might feel jealous, though nothing's going on – how could it, with you and the kids always here, too?'

'You'll have to gag your David, then. He's got a mouth like the Dartford tunnel.'

A horrified expression crossed Gwen's face. 'I hadn't thought of that.'

After a moment's concentrated thought, Marge burst out, 'I've got it! We could tell him it's against army rules for any soldier to visit another soldier's home.'

'But that would be a downright lie!'

'Lying's not a criminal offence, and it's either that or tell

238

Alistair the truth. David won't question it, not if I say it's a grown-up secret and he'll have to keep his mouth shut so Ken won't get into trouble.'

'What about Leila?'

'I think she'll fall for it, too, and nobody else knows Ken comes here. I've never said a word to a soul in the village, have you?'

'No, it was nobody's business.' Gwen eyed her sister as if begging for assurance. 'Do you really think it'll work?'

'I can't see why not.'

On his first night home, Alistair had done so much travelling and hanging around railway stations over the previous twenty-four hours that he tumbled into bed and was asleep in a few seconds, and Gwen, curlers in and skin shining from the cold cream she had rubbed in and wiped off, felt her heart turn over at how vulnerable he looked. She loved him so deeply it hurt. They'd all been in the house when he arrived, and he had only kissed her once before David and Leila clamoured for his attention, and the moment had passed, the moment he should have taken her in his arms and shown her how much he'd missed her.

Of course, it was natural that he wanted to hug his children, and he'd said he had fourteen days' leave altogether, but the army didn't allow for the time it would take to travel from the south of England and back. That meant she would only have him for twelve days . . . maybe just eleven nights, and he was sleeping through one of them.

Awake first in the morning, Alistair felt ashamed that he'd been too tired the night before to make love to his wife, but surely she would understand? Something else was niggling at the back of his mind, though, if only he could remember what it was. It had nothing to do with Gwen, nor Marge . . . nor Leila, even if she *had* been a bit reserved with him.

That left David, who had definitely been different towards him after the initial joyful welcome. Of course, it was months since they'd seen each other – when he'd been David's age, the two months between his birthday and Christmas had seemed like a year – but it wasn't just that. There was an excitement, a nervousness, about him. Had he done something really bad and his father was being left to administer the punishment?

Feeling Gwen stirring now, Alistair leaned across to kiss her, then everything else was blotted from his mind as he made up for lost time. It was wearing on for an hour later, and thankfully they were lying peacefully, when the bedroom door crashed back against the wardrobe and David leapt in.

'Dad, Auntie Marge says to ask if you're needing the bathroom before me and Leila go in to wash?'

'Maybe I'd better.'

Gwen sat up. 'I'll go after you, then, because they take ages.'

'And Auntie Marge says your breakfast's ready and just go down in your jim-jams.'

Her face reddening, his mother said, 'Off you go, my lad, and make sure you brush your shoes before you go to school.'

Listening to him running down the stairs, Alistair burst out laughing. 'Go down in our jim-jams,' he spluttered. 'Just as well she didn't say to come as we are.'

Swinging his feet to the floor, he went over to the chair by the window to get his underpants and trousers, his naked body more muscular than it used to be, his stomach muscles taut from the discipline of drills and marches.

David and Leila off to school, Gwen upstairs in the

bathroom, Alistair took the chance to have a private word with his sister-in-law. He hadn't said anything to his wife, in case he was being oversensitive because of what he would have to tell her soon. 'Is David in trouble of any kind, Marge?'

'Not that I know of. What made you think that?'

'It's ... I dunno, the way he looks at me, I suppose, as though he was expecting me to get on to him for something.'

Marge gave a low chuckle. 'Somebody's always having to get on to him for something, at home and at school, but I'm sure his conscience is clear just now. He's growing older, maybe that's what it is? Maybe he wants you to show him how to do things, like ... um, like other fathers show their sons.'

Alistair didn't notice her slight hesitation to cover the gaffe she had been on the point of making. 'That'll be it,' he smiled. 'Well, I'll kick a ball around with him for a while when he comes home, how would that do? And I could take him to the burn where Dougal and me used to guddle for fish.' Noticing her puzzled expression, he laughed loudly. 'It means catching them with our hands.'

'Great!' she enthused. 'That's the kind of thing he'll enjoy.'

'How are you and Gwen coping here?' he asked now.

'Like old stagers,' she smiled. 'I was bored stiff before the dances started, but one evening's dancing sees me through the four weeks till the next one.'

Alistair frowned. 'Dances?'

'The vicar or whatever they call him puts on a dance once a month for the men at the camp, and he gets a three-piece band from Aberdeen to play. They're quite good, the band and the dances, though everything stops at half past eleven.'

'You mean you go every month? What about Gwen?'

'She doesn't want to go, you know how she is, but she doesn't mind me going.'

'Does Dougal know? I wouldn't be happy about it if you were my wife.'

'I've told him. All the boys know I'm married and out of bounds, so we just have a few laughs. Besides, with a dozen pairs of beady eyes watching my every move, I wouldn't dare to misbehave even if I wanted to, which I swear I don't.'

'What about Gwen? Does she not mind being left here on her own?'

'It's only once a month, Alistair, for goodness' sake, and you know she's a home bird. She wasn't happy to start with, but only because she was afraid I'd meet somebody. She keeps an eye on me, though she knows I'm a one-man girl, like her. I would never want anybody but Dougal, my big Scottish he-man.'

Alistair's leave flashed past. He was glad that he had taken Marge's advice, for he *had* got to know his son better, showing him all the old haunts he had frequented when he himself was a boy, spending maybe half an hour before teatime every day fooling around together with a football, hunkering down with him at the back door to play marbles. Yet he hadn't neglected his wife and daughter. On the Saturday, he had taken them on the bus into Aberdeen and while Gwen was contentedly looking round the stores in Union Street, he had taken the children to the beach by tramcar, a first for them in both cases.

On the Sunday, they'd had a picnic at the tower, and while he and the two women had lain on the grass lapping up the sunshine, Leila had tried to find as many different kinds of wild flowers as she could, and David searched for insects. Watching them as they darted hither and thither brought a lump to Alistair's throat. He was a lucky man, a truly lucky man, with a beautiful wife who loved him as much as he loved her, and the two bonniest bairns in the world. If only he could be here with them all the time!

On his last evening, Gwen persuaded him to cycle to the village. 'You might see some of your old friends in the hotel bar,' she added, not really wanting him to spend precious time away from her, but trying to let him rekindle old acquaintances and give him something else to remember when he went back.

He had intended to stop at the shop for cigarettes but the shutter was up and he carried on to the hotel. He was out of luck there too, the supplies having run out the day before. It was Dod Tough – husband of Doodie and regarded by her cronies as henpecked, but a force to be reckoned with in discussions and arguments in the bar – who came to his rescue. 'Lexie aye keeps a puckle packets under the coonter for special customers, and you and her being . . . eh, good *friends*, heh, heh . . .' He gave a loud snigger. 'Go roond the back and knock on the hoose window.'

Ignoring the knowing glances and winks being exchanged by the other men, Alistair said, 'I need fags if I'm to be sitting here drinking for a couple of hours.'

Lexie didn't seem surprised to see him as she ushered him inside. 'I heard you were home.'

'I leave tomorrow.' He shook his head as she gestured towards the sofa. 'No, Lexie, if I don't get back to the bar, they'll think . . .'

She regarded him clinically. 'You wouldn't have worried at one time.'

Embarrassed, and more than a little apprehensive, he was unsure what to say. 'At one time maybe, Lexie, but a lot of water's passed under the bridge . . .'

She gave a reassuring laugh. 'And you've got a wife and two fine bairns. You needn't look so worried, Alistair. I'm not going to jump on you.'

'I never thought . . .'

'No? Look, I admit I was hurt when you went off to London and left me, and I did hanker after you for years, but I got over you.'

'You never married, though?'

'Not yet, but I'm still looking.' She gave him a playful punch on the arm. 'There's plenty of men around Forvit now, you know, and dances every . . .'

'Every month, Marje told me.' After a moment's hesitation, he asked, 'Is there any . . . gossip about Marge?'

'Show me one girl in Forvit there's no gossip about . . .' She shook her head, giggling. 'You must remember what Doodie Tough and her lot are like? If we as much as smile at one of the Ardley boys, we're making up to them. But you can tell Dougal he's got nothing to worry about with Marge. She tells each and every one of them she's a married woman and they respect her for it, and they still have a good time and so does she. Now, you'd better come through to the shop and I'll miraculously produce a packet of Capstan out of the air for you – that's all I've got, and I've to keep them hidden.'

He followed her through, insisted that she take the money for the cigarettes she gave him. 'Thanks, Lexie . . . for everything. You're a good friend.' After a slight hesitation, he added, 'I won't be seeing you for a while, we're being sent overseas when I go back. I'm going to tell Gwen tonight.'

'You haven't told her yet?'

'I didn't want to spoil our time together, but tonight's my last night.'

'You'd better make the most of it, then. Well, cheerio, Alistair, and good luck!'

He put both hands round the one she held out and clasped it tightly for a moment. 'Thanks, I'll need it.'

He did not see the wistful look she gave him as he made his way out, and walked into the bar to the accompaniment of loud cheers. Dod Tough leaned across to him when he sat down. 'I didna think you'd get awa' withoot . . . you ken?'

Alistair's laugh was guilt-free. 'Lexie and I have never been more than friends. No matter what anybody thinks.'

'Good enough friends for her to gi'e you a packet o' Capstan, I see.'

Alistair let that pass, he had done nothing that needed justifying, and his companions returned to their previous topics – the weather, the price of beer and cigarettes when they could get them, the progress or otherwise on all the war fronts. He put forward his opinions when they were asked for, but he backed out of commenting on the war. 'Don't ask me. The rank and file are the last to hear what's going on.'

'That's right enough,' agreed Bill Mennie, sitting in a corner with a man Alistair recognized but couldn't name. 'It was the same last time. Them at the top made the decisions, never mind if it was dangerous for the poor bloody infantry. We were . . . expendable, that's the word. We're the ones that had to go over the top though we knew Fritz was waiting for us, and we got mowed down like . . . rats in a trap.'

'. . . like rats in a trap,' echoed his companion.

Dod Tough clicked his tongue. 'Dinna heed them, lad. They mak' oot they saw a lot of action, but they werena five minutes ower there when the Armistice was signed.'

Alistair laughed along with the others, then said, 'I hope it's the same for me. We're being sent overseas – I don't know where.'

He should have known better. He was now plied with drinks to wish him well, and he felt increasingly uneasy – not for his own safety, but because he still had to tell Gwen. After an hour, his head beginning to swim, he took his leave of the group of men and cycled back to Benview.

'You haven't been long,' Gwen greeted him. 'Didn't you see anyone you knew?'

245

'I knew most of them, but none of my old pals were there.' He took out his cigarettes, and fished for the lighter he'd made from a bullet shell. 'They didn't have any fags left in the bar, though, and I'd to knock at Lexie Fraser's house door to get some.' He could sense a change in the air at this, and he wondered why everybody, even his own wife and her sister, took it for granted that there was still something between him and Lexie. The drink he had consumed was enough to fan his pique into anger. 'Well, I see I've been convicted, judged and tried, so I won't bother denying it. Think what you bloody well like, I'm off to bed!'

He stamped upstairs, threw off his clothes and was asleep in minutes . . .

Gwen looked imploringly at her sister. 'D'you think he was with her all the time?'

Marge screwed her mouth to one side. 'Um, no, I shouldn't think so. He's had a few too many by the look of him, so maybe he doesn't like being questioned.'

'But if he's nothing to hide . . .'

Marge regretted ever having voiced her own suspicions. 'He'll feel guilty for drinking so much. He'll probably tell you in the morning, but if he doesn't, just let it drop.'

Even after resolving to take Marge's advice and not question her husband, the first thing Gwen did when he opened his eyes the following day was ask, 'Were you with Lexie Fraser all the time you were out last night?'

'Oh, Gwen,' he groaned, gathering her into his arms, 'my darling, darling Gwennie, I was only with her for . . . not much more than five minutes. Look, I'll be perfectly honest with you. I've known her all my life, I like her quite a lot,

246

but I do – not – love her! I wouldn't have seen her at all if I hadn't needed fags.'

They were just reaching the point when passion would no longer be denied, when their son barged in. 'Oh!' he exclaimed in disgust. 'Do you two never get tired kissing?'

Trying to control his laboured breathing, Alistair managed to laugh, 'No, and we never will.'

'Well, you'd better stop now, for Auntie Marge says you'll need all your time if you don't come down for breakfast right now.'

There was something of a scramble until they were all seated round the table having breakfast. 'How long will it be before your next leave?' David asked, his mouth full of toast.

A silence fell now, an electrifying silence during which even David didn't speak, then Alistair laid his hand over his wife's. 'I'm sorry, darling,' he murmured, looking deep into her eyes, 'I shouldn't have left this till the last minute, I meant to tell you last night, but ... things happened. I've been on embarkation leave, we're being sent overseas when I go back, so it could be long enough before I get home again.'

It was left to Marge to dam the hole in the dyke. 'They'll be needing reinforcements somewhere,' she told David, 'and your Dad has to go where he's told.'

'Where, Dad?' the words were croaked, as the boy took his cuff across his eyes.

'I don't know yet, son. It could be anywhere – Far East, Middle East ...'

'Near East?' Marge was trying to make a joke.

'Anywhere.' Alistair got to his feet and pulled Gwen off her chair, too. 'Give me a hand to fasten my bags.' He took time to hug his son and daughter before he turned away with moist eyes, and Marge cleared the obstruction in her throat in order to reassure the children. 'He'll be fine, don't worry, my pets.

He won't have to fight Germans wherever he's going, that's good, isn't it?'

She managed to shoo them off to school – David crowing 'Wait till the boys at school hear my Dad's going overseas!' – and sat down with another cup of tea. Only a few minutes later, Alistair and his wife came downstairs, Gwen's eyes red from weeping.

'I hope you're pleased at what you've done, Alistair Ritchie!' Marge couldn't help herself. 'Fancy waiting till the very last minute before you told your wife and kids you're on embarkation leave. Can't you see how hurt she is?'

Gwen shook her head. 'I'm all right, Marge. He's explained why he didn't tell me before, and it was my own fault that he didn't say anything last night.' She slid her arm through her husband's. 'I'll walk to the road with you, Alistair.'

'You'll have to put a step in, then.' Marge stood up and kissed her brother-in-law's cheek. 'I'm sorry, Alistair, I'd no right to say . . .'

'You have every right, Marge, and I'll regret being so stupid to my dying . . .'

'No!' Gwen burst out. 'There's no need for regrets. We had a wonderful time while you've been home. Don't let's spoil it now.'

'Well, 'bye, Alistair,' Marge murmured, 'and God bless.'

When Gwen returned, her face ravaged by tears, Marge said, sympathetically, 'I know how you must be feeling. I'd never speak to Dougal again if he did that to me.'

'I was the one who made him go out last night,' Gwen reminded her, 'and I shouldn't have said anything when he came home. It was asking for trouble when I could see he'd had too much to drink.'

'I suppose he told his friends he was being sent overseas,'

Marge offered, 'and they'd been dishing out the booze to him.'

Gwen nodded. 'Yes, that's what he said.' Squaring her shoulders, she added, 'He told Lexie, too.'

'Before he told you?' Marge was outraged.

'He said it didn't matter to him. I mean, he wasn't worried about telling her. She was just a friend, like the men in the bar, but I'm his wife, and he didn't want to spoil our time together. There's nothing between them, Marge, it's just me he loves.'

'Of course it is.'

Not quite believing her own assurance, Marge wasn't surprised at Lexie's first remark when she went to the shop that afternoon. 'Did Alistair get away all right this morning?' Receiving only a slight nod in answer, she went on, 'He wasn't looking forward to telling his wife, you know. I nearly said he wasn't being fair to her, but it wasn't really any of my business.'

'No,' agreed Marge, tersely, 'it's not any of your business.'

'Listen, Mrs Finnie, you know Alistair and me were ... well, I looked on him as my boyfriend but he didn't feel the same way about me. So if you and your sister think there's still a spark of something between us, there never was ... not on his side anyway.' She smiled brightly. 'And only friendship on my side now, as well.'

There was something about the woman that got through to Marge at this point. She had heard the gossip about her looking for a lad at the dances, although she didn't seem to have succeeded, but she was positive that it wasn't because of Alistair. Whatever Lexie had felt for him at one time, and perhaps for years after he left Forvit, there was only friendship now, perhaps slightly more ... affection? Certainly not love.

Marge related the conversation and her conclusion to

Gwen when she returned to Benview, and her sister's spirits were raised even more when she received Alistair's letter two days later, penned as soon as he returned to his base.

My Darling Gwen,

I had to write to let you know how deeply I regret drinking so much on my last night at home, and how ashamed I am for not telling you as soon as I arrived that it was embarkation leave. I could see how hurt you were that I had told Lexie first. I did try to explain how I felt about her, but I don't think you believed me.

My dearest darling, you have no need to feel jealous of her. We grew up together, we had some good times together, but only as pals, nothing more than that. We are adults now, of course, but still friends, close friends, but I treat her the same as I treat the men I've known all my life. I hope you understand.

Thank you for the other nights we spent together, at least I have all those lovely memories to take out and relive when I feel down. You mean everything to me, my darling, and I bless the day Dougal decided to marry Marge, otherwise I might never have met you. By the way, give her my regards.

We are being issued with light kit, and the rumour is it's North Africa, but keep your chin up. Wherever I'm sent, I promise to come home to you. All my love, my dearest, and kiss the kids for me every night, so they won't forget me.

Your ever loving husband,
Alistair. XXX

Gwen handed the epistle to Marge, who gave it a cursory read then said, 'Well, I think you can take it that he loves you.' She regarded her sister with twinkling eyes. 'How was it between you two the rest of the time he was here?'

'Perfect,' Gwen sighed, 'but I wonder if we should . . .'

'If you're going to say we should stop inviting Ken when he gets back, put it out of your mind. He's as straight as that broom handle and he's got no designs on either of us. Being part of our family reminds him of his own, I suppose, and we can't deny him that. Maybe we should have told Alistair about him while he was at home, but there's no sense telling him now, not when he'll soon be in the heart of the fighting. It would just worry him. You know, my Dougal's been saying in his letters for ages that he's fed up still being on this side of the Channel. I ask you! After what he went through at Dunkirk! Funny creatures, men, aren't they?'

On Saturday morning, David asked when Ken would come to see them again. 'They haven't found out he was coming here before, have they, and punished him for it?'

It took both his mother and his aunt a second or two to realize what he meant, then Marge said, 'No, no, nobody found out. He's on leave, like your Dad was, and he's gone home to see his own family.'

'I love my Dad,' David stated, with a touch of embarrassment, 'but I miss Uncle Ken, and all. We can speak about him now, can't we?'

'Not to anybody outside this house,' Marge cautioned. 'You never know, one of your school friends might tell his mother, and she'd tell somebody else, and it could easily get back to Ardley.'

'OK!' David gave an exaggerated salute before picking up

the bag containing his football strip. 'I'll keep my mouth buttoned up, and so'll Leila. You can depend on us. You coming, then, Lei?'

His mother and aunt couldn't help laughing when the two children went out. David's words and actions came as a result of reading the *Wizard* and the other comic strip magazines for boys which he and his chums circulated amongst them. 'I hope we're not being stupid,' observed Gwen in a moment. 'Encouraging them to tell lies.'

Marge cocked one eyebrow. 'It's not lies, just ... well, a way of saving trouble, really, though we're not doing anything wrong. You're not thinking of being unfaithful to Alistair are you?'

'I should think not!' Gwen was horrified at the very idea.

'If you ever do, let me know,' laughed Marge, 'so I can be on the lookout for someone, too. I don't want to miss out on any fun.'

Chapter 17

❧

'I hope Uncle Ken remembered to buy me a cricket bat.'

Gwen shook her head reprovingly at her son. 'He gives you far too much, Leila too, and don't ask him about it. It's not manners to ask for presents.'

'I didn't ask,' David protested, bright blue eyes flashing indignantly. 'It was him promised to get one so he could teach me how to play proper cricket.'

'If he promised, he'll likely have it, but if he's forgotten, don't get in a paddy.'

The boy looked hurt now. 'I never get in a paddy . . . only when Leila makes fun of me, her and her chums. That Kirsty Droopy-Drawers . . .'

'That's enough, David! Her name's Kirsty Kelman, and it's no wonder the girls tease you if that's the kind of things you say about them.' Becoming aware that her sister was chuckling in the background, she snapped, 'It's not funny, Marge! He's getting worse and he'll have to learn some manners, else people will think I can't control my children.'

'Calm down, Gwennie, he's just a kid, but . . .' Marge gave her nephew a poke in the ribs, '. . . you *will* have to learn how to behave, David. You don't want to make your Dad ashamed of you, do you? He wants to come home to a boy people respect.'

His head drooped. 'I'm sorry, and I won't say anything to Uncle Ken if he hasn't got a bat . . . but Auntie Marge, is it OK if I ask him when we'll be playing cricket?'

She had to turn her head away to hide a smile, but Gwen heaved a lengthy sigh of exasperation, 'David Ritchie! Don't you dare mention cricket!'

Keeping her face straight with something of a struggle, Marge coaxed, 'Why don't you come outside, my boy, and help me tidy up the tool shed. It'll be something for you to do till Uncle Ken comes, and keep you out of your Mum's way.'

'This isn't his weekend on duty, is it? I don't like the Saturdays he can't come.'

David was still chattering when the back door closed behind them, leaving Gwen wondering what would happen when Ken Partridge was posted away from Ardley Camp, as was bound to happen sooner or later. He had been spending three Saturdays out of every four with them for almost a year now, and she had an uneasy feeling that David had begun to regard him as a father-figure. It wasn't surprising, really, when his real father wasn't there to guide him through his formative years. And Ken was so good with him and Leila, giving them the affection and attention he should be giving his own children. It was a terrible world, she reflected morosely, when families were kept apart like this.

She dabbed away an unwelcome tear that had edged out. She mustn't let herself wallow in misery, even though her sadness wasn't just for her own family and Ken's, it was for families everywhere. There must be hundreds, thousands, of wives praying every night for the safe return of their husbands, quaking every time someone came to the door in case it was a telegraph boy bearing the news they dreaded.

'Are you all right, Mum?'

Her daughter's concerned voice shook Gwen out of her reverie. 'Yes, dear, I'm fine. I was just feeling a bit sad, missing your Dad.'

'I miss Dad, too, but Uncle Ken won't be long now and

he'll cheer us all up . . .' Leila paused thoughtfully, then went on, '. . . though he must be missing his wife and children, too. Hardly any of my friends at school have Dads at home. Most of them are in the army, and there's a few in the RAF, but there's only one in the Navy. Why's that?'

'Probably because Forvit is nowhere near the sea. The men haven't got the sea in their blood like people from towns and villages on the coast.'

'It must be ever so dangerous on the sea, and up in the air,' Leila observed. 'I'm glad my Dad's a soldier on dry land.'

Gwen was only glad the girl hadn't realized that her father was in just as much danger on land as in the sky or on the waves. She was better not having that worry.

The shrilling of a bicycle bell made Leila jump up in excitement. 'That'll be Uncle Ken,' she cried, rushing to the door.

Gwen's heart contracted when she saw how the man scooped her daughter up in his arms. He was always so attentive to the children, showing more affection than Alistair, a reserved Scotsman, had ever done, yet she wished that it was he who had just come in.

'How are things, Gwen, girl?' Ken was standing looking down at her anxiously.

'Fine.' Even to herself her reply sounded listlessly insincere, and she tried to correct the impression she must be giving. 'I *am* fine. Just a bit down, thinking of Alistair.'

'Have you heard from him lately?'

'It's been nearly five weeks.'

'Given the state of the army postal service,' he smiled, 'that's not too bad. You'll get a whole bunch at once, no doubt.'

The door banged open as David burst in. 'I knew you were here, Uncle Ken! I saw your bike outside.'

'Did you take a good look at it?'

255

'No. Why? Should I have?'

'It might be a good idea.'

David whipped round and scampered out, almost knocking Marge off her feet as she came in. 'Where's the fire?' she gasped, but he didn't hear.

In less than a minute, he was back, grinning from ear to ear and brandishing a shiny cricket bat and a set of stumps. 'You did remember!' he crowed.

'Manners,' Gwen prompted.

'Thanks, Uncle Ken, thank you, thank you, thank you. I knew you wouldn't forget.'

With David on heckle pins at his side, Ken took time to drink the cup of tea he'd been given before he got to his feet. 'Well, I guess now's as good a time as any, David. Have you got a cricket ball to practise with?'

'Won't the sponge ball do?'

Ken put his hand in his trouser pocket and drew out a brand new cricket ball. 'I think we should keep this for a while yet, though. It's a bit too hard, and we don't want you breaking any windows. We'd better use the sponge ball till you've had some practice.' He still didn't move, however, but extricated a small package from his other pocket and handed it to the girl with a flourish usually executed by conjurers. 'Can't give to one and not the other, can I, Leila?'

'You shouldn't give either of them anything,' Gwen admonished him.

'I want to,' he said, simply, thus putting an end to her protestations.

'Oh, gosh, Uncle Ken!' Leila held up a little brooch in the shape of her name for them all to see. 'It's lovely! Thank you ever so, ever so much.'

'It's made of gold wire, and the boys are all making them for their daughters.' Gwen's frown made him smile broadly.

'I made one for my own daughter first, then I thought Leila might like one, too.'

'It's very kind of you.'

His ruddy face even redder than usual, he cleared his throat. 'Right, then! Who wants to come and field for us?'

They all trooped out, Leila proudly sporting her 'identity' brooch, and each one participated in the fun game until Gwen said she should go in to organize tea, and Marge and Leila offered to help. So now Ken was free to give young David some lessons on holding the bat, how to stand properly, how to keep his eye on the ball – the serious business of coaching. He called a halt when the picnic meal was carried out by the 'three ladies' as he called them, making Leila straighten her back proudly and Gwen glance at him in gratitude. It was a beautiful day, exceptionally warm even for September, so they lingered over their makeshift meal, taken on the 'drying-green', the only spot in the whole garden not given over to growing vegetables.

Looking around him with satisfaction, Ken suddenly said, 'Fetch the camera, David. I'd like to have some reminders of this day.'

The boy dashed off and returned with the box Brownie Ken had given him a few weeks earlier. 'It's showing eight,' he said, seriously, 'so that means there's still four left to take.'

Ken unwound his long legs and rose to his feet. 'Sit down so I can get you all in.' He waited until they arranged themselves as Marge considered best, then pressed the catch. 'You all look too posed,' he laughed. 'Can't you pretend to be doing something, so it'll look more natural?'

David flung his arm round his sister's neck as if he were about to strangle her, and Marge lolled drunkenly against Gwen. 'How's that?' she asked, grinning.

'That's better.' Ken took another snap, then handed the

camera to her. 'Take one of me and the kids. I'd like to have a keepsake of them.'

'There's still one left,' she smiled, after taking him capering with the two children.

David ran over. 'Let me take the last one, Auntie Marge. Uncle Ken, get in the middle between her and Mum. No, that looks too stiff . . .'

Ken obliged by putting his arms round the women, and David pressed the button while his mother and aunt were still laughing. 'That should be a good one,' he crowed.

'I'd better go inside the shed to take the film out.' Ken held out his hand for the camera. 'The photos'll be spoiled if any light gets in.'

David went with him. 'I want to see how to take the spool out,' he told his mother, who had frowned at him for dogging the man's footsteps.

A few minutes later, when they rejoined the others, Ken said, 'I'm being sent to London on a two-week course next Thursday, so I'll get it developed and printed there. In fact, I'll get two sets, one for myself as well, but you'll have to wait till I get back, David, before you can see them, I'm afraid.'

David looked crestfallen. 'That'll be three weeks, won't it?'

'It'll soon pass, and anyway, you'll have your Uncle Dougal for most of the time.'

'I'd nearly forgot about that.' The boy perked up again. 'Can we have another game now? Mum will want to clear up, so Leila and Auntie Marge can . . .'

'Hold your horses, David, my lad.' Marge got stiffly to her feet. 'I'm not doing any more running after that ball. I'm going to help your Mum.'

They all shared in the clearing up, then the two ladies were left in the kitchen to do the washing-up while the other three went back outside. After a few moments of silence, Marge said, reflectively, 'It's funny Ken having to go on a course just now, isn't it?'

Gwen looked up in puzzlement. 'What d'you mean?'

'I think he's volunteered to go. It's a year and a half since he first came here, and he always stays away when Dougal's on leave. Always some excuse.'

'But he can't plan things like that. He's got to go where he's told . . . when he's told. Anyway, I never asked him not to come while Dougal was here.'

'Neither did I,' Marge said, sharply. 'I'd have been quite happy for them to meet. I'm sure they'd like each other . . . Alistair, too.'

'I wish he would write more often.'

'He's fighting a war, remember, not having a holiday by the Mediterranean. He hasn't got time to write to you every other day.'

'I know that, but . . .' Gwen tailed off, forlornly.

'Getting back to Ken, I don't understand why you want him kept secret. He's only a friend, after all, and he's been jolly good with the kids.'

Not quite sure why herself, Gwen floundered a little before saying, 'I've the feeling Alistair would be hurt if he knew . . . because he can't be here to give them presents or play games with them. It's almost as if they look on Ken as their father, and that's . . .'

'Yes, but when Ken's posted away, they'll soon forget him and look forward to their real Dad coming home . . .'

Another few moments elapsed before Gwen murmured, 'I don't know how David's going to take it when Ken does have to leave Ardley. He dotes on him.'

'He'll cope. He was all right when Alistair went away, wasn't he? Now, can I go, or are you going to make me wait half an hour before you hand over that plate you're trying to scrub the pattern off?'

The last plate duly dried, everything tidied away, the sisters went to join the others, who, exhausted now, were sprawled out on the grass. The women sat down beside them, letting the newly-sprung cool breeze help them to recover from their exertions and ruffled emotions.

At nine o'clock, the usual hour for the children's bedtime on Saturdays, Marge said, 'I'll see these two settled, Gwen, then I think I'll go to bed myself. I've got a blinder of a headache with sitting in the sun too long, but it's too good a night to be cooped up inside. Why don't you two go for a walk?'

Ken beamed at her. 'I'd love to. What about it, Gwen?'

She cast a glance of appeal at her sister, who interpreted it correctly and gave her the push she needed. 'Go on, Gwennie, it'll do you good and nobody'll see you.'

'Even suppose someone did see us,' Ken remarked as they strolled up the track a few minutes later, 'we're doing nothing wrong, are we?'

'We know that,' she murmured, 'but other people wouldn't.'

'Forget about other people. Why can't you just relax and enjoy the walk? I've always felt easy in your company, though I know you took quite a while to feel completely at ease with me. I can assure you I've no intention of doing anything out of place, I respect you far too much, and I know you miss Alistair as much as I miss Rhoda. A man and a woman *can* have a close platonic relationship, Gwen. They can feel affection, even love in a kind of way, without anything . . . physical, if you get my meaning.'

She got his meaning, and the thought of what *could* happen made her nervous, but Ken was a decent man, and Marge must trust him, otherwise she wouldn't have suggested them taking this walk. Besides, Alistair couldn't object if he knew how innocent it was.

Because it wasn't too far, they made for the tower, and

while they stood looking down on the panorama spread out below them, and across at the snow-capped mountains in the distance, she thought of all the men and girls who must have stood there over the years, had perhaps consummated their love there, and gave an involuntary shiver.

'You're cold!' Ken exclaimed, removing his battledress blouse and wrapping it round her. 'We'd better put a step in going back. I don't want you ending up with pneumonia.'

'I'm not cold,' she protested. 'I was thinking of all the people who had stood here – since the tower was first built, and it gave me a queer feeling.'

His arm was still round her waist when they returned to the house, and she was quite relieved that Marge had gone to bed and didn't see. 'I'll make a pot of tea,' she said, her voice low and breathy.

'No, I'd better go.'

She didn't want to let him go just yet. 'It won't take long.' She lifted the kettle and held it under the tap.

'I'd better go. Believe me, Gwen, it *is* better.' He retrieved his jacket and put it on, then said, 'Good night, I've really enjoyed my day . . . as usual. I won't see you next week or the week after, of course, but I should manage the week after that . . . with any luck.'

He was gone before she could set the kettle down, and the rattle of the old bike told her that he hadn't waited for her to see him off. She lit the gas ring and sat down to think over what he had said. They did have a close relationship, she did feel affection for him, but not love. Not any kind of love – well, maybe just a touch. Why did he have to be so nice? Why did Marge have to pair them off? Why was she trembling at the memory of his arm around her?

The hiss of water on the gas flame made her jump up. When the tea was infused, she poured out two cups, one for herself and one for Marge. Her sister would likely wonder why Ken hadn't stayed for a cup, too, so she'd have to think of a reason to explain it.

Marge's light was still on, so she went straight in. 'How's your head now?'

'A bit better. I took a couple of aspirins and I dozed off for a while. Did you and Ken go up to the tower?'

'Mmm. It was lovely up there, so clear we could see for miles.'

'Um . . . he didn't stay very long when you came back?'

'No, he thought I'd caught a cold, because I was shivering. It was only somebody walking over my grave, but . . . he insisted on giving me his jacket.'

'You look kind of guilty, Gwennie, so you'd better tell me. Did he try anything?'

'No, he didn't!' Gwen was truly indignant.

'He didn't even kiss you?'

'No, he didn't.'

'Did you wish he had?'

'No, I didn't.'

Marge's eye hardened. 'Change the record, Gwen. I can read you like a book.'

'Well, you're wrong tonight. Nothing happened, and I wasn't sorry. Ken said ours was a platonic relationship, and that's how we both want it.'

'I'm glad to hear it. I did wonder, after I sent you out with him, if I was stirring up a hornets' nest, so I'm pleased you're both so adult and sensible about it.'

'Well, we're both married and love our . . .'

'Spouses, that's the word. Now you'll maybe understand how I feel when I'm out dancing. It's nice to be in a man's company again, especially when there's no chemistry to foul things up. I won't feel so bad now about leaving you on your own. And that's another thing. Would Ken have volunteered to be the permanent bus driver taking the soldiers to Forvit?

262

He always makes a point of staying in the hall all the time, nowadays, but he never asks any girl up to dance ... not even me.'

In her own bed, Gwen turned Marge's last remark over in her mind. Ken probably *had* volunteered to ferry his friends from the camp to the village and back, and had remained in the hall to save even her sister getting any wrong ideas about her.

Because the monthly dance fell on Dougal's second night home, Marge said she couldn't desert him, but he pulled a face. 'I don't want you giving up your night out ... d'you think any of the boys would mind if I went with you?'

'I don't see why they should. You're in the forces, the same as them.'

The minister was delighted to make Dougal's acquaintance and, after his usual few words of welcome to the 'boys from Ardley', he made a point of introducing 'Marjory's husband'. There were shouts of 'Good old Marge!' and 'Good luck, mate!', and even one cheeky 'He's why we only get to dance with her,' at which she beamed happily.

At that moment, the band struck up, and a laughing Dougal swung her into their first lap of the church hall to the strains of 'You Are My Sunshine', played with gusto on sax, piano and drums by three ex-members of a quite well-known dance band.

Dougal forgot everything and everyone else in the pleasure of holding his wife in his arms, their bodies moving in unison to the pulsating rhythm. 'You'll never know, dear, how much I love you,' he sang softly into her ear.

'Oh, Dougal,' Marge sighed, her heart performing all kinds of somersaults, 'I didn't know you were such a good dancer.'

'We never went dancing, did we? Some of the other girls I took out were dancing mad, so I went with them, and I used to go to all the dances round here before I went to London.'

'Sowing your wild oats?' she teased.

He chuckled at this. 'What we thought was wild oats at the time, I wasn't long sixteen when I left, remember. I looked on myself as a proper Romeo, you know, and if a girl let me kiss her when I saw her home, I thought I was the bee's knees.'

'Did you never . . . ?'

'I used to boast to Alistair I'd gone all the way, he was a lot quieter than me, but it wasn't true. Oh, I admit I made some feeble attempts, but I'd have dropped flat on my face with shock if any of them had let me.'

The quickstep ended with a flourish and was followed by a modern waltz, then a Paul Jones, where, miraculously, they ended up with each other every time the music changed. After the energy expended in most of this, they were glad of the dreamy slow foxtrot to which Dougal substituted the words 'A Nightingale Sang in Russell Square' instead of the proper Berkeley Square, but he broke off when he realized that his wife's eyes had filled with tears. 'I'm sorry, Marge, have I made you homesick?' he asked, anxiously.

'No, it's not that.' She dragged the back of her hand across her cheekbone. 'It's just . . . that Russell Square reminded me of Guilford Street, and the hotel . . . and Dad.'

'I didn't think – I could bite my tongue out. Will you be all right?'

'I *am* all right. I was being silly.'

Next, they were told to form into lines for the Lambeth Walk, which was all she needed to banish the nostalgia, and she joined in the fun right to the final 'Oy!' Spirits were high as the band took a well-deserved break, and the ladies of the Women's Guild took up their positions on the small stage round the tables which held huge tea urns and dozens of plates of scones and pancakes, baked by the ladies themselves. The minister now said a brief grace which doubled as a prayer for absent friends, adding after the Amen, 'Pray silence for the vice-president of the Women's Guild, Mrs Georgina Tough.'

Dougal couldn't trust himself to look at Marge as Doodie stepped forward. 'I just want to say,' she began, in her best speechifying-English, 'how sorry we are that our president is nae able to be here the night, and I think I spikk for yous all when I say we hope her operation's a great success.' She looked round the assembly and then observed, to the minister's very obvious embarrassment, 'Piles is nae a fine thing to ha'e – I ken that, for my Dod's suffered wi' them for years – and I'd be obliged, Mr Lennox, if you'll pass on oor best wishes to your lady wife. Now, that's me finished, so jist come up and help yoursel's! There's plenty, and you can come back for seconds if you want. Like my aul' Granny used to say, "Stick in till you stick oot."' With a toothy smile, she returned to her station, ready for the rush.

Surprisingly, the dancers made their way on to the stage in an orderly line, which resulted in a smooth operation where everyone was served in no time at all. Dougal was astonished by the amount on offer, but didn't heap his plate like most of the other men. 'These pancakes are out of this world,' he enthused when he and Marge were seated. 'How do they do it when everything's rationed?'

'All the women chip in a little something,' she smiled. 'Flour, sugar, eggs ...'

'Dried eggs? I heard they were awful.'

'A lot of wives here keep hens, so we hardly ever have to use the dried stuff, though it's not too bad when it's reconstituted ... not good, but bearable. And Lexie's quite good at giving the committee a bit of Stork margarine, or Echo, no butter, of course.'

'Does she ever attend these dances?'

'Not every one, and she's not here tonight. She'd a bad cold on Thursday when I saw her, so she probably didn't feel up to it.'

Dougal eyed his wife reflectively. 'I don't suppose you and Gwen ever made friends with her?'

Marge lifted her shoulders in a small shrug. 'Not friends as such. We talk to her in the shop, that's all. I've never really taken to her, you know.'

'If that's because of Alistair, I'm nearly sure she gave up on him long ago.'

Their little tête-à-tête was interrupted by a roll on the drums, and the first few bars of 'Jealousy' on the saxophone. A tall captain appeared in front of them now. 'I hope I'm not intruding,' he began, 'but I really must have this tango with Marge. She's the only one in the place who can do it properly. I hope you don't mind ... Dougal?'

Marge jumped to her feet. 'Of course he doesn't mind.'

As Dougal watched them, he thought what a stunning couple they made, their steps gracefully synchronized, as if they'd been partners for years. He felt slightly jealous, only very slightly, he told himself, but was it any wonder? Not only an officer, this man was devilishly good-looking – tightly-curled blonde hair, piercing blue eyes, dimpled cheeks – and Marge was laughing as she looked up at him.

When the tango ended, she pulled the captain back to be introduced properly. 'Dougal, this is Percival Lamont. Percy, this is my beloved husband.'

The attractive smile widened. 'I'm very pleased to make your acquaintance, Dougal.'

The lilting Highland accent would be another point in his favour with the women, Dougal thought, but he shook the man's hand as warmly as he could. 'Pleased to meet *you*, Captain.'

'We don't bother with rank at these dos. But I must tell you how much I envy you, Dougal, having this lovely lady for your wife, a faithful wife, at that. There are very few of them around now.'

Blushing faintly, Marge giggled, 'Get on with you, Percy. You could charm the birds off the trees if you tried.'

'But not you, I fear.' He winked at Dougal to show that he was only fooling. 'Now Dougal, I must spread myself around – I wonder who will be the next lucky lady?'

He turned away and headed for a small brunette at the other side of the hall as the band struck up a slow foxtrot, and Marge said, 'Don't mind Percy, Dougal. He's an awful tease, but it's all in fun. He's very happily married, his wife had a baby a couple of months ago, and for all his flirting, he wouldn't do anything to hurt her.'

Her husband led her on to the floor. 'I just wish he wasn't so handsome . . . like a blinking film star.'

'I like my men rugged,' she said, softly, 'with dark hair and called Dougal, not a cissy name like Percival.'

The rugged, dark-haired man called Dougal tightened his hold on her. 'I love you, Marjory Finnie,' he whispered in her ear, 'and I'm glad I came with you tonight.' She looked so lovely, so happy, that he couldn't resist kissing her. It didn't go unnoticed, however, and they jumped apart as various teasing comments were made, but, because of the minister's presence, nothing out of place.

'We'll have to excuse them – they haven't seen each other for months.'

'Couldn't you two wait till you went home?'

'I hope my old lady kisses me like that when I'm on leave.'

And so on, the Reverend James Lennox's face never changing its affable expression, although he did unbend a little when the other dancers moved away and left Marge and her husband on their own. 'Oh, God,' Dougal muttered, 'I don't like everybody watching every move I make.'

'It's a compliment,' she giggled, 'so let's show 'em!'

Their intricate scissors-steps to 'I'd Like to Get You on a Slow Boat to China' drew frenzied applause from the onlookers, but Dougal was glad when they could return to their seats. 'I felt awful,' he groaned, while they watched the more energetic Eightsome Reel which followed, 'like a goldfish in a bowl.'

'Tell the truth now,' Marge chuckled, 'you really liked being the centre of all eyes, didn't you?'

'Aye, I suppose so. I always did like to show off.'

At the end of the evening, several of the men shouted goodnight to them as they made their way outside, one even saying to Marge, 'Have you got your bike tonight?'

She hadn't, there was only one adult bicycle at Benview, Alice's old rattler, and the thought of having to walk three miles home after dancing all evening was not a pleasant one. The bus was waiting outside to take the soldiers back to Ardley, but the driver – not Ken, Marge was glad to see – came up to her and said, 'It's back along there, isn't it? Hop in, it's not taking me much out of the way.'

As they plodded up the track some minutes later, Dougal observed, with deep feeling, 'Thank goodness we got a lift a bit of the way. My legs feel like telephone poles with dancing so much, but I really enjoyed myself.'

'That's good, 'cos so did I.'

He waited until they were in bed, until he had demonstrated how much he loved her, before he gave her the bad news. 'This is embarkation leave, I'm afraid, darling, and the word is it's the Far East, so God knows how long it'll be before I get home again.'

Marge frowned. 'I know you've been dying to get back into

it, but you did your bit in 1940, more than your bit. Why can't you be satisfied with that?'

'I wasn't the only one, and we were just doing what we were trained for.'

'When I remember how you were when you got back from Dunkirk . . .' She broke off, her eyes softening. 'I know you've got to obey orders, but you're not really sorry to go, are you?'

'I'm not sorry in one way, but I hate the idea of being away from you for . . . well, it's indefinitely, isn't it?'

'I'll survive, my darling, but I'll never stop thinking about you, and praying for you.'

He drew in a long contented breath and let it out slowly. 'Marge, I'm really glad I went to that dance with you tonight. I've always known you liked to enjoy yourself, and no matter how often you said in your letters I could trust you, I couldn't help wondering. But what those men said about you . . . it made me realize what a jewel you are. I love you so much, Marge Finnie, I'd bloody die for you if I had to.'

Her eyes flashed in alarm. 'No, Dougal, don't say that! Please don't say that!'

He held her trembling body in his arms, as she sobbed out her fear for him, the fear that she had planned to hide if this moment ever came, but couldn't when it had actually arrived, and when she pulled herself together at last, he made love to her again.

'I know you'll worry about me,' he said afterwards, 'but there's no need. I'll be back. I swear to you I'll come back. Don't ever forget that, my darling.'

Marge's heartache was almost unbearable, yet she was glad that Dougal hadn't waited until the last minute before telling her his news, like Alistair had done. At least *she* could make the most of the ten nights she had left to enjoy her husband, but even when Gwen took her children to Aberdeen to let them be alone on his last Saturday, it didn't seem long enough.

When Ken Partridge put in his next apperance, the first thing he did was to hand David a slim wallet of photographs. 'They're all quite good,' he observed, smiling at the boy's haste to take them out and look.

'So they are!' David exulted. 'Look, Mum, and Uncle Ken only took three. I took the rest myself.'

The snapshots duly inspected by Gwen, Marge and Leila, and praise given where it was due, David wanted to play cricket again, so they all trooped outside to get some exercise and then soak in some sunshine while they recovered. Both Gwen and Marge had a feeling that Ken was holding something back, but neither of them said anything. If he had something to tell them, it was up to him to choose his moment.

They had another picnic tea, but as soon as a move was made to gather the dirty dishes, Ken said, 'Leave them for now. I'm not going to make a speech, exactly, but there's a few things I'd like to say before I leave Forvit.' He held up his hand to stop any comments on this, and continued, 'First, I want to thank you two ladies for the pleasure you've given me over the past eighteen months. You always made me feel I was part of your family, and as for you two . . .' he ruffled David's hair with one hand and touched Leila's cheek with the other, '. . . well, it was like being with my own kids.'

David knuckled his eyes. 'You're not going away, are you, Uncle Ken?'

'I'm afraid I have to. We're being posted down south somewhere.'

'But you'll come back to see us?'

'I don't think we'll ever be sent back to Forvit.'

'Will you write to us?'

Ken glanced hopelessly at Gwen, then clasped the two children closely for a second. 'No, I don't think that's . . .'

'No, of course, you're not supposed to be friends with another soldier's family, are you?' David still believed the tale Marge had once spun him, but Ken was too involved in making sure he expressed his sentiments clearly to notice.

'I'll never forget you, though . . . any of you.' The man's voice was strained now, and he said nothing more until he composed himself. 'What about a last shot at cricket, David? You learned pretty quick, you know, so maybe, if we promise to be careful, your Mum'll let us use the proper ball?'

It was Marge who jumped in. 'Fifteen minutes, then, to let us get the dishes done, then it's off to bed with you.'

When Gwen finally managed to haul her son upstairs, still begging to stay up a bit later since it was the last time he would see Uncle Ken, Marge took advantage of her brief absence. 'I'm going to tell Gwen I've got another headache,' she told Ken, 'so would you be a dear and take her out for a while? She won't admit it, but she's really worried about Alistair, and she must miss a man's company.'

'It'll be my pleasure, Marge, but are you sure you'll be all right?'

'There's nothing wrong with me, but don't let on to Gwen. Ssh, here she comes.' She raised her voice now and went on, 'Well, I suppose it's goodbye, Ken, so all the best, and take care of yourself.'

'You're not leaving already?' Gwen asked, anxiously.

'No, he's not, but I've got another of my headaches so I'll leave you to entertain him. Good night, Ken dear, and God bless.'

'I'm sorry,' Gwen murmured, uncomfortably, when her sister closed the door, 'she could surely have managed to stay with us till . . .'

'It's all right, it gives me a chance to let me have one last stroll with you.'

'Oh, Ken, I don't know if I should . . .'

'Please, Gwen?'

The entreaty in his eyes was too much for her. 'All right, but just for a little while.'

They walked up the hill again, making light conversation and scrupulously keeping their bodies from touching, but when Gwen stumbled over a bigger-than-normal stone and Ken's arm shot round her waist to steady her, she didn't object. Nor did she protest when he tucked her arm through his instead, and this is how they carried on walking.

'You *will* hear from Alistair,' Ken assured her. 'I'm sure you will.'

'I wish I could be so sure.' Feeling a wave of sadness wash over her, she wished that he hadn't mentioned her husband. It was bad enough that she was about to lose *him*.

As if he knew what was going through her mind, Ken said, softly, 'This is the last time we'll be together.'

She could think of nothing to say. She had known it would come some day and had thought she would be able to wish him luck as she waved him goodbye, as Gracie Fields sang, but she couldn't get it out. She had even planned to ask for his home address, so that she could write to his wife and tell her how good he had been to Leila and David, but perhaps that wouldn't have been such a good idea. In any case, she was struck dumb, unable to wish him well, unable to tell him how much she would miss him.

'Are you OK, Gwen? You're not upset because I'm going away, are you?'

'Yes,' she managed to croak, 'I *am* upset . . .'

Tears welling up, she turned blindly to him and he took her in his arms. 'Oh, God,' he moaned, 'are you crying for me, Gwen? I didn't dream you felt . . . I've steeled myself for months not to let myself get too fond of you.' His murmured words of affection became words of love, of passion, and before they knew it, they were lying on the heathery scrub kissing as if there would be no tomorrow. And neither there would . . . for them.

'Come here, Floss.' Lexie had thought the collie would be all right off the leash, but she was determined to get into a rabbit hole, burrowing away as if her life depended on it, but she did stand, a little impatiently, as the lead was fixed to her collar again.

Lexie had never cared much for dogs, but when old Mary Johnston had asked her to look after Floss while she was in hospital having her varicose veins stripped, she hadn't liked to refuse. The poor woman hadn't long lost her husband, and having always kept herself to herself, she had few friends. Still, walking the collie took a person out, Lexie had told herself, and set out for the tower without thinking. It was the only walk she had ever taken when she was younger, and it aroused memories of happy times with Alistair. But she shouldn't dwell on that; it was long behind her.

She had to pull the dog back suddenly, for she was straining to bound towards a couple lying at the foot of the tower. Lexie didn't consider herself a romantic, but it seemed a shame to disturb the young lovers, though she would have liked to know who the girl was. The snag was, she couldn't see their heads, and she could hardly walk right up to them to find out. Just before she turned to walk back, however, a low voice made her strain to hear what was being said. 'Oh, Lord, I'm sorry!' That was all. It was an Englishman, but a lot of the lads at Ardley were from somewhere in England. 'I didn't set out tonight to do that. I'm truly sorry.'

'It was as much my fault as yours.'

Lexie drew in her breath. She'd know *that* voice anywhere. Alistair Ritchie's wife! Up at the tower, making love with a soldier!

'It just happened because you're going away.'

'That's no excuse. Can you ever forgive me?'

'There's nothing to forgive. We'd better go back now. It must be late.'

Lexie didn't wait to be caught eavesdropping. Stepping off the stony path, she padded as swiftly and silently as she could until she reached the trees and was sure she wouldn't be seen. Making her way obliquely towards the road, she could hardly believe what she had seen and heard. Gwen Ritchie with a soldier? It was manna from heaven!

It didn't matter that she'd have to wait till Alistair came back from overseas. What she had to tell him would blast his marriage apart. To be absolutely sure, she would say she had seen the couple making love. It was only half a lie, for that *was* what they must have been doing. Why else would the man have been pleading for forgiveness? Not for just a few kisses.

Lexie breathed a long, contented sigh. Everything comes to he – she – who waits. God bless old Mary Johnston's varicose veins! God bless the dear old soul for having a dog that needed to be walked at nights! God bless everything and everybody, especially Lexie Fraser!

Chapter 18

❧

It was on the Wednesday of the following week that Sandy Mearns said, as he handed a buff envelope to Gwen, 'Is your sister in? If she's nae, you'd best wait till she comes back afore you open that.'

It took a moment for the meaning of his remark to penetrate, then she muttered, her voice quivering a little, 'It's OK. She's in the kitchen.'

When she went inside, Marge said, 'Is something up? You look kind of ... funny.'

'The postman thinks it's bad news.' Gwen was fumbling at the flap of the envelope.

Understanding now, Marge said, softly, 'D'you want me to open it?'

'No, I want to do it myself.'

Marge didn't have long to wait to satisfy her curiosity. 'Oh, no!' she exclaimed, when her sister passed the single sheet over without a word. 'But ... it's not as bad as it could ... it just says he's missing. That means they must think he's OK. If they didn't, they'd have said "Missing, believed ... killed."'

'I knew something was wrong! I just knew it!'

'Don't give up hope, Gwennie. I've read of some men going missing for weeks, months sometimes, and then they turn up again – maybe lost their memory, or been wounded and taken in and cared for by some family, or ... oh, there's lots of reasons.'

'But there's always some who don't turn up,' Gwen pointed out, her voice flat.

Forced to concede that this, too, was true, Marge happened to glance out of the window. 'Sandy's still fussing about at his bike. He'll be waiting to hear what was in the letter. I'll go and tell him.'

When she came in again, she said, 'He's a nice old stick. He said to tell you he'll be praying for your husband's safe return. Wasn't that thoughtful of him?' She paused, then asked, 'Are you going to tell Leila and David?'

'I don't know, I don't want to upset them. The thing is, if it gets round the village, one of their friends at school might tell them.'

Marge's nose crinkled. 'I asked Sandy not to tell anybody.'

'He's bound to tell his wife, and Mrs Mearns is a real gossip. I know, I've heard her in the shop.'

Marge couldn't hold back a slight smile. 'He knows that. He said, "I'll nae tell a soul, lass, specially nae my Aggie." But I suppose it would be best not to tell the kids – not till . . . we hear something definite.'

And so, every morning around nine fifteen, whether he had a delivery to make or not, Sandy Mearns was to be found in the kitchen at Benview, making droll comments in the hope of cheering up the 'poor English lassie'. Marge would laugh hilariously for a moment at something she thought was comical, then quieten down when she noticed that Gwen, the true object of his wit, was scarcely smiling.

It was quite an effort for the two young women to keep up an appearance of normality in front of the children, whose first question when they came in from school was always, 'Is there a letter from Dad?', but Marge managed to paper over any cracks in her sister's manner that might have caused them to fret.

276

It was an afternoon almost six weeks later – with Gwen's limbs becoming more and more leaden, her face more and more peaky, her temper shorter than even the more volatile Marge's had ever been – before the telegram came, the telegram which Gwen was powerless to bring herself to open, but Marge seized as soon as the door was shut on the telegraph boy.

'He's all right, Gwennie!' she screamed, in a second. 'He's been taken prisoner.' She grabbed her sister's arms and pulled her to her feet to waltz her round the room.

But Gwen was not yet in a dancing mood. 'I want to read it for myself,' she protested, picking up the scrap of paper with the information pasted on in narrow, typed strips. 'I don't know what to think,' she sighed after a while. 'I know it means he's alive, but aren't prisoners sometimes badly treated?'

Tutting at this, Marge said, perhaps more snappily than she meant, 'Stop going on, Gwen, for goodness' sake! At least you know he's alive, and he'll be safer in a prison camp than anywhere else, won't he?'

'I suppose so.' She sat pensively for a few moments, then burst out, 'Yes, I'm being silly. Of course I'm glad he's a prisoner, and now all we have to worry about is Dougal's safety.'

'It's hellish, isn't it?' Marge commented, bitterly. 'I'd feel much better if I could be doing something, instead of being stuck up here at the back of bally beyond.'

'You're not thinking of going back to London?' Gwen asked, looking worried.

'No . . . no, I'm not. I promised Alistair I'd never leave you here on your own.'

The children came home at the usual time, David bursting in like a wild animal to let them know what he had been told.

'They're all saying our Dad's been taken a prisoner. It's not true, is it?'

Marge jumped in. 'Yes, isn't it good news? We just heard this morning, how did your pals hear?'

'Petey Rae said Dad's name was on the list of prisoners Lord Haw-Haw read out last night on the wireless. His Mum listens every night, and she said she was sure it was the same Alistair Ritchie she was at school with.'

He lapsed into silence now, making Marge realize that he, like his mother, was not sure whether to regard this as good or bad news. 'He's out of the fighting now, that's the main thing, David, and there are rules laid down about how prisoners of war should be treated. He'll be all right, dear.'

In the background as usual, Leila made a sudden mewing noise, and flung herself at her mother. 'I knew something was wrong,' she sobbed. 'Dad hasn't written to us for weeks and weeks and weeks, and I thought he . . . I thought he'd been killed.'

Watching Gwen comforting her daughter, Marge marvelled at how quickly a mother could summon up such strength. Having her children to consider would help to take her mind off herself.

Sandy Mearns's smile was a little wry the next morning. 'The news is out, Mrs Ritchie, and it wasna my doing. It seems . . .'

She smiled to put him at ease. 'We know. Somebody listened to Haw Haw.'

'That bloody traitor!' His hand jumped to his mouth. 'Ach, I'm sorry, ladies, but if I got my hands on him, I'd . . . damn well throttle him. But at least you ken your man's safe, Mrs Ritchie. It must have been real hard on you when you was tell't he was missing.'

'It wasn't easy,' she agreed – a vast understatement if ever there was one.

*   *   *

Another few weeks passed before a guilty Gwen suspected that she might have more to worry about than her husband's and her brother-in-law's wellbeing. The first time she missed, she had put it down to the ordeal of waiting to hear about Alistair, but this second time, well, there was no excuse. Feeling that she couldn't confide in anyone, not even her sister, she became withdrawn and tearful.

'Luv-a-duck, Gwen!' Marge exclaimed when the children left for school one morning another month later, after a somewhat fraught breakfast. 'You've been snapping their heads off since they got up. What's wrong? It's not as if you got out of bed the wrong side today, it's been going on for weeks.'

That was enough. Gwen burst into a torrent of tears.

'Oh, come on, now. I know you've only had one little card from Alistair since he was taken prisoner, but surely . . .'

'I'm . . . pregnant.' The whispered words were almost lost in the weeping.

Marge's head jerked up as her eyebrows shot down. 'You're what? You can't be! It's months since Alist . . .' She broke off, comprehension hitting her like a punch in the face. 'Oh no, Gwen, tell me you didn't . . . ?' Her sister's bent head, bobbing in time with her sobs, told her all she needed to know. 'Dear God! I trusted Ken! I never dreamt he'd take advantage of you! Did he rape you?'

Getting no answer, she continued, 'Obviously not! So you let him! How could you?'

Gwen looked up, her eyes dark with shame. 'I . . . I can't . . . it was . . . his last . . . night, and he was missing his wife, and I was missing Alistair, and we were . . . it just happened.'

'But servicemen are issued with thingummies. Why didn't he use one?'

Her sister shook her head. 'It wasn't planned . . . it happened so quickly . . .'

'But you must have known the risk? Good Lord, you're not a child!'

Gwen dissolved into a fresh bout of weeping, and Marge shook her head hopelessly. 'So what are you going to do?'

'I don't know. I . . . can't think. Alistair'll kill me when he finds out.'

Marge pulled a face. 'He's not that type, but he's bound to . . . oh, what a thing for a man to come home to. His wife with another man's child.'

'Stop it, Marge! I feel bad enough without you making it worse.'

There was an uneasy silence, broken only by Gwen's hiccuping sniffs, until Marge said, 'Have you tried to get rid of it?'

'I'm too scared. I've heard it's dangerous, and anyway, I don't know what to do.'

'Poking things up's dangerous, but there are other ways. Drinking gin's supposed to do the trick. Or a good dose of castor oil or liquid paraffin, so I've heard.'

'I . . . don't think . . .'

'It would be difficult to get any of that, in any case. We'd have to go to the pub for gin, which would start tongues wagging, and if you ask in the shop for castor oil or liquid paraffin it'd be a dead giveaway.'

'Oh, Marge! What am I going to do?'

'It'll be OK, Gwennie. I'll think of something, but I need absolute peace for my little grey cells to work, as 'Ercule Parrot says, so I'll make a start on tidying up David's room for you. He leaves it like a pigsty. Just give me a shout when it's dinner time.' An idea had already occurred to Marge, but it would have to be well planned, every wrinkle ironed out, before she mentioned it to her sister. Gwen had a more analytical mind than she had, and would be sure to pinpoint snags if there were any to be found.

While she gathered up the clothes David had dropped on the floor the night before, and arranged things so that drawers would shut, she looked at her idea from every angle, explored every avenue where there could be a trap for the unwary, and eventually decided that it was quite feasible ... if they were careful. The main problem, of course, was Gwen herself. Would she agree, or would she think that her sister was taking advantage of her plight? In fact, Marge mused, was that what she really *was* doing? Her solution would benefit herself as much as ... no, more, a thousand times more, than Gwen. But it was the only way.

When she was called downstairs, she burst into the kitchen and sat down at the table with a thump. 'I've got it! I've got it!'

Gwen regarded her miserably. 'Not one of your silly ideas, please. I've done some thinking, too, and I've come to the conclusion that I'll just have to face up to it, but I won't tell Mum till it's all over. She'll be so disappointed in me.'

Marge said nothing until she had forced down a few mouthfuls of the detested, not rationed, corned mutton. 'My idea isn't silly, Gwen, and you won't have to tell anybody anything. Not Mum, not Peg, not Alistair when he comes home, not a soul.'

Her sister's face blanched. 'You're not going to tell me to get an abortion? I couldn't do that, Marge, not even if you found a woman who's done dozens.'

'You know this? You're a blinking pessimist, Gwen Ritchie! Maybe you can't see a way out of the mess, but never fear! Marge is here!'

'Stop fooling! I'm not in the mood.'

'I'm not fooling, believe me! Just listen.'

Over the next twenty minutes, Marge laid out her plan and satisfactorily, she hoped, fielded off each attempt to pick holes in it. 'It's foolproof!' she crowed at last. 'I've thought of everything, and though we wouldn't get away with it in London, it'll be a cinch here. Nobody near us . . .' she broke into song, '. . . to see us or hear us. Gwennie, it's perfect, so why can't you look happier about it? I've nearly worn my brain to the bone for you, and I get no thanks for it.'

'I *am* grateful, Marge, but d'you honestly think . . . ?'

'I don't think, I know. We'll have to take things stage by stage, of course, so we don't raise any suspicions, but I'm a good actress and I'll carry it off.'

'I don't doubt that,' Gwen muttered, 'it's me I'm worried about. I can't tell lies, you know that. I get all guilty and flustered, and people know . . .'

'You won't have to tell lies, just go along with the lies I tell. I'm going to leave it for now, and we'll discuss it again tomorrow. That'll give you all night to think it over and to . . . realize it *will* work. In the meantime, don't let Leila and David see there's anything up. We don't want them upset, as well.'

For the rest of the day, Gwen went about her usual chores silently, only opening up when her children came home from school and apologizing for being so bad-tempered in the morning.

David nodded vigorously. 'Bad-tempered? I'll say! I was scared to open my mouth in case you jumped down my throat.'

Marge jollied them along. 'It'll maybe teach you to keep your mouth shut, then,' she chuckled. 'You should know by this time it's not sensible to argue with anybody who's in a bad humour. Your mum and me keep well away from you when you're in a paddy.'

'I only get in paddies 'cos it's always me you and Mum pick on.'

'Because you're the only one who needs to be picked on.'

David saw the truth of this and grinned mischievously.

'We calling pax now, are we?'

Marge pretended to punch his arm. 'Till the next time.'

Gwen gave Marge's plan a great deal of consideration that night. At first, it had sounded so outrageous that she'd been sure it couldn't possibly work, that it was just another of her sister's harebrained schemes, but the more she mulled it over, the more she came to think that it might work, with any luck. The one big snag as far as she could see was that, although it would be Marge who was supposed to be expecting, *she'd* be the one growing fat. But Marge had thought of that, too, positive they could overcome even that hurdle.

Having their usual, most appreciated, cup of tea after the children went off to school next morning, Gwen broached the subject first. 'I've decided to play along.'

Marge clapped her hands. 'Thank God for that! I don't know what we'd have done if you hadn't. Now, the first thing to do is for me to tell people you're not very well. I'll do all the shopping from now on, and as you get bigger, you'll have to keep out of the postman's sight, and young Barry's. They're the only ones who come here. And you'll have to keep me right on how fat I'm supposed to be at the different stages.' She beamed expansively. 'You know something, Gwennie? I'm looking forward to this. It's a real challenge to my ingenuity.'

'There's just one thing we've never mentioned,' Gwen said, cautiously. 'When we go back to London, who takes the baby?'

Marge looked a little uneasy. 'If you don't want Mum and Alistair to know ...' She came to an abrupt decision herself and took the bull by the horns. 'It'll be best all round, Gwennie. Dougal went back off his last leave just a week ... no, two weeks before you and Ken ... He'll be jumping his own height thinking he actually hit the jackpot after all these years, so there'll be no doubts in his mind that he's the father.'

Eager to make a start to the long series of deceptions she was instigating, Marge cycled to the village that morning to cash her army allowance. 'Is it possible for me to collect Gwen's as well?' she asked Lexie.

'Is she not feeling well?'

'She's got a blinder of a headache, and I told her to go back to bed. Migraine, likely.'

'Tell her I hope she gets over it soon, and . . . well, I suppose it'll be all right.'

While she served her customer with the groceries she needed, Lexie said, a little slyly, Marge thought, 'I thought I saw her with a soldier up at the tower, one night a few months ago. About half past nine, it would have been.'

'It couldn't have been Gwen!' Marge stated firmly. 'She never goes out at nights, just with me and the kids, and they're in bed by nine.'

'I must've made a mistake then.'

Cycling back to the cottage, Marge decided not to tell Gwen about it. She'd only get more worried, and the success of the whole thing depended on them both staying calm. In any case, Lexie Fraser hadn't seemed sure it was Gwen. She'd probably said it for effect more than anything, maybe she'd been there with a soldier herself, and had wanted her, Marge, to ask what she'd been doing at the tower at half past nine at night. She'd been wanting to prove *she* had a man friend. That was all.

Lexie smiled craftily to herself when Marge went out. Did that Cockney think she'd come up the Don in a banana boat? Maybe – a weak maybe – it was just a coincidence that Alistair's wife was feeling off colour, but more likely it was because her lover-boy had put her up the spout. Judging by the time that had gone past, she would be due to feel sick and that kind of thing. It all fitted in, and the situation should be monitored as closely as possible. If she *was* expecting, Gwen Ritchie hadn't a hope of hiding it.

In London, maybe, but not in Forvit. Not a hope! Definitely not!

Chapter 19

❧

Marge was greatly relieved that Lexie Fraser, usually sub-covertly inquisitive about all her customers' lives, especially Alistair's wife's, had never commented on how pale and haggard Gwen was beginning to look. In fact, the shopkeeper seemed quite surprised when Marge said that her sister was going to see a specialist the following week. 'It's a woman's problem, you see, and she was too embarrassed to go to the doctor here, so I took her to a lady doctor in Aberdeen a few weeks ago. *She* made all the arrangements.'

Lexie just nodded half-heartedly and said, 'So she would. Now, that's one pound, sixteen and four pence, please, Mrs Finnie.'

Marge picked out the correct amount from the money she had just received as her army allowance, and as she packed her purchases into the shopping bag, she wondered what God-sent problem was keeping Lexie so preoccupied. The thing was, she thought, while she cycled back to the cottage, it might not last long, and it was better to face all possible snags before they arose. That was why she had given the first hint of something brewing . . . but leading the shopkeeper, naturally, in the wrong direction.

'You'd better not go to the shop again,' she told her sister when she went in. 'I've told Lexie you're going to see a specialist next week, and even if I'm not sure if she took it in, it's better that you stop going to the village till after . . .'

Gwen looked up sadly from preparing the vegetables. 'But

if you're going to pretend it's you who's having the baby, you can't go either. She'll see you're not expecting.'

'It's going to be OK. I'll stick a cushion up my jumper . . .'

'But you'll need two cushions when it comes nearer the time, and you won't have any clothes to fit over that.'

'I think I will. D'you remember, before Alice left, she said she'd never thrown out any of her mother's clothes? She said they were in an old trunk in the attic, and Mrs Ritchie was quite stout, remember? I'll go up this afternoon and sort something out. It'll work, Gwennie, I promise it will.'

'Oh, Marge, I don't know what I'd do without you.'

Marge pulled a face. 'You wouldn't be in this mess, for a start. You'd never have gone out with Ken Partridge if I hadn't made you.'

That afternoon, while Marge was up in the attic, Gwen went into her son's room to look at the photographs again. David had got some nice snaps of the tower, of the house, of some of his chums, but those taken at Benview were really good. Of course, Ken had taken two and Marge had taken one, but the one David had taken was by far the best – Ken standing between her and her sister with his arms round their shoulders. David had told them not to be so serious, she recalled, so Marge, grinning up at Ken, had passed some silly remark, he was smiling broadly at her, and she, herself, was laughing.

Gwen studied this print for several seconds, waiting to see if what she'd felt for the man on that last night would return, the powerful emotion that had led to her present predicament, but there was nothing. She still felt an affection for him, missed him coming to the cottage, but that was all. Her heart hadn't speeded up in the slightest. It was Alistair she loved, and God knows what he would think of her if he ever found out what she had done.

She returned the slim wallet to the shelf when she heard

287

her sister creaking down the rickety ladder. 'Did you find anything?'

'A few skirts and some knitted jumpers and cardigans, and a coat, so we're OK. It's a good thing we went to Aberdeen last Thursday. If Lexie does start asking questions about us, she'll find out *that* was true, though she'd have a fit if she knew it was for a maternity skirt for you. We'll have to go again next week to keep to my story, but we can buy some baby things. Nobody'll think it's queer that you couldn't ask the local doc about your "problem". They all know how shy and easily embarrassed you are.'

Gwen sat down with a thump when they returned to the kitchen. 'You said I wouldn't have to tell any lies, but I've still got to go along with this awful deception.'

'If you don't,' Marge snapped, in exasperation, 'you'll lose Alistair. So what would you rather do? End your marriage, or listen to me tell a few whoppers?'

'Don't try to make me laugh. I never felt less like laughing in my whole life.'

Gwen could see that Marge was enjoying the masquerade. She came down to breakfast every day already padded in case the postman came, and if he did, she took him in for his usual 'cuppa' as bold as brass. Real pregnant women tried to hide their condition, not flaunt it in front of people like she was doing. Being Marge, of course, she could get away with it, Gwen mused, a trifle enviously, whereas she was so scared in case Sandy Mearns suspected anything that she wrapped herself in a blanket before he was due, and sat in an armchair until he left. As if that wasn't bad enough, she was worrying more and more about what had still to come.

'I can't leave it too long before I go . . .' she began one day. 'Travelling so far wouldn't be good for the baby.'

Marge wrinkled her nose. 'Safe up to the end of your eighth month, I'd say.'

A little put out, Gwen said sourly, 'What do you know about it? You've never had any.' The minute the words were out, she regretted them. 'I'm sorry, Marge, but I'd like to make up my own mind sometimes.'

'Go when you like!' Marge retorted, 'I thought . . . if you're away too long, the kids'll wonder what's up.'

'OK, I'll wait a month, though Ivy said to go any time I wanted.'

Ivy Crocker had been another of Marge's brainwaves. 'You don't want to let Mum and Peg know,' she had observed, 'and it's safer not to ask Alice. Ivy was the only other person I could think of, and she'll likely be glad of some company for a while. She's had a pretty rough time this last year, what with her sister dying and then Len, so she'll likely be glad of some company for a while. Besides, she's not the kind to condemn you.'

For the next two weeks, the pseudo-pregnant Marge cycled into the village to collect their army allowances, and to stock up with groceries for the week, answering, when anyone hinted that she shouldn't be on a bike and her so far on, 'It's good exercise for me, and I'm as fit as a fiddle . . . a dashed big fiddle, but still fit. It's Gwen who's . . . she's to go to London to see some kind of specialist. She's just waiting to be told the date.'

At last, noticing one day how awkwardly Gwen was walking, Marge decided it was time to implement the next stage of her plan, and asked Lexie if it was all right if David and Leila handed in a shopping list on their way to school each Monday, and collected the items on their way home. 'Gwen's annoyed at me for carrying on biking so long,' she explained, 'and she's not fit for it ... she's got some woman's trouble, you see. Her hospital appointment's on the second of May, so that's less than a week to go, thank goodness. I just hope the London surgeons can cure what's wrong with her.'

Lexie appended the official Post Office rubber stamp to the two allotment books, and said, 'If you sign your book every week, I can let the bairns have the cash, as well. It's against the rules, but ... under the circumstances ...'

'Thanks, that's ever so kind of you,' Marge exclaimed, having been rather worried as to how she would manage if there was no money coming in.

'Get Gwen to sign hers for however long she thinks she'll be away,' Lexie offered, 'and I'll give it to Leila week by week along with yours.'

'Gee, thanks!' Marge's opinion of her rose. 'Hopefully, she should be back before I ...' Winking, she patted the area of the cushions.

Through the window, Lexie watched Marge placing her purchases into the bag behind the saddle of her bicycle. She was a fly one, every move thought out, covering up for her sister. Some woman's trouble? Tosh! What ailed Gwen Ritchie was what that soldier had put in her belly, and it was well over a year since Alistair had been home. She hadn't been in the shop for months, and nobody had seen her. Wait, though! Sandy Mearns must have seen her – he said he always got a cup of tea at Benview when he was there.

Strangely enough, Aggie Mearns walked into the shop not long after Marge had left and said, in her tinny voice, 'Was that Dougal Finnie's wife I saw biking off?'

Smiling inwardly at how fate was playing into her hands, Lexie nodded. 'She was asking if she could send a list with Alistair's kids.'

'It was aboot time she stopped comin', that track's full o' humps and muckle stanes, and it must be eight month since Dougal was hame. She coulda lost that bairn. I'm nae needin' much the day, Lexie, just a loaf, and a pair o' laces, and a packet o' envelopes.'

As she selected the requested items, Lexie manipulated the conversation to suit her. 'She was telling me Alistair's wife has to go to London for some special operation.'

'Sandy says she's a poor thing, aye sitting in a easy chair rolled up in a blanket.'

'Well, I hope the operation's a success. Now, was there anything else, Aggie?'

'No, that's the lot.'

After Mrs Mearns had paid and gone, Lexie considered what she had learned. Sandy hadn't actually seen Gwen walking about, so she could be as fat as a pig and he wouldn't know. Like most men, he probably wouldn't realize she was expecting unless she dropped the bairn at his feet.

But suspicion wasn't proof. Gwen *could* have some woman's trouble that needed a special operation, it was possible, so it was just a case of waiting to see whether one or two babies turned up at Benview in the next few weeks.

The stage had been set, but young David forestalled the final act by two days. Squeezing past his mother one morning, he muttered, 'Mum, if you and Auntie Marge get any fatter, there won't be room for both of you in this kitchen at one time.'

Marge saved Gwen's stricken face by roaring with laughter. 'It's all the country food, and the working outside gives us big appetites.'

But the boy had made the sisters think, and when they were alone, Marge said, 'I'm afraid you'll have to go today, Gwennie. I'll write out a pretend letter from Peg, saying

291

Mum's ill, so we'll have that to show if David or Leila ask any awkward questions when they come home from school. I'll see you on to the train at Aberdeen, so don't panic about that, and I'll carry your case down to the bus. Will you manage to walk that far?'

'Yes, I'll manage.' Gwen's mind was one big whirl. She was worried that her son and daughter might suspect the truth; she was dreading having to walk to the main road; she was scared that someone who knew her would be on the bus; she was petrified at the thought of travelling as far as Newcastle on her own in her present condition.

'It'll be all right,' Gwennie,' Marge assured her, 'but we'll have to get a move on. I'll phone from the station to let Ivy know you're on your way, and I'm sure she'll meet you at the other end.'

By the time she arrived in Aberdeen, Gwen was shivering with apprehension, and she followed Marge gratefully into the station tearoom. 'I'll go and phone Ivy,' Marge said, brightly, when she came back from the counter with a cup of tea and a sandwich. 'You'll be OK till I come back?'

Gwen nodded, afraid that the tears would come if she said anything, but she did manage to eat half the sandwich and drink the tea before her sister showed up again.

'That's all settled,' Marge said, a little breathlessly. 'I told her when you'll arrive, and she'll meet you at the station. Everything's organized, so don't look so scared. It's not your first, for heaven's sake.'

Gwen shook her head wretchedly. 'But Mum and Peg and you looked after me when I had Leila and David, and Alistair . . .' She broke off, biting her bottom lip.

'Ivy'll look after you. I'd have come with you like a shot, but we've the kids to think of. I wish there was some way we could . . . somebody we could trust to look after them, but it's best that nobody in Forvit knows what's going on.

Now, there's still two hours till the London train leaves, so why don't we go to a bank and ask if you can get some money out of that account Alistair set up for you when we came up to Scotland first?'

Gwen had made up her mind at the time that she would never touch a penny of that money, but Alistair had said she was at liberty to draw out as much as she wanted in an emergency. 'I suppose I could call this an emergency,' she muttered, 'and I *will* need cash to pay Ivy for keeping me, and for my fare home.'

This errand accomplished, they did some window shopping until Gwen spotted a clock above a jeweller's window. 'Look at the time. You'll have to get back for David and Leila. What'll they think if you're not there when they get home from school?'

'I left a note, and the pretend letter from Peg, so they think you're on your way to London because Mum's been taken ill, and if Lexie ever asks them where you are, that's what they'll say.'

'But you told her I was going to hospital . . .'

'She'll think I've told them different to stop them worrying about you. You know, my girl, you've got a dashed clever sister.' Marge gave a wicked grin. 'I've thought of everything, and I'll make ready that pram Alice said she had for Morag. It'll be all clean and sparkling like a new pin before you get back with . . . whatsisname.'

'D'you think it'll be a boy?'

'I haven't the faintest, but I'll love it whatever it is.'

Gwen had to swallow the lump which had risen in her throat at this. She had forgotten that the baby wouldn't be hers once she got back to Forvit. Marge would have to look after it otherwise David and Leila, Leila especially, would think it strange.

When they returned to the station, she said, 'Marge, I know

you're hanging about here to make sure I'm all right, but I'll be a lot happier if you just go home to the kids now.'

Not wanting to upset her sister at this stage, Marge said, 'OK, don't go lifting that case. Ask a porter to look after you when it's train time.'

Feeling anything but comfortable about the whole business, Gwen would have panicked altogether if she had known what a narrow escape she'd had from discovery. They had left Forvit at five past eleven, quite unaware that Mrs Mearns, the postman's wife, had come to Aberdeen by the next bus on her way to see a friend in Laurencekirk. She had arrived at the station while they went to the bank and, when the gates opened to let passengers in, had found a seat in a carriage near the engine because she was always afraid that the back end of the train might stop short of the platform.

Only five minutes later, the porter helped Gwen into the first empty compartment they came to, unwittingly enabling Gwen to escape detection.

The meeting on the platform at Newcastle some hours later was too much for her. Despite her abhorrence of bringing attention on herself, she burst into tears and rushed into Ivy Crocker's welcoming arms, heedless of the people milling around them.

'Hush, love,' the older woman crooned, 'hush now. It's going to be all right. Ivy'll look after you.'

When she composed herself, Gwen noticed that her old friend was looking much older. She still wore too much make-up, still bleached her hair, but there were lines on her forehead that could not be hidden. There was a sadness in her black-outlined eyes, a sadness that told how much she missed her life's partner.

Ivy was looking at her compassionately. 'All right now, dearie?'

'Yes. I'm sorry, I made a proper exhibition of myself.'

'Nobody noticed, but we'd better get on. I'll carry the case, if you can manage the bag? Won't be long now, less than half an hour on the bus, then a few minutes' walk.'

In just over the half hour, Gwen was sitting in the kitchen of an old cottage in the village of Moltby. 'Put your feet up on that pouffe till I pour you a drop of my plum wine.' Ivy pushed a squashed round pouffe towards her. 'I bet you're exhausted after such a long journey,' she observed in a moment, handing over a glass.

Gwen nodded wearily. 'I am a bit tired.'

'Your room's all ready for you, so you can have a lie down any time you want.'

'Oh Ivy, you've always been so kind to me.' Gwen's voice was trembling now, the tears perilously near the surface again. 'What must you think of me?'

Ivy stepped in before she broke down for the second time. 'Gwen, I make it my business not to mind anybody else's, and I wouldn't presume to judge you, but I would like to know . . . why?'

Knowing that Ivy had thought the world of Alistair, Gwen did her best to explain, in low, shamed monotones, beginning with Ken taking Marge and the bicycle home from the 1941 Hogmanay Do.

'Sexual attraction,' Ivy said, when the tale ended. 'That's what it had been, because you were both vulnerable to your emotions. I don't condone what you did, but I do understand. I had my own moments, you know, I wasn't always this old and this ugly.'

'Oh, Ivy, you're not ugly, and I don't know what I'd have done if . . .'

'That's enough of that. I think you're being very noble letting Marge have the baby.'

'I'm not being noble. I'm only thinking of myself – I could lose Alistair if he found out. That's another thing I'll always worry about. I can't tell lies without blushing, or giving the game away somehow. So how will I manage when Alistair and Dougal come home? One slip, and I throw a spanner into the works and burst up two marriages.'

'You'll have to harden yourself. Think of it as Marge's, right from the start . . .'

'But I'll be feeding it and caring for it for the first two weeks . . .'

Ivy leaned forward and gripped her hand. 'We'll sort something out. Have you seen a doctor, or anything?'

'No, I couldn't let anybody in Forvit know.'

'I'll get Tilly Barker to check you over tomorrow. She's our local midwife, and she's been a good friend to me. When it's born, we'll put it on the bottle, so you won't get too fond of it.' Gwen's frown made her add, 'Believe me, it's best. If you're not suckling it, you won't bond with it. You must look on it as something you're doing for your sister. A sacrifice, if you like, to please her and Dougal.'

Gwen sighed, but did not reply to this, and Ivy carried on, 'I had a baby, you know, before I met Len, and he loved that boy like it was his own. We both doted on him, maybe too much . . .' Her voice faded, her eyes misted.

Gwen leaned across and took her hand. 'What happened, Ivy?'

'Our little Billy was taken from us when he was just three and a half. The doctors never said what it was – I don't think they knew – but one day he was running about, laughing and tossing his curly head, the next, he was fighting for life in a hospital bed.' She stopped for a moment, then said, 'Two days later, he was dead.'

'Oh, Ivy, how awful. I don't know how you could have got over that.'

'I don't think we ever did, not really. Len was in the Navy at the time, so I was mostly on my own, and it was really bad

296

for a long time.' She straightened her back abruptly. 'But it's surprising what you can survive if you have to.'

'Maybe I shouldn't have come,' Gwen murmured, unhappily. 'It might upset you . . .'

'No, dearie, I'm as hard as rock, I am. Nothing upsets me nowadays.'

'I was very sorry about Len . . . and your sister. I bet that upset you?'

'Ah, yes, that did upset me, but I'd been expecting it with Len. He'd had two slight heart attacks, you see, so I knew it was coming.'

In Ivy's back room that night, Gwen wondered if Alistair would have accepted Ken's baby as his if she'd given him the chance, like Len Crocker had done. But . . . Len hadn't been married to Ivy at the time of her pregnancy, so he had nothing to forgive, whereas she had committed adultery while Alistair was fighting for his country, worse, while he was a prisoner of war. There was no comparison.

Ivy and Marge were both right. It was better this way. She, Gwen Ritchie, was the only one who would suffer, but that was as it should be, since she was the one who had sinned.

Chapter 20

∾

Gwen was shocked out of her misery and self-condemnation by her old friend as they sat by the fire one evening. She had just said, for the umpteenth time, that she deserved to be punished for the awful thing she had done and Ivy had burst out, 'Good God, girl! I'm sick of hearing you running yourself down like that. You surely don't think you're the only wife in this world that's ever had a little bit of fun on the side? Wives all over the country are doing it, and quite a few of them have landed the same as you. It's natural to miss the loving when your husband's away, and it's hard to resist if another man lights a spark in you. You're just one of the unlucky ones, that's all – too fertile. You had two children by the time you were two years married, remember?'

Scarlet-faced at what she took for implied criticism, Gwen hung her head, and Ivy went on, softly, 'I'm not getting at you, I'm trying to make you see things in perspective.'

'You can't understand. You were never unfaithful to Len, were you?'

Ivy rose to put some coal on the fire, then observed, 'I'll likely regret telling you this, but, after my Billy died, I felt life was passing me by. Len was away in the Navy, and I took a job as a caretaker in a block of offices, for the company as much as the money, and there was a basement flat that went with it.' She hesitated and then went on, 'I was only sixteen when I had Billy, and seventeen when I married Len, so I missed out on an awful lot. I didn't realize it at the time, of course, for I loved Len, but he was away so much.'

'What made you change?'

Ivy shrugged. 'Nothing really. I still loved Len, always have, but when young Mr Gerald, the boss's son, put his arm round me in the passage, I didn't push him away.'

She stopped again, smiling. 'He was so handsome, and I'd gone all wobbly at the knees any time he as much as looked at me, but he didn't take advantage of me. It was me – and it went from kissing in the corridor, to cuddling, then downstairs to my flat, and that's when it happened . . . as I wanted.'

Gwen gasped in astonishment. 'You planned it?'

A little sadly, Ivy said, 'He was only a boy, maybe seventeen, and I was well over twenty. It only happened that once, but I never forgot him, and I never regretted it. *And* it never made any difference to how I felt about Len. Can you understand that?'

'Oh yes,' Gwen breathed. 'It was the same as me, in a way, not love, just . . .'

'Just a need,' Ivy finished for her. 'It wouldn't have happened if Alistair had been at home, any more than if Len had been at home with me, but I was lucky. I don't know if his father suspected anything, but he sent Gerald off to their branch in Edinburgh, and I never saw him again.'

'Did you ever tell Len?'

'Gwen, I might have been a fool, but not as big a fool as that. He had accepted Billy without a murmur, but I couldn't expect him to forgive that.'

'And he never suspected anything?'

'Why should he? So, Gwen, dear, if you're thinking, as I believe you are, of telling Alistair the truth, put it out of your head. Marge wants to give Dougal a child he thinks is his, and Alistair will be none the wiser, so why upset the apple cart? And clear the shame and guilt right out of your system before you bring this child into the world.'

Trying to do as Ivy said, Gwen assured herself that, if there hadn't been a war on, she would never have . . . She wouldn't have *met* Ken Partridge in the first place. It was this awful war that was to blame, yet . . . if she hadn't been worried about Alistair . . . if Ken hadn't been leaving the next day for good . . . if Marge hadn't encouraged them . . .

She drew in a long breath and let it out slowly. She must forget all the ifs. She was the only one to blame, no matter what anybody said. Ivy was made of different stuff . . . but maybe it was losing her son that had made her start painting her face and bleaching her hair . . . and seeking affection, if not love, outside her marriage. Gwendoline Ritchie didn't have any excuse. Ken Partridge had treated her like a lady, of course, done things for her and made her feel ten years younger, so was that why? She wished with all her heart that she could look back on her time with him as a pleasurable interlude, not the shameful incident which was overshadowing everything else.

'Do you ken what kind o' operation Alistair Ritchie's wife's getting?'

Lexie shook her head. 'No, Aggie, I'm sorry. Dougal's wife just said it was some woman's trouble she had.'

'But naebody's seen her for months,' Mrs Mearns persisted.

Doodie Tough, waiting to be served and ever anxious to winkle out the last drop of any gossip or scandal, said now, with a touch of sarcasm, 'Your Sandy musta seen her.'

'Sandy? A magenty horse wi' a sky-blue tail and purple wings could knock him aff his bike and he'd never tell me.

I couldna get a thing oot o' him, except she aye sat in a chair rolled up in a blanket.' Aggie picked up her change and left.

Lexie weighed her next words carefully. 'That seems a bit queer, don't you think?'

Sensing something of interest, Doodie's eyes glittered. 'What d'you mean?'

'I wouldn't think you'd need to sit about in a blanket if it was just woman's trouble.'

Not particularly quick-witted for all her garrulity, it was a few seconds before Doodie got the meaning of this. 'You think she's expectin'?'

'Oh, I never dreamt it was anything like that, Doodie.' Not wanting it to be known that the idea had come from her, Lexie was glad that the woman had figured it out with so little prompting. 'Though now I come to think about it . . . I suppose she could be.'

'But . . .' Mrs Tough pursed her mouth and lowered her brows in thought, and at last she whispered, 'But Alistair hasna been hame for . . .' Her eyes dilating, she stopped with a satisfied smirk. 'She musta took up wi' ane o' they sodjers afore they was shifted.'

Lexie's face registered shock. 'But she was so quiet, not like her sister.'

'Still waters run deep,' intoned Doodie, narrowing her eyes now to emphasize this, 'but I must say I'd never . . . she's a dark horse, right enough.'

'We'd better watch what we're saying, though. We've no proof.'

'What else could it be, an' her needin' a blanket to hide her belly?'

Wondering if she had gone too far by implanting the suspicion, Lexie now did her best to erase it. 'We're letting our imaginations run away with us, Doodie. She must have something far wrong if she needs special equipment they haven't got in Aberdeen.'

Susceptible to anything, Mrs Tough digested this new concept with the same intensity as before. 'Aye . . . we'd best gi'e her the benefit o' the doubt.' She paid for her purchases and went out, clearly trying to decide which of the two versions she should pass on.

Lexie felt a little uncertain herself now. She had been so sure that Gwen Ritchie was expecting, but voicing it to somebody else had raised doubts in her own mind. Maybe the woman was *really* ill – but she *had* been with a soldier, there was no getting away from that. Yet . . . how would she have met him? That was the sticking point.

Gwen's labour started one afternoon only days later, three weeks early. 'Is a premature baby less likely to survive?' she asked, anxiously, during a pain-free interval.

Ivy pulled a face. 'They used to say a seven-month baby was all right, but an eight-month wouldn't have any nails – old wives' tales. Anyway, you're into the ninth month, and we'd best get Tilly. I'll ask Mona next door to go, she's quicker on her feet than me.'

Both in their thirties, Gwen and Tilly Barker, the midwife, had taken to each other as soon as they met, and had gone walking together in the cool of the evenings, when Ivy was too tired to go out. Gwen had even told Tilly the truth about her pregnancy, which the other woman had laughingly shrugged off. 'It's happening all over, lass.'

It hadn't been as bad as Gwen remembered, and it was a boy, which should please Marge, although she had always said she didn't care one way or the other.

'He's all right, isn't he?' she asked, while Tilly was cleaning him.

'Oh, you mothers,' the neat little woman smiled. 'Why wouldn't he be all right? He's perfect, got all his important little bits. Look.' She held him up for inspection.

His face was a bit redder than either of her other two had been, Gwen thought, and his tiny mouth was screwed up like he had a pain somewhere, but he was still lovely. Only one thing jarred. His head wasn't bald like David's had been, nor covered in fair down like Leila's. He had bright ginger hair! Like Ken Partridge's! Would this make Dougal start wondering, when he came home? Could two dark-haired people make a red-headed baby? It would be a problem for Marge and her, at any rate; for it would always remind them of who his father had been.

Marge was delighted to get Gwen's letter saying she'd had a boy. He had come early, all to the good, and mother and child should be fit enough to travel in a couple of weeks. Once she held the infant in her own arms, she'd feel that the Finnies were a proper family at long last. She read the letter again, smiling a little because her sister seemed worried about the colour of his hair. Any couple could have a red-headed child whatever theirs was ... couldn't they?

She took out the letter Gwen always enclosed, to be sent to their mother. Mum would have wondered what was up if she didn't get a letter from her eldest daughter for over a month, and although the place where it had been posted wasn't supposed to be franked on an envelope in wartime, maybe they did in the cities. That would put the cat among the pigeons with a vengeance. Mum would go on her high horse and demand to be told why Gwen was in Newcastle, and what was all the secrecy about?

After addressing an envelope for her own letter to her mother, Marge laid them both down on the ledge in the front porch, ready to give to the postman next morning. Thank goodness the final stage of her plan would soon be in motion, because Sandy Mearns was always saying, 'Not long now, eh?'

He had no idea that she wasn't really pregnant, which was why she couldn't have a doctor or midwife coming to the house, not that he'd have known that. She had told him, so that he could pass it on to anyone he liked, that she was going to have the baby in a hospital in Aberdeen. She had already provisionally booked a hotel room for fourteen days, so she'd have to confirm it now she knew the exact dates it would be used. She'd been a bit worried about this end of the procedure, she hadn't really planned it properly because she hadn't been sure if Ivy would agree. She needn't have worried.

'Gwen wouldn't manage taking her case and bag on and off the train, as well as the baby,' Ivy had written, 'and I'll be delighted to see her all the way back to Forvit. I can stay for a week or two, if you need me, I wouldn't mind a little holiday.'

Ivy was going to save their bacon, Marge gloated. She had been really worried in case her sister got too attached to the baby, but Ivy had said that she had been doing as much as she could to prevent any bonding. Gwen would have less than two days in the hotel on her own with it, then maybe another couple of days letting her sister get accustomed to looking after it.

Marge's plan was carried out. Ivy saw Gwen settled into the hotel with the baby, and followed her instructions on how to get to the bus terminus. Marge met her at the end of the

304

track, and insisted that she take a rest before Leila and David came home from school.

When they did, of course, they were overjoyed to see their Auntie Ivy again, and she invented a little fib to set their minds at ease about their mother. 'One of my friends in London went to see your Grandma and she says she's looking much better. It shouldn't be long before your Mum's home.'

That night, when the youngsters had gone to bed, much happier because of what Ivy had told them, Marge said, with a broad grin on her face, 'I didn't realize what a good liar you are. Almost as good as me.'

Ivy pulled a face. 'Only when it's necessary.'

Her expression sobering, Marge said earnestly, 'Me, too.'

The only sticky moments came when they went to the hotel next day. Although Gwen had agreed to it, she wasn't happy at having to hand the baby over to Marge, who was determined to take over right from the start.

'You'll have to get used to it,' Ivy sympathized, 'so just let him go. Look, I'll have to leave, can't keep that car waiting any longer.'

When she had gone, Marge said, 'She insisted we took the car the Bankside garage hires out. She said it would look better than me going by bus when I was supposed to be in labour. I suppose she was right, at that. Now, let me see my little darling.'

Once the ball had been set rolling, things went relatively smoothly, although Gwen was quite tearful when her sister refused to let her even hold the baby.

'Look, Gwennie,' Marge pointed out, softly, 'you have to give him up some time, and I have to learn how to deal with him as long as you're here with me.' She paused for a second, then said, 'Have you given any thought to a name for him yet?'

'If you're so determined to have him right now,' Gwen said, miserably, 'you'd better choose it yourself.'

'Dougal and I used to discuss names . . . before we realized we'd never have a family, and it was to be Nicholas for a boy and Louise for a girl.'

'Nicholas? I like that.'

'Good, then Nicholas it is.'

Marge considered that little Nicholas was an absolute darling. At just over two weeks old, his face was no longer wrinkled and red like Gwen had said it was at first, and his hair, a beautiful, thick, gingery auburn, had a little curl in it already. His infant-blue eyes would likely change to brown, the same colour as Dougal's and hers, which would allay suspicions from all directions – though there shouldn't be any after the trouble she'd taken to pull the wool over innocently inquisitive and downright nosy eyes.

After three days of togetherness, Marge told her sister that it was time she went back to her own children, a turn of phrase which she saw had upset her, but it was how it had to be now – Gwen only had two children, Nicholas wasn't hers any longer.

Thus it was that Gwen returned to Forvit alone, and sat with Ivy waiting for David and Leila to come home from school. She knew they would ask how their grandmother was, to which she could answer, honestly, that Grandma was as fit as ever.

'You'll have to be careful,' Ivy warned her. 'They're going to be all over you since you've been away so long, and you're still in a post-natal condition, so you won't have to let your emotions get the better of you.'

'Yes, I know, and I think I can cope.'

She coped very well. David let out a whoop of delight when he came in, and almost knocked her over with the force of his bear hug. Leila was less exuberant, but Gwen knew that her relief at having her mother back was just as great.

'Auntie Marge has gone away to get a baby,' David confided loudly, when they were all seated at the table. 'I don't know why she wants one, though. They're noisy smelly things, aren't they?'

Gwen summoned up a smile. 'Not all of them. Some of them are really beautiful . . .'

'Auntie Marge's will be beautiful,' Leila observed dreamily. 'I'm looking forward to when she brings it home. A real live baby'll be better than a doll.'

'Soppy!' David glowered at her. 'All girls are soppy! All they think about's getting married and having babies. Yeugh!'

Ivy chuckled as she stood up to clear the table. 'You'll change your mind about things when you're a bit older. Once a boy really falls in love, all he wants is to marry the girl and have babies with her.'

'Not me! When I'm grown up we'll be back in London and I'm going to go in for motor cycle racing. Vroom! Vroom!' He turned the throttle on his pretend steed and looked defiantly round the others.

Deeming it best not to rise to the challenge, Gwen said, 'I hope you behaved for Auntie Marge while I was away?'

'I always behave!' He looked put out that she could doubt it.

'He did behave, Mum,' Leila put in. 'She wasn't feeling well enough to bike to the shop, so we've been getting the groceries for her. Miss Fraser said we were very good messengers, but Auntie Ivy did the shopping on Monday.'

'I wanted to see the village,' Ivy explained, not wanting to admit that it had been the shopkeeper she had wanted to see, having heard about her from Marge. 'It's quite a nice little place, and I love this house, but it's a bit far away from everything for my liking.'

'When we came here first, Marge said it was at the back of beyond,' Gwen smiled, 'but you get used to it.' And it had been ideally situated for the conspiracy that was now taking place, she thought. But it would soon be over, and things would be as they were before . . . with the addition of a new baby.

When Marge's allotted fourteen days were up, Ivy went to Aberdeen to collect her and her 'son', and Gwen, to take her mind off it, cycled into the village. 'My aunt's gone to fetch Marge and the baby,' she informed Lexie.

'They're all right, are they? Dougal'll be pleased when he comes home. I bet he'd given up hope of having any children. It's twelve years since they married.'

Gwen did wonder why she was so sure of that, but presumed that Marge must have mentioned it. What worried her was the peculiar way Lexie was looking at her. It was almost as if she suspected something, some wrongdoing, but surely she couldn't have any idea . . . ? No, of course she couldn't.

'Are you keeping better yourself?' Lexie enquired, suddenly. 'Your sister said you were in London having an operation. No complications?'

Having practically forgotten this reason for her being away, Gwen felt flustered, but said, steadily, 'None. Everything went smoothly, and I don't have to go back.'

'That's good. Have you heard from Alistair lately?'

'Not for a few weeks, but I suppose no news is good news.'

'So they say.'

Lexie didn't move for some time after Alistair's wife went out. The woman certainly looked better than she'd done before the operation, but she herself still wasn't convinced about that. She'd been sure it was Gwen Ritchie with the soldier at the tower, and the length of time was right for her to have had a baby, yet it was Marge Finnie who was bringing home a son.

There was something dashed fishy going on. If Gwen *had* been in London giving birth – though maybe she hadn't gone as far as London – the child would be illegitimate, and maybe she'd had it adopted? But she shouldn't get away with it. It wasn't fair on Alistair. If she, Lexie, could plant even a tiny grain of doubt in his mind when he came home from the war, she would be doing him a service ... though Alistair Ritchie wasn't as gullible as Doodie Tough. It wouldn't be easy to make him believe ill of his wife.

Even David fell under little Nicholas's spell. 'Look at the size of his nails,' he crowed. 'His hands are so small, I wouldn't have thought there was room on his fingers for nails at all, but they're the same as everybody else's.'

'What did you expect?' Marge laughed. 'Babies *are* the same as everybody else, just a lot smaller.'

'He's so small, I'm afraid to touch him,' Leila murmured.

'You can hold him, if you like. He won't break. Just be careful.'

The girl sat down in one of the armchairs and let her aunt hand her the infant, who burped loudly. 'Is he all right?' she asked in alarm.

'Of course he is,' Marge assured her. 'It's natural for babies to burp more than we do.'

Nicholas's next breaking of wind had David doubled up with mirth. 'I didn't know he could do it from that end as well!'

'Just like you!' Leila said, dryly, which made them all laugh.

Everyone was sorry when Ivy said she had better go home. While she'd been there, Benview had been a place of love, of laughter, of a general feeling of satisfaction with life, and the sisters were afraid that her departure would change everything. But she suggested that Gwen and her children should see her on to the train at Aberdeen, and David was excited at the thought of spending an afternoon in the city. Gwen, of course, was a bit apprehensive at leaving Marge alone with Nicky, as David had called him and it had stuck, and Marge, too, wondered how she would cope, but all went well.

Life soon returned to normal, with Nicky a well-loved addition. A large bundle of letters arrived for Gwen, though they contained little but assurances of love for them all. Marge got letters from Dougal at irregular intervals, and it was several weeks before she received the one saying how he could hardly bear to wait to see his son.

'I thought we'd never manage,' he wrote, 'but we must have done something right that last night we were together.'

Marge showed her sister this letter. 'I said it would be OK. He's sure Nicky's his.'

Gwen nodded, but remained uncertain. Once Dougal saw the bright ginger hair and green eyes, would he be so sure?

Chapter 21

❧

Life in Benview was not quite as joyful as it might have been. The two older children were, naturally, delighted that the war looked to be almost over and they would soon see their father again, yet the prospect of leaving the friends they had made at Forvit School was quite depressing. As for Gwen and Marge, they were becoming more and more apprehensive about their return to London, although neither admitted it to the other. Their personal D-Day would soon be upon them, or, as Gwen had come to regard it, her Armageddon. As soon as hostilities were over, they would have no excuse to hibernate in this isolated cottage, and their mother, with the uncanny knack of knowing when they were keeping something from her, would do her best to ferret it out.

The summons came at the end of April. 'This is it, Gwennie,' Marge observed as she folded up Rosie's letter ordering them home and asking what they thought they were playing at staying away when there was no danger now. 'Last hurdle coming up!'

'Not the last,' Gwen sighed. 'After her, we've still got to face Dougal and Alistair.'

'We don't have to worry about them. Dougal's going to be hooked on Nicky the minute he sees him and he'll spoil him rotten, and Alistair's not likely to question my son's parentage, is he?'

'No, of course not.' Gwen tried to sound positive.

Marge went to bid Lexie Fraser goodbye before they left.

They owed her that for the help she had provided. 'We really enjoyed our stay in Forvit,' she gushed. 'It was so peaceful after the bombing in London, but Alice and Sam will want their house back. Besides, my mother's desperate to get all her chicks under her wing again.'

Trying not to show her sadness at the thought of not seeing him again, Lexie said, 'But will Alistair not want to come back to the peace of Forvit?'

'I've no idea.' Marge shrugged then held out her hand. 'It's time I was going, but thanks once again for all you did for us.'

Lexie smiled. 'You'd a pretty rough time for a while, what with you expecting and your sister having to go to London for whatever kind of operation it was.'

Marge had to do some quick thinking. She had blithely mentioned some woman's trouble at the time without specifying which, and the village gossips had likely spent hours speculating over it. None of them had ever gone out of their way to be friendly. She had even heard one calling them 'stuck-up Cockneys', but she hadn't bothered to correct her, and perhaps she and Gwen *had* kept themselves too much to themselves. They had never really felt as if they belonged, that was the trouble.

'Gwen didn't want anybody to know,' she said at last. 'It was an ovarian cyst, as big as a melon, the surgeon told her. It wasn't cancerous, thank goodness, but she still hasn't recovered properly.'

'I hope she improves once she's back with her mother. Say goodbye to her and the bairns from me. I got quite fond of Leila and David, you know.'

As Marge cycled back to Benview, she congratulated herself on remembering what had happened to one of her neighbours in Woodyates Road a year or so before the war started. Etta Smith had been a widow for many years, so when a bump appeared on her stomach, the rumour went round that she'd been having a secret affair with a married man and been left to have the baby on her own. The bump had grown as the months passed, as such bumps do, and when Etta's sister Vi turned up to look after the house and feed the cat, the sniggering gossips told each other that Etta had gone to hospital for her confinement. Then Vi had mentioned one day that her sister was having an ovarian cyst removed, which had made them all feel rotten. It would be best, Marge decided, not to let Gwen know the story she had spun about *her* 'operation'. This final, unnecessary lie would only worry her.

Lexie couldn't help wondering about Marge's version of her sister's trouble. She had seemed a bit put out at being asked, and she'd obviously had to invent something on the spur of the moment . . . not all that convincing, either. Gwen Ritchie wouldn't have had to go to London to have an ovarian cyst removed when the Royal Infirmary in Aberdeen was classed as among the best in Britain. She had definitely had a baby, but it was anybody's guess who was the father, and whether it had died at birth or been adopted. Still, Lexie mused, what did it matter now? It was a shame, though. Alistair would go back to London when he was repatriated, to the wife he believed had been faithful to him, and live in happy ignorance for the rest of his life.

Poor Alistair!

That evening, probably as a result of the frustration of her earlier thought, Lexie was beset by a memory she had done her best to ignore any time her mind touched on it, but this time it refused to go away. It had happened a few months ago, and was the last time she had gone out with any man. Ernie Paul was an old schoolmate, a cheeky devil, he'd once put his hand up her knickers when they were climbing the wall bars in the gym. He'd been quite keen on her, but at the time, she'd only had eyes for Alistair Ritchie. Ernie had got a job in Aberdeen as soon as he left school, and some years later, like most of the other young men she knew, he'd been called up.

He had come into the shop once or twice on each of his leaves, the same bantering lad he'd always been, but there had been a change in him the last time he was home ... more serious, more intense about things, although there was still the occasional twinkle in his eyes. She had found herself warming to him, and when he asked her out, she had agreed to meet him after she shut the shop. He had taken her by bus to the Capitol Cinema in Aberdeen, and though she half-expected him to slip his hand up her leg while they were watching the film, he had been a proper gentleman, even when he saw her home. He wasn't cheeky any more, and it was only after their third date that he kissed her good night at her door.

Completely at ease with him now, she had asked him in the next time he saw her home, and as soon as she closed the door behind them, he put his arm round her waist and drew her towards him. This kiss was different from the first, a kiss that made her whole body quiver. He had pulled her down on the sofa beside him, and she had given herself up to the thrill of his caresses. His kisses had become more urgent and she hardly noticed that one of his hands had slipped down until she felt his fingers touch her most private part – she grew hot at the memory of it. Then for some inexplicable reason – for she had wanted him to go on – she had shoved him away and burst into tears and screamed at him as she jumped to her feet. 'Get out! Get out! Get out!' She couldn't stop herself, and had even lashed out at him with her feet.

'Good God, Lexie!' he had shouted, standing up and stamping to the door. 'I wouldn't have touched you ... honest, but I thought you wanted it.' He had slammed out.

Ernie had been the only one who had ever got as far as that. She had never let any of the others, over the years, touch her in an intimate way ... not even Alistair. She had encouraged *him*, yes, but if his hands wandered below her waist it was as if she froze with fear – and what had she to fear from him, for goodness' sake? From anybody, for that matter? It was only natural for men to try, and for girls to try to stop them. But her reaction wasn't natural. It was violent, intended to hurt. Why?

A tiny sliver of what may have been a possible explanation shot through her, but it was gone before she could make anything of it, and in any case, she wasn't sure that she wanted to understand, after all. It was quite obvious that something so bad had happened to her at one time that she couldn't bear to think about it. It had crossed her mind before that her father might have interfered with her and run away because of shame, but she couldn't remember him ever touching her where he shouldn't, not even accidentally. He had loved her as a father should love a daughter, nothing else. Yet there was still this awful sense of an impending revelation that would turn her world upside down.

Rosie couldn't get over how tall Leila and David had grown in the four and a half years they had been away, and she was moved to tears at the sight of little Nicky exploring her living room on his tottery podgy legs. 'When Dougal came to see me last,' she told Marge, 'he said he wished he had a child to leave behind if he was killed, and now it's all over bar the shouting, and he's got a son! You girls will never know how often I prayed for your husbands to come home safely and for these three houses to escape the bombs.'

'Yes, I know you had it pretty bad, Mum. I felt really guilty that I was up there when I'd no kids to worry about.'

Rosie grinned puckishly. 'But if you hadn't been up there, you wouldn't have had Nicky, would you?'

Marge felt her stomach heave at the truth of this. 'N . . . no, that's right, of course.'

Noticing the peculiar glance Marge gave Gwen, and knowing her daughters inside out, Rosie was sure that they were hiding something. What had happened in Forvit? Had one or both of them been misbehaving? No, she couldn't think that of Gwen, but Marge had gone dancing there, and she must have met lots of servicemen. Had she had a fling? No, she loved Dougal. She wouldn't have put her marriage in jeopardy. All the same, something was definitely not quite as it should be, and she would have to persevere until she found out what it was.

Over the next week or so, Rosie watched and listened to her daughters, trying to pick up even the slightest hint that would put her on the right track, but although Marge talked freely about their time at Forvit, the gossips in the little shop, the strange way the people spoke, Gwen scarcely said anything, especially about the last year of their stay. She clearly found it too painful to speak about.

Increasingly unsettled, Rosie puzzled over it constantly; positive that she wasn't making something out of nothing. Then one afternoon, when the house was quiet – the family, including Alf, having gone to the Heath – it struck her, like a bolt of lightning, so devastating that she felt faint. She shied away from it and tried to read the morning paper, but the print jumped all over the page and nothing registered, so she gave herself up to considering the awful suspicion.

Was it possible that Dougal was not Nicky's father after all? Had the monotony of Forvit made Marge have more than just a fling with another man? That must be what was wrong with Gwen. She wouldn't have approved what her sister was doing, but even if she had tried to stop her, Marge wouldn't have listened.

Rosie found herself latching on to stronger evidence. Marge and Dougal were both dark-haired and brown-eyed, but little Nicky's hair was the brightest red she had ever seen, his eyes a piercing green, both of which were highly unlikely in the normal run of things. She didn't know much about that kind of thing, of course, so it could be possible, though she doubted it in this case.

She kept her thoughts to herself when her family returned, and it wasn't until the following morning, when Peggy came in to see how she was, as she did every morning before going to work, that she decided to test the waters. 'Peg,' she asked, carefully choosing her words, 'does Nicky's colouring strike you as odd?'

'His hair, you mean? I think it's a lovely colour.'

Rosie lay back against her pillows with a sigh. Peggy wasn't all that perceptive, so it wasn't surprising that she hadn't twigged.

When she went downstairs at just after ten, the children were playing in the garden and Gwen was tidying up. Rosie decided that this would be a good time, with Marge still in her own house, to ask a few pertinent questions. 'I expect you and Marge were bored up in Scotland, with Alice's house so far from the village?'

'It wasn't too bad.'

Gwen's face, however, had a definite pink tinge, further proof to her mother that she wasn't comfortable speaking about it. So there was something! 'What did you do for entertainment?' she pressed on, but at that moment, with Gwen clearly struggling to think of an answer, Marge opened the back door and took in the situation at a glance.

'We ought to take the kids out for a while,' she said, giving Gwen a warning look. 'We'd better make the most of this lovely weather before David and Leila start their new school. Will you be OK on your own, Mum?'

'I was on my own for . . .' Rosie began, sarcastically, then thought better of it. 'I'll be fine. If Alf sees you going out, he'll likely pop round some time. He was very good at looking after me when you were away, you know.'

The stir over, Rosie picked up the telephone. 'Alf? Can you come round for a few minutes?'

'Delighted to. There's nothing wrong, I hope?'

'Not exactly. I want to ask your opinion on something, and I'm on my own for a while. They've taken the children out.'

'Righto, Rosie, my old dear. I'll be with you in two shakes of a lamb's tail.'

She replaced the receiver with a smile. She'd come to depend on Alf. He'd been there for her almost every evening during the air raids, making sure she and Peg went inside her Morrison shelter, while he sat by the fire if he wasn't on duty fire watching. If a doodlebug had fallen on the house, the survival of his wife and her mother would have been questionable, but there was no doubt that he'd have been a goner himself.

He was with her in no time. 'What's up, then, Rosie? I thought everything would be perfect for you now, with your brood all around you?'

She regarded him affectionately. His back was a little bowed, and he just had a semicircle of grey hair at the back of his head. His face was lined from the chest pains he suffered periodically, but he was always cheery, no matter what.

'I've got a bit of a problem,' she admitted, 'and I want to hear what you think.'

'I'll do my best, if you fill me in.'

'Do you know . . . how . . . people's genes affect . . . their children?'

A brief frown crossed his face. 'Genetics can be . . . but if you're thinking what I think you're thinking, Rosie, I'd advise you to forget it.'

'So you've spotted it, too? It's his colouring.'

'His hair's a lovely colour.'

'But it's his eyes, and all. I didn't think two browns could make green.'

'I know you're in deadly earnest, but put it out of your mind.'

'But it's not fair to let Dougal think . . .'

'Rosie dear, please don't say anything. It will only cause trouble. Even if it's true, I'm sure Marge regrets it now, and Nicky's a permanent reminder. Don't you think her guilt will make her suffer enough without you making it worse for her?'

She heaved a shuddering sigh. 'I know you mean well, Alf, but I can't overlook the fact that one of my daughters has committed adultery.'

He leaned towards her and took her hand. 'Listen, my dear sweet Rosie, I know your conscience tells you she should be punished, but try to see beyond that. What is to be gained by denouncing her? You will also be punishing Dougal and her innocent young son, and the strife will rub off on every one of us. Dougal will blame Gwen as the older for not taking better care of his wife, and even Alistair might put some of the blame on her. Leila and David are both old enough to sense if something's wrong. You would be opening Pandora's box, Rosie, stirring a hornets' nest, splitting up your family.'

Her soft sniff made him murmur, 'Don't upset yourself so,

my dear. You may be worrying for nothing. I think I read somewhere that red hair can be passed down from some generations back, and that could be what's happened.'

Rosie let the matter drop. Perhaps what he had just said was true, perhaps it wasn't and he was trying to plug a hole in the dyke, but he was right to tell her to say nothing. In order to be sure of having her family happily around her, she would have to keep her suspicions to herself. It was just a good thing Tiny wasn't here to put his oar in. He'd have muddied the waters, all right.

Alistair was home first. His camp had been freed in April, but he had to undergo some medical and other tests in Germany before he was pronounced fit to travel to Britain, and more tests on this side, so it was into December before he reached Lee Green. There was great jubilation, of course, and after about three quarters of an hour, Alf, realizing that Gwen would want to be alone with her husband, swept Rosie and all the rest of her family into his house for the afternoon. Even David, complaining that he wanted to be with his Dad, was persuaded that his parents deserved some time on their own.

Gwen had been shocked at how painfully thin Alistair looked when he walked in, how his cheekbones stood out, how grey his skin, how white his hair, so it came as no surprise when he kissed her only a few times and then muttered, apologetically, 'I'm sorry, my darling, but all I want to do now is sleep, sleep, sleep. In a decent bed with soft blankets and an eiderdown, with nothing at all to worry about.'

In a way, she was relieved, and when she went upstairs with him and watched him undress, her heart cramped at the sight of his skeletal body, she could have counted his ribs without touching him. There was no way she could ever willingly hurt him. She would have to make absolutely certain that nothing of what she had done ever leaked out, that he never learned that she was young Nicky's mother. It would tear him apart.

At six o'clock, when Marge came to say that Alf had prepared as good a feast as rations would allow, she had to explain that Alistair was sound asleep and she didn't want to disturb him. Marge, of course, teased her about tiring him out already.

'No, there was nothing like that. He was almost dead on his feet, and all he wanted was to sleep. Tell Alf I'm sure Alistair will appreciate the effort he's made, but I'm afraid we'll have to pass on it. Say we'll have it tomorrow, if it'll keep.'

So Alistair's real homecoming took place the day after he came home, and even though he was still exhausted, he did his best to enter into the celebration that his in-laws seemed to be bent on having.

That night, once again he wanted only to sleep, and Gwen lay by his side, thanking God that he'd come home safely to her, and praying that his health would soon improve.

Chapter 22

❧

Alistair had been withdrawn and uncommunicative ever since he came home six months earlier. Marge had told Gwen repeatedly that she shouldn't try to push him. 'It must have been awful for him in that Stalag whatever, and he won't feel like speaking about it just yet. It'll take a while, but I'm sure he'll tell you all about it in his own good time.'

Gwen felt like saying that she didn't care if he never told her about the prisoner-of-war camp. He had been gone from her for so long that all she wanted was to be told how much he'd missed her, how much he loved her. Instead, he hardly spoke when they were alone together, which wasn't often, what with Marge, Peggy or their mother popping in whenever they felt like it, and Alistair himself going out every morning and sometimes not turning up again until just before the children were due home from school. What was more, he never told her where he had been or what he had been doing.

When he knew that Dougal was to be demobilized soon, however, and would be coming home, he seemed to ease fractionally out of his cocoon. 'We're lucky,' he observed one evening as he sat at the fireside with his wife, her mother and Marge. 'Dougal and me, I mean. I never dreamt . . . we'd both come through without a scratch. I thought about him all the time, you know, wondering what was happening to him.'

'Me, too,' Marge smiled. 'The silly devil could have been

volunteering for all kinds of dangerous missions without a thought to his own safety, you know what he's like.'

Alistair nodded gravely. 'Of course I know what he's like! Better than anybody! We were like brothers all our lives, we'd have done anything for each other. Like that other war song said, "Comrades, comrades, ever since we were boys," but we didn't end up the same way. The last line went, "When danger threatened my darling old comrade was there by my side," and we weren't there for each other, were we?'

'Neither of you was to blame for that,' Rosie pointed out, 'so just be glad you both survived.'

He lapsed into morose silence for about ten minutes, ignoring the conversation around him, and then mumbled, 'I'm whacked. I'm off to bed.'

Rosie patted Gwen's shoulder when the door closed behind him. 'Don't upset yourself, dear, it'll take him a long time to get over what he's been through.'

'I know, Mum, but he said he'd only thought about Dougal when he was a prisoner, and he's never said he . . .' She halted, then ended, shakily, 'He's never said he thought about me. He's never even said he missed me.' The tears she had pent up for months came out at last. 'I sometimes . . . wonder . . . if I'm being . . . punished for . . .'

Marge jumped in before her sister revealed their dark secret. '. . . for going to Scotland and leaving him? It was his idea, remember? Then he lost Manny, a man he practically looked up to as a god, and he didn't have a job any longer. He was concerned for your safety, and the kids', but he'd have joined up even if you hadn't been away. You've nothing to reproach yourself for . . . about that,' she added.

As soon as Rosie went to bed, Marge turned angrily on Gwen. 'What the devil were you thinking about? Do you want everybody to know?'

'I'm sorry, it was when Alistair said he'd just thought about

Dougal . . . He's been so distant to me since he came home, and . . . well, that got to me.'

'Look, Gwennie,' Marge's voice was softer now, 'you've got to make allowances for him. He's been through hell, things that he'll maybe never tell you about, and with nothing to take his mind off it, he can't help brooding. If he had a job . . .'

'I wish I could tell him that, but I don't want him to think I'm criticizing.'

'He's out every day, so maybe he *is* looking and can't find anything. Maybe that's why he's so down? There's so many men looking for jobs now. Dougal'll chivvy him on, though. Once *he's* home, Alistair'll soon get back to normal.'

Everyone, in all three houses, felt better once Dougal Finnie came home. His joy at holding the son he thought he would never have was 'indescribable', as Rosie told one of her friends, and even Alistair joined in the celebration round the Pryors' large table the day after this homecoming.

'I didn't fully realize how much Dougal wanted children,' he remarked to Gwen as they undressed for bed at the end of the convivial evening. 'He must have been jealous seeing us with our two every time we came to visit.'

Thankful that her husband was discussing something with her at last, Gwen said, 'I don't think Dougal's the jealous kind. He wouldn't be the slightest bit jealous even if somebody he knew won a fortune on the football pools.'

His eyes narrowed. 'You think I would?'

'I didn't say that!'

'It's what you were thinking, though, wasn't it? You believe I'm jealous because he's got everything he wants now – a wife, a son, a house he owns, a job to go back to?'

She summoned a smile. 'You've no reason to be jealous.

324

You've got a wife who loves you, a son and daughter who love you, a good home, your health's improving . . .'

He puffed out his breath from pursed lips as he lay down beside her. 'Yes, I've got all that, Gwen, and believe me, I count my blessings every night, but I just can't seem to get out of this . . . rut, I suppose you could call it. I want to be doing something, and I can't make up my mind what I want to do. What is there for me?'

'Alistair, darling, have you forgotten that Manny taught you how to mend clocks and watches? And what about all the jewellery he left you? And the money?' She could mention that without fear, she reflected, because she had paid every last penny back that she had used at the time of . . . her trouble. 'Maybe a pawnshop isn't what you want, but what about an antique shop, or a watchmaker and jeweller, something along that line.'

'I can't summon up enthusiasm for anything,' he admitted.

'Have a word with Dougal. He'll be able to point you in the right direction.' She wished she hadn't said it. It could be construed as meaning that she had every confidence in her brother-in-law and none in her husband, so she felt great relief when he merely nodded his agreement.

Meanwhile, in a bedroom only the width of two driveways away, Mr and Mrs Finnie were relaxing after a rather hectic half-hour of lovemaking. 'I don't like seeing Ally as down as he is just now,' Dougal observed, as he flicked his cartridge-shell lighter.

'He's been like that ever since he came home,' Marge answered.

'I felt like shaking him, but Gwen was trying to shield him from any questions.'

'She doesn't want him to think anybody's criticizing him.'

325

'That's a bloody stupid way to look at things. He needs to get off his backside and look for work. I could maybe get him in with me . . .'

'Don't suggest that, he'll just resent it. He needs to make up his own mind, or at least to *think* he's made up his own mind. Why don't you ask him out for a walk tomorrow? You might find out what's eating at him.'

Dougal took one last pull at his cigarette and stubbed it out in the ashtray beside the bed. 'Good idea, my precious, but why are we wasting time speaking about Alistair? We have years to make up yet. Show me again how much you missed me.'

'So, how're you doing, me old mate?'

Alistair's smile was somewhat wry at his friend's attempt to cheer him. 'I suppose Marge told you I've been vegetating since I came back?'

'She didn't have to, I gathered it myself from odd things that were said, and the way Gwen and Rosie watch you like hawks in case you get upset about something. Look, if you'd like to tell me what's bothering you, I'm willing to listen for as long as you want. On the other hand, if you want me to shut up, I'll do my best, but you know me.'

They were strolling across Blackheath in the direction of the Greenwich Observatory, but neither of them paid any attention to the view below them, where the River Thames sparkled in the sunshine as it meandered towards the sea, nor to the old sailing boats which were moored to the quay. A few moments passed before Alistair muttered, 'OK. We could have a seat on the grass, if you like.'

He smoked as he talked, lighting one cigarette after the other, and Dougal did the same while he listened, because he, too, had memories that he would never tell his wife. Thus, for the next two hours, Alistair spoke of being captured at Anzio on February 28, 1943, when the Germans made their big push. 'Some of our boys had gone to HQ for rations, but the Company Commander and all the rest of us were captured, surrounded by the Herman Goering lot. They were on the run by that time, of course, with Monty and the Yanks both at their heels, and they made us carry their wounded out on stretchers, for about eight to ten days, I can't remember exactly.'

He stopped to light another full-strength Capstan. 'We were under our own shell fire, of course. They ordered us to shove one of their trucks out of a ditch, and when we got it out, four of us climbed aboard it. We'd hoped we could escape along the way, but it went straight into German Headquarters. The driver got a right surprise when he found us in the back, and we were held in caves for . . . four, five days. We lost track of time.'

He went on to describe being taken in various modes of transport to Rome, where they were held in what had been a film studio, and then to Florence, until, at the end of May 1944, they were taken by rail in goods trucks into Germany itself, to Moosburg. 'It was a huge camp, held 40,000, Russians, Yugoslavs, all different nationalities. We stopped in a siding, and the SS guards gave the political prisoners a helluva beating. Then they took us to Bavaria, right up in the hills, to build a factory for them. We didn't know at the time, of course, but it was intended for making V2s.'

He glanced at Dougal for a moment, trying to explain. 'We'd to get the stone out of quarries and take out the foundations, no diggers, just barrows and spades and graips. The SS were running things, their secret police came up every now and then to see what was going on, but because we were always indulging in sabotage and trying to escape, that factory never started working.

'Fifty of us were working there, but we were moved out in April 1945, back to Stalag 7A, and General Patton liberated us on the 29th. Came roaring into the camp! You never saw anything like it! Some day!' He relaxed with a huge smile, recalling the thrill of it.

While Alistair had been talking, Dougal mentally filled in the gaps in the story. He could imagine the treatment the prisoners had received, the British as roughly handled as the others, if not worse in some instances. 'What about the food?' he asked.

'It was pretty poor in Italy, that was the worst. There was no Red Cross stuff coming in at all and there were German cooks and Italian, so we never knew what we were going to get. Usually it was a slice of black bread in the morning and a cup of substitute coffee, ersatz, the Jerries called it. At dinnertime, they filled your steel helmet with some sauerkraut, that was the rations. Night time, coffee again, and a bit of bread and jam, put on and scraped off again. Sometimes you got a wee drop macaroni.'

He paused, the memories inching back to him now that he had opened the gate a little. 'I was about a month there when I collapsed and they sent me to hospital. It was funny – the guardsmen who were there, big sturdy men, you know what they have to be, well, they didn't manage to stick it out as long as the rest of us. They caved in after two weeks, they must have needed more vitamins than we did. Once we were in Germany, though, we got our Red Cross parcels, which helped a good bit.'

'Did *you* ever try to escape?'

Alistair rubbed his chin. 'A few did try to get out of the film studios in Rome, but they were found and shot. Stalag 7A at Moosburg was considered 100% secure, but some prisoners tunnelled right under the wire, and the Jerries had got word of what they were up to, God knows how. They put Alsatians through from the camp side, and they waited at the other end till the men came out and shot the lot – seventeen of them. They hadn't a chance, Dougal, and I didn't want to end up dead meat, I'd my family to come home to, so like the coward I am, I never took one step out of line.'

'There's nothing cowardly about wanting to stay alive,' Dougal said firmly. 'I'd have been exactly the same.'

Alistair visibly perked up. 'Would you? Honestly?'

'Cross my heart and hope to die,' Dougal smiled, 'and I don't consider myself a coward.' Deciding to take the step Marge had warned him against, he went on, 'So what's your plans now?'

'I haven't got my thoughts together long enough yet to make any plans. I'll have to start earning something soon, but I don't know how. I went round the markets without thinking when I came back first, then one of Manny's old contacts let me work on his stall and that's what I've been doing for the past few months. I haven't told Gwen, because . . .'

'. . . because you're ashamed of being a barrow boy?' Dougal supplied. 'But how have you been living? You can't be making much, and Gwen can't buy food and clothes for the kids if you don't . . .'

'I told her I was drawing from the account I set up for her when she was in Forvit. She didn't use any of it, but . . .' He shook his head. 'Oh God, Dougal, I should make a proper effort to get a job, shouldn't I?'

'What kind of job do you fancy?'

'Would you think I was off my head if I said I'd like to carry out Manny's dream and open a jeweller or an antiques shop?'

'No, I'd say go for it! If you've got the money to start you off . . .'

'The thing is . . . I'm not happy about living at Rosie's. I'd like a place of our own and that'll take every penny I have, including what I'd get if I sold all the stuff the bank's had in safekeeping.'

'You'll have to make up your mind.' Dougal sounded exasperated now. 'Either your own house or your own shop, and I can't see your problem. Rosie's got tons of room, and she's not going to last for ever, is she? I don't mean that in a nasty way, I love the old dear, but you'll have to think ahead. She'll likely have left the house to Gwen, seeing Peg's settled with Alf and Marge has the best husband in the world.'

Alistair was too agitated to rise to this quip. 'I couldn't let Gwen accept the house. When the time comes, it should be sold and the money divided between . . .'

'When the time comes, you could pay Marge and Peg a third each of what it's worth, if it would make you feel any better, but for God's sake, man, take the plunge and get your shop.' Dougal rose to his feet, flexing his legs to get the circulation going again. 'Come on, Ally. They'll be expecting us back for dinner.'

Alistair looked at his watch in dismay. 'Oh, Lord, and I've done nothing but bleat on about myself. Why didn't you stop me? I'd have liked to hear what you'd been doing.'

'Nothing very exciting, I assure you, and, anyway, we've got the rest of our lives to talk to each other.'

Alice burst out with her news as soon as she entered the shop. 'Gwen says in her letter that Alistair's looking for premises so he can open a wee jeweller's or an antique shop.'

'Oh, aye?'

So excited herself, it didn't occur to Alice that Lexie might have other things on her mind. 'He's speaking about London, of course, or the south of England somewhere, but my Sam came up with a better idea when he read the letter. You see, he's never settled down since we came back, and now he's learned about the government offering assisted passages to Australia, he wants us to emigrate and let Alistair move into Benview. So I'm going to write and suggest he could open his shop up here somewhere. It's just a case of waiting to see what he thinks.'

Suddenly noticing Lexie's sunken eyes and drawn face, she said, 'Are you feeling well enough? You look ghastly.'

'I'm not all that good, to be honest.'

'See the doctor, then. It's stupid to let it run on. It could get worse, whatever it is.'

'I'm not sure about this new doctor we've got. I liked old Doctor Geddes, but this one's too young for my liking.'

'He's still a qualified doctor, Lexie, and you really need to get him in.'

'I'll see how I feel tomorrow.'

'Don't wait longer than that then. I'll have to go, but mind what I've said.'

Left by herself, Lexie leaned weakly against the counter. No doctor could cure what ailed her. Her trouble wasn't medical, it was mental. She couldn't stop wondering about what had happened to her father. She had spent nights trying to remember more of what happened before and after the time of his disappearance, but just when she thought she had something in her grasp, her mind always seemed to shut down, and she was coming more and more round to the idea that it might be best if she didn't remember. That was why she didn't want to see the new doctor. He might make her see a psychiatrist, and God knows what he would dig up. Over the last two days, she had done her best to keep her thoughts at bay, but she couldn't go on much longer like this.

Having made her decision, she went over to the small telephone exchange which had recently been installed by the Post Office. Before the war, there were only a scattering of phones in the whole of the parish, not enough to warrant an exchange, but the number of subscribers had more than doubled now. After plugging in, she waited for her call to be answered.

Since shortly after Dougal came home, a question had arisen in Alistair's mind, and no matter how hard he tried, it wouldn't go away. In fact, it grew stronger every day until it no longer needed to be answered. The proof was there every time he saw Dougal, Marge and little Nicky together. There was no resemblance between the boy and either of his parents, and when he had mentioned this casually to Gwen one day, she had flown up in the air. That was when it had dawned on him – two dark browns don't make a ginger, two browns don't make a green. As the old saying went, there had been dirty work at the crossroads! Had Marge been . . . ? Was Dougal not Nicky's father?

His mental health still in a somewhat fragile state, Alistair nibbled at this concept for hours, feeling sick at the thought of Marge being unfaithful to the finest man in the world. Should he tell Dougal? Was it fair to let him go on thinking . . . ? Why hadn't he seen it for himself?

Maybe he should ask Gwen? But would she tell him the truth? She had kept her silence about it. She wouldn't tell him a lie. She had never lied to him. When he put his question later, however, he wasn't so sure about that. 'Did you never wonder about Marge when you were in Forvit?' he began, and could see her go on the defensive.

'Wonder what about Marge?' she snapped, her eyes wary.

'If she was . . . being unfaithful to Dougal, for instance?'

Her eyes wavered for an instant, then held his. 'Marge

was never unfaithful! She did go to the dances, but she told Dougal and he trusted her.'

He didn't want to push it too far. 'Oh, well . . . I just wondered.'

Recalling it in bed, Alistair was nearly sure that his question had upset her. She had never told him a lie before, but she had told him one then – no doubt about it.

The more he turned it over in his mind, the more positive he became that Dougal was not Nicky's father, and watching them teasing each other the next day, lovingly like any father and son, but one so dark and the other so bright, he wanted to take his long-time friend aside and tell him the truth. The only thing that stopped him was the knowledge that it would break Dougal's heart. What worried him was that he was so upset himself that he was afraid he might let it out accidentally. There might even come a time when he wouldn't be able to keep it back any longer and would let fly at Marge, and even if it *was* all her fault, it would cause ructions between him and Gwen, and he didn't want that. It was like living on a razor's edge.

'What's up with Alistair?' Marge eyed her sister curiously. 'He's been snapping my head off lately and I can't think of anything I've said or done to . . .'

'Something's bothering him,' Gwen interrupted, not wanting to tell her what. 'Um . . . has Dougal ever said . . . has Alistair ever asked . . . ?' She stopped abruptly.

'The day they took a walk together, he spoke about what it was like being a prisoner of war. Dougal won't tell me anything more than that.'

Gwen's concern that her husband might have stumbled on the truth was so great that she had to find out, and so she tackled him that evening when they were sitting

333

by the fire. 'Marge is wondering what she's done to upset you?'

'Is she, now?'

His tone was so sarcastic that her determination faltered a little, but she knew she had to get to the bottom of things. The air would have to be cleared. 'Alistair, I wish you'd tell me what's wrong with you. Did something happen to you in the prison camps that's made you change? I know it must have been a terrible time for you, and all I want to do is help you to forget.'

'And all I want is for you to tell me the truth,' he snapped. 'I hate to see my best pal being tricked, though if he wasn't so bloody besotted by the kid, he'd see it for himself.'

Gwen felt herself go cold, but she answered honestly. 'If you're still thinking Marge was unfaithful, you're wrong. I can swear with my hand on my heart – she never took one step out of line the whole time we were in Forvit. She was as true to Dougal as . . .'

He took up where she left off. '. . . as you were to me?' He thought nothing of her hesitation. Gwen had always found it difficult to speak from her heart.

Thankful that he hadn't noticed anything, she tried to coax him out of his mood. 'You've got a wrong idea in your head, darling, and if you don't get rid of it, it's going to cause a lot of trouble.'

'For Marge? You would stick up for her, of course, seeing she's your sister.'

'I'm sticking up for her because I know she's not guilty of what you think. Yes, she enjoyed herself at the dances, but if her own husband can look on that as innocent fun, I don't see why you can't.'

'You think I'm jealous, do you? You think I want Marge?'

'Of course I don't, that's silly.' Gwen was angry now. 'I think you're . . . twisted. You've never been right since you

334

came home, and you've been worse since Dougal came back. No matter what you think – and I tell you you're making a big mistake – for God's sake don't say anything to him. He's so proud of his son, it would destroy him to think he wasn't . . .'

'I'm not heartless,' Alistair said, bitterly. 'That's the only reason I *haven't* told him. But I warn you, if he ever hints at having doubts, I won't hesitate.'

'But there's nothing to tell,' Gwen wailed. 'It's all in your . . . warped mind.'

'Thank you very much. It's nice to know where your loyalties lie.' Alistair stood up and walked towards the door.

'Where are you going?' she asked, anxiously.

'Out.'

'I'm sorry, darling, I didn't mean the things I said about you. I'm just upset at you for thinking Marge would . . .' She stopped and drew a deep breath to calm her ragged nerves. 'Can't we forget about it? You're not doing anybody any good by carrying on like this. Can't we get back to the way we were before the war?'

'One big happy family?' he sneered. 'With a cuckoo in the nest?'

His wife's cry of anguish made him halt with his hand on the door knob, and the ensuing torrent of tears, sounding as if they came from the innermost core of her, made him dart to her side. 'Oh, Gwen, my dearest darling, I'm sorry! I'm sorry! I didn't mean to hurt you. You're quite right, my mind must be warped, but I shouldn't take it out on you. I shouldn't have said anything. I know I'm wrong about Marge, but I couldn't help . . . Can you forgive me? Please?'

She looked up at him, her eyes still streaming, the sobs still racking her whole body. 'I do forgive you, Alistair. I can understand that what you went through in the war has changed you, but I wish ... oh God, how I wish ... I had my old husband back.'

Much later, as she lay cradled in his arms, their love having been re-avowed and demonstrated, Gwen wondered if she had been correct in her summing up of him. Had his suspicions of Marge and his desire to protect Dougal really twisted his mind? Could it be the result of the dreadful beatings and kickings he must have received in the POW camps? Or ... was he going insane? Was he edging down a slippery slope towards utter madness? Was it possible for him to reverse?

Salvation for Alistair came at the end of January, with the arrival of a letter from his sister, addressed to him, not to Gwen as was usual.

Dear Brother,

You'll likely have a fit when you read this, so sit down and take it slowly. Gwen tells me you can't settle since you got home, and my Sam's exactly the same, but he's doing something about it. He's applied for us to go to Australia on this assisted passage scheme. The fare's only £10 if you agree to stay for at least two years, and he says it's too good a chance to miss.

The trouble is Benview, and that's why I'm writing. You've said you want to open a jeweller's shop or something like that, so why don't you move up here? It would save us the bother of trying to sell the house. It's too far from civilization for most people, and it's really yours, anyway, remember? You could get a shop in Aberdeen, it's not that far if you have a car.

What I'm saying is, we would leave everything, furniture, etc., so you wouldn't have to worry about that. Sam says it's a wonderful opportunity for all of us, so please think about it and let us know by the end of the month.

Give my love to Gwen and the kids, and to all the rest of the folk at your end. I bet Dougal's still in seventh heaven having a son after all this time.

Your hoping-to-emigrate-soon sister, Alice

'Well!' exclaimed Gwen, after she read it. 'That's a surprise!'

'What do you think, though?'

'I haven't had time . . . and it's up to you. I'll fall in with whatever you want.'

'We'd better discuss it with the kids. It's their future, as well.'

And so, for the rest of that day, fortunately a Saturday when thirteen-year-old Leila and David, twelve, were at home, the topic was, 'Should we move up to Forvit for good?' Later, when they were joined by the rest of the clan, as Dougal laughingly referred to them, and after much deliberation and tossing around of opinions, the final consensus was that Alistair should make up his own mind.

Lexie's visit to the new doctor had a result she had not expected, although she should have known. Not that he did or said anything out of place – he took her blood pressure and pulses, tested her reflexes, then sounded her chest. 'Your trouble isn't physical as far as I can make out. Are you worrying about something? That is often . . .'

She had shaken her head – how could she tell him what she suspected? – but as she looked at him, her senses began to swim, and she felt herself going back to that awful night. 'Stop it,' she moaned, 'I don't like you doing that.'

Straining against the arms now trying to pin her down, she could again feel the pain of the object being forced inside her. 'It's too sore!' she screamed. 'You're hurting me! Stop! Please stop!'

She could see the sweat running down a horrible, unfeatured red face until, as abruptly as it had begun, the horror came to an end and she was able to stop struggling against it.

'That's better.' The voice was soft, the touch was gentle, and she smiled tremulously into the puzzled face of young Dr Geddes. 'I hope I didn't hurt you, but I was forced to hold you down, you were in such a state, fighting like a tigress.'

'I'm sorry,' she whispered, deeply ashamed. 'I was remembering something ... I thought ... you were somebody else.'

'Obviously somebody who terrified you half to death. Tell me about it. It happened when you were quite young?'

She was still trembling. 'Not quite sixteen, and I can't speak about it. To tell the truth, I'm not quite sure if it happened at all, or if it was just a horrible nightmare.'

'It would help to tell me, whether or not it actually happened. You need to get it out of your system. Facing up to it should stop the nightmares for good.'

'It was ...' She stopped, shaking her head determinedly, knuckles white as she gripped the seat of her chair. 'I can't speak about it. I can't!'

'It's all right, don't force it. You seem to be at the limit of your endurance, and if you could only bring yourself to talk through it for me, I'd be better able to ...' He stood up and unlocked one of the glass doors of the cabinet against the left-hand wall. 'All I can do, meantime, is give you some tablets to help you to sleep.'

And they had for as long as they lasted, Lexie thought now, though they weren't as potent as the ones Doctor Birnie had given her all those years before – they had knocked her out in minutes. But now that she knew what her father had put her through – for it *had* been her father – she could understand why she couldn't bear to let anybody else near her in that way.

She couldn't even think of Alec Fraser as her father now, but it was no wonder he had cleared out of Forvit. He had abused her so badly as to make her bleed, actually torn her. How could they have faced each other after that?

1947–1949

Chapter 23

❧

Waiting in Benview's large kitchen for David to come home from school, Gwen Ritchie wondered what had possessed her to come back. She had wanted to watch young Nicky growing up, even though it pulled at her heartstrings to be powerless to claim him as her son. Yet . . . probably it was best this way. Alistair was so unstable that, if they'd stayed in Lee Green, she couldn't have trusted him not to blurt out his suspicions to Dougal, and she'd have been duty-bound to confess the whole sorry tale. She couldn't let Marge take the blame for what *she* had done.

Although the move to Forvit had not been made without due consideration, it was effected far too quickly for her liking. Rosie, of course, was against them going, and so, too, was Peggy, who would have to take on some of the responsibility for her mother. Alf Pryor had said it wasn't his place to put forward an opinion, but, when pressed, he had admitted that he wouldn't mind cooking Rosie's meals again. It would leave Marge free to concentrate on her husband and son, and it would give him something to occupy his time other than tending the two gardens. He had come down firmly, if just a little shamefacedly, on the opposite side from his wife.

Marge had been torn between the need to have her sister next door for company and relief that she wouldn't be there to criticize the way she was bringing up Nicky. Dougal, as Alistair's close friend, had no inhibitions about voicing *his* opinion, and had urged him to jump at the opportunity and not be so bloody stupid.

As for the younger members of Rosie's flock, two-year-old Nicky's unnatural silences let everyone know how much he would miss his two 'cousins', especially David, who had been teaching him all kinds of boys' games. David himself was keen to go back to Forvit, where he had left many friends and where there was space to roam around and act out the stories they read. Leila, however, was the one who astonished them. They had all expected her to prefer living in London because of the cinemas, dance halls and all manner of places where a young girl could meet the opposite sex, but when she was asked what she wanted, she said, 'I'd like to go back to Forvit.'

Her grandmother had reminded her that she would be leaving school at summer – she would be fourteen in May – and that Forvit would have little to offer in the way of employment.

Dougal had got round that. 'She can keep her father's books,' he crowed, then turning to Alistair, he went on, 'Your best bet's to look for a place in Aberdeen. More chance of succeeding there, and it's only twenty-eight, twenty-nine miles. You could do it in under an hour if you bought a decent car.'

That Saturday evening, the day after he got Alice's letter, Alistair had replied that they would take up the offer of the house, and in two days, she wrote back to say how pleased she was and not to worry about anything.

'We'll leave everything as it is,' she had continued, 'furniture, dishes, the lot, so all you'll need to bring, apart from your wife and kids (ha-ha) is clothes and any personal things you feel you need.'

'That's a blessing,' Alistair had grinned, 'seeing we've never had any household goods of our own, anyway.' Then he had looked at Alf somewhat apologetically. 'I nearly forgot. There's all the stuff you and your friend stored for us.'

Alf was an understanding man. 'That's all right. The Salvation Army's always looking for things for the needy, so I'll ask them to collect it ... unless you want to have a look through it first, in case there's something you want to keep?'

Rosie had given a sarcastic laugh. 'There's nothing there worth a brass farthing. The furniture was second-hand when Tiny bought it.'

Three months later – the time it took for the Guthries' documents to come through from Australia House – the Ritchies had returned to Benview. The first three days were a sort of 'handing-over' period, with Gwen helping Alice to turn out her cupboards. The men made a bonfire of the useless items from the outhouses and also burned what Alice was throwing out.

The final leave-taking had not been as emotional as Gwen had feared, though she should have remembered that the Scots were not as demonstrative as the English. The brother and sister hadn't even kissed each other's cheeks, yet they must have known it was most unlikely that they would ever see each other again.

And now, only two days on, it was as if she had never been away, except that there was no Marge to keep her from getting depressed. Being on her own every day from morning until David came bouncing in from school around five was like a punishment – likely *was* a punishment, and she shouldn't complain. After what she had done, she had got off lightly.

She couldn't get over how attitudes had changed in the village, however. Only one or two of the village women had ever spoken to Marge and her in any sort of friendly way before, and now they all smiled and commented on the weather, or said how glad they were to see them back as a complete family.

When she mentioned this to Alistair, he had said, 'It's because you're here for good this time. They'd been timid of you and Marge before because you didn't belong and they couldn't understand what you were saying. When I went to London first, it sounded to me like they all spoke with a marble in their mouths and thought they were better than Dougal and me. So that's what the folk here had thought about you and Marge. No,' he added hastily, 'I know you wouldn't have looked down on them, but . . .' He shrugged off the prejudices of the country folk.

Gwen sighed – she would never understand. It was Lexie Fraser, who had always been quite friendly, who now seemed to give her the cold shoulder. She had never asked about Alistair, yet during the war, her first question had always been, 'How's Alistair? I saw you had a letter from him this morning,' or whenever. She looked much older, too, as if something dreadful was preying on her mind. It was a pity she couldn't meet a nice man. Marriage would do her the world of good.

Lexie watched Gwen Ritchie as she went out of the shop and cycled off. She didn't look as happy as she used to, but no doubt she hadn't wanted to come back to Forvit. What was there here for her, for goodness' sake? She, herself, would leave like a shot if she thought she could survive out in the big world, but she had a sense of security here, of being safe, as if something terrible would happen if she ventured out of her cocoon.

She had vowed, time and time again, never to think back, but she couldn't help it. She couldn't stop herself. It would

346

haunt her for the rest of her life . . . or until her father came back and admitted what he had done. She had this other worry as well, now. Every time the doctor came into the shop, she could hardly bring herself to look at him, and he had done nothing wrong – that had been all in her mind. She had come perilously near to losing her sanity altogether at that time, and even if she was relatively calmer now, it wouldn't take much to push her over the edge.

Two other people she thought about sometimes were Nancy Lawrie and Margaret Birnie. She was sure that what Doodie Tough said about Mrs Birnie and another man couldn't be right, although Doctor Tom had told a few folk that she had never been totally happy in Forvit, and he had given in to her pleas to find a practice somewhere near Stirling so that she could look after her mother. She had gone on ahead of him, leaving him to attend to the sale of the house and the removal of their belongings. It had been a blow to the local community when he left, about three months after her father, and he'd been presented with a lovely gold watch in appreciation of his seven years' dedicated service.

It was a shame, really, because Mrs Birnie had been a lovely woman, a bit reserved maybe, but she'd likely just been shy. She'd been quite well-liked, had sung in the kirk choir and was president of the Guild, so folk couldn't understand why she hadn't been happy. Still, nobody knew what went on behind closed doors, did they? How a person behaved in private could be completely at odds with his or her public image.

Replacing the lid on a tin of the mixed biscuits she had been weighing out for Alistair's wife, Lexie's thoughts turned to Nancy Lawrie. She'd been so different from Margaret Birnie, a go-ahead girl, full of fun and always flirting with the boys. She wasn't the type of person Alec Fraser would be drawn to. He had been reserved and quiet . . . it was really just as unlikely that he had taken up with Nancy as that he had raped his daughter. An iciness clutching at the pit of her stomach, Lexie took a deep breath. If she carried on like this, they would haul her off to the nearest asylum and put her in a straightjacket ...

Picking up her duster, she made a desultory attack on a side shelf. Gwen Ritchie didn't know when she was well off, that was her trouble. She didn't have a dark secret that ate at her very innards while she had to smile and pretend that nothing was wrong. Not only that, she had a lovely husband, two lovely children ... everything that Lexie Fraser had ever wanted.

Leila Ritchie had walked past the house three times, hoping to catch a glimpse of Barry Mearns. She had always had a crush on him, from the first day he'd come to help with the garden, back in 1941 when she was just a little kid.

She wouldn't be a kid much longer, though she'd have to stay on another year at school because the leaving age had been raised to fifteen. The year after that, she would be old enough to get married in Scotland, so she had heard.

'Well, well! It's young Leila, isn't it?'

She looked round in surprise to find the postman, Barry's father, regarding her with an expression she was just beginning to recognize. Since she'd started wearing nylons, the latest in stockings, and putting a touch of make-up on, men as well as boys had begun to look at her like she was good enough to eat, and she couldn't help flirting a little. 'Yes, Mr Mearns, we're back. Dad's looking for a place in Aberdeen to open a jeweller's.'

'So he was saying when I handed in his letters the other day. Barry was asking if I'd seen you, so I'll need to tell him you're bonnier than ever. He's nearly finished his apprenticeship at

Bill Rettie's garage in Bankside, but he still does a bit o' gardening in his spare time, so if your Dad needs some help . . .'

'I'll tell him. I'd better be going, Mr Mearns, else Mum'll wonder where I've got to.'

'She'll need to keep her eye on you, or the lads'll all be after you. Cheeribye, lass.' Sandy gave her a laughing salute as he turned away.

Leila walked off feeling very pleased with herself, retrieved her bicycle from where she had set it against the gable wall of the Jubilee Hall and sped along the road. Barry had asked about her! And his father thought she was bonnie – it sounded even better than being pretty. Coming up for fourteen was a perfect age to be!

Leila was even more pleased with herself that evening. Her father had come home in a state of high excitement. 'I've found a wee place off Union Street!' he exulted. 'It's not ideal, a wee bit cramped, but it's right in the heart of the city and it'll do till I get on my feet.'

All through their evening meal, he told them his plans, so animated that Leila glanced at her mother who was looking happier than she had done for some years – even before Dad came home from the war, really. He'd been different then, not like he'd been before, and she'd been as upset as her mother about that. Of course, he must have had some bad experiences, and it would have taken him a long time to get over them, so they should be grateful that he was getting back to normal, though it had taken a long time.

They had just finished eating when someone knocked at the porch door, and Leila, being nearest, went to open it. 'Barry!' she gasped, her face flooding with colour.

The twenty-year-old was also embarrassed. 'I've come to see if your father needs any help with the garden. Da said . . .'

Curiosity about the caller had brought Alistair into the porch, too, but the youth was a complete stranger to him. 'You're a gardener, are you?'

'He's Barry Mearns, the postman's son,' Leila explained.

'I'm serving my time as a motor mechanic, Mr Ritchie.'

'He helped Mum and Auntie Marge with this garden when we were here before,' Leila said shyly, 'and he's really good, Dad.'

Feeling a sense of goodwill towards all men at that moment, Alistair smiled broadly. 'A reference already? That's good enough for me, and I shouldn't think I'll have much time myself to spare on the garden for a few years yet, so when can you come?'

Barry cast a grateful glance at Leila. 'I've been helping the doctor for the past few Mondays. He's wanting to change the whole layout of his garden, and we're digging out everything so he can start from scratch. The trouble is, he's often called away and I'm mostly on my own. Tuesdays, I tidy up at Mrs Wilkie's, and do a quick job on Lexie Fraser's wee square. Wednesdays . . .' he paused, then said, bashfully, 'it's choir night. I don't like to let the minister down.'

Alistair nodded appreciatively. 'Good lad.'

'Thursdays,' Barry continued, 'I've been giving my boss a hand to dig a foundation for a wash-bed he wants to put in, and a bigger area round the petrol pumps. That'll take another couple of months, maybe. I could manage you Fridays, though, if that's OK?'

'Fine, but are you sure? You're not leaving yourself much time for enjoyment.'

'There's not much to enjoy round here . . . up to now.' Barry shot another glance at Leila, whose face went crimson at what he was implying.

This was not lost on her father, who, however, decided to ignore it. 'So you'll be here on Friday at . . . ?'

'I stop at five, so I can manage by six, if that's not too early.'

'I probably won't be home, but you'll manage?'

'I know where everything is, Mr Ritchie.'

'Right! Shall we say ... a couple of hours till we see how it goes?'

Alistair took the overnight train to London on Wednesday, to close his bank account and collect the items he had deposited in Manny's name but which were now his. He went to Lee Green after his business was over, to acquaint them with the progress he was making, and to find out how everyone was. Peggy and Dougal, of course, were both at work, but Marge, Rosie and Alf were delighted to see him, and interested in his plans. He resisted Marge's pleadings for him to stay over. 'Dougal's going to be so disappointed if he doesn't see you,' she wailed.

'I'm desperate to get home, Marge,' he excused his hurry. 'I can't wait to get started.'

It wasn't only his business that pulled him away, however. It was seeing young Nicky again. As he told himself after he settled into the window corner of the railway carriage, there wasn't a chance in hell that that kid was Dougal's. What was every bit as bad, as far as Alistair was concerned, Gwen must have known what Marge got up to. Pregnancy could be hidden up to a point, but not between two sisters who were living in an isolated cottage in the middle of a war.

To be fair to his oldest friend, he should make his own wife admit the truth and not let the deception carry on any longer, but ... he had other things to concentrate on. He had a shop to set up and get running, and he should really try to get some sleep tonight, to be fit to see the solicitor in Aberdeen in the morning. There were papers to sign, advice

351

to ask for . . . and he'd be better to open a current account at the bank. It was more businesslike to hand over a cheque for any stock he had to buy than a bulky wad of notes.

Everything accomplished that he had set out to do, Alistair came off the bus outside the shop/post office, and decided to go in and have a few words with Lexie. He hadn't seen her since he came back to Forvit, and . . . by God, yes! *She* would know if there had ever been any gossip about Marge. He was dismayed at how ill she looked when he went in, but it wasn't policy to say that kind of thing to a woman. 'Here's me turning up again like a bad penny,' he laughed.

'I thought you might have come to see me before,' she muttered, accusingly.

'I've been looking for premises in Aberdeen. I'm opening a shop, jewellery, new and old, watches, clocks . . .'

'You'd learned all that from your Jew, of course,' she said, listlessly now.

'Manny was the best teacher I could ever have had. I still miss him.'

For some moments, he asked about people he used to know, then he plucked up courage and came out with his question, the answer to which should settle the burning agonizing he'd done over the past months. 'Did you ever hear any rumours about Dougal's wife when she was here?'

Lexie's eyebrows lifted briefly. 'What d'you mean? What sort of rumours?'

'About her . . . going out with any of the men from Ardley Camp?'

'I never heard anything about her. It was Gwen I saw up at the tower one night with a soldier.' She hesitated briefly, regretting having said anything, and conceded, 'I could've

352

sworn it was her voice, but I suppose it could have been Marge.'

He had fixed on one unsavoury sentence. 'It couldn't have been Gwen you saw, she wouldn't have done anything wrong. Why did you think it was her? She's blonde and Marge is dark. You'd have noticed which one it was, surely?'

'I could only see from their waists down ... caught them in the act, though I didn't stand and watch. It was the voice that made me think it was Gwen, but they're both Cockneys, of course.'

'They're not Cockneys,' Alistair began, but didn't waste time explaining, 'and it *had* been Marge. I knew it! Dougal and her are both dark, and Nicky's bright red!'

'I suppose that could happen.'

'Not in this case, now I know what she'd been up to.'

'You should ask Gwen,' Lexie murmured. 'She must have known what was what.'

Alistair felt obliged to cover up for his wife. 'Marge wouldn't have let her know. She'd always have met the man away from the house.'

'But she couldn't have hidden ... no, Al. Marge grew so big, I wondered if she was having twins, and it *was* born nine months after Dougal had his embarkation leave.'

Alistair was glad when she fell silent. Had his suspicions been groundless? They must have been. His wife would never have agreed to anything underhand, and Nicky must be Dougal's after all. Unless ... he had never once heard Marge telling a lie, but she was far more capable of it than Gwen. She could have been carrying on with a soldier and been lucky that Dougal had been on leave about the right time, or near enough for her to swear it was his baby, and Gwen wouldn't have suspected a thing.

Lexie cut into his deliberations. 'I've just remembered.

Gwen was quite ill at the time, as well. She'd to go to London for an operation.'

'An operation?' he gasped. 'She never told me that in her letters – nobody did.'

'They hadn't wanted to worry you. You were in a prison camp, after all.'

'But I'd have liked to know. Was it serious? What if she'd died?'

'Marge said it was woman's trouble, a cyst that turned out to be benign. I was a bit worried about Marge being there on her own while Gwen was away, but an auntie came up from England in time to take her to the hospital, and Gwen was home before she came back with the infant.'

His mind in a state of turmoil, Alistair bade Lexie goodbye and walked pensively along the road, going over what he had heard. By the time he reached home, he had convinced himself that what Lexie had told him didn't prove he was wrong. It didn't prove he was right, either, that was the only thing.

'Why didn't you tell me about your operation?' he asked Gwen when he went inside.

By the expressions on his children's faces, he could tell that they hadn't known either, and he regretted not waiting until he and his wife were alone. But it was done now, so he persisted, 'Why didn't you let me know?'

Gwen's face was chalk white. 'Marge said . . . it would be best . . . not to worry you,' she said, haltingly, obviously upset at the accusing way he had spoken to her.

He took a deep breath, and his next words were more gentle. 'Didn't it occur to you I'd want to know?'

'You couldn't have done anything, Alistair, and . . . maybe I should have told you once it was all over, but . . .'

'You didn't tell us either, Mum,' David said loudly.

Leila was looking puzzled. 'Was that the time when you were supposed to be looking after Grandma?'

Gwen's sigh was a little tremulous. 'We only said that to save you worrying, dear.'

'But why did you have to go to London to have an operation?' David demanded. 'Isn't there a hospital in Aberdeen that could have done it?'

'It was ... it was ... how can I put it? They wanted to try out a new piece of equipment.'

Alistair's face darkened. 'They were experimenting on you?'

'It wasn't dangerous. It had been tested and tested, and I was all right, so can we just forget it? It's all over, and I'm as fit as a fiddle. Tell us how you got on in London.'

When Alistair left, Lexie wished that she hadn't mentioned Gwen in connection with the soldier at the tower – she could tell it had upset him. It would be better to let him think it was Marge, though she was absolutely positive that it hadn't been. He had suffered enough as a prisoner of war, it would be a crime to stir up trouble for him when he was getting his life back together again.

What Lexie told Alistair, however, had farther-reaching effects than she realized. Leila, who had only been ten at the time, was old enough now to put two and two together and make sense of what had gone on. Her mother had told a lie about going to London to look after Grandma, so the rest of it could have been a lie, too. It was too much of a coincidence that Auntie Marge and Mum had both grown so fat at that time. Now that she came to think back, they could both have been expecting babies. Uncle Dougal had been on leave about the right length of time before Nicky was born, so that was OK, but Dad had been away for a year and a half, if not more, so if Mum *had* had a baby, it must have been to somebody else.

Every time her mind touched on this, Leila felt sick, but there was nothing she could do. She couldn't accuse her mother, not unless she had proof, and in any case, she could be wrong.

Gwen felt she was living on the edge of a crumbling precipice and could do nothing to save herself if it gave way. If it ever crossed Alistair's mind, she kept thinking, that saying she'd had an ovarian cyst removed could be an excuse for going away to have a baby conceived in sin, he wouldn't have anything more to do with her. Nevertheless, even if he didn't suspect her of being Nicky's mother, if he ever accused Marge to her face of being unfaithful to her husband, or told Dougal that he wasn't Nicky's father, she would have to tell the truth. She couldn't let her sister shoulder the blame.

She had hoped that by moving to Forvit, Alistair would never have the opportunity to air his suspicions to Marge or Dougal, but he was speaking of making occasional trips to London to buy stock for his shop. Yet, even knowing that it was bound to come out some time, she was too much of a coward to confess unless she was forced to.

She would have to exist in this awful state of limbo until . . . the end.

Chapter 24

'Are you feeling well enough, Alf?' Rosie studied her son-in-law in some concern. 'You look ghastly.'

He gave a faint smile. 'Thanks, Rosie. That makes me feel absolutely tip-top.'

She shook her head at his sarcasm. 'You didn't need to cook anything for me if you didn't feel up to it. I could easily have slapped two slices of bread round a chunk of cheese. Or Marge would have done something for me, if you'd asked her.'

'No need, Rosie, old girl, though I don't feel quite up to scratch, if you must know. Age catching up with me at last, I suppose.'

'Oh, poof! I can give you fifteen years and there's nothing wrong with me . . . apart from my stupid legs. If I got a new pair of knees, I'd be on top of the world.'

'You always *are* on top of the world, Rosie, dear. I wish I'd half your spirit.'

'No sense in moping like a dead duck all the time,' she laughed.

He ate little of the steak and kidney pudding he had prepared, and not a single spoonful of the apple pie with the melt-in-the mouth pastry almost as good as Tiny used to make, but Rosie passed no comment. He'd be upset if she fussed.

She lay back in her chair when he had gone, her feet on the brown plush pouffe she kept handy to ease the pain in her legs. Should she say anything to Peggy, or would it worry her? Well, of course it would worry her, Rosie scolded herself, so she'd better see what Marge thought first.

As she always did, Marge went to check on her mother at half past three on the dot, having given her time for her afternoon nap, and Rosie, who hadn't slept at all that day, jumped straight in. 'I'm worried about Alf, Margie. He doesn't look a bit well, and he hardly ate any of the steak and kidney pud he cooked for me.'

'He loves cooking,' Marge smiled. 'You should think yourself lucky having at least one domesticated son-in-law. Dougal wouldn't know how to boil an egg, and neither would Alistair, I shouldn't wonder.'

'I wish you'd stick to the point,' Rosie sighed. 'It's not like Alf. He was so pale, and there was sweat on his brow like he had a fever.'

'Shall I go and have a word with him?'

'Have a look at him anyway, then come right back and tell me what you think.'

'I can't just look and walk out,' Marge objected.

'You can surely think of some excuse.'

The distance between the two back doors was not sufficient to give Marge time to think of anything, but as it happened, she didn't need an excuse. When she went into his kitchen, her brother-in-law was slumped over the sink. 'Oh, dear God, Alf!' she cried. 'What's wrong?' He patted his chest and, remembering that he had medication for his angina, she asked, 'Have you taken a pill?'

His nod made alarm course through her. If the pill wasn't helping, it must be bad – a proper heart attack. She helped him into the living room and, while she settled him in a chair, she said, 'I'll phone for the doctor. I'll just be a jiffy.'

Rushing through to the hall, she was glad that Alf had made them all have telephones installed. It was her mother they had feared for, of course, but it might be his life she could be saving now.

Having caught the doctor towards the end of his afternoon surgery, she was back in no time, not even popping in to let her mother know what was happening. 'He'll be here as soon as he can, Alf, so I'll wait with you till he comes.'

'It's a good thing your Mum told you to have a look at Alf,' Dougal said, that evening. 'He could have been dead by the time Peg came home from work.'

'I know,' Marge muttered, 'and I nearly didn't go. I thought Mum was fussing about nothing, you know what she's like, but . . . oh, Dougal, I thought it was all over before the doctor even turned up, and he was there in less than ten minutes and took him to hospital himself. How was he when you saw him?'

'He's not too good, but we'll have to play it down in front of Peg. She's worrying herself sick about him.'

'I'd be out of my mind if it was you. Um . . . do you think he'll pull through?'

'I wouldn't like to say.'

'Thank goodness you've the car. It'll save Peg having to take buses . . . or taxis, if the worst comes to the worst.'

Dougal frowned now. 'Take things as they come, eh? Don't look on the black side.'

The black side, unfortunately, came looking for them. At five minutes to five the following morning, they were roused out of fitful sleep by the slam of a car door, and when Dougal jumped to look out of the window, he gave a feeble groan. 'It's the police at Peg's!' he told his wife, pulling on his trousers and jacket over his pyjamas. 'We'd better get round there.'

When he left his house, his heart sank even more. One policeman was hammering on the Pryors' door while another was knocking on Rosie's. 'No, no!' he called to the nearest man. 'She's an old lady. You don't want to frighten her out of her wits.'

'We thought Mrs Pryor should have a neighbour or someone with her when we told her. Her husband has just died in hospital.'

Marge came running up now, trying to get her arm into the sleeve of her coat. 'Oh, no! Poor Alf ... and poor Peg.' With an effort, she kept hold of her senses, and explained, 'I'm her sister and this is our mother's house, and she'll be wakened now anyway.'

'You'd better go in and tell her,' Dougal advised, 'I'll look after Peg.'

The next few hours were horrendous for the inhabitants of all three houses. While Dougal was running Peggy to the hospital, Marge was attending to Rosie, who had been rigid with fear when she went in. 'A burglar was trying to break in,' she whispered, her teeth chattering, her face grey, 'and I was sure he'd kill me if I made a sound.'

'It wasn't a burglar, Mum,' Marge soothed. 'It was one of the policemen. They came to tell Peg that Alf had ... passed away, and they were trying to get a neighbour to be with her. They didn't know ... you could hardly walk ...'

'Oh, dear Lord! Poor Alf, I knew he was ill! He shouldn't have cooked lunch for me. It's my fault he's dead.'

'Don't be silly, Mum. He loved cooking, and oh, it's awful, really awful. I don't know what Peg's going to do.' Noticing then that her mother's face was an even more peculiar colour and that her breathing was so shallow she scarcely seemed to be breathing at all, Marge exclaimed, 'Mum! Take it easy! We don't want you ...'

Marge was too late. Rosie, like Alf, had suffered a fatal

heart attack, but unlike his, hers had given her no warning.

Only David was his normal self at breakfast time, the other three were so quiet that he said, grumpily, 'Don't know why you lot are so miserable. Just think about me. Even if that blasted rain goes off, the pitch'll be waterlogged.'

Not receiving the reprimand he expected from his mother for saying 'blasted', he drained his cup and pushed back his chair. 'I'm going upstairs again. There's nothing to do down here.'

'You could help with the dishes,' Leila suggested, but he pretended not to hear her. Washing and drying dishes was women's work, not men's. His father never dried as much as one measly teaspoon, and *he* wasn't going to let the side down.

In his room, he sifted through his comics listlessly; he'd read them all dozens of times. He didn't care much for books, though he quite liked the William series, by Richmal Crompton. He gathered the *Wizard*s and *Boys' Own*s into a semblance of neatness and stuffed them back in his cupboard. He was bored, bored, bored.

Then his curiosity was aroused by something hanging down the back of the shelf; it must have been under the comics and he'd pushed it back when he put them in again, but he'd no idea what it was. He couldn't remember ever putting anything there. Stretching over the sundry items that he regarded as treasures, he pulled out a slim paper wallet. Then it came back to him.

Rushing downstairs, he said, 'Dad, I just found something you've never seen. I forgot all about them.'

Alistair turned round with a smile, and held out his hand for whatever he was meant to look at. 'Oh, it's photographs.'

'I took them when we were living here before and the packet must have got jammed at the back of the shelf.'

'*You* took them? They're really good. Are these boys still at school with you?'

'He's left,' a grubby finger pointed, 'but the others are still there. And that's Auntie Marge digging up potatoes. She was sweating. And here's one of Mum speaking to the postie. Uncle Ken took this one of us all having a picnic at the tower, and he took that one of me another day, after he'd been teaching me how to bowl. This was the last one in the film – Uncle Ken standing between Mum and Auntie Marge.'

Gwen's gasp made her son look at her anxiously. 'It's all right to speak about Uncle Ken now, isn't it, Mum? I forgot it was supposed to be a secret, and anyway, it surely doesn't matter when the war's been over for so long, does it?'

He was astonished to see that his mother's eyes were round with what looked like terror, her mouth gripped in her chalk-white face, and he knew that it *was not* all right. He switched his eyes back to his father, who was angrier than he had ever seen him.

'Why had it to be kept a secret?' Alistair asked, very quietly.

'Well, you know . . .' the boy began, then believing that his father didn't know, that maybe the rule hadn't applied to servicemen overseas or even in other parts of Britain, he gathered confidence and went on, '. . . because soldiers weren't allowed to visit other soldiers' families. He'd have got into trouble, maybe been stuck in the glasshouse.'

Alistair studied the picture once more, and when he raised his head, his eyes were icy and his voice was clipped as he addressed his wife. 'And who is Uncle Ken?'

'He was a soldier who drove Marge home from a dance one night,' Gwen muttered, through lips almost frozen with fear, then, realizing what her words implied, she added, 'He was only a friend.'

'A bloody good friend, going by the amount of times he must have come here!'

She pulled her senses together with a great effort. 'Stop it, Alistair! If you want to pick a quarrel, please don't do it in front of the children.'

His face dark with anger, he snapped, 'Go to your rooms, you two! I want to have something out with your mother!'

They were only halfway up the stairs when he called, 'David, what colour was Uncle Ken's hair?'

'Um ... red, or ginger, or whatever it's called. Can I go now?'

Waiting until he heard a door closing, and guessing that they had both gone into the same room, Alistair's bottom lip curled. 'So that's why young Nicky's hair's red? Yet you swore to me Marge hadn't been unfaithful!'

'She wasn't! She really wasn't! Ken was only a friend. He had a wife and two children in Birmingham and he missed them something awful. We asked him here because we could see he was a decent man, not like some of the single boys who left a lot of sore hearts when they were posted away. He was so grateful to be part of our family.'

'He'd had a lot to be grateful for,' her husband sneered. 'He'd two kids on tap to replace his own, and a woman ready and willing to be a substitute wife!'

'It wasn't like that! We treated him like a brother, and he brought presents for Leila and David, and sometimes something for us from their cookhouse, and ...'

'And you're still trying to tell me it was all above board? What d'you take me for, Gwen? A bloody fool?'

'You are a bloody fool!' Gwen couldn't help saying it. She had to protect her sister's marriage ... as well as her own. 'You won't listen to reason, but please don't go telling Dougal what you've got in your stupid mind! You'll only turn him against Nicky ... and Marge never did anything wrong. I swear, Alistair, swear!'

Nostrils flaring, he inhaled deeply, then said, his finger on the photograph and enunciating each word clearly, 'Do you swear that Nicky is not that man's son?'

In her desperation, Gwen would have sworn to almost anything ... except this, and she had to fight her rising nausea before she could say, 'Marge wasn't unfaithful to Dougal. Never, Alistair. I've sworn it dozens of times and it's the honest truth. Believe me, all Forvit would have known if she had been.'

'Maybe they did! Maybe it was only you that didn't know. I promise you, Gwen, if I ever see Marge again, I'm going to have it out with her. Now, I'm going out for a while to clear my head. I need to think.'

The door slammed behind him and she turned guiltily as David ran down the stairs. 'I'm sorry, Mum. I didn't think ... I should have remembered.'

'It wasn't your fault, dear,' she said, wearily. 'Your father's been different since he came home from the war, and he doesn't like the idea of us keeping secrets from him. Don't worry about it, David. Everything will be all right.'

His clouded eyes cleared. 'Can I go out now? The rain's just about off.'

'It might be a good idea to tidy your bedroom a bit, the cupboard, at least. I'm sure there's a lot of stuff that you've grown out of and could be thrown out.'

She was relieved that he went back upstairs without arguing, and hoped that he and Leila wouldn't start discussing what had happened. The girl was old enough to see what had caused her father's anger, and perhaps wise enough to work out that her mother was not telling the truth. To take her own mind off things, Gwen cleared the table, washed up the dishes and then wielded the sweeping brush on the kitchen floor as if repelling an army. Why hadn't she remembered about the photographs? She didn't blame David, he hadn't dreamt . . . Nevertheless, the evidence of Ken Partridge's visits was there in black and white and there was no denying that.

Her innards tight with worry, she took a duster and the tin of Jamieson's wax polish from the cupboard and attacked the floor again. Some moments later, perhaps as a result of this physical effort, her fears eased a little. Even if Alistair asked the entire population of Forvit, no one could give him any scandal about Marge, not even if he went to the shop, because Marge had done nothing to give rise to any. It was *she*, his own wife, who could have set tongues wagging . . . but not a soul could have seen her on either of the nights she had been with Ken. They had been well away from the village.

Alistair stumbled slowly down the hill. He had sat by the tower for hours, agonizing, but he needed someone to talk to, so, still shaken by what he had learned, he now took the path towards the village. He had to find out whether or not Nicky was indeed 'Uncle Ken's' son, and the only person who could – or would – tell him, was Lexie. Glancing at his watch, he was pleased to see that she would be closing the shop in five minutes.

He walked a little quicker when he reached the road, and arrived at the shop as the last customer was leaving. 'Can I have a word with you, Lexie?' he asked, anxiously.

Nodding, she locked the door and led him through to the house. 'What's up, Alistair?' she asked when they were seated. 'I can see something's happened.'

Before he could tell her about the photographs David had unearthed, someone rapped loudly on the shop door. 'Ignore it,' she sighed. 'Somebody always tries it on, and whoever it is, they'll just have to wait till tomorrow.'

But the caller, after another assault on the shop door, tramped round the side of the house, making them look at each other in dismay. 'I'd better answer it,' Lexie muttered when the heavy knock came at the porch.

'It's the bobby,' she said, unnecessarily, in a minute, ushering the tall policeman inside. 'He wants to use the phone, and I'll have to show him how the exchange works.'

Through the open door, he watched her fitting the bulky earphones on her head, picking up a lead and plugging it in and then winding the handle at the side for a few seconds. When the call was apparently answered, she handed the earphones to the constable and waited for him to end his call before unplugging and switching off. Too far away to hear what was being said, Alistair did not have to contain his curiosity very long before they came through from the shop again, both looking somewhat agitated.

'He had to report to Aberdeen,' Lexie said, her voice trembling. 'They've found a body in the moor, not far from the back of the Jubilee Hall.'

'Good God!' Alistair exclaimed. 'I did hear somebody saying there were diggers working there. What . . .'

'They're clearing a site for building new houses, but . . .' She broke off, then added, 'They say it's not big enough for a man, so it must be a woman.'

Relief coursed through Alistair. For a moment, he had feared that they had found her father. He turned to the policeman. 'Have you any idea who it is?'

'Not yet.' Magnus Robbie, from the Police House in Bankside and usually referred to behind his back as Bobby Robbie, sat heavily down on a chair. 'It'll need to be examined first, afore they can say for sure it *is* a woman and how lang she's been there.' He took out his handkerchief and mopped his brow and neck. 'I'd a right turn, I can tell you. It's my first murder, and she's nae a bonnie sight. I'd say she's been

366

there for a good few year, though I could be wrong. They'll need to ken if any women ever went missing.'

Alistair looked at Lexie apologetically. 'What about Nancy Lawrie? You always said your father wouldn't have run away with her.'

'It ... might be her.' Lexie sounded somewhat hesitant. 'She did disappear, but that was nearly twenty years ago.'

'I've only been up here for about ten year,' observed Robbie, 'so I dinna ken what went on afore that. Did any other women ever disappear?'

After considering this carefully, Lexie shook her head. 'Nobody that I know of.'

Robbie shook his head hopelessly. 'I suppose it could be a gypsy. I've heard they used to come to Dotterton, and that's nae far ... five mile at the most. Less, if somebody wasna wanting to be seen and come through the woods.'

Looking a bit happier about things, he stood up. 'That's what it must be. Them gyppos have quick tempers, and ... well, if one found his woman wi' another man, he might have stabbed her in the heat of the minute and then had to get rid o' the body.'

Alistair nodded. 'If it was years ago, you might never find out who she is ... was.'

'No, they shift aboot like ants, but a Detective Inspector's coming up from Aberdeen, so it's nae up to me to find out who did it. I'd better get back to the scene o' the crime.'

When Robbie left, Alistair regarded Lexie in some concern. 'You're as white as a sheet. D'you want me to stay with you for a while till you get over the shock?'

She gave a semblance of a smile. 'I'm all right. I thought at first it might have been my father's body, so I was glad when Robbie said it was a woman, but it can't have been anybody from round here. Who'd have wanted to kill Nancy Lawrie? She was only about seventeen, and nobody else went missing.

Go home, Alistair, I'm OK, and Gwen's likely wondering where you are.'

He hadn't the heart to mention his own problem, not after what she had just been through, and so he took his leave, giving her a comforting pat on the shoulder as she saw him out. He didn't really believe that she was all right; he was far from all right himself. Hearing about that body had given him a bit of a shock, too. Whoever she was, the dead woman had been somebody's daughter, or girlfriend, or wife, and even if she *had* been a gypsy, being murdered and buried in a moor was no way to end up.

His mind jumping like a grasshopper, he wondered if he had made something out of nothing with regard to the snap of the man his son had obviously been quite fond of. While he, himself, had been far from home, he had accepted invitations to the homes of a few girls he had met, had been made very welcome by their parents, had felt happy to be part of a family for even a short space of time. He had done nothing out of place with any of them, so why should he think the worst of this 'Uncle Ken'? And, now that he came to think of it, he had never told Gwen about those friendships, either, so she wasn't the only one to have kept secrets. It was Marge who had betrayed her husband, and although he didn't like the idea of Dougal being cuckolded and even worse, fooled into believing he was a father, it was probably best all round for him to hold his tongue.

Gwen was still sitting by the fire when he went in, her face showing evidence of prolonged weeping. 'I'm sorry, darling,' he said, holding out his arms to her.

She jumped up and ran into them, and while he held her tightly, he told her that he had spent a long time at the tower thinking, then he'd gone to see Lexie.

'I thought that's where you'd go,' his wife said, tremulously. 'What did she say?'

'I didn't get round to asking her,' he admitted, and told her about Magnus Robbie's visit. 'He'd to report a body being found.'

'A body?' she gasped. 'Do they know who . . . ?'

'I thought it might have been Alec Fraser – Lexie's father – and so did she at first, but apparently it's a woman, and the bobby says it could be a gypsy.'

He told her about the platonic friendships he had made during the war and went on, 'So you see, I wasn't any different from that Ken, was I? It was . . . well, Marge . . .'

'I told you, Alistair,' Gwen said, relieved that he had stopped being so aggressive, 'there was never anything other than friendship between Marge and Ken. I swear it! And she never wrote to him after he was posted.'

Going by the years of the Finnies' childlessness, the colour of the boy's hair, plus the fact that Lexie had said it could have been Marge with the soldier, Alistair was more convinced than ever about her guilt, but he said, 'OK, we'll leave it at that.'

In bed that night, listening to Alistair's deep steady breathing, Gwen was thankful that he had dropped the subject, but she was well aware that he hadn't changed his mind. The problem was, although he obviously hadn't the slightest suspicion that it was his own wife who was Nicky's mother, if he ever told Dougal that *he* wasn't the boy's father, she would have to own up, and take the consequences.

Unable to sleep, Lexie was turning things over in her mind. Nancy Lawrie, out of all the women who had ever left Forvit, was the only one unaccounted for. If, as the gossips had said at the time, she had been expecting Alec Fraser's baby, had

369

she told him about it? If she had – Lexie's blood ran cold at the thought – would he have killed her to keep it from his wife and fled in shame? It would be the natural reaction . . . but her father would never have killed anybody . . . whatever else he had done.

But . . . he *had* run away. With no clothes. No money. Not even his bank book!

Chapter 25

∾

The funerals – Rosie being interred with her beloved Tiny, and Alf in the adjacent part of the double lair which she had thoughtfully purchased to accommodate her entire family – had been heart-wrenching for all of them, but Peggy, having lost her husband as well as her mother, was harder hit than her sisters. Dougal and Alistair did their best to comfort all three, but there were also the younger members of the family to consider.

Although no longer a child, and blossoming out as a woman, Leila couldn't stop crying. She had loved her grandmother and had missed her deeply when they moved away from her again. But she had also thought a great deal of her Auntie Peg and Uncle Alf, and couldn't bear the idea of one without the other.

David, still a boy, had tried to behave like the man he wanted to be, and had successfully hidden his grief until his grandmother's coffin was being lowered into its final resting place beside the grandfather he could not remember. Then he had to let it out, scrubbing his checks with his handkerchief in great mortification until he managed to stem his tears.

Nicky could not quite take in the fact that he would never see his Nanna again, nor his Uncle Alf, who had often slipped him a tanner to buy sweets, but the strained atmosphere in whichever house he happened to find himself over the past few days had effectively subdued his loud boyish treble.

At the funeral tea, Gwen was in constant dread that Ivy Crocker – who had come all the way from Newcastle on her own – would let it slip that she had been present at Nicky's birth and lay bare the secret his biological mother was struggling to keep from Alistair and Dougal, and she felt faint with relief when the seventy-year-old just clasped her hand for slightly longer than was necessary before leaving. She should have known that she could depend on her old friend not to let her down.

She desperately wanted to warn Marge that David had let the cat out of the bag about Ken Partridge's visits, but they never had a chance to be on their own. If their husbands took the children out of the way for a while, Peggy was always hovering somewhere near and she, too, had to be kept in the dark. She had more than enough to cope with already.

Gwen's worst fear, however, was that Alistair might inadvertently say something to Dougal about Ken, perhaps mention that he had ginger hair and thus sow suspicion in his friend's mind, even though he had promised not to.

Despite her sorrow, despite not wanting to leave Peggy just yet, she was glad when Alistair said, on the second evening after the funeral, 'We'd better go home tomorrow. If the shop's shut too long, customers might think it's shut for good.'

'You put a card in the door saying "Closed due to family bereavement",' Leila reminded him, 'so they'll know you'll be back.'

'But it's best not to stay away too long.'

The leave-taking was the hardest any of them had ever had to endure, the emotional kisses and long embraces seemed to go on for ever, even David lingering inside the group as if that would delay the parting, and it took the arrival of the taxi Alistair had ordered to take them to King's Cross to finally make the split.

*   *   *

372

Lying back in the carriage, Alistair closed his eyes and, because of the tension of the past few days, he soon fell asleep, and it was some time later, he didn't know how long, when he became aware of where he was and why. Reluctant to talk, however, he kept his eyes shut and let his thoughts return to Lee Green. Each time he had been alone with Dougal, he had been sorely tempted to tell him the truth about Nicky, but it would have been barbaric to inflict further heartache on the family – it would have affected every single one of them. He had tried to keep his manner to Marge as civil as he could, and even if he'd had to count to ten occasionally, they'd all been too upset about Rosie and Alf to notice.

If he'd been there any longer, though, the slightest thing could have lit the fuse of his anger at Marge for betraying her husband. It wasn't fair to Dougal to let it run on, and there would come a time when he wouldn't be able to hold his tongue, but it hadn't been possible to say anything in the circumstances. Besides, he had given his promise to Gwen.

'Mum, d'you think Auntie Peggy'll ever get over losing Alf?'

Leila's voice suddenly got through to him, and he listened listlessly to see how his wife would answer.

'She'll never forget him, if that's what you mean,' Gwen murmured, 'but she will get over his death eventually.'

'It was awful Grandma dying like that, too. Auntie Marge must have had a terrible shock.'

'Your Auntie Marge is a much stronger person than Peg. She can cope with anything, and she'll help her baby sister to get over things.'

'Baby sister?' Leila laughed. 'Auntie Peg's not a baby now.'

'Marge and I always looked on her as our baby sister, and it annoyed her. When she was still at school, she wanted to do the things we did, but our Dad wouldn't allow it.'

'Boyfriends and that, d'you mean?'

Gwen laughed softly. 'You probably won't believe it, but Marge never had a boyfriend till she met Dougal.'

'What about you, Mum? Was Dad your only one?'

After a brief hesitation, Gwen said, 'No, I did go out with another boy first, but it was all over before I knew your Dad.'

Having known this anyway, Alistair was glad that Gwen was being honest with their daughter. That was the difference between her and Marge. *She* would never tell lies, or do anything she might be ashamed of later ... whereas Marge ...

The low voices carried on, but it was only when Nicky's name filtered into his semiconsciousness that he listened properly, wanting to know what Leila was saying about the boy. 'He's not so naughty as he was in Forvit. Don't you think so, Mum?'

'He's that bit older,' Gwen explained. 'I thought he was going to be a ragamuffin like David used to be, but he was never as bad as that, I don't think.'

Wondering why David wasn't objecting to this slur on him, Alistair took a cautious peep out of the eye farthest from his wife. David was fast asleep, which was why his mother had said what she did.

Nothing was said for another few moments, then Leila murmured, 'Mum, can I ask you something? About Nicky.'

'Yes, dear, of course you can.'

Discerning a hint of apprehension in his wife's voice, Alistair strained to hear.

'I couldn't help thinking...' Leila went on, '... he's awfully like ... Uncle Ken.'

'That's only because of his red hair.'

'But his eyes are the same green as Uncle Ken's, and he ...'

What Leila was about to add was never said, because Gwen interrupted. 'Wake up, David, we're coming into York. If

374

you're thirsty, you'll get something at the trolley on the platform.'

The boy jumped up at once. 'Are you coming, Leila?'

'No, I'm too sleepy.'

Through all the squealing of brakes, banging of carriage doors and other loud noises, Alistair still feigned sleep. What he had just heard had convinced him that his suspicions were well founded. Gwen's abrupt interruption of Leila's questioning had been too fortuitous to be coincidence. She'd been afraid of what the girl might say, and if they hadn't arrived in York, she'd have roused David on some other pretext. It dawned on Alistair now that Leila might have been old enough at the time to twig that something was going on between Marge and her soldier 'friend' – kids were a lot more perceptive than adults gave them credit for – and was only just beginning to understand what it was. But he had better not ask her anything.

It was Leila and Gwen who slept all the way to Edinburgh, although Alistair suspected that his wife was shamming, as he had been earlier, but David, his usual inquisitive self again, kept asking about the places they were passing and gave him no space to think.

Lexie's heart sank when Magnus Robbie walked into the shop for the first time since the discovery of the body. 'Have they found something else?' she asked, still not convinced that it wasn't her father. 'Are they still sure it's a woman?'

Robbie took off his hat and gave his head a thorough scratch before answering. 'They are that, and the coroner's report says she's been dead for anything from ten to twenty years, so they're putting out an appeal to find that lassie you spoke aboot.'

'Nancy Lawrie?'

'That's her. Apparently, she disappeared in 1929, so I dinna ken aboot you, Lexie, but my money's on her.'

'No, I'm nearly sure it's not her, I don't know why. It's just a feeling I've got.'

The policeman regarded his chubby fingers for a second, then pronounced, in his more official tongue, 'But the law doesn't work on feelings, Lexie. It's facts that's needed – indispupital . . . indist . . . facts that naebody can argue aboot. Proof! Absolute proof!'

She managed to ignore his lapse in pronunciation, if lapse it was; he wasn't very bright at the best of times. 'How do they expect to get proof, then?'

He looked somewhat put out at being expected to know this. 'The proof . . .' he began, stopped and started again. 'The proof is in the eating.'

'What?' Lexie took a moment to fathom out this ridiculous statement. 'Oh! It's the proof of the *pudding* that's in the eating,' she corrected, gathering that he must have been in the bar earlier. 'The proof of a crime . . .'.

'The proof of a crime is the body,' he butted in, stiffly. 'A buried body suggests a murder, and murder . . . is . . . a . . . crime.' He looked at her triumphantly.

'Yes, I know, but you need . . .'

'We need proof of . . . um . . . identity. You wouldna happen to know where that Nancy's folk flitted to, would you?'

'No, they didn't tell . . .' Lexie glanced at the door as the bell tinkled. 'Oh, it's you, Aggie. Do you know where the Lawries went? Nancy's Mam and Dad? The police want to find them.'

Clearly flattered at being asked, Mrs Mearns drew herself up to her full, well-padded four feet eleven. 'No, it was like they disappeared off the face o' the earth and all. Of course, Nettie was black affronted that Nancy'd got hersel' in the family way . . .' It occurring to her who the presumptive

376

father had been, she slid easily into another tack. 'I tell you what, though. If I mind right, somebody once tell't me Ina McConnachie up at Leyton kept in touch wi' Nettie, so you'd better ask her . . .' The policeman having already gone, she stopped in mid-sentence and turned to Lexie with a sigh. 'He's useless, that ane. I coulda tell't him that days ago if he'd asked.'

'He's doing his best. Now, what can I do for you today?'

The door opening to admit Mattie Wilkie, Mrs Mearns laid a scribbled shopping list on the counter and left the shopkeeper to get on with it. Lexie couldn't help smiling at her exaggerated version of her brief encounter with Bobby Robbie, and kept her ears open when they lowered their voices.

'It must be Nancy Lawrie,' Mattie said, in a hoarse almost-stage whisper. 'The time's aboot right. D'you think . . . um . . . he . . . could've . . . ?'

Aggie gave this idea, new to her, her deepest consideration for a few moments. 'It hardly seems like him, but you never ken. They said yon Dr Crippen was as nice a man as you could meet.'

Outraged at this, Lexie felt like letting fly at them, but they were customers, after all, and she had been taught that the customer is always right. Not these two, though.

Fortunately, Mattie came up with another rumour which was circulating. 'I heard ane o' them tecs saying it could be a gypsy woman.'

'Ach!' Aggie snorted. 'They're aye saying something, and they ken damn all!'

'Lizzie says she heard somebody had seen a couple o' gypsies fighting one night up by the moor, a man and a woman, aboot the right time, it was.'

'How could onybody mind what happened twenty year ago?'

Lexie gathered from Aggie's tone that the idea of it just being a gypsy's body wasn't nearly as exciting as the possibility of having known the person concerned.

Mattie gave it one last try. 'It could be onybody. If he'd a car, a man could bury a body hunders o' miles away from where he killed it. Look at that Buck Ruxton doon in England some place. He killed his wife and their maid and drove them up to Scotland to dump them in a burn.'

'They wasna lang in being found, though, and he was a foreigner, an Indian or something, nae English.' Having lost interest in the discussion, the postman's wife turned to Lexie. 'Is that it?' She handed over a pound note, then said, 'If you're nae needin' a lot, Mattie, I'll wait and walk along the road wi' you.'

They had not been gone long when Detective Inspector Roderick Liddell walked in. In charge of the case, he had been using Lexie's parlour as a makeshift incident room. He hadn't bothered her much, but she didn't think she would have minded if he had.

'May I use your phone again, Miss Fraser?' he asked. 'I expect you know we've been trying to trace Mr and Mrs Lawrie, the parents of . . .'

'Nancy. Yes, I know. Did you get anything from Mrs McConnachie at Leyton?'

'She gave us an address, but she wasn't sure if they were still there, or if they were still alive. It's some years since she was in touch with Mrs Lawrie.'

'I hope you find them.'

'Yes, I suppose you must want to know, one way or the other.'

She nodded, not actually sure that she did want to know, after all.

*   *   *

Gwen Ritchie was anything but contented – she was alone at Benview for most of the day and missed Marge's cheery chatter. Leila was working with her father in Aberdeen, and the shop didn't close until six. This meant making something for David, who came in from school around five and went out about half an hour later on some pretext or other, and having another meal ready at seven for herself and the 'workers'.

Leila generally hurried through hers, then gave herself a quick wash, a puff of powder and a dab of lipstick before cycling off to meet her friends. Which left her, Gwen mused, the cook, the laundress, the cleaner, alone with her husband, which was anything but comfortable for her. She could tell that something was smouldering under the surface of his overpolite exterior. He hadn't mentioned Marge, nor Nicky, nor Ken Partridge since they came back from Lee Green, but something about him made her edgy; nothing definite, nothing she could challenge him with, just the suggestion of doubt on his face at times and, more often, the almost-accusing way he regarded her.

The peculiar looks Leila gave her occasionally also disquieted her, as if her daughter was turning something over in her mind, and that, too, could only be to do with Nicky. Sure that things were building up against her, Gwen seriously considered making a clean breast of everything to her husband and facing up to the consequences – they couldn't be worse than this constant dread of an eruption that would blow everything sky-high.

Detective Inspector Liddell looked apologetically at Lexie when she opened the door to him for the second time that day. 'I hope I'm not disturbing you, Miss Fraser?'

'Is there some news at last?' she asked, anxiously.

'A bit of a setback, actually. According to the coroner the

woman was between thirty-five and forty, so that rules out Nancy Lawrie. We haven't managed to trace her parents yet, I'm afraid. They had moved from the address we were given. We still hope to get a result from our appeal for information on her, of course, even if it won't help us to identify the body. We have begun the next line of enquiry – the gypsies – but they have their own methods of punishing the wrongdoers amongst them, which do not include bringing in the police. I've the feeling that we're wasting our time there, but I'll keep you informed if anything does transpire. I'm sorry to have intruded, Miss Fraser.'

He turned to go, but Lexie said quickly, 'You're very welcome to stay for a cup of tea, Inspector, I'd be glad of the company. That is, if you don't have to go somewhere else?'

'Nowhere else tonight, but if we're to be drinking tea together, wouldn't it be more friendly to call me Roddy?'

'Only if you call me Lexie,' she smiled. Their eyes suddenly locked, but in a moment, she dropped hers in confusion and rose to put the kettle on to boil. She had felt drawn towards this man from the first time he came asking the questions he had to ask. He couldn't believe that no search had been made for her father and Nancy at the time, even when she said she'd been told it was such a common occurrence it was a waste of police time.

'You have never believed that your father was with the girl?' he asked, as she set out the cups and saucers.

It was as if their minds were on the same planet, she thought. 'Never, and I never will, unless he comes and tells me himself.'

'Maybe he will, Lexie, some day. There has been no response yet to the posters that have been put up in every police station in Scotland for information about her. They say that she went missing from Forvit, Aberdeenshire in May 1929. It's better that we concentrate on her for now,'

380

he explained, 'because, if they *are* together, there's the chance that if we find her, we'll also find him, but if that fails, we will make a separate search for your father, in the hope that he can tell us where she is.'

Noticing how grim his expression was now, a wave of horror swept over her, and she was almost afraid to ask, 'Roddy, you think he . . . killed her, don't you?'

To her immense relief, he shook his head. 'It's a possibility, of course, but somehow I don't think so.'

The shrilling of the telephone startled her, and she ran through to the shop, the Inspector at her heels. 'It's for you,' she said, handing him the earphones.

He listened intently for some moments, then said, crisply, 'I'll be there as soon as I can.' He turned to her. 'I'm sorry, Lexie. Something has cropped up.'

He didn't say what, and she didn't like to ask.

Chapter 26

❧

With David also working with his father, Gwen was alone from 7.15 a.m. until 6.45 p.m. five days a week, and until 1.30 p.m. on Saturdays, wondering sometimes where the years had gone. One minute, her son had been a tousle-headed, cheeky-faced podge, the next, it seemed, he was a tall, slim young man, hair slicked back with his father's Imperial Leather brilliantine, his voice varying from treble to bass. But she eventually got more or less used to the change in him and to the long days without a soul for company.

One balmy August day, she had her usual lonely sandwich at half past twelve, then went out to wage war on the weeds in the garden, and had been at it for less than an hour when she heard a vehicle coming up the track. Apart from Alistair's old Austin and the postman's van – Sandy Mearns didn't have to do his round on a bicycle any longer – this was so unusual that she stopped what she was doing and waited for it to come into sight. It turned out to be a big black car which reminded her of the one Dougal had driven when they were in London for the funerals, then her heart leapt. It *was* Dougal's Ford. Marge was in the front passenger seat, waving excitedly to her, and Nicky was in the back seat with his head poking out of the window, and . . . yes! Peggy was sitting beside him.

She rushed forward to embrace her sisters, then she was hugging her secret son close to her, smiling somewhat wryly at his, 'Are you glad to see us, Auntie Gwen?'

'Of course I am, dear. Oh, Marge, why didn't you let me know you were coming?'

'Didn't know myself,' Marge chuckled. 'We were just touring and Peggy mentioned she'd like to see Edinburgh, and being so far north, Forvit kept calling to me.'

By the time Alistair, Leila and David came home, furniture had been shuttled around, beds changed, sleeping arrangements made and – Dougal and Nicky having gone to the village for more supplies – a huge meal had been prepared.

Nothing of any consequence was said while they dined, and as soon as they finished, Leila jumped to her feet. 'I'm meeting Barry at eight, Mum, but I won't be late home.'

It was Marge who grinned, 'The postman's boy? Don't keep him waiting, dear, but just make sure you don't do anything I wouldn't do.'

'That gives her a pretty wide scope.' It had come out without Alistair thinking, and he tried to pretend he'd been joking by giving her a broad wink.

'We'll take the boys out for an hour to let you tidy up.' Dougal's voice had a tightness in it. 'That's if you haven't got a date, as well, David?'

'A date? With a girl? Who, me?' David's shocked expression made them all laugh.

Desperate to get Marge on her own, Gwen said, 'Why don't you go with them, Peg?'

'No, thanks,' Peggy retorted. 'I'd rather do dishes than plough through heather and ladder all my stockings.'

The three sisters had plenty to discuss – Rosie had left her house to Gwen, and both Marge and Peggy wanted her to persuade Alistair to come back to London. 'It would be a waste of time,' she told them, 'his shop's established now, and this is where he wants to be. He was born and brought up in this house, and . . .'

'Oh, Gwennie!' Peggy burst out. 'It would be lovely if all

three of us could be together again.' Emotional tears coming to her eyes, she murmured, 'I'd better go to bed. See you in the morning.'

Gwen waited until she heard the upstairs door being closed. 'She still hasn't got over Alf and Mum, has she? But I'm glad she's gone, so I can tell you the bad news at last.'

A crease furrowed Marge's smooth forehead. 'What bad news?'

'Do you remember Ken Partridge giving David a camera?'

'Yes of course, and he took some jolly good snaps.'

'Yes, of all of us . . . including Ken.'

It took a minute for the significance of this to sink in. 'You mean he showed them to Alistair? How awful for you. What did you . . . ?'

'He got it all wrong. He asked David what colour Ken's hair was, and he's convinced it was you and Ken . . .'

'Good Lord, Gwen! Good Lord!'

'I swore to him that you'd never been unfaithful to Dougal . . .'

'Which was the truth.' Marge's smile was a little crooked.

'But he won't believe it. He's positive . . . you and Ken . . .'

'He's not likely to tell Dougal, is he?'

'I don't know, honestly. When we were there for the funerals, he promised me he wouldn't say anything, but now they're out together, God knows . . .'

'He wouldn't say anything in front of the boys?'

'He's been so different since he came home from the war, I don't know what he'll do.'

'Well, Gwendoline, I'm afraid the only thing we can do is keep our fingers crossed. I doubt if even God would help us now, after the things we did.'

'Oh, Marge,' Gwen gulped, 'I don't know how you can be so calm.'

'Getting in a paddy's not going to change anything, is it?'

*   *   *

384

With David pointing out rabbit holes to Nicky, explaining about the lichen on the trees, showing him a badger's sett, and generally keeping well away from the two men, Alistair decided to take the bull by the horns. It was now . . . or never!

'Nicky's getting to be a nice looking lad,' he began.

'Aye,' laughed Dougal, 'nothing like his father, eh?'

'No, nothing like *you*,' Alistair said quietly, then added, 'but very like his father.'

Dougal's face darkened. 'What the hell d'you mean by that?'

'I'm sorry, but I think it's time you knew. His father was a soldier Marge met during the war. He was stationed at Ardley House and they . . .'

· 'For Christ's sake, man! You're mad! Absolutely raving. I was home on leave . . .'

Alistair nodded morosely. 'Round about the right time? What if you were? How long had you been married without having any children? Have you never had doubts?'

'Never. Christ, Ally, I trusted Marge. She wouldn't have been unfaithful . . .'

'Wouldn't she? I'll have to get David to show you the snaps he took.'

'Photographs won't prove anything.'

'Wait till you see them.' Alistair had heard the doubt creeping into Dougal's voice and recognized it dawning in his eyes. He didn't relish what he was doing, but it had to be done. No man worth his salt could let his best friend go through life thinking he had a son when he hadn't. He should be grateful.

Each wrapped in his own thoughts – Alistair in self-righteousness, Dougal in outraged disbelief and anger – they made the walk back without saying another word, except if either of the boys asked them something.

*   *   *

385

The minute the men walked in, both wives could tell that something was wrong between them, and when Alistair asked David to bring down his old snaps, Gwen knew that this was it for her. She sought for Marge's hand to reassure her that *she* had no need to worry, but when Dougal went to the bathroom and Alistair's attention was on David, who had brought down the photographs, her sister managed to whisper, 'Leave all the talking to me, Gwennie.'

Waiting until Dougal came back, Marge said, brightly, 'May I see those snaps after you, please? David took them during the war and I'd completely forgotten about them.'

Gwen held her breath. Dougal's expression had lightened, but Alistair's was darker than ever, and he said, harshly, 'I'm surprised you forgot about your lover.'

Marge laughed gaily. 'My lover? Ken Partridge? He was never my lover. Yes, he came to the cottage nearly every week when he was stationed at Ardley, but only as a friend. He told us about his wife and family, and we told him about you two. And he was ever so good with Leila and David, giving them presents and . . .'

Trying to dispel the unpleasantness he could sense but couldn't understand, David butted in. 'He taught me how to hold a cricket bat properly, and how to bowl, and . . .'

His father turned on him angrily. 'Stay out of it, David! You don't know anything about this, so go upstairs and keep Nicky from coming down.'

The boy blanched and spun round, giving a last appealing glance at his mother before slamming the door behind him, but before she could say anything, Marge, who had been flicking through the photographs, held up the one which had caused all the trouble. 'Is this what's bothering you, Alistair?'

He seemed uncomfortable now. 'Well, do you see how he's looking at you? Like you were the only person in the world to him?'

'We were playing the fool for David,' she laughed. 'I said something funny and Ken was laughing at me, that's all.'

Alistair scowled. 'That maybe explains the photo, but it doesn't explain ...' He broke off to take a deep breath. 'Can you deny that *he* ...' he jabbed his finger on the shiny black and white card, 'is ... Nicky's ... father?' He turned desperately to Dougal. 'Look at it, man. Can't you see the resemblance? And David says *he* had ginger hair, as well!'

Gwen could stand it no longer. 'That's enough,' she said quietly. 'You're absolutely right. Ken *was* Nicky's father, but it's not Marge you should be accusing, it's me.'

Her husband whipped round to face her, the wounded shock in his eyes tearing at her heart. 'You? What in God's name are you saying?'

Marge stepped in again. 'Don't listen to her, Alistair! She's covering for me, but I admit it! Ken Partridge *was* my lover!'

'It's not true!' Gwen cried. 'It was me!' She gulped and ended, 'I'm Nicky's real mother, and ... Ken Partridge is his real father.'

The two men exchanged utterly shocked, perplexed looks, obviously wondering which of the women to believe, then Alistair said, bitterly, 'Gwen's telling the truth, Dougal. She wouldn't tell a lie like that.' His head drooped for a few seconds before he addressed himself to his sister-in-law. 'I can't tell you how sorry I am for causing you all this trouble, Marge, but I honestly did think ...'

'It's all right,' she told him, 'I can see why you made the mistake, but Gwen wasn't to blame for what happened. I made Ken take her out for a walk, and I should have realized they were both too vulnerable. He was going home on embarkation leave so it was his last night here, and ... well, she was upset about not hearing from you for so long, and surely . . . you can understand . . . and forgive?'

He glared at her and spat out, 'I can neither understand, nor forgive. The pair of you have made a fool of me all this time, and . . . oh God!' He shot a look of what might have been apology at his old friend and barged out.

Dougal regarded the two women with distaste. 'What am I supposed to do now? I've just learned that my son's not my son, and my wife isn't even his mother.' He glowered at Marge. 'That *is* true, I take it?' Her mute nod made him continue, 'Am I expected to carry on as if nothing had happened? Or am I meant to hand the boy over to Gwen? Damn it all, Marge! I love that kid! I can't just turn my back on him because you two played silly games when he was born. If Alistair hadn't seen that snap and stumbled on the truth, he wouldn't have been any the wiser, and no more would I.'

'That's true,' she admitted. 'And don't blame Gwen for that, either. It was my idea that she should hand her baby over to me – in fact, the whole plan was my idea.'

'I'll leave you to explain everything,' Gwen interrupted. 'I'd better go after Alistair.'

Guessing where her husband would be headed, she went up the rough track. She had been relieved when Dougal said that he loved Nicky – it meant that he wouldn't need much persuading to take the boy back to London – and she was almost sure that he and Marge could sort out their differences. After all, *she* hadn't been unfaithful. Her only sin lay in claiming that the child was hers and Dougal's.

Gwen had to go all the way up the hill before she saw Alistair, squatting on the stony ground beside the tower. 'I'm so sorry,' she muttered, stroking the crown of his head.

'Don't touch me!' he growled, jumping up and pushing her. 'How could you let me go on believing it was Marge, when all the time it was you! You and a ginger-headed soldier!

Get out of my sight, for I don't want you anywhere near me! Ever again!'

He gave her another shove, and knowing that any argument or attempt at explanation would be useless, she turned and retraced her steps. She deserved his scorn, his disgust. She had known all along, right from the night it happened, that Alistair would never forgive her if he found out.

She would have to face up to life without him ... and probably without her children, too. All three of them.

Chapter 27

❧

Lexie was on her way to lock the shop door when a woman with a vaguely familiar face walked in. 'My goodness!' the incomer exclaimed. 'It's not Lexie, is it?'

'Yes, I'm Lexie Fraser, but . . . ?'

'You likely won't remember me. Nancy Lawrie . . .'

Her legs buckling, Lexie grabbed at the wooden counter. This was something she had never imagined, not in any of the various scenarios she'd played over in her mind. Was she about to learn where her father was?

The other woman was looking at her in some concern. 'Are you all right? I heard the police want to talk to me, but I wanted a quick word with Alec first. Is he handy?'

With a low moan, Lexie slid to her knees and, Nancy, running round the counter in consternation, half-lifted her on to the courtesy chair. 'I don't know what's wrong, but . . . look, I waited till nearly closing time, so what if I lock up and make some tea for you?'

Not waiting for an answer, she stepped back to turn the key in the lock, and then led her charge through to the house. While the tea was being made for her, Lexie took stock of her visitor. Nancy's figure was fuller than when she was a girl, but she still had the same almost jet black hair, with just a few silver strands showing in it, although it had been cut into a neat bob instead of hanging loose to her shoulders. Her face was rounder than Lexie remembered, her cheeks not quite so rosy, but her brown eyes were still as dark, with perhaps a hint of sadness in them now. That was natural, Lexie mused, for this must be the first time she'd come back to the village which had once been her home, and twenty years was a long time to be away, however well she was wearing.

'Are you feeling any better?' Nancy asked, handing her a steaming cup.

'Yes, thanks. I'm sorry I was . . .'

'It was my fault, a ghost from the past, but I only want to see your father.'

Lexie's mouth went dry again. 'He's not still with you?'

'Still?' Nancy was clearly puzzled. 'He never *was* with me, you should know that.'

Trying to swallow the bitter bile burning her throat, Lexie whispered, 'Didn't he run away to be with you?'

'Me and Alec? What on earth made you think that, Lexie?'

'They all said you were expecting to him, and that's why . . .'

'So the gossips got it cockeyed as usual. I *was* expecting, that was right, but not to Alec. He's the finest man I ever knew.'

This was not how his daughter regarded him, Lexie thought. He had abandoned his wife and child, whoever he had gone off with. There was still something she wanted answered, however, although she could scarcely bring herself to speak. 'But . . .,' she croaked, '. . . who was the father?'

Her face flushing, Nancy murmured, 'Tom Birnie.'

'The doctor?' Lexie gasped, unable to believe this.

So the story was told of how a forty-year-old doctor had taken advantage of a naïve seventeen-year-old girl, had sworn that he loved her, and she had believed every word.

'A month or so after I told him I was pregnant,' Nancy went on, 'he rented a room in Edinburgh for me, and said he'd come to see me as often as he could. He promised to marry me and buy us a decent house after his wife divorced him.'

'Did he keep any of his promises?'

'He came to see me once, then his wife's mother took ill, and she went to Stirling to look after her, so he wrote saying he couldn't tell her about me till the old woman was better. That was the last I heard from him.'

'I wouldn't have thought Dr Birnie would be so ... after he said he loved you?'

Nancy blew a derogatory raspberry. 'Some men swear they love a girl to get their evil way with her, but I was lucky, in a way. Tom had paid three months' rent for the room, and I got a job at the sheet music counter in Princes Street Woolies – that paid my keep and let me save a wee bit every week. The landlady, Mrs Will, was really good. When I'd to stop working, she let me have free board for helping in the house – she had other lodgers, you see – but she didn't really need help. She was a wee ball of energy.'

The tale went on and Lexie learned that when the baby was born, Mrs Will had looked after it so that Nancy could take another job. 'Was it a boy or a girl?' she asked.

'A boy. I called him Alexander, after your father.'

Lexie's heart, and her stomach, plummeted rapidly. If people knew that Nancy had called her son Alexander, they would be in no doubt as to who the father had been, but Nancy had noticed her discomfiture. 'I didn't know what to do when I found out I was expecting,' she explained, hastily. 'Tom swore it couldn't be his and I knew Ma and Da would wash their hands of me if they knew, so I was at my wits' end. Alec noticed I was crying one day and when he asked what was wrong, I just came out with it. He took me to Tom's house and threatened to tell his wife if he didn't take responsibility for what he'd done. That's what made

Tom get me the room, and I want to let your father know that things didn't turn out too badly for me, after all.'

'But he's not here!' Lexie burst out. 'He never came home from choir practice the night after you disappeared. That's why we all thought he'd gone to be with you.'

'But . . . but . . .' Nancy floundered, 'I didn't know. You've never heard from him?'

'Not a word, and it was really the finish of my mother. She was never very strong, if you remember, and after Dad went away, she just pined and pined. She'd nothing left in her to fight the cancer.'

A silence fell between them as her words dried up, each trying to find a reason why Alec Fraser had left his family, and two full minutes had passed when a loud rapping on the porch door made them both jump. 'I can't speak to anybody now,' Lexie whispered.

A second knock was followed by a man saying softly, 'Lexie?'

'It's the Detective Inspector,' she said in relief, rising to let him in.

Roddy Liddell came straight to the point when he saw her companion. 'You're Nancy Lawrie, I take it?'

'How did you know . . . ?'

'Someone told Constable Robbie that she had seen you going into the Post Office, so I came to make sure there was no mistake.'

'No mistake.' Nancy's smile, however, was somewhat forced. 'I can't think why the police want to see me, though, not after twenty years.'

'Yes, a search for you should have been instigated at the time,' he admitted.

With no prompting, Nancy launched into a brief outline of her story, after which he leaned back, sighing. 'I originally thought it was your body we'd found.' Nancy's strangled gasp made him add, 'I'm sorry. You obviously don't know about that.'

'I hadn't got round to telling her,' Lexie defended herself, 'and I always hoped it wasn't Nancy's, because it could have meant my father had killed her.'

Nancy took hold of her hand before saying, 'Alec hadn't it in him to kill a spider, let alone another human being. Your father was a gentleman, Lexie, a truly gentle man.'

Liddell politely refused Lexie's offer of tea, his mind too occupied with solving the crime. 'I wonder . . . ?' He looked at Nancy speculatively. 'Would there be any likelihood of the doctor – Birnie? – paying Lexie's father a large sum of money to keep his mouth shut and leave Forvit altogether?'

'I wouldn't put it past Tom to have tried,' Nancy said, 'but I can't see Alec taking it.'

'He wouldn't have taken money from anybody,' Lexie agreed.

'I remember you telling me that he hadn't even taken his bankbook with him,' the Inspector pointed out, 'and no money was missing from the shop or the church. Does that not suggest that he'd had ample funds to live on for some time? Of course, there's another side to the coin. Alec Fraser himself may have seen an opportunity to make some money. He could have blackmailed Birnie, threatened to get him struck off the medical register . . . a very lucrative, ongoing . . .'

He broke off, regarded the two outraged faces for a moment, then shook his head. 'I can see you don't think much of that idea, but you must agree that my best bet now is to find Birnie, and get the truth out of him.'

'If you're lucky,' Nancy put in. 'He doesn't know what truth is.'

Liddell turned to Lexie. 'We will keep up our appeal for information on your father's whereabouts . . .' He pulled pensively at his ear lobe. 'The thing is, twenty years on, it's going to be difficult, especially if he doesn't want to be found . . .' He got to his feet. 'I'll keep in touch, Lexie, and if either you or Miss Lawrie hear anything that could be of use, please let me know. No, don't get up, I'll see myself out.'

'He's nice,' Nancy remarked after he was gone, 'and he fancies you.'

'Don't be daft,' Lexie mumbled, but her blush revealed that she quite fancied him. 'It's getting late, you won't get a train back to Edinburgh from Aberdeen tonight. I'll make up a bed for you here, if you like.'

'No, it's all right. With that Inspector coming, I didn't get time to tell you the end of my story. After Alexander was born, I got a job in the office of a big furniture store, and . . . well, I married the manager a year later.'

Lexie clapped her hands. 'You're still together, I hope?'

'Still together and still in love . . . even after nearly eighteen years. We had a daughter – she'd have been fourteen in three weeks if she'd lived, but she died at three months.'

'Oh, Nancy, I'm so sorry.'

'It was hard at the time, but we got over the worst of it, and we had Alexander. Greig has been a wonderful father to him, and put him to George Herriot's and then on to St Andrews' University. He's studying law now, and seems to be doing very well.'

'So you're Mrs Greig . . . what?' Lexie wanted to know.

'I'm Mrs Greig Fleming, and proud of it.' Nancy gave a slightly embarrassed laugh. 'He's waiting in the hotel bar. He took me to Oldmeldrum to see my mother before we came to Forvit. You see, I started buying the *Aberdeen Press and Journal* to keep up with the north news, and I saw my father's death in it a few years ago. I took a note of the address, but I couldn't pluck up the courage to write to

Ma. Then, when I heard the bobbies were looking for me, Greig said we could do the two things in one go.'

'What did your mother say when she saw you?'

'She broke down, Lexie, and everything's just fine between us again. She asked us to go back and spend the night there.' She swallowed then continued, 'I'll only need to find out where Alec is to make my happiness complete.'

'The police are doing all they can.'

'Aye. Anyway, I'd better get going. Cheerio, Lexie, and I'll keep in touch.'

Of the six persons in Benview that night, one slept soundly, three somewhat fitfully and two didn't even try. Nicky was completely ignorant of the trauma which had laid bare the true facts of his birth, David and Leila suspected that trouble was brewing and Peggy had been aware before she went to bed that something was not as it should be. She would have been horrified to learn that her sisters had sat up all night wondering when their men would return, and, as time went on, *if* they would return at all.

'I'm nearly sure Dougal won't hold anything against me,' Marge observed at one point. 'He'll come round once he's got over the shock. He loves Nicky like he *was* his father, and that won't change.'

Gwen shook her head. 'Did you see Alistair's face when I said . . . He'd been so sure it was you who . . .' A sob came into her voice now. 'He thought it was his duty to let his old friend know the truth, and he didn't consider how Dougal would feel.'

'He knows how it feels himself now, though,' Marge said, somewhat drily. 'If only I hadn't interfered. I should have guessed what would happen. Both you and Ken in an emotional state and being paired off like that . . . it *had* to come. Don't blame yourself, Gwennie. If it had been me, I'd likely have done it months before.'

Gwen dabbed her eyes with the tight wad of damp handkerchief. 'I know you're trying to make me feel better, Marge, but it's not helping. There's no excuse for what I did and I'll have to take my punishment for it.'

'But it was me who made you hide it,' Marge burst out. 'I made you play along with a stupid plot that couldn't possibly stay hidden for ever . . .' She paused, then added, with a glimmer of a smile at her lips, '. . . though we might have got away with it if David hadn't kept those dashed snaps.'

'No, that wasn't what did it. Alistair has suspected for a long time that Dougal wasn't Nicky's father, but he never had any doubt about you being his mother. He . . . he trusted me, that's why he's so upset.'

Raising her eyebrows, Marge asked, 'Would you rather we hadn't pretended? Would you have preferred if I'd let you write to Alistair to tell him you'd had a baby to another man? Or would you have waited and sprung it on him when he came home?'

'I don't know. It would have hurt him just as much whenever I told him, wouldn't it?'

'Since we're being honest, I guess you're right. On the other hand, maybe it hit him harder because he practically found out for himself. The only difference I can see is that if you'd told him at the time, he might have learned to accept it before he came home. Time does blunt . . .'

'But he was a prisoner of war and I couldn't . . .'

'You didn't know he was a prisoner. You just hadn't heard from him for a long time, then you were told he was missing and you thought he might have been killed. Maybe you hoped . . .' She clapped her free hand over her errant mouth. 'I'm sorry, Gwennie, I didn't mean that.'

'I never wished him dead, if that's what you were going to

say, but I ... did sometimes wish the baby wouldn't live. I know I wouldn't hear of an abortion, but now you know.'

Marge looked her straight in the eye. 'I'd better tell you that I often wished the same thing, so now *you* know, too.'

Needing both shaking hands to steady the glass Marge had given her some time ago, Gwen took a good gulp of the neat whisky, hoping that it would give her the strength to survive this terrible ordeal. Not being a drinker, however, the fiery liquor almost took her breath away, and a few seconds passed before she managed a hoarse, 'Marge, do you think Alistair will ever forgive me?'

'I'd love to say yes, but I doubt it. Maybe you should come back to London with us for a while, to let him ... you know, start missing you. That might do the trick.'

Gwen mulled this over for a few moments, then shook her head. 'I'd rather not leave him, not in the state he's in. Mind you, I wouldn't be surprised if he throws me out when he comes back, but I don't want to depend on you and Peg.'

'Are you forgetting Mum's house is yours now?' Marge's voice now became sharply sarcastic. 'You can settle in there and brood for as long as you like.'

They sat back, thoughts running on much the same lines, although one was confident that her husband would forgive her for her part in the deception, while the other was equally positive that hers would not.

Dougal picked up a stone and flung it as far as he could. 'What are you thinking, Ally?'

'What d'you think I'm thinking? God Almighty, man, you've no idea how it feels to find out my wife's had a son to somebody else when I was rotting in a prison camp!'

'I do know, Ally. The same as I felt when you told me it was Marge – like the bottom of my stomach had fallen out, like somebody had stuck a dagger in my bloody guts and was twisting it round and round to dig out my heart. That's it, isn't it?'

Alistair's head-shake was an agreement. 'I never thought how it would affect you. I was positive it was Marge ... and I thought you should know. I'm sorry. I wish to God I hadn't opened my big mouth. Your life would have gone on as usual and I'd have been glad it wasn't my wife that ...'

'Stop tormenting yourself, Ally. Things were different during the war. Didn't you ever have a wee fling yourself?'

'Never. Did you?'

'A bit of flirting. I did go all the way once, but we'd both been soaking up the drink like sponges and it didn't mean a thing.'

'I'm not like you,' Alistair said, morosely. 'I never let myself get in a position to be tempted.'

Shrugging at this, Dougal picked up another stone and sent it flying down the hill. 'We'd better get back. They'll be wondering where we are.'

'Before we go, are you going to ... the boy, now you know he's not yours?'

Dougal's head swivelled round abruptly. 'Why? Do you want him?'

'God, no! I'll never be able to live with Gwen again, never mind her ... bastard.'

'Come now, Ally, that's a bit much. You're not going to leave her, are you?'

'Why should I leave? She's the one who did wrong.' Alistair reflected for a short time, then said, 'You go on back. I've still a lot of thinking to do.'

Dougal got to his feet reluctantly. 'You're not going to do anything stupid, I hope?'

'I'm not that daft. Go on, and say I want to be on my own for a while.'

Listening to the steadily diminishing sound of Dougal's feet, Alistair knew that he should make a decision, but his whole body was ice-cold and his brain was frozen solid. New thoughts were an impossibility. All he could do was go over what had happened a few hours ago ... though it felt like a lifetime.

Recalling it only increased the ache in his heart, brought nausea and a desperate wish for oblivion. He couldn't cope with this. What was he supposed to do? Gwen couldn't really expect him to forgive her. Conceiving another man's child was bad enough, but letting her sister pass it off as hers was a thousand times worse. It was the deception that stuck in his craw, and the years they'd kept him in ignorance, made a proper fool of him.

Small flecks of light in the sky foretelling imminent dawn, he stood up stiffly, flexing all his joints to get them to move. He couldn't go home. He couldn't face any of them. He wouldn't be able to face anybody ever again. After a few tottery steps round the tower, he took up his stance at the other side, looking across at the dark silhouettes of the mountains in the distance, the bens he knew and loved, waiting for some sign of what he should do.

Dougal shook his head when he returned to Benview. 'You'd better get some sleep, Gwen. He said he needed time to think, and I doubt if he'll come back tonight.'

'Tonight's past already,' Marge muttered. 'It's nearly five tomorrow morning.'

He turned on her angrily. 'Trust you to make a joke at a time like this. And you'd better go to bed as well, because I'm going out again, and I probably won't come back till some time tomorrow either – later on today,' he added, to make sure she understood.

Outside again, shivering, he took his coat from the boot of his car, but in the act of putting it on, he wondered if he should go back inside to take one for Alistair, who was also out there in the cold, coatless. But if he went in again, he might say things in his bitterness that he would later regret, though both women deserved all the venom he could hurl at them.

As he stumbled up the uneven path again, it occurred to him that he should be thankful that it wasn't *his* wife who'd been unfaithful, but the thought didn't ease the aching void inside him. The circumstances had been such that Gwen's adultery was understandable, if not excusable, but what Marge had done had taken hours of planning. She had calmly plotted out a way to deceive not only her sister's husband but also her own, and would have got away with it if it hadn't been for some old photographs.

He could hardly believe how gullible he'd been. Fancy believing he'd managed to father a child after all the years he'd tried ... but Marge wasn't Nicky's mother, either. If he was sterile, she was barren. What a combination! Yet ... he was sure that she loved the boy as much as he did. They couldn't give him up, even if Alistair was willing to accept him, which wasn't likely. There was, of course, the inevitable doubt. Could *he* still look on Nicky in the same way as before? Could he maintain the same relationship with his wife? Wouldn't the thought of her scheming always come to the forefront of his mind, to cast up if she did anything to displease him in future?

He looked up, expecting to find his friend sitting by the tower, but there was no one there. In any case, would they still be friends, or would Alistair cut himself off from all further contact? The only way to find out would be to ask him, but where was he?

For God's sake! Where was he?

Chapter 28

❧

Nancy Lawrie had left hours ago, yet Lexie Fraser still couldn't get over the shock, a double shock, in fact. Her first thought was that she would learn where her father had been all those years, that he was alive and well, and it had been a terrible disappointment when the woman couldn't tell her. Despite having always voiced her belief that he hadn't run off with a young girl, as Nancy had been then, it was worse to have it proved and not to know why he had vanished so abruptly . . . so completely.

After striving for some time to find an acceptable answer, it had crossed her mind that he might have been involved with a woman nearer his own age, but it couldn't have been anybody from around Forvit – nobody else had ever gone missing. The thing was, he had hardly ever gone anywhere, just a day in Aberdeen now and then on business. He could have met somebody there, of course, but it didn't seem likely – he had never stayed away long enough.

Lexie had convinced herself once more, however, that there had been no other woman. There must be some truth in her nightmares, but why had he raped her? Had his wife's illness affected her before they knew she was ill? If she'd been refusing him his rights, would his growing frustration have culminated in turning to his daughter? He had always been a loving father, had cuddled her much more than her mother ever had, had only stopped taking her on his knee when she left school at fourteen. She had accepted it as natural, but now she came to think about it, none of the other girls had ever said *her* father still took her on his knee. Her stomach lurching, Lexie mentally scolded herself for being so naïve, and for so long. She was thirty-six now, for goodness' sake, and it should have dawned on her years ago.

Another possible reason for his disappearance struck her now – more sinister but less hurtful to herself. When Roddy Liddell learned that Nancy was alive, he had jumped to the conclusion that the body unearthed by the excavators must be one of the travelling people, and working on that might be worth a try. Her father had been a compassionate man, so if he'd come across a gypsy girl in some sort of trouble, he would have tried to do something to help her, and it was well known that gypsy men were jealous-minded and fiery-tempered. If one of them found his woman with another man, no matter how innocently, that could have been enough to make him kill her.

Lexie took in a shuddering breath. That would explain the female body, and it was just possible that the man might have . . . she'd heard of people being abducted by the gypsies. Or they could have threatened to kill him, which would explain him running away. Trying to moisten her lips, she discovered that her tongue was just as dry, but she was sick of tea; she must have drunk gallons over the past few hours. She needed something stronger.

She never kept spirits in the house – Roddy Liddell wouldn't drink on duty and he was the only man who came to see her nowadays – so she made her way through to the shop on legs that felt as if they were attached to her body by pieces of elastic. She switched on the light and was so engrossed in choosing between Glenfiddich or 5-Star Cognac that the imperative knock on the shop door almost made the two bottles slip through her fingers. Her nerves were in such a state that she couldn't face speaking to anyone – whoever

404

it was shouldn't expect to be served in the middle of the night even though she was behind the counter – but a hoarse voice hissed through the letterbox, 'It's Alistair, Lexie.'

Her hand shook as she turned the key in the lock, and he barged right past her and through to the house before she could utter a word. Locking the shop door and switching off the light again, she supposed that he had heard what had happened and had come to discuss what it meant to her.

'Oh, God, it's awful!' he moaned, when she joined him in her kitchen.

'I still can't take it in properly,' she agreed, before she noticed how strangely he was looking at her. 'How did you find out?'

His expression hardened. 'How long have *you* known?'

'Since just before six, and when the police inspector came . . .'

'Police?' he exclaimed. 'What have the police got to do with it?'

'He thought the body was Nancy Lawrie, so when somebody told him they'd seen her coming here . . .' His stunned expression made her say, sharply, 'You didn't know about her turning up again? What did you come for, then?'

He seemed to search for a reply, then, his voice hoarse and strained, he put forward another question. 'Didn't your father come with her?'

'You'll never believe this . . .' she began, but before she could tell him anything, her knees gave way and she thumped down on the sofa.

'Lexie, I'm sorry,' Alistair muttered. 'I wouldn't have forced my way in if I'd . . .'

Her attempted smile didn't reach her eyes, 'I need a drink. That's why I was in the shop . . . will you get the bottle of brandy I left on the counter?'

He dashed through to fetch it, took two glasses from the

cupboard she indicated with her hand, and sat down beside her. 'Has something happened to Alec – is he ill? Is that why she came?'

She took one good sip to fortify her, and let it swirl around in her mouth before swallowing it with a grimacing shudder. 'He was never with her. He never had anything to do with her. It wasn't his baby she was having, it was Doctor Birnie's.'

His own troubles fading, Alistair's eyes widened in disbelief. 'Doctor Tom? All I can remember about him was he was tall, and kind of good-looking, and he surely wouldn't have needed to take up with a young lassie. His wife was a right bonnie woman, though she was middle-aged. Her hair was a lovely wavy chestnut, and her eyes were dark brown and looked at you as if you meant something to her. I'd a bit of a crush on her when I was about thirteen or so.'

Stuck for something else to say, he added, 'Maybe she wasn't as old as that. I suppose everybody over twenty was middle-aged to me at that age.'

At that moment, someone knocked on the kitchen window and, noticing Lexie's apprehension, he asked, gently, 'Will I open the door, or . . . ?'

'It's Dougal Finnie, Lexie,' came a deep voice. 'Is Alistair there?'

Alistair rose and went to the door, but to save Dougal blurting out what had happened at Benview earlier, he said, as he let him in, 'Lexie's had a bit of a shock. Nancy Lawrie came to see her today and Alec didn't run away with her, after all.'

'My God! So where did he go?'

Her mind and emotions in utter turmoil, Lexie accepted Dougal's presence without question and answered him herself. 'She thought he was still here. She wanted to speak to him. I was just going to tell Alistair . . .'

The two men listened, spellbound, as the sorry tale

unfolded, not saying a word in case they dammed the flow, but when she finally said, 'And that's all I know,' Dougal murmured, 'It's a funny business, isn't it? You've no idea what made your father . . . ?'

She related what had been going through her mind during the hours she had been sitting alone, but when she mentioned the likelihood of him being threatened by an angry gypsy, Alistair soothed, 'No, Lexie! Your father wouldn't . . . there must be some other explanation. Maybe he *did* meet a woman in Aberdeen . . .' He stopped abruptly. 'You said the police inspector had been here last night again. What did he have to say?'

'They're going to start a proper search for him, but I don't think they'll ever . . .'

Dougal gave a slightly anxious cough. 'Ally, I think it's time we were going. We've still some things to sort out ourselves.'

Alistair scowled. 'We can't leave Lexie in this state.' He turned to her solicitously. 'We'll stay as long as you want.'

'Your wives'll wonder where you are.'

The two men exchanged cautious glances, then Dougal said, 'There was a wee bit a row, that's why we came out, and they won't expect us till we show up.'

'No, off you go,' she murmured. 'I'll be OK. I'll have to open the shop in a couple of hours anyway for the newspapers. The van'll be here any time now.'

Alistair was not particularly keen on returning to face the music, but he bowed to Lexie's wishes and left quietly, for which she was truly grateful. She was glad she'd had someone to talk to, more than glad that it had been Alistair and Dougal, but was relieved that they had gone now. She had to open the shop soon; she couldn't let her customers down.

She busied herself tidying up the kitchen and giving the room a perfunctory sweep and dust before she went upstairs to wash herself and change her clothes. Downstairs again, she felt a bit peckish and made a couple of slices of toast and a cup of cocoa to wash them down. It was while she was rinsing her dishes that the question arose in her mind. Why had Alistair come to see her? He hadn't known about Nancy Lawrie, and Dougal had said something about a row. But who had the row been between? Not Alistair and Dougal, they had still been very friendly. Gwen and Marge?

Come to think of it, though, it was Dougal who had been most eager to get back to Benview, so maybe the quarrel had been between him and Marge. Maybe he'd walked out on his family, just like her father had walked out on his twenty years ago? Maybe poor Marge was crying her eyes out right now. But that wouldn't have made Alistair come to see her ... unless he and Gwen had fallen out about it.

Everything tidy, she went to the mirror to give her face a light rub of pancake make-up and apply a touch of lipstick before opening the shop. Whatever had happened in the past, she reflected as she turned the key in the lock, all she could do now was to wait and see if anything came of the police search for her father.

'Look Ally,' Dougal observed as they walked along the road, 'I know you feel sorry for Lexie, but you'd better steer clear of her. You've your own life to sort out.'

'Aye.'

'What are you going to do about Gwen?'

'God knows.'

'It's not up to Him, though, it's up to you! Either you let things go and carry on as you were, or ...'

'Or?'

'For any sake, Ally! Do you want me to make your mind up for you? If you can't bring yourself to understand how it happened and forgive her, you'll have to leave her, or tell her to get out. Gee yourself, man!'

Alistair stopped walking and looked pathetically at his friend. 'I can't forgive her, Dougal, and I'll never forget what she did.'

'Nobody's asking you to forget, but if I can forgive Marge for telling me lies . . .'

'That's a different thing! She didn't have another man's child.'

'Granted, but telling me I was the father of another man's child was just about as bad, wouldn't you say?' Dougal stretched out his arm to pat his friend on the back. 'Let it go, Ally. Don't ruin your children's lives as well as your own and Gwen's. Be . . . what's the word? Magnanimous, I think. Try, I know it'll be hard, but it's the best way.' Getting no reply, he deemed it wise to leave Alistair to work it out for himself.

As it happened, the decision was taken for him. When they went into the house, a row of cases and bags was sitting in the porch, and the three women were silent and tearful.

'What's going on?' Dougal asked Marge.

'Gwen's coming back with us . . . and no arguing!'

He turned to Alistair, waiting for him to plead with his wife to stay, but he snarled, 'Good! That saves me throwing you out!' Then he spun round and stalked through the door again.

'It's OK, Dougal,' Gwen muttered, 'he's made it plain that he wants me to leave. I know what I'm doing, and Leila and David will be all right. Their lives are here. Now there's no more to be said, but if you want some breakfast before we go . . . ?'

'I'm not hungry.'

'Let's get the car packed, then. That's if . . . will it be too tight a squeeze with an extra passenger and more luggage?'

'We'll manage.' Dougal's voice was gruff.

Everyone was upset by the time the car was loaded, including little Nicky, who could sense the drama around him, and as they drew away from the house, even the four adults had to fight back the tears.

Chapter 29

∽

In bed by herself for the first time since Alistair had come home from the war, Gwen lay staring at the ceiling, the ache in her heart too great for sleep although she was physically exhausted. She would have liked to forget the past twenty-something hours – or thirty-something or forty-something, whichever it was – to expunge them from her memory for ever, but she couldn't. It was like having a cavity in her tooth and, in spite of the pain it caused, being unable to keep her tongue from probing inside, or, when she was small, like picking at the scar of an earlier injury and making it take all the longer to heal.

After trying everything she could to make her change her mind, Marge had conceded that it was Gwen's choice and let the subject drop, and Dougal had carried the bag out to his car. He, too, had been against her running off, urging her to wait until she had talked things over with her husband at least one more time, but she couldn't bear the idea of having to face Alistair again. And, unable to budge her on this, Marge had made her family's breakfast before rousing Peggy.

Their youngest sister had been horrified at what had gone on while she was asleep, but her fury was directed at Gwen for what she had done, not at Alistair for not trying to understand. The quarrel which had ensued had wakened Leila, whose face had blanched when she heard the reason for it. 'When I saw Nicky at Grandma's funeral, I said he was like Ken. I told you on the train home, remember, Mum?'

Recalling it, Gwen felt worse than ever. She had never dreamt that her daughter suspected anything, but, bless her heart, Leila hadn't turned against her. Through her tears, she had said, 'If it wasn't that I don't want to be hundreds of miles away from Barry, I'd come with you.'

At this, Dougal had pulled a face. 'There wouldn't have been room for you, Leila. It's going to be hard enough to pack everybody in as it is, plus all the luggage.'

By the time two cases had been strapped to the roof rack, and as many of the bags, cases and parcels as possible in the boot, the two boys had appeared, and Leila, guessing that the adults wouldn't want Nicky to hear anything, took him upstairs again to make sure he hadn't left any of the comics and toys he had arrived with.

It had been left to Gwen to tell David, and her fragile composure had almost snapped at the sight of his stricken face. 'I don't know if you can understand why,' she ended, 'but I'm going back to London to live in Grandma's house. She left it to me.'

'Yes, I understand.' His voice, beginning to deepen anyway, had cracked. 'But what about us? Leila and me? Where are we going to live?'

'I'll let you make your own choice,' Gwen had said, her own voice perilously near breaking. 'You both work in Aberdeen, so . . .' She had been unable to go on.

Because the car was packed to capacity and more – Gwen's travelling bag ended up sitting on the floor with Nicky's feet resting on it, and both she and Peggy nursing large carrier bags – the choice did not have to be made immediately, and Leila and David stood at the gate, white-faced and forlorn, as they waved goodbye.

They met Alistair halfway down the track, but he kept his head down even when Dougal drew his car to a halt. 'Drive on,' Gwen whispered, her heart so full she had nothing to say to her husband on perhaps the last time she would ever see him.

Dougal, however, obviously wanted to make Alistair squirm. Rolling down his window, he called, 'Your wife's in my car, man, heartbroken at having to leave her home and her children. I hope you're pleased with yourself.'

The other man making no sign of having heard, Dougal continued, 'Damn you, you selfish son-of-a-bitch!'

He had driven on then, his face scarlet, and they had soon left Forvit far behind, but cramped as they were, only young Nicky ever complained. They made the whole journey, all five hundred plus miles of it, in eighteen hours – including the stops due to the call of nature and to buy some sustenance to keep them going – with only a modicum of conversation between them.

Turning to her other side now, Gwen wondered if the pain in her limbs would ever go away. They had almost seized up when Dougal helped her out of the car, and no doubt Peggy would be the same. Her youngest sister hadn't spoken to her since they set out, and, quite possibly, Marge, too, would start resenting her for upsetting their lives. It was going to be hard on all of them with her living in the middle house, and how was she going to cope with seeing young Nicky every day and his carroty nob reminding her of who his father had been?

Marge had said they would leave her alone if that's what she wanted, and right now that's exactly what she wanted. She would have to come to terms with herself before she could face anyone else, and that was going to take some time. Then! What then? She couldn't expect Alistair to send her any money, so she would have to get a job of some kind, and she had never gone out to work before.

Dougal had made a stop in Lewisham to let them stock up on provisions, so she rose to make a cup of tea. She wasn't hungry, but she needed something to refresh her mouth. Looking at the little clock her mother had always had on the bedside table, she found that it was still only two o'clock – five hours short of two days since she left home. No, she corrected herself, home was here now ... but her thoughts were still in Forvit. Alistair would be getting up in a few hours, and Leila and David, breakfast would be the usual rush, without her to make sure they had everything, then they would all get in the car ...

She would have to stop this. She would never get over things if she carried on like this. Gulping down the lump of self-pity in her throat that threatened to choke her, she came to the conclusion that she would never get over anything anyway, not on her own. She couldn't appeal to Marge or Peggy for sympathy or advice, so who ...? Dear old Ivy had died over a year ago, and now there was absolutely nobody.

Then it struck her – Tilly Barker! After delivering Nicky, the midwife had become a good friend, and they had exchanged Christmas cards ever since. She had also written when Ivy died. Yes, Tilly would help her, Gwen decided ... if she had remembered to take her address book with her. Grabbing her handbag, she rummaged inside, casting aside letters from Marge as well as old electricity and gas bills. It flitted across her mind that Alistair would have to look after those now, but it didn't put her off her search. Just as she was thinking that she must have forgotten to put the little book back after she wrote her cards last Christmas, her fingers touched its imitation leather cover.

The decision made, she deemed it best to leave before the households on either side of her were stirring, and so it was that, if anyone had been in Woodyates Road ten minutes later, he or she would have seen her closing her house door very carefully to prevent any noisy click, creeping furtively down the garden path and being equally cautious opening and closing the gate. Then, carrying the travelling bag she hadn't yet unpacked, she strode purposefully towards Burnt Ash Road and the railway station. She would be in King's Cross in no time, and even if she had to wait hours for a train to Newcastle, at least she wouldn't be seen there.

Alistair studied his son and daughter as they ate the toast he had made for them. By the look of them they'd had as little sleep as he had. Although he had found out, only by asking a direct question, that they knew everything, they hadn't mentioned their mother again, not even to condemn her or take her part. What was more, they had neither accused him of being cruel nor agreed that he had done the right thing. It was difficult to know what they were thinking, where he stood with them.

When he'd arrived back in the cottage two mornings ago, he could see that they were very upset, but they had kept themselves under control, even David, who was normally quicker to air his true feelings than Leila. They had both expressed their desire to go to work as usual, and he'd had to wait until evening before Leila told him that they were going to stay with him until they made up their minds what to do.

'I'm going steady with Barry Mearns,' she had told him with no sign of shyness, 'so I don't really want to leave, and David's in Forvit football team, so . . . well, we'll just wait and see what happens.'

And that was it – she wouldn't say another word. That evening, she had gone out to meet her lad as soon as she had tidied up the supper things, and David had gone out with his friends, so he himself would have been free to go to see Lexie, but it didn't feel right. It wasn't that he didn't want to see her, because he did, more than he had ever done in his whole life, but he was just managing, by the skin of his teeth, to keep himself under control at the moment, and it would only need one word of encouragement from her . . . If she gave way to her emotions and all, anything could happen, and he wasn't ready for any more complications in his life.

Of course, Lexie didn't know yet about Gwen, but no doubt it would soon get round the place that his wife had left him, and he'd have to make it known that *he* was the innocent party and had wanted her to go. It made no real difference, of course, for either way, they would know that another man was involved. He could practically hear Lizzie Wilkie's mother and her cronies. 'That's what comes o' takin' up wi' they English dirt.'

And the reply would be, 'Aye, they're nae like Forvit lassies.'

But surely at least one of the women would stick up for Gwen? Say something like, 'But Alistair Ritchie's wife wasna as flighty as her sister.'

That was what kept niggling at him, eating away at his self-esteem. Gwen had always been content to sit at home every night with her husband and children, both before and after the war. She had never looked at another man . . . so what had been so special about 'Uncle Ken'? It probably hadn't been all her fault, of course, the man could have put pressure on her. Knowing how genuine she was, he could have set himself out to push down her barriers, to get her to fall for him. Making up to her children would have been the first step, and sympathizing about not hearing from her husband, until, being the kind of person she was, the liking had turned to loving and she'd have been putty in his hands. That was how it had been, and nobody could tell him they'd only been together once. Marge was as bad, of course, thinking up lies to cover up for her, and spinning absolute whoppers after the child was born. He still couldn't understand Gwen agreeing to a deception like that.

Yet ... if she had written and told him instead of letting him find out for himself, would he have forgiven her? He didn't think so. He'd have been taken prisoner before he got such a letter, as low as he could be, so what would that have done to him? He'd have felt like doing himself in, that was what – so he should be grateful that she hadn't mentioned it. What if she had told him after he was repatriated? How would he have felt then? He would have arrived home a physical wreck to a wife he hadn't seen in three years to find her holding a two-year-old kid. It might have taken his befogged brain a few minutes to figure out it was another man's child, but once he did ... Christ! He'd have felt like doing *her* in!

His hands had been tied by the way it happened – to learn a thing like that in front of your best friend and his wife, in front of your own kids! Oh, he'd yelled at her, but if they'd been on their own it would have been different. He likely *would* have killed her, he'd been so angry. Any man would have been the same, especially when he had kept on the straight and narrow himself before he was sent overseas and captured.

God, what a bloody mess!

Having been half expecting Alistair to put in another appearance, Lexie answered the door with a smile which slipped a little when she saw Roddy Liddell. His visits were beginning to disconcert her, in more ways than one. 'I'm sorry to be bothering you so late,' he said, 'but there's something I must ask you. May I come in?'

She wondered what on earth he wanted to find out, for she had told him everything she knew, which wasn't much, but she didn't want to make him feel he was intruding. He had been a bit stiff towards her lately, for some reason.

When he was seated, he said, 'I know I've made a nuisance

of myself already, but I was going over the information we have so far, when something struck me.'

'Yes?' she ventured.

'When the body was found, the constable recorded that you were very shocked, that before he told you it was a woman, you thought it might be your father.'

'Yes?' Her deepening apprehension was evident in her voice.

'Had you any reason to think that it could have been your father?'

'Not really, but . . . he disappeared the day after Nancy, and everybody thought . . . but it wasn't my father's child she was carrying, it was the doctor's.'

'Yes, I remember – Tom Birnie.' Liddell rubbed his left hand across his mouth. 'Could there possibly have been anything between Mrs Birnie and your father?'

'Oh no! They knew each other, of course. He was choirmaster at the kirk, and she was one of the contraltos, but that was all. There was never any gossip about them, and she went to Stirling to look after her mother.'

'So her husband made out, but he wouldn't want it known that she had left him.'

'No, I'm positive my father wasn't carrying on with Mrs Birnie.' Gulping, she went on, 'I wish I knew where he was and why . . .' She broke off, too overcome to continue.

'I didn't mean to upset you,' the man began, 'that's the last thing I'd want to do, Lexie.'

'Is it Roddy?' she managed to whisper, her heart hammering against her ribs.

'Yes,' he replied, and then his manner changed abruptly. 'I must get to the bottom of the mysteries surrounding this murder. I must keep an open mind. I hope you understand.'

When she locked the door behind him a few minutes later, she sat down at the fire again. She did understand.

She, too, felt that the slate would have to be wiped clean, otherwise there would always be a restraint, a barrier, between them.

Gwen hired a cab to take her from Newcastle to Moltby, praying as it took her out of the city that Tilly hadn't moved. Her limbs were trembling as she pressed the doorbell, but Tilly's smiling welcome, astonished but warm, dispelled her fears. 'Gwen Ritchie! Oh, my dear, what's happened? I can see there's something.'

Despite feeling that what she was about to confess could turn Tilly against her, too, Gwen told her everything, the tears coming in fits and starts as she spoke, and she was grateful that her listener did not interrupt. 'I don't know what you think of me now,' she ended. 'I'll understand if you tell me to leave.'

'Leave?' Tilly cried. 'Why would I do that? You told me at the time that the baby wasn't your husband's. Quite a few of the children I brought into the world during the war were mistakes, and . . .'

'But the lies I'd to tell?'

'I can understand the need for them. I was lucky, you know. I got involved with an American marine not long after you went home. He was a real film-star type, and it was his voice that got me – such a gorgeous drawl, deep and sexy.' She laughed at the astonishment on Gwen's face. 'I met him at a dance, his name was Grover, he must have been six foot five or six, and I fell for him like I was a teenager again, and me in my thirties.'

'But you didn't . . . ?'

'Lots of times, but, like I said, I was lucky, which was a blessing. I couldn't have passed a child of his off as Fred's.' She stopped, then finished with a twinkle in her eyes and a

419

huge grin all over her round face, 'You see, he was black.'

'Oh, Tilly!'

'That shocked you? I bet you don't feel so bad now about your little affair, eh?'

'I can't believe you actually ... Don't you feel guilty at all?'

Tilly pulled a face. 'I did at first, but Fred was a warden and often out all night, and in any case, I discovered ... well, to put it bluntly, it had put a bit of ginger into my relations with Fred. So, good came from ... I was going to say, from evil, but I never felt I was doing anything wrong.'

'What I did was a lot worse. It was the lies that got to Alistair, the not owning up to Nicky being mine. I was scared to tell the truth in case I spoiled my marriage, but in the end, I destroyed it completely, and very nearly Marge's, as well.' She fell silent, then, after a few moments, she asked, 'Did your Fred never suspect anything? Didn't he wonder why ... like you said, there was more ginger in your relationship?'

'If he did, he didn't say anything, just enjoyed it.'

Gwen managed a weak smile. 'Tilly, I hope you don't mind, but ...'

'Yes, you can stop here for as long as you like.'

'How did you know ... ?'

'I'm not psychic, it was just a matter of logic. You hadn't anywhere to go when your husband put you out ...'

Gwen told her about the house in Lee Green and went on, 'But I couldn't stay there with my sisters so close, and Peggy wasn't very friendly, and I needed somebody to talk to ... but what will Fred say?'

'Fred won't say anything. He's not a bad old stick, though he sometimes goes down the pub and comes back smelling like a knocking shop. You're welcome to stay here till you sort things out.'

'I don't know if they'll ever sort out,' Gwen muttered.

'It don't matter,' Tilly beamed. 'You can move in altogether if you like.'

Lexie wasn't surprised by the phone call from Nancy Lawrie – she'd never be able to think of her as Mrs Fleming – but she *was* surprised by what she said.

'I've just thought, Lexie . . . oh, you'll likely say I'm off my rocker, but it's worth a try.'

'But . . . but . . . ? I don't understand.'

'Listen. Why don't I put an advert in one of the Scottish papers for information as to the whereabouts of Alec Fraser, at one time resident in Forvit, Aberdeenshire?'

'But the police haven't had any reply to their appeals.'

'That's the point! Some folk are scared to have anything to do with the police, but they might answer a newspaper ad. D'you see what I mean?'

At a loss to know what to think, Lexie said, miserably, 'I'm not sure.'

'You don't sound very keen. Don't you want to find your father?'

'I do, but . . . shouldn't we leave it to the police?' Lexie couldn't understand what was wrong with her. Was she afraid to know the truth? Was that why she was holding back?

'They haven't done very much so far, have they? Look, I'll put in a full description. Somebody must know where he is, even if he's changed his name.'

She couldn't catch Nancy's enthusiasm. She *wasn't* keen on finding her father . . . not after what he had done to her . . . or what she thought he had done to her. She had read once that a dream meant the opposite of what had happened or was going to happen, so maybe her nightmares didn't mean a thing. She had never actually remembered a face, or anything definite, and she could be wrong. She had taken a sleeping tablet, and it could all just be her imagination. 'All right, Nancy,' she mumbled.

'You want me to go ahead? I'm sure it'll work, Lexie, I know somebody's going to get in touch with me, and I'll let you know the minute they do.'

Disconnecting the line, Lexie guessed that Nancy would have carried out her plan whether or not it had been agreed on. As she had said, it was worth a try, and no harm would be done if nothing came of it.

Chapter 30

❧

If she hadn't left a note saying that she was going away and didn't know when she would be back, Marge Finnie and Peggy Pryor would have been extremely worried about their sister. As it was, they couldn't understand her reason for it.

'What does she mean she needs to get some peace?' Peggy wailed. 'We weren't going to pester her.'

'She should have known that. I told her we'd leave her alone, if that's what she wanted, and we didn't go near her.' Marge looked pensively at the small sheet of paper. 'Should I let Alistair know she's gone?'

'It's up to you, but I don't think he'd care – not the way he was when we left.'

'He's had time to think, though. He'll blame us if anything happens to her.'

Peggy scowled at this. 'It's not our fault. She's thirty-six, for goodness' sake . . . old enough to look after herself.'

'That's just it.' Marge shook her head sadly. 'She's never had to look after herself. She'd Mum and Dad at first, then she'd Alistair, and it was up to me in Forvit.'

Casting her eyes heavenwards, Peggy sneered, 'You didn't make a very good job of it, did you? You said yourself she wouldn't have gone out with that Ken Whatsit at all if you hadn't made her.'

Stung by her younger sister's sarcasm, Marge spat back, 'Well, if you're going to start casting things up, there's no more to be said, is there?'

They flounced back to their own homes and tackled their household chores with much vigour but little awareness of what they were doing, and it took Marge only about ten minutes to think better of her high-handed attitude. Gwen had every right to be alone if she wanted to; she certainly had a lot to think about, and she probably felt hemmed in having a sister living on either side of her, not that they would have pressurized her in any way, Marge assured herself. But it was easier for her. She had come off lightly, after all. Dougal was still a fraction cool towards her, but she was practically sure that he would understand the reason for what she did and would come round soon. He hadn't discussed it with her yet, of course, hadn't even mentioned it, but it was early days, and at least he hadn't changed towards young Nicky. That was the main thing.

As she so often did, Marge made an abrupt decision. What was the point of falling out with Peggy when they couldn't do anything about anything? What was done couldn't be undone, as their Mum used to say. If Gwen didn't want advice from her own sisters, that was that! They'd have to let her take her own time to come to terms with herself, wherever she was ... which was a mystery, for she didn't have Ivy to run to now.

Marge was about to pick up the telephone when it rang, making such a pang of guilty fear shoot through her that her hand hovered in the air for a second before she lifted the receiver, and she had never felt as thankful as she did when Peggy's voice said, 'I've just made a pot of tea ... are you coming round?'

Alistair's mind could cope with only one thing, and no matter how many angles he viewed it from, he couldn't bring himself to excuse his wife for what she had done. If only he'd had more time to talk it over with Dougal . . . though Dougal was bound to be biased. Gwen's adultery had given him the son he had longed for, so he wasn't likely to condemn her. He hadn't even condemned his own wife, in spite of her trying to shoulder the blame . . . and she *did* have a lot to answer for, both before and after the event, which, of course, could only be laid at Gwen's door.

A customer interrupted his thoughts at this point, and he gladly entered into a discussion about the watch she had brought in for repair. 'It hasn't varied a minute in the three years since my mother gave it to me for my twenty-first,' the smart young woman told him, 'and it just stopped with no warning, and I didn't overwind it. I've always been very careful about that.'

'It could be a speck of dirt,' Alistair suggested. 'That's the usual reason for a watch stopping. Or . . . what line of work are you in? It might be . . .'

She gave a wry laugh. 'You've probably hit the nail on the head, Mr Ritchie. I've only been teaching for six months, but I suppose it could be the chalk.'

Alistair forced a reassuring smile. 'Quite a few teachers come in with their watches clogged with chalk dust, and it's easily remedied. I'll give it a good clean and blow out and you can collect it in . . . say thirty minutes?'

'I'm on my dinner hour, so is it all right if I come in after school?'

'Yes, of course.'

'I'll be here about ten to four, then. I say, I like what you've done to your shop. It's much brighter now. See you.'

With the click of the door closing, his smile faded, and he looked around him with little interest. It was Leila who had gone at him for weeks about the front shop looking dingy. Neither he nor David had noticed; men didn't set the same store by appearances. The fittings were as they had been when he bought the place – previously a small wool shop – a solid wooden counter, wooden shelves on the walls, and it really had been dingy compared with what it was now.

It had all happened so quickly. Less than a month ago, a customer had happened to mention that another jeweller was about to retire and was letting all his glass cases go cheap for a quick sale. Leila had bullied him into buying the lot, and Barry and his cousin, an apprentice joiner, had worked the miracle. After painting the doors and walls, making the place look 100% better already, they whipped out the old wooden counter and shelves and fixed up their replacements over one Saturday evening and Sunday morning, and stayed all afternoon to help get all the glass cases spotlessly shining. Mickey, the cousin, had then gone off, whistling, to meet his girlfriend, but Barry had helped to set the stock of timepieces and jewellery out on display. It was a great improvement, Alistair conceded now, though it was a pity Gwen had never seen it.

He was kept fairly busy for the rest of that day, so it was not until he was home in Benview, and both Leila and David had gone out, that he had the chance to get back to his problem ... though he didn't look on it as a problem. Problems needed to be worked out, answers had to be found, decisions had to be taken, but ... he had already taken the decision, which was why he was sitting by himself in this remote cottage, sick to death of his own company and wondering if there was any point to life. Maybe he should have a night in the bar, drink until his brain was so pickled it wouldn't be able to think at all. But it probably wouldn't help. Nothing would help. That was the bloody awful thing!

He kept brooding for some time. He needed somebody to talk to, somebody who would listen and sympathize, somebody who could be objective, but he wouldn't find anybody like that in the bar. There was always Lexie, of course, but had she got over the shocks she'd had herself recently? In any case, wouldn't this give her the chance to sneer at him? His beloved wife giving herself to another man as soon as his back was turned?

But was it true? Marge had said she was the adulterer, and Gwen, being the older, had wanted to shield her. That was it, wasn't it? That was the kind of thing Gwen would do, and Marge had always been ... the flighty one, going dancing, having a good time. Marge wouldn't have pleaded guilty just to save her sister's marriage.

It was over an hour later, his mind having gone round and round so many times that he hardly knew what to think or what to feel, before it touched on something he should have remembered before. He hadn't long come back to Forvit to live, he had gone to the shop for cigarettes, and Lexie had flung it at him that she had once seen Gwen lying with a soldier up at the tower. When he refused to believe it, she had quickly said it might have been Marge, but he knew now. It *had* been Gwen.

He'd been a bit annoyed at Lexie for telling him at all, had put it down to yet another attempt to get him back – that was why he had buried it as deeply as he could – but she had only wanted him to know the truth about his wife. So that was it! No more touching on the possibility that she was innocent and he should ask her to come home; no more dreaming of a loving reconciliation; only the prospect of a long, lonely life without her.

He banked up the fire with dross, put on his jacket then remembered that he should leave word for Leila and David to let them know he had gone for a walk ... in case they got home before he did. If he came home at all.

* * *

427

Downhearted because she had heard nothing from either Nancy Lawrie or Roddy Liddell for a couple of days, Lexie wondered if the latest rumour she'd heard was true. It all stemmed from the postie claiming to have seen Dougal Finnie and his family early one morning that week in a car going towards Aberdeen. This in itself was strange, since Dougal had told her himself, when he came to buy some groceries, that they'd be here for the last week of his holidays and they'd brought Marge's other sister with them. What was even more peculiar, though, was what else Sandy Mearns had told his wife.

'He says there was twa cases strapped to the roof,' Aggie reported, 'an' the door o' the boot was held doon wi' string, so it had been packed that full they surely couldna shut it. Dougal's wife was sitting in the front, an' the youngest sister was in the back wi' Dougal's laddie in the middle, atween her and . . .' She gave a quick glance round to make sure that no one else had come into the shop before whispering, with obvious delight at having such juicy news to impart, '. . . atween her and Alistair Ritchie's wife.'

She paused to give her listener time to digest this, then added, 'Sandy says she could hardly see ower the top o' the bag she had on her knee, so me an' Lizzie Wilkie thinks she's left Alistair . . . for good.'

She had waited expectantly for a reaction, and then, disappointed at getting none, she had dropped her purse into her shopping bag and left, no doubt to pass on her gossip to the first person she met. But, Lexie thought now, it couldn't be true. Gwen wouldn't leave Alistair, and she certainly would never leave her bairns. Besides, if the car was as packed as Sandy had made out to Aggie, they couldn't be going as far as London; they wouldn't have room to move. Dougal must have been giving Gwen a lift to Aberdeen to do some shopping, that was all. As Nancy had complained the other day, gossips – and in particular, Forvit gossips – nearly always got things twisted.

The whole business was queer, though. Why would Dougal leave so soon? He had mentioned a row the other night – between him and Alistair? It couldn't have been the sisters, not when they were all squeezed in the car together. Had Alistair found out about Gwen's supposedly-non-existent baby and thrown her out? It was the only thing it could have been, and Marge had made Dougal take her back to London with them . . .

Lexie was mulling this over – she'd always been sure it was Gwen she had seen with a soldier – and feeling sorry for Alistair, when someone came to the door. With him uppermost in her mind, she jumped to the conclusion that he had come to confront her about what she had said, and wondered if she should let him in. There would likely be no reasoning with him, he might attack her. He might . . .

Her old nightmare returning, her heart palpitated wildly. She was back in that awful night, when another man – about the same age as Alistair was now – *had* raped her. That was why she couldn't bear anybody to touch her.

She didn't push the half-memories away now. She mentally laid them out and confronted them. She had to know all the whys and wherefores, but it was so long ago, it was difficult to separate fact from imagination. She had been in bed, that was fact. She had been naked . . . but was that imagination? It had seemed to her at the time that there were dozens of hands, touching, poking, prodding . . . then that thing . . . No, face up to it. She was old enough now to know what had been rammed inside her, that was fact, also the excruciating pain she had suffered. No one could imagine that!

She still couldn't picture a face, because she hadn't been able to open her eyes. Recreating the scene, she closed them now, and that was when she heard the hoarse whisper.

'*The sins of the fathers shall be . . .*' She couldn't make out the next bit, but it had ended, '*until the third and fourth generation.*'

What did it mean? Had her father been chanting about the sin he was in the act of perpetrating at the time? He'd certainly known the Bible inside out.

A chill seemed to settle over her; it wasn't only her limbs that were trembling. She pulled her cardigan closer round her and huddled nearer to the fire but still felt cold, and when she heard another knock, she had to suppress a scream of terror. Unable to make any move, she couldn't tear her eyes away from the door handle as it turned, and flung her arms over her head as the door itself was pushed open.

'Lexie! I'm sorry if I've scared you. I did knock a few times. What . . . ?'

She lowered her arms with relief. 'Roddy! Thank God it's you.'

He hurried forward as if to take her in his arms, but her stony expression halted him in his tracks. 'What is it, my dear? What's happened?'

He sat down at the opposite side of the fire while she told him why she'd been afraid to open the door, ending by saying sorrowfully, 'But Alistair's not really like that and I don't know what came over me.' She couldn't possibly tell this man about the loathsome memories that had flooded back to her. 'I was just being stupid.'

He kept looking at her so enquiringly that she burst out with it. 'I was remembering the night my father went away . . .'

Slowly and painfully, he got it out of her, not interrupting in case the confidences dried up, but when she stopped speaking, he said, gently, 'You can't be sure it was your father, though?'

430

'It must have been, and he ran away because he was ashamed of what he did.'

Roddy's mouth twisted. 'We've had no luck with our search for him.'

She wondered fleetingly if she should let him know that Nancy had already sent letters to two Scottish newspapers, the *Scotsman* and the *Daily Record*, but decided against it. Time enough if anything came of it. 'Are you any nearer finding whose body it is?'

'No, but that reminds me. We did find a ring just below where the body was lying – that's what I came to tell you.'

'What kind of ring was it? Wedding? Engagement?'

'Just a plain signet ring, but it has an inscription inside, which should help us to identify her. The initials M.M.McL, and the date 30.6.1906, which may be a special birthday or anniversary of some kind. Whoever buried her may have removed any other rings but had, perhaps, not known about this one.'

To enable her to pass on the information to Nancy, Lexie made a mental note of the initials then offered her visitor a choice of tea or something stronger to drink, but Roddy pleaded pressure of work and left shortly afterwards. With peace to think, she tried to remember if there had ever been anyone living in the neighbourhood with the initials M.M.McL., but the only two she could think of had to be ruled out. Old Maggie McLennan had died a natural death about fifteen years ago at the age of eighty-three, and Molly McLaren had been killed in one of the air raids on Clydebank during the war. It was a terrible tragedy, for she'd only been eighteen and just started her training as a nurse.

When Lexie called Edinburgh to tell her about the ring, Nancy had important news of her own to pass on. 'I've just finished speaking to a Mrs Chalmers in Aberdeen, and I'm still all excited. She saw my advert and said she wanted to ask me some questions about it. She wouldn't tell me anything, but she must know your father, or she'd known him at some time. She's coming to see me tomorrow forenoon, and I'll give you a call as soon as she leaves, and let you know what's happened.'

Lexie did not hold out much hope of learning anything from such an unlikely source, but she urged Nancy not to forget to mention the ring that had been found, in case there was some sort of connection.

When Roddy Liddell walked into the shop the following morning, she felt somewhat annoyed – she wouldn't feel free to talk to Nancy if she phoned while he was there – but what he had to tell her left her reeling with shock.

'We're on to something at long last. I've just heard from Glasgow that a Thomas Birnie has contacted them.'

'Doctor Birnie?' She could scarcely credit it. 'But why? He wouldn't know where my father is.'

'He told them that his wife had run off with another man many years ago, and he'd been shocked when he called at Police Headquarters yesterday to ask about an attaché case which had been stolen from his car, and saw a photograph of this same man on a Missing poster. "Alec Fraser ran off with my wife," he told the desk sergeant.'

Lexie's gasp was genuine. 'I don't believe him. He told Nancy and everybody here that his wife went to Stirling to look after her sick mother, and she forced him to give up his practice and move down there to be with her.'

'Like I suggested once, he was too ashamed to let people know she had left him, and he spun that story when a patient said she hadn't seen his wife for a few weeks.'

Lexie leaned forward so that her midriff was supported by the counter, then looked accusingly at the detective. 'He'd been pulling the wool over their eyes, the Glasgow police, I mean. Nancy said he could make his lies sound like the

432

gospel truth. Mrs Birnie wasn't the kind to run away with anybody, and no more was my father. They knew each other, of course, she was in his choir, but that was all.'

'That may have been all anyone knew about, but there could have been more.'

'No, not here, not in a wee place like this. Whatever anybody does, however much they try to keep it secret, somebody else always gets to know about it.'

She hesitated for a moment, then said, 'D'you know what I think? Nancy said Tom Birnie wasn't pleased at my father for making him admit to fathering her child, so I'm nearly sure this is just a story he's made up to get back at him.'

'What good would it do Birnie, though?'

'I don't know, just the satisfaction of blackening my father's character, I suppose. In any case, whatever he said, it hasn't taken you any nearer to finding my Dad, has it?'

Roddy smiled wryly. 'No, it hasn't.'

He had only been gone from the shop for five minutes when Nancy rang. 'Take the chair round from the end of the counter,' she ordered. 'You'll need a seat when I tell you the latest.'

Stretching as far as she could, Lexie managed to hook her toes round a leg of the chair provided for elderly customers and pull it towards her. 'Right, hurry up and tell me, for I've got something to tell you, and all.'

'OK. You know that woman from Aberdeen I spoke about? She's Mrs Birnie's sister. She says she didn't know Alec Fraser, but according to Tom, he was the man Margaret ran away with in 1929. She has never heard a word from her since.'

The wind having been taken out of her sails, Lexie mumbled, 'I still don't believe it.'

'What d'you mean still? Has somebody else told you the same thing?'

433

'Roddy Liddell's been in to tell me the doctor contacted the police in Glasgow and told them that same story, but you said yourself he was a liar.'

'Oh.' There was a wealth of meaning in the word, then silence.

Lexie waited for a few moments, then said, 'Are you still there, Nancy?'

'Yes, I'm thinking, and you're right. I wouldn't trust that two-faced swine supposing he'd a halo and wings – though he's more likely to have horns and a tail. Anyway, Mrs Chalmers gave me her mother's phone number – she was going to Stirling to see her after she left me – so I'll give her a tinkle there in the afternoon and ask if her sister ever divorced Tom. I wouldn't put it past him to have lied to me about her refusing, as well. He could have been free to marry me and never let on . . . though I'm glad he didn't, as things turned out.'

'Did you remember to tell Mrs Birnie's sister about the ring and the initials?'

'Oh, damn! I clean forgot, I was so surprised at what she was telling me. I'll mention it when I phone her at her mother's, though. I'll speak to you later.'

Lexie was kept busy that afternoon and old Mrs Wilkie came in just on six to complain in her best English, 'All yon biscuits I bocht yesterday was broken, and I'd to crummel them ower my stewed rhubarb. You'll need to replace them . . . free.'

Fly to all Lizzie's mother's tricks, Lexie said, firmly, 'If you haven't taken the other packet back, Mattie, I can't replace it, I'm afraid.'

The old woman stamped out in high dudgeon at being refused, and Lexie was locking up for the day when the telephone shrilled. Presuming that Nancy would only be ringing to vent her fury about Tom Birnie, whose wife had probably divorced him and thus left him free to marry whatever paramour he had by that time, Lexie plugged listlessly into the small exchange. Her eardrums were assaulted by the shrill voice.

'Oh, God, Lexie, I wanted to ring you hours ago, but I knew you wouldn't have peace to listen. I've nearly bitten my fingernails right down to my knuckles waiting till you shut the shop.'

Knowing Nancy well enough by now to realize that she was excitable and prone to exaggeration, Lexie held little hope of hearing anything of importance. 'If you'd stop yapping,' she said, quietly, 'you'd be able to tell me now, whatever it is.'

Nancy's voice slid several points down the vocal scale as she held her emotions in check. 'D'you know what Margaret Birnie's mother's name is?'

'I've no idea, but I bet you're going to tell me.'

'She's Mrs Tabitha McLeish.'

'And . . . ?'

'She had two daughters – Mary, the oldest one, married a Bill Chalmers, and Margaret married Tom Birnie. Do you get it?'

Lexie felt quite exasperated by this guessing game. 'Yes, I realize that Mrs Chalmers is Mrs Birnie's sister, and their mother's a Mrs McLeish, but . . . ?'

'Mrs McLeish's maiden name was Martin, and both daughters have that as a middle name. Mrs Chalmers was once Mary Martin McLeish. Now do you get it?'

'Mary Martin McLeish?' Lexie repeated it slowly, taking time to consider what it signified, and then light dawned in a blinding flash. 'Oh, I see now! Mrs Birnie would have been Margaret Martin McLeish! M.M.McL. It's her ring! Her body they found!'

'The penny's dropped at last! Now, Mrs Chalmers said she would get on to Aberdeen police as soon as she stopped speaking to me, and arrange to go and identify the ring when she got home, which would have been around five. So you can expect a call from your friendly Detective Inspector some time this evening. Look, I'll have to go. Greig'll be home in a few minutes, and I've nothing ready for him to eat. I've been too excited to cook, so it'll be fish and chips, I'm afraid. Give me a tinkle as soon as you can, to let me know what's happening.'

Leaving her telephone exchange ready for other calls, Lexie went through to the house and tried to think how this new development would affect her. If the body did turn out to be Margaret Birnie, it meant that she had never left Forvit at all. She hadn't run away with any other man. The doctor had told lies about that, though he'd pretended it was to save his own face, so . . . was it possible . . . had he killed her? He must have!

Lexie was still going over and over this possibility, when Roddy Liddell arrived. 'I suppose Nancy has told you what was going on?' he asked, plumping down on the vacant arm-chair. 'It is . . . was . . . Margaret Birnie's ring. Apparently both sisters were given a signet ring on their eighteenth birthday, and according to Mrs Chalmers, Mrs Birnie had to wear hers on the cranny of her right hand when she was older. I believe that whoever killed her had removed her wedding ring, but hadn't known, or had forgotten, about the other one.'

'She could have lost it herself . . . how can you be sure it's her body?'

'Mrs Chalmers told us that her sister had broken her left leg just below the knee and her left arm just above the wrist in a cycling accident when she was about fourteen, and our surgeon has confirmed that it is definitely Margaret's body. All we have to do now, is to pick up the doctor.'

Without warning, a horrible thought struck Lexie. 'What if it wasn't him?'

Roddy regarded her in some surprise. 'Who else could it have been?'

Swallowing nervously, she muttered, 'Suppose she *had* been having an affair with my father and he'd made her pregnant? Suppose he got angry when she told him?'

The detective stretched across the fireplace and patted her hand reassuringly. 'From what I've heard of him from you and Nancy and other people I've spoken to, he was definitely not an aggressive man.'

'But, he might have wanted to stop her telling anybody, my mother, or the doctor, and he could have killed her. Then he'd have had to bury her, and he wouldn't have been able to face my mother, and that could be why he disappeared.'

Her visitor sighed deeply. 'Do you honestly think he had it in him to murder another human being?'

'He hadn't meant to kill her. He could have given her a push or a shake that knocked her off her feet and she hit her head on a stone, or something like that.' She halted, then shook her head. 'But if he hadn't meant to kill her, he wouldn't have buried her. He'd have reported it ... wouldn't he?'

'I'm sorry, Lexie, but I must point out that people who kill without premeditation, accidentally or otherwise, become so agitated that all they are concerned with is how to dispose of the body. Once they've left the scene of the crime and can think rationally, they are too scared to go back and own up to it.'

'But ...' Lexie's face puckered up and she held out both arms to the detective as if appealing for comfort.

'Don't upset yourself, my dear,' he murmured, rising to pull her to her feet and then holding her tenderly. 'At the moment, we're still guessing, and we can do nothing more until we hear what Doctor Birnie has to say.' He glanced at the clock. 'I thought I'd have heard by this time. I gave them this number.'

Right on cue, the telephone rang, and dropping one arm, he pulled her through to the shop. She made the connection for him then stood by his side, her eyes following every movement of his lips.

'What? Oh, no! For God's sake! It proves he did it, though, doesn't it? I take it the heat's on to find him? Let me know as soon as you hear anything.'

'Birnie's vanished,' he announced as they walked back to the kitchen. 'His wife says he told her he'd found somebody else, and went out on his round next morning and never came back. She says she doesn't know where he is, but they think the other woman was just a blind and that she's protecting him. Still, it's a good thing for us that he did take off, for it proves he's guilty. We'll find him, don't doubt that, Lexie.'

Her feelings having seesawed so much over the past hour or so, she couldn't hold back a sob of relief. 'Thank goodness it wasn't my father.'

Liddell's arms went round her again, more purposefully than before. 'My poor, poor Lexie. I had hoped the case would be finished tonight, everything solved, but . . .' He lowered his head towards her and brushed her lips with his. 'I won't rest till Birnie's under lock and key, but I wish I could find your father for you. I'll do all I can to trace him, believe me.'

'Roddy, you've been so kind . . .'

Her voice was so tremulous that it came as no surprise to him when she burst into tears, and his arms tightened round her. 'Let it out, Lexie. It'll do you good.'

He held her until she calmed, and then looked deeply into her eyes. 'Will you be all right on your own tonight, or would you like me to stay with you?'

Not having the nerve to say she would prefer if he kept her company, she assured him that she would be fine.

'Lock the door behind me,' he instructed, as he took his leave, 'then try to get some sleep, though I know that's easier said than done at a time like this.'

Rising to obey his first order, she thought she may as well go to bed when she was at it, but before she reached the bedroom someone knocked at the outside door. Knowing it couldn't be Roddy, her legs shaking, she turned and shouted, 'Who's there?'

'It's Alistair, Lexie.'

'Go away! I don't want to see you. I'm going to bed.'

'I've something to tell you.'

'If it's about Gwen, I know she's left you.'

'You were right, Lexie. It was her you saw with the soldier. I need somebody to talk to and there's nobody else.'

His last three words were his undoing. 'Leave me alone. I'm not letting you in!'

She held her breath until she heard his feet going round the side of the house, then she relaxed, but she couldn't help thinking how much things had changed. At one time, she'd have rushed to let him in. She had practically offered herself to him more than once . . . but that was before she had remembered being raped. If she had let him do what he wanted the night before he went to London, would the awful memory have come back then, or would he have obliterated it for good? And all those other young men she had stopped after egging them on, had it been stirring in her mind then too? Had she been scared, though she didn't know why?

Well, now she knew why . . . and who . . . and it was awful, unbearable. Alec Fraser hadn't run off with Nancy Lawrie, or Margaret Birnie, or any other woman, and the only explanation was his shame at raping his daughter.

Having walked for hours trying to think straight, and getting no respite at Lexie's house, Alistair's walk back to Benview was slow and laboured. It was maybe just as well she hadn't let him in, he mused, with a sob in his throat. He was still upset by what Gwen had done; the showdown had taken him by surprise, his heart still felt leaden. Coming to a smooth stretch of grass at the roadside, he sat down to have a breather. Everything was going wrong for him. Every-bloody-thing in his life. He'd been away from his wife and family for five years, two of them spent in a prisoner-of-war camp, and round about the time he was captured, his wife had been consoling herself with another man. Ken Bloody Partridge – it was a name he would never forget.

He fished in his jacket pocket for his packet of Capstan, and couldn't stop his hand from shaking as he snapped his lighter, but the first long draw of the cigarette did help him. The pain in his heart eased a fraction, the obstruction in his throat disappeared – maybe the effects would only last as long as the cigarette itself, but at least he was getting some benefit from it.

Chapter 31

❧

Two weeks on, Alistair was no nearer to forgiving his wife, despite recalling what *he* had almost done while she was giving birth to their daughter sixteen years earlier. There were times when he came close, but he always excused himself on the grounds that the circumstances had been entirely different. His lapse had come of a weakness, weakness born of heightened emotions and pique at Lexie's negative reaction.

The atmosphere at Benview was still distinctly chilly; Leila in particular making it clear that she held him responsible for breaking up the family, which was ridiculous since he had done nothing wrong. Life wasn't fair. It never had been. Not for him.

He was beginning to realize, however, that such self-pity could not continue for ever. His business was suffering because of his lack of concentration and that was bad. He would have to pull himself together and face up to being an unattached man. Not that he wanted to be attached again, but he should at least try to lead a more or less normal life. He wasn't the only one whose wife had borne a child to another man while he was away. The damned war had a lot to answer for, though it was no excuse for being unfaithful . . . for a woman or for a man, though just as many husbands as wives had done a bit of philandering . . . more probably.

That evening, as he sat down with his children to their evening meal, Alistair decided that it was time to make them understand how deeply their mother had hurt him. He had never defended himself to them, and they needed to be told. Waiting until David had finished his second helping, he motioned to them to remain where they were.

'But I'm in a hurry,' David pouted. 'I'm going out with my pals.'

Leila scowled at her father. 'I'm meeting Barry, and I don't want to be late.'

Impatient at their self-absorption, he barked, 'What I'm going to say to you is far more important than pals or lads.'

They glanced at each other, silently apprehensive, yet obviously resentful, so he went straight into the little speech he had planned. 'I know you both feel I was too hard on your mother, but let me give you my side.' He started by relating his experiences in the war, the deprivations of being part of an invading force in alien territory even before he was caught and put behind the barbed wire of an Italian prison camp. Then had come the transfer to the first of several German Stalags, and the long hazardous treks from one to the next, with only the thought of his loving wife and children to keep him sane when there was no food, no kindness, and seemingly, no hope.

'I loved your mother,' he told them, 'and I prayed that it wouldn't be long till I'd be going home to her again. I trusted her to be faithful to me because I stupidly thought she loved me just as much as I loved her.'

'She did, Dad,' Leila burst out. 'She did. She just made one silly mistake.'

Alistair shook his head mournfully. 'Young Nicky was the result of that one silly mistake, and that kind of thing can't be hidden, Leila, though she and her sister did their best.' He looked at each of his listeners in turn now. 'I don't suppose you know how they managed to pull the wool over everybody's eyes?' Their blank expressions telling him that

442

they didn't, he detailed the plot Marge had hatched, and was pleased to see his daughter's eyes widen, her expression soften a little.

'I never knew,' she whispered.

'That's what I can't forgive,' he admitted. 'If she'd confessed to me at the time, I'd have been hurt, naturally, but I could have coped with it like I learned to cope with all the other things fate threw at me. But learning like I did, years after . . .' He ran his hand across his perspiring brow. 'Right from the minute I saw him, I knew Nicky couldn't be Dougal's, but I thought it was Marge who had misbehaved, and your mother let me carry right on believing that.'

'It was all my fault, wasn't it?' David muttered suddenly. 'If I hadn't let you see the old snaps, you'd never have . . .'

'No, that wasn't what did it. They just proved to me I'd been right about Marge. I never dreamed that . . .' He swallowed before going on, '. . . that it was your mother.'

'Auntie Marge was willing to take the blame,' Leila reminded him, 'and Mum didn't need to tell you the truth. You'd never have found out if she hadn't.'

'Truth will always come out, and I had the right to know, hadn't I? My heart was ground to dust that day, and I've only been half a man since. It was like a part of me had been taken away, a part I needed to keep me alive.'

'Dad,' Leila said, gently, 'I can imagine how badly you feel, but Mum does love you and if you loved her as much as you said, you'd have understood that she didn't mean to do it, it just happened. Ken and her . . . their feelings, emotions, were all upside down, and their bodies needed each other. Don't you see? I've got to go, but think about it.'

She grabbed her coat from the back of the chair where she had thrown it when she came home and ran out, and David, his face red because of the nature of the conversation, stood up. 'I'm late, as well, Dad, but I think Leila's right. Not that

443

I know about feelings and emotions,' he added hastily, 'but it makes sense . . . doesn't it?'

Left alone, Alistair wondered if he should have resisted the urge to make them see things from his point of view. He had uncovered something else for him to worry about. Had his sixteen-year-old daughter been speaking from experience? Had Barry Mearns been . . . ? It was agony to think that the postman's son's rough paws had touched her, caressed her, knowing it would arouse her passions as well as his own.

'I'm surprised we haven't heard one word from Gwen.' Marge eyed her husband warily, because she sensed that he didn't like speaking about her older sister now. 'She's been away for well over a week.'

Dougal drained his teacup and got to his feet. 'She'll be all right. Don't fuss!'

'It's not like her, that's all.' But she said no more about it, and kissed him before he left for work, Nicky running out to wave him goodbye as he drove off.

When her son came in again, Marge said, 'Mummy has to go to the dentist this morning, remember, so be a good boy for Auntie Pam.' The courtesy title was given to Pamela Deans, who lived in the other half of the semi-detached villa. She was a widow who lived alone, but she had brought up a family of three and knew how to amuse little boys, even little boys as active as Nicholas Finnie.

'Auntie Pam found a box of tin soldiers in her attic,' Nicky observed, fidgeting with impatience to get his hands on them. 'She says they're her Frank's, but he's in Australia. Her Frank must be a funny man if he played with soldiers, what d'you think, Mummy?'

Marge couldn't help smiling. 'He'd just have been a boy

444

when he played with them. He was grown up when he went to Australia.'

'Where's Australia, Mummy?'

'On the other side of the world, darling – a long, long way from Lee Green.'

'When I grow up will I go to the other side of the world, Mummy?'

'I can't tell you that. It depends on a lot of things. Now stop asking questions and put on your jersey.'

It was one of Dougal's busiest days. They'd had a long weekend off because of the Bank Holiday, and there was a mountain of paperwork to catch up on. He had told the girl in the outer office that he didn't want to be disturbed, so he glared at her when she gave a timid knock and walked in. 'I told you I didn't want . . .' he began, but stopped, his face paling, when he saw the uniformed man behind her.

'I'm sorry to disturb you, Mr Finnie,' the policeman said, 'but . . .'

Dougal held his hand up. 'It's all right, Jane, you may go.' Only one explanation had jumped to his mind, so when the girl shut the door behind her, he said, 'I suppose this is about my sister-in-law? What has she done?'

The other man turned an embarrassed pink. 'No, Mr Finnie, it's not about your sister-in-law, it's . . . about your wife. There has been an accident . . .'

Dougal could feel the blood draining from his face. 'An accident? How bad is she? Which hospital did they take . . . ?'

'I'm afraid . . . she died on the way to hospital. It seems she was standing at a junction speaking to another lady when an articulated lorry carrying sewage pipes took the corner too quickly, and . . .' The young policeman licked his dry lips. 'The load slipped and . . . it all happened in a matter of seconds, according to witnesses.'

'Where is she? I have to go . . .'

'Look sir,' the uniformed man looked most uncomfortable, 'I know how anxious you must be, but another ten minutes or so won't make any difference, and I really think you should give yourself a little time . . . to steady your nerves.'

'I'm perfectly all right!' He couldn't help being curt.

'If you say so. Your wife's identity card was in her handbag, that's how we knew where she lived. There was no one in when we called there, but a little boy was playing in the garden next door . . .'

'That had been my son,' Dougal managed to croak. 'Mrs Deans was looking after him to let my wife go to the dentist.'

'So I believe. Your son said his Mummy had gone to the tooth man, and Mrs Deans gave us your office address. Is there anyone I can contact for you, Mr Finnie, someone to give you some support through this dreadful time?'

'Will you please notify my sister-in-law? Mrs Pryor.'

'Would she be the lady you were referring to earlier?'

'No, there are . . . were . . . three sisters. Gwen, the one who went away without leaving any address, Marge, my wife, and Peggy, the youngest, Mrs Pryor.'

As he and Peggy sat by his fireside, Dougal couldn't remember half of what he had done that day. 'It's been a nightmare,' he groaned, 'and I kept wishing I'd wake up.'

'I was the same,' she admitted. 'I still can't believe it.' She looked at him pensively, noting how grey he looked, how absolutely done in. 'Do you want me to phone Alistair? You might feel a little bit better with another man to lean on.'

'I don't know if he'd want to come.'

'Because of . . . Nicky, you mean? But surely he'd put all

446

that out of his mind at a time like this? I'll tell him Gwen's not here . . .' Peggy broke off, her eyes misting. 'I wish I knew where she was, though. She'd want to know about Marge. She'd want to be here.'

Dougal patted her hand. 'I'm truly sorry she's not here for you. I've been so wrapped up in myself . . . but you've lost a sister. You likely think you've lost them both, but I'm sure Gwen'll come back.'

A little of the hopelessness left Peggy's eyes. 'Do you really think so?'

'I do, Peg, but are you sure you've no idea where she could be? Marge couldn't think of anybody she'd have gone to, not with dear old Ivy gone, but maybe you can remember somebody else she'd been close to.'

'I've racked my brains, Dougal, and I just can't think of anybody else.' She stood up wearily. 'I think I'll go home and phone Alistair from there. He should know . . . about Gwen, as well as Marge.'

She had to get away for a few minutes. The pain in Dougal's eyes, the change in him from a bright, upright, healthy man to a bowed, haggard wreck with stubble on his chin and upper lip, his hair uncombed since he'd gone to work in the morning, was too much to bear on top of her own grief. She needed a short respite, to charge her batteries.

Once inside her hallway, her hand trembling, she dialled the number and glanced at the clock while she waited for an answer. Good grief! She hadn't dreamt it was half past nine already. Thinking that everyone at Benview must be out, she was on the point of laying down the receiver when a rather weary 'Hello?' came over the line. 'Alistair?' she said, huskily, 'it's Peggy.'

'What is it? Is something wrong with Gwen?' She was gratified to hear a touch of anxiety in his voice. 'Nothing's wrong with Gwen as far as I know, but Marge was . . . killed in an accident ... this forenoon.' It wasn't easy for her to say. It turned the prolonged nightmare into stark reality.

'What?' His gasp was followed by a short silence, then he murmured, 'No, no, Peg, say that isn't true.'

'It is true.' Peggy fought down the lump in her throat. She had to keep calm, she couldn't let herself go to pieces on the telephone. 'I can't talk any more, Alistair, I'm too upset, but Dougal needs you.'

'Tell him I'll be there as soon as I can. Wait! What did you mean nothing was wrong with Gwen ... as far as you know?'

'We ... don't know ... where she is.' The tears spilling out, her throat constricting, she put the instrument back on its rest, and sat down to give way to the sorrow she'd had to deny in front of Dougal.

On the early morning train to London, Alistair couldn't help feeling as upset about Gwen being missing as about her sister's death, but he tried to concentrate on what Peggy had said. An accident? She might have explained and not left him wondering? Had it been anything to do with Dougal? Had he fallen out with Marge over young Nicky? Had he finally let out the fury he must have nursed since her deceit was uncovered? Had he lost control ... and killed her? Oh God, not that!

The noises in Edinburgh's Waverley Station brought him reluctantly out of the exhausted sleep he had succumbed to. He didn't want to remember, but he couldn't banish the memory of the awful event in Benview he couldn't remember how long ago – sometimes it felt like for ever, at others it was as if it had only just happened. He drew in a ragged breath. The pain Gwen had caused him was still too raw to dwell on. Maybe, like the pain of bereavement, it would ease with time, but he didn't think so; the deception she had played was far worse than any bereavement. He had blamed Marge, as well, at the time, but . . . oh, Lord, how he wished now that he had made his peace with her.

Roddy Liddell didn't relish what he had to do. Lexie was distressed enough already, but it was better that she knew. 'I'm sorry,' he said softly, when she let him in, 'it's more bad news, I'm afraid.'

She motioned him to a chair. 'You'd better tell me.'

The resigned acceptance on her face made him revise what he had said. 'It's not all bad, a sort of mixed bag, actually. The good news is that we managed to trace Doctor Birnie for the second time, purely by accident. One of his patients happened to be in another part of Glasgow yesterday, at the opposite side of the city, when she recognized him going into a small villa. Word having got round her own area that he was wanted by the police, she gave the address to her nearest police station. The Investigating Officer presumed that he'd been visiting another patient, but it turned out that Birnie hadn't had time to find another practice.'

'So that's it?' Lexie, breathed. 'You've got him?'

Roddy shook his head angrily. 'No, he's too clever by far, and here's the bad news. He professed deep sorrow on hearing that his first wife's body had been found in Forvit, but swore that he knew nothing about her death.'

'He would say that, wouldn't he?' Lexie muttered.

The detective nodded. 'It would be only natural, whether or not it was true. On the following day, however, he contacted the DI and told them that, after much deliberation, he had concluded that . . .' He stopped. 'Oh, Lexie, I don't think I should go on.'

Steeling herself, she whispered, 'Whatever it is, you'd better

449

tell me. You can't leave it at that.'

Standing up, the detective moved swiftly to sit beside her on the sofa. 'Yes, you're right. It would be insensitive of me not to tell you now. Birnie said that he had been thinking, and it had occurred to him that Alec Fraser, the man he thought Margaret had run away with, must have killed her, possibly she'd been pregnant and he hadn't wanted anyone to find out. Birnie also said he had probably buried her there to cause most heartache to him, her husband.'

'Oh, Roddy!' Lexie burst out. 'That couldn't be true . . . could it?'

Taking her hand, he clasped it reassuringly. 'I doubt it. It sounds to me more like the invention of a desperate man . . . a guilty man. Please, Lexie, don't distress yourself.'

'I'm all right,' she whispered, but she obviously wasn't. 'Did he say anything else?'

'When he was told there had been no evidence of pregnancy, he shrugged it off and said they must have quarrelled. He made a point of saying that his wife was an even-tempered woman, but hinted that your father could be "quite volatile if he was angered."'

This was too much for Lexie. 'Nancy said he was a liar,' she sobbed. 'You don't believe him, surely?'

'Absolutely not!' Wishing that there was more he could do to put her mind at ease, Roddy added, 'If Birnie thinks he's got away with it, he has a nasty shock coming to him. The case is not closed, not by any means.'

'They didn't let him go?'

'With no proof of his guilt, we have to presume him innocent, but he's obviously on the run, and we *will* get him!'

When Lexie recovered her composure, Roddy said he had to report at HQ that night, and although he did feel guilty at leaving her, she vowed that she was perfectly all right.

*   *   *

It was almost nine the following night when Alistair rang Dougal's doorbell. At one time, he would just have walked in, but their last parting had not been on the best of terms and he was feeling uneasy about this meeting. Peggy let him in, and he was relieved that she, at least, had no reservations with him, giving him a kiss and a warm hug before he went into the living room.

Dougal, his eyes puffy and red-rimmed and surrounded by dark circles, jumped to his feet and came towards him as though they hadn't seen each other for years. 'Oh, Ally, I'm right glad you're here.'

Alistair could tell that every word was heartfelt, and his own emotion was such that he could hardly speak for a second or two, then he flung his arms round his old pal and held him, their cheeks running with tears, and Peggy, her own eyes streaming, withdrew to the scullery.

Scarcely noticing when their sister-in-law excused herself and went home to bed, the two men sat for hours, reminiscing about the early, happy, days of their marriages, of the hotel in Guilford Street, of Tiny and Rosie, even of Manny Isaacson, who had also been a big part of their lives at that time. They avoided talk of the war and the years following, afraid to come anywhere near to the 'trouble' and having to skirt around it, which would draw more attention to it.

It had to come, of course, and with one careless slip, Dougal uncovered it. 'Marge and Peg were both worried about Gwen . . .' Too late, his hand flew to his mouth. 'I'm sorry,' he mumbled, 'I forgot . . . you haven't asked about her, so I thought . . .'

'I didn't know what to say,' Alistair interrupted. 'I don't want to see her, but I didn't realize there was a problem.'

Dougal filled him in about his wife's disappearance then said, 'I think they were fussing about nothing. She said she wanted peace to think, and I can understand that.'

Surprised at the alarm that came to him, Alistair muttered, 'So you think she's OK?'

'I can't be sure, of course, and it's nearly two weeks since she . . .'

'Two weeks?' A light cramping had started round his heart . . . as it would do for anyone he knew who had just walked away from her home and sisters. 'She couldn't have been here long when she . . .'

'Not more than a couple of days, and the thing is,' Dougal explained, 'we don't know where she is. We can't think of anybody she'd have gone to now she doesn't have Ivy.'

Alistair extracted the last cigarette from his packet, snapped his lighter and leaned back to think. No Manny, no Ivy, the two people Gwen had been closest to at one time. She'd never been as friendly with anybody else, not that he knew of. Then the answer hit him square on, making an iciness shoot through him and settle in his very bones. 'Ken Partridge!' he said, harshly. 'I bet that's where she'll be. He's the only one she *could* go to. Did Marge ever mention where he came from?'

'Not that I can remember. Don't you know?'

'No, and I don't want to.' Alistair's lips pressed together, and no more was said on the subject.

'What's on your mind, Tilly?' Gwen asked suddenly. 'Something's been on the tip of your tongue for ten minutes at least, so you'd better come out with it, whatever it is.'

The woman heaved a sigh. 'Don't get me wrong, Gwen, love, I don't want rid of you, and I know you've had a bad time, but . . . you should be with your husband and children.'

'But Alistair doesn't want me. He wanted me to leave.'

'It was what he'd wanted at that specific moment, any man would after what you'd just told him, but he's had time to think. He's had two whole weeks of coming home to an empty house, having to cook his own meals and do his own laundry . . .'

Gwen felt her hackles rising at the criticism. 'He'll have Leila doing everything for him, or . . .' She gave voice to a thought that had been niggling at her ever since she left Forvit. '. . . or he'll get Lexie Fraser to do it. She was his girlfriend before he ever came to London, and I think he still loves her.'

Tilly shook her head. 'I doubt that very much. I don't know him, but from what you've said about him, I wouldn't think he was the kind of man to . . .'

'You'd have said I wasn't the kind of woman to be unfaithful, either, but I was, though I'll regret it to my dying day. If only I'd stood up to Marge and told her to mind her own business, I wouldn't be in this mess now.'

'You did what you did, love, and you can't change things by wishing, but it's time you did something to sort out your life. For a start, why don't you write to one of your sisters to let them know where you are, they must be worrying, then I think you should write to Alistair. Don't ask him to take you back, just ask how he is and how Leila and David are. Leave it up to him to tell you how he feels, don't force him.'

Pulling a face, Gwen said, 'It's too soon. Is it all right if I wait till I've been away for . . . say two months?'

'You're welcome if that's what you want. Maybe you're right about it being too soon. Another six weeks might be best.'

The funeral had been an ordeal for the three chief mourners. Both Dougal and Peggy had been inconsolable, and Alistair had been hard pressed to stop his emotions from getting the better of him. He had been truly thankful that he hadn't had to see much of young Nicky. Mrs Deans, Dougal's next-door neighbour, had kept him until they came home from the service, and he'd gone to bed about eight, asking for his Mummy, which had upset them all over again.

Back at his own fireside again, Alistair wondered what was going to happen about the boy since Dougal wasn't his real father, he hadn't liked to ask his old friend about it, but Peggy seemed to think he would keep him, which was a blessing. *He* certainly didn't want him, reminding him of his wife's faithlessness. His mind refused to veer from the subject of his wife now, and he wondered where she was. He had asked David and Leila if they knew where 'Uncle Ken' lived, but neither of them could tell him, and anyway, what did it matter? If that's where she was, he didn't want her back.

Chapter 32

❧

Lexie felt she had no one to confide in now. She could talk quite easily to Roddy Liddell these days – they were quite close now – but how could she tell him that she didn't believe her father was a murderer, just an incestuous rapist. Just? she thought, grimly. Incestuous rape was every bit as bad as murder . . . worse, for the person at the receiving end, at any rate.

She was almost certain that this was the reason for her father's disappearance. Whatever had made him do it, the shame and guilt had been too much for him to bear, for he was a decent man at heart, everybody had said so. One thing she was absolutely sure of was that he hadn't been having an affair with the doctor's wife, no matter what Tom Birnie had told the police. And there had been no evidence of pregnancy when they did an autopsy on the body, so that was another of his lies exposed.

Constantly wondering if she would ever learn the truth, Lexie was quite glad when Nancy Lawrie phoned her one evening to ask if there had been any further developments. 'Not a thing,' she told her, morosely, 'and the waiting's getting me down.'

'Well, I've been thinking.' Nancy's voice held a hint of excitement. 'Do you know if the police ever asked Margaret Birnie's mother if she'd heard from her at all since she left Forvit? Mrs McLeish, wasn't it? She must be in her eighties, I'd think, and if they didn't ask her, she likely wouldn't have thought it was important.'

Lexie had to be perfectly honest. 'But we know where Mrs Birnie is . . . was.'

'That's where she ended up, but maybe she'd come back to see *him* before he got everything sold up and he killed her in a temper. Now d'you see?'

'I can't think properly, Nancy.'

'Sorry. What I'm getting at . . . maybe the old lady can tell us where your father is . . . or was at some time. If we got his first address, we could maybe trace him from there.'

Lexie's spirits lifted for the first time in weeks. 'I suppose . . . it's possible. At least we know Mrs McLeish is still alive. Will I tell Roddy . . . the Detective Inspector . . . ?'

'Ah-ha! So it's Roddy now, is it? But no, I don't think we should involve the police just yet. Leave it to me. Greig's taking me to Stirling on Sunday to see her.'

'I wish I could do something. I'd love to go with you, but I'm not free on Sundays till dinnertime – I've to open for the papers, you see – and that wouldn't give me time.'

'No, I'm afraid not, but don't worry. I won't upset the old lady, and she'll maybe be glad to speak to someone about her daughter . . . and her son-in-law. You never know, I might learn a few interesting things about him. Any family scandals would have been swept under the carpet at the time, but she mightn't be so discreet now.'

'Let me know what happens as soon as you can. I'll be all on edge.'

'It could turn out to be a waste of time, Lexie, but it's worth a try, isn't it?'

'Oh, yes, and thanks, Nancy. At least you're doing something. I feel so useless.'

She had only just hung up when Roddy Liddell appeared. 'Nothing new to report,' he began, looking slightly embarrassed, 'but I thought I'd come to see how you were.'

'Not too bad.' She found it hard to disguise the hope that Nancy had raised in her.

'I should have come before. Did you think we'd stopped bothering?'

'I knew you'd tell me if you'd found out anything.'

'Police all over Scotland are trying to trace your father, and nothing's turned up.' He eyed her uncertainly. 'I'm trying to persuade the powers-that-be to give the builders the go-ahead to excavate the whole of the site.'

The hope disintegrated. 'You think *his* body's there as well?'

'It's a possibility, Lexie.'

'Oh, but . . .' This was a new idea to her, loathsome, alarming, and despite wanting to appear composed in front of this man, she couldn't stop the tears from edging out.

He handed her his handkerchief. 'Don't you think it would be best for you to know, one way or the other?' he said gently, his eyes holding deep compassion. 'The answer is either that he's been murdered, or that *he* was the murderer. I realize it's not much of an option, but there doesn't seem to be anything in between.'

'I suppose not.' Her knees were shaking as she contemplated telling him the option Nancy had put forward, but she thought better of it. He might be glad of the suggestion, might even have it followed up, but speaking about it might bring bad luck, and she didn't need any more of that. She needed to believe she was on the verge of finding her father and learning the truth of what had happened all those years ago.

'D'you want some brandy?' He was even more solicitous now.

'No, I'm OK . . . Oh, I'm sorry, Roddy, I should have offered you something . . . ?'

'No, I'm OK.'

Wondering why the corners of his mouth had twitched, it

dawned on her that he had repeated her own words. Poor soul, he was doing his best to cheer her, and she was making his job harder by persisting in feeling sorry for herself. She attempted to make amends. 'It's good of you to call to tell me yourself, Roddy. You don't have to, you know.'

'I know I don't, I just want to. You don't mind, do you?'

His appealing eyes – as if he were afraid of being rejected – and his attractive boyish grin were enough to tell her he meant it. 'No, you can come as often as you like, you know that. I'm always pleased to see you.'

'Are you? Are you really, Lexie? I sometimes get the feeling you'd rather I didn't . . .'

'No, it's not you,' she interrupted. 'It's worrying about what you might have come to tell me.'

He grinned again. 'Will I arrange a signal? I could give three taps on the window and say, "Me . . . friend . . . open sesame." How would that do?'

She had to laugh. 'Oh, Roddy, you're so good for me.'

'I aim to please.' The teasing light left his eyes. 'I'd like to be . . . your friend.'

'You *are* my friend, a very good friend.'

'Good. I mean . . . to tell the truth, Lexie, I'd . . .' His face colouring, he stopped short and stood up. 'Now, remember, I'll never let this investigation drop. I'm as anxious as you to get to the bottom of it, so you'll tell me if you think of anything that might help us, won't you? Promise?'

Crossing her fingers, she muttered, 'Yes, of course.' She couldn't look him in the eye and make a solemn promise, not when she knew she would break her word if Nancy's visit to Mrs McLeish paid off. They didn't want the bobbies jumping in with their size thirteen boots and spoiling everything. In an attempt to pacify her protesting conscience, she jumped to her feet. 'Thank you for what you're doing, Roddy, you really are a true friend.' She pulled her hand out of his clasp, and added, breathily because her heart was racing. 'And you'll let me know the minute *you* hear anything?'

'Definitely, and that's a promise, too!'

Mrs Deans had offered to look after young Nicky during the days in order to let Dougal go back to work, and Peggy came in every evening to give him his bath and see that he got to bed at a decent time, because his father seemed to have lost interest in everything, including the clock. The passing weeks, however, had made the boy more and more fractious, demanding to see his mother although all three of the adults attending him had tried to break it to him in their own different ways that he would never see her again – not in those basic words, of course.

It came as no surprise to the other two, then, when Mrs Deans said she was leaving to stay with her son in Southampton. 'I'm sorry, Dougal,' she went on, 'but I'm wearing on for seventy and I can't manage him when he goes into one of his tantrums, and Gordon's been telling me for years I should sell my house and go and live with them. I feel I'm leaving you in the lurch, but, honestly . . .'

'Don't feel like that,' Dougal assured her, his stomach slowly returning to its normal position. 'You've your own life to lead and I'll easily find somebody else.'

When she left, he grimaced to Peggy. 'I knew that would come, but I didn't expect it just yet, and who on earth's going to look after an uncontrollable five-year-old?'

His sister-in-law, however, having also known that it would come some day, had a solution ready for him. 'What would you say to a thirty-five-year-old widow who knows him and loves him in spite of all his going-on?' Seeing the perplexity on Dougal's face reddening to comprehension, she gave a little chuckle. 'It makes sense, doesn't it?'

He shook his head. 'It might make sense, but it's not practical. You can't give up your job to look after my child.'

It crossed neither of their minds that Nicky wasn't Dougal's biological child, nor even his late wife's, and Peggy said, very firmly, 'I don't have to work, you know. I could live quite comfortably on what Alf left me.'

'No, Peg, I can't expect you to ... you've a life of your own to live, as well.'

'... to do with as I choose,' she grinned, 'and if I choose to look after a little boy who only behaves badly because his heart is aching for his Mummy, that's my own business.'

Burying his head in his hands, Dougal groaned, 'Oh, Peg, I can't let you ...'.

'And there's another thing,' she stated. 'This little boy has a Scottish father who's as stubborn as a mule, and he needs looking after, too.'

Dougal's head jerked up. 'Oh now, wait a minute! I'm maybe no great shakes at seeing to Nicky, but I can look after myself.'

'Can you cook? I haven't seen any evidence of it.'

'I never get the chance. You've made all our meals since ...' He swallowed before going on, '... since Marge died, and Mrs Deans baked cakes and biscuits for Nicky, but I'm sure I could manage.'

Peggy shook her head. 'I despair of you. Why can't you just be grateful and accept my offer? You can pay me what you paid Mrs Deans, if that would make you feel any better, but it's just as easy to cook for three as for one, easier in fact.'

Taking one of her hands, he pressed it hard to show his gratitude, then swung away from her to hide his tears, and knowing how mortified he was at crying, she just said, 'I'll start the day Mrs Deans leaves. See you in the morning.'

As she strode past what was now Gwen's house, still empty, Peggy wondered when all the worry and upsets would end.

She had definitely lost one sister, and it looked as though the other one was lost to her, as well, whether by choice or by some accident. If only she knew what had happened.

Tilly made up her mind to give it one last try. The longer Gwen stopped on there, the harder it would be for her to go back. No matter if what happened had been her fault or her sister's, her Alistair should have done the proper thing and forgiven her. Of course, she still loved him, that was quite obvious. She was always making excuses for him, that he was a changed man when he came home from the prison camp and had never got back to his old self again, but, surely he still had some of the milk of human kindness in him?

Gwen's woebegone face when she came down to breakfast almost made Tilly change her mind, but she drew in a deep breath to give her strength and said, 'Now, I hope you won't be offended, love, but I do think it's time you went home . . . for your own sake.'

'Home?' Gwen's voice was listless. 'I don't have any home . . . except here.'

'This is not your home, Gwen, and if you feel you can't go back to Forvit, you should go back to London. Your sisters must be out of their minds worrying about you.'

'I left a note telling them I needed peace to think . . .'

'That was nearly four months ago. Write to them to let them know you're all right.'

Gwen gave a resigned sigh. 'I suppose I should write, but I can't go back . . . not yet.'

'Don't fret, then, lovie. If that's how you feel, I won't throw you out. You can stay here for as long as you need me. Fred won't mind.'

Listening to Gwen trailing upstairs to tidy her room, Tilly banished all thoughts of lazy evenings by the fire with her husband – Fred hardly spent any time at home these days – or an early night when they felt like it, even a late morning if *she* took it into her head. It looked as if they had a lodger for life.

Giving herself a mental shake, she went to the kitchen for her carpet sweeper. What was she going on about? Gwen helped with the housework. She was good company . . . most of the time. It wasn't so bad. It was just that Fred . . . well, he was just being Fred and hinting that he could do with a bit of peace and quiet in his own home.

Chapter 33

David Ritchie couldn't get home fast enough. He and his pals had been, not exactly rampaging through the woods between Forvit and Bankside, just giving vent to their youthful high spirits by racing about and yelling at the tops of their voices. That, of course, had led on to acting out a Tarzan film they'd seen – there had been a film show every Friday and Saturday in the village hall for a few months now. The boys took it in turn to be the hero, yodelling, or trying to, the famous call as he swung on a low branch, while the others were either 'baddies' or apes . . . or, most reluctantly, Jane.

None of the fourteen/fifteen-year-olds wore watches, but being winter, the onset of dusk told them when it was time to go home, and they made their way back to where they had left their bicycles. This was the point at which they split up and went in various directions, David and his best friend, Eddie Mearns, younger brother of Barry, wheeling their bikes back to Forvit. They preferred to walk to Eddie's house, because it gave them time to talk over anything they felt was worth discussing, just the two of them. As soon as their friends had left them this particular evening, Eddie said, 'They've dug up another body.'

This was much more interesting than the usual kind of titbits he gleaned from his father, whose job as postman let him in on many little secrets, and almost dropping his cycle in surprise, David asked, 'Do they know who it is?'

'One of the workmen told my Dad it's Alec Fraser, Lexie

from the shop's father. He run off with a young girl, or somebody else's wife, years and years ago ... or everybody thought he run off, but he couldn't've, could he? I'm nae supposed to tell anybody, mind, for the police havena made it public yet, so you'd better keep it to yourself.'

It was a meaty topic, however, and the two boys made the most of it, speculating on why this man – a man who had disappeared long before they were born – had been killed, and more exciting still, who had done the dirty deed. By the time they came to Eddie's house, they were agreed on one thing – the murderer must be somebody from the village or quite near to it. Who else would want to kill the man who had just been the local shopkeeper? But neither of them could come up with any kind of motive.

'My Mam says Alec Fraser was a decent man,' Eddie remarked, as they stood at his gate for a few moments, 'and my Dad says he was well respected, for he took the kirk choir and that, but there musta been something bad about him afore somebody'd want to murder him.'

'That doesn't follow,' David pointed out. 'He could have found out something bad about the murderer, and he got killed to stop him telling the police.'

'It's like that picture we saw a few weeks back. James Cagney, or was it Raymond Massey? I canna mind the name o' it, though.'

'Neither can I, and I'd better be going, Eddie, or my Dad'll be yelling his head off at me for being so late. See you on Saturday, usual time?'

'Aye, it's a Western wi' Joel McCrea, and it's a Boris Karloff next week.'

'Good, I like creepy pictures better than Westerns.'

As David swung his leg over the bar of his cycle, his mind returned to the more fascinating business of the murder ... a real murder! This, then, was the reason for his haste as he pedalled hell for leather along the road in his anxiety to get home and tell his news. He hadn't actually promised Eddie that he would keep it to himself, and his father was friendly with Lexie Fraser, so he'd be pleased to hear the latest about her father.

Throwing his bicycle down, he burst into the house. 'You'll never guess, Dad!'

His father and sister had been reading quietly by the fire, so Alistair looked up in some annoyance at the noisy intrusion. 'Must you come barging in like that? And you haven't left your bike outside, have you?'

Only then remembering the strict instructions he'd been given when he got this new Raleigh three-speed for his birthday, David dashed out again to put it under cover in the shed. It didn't look like it was going to rain, but he didn't want to chance it getting rusty. In his excitement, his fingers fumbled with the lock before managing to get it back in the hasp and snapping it shut, then he darted back inside to impart his red-hot scoop.

Closing the door quietly behind him, he said, as nonchalantly as he could, to see what the effect would be, 'They've dug up Alec Fraser.'

His father's first reaction did not disappoint him. Leaping to his feet, Alistair cried, 'What? When? Who told you?'

'One of the workmen told Eddie's Dad . . .'

Before David could give any further details, not that there were any more to give, just his and Eddie's speculations, Alistair was hauling on his jacket and going through the door. 'Poor Lexie, she'll need me.'

In another few moments, brother and sister heard an engine being started and the noise of the car's tyres crunching down the stony track. 'Is something going on between Dad and Lexie?' David asked sadly, wishing that his father had at least stayed long enough to pass some kind of comment on what had happened – his bombshell had fizzled out.

Leila shook her head. 'I don't think so. They've been friends since they were at school, that's all it is.'

'But he goes racing off to her every time anything goes wrong. He went there after the row with Mum, remember? That's where Uncle Dougal found him, and there's been other times.'

'He needs somebody to talk to.' Although only a little over a year older, Leila could look on things from an adult point of view, whereas her brother's outlook was still that of a child. 'Mum always said he was never the same after he came home from the war. We were too young to remember how he was before, but she said he was even-tempered and full of life whereas after he came back she never knew how he'd be, fine one minute and grumpy and short-tempered the next. Mind you, after what he told us he went through as a prisoner of war, it's not surprising he changed. I'm sure there's nothing between him and Lexie Fraser, though. He still loves Mum, I know he does.'

Neither of them feeling the need of anything to eat or drink, Leila made David tell her exactly what Eddie Mearns had said, and felt somewhat let down when he couldn't tell her anything more. They went to bed about a quarter of an hour after their father had gone out, but when, in their separate rooms, they heard him coming in just minutes later, they each decided against going down to ask him why he was home so soon.

Earlier that same evening, Lexie Fraser was making herself some cheese sandwiches as she listened to the end of the six o'clock news on the wireless, but she was interrupted by the bell shrilling on the shop's small telephone exchange. Laying

466

down the knife, she ran through, plugged in and put on the headpiece. 'Forvit Post Office.'

'It's Nancy, Lexie. Listen, this is going to warm the cockles of your heart. You know I told you Mrs McLeish said she never reported Margaret missing because Tom had said she'd run off with another man? And you said that's what he'd told the police, as well, but now they're looking for him again?'

Utterly mystified, Lexie murmured, 'Yes, I know all that, but what . . . ?'

'Well, I've just had a phone call from Mrs Chalmers in Aberdeen, the other daughter, remember, and speak about blinking coincidences!'

'Nancy!' Lexie felt exasperated by the other woman's habit of spinning out any information she had to give. 'Will you just tell me what she . . .'

'Sorry, I get carried away. She's just back from a touring holiday on the west coast, and on their way back, they stopped in Inveraray to take a look round, and who do you think they saw coming out of a shop? This is where the coincidence comes in – it was Tom Birnie himself – he's her brother-in-law, remember. She said her first thought was to confront him there and then, but she knew he'd have bluffed it out and spun her some weird story, so she went into the shop and asked where the nearest doctor lived, because her husband had cut his foot on a piece of glass.'

'But . . . but . . .' Lexie was absolutely mystified. 'That wasn't true, was it?'

'Of course it wasn't true. She made it up on the spur of the moment, and I think it was pretty clever of her. Anyway, the shoplady said that Doctor Balfour had been in just a few minutes ago, and he was on his way home, so she gave Mrs Chalmers his address.'

'So it wasn't Tom Birnie . . . ?'

467

'Lexie, would you use your brains?' Nancy sounded disappointed with her. 'He must have moved from Glasgow after the police spoke to him that second time, and changed his name to make it more difficult for them to find him again. He'd likely have got away with it if Mrs Chalmers hadn't been in that particular place at that particular time. It was fate, Lexie, and don't you see? Tom Birnie must have something to hide, or he wouldn't change his name and hide away in a wee place like Inveraray. And now I'm surer than ever that we'll find Alec, even if he's changed his name, and all. Somebody's bound to see him somewhere and recognize him.'

Despite her head still being in a whirl, it occurred to Lexie that Nancy had omitted one vital factor. 'What'll happen now, then? Has Mrs Chalmers given Tom's address to the police . . . ?'

'I asked her not to. I thought you'd like to tell your detective friend yourself.'

'I don't know when I'll see him.'

Hearing a trace of wistfulness in the words, Nancy said, 'Friend Birnie won't be going anywhere – he doesn't know he's been spotted – so a few days' wait won't matter.'

A sudden strength surged up in Lexie now. 'I'll tell him as soon as I can, he comes in quite a lot. Um, Nancy, do you think Tom Birnie would know where my father is?'

'He might, but don't bank on it, Lexie.'

'I won't. I don't suppose he'd tell anybody, anyway.'

'Not likely. Now, you'll let me know what happens?'

'Of course I will, and thanks for what you've done, Nancy.'

'My pleasure. I'd like to see that lying devil get his comeuppance for what he did to me, and to other girls, as well, for all I know. Speak to you soon.'

Lexie had just got back to her sandwich-making when Roddy Liddell knocked on her kitchen window, and she signed to him to come in. 'I've got news for you . . .' she began, but stopped when she saw how grave his face was. 'Has something happened? What have you come to tell me?'

'Let me get you some brandy first, Lexie.'

'No! Tell me now! It's about my father, isn't it?'

'I'm truly sorry. The excavators turned up another body first thing this morning, but I was under strict orders not to tell you until we learned a bit more about it. The police surgeon's report on his first examination was that it's male, probably about five feet eleven in height and around forty years of age . . .'

'Oh, God! It *is* my father, isn't it? Will I have to . . . identify him?'

Liddell's eyes rested on her pityingly. 'There's little hope of positive identification, as you might understand after so long, but they kept searching for something that could either point to it being your father, or rule him out altogether, and they were ready to stop for the day when one of the men saw this.' He took a gold pocket watch from his pocket and held it out to her.

She took it with trembling hands, opened the back with some difficulty and looked at the inscription through a mist of unshed tears. 'To AWF with all my love CRS, and the date 18.6.1907,' she read out. She gulped to hide her emotion, but her voice broke several times as she added, 'My mother gave it to him on their wedding day. His full name was Alexander William Fraser and . . . he was twenty at the time. Her name was Caroline Ross Shewan and she was nineteen.' She stopped to clear her throat, but was overcome with the tears she could contain no longer.

Gathering her into his arms awkwardly, he let her weep, murmuring gentle words of comfort against her hair, and when the dreadful heaving sobs eased, he kissed her cheek, the salt taste of her tears making him ache with pity for her.

469

'I feel as if I'd betrayed you, Lexie,' he murmured. 'If it had been up to me, I'd have come straight here when I was told they'd found him, but my Super was there, and God knows who else, and they watched me like a hawk so I couldn't slip away. They said they weren't sure whose body it was, but I knew right from the start, and I'm so sorry, my dear.'

Her thoughts were so concentrated on the news he had given her that the endearment was lost on her. 'It's all right, Roddy. I know it wasn't your fault, but I'm so mixed up I don't know what to think about anything.'

The exhaustion of her torrent of weeping sounded in her voice, and he said, 'Don't think about it yet, Lexie. Wait till you're . . .'

'I can't help thinking about it. I'm glad they found him, it proves he didn't kill Mrs Birnie, but on the other hand . . . well, he's my father, and he's dead, and . . .'

'Isn't it better to know for sure than to keep on wondering? At least, as you said, we know he's innocent, but we still have to find Birnie. He's the only suspect now.'

Her head snapped up. 'I forgot! That's what I was going to tell you. Nancy Lawrie rang up and gave me his address.'

He listened, amazed, as she told him how Mrs Birnie's sister had accidentally run him to ground, and then he said, 'Well that's good news. Thank goodness we've got something positive on him at last. We'll get the bugger now. I'm sure it was him. I felt it all along. May I use your phone to let my Super know?'

'I'll put you through.'

Once she connected him, she left him to pass on the most important piece of information they'd had so far, and went back to sit by the fire. It was a mild evening so she wasn't cold, but the heat gave her some comfort, and as her feelings metaphorically thawed out, she was ashamed for having broken down so completely in front

470

of Roddy, though he'd been like a rock to her. She wouldn't have been able to stop crying at all if he hadn't been there.

She felt a little shy with him when he came through from the shop again, beaming as he sat down beside her. 'Well, that's the last stage set in motion, but I'll stay on with you for a while, till you get over the shock a bit. The Super understands how upset you must be, and said I can stay for as long as you need me. I parked the car at the other end of the village, so the neighbours won't have any cause to gossip. How are you feeling now?'

'Much better, thanks to you. I'd have gone to pieces if you hadn't . . .'

'Lexie, I know this isn't an appropriate time, but I have to know if . . .' He looked away in some embarrassment, and his voice was barely audible as he went on, 'I need to know if there's any chance for me. If there's not, don't be afraid to say, and I'll never mention it again.'

It took a moment for her to understand what he meant, and it was surprise as much as shyness that held her back from throwing her arms round his neck. 'It's OK, Roddy,' she said, cautiously, 'I've been hoping you'd . . .'

Taken abruptly into his arms, she gave herself up to the thrill of his kisses, but they ended just as abruptly. 'No, Lexie dear,' he murmured, as she tried to kiss him again, 'now I know how you feel, this can wait . . . till we get Tom Birnie safely behind bars.'

As usual while driving down the track, it took all Alistair's concentration to avoid the sharp stones which could slash his tyres, so he was on the road before he could do any thinking. If it really was Alec Fraser's body that had been found, everything pointed to Tom Birnie being the killer.

There was nobody else it could have been. Poor, poor Lexie. What a state she must be in.

It didn't take long for him to reach the village, and he drew into the little side lane some distance from the shop. The only other vehicle in sight was the little red Post Office van at Sandy Mearns's gate, and he didn't want Aggie or Doodie Tough or any of the other scandalmongers, to see his A40 outside the shop and make something out of nothing. It wouldn't be fair to Lexie.

He closed his car door quietly and walked along to the opening through to her house. It was getting quite dark, yet her light wasn't on and he hoped that she hadn't gone out, though she would be needing company after what she'd been told today. As he stood uncertainly, wondering what to do, he could see the flickering of the fire through the curtains, so she couldn't have gone far. She had told him once that she didn't lock her porch door if she wasn't going to be out long, so she likely wouldn't mind if he went in to wait for her.

In case she was inside sleeping off the effects of long bouts of weeping, he made no sound as he turned the handle with great caution, stepped gingerly over the threshold then closed the door carefully behind him. The door into the kitchen was half open, and there she was on the couch ... but not asleep. For a few moments, transfixed by the sight of the detective with his arms around her, Alistair stood with his mouth agape, until a weird sensation started in his innards. If he had loved Lexie, he'd have sworn it was jealousy, but he didn't, so it wasn't – it couldn't be? It was just shock at seeing her being kissed so ardently by a man ... especially this man.

The pair were so absorbed in each other that they weren't aware of his presence, so he backed out on tiptoe, took time to close the door silently again and stumbled to his car on legs that felt as heavy as tree trunks. Then he plumped down

472

in the driver's seat to start the engine. He had to think, but not here – not so near.

Arriving back at Benview, he went straight to bed to consider what he had seen. It was strange, really, that Lexie hadn't met somebody long before this. But that 'tec? He wasn't a good choice. What could she see in him? Had it been reaction to what he'd told her? Or had he taken advantage of her vulnerability?

Alistair stretched out to the chest of drawers for his cigarettes and lighter, but as the flame ignited, it dawned on him that, although he had never actually loved Lexie, he had always been sure that she loved him. Was that why he felt so betrayed?

David was surprised to hear his father's car coming back after just twenty minutes. What had happened at Lexie Fraser's house? If only Mum was here. If he knew where she was, he'd write and beg her to come home. She wouldn't know about poor Auntie Marge, of course, and she'd be terrible upset when she did.

Oh, this was awful! How could he sleep with all these thoughts jumbling round in his head? Maybe he should try reading? He'd read all his comics, though, and Mum had made him put all his books in the cupboard on the landing on the shelf under hers and Dad's. He might as well take a look. There might be one he hadn't read.

Jamming his feet into his slippers, he crept across his bedroom and inched the door open to save it squeaking, then stepped along the landing to the next door, which was a bit trickier. He held his breath at the three long creaks it gave before he got it open, but nobody shouted at him so he felt for the flashlight Mum kept there because there wasn't an electric point. The weak beam wavered along the row,

Treasure Island, Huckleberry Finn, The Last of the Mohicans, Children of the New Forest, two of the *Biggles* series. He'd read them all ... two or three times. Looking up at the shelf above, he didn't fancy any of Dad's books, Dickens and that crowd would be dull and boring. C.S. Forester's *The African Queen* sounded a bit more promising, though, at least it looked action-packed.

Settling down in bed again, he pulled out a bookmark and wondered why Dad hadn't finished the book. Then he remembered seeing Mum reading it. She probably hadn't finished it when she went away, and Dad must have put it back in the cupboard.

The bookmark however, wasn't a bookmark, he discovered. It was a letter from somebody called Tilly to his mother, dated 1 March 1948, telling her that Ivy Crocker had died. It ended, 'Remember, if you're ever anywhere near Newcastle, Fred and I would love to see you again.'

The name Tilly was vaguely familiar, and he pondered over where he could have heard or seen it before. She lived near Auntie Ivy ... where Mum had gone when she had the baby. Did Tilly know about that? He hadn't known himself at the time, not till Dad had told him and Leila what had happened. He still couldn't fathom out all the ins and outs of it, some things still puzzled him. Was Nicky his brother, for instance? They had the same mother, but apparently Uncle Ken was Nicky's father. That's what had caused all the trouble.

Out of nowhere, it suddenly struck David where he had seen the name Tilly before. She sent Mum a Christmas card every year. 'Love from Tilly and Fred', she always put, the same as the letter. His heart skipped a beat. Was that where Mum was? Dad said he had no idea, nobody had.

A warm excited glow began to spread through the boy's rapidly-cooling body. If he could trace her and get her to come home, it would make up for being to blame for the burst-up in the first place. If he hadn't shown Dad those snaps . . .

Yes! It was all up to him now.

Chapter 34

∾

Roddy Liddell had spent an almost sleepless night, but it wasn't the murder investigation which had kept him awake. Yesterday had been quite a momentous day for him, apart from the unearthing of Alec Fraser's body. He had more or less told the dead man's daughter how he felt about her, and wonder of wonders, she had said she felt the same. Perfect result, despite the bad timing.

But he'd have to put it on a back burner meantime. For now, he had to concentrate on tracking down that damned murdering doctor, whatever name he was calling himself. He had contacted Mrs Chalmers first thing this morning, and was inclined to believe, from the way she spoke, that it really was Tom Birnie she had seen, and that she wasn't one of the cranks they sometimes had to put up with. She had understood that she would be called as a witness at the trial, and said she would be happy to let the whole world know the kind of rotter her brother-in-law had been and obviously still was.

Of course, Liddell warned himself, the case might never come to trial if the man was as accomplished a liar as it appeared. Mrs Chalmers' evidence was only second-hand; it was her deceased sister's word against a desperate Birnie's. It would be impossible to make people believe that a doctor as well respected as he had been in Forvit, and likely in Glasgow and Inveraray too, would have illicit associations with young girls. He would deny it, no doubt about that, and look suitably horrified that his wife's sister would even think such things about him. What Nancy Lawrie could say would be more effective, if she was willing to testify, although, again, the swine would probably deny everything, and accuse her of telling lies out of spite because he had rebuffed her advances.

In any case, would she be capable of describing to a crowded court what he had done to her? Could he put her through such an ordeal ... even for Lexie's sake? Infidelity was not enough to convict a man for murder, nor was fathering a child on a woman not his wife, nor was breach of promise. The whole investigation was liable to collapse, with not even the smallest piece of circumstantial evidence to go on. What could anybody expect after twenty years? Tom Birnie's method of killing his two victims and his reason for so doing were likely to remain his secret for evermore.

Since Nancy Lawrie had miraculously appeared again, the Forvit women had reversed their opinion of Alec Fraser. Yesterday afternoon, he'd been hard pressed not to laugh out loud.

'I never thought Alec Fraser would've run off wi' her.' This was the postman's wife.

The one they called Doodie had almost nodded her head off. 'Me, either. Didn't I say, Mattie? I said no, no, nae Alec. He's a decent man and he would never've ta'en up wi' a lassie young enough to be his dother.'

Mattie had added, 'As for him and Mrs Birnie! Well, there was nae wey there would be ony scandal aboot them. They was pillars o' society, baith the two o' them.'

Not that that was conclusive, Roddy mused. Pillars of society had been known to stray, even to commit heinous crimes, they were only human, after all, with human feelings and failings.

Glancing at his alarm clock, which he had set for six

but switched off at five thirty because he was wide awake, Roddy was astonished to see that it was now almost quarter to seven. Good God! He'd planned to collect Gaudie and be on the way to Inveraray before seven, and it would take him all his time to be ready for half past.

First telephoning to tell his sergeant that he was running late, Liddell gave himself the quickest wash and shave he'd ever had, rummaged in his chest of drawers for a clean shirt and uncrumpled tie till the kettle boiled, and drank his cup of tea while he dressed. It was twenty-nine minutes past seven when he went out to his car, his brown wavy hair flopping over his eyes because he'd forgotten to brush it, two small pieces of toilet paper attached to his chin to staunch the blood where the razor had nicked it.

Alistair's thoughts were so tangled when it was almost time to get up that he knew his work would suffer. Maybe he should just lie there in the hope that exhaustion would overcome him eventually and he could sleep for a few hours?

He had more or less decided that what he felt for Lexie now stemmed from pity rather than love, but he still couldn't make up his mind about his wife. What he felt for her wasn't so easily defined. This not knowing where she was had blunted the earlier hatred and resentment for the pain she had caused, and what was left was an aching anxiety to know that she was safe and well. What she had done while he was a prisoner of war still rankled, and he wasn't sure if he could ever forgive her, but his children needed their mother and for that reason alone, he would ask her to come home. The thing was, where the devil was she? She had made it quite clear to her sisters – just Peggy now – that she wanted to be on her own, but that was almost six months ago. Surely she had done all the thinking she needed by this time.

Oh, hell! He couldn't carry on like this, going round and round and getting nowhere. He'd be as well going in to work to take his mind off it.

After a quick wash and shave, he came out of the bathroom and called, 'Come on, troops, time to get up,' before going downstairs.

The first meal of the day had deteriorated into a cup of tea and a slice of toast each, but neither his son nor his daughter had complained . . . so far. A flurry of raised voices overhead made him smile. David would be accusing Leila of sneaking into the bathroom before him, and she would be retaliating by saying she couldn't let him go first because he splashed soapy water all over the floor and left the basin in such a mess. But they were good kids, and David seemed to have a talent for repairing old clocks and watches. Leila, of course, wasn't quite so dedicated. She appeared to be serious about Barry Mearns, so she probably had her mind set on marriage and babies, not a career in a small watch-maker/jewellery shop in a side street.

Leila came downstairs first. 'David thinks Mum's with the Tilly Something who sent her a card every Christmas.'

Taken aback, he stammered, 'I . . . I never knew her.'

'Are you going to get in touch with her? She lived beside Auntie Ivy, so it must be in or near Moltby somewhere.'

'But she might have moved . . .' The accusation in his daughter's eyes made him get to his feet. 'I'll tell you what. If you and David clear everything up when you're finished, I'll go and phone Auntie Peggy. I'm not saying she knows that address, but she could possibly find out for us.'

*   *   *

479

As David grudgingly dried the dishes, his ears were fine-tuned to catch what his father was saying on the phone in the little porch at the front door, but, unfortunately, all he could hear was an odd phrase here and there, and only one side of the conversation.

'... I should know myself ... yes, yes ... paid more attention ...'

David nudged his sister. 'Auntie Peggy's getting on to him for not remembering himself.'

'What? ... Gwen's address book? ... I don't know. I think she kept it in her handbag.'

'She doesn't know either,' David muttered in disgust.

'She didn't know Mum ever went to Auntie Ivy's ...' Leila stopped speaking at David's imperative 'Ssshh!'

'Yes? ... it doesn't matter ... but I'd be grateful if you or Dougal remember anything ... Yes, I know he wasn't at home, but Marge could have said something in a letter ... OK, thanks anyway.'

He came back into the kitchen, shaking his head. 'She doesn't know. Well, that's it, I suppose.' Alistair gave a long sigh and shook his head again. 'Look at the time! The shop won't be opened at eight o'clock this morning.'

'Nobody ever comes in as early as that, anyway,' Leila consoled.

'This'll be the day somebody does,' her father said, dolefully. 'Have you both got everything, now?'

David gave an annoyed exclamation. 'No, I've forgot a hankie. Just be a tick.'

With his father and sister on their way to the car, he ran to the sideboard and extracted a sheet of notepaper and an envelope from the left-hand drawer. He wasn't going to be stumped because he didn't know exactly where this Tilly lived. He was desperate to see his mother, and the only way to find her would be to write ... to any sort of address. He was often left on his own in the little back workshop, and surely he'd have a chance to scribble a few lines, and Dad wouldn't miss a stamp if he took one.

'Thomas Birnie?'

The tall, white-haired man frowned, then gave a light laugh. 'No, I'm sorry, you've got the wrong man. My name is Charles Balfour and I've never heard of this ... what was it you called him? Birnie?'

'I am Detective Inspector Liddell from Aberdeen City Police, and this is Detective Sergeant Gaudie. There is no mistake and we are taking you to the Police Station here ...'

'Are you arresting me? On what charge, may I ask?'

His insolence got under Liddell's skin. 'No charge ... yet. We are merely taking you in for routine questioning.'

'Questioning? About what? A robbery, a paternity suit, ha ha? You've got the wrong man, I tell you. I have committed no such crimes, Inspector.'

Having to hold himself back from punching the man in his supercilious face, Liddell said, 'It is nothing like that. Fetch your coat, please, and come with us now.'

'Am I allowed to tell my wife where I am going?'

Gaudie's restraining hand on his sleeve made Liddell take a deep breath, and he managed to keep his voice steady. 'Yes, of course.'

Birnie disappeared into what they took to be the kitchen, and came back in a few seconds, followed by a brown-haired, pleasant-faced woman who looked to be in her late forties, much younger than her husband, if he was her legal husband, which was doubtful. 'What's wrong, Inspector? What is Charles supposed to have done?'

The soft, lilting Highland tongue made Liddell feel even

481

more sorry for her. Poor soul, he thought, she's in for a shock when everything comes out. 'We want to question him regarding his first wife, Ma'am.'

Her unlined brow wrinkled. 'His first wife died many years ago.'

'Yes, Ma'am, we know. Are you ready, sir?'

With a sneering smile at Liddell, the doctor kissed her cheek. 'I'll be back before you know it, my dear. There's been some terrible mistake, but I'll soon clear it up.'

They hadn't far to go, and within minutes, the three men were seated at a table in a small room in Inveraray Police Station. Giving his sergeant time to produce his notebook and pencil, Liddell regarded his suspect. The man must know he was about to be accused of murder, but his eyes – a startlingly bright shade of blue – held no indication of worry or apprehension, and his hands were as steady as a rock when he took out a packet of cigarettes. 'May I?' he asked, as he extracted one and fished in his pocket for his lighter.

Silently, Liddell pushed the ashtray over to him. 'If you're ready, we can begin. As your present wife mentioned, your first wife died some years ago. Is that correct?'

The silver head nodded, the mouth turned up briefly in a sad little smile. 'Yes, that is so, Inspector. Sadly, Margaret caught a chill one night, which developed into pneumonia. She'd had a bad chest since she was a child, I believe, and I did advise her not to go out that night, it was so cold and damp, but she wouldn't listen.'

'She was, perhaps, going to choir practice at the church?'

Liddell thought he could discern a flicker of anxiety now, but Birnie said, quite calmly and with a sarcastic smile on his long lean face, 'No, Inspector, Margaret had a voice like a corncrake. As I told you before, you have the wrong man.'

'No, sir, I think not. You have been definitely identified by a witness as Thomas Birnie, medical practitioner.'

'A case of mistaken identity, Inspector.'

'She swears . . .'

'She? Oh, Inspector, never, never trust a woman's judgement. If you ask any woman if she has seen a certain man, of course she will say yes. It is part of their nature.'

'Is it part of their nature to provide that certain man's address?' Liddell was growing increasingly irritated by the doctor's attitude. 'Furthermore, this lady had not been asked anything about you. She did, of course, know that we were trying to trace you, but she came to us of her own accord to tell us where she had seen you, and how she discovered where you lived . . . under an assumed name.'

'I am afraid your witness picked me at random, Inspector. I had never heard the name Thomas Birnie until you mentioned it to me earlier. Where, if I may dare to ask, does your witness live?'

'She and her family were on holiday in Inveraray from Aberdeen when she spotted you. She knew you very well at one time, and I have every faith in her. She made no mistake.'

'I have never known anyone from Aberdeen, Inspector. I cannot understand this.'

Liddell was pleased to detect a tremor in the voice now. Birnie was getting edgy, though he would still brazen it out. 'How long have you been practising in Inveraray?'

There was a slight pause. 'Um, we moved here only a few weeks ago, on account of my wife's health. Prior to that I was almost twenty years in the heart of Glasgow.'

That could be true, Liddell thought; since he left Forvit, but it would have to be checked. 'And before that?' This was the crucial period.

'Dunoon. From the time I qualified until Margaret died ... almost eight years.'

'Not Dunoon, Doctor. Well over a hundred miles from there, wasn't it?'

'What are you getting at, Inspector?' The mask was beginning to slip, the voice was sharper, higher. 'Where am I supposed to have been?'

'Do you know Aberdeenshire at all, Doctor?'

'No, I have never been as far north as that.'

The questioning went on for hours, over and over the same details, with Birnie obviously trying to remain calm, but there was an odd second or two when Liddell knew that perseverance would pay off. The man would crack ... if they kept at him.

It was almost midnight, with all three men on the verge of collapse, when, after Birnie had again denied ever being in Aberdeenshire, Liddell said, wearily, 'So if we take you to a small village some miles to the north of Aberdeen tomorrow, you will be confident of not being recognized?'

At this, Birnie jumped to his feet, his face crimson with anger. 'Can't you get it into your thick police skull that I have never – ever! – set foot in Forvit?' His colour draining, he thumped down on his seat again.

Almost simultaneously, Gaudie threw down his pencil with a smirk on his face, and Liddell himself leaned back with a tremendous feeling of satisfaction. He had known Birnie would put his foot in it eventually.

Tilly was smiling as she came in with the post. 'It's for you, Gwen, but just look at how it's addressed. Mrs A. Ritchie, care of Tilly and Fred, Somewhere in Moltby, Near Newcastle,

484

and somebody in the post office has written, "Try Barker, Jasmine Cottage." Just as well, or you mightn't have . . .'

Grabbing the letter, Gwen gasped, 'It's David's writing. Oh, God! Maybe Alistair's ill, or Leila.' Her nervous fingers made a sorry mess of the envelope, but at last she drew out the single sheet. '"Dear Mum,"' she read out, '"if you ever get this letter, please come home as soon as you can. Your loving son, David." Oh, goodness, something must be far wrong up there.'

Tilly shook her head. 'David must be missing you, he's still very young.'

'He knows I can't go back. His father as good as threw me out.'

'Alistair likely didn't want to climb down, so he let David do the pleading.'

'D'you really think that's it?' A note of hope came through the question.

'It's how it looks to me.' Tilly's brow suddenly furrowed. 'But Alistair knows where you are . . . doesn't he?'

'I never told Marge or Peg where I was going,' Gwen muttered, guiltily.

Gasping, Tilly said, 'No wonder nobody's written before. They must be frantic with worry, and it's high time you got in touch. Go and phone right this minute.'

It was with some reluctance that Gwen went upstairs for her purse, but she was down in seconds pulling on her coat. 'I'm not going to be bulldozed into going home, though, if I don't think Alistair wants me.'

The nearest telephone kiosk being in the village proper, Tilly knew that she would be gone for at least twenty minutes, and busied herself by sweeping the flagged kitchen floor, sluicing down her back doorstep and emptying the teapot on to the rose bush under the bedroom window. Then she went back inside, filled the kettle and put it on the stove.

Gwen would likely be glad of something to heat her when she came in out of that cold wind.

Gwen timed it perfectly, running in, her face ashen, as the kettle started to warble.

'What's up, love?' cried Tilly, jumping up to take her in her arms.

'Marge is dead! And I didn't know! Oh, Tilly, it's awful!'

'There, there, my lovie. Don't upset yourself.'

'But I didn't know, that's what hurts. A big pipe fell off a lorry and hit her, and she died on the way to hospital, and Peg said they'd all been worried stiff about me.' She took in a deep gulp of air and went on, 'Alistair had phoned Peg to ask your address, but she'd never heard of you, and I took my address book away with me.'

'You should have phoned his shop when you were at it. I'm sure he'd have dropped everything and come to you.'

'I just had the two pennies, but Peg said she'd ring him and tell him I'd be at Lee Green. She wants me there as soon as I can ... to talk about ...'

Tilly's sympathy metamorphosed into brisk efficiency as she organized her soon-to-be-ex-lodger and looked up the LNER timetable. 'There's a train at ten past two, so you'll need to catch the 12.45 bus from here. You'll just have time to get your things together and have a bite of something to keep you going.'

Gwen was glad that she'd have no time to brood over her sister's death, although Marge's cheery face still flashed into her mind occasionally.

Their leave-taking was harrowing, because Tilly, as close to Gwen now as Ivy had been, couldn't hold back the tears, which set her off, too. Everything bad, as well as good, comes to an end, however, and at last she was sitting on the bus with her bag at her feet and her hands clenched.

She was on her way to Lee Green again, but even though Peggy had said she would tell Alistair to drop everything and come to London, too, it would be anything but a happy homecoming.

Chapter 35

❧

The welcome in Lee Green was even more traumatic than the farewell in Moltby. Hours were spent in the telling of, and the mourning for, Marge's death. Over the months since it happened, Peggy had learned to hide her sorrow, to profess acceptance, but the fragile veneer was scraped away by the depth of Gwen's grief. 'I should have been here,' she sobbed. 'I can't bear to think she died and I didn't even feel something inside me.'

Peggy put extra pressure on the hand she was gripping. 'It wouldn't have made any difference, Gwennie. She never regained consciousness. She wouldn't have known that none of her family was with her at the end, only two ambulance men.'

And so it went on, the tearing apart of one heart and the desperate struggle of the other not to let the wound open again, and when Dougal came home from work it began all over again, with him doing his best to console his wife's sisters while he, the bereaved husband, was equally in need of comfort – even more so, in fact.

It was almost time for bed when Gwen remembered. 'Where's Nicky? Who's been looking after him?'

'You remember Eth Powell, three doors down? I asked if she'd take him today and keep him overnight, till I saw how you were.' Peggy glanced at Dougal now and, a slight nod telling her it was all right, she continued, 'Pam Deans looked after him at first while we were at work, till one of her sons persuaded her to go and live with him and his wife. Then . . . well, I gave up my job and took over.'

'And *you* bath him when you come home, and put him to bed?' Gwen asked Dougal.

'That's how it was for a while,' he answered, carefully.

'But not any more?'

'Let me tell her.' Peggy regarded Gwen apprehensively. 'For the first few weeks, I went to my own house as soon as Dougal came in, but it seemed so silly to be burning two lots of electricity and gas, so . . . I more or less talked him into letting me move in here.'

Dougal took up the explanation. 'Gwen, I can see by your face what you think, but it wasn't like that. We stuck to the rules and slept in different rooms, but we had all our meals together, and sat together in the evenings, remembering things Marge used to say and do, and . . . we gradually began to feel closer to each other. I suppose it was inevitable, really, two lonely people brought together by one vulnerable little boy. We still sleep in separate rooms, Gwen, we haven't done anything wrong. We were hoping and praying you'd come back, because we want your blessing on us getting married in another six months or so. It's the only way it would feel right for us.'

She looked down at her hands, uncertain of how she felt. It seemed awful that Dougal was thinking of taking a second wife so soon, yet . . . why shouldn't he? He was a decent man. He hadn't jumped straight into bed with another woman, and if he did feel the need of somebody else, he couldn't do better than Peggy. Gwen lifted her head again, and her heart went out to the two people waiting so anxiously for her verdict. She had been on her own for months now, yet she had always cherished a faint hope that she could go back to Alistair one day. They didn't have that – Alf and Marge were gone for good.

The thing was, if Peg was wrong about Alistair, it would be difficult to live where she would see Nicky every day. She would have to keep her distance, be an aunt not a mother . . . which was probably just as well. If Alistair ever did want her back, he wouldn't want Nicky thrown in.

'Dougal,' she began, 'don't think I'm against you two getting married. It's just I'll have to get used to the idea – it's been quite a shock on top of . . .'

'We discussed it night after night,' Peggy said, quietly, 'and we've decided to put both houses on the market and move to another district altogether.'

'Either that,' added Dougal, tentatively, 'or . . . my mother's getting on now, and I'd like to see her and my sister again. Once we sell up here, we could easily afford a holiday in America for the three of us, and there's always the chance I could get a better job and settle over there. What do you think?'

'It's up to you.' Gwen's throat had tightened. She was happy for Nicky that Dougal was including him in their plans, although, if they remained over there, she would never see her younger son again, and her last sister would be lost to her, as well.

Seeing how their news had affected her, Peggy said, 'Leave it just now, Dougal. She still hasn't got over Marge.'

'None of us'll ever get over Marge,' he said sharply, 'but you're right. It's too soon for us to be making definite plans.' He paused, then said, 'Peg, did you remember to phone Alistair?'

'Yes, just after I phoned you, and he said he'd get here as soon as he could. They've all missed you, you know, Gwen.'

'David and Leila probably have, but I'm not so sure about Alistair.'

'He's had time to cool down and think,' Peggy said hastily,

to avoid the subject being dragged up and dissected again. 'I'm almost sure he wants you to go home.'

'I'll believe that when he tells me himself. Being a prisoner of war changed him, you know. The old Alistair would have been shocked at what I did, but he'd have got over it. This Alistair broods over things, and . . .' She broke off with a sigh. 'I'll just have to wait and see what happens.'

The phone call put Alistair into a state of flux. He didn't know whether to be glad or sorry that Gwen had materialized again. He had been out of his mind wondering if she was all right, yet he couldn't forgive her. She apparently wanted to come back, but it was all very well for her. She wasn't the one who had been betrayed. It wasn't her heart that had come within a hairsbreadth of being ground to dust. She wouldn't have to cope with nightly images of her spouse making love with somebody else.

What worried him more than anything, though, was the fact that David had felt driven to write to his mother. If the boy missed her as much as that . . . ?

'Who was that on the phone?' Leila was looking at him in some concern.

'Your Auntie Peggy. Did you know David had written to your mother?'

'Where did he get her address?'

'God knows.'

'What are you going to do, Dad? Are you going to let her come home?'

He gave a doubtful shrug. 'Do you and David want her home?'

'Of course we do. Don't you?'

He avoided her eyes. 'I don't know, Leila, and that's the

truth. She . . . no, I still can't speak about it, not yet and especially not to you.'

'Don't be too hard on her, Dad. She's been punished for what she did – she must have spent years wondering when the axe was going to fall. She's not a bad person.'

'I know that, but . . . no, you can't understand, Leila.'

'Maybe I can't, but . . . please, Dad, make her come home.'

He raised his head again. 'I said I'd go to speak to her, and we'd see what happens. Will we shut up the shop for a few days, or will you two manage to keep things going till I come back?'

'We'll manage.'

'Just take a note of anything I need to do, and I'll attend to it when I get back. I'll have to go and pack a few things, so you and David will have to take the bus home.'

'I bet he would crawl home on his hands and knees if it would bring Mum back.'

Her trill of laughter was music to his ears; neither she nor David had so much as smiled for some time, and his own heart lightened a little as he went out to his car.

On his way to Forvit, he decided that he might as well tell Lexie that he was going to see Gwen. Whatever she said, even if she told him he was being a fool, it wouldn't make him change his mind, but it was best that she knew.

It proved difficult to speak about personal matters in the shop. He was forced to stop each time a customer came in, and he had only got as far as telling her how David had worked out where to contact his mother, when they were interrupted again.

This time, it was Detective Inspector Roddy Liddell who walked in, his face so grave that they both knew he had something seriously bad to impart. 'I'd advise you to shut the shop, Lexie,' he began, then looked at Alistair. 'I'm glad you're here, too. She's going to need somebody and I'll have to get back after I say what I have to say.'

Noticing that the blood had ebbed from Lexie's face, Alistair took it upon himself to walk across to the shop door, turn the key in the lock and push down the snib. 'What is it? Has there been a new development?'

Liddell was already shepherding her through the connecting door to her house, his arm protectively round her waist, and all thoughts of going to London flew out of Alistair's mind as he followed them. Whatever the 'tec had to tell Lexie, he appeared to be quite sure that it would knock her for six.

In the kitchen, Liddell sat on the sofa with her, taking her hand between both of his, but Alistair, waiting to hear the bad news, remained standing.

'I wish I didn't have to do this,' Roddy said, after a moment. 'And I don't know where to begin.'

'It might be a good idea to begin at the beginning.' Alistair couldn't help the sarcasm.

'Yes, of course. Yesterday, my sergeant and I went to the address in Inveraray given by Mrs Chalmers. The man who answered the door denied that he was Tom Birnie, but we took him in for questioning anyway.'

With both his listeners' attention riveted on him, he told them of the long hours of questioning before the man made his fatal slip and his interrogators knew for certain that he *was* the man they were after.

An important question occurred to Alistair. 'If he hadn't shot himself in the foot, so to speak, would you have let him go?'

Liddell gave his head a firm shake. 'No, I was one hundred per cent positive that we had the right man and we'd have kept on and on at him until he did crack. He gave the game away by naming Forvit, which we had avoided mentioning,

493

so we brought him up to Aberdeen to get his full statement, and believe me, once he started, he didn't want to stop. He boasted about all the young girls he had seduced – that was the word he used, but we did get him to admit that in most cases it had been rape – and then he came to Nancy Lawrie. I'll read a bit of my sergeant's notes. He's good, got it almost verbatim.

'I'd actually grown quite fond of the girl, but when she collared me one day and said she was in the family way and what was I going to do about it, she got me on the raw. I thought she was trying to trap me and I got really angry. I said it wasn't mine, and I could take no responsibility for it. She had got herself into the mess and she could bloody well get herself out of it.'

At this point, Lexie spoke for the first time. 'Nancy said he promised to marry her when his wife divorced him, though he never did, but he got her a room in Edinburgh.'

The detective nodded his agreement with this. 'That came later. At first, she was so upset by the doctor's attitude, and scared that her parents would find out, that when your father asked her why she was crying, she burst out with the whole sorry story.'

'Yes, she told me all that, and Dad went to Tom Birnie and threatened to tell his wife what he'd done if he didn't support Nancy and the child.'

Liddell hesitated before saying – softly wary and obviously ready to stop if Lexie's reaction was too strong – 'This is when it turned really nasty, I'm afraid. He fooled Nancy into believing that he would marry her when his wife divorced him, but he says he never had any intention of leaving her. It was she who had the money, you see, and he didn't want to foul his own nest by admitting what he had done.

'Unfortunately, he hadn't fooled Margaret. She had known for years the kind of man he was and hadn't been particularly

494

worried because she knew he wasn't serious about any of them ... until Nancy. So she tackled him one night and they'd had a ding-dong row that went on for hours, he said, and was still raging when they went up to bed. She had thrown every bad name she knew at him, and at first he laughed it off, but when she started to say foul things about Nancy, he lost his temper and hit her to shut her up. It didn't stop her, though, and she kept on, pummelling into him while she spat out more filth and ...'

Liddell glanced briefly at Alistair before he went on, 'He says he didn't mean to kill her, but he lost control altogether, and one of his punches knocked her on to the bed and he lifted a pillow without thinking and suffocated her.'

Lexie rendered speechless by this, it was left to Alistair to say, 'You can't suffocate somebody without meaning to, though.'

'No, it was definitely murder, but probably unpremeditated. At any rate, he panicked, and sat for a while wondering what to do, till he realized that the longer he waited, the worse it would be for him to shift her – rigor mortis sets in after so many hours. Of course, it disappears again after about another twenty-four hours, but he couldn't wait that long to dispose of the body. So he wrapped it in the bedspread, bumped her down the stairs and through the kitchen, but unluckily for him ...'

Liddell's voice had begun to waver before he stopped speaking, and now he put one arm round Lexie's shoulders. 'This is the worst bit for you to hear, my dear, and I should probably have told you this first, but ...'

He looked round at Alistair, who said, 'Aye, it was my fault you didn't. But go on, tell us now, for God's sake. Has this something to do with Lexie's father?'

'Yes. I'm afraid so. Birnie said that when he opened the back door, Alec Fraser was standing on the step with his hand raised ready to knock. He said he'd come to ask if Margaret was well enough, because she hadn't turned up for choir practice that night, then, according to Birnie, Alec looked past him and saw what he shouldn't have seen. A strand of Margaret's hair had worked its way out at the top of the bedspread.'

Roddy paused with a sigh. 'I'll give you his account of what happened next, if I can find the place. Ah, here it is.'

'Fraser froze with shock, but I couldn't chance him recovering and running off to report me, so I punched him in the solar plexus and knocked him out. Then I ran up to the bedroom and got the pillow . . .'

Out of consideration for Lexie, Liddell stopped there, but she muttered, 'No, Roddy, I want to know everything. What did he do after he smothered my father?'

'He wrapped him in a sheet and had two bodies to dispose of. He was telling me all this without batting an eyelid, boasting about it, but he admitted he'd had quite a struggle to drag them, one at a time, through the back door. He wondered if he should put them in his car and hide them somewhere miles away, until it struck him that the handiest place would be best, the nearest, the one it would be least likely for anyone to look, even if the police did make a search for them as missing persons. At the other side of the wall was a moor which had been shown on maps as early as the sixteen hundreds, an ideal burial ground, although it needed a Herculean effort to get them over the wall.

'I'll quote here – "*I didn't bury them in the same grave. I couldn't have Fraser lying on top of Margaret for all eternity, but I had to get rid of the sanctimonious bastard.*"

'That was how he put it,' Roddy said apologetically. 'The hue and cry went up next day about Alec Fraser having disappeared, but Mrs Birnie wasn't missed until one of her

496

friends realized that she hadn't seen the doctor's wife for some time and asked him if she was well enough. That was when he put out the story about her going to Stirling to look after her sick mother, the story he'd had time to manufacture.'

Roddy waited for a moment to see if Lexie wanted to say anything at this point, but she seemed to have sunk into some kind of morose reverie, so he went on, wanting to get it over. 'The day after the murders, Birnie was called in to attend to your mother, and he went back that night with the excuse that the two of you needed something to help you to sleep. What he gave your mother had her out like a light in minutes, he told me, so he took you through to your room, Lexie, gave you the same sleeping potion or whatever, and waited to see if it took effect. Of course, we know now that he was easily aroused by young girls' bodies, and as you took off your clothes it occurred to him how he could get his revenge on your father for interfering in things that didn't concern him.'

Only then did Lexie give a start and her eyes darkened as she exclaimed, 'It was the doctor that raped me?'

'Yes, it was Tom Birnie, adulterer, seducer, rapist and murderer . . . and liar, of course. Accomplished liar. You weren't the only one, Lexie, just one of many.'

'That doesn't make much difference to me, though.' She made a loud gulping noise and then muttered, 'No, I'm wrong. It does make a difference. I can think of my father as a decent man now, after all the years of hating him for what he did to me.'

'You can be proud of him,' Liddell pointed out. 'He wasn't afraid to do what he felt needed to be done. He did what he could for Nancy Lawrie, and if he'd arrived at the doctor's house half an hour earlier, he'd likely have tried to help Margaret Birnie. As it was, he didn't even get a chance to accuse her husband of murdering her.'

'Everybody always said Alec Fraser was a gentleman,' Alistair put in here. 'People could hardly believe he'd run off with anybody, never mind a girl like Nancy, but that was how it looked, and I'm glad his name's been cleared at last.'

Lexie released a shuddering sigh as Liddell got to his feet. 'Don't leave me, Roddy.'

He bent down and kissed her brow. 'I have to, Lexie, my dear. I've overstayed the time I was allowed, as it is.'

'She'll be all right,' Alistair stated, firmly. 'I'll stay with her . . . all night if necessary.'

'Thanks, I hate having to go like this, but my Super wants me back right away. I'll come back as soon as I can, Lexie, but I can't promise any definite time . . . or day, even. There's still a lot of work to be done before we get things properly tied up.'

'I understand, Roddy.' She was plainly trying to keep her voice steady, but she couldn't disguise its slight tremor. 'I'll see you when I see you.'

She controlled herself until his footsteps faded, and then the floodgates opened. 'Oh, Lexie,' Alistair begged, 'please don't cry like that. I know how upset you must be, but it tears me apart hearing you . . .'

She stretched out a hand and pulled him down beside her, and he had no option but to take her in his arms – not that he didn't want to, because he felt more genuine love for her at that precise moment than he had ever done before. Over the past few weeks, too, he had found himself recalling, with deep fondness, the evenings they had spent together in the shadow of the tower when they were young . . . before her father . . . before she thought Alec had abandoned her. Not only that, it had just transpired, she had thought that it was shame at raping her which had made him leave, and that wasn't true either. But it explained her peculiar behaviour. That was why she'd been like she was, why she had suddenly started fighting him off after making him believe she wanted him to make love to her, after she'd succeeded in making *him* desperate for it. But it was no wonder she had changed. Being raped at sixteen would be bad enough, but thinking it was her own father . . .

How could any doctor, in a position of trust, take advantage of young female patients like that? It was . . . despicable, though that word wasn't really strong enough, and there was no excuse for it. And then, to top it all, he had killed his wife in a fit of rage, also an innocent well-meaning man . . . Christ Almighty! How low could a human being sink?

It dawned on him now that Lexie's almost hysterical sobbing had eased. 'Do you fancy a drink to steady you?' he asked her.

She drew in a long, quivering breath. 'I'll go through and get a bottle of brandy from the shop. Roddy and I finished one the last time he was here.'

He let her do it. It was something to occupy her for a wee while, but it gave him, unfortunately, time to imagine what she and the 'tec had got up to after finishing off a whole bottle of brandy. Had she let *him* go all the way? But maybe the bottle hadn't been full when they started? He sincerely hoped not, for even if Lexie wasn't a young girl any longer, she had kept her figure. Of course, she hadn't borne any children, so it had been easier for her than for Gwen, whose waist was thicker than it had once been, and her breasts more flabby.

A lead ball hit him in the gut. With everything that had happened, he had forgotten all about Gwen. She would be sitting in Lee Green tomorrow on her own waiting for him to show up. Of course, she might spend the night in Peg's house, or Dougal's, though that wouldn't make it any easier for her. But he couldn't help it. He had promised to look after Lexie tonight, and he couldn't let her down. He couldn't even phone Dougal to explain. If Lexie knew he had promised to go to Lee Green, she would make him go.

He raised his head with a smile when she came back with a bottle of Five Star Cognac, and watched while she took out two goblets and almost filled them. Then, after sitting down beside him again, she murmured, 'I don't know what I'd have done tonight without you, Alistair, d'you know that?'

'I'm just glad I was here, though I'm sure Liddell wouldn't have gone back on duty if you'd been on your own.'

She gave a tremulous smile. 'I wouldn't be too sure of that. Doesn't duty come first, last and always with a cop?'

'Do you ... is it serious between you?'

Shrugging sadly, she said, 'I wish I knew. I don't know what's wrong with me, but I always pick men who can't make a definite commitment to me.'

He took this as a hit at him. 'Lexie, we were far too young ...'

'Forget what I said, I'm not thinking straight. You know, you don't have to stay with me all night. I've got over the worst, and I'll be all right.'

'No, Lexie, if I leave now, you'll go over and over things in your mind till you're in a right old state.'

She looked at him cautiously. 'I need to go over it again, Alistair. I want to remember how it happened. Now I know it wasn't my father, maybe other details will come back to me. As a matter of fact, just a few minutes ago, something that man said came into my head. It was while he was ... actually doing it, and he must have thought the sleeping pills he gave me had taken effect, but if he'd only realized, he was keeping me awake with the pain he was causing.'

'I think you should try to forget,' Alistair muttered, uncomfortably.

'No, Al, I have to remember everything that happened that night, to lay it all out and see the truth of it, before I can let myself forget. Please don't try to stop me.'

His heart aching with pity for her – or could it be that love was blossoming after all this time? – he put an arm around her and pulled her against him so that her head was resting on his shoulder. 'Get it off your chest, then, but remember, I'm here to catch you if you feel you're falling into a bottomless pit.'

She fished for his free hand and gripped it tightly, reassuring herself and drawing comfort from him before she began. She told him how happy her childhood had been, how her father had been everything a child could wish for, how he had given her a love of music. 'I'm sure he was disappointed that I couldn't sing for peanuts, but he never said anything. He was always loving towards Mum and me, and she was quite happy for him to be helping people out of little troubles they couldn't see a way round themselves, men as well as women, and girls. Mum trusted him, that's why it came as such a shock when he just went off. He hadn't told her about Nancy, I don't know why. If he had, things might have turned out differently. As it was, she couldn't bring herself to believe he'd run away with a young girl, but there wasn't any other explanation.'

Lexie suddenly twisted round to look up into Alistair's face. 'That's really what killed her, you know, the thought of him betraying her and the nagging suspicion he could have been carrying on with other females for years.'

Her lovely blue eyes were pleading, her trembling lips only inches away from his as he looked down on her, and he was overcome with love for her, but he knew better than to kiss her – not yet. He had to let her work out the sequence of events, had to listen if she wanted to describe every move the evil doctor had made. 'I'm sorry, my dear.' It was all he could say.

She *did* go into every last detail which had flooded into her reawakened mind, describing Birnie's lascivious face – although she said 'drooling' – as she undressed after taking the sleeping tablets. 'He even unfastened my bra because my fingers wouldn't work. I don't think he put my pyjamas on for me. I think he wanted me naked ...' She shuddered. 'Wait, though, something else is coming back ...' She closed her eyes for a few moments then whispered, 'He was gripping my ... breasts and moaning, not words, just sounds, then he muttered something about the sins of the fathers. It was after that, when he was fastening his trousers, that he gave a horrible, cackling laugh and said, 'That's paid you back for sticking your nose in where it wasn't wanted, you interfering slimy bastard.' I thought it was me he was calling names and I was too young to understand what they meant, but now I do.'

Alistair felt really uncomfortable at hearing what Lexie had gone through, but he had promised to listen and he supposed it was good that she could talk about it. Luckily for him, having satisfied herself as to what had been done to her and by whom, she didn't want to go any further down that particular path.

For the last minute or two, she had been looking into the fire, but she swivelled round once more. 'Maybe now you'll see why I couldn't let you do what you wanted, nor any of the other boys I went out with, locals and boys from Ardley Camp during the war. Not only that, I couldn't forget you, Al, you were always there in my mind. Even after you got married, I still believed I could get you back. After I met

Gwen, though, I knew I'd just been fooling myself. That reminds me, have you heard from her yet?'

He shook his head vehemently. It was true – he hadn't heard from Gwen. He'd only heard of her through Peggy when she phoned. 'Since she went away, I've been thinking more about how things used to be between us, Lexie. I think I did love you, but ...'

'But I was too eager?'

'Aye, that was it. We ... I've wasted a lot of years, Lexie ... darling.'

She gave him no encouragement – he had to lift her chin with his thumb – but the minute their lips touched he believed that he could sense the electricity between them. 'Oh, Lexie,' he groaned.

Strangely, he didn't even think of going any further than that. It wouldn't have been fair to her after what she had learned earlier, and he was content just to hold her in his arms and stroke her fine blonde hair.

They stayed like that until the fire died down. 'Will I put on more coal?' he asked.

'It's hardly worth it. It's ten to ten.'

'Yes, it's time you went to bed. I'll sleep on the couch, if you look out a couple of blankets for me.'

She propped herself up on one elbow and looked deep into his eyes. 'I don't want you to sleep down here. Come upstairs and just be there for me – if that's all right?'

He wasn't too sure of the wisdom of this – in such a situation wouldn't he be tempted? – but if that was what she wanted, he would do his best.

Later, lying on top of the bedcovers while she slept in fits and starts in the crook of his arm, he thought of his wife, who would be expecting him in the morning; of his children, who would believe that he was on his way to London until Peggy or Gwen phoned to let them know

503

he hadn't arrived. But he resolutely put all thoughts of them out of his mind. What did anything matter? He had been reunited with Lexie and she would never, ever, let him down.

Chapter 36

❧

Chilled to the bone despite the electric fire which Lexie had switched on so that he wouldn't be cold, Alistair regarded it doubtfully; he could just make out the faint glow of the spiralled strip of its single element; there didn't seem to be any heat coming from the damned thing. Shouldn't it be brighter than that? Lexie must be warm enough, though. Astonishingly, despite what she had learned last night, she was fast asleep, not, however, an altogether peaceful sleep. Her body was restless, moving, jerking involuntarily every now and then.

Poor lass. She hadn't had an easy life, especially with that awful suspicion about her father at the back of her mind for so many years. Thank goodness she knew the truth now, which, he had to admit, much as it went against the grain, was entirely due to the efforts of Detective Inspector Roderick Liddell. Still, there was no need to be jealous of him now. With the case solved, he wouldn't be bothering Lexie much longer. She'd be free to get on with her life, a life that she had dreamed of for twenty years, a life with her first and only love.

Alistair's sigh came out louder than he intended, so loud that his companion stirred and opened her eyes. 'Are you OK, Al? You look cold.'

'I'm not too bad,' he fibbed. 'Go back to sleep. You need all the rest you can get.'

'I haven't really been asleep, just dozing off and on. I've

been conscious of you there all the time, thank goodness. Come under the blankets and speak to me.'

Ignoring the warning bell ringing in his head, he hoisted himself up then slid in beside her. 'You *are* cold!' she exclaimed. 'You're shivering. Come closer till I see if I can get some heat into you.'

She moved over and he obediently lay in the spot she had vacated for him, his temperature shooting up with the heat of her as she snuggled against him. Good God, he thought, that wasn't bad going – from well below zero to well above boiling point in a couple of seconds – but he said nothing, for fear of breaking the spell.

'I've something to tell you, Al,' she murmured after a while.

His limbs feeling as if they belonged to him again and wouldn't cut off her circulation if they touched her, he put an arm round her and ran his hand gently down her back. He wanted to show that he loved her, too, that he had come to his senses at long last. Her little intake of breath showed that the caress had pleased her, but he wanted to hear her say what he was sure she was going to say. 'Yes? What is it, my darling?'

She kissed him first. 'Oh, Al, my dear, dear Al. All my life it was you I wanted . . .'

'Yes,' he breathed, 'and you've got me now.'

'But that's just the point,' she whispered. 'Now I know I can have you . . .'

His kiss was tender. It wasn't time yet for passion. 'There's no need for you to worry, my darling. I know what you're trying to say.'

'Do you?' She sounded surprised. 'How could you? You can't have guessed?'

'Yes, it wasn't difficult, all the signs were there.'

'But we tried to keep it a secret till . . .'

506

This wasn't going as he thought. In fact, his mouth had dried up, the chill had settled on him again. 'We? You and who else? Oh, no!' The understanding almost crushed him. 'Don't tell me that bloody 'tec's been at you, got you fooled.'

She pulled away from him. 'Alistair, that's not fair. Roddy's been very good to me, very considerate, and I love him ... more than I ever loved you.'

He didn't believe her. He had caught her on the raw, and she was trying to get back at him by saying that. 'You hardly know him. How long is it since you met him?'

'Long enough. It doesn't take long to fall in love, and it doesn't take long to be sure if the other person loves you back.'

'You can't know that for sure.' Alistair was fighting against the intrusive feeling that it wasn't only Gwen who had betrayed him. 'I bet he's married and you're just a bit on the side for him.'

Her open hand slapped his cheek, and as he jumped back, she spat out, 'Thank you for those kind words!' Her voice was icy. 'But let me tell you, his wife died over five years ago, and I would trust him before you, any day! Get out of my house, Alistair Ritchie, and I don't want to see you ever again!'

Needing no second telling, he leapt out of bed, scuttled down the stairs and slammed out of the house. His mind was in such a state of torment that he completely forgot parking his car at the shop door the day before and walked in the other direction ... and carried on walking, sheer instinct alone guiding his feet. All he was conscious of, apart from the jagged pain of rejection, was self-pity, an overwhelming deluge of self-pity. Why did all these bad things have to happen to him? What had he done, for God's sake, that he had to be punished for it? Hadn't he fought for his King and country? Hadn't he endured over two years in

507

a prisoner-of-war camp? Hadn't he worked his gut out to run a business successful enough to keep his family in a decent style?

And then he'd been felled by learning that his wife had cheated on him while he was away, that she had filled her lonely hours with another man, that she had even let this other man make love to her and plant a child inside her. All that of course, according to her, was Marge's fault, and God had certainly punished *her*. One smack with a sewage pipe and poof!

Poof? Why did that remind him of something? Somebody? Somebody who said 'Poof', and snapped his fingers? *His* fingers. Yes, it had been a man. *Manny!* Manny Isaacson. Oh, if only those happy days could come back again. If only there had never been a war. If only he had never made Gwen take their children to Forvit. If only he'd never left Forvit in the first place. He would likely have married Lexie, and they'd have been happy ever after. *She* wouldn't have broken her marriage vows.

Alistair had no control over his thoughts, which were leading him to ridiculous heights of improbability ... nor over his feet, which were taking him towards the tower, his old trysting place with Lexie. They were averse to going home, where, his subconscious mind told him, lay decisions to be taken, explanations to be made, neither of which he was capable of at the present time.

There was a light layer of frost on the stony path, making his footsteps crackle as he made his way up the hill, and the scrub and clumps of heather on either side of him seemed to be ghostly, uneven, white shapes in the dim light of the half moon. When he reached the track which branched off to the right, the way to his own house, he stomped past it, firmly set now on getting to the old tower which had deteriorated even further since he was a youth, to the place where he could be

508

sure of peace to think, to confront whatever it was that had been bothering him, ripping him apart.

Reaching his goal, he sat down on the far side, leaning against the crumbling stone wall, drawing his feet up and putting his arms round his knees. Why was he in such a state? What had happened to him? He felt completely and utterly lost, with no friends, no family, to guide him. Oh, Manny, if only you were here. You would advise me. You would keep me right. You would help me to make my decision.

What decision, though? That was the point. The ache inside him was growing angrier at the thought of having to make it. Clearly, whatever choice he made would not be a happy one. Nothing in his life would be happy now. Nothing could be even the least little bit happy any more. It was to do with . . . two women. That was it. One woman he loved, and the other woman he . . . also loved?

He sat up with a start. Where was Lexie? Why had she left him up here on his own, with these big boulders all round him. What if more bits fell down? Would anybody care if he was hurt, or killed? Nobody!

Gradually, however, as he sat regarding the surrounding stones with distaste rather than fear, a picture of two small children returned to him. Two fair-haired children – a boy and a girl. But there was another child's face intruding – a face topped with bright ginger hair, an appealing face but one he didn't want to see.

He closed his eyes, and tried to conjure something else up, and thankfully it was Lexie who came into his inner view. But where was she? Something was wrong somewhere, something far wrong. He had to find her . . . as soon as he could, before she . . .

Rising unsteadily to his feet, he skirted the debris and set off down the hill again, his feet, this time, scarcely taking time to touch the ground. But it wasn't dark now. It was morning, early morning. His mind on what he knew was an urgent quest, he broke into a desperate run, gaining further momentum on the last steep slope before the track joined the road.

He didn't see the single-decker bus coming, and even if he had, he would have been unable to stop.

'Something could have happened. Why don't you phone the shop and find out . . . ?'

'No, Peg, I know exactly what's happened,' Gwen interrupted. 'He's changed his mind. He's had time to think, and he still can't forgive me.'

'Go home, anyway,' her sister pleaded. 'For David's sake, and Leila's.'

Shaking her head, Gwen murmured, 'It's for their sakes I'm not going back. Alistair can be very nasty, as I found out, and there would likely be another big scene. I can't put them through that again. In any case, he probably wouldn't let me in.'

'Haven't you got the doorkey with you?'

'I didn't think . . .'

'I don't suppose it matters.'

After a few minutes' silence, however, Peggy suddenly said, 'Don't you love him any more, Gwennie?'

She didn't have to think about this. 'I've never stopped loving him, but it's obvious he doesn't love me now, so what's the point?'

'The point is,' her sister said brusquely, 'that you are his wife, and not only that, you have two children to think of.' She paused, then went on, cautiously, 'Yes, just two. It's easier all round if you forget . . . Once we take Nicky to America, Alistair might come round.'

'Do you think so?' A trace of hope appeared in Gwen's eyes.

'It's possible.'

*   *   *

'It's funny Dad hasn't phoned yet,' David said, as he and his sister were walking down to catch the bus. 'He should have got to Lee Green by now.'

'Maybe Mum and him were too busy talking to notice the time,' Leila comforted. 'One of them'll likely phone the shop this forenoon.'

'Leila, what if she doesn't want to come home?'

'She's probably still getting over Auntie Marge. She wouldn't have known anything about that, remember.'

'No, I forgot. But Auntie Peggy could have let us know what was going on?'

'She won't want to interfere. Mum's got to make up her own mind.'

'I'd have thought she'd be desperate to see us.'

'You're still too young to understand, David. Come on, we'd better hurry or we'll miss the bus and we'll have to wait an hour for the next one.'

He dutifully speeded up, but his face told of his inner dissatisfaction with the way things were turning out. They waited at what was recognized as a courtesy bus stop, but the bus didn't arrive on time, and they argued for some minutes over whether to go home and come back in an hour to get the next bus, or, as David wanted, to start walking in the hope that this bus had been held up and would catch up with them. Leila had finally given in, and they were twenty minutes on their way when a car drew up alongside them.

They knew the driver by sight and he explained that the postman had told him there had been an accident about a mile and a half back. 'Somebody apparently ran on to the road in front of the bus. Goodness knows how long it'll be before you'll get one, so you'd better hop in and I'll give you a lift into town.'

They accepted gratefully, and while they were speeding

511

towards the city, he said, 'You're Alistair Ritchie's two, aren't you? I was at school with him, a year younger – Sid MacConnachie.' Gathering from their animated faces that they would be interested in hearing about their father's boyhood, he told them of the mischief Dougal and Alistair had got up to, but he changed the subject when they came to the outskirts of Aberdeen. 'I was sorry to hear about your Auntie Marge. I only met her once or twice – at the dances for the boys at the camp during the war – but she was full of fun. I wasn't called up for service, you see . . . graded 4F at my medical.'

'4F?' asked David, his curiosity aroused. 'What was that?'

'Well, you know what A1 means?'

'The best there is?'

'Right, and they graded you down from that. 4F was the lowest, practically branding you ready to kick the bucket.' MacConnachie gave a throaty chuckle. 'They failed you for deafness, flat feet, asthma and that kind of thing . . . and I had the lot.' He grinned at Leila through the mirror after negotiating the intricacies of Queen's Cross, a meeting of five streets. 'Where do you want me to drop you? I turn down Holburn Street.'

'That's fine,' she smiled. 'Let us off when you come to Holburn Junction. We haven't far to go from there.'

As soon as the car stopped, David started to run, anxious in case his mother or father phoned to tell them what had been decided, while Leila hurried behind him.

It was, however, almost noon before the telephone rang, but when David dived to answer it, it was Lexie Fraser to tell them that their father had been in an accident with the early morning bus and was in the Aberdeen Royal Infirmary, although she was so upset that the boy had difficulty making out what she was saying. 'Lock up the shop,' she instructed, after obviously pulling herself together, 'and get a taxi to the hospital, you and Leila. Tell the driver I'll pay when you get here.'

David looked at the receiver for a moment after she rang off, and Leila asked, 'Well? It was Mum, wasn't it? What did she say? Is she coming home?'

He burst into tears now. 'It was Lexie. Dad's in hospital . . . it was him that was in that accident . . . but how could it be? He's in London with Mum, isn't he?'

'How is he?' Leila asked Lexie, thankful that the woman had appeared quickly, because the man at the door had been most unwilling to let them in without visiting cards, and the taxi driver had displayed obvious disbelief that he would be paid.

'He's still unconscious, but I thought you should be here in case he comes round.'

'Have you told my Mum?' David wanted to know, finding his voice at last.

Lexie looked puzzled. 'I thought nobody knew where your Mum was.'

'She's back in Lee Green,' Leila cut in, to avoid David going into a long explanation.

'Do you know her telephone number?'

'I know the three of them,' Leila said proudly, her voice trembling just a little. 'Should I go and find a phone?'

'If you don't mind. I'll wait with David till you come back.'

Leila had rung her grandma's number and her aunt's before she found Gwen at Dougal's, but it was Peggy who took control of the situation when she heard what had happened. 'Leila, is anybody there with you . . . an older person, I mean?'

'Yes, Lexie Fraser's here. I don't know yet how she found

513

out about the accident, but it was her that phoned us. We're all at the hospital, and Dad's still unconscious.'

'I'll let Dougal know, and he'll likely want to take your Mum up on the train. I'll stay here with Nicky, and I won't leave the house at all, so phone me the minute there's any change in your Dad.'

When Dougal and Gwen walked into the hospital waiting room the following day, both Leila and David looked ready to collapse, but stood up to hug their mother. Then Lexie rose to shake her hand.

'I'm glad you're here, Gwen,' she murmured, 'and you, too, Dougal, but we'd better leave the explanations till ... later. I'll take you along to see Alistair, but I'd better warn you, he's not a pretty sight.'

All five of them remained in the hospital for the rest of that day, taking it in turns to go to the small tearoom for a cup of tea and a biscuit, while the others kept vigil in the corridor outside Alistair's ward. Dougal sought out one of the doctors to find out how hopeful they were of the patient's recovery, and the elderly man, utterly worn out as he appeared to be, spent several minutes talking to him and Gwen.

'He seems to think Ally should come round any time,' Dougal observed cheerfully, when the doctor had left. 'They can't do much about anything till he does, so we'll just have to wait to find out how the injuries will affect him.'

Lexie insisted that she should take Leila and Dougal home that night, but it was three days later before Alistair regained consciousness and was pronounced out of danger, and another few hours before Dougal could persuade Gwen to leave the hospital.

Not until they arrived at Benview, however, did she let her thoughts touch on the accident, and why Alistair had been in that particular spot at that particular time, a time when both Leila and David were under the impression that he had gone to Lee Green to fetch her home. 'I'm sure Lexie Fraser knows something,' she said to Dougal, when they were seated by the fireside. 'She said explanations could wait, so . . . d'you think Alistair had been with her all night?'

'Don't torture yourself, Gwen. Look, why don't I go and ask her to come and see you as soon as she can? It's Sunday, and the shop'll be shut by now. I'll take Leila's bike.'

He had just tucked his trouser legs into his socks when they heard a vehicle drawing up outside. 'It's our car,' Gwen muttered, looking out of the window. 'Sandy Mearns is driving and Lexie's coming out. So Alistair must have left the car there for some reason.'

'Don't upset yourself. Wait till you hear what she has to say.'

They had to wait a further few minutes, Barry arriving to take his father back, before Lexie told them anything, and even if some of her story bordered on the unbelievable, it did go a long way to allay Gwen's fears, though there were still a few things that niggled at her.

'I wouldn't have got through that night if he hadn't been there with me,' Lexie assured her. 'Roddy had to go back on duty, so he was glad Alistair could stay. Look, Gwen, nothing went on between us, absolutely nothing. I don't know why he came to see me, he didn't get a chance to say because Roddy came to tell me they'd arrested Tom Birnie. He's admitted to killing both his wife and my father, and as you can imagine, I was in such a state, I think Alistair was scared I'd do something silly . . . and maybe I would have, if he hadn't been there.'

Gwen still looked puzzled. 'I understand all that, but why

was he coming down from the tower at that time of morning? That's what I can't understand.'

'To be honest, neither can I.' Lexie met her eyes squarely. 'Maybe he was trying to make up his mind about taking you back, and he'd decided he would. That would explain him rushing back . . . to pick up his car.'

This bolstered Gwen's flagging hopes of reconciliation with her husband.

Roddy's face told Lexie that something dreadful had happened, and he burst out with it as soon as he closed the door. 'Tom Birnie committed suicide last night! Poisoned himself! We don't know exactly what it was he used, we'll have to wait for the autopsy report.'

'But where would he have got poison? Wasn't he searched?'

'You're as bad as my Super. He was stripped and searched, and nothing was found on him or his clothes, but he left a note . . . to rub my nose in it.' Roddy's long-suffering sigh told of the scorn his superintendent had heaped on him. 'He said he had always known he was bound to be caught some time, and he had taken the precaution of making ready for it. He'd hollowed the heel of one of each pair of shoes he bought over the years, hidden a capsule of poison in the cavity then fixed a rubber heel on top.'

'He'd been doing that for twenty years?'

'It would always have been at the back of his mind, though nobody noticed anything odd about him. His wife says he was the kindest of men. She's totally shocked, can't believe the things he confessed to. He even boasted he'd married her bigamously, after running out on his second wife.'

'Poor woman!'

'It's her I feel most sorry for, and all the other poor women he brutalized, including you. How are you, now, my dear? Have you got over . . . ?'

'I didn't have time to think about that for days . . . but you don't know, of course.'

She told him about Alistair's accident, about him still being in hospital in Aberdeen, then continued, 'He stayed with me all night, you know, after you told us you'd arrested Tom Birnie.'

Roddy looked at her questioningly. 'You said he was running down from the tower and came out on to the road in front of the bus. What had he been doing up there?'

Lexie took a moment to answer. 'We'd had a disagreement, and he rushed out . . .'

'A disagreement? Good God! At a time like that? What was going on, Lexie?'

Having resolved to keep nothing back from him, she murmured, 'I told you he never felt the same about me as I did about him when we were younger, but that night . . .'

'You mean . . . he tried something on . . . after what I'd just told you?'

'No, no, it wasn't that. He wouldn't believe that I didn't love him, and he said I was a fool for . . . he said I was just a bit on the side for you, so I slapped his face. He wasn't stable, you know. Being a prisoner of war changed him, and then Gwen leaving him . . .'

Roddy bit his bottom lip. 'I always had the nasty feeling there was still something between you.'

'There wasn't, just . . . a girl always has a sort of soft spot for her first love, no matter how he treated her. But he was mad at me for hitting him and he just slammed out.'

A rather uncomfortable silence fell then, while she frantically thought of some way to change the subject. 'Does Nancy know about Doctor Birnie?' she asked, at last.

'Last time we talked to her, she was told that he'd been arrested, but she doesn't know that he killed himself.'

'Oh, Roddy!' Lexie burst into tears now, and as he held out his handkerchief to her, he said, 'I know how you feel, my dear. You wish he hadn't been such a coward. You wish he'd lived to be hanged for what he did. Am I right?'

She nodded, but after a moment, she said, in a contrite little voice, 'Is that bad of me?'

'Not in the slightest. He was a monster, and even if he could turn on the charm and be a model husband, like this last "wife" says, it doesn't excuse the anguish and agony he put his victims through, including his first wife. You should think of yourself now, put the past behind you.'

Her heartbeats speeded up, but she couldn't say what she knew he wanted her to say. There was still something holding her back, still the fear of being manipulated into something that would end in tears.

'What's wrong, my darling?' His arms stole round her, and his eyes, and his voice, softened. 'Is it still too soon for you? If it is, it's all right. I love you, my darling, and I'm willing to wait.'

She shook her head sorrowfully. 'Oh, Roddy, I'm sorry.'

'No need to be sorry, Lexie. As usual, I've jumped in with my size thirteen boots and made a muck of it.'

'No, no! It's not you . . . it's me . . .'

There was something in his face now, a quirkiness that banished all her fears. This man could never hurt her. She would be safe with him . . . wouldn't she?

As if he sensed that the love blossoming within her was still quite fragile, his lips touched hers reverently, brushing, lingering, until, with a soft sigh, she gave herself up to the magic of his kisses, the magic of him.

'Lexie,' he murmured after a minute or so, 'I want you to be quite, quite sure, before you commit yourself . . .'

'I am,' she whispered into his ear, 'quite, quite sure.'

With a quick intake of breath, he took her face between his hands. 'Isn't it about time you told me how much you love me?'

Needless to say, it was some hours before Detective Inspector Roderick Liddell left the house behind the general store-cum-Post Office, during which time everlasting love had been sworn, a proposal of marriage had been made . . . and accepted.

1950

Chapter 37

❧

After going over and over it in her mind, Gwen decided that she'd have to tell Alistair about Lexie and Roddy Liddell. Once he started going out again, he would hear it for himself, and it was better that it came from her. The trouble was, he was so unstable, how would he take it, and when would be the best time?

She waited until afternoon. She generally sat with him for a couple of hours after lunch was over and her housework was done, and before she had to prepare the evening meal. It was a peaceful time, a time to discuss what was in the newspaper and on the wireless, a time to talk about anything she was sure would not upset him. Even after six months, he was still fragile, in mind as well as body, and had to be treated with kid gloves.

'The new man's taking over the shop today,' she began, carefully.

'Aye,' he said, in his usual expressionless voice, so that she could never be certain if he had actually taken in what she said. 'Sandy Mearns told me this morning.'

The postman had been a lifeline to Gwen. He had arranged that their delivery be the last of his morning round, which let him have half an hour or so to sit and speak to Alistair over a cup of tea and a biscuit. Perhaps it was because he was older, on the verge of retirement, that he was the only one who seemed to get through to him. Not even David, nor Leila who was his favourite, could hold his attention for more than a few minutes, yet he chatted away to Sandy all the time he was there, which gave her freedom to do things she couldn't get at otherwise. If she was out of Alistair's sight for longer than it took to go to the bathroom, he was shouting for her.

Dragging her thoughts back to the matter in hand, she said, brightly, 'I'm glad for Lexie. She waited a long time, and she couldn't have picked a nicer man than Roddy.'

Alistair's brow wrinkled. 'Roddy? The 'tec? But he hasn't taken over the shop?'

She couldn't help wondering, not for the first time, why he seemed to have such a down on the man, but she let it pass. 'No, it's a Bill Munro, and I don't know where he comes from. I meant . . . Lexie's marrying Roddy on Saturday in Aberdeen and I wish I could go and see her. She'll make a lovely bride.'

Her husband was silent for so long that she wished she hadn't raised the subject after all. Lexie was one of his closest friends, and besides helping Leila and David at the time of their father's accident, she had stayed at his bedside until his wife managed to be there with him. Had there been more than friendship between them? Had the romance of their childhood carried over into adulthood, or had it lapsed when he went to London and been revived again when he returned to Forvit? There had been other occasions when she had been suspicious, had felt jealous of Lexie, but it had always blown over. Not this time.

Yet . . . if he loved Lexie, why had he been so upset when he learned about . . . his wife's one and only slip? It would have been an ideal let-out for him, a perfect reason to file for divorce, but he hadn't taken it. That was why she had always hoped . . .

'Aren't you happy for Lexie?' she asked, wanting to get at the truth once and for all. In his present state, he wasn't capable of carrying off a downright lie. 'You thought quite a lot of her at one time, didn't you?'

His eyes, when he turned them on her, were accusing, as if he knew exactly what she was up to. 'Yes,' he said, slowly and very deliberately, 'I've always thought quite a lot of Lexie, and if Dougal Finnie hadn't whisked me off to London, I'd likely have married her. Is that what you wanted me to say?'

Disappointment almost choked her. She'd wanted him to tell her that it had only been puppy love between him and Lexie, that it was his love for *her* that was the real thing, the true love, but she had been deluding herself all these years. 'So ... you're not happy for her?' she got out with great difficulty, laying herself wide open to further heartache.

At that moment, the telephone rang, and she jumped up, relieved yet angry at being interrupted. He watched as she listened intently for a few seconds, and then without having said a word herself, she held out the receiver to him. 'It's Dougal,' but held her ear as near to it as she could.

'Before I tell you anything, Ally,' came the loud metallic voice – unnaturally loud with the possible intention of letting her hear, too? – 'I hope you're a lot better than when I left you. Gwen's letters say you're coming on nicely, but I want to hear it from you, and I want the truth, mind.'

'The truth is I'm fine, so you'd better hit me with whatever it is you're hedging about, for I know it's nothing good.'

'Depends how you look at it, Ally boy. I don't know if Gwen told you, but I made up my mind to emigrate to America ...'

'No, she didn't tell me.' Alistair's voice was clipped, Gwen noticed, his face closed.

'Well, I filled in all the forms, and everything's cut and dried. We're ready to leave now for Southampton and we sail tomorrow.'

'We?'

'Oh God, did she not tell you that, either?'

'She thinks she's shielding me from getting hurt.' Alistair sounded bitter, now. 'So . . . who's we?'

'Peg and me, of course. We didn't know if I could marry my sister-in-law in this country, and we didn't have time to make enquiries, so she changed her name to mine by deed poll, and we're travelling as man and wife. If it's possible, we'll make it legal when we get to the other side. If not . . . well . . . it won't matter.'

Alistair glanced at Gwen, who gave his hand a reassuring squeeze. 'What about . . . ?' he whispered to her, his hand over the mouthpiece.

'It's all right,' she whispered back. 'Just listen to what he's got to say.'

'If you're wondering about Nicky,' Dougal continued, 'we're taking him with us. He is our son, after all.'

Seeing the haunted look in her husband's eyes, Gwen took the instrument from him. 'Thanks for telling him yourself, Dougal, but I think he needs time to digest it. He's still not quite . . . you know. Bon voyage, dear.'

'Thanks, Gwen, but somebody else wants a word.'

'Hi, Gwennie, it's your baby sister. How are you coping?'

'Better for hearing you. Oh, Peg, America's such a long way off.'

'We'll keep in touch.'

The sound of a slight scuffle came across the wire now, then a treble voice piped, 'It's me, Auntie Gwen. Isn't it exciting? Dad says we'll be going on a great big boat all the way across the Atlantic Ocean, and I've to make up my mind not to be seasick.'

'That's good,' she breathed, her raw emotion scarcely letting her speak. 'You won't forget me when you're over there, will you?'

'Of course I won't. I'll write as often as I can, but I 'spect I'll be awful busy for a good while.'

'I 'spect you will,' she managed to laugh. 'Never mind, drop me a note any time you can manage it.'

'Can I say goodbye to Uncle Alistair, please?'

She turned round. 'Nicky wants to say goodbye.' She didn't know what to expect, a tantrum perhaps, or hurling the telephone across the room, but she didn't flinch, and after a very slight hesitation he took the instrument from her. She could still hear both sides, the boy's voice coming across loud and clear.

'Is that you, Uncle Alistair?'

'It's me, Nicky. You're ready to go, then?'

'Our luggage is all sitting ready for the cab to take with us to the station, and I can hardly wait, but I couldn't go without saying goodbye to Auntie Gwen and you.'

Alistair's eyes searched his wife's now. 'I haven't known you very well, Nicky, but I know she's going to miss you. I hope you have a good journey; I bet you're looking forward to it, aren't you?'

'Not half! I didn't sleep last night for thinking about it. I'll have to say cheerio now, though. Mum wants to speak to you, too.'

'Goodbye ... Nicky.'

'Hi, Alistair. This is it, then.'

'Yes, this is it. Um ... Peg, you'll take good care of the boy, won't you?'

'You don't need to ask. He's in good hands.'

'Yes, I know. Sorry for ...'

'It's all right, I understand. Look after yourself, Alistair, and we'll write and keep you up to date with ... everything.'

'Thanks, Peg, and ... safe crossing.'

'Bye, Alistair.'

He laid the receiver back in its cradle. 'Gwen, would you mind if I went out for a wee while? I need space.'

'Are you sure you're fit to be out by yourself? Would it

527

be better if I went out instead? I could bike to the village and get another magazine for you. It would give me a chance to see the new man.'

'Well . . . if you don't mind?'

She was on her way in minutes, glad of the fresh air and the light wind fanning her cheeks. She did feel a bit anxious about leaving him alone, but she could understand his need to think. In addition to Lexie's marriage, he now had to cope with the thought of his wife's illegitimate son being whisked across the Atlantic out of her reach. What would he make of it all?

Lexie Fraser, of course, was not in the shop. She had spent a week with the new owner to help him get to know the customers, but she had stopped working on Saturday. So that was that, Gwen thought. She'd have liked to tender good wishes for the future, but maybe it was just as well she wouldn't have the chance, feeling as she did about Alistair's relationship with her. After exchanging a few remarks with Mr Munro about the way prices were going up, she paid for the *Titbits* she had bought for Alistair and the other items she had purchased and went outside. As luck would have it, she was still putting her groceries into the basket of her cycle when a bus stopped beside her and Lexie Fraser stepped off.

'Thank goodness I've seen you, Gwen,' she smiled. 'I didn't want to leave without saying goodbye, but I didn't want to come to Benview in case it upset Alistair. Come on round and have a cup of tea. You'll have to excuse the mess. I'm still packing.'

Feeling trapped, Gwen followed her. 'I thought you'd moved out already.'

'No, the removal van's coming on Friday to take my things to Edinburgh. Roddy put in for a transfer. He thought it would be best for me to be away from . . . Forvit, and the

528

house he's bought isn't far from where Nancy Lawrie lives. I told him not to go to the expense of buying furniture. What's here is in reasonable condition, because I replaced my mother's stuff bit by bit over the years.'

Lexie unlocked the house door and ushered Gwen inside. 'Sit down if you can find a decent place to park yourself, and I'll put on the kettle. How's Alistair keeping?'

Shifting a large carton on to the floor, Gwen sat down in one of the easy chairs. 'He's coming on nicely, still a bit unstable, you know, but not too bad, considering.'

'How are you keeping yourself, though? You've been going at things like a beaver ever since you came home.'

'I have to keep busy, otherwise I'd . . .' Gwen stopped with a little sigh. 'I don't mind doing everything for him, if only he wouldn't . . .' She halted again, then continued with a smile. 'No, you don't want to hear me moaning.'

Sitting down at the opposite side of the fire, Lexie stretched out her legs. 'If you want to moan, Gwen, carry on. It's time I thought of somebody else for a change.'

'It's all right. I'm making a mountain out of a molehill. I get so tired at times I feel a bit resentful, if you understand.'

'I should think you would. How long's that now? Nearly six months, isn't it?'

'It won't be for much longer, he's well on the way to recovery. The doctors were very pleased with him when he had his last checkup.'

'I'm glad. You know, when I saw him that first time . . . I thought he'd had it.'

'I'll always be grateful for what you did at that time, Lexie. I don't know how Leila and David would have coped without you.'

'I was glad to be able to help.' Lexie got to her feet again as the kettle lid began to dance. 'They're nice kids, and I've always thought a lot of them.'

'And Alistair?' It was out before Gwen could stop it.

'Yes, Gwen, and Alistair,' Lexie murmured, filling the teapot. 'I loved him once, or thought I did. After what had happened to me, I needed him, though I didn't realize why, and then my mother died, and I clung to him in my mind. It was like an obsession, and it wasn't till I met Roddy that I fell in love properly.'

Watching her take a second mug out of a box – she had kept only one out for her own use, presumably – Gwen said, 'I know I asked before, Lexie, but have you any idea what Alistair did after he left your house that morning ... the morning of the accident? Where he went? Why he was coming down the hill on to the road?'

'I'd say he'd been up to the tower to do some thinking.'

The other woman's eyes refused to meet Gwen's now, so she persisted, 'What did he have to think about, that's the point? He was with you all night, wasn't he? Did he do something he shouldn't? Don't be afraid to tell me – he'd thrown me out before that.'

Lexie waited until she was seated again before answering. 'You know, Gwen, he never loved me, not really, but he took it for granted that I'd always loved him, and he turned a bit nasty when I told him I loved Roddy. He said I was fooling myself, that I was only a bit on the side for Roddy, so ... I slapped his face and he stormed out.' She paused momentarily, then went on, 'I suppose I should have gone after him in case he did anything silly, but I was in such a state myself it never crossed my mind.'

'Oh, I'm not blaming you for anything. I just wanted to know.'

'But you've got to believe me, Gwen. He never loved me, never ever. It was you he loved, and it was pride that held him back from trying to stop you leaving, and pride that wouldn't let him write and ask you to come back. It's a good thing that young David took the initiative. He could be a detective some day with his powers of deduction.'

'Yes, it was all down to him that Alistair took me back, and I suppose we'll manage to get over things eventually and learn to live in peace together.'

'Listen, Gwen, and don't take this the wrong way. I'd really like if you could persuade him to come to the wedding. I've asked Nancy Lawrie to be matron-of-honour because I didn't have anyone else, and she's the only one on my side apart from her husband if you two aren't there. I couldn't ask any of my customers, because only a few people are allowed in Aberdeen Register Office, and the ones I didn't ask would be offended, so ... please Gwen? Take David and Leila, as well. You're ... my family.'

'I'll see what I can do, although I'm not sure if he's well enough to ...'

'You've been taking him on the bus to Aberdeen for his checkups, haven't you?'

'It's not the travelling I'm worried about. It's his mental state.'

'Trust me, Gwen. I'm sure it'll make him see sense and get over everything.'

On her way home, Gwen mulled over Lexie's last statement. Was she right? Would seeing his first girlfriend, the woman he still had a soft spot for if nothing more, being married to another man straighten all the kinks in Alistair's mind? Wasn't it more likely to send him off the rails altogether? But she had better ask him and let him decide whether or not to put himself through this fresh torture.

It had taken some persuasion, but the Ritchie family caught the second bus on Saturday morning to give Gwen and Leila time to buy clothes suitable for a wedding. David, chattering unceasingly, and Alistair, strangely silent all the way to the city, already had decent suits to wear, although as they all trooped into Falconer's store, Gwen detailed her husband to go to the men's department and buy a more presentable tie for each of them.

'We'll meet you in the restaurant about half past ten,' she instructed. 'We can have a cup of tea and a scone or something before we go to the Registrar.'

The ties were chosen in less than five minutes, so Alistair suggested that having a look at the harbour would fill in the remaining fifty-five minutes before they had to meet their womenfolk. It was a cold day, but quite pleasant as long as they kept moving, so they stepped smartly down Market Street towards Regent Quay, where there was always some activity going on, the loading or unloading of the large cargo vessels.

David, however, had other things on his mind. 'Dad,' he began, as they passed the Labour Exchange and rounded the corner, 'are you going to let Mum stay with us once you're right better?'

Alistair's eyebrows shot up. 'Do you think I shouldn't?'

'I think you should! I know what she did wasn't right, but if you love her, you'd be able to forgive her.'

Evading the implied question, Alistair said, 'Look, there's a Norwegian boat. It's likely brought in some timber – pine, possibly.'

His son wasn't to be sidetracked. 'Don't change the subject. Is it Mum you love, or Lexie? Why have you come here today? Are you hoping to stop the wedding?'

Alistair felt a sudden spurt of anger. How dare his son say things like that to him? Where on earth had he got the idea that . . . ? God Almighty! How many other folk had got that impression? Had Leila? Worse still, had Gwen?

'Dad? I'd like an answer.'

'Leave it, David. I can't think properly just now. We have to get back.'

While they completed the rest of what was a rectangle – along Regent Quay, up the even steeper Marischal Street, along Union Street back to Falconer's – Alistair turned the question of what he felt for his wife over and over in his mind. Gwen probably did know how he felt about Lexie, yet she had almost forced him to attend the wedding. Was she hoping that he would give up on his first love when he saw her marrying the 'tec?

He didn't care about anything these days, so why the hell had he come? He hadn't had the strength, the willpower, to refuse, that was why. Gwen had said she would like to see the wedding, but she wouldn't have gone and left him on his own, so it had been easier to agree. Yet . . . was that all it had been? He could remember now how he had briefly felt ashamed of himself, not so much for being a burden to her – which he was – but for resenting her getting her own way, when she'd had precious little to be grateful for over the past few months. He'd had everything his way.

He and David had only a few minutes to wait on the store's top floor before Gwen and Leila joined them and they all went into the restaurant. His wife looked at him anxiously as they sat down. 'Are you all right, Alistair?'

'Perfect,' he said, sarcastically, because he was absolutely done in. It wasn't just the effect of the physical exercise, it was all the concentrated thinking he was having to do.

He knew that his brain wasn't anything like back to normal – it might never be – but surely he knew what was what? No, even that was debatable. Unable to banish the picture of his wife with that Ken Partridge, he had put her through hell since she came back. Would he ever be able to forgive her?

Unaware that she was watching him, he gave a slight start. Would he *ever* be able to forgive her? He usually thought

533

that he would *never* be able to forgive her. It must be a step forward? He did feel that bit different today. Lexie had apparently sat with him during his first few days in hospital, but it was Gwen who had tended him day and night since he was discharged, Gwen who had comforted him when his darkest demons were tormenting him, Gwen who smiled even when he was shouting for attention. Only a woman whose love was unshakeable could have put up with him.

It had been some time after he was home before he started wondering about his accident, and why he'd been coming down from the tower so early that morning. It had been like trying to dig up an irremovable stone, however. Maybe it was better for him not to know, just to accept things as they were. He should praise Leila and David for coping so well in the shop without him, instead of resenting that, too. Life would be much easier for all of them, himself included, if he mended his ways. He stood in danger of losing his wife if he carried on the way he was doing.

Testing his feelings further, he decided that he could live quite happily without Lexie in the background, but he couldn't visualize spending the rest of his life without Gwen. The question he should be asking himself was, *Would she ever forgive him?*

In the Register Office, part of a row of granite buildings with shops at street level, the wedding party was shown into a drab, uninspiring room, where sat an elderly gentleman with a high, Victorian-type collar. He gave them a weary, harassed smile as he motioned to the main participants – bride and groom and their attendants – to come forward, and to the Ritchies and the only other man to take a seat.

Noticing how drawn Alistair was looking, Gwen wished that she hadn't made him come. Was he stable enough to

534

watch Lexie Fraser marrying Roddy Liddell? Was he planning to do something to stop the wedding? He was obviously deep in thought, and she primed herself for the explosion she was almost sure would come, but everything went smoothly. The vows were affirmed, the ring placed on the third finger of the bride's left hand, and the ceremony was being brought to a close.

'I now pronounce you man and wife,' the registrar intoned, constant repetition of the words over many years depriving them of any real meaning. 'You may kiss the bride.'

It was then that Alistair jumped to his feet, taking everyone by surprise, even his own wife, but it was nothing like she had feared. 'I love you, Gwen,' he said, articulating each word in a loud clear voice that rang round the room, 'and I always will!'

The registrar's head jerked up, Lexie and Roddy whipped round grinning; Nancy Fleming was beaming when she turned; Leila, although scarlet with embarrassment, wore a beatific smile of sheer happiness. The best man, another police inspector, and Greig Fleming, Nancy's husband, not understanding the poignancy of the statement, were both staring at Alistair as if he had taken leave of his senses.

David seemed to be the only one to have retained the power of speech. Barely able to contain his excitement, he chortled, 'Atta boy, Dad! Close your mouth, Mum, so he can kiss you, and all.'

The House of Lyall

To Jimmy – chief cook, cleaner and bottlewasher since I started writing. Until then, I had no idea that husbands could come in so handy. They can't half hide their lights under bushels.

Thanks to Susan Opie, my editor, who sorted out the muddle in which I managed to find myself. *The House of Lyall* would have been far less readable without her help.

PART ONE
1894–1903

Chapter One

It had never crossed Marion Cheyne's mind before, but then she had never seen so much money before, and she didn't recognize what she was feeling as temptation, never having come across that before, either. So her hand was as steady as a rock when she picked up five sovereigns and dropped them into the pocket of the apron which enveloped her from neck to feet. Some inborn sense of preservation, however, made her stir the silver and copper around the remaining golden coins with her finger, so it wouldn't be noticeable at first glance that any had been removed from the shallow china dish. This was actually meant to hold bonbons, but Mr Moodie deposited his small change in it every night – farthings, ha'pennies and pennies as a rule, with the odd thrupenny or sixpenny bit amongst them, sometimes even a shilling or a florin, but never gold, and certainly never a heap of gold like today.

Finished here, she walked to the door, but the telltale jingle accompanying each step made her stop to tie the coins tightly inside her handkerchief; then to be doubly sure they would not betray her, she stuffed the solid little bundle into the pocket of her drawers. This act of secrecy, an admittance that what she had done was wrong, didn't bother her as much as it should have done. If the gentry were as stupid as leave big amounts of money lying about, they deserved to be robbed.

Not that the Moodies were true gentry. Even if their house stood on its own, hidden from curious eyes by the spreading trees that had given it its name, Oak Cottage wasn't much different from the rest of the houses on that stretch of the turnpike – most of them built of the pink granite quarried in Peterhead. Of course, he *was* manager of the North of Scotland Bank's branch in the Square, and went to work every morning in a black suit and a white shirt with a winged collar, and a moleskin hat jammed on his head, but that didn't give him the right to think he was better than his neighbours. Apart from Mary McKay – who was employed by the council to assess the old and infirm inhabitants of Tipperton with a view to putting them in the poor's house – they were mainly shopkeepers, and most of them could buy and sell him.

Her mind returning to matters in hand, Marion realized that she would be under suspicion the minute he discovered the loss of his five pounds – there were only herself and the mistress who could have taken them, and he wouldn't blame his wife. Well, it didn't matter, for Marion Cheyne would be well away by the time he came home. She'd been thinking of leaving anyway. It wasn't that Mr Moodie had done anything out of place, but with him sleeping in a different room from his wife, their servant was taking no chances of being roped in as his bed-warmer . . . or maybe worse! She would be fifteen next week, old enough to fend for herself, so why shouldn't she go to Aberdeen and look for a better job? No one would miss her at home – her father was too much taken up with his new wife to care a docken about his daughter, and Moll, her stepmother, couldn't stand the sight of her, which didn't really matter because *she* hated *her*. They'd already got rid of her young brother by sending him to work for a horse-breeder in England somewhere, though it had pleased Kenny, for he'd always been mad about horses and wanted to be a jockey some day.

When Marion went into the kitchen, Mrs Moodie was dampening the first lot of clothes they had washed earlier and rolling them up for her servant to iron in the afternoon with the rest. The girl had nothing against the woman, but she could feel her cheeks reddening at the thought of what lay hidden under her skirts, so when her mistress looked up and said solicitously, 'You look flushed, Marion. I hope you're not coming down with something,' she was quick with her reply.

'I'm not feeling very well.'

The result was surprisingly gratifying. 'You had better go home,' Mrs Moodie said, 'and don't come in tomorrow unless you feel better.'

Presented with a perfect means of escape, Marion had the sense to take advantage of it, and within minutes was walking through the back gate and round on to the drive. It had happened so quickly she had no time to make plans, but one thing she did know – she couldn't go home. Her stepmother would see she wasn't really ill, and would go on and on at her till she was trapped into saying something she shouldn't. If she owned up to the stealing, she would be hauled back to Oak Cottage to confess. The only thing she could do to avoid that was to go with just what she was wearing, but the five sovereigns, now beginning to weigh on her conscience as well as on her hip, would be enough to pay her fare and buy some new clothes.

Squaring her shoulders, she flung her head back, and with her long copper-coloured hair streaming out behind her, she strode out as if she hadn't a care in the world. And neither she had, she assured herself, for she had burned her boats and there was no use worrying. As she walked past the cemetery, she remembered some boys at school telling her the spirits of the dead lurked near the gates to catch sinners and criminals, and even though it was only ten to eleven on a bright October morning, icy shivers ran down her spine and her heart seemed to be beating inside her mouth. Terrified, she pulled up her skirts and sprinted well past the danger area, until common sense told her she was being daft. Only bairns believed in ghosts. There were no such things, in the cemetery or anywhere else.

She slowed down a bit, but kept running because the track branching off to the left led down to the sawmill where her father worked and she wanted to get past as quickly as possible. She couldn't chance being seen by any of his workmates or their wives, though there wasn't much risk of that with all the trees in between the cottages and the road. In a valiant effort to bolster her conscience, she started to whistle – her poor dead mother used to say that whistling maidens and crowing hens weren't lucky, but it had never broken her of the habit – stopping only when she neared the first houses in the village proper. She didn't want to draw attention to herself in case any of her stepmother's cronies saw her. She had often moaned that the whole of Tipperton might as well be a burial ground for all the life there was in it, but today she was thankful that it was so.

Long before she came to the smiddy she could smell the smoke, and feel the heat of the almost molten metal, and hear the clang as the smith shaped another horseshoe. She used to watch him on her way home from school, fascinated by his skill yet shuddering at the thought of the agony the horses must suffer when he shod them, but this time she hurried quietly past.

Reaching the crossroads, she dithered over whether to turn left over the river in the hope of being picked up by a carter taking a load of vegetables to Aberdeen – she didn't know when the coach ran, and in any case, she could hardly stand about here where everybody would see her – or to turn right and make for the railway station. She would certainly be out of sight there, for it was well out of the village and she had often played there with the other bairns in the school holidays. The sight of a stranger getting off was a source of endless diversion and speculation for them.

It occurred to Marion that a train for Aberdeen came through about half-past eleven. She wouldn't have long to wait, and she had more than enough money to pay the rail fare, so she turned right.

She was on heckle-pins while she passed the shops, but strangely, there weren't many women about that morning, and nobody she knew. Then she remembered that it was Monday, washing day for most housewives – she couldn't have timed this better if she'd tried.

There was quite a commotion inside and outside the Mart, where farmers from miles around came to buy and sell beasts and grain, and to have a news with old friends, but she didn't recognize any of them and, in any case, they were all too busy to notice her. In another few hundred yards, she hurried past the tall, grim building which had a brass plate on its gate proclaiming it to be 'Tipperton Institution for the Aged, Destitute and Incurable', an awful grand name for what everybody in the place knew was really the poor's house, only steps away from the entrance to the station.

She was about to turn in, congratulating herself on getting there without being seen, when, coming towards her, she spied a sight familiar to the whole village: Mary McKay on her bicycle, her hat jammed down on her head, her skirts flapping about her legs. She was the very last person Marion wanted to see, a terrible gossip who kept everybody informed about everybody else's business except her own and, crossing her fingers, the girl prayed she would go past without stopping. No such luck!

'What are you doing up here at this time of day, Marion Cheyne?' Mary asked breathlessly, as she drew up alongside.

'Mrs Moodie sent me with a message to . . .' the girl cast about for a name that would sound plausible, '. . . to Miss Fraser up the moorie.'

The nurse noticed her hesitation but did not remark on it. 'I'll not waste your time, then, for she'll be expecting you back.'

Unaware that the woman had suspiciously moved into the lane to the poor's house from where she could check unseen whether she carried on along the road to the moor, Marion turned into the station with relief that nobody would know where she had gone. Tipperton being little more than a halt, there was only one railway employee. Dod Cooper was station master, issuer and collector of tickets, porter, signalman, post office sorter and general dogsbody . . . but not a nosy parker. He kept his tongue between his teeth, as the saying went, and Marion was sure that he wouldn't say anything to her father or anybody else about her presence at the station.

Glancing at the big clock on the back wall of the wooden shelter, she saw that she had still ten minutes to wait, and to pass the time and keep out of sight, she paid a visit to the WC, which reminded her to resurrect what was the sum total of her possessions . . . five gold pieces. Then she caught sight of her reflection in the mirror – her face white and strained, her hazel eyes wide and anxious, her coppery hair carfuffled from hauling off her big apron before she left Oak Cottage. She hadn't a comb, so the only thing she could do was to run her fingers through the tangles until they looked smooth. Thank goodness her hair was dead straight, and so easily tamed. Moistening a corner of her handkerchief with her tongue, she scrubbed her cheeks to bring some colour back into them, and was quite pleased with the result. Surely Dod Cooper wouldn't notice anything strange about her now.

Ten minutes later, after concocting a lie about why she had handed over a sovereign for a ticket that cost less than a shilling – she said one of her aunties had given it to her so she'd have something to spend when she went to Dundee to see her mother's other sister – Marion almost collapsed into a seat in an empty compartment. Not a soul knew where she was going . . . even Dod Cooper couldn't tell the bobbies if they started asking, for he thought she would buy another ticket in Aberdeen to take her to Dundee. She could hardly believe how easy it had been, right from the beginning, as if fate had guided her, encouraged her, and she hadn't strayed far off the straight and narrow when all was said and done. She had grasped at an opportunity, and who could blame her for that?

Her thoughts now ventured further ahead. She hadn't had the cash for very long, but it gave her a feeling of power, of not being at anybody's beck and call. It was a good feeling, and she wanted to be like this all her life. It wouldn't be easy to get a position where she would come in contact with the upper classes in Aberdeen, but she was prepared to work her way up until she landed amongst people with lots of money, and then ... then she could marry a rich man and live in luxury until she died. Love didn't come into her scheme of things – though it would be nice if it did turn up somewhere along the way. Whatever, in future Marion Cheyne would make sure that her every action would be to her own advantage.

When Alfie Cheyne went home at mid day, looking much older than his forty-one years after six hours' hard work at the mill, his wife, nudging thirty but with the hourglass figure of a twenty-year-old due to the tight lacing of her stays, was not her usual flirtatious self.

'That lassie o' yours has run off.'

His greying brows plummeted. 'Run off? Dinna speak daft, wumman! She's at the Moodies' where she's supposed to be ... is she nae?'

'She left there this morning. She was goin' into the station this foreneen when Mary McKay saw her, an' she never come oot again, for Mary waited half an hour an' more, so she said. An' when she went up an' asked Dod Cooper, he hummed an' hawed then said she was awa' to Dundee. So I went an' asked Mrs Moodie if she kent onything about it, an' she said there was money missing.'

'But my Marion wouldna steal!' Alfie gasped.

'Well, Mr Moodie had left twelve sovereigns for his wife to pay for a new table an' chairs she was gettin' delivered, an' when the cart came from Aberdeen an' she went to pay the man, there was only seven left. Marion must have ta'en the other five, for there was naebody else there. Oh, she'd said she wasna feeling well, an' Mrs Moodie sent her hame, but she didna come back here.'

Her triumphant sneer annoyed Alfie. Why had she thrust this worry on him when all he wanted was to eat his dinner in peace and have a wee nap before he went back to work? He'd got precious little sleep at nights since he'd wed Moll. He'd thought he was the luckiest man on God's earth the first month or so, and told himself many a man would give his right arm to change places with him, but by Govie, you could get too much of a good thing.

'Have you nothing to say about her?' Moll demanded suddenly.

'What can I say?' he mumbled. 'If it was her that took that money, an' it looks like she must have . . .' He halted, rubbing his hand over his wiry beard. 'If it was just a shillin' or two, it wouldna be so bad, but five sovereigns! That's near what I get for a twelve-month slaving in the mill an' filling my lungs wi' sawdust.' Thinking that it might be as well to keep on his wife's good side – he might fare a lot worse if he got her dander up – he said quite decidedly, 'Well, a' I can say is good riddance to her!'

That made her beam with pleasure. 'It'll just be me an' you, noo, Alfie.'

He nodded. 'Aye, Moll, just you an' me.' And if she carried on the way she'd been doing, he thought morosely, he'd be a wizened old man before he was fifty, his manhood drained off him. Looking at it from the other side, though, she was a damned good-looking wench who knew how to please a man, and there were worse ways to end his days than taking full advantage of what was legally his.

'You'll be ready for your stovies now, then?'

She had almost purred the words, and Alfie's saliva was flowing as he watched her filling a bowl with creamy milk, heaping his plate and then sticking a quarter of oatcakes in the middle. This was the traditional way to eat this dish, the milk being necessary to wash down the dry triangle of oatcake and barely moist stoved potatoes. For dinners like this every day he would gladly put up with Moll's nightly appetite.

Something else struck him as he took a quick sip of milk to clear his gritty mouth. 'Are the Moodies going to report her to the bobby?' he asked, wiping his moustache and picking up his fork.

'She says he'll likely want to, but she's goin' to tell him it was his ain fault for leaving so much money where Marion could get her hands on it, an' ony young girl would have been tempted. Eat that up afore they're caul' now, for I've got a apple dumpling for after.'

When Marion came out of Aberdeen railway station, her ears were assaulted by the bustle and din, and her nose by the strong smell of fish. Not that she didn't like fish – she got it once a week at home – but she wasn't accustomed to the stink of it all around her. Horses clopped over the granite setts, their carts piled high with wooden fish boxes leaking streams of brine on the road, or loaded with big beer barrels looking as though they would come toppling over at any minute. The leather-aproned carters whistled blithely, and mostly untunefully, as they flicked the reins to show their trusty steeds who was master.

Errand boys flashed past her on their bicycles as she stood gaping, the parcels in the baskets on their handlebars wobbling precariously when they rounded the corner, bells shrilling in warning. The pedestrians must have been aware of the danger, but the women were more concerned with striving to hold their skirts down against the wind, which made Marion recall a rhyme one of the old men in Tipperton had taught her brother.

> The devil sent the wind to blow the ladies' dresses
> high,
> But God was just and sent the dust to blind the bad
> man's eye.

Eight-year-old Kenny had kept chanting it till their father had given him a good clout on the lug. Memories of Kenny made Marion think fully about what she had done. If she hadn't run off – if you could call going on a train running off – she could have gone back and returned the five sovereigns before anybody noticed they were gone, but it was too late now. She had left her home and would have to stay in this huge unfriendly city, and she had no idea of where to go or what to do, though it might be wise to get away from the horrible stink of fish.

She had noticed that most of the carts coming from her right were empty, while the ones going in the opposite direction were piled high, so it didn't take very much gumption to tell that the docks were to her left. To be certain, however, she went to the edge of the pavement and craned her neck leftwards. Yes, she could see an array of masts with their sails tied up, so there *were* ships there, loading or unloading.

She set off now away from them, turning a corner in seconds and going up a street of shops with houses above them, but even with money in her pocket, she resolutely kept her eyes away from the windows; she might need every penny before she got settled.

At the top of the hill, a black and white tiled sign on the wall of the last granite building told her this was Bridge Street, which didn't surprise her, though there was no water under the bridge she'd just crossed, only another road. The thoroughfare she had reached – it was the only way to describe it, it was so grand – was Union Street, according to the nameplate on the far side, and having heard of that before, she knew it was more or less the backbone of Aberdeen.

Curiosity overcoming all her other senses now, Marion turned right and wandered round several of the large shops, stores really, and it was very much later when, emerging from one absolute wonderland, she caught sight of a clock on a building some way ahead. Twenty-five past five! No wonder it was getting dark and her belly was rumbling. She'd had nothing to eat since breakfast time. She was considering going back to the last place she'd walked round, where she'd seen people sitting having meals at the tables, when it dawned on her that all the shops she could see were now emptying before the doors were closed for the day.

Disappointed, and hungry, she trudged on, Union Street changing to Castle Street and widening into a kind of large square, which soon narrowed again and became Justice Street. Halfway down here, wonder of wonders, she came across a pie shop, where several men in working clothes were waiting to be served. They were obviously buying things to eat somewhere else, and came out in ones and twos, each carrying so large a bundle that it looked as if they were preparing for a siege, but she went inside when one of them politely held the door open for her.

The short stout man behind the counter saw her perplexed expression. 'They're night shift at the gas works,' he informed her. 'If you want, you can sit down an' eat yours here,' he added kindly. 'You look worn oot.'

'I've been walking a lot,' she admitted, sinking down gratefully on one of the benches at the side. She was even more grateful when he set a plate down on the stained table in front of her, for there was a large mouth-watering pie on it, smothered in gravy and a big mound of juicy peas. There was also a big chunk of bread on the side for mopping up the last drops of moisture.

'Was you makin' for some place in partikler?' the man asked, having no one else to serve at that moment.

Dog-tired physically, Marion was as alert as ever mentally. 'I was supposed to be goin' to my auntie in Bridge Street,' she fibbed, naming the first place that came to mind, 'but she wasna in. She musta forgot I was comin', so I've been shovin' in time till I was sure she'd have to be hame for my uncle's supper. But, if she hadna minded aboot me, she'd only be cookin' for the two o' them, and that's why I come in here.'

The man nodded, satisfied that she wasn't in any kind of trouble, but the entrance of more customers took his attention off her. When a quarter of an hour later, she stood up to leave, he said solicitously, 'You'll manage to find yer wey back to yer auntie?'

'I'll go back the wey I come,' Marion assured him, holding out a shilling because she didn't know how much he charged.

He waved it away. 'Na, na, lass, that's a' richt.'

'But I must pay for the pie.'

'My treat, m'dear. Us Aberdonians are nae as mean as folk mak' oot.'

'Well, thank you very much then.' It crossed her mind to ask if he needed any help in the shop, but he'd been so good to her already it wouldn't be right to take advantage of his good nature.

Of course, she did not go back the way she had come, but went on down Justice Street, then turned into Constitution Street, lined with an assortment of houses, big and small, but sadly she discovered in a few minutes that it took her down to the beach. It was much darker now, with just a scattering of tiny stars twinkling over the wide expanse of water. She'd heard more than one person in Tipperton saying that it didn't matter what kind of weather it was, or what time of day, when you went to Aberdeen beach you'd be sure to find other folk there, but *she* couldn't see a blessed soul!

October was long past the season when the well-off from Glasgow and Edinburgh took holidays, and who on earth would come here at the back end of the year if they didn't have to? Well, she was too tired to trail back to find a place to stay the night, but she'd have to have a rest. She'd feel better in the morning, more able to look for lodgings, and maybe a job, though she did have enough money to keep her going for a few weeks – months if she was careful.

She was lucky to find, a short way along the front, a three-sided brick erection, likely for the use of mothers or nannies to keep a·watch on their children playing on the sands, which afforded some shelter although it was fully exposed to the icy night wind howling in across the North Sea from the Arctic. It was bitterly cold, but she was so exhausted that she did eventually fall into a deep sleep from which she was rudely awakened in a few short hours by the screaming of the gulls circling overhead, probably hoping she'd some scraps to give them.

'You're unlucky this time,' she shouted at them to scare them off. 'I haven't anything for myself to eat, so you'd better go and look somewhere else.'

Standing up was an almost impossible task. Her whole body felt as if it were frozen stiff, and once on her feet, she stood looking miserably around her. With the dawning of the day came the realization that she would never survive if she didn't find somewhere to live, and she didn't know how to do that. She'd made a dreadful mistake when she ran away from Tipperton, an even worse when she stole the money. Was this God's way of warning her that unless she went back and confessed to her crime, He would have to punish her? Deciding that it was better late than never to do the right thing, she still felt a great reluctance to move. Why didn't she just lie down again and let the elements finish her off?

But Marion was not a pessimist by nature, and it wasn't long before she shook off her despondency. Far better to face up to her sin than cause trouble by practically committing suicide on a deserted beach.

Nevertheless, by the time she had retraced her steps of the day before, her feet and legs still aching agonizingly, her spirits had taken another downward spiral. How could she face the Moodies again, after the banker's wife had been so kind to her? And what about her father? He'd never been a violent man, though he'd often given her brother a wallop when he misbehaved, so what if he lost his temper with her? What she had done was an awful lot worse than anything Kenny ever had.

To stop her imagining the leathering she would get, Marion came to a halt to find out where she was. Without noticing, she had got back to Union Street and, if her memory served her right, she wasn't far from the top of Bridge Street. Should she go home . . . or not? Still a child at heart, she gave herself a choice. If the next street she came to was Bridge Street, she'd go down to the station. If it wasn't, she wouldn't. That was fair, wasn't it? Surely God wouldn't argue with that?

Not sure whether to be pleased or not, she found that the next street was indeed Bridge Street and, resigned to her fate now, she turned down it, her steps determined. At the entrance to the station, however, she was assailed by sudden misgivings. She had told Dod Cooper at Tipperton that she was going to her auntie in Dundee, and maybe that's what she *should* do. Her mother's sister did live there, and it would be a lot easier to confess to Auntie Bella than to her father.

Unfortunately, after running down the steps and going to the ticket office, she was told that trains from there ran north only, and she'd have to go to the station at the other side of Guild Street to get a train to the south. She trailed back up to the street level, turning left as the ticket man had directed her, but – although it was only a matter of crossing the street and going along a wee bit – by the time she reached the LNER station, she was confused and completely demoralized once again.

After taking a few faltering steps, she came to a trembling halt with tears streaming down her cheeks and her hands over her ears to blot out the cacophony around her. She stood thus for at least five minutes, nobody taking any notice of her until a gentle hand on her shoulder made her look up into the concerned face of a young man in a flat black hat and a priest's flowing robe.

'Are you lost, my child?' he asked. 'Where do you want to go?'

Marion couldn't answer that. She *was* lost, but not in the sense that he meant. 'I've run away,' she whispered at last, compelled by his calling to tell him at least part of the truth. But not wanting him to be under any misapprehension, she added, 'I'm not a Catholic.'

'Priests help all God's creatures,' he smiled, 'even if they are not Roman Catholics. What is your religion, my dear?'

'I went to the parish church at hame.'

'Can't I persuade you to go home again?' At her tearful, mute shake of the head, he took her by the arm. 'If you have nowhere to stay, the Church of Scotland, like us, runs a place where young girls may have a bed for the night. Would you like me to show you where it is?'

They had just turned into Bridge Street when he said, 'I haven't asked your name yet. Mine is Father Bernard.'

Marion wished that hers was more in keeping with the life she wanted to lead, and with a feeling of destroying all bridges behind her, she said, 'My name's Mar . . . Marianne . . . Marianne Cheyne.' It wasn't such an awful lie. She had just changed one letter and added another two, but it sounded so much better. It was just a pity she hadn't thought of changing her last name as well.

'Would you be looking for work, Marianne?'

'I've been in service before.'

'I wasn't suggesting you go into service. I know some

ladies who run a children's wear shop in Holburn Street, and they have been speaking of taking on a smart young girl to help them. Would you manage that?'

'I'm sure I could.'

'I shall take you there first.' Father Bernard took her across the street and up a long flight of stone steps. 'It's shorter this way than going by Union Street,' he smiled, as they made their breathless way to the top.

After passing a beautifully turreted granite building which she took to be a castle but which he told her was the main post office, he led her into a narrow street which eventually led them out on to Holburn Street, where the shop was.

While they walked, he told her a little about the ladies who ran it. 'There are three unmarried sisters, but Miss Esther keeps house for Miss Emily and Miss Edith. They live in Strawberry Bank.'

'What a lovely name for a house!' Marianne exclaimed.

'Strawberry Bank is the name of the street,' he grinned. 'Miss Esther, the youngest, seems quite happy to be the homemaker. Miss Edith, the brains behind the business, is the eldest, and Miss Emily, the middle one, is the quietest. They are dear ladies, all three.'

The sign above the shop window read 'E. & E. Rennie, Children's Outfitters'. The two elderly ladies within raised their heads when the doorbell tinkled, their faces lighting up when they saw the priest. 'Father Bernard!' they chorused. 'How nice to see you.'

Marianne lost track of the order of events then, everything happened so quickly, but when she lay down that night in the attic room in the Rennies' cottage in Strawberry Bank, she had an assistant's job, she had two serviceable serge skirts and two plain blouses for work, and was also the proud possessor of a barathea skirt, and a cream silk blouse for Sundays ... with a frill at the neck. These had been purchased for her by Miss Esther on Miss Edith's

18

instructions after Marianne told them that she had run away from home without any clothes because her father's new wife made her life unbearable.

As the priest had said, they were dear ladies, all three. Miss Esther was inclined to twitter a bit, probably because she was on her own all day and was glad to have someone to talk to. She was plumper than the other two, the result of testing her cooking for seasoning, likely. Her rosy face was round, her full lips nearly always turned up in a smile. Her white hair was often rather untidy, except on Sundays, she said, when Miss Edith put in her hairpins for her so that they would not fall out in church. Miss Esther could be classed as happy-go-lucky, Marianne decided.

Miss Emily was indeed the quiet one, listening to what her sisters said when she was at home, yet able to keep up lengthy conversations with customers in the shop, or maybe it just seemed that way and it was the customers who did most of the talking. Not only was she the middle of the three in age, she was also middle in height, about two inches taller than Miss Esther, who was barely five feet, but shorter than Miss Edith, who was about five feet six. Miss Emily, although she had a pleasant heart-shaped face, was inclined to be rather prim and occasionally showed her displeasure by gripping in her mouth if anyone made a remark which she considered not in the best of taste. She was slim, but not too thin, and particular about her appearance, her black dresses immaculate and the soft, silvery coil of hair on the crown of her head with never one strand out of place. Miss Emily was . . . well, daintily quiet was the only description for her.

Miss Edith had the strongest personality. She had a long face with clean-cut features and sharp blue eyes. Her hair, dragged back into a tight bun at the nape of her neck, was steel-grey, and her body was verging on the scraggy. Her words were clipped when she spoke, she gave the impression of being stern and forbidding at times, but Marianne soon got to know that it was just a veneer. Miss Edith was a sheep in wolves' clothing.

Marianne didn't feel that she had deceived the Rennies. They were pleased to have an assistant – they would have fitted her out with clothes for the shop anyway – and she would work hard to repay them. Best of all, she still had four pounds nineteen shillings plus a few coppers left of the five sovereigns. She had better hang on to that in case ... well, just in case. But come what may, she wouldn't dream of stealing from her benefactors, or whatever the female version of that was.

She had been really lucky this time. God had given her a wee taste of what he could do to her if she ever stole again ... but she wouldn't have to, would she? She'd been weak yesterday but she felt different now. She would work hard and make something of herself, do anything she had to, to make a success of her life – but she wouldn't do anything dishonest.

Chapter Two

Trade had been very brisk in the weeks leading up to Christmas, but the lull during the first three months of 1895 gave the Rennies and their assistant time to clean shelves and glass cases properly and arrange their replenished stocks to Miss Edith's satisfaction. It being found that Marianne had a penchant for setting out an eye-catching window display, she was allowed to carry out this important task at least once a week, more often if any of the items on show were removed and sold, which became a more regular occurrence as March came to an end and April brought sunshine along with its showers.

The shop was extremely busy on Saturdays, but as Marianne – this was how she always thought of herself now – decided one Saturday in early April, while she went to fetch another batch of white wool from the storeroom at the back, the premises were so tiny that even four customers filled the shop and six made it look crowded. There had been a steady stream all afternoon today, though those who had to wait to be served showed no impatience. In fact, the eyes of the young mothers or elderly grandmothers were usually caught by something other than what they had come to buy, which meant extra sales, and was it any wonder with the Rennie sisters being so obliging and polite, no matter what?

They darted about their little emporium like birds, from counter to shelves, or to drawers, or to stands, even to the window display, and didn't mind laying out dozens of items for someone to choose from, be they expensive christening robes (lovingly and beautifully stitched by Miss Esther), or the cheap woollen mittens and bootees knitted by Miss Emily in the evenings while Miss Edith wrote up the books.

Marianne could still scarcely believe her luck in being part of it. The Rennies had taken her completely under their collective wing; they had given her room and board as well as wages, and they were so clearly glad of the extra pair of hands in the shop that they never made her feel under any obligation to them. They had taught her by example how to deal patiently with members of the public bent on being difficult, although there were very few of them; how to remove – surreptitiously and with no change in gracious manner – sticky little fingers that were exploring the garments within their reach; how to suggest, without making it too obvious, that a pale green coat and hat set would suit ginger (this word was never mentioned, of course) hair much better than a bright scarlet.

It was all very exciting to Marianne, but the most exciting thing that had happened to her was meeting Andrew. When the three sisters had been in such a state of chirping nervousness about the nephew who was coming for Christmas dinner, she had known he was someone really special. Miss Esther had told her he was the son of their darling brother Edward, who had gone to live in Edinburgh many years before.

'Sadly,' she had continued, 'he died not long after his only child was born, and Annette, his wife, was so afraid that anything would happen to Andrew that she hardly let him out of her sight. We didn't see him at all when he was a child, but we met him at her funeral, and again . . . oh, it must have been last August, when he came to tell us he had been accepted for Aberdeen University and would be starting there at the beginning of October. He can't really have had time to settle down, yet he's coming to visit us already. He's a dear boy.'

Believing that anyone under fifty would be a boy to Miss Esther, Marianne had paid little heed to this, but Andrew had definitely been under fifty, more than thirty years under, and his clear grey eyes had lit up when they fell on her. Marianne, not long fifteen, had felt deeply flattered by the warmth of his smile when Miss Edith introduced them, and the strength of his handclasp had made her heart speed up in a fluttery manner for the very first time in her life.

Concentrating on every word spoken in case she missed any relevant information about him, she'd learned that he was eighteen, a first-year law student. By dint of an arch question asked by one of his aunts, Marianne had even got to know that as yet he had no lady-friend, and the knowing look exchanged by Miss Esther and Miss Emily had not escaped her; they were planning some matchmaking in a year or two, with her as the lucky girl.

Andrew had turned down his aunts' frequent invitations to Sunday tea by saying he hoped they would understand that he had to study every minute he could, but he did promise to take an afternoon and evening off at Easter, which was why, at five to one on the afternoon of Easter Sunday, Marianne was sitting decorously on the edge of the sofa so as to make a good impression. At the other end sat Miss Esther, strands of fluffy white already escaping from the chignon Miss Edith wanted her to adopt but which wouldn't stay pinned, her blue eyes expectant, cheeks flushed, hands fidgeting ever so slightly against the dark blue crepe of her Sunday dress. Still persisting in tasting what she cooked, Miss Esther's girth had gradually increased, and Marianne couldn't help thinking that she would soon be a proper roly-poly . . . though that was a bit unkind.

The other two sisters were occupying the armchairs by the fireside, consciously or not staking their claim as bread-winners to the best seats, but while Miss Emily – a faint wave at the front of her immaculate silver coiffure –

nervously crossed and uncrossed her black-stockinged legs under cover of her skirt, Miss Edith appeared to be in perfect control of her emotions. She had hidden the deep hollow at her neck with a stand-up collar, but she could do nothing to camouflage the hollows in her cheeks, which made her long narrow nose appear even longer and more pointed. Children with vivid imaginations would see her as a witch, Marianne reflected, especially in that black bombazine dress which did nothing for her. It fell straight from shoulder to hips, her bust, if she had one, lost under heavy tucks of material.

A barely discernible tic at her jawline, however, showed that she was not as composed as she looked, and Marianne couldn't help but pity all three sisters. The nervousness, the preparations for the elaborate meal and the production of best china and tablecloth, and all because there would be an unaccustomed male presence in the house – a young man who likely had to eat off unmatched china in his room at the varsity. Still, as he had proved the last time he was here, Andrew Rennie was a perfect gentleman who wouldn't spoil his aunts' pleasure by telling them so.

He arrived at one o'clock exactly, making Marianne suspect that he had waited outside so as not to be early. That was the kind of boy he was, she mused, wondering if gaining his degree and then training to become a solicitor would make him rich enough for her to consider as a future husband. She liked the way his brown hair waved at the front, and his neat, rather gingery moustache; she loved his grey eyes and the strong lines of his face. He was a good bit taller than she was, at least seven inches more than her five feet three, and very handsome. She wouldn't mind marrying him ... but she wasn't going to jump at the first boy she met. There was plenty of time yet, and who knew, she might come across somebody with more money than Andrew could ever earn. In any case, once he was soliciting, or whatever solicitors did, he wouldn't want to tie himself to a country quine with little education.

During lunch, he told his aunts about life in Marischal College and Marianne found herself transported to a magic world of books, of lectures, of theses demanded on time by grim-faced professors. Then his expression lightened, and he made them laugh about the tricks his fellow students got up to, especially how they got the prescribed work done and still had time to go out and enjoy themselves. 'They take it in turns to do the research and revision, and then they all make copies with slight variations.'

'Oh, Andrew!' exclaimed Miss Edith. 'I hope you do not take part in those deceptions?'

'No, Aunt Edith,' he assured her. 'I appreciate my good fortune in being given the chance to make something of myself, although I have a struggle to get through the work in time.'

'I am glad to hear that you behave honourably.'

It was Miss Esther who said, when they were clearing the table, 'It is too nice a day for young people to be cooped up inside. Why don't you take Marianne for a walk, Andrew?'

He jumped to his feet eagerly. 'I would love to, Aunt Esther, but perhaps she does not care much for walking?'

The girl stood up quickly. 'I do, I love it.'

'She is only fifteen, remember,' Miss Edith cautioned him. 'Do you think it seemly to . . . ?'

'Seemly my foot!' exclaimed Miss Esther. 'Her head is screwed on the right way, and Andrew knows how to behave. I am not suggesting he takes her to the Tivoli, or anything like that.'

It was the first time Marianne had heard any of the sisters arguing and she hoped that they wouldn't end up fighting, but Andrew led her outside before anything else was said. 'Don't take it to heart,' he smiled. 'I do not think their disagreement will last long.'

'I dinna like the idea of them quarrelling over me,' she murmured.

'They're not really quarrelling, and what would you rather do? Go back and sit with them, or walk along the Dee with me?'

'That's nae fair,' she smiled. 'You ken fine I'd rather walk with you, wherever you take me.'

'We might meet some of my fellow students. Quite a few take their lady-friends that way, as well.'

Marianne wondered if he realized what he had said. Did he really want her to be his lady-friend? Or did he mean lady friend, which wasn't the same at all? She didn't ask; the thought of meeting other boys, whether alone or accompanied by lady-friends, was too exciting to jeopardize.

There were indeed several couples promenading when they reached the path which ran along the riverbank, but no one Andrew knew. 'I hope you won't be bored with just my company,' he smiled, after they had been ambling along for about fifteen minutes. 'I'm often accused of being a dull old stick.'

'Oh, you're nae dull,' she protested automatically.

'It's what comes of not knowing any girls, and I get the feeling you haven't known any boys, so we can learn together . . . if you like?'

'Learn what together?'

He laughed at her wary expression. 'Nothing bad. Just the art of making conversation with the opposite sex.'

Relieved that this was all he had in mind, she said, 'I didna ken there was an art to that.'

'There's an art to everything, Marianne, and it would help us to find out more about each other.'

She had no intention of telling him anything about herself, other than giving him the 'cruel stepmother' reason for her leaving home, but as time passed, with him confiding that he hoped to set up a law firm of his own eventually, she let it slip that she wanted to marry someone rich. As soon as she said it, she wished that she hadn't.

'I suppose you think I'm awful?'

He took her hand and stroked it gently. 'Not at all, my dear. It is probably every girl's dream to marry money, but the majority never do. They fall in love with a boy who hasn't a penny to his name, and live in a poky little house, and raise a large family on next to nothing . . .'

'. . . and they end up hating each other,' she burst out. 'I've seen it happening time and again at hame.'

'It doesn't always happen like that. Didn't your parents keep on loving each other until your mother died?'

She considered briefly. 'I never heard her saying she loved him, but I suppose she must have, deep down, and he was that cut up when she died I was sure he loved her.' After a pause, she added, somewhat bitterly, 'But it didna take him long to find another wife.'

His grasp tightened. 'It's different for men. Most women can face years and years of widowhood, but a man needs someone . . . to care for him, to look after his children . . . to satisfy his needs. Do you know what I mean, Marianne?'

She coloured and snatched her hand away, her outrage making her speak in the dialect she had been doing her best to forget. 'Aye, I ken, and I'm sure decent men dinna speak to young girls about things like that.'

'I'm sorry. I told you I had never had anything to do with girls. I was only trying to save you pinning your hopes on a dream which may never materialize, but I'm beginning to suspect that you are one of those people who will succeed in everything you set out to do. I will not, however, cast it up if you do marry a poor man.'

They said nothing for some time, and she found it very pleasant to be walking so close to him, the gentle sound of water lapping against the bank disturbed occasionally by the screech of the swans sailing majestically a little farther upstream. If he wanted her to be his lady-friend . . .

'Well, well! Rennie, you secretive old dog!'

The strident voice startled them both, their heads swivelling to see who was talking. A broad young man in grey breeches, and with a peaked cap set on his head at an absurd angle, had come up behind them.

'Oh, it's you,' Andrew said unenthusiastically.

'Won't you introduce me to your paramour?' Without waiting, the other man turned to Marianne with his hand outstretched. 'My name is Douglas Martin, and this . . . is Vi . . . um . . .' He looked enquiringly at his companion with a barely suppressed lewd giggle.

'Vi Collie,' she supplied, rolling her eyes sideways.

Shaking the proffered hands one after the other, Marianne murmured, 'Pleased to meet you.' There was something about Douglas Martin she didn't like, but since he seemed to be Andrew's friend, she would do her best to be polite to him . . . and the common-looking girl clinging to his arm like a sticky-willow. It dawned on her that Andrew hadn't introduced her to them, and she hoped he wasn't ashamed of her.

Catching her accusing eye, he looked at the other man and said, very coldly, 'This is Marianne Cheyne. She works in my aunts' shop.'

The underlying message was received and acted upon. 'Ah . . . yes . . .' Douglas mumbled, moving away. 'We'd better be getting on, eh, Vi?'

When the ill-matched pair were out of earshot, Marianne asked, 'Why did he go off so suddenly? Did he not want to speak to a girl who works in a shop? That Vi looked as if she . . .'

Andrew laughed at her confusion. 'Yes, Martin is a snob of the highest degree, yet it wouldn't surprise me in the least if he had spent most of last night with her.'

She was shocked. 'Do students do that sort of thing? Have you?'

'Have I been with a lady of the streets? Not yet, but I

sometimes feel I should, just once, to see ... to learn ... the ropes.'

They both laughed, he self-consciously, she in embarrassment, and they turned to make their way back to Strawberry Bank.

At his Aunt Esther's behest, Andrew's visits became weekly once his preliminary examinations were past, and throughout the summer, he and Marianne went out walking every Sunday afternoon if the weather was suitable. Sometimes, they met other students who stopped and were introduced to Marianne, who was pleased that they seemed as decent and polite as Andrew was. In fact, she was quite attracted to one in particular, and when they happened to run into Stephen Grant too many times to be coincidental, Andrew didn't seem to mind. 'You've made a conquest,' he teased, making her blush.

Nevertheless, it was well into September before this was proved to be true. As Marianne waited for Miss Edith to lock up the shop one night, with Miss Emily fussing silently round her sister as usual, she was astonished to see the lean six-footer standing in the next doorway. When he came forward, she said timidly, 'Miss Edith, Miss Emily, this is Andrew's friend Stephen Grant.'

'You are his aunts, I believe,' he smiled, showing a dimple in each cheek. 'I hope you don't mind if I ask your permission to take Marianne out one evening? Andrew will vouch that I do not drink, and I have no other vices which would blacken me in your eyes.'

Marianne held her breath, but she need not have worried. Both sisters were bowled over by his boyish charm, and Miss Edith, the decision-maker, was beaming as she said, 'We have no objection to you taking Marianne out for a short walk occasionally, Mr Grant, as long as you do not keep her out late. You may call for her at half-past seven tomorrow night.'

Taking this correctly as a dismissal, Stephen gave a small bow, cast a delighted glance at Marianne and walked away. Before she had time to make up her mind whether to be pleased at his dexterity in dealing with the elderly ladies or offended that he hadn't asked her first, Miss Edith said, 'He seems a very agreeable young man. I take it you like him, Marianne?'

'I don't know him very well, but I've nothing against him.'

'I don't know what Andrew's going to say about this,' Miss Emily put in. 'I thought he and Marianne –'

Miss Edith tutted impatiently. 'She is too young to be serious about any one boy – it will do her good to get to know others. She can come to no harm as long as we vet her escorts.'

Too young – as Miss Edith had said – to appreciate what could happen to her, or to have any deep romantic thoughts about either Stephen or Andrew, Marianne slept soundly that night, and did not feel at all nervous about the assignation until about five minutes before Stephen was due.

When the expected knock came, Miss Edith motioned her to stay where she was and went to the door herself. 'Ah, good evening, Mr Grant. You must come in and meet my youngest sister, and then we will hinder you no longer.'

'They all like you,' Marianne told him a few minutes later, as they walked away from Strawberry Bank. 'You made a good impression on them.'

'Your aunts are dear old souls,' he smiled.

She didn't correct him. What difference did it make if he'd made a wrong assumption? 'Have you seen Andrew today?' she asked.

Blushing, Stephen looked squarely at her. 'I made a point of seeing him. I didn't want him to think I was keeping our meeting a secret.'

'What did he say?' she asked conversationally, although she wasn't really interested in what Andrew had said. It had nothing to do with him who she went out with.

'He said he was glad someone else was taking an interest in you.'

This put a different slant on things. How dare Andrew palm her off like that? Had he another girl in mind for himself? She couldn't let Stephen see that she was angry, however. It wasn't his fault.

They kept on walking and talking, her anger faded, and the more she was in his company, the more she came to like him. When he told her that his father was one of the top surgeons at the Infirmary and his mother had been a Drummond of Drumtocher, she could tell that he wasn't just trying to impress her.

'Are your parents still alive?' he asked her then.

The abrupt question took her by surprise. If she told the truth, he would want to know where her father lived and what he worked at, and she couldn't tell him about the ramshackle house where she had been born and brought up, the sawdust from the mill lying thick over the bits of furniture her mother had dusted lovingly several times a day until her lungs had been contaminated. 'They both . . . died,' she said presently. 'That's why I had to come to Aberdeen.'

'Where did you live before that?'

'We'd a lovely big house in its own grounds.' For a moment, she felt sick at the lies she was concocting, but she had started now and it was quite good fun really. Carried away by her imagination, she went on, forgetting to be careful with her speech, 'It had oak trees a' roon' it, an' it had six lums an' a orchard at the back, an' . . .' Her inventiveness giving out, she looked guiltily round into Stephen's face.

Fortunately, he thought he understood the reason for her sudden stop. 'I'm sorry, I shouldn't have made you speak about it. I can see you still haven't got over losing your parents and your home.'

She dropped her eyes in a suitably overcome way, and they walked on for a time without saying anything. They were in Albyn Place, where each house was a veritable palace to Marianne, when Stephen observed, 'D'you see this house we're just coming to? That's where I live.'

She was shocked. He couldn't live in a place like this? It was huge! There were dozens of lums, and turrets at the corners, with tiny leaded windows which wouldn't let in much light but were real quaint; there was a curved drive up to the entrance; it was too big to be called a door. Before she had time to absorb any more details, they had passed the vantage point and her view was obscured.

'That's funny-looking trees,' she observed, never having seen anything like them, their feathery branches sweeping down to the ground.

'I can't remember the Latin name for them,' Stephen smiled, 'but most people call them monkey puzzles. I hope you don't think I took you this way to boast about my home, it was just that it's a pleasant way to get out of town – right out Queen's Road.'

Queen's Road being a continuation of Albyn Place, she had to agree with that. All the houses they passed before they came to the open countryside were every bit as grand as the Grants', and all built from the silver granite taken out of Rubislaw Quarry, so Stephen told her when he took her up the grassy bank to show her the vast, gaping hole. It was so deep that her legs started trembling and she felt a sickness deep in her stomach, and she was extremely grateful that he didn't make her stand so near the edge for long.

They had been walking for almost an hour when he asked, 'Do you want to sit on this dyke for a minute?'

She shook her head. 'I'd like a wee seat to rest my feet, but I'd best be getting back.'

'Yes, if you're late, your aunts might not let you come out with me again, and we can't have that.'

Until then, Stephen had been doing most of the talking, mainly about his fellow students and their squabbles, and had told her how disappointed he had been at not getting into Oxford, which had made her realize the vast difference between them, and when he asked which kind of books she read, she was too ashamed to confess that she couldn't read very well.

'What kind of books do you like?' she countered, hedging.

He shrugged wryly. 'I used to like Sheridan and I quite liked Oscar Wilde's stuff, but I don't get time to read anything these days except law books . . . so dry they turn your brain to sawdust.' Then he laughed. 'I expect you're like my mother. She loves novels – romances and tragedies, you know. She cried all the way through Mrs Wood's *East Lynne*.'

'So did I, and I love romances, and all.' Marianne hadn't read any novels, romantic or otherwise, but if Stephen's mother loved them . . .

'How old are you, Marianne? I didn't think of asking before.'

'I'll be sixteen next month.' His involuntary gasp, 'God, you're only a baby,' made her ask, 'How aul' are you?'

'I was twenty-one in July.'

From then on, Marianne could sense a difference in him, and tried to think what had caused it. Did he think she was too young for him? Or had he seen through her attempt to sound well read?

At her door in Strawberry Bank, he remarked, very correctly and not at all convincingly, 'Thank you for walking with me, Marianne, I have enjoyed your company, and no doubt I shall see you again some time. Good night.'

She managed to hide her disappointment that he so clearly didn't want to take her out again. 'Good night, Stephen.' She had to force her legs to move as she went into the house, only to find that her ordeal was just beginning, because the sisters were waiting eagerly to hear how she and Stephen had got on together. Too vain to say something had gone wrong, she told them about the first half of the evening, letting them believe that things had been the same on the way home, and, urged to tell them as much about his house as she could, she embellished her description until they were satisfied and she was free to go to bed.

Miss Esther and Miss Emily retired to their room happy that their young friend had enjoyed her entire evening, but Miss Edith, sharper and more observant, had a feeling that this was not the case. Sorry for the girl, she kept her suspicions to herself.

Marianne felt reluctant to go out with Andrew the following Sunday, but once away from the house, and sure that he would be sympathetic, she asked him if Stephen Grant had said anything to him about her.

'He didn't say anything about anything. Why? Didn't you get on together?'

'We did at first, then . . . oh, I dinna ken what happened. I couldna tell him the names of any books because I've never read any, and then he asked how old I was, and after that, he hardly spoke.'

Andrew pursed his mouth for a moment. 'Would you like me to tell you the novels my mother used to read?'

'Would you, Andrew? I hated having to read books when I was at the school, but I might enjoy novels with good stories. Another thing, though – maybe he didna . . . didn't like the way I speak.'

'You have a very broad country accent,' Andrew smiled, 'but that's nothing to be ashamed of.'

'I hear myself broader than folk in the town, and I dinna ken any big words. And when I get mixed up, it gets worse. Could you help me with that, and all?'

'You want me to prepare you to be a lady, is that what you mean?'

34

'If I do find a rich husband, I wouldn't want to let him down by not speaking proper.'

'If he loved you, he wouldn't care how you talked.'

She shook her head. 'Like I told you before, I'm not interested in love. Will you help me, Andrew?'

'All right, I'll give you lessons in speech and deportment, so that you will be able to hold your head up in any company. I'll make you read certain books in set times, and I'll give you others to help you to improve your vocabulary. But once we start, young lady, we'll go on until I'm satisfied with you, so there must be no complaining.'

'I won't complain, Andrew, and I'm really grateful. I'll show that Stephen Grant I'm as good as him . . . and his mother.'

'Ah, so you're doing it for him, are you? Well, I can promise you that when we are finished, you can set your sights much higher than Stephen Grant.'

Her eyes were dancing, her face agog with enthusiasm for what she hoped to accomplish. 'I'll maybe end up among royalty,' she giggled, her expression sobering when she saw how Andrew was looking at her.

'I'd prefer if you stayed just the way you are right now,' he said softly.

Chapter Three

At first, Marianne's eagerness to improve herself had amused Andrew, but, looking back, he was amazed by her quick assimilation of all he had taught her over the past year. He had given her a list of books he thought would appeal to her as well as add to her vocabulary, and by the middle of 1896, there was a marked improvement in her self-confidence, especially when she was introduced to his friends. What bothered him was that they obviously liked talking with her and lingered on while he wished them at the other end of the earth. But he could not tell her so. She clearly didn't feel the same way about him as he did about her.

Another summer coming to an end, the weather turned progressively colder. Sunshine gave way to winds and showers, then to mists and rain and then to sleet and snow . . . accompanied by gales. The young people did not forego their afternoon walks unless the weather was too bad, but come Marianne's third November in Aberdeen, they were more often inside than out. This put a temporary end to the lessons, but Marianne surprised the sisters by her newly acquired ability to enter into discussions on current affairs. As Miss Edith observed, 'Andrew has worked wonders. Except when she is under stress, Marianne has practically lost her country accent, and she can carry herself quite gracefully. And she has grown since she came here; she is almost as tall as he is now.'

'I think they're a perfect couple,' Miss Esther beamed, 'just made for each other.'

'No, no,' cautioned Miss Emily. 'I think that our Maid

Marianne is looking for someone with better prospects than Andrew.'

Very much out of character, Miss Edith gave a long sigh. 'Can't you see that he already loves her? I am afraid she will break his heart, not deliberately, but he will be hurt, nevertheless.'

Sighing too, Miss Esther murmured hopefully, 'She is young yet. By the time she is old enough for marriage . . .' The return of the young people at that moment put an end to their conjecturing.

It soon became noticeable, to Marianne herself as well as to her benefactresses, that her relationship with Andrew had changed; although they were still just friends, a new element had crept in of his wanting to touch her, to brush hands or shoulders, to sit closer to her on the sofa, which made Miss Esther nod happily.

Marianne herself did not know how she felt about it. While she liked the way that she sometimes caught Andrew looking at her, his eyes soft with admiration . . . or more? . . . it made her uneasy. She had now made the acquaintance of several of the students who were at Marischal College with him, and she was hoping that one of them would ask her out so that she could make some comparisons. She did wonder how Andrew would take it, but surely he'd want her to enjoy herself? A few hours of innocent pleasure – what would be wrong with that?

Andrew sprung his surprise as soon as he arrived on the first Sunday in December. 'There's a Hogmanay Ball being laid on for the Law Faculty,' he announced, his eyes going round the four smiling faces. 'I want to go, but . . . I need a partner.'

'Take Marianne,' beamed Miss Esther. 'She won't have to worry about a ballgown, because there's plenty of time for me to –'

'I can't let you make one for me!' the girl gasped, scarlet-faced.

Miss Edith, the decision-maker, stepped in. 'That is not the point in question, Marianne. Do you really want to go, or do you feel that you had better go for the sake of appearance, since most of Andrew's friends will have seen him out walking with you?'

'I want to go,' Marianne cried, 'but it'll be an awful lot of work for you and such an expense . . .'

Miss Esther stood up. 'I was not meaning to make a dress. I am sure one of the old gowns in the trunk in our cellar would fit without too much alteration. Emily, will you come down with me to hold the candle while I look?'

After her sisters left the room, Miss Edith got to her feet. 'I may as well go with them. I would quite like to see our gowns again. Mamma had them made for our one and only ball, but . . .' She shrugged this off as though she did not regret it, but her wry smile and rather sad eyes told a different story.

'Your one and only ball?' echoed Marianne. 'Why was that?'

'Father did not approve of dancing, but he was away at the time when Lavinia Tennant – Father Bernard's mother, you know – invited us to her twenty-first birthday ball, so Mamma let us accept. She said we would never meet any young men otherwise, but when Father came home and found out, he locked the gowns up in his old trunk, and took it down to the cellar. Then Mamma died, and . . . well, we didn't feel like dancing after that, and by the time Father passed on, we were all past marrying age.' Miss Edith dashed away the solitary tear that had edged over her bottom eyelid as she closed the door behind her.

'I don't think I'd better go to the ball with you, Andrew,' Marianne whispered. 'It would likely upset them to see me wearing . . .'

He came towards her, eyes wide and pleading. 'Please, Marianne? I can't go unaccompanied. Please?'

A flash of irritation made her say, 'You just want me to come with you because you can't find another partner, that's all! Why don't you ask that Vi, or one of the other ladies of the street? You told me once you wanted to –'

He stepped back like a wounded animal and lashed out in the only way he knew how. 'Maybe I will.'

'Go ahead, then, and see if I care!'

'Oh, how stupid I've been, thinking you . . . liked me a little bit.'

Her conscience smote her. 'I do like you, Andrew! Quite a lot! But I don't want to bring back bad memories to your aunts, they've been so good to me. Can't you understand that?'

'Yes, of course I do, and I'm sorry. All right, if you think even one of them will be upset if you wear her dress, I won't try to make you change your mind.'

They left it at that, and he sat down to await his aunts' return.

The elderly ladies, whispering excitedly, came in with their arms empty and explained that they had taken the dresses up to Marianne's room. 'You can try them on when you go to bed,' Miss Edith told her.

Andrew smiled broadly. 'I get the impression you don't want me to see them.'

'Of course we don't, not yet!' declared Miss Esther, who was now harbouring secret dreams of him taking one look at the girl in her chosen gown and being so overcome by love that he would gather her into his arms and shower her with kisses in front of them all.

Pretending to be offended, he got to his feet. 'I suppose I'd better get out of the way.'

'You don't need to leave yet,' Marianne protested, although she was desperate to see the gowns.

'I have a lot of revision to do for the end-of-term assess-ments,' he assured her. 'I wasn't intending to stay anyway.'

As she had been doing for some weeks, she saw him to the door, but tonight, instead of his usual joking farewell gesture of tipping his forelock, he took her hand in both of his. 'Choose the dress you want, Marianne, and don't worry about the aunts. They're not as vulnerable as they look; they're really tough old birds.'

'I still wouldn't want to hurt them,' she said gently. 'You wouldn't be angry if I didn't go with you, would you?'

'I wouldn't be angry,' he said softly, 'I'd be broken-hearted.'

His eyes held the same strange look she had noticed briefly before; a serious look that she couldn't have described if anyone had asked her; a look which, combined with the squeezing of her hand, had made her heart speed up, her stomach turn over with a pain that wasn't a pain, the kind of feeling she welcomed and wished would never go away. Hoping that he was about to kiss her on the mouth, she was disappointed when he raised her hands to his lips. 'Good night, my dear Marianne,' he murmured.

'Good night, Andrew.' She closed the door and leaned against it. She couldn't be falling in love with him? She couldn't be! She certainly hadn't counted on anything like that! The rich man of her dreams still hadn't materialized . . . but he would!

When she went back to the parlour, Miss Esther said, 'Shall we go to your room now?' and at Marianne's nod, they all trooped upstairs.

When she saw the array of shimmering loveliness spread across her bed, she gasped with awe and glanced helplessly from one to the other of the elderly ladies. 'I'll never be able to choose one.'

'We will leave you to try them on,' Miss Edith said, in the brisk manner she used in the shop, pushing her sisters towards the door.

'Yes, take your time, dear,' Miss Esther smiled. 'Move around and see how you feel in them. Nothing is worse than spending a whole evening in something uncomfortable.'

Miss Emily nodded. 'When you've picked the one you feel happiest with, Esther will do any alterations it needs.'

Ignoring the smell of camphor emanating from the gowns, Marianne tried to judge, while she tried them on in an imaginative euphoria, which suited her best. First, she wriggled into Esther's soft peach – tulle underlined with stiff taffeta – with layers of ruffles looped round the hem of the huge skirt, and so narrow in the waist that she would have to be laced in very tightly before the buttons down the back would fasten; Miss Esther must have been much slimmer when she was young. Holding the back together as she twirled in front of the long cheval mirror, she gasped at the way the yards and yards of material moulded into her body instead of looking bulky as she had believed they would. She had never given a thought to her figure before, but her curvacious reflection elated her - this was the one!

In case Miss Esther's sisters would be offended, she decided to try on theirs too, and so, lifting the deep rose which had been Miss Emily's, she slipped it over her head and turned back to the mirror. It was not a girl she saw this time, but a tall, elegant woman, the décolletage displaying every inch of her neck and shoulders . . . and most of her bosom. The front of the skirt flowed to the floor, but the back was padded out by a bustle, not big, but enough to be a talking point these days. She considered for a short time and came to the conclusion that she didn't have the nerve – nor the figure, if it came to that – to wear this gown. Maybe when she was older . . . ?

The ice-blue creation that was Miss Edith's seemed at first glance to be too cold a colour, not what Marion had thought would appeal to her, but as soon as she put it on and pirouetted to get an idea of how it looked from behind, she knew that *this* really was the one. There was just a shadow of cleavage showing at the bust, much more demure, though the bodice was constructed so as to make the most of small breasts. From the waist, which was not quite so small as the peach, the skirt billowed out over a wide crinoline. It was ... oh, perfect didn't do it justice, but it was the best word she could come up with.

A quiet tap at her door made her call, 'Come in.'

Miss Edith opened the door and asked, 'Have you decided yet? Please don't laugh at my haste, but I had to find out.'

'I'm not laughing. They're all lovely, but I'm going for yours.' Although Marianne had told Andrew she would give up the idea of going to the ball if any of his aunts seemed distressed, she knew now that she wasn't so self-sacrificing. Whatever happened, she would be there as his partner.

Miss Edith, however, did not appear at all distressed. 'Do you not think it too old-fashioned?' she asked, as she began to fasten the tiny cloth buttons. 'Crinolines of this size were going out even when I wore it, and that's ... great heavens, almost forty years ago!'

Marianne shook her head. 'I don't care how old-fashioned it is!'

'It certainly suits you ... much better than it did me.' Miss Edith said nothing more until she had done up the whole twenty-four, then she stepped back to get a better view. 'You look exactly like one of the illustrations in a fairy-tale book we once had.'

She called for her sisters to come and see, and when they ran in, Miss Esther clapped her hands in delight. 'Oh, Marianne! You're like the fairy in –'

'I've told her,' Miss Edith said drily, but smiled just the same.

'I hope nobody's offended because I've chosen this one,' Marianne murmured. 'I couldn't make up my mind when

42

I saw them first, but this one fits me best. It won't need any alterations.'

Miss Emily gave a long deep sigh. 'Seeing you standing there like a graceful swan . . . it takes me back –'

Not wanting any of them to become nostalgic, Marianne interrupted, 'I can't get over what a difference a dress can make.'

'People used to say, "Manners maketh man",' Miss Esther smiled, 'but our mamma always added, ". . . and the proper clothes maketh woman."'

'I can't get over Father taking the trouble to put camphor in the trunk when he packed these away,' Emily observed. 'I was afraid they would be moth-eaten, but they look as good as new. We shall have to give them a good airing to get rid of the smell of the mothballs, and we should hang them in a closet so that Marianne can have the use of any of them any time she wants. Andrew will probably take her to other balls.'

'That's true,' Miss Esther beamed. 'Oh, this is all so romantic.'

Edith brought their matchmaking to a halt. 'If not Andrew, someone else. We must not rush the girl into anything, and I think she wants to get to bed now.'

She helped Marianne out of the blue gown while her sisters went out with theirs over their arms. Crossing to the door carrying hers, she said, gently, 'Those two have made up their minds that you and Andrew are right for each other, and I have the feeling that he would agree, but you must not marry him just to please us, or because you feel you owe us something. Think of your own happiness, my dear.'

'Thank you for understanding, Miss Edith.' Marianne sat down on the bed when the door clicked. In spite of being so tired, and so excited, she had to think. She liked Andrew, was possibly on the verge of loving him, but she wanted more than that. She wanted wealth, a standing in society. She wanted to be the wife of a man with power, a man other people looked up to and admired. Andrew would never fit that bill: he was too honest, too considerate of his fellow men and women. He might be successful as a solicitor, but he would never make a name for himself at that or anything else.

Feeling suddenly chilly in her undergarments, she stood up to change into her nightie, then got into bed and snuggled down. In her last thoughts before sleep claimed her, she pictured her spectacular entry to the ballroom on Andrew's arm in the magnificent ice-blue gown, imagined all eyes turning to watch her progress into the room, conjured up dozens of handsome, eligible bachelors begging her to dance, gold cravat pins gleaming a few inches above the chains of their gold pocket watches.

Drifting off into slumber, her dreams followed the same pattern, and strangely, in the morning she could remember them distinctly.

When she was thirteen, there had been a special celebration put on in Tipperton for some occasion now forgotten, and her mother had allowed her to stay to watch the dancing after the concert. Marianne had been enthralled by the energetic Lancers and in her dreams had seen herself performing the intricate steps with this stranger or that, their eyes telling how much they were attracted to her, her crinoline floating out around her. Each time the music had come to an end, her partner – a new one every time – had taken her to another room on the pretext of finding her a comfortable seat. Then her supple body had been pressed against a manly chest, firm hands going round her waist, but each time she'd looked up to smile at a hopefully prospective suitor, it had been Andrew's face she'd seen, his lips within a fraction of hers.

During breakfast, she assured herself that he'd been the one she'd seen because he was the only man she knew for certain would be there. He was too shy to kiss her; it was more likely to be Stephen Grant or any one of the men she had been introduced to over the past year and a half.

It could even be the boy – the rich man – who was to be her future husband. She didn't have a picture of him in her mind; she didn't care what he looked like . . . as long as he was taller than she was. She was five feet seven already and maybe hadn't stopped growing, so he might need to be over six feet.

Tall and wealthy? Surely that wasn't expecting too much? He didn't need to be handsome.

Chapter Four

❦

In order to be seen at her best, on the evening of the ball Marianne waited until Miss Esther, chirping delightedly, had taken Andrew inside before she came slowly down the stairs. His stunned expression, the admiration which sprang to his eyes, more than compensated for the awkwardness of holding up a crinoline so that she wouldn't fall over it, but the shocked faces of his aunts told her that her petticoats were showing. Well, it was better to be a little immodest, she thought, in some irritation, than to pitch headlong down the stairs and display a much more intimate garment.

Miss Esther sidled up to her before she reached the floor. 'Let me remove the hoop,' she whispered. 'I had quite forgotten that Edith had trouble with it. All I have to do is snip the holding stitches, so it will not take long.'

'No,' Marianne whispered back, 'I want it left in. It's a talking point, isn't it? No one else'll have one.'

'That is true. Well, if you are sure.'

Miss Esther helped her down the last two steps, where Miss Edith flung a hooded cloak round her shoulders, and before Andrew led her out, all three sisters kissed her on the cheek. She needed Andrew's assistance to negotiate the high step of the cab he had waiting, but once up, she had the presence of mind to lift the back of the hoop before she sat down, albeit rather gingerly.

When Marianne finally walked majestically into the Mitchell Hall on Andrew's arm, her reception was all that she had hoped for . . . at first. All eyes turned to her, and those of each young man brightened at the sight of her fairy-tale loveliness. Savouring this, it took her a few minutes to realize that the girls – there as partners to the law students – were whispering to each other, and giggling as they pointed at her. One of them – all skin and bone in a hobble-skirted gown – didn't bother to lower her voice. 'Doesn't she know these things have been out of fashion for decades? My grandmother speaks about wearing them when *she* was a girl, for goodness' sake.'

This raised a laugh from the girls standing nearest to her, until they caught sight of Andrew's scowl. 'I think I should take you home,' he said loudly to Marianne. 'I don't want you mixing with these ill-mannered people.'

Sick at heart, but determined not to show it, she shook off the hand he had laid on her arm. 'It's all right, Andrew,' she declared as staunchly as she could. 'They can't help being badly brought up, and they didn't bother me. In any case, I don't need to go anywhere near them. They'll be in the minority here, I'm sure.'

The girls' mouths gaped, their eyes widened in shock, but several of the young men clapped their approval at her show of spirit, and Andrew was left standing at the side while she went off with one after another of those clamouring to claim a dance. As in her dream, she was often asked to go to another room, a secluded room, to have a rest after an energetic romp, but she always said that Andrew was her escort and asked to be returned to where he was waiting.

'I'm sorry,' she puffed, nearly an hour after they had arrived. 'I don't like saying no when somebody asks me, so if you want to dance with me, you'll have to make a stand against them.'

He had been watching her closely while she was on the floor, noting her too brilliant eyes, her deeply flushed cheeks, the white around her pinched nostrils, all of which gave the lie to the impression she was trying to give, that of enjoying herself. 'I'd prefer if you'd sit this one out with me,' he said.

47

'Oh, thank you, Andrew,' she said gratefully. 'It's been an awful strain.'

'It must have been.' He could not let her know that he was well aware of the effort she had been putting into appearing free of care.

During one of the previous dances, he had looked for a place to take her if he got the chance, and led her now to the little alcove he had found. It was screened from the rest of the hall by two large plants in tubs, and even better, as far as he was concerned, the only place to sit was a small chaise longue.

Flopping down in utter exhaustion, Marianne was horrified that the crinoline made the front of her skirt shoot into the air. She looked at Andrew in dismay. 'I should have listened to Miss Esther,' she wailed. 'She wanted to take the hoop out, but I wouldn't let her. I thought . . .'

His heart went out to her when he saw the tears in her eyes, and he longed to hold her, to stroke the soft coppery hair one of his aunts must have dressed for her, it was so beautifully pinned up. But he did not want to take advantage of her present vulnerability. He tried to think of an answer to her latest problem – it wouldn't do for her to be caught in such an undignified position – and then he took hold of both her hands. 'I'll pull you up, but you'll have to be careful when you sit down again.'

With Marianne decently covered, he felt free to sit down beside her. 'I wish I hadn't made you come,' he murmured, taking her hand. 'I had no idea that any girl could be so rude about another's dress. In any case, I thought you looked . . .' He paused, swallowed, and then said reverently, 'I had never seen anything so beautiful in all my life as the picture you made walking down my aunts' stairs.'

'Oh, Andrew.' It was all she could say with her throat so tight.

'And I'm sure all the men here tonight felt exactly the same when they saw you come in. You outshone every girl in the hall. That's what was wrong. That girl was jealous. It was a compliment, really, when you come to think of it.'

'Was it? Are you sure?'

'Yes, I'm sure. And the rush of men to dance with you, that was a compliment too. Now, have you rested enough, or do you want to dry your eyes and give me at least one dance before I take you home?'

Turning towards him, she leaned forward and kissed his cheek. 'You're such a dear, Andrew. I'm sorry I neglected you, and I feel better now.'

As soon as they emerged from their haven, Marianne was besieged once more, but she shook her head. 'This dance is Andrew's.'

When the military two-step was over, they made for the seats round the wall, and noticing two young men heading in her direction, Marianne waved them away.

'I won't hold you to the next dance if you –' Andrew began, but she broke in, 'I want to dance with you.'

Waiting for the music to start again, she let her eyes rove round the hall and when she noticed a small knot of girls at the opposite side looking up flirtatiously at a tall, fair-haired young man, who was paying no attention to them, she gave Andrew a nudge.' 'D'you know who he is?'

'I can't see his face, but he must have more charisma than I have,' Andrew grinned. 'Girls do not mill round me like that. Do you want me to find somebody to introduce you?'

'Oh, no! I'd be too embarrassed.'

The next dance was stopped before the end, so that everyone could hear the bells chime midnight, and after the hand-shaking and well-wishing had died down, most of the men kissed their partners, and so Andrew felt emboldened to kiss his. 'Happy New Year, dear Marianne,' he murmured bashfully, taking her in his arms.

As with several other couples, the first kiss was quickly

followed by another of longer duration, and when Andrew drew away, he was confused by the depth of his feelings and too shy to declare himself.

Striving to understand her own emotions, Marianne said breathily, 'We'd better get off the floor before ...' Not knowing why she wanted to sit down, she broke off.

Acutely conscious of each other now, they sat through the next dance without uttering a word, but at last Andrew said, 'I think I should be getting you home, in case the aunts are worrying.'

When he helped her to her feet, she said, 'I'd like to walk home, if that's all right? My head needs clearing.'

'Mine, too.'

Although the night air was bitterly cold and frost was glittering on the granite setts of the street, they ambled along silently for quite a time before Andrew summoned enough courage to say what was on his mind. 'Marianne,' he began, 'we've known each other for two years, and I was drawn to you from the very first. No, don't say anything yet,' he warned, as she opened her mouth, 'I want to get it off my chest, and I need to know where I stand. I said "drawn to you", but I really fell in love with you the minute I saw you. I meant to wait till I'd something to offer you, until I had set up as a solicitor, which won't be for a few years yet, but I know my aunts would be pleased if you ... if we ...'

They had stopped walking, and Marianne put her hand up and stroked his cheek. 'We're too young to make our minds up on something as serious as marriage, Andrew.'

'We could just be engaged ... and my mind was made up months ago.'

'It might change in a few years, and if you remember, I told you on our very first walk I was going to marry a rich man. Maybe you thought that was a silly girlish dream, but I still mean it.'

He eyed her mournfully. 'So you don't love me?'

'Maybe I do, maybe I don't. I just don't know, Andrew.'

'If you did, you'd know,' he said, his voice throbbing with the pain eating at his innards. 'I fall asleep every night thinking of you, and I wake every morning thinking of you, and I think of you every minute of the day. That's love, Marianne!'

'I often think of you, Andrew, and if you went away, I'd really miss you, it would probably make me miserable for a long time, but I can't be sure if it's love or not. I'm sorry.'

'It's all right,' he said gruffly, although clearly it wasn't. 'We'd better go.'

Pulling up the hood of Miss Edith's cloak, she held the body of it closely around her. 'I didn't mean to hurt you, Andrew,' she told him as they walked on again. 'I told you the truth, but remember, as your aunts keep saying, I'm only seventeen. I do like you an awful lot, more than anybody I've met yet, and maybe I will fall in love with you and marry you . . . some day.'

'What about the rich man you're looking for?' he sneered.

'If I meet one and he asks me to marry him, I'll say yes. You see, Andrew, I never had any money to spend, that's why –' Her hand flew to her mouth, but after a moment, she went on, 'I may as well tell you.'

For the very first time, she confessed to being a thief, and was most surprised when Andrew said, 'Not many young girls would have denied the temptation when confronted by a heap of sovereigns like that; most of them would have taken the lot. But tell me, what did you spend them on? What did you reward yourself with as a counter-effect to your guilt?'

She drew a deep breath. 'Do you know something, Andrew? I never did feel truly guilty. I thought it served Mr Moodie right for leaving his cash lying about, and all I bought was the railway ticket to Aberdeen. I still have four pounds, nineteen shillings and a few coppers left. Now, how does your love stand up to what I did?'

Coming to an abrupt halt, he grabbed her by the arms and turned her round to face him. 'I don't condone it, Marianne, but my love for you is strong enough to withstand any sin you care to commit. Don't forget that, do you hear? Even if our paths diverge in the future, any time you are in trouble, you have only to come to me. I will always be there for you.'

Feeling humbled, tears came to her eyes. 'Andrew, I'm all mixed up. When you say things like that my heart aches with what I suppose is love, and I want you to kiss me, but you won't want to . . .'

'I'll always want to, my darling.' His kiss was tender, a pledge of undying devotion. 'I've been a fool tonight. I shouldn't have said anything; it was much too soon. You must wipe it from your mind and not let it spoil the close companionship we had before.'

When they reached Strawberry Bank, his aunts wanted to know how their evening had gone, and only Miss Edith saw the shadows in Andrew's eyes, the heightened colour in Marianne's cheeks, as they described the four-piece ensemble which had provided the music for the more sedate dances, and the three students who had volunteered to play, with gusto, for the others. At last, putting an end to the questions still being asked by her sisters, she shooed the young man away and ordered the girl to bed.

'Something went wrong,' she whispered to Miss Esther when Miss Emily had also gone upstairs. 'Something they kept from us.'

Miss Esther frowned. 'They said they had a marvellous time.'

'Yes, and maybe they did, most of the time,' Miss Edith nodded, 'but they were definitely holding something back.'

Her sister eyed her thoughtfully. 'Would it have been the crinoline? Remember the trouble you had with it?'

Miss Edith smiled triumphantly. 'That's it! Marianne must have had trouble sitting down. I just hope she was not as bad as I was – even my drawers were in full view, if you recall.'

'They would have been embarrassed, but they would have got over it quickly. I'm sure they enjoyed themselves as much as they said.'

Marianne heard the murmur of their voices as they said good night and went into their separate rooms, but she knew that she wouldn't sleep. How could she, after what had been said earlier? It was all very well for Andrew to tell her to put it out of her mind, but she'd been cruel to him, hurt him badly, yet, in spite of that and the theft she had confessed to, he still swore that he loved her, would love her for ever. How could anybody love like that? If he landed in trouble by committing a crime and came to her for help, would she stand by him? She didn't think she would! But then, she had never professed to love him – that was the difference.

She wasn't interested in love. She wanted the safety, the power, of money around her, the wherewithal to buy enough clothes to fill closet after closet – and have some little saleswoman falling over herself to give advice on the proper outfit for the occasion. She could do without cuddles and kisses, she hadn't had many up to now anyway ... though she'd the feeling she could grow to like Andrew's. But he could never take her into the realms of the upper classes, where no one would ever dare speak to her the way that stuck-up pig of a girl had tonight. If it hadn't been for that, she might have let herself be swept away by his declaration of love.

She was getting weak.

The New Year of 1897 was only days old when the snow started, and for the next three weeks there were no walks for Marianne and Andrew, which, if they were perfectly honest, was a relief to both of them. By the time the storm came to an end, and the streets had cleared, the two upsetting episodes of the night of the ball were past history and were never mentioned, and Marianne and Andrew slipped back naturally into the easy relationship they had had before.

Marianne, however, was still longing for a chance to compare him with another man . . . or more than one . . . and so, if they met any of his friends when they were out, she deliberately flirted with them. Her efforts came to fruition one Sunday early in March, when they ran into Douglas Martin, whom she had met only once before, with his common 'friend', Vi.

He was with a young man this time, one who greeted Andrew like a long-lost friend. 'Oh, Rennie, you don't know how glad I am to see you. Could I possibly have a few words with you, or . . .' He tailed off, looking apologetically at Marianne. 'I'm sorry. I didn't realize . . .'

'I don't mind,' she assured him, walking on to give them privacy.

Douglas seemed to have the same idea, because he hurried to catch up with her. 'You don't mind if I keep you company until they . . . ?'

She smiled encouragingly. 'I don't mind.'

He waited until they were well away from their companions before he said in a low voice, 'I've seen you out with Rennie a lot, though you haven't seen me, and I hoped I'd get a chance to speak to you on your own some time. Maybe I'm saying something I shouldn't – if you and Rennie are . . . I don't want to trespass.'

She was mystified, but intrigued. 'Andrew and I are only friends.'

'Thank God! I'll have to grab my chance, so . . . will you come out with me tomorrow night?'

She did not take long to consider. She couldn't say she cared for him much, but Andrew had told her some time ago that Douglas Martin had given up Law and was now studying for the ministry, so an evening out with him would be interesting . . . yes, it would be very interesting. 'I'd love to,' she murmured.

'Seven o'clock at the Junction?'

'All right, but I might be a few minutes late. I don't finish work till six.'

'I'll wait,' he grinned, turning as the other two came alongside.

They split into their original pairs, and Marianne's curiosity made her ask, 'What did that fellow want with you, Andrew?'

'He wants me to help him with some written work he should have handed in, so I said I'd go over it with him tomorrow night.' He hesitated for a moment, then said, 'What was Martin saying to you? You looked very serious.'

'He asked me to go out with him tomorrow night and I said yes.' Why should she keep it a secret? There was nothing to hide.

Andrew's open face closed abruptly. 'I'd rather you didn't go, Marianne.'

She felt outraged at his attitude. 'You don't own me, Andrew Rennie! I'll go out with anybody I want!'

'But I know what he's like. Remember the kind of girl he was with when – ?'

'I know you said she was a lady of the streets, but that doesn't mean Douglas is a . . .' Not knowing the word 'libertine', she stopped.

'He boasts about the girls he's . . .' Too much of a gentleman to repeat the things the other man said, Andrew ended lamely, '. . . been out with.'

She thought she knew what he meant. 'I can look after myself. You should know by this time I'm not a shrinking violet.'

He said no more, though aware that she had no idea

what men like Douglas Martin could do, and she wouldn't believe him if he told her.

Monday was several degrees colder than Sunday yet Marianne's temperature was higher than usual. Andrew wasn't the only one who had shown displeasure at her making a tryst with another man: all three of his aunts had let her see how they felt at some time during the day, but she didn't try to defend herself. They didn't own her either, and they couldn't interfere in her private life.

Supper that night was eaten in an uncomfortable silence, but neither the sisters' stony glances nor occasional accusing looks made any difference to Marianne, and when the time came for her to set off, she decided that she couldn't keep up the animosity any longer.

'I know what I'm doing,' she said as she put on her jacket.

Miss Edith's mouth twisted in disbelief. 'You are far too young to know what some young men can do. You have only ever been out with Andrew, who is a proper gentleman. He would never –'

'I was out once with Stephen, remember?' Marianne pouted. 'Douglas is a nice boy, too.' Andrew had made her suspect that Douglas wasn't as decent as he or Stephen Grant were, but that was half the fun of going out with him, as far as she was concerned. She wanted to find out what he would do, and she would easily stop him if he tried to do anything wrong.

Miss Esther took over the cautioning. 'Be careful, Marianne dear. I remember, when I was about your age, a boy –' Her face turning deep crimson, she came to an abrupt halt, then went on, her voice trembling a little, 'No, no. You do not want to hear that.'

'Times have changed,' Marianne murmured. 'Things are different nowadays.'

'Not all that much,' Miss Esther said sadly. 'So be on your guard.'

Miss Emily added a rider. 'It is best not to let boys know how you feel; it only encourages them.'

'Do not let him keep you out too late,' was Miss Edith's farewell.

Douglas was waiting at the Junction, where Holburn Street met Union Street. 'I thought of taking you to see the show at the Music Hall,' he observed. 'It's a bit too cold for a walk, isn't it?'

If they were in a hall among other people, Marianne thought, he wouldn't have the chance to do anything to her, wrong or otherwise, and she dared to say quietly, 'I'd rather go for a walk, if you don't mind?'

They set off into the dimly lit evening.

Smiling at the effort her sisters were making to camouflage their tiredness, Miss Edith remarked, 'For goodness' sake, off you go to bed, the two of you. I'll wait until Marianne comes in.'

They jumped up with surprising alacrity, Miss Esther saying, 'I seem to need more and more sleep as I grow older.'

Stifling a yawn with her hand, Miss Emily nodded. 'I am the same.'

As the eldest, Miss Edith shook her head reprovingly. 'If you give in to your years, senility will come on you all the sooner.'

Miss Emily paused at the door. 'Oh, do you think we should not . . . ?'

'One early night will not harm you, but do not make a habit of it.'

Edith lay back against the cushions of what had been their father's seat, a wide, leather-covered armchair with a high, buttoned back. She was concerned for their protégée.

Marianne looked older than seventeen and she had no experience of the big, harsh world, where men, even young men, lay in wait for those such as her, to ravish them, to defile them and leave them afraid to trust any other man. She cast her mind back almost forty years. She had been seventeen, the same age as Marianne, when she met Sandy Raitt. She would never forget him. Sandy! He had been so handsome in his blue uniform, and looked such a gentleman that even her father had been taken in . . .

The elderly lady was startled out of quite a deep sleep by the silvery chimes of the domed clock on the mantelshelf. Eleven o'clock! What could have happened to Marianne? Wide awake again and, in her anxiety for the girl, more finely tuned to any noises, Edith became aware of a sound outside in the street. Thank heaven! But it was far too late for Marianne to be staying out with a boy! She would have to be told . . . but why hadn't she come in?

Absolute silence fell again, and after another five minutes, Edith could stand it no longer. She had to find out what was going on.

Striding to the front door, she opened it quietly and was astonished that she could see no one in the flickering light of the gaslamp a few yards along. Thinking that she must have heard a cat prowling about, she was on the point of going back inside when her eye was drawn to a slight movement to her right.

'Is that you, Marianne?' she said softly, not wishing to rouse her sisters.

Skirts rustling, a figure trailed round from the side of the cottage. 'Good gracious!' Edith exclaimed. 'What were you doing round there?'

'I was . . . I was waiting . . . for you to go to bed.' The unsteady words ended in a torrent of tears, and Marianne gladly allowed herself to be led inside.

Her story came out as if she were in a trance; the walk down to the river and along the banks. 'He wasn't doing anything bad,' she went on, gulping, 'till we came to the cemetery . . .'

'Trinity,' murmured Miss Edith, wondering what was coming.

'Is that what it's called? Well, he took me over and pulled me inside the gate . . . I was scared to go . . . and then he . . . started . . .'

'I can guess, my dear. Do not distress yourself by telling me.'

But now she had started, Marianne felt compelled to get it all out. 'He was only kissing me at first, and stroking my neck, but something aboot him made me fear't, so I started fightin' him aff, but it was like fightin' a raging bull and I couldna stop him – nae even when he started touchin' me on my . . . bosom. But when he lifted my skirts and tried to force me down on the ground, I went right mad.'

Her voice was rising, so Miss Edith grasped her hand. 'My dear girl, I know exactly what happened. It happened to me once, when I was about your age.' She gave a tight smile at the incredulity on the white face. 'I was quite pretty in those days and I was very lucky that the boy did not make me pregnant, otherwise my father would have thrown me out. The best thing for you to do now is to give yourself a thorough wash . . . down there, and go to bed. We can do nothing else but wait until –'

'You don't understand!' Marianne cried. 'I didn't let him! You see, I've always been scared of cemeteries, and it was being so close to the gravestones as much as him mauling me . . . that helped me to . . .'

'You actually stopped him?' Miss Edith could scarcely believe it.

'I twisted awa' and kicked him right in the balls! An' when he was holdin' himsel' and swearin' like a trooper, I took to my heels and ran.'

Her eyes wide with shock at the coarseness which had come from the trembling young mouth, Miss Edith overlooked it since the girl was in such a state. 'All I can say is thank heaven you got away from him. It was a brave thing you did, but you might easily have been overpowered. Your escape was lucky indeed! Now, off you go to bed, but remember, do not arrange to meet any more boys until I have vetted them. Good night, my dear. You are quite safe now.'

'Good night, Miss Edith.' Marianne stood up and, on impulse, bent down and kissed her cheek. 'Thank you for not being angry with me.'

'Is that why you waited outside? You were afraid I would be angry? I am angry at the boy for taking advantage of a naïve young girl, but it was not your fault, although . . .' she paused for a moment, a twinkle in her eyes, '. . . we tried to warn you, if you remember? But we must let bygones be bygones. I shall never mention it again, not even to my sisters . . . and especially not to Andrew.'

Miss Edith did some thinking while she made sure that the fire was left safe before she went to bed. Was it fate that had made the seducer choose a graveyard in which to perpetrate his vile deed? Had Marianne been given divine protection? Or was it sheer good luck? Whatever the reason, her ordeal had not been as bad as it could have been. At least it was over. She would not have the worry of waiting to see if her show came. Nor was she suffering from a broken heart, as she, Edith, had been, for she had loved Sandy Raitt. They had kept company for almost three months while he was stationed in the Torry Point Battery, close to Girdleness Lighthouse – he had been one of the first volunteers who made up the Aberdeenshire Royal Garrison Artillery – but after that night, she had neither seen nor heard of him again.

She laid down the poker and straightened up. He had professed to love her, which was why she hadn't stopped him . . . and it hadn't been an altogether dreadful experience because she loved him. Even after all those years, there was still a soft spot for him in her memory. She may be an old maid, but unlike many of the breed, she *had* tasted of the sweet fruit which was forbidden to unmarried girls.

One pleasant Sunday afternoon in late March, when Marianne was walking along the beach promenade with Andrew, the sea looking much more friendly than on her first visit, she was surprised to see Stephen Grant coming towards them. She hadn't seen him since the night he dropped her like a hot brick, a year and a half ago, and she was elated by the change in his expression when he heard her talking in such a refined manner. She laid it on thickly. 'It's so nice to see you again, Stephen,' she gushed. 'I often wondered if I had done something to offend you.'

'I've b-been b-busy swotting,' he stammered.

'All the time?' Her eyes twinkled mischievously, causing Andrew to step in to save his friend embarrassment. 'Pay no attention to her, Stephen. She is just teasing.'

'May I walk along with you?' Stephen mumbled. 'Dick Thorne started off with me, then he met a girl he knew, and –'

'You're very welcome to join us,' Marianne smiled.

For a time, conversation centred round the weather, always a good talking point, then Stephen looked hopefully at Andrew. 'My parents are abroad until the middle of July and I was thinking of asking some friends to dinner one night next week – Dick and his girl if they'll come, another three chaps with partners, and there's my young sister and me, of course. Would you and Marianne care to come? Our cook is a true gem, so you'd be guaranteed a sumptuous meal.'

Before Andrew could answer one way or the other, Marianne said, 'We'd love to come, wouldn't we, Andrew?'

'Yes, thank you, Stephen. We'd be delighted.'

'I'll let you know which day when I've got everything arranged.'

Satisfied that his invitation had been accepted, Stephen bade them good night and left them, and Andrew turned to Marianne. 'What are you playing at?' he demanded disapprovingly. 'I'd have thought you wouldn't want anything to do with him after he –'

'He lives in one of the biggest houses in Albyn Place.'

'Oh!' His face fell. 'Is he rich enough for you, then?'

'His father is. Oh, I just want to see inside their mansion.'

'But you wouldn't say no if Stephen popped the question? He's not a brilliant student, you know, and he'll probably end up being an ordinary solicitor like me, with hardly enough money coming in to keep himself, never mind a wife.'

'He'll still have a wealthy father,' she retorted, 'and a mother out of the top drawer. I never made any bones about what I wanted, Andrew. You've known that all along.'

'Yes, you're quite right.' He appeared chastened now, and held his head down for most of the way back to Strawberry Bank.

When they neared the house, he mumbled, 'Will you please tell my aunts I've a lot of notes to write up? I can't face them right now.'

'I'll tell them, and ... Andrew, I'm sorry. Anyway, Stephen might not want to marry me. He was quick enough to drop me before. It's a long way from dinner to marriage and maybe he asked us to make up the numbers.'

'Oh, he already has his eye on you. I'm sure the "dinner for friends" was a spur-of-the-moment thing just to get you into his home.'

Marianne deemed it wisest not to continue on that topic. 'Will I see you next Sunday?' she begged.

'If you want me to come.'

'Of course I want you to come. I'll always be your friend, no matter who I marry.'

He turned away hastily, making her regret being so

insensitive. He had made it clear so often that he didn't want to be just her friend.

When she went in, she passed on Andrew's message and then pleaded a headache so that she could go to bed. She didn't care that his aunts would suspect something was wrong between them – she couldn't please everybody and she wasn't going to try. She would please herself. It was her life, after all.

The doubts started creeping in after she undressed and lay down. Was she being foolish? She knew nothing about Stephen Grant except that he was an out-and-out snob, so his parents would likely forbid him to marry the likes of her. Why couldn't she be content to marry Andrew when he'd got his degree? She would be better off than she was now, financially and emotionally, because nobody else would ever love her as much as he did. And she . . . nearly loved him. It hurt to think there might come a time when she would no longer see him. It would depend on the partner she chose, though not many husbands would permit their wives to remain so friendly with another man.

It all depended . . . it all depended . . . was it to be Stephen? Or Andrew? Or somebody she hadn't yet met?

Chapter Five

❦

'Andrew is asking for trouble,' Miss Esther remarked. 'Marianne will meet a different kind of people at Albyn Place.'

Miss Edith shrugged. 'He is afraid that if he doesn't take her, she might come to resent him for spoiling her chances.'

Miss Esther said no more, but when Andrew said the next Sunday that the dinner was to be on Wednesday, his pale face and sad eyes pierced her heart and she longed to reassure him. As she whispered to Miss Emily when they went to bed, 'She cannot possibly meet anyone nicer than he is, so he need not upset himself.'

On the evening of the dinner, wishing that she had something more elegant to wear, Marianne put on a skirt and blouse she had bought the previous summer and, it still being cold in the evenings, she was forced to cover the pastel pink with a muddy-grey woollen cardigan, felted after being washed so often. She didn't care so much that her well-worn coat was bordering on the threadbare – she would be taking that off – but while Andrew walked with her to Albyn Place, she wondered if anything would be said about her lack of dress sense. But surely Fate couldn't be so cruel as to have the horrible girl of the Hogmanay Ball at Stephen's house tonight?

She soon discovered that Fate could. Stephen himself admitted them to his home and detailed his sister, Myra, to show Marianne where to leave her coat. Then, when she was taken into the drawing room, the first person she saw was the stuck-up pig, as she had designated her.

Only too conscious of her matted cardigan, Marianne

stepped forward to shake hands when Myra made the introductions. 'Marianne, meet Sybil and Barty, and Ethel and Richard. Hamish and his partner haven't arrived yet.'

Taking in only one of the names, Marianne sat down in the chair Myra indicated. So she was called Sybil, was she? Well, if she started anything here, she would get more than she expected. Another man coming in at that moment, there was a renewed flurry of hand-shaking, and when that was over, Sybil leaned across her partner and said to the girl on his other side, in a clear voice that echoed round the room, 'Do you see what I see? It's the crinoline creature from the ball – and she is no better dressed for the occasion tonight than she was then.'

Her blood boiling, Marianne strove to keep calm. 'We do not all have the money to dress in the height of fashion,' she said quietly, into the deathly hush that had fallen. 'I have to work for a living, though I don't suppose you'll ever know what that means.'

Sybil turned a scarlet face towards her. 'You . . . you . . . insolent . . . guttersnipe!' Barty, her partner, tried to calm her, but she went on, 'Who do you think you are talking to?'

'To a bad-mannered, spoiled bairn that should ken better!' Marianne spat out, the speech lessons forgotten in her white-hot anger, the good impression she had wanted to create killed off in the first few minutes. 'I'm nae as well-educated as you, but I wouldna dream of doing to onybody what you just done to me!'

Tears stinging her eyelids, she stood up to go to look for Andrew, who had disappeared somewhere with Stephen, and the tall, fair-haired stranger who had come in behind her stepped aside to let her pass. 'Good for you!' he murmured, patting her on the back. 'I have been dying to take Sybil down a few pegs for a long time.'

Recovering some of her equilibrium as he followed her out of the room, Marianne sighed, 'But being a gentleman, you couldn't, so it fell to an ignorant peasant like me.'

'No, no, do not degrade yourself like that. I just wish I had your spirit.' After closing the drawing-room door behind him, he gave her arm a brief, reassuring squeeze. 'I do not suppose you will feel like staying here now, so if you go and fetch your coat, I shall take you home.'

Still too upset to think, she was halfway to Strawberry Bank with him when she exclaimed, 'Oh, Andrew'll be wondering where I am! And what about your partner?'

One corner of his mouth lifted in a smile. 'She had not come out of the cloakroom when we left, but I should think they have both been told by this time that I whisked you away. And if it was Andrew who was talking to Stephen on the stairs, Hester won't mind being left with him. The question is – will he mind being left with her?'

'No, I don't think so.' She knew Andrew would be hurt that she had run out on him, but she couldn't have stayed a minute longer.

'Perhaps I had better introduce myself. Hamish Lyall, your very good servant, Miss . . . ?'

'Marianne Cheyne,' she laughed.

'Are you and Andrew . . . ?'

'We're just good friends. I work in his aunts' shop, and I've got a room in their house.'

'I hope you do not think me too bold on such short acquaintance, Miss Cheyne, but I would be honoured if you let me treat you to a meal one night, to make up for tonight's disaster.'

'But it wasn't your fault, and I don't know –'

'I will ask your employers' permission, if you think it necessary.'

Her temper having completely cooled, she looked at him appraisingly. He was very tall and not particularly handsome, but he was dressed in the latest style – a cut-away coat and brimmed hat, which must have cost a pretty penny. Slim, with a longish, leanish face and straight blond hair combed well back, his chin was clean-shaven, but his top lip sported a neat moustache. She was sure that this was the first time she had seen him, yet there was something familiar about him.

'Have we met before, Mr Lyall?' she asked.

'Not met, exactly,' he smiled, 'although I have seen you before. At the Hogmanay Ball,' he added, noticing her perplexity.

It came to her suddenly. He was the man who had been surrounded by adoring girls! Well, well! If she were to be seen out with *him*, it would be one in the eye for the obnoxious Sybil. 'You don't have to ask anybody's permission,' she said. 'I'll be happy to go for a meal with you, thank you for asking me . . . and for rescuing me.'

'May I call for you tomorrow at . . . half-past seven?'

'Half-past seven's fine. Good night, Mr Lyall.'

'Hamish, please . . . if you will allow me to call you Marianne?'

'Good night . . . Hamish,' she smiled.

The sisters were surprised to see Marianne home so early, and although she confined her tale to Sybil's nasty remarks of that night and did not mention her criticism of the crinoline, they were outraged that anyone could treat their protégée in such a barbaric manner.

They were still discussing it when the door opened and Andrew came in, having run all the way from Albyn Place. 'I'm sorry,' he panted. 'I was having a quiet chat with Stephen and I didn't know what had happened until we came downstairs.'

Miss Edith gave a start. 'Then who took you home, Marianne, if it wasn't Andrew?'

'One of the other guests,' she smiled. 'His name's Hamish Lyall, and he's very nice. He's taking me for a meal tomorrow night.'

Andrew's concerned face turned an even deeper shade of red. 'Is that what he said his name was?'

'Oh, no!' Miss Esther fluttered. 'Did he give a false name?'

Marianne's stomach plunged. She might have known he was too good to be true. 'What *is* his name, then?'

Andrew was obviously reluctant to tell her, so she repeated, 'What *is* his name, Andrew? Tell me!'

He looked at the floor for a few seconds. 'It wasn't really a false name,' he mumbled, then stared defiantly at her. 'He didn't tell you his full name, that's all. He's the Honourable Hamish Bruce-Lyall, and his father is Lord Glendarril, an old friend of Stephen's father.'

Miss Edith was first to recover. 'Ah, yes. I have read about the Bruce-Lyall family, and if my memory serves me correctly, there were twin sons. One suffered from some kind of debilitating disease and died when he was still quite young, and it would appear that Hamish stands to inherit the title.'

Miss Esther clasped her hands together in pleasure. 'Our Marianne will be sharing a table with an honourable tomorrow night.'

'Fancy that!' Miss Emily looked awestruck.

'Yes, just fancy!' Andrew said dolefully. 'I'll have to go now.'

'But neither of you could have had anything to eat?' Miss Esther was a willing hostess. 'We have enough ham and vegetables left over to make a decent meal for two.'

'I couldn't eat a thing,' he muttered. 'Thank you all the same.'

'Neither could I,' Marianne said. 'I'll see you to the door.'

Outside, she started to apologize, but Andrew had worked himself into what bordered on a frenzy of jealousy. 'You could have waited for me. I came down a few minutes later, but you had found your rich man! Is he the one, Marianne? Is an honourable good enough for you? I don't believe you could do much better than him. He will be a lord one day!'

Marianne's temper flared once more. 'Andrew Rennie! I didn't know who he was. I only agreed to see him once because I thought it'd be bad manners to refuse when he'd rescued me from your snob friends, but if he asks me to meet him a second time . . . or a third or fourth, I will! I'm sure he would never sneer at me, for he's honourable in every sense of the word, and you needn't think I'll take a walk with you on Sundays again, for I won't!'

She slammed inside, and barged past the sisters, who looked at each other in dismay as she stamped upstairs.

'Oh dear!' moaned Miss Esther. 'It looks like Andrew has put his foot in it somehow.'

Miss Emily was wringing her hands. 'Poor boy! Poor boy!'

'Perhaps we should consider this more,' Miss Edith observed wisely. 'Is it fair of us to want Marianne to stick to Andrew if she will be happier with young Bruce-Lyall?'

Her head on one side, Miss Emily murmured, 'But she only met him tonight.'

'It could be love at first sight,' romantic Miss Esther put in.

Miss Edith snorted. 'I think it is love of money with Marianne. I've had the feeling, from little things she let drop, that she has always wanted a rich husband. I hoped that she was growing out of it, but Andrew's jealousy, understandable though it is to us, may have pushed her into this other man's arms.'

Miss Edith was very near the truth. Marianne had wounded Andrew by what she had done, but he had wounded her every bit as much. She had expected him to sympathize, not to upbraid her for making her escape from a terrible situation with the only person available. Andrew had left her on her own with a roomful of strangers and he hadn't been there when she needed him, after all his promises. She couldn't rely on him, whereas Hamish knew the right thing to do at the right time . . . and he *was* rather nice. Besides, according to Miss Edith, he had a lineage to be proud of, and *she* hadn't objected to him as a suitor.

In the dining room of the comfortable inn where he had a room, Hamish told Marianne that Ma Cameron – as the hostess was affectionately known – was famed for the meals she provided. 'I always stay here when I'm in Aberdeen overnight, though I don't like leaving home for long these days. My father's health is none too good, and –'

'Hamish,' she interrupted, 'why didn't you tell me who you were? I got an awful shock when Andrew said your father was a lord.'

He smiled enigmatically. 'He came to check if you got home safely? Did he think I would seduce you on the way?'

Shocked, she said, 'He wouldn't have thought anything like that.'

'But he wasn't pleased?'

'No.'

'Is he in love with you?'

'He says he loves me.'

'Do you love him?'

'Why are you asking all these –'

'Do you?'

'I don't know.'

He leaned back now. 'I am pleased to hear that, Marianne. You would certainly know if you *were* in love with him, and it encourages me to . . . get to know you better, if I may?'

Overwhelmed by astonishment as well as shyness, she could only whisper, 'I've no objection.'

So Hamish called for Marianne every Thursday for three weeks, taking her first to His Majesty's Theatre where her awe at the magnificence of her surroundings was dispelled as soon as the first act came on. She was totally unaware of Hamish, who spent his time watching her rather than the performers on stage. In the second week, he introduced her to the Music Hall, where, although the acts were of much the same standard – men and women singing or dancing, jugglers juggling with an assortment of items – the sketches were humorous instead of dramatic, and the interior was not quite so impressive.

The third week saw her at the Tivoli, laughing at the jokes delivered at speed by the comedians and the slightly naughty ditties sung by women – one dressed as a man – who encouraged the audience to join in the choruses. There were also some acrobats, young men and girls in scanty costumes contorting their bodies in unbelievable ways. She loved every minute, as she told her escort while he walked her home.

'I must apologize for the rowdiness of the audience,' Hamish said. 'The people up in the gods are a rough bunch – that's the top tier of seats,' he added in explanation.

'Oh, I didn't mind that,' she smiled, 'though I did wonder at first why they were shouting. You've opened my eyes to things I never knew went on, you know.'

He gave a sad little smile. 'Perhaps that was not such a good thing, but next Thursday, if you will allow me, it would give me great pleasure to take you to Ma Cameron's for a meal.'

'But you took me there already – to make up for the meal I missed at Albyn Place, and you've taken me to all these other places, so you've more than made up for –'

'None the less, I need an opportunity to talk to you properly, to ask –'

He broke off, but she was so involved in thinking of all the things she had to tell the Rennies that it didn't occur to her to wonder what he meant to ask.

As he had done every week, he bade her good night at her door and waited until she went inside before walking away. Marianne always felt uncomfortable about that – it made her feel self-conscious to know his eyes were on her every step. But as she had known they would be, the sisters were waiting eagerly to hear where she and Hamish had gone that night, so it was some time before she managed to get to bed, to dream, naturally, of all the wonderful things she had seen.

There was something different about Hamish, Marianne thought the following Thursday as they sat down in Mrs Cameron's dining room. His face was just a trifle flushed, his voice was pitched a little higher as if he were excited about something and, recalling that he'd said he would have something to ask her, she waited for him to ask.

She was beginning to think he had forgotten, or had changed his mind and wasn't going to bother, when he said, hesitantly, 'Marianne, when I asked you a few weeks ago if you were in love with Andrew, you did not know. Have you come to any conclusion yet?'

She shook her head. 'I haven't given it any more thought, but like you said before, if I *was* in love with him, I would know, so I suppose I'm not.'

'Good! That enables me to come to something I have been mulling over since the night I met you. If I asked you to marry me, what would you say?'

She grinned now, sure that he was joking. 'I'd say you were drunk ... or mad ... or both.'

There was no answering humour on his face. 'I am neither,' he said gravely. 'My father is obsessed with getting me married so that he will know, before he dies, that I have a son to succeed me. To let you understand, the title always goes to the next *legitimate* male – even those born through the female line – and he is afraid that ...' Hamish halted briefly, then changed what he had been about to say. 'He has also stipulated that I find a woman who is fit enough in mind and body to be the perfect mother, and who will be less likely to give birth to puny weaklings –

his words. You see, with so much inbreeding over the centuries, very few of my ancestors lived to a ripe old age ... indeed, some were bordering on idiocy.'

'Oh, surely not!'

He clicked his tongue. 'Not literally perhaps, but quite near. I am making heavy weather of this, I am afraid, and I have said enough at present. I will give you ten days to think it over, and if you are interested, we can discuss it further.'

'Yes, I need time. I don't know what to think right now, my mind's in a complete whirl.'

Hamish laughed. 'I had better take you home.'

On the way, Marianne was too stunned to speak and was thankful that he expected no answers to the inconsequential remarks he was making. But when they reached the end of her street, he said, 'I shall meet you here at the same time a week on Saturday ... so be ready with your answer.'

When she went in, her benefactresses were waiting anxiously to hear how she had fared, so she described the inn, the room, the food she had eaten and some of the things they had talked about, but she could not bring herself to tell them about Hamish's proposal. She was still too dazed by it.

Unable, even after two whole days, to make up her mind, Marianne felt the need to discuss it with someone, and during a restless Saturday night, she hoped that Andrew would turn up the next day, to see his aunts, if not Marianne herself. She had never made any secret of her ambition, and surely he'd have got over his pique by then – he might even be pleased that she had got the chance to fulfil her dream – and she had always been able to tell him more than she could tell his aunts.

Unfortunately, she rose on Sunday morning to the sound of heavy rain battering against her window, and although she put up a silent prayer that it would clear by lunchtime, it had not eased off at all by the time Andrew arrived. She had meant to ask his advice and be guided by it, but it seemed that there would be no opportunity for private talk.

When he came into the parlour, however, and Marianne saw how pale and drawn he was, she was quite glad that she would be unable to discuss anything with him. It would be too cruel to let him believe, even for a few minutes, that she wasn't sure. She had been offered the chance of a lifetime – how many girls got the opportunity of being a real lady with a title? – and even if there were no family fortune, how could she turn the rest down? Her very position would give her access to the wealth she craved, and a title would give her power.

She tried, by addressing most of her remarks to him, to let Andrew see that she was still friends with him, and she wasn't the only one who was relieved to see him brighten as the afternoon wore on. The weather had faired by the time he was leaving in the evening, so she walked a little way with him, 'to blow the cobwebs off me'.

As soon as they were outside, Andrew sighed, 'I shouldn't have said what I did when I last saw you, and I'm truly sorry, Marianne. I was angry at you for leaving without me, and when I learned who had seen you home, I was afraid you would prefer him to me, might even see him again. But that does not excuse me for . . .'

'Andrew,' Marianne said softly, 'you've nothing to be sorry for.' She hesitated, then added, 'I'd better tell you, though . . . he has asked me to marry him.'

He grabbed her arms and pulled her roughly to a halt. 'I thought you only dined with him once?'

'I thought that would be all, but it was more than that and he proposed last Thursday and gave me ten days to think about it. I've thought and thought . . . well, I'm going to accept.'

'But you can't, Marianne! You don't know anything about him!'

'I know enough.'

'Oh God, Marianne! You can't do this! You know I love you, and you can't love him!'

Her heart was cramping at the anguish in his eyes, but she said stoutly, 'Who said anything about love? I told you a long time ago I didn't care about love. He wants me to . . . give him the son he's got to have to continue the Bruce-Lyall line.'

'Good God! Do you realize what you are saying, Marianne? He must know dozens of suitable girls; he doesn't need you. Not like I do.'

'Andrew, my mind's made up. I've always said I wanted a rich man, but even if he's not rich, I'll still marry him for the title.'

He flung her from him. 'I'd better not argue any more. I thought I could have persuaded you to . . . but when I asked Stephen, he said the Bruce-Lyalls were one of the wealthiest families in Scotland.'

'There you are!' she snapped, rubbing her arms where his nails had dug in. 'It seems I picked well, after all.'

Chests heaving with the anger they felt, they glared at each other for several moments before Marianne said, with a catch in her throat, 'Andrew, I know you don't think much of me now, but I still want you for a friend. You're the only one I could turn to if –'

'You're beginning to have doubts?'

'No, I don't have any doubts, but even the best marriages go wrong sometimes, and I'd like to know I had someone . . .'

'Oh, Marianne!' The words were wrung from him. 'I let you down on that evening at Stephen's, but I'll never let you down again. I'll always be there for you. I'll run at your bidding, and I'll do anything you want, whatever it is. I'll never stop loving you.'

She was surprised by the tears which sprang to her eyes. 'I wish it could be different, Andrew dear. I wish I could love you like you deserve to be loved.'

He put his hand up to dry her cheek. 'Tell me something, Marianne. Do you love Bruce-Lyall?'

'No, I don't love him, but I do like him and he can make my dreams come true. Can't you feel happy for me about that?'

He held her face between his hands now. 'I do, Marianne, though I would feel happier if I had been the one to make your dreams come true.' His lips touched hers lightly. 'It does help a little to know that you do not love him either, but it is still going . . .' A slight tremble in his voice made him clear his throat determinedly. 'Do not forget, if you ever need me you have only to let me know.'

'Thank you, Andrew. I won't forget, but why don't you find another girl? You must know some.'

'None of them can compare with you,' he sighed.

'That's just because you don't want to compare them. I'd better go back now, or else your aunts will be thinking I'm lost.'

Because Marianne had taken almost half an hour to come back from seeing Andrew to the end of the street, two of his aunts had presumed they had made up their quarrel, and so were not averse to the girl meeting Hamish again.

'It will do her good to mix with people like that,' Miss Emily said, feeling free to state her opinion because she knew that Miss Esther felt the same.

'It should do us good, too,' the youngest sister pointed out. 'He must have young married friends who might need a layette for a coming infant, or want to buy something for a toddler.'

Perspicacious Miss Edith said nothing. She knew that something had happened between their nephew and the

76

girl, something drastic, which had not been resolved. She also wished she knew how to stop Marianne from seeing more of young Bruce-Lyall; a liaison between them could be dangerous. Marianne's head could easily be turned by the thought of having a title and acting the gracious lady . . . and where would that leave poor Andrew?

On Saturday, Marianne was rather pleased that Hamish had asked Ma Cameron if they could have dinner served in his room, away from the possible eavesdropping of her other customers, but he waited until their meal was over before he broached the important subject. 'Have you made your decision yet?'

'Didn't you say there were further details to discuss?' she hedged.

He looked at her over the rim of his brandy glass. 'I think we could safely leave the other details until you give me your answer. I have already told you my reason for marrying you, so you should be under no misapprehension.'

She felt a twinge of what she hoped was '*mis*'-apprehension. There was something here that she couldn't fathom, something he was keeping from her, but surely nothing bad? There was no love between them, she was content to have it that way, and there couldn't be anything else unless . . . 'Are you preparing me for a divorce after I give you the son you want?'

'Oh no, my dear, nothing like that. Our marriage will last until the day one of us dies . . . as long as you are happy with it.'

It wasn't a truly satisfactory answer, suggesting as it did that she might not be happy, but the lure of becoming a member of one of the wealthiest families in Scotland was too great. 'I have decided, Hamish. I'll marry you whenever you want.'

He poured himself another brandy and gestured to her

to lift her glass. 'We will drink to that and then we can get down to business.'

She took a small sip, shuddering as the spirits set her throat on fire, and watched in amazement when he tossed his down in one go like a dose of cough linctus, and poured another.

The brandy seemed to help him to present his case. 'First, I had better tell you that my mother was not at all happy about this, but my father made her see that it is best . . . all round, and so you will be summoned to Glendarril very shortly.'

'To see if I pass muster?' Marianne was outraged at being ordered, not invited, to meet his parents.

'There is no suggestion of passing muster,' Hamish smiled. 'I have made my choice and they will stand by that. As is only natural, my mother wants to meet you and you will be expected to live with us so that she can prepare you for –' he broke off, his tone softening. 'I can tell by your terrified expression that I am not explaining things very well.'

'It *is* a bit terrifying,' she admitted. 'You know I don't exactly shine when I meet snobs . . .' Her hand flew to her mouth. 'Oh, I don't mean your parents or their friends are snobs. How could I, when I haven't even met any of them yet?'

Hamish did not appear in the least put out. 'They *are* snobs, my dear Marianne,' he grinned, 'my mother the worst of all. But you will soon learn how to talk to them, and to the servants. That is why Mother wants you to move in with us as soon as you can. It will take her time to arrange the wedding to her liking, with goodness knows how many guests – five hundred, I shouldn't be surprised.'

'So many? And what about my wedding dress? Miss Esther will want to make it . . .'

'Mother will whip you up to London or Edinburgh for an exclusive, if I know her. There will be no need for you nor Andrew's aunts to worry about anything. It will all be taken care of – invitations, your whole trousseau, the bridesmaids' dresses, the floral arrangements, the wedding breakfast, the hiring of the musicians.' He stopped, laughing at her bemused face. 'Yes, I know every step, every inch of the way to the altar. A young friend of the family was married last year, and Mother wouldn't let the bride's mother – her closest friend – do a single thing. She took over the wedding completely, and I must say, she did a wonderful job.'

'I never dreamed it would be anything like that,' Marianne sighed, 'but it's maybe good that your mother will be choosing my wedding gown. You know how some people criticize my taste in clothes.'

'Shall I tell you something?' Hamish murmured, slurring the words ever so slightly. 'It was hearing you stand up to Sybil at Hogmanay that started me thinking . . .'

'Oh,' she gasped. 'You saw that business as well, did you?'

'That's when I began to consider you as a wife, and when I told Father how you fended off Sybil and her cronies, he agreed that you would be ideal for our purpose, but I knew nothing about you – your name nor where you lived. So I could hardly believe my luck when I saw you at Albyn Place. Now, I had better take you home.'

Hamish got to his feet and came round to pull Marianne's chair back for her, and when she was standing in front of him, he muttered, 'I suppose I should have kissed you earlier, when you accepted me?'

'It doesn't matter,' she said, although she *was* quite disappointed that he hadn't, then or now.

'You will be receiving a letter from my mother in a few days, I suppose, to tell you when she expects to see you.'

'You'll have to meet the Rennies before I leave them. Will you come in with me tonight?'

'I have had a little too much to drink tonight, I am afraid.

79

I do not want them to get a wrong impression, because I do not normally indulge, but . . . well, I had to boost my courage. I do, however, want very much to meet them. Shall I come tomorrow?'

'I'll let them know, though I'm sure it'll be all right.'

He left her at the end of her street, and Marianne went in to tell the sisters of her good fortune. They should be pleased for her . . . unless they couldn't forgive her for not marrying Andrew.

When the summons arrived, Marianne was awestruck. The coat of arms itself at centre top was very impressive, and the gold deckled edging, but it was the embossed heading at the right-hand side which took her breath away. Castle Lyall, Glendarril! Hamish hadn't said he lived in a castle and Miss Edith hadn't mentioned it. But everything was going to be all right. In the ten days since he had met them, Hamish had charmed his way into three elderly female hearts, Miss Edith's being the last to succumb. Even Andrew, sure that he would hate the man as soon as he was introduced to him, had admitted to her that Hamish was a decent fellow.

Marianne was relieved that there was no sign of rivalry between them. In fact, they got on so well that she hoped Hamish wouldn't object to her inviting Andrew to the castle occasionally after the wedding. She couldn't bring their friendship to an end and leave him as if he meant nothing to her. It wasn't true. She had *always* felt something for him . . . though it wasn't love.

Chapter Six

❧❧❧

On the southbound train, Marianne felt quite down-hearted. She had hoped to be sent off with good wishes ringing in her ears, but at the station Miss Esther and Miss Emily had barely touched the tips of her fingers with theirs before they turned away, and when Miss Edith stepped forward her opening words were anything but encouraging. 'I trust you have considered all aspects of the union you are determined to make? You will be far removed from your friends –'

'When I came to Aberdeen,' Marianne butted in cautiously, 'I was all alone and I didn't know a soul. I wouldn't have known what to do if it hadn't been for that priest.'

'Ah yes, Father Bernard. When his mother was alive, she was a great friend of ours, and we all missed him when he took up his missionary post in East Africa. But you are unlikely to meet anyone like him in a long glen with little habitation, according to what I have read.'

'I'll have proper relations, though.' Realizing that she might have offended Miss Edith, Marianne hurried on, 'I've thought of you and your sisters as my aunts as much as Andrew's, but when I marry Hamish, I'll have a mother and a father – just in-laws, I know, but still relations – as well as a husband. I won't forget you, though. I'll come and visit you as often as I can.'

Miss Edith – stern, inflexible, disapproving Miss Edith – swallowed her emotion before she said, her voice quavering ever so slightly, 'I will pray for your happiness, Marianne.'

'I know *you* will, but I wish Miss Esther and Miss Emily could see past the ends of their noses.'

'It is their love for Andrew that they can not see past, but I am sure that in the fullness of time they will forgive you for breaking his heart.' The noise of steam pressure building up made Miss Edith step back, satisfied by Marianne's stricken face that the last barb at least should make her think again.

The girl held out her hand in appeal – to be understood, to assure these dear ladies of her love for them – and cried out, 'I'll write to let you know the arrangements for the wedding.'

The guard's whistle shrilling, the two younger sisters turned back to see her being borne away, and three hands kept waving until they were out of Marianne's sight. Only then did she sit down. There was so much to think about, so much had happened in so short a time, that she still couldn't take everything in.

First, there had been the strange proposal and Andrew's reaction when he'd been told, then her acceptance – with no sign of elation from Hamish – and how the Rennies had taken her decision. Perhaps she had gone the wrong way about telling them, but she'd had no time to plan it, and finding an easy way was impossible. She had announced it the minute she'd walked into the house . . . thrown it at them defiantly.

'I'm going to marry Hamish!'

There were three separate gasps, holding different degrees of horrified astonishment, and then Miss Edith – why was it always Miss Edith? – her nose twitching, said, 'It is obvious that you have been drinking, Marianne. I can smell the brandy on your breath, but you should have thought before coming out with a remark like that. It was enough to give any of us a heart attack. If it was meant as a joke, it was in very poor taste.'

'It's not a joke,' she burst out, thinking fleetingly that Miss Edith's heart would not be so easily attacked. 'He asked me last week and I said yes tonight. That's why we had the brandy.' Hamish had ordered the brandy before she gave him her answer, but it made no difference. It was a good excuse.

Miss Esther's hand had jumped to her chest. 'Oh dear! My heart's still thumping with the shock,' she wailed. 'You can't marry anyone else, Marianne! You love Andrew . . . don't you?'

'Yes, I do love him . . . like a brother.'

'Unfortunately, he does not look on you as a sister.' It was Miss Edith again, her eyes and voice holding a sharp censure now. 'I have never seen any boy love a girl as much as he loves you. Does he know about this . . . charade?'

'It's not a charade. I told him on Sunday, and . . . well, I suppose he took it the way you'd expect him to take it.'

'Poor boy!' murmured Miss Emily, dabbing her eyes with a square of lace-edged lawn.

'It's so cruel!' moaned Miss Esther.

'You don't need to tell me I'm being cruel! I know that perfectly well, and I wish it could have been different!'

'When is this wedding to be?' Miss Edith asked. 'Will there be time for you to see sense and change your mind?'

'I won't change my mind! You'll likely be worse shocked when I tell you I'm marrying him because it won't be long till he has a title. I suppose I'd be happy if I married Andrew but . . . having wealth and a standing in society, I'll be ecstatic!'

Miss Edith shook her head. 'Wordly possessions are not everything, and I have not heard you say that you love young Bruce-Lyall. The prestige of being even the highest lady in the land is worth nothing if there is no love there. Perhaps it would satisfy you for a year or so, then the rot would set in.'

Marianne was almost weeping with the futility of trying to explain. 'I haven't known him long, but I do like him an awful lot.'

'I grant you that he is nice, but does he like you "an

awful lot"?' Miss Edith's lips were almost in a sneer.

'Yes, he does!' Marianne burst out. 'So you see!'

The argument had ended there, Marianne recalled. It was evident that the sisters had not understood what they were meant to see, and, to be quite honest, neither did she now. Hamish had only said that he admired her spirit. He had never mentioned liking, let alone loving. But she didn't want love. She'd be more than content to spend his money in exclusive gown salons, or having her clothes made specially for her by a world-renowned ... whatever dressmakers were called in high circles. Nobody would ever laugh at her again for what she was wearing. People would bow and scrape to her. Men would worship at her feet ...

The train drawing to a screeching halt, she was laughing as she looked out to see where she was. Stonehaven. Halfway there.

The short stop, the stir of the small station, the different accent she could hear, though this was only fifteen miles or so south of Aberdeen, all served to wrench her mind away from the pleasant plane it had reached. Her thoughts went now to Andrew. Poor, dear Andrew. She would miss him, truly miss him. An ache for him was already beginning deep down inside her. Would it lessen as time went past, or would it be a case of absence making the heart grow fonder? Would she come to regret being so impetuous? Should she back out before it was too late?

She banged her fist on the window frame. No, she wasn't going to back out! She had made her choice, she had survived the ordeal of wounding the four people she cared for most so that she could have a wonderful new life – the life she'd had her heart set on since she'd seen a heap of sovereigns lying in a dish. And whatever she had to suffer in future years – supposing the Bruce-Lyall family lost every ha'penny and she was forced to go out to work again – she'd have been part of Society with a capital S for a while, and she would never go crawling to anybody. She would never admit she'd been wrong.

The next stop was Laurencekirk, another fifteen miles farther on. As soon as Marianne stepped down on to the platform, a porter – or possibly he held down all the jobs like Dod Cooper at Tipperton – came forward, touching his hat respectfully. 'Miss Cheyne? His Lordship's carriage is waiting. I'll take your luggage out for you.'

He did his best to hide his surprise at learning she had only the valise she was carrying, but it was obvious that he thought she fell far short of the usual standard of visitors to Castle Lyall.

'Thank you,' she said, as graciously as she could. She was tempted to add 'my man', but decided that such an embellishment would best be kept until she was actually married to Hamish.

She followed him out to the waiting carriage, where the coachman, a man about forty with an almost completely bald head, also stared doubtfully at her, but the coat of arms on the door gave her fast-sinking morale a great boost. The coachman, looking down on her from his lofty perch as the railway employee helped her aboard, was just a servant, *her* servant . . . or would be very soon.

Nothing was said while the high-stepping horse trotted out of the village at a gentle pace, turning, without any directions from the man, into a much rougher side road marked 'Glendarril'. Proceeding into the glen, they came, in what she judged to be about three miles at least, to a wide, low building with a high, smoking chimney stack. She didn't like to ask what it was, but when they passed it, she saw a huge sign above the gates – 'Glendarril Woollen Mill'. So that was how the Bruce-Lyalls made their money? She hadn't given a single thought to that before now.

They penetrated deeper and deeper into the narrow glen, lined for the next few miles by silver birch and horse chestnut trees, with a wealth of wild flowers growing around them – ragged robins, lords-and-ladies, small blue orchids, bluebells swaying in the gentle breeze. The road was climbing, she realized, and with the thinning out of the trees she could see dozens of sheep grazing on the hills rising on either side, and beyond them, in the distance, the snow-capped peaks of mountains pierced the sky. With so little sign of habitation as yet, Marianne had a strange feeling that they had left civilization behind, and she wondered how much further they had to go. Eventually they came to some small cottages, each with a neat strip of garden in front, and, she could see as they approached at an angle, a stretch of cultivated ground at the rear. She brightened now, and felt considerably better when she saw another cluster of houses and farther on, a small church with a large bell in its tiny steeple. Alongside, within the area of yew trees which surrounded the kirkyard, poked the chimneys of what she took to be the manse.

'That's the school,' the coachman announced shortly, pointing to what looked like another cottage on their left. He gave a cackle at her astonishment. 'It's the dominie's house, and all.'

Tipperton having had a large population of children, sometimes nearly a hundred and fifty at a time, its two-storeyed granite school had a good-sized, separate building at the side for the headmaster. The County Council employed one assistant for him, usually a product of Aberdeen University who had failed to graduate, and another helper known as a pupil-teacher, unpaid because he or she was learning a profession. So this tiny place seemed to be most inadequate.

'Just a dominie for the whole school?' she asked. 'No other teachers?'

'No teachers, just Mr Wink.' He turned round and grinned at her. 'Is that no' a funny name for a dominie? William Wink. He's been here all his life, and he's awfae

86

good wi' the bairns. There's only five the noo – Jeannie and Maggie McDonald, wee Kirsty Bain, Chae Rattray and ... oh, aye! The dominie's ain laddie, Peter. He's mair like his mother than his father, though! Mistress Wink wouldna be pleased if she kent folk ca' the dominie Wee Willie Winkie behind his back, for she thinks she's better than ... oh!' His large brown hand thumped the side of the carriage. 'I shouldna say that to you, for I hear tell you're Master Hamish's intended?'

So caught up in his gossip, Marianne had practically forgotten how she would appear to the men and women on the estate. It wouldn't do for the future Mrs Bruce-Lyall to be seen hobnobbing with any of them, least of all the coachman. 'Yes,' she said, primly. 'We are engaged to be married, Mr ... um ...'

'I'm Carnie, miss. Just Carnie.'

'Carnie. I'll remember that.'

The next small collection of buildings boasted a shop, actually the front room of one of the houses, and judging by the vast selection of items packed into the window, it sold everything. One much larger house stood out from the others.

'That's the doctor's,' Carnie told her. 'Auld Dr Tyler retired just six month ago, and some folk havena got used to Robert Mowatt treating their ills, for he was born and brought up here in the glen and they still think of him as a laddie.'

In another hundred yards, the horse turned, once more of its own accord, into a wide drive with huge metal gryphons perched atop the gateposts, one on each side of the entrance. She knew they were gryphons because she had come across them in one of the books Andrew had given her to read to broaden her knowledge. But Andrew had no place in her mind here. Her eyes were drinking in as much as they could as she was borne between two lines of larch trees, their feathery boughs caressing the edge of the long curved drive. They were lovely to look at, though she couldn't help thinking that more daylight would filter through if there were fewer of them.

She hadn't realized that they were still going uphill until they emerged into an area of landscaped gardens that took her breath away with their splendour, neat low hedges breaking the huge expanses of lawns on the down slope into symmetrical designs, with flowerbeds in regular patterns. And then she saw it – the castle itself.

Her initial impression was one of disappointment. This wasn't the fairy-tale castle she had imagined, with quaint turrets and tall thin windows where an imprisoned Rapunzel might have let her hair down for her lover to climb. It seemed to have been built quite haphazardly, with no definite plan, and it was much smaller than she had expected. On closer inspection when they drew nearer, however, she found that it had been built in a series of wings, and stanchions, and – glory be! – there *were* some turrets after all, almost out of sight among the welter of stonework. It must be an awful old place, she decided, for it was just built of big boulders, probably carried down from the mountains and added to at various times. It wasn't nearly as grand as Balmoral – where Andrew had once taken her on the train – which was granite-built and sparkled in the sun as if it were studded with diamonds. But that had been rebuilt for Queen Victoria by her loving Prince Albert, God rest his soul, and Marianne Cheyne shouldn't be critical of Castle Lyall. At least it *was* a castle!

The horse came to a standstill at the steps up to a massive oaken door, and Carnie jumped to the ground to come hurrying round to help his passenger down, but Marianne was too rapt in discovering all she could about the higgledy-piggledy building to notice him. When she did, she got to her feet but was sidetracked by turning her head and seeing the panorama on that side of her. From this high vantage point, looking over the larches they had passed on the way up, she saw the mountains much better, range after range, some so tall that, judging by the amount of snow huddling in the passes between them even in May, it must come at least halfway down them in winter. What she could see of the most distant seemed to be truncated masses of dark blue rising mistily to blend into the hovering cumuli, but the lower slopes of the nearer ranges tended to be brown, probably with dead heather, for it wouldn't burst into glorious purple until August or September.

She shifted her attention to the foothills – nearer but still miles off – green for most of their height from the grass and undergrowth where there were no pines and firs, and from the trees themselves up as far as the tree-line.

She was surprised at how much she remembered of the natural history books Andrew had given her. Brought up in the heart of an area of low-lying farmland, windswept and bare, she had never seen mountains like these, and what she used to think were hills had been little more than mounds, touched with white only in the severest winters.

'Are you ready, miss?'

Carnie's voice brought her out of her reverie, and grasping his rough hand, she let him half lift her down on to the gravel driveway. Only then did the front door open, but it wasn't Hamish who stood waiting to welcome her, and she climbed the dozen or so steps with a heavy heart. If he couldn't come to the station to meet her, he should at least have been here to welcome her.

'Her Ladyship is waiting to receive you,' announced the stiffly erect maid, black-clad apart from a strip of white lace round her head.

'Thank you.'

'You're a bit late.'

Marianne wasn't going to start by apologizing for any-thing . . . to anyone. She followed the woman along a corri-dor until she halted outside one of the oak-panelled doors. After giving a small tap, the servant opened it just wide enough for Marianne to walk through, and closed it silently behind her, leaving her to stand uncertainly.

The elegant woman sitting in a chair by the window stared at her, giving her no indication of what she was expected to do. If this was meant to cow the girl, however, it had the opposite effect. Marianne reacted to the cavalier treatment by deciding not to knuckle under. At some date in the future, *she* would be Lady Glendarril and this ill-mannered woman in her silk dress and rope of pearls (for she *was* ill-mannered, even though she was an aristocrat) would be a dowager.

Smiling at this comforting thought, Marianne advanced into the room, and held out her hand. 'You must be Hamish's mother? I *was* expecting him to come to meet me at Laurencekirk – or at least one of the family – but it seems none of you has even a nodding acquaintance with mannerly behaviour.'

The last part came out before she realized what she was saying. She had no right to speak to a titled lady like that, and although she derived great satisfaction from seeing the woman's jaw drop as far as it would go, she whirled round in dismay at a sound behind her. The man in the doorway, however – quite short and unheathily thin, wearing old corduroy trousers and a battered tweed hat and jacket – wasn't scowling at her as she deserved, but was softly clapping his hands.

'Good for you!' He grinned at her impishly. 'Hamish said you had a lot of spunk. I am his father, in case you were wondering.'

'I thought you must be,' Marianne smiled, still determined never to fall into the trap of apologizing. 'I'm very pleased to meet you.' She turned again to his wife, and this time, after a slight hesitation, her hand was touched by the heavily ringed fingers. 'I'm pleased to meet you, and all, Lady Glendarril,' she smiled, doing her best to put things right between them. She should have thought before saying what she had; she would be wise not to make an enemy of her future mother-in-law.

Lord Glendarril looked accusingly at his lady. 'Hamish said he was going to collect Marianne. Where is he?'

'I have had frightful indigestion since Sunday – I didn't tell you, Hector, in case it alarmed you – so I asked him to get some magnesia for me from the pharmacist in Montrose. He left early enough to be back in time to meet ... the train.'

Her husband frowned. 'You did not need to send him to Montrose, surely? Robert could have given you something?'

She glared at him defiantly. 'I always get it from Montrose, but I have just remembered ... the old man died some weeks ago, and I do not know if anyone has taken over from him yet.'

Marianne glanced at the man to see if he had been fooled by this blatant ploy to keep Hamish from going to the station, and was glad to see that his lips were compressed in a thin hard line.

When he caught her eye, he said, 'Would you like me to show you round some of the gardens, my dear? Or are you too tired after your journey?'

'No, it wasn't far and I'd love to see the gardens.'

He waited until they were clear of the house before he said, in a low voice, 'I am afraid that Lady Glendarril is against Hamish taking you as his wife.'

'I gathered that.'

'Since our other son died, she has pinned all her hopes on Hamish, and even if he wanted to marry one of the royal princesses, his mother would not consider her good enough. In any case, I have always believed that this family needs a new strain in it to set healthier blood running through its veins, and when he told me how well you had stood up to a girl who was nasty to you, I knew you were the one for us.'

'Well, I'm prepared to do my duty as his wife . . .' She decided to be brutally honest – there was something about this man that demanded it. 'I suppose he told you that love was never mentioned between us, so you won't be surprised to know I'm marrying him for the money?'

His expression saddened. 'I was afraid of that . . . but perhaps . . . in time you will . . .' He broke off. 'We should go back. Hamish is probably here and will be wondering where you are.'

While they strolled along he said, 'My wife is a woman who likes her own way, and I would advise you not to cross swords with her. For instance, however much you want the wedding to be to your liking, let her arrange it. She will derive great pleasure from letting it be known that she was responsible for everything. She has her mind set on making a great splash, the kind of show she was denied herself because her father, titled although he was, could not afford it. It was a pity you got off to such a bad start with her, but I am sure she will come round to you. Ah, here is Hamish now, and I would be obliged if you kept our little talk a secret.'

The length – and strength – of Hamish's apologies for not meeting her did much to soothe Marianne's ruffled feelings. It wasn't his fault that his mother had manipulated him. What was more, she had most likely smothered him with love after his twin died, and she would be to blame for Hamish being the way he was now. That was something *she'd* have to remember, Marianne told herself, when her son came along . . . When she arrived she had been pleased that both Hamish and his father were casually dressed, remembering her previous dress mistakes, but when she entered the dining room at seven that evening and saw them in evening dress and Lady Glendarril in a beautifully embroidered gown, with her greying hair coiled up in a deep swathe, Marianne's heart sank.

The maid assigned to Marianne had asked about a dress

but Marianne hadn't understood the situation and had shrugged off – foolishly, she now knew – suggestions that she change.

The woman pounced on her immediately. 'Why have you not changed? Did Hamish not tell you that we always dress for dinner?'

Hamish jumped to his feet. 'I'm sorry, Marianne, I didn't think.'

'It wouldn't have mattered anyway,' she shrugged, struggling to keep her temper under control. 'I don't have any dresses – just blouses and skirts.' And not many of them, she thought sadly.

He came over and took her hand, squeezing it comfortingly as he led her gently to her place. Unfortunately, his seat was at the opposite side of the table and during the meal, he scarcely had a chance to say a word to her, his mother skilfully manoeuvring the conversation to exclude the interloper. Trying not to show how hurt she was, the girl took the opportunity to study as much of the room as she could see without twisting round. Facing her was a fireplace so immense that you could roast an ox in it, she thought, then smiled as she realized that any roasting of oxen or other beasts would be done in the kitchen, not in the dining room. The andirons, the poker, tongs and long-handled shovel, looked to be made of silver but surely they couldn't be? Heat would melt silver, wouldn't it?

The two magnificent portraits on either side of the chimney breast must be Bruce-Lyall ancestors. The man, resplendent in a maroon velvet jacket with a cream cravat at the neck, had a look of the present Lord Glendarril – the same penetrating blue eyes and silver hair receding from his deep forehead; the same brownish eyebrows and bushy moustache, though the beard was much bushier – his father, or grandfather? The woman at the other side would be his mother, or grandmother. Her attire was more sombre, her black dress, moulded to her body, showing a bust of large proportions. Her long face was sharply featured and her hair was metallic grey, pulled severely back off her face. The one redeeming feature in what would otherwise be a mundane representation of a serious, plain woman, was the twinkle, the sparkle, the artist had caught in her grey eyes.

Hoping that no one had noticed her absorption with the portraits, Marianne stole a glance at Hamish, and was astonished to find him looking at her with the same sparkling twinkle in his eyes, more blue than grey. His mother seeking his attention again, he turned away at once, and Marianne was free to continue her appraisal of the room.

Above the mantelshelf was another portrait, a younger man posing in a bright red uniform, his blond hair partly covered by a shako with a red hackle at the side. He was so like Lord Glendarril that he must be his brother.

To her left, she saw a pair of smaller paintings on the wall at right angles to the fireplace wall, again of a man and woman she took to be husband and wife, dressed in what could only be Regency style, very elegant and ornate. Beside the door, she noticed for the first time a row of miniatures, oval in shape and with narrow gold frames. She came to the conclusion that the only way she would find out who was who would be to ask Hamish . . . if she could get him away from his mother long enough.

By the time dinner was over, the strain was beginning to tell on Marianne, and when Lady Glendarril remarked on how tired she looked, she gladly took up Hamish's suggestion that she go to bed. She did need a rest, and a good night's sleep would help her to withstand all the jibes the woman cared to make tomorrow.

Chapter Seven

❦

Perhaps it was the euphoria of organizing on such a large scale in such a short time, or perhaps Lady Glendarril had been warned by her husband to be more friendly towards her future daughter-in-law, but whichever it was, Marianne was very thankful that the woman grew less antagonistic towards her as the days went past. The only friction, a slight contretemps, was the compiling of the guest list for the wedding.

'Have you decided whom you wish to invite?' Clarice asked. 'If you have, I would like a list of the names and addresses as soon as possible . . . not more than two hundred, if you can avoid it.'

Marianne burst out laughing. 'I can give you my list right now, Lady Glendarril.' She stretched over for a piece of paper and a pencil, wrote for a minute or so and then handed it over.

Clarice scowled. 'I do not appreciate your sense of humour.'

'It wasn't meant to be funny. I just want to ask four people to my wedding, that's all, and surely there's nothing wrong in that?'

'But have you no other relatives?'

The smile was wiped off Marianne's face. 'No, and the Rennies are no relation either.' She hesitated, wondering if she should divulge her early life to this out-and-out snob, and came to the conclusion that the least said about it the better. She had given Andrew the four sovereigns and the silver and copper before she left Aberdeen and asked him to put them in his church collection, and that, as far as she was concerned, was the end of that! Her conscience was clear . . . though she still had to account for her non-relationship to the Rennies.

'They're just three sisters who took me in when I arrived in Aberdeen, homeless and friendless after I ran away from my cruel stepmother. They gave me a job in their shop and a room in their house.'

Lady Glendarril gasped. 'When Hamish told me about you, I asked my solicitor to make inquiries about them, to satisfy myself of your . . . and he said that their father had been a sea captain who had left them some money when he died. This was how they bought their shop – selling children's wear? – which, I understand, is quite successful. I had no idea . . . Hamish let me believe that they were your aunts –'

'They're Andrew's aunts,' Marianne interrupted, 'and maybe Hamish didn't realize –' She broke off, then murmured, 'I'm sorry, but they're the only real friends I've ever had.'

'But,' floundered the older woman, 'you must know a few girls . . . ?'

Marianne snorted. 'Them that I met would be the last folk I'd invite.'

'But there are already more than a hundred and fifty on my list.'

Hector stepped in now, his eyes resting pityingly on Marianne before he addressed his wife.

'You must crop your list, Clarice. Why can you not settle for the quiet ceremony Hamish said he would prefer?'

Quite clearly averse to the idea of having to tone down her plans, but an aristocrat to her fingertips, she ignored his last question. 'I presume you will want to invite the Mowatts, the Peats and the Winks?'

This annoyed him further. 'We must ask the whole glen,' he scowled. 'The workers would be deeply hurt if they were not allowed to see their future laird being married.'

'Then I shall have to book Brechin Cathedral instead of St Giles's,' she declared, giving a resigned sigh, 'and we shall have to provide transport for them. In the face of that, you must at least let me invite all my relatives.'

'Just your sisters and their husbands,' he stipulated. 'That makes four for you and four for Marianne, and I suppose to be fair we should invite four of Hamish's friends too.'

'I did ask him, but he said there was no one in particular that he wanted to ask.'

Marianne was disappointed at the turn events had taken. She didn't want to be married in a small place like Brechin, even though it *was* in a cathedral. She wanted to be the main attraction at a big society wedding in St Giles, the most prestigious place of worship in Scotland's capital city. On the other hand, though, now she came to think of it, she might make more of an impact as a big fish in a small pond.

When Hamish came home that evening from a trip to Aberdeen, he was pleased to be told of the change in wedding plans. 'That suits me,' he grinned. 'I was not at all keen on us being the focus of all eyes in Edinburgh, were you, Marianne?'

'Not really.' She had actually been looking forward to seeing the bystanders' mouths drop open in reverence at her beauty, to having them whisper to each other that she was the next Lady Glendarril . . . but surely it would still happen like that, if on a smaller scale. After all, she could make a proper splash when she accompanied her husband and his parents to London for the Queen's Jubilee on 22 June. Lady Glendarril had promised to help her choose some dresses for that occasion, too, and it was to be only two weeks after her own big day. She was bound to meet hordes of the nobility there.

Excitement pulsed throughout the castle as the young Master's wedding drew nearer. The servants were avidly looking forward to the trip to Brechin in the laird's crested carriages and being guests in the cathedral along with the nobs. By early June, Lady Glendarril had taken Marianne to Edinburgh several times to select and fit a gown for the bride, and an outfit for herself, and although Marianne had been given no choice in hers, she didn't care. The creation her future mother-in-law had plumped for was absolutely perfect. Its foundation was a plain ivory silk shift, and at the final fitting, when her waist was confined in a high corset which pushed up her bosom, Marianne was delighted with her new figure. The frothy Chantilly lace overdress had dozens of minuscule seed pearls sewn on, and the matching train trailed yards behind her as she paraded around the small salon in the Royal Mile, which, according to Lady Glendarril, was patronized by all the royal princesses when they were at Holyrood.

It was at the final fitting, when Marianne first saw the headdress – which could have passed for a tiara with a veil – that she wondered if she would ever have the dress sense that Hamish's mother seemed to have, a talent for instinctively going for what was most suitable ... and most expensive.

While Lady Glendarril was having some last-minute alterations done to her own ensemble – a straight, powder-blue dress with a long jacket to be worn with a huge straw hat with deeper blue fringing round the brim – Marianne was taken to another room for silk underwear, silk stockings and ivory-coloured satin shoes.

'Nobody'll see what I've got on underneath,' she laughed.

The assistant who was attending to her – the manageress was fussing around Lady Glendarril – did not smile. 'Knowing that she is dressed to perfection, underneath as well as on top, gives a bride confidence.'

Her hands slid down the hour-glass figure, then up again

98

to make a small tweak at the neckline which then showed less bust.

On the return journey in the train, Marianne noticed that her companion looked deathly pale and beads of sweat were sitting on her upper lip – though it would offend her dignity to be told so. 'Are you all right, Lady Glendarril?' she asked anxiously.

'To be honest, Marianne, no, I am not. A dreadful tiredness came over me after we had lunch, and it has grown worse and worse.'

'You should have told me. We could have come home hours ago.'

'I did not want to have to come back again.'

She said no more, but Marianne kept a wary eye on her, watching for any further sign of exhaustion or illness, and she was glad when Lady Glendarril's eyelids drooped. A short sleep should help her.

When they arrived at Laurencekirk station, she was relieved to see Hamish standing on the platform. He came forward to give them a hand down, and then helped them into the landau while Carnie saw to their parcels.

'Your mother's not feeling well,' Marianne whispered. 'I think we should stop at the doctor's.'

But the woman had heard. 'You will do no such thing,' she said weakly. 'It has been a long day and I am very tired, that is all. I will be back to normal by morning.'

Her personal maid having been given the day off and not expected back until 10 p.m., Marianne saw Lady Glendarril to bed as soon as they entered the castle, and his Lordship himself carried up a tea-tray to her. 'She does not want anything,' he said, when he came down five minutes later. 'And that is most unlike her.'

Marianne tried to stop him fretting. 'I'm tired myself, and I'm a lot younger than she is. Leave her to sleep.'

Immediately after dinner, when Lord Glendarril took

himself off to bed, the girl looked at her young man apologetically. 'I hope you won't be offended, Hamish, but I'll have to get some sleep, too.'

'I'd like to talk to you for a few minutes first.'

'Make it quick, then. I'm dropping on my feet.'

His eyes averted from her, he said, 'I trust that you still want to go ahead with the wedding? I know that you do not love me, and I wondered if you had changed your mind . . .'

She sighed. 'You told me why you wanted me to marry you, Hamish, and I told you why I accepted you. It is a business arrangement – agreeable to both parties – nothing more than that.'

'Yes, but . . .' He hesitated, then burst out, 'I had the feeling you were in love with Andrew Rennie, so if you want to carry on seeing him after we're married, I won't –'

'I *will* carry on seeing him, Hamish, but I'm not in love with him either. I don't need anybody to love, I'll be quite happy the way we'll be . . .' She paused briefly then sighed. 'Now, if that's all you wanted to talk about, can I go to bed?'

'Yes, of course.' He held his hand out and squeezed hers briefly as she stood up. 'Thank you for being so honest with me, my dear, and remember, if ever you do fall in love, I shall sort something out.'

'Divorce, you mean?'

'Oh, no! Divorce would be unthinkable for a Bruce-Lyall, but we could arrange something, I'm sure. Something that would suit both of us. Now, off you go!'

The early morning peace of Castle Lyall was shattered by a loud wail of anguish. 'No! No! Oh dear God, no!'

Marianne jumped out of bed and, not stopping to put on a wrap, hurried along the corridor. Servants were appearing in various kinds of night attire, converging at the point where Lord Glendarril, wild-eyed and ashencheeked, was standing in his nightwear at the door of his wife's room.

Gripping his silk dressing robe together on top of a nightshirt that was too short to hide his bare legs, Hamish pushed to the front and grabbed his father's arm with his free hand. 'What's wrong?'

'Your mother! I came to see how she was, and she did not answer me. I think she . . . is dead!'

This galvanized the entire gathering into action. Carnie said, 'I'll get the doctor,' and he dashed downstairs. His wife, the cook – her hair hanging like a grey-flecked black blanket down her back instead of being pinned neatly on top of her head as it was normally seen – gathered her staff together to go down to make some tea and have some sustenance ready for his Lordship and his family; the chamber maids – looking uncomfortable in the dozens of little rags they had put in their hair in order to curl it – looked at each other in helpless blankness until Mrs Carnie told them to light the fires in all the public rooms and to have them spotless for the many callers who were certain to come. She also took one look at the mistress's personal maid and said, 'You'd better come down and all, Thomson, and get some brandy in you afore you land on the floor in a faint.'

The gardener and his underlings went to waken the young lads who slept in a room above the stables, so that they could get the other carriages and equipment ready before Carnie came back.

Having had a quick but close look at his mother to make sure that she really had stopped breathing, Hamish turned to Marianne. 'I'll take my father downstairs and give him a dram to steady his nerves, and I'd be obliged if you'll stay with Mother until the doctor comes. You won't be frightened, will you? Thomson is in no fit state but I could send up one of the other –'

Despite the chattering of her teeth, Marianne said

bravely, 'No, I'll be all right; it's your father that needs the attention now.'

She watched him helping the older man as far as the landing, then turned round and advanced slowly into the chamber of death. She made it to a chair and, her knees refusing to bend, sat down with a thump. She had no idea when Lady Glendarril had died, but already there was that unmistakable sense of another presence in the room. She'd had the very same feeling after her own mother died, and hadn't been comforted by a neighbour's doom-laden observation, 'It's the Grim Reaper letting you ken he's been.'

When the doctor arrived, almost an hour later because he had been at a difficult confinement, Marianne was stiff with cold and fear, and was glad to be packed off to bed with a sleeping powder. She was asleep in no time and heard nothing of the ensuing commotion, or the visits Hamish made to check on her.

It was late afternoon when she came to her senses again, and she lay for some minutes remembering and conjecturing. This was Tuesday and the wedding had been planned for Saturday, but no doubt it would have to be postponed. It was ludicrous, she knew, but she couldn't help feeling that Lady Glendarril had planned this as well, hoping the wait until the end of the recognized period of mourning would make her change her mind about marrying Hamish. But Marianne Cheyne certainly wasn't going to give up the chance of the best marriage she would ever be offered, and if she did have to wait a year, she would hold out for St Giles's and resurrect Lady Glendarril's original guest list. Best of all, she would ask Andrew to find out the addresses of those horrible girls who had belittled her in Aberdeen and invite them all, rub their snooty noses in the splendour of her wedding gown and her castle home. Yet, even with the thought of an Edinburgh wedding enabling her to get her own back on Sybil and friends, she didn't really want to wait. She would rather be married sooner than later.

She got out of bed languorously and went over to the washstand where the willow-pattern ewer had been filled with water, probably hot at the time but now stone cold. Pouring some into the matching bowl, she splashed her face several times, which took her breath away but gave her the invigoration she needed. Selecting one of the lawn blouses Clarice had bought for her on their first visit to Edinburgh, she dressed herself with more care than usual, because she could hear strange voices wafting up, and guessed that the house would already be full of people come to pay their respects to the dead woman.

She discovered that they were well past the respects stage, and had progressed to airing their views on when the wedding should now take place. No one noticed her as she circumnavigated the large group in the ballroom, her ears taking in every argument put forward for the postponement of the wedding, yet hoping that someone would advocate letting it go ahead as planned. After a time, concluding that this was too much to hope for, she moved into the vast library – walls lined with shelf after shelf of leather-bound tomes, with busts of famous authors placed in a seemingly random manner on all available surfaces – where another heated discussion was going on.

Those assembled here were clearly relatives of Lady Glendarril, her sisters and their husbands amongst them, likely, who were not afraid of saying what they thought, no matter what. Here, also, were Hamish and his father, both scarlet in the face and looking ready to erupt at any moment.

'Oh, no, Jarvis!' exclaimed one whale-boned, silver-haired matron to a man who may or may not have been her husband. 'They cannot be married as soon as that. Three months is not nearly long enough for –'

'A year at least,' agreed another high-bosomed lady who

could have been her twin. 'And it should be St Giles, like poor dear Clarice wanted. I simply cannot understand why she cancelled that. It was so inconsiderate! I had my dress made long before the letter came to say she had changed it to Brechin and we were not invited after all.'

Hector could contain himself no longer. 'No, and you will still not be invited, Priscilla, whatever I decide. And I hope all of you heard that! Whatever *I* decide, I said, for it is my decision that counts, not what any of you think. I have been mulling it over ever since you descended on my house like a plague of locusts and I am sure Hamish and –' He broke off to look round, then, spotting Marianne hovering near the door, he held out his hand to her. 'Come here, my dear, and tell me what you think of *my* idea.'

He put his arm round her shoulders when she went to him. 'I see no reason to postpone the wedding for a year, not even three months. We could have the funeral on Friday and the wedding could go ahead in Brechin on Saturday as planned. *Or.* . . and this is what I believe we *should* do . . . we can have both wedding and funeral on Saturday in our own kirk here in the glen.'

Shocked gasps and dismayed exclamations greeted this. 'Hector, you simply can *not* have a wedding and a funeral . . .'

'It isn't done, Hector, old boy.' This from a stout man with such a purple complexion that Marianne feared he was about to have a heart attack there and then.

Hector looked at her. 'What do you think, my dear? Would you be willing to . . . Do you feel you could cope with that?'

'I'll do whatever you say,' she quavered, 'as long as Hamish –'

Her bridegroom-to-be drew in a long breath and let it out noisily. 'I don't see why not, if Duncan doesn't object. The Reverend Duncan Peat,' he added, for the benefit of those not familiar with the name.

'Duncan won't object,' Hector said, waving his hand airily. 'He is a product of the glen.'

At this, several dissenting voices pointed out that his place of birth should have no bearing on his beliefs, and Hamish waited for silence before he said, 'My father financed him while he studied for the ministry.'

Embarrassed that his largesse had been made public, Hector mumbled, 'That does not mean I expect him to kowtow to me. He is quite free to refuse to conduct one or other of the ceremonies, or both if he so wishes, but he holds liberal views. I think he will agree.'

With barely concealed ill grace, the members of this gathering split into small groups to discuss the matter further, although some, out of curiosity, followed their host to the ballroom, where, with his arm still round Marianne, he made his announcement again. It was received in exactly the same way as before.

Head held high, and leaving his son to deal with irate relatives and friends, Hector shepherded the girl upstairs to the room where his wife lay, and only then gave way to his true feelings. 'Clarice, oh, Clarice,' he moaned, plumping down on a tapestry-cushioned chair. 'I know you tried to be a good wife to me, but I'd have been happier if you had not tried to run my life. If I had let you, you would have strangled me with affection like you did Hamish. That was why I went away so often – to get away from you. I felt free when I was in Edinburgh and London, free to find a woman to give me release from the eternal frustration of bowing to your wishes.'

Somewhat shocked and very embarrassed by what he was admitting, Marianne let him ramble on. It was probably the best thing he could do.

'You would have been hurt and puzzled, Clarice, by the length of time I spent in the arms of those ladies of the streets, but I was determined not to be like my ancestors, most of whom, according to legend, were more interested in other men than in women. Mind you, for a time in my teens, at school, I did have a preference for masculine company, but once I left I did not take long to discover the delights girls could provide.'

He took his handkerchief out to mop his perspiring face, and as he returned it to his breast pocket, he muttered, 'I should not have betrayed my wife. Thank God she never knew.'

He fell silent, and Marianne still couldn't think of anything to say. She wished with all her heart that she could sneak out and leave him to his tortured thoughts, but she couldn't bring herself to move. She was hardly aware of Hamish coming in almost twenty minutes later, but gratefully accepted his arm to help her to stand. When he took her into her own room, she said, 'You should get your father out of there. It's not good for him.'

'I'll see to him in a minute, but I wanted to tell you Miss Glover has told the chamber maids to make rooms ready for those relatives who live furthest away. If they do not arrive until tomorrow, they will likely want to stay over until Saturday. I sent the trap for Duncan Peat and he came up with a solution that everyone finally agreed to. He'll have the funeral service first so that those not invited to the wedding can leave before it starts, but . . .' he stopped with a wry smile, 'I am afraid they will all stay on out of curiosity, though there won't be many asked back to the house. Marianne, are you still sure about this?'

'I'm still sure, though I wish it was all over. Now, for any sake, Hamish, go to your father.'

Left alone, she sank back on her bed to think. The society wedding in St Giles she had longed for was only a pipe dream now. She had been prepared to settle for making a ripple at Brechin, and that, too, had been knocked on the head. Nevertheless, being married in a wee kirk in a sparsely populated glen, with members of the nobility mixing with the castle staff and estate workers, would most likely be unique particularly since it was to follow a funeral where some of the mourners would be wedding guests once the coffin was interred in the kirkyard. It would be a talking point for years, Marianne mused happily.

Her first priority would be to let Andrew and his aunts know of this latest development. They had declined to attend at either St Giles or Brechin Cathedral – no doubt they felt such places would be too grand for them – but surely they wouldn't refuse to come to a wee kirk where most of the people in the pews would be workers in the Glendarril mill and their families, and tenants of the wee crofts on the estate. The four Rennies would have to come! They were her only guests . . . and she had the feeling she would need them.

Chapter Eight

❦

'Well, I never!' exclaimed Edith Rennie in some irritation, when she read the short note Marianne had enclosed with her letter to Andrew. 'How can she and Hamish be so callous?'

Esther was not quite so quick to criticize. 'They could hardly have carried on with their original arrangements ... not with a death in the family.'

Edith nodded vehemently. 'That is precisely what I meant. They should be showing more respect and not turning his mother's funeral into some sort of circus. His father must be cut to the quick that they have not cancelled the wedding ... nor even postponed it.'

'I gather from what she said in her letter to me,' Andrew put in, 'that it was Lord Glendarril himself who suggested it, Aunt Edith. She said he was angry at his wife's relatives for dictating that the couple should wait anything from three months to a year.'

Esther and Emily exchanged troubled glances, but it was left to Edith to ask the question. 'Andrew, you do not think ... ? Marianne could not be ... ? Surely Lady Glendarril would not have let her son make free with the girl?'

Amused by her spinsterish euphemistic term for seduction as much as by her calculated refusal to use any of the words usually associated with pregnancy, Andrew was still appalled at the suggestion that this was the reason for the hasty tying of the knot. 'Oh no, I shouldn't think that!'

'Poor girl,' murmured Emily, joining into the discussion

at last. 'Marianne was so happy . . . and now . . . oh dear!'

Esther nodded. 'Yes, immediately after she becomes Hamish's wife, she will have to stand at his mother's graveside and comfort him! Solemnizing a marriage and consecrating a body to the grave at more or less the same time sounds very heathenish to me, and it does not bode well for their future happiness.'

Knowing why Marianne was marrying Hamish, Andrew let out a deep sigh. Even before the unexpected death of the bridegroom's mother, he had not foreseen the girl being truly happy on her wedding day, never mind in the future, and as it was . . . 'It's the other way round, Aunt Esther. They have arranged to have the wedding ceremony after the burial, and I'm sure Marianne will cope, whatever happens.'

Edith regarded him shrewdly. 'You are not thinking of attending, are you, Andrew?'

He gave an apologetic smile. 'I thought she might need someone on her side, someone she could turn to if anything goes wrong. She has nobody down there, nobody at all.'

Edith was about to point out that she had Hamish, but something in her nephew's eyes stopped her.

'If there's any bad feeling amongst the mourners,' he carried on, 'and I fear there will be since Lord Glendarril has stipulated that only the estate workers will be looked on as wedding guests, Marianne will need me . . . all of us, Aunt Edith. That's why she wrote. We are invited back to the castle afterwards as her guests . . . her *only* guests.'

'In that case, we had better accept, but it scarcely gives us time to find clothes suitable for both ceremonies – a Herculean task.'

When Andrew was leaving, Edith walked a little way along the street with him, and he guessed she meant to give him a lecture. Her first words proved him right.

'I hope you have thought carefully about what you are doing, Andrew. I know how you feel about Marianne, and

I am rather afraid that watching her being joined in holy matrimony to another man will be too much for you.'

'It's because I love her that I want to be there for her, though it'll turn the knife deeper into my heart. I'll never stop loving her, Aunt Edith, so I'll have to get used to her being someone else's wife. I'm a grown man now so stop worrying about me. Marianne said one of their carriages would pick us up at Laurencekirk station if we did decide to go, so I'll send her a telegram to let her know we will be there.'

Before she turned away, his aunt stroked his cheek. 'You are a dear boy, Andrew, and I hope with all my heart that some day you will find a –'

He interrupted her there, to stop her hoping for the impossible. 'We have to take the nine forty train on Saturday forenoon, so I'll meet you at the station around half-past.'

Saturday dawned bright and fair, but the tension at Castle Lyall became more fraught as the morning progressed, resentment running high amongst those who had stayed overnight and still had not been invited as guests at the wedding. Fortunately, Lord Glendarril had taken the precaution of having Carnie and his wife set up tables in the ballroom as well as in the dining room, so that his relatives – a few ancient aunts and spinster cousins – and the army of relations on his wife's side could be kept separate while they had breakfast . . . not that it was really necessary. The majority on both sides agreed that the wedding should have been put off, and all were outraged that they had been ordered to leave after the interment. They whispered to each other that Hector's loss had temporarily deranged his mind – why else would he ban them from the wedding reception? – but one look at his set face prevented even the most stout-hearted from saying anything.

Marianne, aware of the atmosphere there would be

downstairs, kept to her room – she was nervous enough without getting involved in any arguments – but she was quite glad when Lord Glendarril himself appeared with a cup of tea after her breakfast tray had been removed untouched.

'You need something in your stomach to see you through this day,' he said, sitting down on the edge of her bed. 'How are you feeling?'

'Not as bad as I thought I'd be.'

'Only another few hours to go and then we can relax. We will still have the reception to get through, of course, but the workers will likely clear the tables of food in no time, and I have told them there will be no dancing or celebrating afterwards . . . not in the castle. I have made several crates of spirits and porter available to them, and what they do in the privacy of their own homes – or in the school hall – is up to them. I know some people think I am showing no respect for Clarice, but I have had to steel myself, and I know I shall give way when everything is over.'

'It would be only natural,' Marianne murmured although privately wondering how natural anything could be in such an unnatural situation.

'Natural, perhaps, but as a Bruce-Lyall, I cannot let that sort of weakness be seen by the minions. I must say, I have been impressed by how Hamish has been taking his mother's death. He was so devoted to her I would have thought . . . but he must have more backbone than I gave him credit for.'

He laid her empty cup on the table by the bed and patted her hand. 'I suspect that he, too, will give way when the pressure is off, so you will have to be strong for him, my dear.'

'I will,' she promised. 'I know it sounds awful, but I didn't know your wife very long, so I'm not so affected as everybody else.'

'That is good. After today, you will take her place as Lady of the . . . but we will say no more about that at present. I shall send Thomson up to help you dress. She will be *your* personal maid now.'

Something he hadn't considered before suddenly struck him. 'Um, Marianne, I trust you will wear the wedding gown Clarice chose?'

'Oh, Lord Glendarril, I couldn't turn up at her funeral dressed like that! What would folk say?'

He gave a half-smile. 'My dear girl, we Bruce-Lyalls do not give a damn for what people say, especially the upstart *nouveaux riches* who bore their way into everything. As for *my* workers, every man, woman and child is dependent on me for the roofs over their heads, for the food they eat, for the clothes they wear. Not that I ever cast that up to them, but whatever they think of today's arrangements, they are unlikely to voice their opinions aloud.'

'But I wouldn't feel right about it myself,' Marianne pointed out. 'I could wear the navy costume she had made for me, that would –'

'You cannot get married in a navy costume!' he frowned. 'I know how these women's minds work. They will be wishing they could have seen the wonderful gown our maids told them about.' He tapped his fingers on the jamb of the door for a few seconds then brightened. 'I know! I shall tell Thomson to pack it carefully in its box, and one of the young lads can take it to the church as soon as possible. You will wear your navy costume when you leave here, but after the funeral, she will help you to change in the vestry, and I guarantee that you will cause quite a stir when you walk down the aisle.'

That settled it for Marianne. He was arranging it so that she could have her big moment after all, although she would have preferred more people – especially more of the aristocracy – to witness it. But why was he rushing the wedding like this? Was he afraid that Hamish might change his mind, or was he afraid that he, himself, would die unexpectedly?

Andrew was astonished when Hamish himself met them at the station. 'I got orders from Marianne to take you to the house first because she has something to ask your aunts.'

After being helped into the impressive landau, the ladies settled back to enjoy the scenery, and Hamish turned to face the other man. 'I have something to ask you, too, Andrew. I would be honoured if you would act as best man for me. I'm glad you could come, and since we are keeping the numbers to a minimum . . .'

'Of course, and I'll be honoured to do it.' Nevertheless, Andrew's heart was aching at the thought of what this would entail.

His aunts were much happier at what Marianne asked of them. She had decided, when she first knew they were definitely coming, to ask Andrew if he would give her away, but Hamish had appropriated him to be best man, and she had enquired of the minister if she could have a woman to take over this duty.

Duncan Peat had said he didn't see why not, although it was most unusual, and so she had asked Miss Edith to do this, and Miss Emily and Miss Esther to be bridesmaids.

The small church was absolutely packed for the funeral service, with many of the gentry left fuming outside. The hymns were played on a small wheezy harmonium by an elderly woman who seemed to be crouching over the keyboard as her feet pedalled madly, but the music could be heard even above the lusty singing. After Duncan Peat spoke a fitting eulogy for the laird's wife, he put up a shorter prayer than usual before the last hymn was sung. The six pallbearers now stepped to the front and hoisted the brass-handled coffin up on their shoulders. In a slow march, they carried it outside to where the beadle, who was also gravedigger, had the family lair – the largest and most ostentatious in the kirkyard with a huge marble angel standing guard at its head – open to receive its latest occupant.

Still frightened of cemeteries and gravestones, Marianne kept her eyes on Hamish, and saw his pallor change to a horrible grey. Alarmed that he was going to faint and fall into the grave, she was about to run forward to him when she noticed that his father was exactly the same colour. She should have expected it. After all, they were saying goodbye to a woman they had loved. She herself, mindful of what she had to do immediately after the service, had purposely kept in the background, and when the Reverend Duncan Peat ended his closing prayer, she signed to her maid and to Esther and Emily to follow her to the vestry.

Some ten minutes later, she was asking, 'Do I look all right? Is my veil on straight?'

Thomson, a small woman in her late forties, seemed to be struck dumb by the transformation of the robust young girl into this elegant woman, but Miss Esther breathed, 'You are absolutely lovely, my dear. I do not think I have ever seen a more beautiful bride.'

Thomson slipped out to give the organist the signal and then sat in the seat Mrs Carnie had kept for her. When the Wedding March rang out, Marianne made sure that her two maids of honour had a firm grip of her long train before going forth to link arms with Miss Edith, who had been waiting just inside the church door for her moment of glory.

The little procession moved slowly and gracefully down the aisle – Miss Esther and Miss Emily in the midnight-blue shantung dresses they had considered suitable for both funeral and wedding, though they had not known before-hand that they would be bridesmaids, and Miss Edith regally tall and erect in a clerical-grey moire two piece, as if she had known she was to act as 'father of the bride'. The gasps from those in the rear pews were enough to make all heads swivel in order to have a good look at the bride, the girl who had flouted convention by wearing a gown fit for a princess when she should be in unrelieved black to show respect for the woman who had died before becoming her mother-in-law.

As though to the manner born, Marianne kept her head aloft and her step slow and measured. She knew that this day would be spoken of in the glen for many years, and hoped that these women would not hold it against her. Surely they would realize that she'd had no option?

'You are very quiet, Andrew,' Edith observed when they were homeward bound in the early evening. 'I hope that you are not –'

'I'm all right, Aunt Edith. I must admit it was an ordeal, but not quite as bad as I expected. I was really proud of you three, though. You carried out your duties to perfection.'

As he had hoped, this took their minds off him, and they proceeded to discuss the funeral, the wedding, the meal, the friendliness of the glen folk, leaving him free for his own thoughts. The sight of Marianne walking so determinedly down that aisle would have amused him in other circumstances, but he had been overcome with love for her, she looked so ethereal, so virginal, swathed in yards of ivory lace, and he had been hard pressed not to fold her in his arms and defy anyone to take her away from him. But . . . she was not his!

He had known, of course, that Marianne did not love Hamish – which was what had made it easier for him to bear his heartache – but he hadn't realized until today that Hamish did not love her. Hamish had stood like a statue while she came nearer, had shown no sign of emotion when she reached him, had not had the slightest tremor in his voice when he made his vows. The minister had to tell him to kiss his bride, and the kiss itself was a token gesture. Andrew didn't know whether to be glad at Hamish's lack of response or sorry for Marianne. Most girls would want to be loved, for that love to be proved in front of the congregation, but Marianne was not most girls. The thing was, would she be satisfied to spend the rest of her life with a man who had come across as completely indifferent to her?

There was a suggestion of dawn in the sky, yet Marianne Bruce-Lyall was still lying wide awake, remembering, conjecturing, but not, for one single moment, regretting. She had savoured to the full the impact she had made. Apart from the thrill she had got from the audible reactions in the church to her gown, there had been the standing inside the ballroom to be introduced to the handful of relatives present and better still, to every resident of the glen. Although nothing specific had been said or done, she had been left with the distinct impression that Hamish's kinfolk looked down on her, but the estate workers, those she would be most likely to come in contact with, had made her feel welcome amongst them . . . as their better.

Her mind now went over her leave-taking of the Rennies. She had expected Miss Emily and Miss Esther to be weepy, but she had been astonished that Edith had openly dabbed her eyes and then hugged her closely. 'You know I wish you happiness, Marianne dear,' she had whispered, 'but I would like you to look on us as aunts to whom you can come if you need advice, or if . . .'

Her voice breaking there, Marianne had said shakily, 'Thank you, I'll not forget.'

Then Andrew had taken her hand, his eyes dark with the hurt she had inflicted on him. 'I'm truly sorry, Andrew,' she'd murmured, his pain reaching out to clamp around her heart.

His finger had risen to dash away the tear that she couldn't stop edging out. 'No tears, my dear,' he'd told her. 'I am happy that your wish came true, and I sincerely hope that you will find happiness as well as contentment in your new life ... but remember, Marianne, if things do not work out the way you envisaged, I will gladly come and take you away from him.'

Before she realized what he was doing, he had swept her into his arms and given her a kiss that came within a hair's-breadth of being passionate. Then, with a stifled moan, he had jumped on the landau and it had moved away. She had gone back to Hamish, who had been standing in the doorway to give her privacy to say her goodbyes. He'd looked even greyer than before, despite the feverish spot in his cheeks.

'There's still a few left,' he'd muttered, 'but my father is helping them to gather all the left-overs ... Ah, here they come.'

The few he mentioned – about ten over-happy men and perhaps six women – had reached the foot of the curved steps as the first of the traps returned, and Marianne had had to smile when she'd noticed the boxes that clinked being loaded much more carefully than the ones which presumably held the left-overs from the meal.

'Thank you for everything, your Lordship,' the oldest man had grinned and, after shaking his employer's hand, he'd turned to Marianne. 'My best wishes to you and your man, m'lady, and dinna tak' lang to gi'e us the heir we need.'

The sturdy woman who was obviously his wife had pulled at his sleeve. 'Behave yoursel', Tam! Get up on the coach, for ony sake.'

The drive empty at last, Hector had turned unsteadily, and Marianne had helped him up the steps, smiling as she noticed how high he was lifting each foot, as if uncertain where to set it down. Recalling having seen Dick, his valet, staggering around in an advanced stage of inebriation quite early on, she'd realized that the servant would be totally incapable by this time of attending to his master. 'Will Hamish help you get undressed?' she'd asked her father-in-law inside.

'I can manage to take off my own clothes,' he'd said, but it was the bridal couple themselves who had half carried him up to his room, where, giving up all pretence of joviality, he'd sat down on his bed with tears streaming down his face. Never having seen a grown man cry, Marianne had felt most uncomfortable. 'I'll leave you to deal with him,' she had whispered to Hamish, and withdrew before he could say anything.

She'd felt pleased to have the chance to undress without being seen, but had forgotten that she could not unfasten the hooks and eyes down the back by herself and she had not wanted to ring for Thomson. Sighing, she'd sat down at her dressing table to wait for her bridegroom.

It had been twenty minutes before he'd appeared. 'Too much whisky made Father very emotional,' he'd muttered, 'but he's fast asleep now.'

'That's the best thing for him. Hamish, will you help me out of this gown?'

When he'd come closer, she'd seen that his face was ravaged by tears. 'Hamish, I'm sorry. I should have known how upset you'd be. I'll ring for Thomson.'

'I'll manage!' With what was almost a grunt, he'd grabbed her by the shoulders and spun her round with her back to him, so that he could undo the tiny fasteners. Letting her go abruptly when they were all open, he'd burst into tears and she'd thought it best to let him get it out of his system. Eventually, he had said brokenly, 'I am truly sorry, Marianne. I don't know what you must think of me, but I couldn't help it.'

Knowing that he was ashamed of himself for giving way, she'd tried to reassure him. 'I was the same when my mother died. Everybody's the same. After all, your mother's the person who feeds you and takes care of you when you're small . . .'

'I can't even use that as an excuse,' he'd hiccuped. 'My brother and I had a succession of nurses to feed us and care for us.'

She could have bitten her tongue out. 'Your mother gave birth to you, Hamish, and there's always a close bond between children and their mothers, especially boys, I've been told.'

'Perhaps that is it, then. Ever since my brother died, I have felt it my duty to make it up to her. She was almost inconsolable at the time, and made such a fuss of me after she recovered.' He'd stopped, and there was a long pause before he had whispered, 'I know what you are expecting of me, Marianne, but I can't, not tonight!'

'I understand,' she'd soothed, but to his rapidly retreating back.

It shouldn't have come as any surprise to her, but she could not help feeling let down. It was their wedding night and he had left her in this huge bed on her own.

Because of the ill-feeling he had engendered by having the wedding immediately after the funeral, Hector had decided to offer a kind of sop to the offended relatives who had stayed all night.

Sitting down to breakfast the following morning, he looked around the table with a somewhat shamed expression. 'I have been thinking more clearly since my beloved wife was laid to rest,' he said sadly, wiping away a non-existent tear, 'and I realize that I ought to have listened to . . .' He cleared his throat noisily. 'I should have let Hamish and Marianne postpone their marriage as they wanted to, but what is done can not be undone, and I pledge, before all of you here, that my entire household will observe the customary full year of mourning. We will not, therefore, attend the Queen's Jubilee on the twenty-second as we had planned.'

The satisfied murmurs proved that his strategy had worked. Only Marianne's disappointed expression pricked his conscience and, as soon as he got her alone, he murmured, 'I am very sorry, my dear. I know how much you were looking forward to going to London to join the celebrations, but it is best that we do not flout convention again.'

Marianne nodded her head. 'I *am* disappointed, but I do understand. I heard Lady Glendarril's two . . . cousins, I think, say yesterday that they were shocked at you for . . .'

'If I tried to count the times I have shocked Eunice and Rosemary over the years,' he chuckled, 'it would be in the hundreds, perhaps even the thousands. They are sour old maids – they were sour even when they were young. It would have done them the world of good if one of their brother's friends had ravished them.'

Marianne's smile vanished when Hector went on, 'Speaking of which, I hope you will soon be telling me that I am going to be a grandfather.' He clasped her hand tightly for a second and then walked away.

Wondering what he would have said if she told him what had happened the night before, Marianne went upstairs to the room where she had lain alone in the darkness. The vast bed had curtains all round, which she intended to remove as soon as she could. She had left them open last night, but she had still felt as though they were smothering her when she tried to get some sleep.

When would Hamish come to her bed and make them truly husband and wife? Surely he wasn't such a Mammy's boy that he'd take weeks to get over her death?

She took a deep breath. What was the good of looking on the black side? It was early days yet.

∗　　∗　　∗

Moll Cheyne had waited impatiently all forenoon for her husband to come home, and the minute he walked in, she burst out, 'Have you seen the day's paper, Alfie?'

'I havena time to sit about readin' papers,' he growled, setting his hard backside on the equally hard chair at the table. 'I hardly get time to draw breath.'

Always worried that the sawdust he breathed in would eventually clog his lungs completely, Moll let him finish his soup before she handed him the *Aberdeen Journal* and pointed to the photographs accompanying a prominent article. It had been written by a cub reporter on the *Observer* – the local paper for Laurencekirk and most of the county of Kincardine – whose editor had deemed the Bruce-Lyall funeral-cum-wedding worthy of much wider circulation.

Peering at the pictures short-sightedly, Alfie suddenly exclaimed, 'Lord preserve us! It's my Marion!'

'Read it,' his wife urged. 'Read it an' see why she's never wrote or let us ken where she was.'

Still only concerned with the photographs, he studied the first – a host of black-clad men and women over-shadowed by a girl in a dark costume standing at the rear of the group but in the foreground of the picture – then read out the caption: 'Marianne Cheyne is one of the mourners at the burial of Lady Glendarril of Castle Lyall, in Glendarril churchyard on Saturday.' Alfie's head shot up. 'She must be in service at the castle.'

Moll shook her head then pushed back the greasy lock of hair that had fallen over her face. 'It doesna say onything aboot her bein' in service, but maybe that's where she met him.' Her husband's puzzled expression made her snap, 'Get on, Alfie!'

His eyes moved slowly to the other picture – the same girl emerging from a church wearing a wedding gown and accompanied by a tall young man with a sombre expression. ' "The Honourable Hamish Bruce-Lyall leaving

Glendarril church on Saturday with his bride, the former Miss Marianne Cheyne," Alfie read out. His brows crawled together in puzzlement. 'There's some mistake here. It says the frunial was on Saturday, so the wedding couldna have been on Saturday an' all?'

Moll stood up. 'For ony sake, read it a'!' She moved over to the fire to make a pot of tea for him. It's all he would feel like after reading the rest.

At last, Alfie took a look at the headline: 'GLEN MINISTER CONDUCTS WEDDING IMMEDIATELY AFTER FUNERAL OF GROOM'S MOTHER.'

The reporter may just have been learning his profession, but he knew how to attract attention . . . and how to hold it. Much was made of the fact that Marianne had been befriended by the Rennies when she arrived in Aberdeen, and that she had shown her gratitude by asking them to take on the duties of bridesmaids and of giving her away. This information had been gleaned mostly from those of Hector's relatives who had been denied the privilege of being wedding guests, and thus were loud in condemnation of Hamish and Marianne for not cancelling their marriage, but the journalist had taken great pains to cast no slur on the bridal couple. In fact, he made it appear that Clarice herself had begged them before she died not to change their plans, and that they had agreed reluctantly.

This was how he explained the seriousness of their expressions after the nuptials were tied, creating a tide of sympathy for them by saying that each anniversary of their wedding would remind them of Lady Glendarril's death. He ended with, 'And so, as the Honourable Hamish Bruce-Lyall and his bride start married life with sorrow dimming the joy they should be sharing, let us wish them every happiness for the future.'

Alfie laid down the newspaper as Moll set an enamel mug of tea before him. 'Well?' she demanded.

'Well, what?' Alfie was not particularly bright at the

best of times, but what he had just read had completely flummoxed him.

'Are you to be writin' to her?'

'Writin' to her? What the devil for?'

'For God's sake, Alfie! Can you nae see what this means? Here's us, countin' every ha'penny an' never having enough to go round, and there's her, rollin' in it!'

He banged his clenched fist on the table top, making the tea splash out of both mugs. 'If you think I'd beg fae my ain lassie, you're softer in the heid than I thought you were.'

'But she's got plenty, an' you *are* her father.'

'I used to wonder what had became o' her, an' I'm pleased she made something o' hersel', but a father's supposed to provide for his bairn, nae the other wey roon'.'

'Aye, well, but . . . maybe we should let her ken the Moodies never did nothin' aboot that money she took, an' tell her she's welcome back ony time she –'

Alfie's face darkened even further. 'She'll nae be welcome back! I'm having nae trock wi' a thief though she *is* my ain lassie. And dinna you think on writing to her, for you'll nae get me to speak to her supposing she's got the nerve to show her face here!'

Recognizing that nothing would make him change his mind, Moll gave up, but she cut out the item about the wedding and hid it away for future reference. Should Alfie ever have to stop working because of his chest, she would write and ask Marion – Marianne, as she called herself now – for help . . . but she wouldn't tell him.

After all the house guests had left, Hector joined the young couple in the Blue Room and said quietly, 'Do you remember me saying you would have to take Clarice's place as mistress of the castle, Marianne? Now, because of her death, I cannot let you take a honeymoon, but I will allow you one week to spend as much time with Hamish as you wish. After that, I expect you to acquaint yourself with the layout of the castle, and what goes on behind the scenes, so to speak. You will probably have noticed that the running of the every day household matters is in Miss Glover's capable hands, but if you do not like her, it will be up to you to find a replacement, and that goes for all the members of our staff. Mrs Carnie is an excellent cook, but if you and she do not get on –'

'I'm sure I'll get on with Mrs Carnie,' Marianne interrupted, 'and Miss Glover.'

'Roberta Glover can be a bit abrupt at times, but she knows her job inside out, and she'll keep you right if there is anything you are not sure of. And now,' he went on, getting to his feet, 'if you two young things do not mind, I must go to bed. I still feel a little off colour after yesterday. I do not make a habit of getting drunk, as Hamish will verify, but whisky was the only thing to numb the ache. Sorrow is not the best of bedfellows.'

'No, indeed,' observed Hamish.

And Marianne said, 'We won't be long in going to bed, either. I didn't get much sleep last –' Her eyes widened as her hand flew to cover her errant mouth.

Misconstruing her embarrassment, Hector gave a great roar of laughter as he went out.

Marianne looked at her husband in dismay. 'I'm sorry, Hamish. I don't know why I said that.'

'Probably because it was the truth,' he said, but not unkindly. 'I feel the need of a good night's sleep myself, and so I shall . . .' He paused, eyeing her warily. 'I shall sleep in my own room again.'

'Your own room,' she echoed faintly.

'You know what our arrangement was,' he muttered self-consciously, 'and the chamber maid knows to keep a bedroom ready for me. My mother and father slept in separate rooms for years.'

Marianne felt like saying, 'But not on the second night

of their marriage,' only what good would it have done? She had entered into this anything-but-ideal contract in order to have wealth and power, and the gates to that world were to be opened for her a week from tomorrow. Love would be an additional blessing.

Alone in the marriage bed again, Marianne boosted her low spirits by thinking that she would soon be in sole charge of everything and everybody in Castle Lyall, and once she had it running her way, both Hamish and his father would see that she was capable of much more than breeding children. She would provide the two sons they needed in order to be sure of an heir, and then . . .

By God, and then! She would make the gentry sit up and take notice of her, fall over themselves to invite her to their homes, be they mansions, castles or palaces. She had the beauty the nobility lacked – horse-faced, most of them. She would be the talk of the glen, the whole of Scotland, even – and England, too.

Chapter Nine

On the first full day of their marriage, Hamish showed his bride the kitchen gardens where all the vegetables were grown, sheltered from frost and winds by the high wall enclosing them, and the flourishing herb patch situated where the kitchenmaid could quickly cut whatever Cook might suddenly decide she needed. Marianne was impressed, although she had never heard of most of the herbs here before.

The flower gardens and lawns also appealed to her – the symmetry of the layouts, the subtle mixing of colours, the more delicate being kept together in patterns around the perimeter, and the shaped beds within graduated up to the most flamboyant. 'I won't remember their proper names,' she whispered to Hamish, after Dargie, the head gardener, reeled off over a dozen, unintelligible as far as she was concerned, before he went off to supervise his undergardeners and left The Master and his wife to carry on alone. 'It sounded Greek to me.'

'It was Latin,' Hamish told her, courtesy forbidding him to laugh.

'We always called *them* red-hot pokers,' she explained, pointing to the tall clump of red and yellow blooms in the centre. 'And that's mappies' mou's,' she went on, indicating the antirrhinums.

'What on earth does that mean?' her husband asked, bemused.

'Surely you ken what . . . ?' She stopped with an embarrassed laugh. 'No, I don't suppose you do. Well, mappies is what we called rabbits at hame, and a mou' is a mouth.

To let you see . . .' She took one of the florets between her forefinger and her thumb to show him. 'If you squeeze a wee bit out and in, like this, it's like a rabbit's mouth opening and shutting.'

'So it is!' he exclaimed, trying it for himself.

A large rockery set with alpine plants held her attention next, and when they moved on to where one of the younger gardeners had been trying his hand at topiary, she was fascinated by the shapes he had created. 'That's a duck! And that's a swan! And that's a . . . stork on one leg!' She clapped her hands in delight. 'Oh, I just love this, and he's done animals down the other side. He must be awful clever with his shears.'

Hamish gave a wry smile. 'I doubt if Dargie will be so happy about it. He has spent years training these hedges to be perfect and this boy has hacked into them –'

'No, Hamish, he hasn't hacked into them. He's done it carefully . . . it's a work of art.'

There were apples, pears, plums in the orchard, and even a small orangery built against a south-facing wall, and strawberries, raspberries, gooseberries and blackcurrants in the soft fruits cages. 'I bet Mrs Carnie makes hundreds of jars of jam with that lot,' Marianne remarked, adding without thinking, 'I used to love watching Mam boiling the berries, and she let me sup the scum before she poured the jam into jars. I liked rasps best, then strawberries, then the goosers, but I didna like the rhubarb, for she aye put ginger in, and I canna stand ginger.'

He let her ramble on, not wanting to let her know that he had asked Andrew where she came from originally, and was well aware that she had been in service to a banker's wife in Tipperton. It was the first time she had ever spoken about her first home, and she was using the words of her childhood. She was like a breath of fresh air to him, even when she did remember to talk and act like a lady. If only he could tell her how he really felt about her.

Next day, he took her along well-trodden paths through the woods outside the family's private grounds, and even where there were no paths. 'I suppose we should really call this a forest,' he smiled as they penetrated deeper into a closely packed mass of tall straight conifers, 'but I'd like you to get to know every bit of the estate and love it as much as I do.'

'I love it already,' Marianne sighed, picking up one of the cones that were lying about. 'I love the smell, I love to feel my feet sinking into the pine needles, it's like a thick carpet, isn't it? And it's so dark in here I can imagine wolves circling all round us, waiting to snarl out on us when they're hungry.'

'You wouldn't be scared of wolves?' he grinned.

She chuckled like the child she really was, for she wouldn't be eighteen for four months. 'I'd be terrified, but it's fun to pretend they're there, and I'd have you to protect me, wouldn't I? Any road, the sun sometimes flickers through between the leaves so I know it's a lovely summer's day outside.'

Her bridegroom took her hand. 'Are you happy, Marianne?'

She looked up into his now serious face. 'Of course I am!'

'You don't regret . . . ?'

'I don't regret anything. Mind you, I *am* a bit worried in case your father'll expect too much of me, but I'll do my best to run the house as good as your mother.'

He smiled at the grammatical error; she only made these slips when she was excited or worried, and she would probably grow out of them, yet he hoped she would always retain some of her naïvety and not turn out like all the other girls he knew.

'This really is a big forest,' she observed presently. 'Would you say we're halfway in yet?'

'I'd say we were more likely to be halfway out.' He tried

128

to keep a straight face but it was difficult when hers was so earnest.

'How do you know?' she asked in all innocence. 'What's the halfway mark when you're coming out?' The truth suddenly striking her, she pulled her hand out of his indignantly. 'Ach, you're making fun of me. Halfway in and halfway out's exactly the same.'

'I'm sorry, my dear. I shouldn't have teased you, but I couldn't resist it.'

When they emerged into the open air again, they carried on uphill for some time until they chanced upon a wide flat boulder. 'I think we have come far enough today,' Hamish remarked. 'I don't want to exhaust you, so perhaps we should take a seat here for a few minutes before we turn back.'

While they rested, he pointed out items of interest in the glen below. 'That's the doctor's house. Robert Mowatt is a good friend of mine, and Flora, his wife, is in her middle twenties, I'd say. She is a sensible girl and would be ideal if you needed someone to talk to.' His finger moved a little to the right. 'The manse is next to the church, there, but you can't see it for the trees. I don't know what to make of Duncan Peat. He's quite dour at times although he is a splendid preacher. But you must make up your own mind what you think about him.'

'He was very good about having the funeral and the wedding on the same day,' Marianne reminded him, 'and Miss Edith always used to say we should take people as we find them.'

'That is probably best, and I am sure you will like his wife. When Duncan is with her, Grace behaves as befits the wife of a minister of the Church of Scotland, but she can be great fun if he is not around, which is surprising in view of the fact that her father was also a minister. Robert and Flora are exactly the opposite. She is the quiet one –

Robert has more go – yet she and Grace Peat are very close.'

'What about the dominie and his wife?' Marianne could not see the school from where they were sitting, but she knew its approximate position.

'Will Wink is much older, a bit over fifty, and he often comes to talk things over with Father. They sit in the study, with the smoke from their pipes curling out into the hall, and discuss which pupils have the ability to carry on their education. They look on it purely from that angle, not whether or not the parents can afford the fees, because Father takes care of the financial side of it for them. He says that it would be a disgrace if any child could not take full advantage of the brains God blessed him with.'

'That's very kind of him.'

'Well, it usually works out to his benefit in the end. Once they get their degrees, he knows he can get a man he can trust if one of the professional posts here falls vacant. As for Agnes Wink, she keeps herself to herself.'

This surprised Marianne. 'Doesn't she mix with the doctor's wife and the minister's? That's what usually happens in small places – they all stick together.'

'Agnes's father, who sadly passed away last year, was a professor at Aberdeen University before he retired, so she considers herself better than either Flora or Grace – better than her own husband, if it comes to that, because his father was just one of my father's crofters.' Hamish shrugged his shoulders. 'Apparently, when she first came to Glendarril, she was most put out that my mother kept her distance, and for over twenty years she has resented being buried in this backwater of a glen, as she has been heard to describe it. However, if you want to be friendly with her, I shall not object.'

'I'll see how things work out,' Marianne smiled. Even having known Lady Glendarril for only a few weeks, she could visualize her reaction to Agnes Wink if she'd thought

130

the woman was trying to insinuate her way into the castle.

The bleating of sheep made them turn round, and coming towards them Marianne saw a man with a black and white collie keeping the sheep together. The dog hesitated, obviously wondering if he should take a closer look at the strangers, then decided to ignore them, but the man tipped his flat bonnet and called, 'A braw day, Maister!'

Hamish responded in the manner of the glen. 'It is that, Fenton. You've met my wife, of course? Marianne, this is Fenton, one of our shepherds.'

Overcome with shyness, the man whipped off his flat cap. 'I saw you at the . . .' he mumbled, stopping short of mentioning the funeral, and began again. 'I saw you at your wedding, and I'm verra pleased to meet you, m'Leddy.'

Embarrassed at being given the title, but unwilling to make things worse by putting him right, the only thing she could do was to hold out her hand. 'I'm very pleased to meet you, and all, Mr Fenton.'

This served to panic him altogether. His fingers hovered briefly over hers, then he gave a sharp nod and turned, sprinting away from them to catch up with those with whom he felt most comfortable, his dog and his sheep.

'Did I do something wrong, Hamish?' she asked anxiously. 'Should I have told him . . . ? I shouldn't have let him call me m'Lady, should I?'

Her husband smiled patiently. 'What do you want them to call you? Mrs Bruce-Lyall is quite a mouthful, and they want you to be their Lady, even if I'm not the Lord . . . the laird, as they say. There is no Lady Glendarril now . . . Let them call you Lady Marianne if they want to.'

'He was shocked at me for wanting to shake hands with him, though. Did your mother never . . . ?'

'My mother was a stickler for protocol and she considered that our workers and their wives were on this earth for the sole purpose of serving her. She would have died rather than shake hands with any of them.' He paused, realizing the irony of what he had said, then went on, 'They respected her and held her in awe, but I believe we should not set ourselves above them, for we are all the same in the eyes of God. I do think, however, that we will have to be careful not to let them be too familiar with us, Marianne. Not only would they lose their awe of us, we would lose their respect as well. We shall have to walk a very thin line.'

She gave him a nodding smile as if she understood, yet she had not quite grasped his meaning. It was going to be difficult to know the difference between being friendly and being too familiar.

On one of their morning rambles, they came across a small hut in the depths of a dense mass of trees. Marianne was intrigued by its position, almost hidden from view. 'Would this be where the charcoal burners live? I've read about them in history books.'

Hamish gave a gurgling laugh. 'As far as I am aware, there never were any charcoal burners here. This is a still. For distilling whisky,' he explained, seeing her puzzlement. 'My grandfather used to tell us stories about the tricks his workers got up to to save the excisemen from finding their stock of illicit whisky. He always said his men were doing no wrong, for they were not making the spirits to sell, only for their own use – and for his, he always laughed – so they should not have to pay tax or duty on it. It hasn't been used for years.'

'It would be against the law these days, wouldn't it?'

Hamish guffawed this time. 'It was against the law in the old days, too. If they had been found out, the men could have been hanged, or at least dispatched to Botany Bay for ever.'

'Yes, the penal colony,' she agreed. 'I've read about that, too.'

The days passed agreeably, and Marianne found herself if not exactly happy, at least settled.

In spite of his father's professed wish for the next heir to be born before he died, Hamish had still not attempted to make a son, but Marianne was quite content with the way her life was shaping, and she was certainly getting to know Hamish better, his likes and his dislikes.

By the end of that first week, her husband had introduced her to most of the folk in the glen, smilingly accepting the title they bestowed on her. It was as if they had discussed it together and decided to so honour her, although they were bound to know she wasn't a 'Lady' in the true sense. Carnie would have told them how little she'd had when she arrived here, or if not Carnie – Marianne had the feeling that he'd be fiercely loyal to the Bruce-Lyall family – certainly the railway employee at the station. They had probably tumbled to the fact that she didn't speak like gentry and maybe that was why they were so warm towards her. She was one of them.

What pleased her most, was when Hamish began to confide in her about how he would like the mill to be run. 'Father's so old-fashioned he can't see that we need to change things. Our spinning machines and looms must have been there since machinery was invented, and the new models are faster and easier to work, so they would pay for themselves in no time. But he won't listen. "What's the point of getting rid of things that still work perfectly well?" That's his attitude. And I keep telling him we should enlarge the buildings so that we can increase our output, but he can't see that either.'

'Maybe he feels you don't have enough people to cope with the extra work,' Marianne ventured, a little timidly because she knew nothing of the workings of a woollen mill.

'We could build more houses and employ more workers. He is well known all over Scotland for being a fair man, a good master paying decent wages, not like some owners, so there would be dozens of men wanting to be taken on.

And their women would help the shepherds' wives with the hand-knitted garments. Plus, if I had my way, I'd install running water in every cottage – not that Father ignores the upkeep of the houses. All the workers, and even the crofters, are encouraged to let the factor know if anything needs to be repaired, but they need to have some sanitation. It can't be very nice not to have an inside WC, and in some cases not even one outside.'

Having been brought up in an old cottage in the last category, Marianne knew that those who were accustomed to it thought nothing of having a dry lavatory, and her thoughts took a different turn. 'You know, Hamish, it might be a good idea to employ somebody to look after the very young children so women who wanted to earn some extra money could work in the mill.'

Hamish shook his head. 'My father would never countenance that.' His sigh was deep and long. 'Anyway, Marianne, I was just being silly, building castles in the air . . .'

'Not castles,' she laughed. 'Just houses to go with the castle.'

He ignored her attempt to cheer him. 'It's no use. He will never agree to that, either, nor any of the other things I want to do.'

The assurance which sprang to her mind that he would be able to do what he liked when *he* was laird remained unsaid, but it hung in the air between them for the rest of that day.

Their 'honeymoon' over, it was time for Hamish to start work again, and once he and his father left for the mill, Marianne thought she had better get to know the layout of the castle as her father-in-law had said, looking at things in more detail. She had been so scared of upsetting Lady Glendarril that she hadn't dared to take more than a cursory glance at any room until now. She decided to start with the ground floor, and went into the entrance hall, but she just had time to notice the row of hooks above the oak chest opposite the front door when the housekeeper came out of the dining room. Miss Glover, whom the new mistress found quite intimidating, was a wraithlike figure dressed entirely in black. She seemed to glide as if she were on casters, silent and unsmiling, terrifyingly forbidding.

'The hooks are for hanging overcoats, ma'am,' she said, her thin mouth forming each word in a way that made her prominent teeth even more prominent. She bent over and lifted the lid of the chest. 'Overshoes and boots are kept in here ... and the guns, of course, in the grouse season.'

'I see, thank you.' Marianne guessed that the housekeeper had been instructed to show her round and explain things to her, and even if she would have preferred to look at things on her own, it wouldn't be policy to antagonize the woman. 'The kist's the same wood as the door, isn't it?' she asked, for the sake of something to say.

'The *chest* is oak, ma'am, the same as the door ... which is restricted to his Lordship, his family and their guests,' she added, in a hushed tone, as if she were speaking about God and His angels.

Marianne determined not to be needled, though the woman evidently didn't include her new mistress in the hallowed company by the tone of her voice. 'The white painted walls give a nice welcome to guests, and the sanded floor's so highly polished ...'

'The floor has never been sanded, ma'am.' There was a ring of pride in what she was saying now. 'It was recorded by his Lordship's grandfather that it had been scraped with broken glass until it took on this fine sheen. Do you see how it reflects the colours from the windows on the staircases, ma'am?'

And so it went on. The secrets of the huge sideboard in the dining room – it took up the whole of one wall – were laid bare to Marianne; the delicate bone-china dinner and tea services and where they had come from; the beautiful silver cutlery in one of the drawers, some with the family crest on the handles, some monogrammed with just a fancy letter L, which, Miss Glover revealed, meant that they had been in the Lyall family even before Marjorie Bruce married into it.

'That was about the middle of the eighteenth century, and she was a direct descendant of King Robert the Bruce, and was named after his daughter, which is why the king of the time granted the family the right to be known as Bruce-Lyall, and the Lord Lyon, King of Arms, approved a new crest.'

Another drawer held silver serving utensils, and a third contained starched damask napkins with the initials B and L embroidered in white to match the tablecloths in the fourth drawer.

The housekeeper reeled off details of the furniture next, the oval table and ten high-backed chairs with tapestry seats, and the carvers to match, one at either end. 'It took three generations of Bruce-Lyall women to finish all the stitching,' she divulged.

'They're absolutely wonderful, though,' Marianne murmured, hoping that she wouldn't be expected to fill her spare time in the same way. Surprisingly, considering how long she had lived with the Rennie sisters, she hated sewing and had never been any good at it.

'As you can see, ma'am,' Miss Glover continued, 'there are numerous small tables, all darkest mahogany like the rest of the furniture in here, for trays to be set down on, or platters of vegetables to be rested on if the dining table is full.'

While the housekeeper gave details of the portraits on the walls, Marianne, having already studied them while having meals here when Lady Glendarril was alive, turned her attention to the Indian carpet square on the floor. It was almost threadbare in places, the pattern scarcely showing. That would be the first entry she would make in the notebook she was intending to keep, she thought – 'See about new dining room carpet.'

The business room, as Miss Glover said it was originally called, was used by Lord Glendarril as a study. To the right of and very close to the fireplace stood a beautiful desk which had belonged to his father, who had been inclined to feel the cold, and his own desk sat in front of the window to afford him more light. Near the door was a desk with four seats at it, which Miss Glover said was the 'rent' desk, where the tenant farmers came once a year to pay their ten-shilling rents to the factor. The floor here was of pine, deeper in colour than usual because of years, maybe centuries, of beeswax polish applied by perspiring young girls, and had a scattering of small rugs to protect it in the most used areas.

The library fascinated Marianne, two of its walls completely lined with shelves from floor to ceiling, some filled with volumes covered in red leather, some with dark blue covers, some linen covers, all of which looked as if they had seldom, if ever, been read, though not one speck of dust could be seen anywhere. On the shelves on the other two walls, on either side of the fireplace and bay window, were books which had obviously been well-leafed – novels, biographies of the famous and not-so-famous, autobiographies, children's and adults' classics. She had never seen so many books and it dawned on her that here was a wealth of reading that would help her improve her still lamentably poor vocabulary – if she got any time to read, that was. She wasn't too keen on the plaster – or alabaster or whatever – busts, which were placed haphazardly anywhere there was room for them.

'The bronzes are celebrated composers,' her guide supplied, seeing her looking at them, 'and the ivories are famous authors.'

Then they entered the Blue Room, most used of any of the public rooms, where the furnishing fabrics were all in some shade of blue, not really to Marianne's taste because it made the room look cold. The chairs here were upholstered in a rough material which felt like hessian but the housekeeper said was hopsack made in the mill – 'A not altogether successful experiment,' she added. Noting the fading and the neat, but still noticeable, patches over what must be worn parts, Marianne could only agree with this, and make re-covering the chairs another of the early jobs to be done. As they left the room, Miss Glover drew her attention to three miniatures on the wall above a whatnot.

'Lady Glendarril's mother, grandmother and great-grandmother,' she observed, pointing to each one in turn. 'His Lordship did not like them and wanted to take them down, but she held out against him. I am surprised, though, that he has not removed them by this time.'

Marianne had guessed that they were ancestors of Lady Glendarril; they all had the same sour faces and flared nostrils, as if somebody was holding a lump of dog's dirt under them, and if her father-in-law didn't take them down soon, Marianne would do it for him. Luckily, she kept her thoughts to herself. Whatever she did when she started making the alterations she wanted, she was bound to upset somebody, so this was another fine line she'd have to walk.

There was also a Red Room – very overpowering with huge paintings of fire-breathing dragons and several luridly coloured urns, so tall that full-grown men could hide in them. Next to that, and probably because there had been too many items to fit into the Red Room, was a Chinese room with disgustingly fat buddhas brooding in every corner, and next to that again, an Indian room with the fire irons set into elephants' feet at the side of the black marble fireplace, and tiger skin rugs on the floor.

All these foreign artefacts, the housekeeper explained with pride, had been brought home by previous generations of Lyalls and Bruce-Lyalls after visits to the east, and

Marianne resolved to do something about these rooms at some time in the future.

Throughout this guided tour, conducted at almost break-neck speed and interspersed constantly by the stressed 'ma'am', she had been genuine in the interest she showed, and grateful for the information the housekeeper had imparted, but at long last, to her great relief, the woman said, 'I hope you don't mind . . . Mrs Hamish, but I shall have to leave you now. There are things I should be attending to.'

The change of title told Marianne that the woman was thawing, was accepting her, thank goodness. 'Oh, I'm sorry, Miss Glover. You shouldn't have wasted so much of your time with me.'

'Not entirely wasted, I hope?'

What was surely a hint of laughter appeared in the housekeeper's eyes, and Marianne suspected that she was not so forbidding as she would like to have people believe. 'Definitely not wasted,' she smiled. 'You've learned me . . .' Remembering Andrew's teaching, she stopped to correct herself. 'I've learned an awful lot. It would've taken me years to find out the things you've told me. Thank you very much, Miss Glover. I really enjoyed it.'

'So did I, Mrs Hamish. Now you'll manage to look round upstairs by yourself? Not that there's much to see, mostly bedrooms.'

In Marianne's next letter to the Rennies, she told them that the bedrooms, both in the east and west wings, were reasonably well appointed. 'I just had a quick look in most of them whether they were being used or not,' she wrote, 'but I went through the cupboards in the passages thoroughly, so I would know where everything is, and I made a note of anything that needed mending or replacing. My notebook is full already, but I can leave most things for a few years. I do not want them to resent me as a new broom sweeping clean.'

It was Miss Emily who observed, 'Shouldn't she think of converting one of the rooms into a nursery?'

Miss Edith gave a small frown. 'I would have thought there would be a nursery there already. She must have recognized it, because in these large houses there are usually bars across the nursery windows to prevent any child falling out.'

Miss Esther smiled mischievously. 'Maybe Marianne thought the bars were to stop the Nanny's men friends from getting in.'

A month after she first took over (or gave the appearance of taking over) the supervising of the household, Marianne knew that she was going to enjoy being mistress of the castle.

'I must have been born to be a lady,' she said to Hamish one night when Lord Glendarril had gone to bed. 'All the servants, even the bootboy and the grooms and gardeners, even the Carnies, saluted or curtsied when I spoke to them, and I loved it.'

'That's what they are meant to do,' her husband smiled.

She screwed up her nose. 'It gets a wee bit embarrassing after a while, though. Could I make it a rule that they just do it the first time they see me every day, and not any other times?'

After considering for a moment, Hamish shook his head. 'Not yet, I think. Give them time to get accustomed to their mistress being so young ... and so beautiful.' As if regretting this compliment, he went on hastily, 'Get them used to doing what you tell them, but you must not order them about like slaves. They will respond much better to kindness and consideration – and you will have to earn their respect before you can relax any of the rules.'

'I can understand that, but I feel awkward with Mrs Carnie; she's old enough to be my granny.'

Grinning at this, Hamish stood up. 'It is time all good

people were in bed.' He held his hand out to help her out of her seat. 'Um . . . Marianne, I have not asked before, I was giving you time to settle to your new responsibilities, but . . . will you allow me to come to your room tonight, or are you too tired?'

She could feel her face grow as scarlet as his was. She had often wondered when he would make her carry out this part of their bargain, but surely he didn't need to ask? She was his wife, after all. 'I'm not tired,' she whispered.

Since the day she had agreed to become his wife, she had worried about how she would cope when this moment arrived, yet she felt a little put out when he said, as they went upstairs, 'I'll undress in my room to give you time to . . . get into bed.'

It was a marriage of convenience, she reminded herself, but why did he have to be so . . . distant, about this? Nevertheless, she hastily cast off her clothes and took a clean nightdress out of a drawer. She had been wearing those included in the trousseau bought for her by Lady Glendarril in Edinburgh, but tonight was special, so she carefully chose one of the shifts made and embroidered by Miss Esther, no doubt with the creation of the new generation of Bruce-Lyalls in mind. Knowing that she was wrapped in the love of her beloved friend, Marianne thought, she would, hopefully, be more relaxed and . . . receptive. It should bring her luck!

She had just got into bed when the door opened and she looked up apprehensively, watching Hamish enter and take off his long silk robe. He folded it neatly and draped it over a chair before sitting down beside her. 'Do you normally go to bed with your hair pinned up?' he asked, smiling.

Even recognizing a hint of humour in his eyes, she felt flustered. 'No, I usually . . . my mother used to tell me never to forget to give my hair a hundred strokes with my brush every night, but I thought . . . I didn't have time.'

'Will you allow me to do it for you . . . please?' He rose

to fetch a tortoiseshell-backed hairbrush from the dressing table, part of the set which had also been bought for her by his mother, and came back to where she was feverishly removing all her hairpins in readiness.

Neither of them said a word until the required number of strokes had been completed, then Hamish let his hand run lightly down her shimmering coppery tresses. 'You have such beautiful hair, it seems a pity to pin it up.'

She turned to face him now, her face pink with embarrassed pleasure at the compliment. 'Only young girls wear their hair down,' she explained seriously.

'It's a crime to hide it away, especially when it suits you so well like this.' Her deepening colour made him smile. 'But you are right, of course. As lady of the castle, it is only fitting that you look dignified in front of others.'

She gave a nervous giggle. 'Dignified? Me? I don't think I'll ever manage to look dignified, but I'm willing to do my best.'

'Given time, my dear Marianne, you will look every bit as dignified as the highest ladies in the land, although I wish that you could . . .'

'That I could what?' she wanted to know.

'That you could remain as sweet and fresh as you are at this moment.' He turned away abruptly to replace the hairbrush in its designated place, and when he came back, it was to the other side of the bed, where he slipped under the bedcovers beside her.

'You are sure about this?' he asked anxiously.

Nodding, she wished that he would get on with it. This shillyshallying was worse than if he just jumped on her. She knew that was what he was going to do eventually, and it wasn't against her will. His first tender kisses quickly became more urgent, his searching hands more insistent, until her body involuntarily rose to welcome him in.

She had long been dreading it, but it was a wonderful, marvellous, exquisite experience which left her puzzling over why some married women hated it, or so she had heard her mother's friends saying when they thought she couldn't hear. And Hamish had seemed to enjoy it, too, for he had kept kissing her and whispering her name, and . . . Oh, dear God, if this was what it took to make a baby, she wanted to have dozens.

He was sleeping now like a child himself, sleeping as though he was exhausted, and maybe he was. Looking at him, she felt a surge of fondness for him. He was a dear man – he'd been really gentle with her, guiding her over the initial pain so that she knew he hadn't meant to hurt her. It had only been for a few seconds anyway, and he had assured her she would never have any more pain during intercourse. That was the word he'd used. He hadn't said 'making love'. He had never mentioned love, but she hadn't expected him to. He didn't love her, like she didn't love him, though she had the feeling it might be easy for her to change her mind.

When Thomson went in the next morning with a cup of tea for her mistress, Hamish had returned to his own room so that she knew nothing of what had gone on the night before. However, when the little chamber maid went up to make the bed after breakfast, she came charging back brandishing a blood-stained sheet. 'He'd been wi' her last nicht! Look at this!'

Miss Glover frowned, but a scowling Mrs Carnie snatched the bed linen out of the girl's hands. 'It's no' decent to let folk see that, Kitty Bain!' she stormed. 'An' it's nobody's business but theirs, so keep your tongue atween your teeth, an' that goes for the rest o' you, an' all,' she added, letting her eyes take in every last one of the trembling girls, who darted off to carry out their assigned duties.

The cook and the housekeeper sat down one on each side of the big range, looking at each other with knowing smiles. 'He took his time about it, though,' Mrs Carnie said grudgingly.

Marianne's plans for refurbishing certain rooms were turned down by Hector. 'I know you mean well,' he said apologetically, having summoned her to his study one morning, 'but I would rather not have the upheaval, and things are better left as they are. I do not take well to change, especially when it would leave me with hardly any memories of my dear Clarice.'

She was contrite. 'Oh, I'm sorry, I didn't think. I wasn't trying to get rid of the things your wife chose, I was only –'

'I know, my dear,' he soothed. 'But bear with an old man. When I'm gone, you and Hamish can do what you like.'

'But you're not old!' she burst out. In the mornings it was easy to forget how tired he often was in the evening, and how bad his colour could be. 'You'll be here for years and years yet, and we'll be walking on bare floorboards if you don't let me get a new carpet for the dining room soon.'

'My grandfather – or maybe it was my great-grandfather – took that carpet home from Persia.'

She had thought it was Indian, but what did it matter? 'Please, Father?' She had been invited to address him as Hamish did and had been highly complimented by this privilege.

He succumbed to the pleading in her lovely young eyes. 'All right. The mill has no dealings with Persia, I'm afraid, but I have an old friend who captains a merchant ship and trades with some eastern countries, so I shall ask him to get an oriental carpet for me.'

'Thank you, Father!' Marianne had to force the enthusiasm into her voice, because she still was not being allowed to choose. Still, whatever the sea captain took back was bound to be better than the carpet in the dining room at present. But she still had another favour to ask. 'What about the pump for the bathroom? Did you look at the information I sent away for? It would save the poor maids having to hump up pails and pails of water.'

'It is a recognized part of their duties,' he frowned.

The twinkle in his eyes, however, told her that he was testing her, so she went on hopefully, 'We could take a bath at any time, not just when somebody's free to fill it. My mother used to say, "Cleanliness is next to godliness," even when she was bent near double filling the old tin bath we had to use.'

Her father-in-law eyed her quizzically. 'That's the first time I have ever heard you speak of your mother. What happened? Did you quarrel with her or . . . ?'

'She died . . . and when my father married again, the woman didn't like me. That's why I ran away.'

Hector could see by the set of her mouth that she did not want to talk about it. 'I am glad you are a strong person, Marianne . . . you know why. And now I have got on that subject, may I ask . . . how are you finding my son?'

It was an odd way of asking, but she knew what he meant. 'I hope it won't be long till I have good news for you.'

'I am pleased to hear it. Tell Hamish not to leave it too long.' Hector was beaming as she left his study.

She was positive that Hector was wondering if they were trying at all, and she herself couldn't understand why she hadn't conceived, because their couplings seemed to satisfy Hamish, though she did wish that he would do it more often and satisfy her. With time on her hands she began to brood about not yet being pregnant.

Despite Marianne's notebook of lists and the suggestions she had dared to voice, Miss Glover had gradually taken over the entire management of the household again. It was done in such a way that it was some weeks before Marianne noticed what was happening, and she had to admit that the woman was more competent than she was. The house-keeper had had years of experience, of course, Marianne told herself, guilty at the relief she felt.

With more time to fill, she asked her husband one morn-ing if he would show her round the mill.

Hamish smiled indulgently. 'There's not really much to see, but if that is what you want ... Give me time to arrange for someone to explain things ... get one of the stable lads to take you down in the trap in about an hour.'

Not knowing what to expect, Marianne was quite impressed by what she saw, made all the more interesting when Mr Gillies, one of the overseers, allowed various workers to tell her what he or she was doing. One of the women at the carding machines told her that the process of teasing the fleece out into yarn had all been done by hand when she was a girl. 'Some of the old women still do it at home,' she smiled. 'My ma thinks a machine cannae dae it as good as her.'

'What do *you* think?' Marianne asked.

The woman shot a glance at the man, then said, some-what defiantly, 'I'd say she was right, but the machines are a lot quicker.'

'Bella Simms is a widow, m'Lady,' Mr Gillies told her. 'His Lordship doesna employ a lot o' women, just them wi' no young bairnies.'

'But is the men's wages enough to keep a family?'

'The wages here are the best in the country, m'Lady, and the shepherds' wives – and any of the other wives that need to – get paid well for the hand-knitting they do.'

'So it's not just cloth, you make, then?'

'Mercy, no! We've got tailors that make the different materials into men's coats and suits ...' – and here the man's pride in his workplace made him forget his careful mode of speech – '... and we sell them a' ower the country. The best o' stuff, mind – nane o' your cheap dirt.'

Marianne looked forward to further amusement when he shepherded her into the next large section, but he was thinking in his best English again. 'This is where the spinners spin the wool into yarn or thread.'

All the machines amazed her, but she was absolutely fascinated by the looms, walking round and asking questions of the men who were deftly making sure that the shuttles were going where they should. She learned from one that the threads going one way were called the warp, and those going the other way were called the weft, and the machines had to be set up to make the shuttle pick up or miss however many threads were needed for that particular cloth.

She discovered also, although she should have realized, that tartan was the most complicated to set up, with the different colours, the different checks, and she couldn't take her eyes off the patterns as they gradually took shape. The foot pedal was only used when the shuttle was in the right position, but the men worked so quickly that there was hardly any delay between each step.

She found that there were several grades of flannel, fine weave, medium and coarse, and the same with the tweeds. She could have remained there all day, but Mr Gillies was anxious to return to his proper duties.

Going more quickly through the place where the wool was spun, put into skeins then dyed, and the smaller room where two men were cutting out at long tables and another two were putting pieces together with meticulous stitching, they came to the huge warehouse where all the finished items, bales of material, hand-made suits, and garments knitted by the shepherds' wives, were stored in readiness for scrutiny by the buyers who came before each new season began.

'We don't deal with the general public,' Mr Gillies told her, 'just retailers, and the orders keep flooding in.' She was glad to hear that. The family's income would be ensured for the future.

He left her at the office, where Hector asked her, 'What d'you think of my domain, then?'

'It's ... it's ... I can't think of the right word. Marvellous, clever, everything's going so well ...'

'So it should be at the wages I pay, and the number of overseers I employ.' His puckish grin belied the menace of his words.

Hamish took her back to the main entrance, saying as they went down the wooden stairs, 'No more visits, Marianne. Father perhaps gave you the impression that he didn't mind, but he does not like any intrusion into his business.'

'I wasn't intruding,' she protested. 'I just wanted to see the inside of the mill, and now I've seen it, I don't need to come again.'

'I'm sorry if I offended you, my dear, but it's best that you know where you stand.'

The stable lad, sitting in the trap waiting for her, jumped down when he saw her coming, but Hamish himself handed her up, which made her feel less upset at him, and by the time she arrived back at the castle, she knew he'd been right to warn her, although she'd had no intention of interfering in the workings of the mill, anyway.

Yet her visit had taught her one fundamental thing. Even if the handful of women workers had been politely forthcoming when she spoke to them, none of them could ever be her friend. The chasm between workers and employers, even employers' wives, was too wide to be bridged. But she missed female company. She missed the Rennies, missed having someone she could talk to, tell her thoughts to, ask advice from. Even if she had lived, Lady Glendarril wouldn't have come anywhere near to filling the bill. The only women – ladies – in the glen who might let her get to know them better would be the wives of the doctor, the minister and the dominie, preferably the first two, after what Hamish had told her, and because they were nearer her own age.

With the intention, therefore, of trying to establish some

sort of relationship with at least one of the other two, Marianne set off the following afternoon to call at the manse. The minister's wife had seemed a friendly person when they spoke at the wedding, even telling her not worry what anyone said about them being married immediately after Lady Glendarril's funeral. She obviously understood how the poor young bride was feeling.

Mrs Peat looked a little flustered when she opened the door – Marianne had forgotten that most ministers' stipends didn't run to employing a maid – so she said apologetically, 'I'm sorry if I've come at an inconvenient time.'

'No, no, come in, please. It's just that I wasn't expecting . . .' She led the way into a cosy room where the doctor's wife jumped up from where she was sitting. 'Lady Marianne's come to call, Flora,' she said brightly, as the other woman's mouth dropped open in surprise.

Not altogether sure if she was doing the right thing, Marianne corrected her. 'I'm not really the Lady, you know, so why don't you just call me by my given name?'

Mrs Peat's hesitation was infinitesimal. 'It seems a bit familiar, but if that's what you want, I'm Grace and this is Flora, the doctor's wife.'

They all shook hands before they sat down.

The conversation was a little stiff at first, both Marianne and Flora leaving most of the talking to Grace, who prattled on gaily about anything that came into her head, but at last, Marianne told them of her visit to the mill and how her father-in-law hadn't been too pleased about it, which began a discussion on how much his family had done for the glen over the years. 'Lord Glendarril put both Duncan and Robert through university,' Grace confided. 'They were at school together, the glen school, and the dominie told the laird it was a great pity that two such clever lads couldn't make use of their brains.'

Flora Mowatt interrupted here. 'It started long before Duncan and Robert, though. It was the present Lord

Glendarril's father, or maybe his grandfather, who first paid for a local boy's education.'

This led to a discussion on the merits or otherwise of helping a boy from a poor family to get on in the world. 'Duncan says if he hadn't been obligated to his Lordship,' Grace said, at one point, 'he might have been called to a big church in one of the cities, instead of mouldering away here, but, to be quite honest, he hasn't the personality to be in charge of a large congregation.' She looked from one to the other of her companions with a wry grimace. 'You probably think I'm not very loyal to my husband, but he gets on my nerves sometimes, being so bumptious. I often wish he was more like Robert.'

Flora shrugged. 'Robert can be annoying at times, too. He's always getting on at me for not mixing with the other women, helping them out, making sure they're not going short of anything, but I tell him that's not our problem. It's not that I'm not sympathetic, it's just ... well, I've always been slow at speaking to people I don't know very well.'

'That's why you never get to know them,' Grace said triumphantly. 'It takes a bit of courage to take the first step. Don't you agree, Marianne?'

'I suppose it does,' Marianne said cautiously, not wanting to offend either of them.

'But you did it today,' Grace reminded her. 'You had the courage to call without going through all the rigmarole of leaving a card first.'

Feeling quite at home with them now, Marianne laughed at this. 'I didn't leave a card first because I didn't know that was expected. I wasn't brought up to that kind of thing, you see, but the difference between Flora and me is that she's shy and I'm not. Neither are you, Grace, so it's easy for us to speak.'

When, in about fifteen minutes, Flora stood up to leave, Marianne also jumped to her feet. 'Oh, my goodness, look at the time! Have I overstayed my welcome?'

'You certainly haven't,' declared Grace. 'We've thoroughly enjoyed your company.'

The doctor's wife nodded vehemently. 'Yes, indeed, and Grace and I usually take it turn about once a week, so you must come to our house next Tuesday.'

And so began a new cycle, with Marianne offering to be hostess at the castle every third week.

When they learned of this arrangement, neither Miss Glover nor Mrs Carnie was happy with it. 'Lady Glendarril never asked any of them to tea,' the cook grumbled.

'There was a garden party every summer, of course,' the housekeeper recalled, a little sadly. 'There were marquees set up for the teas, and a beer tent for the men, but nobody was ever allowed inside the castle.'

'Well, I'm not her Ladyship,' Marianne said hotly, 'and if I want to make friends and invite them for afternoon tea, I'll do it!'

Guessing that Hector, too, would not be at all pleased, nor Hamish, she waited somewhat apprehensively for their reaction when she told them and was taken aback when they looked at each other and burst out laughing.

'You said she would take her own way if she wanted anything,' her father-in-law chuckled, 'and I admire her for it.' He wagged his finger at her. 'Just watch, though, my lass. It may not turn out so easy for you every time, but I can see no harm in giving you your head over this.'

Bolstered by her success, Marianne said, 'And I think I'll start going round the cottages to see if any of the wives need anything, something repaired or replaced –' She broke off, noticing that both men were frowning, and unable to say anything to his father, she vented her annoyance at her husband. 'I don't know why you look so disapproving, Hamish. There could be things they don't like to ask the factor to have done.'

Getting no reply, she stood up and gave it one final shot.

'Well, I'm going up to bed. Are you coming to me tonight, or are you waiting another week?'

She practically ran out, but not before she had seen Hamish's face turn dead white, and once in her room she flung herself on the bed. She shouldn't have shamed him like that in front of his father. He didn't deserve it! But why was he always so reluctant when she knew he enjoyed the matings as much as she did? She knew that because . . . well, because of how he did what he did when he did it. Besides, a girl could tell things like that.

She gave a guilty start when there was a knock at her door a few minutes later and Hamish walked in, but before he could start the telling off she was sure he had come to give her, she said defensively, 'I'm sorry, but I couldn't help saying it.' She came to an abrupt halt, for there was not even the slightest sign of anger on his face when he sat down on the edge of her bed.

'There is no need for you to feel sorry – you were right to let me know how you feel, but, as a matter of fact, I *have* been considering asking you if . . . I may . . . share your bed more often, because . . .'

'Because your father told you to hurry up and make a grandson for him?'

'He did, actually, but I had been intending to ask tonight in any case. However, I do not wish to force myself on you if you would rather –'

'You've the right to, as a husband,' she pointed out, not quite so bitterly.

'Ah, yes, in the eyes of the law, but ours was merely a business arrangement, was it not? Still, I had better put more effort into it –' He broke off, his mouth turning up and a smile making his serious face so much more attractive, she thought. He gave an embarrassed cough. 'My turn of phrase was inappropriate, I'm afraid, but I am sure you know what I meant. I am more than willing to become a nightly visitor as long as you don't mind. I will, of course, depend on you to let me know when ... it is not convenient.'

It took her a little time to understand what he meant by that, then flushing, she whispered, 'I don't mind.'

His eyes now held something she couldn't define. 'Thank you, my dear, and I promise that I will not force my attentions on you once I know ... well, you know what.' He stood up and, not looking at her again, mumbled, 'I shall not be long. I am just going to undress.'

Left alone, she found her heart was doing all sorts of unusual acrobatics. She had had a vague suspicion for several weeks that she felt more towards him than she had done at first – maybe it wasn't love yet, but not very far from it – and judging by the way his eyes lingered tenderly on her at times, surely he was feeling the same. Was their marriage of convenience going to turn out a real love match after all?

Sadly for Marianne, however, Hamish made no mention of love that night or any of the nights thereafter, although his 'efforts', as he had called them, were really quite loving, and sometimes, at the height of his passion, he kissed her like a lover should, and murmured her name and gripped her tightly as if he never wanted to let her go, but she would be much happier if only he could bring himself to tell her what she wanted to hear. And he made matters worse by going to his own room shortly afterwards.

Hector would probably not have been so pleased about his daughter-in-law's choice of friends if he had heard their conversation one Tuesday a few weeks later.

The ladies had been commenting on how strange it was that the wife of one of the shepherds had just had her first baby after ten years of marriage, while a weaver's wife had taken only nine months from her wedding to produce *her* first, when Marianne suddenly said, 'My father-in-law can't wait for me to give him a grandson.'

'What's stopping you, then?' laughed the minister's wife.

'Grace Peat!' exclaimed the horrified Flora. 'You shouldn't say things like that.'

Marianne shook her head. 'It's all right, I don't mind. Nothing's stopping me, Grace, except my body. I must be like the shepherd's wife, because Hamish and I are trying but we've had no luck yet.'

'Duncan doesn't want any children,' Grace sighed, 'but he's got quite an appetite for . . .' She stopped, colouring slightly, then added, 'I'm on tenterhooks every month because he has a vile temper when he's angry.' She looked pointedly at Flora now, as though demanding that she, too, should lay bare the intimate side of her marriage, and at last, her face a deep crimson, the doctor's wife said, 'Robert and I desperately want a baby, too, and I've been pregnant twice, but I lost them both at three months.'

'I'm sorry,' Marianne murmured, but Grace said accusingly, 'You never told me that, you secretive thing. But you shouldn't be depressed about it. Keep trying. If Robert's managed it twice, he'll manage again.'

'Do you really think so?' Flora's expression had brightened. 'He says the same, that two miscarriages don't mean that I'll never carry to full time, but I thought he was only trying to stop me losing hope.'

'He's the doctor, for goodness' sake,' Grace said firmly, 'so he should know. You and Marianne will have to keep trying, and if I can, I'll stop the douching Duncan insists on to prevent me conceiving. Wouldn't it be fun if we all landed in the family way together?'

Her candour about so delicate a subject, and the very nature of their discussion, forged a firm bond between them, which pleased three husbands and at least one father-in-law, who would all have been absolutely appalled had they known the reason behind the closeness.

Chapter Ten

It was August of the following year before Marianne realized what had happened, by which time she had missed
twice, and after she gave Hamish her good news, he completely stopped coming to her room at nights. But there
was no doubt that he was proud of himself, strutting about
like a cock on a muck midden, with a new spring to his
step, and he told his father straight away, though she'd
asked him not to say anything yet. She had also been quite
put out that Hector had taken it on himself to announce
it to all and sundry, for she'd have preferred her condition
to be kept secret until it could be hidden no longer.

News of her pregnancy was the talking point in every
house in the glen within a day of her telling her husband,
mainly because Mima Rattray, shopkeeper and postmistress, had instant access to the ears of all the womenfolk.
'Of course, I never believed yon story that went round about
The Master,' she would say after imparting the exciting
information. 'There was never nothing peculiar about him.'

One of her customers did dare to justify her own cred-
ulity of the rumour. 'Well, right enough, there musta been
some mistake there, but you canna deny it was queer he
never looked at ony o' the lassies here.'

'But, Lizzie, dinna forget, he's gentry,' Mima pointed
out, thus explaining everything, but adding also, 'He'd just
been waiting to find the right wife and what's wrong wi'
that, tell me?'

Lizzie being suitably cowed, one of the other women in
the shop said, 'Aye, there's something to be said for the
groom bein' a virgin as weel as the bride.'

This led to a debate on the benefits or otherwise of such a combination, and ended in such a riot of hilarity that Mima had to put her foot down firmly to keep them in order.

Because of the shame they felt at jumping to their wrong conclusions before, the glen folk were extravagant with their congratulation to the laird and the parents-to-be. Marianne responded to their good wishes with shy embarrassment, Hamish accepted them with a smiling murmur of thanks, but Hector acted as if he alone had worked the miracle. He even began carrying a silver flask of whisky with him wherever he went, so that those he met could drink to the fertilization.

Robert Mowatt having passed on the good news in sympathetic confidence to his wife, Flora confidentially told Grace Peat, and so they actually knew before Marianne told them herself, which gave them time to temper their envy. Nevertheless, she could discern more than a touch of wistfulness in each pair of eyes when they affirmed their rapturous joy at her good fortune. 'Your turns are bound to come,' she told them, gently, 'so don't give up.'

Flora grimaced. 'Robert says we should wait a full year from the time I lost the second one, to give my body time to recover. But I don't know . . .'

'At least he's planning for you to conceive again,' Grace sensibly pointed out. 'D'you know what Duncan said when he heard Marianne was expecting? "Thank God it is not you!" What a thing for a man of his calling to say. It's not up to God to stop His ministers putting a bun in their wives' oven.' She looked pensive for a moment, then gave a little giggle. 'There's such a lot of begetting in the Bible, it seems to me He encourages conception, immaculate or otherwise.'

The shocked Flora now burst out, 'I don't know how you can sit there and take God's name in vain like that, and you married to a man of the Church.'

'Not only am I married to one,' Grace nodded, winking mischievously at Marianne who was hard-pressed to keep a straight face, 'I am also the daughter of one – my father was minister of quite a large parish in the wilds of Aberdeenshire – but what I'm saying is, it might be worth my while to pray a lot more, don't you think? To get in His good books, if you see what I mean.'

Rather belatedly, it dawned on the doctor's wife that her friend was joking. 'Grace Peat, I never know when to take you seriously.'

Grace grinned at her. 'You should know me by this time.'

She stood up to fetch the tray she had made ready earlier, and when she went out, Flora leaned across and whispered, 'There's something not quite right about Duncan, I always think. Grace told me once that when he's in one of his black moods, she's scared to speak to him.'

It was Marianne's turn to gasp in shock. 'She's actually *scared* of him?'

'Oh, don't ever tell anybody I said that,' Flora pleaded, 'but I've seen bruises on her arms when she's wearing short sleeves and I'm sure he hits her. She's never admitted it, mind. Says she banged into a door, or knocked against something, but –' She jumped back at the sound of footsteps coming along the little passageway between the sitting room and the kitchen, shaking her head in warning.

Marianne couldn't put it out of her head, and later, on her way home, she tried to remember if she had ever seen bruises on Grace's arms but she didn't think she had. Going inside, she came to the conclusion that Flora had been imagining things. Duncan was a man of God, for goodness' sake. He maybe had moods, all men did, but he wouldn't strike his wife, and there was no sense in mentioning it to Hamish or Hector. It would only lead to trouble where, more than likely, there had been no trouble at all.

* * *

Life below stairs in the castle was light-hearted now. 'Mrs Hamish has fair made a big change here,' Mrs Carnie remarked to her husband before they went to bed one night. 'There's no' the fear like there was when Lady Glendarril got on her high horse.' She shook her head and corrected her statement. 'No, to be honest, it wasna fear exactly, but we were aye worried aboot what she'd say, for she'd a wicked tongue on her when she got goin'.'

Carnie drew hard on the pipe he was lighting with one of the tapers the chamber maid supplied him with – from the vase in the master's study. 'She were a good mistress, though,' he observed, snibbing the flame between his thumb and forefinger and laying the taper inside the fender.

'Are you tellin' me Mrs Hamish is no' a good mistress?' his wife demanded, ready to be outraged if he even thought such a thing.

'That's no' what I said. She's no' as strict as Lady Glendarril, an' she's mebbe a wee bit ower friendly wi' the young maids . . .'

'She's tryin' to put them at their ease! Some o' they lassies used to be scared stiff at Lady Glendarril. You get better work oot o' them if you treat them right and dinna shout, that's what I aye say.'

Her husband eyed her with scepticism. 'Is that a fact? I've heard you roarin' at them like a ragin' bull . . . mony's the time.'

'Just when they needed it,' she defended herself, then got back to her original topic. 'Ony road, Mrs Hamish didna come o' the gentry. You can tell by the way she speaks she was workin' class, but my faith, she's learned a lot since she come here.'

'Roberta Glover learned her the maist o' it.'

'Na, na, Miss Glover just learned her some o' it, for she wasna ower proud to ask, and she's took her ain road for a good while now.'

Tired of baiting her, though she should be used to it

after near twenty years of marriage, Carnie nodded amicably. 'She's shaped up fine. She's a good heid on her shooders.'

Pleased that he was agreeing with her at last, his wife said, 'You look real tired the nicht, Tam. I'll put a drappie brandy in your hot milk afore we go to oor bed.'

He grinned roguishly. 'I dinna need brandy to kittle me up, as fine you ken.'

She turned a coquettish smile on him. 'Ach you. Behave yoursel'!'

When Marianne went into the dining room one morning in early winter, her husband and father-in-law had finished breakfast, and after Hector went out, Hamish said, 'We were discussing you.'

'And what conclusion did you come to?' The frosty edge to her voice showed her annoyance at being talked about behind her back.

'We think it's time you visited Strawberry Bank. It is almost a year and a half since the wedding, and I am sure the Rennies would be delighted to see you. In fact, Father was astonished that they had not come here again.'

'I've invited them in every letter I write, but Miss Edith says they don't feel easy in the castle.'

'I see, well, all the more reason for you to go to Aberdeen and you had better do it before winter sets in. If you wait much longer, there is a possibility that the journey could endanger your health and the child's, according to Father. You do want to see them?'

Her little spurt of anger evaporated. 'Of course I do! I'll write today and ask which Sunday would be best for them. It has to be a Sunday, you see, it's the only day the shop's shut.'

'In that case,' Hamish said gently, 'you will also see Andrew, will you not?'

There was no sarcasm or jealousy in his voice, so she

felt free to answer honestly. 'Yes, so I will. I'm quite pleased about that, for I've always . . . liked him.'

'I am well aware of that, and he has always *loved* you.'

She could detect a touch of sadness in his eyes now. 'I can't help how he feels about me!' she protested, hoping her husband would admit at last that *he* loved her, too, but she was disappointed yet again.

'As I have said before, I would not object to your . . . seeing Andrew, but as for anything more than that, you will have to wait until you have recovered from the birth of . . . our child.'

She stamped her foot angrily. 'And as I've said before, and all, Hamish High-and-Mighty Bruce-Lyall, I don't *want* anything more from Andrew. Yes, I like him, maybe I love him in a funny sort of way, but I could never break my marriage vows. Us working-class folks were brought up to believe a husband and wife should mean everything to one another, not like you out-of-the-top-drawer folk that have fancy women and fancy men whenever the fancy takes them.' She was unaware of her pun, she was working herself up to such a pitch. 'Or maybe you want me to take up with Andrew so you can have intercourse with somebody else, and all?'

Hamish's face was livid by the time she stopped, even his lips white as he whipped round without saying a word and slammed out, leaving Marianne still shaking.

After a time, recovered slightly, she lifted the silver teapot and poured herself a cup of the now luke-warm liquid, strong as tar with the standing, and braced herself to face whichever maid came in to clear the table. No one appeared, however, which made her feel worse. All the servants must have heard her shouting, and for the life of her she could hardly remember what had started it. They had been speaking about her going to Aberdeen, about the Rennies, about Andrew. Yes, that was where it had gone wrong, and maybe it *had* been her fault. She had been too quick to take offence. Hamish had just been letting her know he wasn't jealous of Andrew, that was all.

Was that why she had exploded? Did she want him to be jealous? Yes, dammit, she did, and saying he wouldn't mind her carrying on with Andrew had been like a slap in the face to her. She didn't love Andrew, not in that way, but she always enjoyed his company and he had taught her so much. If it hadn't been for him, she could never have fitted in at Castle Lyall.

Why could Hamish not understand? Why couldn't he love her . . . as she . . . ? Good gracious, how long had she been in love with her husband? It was something she hadn't foreseen when she agreed to marry him – and what could she do about it?

Recalling Hamish urging her to go to Aberdeen before winter set in – he'd hinted that, if she didn't go soon, she wouldn't be allowed to go till after her confinement – she went upstairs to write to Miss Edith. She couldn't tell the sisters what had happened this morning, of course, but maybe Andrew could advise her.

Strangely, it did not occur to Marianne that it might stretch the bonds of friendship to breaking point and beyond if she asked the man who loved her what she could do to make her husband love her. In fact, she very seldom thought of Andrew as a man who loved her. She preferred to look on him purely as a friend, her best friend.

It was easier for her that way.

The effusive welcome from Miss Esther and Miss Emily the next Sunday – arms flung round her and lips pressed against her cheek – brought tears to Marianne's eyes, and she was glad of Miss Edith's brusque, 'Come, come, no tears today.' A crushingly firm handclasp, however, revealed that the eldest sister was equally pleased to see her.

After Hamish had been given his share of the greetings, Miss Esther said, 'Sit down, for goodness' sake, otherwise lunch will be ruined, and afterwards, Marianne, you can tell us how you are coping with your new role in life.'

The girl glanced at her husband uncertainly. Since that dreadful day, he had not referred to their quarrel, yet their relationship was no longer what it had been. There was a constraint between them, not enough to make other people wonder, perhaps, but certainly enough to make her feel ashamed of having lost her temper. Unfortunately, she'd had no chance to apologize, there was always somebody else around – an older man and woman had even followed them into the first-class carriage when they joined the London train at Laurencekirk. She hadn't wanted Hamish to come with her, but he had refused to allow her to travel unaccompanied, and how could she talk honestly about *his* home, *his* servants, *his* father, with *him* listening to every word?

But he was smiling and shaking his head. 'Thank you, Miss Esther, for your kind hospitality, but I am sure that you did not count on my being here.'

'It is all right,' she protested. 'I always make more than enough food on Sundays. My sisters will tell you . . .'

'It is true, Hamish,' Miss Edith beamed. 'Even after having a meal on Mondays from the left-overs, we often have to feed the remains to the dog next door.'

'If you are sure . . . ?' He sat down now.

Not only had the long-deceased Mr and Mrs Rennie forbidden their daughters to waste good food, they had also taught them that it was extremely bad manners to talk while they were eating, so little was said during the meal, which gave Marianne further space to think. She had hoped to confide her troubles to Andrew later, in the hope that he could advise her on what she might do – Miss Edith shouldn't think it strange if they went for a walk together as they had been in the habit of doing before – but with Hamish here as well . . . ?

No matter how hard she tried, she could think of no way she could get her old friend alone, and finally accepted that she would just have to make the best of her life with no advice from anybody. In any case, maybe Andrew had stopped coming to Strawberry Bank on Sunday afternoons, which would be a relief in the circumstances.

Miss Esther and Miss Emily refused to allow Marianne to help with the clearing up, which provided her with another short respite before giving an account of her time at Castle Lyall, even making her hope, for one brief moment, that they would forget their curiosity, but she knew perfectly well that they wouldn't – not Miss Esther, anyway; she was like a dog worrying a bone when she wanted to know something.

To Marianne's amazement, just as the two younger sisters sat down, Hamish stood up. 'I am sure you ladies would enjoy your talk much better without a man here, so, if you do not think me rude, I will leave you to it.'

'Why don't you wait till Andrew comes?' Miss Esther suggested. 'He always takes a walk on Sunday afternoons, and I am sure he would be glad of your company. He has had to go alone since . . . since . . .' She came to a faltering halt, looking to her eldest sister for help.

Trying to set her at ease, Hamish smiled, 'Ah yes, I had forgotten about Andrew and I have promised to visit a friend for an hour or two. Please give him my apologies and tell him I shall see him when I come back.'

Then, for Marianne, came the biggest stroke of good luck, a virtual miracle, and from the most unexpected source. 'I do not think Andrew will mind,' Miss Emily said, shyly because it was not often that she took part in any discussion. 'He can take Marianne with him, like he always used to do.'

'What a good idea!' exclaimed Hamish, smiling at his wife, who was regarding him doubtfully but nevertheless with a touch of hope. 'It will be like old times for both of you.'

When he went out, Miss Esther said, 'Doesn't he mind?'

Miss Edith saved Marianne's face. 'Why should he mind?

Andrew was her friend long before she met Hamish.'

'Yes, of course.' Miss Esther leaned back, satisfied that all was as it should be. 'Come on, then, Marianne. We want to hear what the mistress of the castle has been doing, before Andrew arrives.'

Once started, she did not find it difficult, and Miss Esther made it easier by asking about the kitchens, which she had never described in her letters.

'When I went to find out what happened below stairs, I got my eyes opened,' she admitted. 'I'd no idea there were so many rooms or so many staff. I thought there would be one chamber maid and one parlour maid, with maybe a couple of young girls to help the cook. I knew there were two footmen, because I'd seen them, and Lord Glendarril has a valet he calls Dick. I thought it was his Christian name, but it turned out to be his last name.'

'And how many staff are there?' Miss Esther prompted.

'There's four chamber maids, three parlour maids, and two still-room maids (who make the tea and coffee and snacks for the servants); they all think they're better than the scullery maids, kitchen maids and laundry maids, two of each, and the poor tweeny who's at everybody's beck and call. Mrs Carnie, the cook, and Dick, the valet, consider themselves above the rest and, of course, Miss Glover, the housekeeper, believes she's superior to the lot of them.'

'You get on all right with her, though?' Miss Esther again.

'We get on fine, in fact, she's been quite a help to me. It was her that told me what all the different rooms down there were for.'

While Miss Esther tried to count the number of servants, with Miss Emily's help when she forgot one, Miss Edith leaned towards Marianne and said softly, 'Are things all right between Hamish and you?'

'What makes you think they're not?'

Her defensive retort confirmed Miss Edith's suspicions,

but she did not pry. If the girl wanted to tell her, she would, in time.

Miss Esther asked about the outside staff next, and Marianne told her about the grooms, the stable lads, Carnie, who was Jack of all trades, from driving the family about to doing any odd jobs in the buildings. 'Then there's Dargie, the head gardener,' she went on. He's got three men under him and two young lads.'

On being asked how many of the staff lived in, she told them who lived in the servants' quarters or over the stables. 'But a lot of them go home every night. You see, the whole glen belongs to the Bruce-Lyalls, and Lord Glendarril's grandfather or great-grandfather built good solid cottages for the workers on the estate and in the mill, and it's their sons and daughters who get all the jobs that's going.'

She was still holding forth about her dealings with those of the staff she saw every day when Andrew walked in, his somewhat solemn face being transformed by a smile the minute he saw her. 'I didn't know you'd be here today, Marianne,' he gasped. 'Nobody told me last Sunday.'

'Nobody knew last Sunday,' Miss Edith remarked drily.

'I only wrote on Tuesday,' the girl said, embarrassed by the naked love blazing from his eyes.

Realizing himself that he was being indiscreet, Andrew looked away from her and sat down to accept a cup of tea from his Aunt Esther. 'How is Hamish?' he enquired in a moment.

'He's very well, thank you,' Marianne replied. 'He did come with me, but he'd promised to visit a friend. He said to tell you he's sorry and he'll see you when he comes back.'

For the second time that day, Miss Emily took the bit between her teeth. 'He doesn't mind if you take Marianne with you on your walk this afternoon, Andrew, and she has plenty to tell you.'

His guard slipping again, he said, his voice practically

begging, 'Are you absolutely sure you want to come with me, Marianne?'

She couldn't tell him that she was desperate to be on her own with him, so she murmured, 'Of course I am, Andrew.'

'Don't go too far, then,' cautioned Miss Edith.

Barely able to contain her curiosity, Miss Esther pounced as soon as the young couple left. 'Why did you not want them to go far?'

Her sister smiled enigmatically. 'Don't say you didn't notice?'

'Notice what?' A short pause, then, 'You mean ... she's ... ?'

'I am almost sure that she will be a mother in a few months.'

While the Rennie sisters were excitedly discussing this possibility, Marianne and Andrew were walking silently towards the River Dee, he longing to reassure her of his undying love but knowing it was not permissible, and she acutely aware of what he was trying so hard not to say. Although it was into December, it was a bright day and not nearly as cold as it might have been, so Marianne ventured to propose that they find somewhere to sit for a while, and within five minutes they were seated on a fallen tree trunk, sheltered from the strong breeze which had suddenly sprung up.

'Marianne,' Andrew said before she could utter a word, 'I know you want to tell me something, but please ... nothing personal. I really could not bear to hear –'

'Please, Andrew, you must listen. I don't know what to do.'

He gave a sigh of resignation. No matter how hard he tried, or how much it might hurt him, he could refuse her nothing. 'Go on, then.'

She poured out the sad tale of how seldom Hamish had shared her bed and how, since she had told him she was going to have his child, he had not come to her at all. 'It's awful to feel your husband doesn't love you,' she wailed. 'I didn't love him when I married him, but I think I'm beginning to love him now, and he doesn't want me, except to . . . give him an heir.'

Andrew did his best to be objective. 'You say he has actually . . . made you pregnant? That seems a complete reversal of what you have just told me.' Unable to continue, he came to an abrupt halt, waiting a few moments before muttering, in despair, 'Oh, Marianne, I can't discuss this with you.'

Intent on getting advice, she was insensitive to his feelings. 'I don't see why not. Surely you've come across this sort of situation before? Hamish actually told me he wouldn't mind if I took a lover; he even thinks you *were* my lover at one time.'

A frown crossed her companion's brow. 'Is that what this is all about? Do you want me to *be* your lover . . . a secret lover?' He gave a deep groan. 'I want to be your lover more than anything else in the world, my darling, but not in secret. I would want everyone to know. I would want you to live with me, to prove to the world that the love was not all on my side.' He looked at her keenly, then ended sadly, 'But it is, isn't it?'

'Oh, Andrew dear, I'm sorry. I do love you, but just as a good friend, my best friend. I shouldn't have told you anything. It was cruel of me.'

After a pause that told of deep inner turmoil, he said flatly, 'I did tell you to come to me if you needed help, so . . . I would advise you to wait until your child is born. That could be the spur Hamish needs; perhaps, although he has had a tendency to be reserved he will be overcome by love for you when you lay his son in his arms.'

Her face had brightened considerably. 'D'you really think so? Oh, Andrew, I'm glad I asked you; I knew you could tell me what to do.'

He stood up and pulled her to her feet. 'It is time we went back. It is growing much colder.'

When they returned to Strawberry Bank, Marianne was conscious of Miss Edith looking enquiringly from one to the other of them, and that Miss Esther and Miss Emily seemed to be excited about something, but before any of them spoke, Hamish knocked at the door. It was evident from the easy conversation the two men struck up now that there was no animosity between them, which made Marianne feel rather put out, though she didn't know quite what she had expected.

Shortly after tea, Hamish said they would have to leave, otherwise they would miss the last train home, and Andrew also stood up. 'I'll walk along with you a bit, if you don't mind.'

His Aunt Edith got to her feet. 'And I shall come to Justice Mill Lane with you, to stretch my legs before I go to bed.'

Naturally, Hamish and Andrew went in front, and Marianne waited for the question or questions that Miss Edith was bound to ask.

'Haven't you forgotten to tell me something, dear?'

'What d'you mean?'

'Surely you do not intend to keep so important a secret from us, Marianne? When is your confinement to be?'

The girl gave a wry laugh. 'I might have known *you* would guess. I'm due in March, and I didn't tell you because I was afraid you'd want to give me all the baby clothes in your shop. I don't want that, for Hamish can easily afford to buy everything we need,'

'Yes, I can understand that he will want to provide for his own child, but Esther will want to make as many things for the infant as she can, and you surely cannot deny her that pleasure?'

'No, of course I can't.'

'One last thing, Marianne. I know something is wrong

between you and Hamish, so won't you tell me about that, as well?'

'It's nothing. We'd a bit of a quarrel a few days ago, but it'll soon blow over.'

Miss Edith was frowning now. 'It is not good to let it run on for long. My mother used to say, "Never let the sun go down on your wrath." She said it was because she had stuck to that rule that her marriage to Father was so happy, and you would do well to remember it, too. In the meantime, I would advise you to apologize to Hamish tonight, then kiss and make up. You will not regret it.'

Miss Edith bade them goodbye first, and when it was Andrew's turn to leave them, Hamish said, 'You must pay us a visit some weekend, Andrew. We would be glad of some younger company.'

'Thank you, I'd like that very much.'

When they were sitting in a first-class carriage by themselves, it occurred to Marianne that she would probably have no opportunity to carry out Miss Edith's instructions once they went home, and that now would be an ideal time. 'Hamish,' she said gently, 'I'm truly sorry for the things I said the other day.'

'No, my dear,' he murmured. 'It was my fault, and you must please accept my apology.'

His kiss was not enough to lift the weight which had been pressing on her, and she came to the conclusion that she would be wise to take Andrew's advice and wait until the baby was born. Surely having his son placed in his arms *would* make Hamish realize that he loved her. Besides, he was probably right to sleep in another room until she recovered from her confinement. She was only six months gone, but she wasn't sure how long into a pregancy a man could ... do it without causing harm to his wife or the unborn infant.

Chapter Eleven

No winter had ever passed so slowly for Marianne. Even Andrew's visit just before Christmas did not lift her spirits, despite assurances from Thomson that she had hardly begun to show. Nevertheless, she had the distinct impression that her old friend was embarrassed at seeing her, which made her so conscious of her condition that she kept to her room as much as she could. This, of course, infuriated her husband, who accused her of being unsociable.

'He was your friend before he was mine,' he snapped after Andrew had gone, 'and you should have made him feel welcome in our home, instead of which you made him so uncomfortable that I would not be surprised if he does not come back.'

She tried to explain. 'I don't like people seeing me like this. Maybe it doesn't matter to you, but I don't want Andrew to see me looking like the side of a house.'

'Yes, it is always Andrew!' Hamish spat out. 'You care what he thinks of you, but I do not matter.'

Because a woman's emotions always teeter on a razor's edge during pregnancy, Hamish's attitude tipped the balance for Marianne now. 'I'll never stop caring what Andrew thinks of me,' she shouted, 'though I know he loves me so much he wouldn't bother how I look.'

'You don't want him to see you with another man's child in your belly! That is the whole crux of the matter, isn't it? Possibly you wish it was his?'

'Don't be so damned stupid!' she screamed. 'You canna have a very good opinion o' me when you're sayin' things like that! You tell't me why you wanted to marry me, and

I was willin' to produce sons for you, and I'd never have agreed to it if I'd wanted Andrew, would I?'

His eyes narrowed. 'You forget what you are getting out of the arrangement. A castle home, a title some day, and wealth you would never have known if I had not come into your life.'

'I haven't forgotten anything, and I'm grateful to you for what you're providing for me . . .' She paused, gulping, and lowered her voice. 'Hamish, why can't you be grateful to me for what I'm doing for you? I'm carrying your child, but it was conceived through your love for your father and the future of the family, not for me.'

He made as if to move towards her, then checked himself. 'We had a business agreement, Marianne,' he sighed. 'Love played no part in it, if you remember, but I am deeply sorry for upsetting you in your condition. What I said was quite uncalled for. Now, I feel the need of a walk before I go to bed, so shall I call Thomson to – ?'

'I'll manage to go to bed myself.'

He held the door open for her, and as she went upstairs, she was conscious of him watching until she reached the top landing.

On Hogmanay, Hector invited some of his business friends and their wives to see in the new year of 1899 at Castle Lyall, and Marianne had been ordered to be there to greet them. She was almost into the seventh month of her pregnancy, and her hackles had gone up when the three over-dressed, bejewelled women had looked at each other knowingly when they saw her. One of them even said, with all the finesse of a bull crashing through a china shop, 'You have put on some weight since you were married.'

Having resolved to be polite to the guests, Marianne smiled. 'Yes, a little.'

A round of puzzled glances followed this unproductive statement, then the same woman, built like a battleship and obviously the leader of the group, coaxed, 'Come now, my dear girl, there is no need to be shy. You can trust us.'

Her persistence goaded Marianne into indiscretion. 'Oh, I can, can I?' she said loudly. 'Well, I'm sure you ken already, for Lord Glendarril's likely tell't you, but I'm six month gone and if you count back on your fingers – likely the only way you *can* count and you've maybe done it already – you'll see the bairn wasna made till long after the wedding night.'

Marianne did not welcome the new year along with the guests. In the shocked silence following her outburst, her husband took her firmly by the elbow and shepherded her upstairs. 'I know they are inquisitive old harpies,' he said, 'but they are under my father's roof and we must observe the niceties of being hosts.'

'I'm sorry, Hamish,' she wailed. 'I couldn't help it. That woman was practically asking me outright if I was expecting, and that isn't very polite, is it?'

'That woman,' he said drily, 'is the sister-in-law of Mr William Ewart Gladstone.'

'Him that was Prime Minister?' she faltered. 'Oh, what have I done? Your father'll never forgive me.'

A grin spread over Hamish's face. 'My father cannot stand her and neither can I, so go to sleep and forget about it. Just remember to be more tactful in future.'

When he closed the door behind him, she plumped down on the stool before the mirror on her vanity table and regarded her reflection with distaste. No wonder those women had been curious about her. Her very face had changed! In the first five months, it had been pale and pinched, which is why Miss Edith had guessed how the land lay, but her cheeks were fuller now, with such a deep rosy glow to them folk would think it was the bloom of good health if they didn't see the rest of her. She considered this for a moment and realized that she *was* blooming with health. She'd had none of the morning sickness other mothers-to-be spoke about; no pains except a slight tenderness in her breasts. Her hazel eyes were bright and clear and her auburn hair had its usual sheen.

The aches and pains came in the last month. Her back felt as if it would break with the extra weight, her breasts were uncomfortably heavy and she couldn't see her feet for the great bump at her front. She waddled when she walked, and it wouldn't surprise her if her legs buckled under her one of these days. It was awful to have no control over her body. But the doctor – she had got to know Robert Mowatt quite well on the fortnightly examinations Hector insisted upon – assured her that there were no problems, that she would sail through the confinement.

And sail through it she did! At 3 a.m. on the tenth day of March, after only about two hours of true labour, he delivered her of a baby boy weighing eight pounds twelve ounces and yelling his head off as he was cleaned.

'He's got a fine pair of lungs, at any rate,' the doctor observed, then raised his voice. 'You can come in now, Hamish. It's all over and you have a son.'

The nurse Hector had been adamant about employing handed the tightly wrapped bundle to the father, who asked only one question before he carried it away: 'Is he all right, Robert?'

The doctor nodded. 'Not a thing wrong with him that I could see, and all his parts are there.'

'Why did you tell him that?' Marianne asked when her husband went out. She was hurt that Hamish hadn't asked how she was, but she couldn't say so to a third party.

Robert looked at her sadly. 'He wanted to know if the child could carry on the Bruce-Lyall line. That's all Hector was worrying about, not just an heir to follow Hamish, but an heir to follow that. So do not be upset that your man was only concerned about the infant . . . no,' he grinned, as she opened her mouth to deny this, 'you can't fool me, young lady. I am sure he'll show more interest in you when he comes back, so don't be angry with him.'

Minutes after the doctor left her, Hamish brought back the son she had not been given a chance to see, and her voice was a touch nippy as she said, 'Is your father satisfied with him?'

'He thinks he's perfect, and so do I. Don't you?'

'Since I haven't set eyes on him yet, I can't really say.'

'Marianne, I am sorry . . . I did not realize . . . I should have . . .' A look of horror crossed his face. 'Forgive me, please. The first thing I should have done was ask how you were. Oh, I made a proper mess of it.'

She did not have the energy to argue, and, after all, she thought, in self-pity, the baby had been the most important factor for both Hamish and his father; it was the only reason for the marriage. 'I'm not too bad,' she sighed. 'The last wee while was the worst, but it wasn't as bad as I'd imagined. Maybe your father was right. Maybe I am the best person you could have found to give you sons.' A devil got in her here, a wish to shock him. 'I was the same as a woman at home. When folk asked her why she kept on having babies, she used to say, "Havin' a bairn's nae bother to me. It's just like havin' a stiff shite."'

His shock was greater than she expected. First, he turned white, then the colour rushed back into his cheeks until they were scarlet, and as he stood gaping at her, she had to laugh. 'That wasn't fair of me, Hamish. I wanted to pay you back for neglecting me, but I don't suppose you've ever heard a girl using language like that.'

He closed his mouth and his face gradually returned to its natural shade, but her coarseness had told him how badly he had wounded her by his cavalier behaviour and he attempted to soothe her. 'Father wants to call him Ruairidh.'

He could not have said anything more likely to rouse

her to fury. 'Your *father* wants?' she burst out. 'Who had this bairn, me or him?'

'Marianne, that's not –'

'Never mind tryin' to get round me. Just go and tell your father I'm callin' *my* son what *I* want.'

'He meant no harm. He is so used to making all the decisions here that he did not stop to think.'

'What about you? You just agreed with him?'

'I was too overjoyed to think rationally about anything. It is not every day that a man has a son, and that was all that mattered to me. I am afraid that I neither agreed nor disagreed with him, and I am practically sure that, if I explain how you feel, he will allow you to choose any name you want.'

This time her devilment was mild. 'What about Dod, then? Or Tam? Or Willie?'

After a brief hesitation, Hamish murmured, 'He would not object to any of these. George, Thomas and William are good, strong names.'

'I was only testing you,' Marianne laughed. 'What did your father suggest, did you say?'

'Ruairidh – it's an old family name, but if you –'

'Rory?'

'Spelled in the Gaelic way, of course. R-U-A-I-R-I-D-H.'

This appealed to her, but having made a stand, she was not going to climb down. 'Tell your father I'll name this one, but we'll call our second son Ruairidh to please him.'

Hamish had forgotten how well she could stick to her guns, a trait in her that his father admired. 'I will make sure that you get your way, Marianne. What name had you chosen?'

Not having chosen one at all, she picked a name out of the air. 'I thought Ranald would be nice.' She had seen it in a poem when she was at school, and she had always liked it.

While she was resting, it occurred to her that she'd had

no chance to test the advice Andrew had given her. It had been the midwife who had handed Hamish his son, and he hadn't given one single thought to his wife till later. After she produced the second son that was wanted, she would likely be left strictly on her own at nights for the rest of her life. She would end up a wizened, unloved old lady unless . . .

Not unloved, though! There was always Andrew.

Marianne came awake slowly and luxuriously. The sun was streaming through the gap she had left in the curtains the night before, the birds were trying to outdo each other with the sweetness of their songs, cows were lowing in the distance . . . yet the small gilt clock by her bed showed only half-past five. June was a lovely month.

Stretching her arms, she decided against rising just yet. Thomson would alarm the whole household if she wasn't in her room when she brought up her morning cup of tea, and she'd have everybody in a proper fankle in no time. Besides, it would be quite nice to have time to consider her life, to set aside the cares of her duties as mistress of the castle. No, her duties didn't actually lie within the castle itself – Roberta Glover took care of the running of the household – but she did look after the needs of, and give advice to, the women of the glen, and they treated her with all the respect she'd ever wanted. They expressed their gratitude in many ways – giving her eggs gathered 'but an hour ago, your Leddyship', a small jacket knitted for her baby, and, from more than one young wife she had coun- selled, a lovely, soft woollen blanket, edged with blue ribbon for the cot or the perambulator. They looked on her as Lady Bountiful, as someone who could sort out any problem for them, or comfort them in their grief if they had lost a loved one.

She had taken to it like a duck takes to water, like an new-born infant takes to the breast, like a dung beetle takes to cows' sharn. She smiled at her own wit, but it was true, though she'd have to watch not to say 'sharn' in front of anybody here. She'd have to find out what the proper name for it was, because she only knew two other words which were even worse. Her mind went back to what she had been thinking about before: her new-found organizing skills. She had surprised herself by her confident dealing with the minor household problems of the crofters' wives, even with her belly starting to swell and her back giving her gyp. Now her confinement was past, she'd be able to attend to the whole glen with one hand tied behind her back, not that she'd ever try it.

She had been annoyed that Nurse Murchie wouldn't let her breast-feed baby Ranald after the first week. 'It's not dignified to be exposing yourself,' the woman had said. 'None of my ladies ever fed the baby themselves. That's why they employ a nurse.'

It did stop her from being tied to the house all the time, Marianne thought, but having her breasts bound tightly to stop the milk hadn't been pleasant. And she'd have to go through it all again at some time in the not-too-distant future, she supposed. It surprised her that Hamish hadn't come back to her room yet – it was three months since the birth.

A bead of sweat running down her nose made her thoughts veer. It was going to be a hot day again, unbearably hot like yesterday. She had meant to do a few odd little jobs this forenoon and then take a walk through the woods after lunch, but it would be even hotter then. She got out of bed to push open the window a little further, and drew the welcome fresh air deep into her lungs. Oh, she'd have to go out; the perspiration was trickling down between her shoulder blades now, but she couldn't be bothered dressing, nobody would see her at this time of morning.

Creeping along the corridor and down the stairs, she heaved a sigh of relief on reaching the door to the garden without seeing a soul. Her heart was singing as she slipped outside and ran lightly towards the gate at the far end of the rose garden. She had forgotten to put shoes on, but what did that matter? When she was a schoolgirl, she had run barefoot every summer, like all the children in Tipperton. Her feet weren't so hardened to stony ground nowadays though, she reflected wryly, picking her way carefully along the gravel path, but once she was in the wood, the going was a little easier. The thick layer of pine needles wasn't exactly as comfortable as a carpet would have been, but when she came to a stretch of moss, her feet felt almost as if there were springs under them.

Her heart was so light that she skipped along for a while, humming an old song her class had been taught by the dominie's wife, and in another few minutes, her exuberance was such that she could contain herself no longer and burst into song.

'Did you not see my lady go down the garden singing,
Silencing all the songbirds and setting the echoes
    ringing?
Oh, saw you not my lady out in the garden there,
Shaming the rose and lily for she is twice as fair?'

Unable to remember what came next, or even if what she had already sung were the right words, she pirouetted and collapsed giggling on the grass verging the small loch she had reached. It was much hotter now, even in the shade of the tall pines and, without considering, she jumped up and waded in. The shock of the icy coldness made her draw a sharp breath, but it didn't take her long to get accustomed to it. It felt so good that she laved water all over herself, soaking her long tresses as well as her thin nightgown.

She cavorted about until she was sufficiently cooled and then got out, hauling her soggy garment off and spreading it over a branch. There was no sense in risking a chill, and it should dry quickly in this heat, and so would she. She sprawled down on the ground, arms and legs spread wide, and watched the birds flying overhead.

She felt wonderful, as though somebody had wrapped her in a warm blanket. She could lie here for ever . . . or anyway, till the sun went down. Her eyes followed a tiny wren for a moment, then a blue tit which landed not far from her and hopped around in search of a grub. A honey bee caught her attention next, buzzing contentedly from one wild blossom to another. Marianne felt totally at peace, with nothing to remind her of duties she should be carrying out. Let them get on with things themselves – they would manage fine without her.

She lifted her breasts so that the skin underneath could have a turn of the warmth – they had returned to their normal size, thank goodness – and then sat up to let her back dry. Some minutes later, she got to her feet and ran her hands down her stomach, as firm as it had been before, then turned round to give the back of her legs a chance to dry. A movement to her right caught her eye. Believing it to be a rabbit or a weasel, she paid little attention until it dawned on her that whatever it was, it was far too big to be either a rabbit or a weasel.

'Who's there?' she called apprehensively.

And rising from where he'd been crouching in the bushes, appeared the most magnificent specimen of a man she had seen in her entire life. His hair was jet-black and curled close to his head and round his ears; his body being bare to the waist, she quickly averted her eyes from the thatch of black curls across his chest. His shoulders were broad, his face lean and tanned to an almost mahogany colour. His eyes were fixed on her, his mouth slightly open . . . as was hers, she realized, snapping it shut and remembering, at the same time, that she was stark naked, which was likely why he was staring at her like that.

'Will you please pass me my shift?' she asked haughtily.

He stepped right out now, placing himself between her and the nightdress she wanted. 'I'd like to look at you a while longer,' he answered, his smile widening into a grin, his eyes twinkling with mischief. 'It's no' often I come across a beautiful damsel wearin' nothin' but her skin, an' by God, you make a right bonnie picture.'

He was so attractive she couldn't help but respond to the compliments he was paying her. 'You make a fine picture yourself,' she smiled.

'Maybe I'd best take off my breeches to make us equal,' he offered, hands going to his top button, but waiting for her to say something before undoing it.

Marianne's reaction to this unpardonable yet fascinating remark surprised her. Her heart had speeded up, deep thrills ran down to her most private place, but, as she took an involuntary step towards him, she came to her senses. 'I'm a married woman,' she declared, with all the dignity she could muster when every fibre of her was aching to be in his arms.

He nodded nonchalantly. 'I noticed your weddin' ring, but it makes no odds to me. Married or single, you're still a bonnie lass.'

'You don't understand!' she burst out, pleading. 'I'm wed on the laird's son.'

'So? I'm pleased to see there's nae difference between a lady an' a workin' lassie when they've naething on, an' your figure's a lot better than mony o' the lassies I've lain wi', the married women an' all.' He undid his top button now, teasing as he said, 'I'm sure you'd like to ken if a tinker's the same as a lord under his breeks?'

'No, no!' she pleaded, somewhat half-heartedly because she *had* wondered about that, although she'd thought he was a gypsy. Then, in her confusion because his eyes were fastened on her bosom, she forgot about being refined and snapped, 'I'm nae a peepshow, so I'll thank you to stop lookin' at me like that.'

Her slip of the tongue made him raise his eyebrows. 'Aye, aye, m'Leddy, I some think you didna start oot as gentry. Was you a skivvy that took the laird's son's eye?'

She was outraged at this assumption. 'No, I wasn't! I worked in a shop in Aberdeen before I met Hamish.'

'But you dinna speak like a toon lassie. What did you dae afore you went to Aberdeen?'

Inquisitive though he was, she couldn't help liking him, and what did it matter if he knew the truth? She wouldn't see him again and he'd have no reason to tell anybody. 'I was servant to a banker's wife . . . in Tipperton.'

He gave a triumphant grin. 'So you *was* a skivvy! I ken't you was mair like me than like a laird's son! Now, bein' on the same level, so to speak, you've nae cause to look doon on me.'

'I wasna lookin' doon on you, but a gentleman would've turned his back when he saw –'

'But I never laid claim to bein' a gentleman, noo did I? An' you was getting' ready to gi'e me my marchin' orders though you dinna really want me to leave.'

She bridled. 'Give me my shift!' she ordered, staring him straight in the eye and speaking as firmly as she could.

Continuing to smile, he passed the still damp item over, then said, 'You could mebbe dae something for me . . . if it wouldna be ower much bother? M'name's Jamie MacPhee, an' me an' my brother's lookin' for work . . . well, it's just me that's lookin', for I'm sick o' sharpenin' knives and scythes. We've just got the one grindin' wheel, you see, an' Robbie's been leavin' me to dae near the lot.' He eyed her hopefully. 'You could get me a job at the castle, couldn't you? It'll nae be for lang, for we'll be goin' to pick berries at Blairgowrie in the middle o' July, dependin' on the weather.'

Marianne knew that Dargie would easily find work for another pair of hands, but she also knew that she wouldn't feel easy if Jamie MacPhee were around the castle for any length of time. His eyes, however, were pleading like a young puppy-dog's, and she cast around in her mind for something to offer him. Thankfully, a solution did crop up. 'I just remembered. The minister's wife told me on Sunday they were looking for a man to keep their garden tidy. Duncan, that's her husband, well, he broke his leg and she's not able to keep the weeds down by herself.'

Jamie's eyes had lit up. 'That's just the kind of thing I was lookin' for, an' I'd best go an' see aboot it afore somebody else gets it.'

'Take that first path on the left there, right down to the road and you'll easy find the manse – it's next to the kirk. They've a fair skelp o' ground, mind.'

'That'll nae bother me.' He touched his forelock in mock respect. 'Thank you, your Leddyship, an' I'm sorry for the things I said afore, but I thocht you was just a servant lassie. If you'd been dressed, see, I'd never have said nothin'.'

Marianne smiled uncomfortably. 'Yes, it was my own fault, but I'd be obliged if you'd forget it, and don't say anything to anybody.'

'I'll nae say a word . . .' he paused, his attractive grin tugging at her heartstrings as he added, '. . . but I'll nae forget.'

'Good luck!' she called as she watched him striding away from her.

She walked home slowly, trying to collect her thoughts. What on earth had possessed her to go into the loch? And worse, to take off her nightgown? Nobody, not even Hamish, had ever seen her naked, and God knows what she had looked like, showing herself off to whoever had chanced upon her. No wonder Jamie MacPhee hadn't been able to take his eyes off her. And what if it had been Lord

Glendarril? Or Duncan Peat? No, he couldn't walk in the woods with a broken leg. But Hamish? He would likely have disowned her.

Another thing, she thought, turning hot at the memory of it, what had made her take to the tinker like that? Was it because he spoke with a north accent, like the one she was still trying to give up, or was it because he had said those nice things about her? Or was it because Hamish had not been in her bed since Ranald was born?

She was less than halfway to the garden gate when she saw Carnie practically running towards her, but there was nothing she could do to stop her damp shift clinging to her, for he'd seen her. 'My God, Lady Marianne,' he puffed, avoiding looking at her now, 'where've you been? They're going aboot mad back there. Thomson came running down the stair about ten past seven screaming, "Somebody's broke in and abducted the mistress!" and all hell broke loose.'

Marianne hung her head. 'I woke up early and it was so stuffy, I went out for some fresh air.'

He took off his jacket and handed it to her. 'You'd better cover yourself, or The Master'll . . .' He waited until she was as decent as possible, then took her arm and hurried her along the path. When they came to the garden gate, he said, 'You were taking a big chance going out in your goonie, though. Somebody might've seen you.'

'Nobody saw me.'

'You'd come out by the garden door? I'd best get you back in that way, and all, afore his Lordship or the Master sees us and thinks I've been trifling wi' your affections.' Carnie gave a great rumble of laughter which she did her best to join, but the thought persisted in her mind that if she hadn't come to her senses when she did, Jamie MacPhee would have trifled with more than her affections.

When they reached the house, Thomson was highly indignant that she had gone out by herself. 'Not even dressed. What were you thinking about, Mrs Hamish? The men are all out looking for you.'

A range of emotions coming to the surface now, Marianne burst into tears. 'I needed a breath of fresh air, and . . . oh, go away and leave me alone. Surely I can do what I like? I'm not a prisoner here.'

Thomson sniffed and tossed her head as she marched out, but Marianne didn't care that she had offended her maid. All she wanted was some peace. She was tired and hot, and she wished that she could go away with Jamie MacPhee and his brother when they left. It wouldn't bother her that he had no money, and was never likely to . . .

But the lack of money *would* bother her! She had achieved her ambition when she married Hamish, and when he became the Lord, she would have, by right, the title of Lady, which most of the glen folk already bestowed on her. In any case, the period of mourning for Lady Glendarril was long over, though Marianne suspected she would likely be made to wait until she produced a second son, however long that would take, before the day she was waiting for – when she could take her place among the nobility.

Half an hour later, she was awakened from a doze by little Daisy, the chamber maid, calling through the door, 'Thomson told me to get a bath ready for you, m'Leddy, so you'd better take it afore it gets cold.'

'Thank you, Daisy,' Marianne called back. 'And thank Thomson for thinking of it.' She didn't feel guilty any more about this, because no one had to carry the water upstairs since Hector had got men to fit the pump for filling the tank for the bath. They had also installed a gas ring under it, and with the work of laying the pipes for that, Hector had decided that they may as well have gaslights fitted in all rooms. One of her suggestions had led to a vast improvement in the standard of life in the castle.

She took her time over her ablutions and did feel much better for the long soak. Stepping out of the tub, she wrapped herself in the huge white towel laid out for her and opened the bathroom door to find Daisy hovering in the passage. 'Would you like me to help you to dry yourself and dress, m'Leddy?'

'No, thank you, I'll manage.'

She had just gone into her room when she heard heavy feet pounding upstairs, then Hamish flung open the door and took her in his arms.

'Oh, Marianne, where were you?' he cried. 'We searched the gardens high and low, although Thomson was determined you'd been abducted. I thought I had lost you.'

'I wanted some air so I went out for a walk. Then it got so hot, I went into the loch for a wee while to cool down and I'd to wait till I was dry, and my . . .' Appalled at having almost admitted how little she had been wearing, she finished, hastily, '. . . till my clothes were dry, too.'

Hamish stepped back and looked at her accusingly. 'Thomson tells me you had no clothes on, only a night-dress? I hope no one saw you.'

'Nobody saw me,' she assured him, her colour rising as she recalled Jamie MacPhee's searching eyes when she stood naked before him, and then, wondering if her husband would react in the same way as the tinker, she let the huge towel slip to the floor.

Hamish said nothing for several moments, but there was no doubt that he was drinking in the sight of her svelte body. She took a step towards him, and because he was her husband, she had no need to break away when his arms went round her again, fiercer than before.

'Dear God, Marianne,' he said hoarsely, 'do you know what holding you like this is doing to me?'

His lips came down hard on her mouth, his knuckles dug into the small of her back, but suddenly, he thrust her from him. 'No, no! I can't! I can't!'

'Why can't you?' she asked, frustration making her unnaturally bold to him.

'If you only knew how much I want to, my sweetheart. I've . . . oh, this is difficult, but I cannot keep it from you any longer. I've loved you ever since I first saw you – standing up to Sybil and her crew during that Hogmanay Ball, but I couldn't tell you before because I was sure that you loved Andrew.'

'Hamish, I told you over and over that I didn't love him in that way, just as a friend.'

His eyes held a trace of sadness now. 'Yet, when I proposed, you said you didn't love me, so what else was I to think?'

'I didn't think I did at first,' she admitted, pausing to kiss his ear before ending, 'but . . . you grew on me.'

He eyed her quizzically. 'Am I to take that as a compliment, or do you mean you got used to me, which isn't the same as loving me?'

'I do love you,' she said, 'but I thought you looked on our marriage as a duty to your father, a duty you didn't really care for.' His gentle but firm push towards the bed made her say, 'What are you doing, Hamish? We can't . . . it can't be long after breakfast time. Somebody might come in.'

He nuzzled her neck. 'Let them all come in. Let them feast their eyes on their master showing his beautiful wife how much he loves her.'

'It's all right for you,' she protested. 'It's me that's naked. You're dressed.'

'I shall soon remedy that,' he smiled, hardly taking time to open buttons as he pulled off jacket, necktie, shirt, trousers, and cast them from him on to the floor.

And now, at long last, came the love-making she had longed for, the caressing, the tender yet meaningful kissing, the exploring hands, the build-up to a height they had never reached before, and she was left in no doubt that he loved her as much as she loved him.

When it was over, she expressed her surprise that no one had come to the door, not even Thomson, and Hamish murmured, smiling at her fondly, 'They are human, my darling. They know what a husband will do to the wife he feared was lost to him.'

'And they likely know you hardly ever slept with me,' she said, embarrassed at reminding him.

He took hold of one of her tresses of coppery hair and twirled it round his finger. 'I wasted a lot of time fretting about you and Andrew.' He put his finger on her mouth as she started to speak. 'Yes, I know that you denied it several times, but a man in love is not always rational.'

'A man in love,' she sighed rapturously. 'Oh, I never thought I'd hear you describing yourself like that.'

'You will hear it over and over again for as long as we live,' he assured her.

This little exchange, of course, only served to keep them in bed, and when they did eventually go downstairs, the two maids in the dining room kept their eyes down. Even Hector didn't look at them, eating his lunch as though he hadn't a minute to spare, but when the servants had withdrawn, he could hold back no longer.

'You might have waited until night-time,' he muttered. 'You know what these lassies are like. It'll be all round the glen in no time that you two spent the whole morning in bed together.'

Stretching out to clasp Marianne's hand, Hamish said, 'We don't care. You maybe will not believe this, Father, but we only discovered today the true extent of our love.'

The suggestion of a twinkle now appeared in Sir Hector's eyes. 'And you couldn't wait?' He gave Marianne a quick glance and then smiled. 'I don't blame you, though. She's a damn fine-looking girl.'

When he, too, went out, Hamish said, 'I'd better go with him, my dear. I don't want to get his back up by staying off work all day, but my heart won't be in it.'

She returned to her room and lay down on the bed to think. So much had happened since she'd woken up and had felt stifled with the heat. She had enjoyed walking barefoot one the carpet of pine needles in the early morning, had enjoyed her cooling dip in the loch, had even, if she was scrupulously honest, enjoyed – revelled in – Jamie MacPhee's flattering remarks.

She wouldn't have been able to look anybody in the face again if she had done what he wanted, especially Hamish. If Duncan Peat ever got to know about it – which he wouldn't for she wouldn't even tell Grace – he would say that God had intervened to stop her from committing adultery. And maybe he'd be right! He was a dedicated minister, she had discovered, having met him in several of the little cottages when someone died or was seriously ill. He had the knack of saying the right thing, of sympathizing as if he truly meant it, of consoling someone who had just lost a husband, a parent, a child, as though that person was the most important thing in the world to him. And they would be, at that moment. It was a great gift to have.

Suddenly recalling what Flora Mowatt had said about him, Marianne shook her head in disgust at the very thought of him hurting his wife. Flora must be mistaken. He wouldn't harm a single living creature!

Anyway, Marianne mused, at least she had done two good turns today. With Duncan having broken his leg – she'd go tomorrow to see how he was – he'd be grateful for help in the garden, and Jamie MacPhee would be glad of the job.

And now, having figured everything out to her own satisfaction, she was free to think about Hamish. It was strange how a misunderstanding on both their parts had caused them to lose two years of real happiness, but they would make up for it. Oh yes, they would make up for it!

Some time later, when she was telling herself that she had better not be too long in dressing for dinner – she wanted to look her best when Hamish came home from the mill – it occurred to Marianne that she owed it to Miss Edith to let her know that their marriage was perfect at last. She had intended inviting them for wee Ranald's christening, but she would write a proper letter instead. Then another, more sobering thought entered her mind. What about Andrew? He was the only other person who knew how things had been between her and Hamish, but would he be more hurt if she told him how things were now? Perhaps it would be better just to say they had improved a little, and tell him the whole truth at some other time.

Chapter Twelve

The summer of 1902 saw preparations for celebrating the coronation in full swing in Glendarril. The dominie and his wife, helped by some of the older children, had freshened up the assembly hall – which also served as a gymnasium, as a sewing room where Mrs Wink showed the older girls how to knit and to stitch, and at other times, where her husband taught the boys woodwork – with two coats of paint, cream from the ceiling to the dado placed well above the reach of even the tallest child, and dark brown from that demarcation line to the floor so that sticky or inky fingermarks would not 'stand out like sore thumbs', as William Wink put it with his usual inability to recognize a pun, although he had made it himself. The same treatment was accorded to the classroom, only one since there were hardly ever more than a dozen pupils on the roll in any one year.

The walls of the hall were then festooned with red, white and blue bunting, and taking pride of place opposite the door were pictures of Edward the Seventh and Queen Alexandra. Trestle tables were to be set up in the playground on 26 June if it was dry, and the whole population of the glen would be sitting down to a repast fit for the Royal couple themselves, which the ladies of the WRI had volunteered to prepare and serve. For weeks, the scholars had rehearsed 'Hearts of Oak' and 'The British Grenadiers' with which to regale the adults between courses, and Mrs Wink was praying that the joyful solemnity of the occasion would rub off on Johnsy Gibb and Davy Marr and make them think twice before tugging any pigtails or, even worse, using them to tie two heads together, which usually resulted in all-out warfare between the sexes.

Still, all in all, it was an exciting time for the country folk, especially for those men who still remembered acting as ghillies at the August shoots Edward had joined as the young and handsome Prince of Wales. One old lady could recall a much more initimate relationship with him but knew that boasting about it, even after forty-odd years, would make some people doubt her son's legitimacy.

Lord Glendarril and family, of course, would be attending the real ceremony in London, and Lady Marianne (as she was still known although not yet entitled to the title) had looked out the robes and coronets – last worn at Victoria's coronation by Hector's parents – and had put them on display in one of the public rooms for a whole day so that anyone who wished could come to see them.

'Marrying into the gentry hasna gone to her head,' the wives told each other, when they were walking back down the long drive, having viewed the robes, 'for there's nae a pick o' side to her.'

Naturally, there were those who disagreed on principle with the decisions made by their employers, as there are in any workforce. Ettie Webster was one such. 'I couldna get ower it when I heard her saying she was putting her laddies to the school here when they're the age,' she sneered the following evening, at a meeting of the Women's Rural Institute in the kirk vestry. 'It just shows she's no' real gentry, for their father and their grandfather, and his father afore him, like enough, was sent to a private school in England some place to be teached, so I thought the laird would've wanted his sons to –'

'The laird did want them to go to his old school,' interrupted Flora Mowatt, 'but their mother wouldn't hear of it. She said she didn't want Ranald and Ruairidh to be brought up thinking they were better than other children in the glen. Mind you, Ranald's just three and Ruairidh's hardly two so she might change her mind when the time comes.'

Grace Peat – president of the WRI – shook her head. 'I don't think she will. In any case, she has been a good friend to me and I do not want to hear anything against her.'

Loud murmurs of agreement to this showed that most of the wives regarded 'Lady Marianne' as a friend. After all, they whispered to each other, didn't she stand and speak to them if she met them on the road any time, even if she'd to come off the bike she'd taken to using for getting around? More to the point, she had started a sort of clothes-exchange for babies and toddlers, even for girls and boys at the school, which was a great help to the mothers with a puckle bairns.

Judging that she had allowed enough time to be wasted, Mrs Peat said, 'Now, we must get down to business . . .'

The meeting proceeded until two committee members rose to make the tea. This was the signal for a hubbub of chattering to break out, discussing the possible consequences of Lady Marianne's boys attending the glen school (a far more important subject to them than the crowning to take place hundreds of miles away), and when they went home, most of the women with daughters under school age were already weaving dreams of being mother-in-law to a Lord one day. Those who had only sons but were still capable of bearing children resolved to produce a girl next time, no matter that they had sworn to their husbands after their last confinement that he need not expect them to have any more.

Grace Peat was no different from her fellow WRI members and was so excited that she didn't stop to think when she went home. 'Oh, I hope it'll be a daughter I have!' The words were scarcely out when her hand flew to her mouth.

Too late! The minister's head jerked up from the sermon

he was preparing. 'Are you trying to tell me that you are
... pregnant?'

His wife flushed, all her dreams for the future disinte-
grating. 'Yes, Duncan. I . . . I didn't know how to tell you.'

'I am not surprised. Have you forgotten how ill you were
when you had pleurisy two years ago? Robert Mowatt as
much as said you were not fit enough to have a child. Does
he know about this?'

'Y-yes . . . and he has warned me that I may have a
difficult time.'

'So! Well, you are taking your life in your own hands
and it will not be my fault if anything happens to you.'

Knowing her husband as she did, Grace let him have the
last word. It was an awful thing for a man of God to think,
never mind say out loud, but at least he hadn't punched
her as he so often did when he was angry with her. It was
fear of his violence that had kept her from telling him of
her condition, made her pull the strings of her corsets so
tight she could hardly breathe, and when he found out that
she was due in three months . . . Thank goodness the baby
seemed small – or at least the bulge around her middle not
so very big. If anything bad should happen to her it was
more likely to be as a result of what he would do to her
than the actual birth.

Marianne was the most excited in the whole of the castle,
with the exception of Jean Thomson, who was to be accompanying her mistress to London. Hamish was looking forward to seeing old school friends again, but his father was
quite blasé about the whole thing.

'We'll get down there in one day, not like in my parents'
time when there was no railway. It took them a week, and
I can remember my mother telling me she felt so faint at
times they had to stop at the first inn they came to, and
some were not fit for decent folk. Of course,' he added

with a smile, 'she was always having fits of the vapours. It was fashionable in her day.'

They were to be staying in his house in Piccadilly, which he used any time he was in the capital on business, which was also when he felt obliged to take his place in the House of Lords. The married couple whom he paid to look after the building while he was not in residence had been advised that he and his son and daughter-in-law would be there for about two weeks and, augmented by several temporary maids and boys, the caretakers had made the rooms ready. In spite of all Marianne's pleas, Hector would not allow Hamish to take her on ahead so that she could see a bit more of London. 'You'll not like it,' he told her.

'Maybe *you* don't,' was her spirited reply, 'but I'm sure I will.'

Hector grimaced at Hamish. 'This wife of yours will be the death of me, too saucy for her own good. I sometimes wish we had picked someone else to be the mother of your boys.'

Noticing the twinkle in his eyes, Marianne just grinned. She was proud of her two sons, and so were the glen wives. When they had been at the castle to view the robes and coronets, the sight of the two fair-haired, blue-eyed little boys racing around the lawns had made them smile, they bore such a striking resemblance to their father. Ranald had more than his share of devilment, but also a great deal of charm, which saved him from being punished for the scrapes he got into, whereas Ruairidh was much quieter, and often the butt of his brother's exuberant pranks. None the less, if either one got on Nurse's wrong side, the other manfully defended him. She was going to miss them while she was away, Marianne mused, on the day before she had to make the journey, but this would be more than counterbalanced by her introduction to London society, the realization of all her dreams.

*　　*　　*

The Bruce-Lyalls arrived in Piccadilly on the evening of 23 June, three days before the coronation, and Hamish forbade Marianne to leave the house the following day. 'You had better take time to recover from the long hours of travelling,' he told her. 'You will want to look your best on the day.'

She was anxious to explore London, but his last sentence made her think. She *did* want to look her best to meet the cream of the nobility, so she had better do as her husband said. She was reclining on a brocaded chaise longue in the drawing room in the late afternoon when Hector burst in and sat down heavily on an uncomfortable-looking chair by the window.

'You'll never guess,' he panted. 'The King...' He stopped to wipe his perspiring brow, then began again. 'They are having to postpone the coronation. Right this minute, the King's appendix is being removed.'

'Is that serious?' Marianne asked. 'How long before...?'

'It is fairly serious in a man of his age, and I really do not know how long it will be before he is fit enough to be crowned... months rather than weeks, I should think.'

'Does that mean...? Will we have to go home and come back?'

'No, no, it is better that we stay in London, just in case...'

Not comprehending what he was hinting at, she felt a surge of excitement go through her. She would have plenty of time now to get to know Hector's titled friends, to do all sort of things she had not expected to do. She would start by exploring this house tomorrow and make friends with the caretaker's wife, who would be able to keep her right on etiquette, etc.

Moll Cheyne had been kept awake all night with Alfie coughing. Deep barks, on and on, till she'd thought he was going to choke, and a cold hand had squeezed at her heart. It was the middle of summer, she mused as she raked out the ashes in the grate, setting aside the cinders which would start the fire today, so it wasn't just a cold he had, and if he died, God forbid, what would she do? He hadn't been fit for the sawmill for a few weeks now, and if he was off much longer, they'd likely be put out of the house, for it went with the job.

Shovelling up the grey dust that was left in the ash-pan, she took it outside to throw on the midden, carefully shielding it from the draught when she opened the door, for she didn't want it blown inside again.

'How is he the day?' asked a voice, as she turned to come back into the house.

She looked up into the concerned face of the foreman sawyer. 'Oh, it's you, Joe. He's nane better. I was up near half the nicht tryin' to ease his cough. I'm right worried.'

'You must be.' Joe Bain was silent for a moment but, realizing that he had no option, he handed her an envelope. 'I'm sorry, Moll, it's nae my doin'. I hope things . . . go a' richt for you.'

He whipped away and she went back inside. She didn't have to open the envelope, she knew what was inside, but she slit the top anyway, and took out the small slip of paper to read the dreaded words.

NOTICE TO QUIT
You are hereby requested to vacate the house you meantime occupy by 26 June. Failure to do so will result in eviction.

She sat down by the flickering coals in despair. What would they do? If Alfie got any worse, she'd have to give up her little cleaning job to look after him, and with nothing coming in, how could they afford to rent a place to live? She had often wished she had some other means of cooking in the summertime when it was too hot with the fire on, but she was glad of it now, for her very bones felt numb with the cold – no, with shock, that's what it was. She'd thought Alec Murchie, the owner of the sawmill, would give them a few months' grace, but the twenty-sixth was less than a week away. She should really keep this bad news from her ailing man, but how could she, when he'd have to be hauled out of his bed in such a short time and made to go God only ken't where?

Mary McKay could likely get him into the poor's house, but it would have to be the last resort, and what about herself? She didn't fancy going back to what she'd been doing before she got wed, though she'd kept her figure, maybe a wee bit more curvy than it was, but most men liked a woman they could get a proper grip of.

While she waited to ask Mary what they could do – the nurse usually called in next door every second day at ten on the dot to see Maggie Burnett's old mother-in-law – she made a start on going through drawers and shelves to see what she would take when she left the house; very little likely, for she'd have no place to put it. She was on the second drawer of the dresser – the furniture all belonged to the mill and would have to be left for the next tenant – when she found a bundle of clippings she had taken from newspapers. She was an incurable hoarder of advertisements she thought might come in handy, corn cures and patent medicines for all kinds of complaints, when a vague memory stirred within her of something else she'd once cut out for future use, something she hadn't wanted Alfie to know she had kept.

Racking her brains, she tried to think what it had been and where she had hidden it, but it was some minutes before she remembered. She gave a satisfied smirk as she removed the lid from the white china hen on the dresser, then lifted out the nest section which could hold one dozen eggs, and nestling underneath, exactly as she had placed it years ago, was the item about his Marion's wedding. It had completely slipped her mind, which showed what a poor housewife she was, for she'd only ever wiped the outside of the white hen, never given it a proper wash.

And then she heard the rattle of Mary's old bicycle and ran out to catch her. 'Will you write a letter for me, Mary?' she asked. 'Once you've done wi' Teenie Burnett?'

'Aye, surely, Moll.' Mary had written many letters for other people in her time as visiting nurse – many of her patients were illiterate, but she knew that Moll Cheyne wasn't. 'Something gey important, is it?'

'Awful important, that's why I asked you, an' it'll need to be posted the day.'

Mary did more than post the letter. After hearing what had happened, she decided to do her best to help the Cheynes. Alfie had slaved all his life at the mill, and it was the sawdust he'd breathed in over the years that had ruined his lungs, but she knew she'd be as well speaking to the wind as trying to get compensation for him from Alec Murchie, for he was a tight-fisted old devil.

She could recommend that Alfie be given a place in the Institute, but he'd likely refuse to go; his mind was still alert enough to shrink from the idea of 'charity'. There was only one alternative left, and she set off on her bicycle to see Jem Park, local businessman and committee member of the Institute's board. He had bought some near-derelict houses a few years back, and let them to people who couldn't afford to rent better places.

Mr Park was a big, rather awe-inspiring man, but very little, people or events, intimidated Mary McKay. 'I'm here to see about a place for Alfie Cheyne and his wife,' she began, bold as brass. 'He's not fit to work now, and they're being put out of the sawmill house, and I know you've got one empty, for I helped to clear it the day before yesterday, after old Jigger Lonie's funeral.'

Jem Park frowned. 'I've got nothing to do with the letting,' he barked. 'You'll have to see my factor, and I would think he's let it by this time. There's a waiting list, you know.'

Mary shook her head in irritation, but went in search of the factor. She had been at school with Greig Lawrie and knew a few little titbits about him that he wouldn't care to reach his wife's ears, so if she had to, she could try a bit of blackmail.

As she had known he would, Greig blustered for a few minutes, swearing that he had already let Jigger's house, then changing, when she said she didn't believe him, to say that she couldn't expect him to let anybody jump their turn. 'There's three after it, and I half promised it to –'

'Then you'll have to take your half-promise back,' Mary said firmly, 'or I'll tell folk about you and Mrs Gill, the doctor's wife.' She had decided to start with his earliest indiscretion and work up to the more recent if the need arose.

His face drained of colour. 'There was nothing atween Mrs Gill an' me! She asked me dae some jobs for her . . . I was only sixteen at the time, for God's sake!'

Mary grinned cockily. 'So you were, but a man for a' that, eh?'

The flattery was all that was necessary.

Moll had still heard nothing from Marianne when the day of eviction came and they were forced to move into the cramped place Mary McKay had managed to get for them. Not only that, she had scrounged a few bits and pieces of furniture – a rickety bed, a couple of chairs and a table. It was anything but comfortable, but at least it was a roof over their heads, Moll told herself, and it would only be till Marion – Marianne – came to their rescue. No doubt it would take her a while to get something organized.

* * *

Marianne soon discovered that she loved the bustle of the capital, watching, when she ventured out with her maid, the elegant carriages conveying well-dressed matrons and their daughters, even trying to guess who sat in the black hansom cabs.

What pleased her even more when she returned from a window-shopping walk with Thomson, was the sight of several calling cards which had been left while they were out. This was the life she had pictured for herself, on the same footing as the barons and earls, although Hamish told her that barons were a lower rank.

In anticipation of returning the calls, she asked the care-taker's wife where the late Lady Glendarril had shopped for clothes, and on being given directions to a very exclusive salon tucked away in a side street practically just around the corner, she set off on her own.

It was the first time Marianne had bought such expensive clothes for herself, but she kept in mind how Lady Glendarril had dealt with the people who served her in Edinburgh, and when she finished her shopping spree, she was highly satisfied with her selection of day dresses and evening gowns, gossamer shawls and substantial capes. She *had* sensed a condescension in the salesladies' manners at times, even in the models who paraded for her, but she didn't care ... the owners of all the establishments she patronized had shown enough deference to satisfy her, practically bowing and scraping as each sale was made.

Her husband refusing to go with her on any of the calls she meant to make, Marianne resolved to go alone. 'But it's not done, Mrs Hamish,' wailed Thomson, who had gone with Lady Glendarril on her rounds and knew the tacit rules under which the gentry operated – not more than an hour in any house being one.

'All right then, you can come in the carriage with me,' Marianne sighed. 'I suppose they'll let you wait in the servants' quarters till I'm ready to leave.'

At the first three calls she made, she sensed that the hostesses felt as awkward with her as she felt with them, although none of them said or did anything to prove that. Wondering if she wasn't dressed properly, she chose carefully from amongst her new outfits for her next venture into the revered company, and plumped for a wine-coloured costume with a narrow skirt which just tipped her black kid shoes, and a hip-length jacket with black frogging. This would have been suitably conservative if she hadn't topped it with a bright blue hat trimmed with ostrich feathers dyed in gaudy reds, greens and yellows, which swept over one eye in a provocative style. 'It'll give me a bit of confidence,' she defended herself to Thomson, whose shocked face told her she had gone too far.

The expressions of the ladies in each of the first two houses she visited that day gave further proof of her *faux pas*, and she wished that she had not worn such a frivolous hat. She had the distinct impression that her hostesses and their friends were inwardly laughing at her, but at least their breeding did not let them ridicule her openly like the girls in Aberdeen who had hurt her all those years before.

She was waiting for Thomson in the hallway of her last call in Guildford Street when she realized that her gloves were still on a small table in the drawing room, and with no warning to the young maid who was seeing her out, she turned and walked back. The door was slightly ajar, enough for the muffled hilarity from inside to reach her ears.

'Oh my, wasn't she awful?' someone was laughing. 'And some of the things she said, I didn't know where to look. Verity Chambers says she was only a shop-girl before she married Hamish Bruce-Lyall.'

'That explains it!' giggled another. 'That hat! Did you ever see anything like it? Her taste must be all in her awful mouth.'

'And her accent!' gushed a third. 'I could hardly understand a word she said.'

Cut to the quick and desperate to retaliate, Marianne threw back the door and marched straight to the occasional table to retrieve her gloves, and not until she reached the door again did she deign to look at any of the young women regarding her silently with their mouths agape. Holding the knob, she said, enunciating each word slowly and with staccato precision, 'I hope you can understand what I am saying now. Yes, I was a shop-girl when Hamish met me, and I was just a skivvy before that, but I was taught manners, something you three obviously weren't.'

Speeding up, she went on scathingly, 'I would never, ever, speak about anybody behind her back the way you were speaking about me.' She opened the door wider, but could not resist a parting shot before going into the hall. 'Let me tell you, I hardly understood a word any of you spoke, either, with your marbles in your mouths and your noses in the air. If you're a sample of London society, I'm glad I live in a wee glen in Scotland.'

Slamming the door, she sailed past the goggle-eyed servant and went down the front steps just as Thomson came up from the basement area. The young groom jumped down hastily to help her into the carriage, and Marianne's dark face warned her maid to ask no questions.

When Hamish and his father returned from the business meeting they had been attending, Marianne told them what had happened, keeping a grip on herself to avoid bursting into tears. Hector had a good laugh at how she had dealt with the situation, but her husband tried to soothe her ruffled feelings.

'Never mind them. They have nothing else to do all day but find fault with others. Is that the hat?' He looked at the offending object which had been thrown in rejection on the seat of a chair. 'Maybe the feathers *are* a teeny bit garish, but that was no reason for them . . .'

Catching the gleam of moisture in Marianne's eyes, her father-in-law said, 'Take her upstairs, Hamish, and see she goes to bed. All the excitement of coming to London has been too much for her.'

Overcome with self-pity, anger at herself for ignoring Thomson's silent criticism, and especially with sharp resentment against her tormentors, Marianne allowed Hamish to guide her to her room.

'Shall I get Thomson to come and help . . . ?' He got no further. The burning tears refused to be contained any longer and burst from her in a torrent which alarmed him. 'They are not worth upsetting yourself over, my dear,' he murmured. 'They are not worthy of licking your shoes.'

He drew away when her sobbing eased, and looked sadly into her face. 'I shall have to leave you again, I'm afraid. I promised to go with Father to see a potential new customer in Brighton. Will you be all right, or should I fetch Thomson?'

'No,' she sniffed, 'I don't want her to see I've been crying.'

'We may not be back until tomorrow, and you need someone. She is very discreet. You can trust her not to tell the other servants.'

When she came in, Thomson clicked her tongue solicitously. 'Would you rather I went away for a wee while, Mrs Hamish . . . till you come to yourself?'

Marianne shook her head. 'It's all right. It's just . . . there was a bit of . . . unpleasantness in that last house I called at. Oh, I might as well tell you.'

The older woman listened to the sorry tale with increasing anger and, when it ended, she said, 'The cook told me her mistress and her two sisters spend most of their time criticising other women, and I think they'd been jealous that none of them has such a distinctive hat. Even if they had, I doubt they could carry it off like you.'

Marianne had to smile at Thomson's staunch loyalty.

'No, I could tell when I put it on you thought it was awful and you were right. I'll ask your advice before I buy any more hats ... not that I'll need any. I'll never come back to London to be made a fool of. Now, you'd better get me out of this costume, and the corset, for it's killing me.'

She stood patiently while her maid undid buttons and unfastened hooks and eyes, turning obediently when instructed to do so, and at last her nightdress was pulled on over her head and she was helped onto the high bed. 'Thank you, Thomson,' she murmured, lying back gratefully.

Left alone again, Marianne's thoughts returned to the glen, and she wondered if her two little darlings were missing her as much as she was missing them. It was the first time she had ever been away from them for any length of time, and the last, if she had any say. Her grasshopper mind jumped now to something else she would be missing in Glendarril, and she smiled as she recalled the way in which she had learned of the two impending happy events.

It had been Flora's turn for the weekly 'afternoon tea', and immediately she had filled the cups and handed round the plate of home-made scones, she burst out, 'I was afraid to tell anybody till after the dangerous third month, but Robert says it's safe now.'

'Oh, Flora, you're pregnant? I'm so pleased for you!' Marianne had exclaimed.

But she had been in for a second surprise, because Grace gave a little cough and got to her feet, tapping on the table in the manner she used as president of the WRI to get the attention of the members before she made an announcement. 'It falls to me,' she declaimed solemnly, 'to express delight at the statement given by our secretary, and to add some news of my own.' She looked at the other two for a moment and then burst out laughing.

Flora's face had screwed up with perplexity, Marianne

remembered, and it had been left to her to say, 'Don't tell me you're expecting, as well, Grace? Wonders will never cease, and when are you due, both of you?'

She had been pleased that both confinements would be in early August, because she should have been home by then, but, as Robert Burns so wisely said, 'The best laid schemes o' mice an' men gang aft a-gley.' Because of King Edward's appendicitis, she was stuck in London. Still, finding out which sex her friends' babies were was a treat for her to go home to, though she would pray every night now that both would be safely delivered.

Robert was cock-a-hoop about becoming a father, but it was difficult to tell with Duncan. He wasn't as forthcoming as Robert, but he was bound to be pleased. Maybe he hadn't cared for the idea of children before – though that might have been another of Grace's jokes – but surely when the infant arrived, he would look on it as a blessing from God.

That was one thing about Hamish. He was a good father, and Marianne did not, and never would, regret marrying him. He loved her as much as she loved him, and as far as the glen folk were concerned, she was a goddess, someone they looked up to and admired for not putting on airs with them. On her first trip to Edinburgh to supplement her wardrobe, as soon as she mentioned that she was the daughter-in-law of the late Lady Glendarril, she had been given honoured treatment, and on the next two occasions she had been recognized immediately she walked in, which had given her a tremendous glow of gratification.

Before she surrendered into the arms of Morpheus, it occurred to her that the only people who had openly not accepted her were the three females (she wouldn't grant them the dignity of thinking of them as ladies) in the house in Guildford Street. She couldn't recall any of their names, except that they were all Honourable Somebodies and probably none of them lived permanently in London. Just the same, they must have known it was her first visit, so what they did was inexcusable.

Let London and all its glories go to the devil, Marianne thought. Hector had been right: she didn't like it, and she would never come back.

Her husband and father-in-law did not return from Brighton until the following day, and she tackled them as soon as they came in. 'I'm going home. I'm not giving anybody else the chance to insult me, and besides, I'm missing my boys.'

Both men were utterly thunderstruck, and it was Hector who rallied enough to say, 'I can understand how you feel, but what about the Coronation? You may never have another chance to see a spectacle like this, and it was the reason you came to London in the first place.'

'Well, I've had enough of it! I just don't want to –'

Hamish interrupted here. 'I know you've been hurt, my dearest, but once you get over it, you'll be all right.'

'No, I won't! I'm sick to the teeth of London and all the stuck-up pigs in it. Look, I'm not expecting you to come with me – I'll manage fine by myself as long as I've got Thomson with me.'

'Well, well!' Hector grinned. 'You've lost none of your pluck, I'll grant you that, and if that's what you're determined to do, I'll book seats for you on the last train tonight. You won't need to worry about your baggage, because Hamish will see to it at this end, and I'll send a wire to Carnie so that he will be at Montrose to take it out of the carriage when he picks you up tomorrow.'

The rest of the day was, therefore, taken up with packing, or rather, Thomson did the work while Marianne paced the floor as if she were champing at the bit to be gone. Every piece of luggage ready at last, the exhausted maid sat down heavily and, her conscience smiting her, Marianne said, 'I'm sorry, Thomson. I know I'm not being fair, trailing you away when I'm sure you're dying to see all the people in the streets on the big day, but –'

'No, ma'am, I've had enough commotion to last me the rest of my life, and all, and I'll be glad to be back home again.'

And so Marianne's dreams of making a good impression and being welcomed into the ranks of the nobility came to nothing. The only impression she made had been much less than favourable – had even been, it could be said, downright ridiculous.

After a hot and exhausting overnight journey, Marianne could not help bursting into tears when her two young sons launched themselves at her in exuberant greeting. 'Oh, do be careful,' Nursie warned them, stepping forward to restrain them. 'Mother is far too tired to be bothered with you just now.'

'Let them stay with me for a little while,' Marianne pleaded.

Thomson, knowing exactly how her mistress must feel, said, 'I know you missed them, Mrs Hamish, but you really should have a rest.'

'Ten minutes . . . please?'

Left alone with her boys, she sat down and lifted them on to her lap. Ranald, always more demonstrative, flung his chubby arms round her neck and covered her face with slobbery kisses, while Ruairidh held on to her fingers as if he were afraid she might go away again. Her seven-week absence had seemed a lifetime to them.

By the time the nurse came for them, some twenty minutes later, Marianne was glad to relinquish them, and went up to her room. 'I was just going to lie down on top,' Marianne protested to Thomson when she saw the bed turned down.

'You'll take a proper rest, Mrs Hamish, or you'll be no

use for anything. Come on, let me take off your things for you.'

'Oh, yes, that's much better,' Marianne sighed, in five minutes. 'I can't understand why women have to be tightened in so much during the day.'

'It's to give us a decent shape,' Thomson said, frowning at the alternative. 'Now just lie back and shut your eyes, and I'll bring your lunch up . . .'

'Take a rest yourself,' Marianne ordered, so near to sleep that she slurred the words slightly. 'I won't need any lunch . . .'

Thomson was smiling as she pulled the curtains together to stop the sun streaming in. She would wake her mistress in time for 'Mother's Hour', when she spent time in the nursery while Ranald and Ruairidh had tea, then played guessing games before settling them down for bed by reading them fairy tales. Nursie, of course, did not approve of this – she was one of the old brigade who felt that mothers had no business interfering in the upbringing of their children – but Mrs Hamish didn't care.

Barely ten minutes later, Thomson burst into the room and ran straight across to let in some light. When she turned round, her mistress was alarmed to see that her face was chalk white. 'What is it? What's happened?'

'Oh, Mrs Hamish, it's awful! Mrs Peat died ten days ago, and the funeral's past and everything! And they say the minister's near off his head with grief.'

Her hand on her palpitating heart, Marianne exclaimed, 'Poor Grace! What did she . . . ? She never looked very strong . . . I'll have to go and see Duncan, he must wonder why I haven't been to offer my condolences.'

'He'll have known you were away. I'll fasten your stays for you, and it'll not take me a minute to get myself ready . . .'

'No, Thomson, it's best that I go myself. He'll not want anyone else seeing him if he breaks down.'

Pushing away the proffered corset, Marianne pulled on a thin skirt and a lawn blouse, then hurried out. To get there quicker, she decided to cycle, although it wasn't far to the manse and walking would have given her time to think what to say. This was the only one out of all of the duties she had to undertake that she didn't care for and she knew Duncan hadn't cared for it either. It was heart-rending to see the sorrow in the eyes of a man who had lost his wife, or a woman who had lost her husband. It was worse when a child died, although women usually bore up better than men.

Grace Peat had been such a lovely person; full of fun and she had never complained about anything. Maybe it would have been better if she had, Marianne mused; maybe the doctor could have cured whatever had ailed her.

As she had expected, when he opened the door, Duncan's face was gaunt, his dark hair dishevelled, his near-black eyes almost lifeless, and as soon as he ushered her into his front room, he held out his arms. Quite taken aback, she held him, letting his shuddering body lie close against hers as great sobs burst from him. She knew not to say anything until he was calmer, but he seemed to take an awful long time, and at last she tried to step back.

'No, don't let me go,' he groaned. 'My parishioners all expressed condolences at the graveside, but Robert Mowatt's the only one who has come to see me since. I need someone to talk to, Marianne, and to hold me! I need you.'

He dropped his head until his chin was resting on her breast, but it wasn't until she realized that his hands were on her buttocks that she felt a tingle of fear. With every second that passed, there came another sign that he was arousing himself by the things he was doing to her, and she wished with all her heart that she had not come out uncorseted.

'Oh, I miss Grace so much,' he moaned, effectively stopping her from trying to wriggle free.

'Of course you will,' she murmured, his words doing a little to reassure her. 'You'd been married for . . . ?'

'For ten and a half years,' he supplied, his fingers caressing her left hip, 'and never once did she refuse me. There are not many men who can say that about their wives. That is why I . . . that is why I . . . I haven't had any release since she told me she was . . . pregnant . . . and she didn't tell me until it was too late.'

'Too late?'

He looked up at her sadly. 'Robert said . . . she was not strong enough . . .' His face crumpling, he burrowed his head into her neck.

His evil intentions soon became crystal clear. His hands were everywhere, one moment pummelling her hips, the next tearing open her blouse and grasping her so roughly that she lashed out with her foot. He had placed his own legs around hers, however, in such a way that she could do him no harm, and in a matter of seconds, he had managed to get her thrashing body down on the sagging leather sofa.

'Duncan!' she pleaded. 'Please stop!'

His only reply was to punch her in the stomach, which proved to her that he didn't know what he was doing. He was past all reason – he had no control over his actions, but, despite knowing it was useless, she continued to fight him. It was an instinctive reaction, but it seemed to make him more violent – he wasn't just touching her in places he shouldn't, he was hurting her, doing his best to make her scream out in agony, and no matter how she tried, she couldn't stop it. But she did stop struggling.

'That's better,' he muttered, his hand less aggressive. Suddenly he said, 'You've only yourself to blame, Marianne. It's your fault.'

She couldn't understand what he meant, but she was

determined not to say anything to set him off again, for he was absolutely raving mad. 'It's your fault,' he repeated, twisting her nipple until she gave an agonized groan. 'It's your fault and you're going to suffer for it.'

In seconds, he had hauled off her skirt and drawers and was clawing at her most intimate part, but when he changed position to open his trouser buttons, she took advantage of her freedom to lash out at him with her fists and slam her knee into his groin. He merely gave a grunt and landed his knee on her stomach with such force that it nearly knocked all the breath out of her.

'You little bitch!' he snarled. 'You common little bitch!'

When he finally drove into her, the excruciating pain made her lose consciousness, and when she came round, he had obviously satisfied himself, because he was sitting on the chair at the fireside, looking at the cinders and ashes that he had not cleaned out from the night before. She made a little move to see if he would notice, but he appeared to be in a world of his own, and so she made her escape as quietly as she could, each breath laboured, as if she had been running.

Chapter Thirteen

On his way to answer the urgent knocking, Robert Mowatt wondered which of his patients had taken a turn for the worse. Old Willie Cattanach had looked a bit better yesterday; surely he hadn't had a relapse? The doctor's eyes widened in astonishment when he opened the door.

'Good God, Marianne!' he exclaimed. 'What happened?'

He had already guessed, however. Her obvious state of trembling shock, her white face, the long strands of chestnut hair dislodged from their hairpins, the way she was holding her ripped blouse together and the bruises on her arms, told him the whole story without her having to say a word. She flinched when he put an arm at her back to shepherd her inside.

'Who was it?' he asked gently. 'Who did this to you?'

Unwilling, or unable, to talk, she shook her head, and Flora, whose mouth had fallen open at the sight of her, came forward. 'Marianne, you must tell us.' She turned to her husband to whisper, 'Go and get a blanket for her,' and when he was out of the room, she bent over the distressed victim again. 'Who was it, my dear? For what he did to you, he must be punished.'

She was still waiting for a reply when Robert returned with the blanket. 'Go and make a cup of tea,' she ordered him. 'I'm sure she'll tell me if you leave us alone for a while.'

With the closing of the door, Marianne looked up at the woman who had come to be as close a friend as she could afford to have amongst her father-in-law's tenants. 'Promise you won't tell him?'

'I can't promise that, Marianne. He has to know.'

'But I don't want it reported to the police . . . Duncan's been through enough already . . .'

Flora Mowatt looked as if she'd been felled with an axe. 'Duncan?' she gasped. 'Duncan Peat? Don't tell me it was *him*? Grace always said he was a violent man, but . . .'

'I only heard about Grace this morning . . . so I went to tell him how sorry I was, and . . . he looked so pathetic . . . and he wanted me to hold him . . .' She paused, then went on, 'I was so hot I'd taken off my corset . . . and I didn't put it on to come out . . . so he . . . so he . . .' Her babbling came to a stammering halt.

Flora's sympathy for her changed to fury at her attacker. 'Losing his wife is no excuse for raping you!'

At last the tears came, noisy ragged sobs seemingly dredged up from the very innermost part of her, and Flora stood back and let her cry. It would help to wash out the shame she must feel, though it wouldn't banish it altogether.

The doctor, who had waited until the storm was over, came in with a tray when Marianne quietened. He looked quizzically at his wife, who said, 'Yes, she's told me.'

'Who was it, then?' he asked, somewhat tetchily, not accustomed to people holding anything back from him.

She lifted the teapot and started pouring. 'She doesn't want me to tell you.'

'Godammit, Flora, I have to report it to the police.'

'Calm yourself, Robert,' she soothed, handing a cup to Marianne. 'It's going to be hard enough for her to face him again without the whole glen knowing what he's done.'

He swallowed, trying hard to contain his irritation at the feminine logic. 'She wouldn't have to face him again. The police would lock him up. At the very least, when Lord Glendarril comes back he will send him away.'

Her face working in agitation, Marianne burst out, 'You

can't put the police on him, not when he's newly lost his wife!'

Robert seized on what she had inadvertently revealed. 'Duncan? But good God –'

'He didn't actually . . . I managed to get away before he . . .'

'That's not the point, though! The intention was there!'

'But he didn't! He didn't, Robert!' She looked imploringly at Flora now, but before his wife could say anything, Robert cried, 'You're not doing him any good by shielding him, you know! He could –'

'I'm not shielding him! Please, Robert, just leave the matter there!'

'I can easily find out. I only need to examine you.'

'Don't touch me, Robert Mowatt!' she screamed, her eyes frantic with apprehension. 'Don't you dare touch me!'

'I only want to know the truth!'

'I'll tell you the truth,' Flora put in quietly. 'Yes, Duncan did rape her but she doesn't want anybody else to know. Finish your tea, then you had better take her home. We can discuss what's to be done when you come back.'

While the doctor went to harness his pony, Flora got a coat for Marianne. 'Cover yourself with this, my dear, and nobody will be any the wiser. I can understand why you don't want the police involved, but think about it when you're calmer. He shouldn't get away with what he's done to you.'

Marianne gave a long uneven sigh. 'I don't want them to know.'

She said nothing to the doctor on the short journey to the castle, but when he helped her out of the trap, she murmured, 'Please don't report him, Robert. He didn't know what he was doing . . .'

She managed to creep upstairs without anyone seeing her, and had put on another blouse and skirt and tidied her hair before Thomson came in. 'I wondered if you were back,' the maid observed. 'How's the minister bearing up?'

It was all Marianne could do to keep her voice steady. 'He's very ... low ... as you'd expect.'

'Yes, yes, of course. Will I tell Cook you're ready for lunch?'

'No, I don't feel like eating.'

'You'll still be upset about Mrs Peat. Well, just ring if you feel like having something later on.'

Having seen Marianne safely inside, Robert took matters into his own hands by going to the manse before he went home. Ever since Grace died, he had felt that the minister was balancing on the fine line between sanity and insanity, and Marianne's visit, well meant though it was, must have tipped the balance the wrong way. Anyway, he wanted to know what the man had to say for himself. He had never cared much for Duncan Peat, not even when they were boys together. Being two years older, Duncan had bullied Robert and threatened him with all kinds of weird punishment if he told anyone. That was why he had believed Grace about a year ago when he had been attending her for blinding headaches and she had confessed that it was fear of her husband that caused them. He had calmed her then, given her powders to help her to sleep at nights, had even had a word with Duncan, but he'd had the feeling that his little talk with the man had only made things worse.

The doctor knew that his hands were tied as far as police were concerned, but he'd have to pass on word of the rape to Lord Glendarril and, more urgently, issue a warning to the offender. He would tell the pervert that it was only Marianne's pleading that had saved him from being reported to the police, and that nothing would save him from jail if he interfered with any other woman in the glen.

When Robert arrived at the manse, he was not really surprised to see the outside door standing wide open –

probably just as Marianne had left it when she ran out. Dreading what he might find, he was reluctant to enter the house, but it was a duty he could not avoid. He was relieved to find the man sitting by his fireside, muttering to himself. He did not appear to be conscious of another presence until he was tapped on the shoulder, and when he raised his head, Robert gave a grunt of satisfaction. His suspicions were correct – there was no recognition in the man's wild eyes, he was dribbling from the mouth, he was sitting in a pool of urine. He was absolutely mad!

There was further trauma for Robert Mowatt the following day when he called at Hillside Mental Hospital to ask if the newest inmate was showing any sign of returning to normal.

The superintendent, biting his lip nervously, led the way into his private office. 'Peat strangled himself with the bed-sheet sometime in the night. It was only discovered when an attendant went to give him his breakfast this morning, and I cannot tell you how badly it has affected all the staff. It is the only suicide in my five years' service here, but there is nothing I could have done. I visited him last evening in the room we keep for very disturbed persons, and he seemed much calmer, so I decided that he could safely be left alone. In my experience, a good night's sleep quite often helps to clear the brain but . . .' The man shrugged his shoulders.

Robert's first reaction was guilt that he had abandoned Duncan at his lowest ebb. If he had spent the night with him, made sure that he did nothing desperate, he might have pulled through.

'Do not blame yourself,' the superintendent said gently. 'I, too, feel guilty. I should have had someone sit with him, but, frankly, I doubt if he would ever have recovered. It is better this way.'

Not convinced of this, the doctor shook the superintendent's hand and went home to tell Flora, who said, 'Of course it's better he killed himself, though it's a terrible thing to say. Once word got round of what he did to Marianne, his life wouldn't have been worth living. His parishioners thought the world of him, but they'd have turned against him, I'm sure. His Lordship would have put him away. God knows what poor Grace had to put up with. You know, Robert, I really miss her – she was a lovely person, wasn't she?'

Robert sighed. 'Yes, she was. Far too good for him.'

It was a nine days' wonder! The good folk of the glen had gossip aplenty to turn over, rumours abounded, speculations ran wild – the minister had tried to hang himself in the manse, that was why he'd been committed to the madhouse, but his head had been taken out of the gas oven just in time; there was even a faction who suspected that some woman had been involved, but the consensus of opinion was: 'Poor man, it was losing his wife and bairn that turned his brain, and them that try suicide and fail usually make a right job of it the next time they try.'

Only two people had any idea of what had actually taken place and they were not saying anything, not even to each other. Robert was nearly sure that it was Duncan Peat's ill treatment of his pregnant wife that had killed her, while Flora thought that the minister had been verging on mad lustfulness for some time. His hands had brushed her breasts once when she'd been arranging flowers in the kirk, and touched her hip another time, accidentally she had believed, but now she wasn't so sure. Maybe she had got off lightly, and she must do something to cheer her friend who had not been so lucky.

Flora went to the castle the day after Duncan's suicide, leaving the large perambulator outside and proudly carrying its tiny occupant inside. 'I thought I'd give you a wee while to get over things,' she announced, when the young parlourmaid showed her in. 'But I thought you'd like to see my daughter.'

Her eyes widening, Marianne gasped, 'Oh, Flora, I'm so sorry! I was in such a state . . . I should have asked . . .'

'It's all right, Marianne, I understood.'

'But I should have asked . . . I'm truly glad it went all right for you this time. Third time lucky, they say. A daughter . . . how nice!'

'She was born two weeks ago.' Flora pulled down the shawl. 'Isn't she adorable?'

'She's absolutely gorgeous!' Marianne gazed entranced at the tiny infant with black hair and dark blue eyes that seemed to have a touch of mischief in them. 'What's her name?'

Flora was beaming with pleasure. 'Esmerelda. Melda for short. Robert let me choose and I've loved that name since I read *The Hunchback of Notre-Dame* when I was just a girl.'

'But Esmerelda was a gypsy.' Andrew had recommended this novel as a favourite of his mother's.

'I know, but it's still a lovely name.'

Thomson came in then with a daintily set tea-tray and, of course, begged for permission to take the tiny babe below stairs, and when the two young women were left alone, Marianne said, 'She's more like Robert than you, but babies change so quickly, don't they?'

'I hope you're none the worse for what happened,' Flora murmured, awkwardly. 'It'll take time to get over it, but at least you won't have to see him ever again.'

'Thank goodness, and I'll have to forget what he did . . . or try to.'

The funeral was over – quite a good turn-out considering – but despite the darkness in the one-roomed house, Moll Cheyne couldn't bring herself to open the curtain. She had missed Alfie since the very second he drew his last struggling breath, and this mark of respect was all she had to remind her of how quickly he had gone.

When she'd had to tell him they'd to move out of the cottage, she had pleaded with him to let her write to Marion – she'd had no reply to the letter Mary McKay had written for her – but he was, had been, a thrawn, independent man, and above all else, as far as his daughter was concerned any road, unforgiving. 'I don't . . . want her . . . charity,' he'd managed to get out.

'She can well afford it.' Moll had wanted to shake him for being so stupid. 'The sawmill's stopped payin' you, so we'll nae be able to rent a decent hoose, an' we've nae money laid by.'

She could still remember how agitated he'd got at that, which was why she hadn't suggested taking another cleaning job although Alfie needed her constant nursing, anything to get a few bawbees. He'd have said she was wanting to show folk he couldn't support his own wife, when, poor soul, he'd put himself in an early grave with being so determined. They hadn't got a decent house, of course, just one garret room two stairs up that Mary McKay had found for them, so damp that if she hung her coat up on the hook on the back of the door after being out to buy what little food she could afford, it had green mould on it before she needed to put it on again.

But there wasn't a soul in Tipperton could say she had neglected Alfie. She'd gone hungry herself so she could give him something he liked – though he hardly ate anything at all – and she'd picked up all the lumps of coal she saw lying on the road, fallen off the cart. She hadn't cared that folk might speak about her, hadn't cared about anything except looking after Alfie, until . . .

Moll let out a hopeless sigh. She had gone begging to the council to help with the shilling rent she couldn't pay at the end of their third week there, and had been told,

'We do not pay rent for anybody. If your landlord evicts you, it will be the Institute for you.'

The Institute, Moll thought angrily. She would have sold her soul to the devil to keep this from her dying man, but while she was out, the factor had called, given Alfie their notice to get out and told him it was the poor's house for them. That was what had killed her husband! He was still alive when she went home, and had managed to tell her, in laboured breaths and with deep shame in his eyes, about his visitor, but had stopped breathing almost as soon as the two dreaded words 'poor's house' had passed his lips.

Her hands came up to her head in anguish. If only she had ignored his pride and written to Marion again . . . but it was too late now. There was no sense in telling her that her father had died. She wouldn't want to know, not after all this time. And the fine lady needn't feel any responsibility for her stepmother, either. Moll Cheyne had a good pair of hands on her, and a sister in Glasgow who wanted her to go and live there, so she didn't need anybody's help . . . especially not Madam High-and-Mighty Marion's.

But, by God, the girl shouldn't get away with ignoring her father's plight. She hadn't done anything for him while he was ill, but she could damn well pay for a gravestone. It was the least she could do.

Marianne's wish to put the rape behind her was doomed to failure. Two days after Duncan Peat's funeral, Robert Mowatt went to Laurencekirk station to collect a parcel from the London train. Seeing Hamish getting off, he thought this chance of a private talk with him was too good to miss. As the future Lord Glendarril, Hamish had the right to know, and his wife certainly wouldn't tell him.

While Carnie was stowing the luggage on to the high-slung carriage, the doctor moved forward. 'I'd like a word with you, Hamish. It's . . . um . . . a bit delicate, so if you tell Carnie to pick you up at my house, you can ride along with me.'

The arrangement made, Hamish got up on the small trap and listened as Robert's story unfolded. 'Grace Peat dead?' he said sadly, when he received the first piece of information. 'Oh, poor Duncan! I had better go and see him before I go home.'

'No, no, Hamish, you can't do that! Wait and hear me out!'

Hamish had been registering sorrow up to this point, but his nose wrinkled in puzzlement at the vehemence in his friend's words, and a look of total incredulity flooded his face in a few moments. 'That can't be true!' he exclaimed. 'For goodness' sake, he's a minister of the Church! He wouldn't lay a finger on the lowest maidservant, let alone –'

'He was a monster at the end,' Robert stressed firmly, 'and there is no blame whatsoever attached to Marianne, I can assure you. She called at the manse with the best of intentions and he flung himself on her. She did try to fight him off, but I very much doubt if any woman could have. The deranged have the strength of the devil, you know. It took three men to carry him out when . . .' Breaking off, he looked at Hamish in appeal. 'I had to certify him.'

'I can't believe that Marianne . . . that he . . . *raped* her.'

Picking up a trace of suspicion in these last words, Robert said hastily, 'Speaking as her doctor, Hamish, I advise you not to let her know I have told you. Perhaps I was wrong in doing so. She feels deeply ashamed although she has no need to be, and the sooner she can erase the attack from her memory the better.'

At the gate of the doctor's house, Hamish professed to be grateful for being acquainted with the facts, however unpalatable, but the thought of his wife being raped by a mad Duncan Peat gnawed at his innards as he transferred to the carriage to make the last leg of his journey. By the time he reached the castle, his mouth was bone dry, his head was pounding, his stomach churned and he staggered slightly when he set foot on the driveway.

Carnie eyed him anxiously. 'Was the doctor saying something to upset you, Master? There's been that many stories goin' round, you'd be best no' to heed any o' them . . . an' if I was you, I wouldna say anything to Lady Marianne. I ken for a fact she'd been to see Duncan Peat the day he was taken away, for she left her bicycle and the doctor got Peter Wink to take it back to the castle, and I've the feeling he did something, the minister, I mean . . .' The old man pulled himself up. 'Ach, I'm just a bletherin' skate, as bad as the rest o' them.'

Marianne jumped to her feet when her husband entered what had been the Blue Room but which was now a delicate shade of cream. The nervous tic at her cheek and the way her hands opened and shut convulsively told him that what Robert had told him was true, and he had to force himself to kiss her cheek. 'I left as soon as I could after the Coronation. Father is still down there, but I was worried about you.'

'I got home all right,' she said stiffly.

The restraint between them was practically tangible; neither could smile at the other and it was as if they were strangers, looking away in embarrassment each time their eyes met.

At last, Marianne said, 'Why don't you sit down, Hamish? You must be tired after your journey. I'll ring for a pot of tea.'

Her mundane manner in the face of what he had learned nudged him out of control. 'I don't know how you can stand there so calmly!' he spat out. 'As if nothing has happened!'

Her face blanched. She had known that the rumours would eventually reach his ears, but she hadn't expected him to have heard before he even crossed the threshold.

'Who's been telling tales?' she asked, her sarcasm a screen for her fear of the consequences.

'So it's true?'

'I don't know what you're speaking about.'

'I'm speaking about Duncan Peat. How could you let him . . . ?'

Shaking her head, she wrung her hands in anguish. 'Hamish, I did *not* let him!'

'No? That's not what I've been told.'

This snapped her self-control now. 'All right, believe what you like and who you like, but I swear I did not *let* him do anything.'

'But it's him! A man of God! It would be against all he ever stood for to . . . fornicate with another man's wife when he had just lost his own.' Giving a gasp as an unwelcome thought struck him, he took a step towards her and stuck his outraged face close to hers. 'I must have been blind. You had been carrying on with him even before Grace died! Perhaps Ruairidh is *his* child?'

Without stopping to think, Marianne gave him a resounding slap on the cheek. 'How dare you speak to me like that? I've never let any man touch me except you.' She couldn't say more. The insult was too great to bear, and putting her hands to her eyes, she burst into a flood of tears.

Love for her overcoming all else, Hamish put his arms around her, and the stiffening of her body did more to convince him that she had been taken by force than further denials would have done. 'I should not have said that, Marianne,' he mumbled, 'and I am deeply sorry.'

Marianne had been fearing Hector's return, fearing the anger he would direct at her; he was bound to blame her. He wouldn't take the word of a shop-girl, even though that shop-girl was the mother of his two grandsons. On the morning of the day he was due to arrive, she asked

Hamish to tell his father about Duncan Peat before he brought him back to the castle. 'He might have cooled down by the time he reaches here,' she explained, thinking that it was highly unlikely.

She worried when they took so long to arrive back from the station, and she trembled with dread at what her father-in-law would say to her when they did turn up, but she never dreamed how he would be brought home.

Lord Glendarril had died of a seizure on the station platform. Robert Mowatt helped Hamish and Carnie to carry him in, laying him out on top of his father's desk in the study rather than in his bed upstairs.

Then Carnie turned to Hamish and astonished them all by saying, 'Will I go to Brechin for the undertaker, your Lordship?' He was the only one who had realized the import of the death.

Hamish looked in horror at Robert. 'Oh, my God!' he moaned, then, gulping back a noisy sob, he hurried out of the room.

The doctor put a hand on Marianne's arm to prevent her following him. 'Leave him just now, your Ladyship.'

'Don't call me that. I'll always be Marianne to you and Flora.'

'Thank you, my dear. Hamish has had a terrible shock, and –'

'Were you there when it happened?'

'No, Carnie came for me, but I was too late.'

'Do you know if Hamish had time to tell him about . . . ?'

'If you think he died because of you, forget it. I've been telling him for months that his heart wasn't up to all the rushing about he was doing, but he wouldn't listen.'

'But if Hamish had told him about Duncan, wouldn't that have been bad for his heart, and all?'

'My dear Marianne, stop torturing yourself. I was expecting it to give out at any time. In any case, I have just remembered. Carnie said Hector hadn't even set foot on the platform when he clutched his chest, and he and Hamish had both rushed to help him down. Then he collapsed altogether and Carnie came for me. Rest assured, my dear, your father-in-law died knowing nothing of what happened.'

Hector looked so peaceful after the undertakers had done their job. Hamish ordered the funeral for a week later, and so began seven days of what Marianne could only think of as the 'lying in state'. What seemed like millions of people – glen folk, relatives, men with whom he had done business, lords and ladies, dukes and duchesses, earls and countesses – milled around the castle before and after the burial service, and if it hadn't been for the self-effacing Miss Glover, Marianne wouldn't have coped. Because a new minister had not yet been appointed to the parish, Hamish had asked Mr Munro from Arbroath, a great friend of his father's, to take the service, a task which the elderly man was only too honoured to shoulder.

Marianne's deep sorrow for the loss of the man who meant more to her than her own father had ever done was made much worse on the day of the funeral by the shaking that assailed her when she neared the church, and when she was passing the manse, it was all she could do to keep moving, for Duncan Peat's lust-distorted face kept swimming before her eyes. Hamish, of course, was too immersed in his own grief to pay any heed to her, and it fell to Robert Mowatt to help her into the kirkyard, between the lines of people from near and far who had known and liked Hector Bruce-Lyall.

Her old horror of graveyards returned at that moment, and she clung to the doctor's arm as a ghostly Hector floated past her, looking at her accusingly and shaking his head. She was practically paralysed with terror before the service ended, and Robert had to whisper, 'Bear up, Marianne, it's all over now,' before she could put one foot past the other.

The glen folk had always accorded her the courtesy of

referring to her as Lady Marianne, but when the mourners returned to the castle and she heard someone calling Hamish 'your Lordship', the realization of her entitlement to the title did much to restore her equilibrium, and to boost her confidence amongst the high-born guests in her home.

She had been pleased to see Andrew Rennie and his aunts in the kirk, but when she invited them to the funeral tea, Miss Edith had said, 'Thank you, your Ladyship, but we must go home,' and Andrew had said, *sotto voce*, 'Well, you've got your wish, Lady Glendarril.'

The line of people had moved on and she hadn't had another chance to speak to them, to tell them that she was still just Marianne, the same as she had always been.

Most of the women, not worthy of the title they held, had talked more to Miss Glover than to her, and even when they did address her directly, their manner was condescending. Only one had singled her out and had a conversation with her.

'I saw them all giving you the cold shoulder,' she had begun, 'but don't you worry your pretty young head about it. I got much the same treatment when I married Clarice's cousin and I've survived. In fact most of them have forgotten by now that I ever was a shopkeeper's daughter and had no right to mix with the likes of them. I'm Lady Matthewson, by the way, Barbara to you, and my daughter's Hamish's age. He used to come to Maxton House sometimes to play tennis with Pam – before he met you – but why don't you get him to bring you over to see us some time? Once the mourning period is past?'

Marianne hadn't known what to say. She was pleased to be invited, but was afraid that, if she did pluck up the courage to go, Lady Matthewson might change her mind about welcoming a shop assistant to her home. 'Is your daughter not with you today?' she enquired.

'Pam's touring Europe at present. She thought a lot of

Hector, though, so she'll be very disappointed at not being here for his funeral.' Barbara Matthewson's eyes were caught then by someone she knew and, excusing herself, she walked away.

The parlour maid seemed ill at ease the day after the funeral when she knocked and opened the morning-room door. 'There's a ... woman at the door asking to see you, m'Lady.'

Marianne raised her eyebrows. 'Didn't you ask who she was?'

'I did ask, m'Lady, but she wouldn't tell me.'

Marianne frowned and began, 'Tell her I do not wish to see anyone at –' but before she could finish, a figure appeared in the doorway, a figure from her past – a past, moreover, that she did not want to be reminded of, especially now.

'Oh, m'Lady, I told her to wait outside,' the maid was excusing herself, but the woman came right into the room saying, 'I think *her Ladyship* will see me.'

If the maid noticed the sneering emphasis, she gave no sign, but scuttled out so quickly that the door swung shut with a thud.

Marianne regarded her visitor coldly. 'What do you want?'

Sitting down as if she were well accustomed to being in such opulent surroundings, Moll said, 'I wouldna have needed to come if you'd ta'en some notice o' the letter I sent a while back.'

Marianne was genuinely puzzled. 'I received no letter from you.'

'Oh, so that's the wey o' it, is it? You're sayin' you never *received* it, are you? Well, let me tell you, *m'Lady*, it was Mary McKay that wrote it for me, an' it was her that posted it, so I ken fine you *received* it, unless you're cryin' Mary a liar?'

Marianne could feel her self-confidence draining away with each sarcastic word. Moll had made her feel like a child again, a silly child who had run away after stealing five sovereigns . . . but surely her father's wife wasn't here because of that? 'When . . . was . . . the letter sent?'

'I can tell you that easy enough,' Moll sneered. 'It was the twenty-second day of June, that's when, just days afore we was put oot o' the hoose.'

'Put out? But why . . . ?'

'Your father had to stop workin' wi' his chest, and we got a notice to quit or we'd be evicted, an' I got Mary to write an' ask you if you could send us some money so we could rent a decent place. A fat lot you cared, for you never answered, but Mary got us a room in Bridge Street.'

She had stopped for breath, but Marianne said nothing. She had never thought of her father since she left, had never even wondered if he was well or otherwise.

'Aye, my fine leddy,' Moll went on in a few moments, 'that's made you think. Here's you in your castle, wi' every blessed thing you need an' servants to run after you, and there was me and your father in one room wi' the damp runnin' doon the wa's.'

Marianne was caught on the raw. 'And little you cared about me when I was at hame,' she snapped. 'Him nor you, you were that ta'en up wi' each other you hadna time for me.' She did not notice that, in her anger, she had reverted to her old tongue. 'I bet you were glad to be on your own wi' him, and it didna bother me. I managed to better mysel'.'

'You did that, a' richt,' Moll spat out, 'but what would your servants think, an' your fine friends, if they ken't you'd once been a skivvy and stole money fae your mistress?'

Marianne was even more infuriated by this. 'Are you threatening me? If I don't give you money, you'll tell them, is that it?'

Losing her temper now, Moll shouted, 'I dinna want your money . . . nae for mysel', ony road. I'll manage to work for what I need, but I think it's only richt that Alfie gets a gravestone, an' you can weel afford it. Mair to the point, it would let folk see his only lassie hadna forgot him.'

Marianne's chest was heaving now. She'd had enough to cope with before Moll turned up, and if the only way to get rid of her was to erect a headstone to mark her father's grave, so be it! 'I'll get my solicitor to arrange it,' she said loftily. 'And I'll get to the bottom of this letter you say you sent. I can assure you, that if I *had* received it, I would not have let my father die in a hovel.'

'Aye, weel, then, just you mind.' Obviously at a loss as to what to say now, Moll decided against saying anything and stalked out, leaving Marianne leaning against the back of her chair with her heart palpitating.

Once she recovered, she went to Hamish's study and took out a sheet of crested notepaper, thankful that he'd been called to London on urgent business – some query about a price which had been quoted and not stuck to, that was all he'd told her except that he would not be home for at least a week – because she didn't want him to know about this. He believed that she had run away from home because she was being ill treated, but neither her father nor her stepmother had ever been physically cruel to her. It was more that she'd resented being ousted from her father's affections by a person she thought was common . . . but Moll had apparently been a good wife, looked after him right to the end.

The tear which plopped on to her hand now made her more ashamed of herself than ever. She *should* have contacted him, found out how he was, if they needed help. He had worked hard for her when she was small, and looked after her single-handedly after her mother died – until he married again. She had never wanted for anything . . . and he had died in poverty.

Then she remembered the letter Moll had said she sent. What had happened to it? Stretching out her hand, she pulled the bell rope at the fireplace and in less than a minute, the little parlour maid appeared at the door. 'Yes, m'Lady?'

'Rosie,' Marianne said, uncertain as to how to word her question because she didn't want to blame the girl if it wasn't her fault, 'I have just found out that a letter came for me while I was in London, which seems to have got lost. Would you know what became of it?'

The girl had been smilingly waiting to hear what was required of her, but at the mention of the letter her face lost every vestige of colour and she looked as if she were about to faint.

'Are you all right, Rosie?' Marianne enquired anxiously.

'Oh, m'Lady, I'm sorry! I can't tell you how sorry I am. I forgot all about it. You see,' she hurried on, desperate to explain, 'Cook asked me to go and get the veggies Dargie had promised her, and I just went out the door when Postie handed me that letter, so I stuffed it in my pocket and carried on. I stopped a wee while to speak to Davey Black, he's assistant gardener since Ben Rogie left and we'd been ... keeping company ... still are,' she confided, blushing a little. Then the haunted look returned to her eyes and a tear trickled out. 'Oh, m'Lady, I know I shouldn't have wasted my time like that, and that's why I forgot about the letter. I'm that sorry. I hope it was nothing important?'

Marianne's smile was rueful. 'It was very important, as it happens.'

'Oh, m'Lady, you're not going to sack me, are you? I didn't mean it . . .'

Marianne hesitated. Her first instinct was to send the girl packing, but she liked little Rosie, who always spoke in her best English and always did what she was told willingly and efficiently. Besides, the poor thing hadn't meant it, yet . . . 'Tell me, Rosie,' she said, as something occurred to her, 'why didn't you find the letter if it was in the pocket of your apron? Surely you would have noticed it when you carried on with your own work.'

'It was pouring rain that day, m'Lady, and I'd put on my coat, and I've never had it on since.'

Her eyes brightened a little. 'It'll still be there! Do you want me to get it?'

'Yes, I *would* like to see what it said.'

While she waited for the parlour maid to return, Marianne dipped the pen into the crystal inkwell, but she had only written 'Dear Andrew' when the girl came hurrying in, holding out a rather crumpled envelope which her mistress grabbed and tore open. It was written in a beautiful script, which astonished Marianne until she remembered that it was Mary McKay who had actually done the writing, likely interpreting what Moll wanted to say.

Marion,

I wish to let you know that your father is very ill. He has not been able to work for some time now, so the mill is putting us out of the house. He needs constant attention, so I can not take a job myself. We will have nothing coming in and I am forced to ask you if you will help us. If you can let us have enough to give him a decent roof over his head and the nourishing food he needs to give him strength to recover, that is all I want from you.

Moll Cheyne

Marianne heaved a somewhat ragged sigh, then realized that the girl was still waiting. 'It's all right, Rosie. I'm not going to sack you, but please be more careful in future.'

The girl did not take the intended dismissal. She had told Cook about the awful-looking woman who was in with the mistress, and knew that Mrs Carnie would expect her to find out who it had been. It was not in Rosie's nature to be bold, or to poke her nose into other people's business, but she was well aware that her life wouldn't be worth living downstairs if she didn't. And so, her face as red as a cock-turkey, she stammered, 'Had the l-letter to do with the w-woman that was here? I know there was a row, for I heard you both shouting.'

Taking a moment to decide how to answer this, Marianne said, 'She wrote it and she couldn't understand why I hadn't replied. But it's all sorted out now, so get back to your duties and we'll say no more about it.'

'Thank you, m'Lady.'

Before knuckling down to writing to Andrew, Marianne couldn't help wondering if it would have made any difference if Moll's letter had been sent to London along with the rest of their mail, and came to the shaming conclusion that it probably wouldn't have, especially if it had followed the afternoon tea fiasco. At that time, she hadn't had even a drop of the milk of human kindness left in her, and she'd had no compassion for anyone else. She would most certainly have torn the letter up. She had never liked her stepmother and she'd have thought it was just a begging letter.

Since coming home, she'd had an even worse trauma to face, one she could never have come through without help . . . from Flora and Robert . . . and Hamish. He was still getting over it himself, and his father's death, which was why she couldn't let him know how callous she had been towards her father and it was time she got this letter written. She meant to do what little she could for her father now, but she needed Andrew's help.

Chapter Fourteen

❧

Andrew had been surprised, and very pleased, by Marianne's letter. Having the Lord and Lady Glendarril as clients would be good for business. She had been married for over five years now, and he had only seen her for a few hours at a time, yet his heart still beat a full drum roll every time he saw her. While the train sped south, he decided that he should manage to cope with seeing her and her husband together for a whole weekend.

Carnie was waiting for him at Laurencekirk, but sadly for Andrew, he was in a talkative mood. 'His Lordship's no' back yet,' he said, as he laid the young man's valise on the seat. 'He's still away in London, but her Ladyship's expecting you.'

This information had the same impact on Andrew as if he had been slapped in the face with a wet fish. Marianne must have known when she wrote that she would be alone. What was she up to? Her indifference to him at Hector's funeral had worried him. He had got the distinct impression that he was intruding on a very deep private grief, but even when he reminded her of his promise to be there for her when she needed him, she swore that nothing was wrong. Perhaps, however, she had been too upset to talk about it then, and she may be ready to confide in him now.

Carnie broke into his thoughts. 'Master Ruairidh was a bit down all day yesterday, but he's brighter the day.'

This did much to ease Andrew's anxiety. He had forgotten about the two boys – they would be around during the day, which would make things easier. 'I have heard that children can be quite ill one day and back to normal the next.'

'That's what Nursie said when her Ladyship wanted to get in the doctor. The bairn's just three yet, of course, so it's little wonder she frets. Master Ranald, now, he's a sturdy wee man, never nothing wrong wi' him, an' it's just as well, for it's him that'll come into the title.' Carnie's weatherbeaten face sobered. 'I sometimes get a queer feelin', though. Old Lord Glendarril had a twin brother, you see, Randolph his name was, and being a couple of hours older, he was the heir, but he caught a terrible chill the winter he would've been twenty-one, and he never saw his birthday.'

The elderly man shook his head mournfully. 'And Master Hamish, the present Lord, was the second son by about an hour, but young Randolph, after their uncle, he picked up some germ and died when he was fourteen.'

'Neither death was caused by a hereditary disease,' Andrew pointed out quietly, 'and if Ranald is as healthy as you say, I should not think there is any chance of Ruairidh ever inheriting.'

'It's the name that bothers me, Mr Andrew. That was two Randolphs that died young, and Ranald's no' that much different from Randolph, is it? I'm sure there must be a curse on the elder sons –' He broke off, then added darkly, 'Things like that comes in threes.'

Andrew had to laugh at this. 'I would not have thought that you were so superstitious, Carnie, and surely you do not believe there are curses in this day and age. We are almost three years into the twentieth century. Ranald will grow to be a fine young man, and with his mother's genes in him, he will be one of the best lairds this glen has ever seen.'

Marianne was waiting outside with the two small boys as Carnie drew the carriage to a halt at the steps. 'Oh, Andrew, it's good to see you again!' she exclaimed, coming forward as if to hug him.

Evading this, and hoping to discourage her from trying again, he bent down to her sons with a smile. 'My, you two have grown!'

'I'm as big as Rannie,' Ruairidh said confidentially.

'You are not!' his brother protested.

'Say hello to Uncle Andrew properly,' Marianne prompted, 'or else he'll think you're always arguing.'

Gravely, they both held out their hands and said in unison, 'Hello, Uncle Andrew.'

'Hello there,' he responded heartily. 'I wish I'd had a brother to argue with when I was young.'

Four large blue eyes regarding him curiously. 'Had you nobody to play with, either?'

'I had a dog . . .' His voice tailed away. He could still recall the awful wrench when he had said goodbye to Duke – far worse than losing his father.

'I'm as clever as Rannie now,' Ruairidh announced.

'No, you're not. I know more than you,' Ranald boasted. 'I can say my catechism, and I can say the alphabet backwards as well as . . .'

'That's enough,' Marianne said sharply, putting her arm through the visitor's to walk up the steps. 'Stop pestering Uncle Andrew. He's tired after his journey and needs a wee rest. You'll see him later on.'

'Oh, good!' Ranald grinned. 'Is he staying for a while?'

'He goes home on Sunday. Off you go, and don't let Nursie forget to give you your syrup of figs tonight . . . remind her it's Friday.'

Both boys pulled faces but scampered off obediently. 'They're not so bad,' Marianne smiled, as she opened the door of the ex-Blue Room, the most comfortable in the house and consequently, the most used.

'They're very well-behaved,' Andrew observed, taking a seat on the couch as his hostess had indicated. 'Carnie was saying that Hamish is down in London.'

'Yes, he did ask me to go with him, but he'd expect me to make the rounds of his friends' wives, and I can't stand any of them. How are your aunts, Andrew? I hope Miss Edith got over her bout of flu?'

'She only stayed off work for two days, but, unfortunately, Esther went down with it, in a much more severe form. Their doctor seemed quite concerned for her but she said last Sunday that she had begun to feel better.'

'I'm glad to hear it. And Miss Emily?'

Andrew smiled fondly. 'She soldiers on. I keep telling her and Edith that they should retire from the shop – they are both over sixty now – but they just laugh at me.'

'The shop's their life. Don't force them into giving it up.'

'I wouldn't dare try,' he laughed.

It was halfway through the afternoon when he said, 'We had better get down to business and have it out of the way. What was it you wanted to see me about?'

'Can I speak about something . . . personal first?'

The pain in her eyes alarmed him. 'Is anything wrong?'

'Not exactly . . . well, you could say there was, but . . . oh, Andrew, I didn't want to let anyone know, but I'll have to tell you.'

She sank down on the couch beside him but before telling him anything, she held one hand out to him and, presuming that she wanted him to hold it to bolster her courage, he clasped it to his chest. 'What is it, my dear?' he asked huskily.

She started with the lost letter and her shame at not having kept in touch with her father, waiting for him to absolve her of all blame, but he looked at her with his head on one side. 'I was afraid that this might happen. In fact, I am surprised that it didn't happen sooner, if this Moll was the kind of woman who ill treated a young girl.'

'Oh, Andrew, I'm sorry,' she wailed. 'I told you that story so you wouldn't think so badly of me for running away. She never touched me, not in anger, at any rate.'

'But you said you ran away because you stole some money,' he reminded her. 'Why in heaven's name did you tell me that and not tell me the truth about your step-mother?'

Her nerves at breaking point, Marianne cried, 'I don't know. It just came out and I can't think about –' She broke off, biting her lip, then blurted out, 'It's all piling on top of me, Andrew!'

The concern in his face changed to uncertainty. 'Is there more that you have not told me?'

'Not about that,' she muttered, averting her head. 'It's just happened so quick after –'

Her abrupt, agitated stop made him say, 'Go on, Marianne. What else happened? Tell me!'

'I was raped,' she stated baldly, 'and don't ask me to tell you anything about that, for I haven't told anybody ... I can't. Not yet. Not ever.'

Pity for her surged up in him as he took her in his arms, biting back the questions he wanted to ask: who, where, why, and how had the opportunity arisen? 'Please don't upset yourself like this, my dear. I know it must have been traumatic for you, but it was not your fault.'

'But *he* said it was,' she moaned. '*He* said it was my fault. When he was ... Oh God, Andrew, you've no idea what it was like. He was like an animal. Oh God! Oh God!' She buried her face in her hands in anguish.

He crooned soothing words to her, patting her gently on the back whilst silently cursing her unknown assailant. At last, when he thought that she was over the worst, he said, 'Does Hamish know about this?'

She nodded, then raised her eyes to him. 'He ... he doesn't know what to do ... he's never had to cope with anything like this, and I didn't mean to tell you, Andrew, but you've got the knack of worming my secrets out of me.'

'I am glad of that, my dear.' He smiled. 'I would hate to think that there were any secrets between us now. Believe me, Marianne, as I told you long ago, no matter what you have done, or do in the future, I will stand by you. I have not stopped loving you and never will, so bear that in mind. All I ask of you is that you will be scrupulously honest with me at all times.'

'I will, Andrew, I promise.'

He drew in a deep breath. 'Now, shall we continue? It will help to take your mind off things. What was it you wanted to see me about? Do you want to divorce Hamish? Is that it?' She had mentioned no such thing when she wrote, but it was the first thing that had occurred to him, perhaps a hope which had lain latent in him since the day of her marriage, although he was not aware of it. Her astonished gasp, however, told him that he was mistaken in his premise.

'No, of course I don't want to divorce Hamish! I love him! I really do, and he loves me.'

'I'm sorry, Marianne. Tell me what it *is* you require of me and I shall do my best to –'

'I . . . need some fresh air. Come on.'

He followed her along the hallway and down to the basement kitchen where she introduced him to Mrs Carnie as the weekend guest. 'We're going to take the dogs out a walk,' she went on, 'but I thought we might have a cup of tea first.'

'In here?' asked the cook, incredulously. She was not accustomed to her domain being invaded in an afternoon, especially by the mistress. Lady Marianne, Lady Glendarril as they should call her now but old habits die hard, usually left everything to Roberta Glover, menus included, and seldom put in an appearance herself at any time of day.

'It'll save you preparing a tray and sending it up.'

'Aye, there's that to it,' the woman smiled, 'and everything's ready, anyway.' She produced a plate of small sandwiches while the young kitchenmaid went to the dresser. 'We won't bother with plates or saucers, Kate,' Marianne told her. 'Just a cup in our hands.'

Andrew made a friend for life of the cook by helping himself to one of the triangles and popping it into his mouth whole. 'Mmmm! This is absolutely delicious.'

Colouring with pleasure, Mrs Carnie beamed at him. 'Eat the lot, I'll easy make some more. There's still half a jar of that plum chutney I made last October. The longer it's kept, the better it gets.'

'There's plenty here,' Andrew said, and while he set about emptying the plate, Marianne smilingly calmed the dogs, who had heard the magic word 'walk' and could hardly contain their excitement.

When they went outside, the two red setters bounding on ahead, Andrew realized that she had been very sensible in taking him to the kitchen first. Talking to the cook, even for so short a time, had cleared the tension which had grown between them, and made it possible for them to behave naturally towards each other. She showed him the circle of stones known to the glen folk as the 'Fairies' Ring', where legend had it that the little people danced at twelve o'clock every Midsummer's Night. About half a mile further on, still climbing the hill, they came across a long mound that she explained was a barrow, a burial ground from Roman times. Being a city person – Edinburgh born and brought up, and now domiciled in Aberdeen – he was fascinated by the extent of her knowledge of, and obvious love of, country lore.

When he spotted a wooden shack half hidden behind two massive firs, he asked, 'The woodcutters aren't going to start cutting here, are they? What a shame, they're such beautiful trees.'

Her gurgling laugh reminded him of those times past when, young and carefree, they had walked along the banks of the River Dee, and he had to stifle the urge to tell her. She had promised not to say anything out of place, and he must not do so, either.

'It's not for woodcutters,' she told him. 'This is a still, where men of the glen made whisky in the olden days, and had to hide from the Revenue men, the Excise men. Hamish says somebody's started it up again . . .' She turned to him, her eyes dancing. 'Will we go in and take a look, Andrew?'

He caught her frivolous mood. 'Why not?' He went ahead of her and shifted a weighty chopper which had obviously been placed there to camouflage the real purpose of the hut, then eased the door open. The large distilling vat with its tapering filter was so shiny and looked so well cared for that they exchanged knowing glances, and Marianne looked around for any sign of recent activity.

Tumbling to what she was searching for, Andrew removed one of the wide flat sticks propped against one wall. 'Look at this!'

'This' turned out to be a collection of bottles containing a clear liquid. 'That's not whisky, though?' he asked.

'I think it is,' she grinned. 'Hamish told me last year they'd given him a taste of their latest batch. He said it looked like water but took the roof off his mouth and the lining off his stomach. I thought he was joking, but maybe he wasn't.' Suddenly remembering her companion's profession, she said, 'I know what they're doing's against the law, Andrew, but you won't report them, will you?'

He flung his head back and his laughter bounced off the rude walls and the empty metal vat. 'I'll not tell, Marianne. I've enjoyed this walk more than anything I've done for years. You're so good for me . . .' He caught himself. 'I shouldn't have said that.'

'Yes, you should. It lets me know you've forgiven me for what I said earlier. We're back to being best friends, aren't we?'

'For ever and ever,' he assured her, 'but I think we'd better go back before Mrs Carnie sends out a search party for us.'

While he closed the door and replaced the axe as he had found it, Marianne called to the dogs, who were poking their noses down rabbit holes, their tails swishing feverishly from side to side. 'Romulus! Remus! Here, boys! We're going home now.'

'What was that you called them?' Andrew asked as he joined her.

She explained that it was how Hamish had referred to them in fun not long after they were born, and the names had stuck.

To make the walking easier, they followed the course of the burn which used the path a glacier had gouged out in its descent from the mountains at the end of the Ice Age. At this point, the water swept over any obstacles in its way in a raging torrent, but by the time it left the glen it had lost its impetus and slowed down, uniting with another stream to make a river which meandered sedately towards the North Sea. 'I love coming this way,' Marianne remarked, 'even though it's just me and the dogs. It's too far for the boys.'

When they arrived back at the house, Marianne said, 'Half an hour till dinner, just time to have a quick wash and change of clothes.'

'Oh, are men expected to change into dinner jackets?'

His concerned expression made her laugh. 'Hector always did, but it depends on how Hamish feels, and since he's not here, you don't need to bother. Put on something you're comfortable in.'

On his way downstairs to join her in the dining room, wearing one of the pullovers his Aunt Esther had knitted for him each Christmas, he hoped that Marianne, too, had put on something comfortable, and was glad to see her in a baggy jumper and equally out-of-shape skirt. She looked up at him and smiled. 'Well, this is nice. I never feel happy when I'm dressed formally, but that's one of the penalties I have to pay for marrying into . . .' She glanced apologetically at him. 'I'm sorry, Andrew. I'd made up my mind not to say anything personal while we had dinner.'

Andrew had also been thinking while he washed and

changed. If she wasn't contemplating divorce, she must be thinking of making a will. Probably Hamish had already made his with the family solicitor, but Marianne, being Marianne, would want to let Andrew do it for her. Thinking about their own death was quite upsetting for some people, and that would be why she had been putting it off. But it couldn't be put off for ever.

'I think we should get your business out of the way tonight, though,' he said. 'That'll give you time to think it over, and if there's anything you want to change, I can alter it before I leave tomorrow.'

'Tomorrow?' she exclaimed, in obvious disappointment. 'I thought you were staying till Sunday. Are you scared of being alone with me in the evenings?'

'I feel it is not proper for me to be sleeping in the castle while your husband is away.' There was a slight pause before he murmured, 'It is not you I am afraid of, my dear, it is myself.'

She coloured, but he could tell that she was pleased by the flattery. 'I suppose we *should* get things over with tonight. We'll get down to it as soon as we finish dinner.'

Over the meal he told her how well the legal firm in which he was junior partner was doing now, paving the way for her to put her faith in his ability, and she recounted stories about the glen folk and the droll things they said when she went amongst them, but, at last, they were wiping their mouths with the starched napkins – embroidered, Andrew noticed, with the Bruce-Lyall coat of arms.

'We'll have coffee in the study,' Marianne instructed the maid, and Andrew jumped to his feet to pull back her chair for her. 'I brought some paper with me to write down what you want to say, so I'll just run up and get some.'

'There's paper in the top drawer there,' she told him, pointing to the massive leather-topped desk which had originally belonged to Hector's father but which he had never used himself. Hamish, however, had taken it as his.

Walking across to it, Andrew cast a covetous eye on the exquisite carving on the burnished mahogany legs and heaved a sigh. 'What a beauty! I wish I could afford a desk even half as good as this.'

'You will, some day.'

The top drawer held a large selection of different sizes and thicknesses of paper, from which Andrew selected a few sheets which did not have the identity of the owner embossed on them, and laying them in a neat pile in front of him, he picked up a pen from the crystal container and dipped it in the matching inkwell. 'Now, what were you thinking of putting in your will?'

Marion seemed taken aback by this, but she answered readily enough. 'Of course, I didn't think of asking you before, but you'll be able to tell me about the jewellery Hector left me. His wife's will had said it had to go to the girl Hamish married.' Her eyes took on a concerned look now. 'It *is* legally mine, isn't it, though the will was made long before Hamish even met me?'

'Oh yes, it's legally yours. Had she lived, Lady Glendarril would no doubt have instructed her solicitor to insert your name.'

'I expect she would,' Marianne said, rather uncertainly. 'Anyway, when I die I suppose it'll go half each to whoever Ranald and Ruairidh marry?'

'Yes, that would be feasible,' Andrew murmured, making a note of it. 'Now, shall I give you a moment to think about what else you want to do?'

'No, I know exactly what I want to do. First, I want you to order a stone for my father's grave.'

Hamish's head jerked up. 'A gravestone? Is that why you asked me . . . ? You do not want to make a will?'

She shook her head impatiently. 'I wasn't pleased when Moll asked me to do it, but the more I've thought about it, the more I want to. A good decent-sized granite stone, not marble, but he wouldn't like an angel or anything like that

243

over his head, so maybe just a wee bit of decoration round the sides. At the top, get them to put "CHEYNE", then underneath that, "Anne Lawrie, dearly beloved wife of Alfred Cheyne, born 24 February 1862, died 12 April 1892".'

'She was only thirty? How tragic.'

'It was, wasn't it? Then below that, I'd like: "Also the above Alfred Cheyne . . ." I'm not sure when he was born, but Moll will have his death certificate and it'll be on there.'

Andrew raised his head again. 'Is that all?'

'Not yet. Down at the bottom, in fancy letters, I want: "Together in love again." And that's all.'

'Your stepmother will probably not be pleased about this, especially the last part. Don't you think it is rather . . . rubbing her nose in it?'

'I'll put what I like, I'm paying for it with my own money. Hector left me a fairly decent legacy, and I'll instruct the bank to let you draw on it.' She was pensive for a moment and then said with a smile, 'I was remembering a gravestone in the cemetery at home – not that I went in there very often, but this one made everybody laugh. I don't remember any of the names, so I'll make them up as I go along. "Annabel Duncan, with her dates of birth and death, dearly beloved wife of William Smith." Then underneath that, "Margaret Ross, also dearly beloved wife of William Smith," and underneath that again, "Matilda Jackson, also dearly beloved wife of William Smith." Then, of course, underneath them all, "Also the above named William Smith." But the funniest thing was what he'd had put on the gravestone, maybe after his first wife died. "Behold, I live for evermore." That was what was inscribed on the pedestal bit. I know it was referring to Jesus or God, but it looked as if he was saying, he'd buried all three of his wives and he would never die. But he did . . .' Andrew's still solemn expression made her break off. 'It's not really funny, though?'

Andrew obliged with a smile. 'Yes, it is. It is just that I

am rather perturbed about what you have asked me to do. You are quite sure about it?'

'Certain.' Watching him put away the unused sheets of paper, she said, 'You know, Andrew, you saying you thought I wanted to make a will has made me think. Maybe we *should* get it done while you're here.'

He turned round to face her now. 'Don't you think that you should talk that over with Hamish first? He may prefer you to use whoever was his father's man of business.'

'I think he'll want you to do it for us, seeing you're a good friend, but maybe I *should* wait.'

'It is entirely up to you.'

'There's one thing I've been worrying about. Hector's twin brother died young and so did Hamish's, that's why they inherited the title, so can you tell me ... if anything ever happens to Ranald *and* Ruairidh, God forbid, who would inherit when their father dies? Would everything go to the Crown?'

'You are worrying needlessly, Marianne. I made inquiries into this while I was still a student, just out of interest, and when the title "Viscount Glendarril" was created, it was stipulated that it must pass to the nearest male relative. This, fortunately, can go through the distaff side – in other words, to the son of a daughter or sister – but not to the woman herself. In the absence of nearer relatives, a search would be made for cousins or second cousins, and should that be unfruitful, the title would lapse. Where the estate is concerned, of course, it would depend on the will made by the deceased peer, and where no will has been made, if a search does not turn up a claimant, then the estate goes to the Crown. But since the last two generations of Bruce-Lyalls have produced only sons, I think both title and estate are safe for many years to come. Does that satisfy you?'

'Yes, thank you very much, Andrew. I knew I could depend on you.'

'And you always will, my dear.' He came over to sit beside her now, taking her hand as he said, 'I know that I should not say this, Marianne, but you mean more to me than –'

'You mean a lot to me, too,' she broke in, 'but I can't . . .'

'I know,' he sighed, 'you can't love me in the way that I love you.' He looked into her eyes, his heart speeding up as it always did when she regarded him with that sad little smile, and he had to force himself not to take her in his arms and kiss her into submission. She would never be his and he must be content with the closeness of their friendship.

She dropped her eyes suddenly. 'Andrew, why don't you try to find another girl? Maybe I'd feel a wee bit jealous if you did, but I'd be happy for you . . .'

The noise of voices outside brought her to a halt, and in the next minute, Hamish strode in, looking surprised to find that his wife was not alone.

'I thought you wouldn't be home till Tuesday!' Marianne exclaimed, a trifle guiltily.

'I finished my business yesterday, but I decided to catch the first train this morning. It's good to see you again, Andrew. If I had known you were to be here, I'd have travelled overnight.'

Andrew gathered from this that Marianne had not told her husband she had invited him, and she broke in now, clearly ashamed of the subterfuge she had employed to get him there, but, just as clearly, determined to brazen it out. 'Hamish, do you remember us discussing making our wills – some time ago?'

'Ah . . . yes.' Hamish's response was only a fraction slow, but enough to let Andrew know that there had been no such discussion.

'Well,' Marianne continued, 'I wrote to Andrew before I knew you were to be away, asking him to come and give us some advice. I thought it would be nice to have a friend as our solicitor.'

The ensuing silence made Andrew wish that he was any-where but at Castle Lyall. 'You must be tired, Hamish,' he said, getting to his feet, 'so I'll make myself scarce to give you peace to talk it over. I'll see you both in the morning.' He looked at neither of them as they wished him good night and, going upstairs, he was thankful that Hamish had the decency to wait until he was out of earshot before hauling his wife over the coals for putting him in such an embarrassing position.

Marianne sat apprehensively until the sound of a door closing noisily released her husband's tongue. 'So?' he began. 'I am supposed to believe that you invited Andrew here not knowing that you were to be alone? Do not deny it – I am not an imbecile!'

'Oh, Hamish, I never thought you were! I wanted some-one to talk to, that was all, and I've always been able to tell my troubles to Andrew. You know that.'

The dark frown eased. 'As you can see, I still have a touch of jealousy where he is concerned, but I should not have doubted you. I am sorry, Marianne. My only excuse is that I am practically dead on my feet. There was some problem with the train, and we were stuck outside Edin-burgh for at least a couple of hours.'

'Do want something to eat before we go to bed?'

'No, thank you. I had a meal in the dining car.'

She let him take her hand and lead her up the stairs, wishing that he could see sense about Andrew. He must know by now that there was not, and never had been, anything more than a deep affection between her and her old friend.

On Saturday morning, Hamish, rested now and trying to make reparation for his boorishness of the night before, suggested that they all go on a picnic since it was such a lovely day. 'Ask Cook to make up a basket,' he instructed his wife, 'and get Nurse to make sure that the boys are wearing suitable clothes. We'll go and see Carnie about a carriage, shall we, Andrew?'

Andrew said no more about returning home now Hamish was back, and was glad of the holiday spirit.

Hamish chose to take them further up the glen, to a large clearing where he spread a tartan travelling rug on the mossy grass for the ladies to sit on, and the forenoon went extremely well, the men playing all sorts of games with the two little boys while Marianne and Nurse just enjoyed the sunshine.

After lunch – and Mrs Carnie had done well in the feast she provided – Nurse said, 'Ranald and Ruairidh usually have a wee nap about now, so if the rest of you want to take a stroll, I'll stay with them.'

It was during this stroll that Hamish voiced his decision. 'I was thinking, early this morning, Andrew, and I believe we *should* have a change of solicitor. Old Bowie is getting on, must be about seventy, and it seems to me that having a friend to look after our business is just what the doctor ordered. What do you say, Marianne?'

'Yes,' she smiled, 'I'd say we couldn't do better.'

'Right, then, Andrew, we can get down to brass tacks after dinner tonight – that is, if my sons haven't exhausted us both by then.'

When the three retired to bed that night, the wills had been made, papers had been drafted for the transfer from Mr Bowie to Andrew Rennie, and Marianne was very glad that the matter of Moll's visit and the headstone had not been brought up. She knew it was worse to keep secrets from her husband than keeping them from a friend, but she didn't want Hamish to know how she had neglected her father, nor what she was prepared to do as atonement.

Chapter Fifteen

It came as quite a shock to Marianne when Flora Mowatt came one Monday afternoon in the early summer of the following year and told her that Robert was thinking of buying into a practice in Dundee.

'But ... you're the only true friend I have in the glen since Grace died,' Marianne wailed. 'I used to think some of the women who come to the WRI knew what happened ...' breaking off, she looked helplessly at Flora and muttered, '... in the manse that day.'

'It had been your imagination, Marianne. Nobody else knows except the four of us.'

'I still need you, though. Tell Robert he can't take you away! I'll get Hamish to have a bathroom put in for you. I'll –'

Flora smiled as she laid down the coffee cup she had been holding in her hand. 'Oh, Marianne, he won't take any bribes. He was born and brought up in the glen and he doesn't want to leave. There's still a lot of folk who remember his father.'

Marianne nodded. 'Yes, Hector used to speak about him. "Old Bob Mowatt didn't often get paid in real money," he told me, one night he was reminiscing, "but his patients gave him vegetables and eggs, and pork when any of the farmers killed a pig, and dozens of other things. He lived like a lord, did old Bob ... better than I did at times."'

Flora laughed along with her for a moment, then her face straightened. 'I'd made up my mind to tell you ... Robert doesn't think I should ... but I couldn't have left ... I don't like keeping it secret from you.'

Marianne eyed her apprehensively. 'That sounds very serious.'

'It is serious. Robert doesn't think he can go on with the deception, that's why he decided to move.'

'Look, Flora, I don't want you to go, no matter what you tell me, but you'd better get it over before I die of curiosity.'

The doctor's wife took a deep breath. 'Well . . .' Shaking her head, she stopped briefly, then lowering her eyes, she whispered, 'It's about Melda.'

'If you think we're annoyed at her being brought here so often, we're not. Everyone likes her even Miss Glover.'

'That's not . . . oh God, Marianne, I can't tell you! You'll never be able to forgive me for . . . living such a lie all this time . . .'

A smile crossed Marianne's face. 'Don't tell me you and Robert aren't married? I don't care about things like that, but we'd better not let anybody else know. Hamish might –'

Her hands almost white with being gripped together, Flora cried, 'It isn't that! We've been married for thirteen years, but Melda's not our child! She's Grace Peat's.'

A shocked Marianne gave a loud gasp. 'Her baby lived?'

'Are you all right? Shall I ring for one of the maids to bring you a glass of brandy?'

Flora stood up to pull the sash at the fireside wall, but Marianne said, 'In the tantalus . . . over there . . .'

Following the pointing finger, Flora hurried across and poured a good measure of the spirits into a brandy goblet. 'Drink that!' she ordered, handing it to her stricken friend.

In only a few minutes, a touch of colour appeared in Marianne's ashen cheeks. 'You were telling me about . . . the baby,' she prompted shakily.

'I'd better leave it for another day.'

'No, sit down and tell me now.'

Flora sat back in her seat and let out a long sigh. 'Poor

wee mite, no mother and no father. Of course, Duncan's parents died some years ago – they were very proud when their son was ordained minister in their kirk – and Robert did everything he could to find out if Grace had any living relatives, but their solicitor said her mother and father had gone to India and they'd both died of some tropical fever.'

'So the poor infant . . . ?'

'She'd have been put in a home and I couldn't stand aside and let that happen. The only thing was for us to adopt her. Robert didn't want to distress you, Marianne, that was why he meant to leave without telling you, but I had to be honest with you.'

Marianne took a small fluttery breath. 'I'm glad you were, Flora, but I wish you'd told me at the time.'

'If you remember . . .' Flora bit her lip, '. . . you were in London and the day you came back . . . you were in an awful state when you came to us, and we thought you knew . . . that Duncan had told . . .'

'He didn't mention the baby, and I never had time to ask what happened. I just took it for granted that it had died, too, and later on, when I started going out again, I heard two of the women agreeing with each other that seeing the tiny coffin being buried with the other one had torn at their heartstrings.' Her mind, which had tensed at Flora's first revelation, was filling now with hateful things she didn't want to remember, preventing her from thinking clearly, but one thing still had to be cleared up. There had been a tiny coffin . . . and if Grace's baby hadn't died . . . She had to ask, otherwise it would nag at her very being for evermore. 'So whose baby was . . . ?' Before she finished her question, the answer hit her. 'It was yours, wasn't it?'

'We shouldn't have done it, I know, but oh, Marianne, it seemed the right thing to do. You see, my baby was stillborn about three hours before Duncan sent young Peter Wink to ask Robert to go to the manse, and when Grace died, in spite of all he did to save her, he could see Duncan wasn't fit to look after the infant, so he took her to me. When he laid the poor little mite in my arms, I lost my heart to her straight away, and when she snuggled round to my breast, I suckled her without thinking. We only meant to keep her till Duncan came to his senses, but . . . well, you know what happened.'

Marianne knew very well what had happened, but her mind refused to think about it. 'I don't know what to say, Flora,' she faltered.

'I'll give you time to think it over. Tell Hamish everything if you want to, and let him know we are prepared to leave Glendarril, that Robert has the chance of a practice in Dundee.'

Marianne let her friend go without ringing for a maid to see her out. Her brain had been taken over by one thing, and one thing only. Melda, the girl she had looked forward to having as a daughter-in-law at some time in the future, was Duncan Peat's child! Duncan Peat!

She sat on by herself for over an hour, wondering what on earth she could do, brooding about the man who had caused her so much misery. If she told Hamish what Flora had said it would be bound to remind him of that terrible day, and possibly rekindle the doubts he'd had that she had let the minister do what he wanted. God, if he only knew how she had fought against the maniac! How she had screamed, and bitten, and kicked . . . and all to no avail.

He had taken her by force, ruthlessly, uncaringly, hurting her as much as he could. How could anyone understand the bitter shame she felt at being treated like an animal by another animal crazed with lust?

Crazed! That was it exactly! Mad! Crazy! Insane! He'd hanged himself in a madhouse, what could be madder than that? A person couldn't go off his head overnight, not even over a week, or a month, or a year. He must have been like that when . . . he made his wife pregnant, and his daughter had the same genes, the same dark hair and dark eyes . . . the same latent madness. Oh yes, it was definitely latent, hiding under the surface until something triggered it off.

Dwelling on this, Marianne's own mind was perilously near to breaking point, but at last, drained, she got to her feet, resolving not to divulge Flora's secret to Hamish. She would tell him that Robert was thinking of moving to Dundee, and, ignorant of all the facts, he would probably try to persuade the doctor not to leave. If he was successful, she would have to steel herself each time she saw Duncan Peat's daughter.

Robert had already agreed to remain in the glen by the time Flora went back to the castle. 'Robert and I are very grateful to you for not telling Hamish,' she said. 'Neither of us wanted to go to Dundee, and I honestly don't think the truth can ever come out.'

'What about Ina Berry? She must have known what happened.' Marianne had only remembered that morning about the woman who usually helped at births, sometimes officiating alone if the doctor was not available.

Flora reddened. 'She wasn't there. She'd been looking after her own mother in Luthermuir on the Friday and Saturday – she'd had a seizure, you see – and Robert told her before she went that she needn't come back till Monday. He thought it would be Tuesday at least before he needed her, but Grace and I were both early. So it all worked out perfectly, as though it was meant.'

'Y – yes,' Marianne said, uncertainly. She had a nasty feeling that Robert Mowatt had engineered the whole thing, though she knew it was ridiculous.

For the next thirty minutes, they discussed glen gossip, then, when she was taking her leave, Flora said hesitantly, 'This will be the last time I say anything about it, but . . . I hope you won't treat Melda any differently now you know who her –'

'Of course I won't,' Marianne assured her.

Flora went away convinced that she had no further need to worry, but once again, Marianne sat thinking for some time afterwards. How could she treat that child the same as before now she knew Duncan Peat had fathered her? Perhaps she should have told Hamish that the girl did not come of a decent family, as they had thought; that she was the seed a deranged fiend had implanted in his delicate wife. A new thought arose now. What if Grace hadn't been as delicate as she had seemed in that last year of her life? Perhaps she liked her husband's sexual assaults, even enjoyed them? The daughter they spawned could have the same genes, and what if she sat her cap at Ranald . . . or Ruairidh? What kind of blood was that to inject into the Bruce-Lyall line?'

At last, Marianne decided that it was not only too late to tell Hamish about the baby nobody knew had survived, it would be like opening an old wound to make sure it wasn't infected. Hamish might not have forgotten what happened that day, but he hadn't mentioned it for a long time, and there was no sense in reminding him.

All she could do was to remove their sons from any temptation before they were old enough to recognize that they were tempted.

PART TWO

1917–1947

Chapter Sixteen

The war, now in its fourth year, had ruptured the slow way of life in Glendarril. Most of the single men – anxious in case they missed all the excitement and adventure if they tarried – had volunteered within a week of it beginning and, tragically, some were killed before its sixth month was over. Instead of deterring others, however, this had fired even married men with families with the desire to settle the score with the murdering b———s. So now, the only males around were either under eighteen or over forty, and a few who could still be safely at home had cheated their ages and gone off blithely to fight the enemy.

With the rapid depletion of the mill workforce, Hamish Bruce-Lyall, Lord Glendarril, had thought he would have to close it down until the men came home, but fate was on his side. In March of 1915, when the foreman was making sure that no one was taking longer than the allowed half-hour to eat his 'dinner piece', he overheard something that made him prick up his ears. Two of the apprentices were discussing what could be done to prevent the rumoured closure.

'The laird should gi'e the wives the jobs,' said one. 'My mother says she could work as good as ony man.'

The other shrugged his shoulders. 'I bet we could work as good as the men, an' all, if he let us.'

Thinking that their repartee would make his boss smile, Hughie Black duly recounted it and was disappointed that not even the flicker of a smile crossed the man's face. It wasn't like him to be so drear, but of course he had a lot of worries on his mind.

Late in the afternoon, Hamish called the foreman into

the office. 'You know, Black, that might not be a bad idea of yours.'

About to say, 'What idea?' the foreman remembered. 'Hiring women?' he asked incredulously. 'But that wasn't my idea, just young laddies blethering. A wife could never do her man's job.'

Nevertheless, when a poster was hung outside the post office the next day, it brought a queue of women to the mill, and Hamish employed the lot. Thus all the adult females became involved, for grannies and widowed neighbours, even those in their seventies and eighties who had never had any children of their own, volunteered to mind the infants and under-fives. With her own two safely away at boarding school, Marianne had made a round of the houses each weekday on a bicycle, in case there were any problems, but there never were, and even if there had been, the elderly women would never have told her. They looked up to her, respected her, offered her tea and home-made girdle scones and pancakes, because they wanted her to see how well they were coping.

The old men, who had worked in the mill since before they left school at twelve or so, were none too pleased at having to waste time showing the newcomers the 'ropes', but the women – glad to be doing something to take their minds off sons, husbands or lovers at the front – learned quickly and soon earned their admiration.

It did not take long, unfortunately, for admiration to deepen into attraction in some cases. Men of fifty were not too old to get a thrill from seeing a shapely ankle or having an unaccustomed view down a blouse when its wearer had opened the top buttons because of the heat. Illicit liaisons were nothing new, of course, for folk in a glen got to know each other better than those in a town, but with husbands out of the way for months at a time, they became a flourishing night-time sideline.

*   *   *

Not yet sixteen, Esmerelda Mowatt – known as Melda – was generally acknowledged to be the prettiest girl in Stonehaven's Mackie Academy. Even the other girls grudgingly admitted it, although some were inclined to be jealous of her long black hair and creamy skin, and the way her black lashes curled away from her dark blue eyes. She accepted the adulation calmly, giving no indication of how she felt, yet she was not a vain person, nor a cold fish. She joined in the other students' pranks and laughed as heartily as any; she bore the other girls' cattiness without losing her temper; she was not above carrying on a mild flirtation but drew the line at going the least bit beyond that. Eventually, apart from those whose skins were so thick that they did not recognize a rebuff unless it was accompanied by a slap in the face or a knee in the groin, they stopped trying to make her forget her principles.

If they had but known, it wasn't just her principles which kept her from taking the biggest step a young girl ever takes – the surrendering of her virginity – but the thought of the two boys who had been her closest companions until they'd been sent to boarding school almost nine years earlier. As soon as she was old enough to think of such things, she had decided to marry Ranald Bruce-Lyall . . . or maybe Ruairidh. She couldn't quite make up her mind which, for they were both so fair and handsome, though Ranald's blue eyes usually held more than a touch of mischievous devilment, while Ruairidh's had become more serious as he grew older.

Last time she had seen them, Ranald had the suggestion of a moustache on his upper lip and had teased Ruairidh because his whiskers hadn't started growing yet. That was the one thing about Rannie she didn't much care for: he was inclined to make fun of his brother, though he jumped to Ruairidh's defence if anyone else dared to criticize him. But she only saw them now when they came home on vacation, as they called their holidays.

They still seemed to enjoy her company, though she was so much younger than either of them. Unfortunately, last time they'd been home, Rannie's seeming need to do things which led to trouble for himself and his brother had involved her, too . . .

They were in the woods, not playing the childish games they had done before, not cycling like mad things until one or other fell off, but sitting on a mossy bank just talking, when Rannie said, 'They've started up the still again. When we were home at Easter, I heard Carnie warning Jimmy Black to watch himself. He said if they were caught, it would mean jail for them, and they did stop for a while, but I took a look last Thursday afternoon and they're at it again.'

'What's a still?' Melda asked.

He jumped to his feet and pulled her up. 'I'll show you. Coming, Ruairidh?'

His brother unwound his long legs. 'Might as well.'

The showing, worse luck, led to the tasting, but what Melda thought was water in the huge container burned her mouth and she spat it out. Rannie, however, was determined to show that he was a man, and Ruairidh struggled hard to keep up with him. After about twenty minutes, the boys began to act strangely, their limbs not behaving properly, their words slurring a little, and in another half-hour, they reminded her of the time she had seen Jimmy Black and two of the old shepherds falling about as they tried to walk along the road, singing at full pitch, and when she told her father, he had said they were drunk.

That was when she realized what was wrong with her two companions. She managed to get them on their feet, and going between them with their arms round her shoulders and hers round their waists, she got them outside, but had to wait several minutes until they stopped being sick before she could take them towards the castle. She couldn't think what to do other than take them home, though she knew that their mother would be very angry when she saw the state they were in . . . and with her, too, probably.

They hadn't quite reached the gate into the rose garden when Rannie's legs gave way, and the three of them landed on the stony path, and this time, no matter how hard she tried, she just could not get them back on their feet.

'I'll have to go and get Carnie,' she told them, aware as she ran off that neither had understood a word.

The coachman collared one of the stable lads and between the three of them they got the miscreants to their feet and more or less trailed them to the stables, where Carnie ducked their heads into the water trough, over and over again, calling them every name he could think of, rough words not meant for female ears. After almost an hour, he gave up and let them sprawl on the cobbled yard, coughing and retching, but miraculously conscious of what was going on. Thankfully, it was a warm April day and the sun soon dried their hair and the necks of their thin cotton shirts. When they went inside the house, they were almost back to normal, apart from somewhat pasty faces, which Rannie excused by saying they had eaten some berries which must have been poisonous.

Melda's mind returned to the present. She'd had hardly any time with them recently. Every time they came home, their mother either had visitors to stay or had accepted invitations on their behalf to the homes of rich families where there were marriageable daughters. Lady Glendarril seemed to be doing her best to introduce her sons to prospective wives. Not that they took it seriously; they just laughed and said they had no intention of marrying anybody just to please their mother, and besides, they were far too young to worry about it.

Melda was counting the days until the start of the Christmas holidays when she was given some bad news.

'You won't see the Bruce-Lyall boys this time.' Becky

Drummond, daughter of the minister, took a delight in saying things to hurt the girl she envied more than any other. 'Oh, goodness! Did you not know they're in the army?' she went on, her sneer deepening.

Melda hadn't known, but was angry at herself for rising to Becky's baiting by showing her surprise. Trying to cover up, she grinned. 'Oh, that! Last time they were home they said they were going to enlist, but they thought they wouldn't be taken till summer.'

She waited until the crestfallen Becky had moved away before she let herself mull over what she'd been told. She knew they had been in the cadets at their college since war was declared. Rannie had said they were training to be officers, but he hadn't said anything about actually joining up and she felt quite put out, for they had never kept anything secret from her before. But maybe Becky had made it up to annoy her.

Unhappily, Melda discovered when she went home that the information was genuine. Her father had been called to the castle to attend to Lady Glendarril that forenoon.

'Her blood pressure was sky high,' Robert Mowatt told his wife. 'It was Ranald's idea, but she's spitting mad at Hamish for buying them into the Royal Scots Fusiliers without discussing it with her first. I can't understand her. She should be proud that her sons are so patriotic.'

'Her boys mean everything to her,' Flora pointed out. 'She's bound to be terrified they'll be killed. I know I would, if it was me.'

The doctor took another helping of mashed potatoes. 'I suppose so.' He turned to his daughter now. 'I bet you're proud of them? They'll soon be off to France to fight for their country.'

Melda fought to banish the fears her mother had aroused in her, and losing the battle, she burst into noisy sobs and ran out of the room. Her father raised his eyebrows. 'What's wrong with her?'

Flora shook her head sadly. 'She's grown too fond of them. I think that's why their mother sent them to boarding school originally.'

'Why? It was a cruel thing to do when they were always together, like two brothers and a sister.'

'Oh, Robert,' Flora sighed, 'don't bury your head in the sand. When they were younger they were like brothers and sister, but it was obvious when Ranald was only about ten that there was going to be trouble.'

'Trouble? Because two boys and a girl liked each other?'

'Because the two boys loved the same girl, because the girl loved both the boys.'

'Melda will choose when she is ready, and whichever one she picks, the other will have to accept it.'

'You're not thinking clearly, Robert. Marianne will want her sons to marry within their own class.'

'*She* was only working class when Hamish married her. The old laird told me at the time he was glad his remaining son had taken a wife who would put some life into the Bruce-Lyall blood.'

Flora laid her hand gently over his. 'That's just it, dear. Have you forgotten whose blood runs through Melda's veins?'

Clearly deeply disturbed, his eyes slid away. 'Surely Marianne would never hold that against her?'

'I wouldn't be too sure. Remember what Duncan did to her?'

The doctor ran his free hand through his thatch of wiry greying hair. 'Does it really matter now?'

After a moment's reflection, Flora said, 'I don't suppose it does.'

Ranald wished now that he had not pressed his father into buying him and his brother commissions in the Fusiliers, in which his grandfather, Hector, had been an officer when

263

his twin brother died. Then he'd been ordered home by *his* father to be trained to run the estate.

But this wasn't the adventure Ranald had thought it would be. He and Ruairidh were both stationed in Inverness yet saw little of each other. The initial zeal, the spirit which had spurred him to train as an officer in the first place, was somewhat blunted now, and, as he wrote to his mother, he was bored stiff up here and wished he had been posted directly to France to see some action.

His boredom was considerably brightened on meeting a very attractive seventeen-year-old at one of the officers' dances. She was a vivacious girl who fixed her sights on the tall, blonde second lieutenant as soon as she was introduced to him. While they recovered from an eightsome reel, she told him her name was Catriona MacLennan and he gave his as Ronald Lyall. He and his brother had both decided that life would be simpler if no one knew that their father was a lord.

At the beginning of the last dance, 'Ronald' suggested going outside for some air, and was flattered at how eagerly she agreed. Her unhidden admiration went to his head, and without having planned it, he steered her towards a dark corner.

It was the first time he had ever been alone with a girl, and his stomach knotted with excitement as Catriona opened her lips to his kisses. Inexperienced, he copied the moves his fellow officers bragged about, and when she arched her back, he knew she was his for the taking.

So he took her, and liked it so much that he took her again.

The following day, he sought out Ruairidh to boast about his conquest, and was deflated when his brother's face broke into a wide smile. 'Oh, great! Now you've got a girl, I'll be free to tell Melda I love her.'

This was not how Ranald saw things. Ruairidh had no right to take it for granted that he wouldn't want Melda now; he wanted her more than ever, really wanted her. Catriona was only a stopgap. Wisely, he kept these thoughts to himself and resolved to arrange his furlough as soon as he could ... before his brother's, that was imperative.

Melda was astonished but delighted to see Ranald Bruce-Lyall waiting for her when she came out of the Academy one afternoon at the end of May, so pleased that she hitched up her skirts and raced to the kilted figure as fast as she could. Grinning, he lifted her off her feet and kissed her in front of everyone, sensuous kisses that took her breath away and had the schoolboys hooting.

Letting her go at last, he whispered, 'It's good to see you, Melda.'

She tried to still her fluttering heart. 'It's good to see you, too, Rannie, but where's Ruairidh? Didn't he come home with you?'

The tiny frown which flitted across his face at this was gone in an instant. 'We don't all get leave at the same time. He'll likely get his when I go back. Now, how do you get home from here?'

'I take the train to Laurencekirk to collect my bike.'

'I thought that would be it, so I left my bike there, as well.'

He put his arm round her waist and they ambled along until Melda said, 'We'd better put a step in. The train won't be long.'

On the fifteen miles' journey, she listened to his humorous accounts of being a raw young officer when the sergeants had ten or twenty years' service behind them. 'They don't think much of us "wet-behind-the-ears-jumped-up gentry", so it's best not to put a foot wrong. They don't know I'm the heir to a title, and I try to learn from them and not to get their backs up by pretending I know better than them, but it's bloody hard going.'

'What about the ordinary soldiers?' Melda asked, guessing that it was from them he had picked up the swearword she had never heard him use before. 'Do they object to having young officers? Do they cast up that you're gentry?'

'Not to our faces, though I bet they resent us. Mind you, there's a few of them came from boarding and public schools themselves. They're the ones who wanted no privileges because of that, whereas I'm happy to have a decent bed at nights and a batman to look after me.' He winked to show that he was joking.

At Laurencekirk, they collected their cycles from the station yard, but before they set off for the glen, Ranald said, 'I've got to see you alone, Melda. We haven't had a chance to talk properly yet.'

Her heart sank. 'If it had been the school holidays, I could have met you any evening, Rannie, but my examinations begin in a week, and I've hours of studying to do. My father'll be really disappointed if I don't pass, for he's set on me studying Medicine at university, and taking over from him one day.'

'Couldn't you say one of your school friends in Laurencekirk has asked you to tea, and she says you'd better stay all night so you don't have to cycle up the glen in the dark?'

Melda saw a big flaw in this. 'Where would I sleep if I said that?'

Rannie didn't meet her eyes. 'I could book a room for us. I'm sure the Western must be used to officers spending the night with one of the local girls.'

Melda shook her head. 'I don't think Father would let me be away for a whole night, and, in any case, I couldn't face a hotel clerk.'

'Don't you want to . . . be with me?'

His wounded look made her say hastily, 'You know I want to be with you, but not like that, Rannie. It's . . . sordid, cheap.'

'Yes, I suppose you're right.' Ranald comforted himself by thinking that Catriona would jump at such an offer if it were made to her. He might try it when he went back. Piqued, however, at being refused by a girl he could have sworn had always loved him, he attempted to punish her. 'I might go and ask Becky Drummond out again. She can give a man an exciting night.'

Having known him for so long, Melda was sure that there was no truth in either of these statements, and decided to ignore them. 'I could get out for a while on Sunday afternoon,' she ventured.

'That means I'd just see you once. I go back on Tuesday.'

A little devil got into Melda now. 'You'll always have Becky to give you some excitement,' she said sarcastically, and putting her foot on the pedal, she hoisted herself onto the saddle and cycled off.

Ranald came racing after her, but he waited until they were well into the glen before he took hold of her rear mudflap and pulled her to a stop. 'I'm sorry, Melda,' he panted, as he cast first his bicycle and then hers down at the roadside. 'I don't know anything about Becky, I've hardly ever spoken to her, never mind anything else.'

'Then why . . . ?'

'To make you jealous.' He grinned at her mischievously. 'You're the only girl for me, Esmerelda Mowatt.'

Her heart flipped over. He had never said anything like this to her before, but . . . she couldn't encourage him; Ruairidh's face, leaner and a little paler than his brother's, had come to the forefront of her mind and was hovering there as if to warn her.

'Come on, Melda,' Ranald coaxed. 'We'll find a place to sit down and have a proper talk.'

'I can't,' she murmured. 'If I'm late home . . .' She raised her eyes to his. 'I *will* meet you at the old hut on Sunday afternoon, though, I promise.' Even as she said it, she wondered if she was being foolhardy. Rannie wasn't a boy any longer, to roll around with on the ground as the three of them had done when they were younger, innocent fun that could never be repeated. He was a grown man now, an officer in the army, so handsome in his dark green kilt and khaki barathea jacket that a pain was gnawing at her insides.

'You're sure you'll be there?' he asked, his eyes, a slightly lighter shade of greyish blue than Ruairidh's, quite serious now, as if her answer was a matter of life or death to him.

'I'll be there.' She lifted her bike and saying, 'Three o'clock,' she cycled off, waving to him airily and feeling cheated that he did't follow her.

When she reached her home and dismounted, she looked back hopefully, but there was still no sign of him, and she propped the bicycle against the gable end and went inside, wondering where he'd gone. She stayed inside the porch for five full minutes, pretending to brush the dust off her boots, but really watching for Rannie going past, and when she gave up, she tortured herself by imagining that he must have gone looking for Becky Drummond.

She thought about Ranald at every opportunity over the next few days, and felt bitterly let down when he didn't turn up outside the Academy again. An awful feeling had risen inside her that he knew Becky better than he professed, and to settle her doubts one way or the other, she sought out the girl at the midday break.

'Have you seen Master Ranald since he's been home?' she asked, trying to sound casual.

The question was a dead giveaway, as even a girl less perspicacious than Becky would have realized, and the minister's daughter wasn't going to pass up the chance to take Melda Mowatt down a peg or two. 'Every day. He's so manly in his uniform, isn't he? He told me his mother got it made by a tailor in Aberdeen, and it's far smarter than the ordinary soldiers get.' She widened her green eyes to feign surprise. 'Why did you ask? Haven't you seen him since he came here to meet me that day?'

Melda's heart cramped. 'He was waiting for you?'

'Of course he was. He apologized later and said we shouldn't blame you for jumping to the wrong conclusion. After all, you always hung round him and his brother before they went away, didn't you?'

Never having come in contact with such an accomplished liar before, Melda took every word as gospel. The colour had drained from her face but she had enough grip on herself to say, 'I'm sorry if I spoiled it for you that day, Becky. Like you said, I used to hang round them and I naturally thought –'

'Oh, it doesn't matter now,' Becky interrupted with a gracious smile. 'And I know you're seeing him on Sunday afternoon, but he'll be with me on Sunday night. He's been with me every night.' She met the other girl's eyes shamelessly for a moment before walking away.

Between then and Sunday, Melda's mind was in deep confusion over what she should do. Should she leave Ranald waiting? Or should she meet him and let him know how sorry she was for butting in when it was Becky he had been there to meet? Yet, every now and then, she suspected that Becky hadn't been telling the truth. Melda would eagerly linger over that until it came to her that Becky knew things that only Rannie could have told her: where he'd had his uniform made, for instance, and the meeting that had been arranged for Sunday. They must have been alone together some time, speaking confidentially, or how would she know?

On Sunday afternoon, she decided to keep her promise. She owed it to Rannie to explain, to tell him that she knew about Becky, to accept his apology for leading her on (if he made one), or to accuse him outright of philandering if he tried to bluster it out.

When she reached the old hut, the still long since gone,

he was already seated inside, and patted the soft floor of golden pine needles to show she was to sit beside him. The scene brought back memories of rainy days during long-ago school holidays, the three of them playing guessing games to pass the time, squabbling if one tried to cheat, laughing hilariously if one made a comic error. She did sit down though, but not as close as he had indicated, and she wasted no time in getting to the point. 'Becky told me.'

Ranald screwed up his nose. 'Told you what?'

'About you and her.'

'There isn't any me and her,' he said, somewhat shortly. 'I only said there was to –'

'To make me jealous,' Melda finished for him. 'I wouldn't have been, you know. I'd have been glad for you, I'd have wished you well, but you lied to me. That's what I can't get over.'

'I didn't lie,' he protested, edging nearer and putting an arm round her waist. 'I really don't know anything about her, but I did meet her once on the road since I saw you, and we spoke for a few minutes, that's all.'

Melda shrugged off his arm. 'Did you tell her where you got your uniform made?'

After thinking about this for a moment, he smiled. 'Yes, I did, now you come to mention it. I didn't know what to say to her, and I was just making conversation.'

'It had been a long conversation,' Melda said sarcastically. 'You'd time to tell her you were meeting me this afternoon, and likely a whole lot of other things.'

'I don't like you in this mood,' he observed.

'Oh? I won't bother you any longer, then.' She made to stand up but he grabbed her arm.

'Melda, what's got into you? I told you you're the only girl for me, so be sensible. If I wanted Becky, why would I tell her about you? I'd the feeling she hoped I'd ask her out, so I told her I was serious about you. I didn't mean to let anyone know that yet, but it's true. I love you, Melda

Mowatt, and I'm going to marry you when the war's over.'

Before her astonished brain could form any words to answer this, his arms were round her, his lips travelling slowly from her ear round to her mouth, and when the long tender kisses began, all she could do was give herself up to the pleasure of them.

But when the mild caressing became forceful fondling, the kisses more demanding, Melda knew that she had to stop him before he went too far. 'No, Rannie,' she gasped, as his hands strayed towards an intimate part of her. 'Please don't!'

'You must let me, Melda,' he begged. 'I wasn't going to tell you in case you got upset, but we're being sent to France when I go back.'

She drew in a ragged breath. 'To France? Oh, Rannie, no!'

'I didn't think we'd have to go so soon,' he admitted, 'but I've got to do what I'm told. I don't want to scare you, my dearest, but . . . well, to put it bluntly, I . . . might be killed, so you have to let me . . .'

She struggled against his insistent hand. 'No, Rannie, I can't.'

He looked at her accusingly. 'You don't love me?'

'I do! I do! But . . . decent girls don't . . . let men . . .'

'They do if they love them.'

She was thankful when he leaned back from her. If he'd kept on, she might have forgotten her principles, or at least pushed them aside. As it was, she wouldn't have to despise herself for being weak. It was better this way.

To take his mind off his biological needs, Ranald began to talk about their childhood, about their schoolfellows in the glen, about those men and women they had thought of as ancient when they were young but some of whom could only have been in their thirties or forties, about those who had passed on. 'There's hardly any what I call "characters" left,' he remarked at one point, and they laughingly recalled the eccentrics of bygone days, the men who had made whisky in the still – Rannie looking sheepish as he recalled his own experience of the raw spirit – the women who, when their husbands were occupied elsewhere, had kept open house – and open legs – for the itinerant tinkers who came to the glen looking for casual work before they went to the Blairgowrie area to pick strawberries and raspberries for Keiller's jam factory in Dundee.

'D'you remember Pattie Raeburn?' Melda giggled, all restraint between them forgotten already. 'She used to hang a pair of red bloomers on her washing line to let that big Highlander know the coast was clear.'

'I remember that,' Ranald gurgled, 'and we bairns timed how long he took to get there and how long he stayed with her. Ruairidh and I once saw him running out at the back when her man was going in at the front.'

Mention of Ruairidh made awareness creep back to Melda. How would she face him when he came home on leave, after what she and Rannie had been doing? How could she tell him it was his brother she loved?

'I think it's time I went home,' she said, her voice a fraction unsteady.

'Must you?' Ranald groaned. 'I'm sorry for what I did earlier, but I'm glad we've had time to get back to a normal footing.'

She looked away. 'I'm sorry I couldn't –' She broke off.

'No, you were quite right, but don't forget, Melda, I do love you, and I will marry you when the war's finished . . . if you haven't fallen in love with somebody else before that.'

'I won't,' she assured him.

'Not even Ruairidh?' he murmured, then immediately cried, 'No, that's not fair of me.' He held out his hand to help her to her feet.

She couldn't have answered his question truthfully, she

was well aware of that. It had always been Rannie *and* Ruairidh, together not singly, that she had played with, laughed with, thought of, and she had the feeling that, if Ruairidh were to kiss and fondle her when he came home, as his brother had done, she might tell him she loved *him*, too.

She didn't protest when Ranald took her hand as they walked towards the path, there was nothing binding in that, and when they came within sight of the road, she let him draw her behind a tree and kiss her. It was a friend's kiss, nothing more, before he took her face in his hands and looked earnestly at her.

'Melda, I shouldn't have tried to make you commit yourself, so don't say anything until after Ruairidh's been home, and if you'd rather spend the rest of your life with him, I'll understand.'

'Maybe he wouldn't want that,' she whispered.

'He told me he loved you, and we agreed to let you decide which of us you wanted without putting any pressure on you.'

She swallowed a lump which had risen in her throat. 'What if I can't decide?' she wailed. 'I feel awful about it, Rannie, but I honestly don't think I'll be able to choose between you.'

'Don't feel badly about it, Melda. We knew it would be hard for you since the three of us were always together, but we've agreed to abide by your decision and the loser will take himself out of your life.' He gave a lopsided grin. 'I'd better warn you, though – I'm not a very good sportsman.'

His eyes darkened again. 'Melda, won't you please let me . . . ? I could be killed, remember.'

Struggling against his tightening arms, she managed to gasp, 'I could easily give in, Rannie, but I mustn't. I don't want to spoil . . . my wedding night.'

The words 'whoever it's with' hovered in the air between

them, and he heaved a long sigh. 'I know you're right, my dearest girl, but I did hope you'd send me off to battle a happy man.' He let her go abruptly, almost pushing her from him. 'I'm not being fair, to you or Ruairidh, so you're at liberty to tell him when he comes home that his brother's not to be trusted.'

Melda felt the tears spring to her eyes. She knew why he was acting like this, and who could blame him? It must be difficult for him to be natural when he knew he'd soon be facing the Huns.

'Please don't cry, Melda,' he said. 'I'm making an unseemly fuss, and I promise I'll dance at your wedding. Come on, I'd better get you home.'

The sun disappeared behind the distant Cairngorms as they walked, and the sky was shot with red, long streaky patterns that changed with every minute that passed. 'I love the sunset,' she said shakily.

'Then I'll think of you each sunset from now on,' he smiled.

Chapter Seventeen

With Ranald in France, Ruairidh Bruce-Lyall was champing at the bit to be in the heart of the fighting, too, and wishing fervently that his furlough at the end of July would be embarkation leave. Never a great letter writer, he sent no word to his mother of when he would be home and was counting off the days until he could surprise her and Melda by just turning up. With only a week to go, he was called to the CO's office, and sure that this was it, he hurried there with a spring in his step, his blood racing with an excitement which held just a trace of apprehension at what might lie in store for him once he was across the Channel.

A mere ten minutes later, he retreated to his billet to be alone, dismissing his batman with a curt, 'I won't need you today!'

He sat down awkwardly, even his bones rebelling at being forced to support him in such circumstances. But it couldn't be true. There must be some mistake. Rannie . . . oh no! Not Rannie!

'Nobby' Clark, a veteran of the Boer war, had seen the same blank eyes, the same stony face, in other men he had served, men whose father or mother had died, or whose sweetheart had just thrown them over, but the mail hadn't arrived that day, so Lyall couldn't have had a letter telling him anything like that; besides, he had never mentioned having a sweetheart. Certain that some dire trouble had befallen the normally cheery young man who had always treated him as a friend, the batman did not move away from the door, and in just seconds, the sound of anguished sobs reached his ears. He steeled himself not to intrude on what must be a truly private grief, but he was a compassionate man who couldn't bear to hear anyone suffering.

Giving a light tap, he walked in, his throat constricting when he saw the huddled figure sitting, head on arms, at the table, a picture of abject misery. 'Go away ... please?' came the muffled voice.

Nobby came to attention. 'Sir!'

'Please leave. There's nothing you can do.'

Ignoring this, the older man moved nearer and laid his veined hand on Ruairidh's shoulder. 'No, sir, you're wrong there. Whatever's wrong, you need somebody to help you through ...'

'Nobody can help me through this.' Ruairidh lifted his ashen face and regarded his batman sadly. 'The CO just told me ... my ... brother's been killed in France.'

'Oh, sir, I can't tell you how sorry I am.'

Ruairidh's bottom lip quivered again and his next words were most unsteady. 'He's only been over there ... less than a month.'

Nobby was almost as shocked as his officer. There was a small framed photograph of the brothers propped on top of the military chest in the corner, proud of the new uniforms they were wearing, probably why the picture had been taken, and he had often thought how alike and full of life they looked ... and now, one of them was lying dead in a rough grave in some French field.

He pulled himself together. 'Do you want me to pour you a spot of brandy, sir?'

'All right ... please.' Ruairidh didn't think it would do any good, but he did feel glad of the other man's presence after all.

In a minute, Nobby handed him a half-filled glass. 'Get that inside you, sir, and you'll feel better.' He stood holding the bottle as he watched the young man forcing the spirits between his frozen lips, and then murmured, 'Another, sir?'

Ruairidh shook his head. 'No, thanks, Nobby. Oh God, I don't know how my mother ... She's not one of those flappy women who can't cope in an emergency, but she thought the world of Rannie ... I'm glad he got home before he ... she'll be grateful to have seen him so recently.'

Thinking that it would do him good, Nobby let him talk about his glen, about his parents, but it was only when he began to reminisce about what he and his brother did in their childhood that the name Melda cropped up. Melda? Nobby thought. It was a funny name, and it could be anything – a dog, a beloved horse – but it soon transpired that Melda was a girl. He gathered that she had been regarded almost as a sister years ago, the only playmate they'd allowed to join their childish games, but they'd both come to care deeply for her, to love her, most likely. He wondered when it would cross the lieutenant's mind that he'd have a clear field to court her now, but after toying with the idea of offering that as a sort of consolation, he thought better of it. It would be insensitive at this time.

When Ruairidh stopped talking, he eyed his batman mournfully. 'I'm sorry, Nobby. I'm ashamed of myself, babbling on like a child.'

'That's all right, sir. It usually helps to talk about it, and I didn't mind. How d'you feel now, sir? There's a bit more colour in your face.'

'Yes, I do feel slightly better. I should have told you when you came in first, but I ...' Ruairidh paused, looking away briefly to compose himself. 'The CO's given me permission to go home tomorrow. I'll be leaving first thing in the morning.'

'I'll have everything packed ready, sir. I'm sure your mother will be glad to see you.'

'Possibly, but I'm dreading it. How can she forget him when he was the one with the charm, the one who had only to smile at her to make her overlook all his naughtiness?'

'I don't suppose she wants to forget him,' Nobby ventured shrewdly, hastily adding the forgotten 'sir'.

Ruairidh shot him a grateful glance. 'I don't suppose she does ... and neither do I.'

Encouraged, Nobby said, 'And the young lady, sir? Melda?'

'Ah, yes! I didn't mean to bring her into it, but ... well ... Melda's two years younger than me, three years younger then Rannie.' He heaved a shivering sigh. 'We spent a lot of time with her when we were at the glen school, then we ... Rannie and I ... were sent south to boarding school and only saw her during vacations, always the three of us together. We both fell in love with her, and last time I saw Rannie, he said we'd have to let her choose between us. He was home before he was sent to ... and he must have seen her, but I don't know ... maybe he didn't say anything to her.'

'She won't have to make a choice now,' Nobby said softly.

Ruairidh either didn't hear, or didn't understand. 'She might have made her mind up already and if it was Rannie, she'll be ... God, I'll be afraid to ask.'

'You shouldn't say anything, sir,' the batman advised. 'Not yet. It's too soon for you and her to be sensible about it.'

'Should I tell her I'm going to France, too?'

'That's up to you, sir, but I think she'd want to know. For one thing, maybe it's you she –'

'Maybe it's me she likes best?' Ruairidh's mouth twisted wryly. 'I doubt it, but you're right – she will want to know.'

Even crouching over the roaring fire, Marianne could feel no heat. She didn't think she would ever feel warm again. Ranald was dead! Her dearest Rannie! She had always loved him more than Ruairidh, though she had tried not to show it. He'd been just that wee bit more mischievous, more affectionate, more outgoing. She had always been glad that he was the elder, that he would inherit the title from his father. His father! Oh, when in heaven's name would Hamish come home to her? He was never here when she needed him.

The woman sitting at the back of the room had been watching her mistress for any signs of distress, and thinking that she could detect a slight change in the stony expression, she leaned forward ready to offer more comfort. But the tears didn't come again.

Marianne's thoughts were still on her errant husband – errant in the sense of not fulfilling his duty as supporter or comforter; he had even been away when his second son was born. Ruairidh's birth had been the worst, two whole days of sporadic pains that escalated in strength and left her drenched with perspiration. Thomson had only allowed the hired nurse to take her temperature and assess the stage of the labour, and had taken upon herself the task of sponging her mistress, changing her nightdress and gripping her hands while her body was bucking in agony.

As if that hadn't been bad enough, Marianne mused, it had been followed by four solid hours of pain so excruciating that she had longed to die, and at its height, Robert Mowatt, summoned by the nurse at the onset of this last stage, had to shove Thomson out of the way to extract the infant. With Rànnie, she'd had twenty minutes of discomfort, slight enough to let her have a degree of rest, and hardly any real pain before he slid out with no help from anybody. It was no wonder that she had always felt more drawn towards him, not that Ruairidh could help what he had put her through . . . nor could he help what she was going through now, even if he did get home.

Her barely audible catch of breath was heard by Thomson, who said, 'Do you want anything, m'Lady? A cup of tea?'

Marianne sighed. 'If I drink any more tea, my skin'll

turn brown. Are you sure you sent that telegram to the right address, Thomson? His Lordship should have been here by now.'

'He hasn't had time yet, m'Lady. He'd only have got the wire about dinnertime, and he'll catch the overnight express, so it'll be . . .'

'. . . tomorrow morning before he gets here? But that's so long . . .'

The sound of a horse's hoofs and the swish of carriage wheels made Marianne sit up straighter. 'This'll be him, thank God. He's caught an earlier train.'

Thomson pulled back the edge of the heavy curtain. 'It's not his Lordship, m'Lady. It's Master Ruairidh.'

Marianne rose shakily, and was holding both hands out when her son strode in. 'Oh, Ruairidh!' she moaned, sagging against him as he swept her into his arms.

Satisfied that she was leaving her mistress in safe hands, Thomson went down to the basement, to let the cook and the housekeeper know the young Master was home. Mrs Carnie had retired at the same time as her husband, three years ago now, and had gone to live in Perth to be near her sister. Miss Glover had left not long afterwards to look after her mother, who was over eighty and not in the best of health. The new holders of these posts were nice enough women, Jean Thomson reflected, but they weren't the same as the two she had worked with for over twenty years and who had become good friends.

'I'm right glad for her Ladyship,' Mrs Ross observed when she heard the news. 'She was needing one of her own to be there with her. Oh, I know she's had you, Jean,' she added quickly, 'and you've looked after her as well as anybody could, but it's not the same as family, is it?'

'I suppose no'.'

In the drawing room, Ruairidh was feeling inadequate. The only family death he could remember, vaguely, had been his grandfather's, and he had been an old man, so it wasn't such a tragedy for any of them. And his arm was getting cramp with holding the weeping woman, the woman who had never been in his arms before, nor he in hers since he was a very small boy.

'Why don't you sit down, Mother?' he murmured.

Drawing comfort from the feel of his arms, the strong young bones, she said, 'I've been sitting all day, ever since the telegram came.'

They were her first coherent words to him, and believing that her quiet weeping had eased her grief, he took hold of her by the elbow and guided her back to her seat. 'When did the telegram come? I heard late last night.'

'The boy delivered it first thing this morning, as soon as he started work, I suppose. Knowing what was in it, he was ill at ease with me and said the postmistress had told him to make sure I had someone with me before I opened it.'

'Father's not here, I take it?'

'He's in London, but Thomson took care of me.' Marianne gulped suddenly, and held a damp handkerchief to her eyes. 'Like she took care of you when I was giving all my attention to your brother. I did love you, too, Ruairidh, but I couldn't show it ... I'm sorry. My only excuse is that Ranald was a name I chose, and Ruairidh was what your grandfather wanted ... though that shouldn't have made any –'

'It's all right, Mother. I understood. Rannie was the bright one, he always got on better with people than I did.'

This was too much for her. 'Oh God, Ruairidh. I can't bear it! I can't! You don't know how I ... !'

Alarmed by her sudden eerily wailing screeches, he kneeled at the side of her chair and put one arm round her waist. 'You're bound to feel that way just now, Mother. I feel exactly the same, but we'll come to terms with it ... some day.'

She burrowed her head into his shoulder, her tears

running down his neck and under his collar, and he felt an upsurge of love for her that made tears come to his own eyes. It was several moments before she sat up and said, 'I don't know why you weren't jealous of Rannie. You must have known I loved him best.'

'I loved him, too,' Ruairidh said simply.

'I feel ashamed of myself,' she muttered. 'It wasn't right of me to make more of one than the other. I did love you, you know.'

'I know, Mother, so don't be ashamed. A woman often feels more for one of her children, so I've heard. And likely a father, as well, though I don't think ours had any great love for either of us.'

She looked outraged. 'Oh, don't think that! Your father's a man who can't show his love properly, not even to me, but I swear he loved both of *you* very dearly.'

'Do you mean . . . he doesn't love you?' Ruairidh asked wonderingly.

'No, I don't mean that. He does love me, but I wish he would tell me sometimes. And he's never here when I need him.'

Mother and son sat silently until Thomson tapped at the door and carried in a tray laden with home-baked scones and cakes. 'Excuse me, m'Lady,' she announced, 'but Cook says you and Master Ruairidh must eat something. "Tell them a full belly keeps the back up", was the way she put it.'

The suspicion of a smile crossed both white faces, and when Marianne shook her head, her son lifted the teapot purposefully. 'You must eat, Mother, to maintain your strength.'

At that moment, there was the sound of another arrival, and before Ruairidh reached the window to look out, his father was inside the room.

Too distraught to notice anyone else, Hamish went straight to his wife, who had tottered to her feet. 'Marianne,' he moaned, taking her gently into his arms and stroking her hair. 'Marianne, I'm so sorry I wasn't here for you . . .' Overcome, he broke off, but not before a large teardrop spilled down his haggard cheek.

Clearly embarrassed by this, he would have drawn back, but Marianne wouldn't let him. 'Hold me, Hamish!' she pleaded. 'I've been waiting for you to hold me.'

At this point, Thomson crept out, but Ruairidh was fascinated by the sight of his normally erect father caving in and kissing his wife as if he had been in London for years instead of days.

'I love you, Marianne,' Hamish whispered hoarsely. 'The trouble was, I was brought up not to show my feelings – Mother said it was unmanly – and I wish I'd let my sons know I loved them, too.'

His heart full, Ruairidh tiptoed out, leaving his father and mother in a passionate embrace.

Chapter Eighteen

It hadn't taken long for the bad news to wing its way round the glen; in fact, most of the inhabitants had known about Ranald Bruce-Lyall's death before his mother did. Mima Rattray – wife of Dougal in whose small general store the post office had a counter – was not by nature a gossipy woman, but by dint of her occupation she had first-hand information on things she felt should be public knowledge; not *aired* in public, of course, but divulged on a one-to-one basis with the stricture that nobody be told that it was she who had passed it on. Although she also warned her eager listeners that it was to be kept secret, Mima knew that, human nature being what it was, the titbit would be told in whispers whenever two or more women got together. But she considered that her undercover tactics in no way broke the confidentiality of her position as a trusted civil servant. She was only keeping the community abreast with local news, after all.

'You'll never believe this,' she had begun every time on this tragic day, leaning towards each woman and murmuring the words in her best English as befitted her position, 'but the young Master's been killed in France.'

And each reaction had been the same. 'Ranald? Oh, no!'

'It's true, as sure as I'm standing here. The word came this morning and Ruairidh's home and his Lordship, though they didn't arrive till long after the telegram was delivered.'

'Poor Lady Marianne.'

'Yes, it's her I'm sorry for. She's not like old Lady Glendarril, she wasn't brought up to face up to death and things like that. She was just a shop-girl before she married, if you remember?'

Her listener on one occasion, however, was a former maid at the castle, known as little Rosie then but now a hefty lump of womanhood. She had information to divulge to the postmistress that she certainly wouldn't have heard before, so she, too, leaned across the counter until their two heads almost touched. 'She wasna aye in a shop, though. She was once a skivvy!'

'A skivvy?' Mima's eyes were as big as soup plates. 'Surely not!'

'God's honest truth! She stole some money an' ran awa'.' Rosie stopped to savour the bemused, practically agonized, expression on the other woman's face. It wasn't often anybody could tell Mima Rattray something she didn't know already, but this . . . !

The eyes narrowed. 'Who tell't you that?' The refined voice was forgotten in her disbelief.

'I'm tellin' you. I was there when her stepmother come to say her father was deid.'

'An' what had her father's death to dae wi' her bein' a skivvy an' stealin' money?'

'It jist come up, like.' Rosie went on to relay all she had heard at the time of Moll Cheyne's visit, but ended, 'I dinna ken if she *did* put a stane on his grave, though, for she wasna pleased aboot the wumman bein' there.'

'Whit wey did you never tell me this afore?' Mima said angrily.

'Mrs Burr said she would sack the lot o' us if we as much as said a word to onybody.'

'I wish I'd ken't.' Mima was relishing the idea of turning this titbit over, and over, and over.

'No, no! You must promise never to say onything. My God, I wouldna like to think what would happen if you did. We'd get thrown oot o' our hoose, but you'd be worse. You'd lose your fine job, an' all.'

This reminder was enough for Mima, and Rosie, satisfied that she had got the better of the postmistress for once, went happily on her way.

It was fortunate for Esmerelda Mowatt, who had gone to Arbroath for the day since Mackie Academy was on holiday for the summer, that she met no one on her way back from Laurencekirk station; to have learned on the road that Rannie had been killed would have been unbearable. As it was, when she arrived home at half-past six and was told by her mother, she had to temper her horror and shock. For well over a year now, she'd had the feeling that her friendship with the Bruce-Lyall boys was frowned on by her father as well as Lady Glendarril – it was almost as if her Ladyship had said something to him, goodness knows why . . . or what.

Nevertheless, Melda could not hide her sorrow for her old playmate altogether. 'Poor Rannie!' she gulped. 'And the poor laird and his wife. And what must Ruairidh be feeling? They were always so close.'

Flora could not help giving a sigh of relief; she had dreaded her daughter's reaction, yet she had used practically the same words herself when Robert told her. 'Yes, it's very sad, and I'm not surprised that Marianne has made it known that she wants no callers. Mind you, as her friend, I'd have liked to let her know that we're all thinking of her. His Lordship wasn't back, the last I heard, and I doubt if Ruairidh will get home. There must be a lot of brothers . . . soldiers . . . oh, you know what I mean.'

'Yes, I know what you mean, but surely . . . ?' Her voice breaking, Melda came to an agonized stop. 'I'm going for a walk.' She had to get away before she lost control of her grief.

'I kept your tea hot for you.'

'I'm not hungry.' She dashed out, knowing and not caring, that her mother would see how deeply she had cared for Rannie.

She ran into the woods, stumbling over stones and rotting old tree stumps in her haste to get to the ramshackle hut, the scene of their last meeting, when she had refused to give in to his pleas.

Feeling unwanted, as he had so often felt before, Ruairidh took the old track through the trees, thinking idly that these silver birches, tall and almost straight, had been there long before he was born. How many of his ancestors, he wondered, had also trodden this path in the throes of sorrow or guilt? People would say his sorrow was natural, that any man would mourn the sudden death of his brother, but what would they think if they knew the truth? His was not a natural sorrow. Oh, there was sorrow there, a gut-twisting sorrow for the boy who had come from the same womb, the boy who had been his constant companion until they went into the army, but there was also overwhelming guilt at how quickly he had realized that with Rannie gone, there was no rival for Melda. He hadn't been thinking clearly when Nobby hinted at it, but it had come to him on the train home from Inverness that he no longer had cause to be jealous.

The combination of emotions was so potent that Ruairidh stopped to give himself the consolation of a cigarette. He hadn't smoked before being in the Fusiliers, but finding himself the odd man out in the officers' mess, he had succumbed to the pressure. Leaning against a tree trunk, he inhaled deeply, his mind forming a picture from the past: two very young, fair-haired boys playing cricket with a dark-haired, chubby-faced girl who never demanded a turn of the bat. The scene changed again: the boys, a little older, were playing tennis, the girl quite content to retrieve the ball for them.

Then had come the split, Ruairidh recalled. Rannie and he had been sent to boarding school, and that was when things started to change between the three of them. As a child, Melda had only shown the promise of being a real beauty, but it was soon plain that Rannie was attracted to her as much as he was. The metamorphosis was gradual; they probably wouldn't have noticed if they had still been seeing her every day, but on each vacation, they saw a different stage of her development. First, her cheeks lost their chubbiness, and her facial bones formed into a perfect oval. Next, her eyes grew a more pronounced blue, her eyelashes lengthened until they swept her cheeks when she blinked. Highlights appeared in her wavy black hair, so long now that it reached past her waist.

Her body lost its childish flatness and her hips broadened just a little, giving curves enough to make any man's heartbeats quicken. But it was on their last visit home together that they'd seen the greatest change, the change which set brother against brother to a certain extent. Her chest had swelled into an upturned bosom, and they could tell by her rounded stomach that she wore no corsets yet. He had felt shy with her, Ruairidh recalled, and even Rannie had been taken aback, but being Rannie, he'd soon got over it.

'My, my, Miss Melda!' he'd grinned. 'Aren't you the young lady?' His tone was light, but Ruairidh had seen that his eyes were fixed on her breasts.

She had coloured becomingly. 'Stop teasing, Rannie,' she'd smiled, but she'd clearly been pleased at the compliment. Then she'd turned to him. 'What about you, Ruairidh? Do you think I'm grown up?'

He'd felt tongue-tied. There were so many things he'd wanted to say to her, but not in front of his brother. 'You're really p-pretty, M-Melda,' he'd stammered.

Now, stamping on the stub of his cigarette with the heel of his highly polished boot, Ruairidh made sure it was properly out before walking on. There had been a long dry spell and the slightest spark amongst the old pine needles, yellowed moss and bracken could start a raging inferno. He caught sight of the old shack after a few moments, the site of so much of their play, when the three of them would act out the stories they'd read, Rannie always taking the hero's role. Was that the onset of his jealousy? Rannie rescuing the fair maiden who rewarded him with a kiss? Not a loving kiss, of course, for she'd only have been around twelve at the time, though they'd been about fourteen and fifteen, old enough to feel the stirrings of manhood.

He couldn't remember properly, Ruairidh mused. He hadn't really recognized the pangs in his heart as jealousy until he was sixteen. He could recall that day very well. It had been during a summer vacation, and fourteen-year-old Melda had met them at the old hut as usual, her long legs bare, her thin dress rather skimpy in length, the bodice, obviously too tight, opened halfway down.

Rannie had suggested that they act out the story of Robin Hood and Maid Marian, and surprised Ruairidh by graciously allowing him to be Robin. He'd had an ulterior motive, of course. 'I'm Will Scarlet,' he had laughed before disappearing.

Melda had looked at Ruairidh. 'What are we supposed to do?'

'I don't know, but didn't Robin make Marian his wife?'

'I can't remember, but we can easily pretend to be married.'

That was when love had hit him, straight between the eyes. Until then, he'd liked her, had wanted to be with her, had even thought he loved her, but it had been nothing compared to what he felt in that instant. That was a love that would have made him lay down his life for her if necessary, or jump to his death from the top of one of the surrounding mountains, if she asked him to. It had also been a love that he was too young to show, and when she told him to put his arm round her like a husband, he had the devil's own job to keep from trembling. 'No, just link arms,' he mumbled. 'That should do.'

He had ambled along with her for a few minutes, his brain so fogged by the touch of her arm that he'd forgotten what they were actually doing, so he got a proper shock when Rannie stepped out from behind a tree, and grabbed Melda. 'Come to me, my Lady Marian,' he boomed.

'You're not supposed to do that,' she exclaimed, struggling.

Taken unawares, Ruairidh could only watch them grappling.

'I want you for my own,' declaimed Will Scarlet. 'It is my right as –'

He came to an abrupt halt, his face scarlet. 'I'm sorry, Melda,' he mumbled. 'I didn't mean to do that.'

'I know you didn't.' But she whirled away from him and ran off.

Rannie had turned to his brother then. 'I didn't mean it, truly.' He looked apprehensive, as if waiting to be castigated.

Puzzled, Ruairidh said, 'What did you do? I didn't see.'

'Just as well.'

This roused further curiosity in Ruairidh. 'Tell me!' he demanded.

'I touched her . . . it was an accident!'

'Where did you touch her?'

'A button must have come off her frock with us wrestling, and I took hold of one of her tits by mistake.' Rannie grinned suddenly. 'I wouldn't mind doing it again, though. It gave me . . . you know . . .'

He had wished Rannie dead at that moment, Ruairidh recalled. Not that his brother had actually made love to any girl at that age; it was just the thought that he might be . . . first with Melda. That had worried him, still worried him. When Rannie was home last time, he'd been alone with her, and he could easily have charmed her into . . .

Almost at the shack, Ruairidh heard someone inside weeping quietly. It could only be Melda, but was she just crying for an old playmate, or breaking her heart over the death of a recent lover? He stood for a second, trying to make up his mind whether to go in to comfort her or to leave her to mourn in private, but the need to share his own mixed feelings decided him.

'I hope you don't mind me intruding . . . ?' he began.

'Oh, Ruairidh!' She jumped up, tears streaming down her face and hurled herself at him in her misery. 'I'm so glad to see you!'

Wrapping his arms around her, he shushed her, patted her, kissed her hair, and when his own tears started, he squeezed her against his chest, wishing that he could build some sort of barrier to protect her from the buffetings of fate. 'Oh Melda,' he groaned, 'I loved him, too, you know.'

'But you don't know . . .' she sobbed. 'You don't understand . . .'

'I think I do. You loved him, and you let him –'

Her head jerked up. 'No, Ruairidh, that's just it, that's what's so awful. He pleaded and pleaded with me, and I wouldn't! I knew he was going to France and could be killed, but I couldn't let . . . decent girls don't do that . . . but I wish I had!'

With her lovely eyes looking sorrowfully into his, tear-drops still dangling from her lower eyelids, all he could do was bend to kiss her quivering lips, a kiss that opened the floodgates and made them forget everything but the craving for the ultimate solace. No words were needed as they lay down on the cushion of old pine needles the winds had blown in through the broken door, and their passion, generated by the conflicting emotions in each young breast, was a revelation which had to be repeated several times before they separated, exhausted, and reality reared its ugly head.

Chapter Nineteen

At daybreak, Melda was still wide awake, unable to sleep because of the questions in her mind.

Why had God let Rannie be killed?

Why had she sent him off to war without proving she loved him?

Why hadn't she stopped Ruairidh?

But that last wasn't fair. It wasn't Ruairidh's fault. It wasn't anybody's fault. They had been locked in each other's arms, seeking desperately for the strength to accept the death of someone they both loved, and what followed had been a natural progression.

But should she, *could* she, excuse it so easily? How could they have thought that it would ease what was champing at the very core of their hearts? Of course, they hadn't been capable of logical thought at the time; they couldn't foresee the weight of the guilt that would descend on them later, crushing them like ants under a tackety boot – for Ruairidh must be feeling the same.

Was it Rannie she truly loved? He had been most fun, an extrovert whose charm could have persuaded any girl to do whatever he wanted . . . yet she had withstood him. Ruairidh, on the other hand, whilst not exactly an introvert, had a quiet appeal about him, an appeal which had succeeded in rupturing more than her morals.

Melda shuddered at the oversimplification, a crude explanation for what had been a wonderful, heavenly experience, although afterwards – after the seeming eternity of the two hours they had been together – when they were drained of all feeling, they had avoided looking at each other and walked silently back to the road. It was as if anything further would have shattered the spell.

And now? She came to the conclusion that her love for the brothers had been equally divided. Life without Rannie would possibly be less exciting, but also less of a strain, because he himself had raised doubts in her as to his trustworthiness. He had teased her about Becky Drummond, or pretended that he'd been teasing, but there had been a touch of mischievous wickedness in his eyes which suggested that it might have been true, or that he wished that it had been. She could not begin to imagine him taking a wife – he would have baulked at the confines marriage would impose – whereas she could see Ruairidh as a perfect husband.

Ruairidh lit another cigarette, grimacing at the overflowing ashtray by his bed. It had been one hell of a night! After seeing Melda home, he had roamed through the woods for hours, agonizing over what he had done. He had taken advantage of her, there was no other word for it. She'd been crying her heart out for Rannie, and had admitted wishing she'd given in to him before he was sent to France, so didn't that prove it was Rannie she loved? And bumbling great fool that he was, Ruairidh Bruce-Lyall had taken what should by rights have been his brother's.

Now, even if she swore that she loved him, he would never be sure that he wasn't second best. Could he be happy with that, or would it cause a rift between them? If he ever dared to ask her to marry him and she accepted, wouldn't he keep thinking that she'd have been his sister-in-law if Rannie had lived, not his wife?

Ruairidh eyed his cigarette with loathing; he had smoked far too many of the blasted things since he was given the God-awful news, and this one tasted absolutely foul. Snibbing the glowing tip carefully so as not to knock any of the old butts or ash on to the floor, and putting the stub behind his ear in the way his batman always did, he lay back to think things over for the umpteenth time.

'We shouldn't have been so selfish last night,' Marianne murmured.

Hamish wound a tendril of her tousled auburn hair round his finger. 'What do you mean . . . selfish?'

'We only thought of ourselves losing a son –' She broke off to steady the tremble in her voice. 'Poor Ruairidh lost the brother he was always so close to, and I ignored him after you came in.'

'You needed me,' Hamish reminded her, 'and I don't think I'd have got through last night if it hadn't been for you, my darling.'

She looked at him gratefully. Last night, after their tears were spent, he made love to her and told her how much he loved her as he hadn't done in years.

'My darling,' he said again, looking at her as if begging her to understand, 'I have been all sorts of a fool. I knew, deep down, that you were not to blame for what Duncan Peat did, but I could not bear to think of him . . . It tore me apart to think . . . Every time I looked at you, I could picture him touching you . . .'

'I know, I know,' she murmured, although, at the time, she had been unable to consider how he had felt, and even yet she could hardly bear to let her mind dwell on that terrible day.

'So many years wasted,' he said softly, kissing her brow, 'and all because I was too obstinate to admit . . . to accept . . .' He heaved a great sigh. 'It had happened, and nothing could change that, and I should have comforted you and helped you to get over it, instead of which, I thought only of how it affected me. Can you ever forgive me, my dearest?'

Her heart full, she whispered, 'Of course I forgive you, Hamish, my dear, but I should have tried to see it from

294

your point of view. I couldn't understand why you turned from me . . .' She broke off tearfully.

'Oh, my dearest dear, I should not have brought it up . . . not now . . . at this time . . .'

He also tailed off, clasping her to him until she thought he would crush her bones to powder, which did a little to counteract the burning grief that had been slowly consuming her since the telegram was delivered. Gradually, however, his grip relaxed and shortly after that, his breathing became steady and deeper, and she knew that he had fallen asleep again. It didn't matter. Most likely none of the maids would dare to intrude on them today. They would be left to console each other, to get up when they felt like it, to eat only if they wanted to.

Her thoughts began to wander now. Their marriage hadn't been altogether an ideal one, though they'd been happy together, up to a point. For many years they had missed out on . . . the deep fulfilment that comes with true, openly expressed, love. If only she had realized why Hamish had closed the door on that. If only she had realized that a man's outlook on things was completely different from a woman's. If only he had been less restricted in his view of what had happened to her. It wasn't her fault. She'd gone to the manse with the purest of intentions, and that vile brute, that – she delved into her memory for a stronger expression and came up with one she had once heard in Tipperton – bugger o' hell! Yes, that's what he was, and she hoped against hope that he would rot there till the end of time. But she shouldn't even think about him.

She drew a shuddering breath. What should she think about? Not about Ranald. Not yet. Not until the searing pain in her heart had subsided. Get back to Hamish, she told herself. They'd have to make the most of whatever time they had left to be together, and at nearly thirty-nine, she surely wasn't too old to give him another heir . . . just in case Ruairidh . . .

Sheering off the unthinkable, she was conscious that Hamish was awake again, and said the first thing that came into her head. 'Like you said a while ago, we had each other to help us through the night, but Ruairidh had nobody. He went out not long after you got home, remember, and I didn't hear him coming in again. Did you?'

'Yes, long after the hall clock struck two.'

'As late as that? I wonder where he'd been.'

'Would he have gone to see Melda? They used to be a threesome with Ranald when they were children.'

Marianne's eyes filled with tears once more, but she didn't voice the objection she had to any liaison between Ruairidh and Melda. It was better not to tell Hamish who the girl's biological father was – she didn't want to remind him of the man, and besides, it was Flora and Robert's secret. 'I never had the chance to ask you, dear. How did you manage to get home so quickly? The telegram I sent wouldn't have arrived until . . .'

He clasped her hand now. 'I probably knew before you, my dearest. A friend in the War Office came to tell me about midnight, so I took the early morning train, but I wish . . . oh, I never want to leave you again.'

'I'd better call at the castle this morning.' Robert Mowatt pushed his chair back and stood up from the breakfast table.

'They don't want any visitors,' his wife reminded him.

'I'm not going as a visitor. I should really have gone as soon as I heard yesterday to see how Marianne was bearing up, but wee Lexie Murison had a bad attack of croup, and by the time I'd drained all the muck from her throat somebody said Ruairidh was home, and it wasn't long before somebody else told me that Hamish was back as well, so I knew she'd be all right.'

Flora's nose had screwed up at the mention of what he'd had to do for the little girl, but she was glad when he went out, giving her the chance to speak to her daughter in private. 'You didn't tell me Ruairidh was home,' she accused her. 'Was that why you raced off yesterday without any supper?'

Melda shook her head. 'I didn't know he was home till . . . I met him accidentally later on.'

'It was after eleven before you came in. You couldn't have been with him till that time of night?'

'Yes I was. He'd just lost his brother, remember, and we were . . . going over old times, when we were bairns running wild in the school holidays.'

'You thought a lot of Ranald, didn't you?'

'I thought a lot of both of them.'

Her mother eyed her calculatingly. 'I think you liked Ranald best, though, but don't forget . . . Ruairidh's the heir now.'

Melda's cheeks flamed. 'I'm not going to chase after Ruairidh to please you. Anyway, you know fine Father wouldn't like it, goodness knows why.'

Fully aware that her husband was afraid of what Marianne would do if he allowed her son to court Duncan Peat's daughter – she was obsessed with the idea of insanity – Flora gave a tight smile. 'I could probably manage to talk your father round.'

She was not going to sit idly by and let something that had happened sixteen years ago spoil her chances of becoming mother-in-law to the future Lord Glendarril.

Not wanting to fuel the hope her mother seemed to have for her, Melda kept away from the old hut all that week, and when she saw Ruairidh helping his mother from their carriage at the church gate on Sunday, she was so taken aback at them for showing themselves in public at such a time that she didn't know what to say. It turned out that, at the laird's request, the minister was holding a memorial service for Ranald. With his body lying in some foreign field there could be no funeral as such, but the Reverend Stephen Drummond's emotional words brought tears to the eyes of every person there and did much to ease the grief of all the men and women who had lost sons in the war.

As was the custom, the rest of the congregation kept seated until the laird and his family left, and when everyone was outside, they stood in small knots discussing the service and the terrible toll that had been taken on the young manhood of the area. Feeling sad enough without listening to so many gloom-laden conversations, Melda walked on when her parents stopped to talk to friends, and was glad she had when she saw Ruairidh waiting for her at the gate.

As she neared him, he doffed his peaked hat and twirled it in his hands. 'Will you meet me in the hut tonight?' he asked shyly. 'I want to tell you something.'

'Yes ... all right,' she mumbled, all she could manage with her mouth so dry.

'Half-past seven?'

At her nod, he moved away to join a man she hadn't noticed before, an older man, probably one of his father's friends though she didn't care who he was. All that concerned her was what Ruairidh was going to tell her.

Andrew Rennie had been shocked to learn of Ranald Bruce-Lyall's death and honoured to be asked to attend the memorial service for him. It had proved a truly moving experience, more so as he had sat behind Marianne and Hamish, both painfully erect in an effort to hide the depth of their suffering. That was the penalty they had to pay for being nobility, he had thought – the duty of maintaining dignity even in the face of heartbreak – watching the woman's hand searching for her husband's, noticing the throbbing vein at the man's temple.

His heart had gone out, too, to the young man next to Hamish, a soldier like the brother whose life was being celebrated. He knew how close the boys had been and could practically feel, himself, the anguish that Ruairidh was enduring at still being alive when Ranald was dead.

When they emerged into the sunlight again, Ruairidh said, 'I won't come in the carriage, Mother. I need a walk to clear my head.'

Also feeling the need of some fresh air before tackling the lunch he had been invited to stay for, Andrew said, 'Would you mind if I came with you?'

'I'd enjoy it, Uncle Andrew.' When the carriage drew away, he added, 'I hope you don't mind, but I want to talk to a girl I know.'

'You should have said. I wouldn't have foisted myself on you.'

'I won't be a second, if you'll just walk on a bit.'

Amused by the boy's subterfuge, Andrew walked on, and it wasn't long until his companion joined him again, his step somewhat lighter. 'Everything all right?' Andrew queried.

'Yes, she's going to meet me in the evening, and . . .' Ruairidh's eyes begged the man to understand, '. . . I'd be grateful if you didn't offer to come with me again.'

'Will this be common knowledge, or should I keep it to myself?'

Ruairidh gave an embarrassed smile. 'I'd be obliged if you'd keep it to yourself, Uncle Andrew . . . please.'

'Yes, of course, and you need not have worried about me butting in again. I am going home in the afternoon.'

At the castle, Ruairidh said, 'I'm going to my room. There's bound to be a lot of people here, and I can't . . .'

As it happened, only Marianne was in the drawing room when Andrew went in. 'Hamish has gone up to change,' she told her old friend.

'Ruairidh thought there would be a lot of people here.'

'I can't face anybody yet,' she said, somewhat shame-facedly.

'You shouldn't have invited me back either. I'd have understood.'

'That's why I asked you; I knew you'd understand. Oh, Andrew, it feels like a part of me has died.'

Longing to show how much he felt for her, he drew a chair up next to her and took her hand. 'I am so very, very sorry about Ranald, my dear, and I wish I could have been here to support you when you ... got the telegram. You must have been devastated since neither Hamish nor Ruairidh was at home.'

She sandwiched his hand between hers. 'It was like I was turned to stone, at first. I couldn't feel anything, and I didn't really take it in till Ruairidh arrived – his CO brought his furlough forward a week – and we were still comforting each other when his father turned up. Hamish has been a rock to me, though he was heartbroken himself ... and d'you know, Andrew, sharing our sorrow brought us closer than we'd been for years.'

Conscious that she was looking at him warily, as if unsure what his reaction would be, he said, 'I am truly glad for you, Marianne.'

As he confided to his Aunt Edith in a few hours, when he went to tell her how the memorial service had gone, 'I *am* glad for her, though I had hoped to be the one to provide the comfort she needed.'

'Andrew,' Edith said sadly, 'I know you have worshipped Marianne ever since you met her, and I have the feeling that she loved you in her own way, but she knew what she wanted. She had set her mind on being rich, and Mammon is a hard taskmaster.'

'If she had waited, I could have given her everything she wanted.'

'You could not have given her a castle, Andrew, nor a title. I am afraid she wanted to get as much as she could out of life, and if she missed out on love, she has only herself to blame.'

Andrew had to admit the truth of this, but when his aunt hinted that Marianne's wealth and her position in the glen community had possibly gone to her head, he said, staunchly, 'She does not put on any airs. I could see for myself that everyone in the church looked up to her, and she treats them all the same, from the lowest maid in the castle to the doctor and the schoolmaster. Hamish's workers and tenant farmers and their wives all showed respect when they told her how sorry they were about her son, yet no one appeared at all awkward with her.'

Edith nodded her snow-white head and smiled. 'She has the knack of getting on well with people, whatever their station in life. I can see you resent me criticizing her, Andrew, but I can assure you that I still care for her, very much. She was like a daughter to us when she was here . . . as you have always been like a son.'

Getting to his feet, he went across and lifted her wasted hand to his lips. 'And I was extremely fortunate in having three such dear ladies to mother me through university and see me through the ordeal of being best man at the wedding of the only girl I shall ever love.'

Tears sprang to the old woman's eyes. 'My dear, dear Andrew.'

He straightened up resolutely. 'No more sentimentality. I have had quite a harrowing day, and it is time I went home to bed, but I shall see you again next Sunday.' He bent to kiss her cheek and then went out, his eyes suspiciously moist.

Aunt Esther had been the first to go, from a heart attack a little over three years ago. That was when the other two sold up the shop and retired, and only a month or two later, Emily had died under the surgeon's knife during an operation to remove gallstones. It was probably fortunate that Edith had outlived her two younger sisters, however, because she had always been the strongest and had made all decisions.

*　　*　　*

All afternoon, Melda fluctuated between wanting to meet Ruairidh and dreading it. What was he going to say? If he wanted her to commit herself to him publicly, she couldn't. She was newly sixteen and her father would not agree to any engagement, particularly not to Lady Marianne's only surviving son. But maybe Ruairidh wasn't going to propose. This meeting could just be a ruse to get her alone, to take his pleasure with her again.

When the time came, therefore, she set off apprehensively, but when she entered the old shack and saw him sitting with his back against the rickety wall, his face serious, his eyes looking straight ahead, she knew that he would never trick her into anything.

He jumped but made no move towards her. 'I should have told you this last time I saw you, Melda, but we were both so upset . . .' He halted, looking down at his feet as if ashamed to remind her of their last meeting. 'You don't know how sorry I am for –'

'What should you have told me?' she interrupted. It was dangerous to speak of that other evening.

'I go back to camp tomorrow and . . . this was embarkation leave as well as compassionate. We're being sent overseas very soon.'

Giving a horrified gasp, and forgetting the promise she had made to herself, she was in his arms and they were murmuring the endearments all lovers make to each other. But it was not long before Ruairidh broke away. 'No, Melda,' he muttered shakily, 'I didn't plan this. I don't want to . . . take advantage of you again. It's not fair when you haven't had time to get over Rannie.'

'I'll never forget him,' she whispered. 'but I've been thinking . . . I've always loved you as two halves of one whole, and I honestly don't know what I'd have done if I'd had to choose between you.'

'You'd have chosen him,' Ruairidh said, but there was no evidence of bitterness. 'He was the one who could make people laugh, he was the one with personality.'

'Oh yes, but I *had* realized that he was turning out to be a bit of a heartbreaker, that he could make any girl think she was the only girl in the world for him,' Melda pointed out. 'You're different, Ruairidh. You wouldn't say anything like that unless you meant it.'

He clasped her hand. 'You *are* the only girl in the world for me, Melda, but it's too soon ... I don't feel happy about saying it myself yet. It's ... oh, I don't know, the world's in such a state. Maybe when we're at peace again ...' He heaved a long, doleful sigh. 'I can't make plans for a future I may not have.'

Raising his hand to her cheek, she burst out, 'Don't say that! Of course we'll have a future, so there's no need to grasp at happiness, is there? Just remember when you're over there that I love you and I'll be waiting for you.'

Determined not to let their emotions overtake them again, they reminisced once more about their childhood; about their fellow pupils at the glen school, some of whom, like Ranald, had been killed, though Melda didn't mention that; about Rannie himself, whose name was not the bogey it had been last time. Well aware of how easy it would be to slip, they kept their kisses as light as they could, reserving their passion for the time when there would be no war, when they would be free to love each other without having a sickening dread looming over them afterwards.

Chapter Twenty

❦

After six weeks, Marianne still had not come to terms with what had happened, but Hamish was being exceedingly patient with her. She knew she was like a fragile piece of china waiting to be knocked down again and smashed beyond repair, yet the way Thomson fussed over her, ready to step between her and anything the least bit threatening, only irritated her.

Why couldn't people see that she was still mourning her son? And how could they carry on with their unimportant lives so soon after Ranald's death, as if it meant nothing to them? Even Flora Mowatt seemed more inclined to tell her how grateful she should be for having one son left alive than to commiserate with her about the one she had lost. It was all right for her – she had no sons.

For as much as Melda had been worrying about Ruairidh's safety, she had a far greater worry on her mind now. When she missed once, she had prayed that it wasn't true, but another month had gone past and she would have to face up to it. She was carrying Ruairidh's child!

She was shivering with cold, yet it was a glorious Indian summer outside, quite a common occurrence in September. The trouble was, she couldn't cope with this predicament on her own, but she couldn't tell her parents.

Her father, an old Victorian patriarch, was loud in condemnation to his wife and daughter of the glen girls who had illegitimate babies. 'It serves them right!' he always said. 'Surely to God they could stop their lad before it gets that far,' and she, in her innocence, had agreed with him

... until lately. Even if she'd wanted to, she didn't think she could have stopped Ruairidh, and it hadn't entered her mind, in any case. If that had been all, if it had been any other boy, she might have braced herself to tell her father of her condition, but because it was Ruairidh, he'd be doubly mad. For years now it was as though he had something truly bad against the laird's sons, which had been reflected in their mother's aloof attitude to her, which had started about the same time. She hadn't been invited inside the castle any more, but it hadn't stopped the boys from letting her join them in their play.

As for her own mother, she was a Victorian-style wife, never daring to disagree with her husband, though she wouldn't do that in this case anyway, because she, too, was dead against unmarried girls landing in the family way. She wouldn't excuse her daughter's plight, no matter who the boy was, so there was no point in asking her for help.

There was no one to turn to. She had no address for Ruairidh – they had never written to each other – and she wondered if his mother would tell her how to contact him if she went and asked.

The next morning being a Sunday, she went to church knowing that no amount of prayers or singing praise to the Lord would help her now. First, she had to find out if Lord Glendarril was at home, for she could never say anything in front of the laird. She was thankful that only his wife and Jean Thomson were seated in the Bruce-Lyall stall. At the close of the service, her shame at what she would soon have to confess made her hold her head down as Lady Marianne went past on her way out, her usual ornate hats replaced by a plain black toque.

Trailing her way home, Melda decided that she had better go to the castle today. This was the first time his Lordship had been away from home since . . . and he might not be away again for months, and by that time the whole of the glen would know she was 'in the family way', and what a scandal there would be.

Fortified by a bite of lunch, she went out for the walk she usually took while her father was having a nap, sometimes not more than forty winks if he was called out, and he needed all the rest he could get. As she walked up the curved drive, she tried to plan what to say; she would have to tell the truth, for she was useless at telling lies. And she'd been heartened by what her mother had said before she came out.

To her dismay, her father had been holding forth about the number of girls who had been 'wronged' by a soldier they'd met at one of the dances being laid on for servicemen in towns and villages for miles around. 'It's a damned disgrace!' he had declaimed. 'But they're as bad as the boys, if you ask me. They must know what they're doing, and who do they think will look after their love children? Their mothers?'

His wife had shaken her head. 'Marianne's always very sympathetic to the girls who shame their families. She finds second- or third-hand prams and cradles for them, and gives them enough money to buy the other essentials, and she never condemns them.'

Robert had snorted. 'It would be different if the blame lay at her own door, though. She wouldn't be so sympathetic.'

Flora had eyed him slyly. 'I know at least one mother who was certain it was Ranald Bruce-Lyall who fathered her daughter's child.'

'Ach! Women's gossip!'

The rest of that story came back to Melda now. The 'shamed' girl had told her, months later, that the laird's wife had paid for the confinement in a small nursing home miles away from the glen, and had found employment for her where she could keep her child. Besides that, long afterwards a farm labourer from somewhere near Brechin had admitted to being the father. Melda had been relieved at the time that it wasn't Rannie, but she had doubts about that now. The Bruce-Lyalls could have paid the farmhand to make his confession to save their faces.

Climbing the nearest set of steps, Melda steeled herself for the confrontation to come and gave two loud raps on the oaken door.

'It's the kitchen door you should've come to,' the little maid told her when she asked to see Lady Glendarril. 'And her Ladyship never sees nobody without an appointment.'

'She'll see me, Jessie.' The sight of her old school friend had given Melda some extra courage.

Jessie shoved her lace cap up off her brow. 'She'll gi'e me a row if I show onybody in the now, for she's havin' a rest.'

'Go in and tell her I have to speak to her – it's important.'

Marianne was sitting in a chair by the fire wearing a silk peignoir over her underclothes when the light tap came at her door. 'Come in,' she called, frowning, because she did not feel like seeing anyone. 'Yes?' she asked, when the maid opened the door. The girl looked scared, but since it was her first week as parlour maid – she had previously been kitchen maid – her mistress could understand how she felt. 'What is it, Jessie?'

'There's somebody asking to see you, m'Lady. I said you wasn't at home to folk, but she says it's important.'

'She? Did she give you her name?'

'She didna need to, m'Lady. It's Melda Mowatt, and we was at the school at the same time.'

'Show her in.' A chill of presentiment made the woman draw her négligée closer around her. Why on earth would the doctor's daughter want to speak to her? When the visitor appeared, she looked every bit as scared as the maid had been, and Marianne, forcing a smile to her lips, prepared for an unpleasant surprise. 'I believe you have something important to tell me, Melda?'

'Yes, your Ladyship,' Melda murmured timidly, wondering if her nerve would hold until she got it out.

Marianne gestured to a chair. 'Sit there and tell me.' The girl sat down, but it seemed that she was unable to come out with whatever had brought her to the castle. 'I won't eat you, my dear. Tell me.'

'I've come . . . I thought I'd better . . . you see . . . I'm expecting.'

The last two words, bursting out like the cork from a champagne bottle, were so unexpected that Marianne did not understand at first. 'But why come to me? What can . . . ?' With comprehension came a violent lurch of nausea that had her gripping herself together in case she was actually sick. Then she felt as if her body was floating away, that she was looking down on a scene which had nothing to do with her. After a few moments, reality returned and, noticing that the girl was looking anxious, she managed to say, 'It is my son's child?'

'Yes, m'Lady, but it wasn't just his fault . . .'

'No?' Marianne was desperately trying to think how to cope with this situation, so similar to many she had dealt with over the past few years, yet so different, the boy concerned being of her own flesh and blood. 'It might be best not to apportion blame,' she quavered.

'But I want you to understand,' Melda said beseechingly. 'It was the night he came home on leave, and we hadn't arranged to meet, but we'd both gone to the old hut in the woods, and . . .'

Marianne was scarcely taking anything in, she felt so angry at her son for putting her in this position, and she said nothing as the girl continued.

'. . . and we were both crying, and trying to comfort each other, and we got to kissing, and then –'

Marianne sat up in astonishment. 'You were trying to

comfort each other? You and Ranald? What on earth for?'

It was Melda who looked astonished now. 'Not Ranald, m'Lady. It was Ruairidh.'

'Ruairidh? But Ruairidh wouldn't . . .' Her head swimming, Marianne had to stop. Much as she had hated to think ill of Ranald, she could easily see him as the culprit, whereas her younger son could never . . . 'I suppose you are going to say he raped you?'

'No! Ruairidh would never harm me, he loves me, and I love him.'

A warning bell started ringing in Marianne's head. Was this talk of love a prelude to a forced wedding? She could not allow Ruairidh to marry the daughter of that madman! It must be all of sixteen years since the minister had made that attack on her, yet she could still see his deranged eyes, still feel his clawing fingers, his hot breath. Oh no! She would have to do something to prevent . . .

She drew a steadying breath and smiled sugar-sweetly to take the edge off what she was about to say. 'You can't have this child, of course. You can't disgrace the Bruce-Lyall name like that. I will have to arrange for an abortion.'

'But it's your grandchild!' Melda gasped, shocked both at the very idea, and that it should come from this respectable pillar of the community.

'I am well aware of that, but with Ranald . . . gone, Ruairidh is heir to the title, and he can not have an illegitimate child hanging over him, possibly dividing the family in future generations and causing embarrassment in this one.'

'But he'll marry me when he comes home,' Melda said firmly. 'I'm sure he will, when I tell him . . .'

Marianne's manner changed completely, her face hardening, her eyes narrowing as she barked, 'You will *not* tell him about this! I will arrange for you to have an abortion, and . . .'

This was too much for Melda. 'I will *not* have an abortion!' she said, firmly but quietly in case Jessie heard. 'It's my baby, and you can't make me! I know you're the laird's wife, and you likely think you own the whole glen, but you don't own me! I won't let you kill my baby!' She glared defiantly at the woman.

Marianne's hand itched to slap her across the cheek, but she would lose control of the situation if she did. Making up her mind that appearing to climb down might be the best policy, she changed tactics again. 'I'm sorry, my dear,' she said softly, 'I was trying to think what would be best for you, but I can understand you wanting to keep the child. The trouble is, I haven't had time to think properly, so I want you to go home now and come back in the evening. Ruairidh's father will not be back until tomorrow, so come round the side of this wing, and I'll let you in by the french window. We don't want the servants to start wondering why you are here a second time, and if Jessie asks you why you wanted to see me, tell her you brought a message from your father.'

When Melda left, Marianne went upstairs to dress for dinner, as she usually did at this time. She must do nothing to rouse the slightest suspicion that something was wrong. The hour she normally spent in answering letters could be used to think how to get rid of Melda or her expected child . . . preferably both.

Her hour of concentrated thought was almost up when a plan occurred to her; a scheme to out-scheme all schemes. It would take a lot of arranging, probably much greasing of palms, but it could be done . . . as long as Andrew Rennie played along with it.

Chapter Twenty-one

❧❧❧

Melda Bruce opened her eyes slowly, hardly believing that the birth was over. For hours there had been brief respites between the labour pains, and then they had accelerated into the excruciating agony that had made her scream and scream until she was sure that her lungs would burst. She had been praying for God to take her, to release her into that heaven where no pain existed, when she was given morphine to help her through the final stage, and the last thing she clearly remembered was feeling ice-cold though she was drenched in perspiration. But she felt better now. Someone had sponged her then told her she had a son, but she couldn't remember anything after that.

'How do you feel now?'

The young nurse who had held her hand and stroked her brow during her labour was by her bed again, and Melda gave her as bright a smile as she could to show how much she appreciated the kindness. 'Still a bit tired, but not too bad.'

'You'll soon get over it.' The girl seemed to be on the point of saying more when the ringing of a bell made her hurry out.

Melda lay back lazily, suddenly realizing that she hadn't asked if her son was all right. That must have been what the nurse had been going to tell her if she hadn't been called away, but she'd tell her next time she came in. Lady Glendarril had said she wouldn't be allowed to see it, but at least she knew which sex it was.

She took a good look around her – she had been in no state to notice anything when she was taken through from the labour ward. Like the rest of the maternity hospital it was disinfectantly clean, but there was a more homely look to this private room. It was furnished with a matching walnut chest of drawers and cabinet, two padded armchairs and a small circular table standing on one beautifully carved leg that ended in three clawed feet. The walnut bed ends supported a firm spring under the mattress, so the bed was quite comfortable, with a plump feather pillow for her head and several fluffy white blankets. She snuggled down into the soft eiderdown that lay on top, and closed her eyes again.

It had all been so unexpected. At first, when she had refused to agree to an abortion, she'd thought that Ruairidh's mother was going to strike her, but only for a moment. She was bound to have been angry, of course, being defied by a sixteen-year-old girl whose condition would cause the glen folk to think that one or both of the laird's sons had seduced her. But later, when the woman had had time to think, she came up with what she'd said was an infinitely better solution. For the hundredth time, Melda wondered how she had ever let herself be talked into it, but it had been the only option open to her. Her mind went back.

Although she had bravely refused to entertain the thought of having her child's pre-life terminated, she had felt anything but brave when she made her second visit to the castle. Her stomach churned, her legs shook, her breath came in harsh gasps, but she kept saying, 'No!'

Suddenly, Lady Glendarril's expression had softened. 'You know, my dear, I can understand how you feel. If I loved somebody, I wouldn't want to dispose of his child either, but there is another way to save all our faces. I could arrange to have it adopted.'

Not caring a fig about saving anyone's face, least of all her own, Melda clung to the back of the nearest chair. 'I told you! I want to keep it! It's mine . . . and Ruairidh's, and when I tell him the things you've been saying, he'll never want to see you again.'

The woman's face turned grey. 'So you would have me lose both my sons? I did not think you could be so cruel.'

'I'm sorry, your Ladyship, it's just . . . you're getting me so muddled, I don't know what I'm saying.'

'Sit down, my dear, and we'll discuss it.'

Melda kept standing. 'There's nothing to discuss. I'm not getting it aborted, and I'm not letting it be adopted . . .'

'Please sit down . . . Melda, you're overwrought, too upset to think clearly. I was not thinking clearly either when I spoke of abortion, but I cannot . . . I can *not* allow you to flaunt my son's bastard –'

'Oh!' Melda gasped, sitting down because her legs gave way. 'What an awful thing to say!'

'It's the truth. A bastard, that's what it will be, and I will not allow Ruairidh to admit being the father, nor take any responsibility for it.' Marianne's eyes hardened. 'If you refuse to do as I say, I shall tell him – and his father – that you do not know whose child it is, that it could be any one of the soldiers billeted in the old hall. That would put an end to any hope you may have of marrying my son.'

'But you can't do that!' Melda wailed. 'A lady in your position? You can't tell a downright lie!'

'I will, if you force me to. I am fighting for my family's good name, remember, and that means more to me than anything. I dislike making threats, but I am prepared to go to any lengths to . . .' Taking in a deep breath, Marianne hesitated before going on. 'On the other hand, if you will only be reasonable, we can work out something to your advantage.'

Melda stared at her. She had gathered earlier that the laird's wife could be devious, so what had she hatched up now? 'What do you mean?'

'Well, you may not have heard, but Jean Thomson is

leaving me at the end of next week. She has been my personal maid since I was married, and I have worried that I may not find another one so dependable.'

'You're offering me her job?' Melda was astounded. 'But wouldn't that . . . ? When they notice I'm expecting . . . it would look like you're admitting it's Ruairidh's.'

'No one will notice your condition. I have told my husband, ever since we heard about Ranald, that I need a decent holiday to help me accept it, but he is always too busy to spare the time. He suggested taking me to London next time he goes, but there are reasons I do not want to go there, and in any case, his trips last for only a few weeks, and we need longer than that.'

Wondering what was coming, Melda decided that nothing Lady Marianne said or did would surprise her – but she was wrong!

'How far on are you?'

'Nearly three months now.'

'Good! I will book a holiday for myself and my companion . . .'

Mystified, Melda murmured, 'Companion?'

'Have you not understood? If I employ you to replace Thomson, it will explain why you have visited me twice in one day, but it will also let me take you away from all prying eyes. We will leave as soon as possible – Thomson will instruct you in your duties first – and no one we know will see you again until after the birth, which, of course, will be in a reputable maternity home or small hospital. Until nearer the time, we can take lodgings somewhere as mother and daughter, and to save tongues wagging, we can say the boy you were going to marry was killed in the war. I'll pay all expenses.'

Almost struck dumb by the thoroughness of this plan, Melda managed to say, 'And the conditions . . . ?'

Shrugging, Marianne smiled. 'You let me arrange for the adoption of the child. You don't ask to see it.' She paused with her eyebrows raised. 'You have not been writing to Ruairidh, have you?'

Melda's head-shake encouraged her to go on. 'Good, but part of the bargain is that you will never tell anyone about this, ever! Your father does not know, I hope?'

'Oh, no, I couldn't tell him – he'd have thrown me out.'

'I doubt it, but it is good that he doesn't know, *and* Ruairidh must never know, either,' she stressed. 'You will stick by that, otherwise . . .' She left the sentence unfinished.

The veiled threat had been the deciding factor, Melda recalled, and in just over three weeks, she had travelled to Aberdeen on the train with her employer. They had been met at the station by the man she had seen with Ruairidh after the memorial service for Ranald, introduced by Lady Glendarril as Andrew Rennie, the family solicitor, who was to pay all expenses incurred by them while they were away. He it was who had organized everything – the booking of their rail tickets to York, the finding of the cottage just outside the city, the booking of the Brightfield Maternity Home for Unmarried Mothers somewhere nearby, even the hiring of a woman to cook and clean for them for as long as they needed her.

'Why York?' she had asked, when they were on their way south.

'I've always wanted to go there,' Lady Glendarril had replied, and Melda had had to be satisfied with that.

She had enjoyed their stay, though. The little house was perfect for their purpose, being set in the lovely Yorkshire countryside and just a short bus ride from York itself. Until Melda became too large to feel comfortable travelling, they took days out here and there; to Ripon to see the lovely old cathedral and, a bonus, the street market which was in full swing the day they went; to Robin Hood's Bay, where they took a walk along the stretch of golden sands before they lay down in the late autumn sun to rest; to Scarborough, much busier, but not so quaint. They also took numerous separate days to explore York itself, taking the bus right into the centre of the city each time. They made for the minster on their first visit, being overawed by the beauty of its architecture as they stood outside, and after walking around inspecting the interior, they sat down for almost an hour, marvelling at the peace which descended on them.

It was when they came out into the sunlight again that Melda said, 'I still don't know if I'm doing right, but this is like a holiday to me and I'm glad I came.'

Marianne patted her arm a little self-consciously. 'I know how much you've been suffering over the decision you made, but believe me, it's best. We have got to know each other better, and I hope you do not think so badly of me now?'

Melda certainly didn't feel so antagonistic towards her, but there was still a bitterness there.

For the rest of their visits to York, to see the castle, to walk the walls, to search out all the ancient buildings, they felt easier with each other, and by the time spring came and Melda was only able to waddle along some of the lanes around the cottage, she was looking on Marianne as a benefactor she was indebted to.

And indeed, when her pains began, the older woman had taken her to hospital in a hired car and the young nurse had told her that her 'mother' would wait outside the labour room until the birth was over. Of course, she had been too drugged to notice whether or not Lady Glendarril was there when she was taken out.

'Now, you understand everything you have to do?' Marianne asked. 'Or do you want me to go over it again?'

The elderly matron bridled a little at this. Never in her life had she needed to be told anything twice. 'Yes, of course I understand, Mrs Bruce,' she said, in a voice as starchy as her uniform. 'But I do not understand why –'

'You are not being paid to understand.' Marianne retorted. 'Just do as I have told you. It really is best for everyone concerned.'

She had no fears that the woman would break her promise. She had seen the greed that lit up her eyes at the first mention of money, and she wasn't being asked to do anything illegal. If it had been against the law, Andrew would have had nothing to do with it.

'We always like to see the couple who are adopting,' the matron said nervously, still unsure.

'I have talked to them,' Marianne said firmly, but untruthfully, 'and the solicitor who arranged the adoption has known them for some considerable time, so you have no need to worry. They will be ideal parents.'

The matron still looked doubtful, but her hand shot out to accept the envelope Marianne handed her. 'Thank you, Mrs Bruce, but I would like to point out that I would not have entertained your plan if I had not needed the money. I am due to retire in just over a month, and my mother is getting to the stage where she will need a lot of medical attention. I was worried that I might not manage to pay the doctor's bills . . . nor for the medication she may need.'

Marianne watched her tucking the envelope into her handbag. Two hundred pounds would keep the mother in medicines for a long time. 'Now that we have settled everything, I will take a peek into the nursery and then I'll have a word with Melda before I leave. When will she be fit to come home? I don't want to risk her seeing any of the other babies and getting upset, and I can have her collected by car.'

'In that case, and since it is a week since her delivery, you can take her away tomorrow, provided you keep her in bed for another seven days. We usually insist on a fortnight's stay, but these are rather different circumstances.'

Going into the corridor, Marianne drew in a deep, shivery breath. That was the worst part over, and the rest was up to Andrew. In the nursery, she stood between the two cots looking down at the sleeping infants with mixed feelings. Neither she nor Melda had thought of the possibility of two babies although there was a long history of twins in Hamish's family – both Hector and Hamish himself being twins – and they were so lovely, so feminine, so tiny, so complete . . . but she must harden her heart. They must be sent away, so that even if Melda had an urge to try to find out what had happened to them, she wouldn't know where to look.

Marianne turned to leave but her eye was caught by a bundle of pillows lying on a cabinet, and what came into her mind then was so awful that she felt faint, and yet . . . and yet . . . Heaving a sigh, she turned and went out. It would have been the best way, but she couldn't do it.

'I still can't believe it!' Melda sobbed. 'Nobody said a word about my baby being ill . . .'

'They hadn't wanted to worry you,' Marianne soothed, trying to ignore the pang of unease that stabbed at her. She had thought that with Melda never having seen her baby – she hadn't been told there were two – she wouldn't be so distressed, but she had been weeping sporadically ever since she'd been told 'it' had died.

'I want to go home,' Melda hiccupped suddenly. 'I want my mother!'

'No, no, my dear. We'll have to wait a week or two, you're not fit to travel yet.' Neither could she be taken home from a supposed holiday in this state, Marianne warned herself. As a doctor, Robert Mowatt would know something was wrong. She had landed in a proper mess with her lies, but that's what she got for manoeuvring other people's lives, and she'd have done anything to save her family's line from contamination.

For the next few days, all Melda could speak about was her dead child. 'If I could only have seen him,' she wailed one afternoon. 'It's awful to think I gave birth to him and never saw him. You should have let me see him, m'Lady. Nobody would have known . . . even if he had lived.'

Marianne swallowed the lump of whatever was choking her, repentance, grief, guilt, shame, she couldn't quite tell which . . . maybe all four . . . and fear? But nobody could find out. Nobody . . . ever!

Melda excused her pallor when she eventually went home by saying she'd had a high fever from something she had eaten while she was away, and her father innocently compounded the lie. 'It must have been botulism,' he nodded. 'That's food poisoning, and it can leave you wabbit for a long, long time.'

Melda searched in vain for an equivalent of the Scots word but she needed more than one to come anywhere near it – pale, sickly, run-down, exhausted. Yes, wabbit was exactly how she felt, and she was thankful for her father's timely remark. She would also remain forever grateful for the speed at which Lady Glendarril had spirited her away. Nobody, not even her father, would ever guess why.

The only person she would have wanted to know, she thought wistfully, was Ruairidh, but if she told him, his mother would spin him that awful lie. She had been cut to the quick by that threat, wondering what her Ladyship had against her, but had realized that she was desperately trying to protect her son. If Ruairidh had found out about the baby, he would have insisted on giving it his name, and marrying her would have been an open admission that he was the father of her child. However loyal to the laird's family the local folk were, they would take it for granted that The Master had raped her, although they might not think any the less of him for it. The gentry did that sort of thing, didn't they? That was their attitude, but it was to avoid this that she had promised Lady Glendarril she would never tell him.

But the infant hadn't lived! So why shouldn't she tell Ruairidh when he came home? It would draw them closer to have made a son together and lost him. If he confronted his mother, though, wanting to know why she had kept it secret, she might still swear blind that the father was an unknown soldier. No, Melda decided, it was probably safer to leave things the way they were.

She was snapped out of her reverie by her mother saying, 'What's up with you, Melda? You're away in a dream.'

Given the afternoon off this first day back to tell her parents about her holiday, she was glad to have plenty to talk about, and described the sight-seeing in great detail. When she ended, however, rather lamely at the point where she had been 'taken ill', her mother looked shrewdly at her but said nothing until the doctor was called away.

'I can't understand why Marianne would want to stay in a little cottage in Yorkshire away from her husband and friends. Not that I've ever heard about many of *her* friends going to the castle, just that man who's supposed to be her solicitor.'

'He *is* her solicitor,' Melda pointed out. 'She'd got him to arrange everything for her, and he'd taken in hand to pay all the bills for the trip, though she didn't run up a lot. I think . . . I know she hadn't got over Ranald's death, and then with Jean Thomson leaving, it was too much for her. That's why I agreed to go with her. She maybe looks a strong woman with nerves of steel, but she's not really. She knows what she wants and makes sure she gets it, but she has a soft side. I couldn't have wished for a kinder person to look after me when I came out of hospital.'

Her mother pounced on this. 'You were in hospital? She should have let us know if you were as bad as need hospital treatment.'

Her face scarlet at revealing part of her secret, Melda tried to laugh it off. 'It wasn't nearly as bad as that. I shouldn't have been in a hospital at all, but she said she was responsible for me and she'd never forgive herself if . . .'

Flora gave a satisfied sigh. 'She'll still be all on edge, of course. After losing one son, she must be worried about the other one, still over there in what was enemy territory.'

Her teeth clenched because she, too, was worried about that one, Melda could only nod at this.

'Is she keeping you on as private maid, or whatever she calls it?' her mother wanted to know now. 'You should never have taken the job on, not when you'd been accepted for Aberdeen University. You know your father always wanted you to follow in his footsteps as a doctor.'

'She hasn't said,' Melda admitted, only realizing it at that moment. She had always dreamed of being a doctor, but what was the point of launching into a long degree course at this time? The war had been over for months now, and surely Ruairidh would soon be home and they could be married. His Lordship had boasted to her that his son was one of the Army of Occupation left in Germany to make sure the Armistice wasn't broken, but Lloyd George couldn't keep them there for ever?

She was so sure that it would work out for Ruairidh and her that it didn't cross her mind to have any doubts.

At the castle, Marianne's mind was also on Ruairidh's return home. With the war over, he was in no real danger now, so she hoped that he would not be demobilized for some time yet . . . long enough for her to persuade Melda to take up the chance of a career as a doctor. Once at Medical School, she might fall in love with someone else, and a battle between Ruairidh and his mother would be averted.

Laying down his newspaper, Hamish observed, 'It'll be good to have Ruairidh home again.'

'Yes,' she agreed. She could sense his unspoken wish that Ranald, too, could have come home, but she couldn't bear to have him say it.

Her husband, if she had but known, was just as unable to mention their dead son as she was, and it took him a few moments to stifle the great sorrow he felt. 'You haven't told me much about your holiday,' he said at last. 'I hope you found the peace you sought? And how did you get on with Melda?'

'It was very peaceful,' Marianne smiled, 'a tiny cottage in Yorkshire, and Melda was an ideal companion. She had lost ... a boy she was fond of, so she had some idea of how I felt.'

'She's a nice lass,' Hamish nodded. 'You know, maybe it's too soon to say this, but I would quite like Ruairidh to marry a girl like her.'

His words cut through his wife's senses like a knife. 'A girl *like* Melda,' she said hastily, 'but *not* her.'

Hamish looked at her sadly. 'Why not? She comes of a good family –'

'She does not!' Marianne shouted. 'She –' She broke off and her voice dropped to a whisper. 'I should have told you long ago, only I thought it wouldn't be necessary, but she's not Robert and Flora's child.' She stopped to lick her dry lips. 'Oh, Hamish, I can't speak about it.'

'You can't leave me in the dark now,' he said sharply. 'If she's not the Mowatts' child, whose child is she?'

Unable to look him in the eye, she muttered, very quickly so as to get it over with, 'She's Duncan Peat's child, the baby everybody thought had died with Grace, but Robert gave her to Flora because she had just lost theirs, and nobody was any the wiser.'

Looking mystified, Hamish stroked his chin. 'But Grace and Duncan were both decent people, too, so why . . . ?'

Seeing remembrance dawning darkly in his eyes, Marianne whispered, 'Now do you understand?'

Aware that the memory of the minister's attack on her had upset him again, Marianne let the matter drop. He would likely recall how the man had taken his life in Hillside Mental Hospital and proved himself to be insane. Surely Hamish couldn't think Melda was a suitable wife for Ruairidh now?

Chapter Twenty-two

❧

Melda could not fathom Lady Glendarril's logic. She would have thought that she would want to keep her maid-cum-companion rather than have her leave after less than a year, but it wouldn't make the slightest difference to the decision she herself had made. She was *not* going to begin a medical degree course even if her employer had promised to finance her throughout her years of study, not now that Ruairidh was coming home. If he had stopped loving her and didn't want to marry her, she might consider a career, but otherwise, no.

There had been an air of excited expectancy in the castle, in the whole glen, since word got out that the 8th Battalion of the Royal Scots Fusiliers was being relieved of its peace-keeping duties on the Black Sea, where it had been posted from the Rhineland some months after the armistice, and the men should be home within the next week or two. Melda lingered over the thought of seeing Ruairidh so soon, her happiness so intense that her heart ached.

She wished she knew exactly when he would arrive – she wanted to look her best for him – but he'd likely be so glad to see her again he wouldn't care how she looked. A softly ecstatic sigh escaped her as she pictured how he would sweep her into his arms and kiss her in full view of whoever else was there ... even his mother? She wasn't too sure about that, but surely to goodness, when Lady Glendarril saw how much they loved each other, she would understand why her personal maid had turned down 'the chance of a lifetime', as she had called it, but it wasn't that as far as *she* was concerned, Melda told herself. The only 'chance of a lifetime' she wanted was to become Ruairidh's wife.

A soft tap at the door of her room at the castle made her sit up. 'Yes?'

'Her Ladyship wants you.'

'Thanks, Ruby. I'll be right down.'

Her heart had speeded up almost out of control. The only reason she'd be summoned at this time in an evening would be if Ruairidh had arrived, so she took a hasty glance in the mirror to make sure that her hair was tidy before running downstairs. She knocked on the drawing-room door as she always did and waited until she was asked to come in, but her spirits sank as her eyes swept the room and found only Lady Marianne there, grim and clearly uneasy.

'M'Lady?'

'Sit down, Melda. I do not relish what I am about to do, but do it I must. You have refused the opportunity I gave you – thrown my goodwill back in my face – so ... I will have to ask you to leave.'

'Leave?'

'I admit I have no fault to find with the way you carried out your duties, but there are other things to consider. My son will be here shortly, and bearing in mind what happened last time he was home, I think it would be best if you were not in the house to lead him into temptation again.'

Melda was outraged at this. 'Oh, m'Lady, that's a horrible thing to say. I told you before, I didn't lead him –'

'Perhaps you didn't, but the temptation will always be there, and will magnify if he sees you every day.'

'But he's going to marry me.'

A peculiar sound, almost a sneering snort, escaped Marianne. 'You cannot for one moment imagine that I will let my son marry the daughter of a madman?'

Melda gasped. 'How dare you say that? My father is a

doctor, a well-liked member of this community. It's you that's mad!'

'Robert Mowatt is not . . .' Marianne hesitated, bracing herself before going on, 'Your father was minister in the glen at one time. He was never a stable man, too easily aroused . . . in more ways than one, and when his wife died giving birth to you it was enough to tip him over the edge into insanity. I had been away and didn't hear about your mother's death until I came back, and when I went to tell . . . Duncan how sorry I was, he . . . attacked me. I did not mean to tell you this, but he was committed to a mental institution where he . . . hanged himself a day or so later.'

Melda's round eyes regarded her in disbelief. 'You've invented these lies to keep me away from Ruairidh, but it's no use. He loves me, and he'll marry me whatever you say.'

'Not when I tell him you were pregnant to one of the Seaforths and didn't even know which, you'd been with so many.'

Her stomach churning with disgusted horror, Melda cried, 'But you made that story up as well, and Ruairidh'll believe me before he –'

Marianne gave an unpleasant smile. 'He will not believe that his mother wanted you to have *his* child adopted, because I will deny it emphatically, and if you persist with your nonsense, I'll tell him you begged me to pay for an abortion. You are breaking the promise you made me, so why shouldn't I break my part of the bargain? As for the facts of your birth, ask Robert Mowatt. He will confirm what I've said.'

Tottering to her feet, Melda made for the door, making no sign that she heard Marianne saying that her wages would be ready in the morning. Nevertheless, when she reached her room on the second floor, she did not, as might be expected, throw herself down on the bed to cry. She was beyond weeping. To have been so near achieving her heart's desire and then have the woman she had thought was her friend tell her something that couldn't, couldn't possibly, be true . . . The other thing, the threat about the Seaforth Highlanders, that wasn't so bad; Ruairidh would have seen it for the lie it was, but she had a strong suspicion that he would be appalled if she really was the daughter of a mentally defective man. However much he loved her, he wouldn't risk the taint of insanity in any children he may have.

She sat for some minutes, torturing herself, unable to lay the blame for her troubles on any one person. She could fully understand now why Lady Glendarril had suggested aborting the baby, why she was so against a marriage, why she was willing to tell lies to prevent it . . . if her story was true. Melda's head jerked up. As the woman had said, there was one sure way to prove it, or preferably, disprove it. She would pack and go home right away – she couldn't stay here any longer – and she would demand to be told the truth.

In less than fifteen minutes, she was carrying her case down the back stairs on her way to tell the other servants – who usually congregated in the kitchen in the evenings – that she was leaving. 'Don't tell her ladyship till morning,' she warned Ruby and rushed out before the astonished women could ask any questions.

Robert Mowatt was sitting alone by the fire. He quite liked when Flora was out at one of her WRI meetings; it gave him peace to think, because he was growing increasingly uneasy. Ruairidh Bruce-Lyall would be home any day now and Robert had a sneaking feeling that the boy would ask him for his daughter's hand in marriage. The thing was, while *he* would be happy to give his consent, Marianne, knowing the truth of Melda's birth and having that unhealthy obsession about Duncan Peat, would do her best to talk her son out of it.

The doctor heaved a noisy sigh. It was such a delicate situation. On one hand, he could easily convince Ruairidh that Peat's madness was not hereditary, just a consequence of losing his wife and . . . as he thought, his child. On the other hand, if he encouraged young Bruce-Lyall to defy his mother, he would be putting his own job in danger. Marianne would not stand idly by and let him make a fool of her. She would get Hamish to send him away from the glen and in all probability ruin his career for ever. Was Melda's happiness worth such a sacrifice? She was a beautiful girl, she would find another man to love . . . but how would she meet any other men when she was tied to the castle? Should he try to persuade her to make use of her education and work for a degree in Medicine? It would likely take some doing to prise her away from Ruairidh, but it would be the best thing all round.

Getting to his feet, Robert took a glass and a bottle of whisky from the sideboard to toast his decision, which he knew would anger most of the people concerned. Flora was pleased at the idea of her 'daughter' being wed to the laird's son, so she would go mad at her husband for interfering, and the boy and girl themselves would feel hard done by . . . but they were young, resilient. They wouldn't take long to get over it. The only person who would thank him, mentally at any rate, would be Marianne.

He was enjoying his third whisky when Melda burst in, her drawn face grey. He jumped up in alarm when he saw her suitcase. 'What's wrong?'

Flinging the case from her, she ran into his arms. 'Oh, Dad, Lady Glendarril says my real father was a mad minister,' she cried, the tears she had been holding back flooding out.

Wishing that he had full control of his senses, Robert stroked her back, kissed her hair and searched frantically for an answer which would pacify her, yet let her see what

328

the consequences to him might be if she and Ruairidh took their own way.

When he said nothing, she looked at him hopelessly, tears still coursing down her cheeks. 'Obviously, since you haven't denied it, the minister *was* my father. Why did you never tell me?'

Her misery tore at his heart. 'Melda, my darling girl –'

'You won't get round me that way!' she cried derisively. 'Tell me! Was my father mad?'

Gathering that she was resigned to being the minister's daughter, Robert felt able to make a definite statement. 'No, Duncan Peat was not mad.'

'How do you know? How can you be so sure?'

'Sit down, my dear, and I'll tell you what happened.'

Sitting warily on the edge of a seat, she listened as he told her of the infant left motherless by Grace Peat's death, of Duncan's total disinterest in the child, of his own wife's inability to bear live children.

'Flora was devastated by losing her third baby,' Robert continued, 'and no one knew the Peat baby was still alive, and . . . oh, I know it was wrong, but I didn't think there would be any harm in it. In fact, at the time I thought it was the only thing to do. I carried it here and told Flora she might have to give it back if Duncan . . .'

'But he didn't want it back?'

It was as if they were talking about a doll, not a living child, the doctor thought before he went on to explain why he had committed the man to Hillside – not naming the girl he had raped.

Melda gasped at this. '*You* committed him . . . and yet you still say he wasn't mad?'

'I was sure he'd recover once he got over . . . He was crazed with grief over his wife's death.'

'But he didn't?'

'He hanged himself.'

After a short meditative silence, Melda asked quietly, 'If he hadn't . . . taken his own life, if he'd got back his senses, would you have told him his child was still alive?'

'That's an academic question.'

'Would you?' she persisted.

'I don't know,' he admitted. 'He killed himself . . .'

'Because he couldn't get over losing his wife . . .' The girl paused and looked at him with her eyebrows raised. '. . . and his child?'

Robert looked away. 'Possibly. I've tormented myself about that ever since.'

After a moment, Melda said, 'If everybody thought the baby had died, who told Ruairidh's mother?'

'Flora felt guilty about it, too, so she told Marianne. That's why –'

Melda straightened up. 'I see now! That's why she tried to keep them from seeing me in their school holidays?'

'Yes, I'm afraid so.' Robert leaned over to pat the girl's hand. 'I'll try to make Ruairidh understand. I'll tell him everything and maybe it'll turn out all right in the end, my dear.'

In view of what she knew of Lady Glendarril, Melda wasn't at all sure of that, and not really having come to terms with what she had just been told, she went to bed even before Flora returned from her WRI meeting.

Ruairidh arrived in the middle of Saturday forenoon, throwing down his kitbag to hug his mother, then shaking hands with his father.

'The first thing I'm going to do is to ask Melda to marry me,' he grinned, not even unbuttoning his greatcoat.

Realizing that he had not seen the girl since he came back from Edinburgh the previous morning, Hamish demanded, 'Where is she? What have you done, Marianne?'

His wife's face turned scarlet, but her voice was quite steady. 'She left on Thursday night.'

'Left? But why?'

'She wasn't really suitable as a lady's maid-cum-companion.'

Hamish frowned. 'Not suitable? Ridiculous! She was the most suitable you were ever likely to find.'

Marianne couldn't hide her agitation, and Ruairidh regarded her quizzically. 'You never said in any of your letters that she was your lady's maid, Mother, but you'll have to find a new one in any case. Like I said, I'm going to marry her as soon as I can.'

His father beamed. 'You couldn't do better, son.'

'He couldn't do any worse!' Marianne screamed.

The two bewildered men glanced at each other, but with no further explanation, she went on, 'I won't allow you to marry her, Ruairidh, and that's that!'

'I'm going to marry her whatever you say, whatever you think you have against her!' His voice had risen, and turning, he strode out.

Hamish rounded on his wife. 'What is all this? What has she done that's so bad?'

'It's not what she's done, it's who she is!'

'Who she is? She is Duncan Peat's daughter, isn't she? She had a good background – father a minister of this parish, mother also the daughter of a minister.'

'Her father may have been minister of this parish, but that didn't make him good. He was as mad as they come.'

'But that was his wife's death –'

'That's what brought it to the surface, but it must have been there ... since he was born. And when I remember your father's insistence on good blood in the family, I can't believe you'd be willing to let Duncan Peat's blood contaminate your son's children.'

With a sinking of his heart, Hamish realized that Marianne was unusually desperate. Her obsession with Peat's lapse, although understandable to a certain degree, was getting beyond what was acceptable, and it would have to be stamped out, faced up to, head on. 'You are being unreasonable,' he said, quietly but firmly.

Before he could say what he had intended to say, however, she burst out, angrily, 'I wish you'd try to understand, Hamish! He *was* mad, raving mad. Robert had to have him certified –'

'Granted, but Robert was also under the impression that Duncan would return to normal once he got over Grace's death, and I say we should bow to his superior knowledge. You must banish all your mistaken, unhealthy certainties from your mind, Marianne, because I am going to agree to our son marrying his daughter.' With that, he turned and walked out.

His wife realized that, for once, her husband was not going to stand for any argument, but wished she could make him understand how she felt. Every time she went to church, or even passed the manse, her stomach churned wildly, her heart beat faster, her mouth went dry, for it wasn't only Peat she hated, but all ministers, everywhere. They were all the same – hypocrites who thought only of their own pleasure. Look at that boy in Aberdeen – he'd been studying for the ministry. Even Mr Drummond, the present incumbent of the glen kirk, looked at all the young girls' legs as they went past. What was worse, as far as she was concerned, was his habit of squeezing past her when it was her turn to arrange the church flowers, and no doubt he did the same to other members of the 'Rural' when their turns came. He possibly got a thrill out of it, but it sickened her, and proved her point.

Melda blanched when she opened the door to Ruairidh, and recoiled when he tried to take her in his arms.

'What on earth's happened?' he asked. 'My mother says I shouldn't marry you . . .'

'Neither you should,' she muttered.

His eyes showed the hurt he felt. 'I don't understand, but we can't talk here.'

Although she was doubtful as to whether or not she could hold out against him if they were alone together, she put on her coat and followed him outside. They had to thresh this out.

Once they reached the woods and she realized where he was heading, she muttered, 'Not the hut, Ruairidh.'

'Why not? That's where we –'

She couldn't tell him the result of their previous visit. She couldn't risk breaking the promise she had made to his mother. 'Not the hut,' she said again.

'I thought you loved me as much as I love you.'

'Things change,' she prevaricated. 'You've been away for such a long time.'

He took her elbow in a vicelike grip and propelled her forward. 'I wish I knew what's going on, but I know you can't have stopped loving me.'

He pushed her through the doorway and, with his hands on her shoulders, turned her to face him. 'You haven't stopped, have you?'

With his blue eyes entreating her, she could only shake her head, and he said exultantly, 'I knew it! Oh, my darling, please tell me what's wrong. If it's something you've done to offend my mother it doesn't matter to me.'

'I didn't do anything,' she gulped, 'it's . . .'

His kiss stopped her, and the love for him that flooded from her eyes, from her mouth, from the closeness of her body, told him all he wanted to know. 'Oh, my darling, darling, Melda,' he whispered, 'I knew you hadn't changed. I knew you still loved me.'

'Yes, I still love you,' she admitted, 'but I can't marry you.' She jerked away from him and ran through the open door, but, pounding after her, he soon caught up and yanked her to a halt.

'You'd better tell me why,' he said harshly.

Unable to stop the tears, she sobbed, 'Ask your mother. She'll be pleased to tell you.'

'I want you to tell me.'

'Let me go! I can't marry you! I can't!'

Letting her go, he watched her speeding away from him.

Chapter Twenty-three

❦

Tempers were frayed in the castle during dinner, the dark moods of the laird's wife and son passing below stairs via those who came in contact with them.

'God kens what's going on,' Ruby sighed, having had to climb up and down to the kitchen several times for unusual items requested. 'The only pleasant face is the laird himsel', and I think it's his smile that's annoyin' *her*.'

The cook, Mrs Burr, red-faced and sweating with the heat from the vast range, tutted in disgust. 'Fancy her getting angry at him for smiling ... of course, we need to mind she wasna born into the gentry like him.'

'True enough,' agreed one of the chamber maids. 'I'd forgot about that, for she's aye so ...'

Mrs Burr had already regretted the reminder. 'She's no' a bad mistress, though – a bittie short in the trot sometimes, but aye fair. She never raged a soul that wasna needing to be put in their place.'

'She sacked Melda for nothing,' Ruby reminded her.

'Aye, that was a funny business. In fact, if you ask me, there's been a lot mair funny business lately, and I was tell't on good authority, no names mind, that Master Ruairidh was seen in the woods wi' Melda on Saturday ...'

This was another eye-opener for Mrs Burr's underlings, who were drinking in her every word. Nodding knowingly, she went on, '... so that could be the reason she got the sack. Her Ladyship couldna let her son take' up wi' the lass that was her maid.'

Ruby felt obliged to stick up for the girl who had been her friend. 'You ken, I never understood why Melda took on being a lady's maid, for she was well educated, bein' the doctor's daughter.'

'That's another thing,' Mrs Burr said triumphantly. 'I've the idea there was more to *that* than met the eye.'

The scullery maid, a fair-haired thirteen-year-old normally as timid as a rabbit, could contain her curiosity no longer. 'What d'you mean, Cook?' she burst out, then turned crimson at having been so bold.

Mrs Burr was too taken up with what she was thinking to give more than a cursory glance of reprimand at this lowliest member of the household. 'Of course I might be wrong,' she began, her set face denying even the possibility of such an event, 'but –' She halted, shaking her head. 'No! It's no' my place to say onything, and I'm saying no more.'

In spite of the chorus of voices begging, 'Oh please, Cook,' she was true to her word, and would only remind them that they had duties to carry out.

Robert Mowatt was rather wary of speaking to Marianne when he called three days later, but unless he made her see sense, as Hamish had requested him to do, there was bound to be trouble of some kind.

He was relieved at her welcome, however. 'I suppose you've been called in to talk me round.'

He nodded. 'You'll have to accept things, my dear. I can assure you that Duncan Peat only suffered from temporary insanity. I know how you must feel about him, but . . .' He stopped and started again. 'There is no tainted blood in Melda's veins. You must believe that, because your prejudice is breaking two young hearts, and you could lose Ruairidh if you don't give in.'

She turned her head away, and he couldn't help thinking, not for the first time, what a handsome woman she had become. Her hair, still a lustrous copper, was piled high on her head in loose waves, her nose was as straight as any of the Greek statues in her rose garden, giving her a strong profile. She had kept her figure, too, her corset nipping in her waist and pushing up her bosom and her hips still boyishly slim, even at the age of . . . she must be forty if she was a day. His eyes travelled down to the shapely ankles which were all he could see below the narrow skirt. She looked every inch the true aristocrat, though she could lay no claim to being of noble birth.

'Robert.'

The soft voice stopping his appraisal of her, he lifted his head and met the full power of her lovely brown eyes. 'Robert,' she murmured again, 'I can't help admiring your nerve, coming to tell me I'm a wicked mother.'

'That's not what . . .' He inhaled deeply, then said quietly, 'I'm going to tell you something I never meant to tell anyone, but I hope it will help you to understand why I took the infant from the manse that night. Duncan said he wasn't her father, and I was afraid he would try to harm her in some way.'

Marianne was taken aback by this information. 'If he wasn't her father, then who . . . ?'

'He thought it was the gardener – you know, the tinker. The man came back for a few years on his way to and from the fruit-picking, to tend the manse garden after that first summer when Duncan had a broken leg.'

Even more shocked at this, Marianne exclaimed, 'But Grace would never have –'

'It was just in his imagination,' Robert pointed out.

Something she had forgotten for many years now made its way to the surface of Marianne's mind. 'Oh, God! That's what he meant! He said it was my fault, and I thought he was blaming me for leading him on, which I never did, but he'd meant –' She broke off, looking at the doctor imploringly. 'Don't you see, Robert? I was the one who told Jamie MacPhee they were needing a gardener at the manse. That's what he'd been blaming me for.'

'More than likely, but don't forget that he was not

responsible for his thoughts at that time. I can only assure you, however, as I have done before, that his condition would have been purely temporary.' He regarded her now with his eyebrows raised.

She smiled wryly. 'You haven't changed my mind about the man, Robert, but you *have* made me realize I'm fighting a losing battle. I've done all I could to prevent his daughter from being the mother of the son Ruairidh needs as the next heir, yet why should I bother when Hamish doesn't seem to care about decent breeding any more? So I'm going to climb down. They can be married in St Giles and I'll take her to Edinburgh before then to let her choose her trousseau, like Hamish's mother did with me.' She gave a dry laugh. 'I only hope I don't die before the wedding, like she did.'

Robert stood up now. 'You won't die,' he grinned. 'You've a constitution like a horse. I'd better go, though. There could be urgent calls waiting for me.'

She rose to her feet and clasped his hand for a moment. 'Thank you for coming, Robert.'

'Thank you for not being too proud to give in. You'll not regret it, Marianne.'

'I hope not. I do like Melda, you know, as a person.'

'I'm glad to hear it. I was a bit worried you would –'

'Take my spite out on her? No, no, I'd never do that.'

He saw himself out and had a new spring in his step as he walked smartly down the avenue. He felt like sprinting as fast as he could to tell Melda the good news and watch the sadness leave her eyes, but he was too easily puffed these days. He'd have to tell Flora to stop making suet puddings, otherwise he'd soon be as round as a ball.

Marianne sat staring into the fire for some time after her visitor left. She felt drained and little wonder. For over a year she'd had a deep fear in her, a fear that she had tried

338

to banish in the only way she knew, yet she had just made it possible for it to flourish and become reality. Plus . . . a new fear had reared its ugly head, a smidgen of fear that could grow into something big if she didn't face it now and stamp it out.

Grace had been quite a delicate woman, shy with strangers despite her outgoing manner, genteel as befitted one who was the daughter of one minister and wife of another, so it was impossible to imagine her breaking any of the ten commandments. So why had Duncan said that? He must have had some reason for . . . but he was beyond all reason that day. Possibly he'd been jealous of the tinker because of his good looks, and that jealousy could have been building up every time Jamie MacPhee was there. He had been left on his own after the funeral, brooding about it, and finally gone over the edge and taken it out on her, the first woman who'd gone into the manse. Whatever Robert Mowatt said, the man had definitely been insane, and that kind of insanity wasn't temporary. It *had* been there from the day he was born, lying in wait for something to trigger it off.

Marianne gave her head a small shake of resignation. No one, not Robert nor Hamish nor anyone else, would ever convince her otherwise, yet she had committed herself to agreeing to a union that was absolutely abhorrent to her, and she would have to abide by that.

When Hamish came home, he strode straight across to her. 'You look worn out, Marianne. Why don't you go to bed, and I shall arrange for your meal to be sent up?' Getting no answer, he said, 'Robert's been to see you, hasn't he? I asked him to call to –'

'To get me to climb down about the wedding?'

'To try to make you see sense. I am sorry to have to say it, my darling, but you were being most unreasonable, and I thought that perhaps he could –'

'He didn't get me to change my mind about Duncan Peat

339

– I'll never do that – but I said I would agree to Ruairidh marrying Melda.'

Hamish bent and kissed her cheek. 'I am so pleased to hear it, and I am sure that you will never regret it.'

'I'm glad your mother gave in,' Melda sighed.

Ruairidh ran his finger gently down her cheek. 'I'd have married you even if she hadn't.'

'I couldn't have gone against her. I'd never have felt easy in the house with her.'

'I'd have taken you away, my darling. I still could, if you wanted me to. We'd be happier on our own somewhere.'

'I know we would, but you're the heir. You can't just go away when you feel like it. Your father would probably disown you and cut you off without a shilling.'

He grinned. 'I'd give it all up for you.' His face sobered. 'I mean that, you know.'

'I wouldn't let you. You've a duty, a role to fulfil and you can't let your father down.'

'I suppose not. He's desperate for us to give him a grandson.'

'Must it be a grandson? Wouldn't a granddaughter please him?'

'A female can't inherit.'

With a twinkle in her eyes, Melda murmured, 'Well, we'll have to see what we can do.'

Forced to succumb to pressure, Marianne was now planning a lavish wedding. Unfortunately for her, both bride and groom were adamant that they would rather be married in the glen kirk than in the big cathedral in Edinburgh. Furthermore, Melda insisted that she wanted a plain, inexpensive gown and that her mother would help her to make one, which did not go down at all well.

Adding fuel to the fire, Hamish laughed off his wife's moans that people would think they were short of money

340

giving the future laird a tuppenny-ha'penny do. 'If you're speaking about all those horsy-faced uppity old frumps who used to be friends of my mother's,' he grinned, 'or the huntin', shootin' and fishin' pals of my father's, let them think what they like. Our son's taking a daughter of the glen for a wife and it's glen folk we want to celebrate with us.'

Marianne's pained sigh made him slide his arm round her waist. 'Why can't you be happy for them, my dear? Surely you can see how much they love each other?'

'I do see, Hamish, and I am happy for them, it's just . . . well, we were married in the glen, as well, and . . .' She stopped, drawing back from the memory of the man who had joined them in holy matrimony.

Her husband swung her round and kissed her tenderly. 'I had not forgotten, my darling, and the only thing I regret is that it took me so long to tell you I love you.'

She looked at his dear face and summoned a smile. 'I'm sure Ruairidh and Melda won't regret it, either.' She felt the coldness coming back into her heart, the coldness she had been trying to dispel for days because she truly did not want to hold the girl's parentage against her.

The wedding was everything that Ruairidh and Melda had wanted. The Reverend Stephen Drummond – the incumbent there for seventeen years now – conducted an impressive ceremony, and it was not only the two mothers who were moved to tears. When the lovely young bride lifted her veil to let her handsome groom kiss her, the 'Oohs' and 'Ahs' echoing from every corner of the kirk were followed by sniffs and the flourish of handkerchiefs, men's as well as women's.

Then the whole congregation was transported to the castle in the Bruce-Lyalls' carriages adorned with the family crest, and though several journeys had to be made, those who were left until last did not complain; they didn't mind waiting.

Extra staff had been engaged to ensure the smooth operation of providing and serving the banquet, all the best china and silver cutlery were on show, and once the guests had eaten as much as they possibly could, the tables were cleared and placed round the walls of the dining room to be set out with the bottles of spirits. All the inhabitants of Glendarril took full advantage of the filled glasses handed round, and with whisky available almost on tap, it was not surprising that many a man thought he was kissing his own wife in the ballroom when it was somebody else's he was dancing with; an honest mistake . . . or so he professed. The women didn't seem to mind, not even Marianne. It had taken one brave soul to give her a swift kiss during a waltz, then she had a steady stream of partners, most of whom gave her a proper smacker on the lips.

'I'm glad she's entering into the spirit of things,' Robert Mowatt murmured to Hamish. 'I was a wee bit afraid she'd –'

'She's got over all that,' Hamish said, watching his wife fondly. 'Your little lecture did the trick, thank goodness.'

The doctor deemed it best not to say that he hadn't convinced her of anything. She had promised that she wouldn't take her spite out on Melda, but even if she fully meant to keep that promise, there was always the possibility that something the girl would say or do might trigger off the paranoia again.

Marianne's thoughts at that moment, however, as she sat down and let her eyes follow the radiant pair, were not on Duncan Peat; she was recalling the two sweet infants she had thought of suffocating. She thanked God that she hadn't, but she didn't regret instructing Andrew Rennie to put them up for adoption. She had safeguarded herself by telling him to keep her identity secret – to prevent them turning up at some time in the future to claim their inheritance. She had also forbidden him to tell her where they had been placed or anything about them, but to salve her conscience had ordered him to send a sizeable allowance to the adoptive parents each month until they came of age – to provide for the twins' maintenance and education.

She glanced at Andrew, standing on the other side of the room, and catching her eye, he came across to ask her to dance. When they got into the rhythm of the Scottish waltz, he said, 'You're looking very serious, Marianne. I hope nothing's wrong.'

'Nothing you can do anything about, Andrew. It's all in the past.'

The slight squeeze he gave her let her know he understood, so she rewarded him with an affectionate smile. 'I don't know what I'd have done without you, Andrew. You've always been there for me.'

'And I always shall be, my dear.'

'But I shouldn't have asked you to ... I don't know what you must have thought of me.'

His love for her was evident as he regarded her earnestly. 'You know what I think of you, Marianne, what I've always thought of you. Nothing will ever change that.'

A lump came in her throat – he was such a good man. She sometimes wondered ... To cover the embarrassment of her thoughts, she said, 'Why don't you find yourself a wife? I'm sure you must meet some eligible young women in the course of your work.'

He shrugged wryly. 'I seldom meet young women. My female clients are generally widows – middle-aged matrons or ancient matriarchs who control their families by threatening to disinherit them. Besides, I'm happy the way I am. What about you? Are you happy with Hamish?'

'Yes, Andrew, I am. He's a loving husband.' Even now, after all this time, she saw the pain surfacing in Andrew's eyes, but it was too late to unsay it.

She wished that Miss Edith had been here for him, but his last aunt had passed away some time before, protesting right up to the last moment, according to the nurse he had paid to check on her every day, that she didn't need a doctor. Poor old dear, Marianne reflected, she was always so independent.

Because the glen folk had not had a celebration like this in the memories of many, they made the most of it, not only the men who clamoured for a dance with the laird's wife or the wife of the future laird, but the women who, their courage also bolstered by the free alcohol – claimed the young Master for a dance, and even the laird himself.

Not until the beer and whisky had almost run out did they show any sign of leaving, and the Bruce-Lyall family, now extended by one, stood outside to wave them off. When they went inside, Ruairidh, with his arm still round his bride, said, somewhat bashfully, 'If you'll excuse us, we'll go up to bed now. It's been a long day.'

Andrew, who had been asked to stay the night, got to his feet a little unsteadily when Marianne and her husband entered the sitting room. 'I had better get to bed, too.'

Hamish grabbed his sleeve. 'No, no, you'll take one last dram with me, surely?'

Marianne left them to their nightcap.

Chapter Twenty-four

❧

When the young couple returned from their three-month honeymoon in France, Ruairidh joyfully announced that Melda was pregnant and, the Mowatts having been asked to the castle to welcome them home, there followed a round of cheek-kissing and back-slapping in which Marianne had to steel herself to take part. Fortunately for her, with so much commotion going on, no one noticed her hesitation ... except Melda, who concluded that her mother-in-law, like herself, was remembering the boy infant who had died.

To banish this from both their minds, she said, turning rather pink, 'The doctor in Paris said my *accouchement* was due in six months.'

Showing none of her embarrassment, Ruairidh boasted, 'He said I must have planted the *enfant* on our wedding night.'

The two fathers glanced at their wives to see how they had reacted to this indiscretion, a breach of good manners especially in mixed company, then caught each other's eye and bellowed with laughter.

'Good for you, son!' boomed Hamish, and Robert added, 'Well done!'

Marianne tried not to show how nauseated she felt, and when Flora leaned over and murmured, 'Well, it was only to be expected, wasn't it?' she nodded stonily.

When Ruairidh attempted to take Melda in his arms that night, she pleaded exhaustion from the travelling and turned away. If he had been too blind to notice that his mother wasn't pleased about the baby, it wasn't up to her to tell him. Not that the woman had said anything, it was a look in her eyes at one point, as if she hated her son's wife. But why? She couldn't still believe that the minister had been afflicted with an insanity which could skip a generation and be passed on to his grandchildren? Yet it had taken her, Melda, some time to believe her father – she would always look on Robert Mowatt as her father – when he swore to her that the man would have recovered from his temporary madness if he hadn't killed himself.

What else could Ruairidh's mother have against her? The boot should really be on the other foot. It was *her* fault that the other baby, her first grandchild, hadn't lived. If she'd just let it be born where it should have been born, everything would have been all right. But maybe it wouldn't, Melda conceded sadly. Maybe it had been meant to die all along. If it hadn't, she would have always been wondering where it was, what had become of it . . . and remembering that it had been conceived on the day she had learned of Rannie's death, which wasn't exactly a pleasant thought. She *had* been grateful to Lady Marianne for seeing her through that pregnancy and saving her from being the butt of gossip in the glen, but she'd only done that for her own sake, to preserve the good name of her family, and its pure blood line.

But she had better not start her marriage off on a sour note by tackling the woman about her present attitude, Melda mused. Ruairidh wouldn't want friction between his wife and his mother, but she wouldn't knuckle under to the woman if she started ordering her about. She was the next Lady Glendarril, wasn't she? With a sob in her throat, she turned to her husband.

When it came to the last month, with Melda's belly appearing to be almost at bursting point, Hamish excused Ruairidh from all duties at the mill to let him be with his wife as much as possible. 'She's just a young slip of a thing,' he explained to his wife. 'She has no idea what childbirth means, and she needs him here with her.'

Marianne couldn't help thinking that she had been little older when she produced Ranald, and that Melda *did* know what childbirth meant, but she didn't feel like arguing with him. She had her old worry on her mind again. She couldn't possibly allow Melda to keep her child if it turned out to be a boy, bringing the possibility of madness into the Bruce-Lyall blood. The problem was, she'd only had Hamish to contend with last time, unobservant and gullible. It had been easy to pull the wool over his eyes and whip the girl out of sight, but Ruairidh was different. He'd been furious, and had refused when his father had told him to book Melda into an extortionately expensive maternity home in Edinburgh rather than trust the local 'howdie' to bring this special child into the world, because he couldn't bear the thought of her being taken away from him.

Robert Mowatt, of course, as the man the whole glen thought was Melda's father, was out of the question, they were all agreed on that, which relieved both Marianne and the young mother-to-be, for the doctor would know as soon as he examined the girl that this was not her first pregnancy. It was he, however, who gave Hamish the name of a highly recommended trained midwife.

A solution to the problem of what to do with the baby occurred to her which made her draw a deep shuddery breath. Could she possibly ask Robert . . . ? Would he do for her what Andrew Rennie had done before? It would be worth trying, and it would only be necessary if Melda produced a boy.

Before the arrival of the trained midwife from Edinburgh, everyone in the castle was affected by the tense nervousness that seemed to pervade the place, but Nurse Crombie, as starchy as her voluminous apron and the cap sitting squarely on her straight greying hair, had an efficient manner that inspired confidence. She organized a special room for the confinement, and when Melda's first pains began, she shepherded the girl there and banned Ruairidh from even opening the door.

'The father can not be present at the birth,' she lectured when he protested vehemently at being excluded. 'It is just not done, and I will look after your wife. Nothing will go wrong, I assure you.'

Marianne, however, categorically refused to be kept out, but was such a nuisance that Melda asked her to go down and keep Ruairidh company.

Having timed the contractions for hours, Nurse Crombie rang for a maid when it was clear that there was some complication, and asked her to send someone for the doctor. Luckily, Robert was on his way and arrived five minutes later, his face grim as he took the stairs two at a time. The tension was building to a climax now, in the room upstairs, in the sitting room, even in the kitchens, where Mrs Burr boiled endless kettles of water to make tea.

Ruairidh's walking up and down irritated his mother, also in a highly emotional state, and she barked, 'For goodness' sake, sit down. You're not helping anything by tramping about like a raging bull. And put out that cigarette. You've done nothing but smoke since I came in.'

'A cigarette might help you, too, Mother,' he snapped. 'You're like a hen on a hot girdle, hodging about on that chair.'

Both realizing that they might say something unforgivable in their agitation, they kept quiet until Robert came in. Holding his hand up to stop the double flow of questions, he sat down wearily. 'It's a girl, a real whopper – 9 pounds 4 ounces, but they're both well. Let Ruairidh go up to see them first, Marianne. You'll get your turn.'

When the door closed behind the young man, the doctor said, 'It's a pity it's not a boy. She had a rough time and

I've told her she shouldn't have any more. I'll leave you to tell Ruairidh.'

Marianne felt as though she had just been set free from a dank prison cell. It was a girl! It would be an only child! She had been worrying for nothing!

Dorothea was the axis round which the world of Castle Lyall revolved. From the laird himself down to the little scullery maid, they were besotted by her. In the nursery, her every move was watched by Nurse Shepherd, who had been employed after Nurse Crombie moved away to attend her next confinement, and when the perambulator was put outside in the sunshine, her slightest squeak had someone running to pick her up. And the tiny red-faced bundle soon became a podgy, golden-haired, blue-eyed beauty who could smile when it suited her but found she got more attention if she went into a tantrum.

'She's got a right wee temper, that one,' Mrs Burr observed one day when the child was barely a year old.

'Aye, Cook,' Ruby smiled, 'but she's such a bonnie wee toot you canna help but like her.'

'They're going to spoil her, though, running after her like that.' She gestured towards the nurse, who was haring across the lawn to lift her charge. 'Still, if I'm right, she'll no' have things all her own way for much longer.'

'Oh, my!' Ruby said in dismay. 'Melda's no' expecting' again, is she? The doctor said she wasna to have another ane.'

'I'd say she was in her third month, by the look o' her.'

'Well, we'll be in for it now. The mistress'll no' be pleased.'

Marianne was definitely not pleased when Melda at last plucked up courage to tell her. 'You stupid girl!' she burst out. 'You know you shouldn't –'

Melda, however, was subservient no longer. 'It was Ruairidh's idea as much as mine,' she interrupted. 'Dorrie's being made too much of, and the only way to stop that is to give her a brother.'

'A brother?' Marianne echoed faintly. 'How can you be so sure it'll be a boy?'

'I can't be sure, of course, but Ruairidh wants a son.'

'But you'll be endangering your life, didn't you remind him of that?'

'No, I deliberately made light of any problems. I want a son as much as he does – a son and a daughter, the perfect gentleman's family.'

'I think you should talk to your father. Um . . . how far on are you?'

'Four months.'

Marianne bristled. 'Why didn't you tell me before?'

'Because I knew what you and my father would say, and neither of you can do anything about it now.'

Their eyes locked, each knowing what the other was thinking, yet bound by old promises not to speak of it.

As Marianne had foreseen, Robert was truly angry when Melda did acquaint him of her condition. 'I told you!' he shouted. 'Your womb . . . oh, I can't explain it to you, but you're going to have to look after yourself. No lifting Dorothea, no running, even hurrying, and you'll have to lie flat for at least the last two months.'

'Is it as bad as that?' Melda faltered.

'I wouldn't have advised you against a second child otherwise. I'd better speak to Ruairidh.' He looked at the pale girl sadly. 'You won't have to let him . . .'

'I can't expect him not to.' She paused, her eyes filling with tears. 'He might look for somebody else.'

'He'd have me to reckon with if he did!' Robert declared hotly.

'Father, don't say anything to him, please. I'll be

very careful till the baby's born and I'm sure I'll be all right.'

'As long as you remember then.'

For the next three months, Marianne and Melda were on the defensive when they spoke to each other, but when the young mother-to-be was ordered to lie flat in bed, her mother-in-law surprised her by being very attentive. Marianne had more or less resigned herself to Fate. What she actually told herself was that there was many a slip 'twixt cup and lip, as she had heard Miss Edith say more than once.

As it happened, the old saying was truly prophetic. Melda lost the baby near the end of the seventh month, and her father pulled no punches when he tackled his son-in-law. 'God knows what you think you're doing, Ruairidh. I advised Melda last time that she should not have any more, but I am going to order it this time. If you make her pregnant again, you will be as good as passing a death sentence on her.'

'Oh, no!' Ruairidh was appalled. 'I'd never do anything to hurt her, Robert, you know that.'

'But you are young and virile, and passion is no respecter of intentions, however sincerely meant, and even if you practise birth control, which is used all over nowadays, there would always be a chance that you'd forget, or something would go wrong, and . . . where would you be? You could possibly get the son I know perfectly well you want, but you would probably lose your wife. I would advise a hysterectomy as soon as possible.'

'A hysterectomy? What does that involve?'

'It is an operation to remove a woman's reproductive organs.'

Ruairidh looked utterly shocked at this. 'Is this a . . . dangerous operation?'

'There is always danger when an operation is performed,

but methods are improving all the time, and I would say there is little chance of anything going wrong. A few weeks in hospital, possibly a month or two of being careful not to do anything strenuous, and then she should be as right as rain.' He hesitated before stating what should have been obvious but which had clearly not occurred to Ruairidh. 'It means, of course, that she can have no more children.'

'I see.' His face blanching, the younger man fell silent, obviously turning it over in his mind, but at last he murmured, 'I'd rather have Melda fit and well than have a son and heir, if that's what you're worrying about. Will it be up to her to decide whether or not . . . ?'

'I will give her the choice, and you must persuade her that if she does not agree to it, her health will deteriorate . . .'

Marianne's relief on hearing this news made her feel as if she would be at peace for ever, though she wished that she had known from the outset that Ruairidh and Melda had been destined not to have a son; she could have saved herself years of fretting. She revelled in the thought that only the purest of blood would run through the veins of future Glendarrils, whoever inherited the title.

It was not altogether surprising that Marianne overlooked the possibility that her granddaughter – also granddaughter of Duncan Peat – could eventually produce a son, who would be heir after Ruairidh, could be the next but one Lord. It had been so long since Andrew Rennie had told her that the title could be passed through the distaff side, and so much had happened in the years between, that she had blotted it from her memory. As far as she was concerned, the danger of contamination was finally over.

The folk of the glen, of course, ignorant of Melda's real parentage and believing the title had to be passed directly to a male, were bitterly disappointed that the Bruce-Lyall line would stop with the present Master. Mima Rattray, as usual, held forth to all who entered the post office. 'It's an awful pity Master Ranald was killed. He'd have made a string of sons to carry on his name.'

One brave soul had the temerity to put her right on one point. 'Only one would have inherited the title, though.'

The postmistress gave her head an irritated shake. 'I know *that*! What I meant was he'd have made sure there was aye a son to follow on. Like, if there was another war.'

'There can never be another war, Mima. The Great War, as they're calling it, was the war to end all wars, wasn't it?'

Feeling that she was coming off worst in the discussion, Mima tutted loudly. 'You never know, Maggie. Nothing on this earth's ever certain, and if there *was* another war, Master Rannie would have had plenty stand-bys.'

Maggie thought it wise to climb down now, but she couldn't resist one last barb. 'Aye, well, you're maybe richt, but Master Rannie's no' here now, is he?'

She had left virtually nothing for the postmistress to take as surrender. 'No,' she admitted, truculently, 'I was just saying . . .'

The entry of another customer brought this difference of opinion to a close, and Maggie went out quite pleased at having beaten Mima for once. The postmistress, however, immediately started up the same subject again, knowing that little Lizzie Black was easily browbeaten.

Dorothea took full advantage of being the centre of attention in the castle, screaming her head off when she didn't get what she wanted, and by her second birthday, she was beginning to get out of hand altogether. Her father, therefore, issued instructions that she must be disciplined, that she would have to learn to control her temper.

Ruby, of course, was loud in protest at this . . . in the kitchen. 'Poor wee Dorrie, she's only two, for goodness' sake. What does he expect?'

Mrs Burr shook her head. 'She'll have to learn. She's that spoiled she thinks the whole place revolves round her.'

'So it should, she's such a bonnie wee thing with her fair curly head and rosy cheeks. She's that like her father, with the same blue eyes and all, but she's got her mother's spirit, if you ask me.'

'Melda had aye plenty spirit,' chimed in Jessie Black. 'I was at the school wi' her, and she was awful clever. We could never understand why she didna go to the university in Aberdeen, for we was sure her father wanted her to be a doctor like him. Of course, she was aye close to the laird's boys, an' maybe that's when she made up her mind on being mistress here some day.'

Mrs Burr, a native of the glen who had married a Glaswegian and only returned to her place of birth when he died, now said, 'Mima Rattray tell't me once there was mair atween her an' Master Ranald than folk kent. Becky Drummond once tell't her that Ranald tell't *her he* was meetin' Melda in the woods – an' that was on the last nicht o' his last leave, poor soul.'

Jessie frowned. 'But a'body kens Becky Drummond tell't lies. I never believed a word she said, though she *was* the minister's lassie.'

Ruby, as Melda's personal maid – although she was more often doing a housekeeper's work – was closer to her than any of them. 'Ranald was a bit o' a rogue though, an' I think she saw through him. Any road, you canna deny she loves the Master.'

'Aye, you're right there,' Mrs Burr sighed. 'And he loves her, and all. They'll make a fine laird and his lady when the time comes.'

With her daughter taken over by the nursemaid, Melda felt time weighing heavily on her hands, and decided one day in the autumn of 1922, to cycle down to the mill to see what exactly went on there. Unlike his father, Hamish welcomed his son's wife's interest in the family business and took her through every process himself. She was intent on seeing everything, but he did notice that she spent more time in the design department than anywhere else. Joking, he said, 'Would you like to try your hand at creating a new patterned cloth?'

'Would I like?' she exclaimed, clapping her hands, 'I'd be delighted.'

Although most of the men in the department had known Melda as a child, and had heard then that she was clever, they were still amazed at the technicality of the drawings she produced and the suggestions she made as to the colours which should be used in the checks. Hamish was absolutely stunned, and said she could come in as often as she liked to give him some more ideas.

The only person who was not pleased about her newly discovered talent was her mother-in-law. 'Your father wasn't happy about me going round the place,' she reminded Hamish.

'I am not my father,' he smiled, 'and things are different now. We have quite a few women workers – some of the men did not come back from the war, remember.'

They both fell silent at that, remembering the tall fair-haired boy with the twinkling eyes and ready charm who had not returned either.

Before Melda took up her appointment, as she thought of it, even if her father-in-law had not meant it as such, she decided to take a day in Edinburgh to see the kind of materials that were most popular in the shops, for ladies' and gents' wear.

'Are you sure about this?' Ruairidh asked. 'You surely don't want to tie yourself down to a job, do you?'

'I'd love to tie myself down,' she laughed, 'especially to a job I'd really love doing. I feel useless at home, you know, spending most of my time out with the dogs, or chatting to one of the gardeners. Your mother does her bit, looking after the needs of the glen folk, so why shouldn't I do something, too? Nursie hardly ever lets me spend any time alone with Dorrie, so . . .'

'I see your point. Well, if you like, I can come with you and we'll make it a little holiday – say a long weekend? What d'you think? Or we could make it London, if you like?'

'I think Edinburgh'll do for a start.'

Somewhat taken aback at first by their proposal, Hamish suddenly became very enthusiastic, sending off telegrams to the managers of several stores asking for their co-operation.

'Looks like Melda's going into the mill,' Mima Rattray observed to the first customer after he had left the post office. 'Her and the Master are having a trip to Edinburgh to look round the big shops to see what sells best.'

Chapter Twenty-five

In late spring of 1925, Melda decided that she would like to try something new. She had introduced many variations of designs for the different kinds of cloth the mill produced, and she needed another challenge.

'I was thinking of finding out about Fair Isle patterns,' she told Ruairidh one day. 'Jean Lambie's cousin's here on holiday from Shetland, and I began copying from her scarf, but there must be other patterns and combinations of colours. So if I go there and –'

Her husband frowned. 'I can't go traipsing up to Shetland with you just now. I've to supervise the worsteds and tweeds we'll offer the buyers for next winter, and Father's trying to set up a better range of light-weight flannels for ladies' costumes.'

'I wanted to go on my own anyway. Fiona goes home next week, so I if I travelled on the boat with her, we could discuss –'

'Can't you discuss whatever you want to discuss with her before she leaves?'

Irritated that he couldn't understand how much better it would be if she saw things for herself Melda said sharply, 'She can't keep dozens of patterns in her head. It took me ages to write down one, and she told me she has a whole set of charts on graph paper at home. She says that's the proper way to knit Fair Isle, not written in words like in the leaflets wool shops sell – two brown, one natural, three white, and so on – and she's willing to let me copy them.'

'Why don't you ask her to do it for you? Or ask her to post them on and you can return them when you've copied them? I'm not keen on the idea of you going so far away by yourself.'

She had to laugh at this. 'I'm not a child now, Ruairidh. I'll be twenty-three soon, and what harm could I come to in Shetland?'

After a moment's reflection, he said, 'I'd be happier if someone was with you. What about Ruby?'

'Oh, you know Ruby. She'd always want to show she's a lady's maid, and I don't want anyone to say I think I'm any different from them.'

'Jean Lambie, then? If I'm any judge, she'd jump at the chance of a free holiday with her cousin.'

'Wouldn't that leave you short of a knitter?'

'Yes, but we'd manage, somehow.'

Ruairidh was not put to the test, however. When Hamish heard of Melda's plan, he pronounced it a dashed good idea. 'And you don't need a guard dog,' he smiled, patting her shoulder. 'No doubt there will be other women on the boat home.' He turned to his son. 'She's a big girl now, Ruairidh. You'll have to let go of her, and there's no need for her to hurry back. She can take the whole summer if she likes. That nurse can keep Dorothea under control.'

Ruairidh gave in, but told his wife later, 'It's all very well for Father, but I can't do without you all summer, my darling.'

Not sure whether to be annoyed that he thought of her as a chattel or to treat it as a compliment, Melda opted for the latter and gave a soft laugh. 'It shouldn't take long to copy down Fiona's charts, but I'd like to ask her friends as well, to get as many designs as I can while I'm there. I'm sure all the shepherds' wives'll be itching to start knitting when they see them, and I won't be more than three or four weeks away.'

'Four weeks?' he groaned. 'That's a lifetime.'

*   *   *

Marianne's air of suppressed excitement puzzled Hamish, but he asked nothing until Ruairidh had left in his new Singer with Melda and her luggage – Jean Lambie's cousin was to be collected on the way.

'What's going on?' he demanded, eyeing her suspiciously as they closed the big oaken door and returned to the dining room to finish breakfast. 'You're up to something.'

After a brief hesitation, she said, 'I'm in the process of creating a grandson for us.'

He tutted his displeasure at what he took to be levity. 'I can't see Melda even looking at another man, and besides, as you know full well, she can't have any more children, sons or otherwise.'

Her finger tapped the side of her nose secretively. 'Not Melda.'

'Good God! You're surely not going to encourage Ruairidh to –'

'I'm just giving him the opportunity. If I can get him to fall for one of the girls I'm going to invite on Sunday afternoons –'

'But, Marianne, even if he makes a son with another girl, it would be illegitimate, and think of the scandal there would be.'

'I thought Andrew could arrange for an annulment of his marriage.'

Hamish snorted. 'On what grounds, may I ask? Ruairidh can't claim non-consummation, not when Melda's already given him a daughter.'

'A divorce, then.' Marianne's sharpness betrayed her irritation. 'Then a son would be legitimate, otherwise there won't be an heir to follow him, unless you're hiding some relatives up your sleeve.'

He shrugged. 'I don't know of any still alive, not even forty-second cousins, and I don't think even Andrew could dig any up.'

*   *   *

On Sunday, the Hon. Patricia Matthewson roared up the drive to Castle Lyall just before three o'clock in a red two-seater sports car with her grandmother looking apprehensive at her side. Marianne, who hadn't seen Lady Matthewson since Hector's funeral twenty-three years earlier, was dismayed to find that Patricia was not what anyone could call a beauty – having what could only be described as buck teeth, and a neighing laugh to match.

Ruairidh did as he had been instructed by his mother and asked the girl to have a game of tennis, but he could not understand why his mother had made contact with the Matthewsons at all. By the time a dainty afternoon tea was served, he'd had enough, and so, pleading a mountain of paper work to clear, he disappeared into the library.

At dinner that night, he turned on Marianne angrily. 'Don't ask me to be nice to that monster again! She couldn't say anything without braying and it went right through my head.'

The following Sunday went much better. Lord and Lady Furness had brought their whole family with them – two sons who had been at boarding school with Ruairidh, and a daughter he and Ranald had both enjoyed seeing when they were in their early teens. Kitty was even more attractive now, and was obviously attracted to him, lying close beside him when he flopped down on the lawn after the exertion of the doubles match. The two mothers were chatting in the shade facing towards them, the fathers were smoking pipes on a bench near the library window but also watching them, and when Edwin and Sydney, both mad about cars, disappeared to the garage to inspect Hamish's new Lagonda, their sister put her lips to Ruairidh's ear.

'Can't we go somewhere a bit more secluded?' she whispered. 'This is like sitting in a goldfish bowl.'

Her perfume had started a flicker of desire in him, her breath fanned it to a glowing ember, and jumping up, he guided her towards the path to the woods. He knew he shouldn't, but he was missing a woman's company. He steered her past the old hut where he and Melda had first made love, and remembering that evening made him realize the risk he was taking now. 'We'd better turn back, Kitty.'

'Oh, Ruairidh,' she pouted, 'don't you like being alone with me?'

'I do, Kit, but . . . it's playing with fire.'

She slid her pointed tongue seductively over her lips. 'And you're scared of being burned? We used to have fun together in the old days and I quite fancy getting a bit singed, myself.'

He was beginning to fancy more than a slight singeing, but he said, 'No, Kit. We're older now, and I've an adult need in me.'

'So have I,' she murmured, turning to press her body against his, 'and it's best to give in to your feelings.'

Her kiss, long and searching, rekindled his inner fire so that his mouth sought hers again, his hands went involuntarily to the small of her back then parted to follow the swells of her buttocks. He would have been lost if Kitty had left him to continue at his own pace, but in trying to hurry him on, she guided one of his hands to where she had opened the buttons of her thin dress. His fingers sank into one breast for only a second before he jumped away from her – alarmed by his reaction to the stimulus. 'We can't . . . I'm a married man.'

'So were nearly all the others I've had,' she murmured huskily. 'I get a bigger thrill knowing the man's another woman's husband, and they say it's more exciting for them, too.'

The knowledge that he was just another married man she wanted to add to her list of conquests sickened him, and although it did cross his mind that he wouldn't be taking advantage of a naïve virgin if he did take her, he pushed her roughly away. 'No,' he said firmly, 'I love my wife and I'd never even dream of being unfaithful to her.'

He walked her back to the castle without saying another word, left her on the lawn, then marched straight past both sets of parents and upstairs to his room. Stretching out on his bed, he wondered if he'd been a fool. Nobody would have known – except himself, and that was what had stopped him. He would never have lived easily if he'd done what he wanted. He couldn't have faced Melda without remembering and feeling ashamed and guilty. A deep remorse flooded through him as he recognized the passion building up in his loins at just the memory of Kitty's softly curved body and the sweetness of her kisses.

Damn it all! he told himself furiously. Melda's every bit as sweet and curvaceous. He had been tempted because he was missing her, and he should be thankful that he'd had the willpower to withstand that temptation. Vowing that he would never again get into a situation like that, whoever the girl was, he wondered why his mother had begun to invite people to the house, something she very rarely did. Worse still, why were they families with marriageable daughters?

'I'm certain something happened,' Marianne said triumphantly. 'He's ashamed of himself, that's why he hasn't come down to dinner.'

'It's nothing to be pleased about,' Hamish frowned, 'and please do not speak about it in front of the servants.'

It took a great effort of will on her part to wait, and as soon as they were alone in the drawing room, she started. 'I could read the signs, you know.'

'You think they'd been fornicating?'

'There's no need to be so crude,' she objected.

'That's the only word for it, the only decent word, that is.'

Marianne scowled at him. 'I can't invite her every week, that would be too obvious, but I'm sure they've started something and we'll have to hope it develops naturally.'

At that moment their son walked in, and without thinking, Marianne said archly, 'Kitty'll make a good wife to some man, won't she?'

Ruairidh's expression was icy. 'I hadn't given it a thought. Melda's the only wife I'll ever want.'

Marianne's face warning him not to say anything, Hamish muttered, 'I'd better take the dogs out.' The two red setters, grandsons of Romulus and Remus, sprang from the hearthrug and dashed through the door as soon as he opened it.

'I just came down to say good night, Mother,' Ruairidh mumbled, 'but before I go up again . . .' His face turning scarlet, he averted his head for a moment and then burst out, 'You're so transparent, so devious, it'd be laughable if it weren't so pathetic.'

She did not seem one whit abashed that he had caught her out. 'You need a wife who can give you a son, and Melda can't now she's been rendered useless. Your father would like to see you with an heir before he dies.'

The slur on his wife made him see red. 'If Father's so desperate for a bloody heir to follow me, why doesn't *he* do the needful? I've seen him eyeing Nursie, so he must still be capable.'

Outraged, Marianne cried, 'How dare you speak of your father like that? He'd never dream of being unfaithful to me.'

'And I'll never be unfaithful to Melda, though I came damned near it today before I saw sense.'

Marianne pounced. 'So I was right! You and Kitty *had* been –'

Hanging his head, Ruairidh whispered, 'That's what you planned, was it? Well, she tried her best, but I did *not* give in to her. All the same, I went further than I should, and if you knew how badly I feel, you'd have some pity for me.'

After a moment's reflective silence, Marianne said softly, 'Shall we let it be our secret, then?'

No more girls were offered as sacrificial lambs, and although Kitty Furness turned up the following Sunday, Ruairidh kept to his room and left his mother to excuse his absence. He was pleased to receive a letter from Melda the following day, asking him to collect her from the North Boat at Aberdeen on Wednesday – pleased, yet apprehensive.

Describing her stay in Lerwick, Melda could sense her mother-in-law's antagonism; Marianne's jealousy of her son's wife was almost tangible. Not only had Melda returned with a huge selection of Fair Isle designs and instructions for knitting them into scarves, ladies' jumpers, men's pullovers, gloves, children's outdoor sets consisting of patterned tops and plain pantaloons, but she had also been told how the various dyes were obtained for the Shetland floss, the two-ply wool in which all true Fair Isle work is carried out.

Having shown her husband and his parents her range of graphs, she produced samples of the fine wool. 'The older women just use white, natural, grey and moorat – this mossy brown – that was traditional, but the younger ones are using other colours as well, not garishly bright like some national shops do under the pretence of them being real Fair Isle, but muted shades of rose, rust, lemon, blue, green, all dyed from woodland plants – lichens, grasses and natural sources.'

She glanced around her three listeners. Hamish was studying the skeins of wool as if trying to visualize the transformation from the dirty fleeces of the mountain sheep to this fascinating rainbow. Marianne had the hint of a sneer on her face as she contemplated the graphs with their explanatory keys at the side. Ruairidh was the only one to meet Melda's eyes, and instead of lingering on her with the love she had expected, he turned his head immediately away.

'They're not all the same,' Marianne observed abruptly. 'Look, a cross on this one stands for natural, but on this one, natural's a blank square, and it's the same with all the colours ... different on every sheet of paper.'

Melda did her best to stifle her impatience. 'That's because I got them from different women. Each one writes them down in the way her mother taught her. They hardly need to look at the patterns now, in any case, they've knitted them so often. They stand outside their doors, their hands working back and forth like shuttles, you'd hardly credit the speed they can go, and everything – from the largest man's pullover to gloves and scarves – is done on four needles ... wires, as they call them.'

Marianne's eyebrows rose in disbelief. 'They can't knit standing up ... not when they're using a lot of colours at a time. The balls of wool would get all tangled up.'

'If you had taken time to look properly,' Melda began, an edge to her voice, 'you'd have seen it's seldom more than two colours at a time, and they break off each colour at the end of the last row it is used, and join it in when it's needed again. I know that sounds as if there'll be an awful lot of ends, but they darn them all in so you'd never notice, and it means there's no long stretches of wool to snag on rings or fingernails when they're being worn or washed. And the wrong side of the work is as neat as the right side.'

'Stop criticizing, Marianne,' Hamish snapped, as his wife opened her mouth again, 'and give credit where it's due. Melda has done a marvellous job, and we'd better have a selection of Fair Isle goods ready for the buyers coming to get their winter stock. Nothing big, of course, maybe gloves and scarves, enough to whet their appetites.'

That night, bitterly disappointed that her husband was lying like a stone beside her instead of loving her as she had hoped, Melda tried to bring him round. 'I can't understand why your mother's annoyed at me. I was just trying to get more interesting work for our knitters and extra business for the mill.'

Having brooded about his own misdemeanour since Sunday, Ruairidh decided he would have to get it off his chest before he could resume relations with his wife. He had not, however, had time to think how to confess without hurting her. 'That's not why she's annoyed at you,' he began. 'She blames you for there not being an heir to come after me.'

Her heart sank. 'We've always known that, so why are you telling me now? Have you done something that needs that as an excuse?'

'I've done nothing ... not really.' It was the first lie he had ever told her, and he could not keep it up. 'Oh, Melda, I've got to tell you. Mother invited the Furness family for afternoon tea one of the Sundays you were away, and Kitty ... I took her for a walk after we'd had a game of tennis.'

'Kitty Furness? Wasn't she one of the girls your mother tried to get you or Ranald to marry at one time? You must have known she was up to something, inviting them here.' Only then did she understand what her mother-in-law had wanted to happen. 'Are you trying to tell me ... you made love to Kitty Furness?' Her eyes brimmed with tears at the thought of how quickly he had betrayed her.

'No, Melda! It's what she wanted, yes, and I nearly did.'

'Nearly did?' Her voice was heavily sarcastic. 'How nearly? Did you kiss her and fondle her, and ... and ... oh, how could you, Ruairidh? I know you can't stop once you're roused.'

'I can't deny I was roused, but I thought of you, my darling, and shoved her away.' He turned towards her in appeal. 'Melda, I could say it was all down to her, but it was as much my fault. I wish you could understand how ashamed I am, though I wouldn't blame you if you can't forgive me ... but ... please try, please!'

Her mouth was trembling. 'You're sure you didn't . . . ?'

'I just kissed her, I swear it, but it's been eating at my innards ever since. I'm so sorry, my dearest! I don't even like her and I've hurt the only woman I'll ever love.'

She *was* hurt, so much that her first instinct was to retaliate by hurting him, but what was the point?

Neither Ruairidh nor Melda tumbled to what was going on that summer. He was pleased to be trusted to deal with so much of the business of the mill on his own, and she was delighted to be allowed to promote the Fair Isle side single-handedly. The fact that they were never away at the same time, that she was sent off perhaps a week after her husband returned, and vice versa, escaped them in the satisfaction of their work, and they spent what little time they had in each other's company discussing plans.

Ruairidh did think it strange that he bumped into Kitty Furness in Edinburgh on one trip, Newcastle on another, but because she appeared to be just as surprised by the meetings as he was, he accepted them as coincidences and didn't mention them to his wife. There was no sense in making her think things that weren't true, because he had learned his lesson and had refused Kitty's invitations in both cities to have a drink at her hotel, nor had he taken up her barely veiled hints that he should take her to his.

When, however, she appeared one Sunday afternoon in September at Castle Lyall while Melda was in Glasgow, he could see his mother's hand in it and determined to call her bluff. He asked Kitty to have a game of tennis, and afterwards, flopped down with her at the edge of the lawn. When, as he had known she would, Kitty suggested going for a walk, he said, in a loud stage whisper, 'Why don't we go up to my room instead?'

His mother's intake of breath satisfied him that she had heard and he prayed that she would be so outraged that she would stop him there and then. She did nothing, however, so he helped Kitty to her feet, put an arm round her waist and let his hand rest on her hip as he steered her past the deckchair.

That was when Marianne's parasol came sharply down on the back of his legs, and never was he more glad of any pain. 'You will not take that girl to your bed!' she said sharply. 'This is not a brothel! Surely you didn't expect me to turn a blind eye to your . . .' She paused briefly, searching for a suitable word, and recalling what Hamish had said earlier, she ended, '. . . to you fornicating under my roof.'

He turned to face her. 'I thought you wanted me to put Kit in such a position that I'd have to marry her?'

Kitty jumped in at this. 'Here, wait a minute! Who said anything about marriage? I'm only out for a good time. I don't want to end up with no waist, varicose veins and a noisy baby tying me down.'

'I know you don't. It was my mother's idea . . .'

'And I thought you'd fallen for my charms,' she murmured, doing her best to look crestfallen.

'Kit, I'm truly sorry for subjecting you to –'

She giggled now. 'Don't be sorry, Ruairidh. I knew you wouldn't say that in front of your mother if you meant it, so I guessed what you were up to. It's a pity, though. I'd have enjoyed finding out how good a lover you are.' She turned to look scornfully at the older woman. 'You obviously don't know how much your son loves his wife, Lady Glendarril, and I wish I knew why you've been trying to use me as a wedge between them.'

'Melda can't have any more children,' Ruairidh explained, 'so there won't be any heir to the title when I die.'

'She could only give him a daughter,' Marianne said bitterly.

Triumph replaced the puzzlement on Kitty's face. 'Well, there you are!' she beamed. 'Dorrie will marry eventually, and she'll surely have a son. Hey presto, there's the next heir.'

'She's right, Mother,' Ruairidh said eagerly. 'And you'd better keep your fingers in your own pies after this. Come on, Kitty, I'll see you to your car.'

Teasing him, she backed away, looking afraid. 'I don't know if I can trust you. You might throw me into the back seat and rape me.' She winked saucily at Marianne as she turned away.

When Ruairidh joined his mother again, she said angrily, 'That exhibition was all for my benefit, was it? I thought you meant what you said. I thought –'

'Mother, we all know what thought did. I knew you wouldn't let me take Kit to bed.'

'I see. You depended on me to stop you? What if I hadn't?'

A boyish grin curved his mouth. 'Kit wouldn't have taken another refusal from me, so I'd have been on top of her right now and you'd maybe have got your wish.'

'You're being very indelicate,' she frowned.

He locked eyes with her. 'You've been far worse than indelicate. I've told Melda about Kitty and luckily for you, she doesn't want any unpleasantness, otherwise I'd have taken her and our daughter away from here altogether. I might yet, if you try any more of your tricks.'

The incident put an effective end to Kitty's pursuit of Ruairidh, and to Marianne's attempt at getting him to provide an heir for the title. Unfortunately, it did nothing to stop her jealousy of her daughter-in-law, who was building up a very profitable Fair Isle department at the mill, and to whom Hamish was referring more and more for advice on current trends in woollen fabrics.

Melda was content with her life and was careful, in her differences with her mother-in-law, not to let them escalate into full-blown rows; she no longer held Marianne in awe, but she didn't fancy making a mortal enemy of her. She did, however, stand up to Marianne if she deemed it necessary, blocking her from getting her own way.

'I used to think Melda was a quiet wee mouse,' Hamish confided to his son while they were having a glass of port and a cigar after dinner one night. 'But she's developed quite a shrewd brain, and she commands a lot of respect from the workers, and the buyers from even the largest of stores. The trouble is, your mother's been cock of the walk for so long I think she's just a teeny bit jealous.'

The understatement of the century, Ruairidh thought, yet oddly enough, it didn't worry him now. His wife could hold off herself, she wouldn't let anyone ride roughshod over her, not even his mother. And that was as it should be.

Chapter Twenty-six

❧❀❧

Just as Marianne had done so many years before, Melda had sent her child to the glen school, but Dorothea didn't fit in as well as her father and mother had done. She was quite bright and outgoing, but her arrogance kept the local children from being friends with her. Nevertheless, with her keen willingness to learn, she soon outstripped others of her own age.

The dominie – forty-six-year-old Philip Stewart, not a product of the glen but the best candidate who had applied on Willie Wink's retirement some years before – even went to the mill one day to talk to her father. 'Dorothea could go to university in time, so I hope you will allow her to go on to Mackie after the holidays. She will be given every bit as good an education there as in any public school for girls that you care to name.'

'Oh, I know that, and her mother would slaughter me if I suggested sending her away,' Ruairidh smiled. 'My wife was a product of Mackie herself, so I am sure she will want Dorothea to follow in her footsteps.'

He made to turn away, then realizing that the other man looked as though he had something else to say, he waited, having a fairly good idea that it would be about Dorrie not behaving properly, and after opening and shutting his mouth a couple of times, Mr Stewart said, very apologetically, 'I do not relish having to say anything like this, but . . .'

'Yes?' Ruairidh encouraged. 'Whatever you have to say, spit it out. What has she done?'

The dominie looked more uncomfortable than ever. 'I am afraid . . . she is developing rather rapidly . . .'

'She's only eleven, for heaven's sake, man. She has hardly started to develop yet.'

'That is perhaps true physically, but –' Mr Stewart broke off, wringing his hands.

This annoyed Ruairidh greatly. Whatever the girl had got up to, it surely couldn't be as bad as ... but Philip Stewart was from a little village somewhere on the west coast, and he was likely easily shocked. 'Has she been swearing, or what?'

'Oh no, her manner of speech in class is exemplary, although she is inclined to use rather colourful language in the playground. It is a different ... oh, this is most difficult, Mr Bruce-Lyall.' He hesitated, but catching signs of impatience in his listener's face, he hurried on, 'She is taking a great deal too much interest in boys.' He paused again for a moment. 'I have caught her myself teasing them.'

'What d'you mean, "teasing them"?' Ruairidh's voice was dangerously calm if the other man could have recognized it.

'She was ... lifting her skirts and showing them her ... thigh.' He stopped altogether now, his face beetroot red, his eyes sliding away.

'I am sure there had been a perfectly simple explanation for it. She could have fallen and skinned her leg or ... or something like that. Was that the only incident, or have there been others?'

'That was the only one I saw.'

'I must assume that you are too ready to jump to conclusions.'

'Mr Bruce-Lyall, I am dreadfully sorry I brought the subject up. You are most likely right in what you said, and I was making a mountain out of a molehill. Please, I can assure you that nothing like this will happen again.'

Thinking that the whole situation was somewhat ridiculous, Ruairidh gave a snorting laugh. 'What did you think she was doing? Letting them put their hands up her knickers? At eleven?'

A subdued impression of a smile crossed the dominie's face. 'Yes, it does sound far-fetched, doesn't it?'

Positive that it was exactly what the man had thought, Ruairidh said sharply, 'Too far-fetched for my liking, and I want to hear no more of this kind of thing.'

He did not tell Melda what had been said – he knew it would just upset her – and he did not approach Dorothea when he went home because he didn't want to put ideas into her head. The dominie was a narrow-minded, dirty-minded fool, and had been making something out of nothing, possibly to titillate himself, and even though he was a good teacher, he would be out on his ear if he ever said anything like that again.

As it happened, it was Kirsty, one of the large clan of Blacks, who reprimanded the girl. 'You shouldn't carry on with the boys like you do, Dorrie,' she told her one afternoon on their way home from school.

'I wasn't carrying on with them!' protested Dorothea.

'Oh, you little fibber! I seen you! You and our Billy and Tommy Rattray!'

'We were only having a laugh. They wanted to see my legs.'

'Well, don't let them see them again.' Just months older in actual age but five years older in worldly wisdom, Kirsty knew what her brother and Tommy Rattray had been after. One of the older boys had tried to get his hand up the leg of *her* knickers last year – she'd kicked his shins – but Dorrie was maybe too much of a lady to do that, though it didn't stop her from swearing like a trooper.

Dorothea had been quite peeved at Kirsty Black. What right had she to tell anybody off for something she likely did herself? Besides, Billy Black and Tommy Rattray had only been kids and she *had* only been having a bit of fun

with them, but now, a year later, it was *Jakey* Black she
was interested in, he was so tall and good-looking. He
wasn't very clever, he'd left the glen school as soon as he
was fourteen, but that made him all the more interesting.
He was a gardener's boy at the castle now, so he was *hers*,
wasn't he – to do with what she liked ... and even to let
him do what he liked to her, as long as he didn't punch
her or anything like that.

It was quite easy to get him alone. She waited till she
knew he'd be inside the stables and then went in after him,
making sure nobody saw her because she knew she would
be in trouble if she was caught. He had looked up in surprise the first time, and she felt so shy all of a sudden that
she couldn't tell him she wanted him to kiss her, just to
see what it was like. She'd been alone with him several
times after that, and it had finally dawned on the big galoot
that she was making up to him.

That was when he grabbed her and pushed her against the
wooden wall. It wasn't as nice as she had hoped. His mouth
was all slobbery and his breath smelled, and she couldn't get
away from him no matter how hard she struggled. To make
it worse, his horrible great hand had touched her chest, and
his knee was trying to prise her legs open.

Dargie, almost retiring age now, had seen Miss Dorrie
coming out of the stable once or twice before, looking a
wee bit guilty, and he'd wondered what she'd been up
to, but he'd never dreamed ... ! 'You filthy bugger!' he
shouted, yanking the lanky boy away from the girl by the
scruff of his neck. 'God Almighty! What the hell d'you
think you're playin' at? Get oot o' here this minute, and
it's the last I want to see o' you.'

Crimson-faced, the youth scampered off, and the old gardener turned to the girl now. 'As for you, Miss Dorrie, I some
think you were askin' for it, but maybe you're no' auld
enough to realize ...' He had to stop, for a sickness was

flooding up in him at the thought of what could have happened if he hadn't stopped it when he did. Jakey Black was just fifteen, but he could easily father a bairn, and the lass was twelve or thereabouts, so she'd be capable of conceiving.

She drew herself to her full height and looked him straight in the eye. 'You won't say anything, Dargie!'

He felt quite shocked, for it was an order not a request . . . the brazen little madam! 'I'll no' say anything, Miss Dorrie, but no' for your sake. I wouldna like to think on the hurt it would cause your mother and father if they ken't their lassie had been lettin' a stable laddie paw at her like yon. But if this kind o' thing happens again, wi' ony o' my men, I'll go straight to your father and tell him. D'you hear me, now? You'll regret it if you dinna heed what I say, for you could easy land in the family way.'

Walking away from him with her head in the air, Dorrie suddenly recalled a conversation she'd heard about a year ago between the two young parlour maids.

'Ooh, Jenny, you never let him?' one of them had asked in a shocked voice.

'Well, I never meant to let him,' Jenny had said, 'but he . . . well, Vi'let, you ken.'

'No, I dinna ken. What did he dae?'

'You ken! My mother aye tell't me no' to let a lad inside my bloomers, but he was kissin' me and strokin' the top o' my leg an' afore I kent what he was daein' he was inside me, never mind my bloomers.'

Violet had given a gasp at that, and then, spotting the girl nearby, had hissed, 'Watch what your sayin', Jenny.'

So that was all she had heard, Dorrie recalled, but a few months later, Jenny left suddenly, and she'd heard the other maids saying she was in the family way. But she could hardly believe what Dargie had said. That couldn't be the way to make babies. There must be more to it than what Jakey had done, but she wouldn't give anybody else the chance to do it.

Chapter Twenty-seven

As the years passed, Dorothea matured more in body than in mind, and she took no interest in the discussions going on around her, mostly concerning Hitler and the trouble he was causing in Europe. She still sulked if she didn't get her own way. At seventeen, having gained the qualifications necessary for entering university, she was determined to take up the opportunity, but she met with opposition from all quarters. The only person who encouraged her was her grandfather, who said it would do her good to knuckle down to the discipline needed in studying.

'Your mother didn't go to university,' Marianne scolded one day at Sunday lunch, 'even though she passed the entrance examinations.'

'That was different!' Melda snapped. 'There were reasons, as well you know.'

On another occasion, another attempt to make him change his mind, Ruairidh told her, 'As my daughter, you do not have to earn your living, and I do not want you to go.'

'What about thinking of what I want for a change?' Dorrie retorted. 'I can't sit around here all day looking decorative.' Giving a laugh at the very idea, she went on, 'Anyway, I'm not a very decorative person, am I? I want to be doing something, something useful, and the only way –'

He shook his head. 'Being a wife and mother is the most useful thing a woman –'

'Why did you send me to the Academy, then, if you didn't want me to use my education? I don't feel ready to settle down and raise kids. I don't think I ever will.'

'You'll feel differently when you meet the right man,' Ruairidh soothed, out of his depth and wishing that his wife hadn't gone to Aberdeen for the day.

'*If* I ever meet the right man,' she said scathingly, 'it wouldn't make an ounce of difference. What's the point of having kids and then rejecting them . . . like you did?'

Her father gasped at this. 'You were never rejected, Dorrie! You got everything you ever wanted, far more than you needed . . .'

'But that's not love! You and Mum were always so busy with the mill, you hardly paid any attention to me.'

'Oh, come now. That's a bit too much, Dorrie. Your mother and I loved you in spite of the spoiled brat you were when you were younger.'

'Thank *you*!' she said sarcastically. 'It's nice to know what you think of me.'

At this, Ruairidh lost his temper. 'All right!' he said loudly. 'Go to university if you want to. You may learn how to behave when you are subjected to proper discipline, but do not expect to come running home here if you do not like it.'

It was while she was home for Christmas at the end of her first term as a medical student, that Dorrie met Archie Grassie. She had gone to the midnight service on her own – her mother and father said they were too tired, and her grandparents had gone to bed early – so she made for the Bruce-Lyall pew. She enjoyed all the old carols she remembered from her childhood, and while the collection was being taken, she had a quick glance round to see who else was there, or rather, who wasn't there, because the little church was quite full. The Black tribe were out in full, she noticed, even Jakey, who had almost given her her first taste of sex. Studying him now, so rough and bucolic-looking, she wondered how she could have borne to let him touch her. Her eyes travelled on again, until she came to where the minister's wife was sitting at the other side of the aisle. The Drummonds had moved to another parish and the popular Mr Mathieson had been called to the glen. Mrs Mathieson wasn't alone today. She had a very personable young man sitting beside her – a very, *very* personable young man.

Dorrie could scarcely keep her eyes off him, and when the service ended, she kept sitting until Mrs Mathieson and her companion rose to leave. He wasn't really all that handsome, but he was well over six feet tall, with dark curly hair, and very smartly dressed. She got to her feet now and joined the moving line of people which had reduced to a mere trickle.

'Nice to see you, Dorrie, dear,' Mrs Mathieson said, as they made their way outside. 'Archie, let me introduce you to Dorothea Bruce-Lyall. Archie's my baby brother, Dorrie.'

'Not so much of the baby,' he laughed. 'I am delighted to meet you Miss Bruce-Lyall.'

'Dorrie, please,' she said breathlessly, wishing that she could sound more sophisticated.

'Then I am delighted to meet you, Miss Dorrie.'

'Oh, damn!' Phyllis Mathieson exclaimed, then covered her mouth in embarrassment. 'It's a good thing that only you were near enough to hear me, Dorrie, but I just remembered that Gil asked me to tell old Mrs Black something. Just carry on, Archie, I'll catch you up.'

He looked questioningly at the girl as they emerged into the crisp winter air. 'May I escort you home, Miss Dorrie? I take it you are going back to the castle?'

She couldn't help giggling. 'I don't usually wander round the glen at this time of night, but I'd be glad of an escort.'

He was extremely easy to talk to, she discovered, and even when he said that he was studying for the ministry, she still felt drawn to him, although, like her grandmother, she didn't much care for men of the cloth. Not that she had ever understood why her grandma was like that, for she was never intimidated by anybody. Still, Archie Grassie didn't look like a minister, didn't speak with the drone of a minister, and, above all, didn't make her tongue-tied like Mr Mathieson did.

Walking steadily along, careful not to step on any of the iced-over puddles glistening at the sides of the road, they told each other their hopes for the future, discussed life in their different areas of study and arrived at the door of the castle much too soon for her liking. 'Thank you for seeing me home ... Archie,' she said, shy now that they were standing alone in the darkness with just a quick flash of moonlight as the clouds scurried across the sky.

'It was a pleasure, Miss Dorrie,' he smiled.

Going inside, she wished that he had asked to see her again, or arranged to meet her in Aberdeen, but contented herself with the hope of seeing him during their next vacation.

Dorothea's Easter visit home – so eagerly looked forward to in the hope of seeing Archie – was a sad occasion. Hamish had been suffering for days with a flu-like sore throat and a racking cough, which Marianne had been treating with a linctus, but his condition worsened on the day after his granddaughter arrived. Robert Mowatt, the girl's other grandfather, was called in, but when he came downstairs after examining his patient, his face was grave.

'I should have been called in earlier,' he said. 'His heart, which was never very strong, as you know, Ruairidh, has been under a great deal of strain from the coughing, and . . .' He looked down at his feet as if unwilling to meet his son-in-law's eyes any longer. 'I honestly can't see him pulling through this.'

Melda drew in her breath sharply. 'Oh, no! Is there nothing you can do, Father?'

'I have done all I can to make it easier for him, but . . .' He raised his head again. 'I think someone should relieve your mother, Ruairidh. She tells me she hasn't left his side for more than a few minutes since he took to his bed, and strong as she is, she can not stand up to that.'

Dorothea jumped up. 'I'll go.'

She went out before anyone could argue with her and ran upstairs anxiously. Of all her grandparents, she loved her father's father best. Both her grandmothers kept so busy that she often felt she should make an appointment to talk to them, and Grandfather Robert, being the only doctor in the glen, was often called out in the middle of a conversation with her, but Grandfather Hamish, no matter what he was doing, had always taken time to answer her questions, to allay any fears she had.

She didn't know what to expect when she went into his room, but his drawn face with the cheekbones jutting out like those of a skeleton, and the effort he was having to make to breathe, tore at her heart. If it hadn't been for the laboured movement of his chest, she might have thought he had already passed over.

'It's me, Grandfather,' she said as brightly as she could with such a heaviness in her. 'I've come to sit with you a while, if you don't mind? To give Grandma a rest.'

Marianne, a gaunt shadow of her usual self, shook her head. 'I'd rather stay here with him.'

The girl forced a smile. 'Doctor's orders, I'm afraid. Off you go, now. We'll get on fine, we always do, don't we, Grandfather?'

A ray of agreement showed in his eyes for a second, then the pain returned once more, and the coughing began. Marianne waited until it was over before she walked to the door. 'I'll have a cup of tea, then, and come right back.'

The girl sat on the chair she had vacated, still warm

from her presence, and leaned forward to take the man's scrawny hand. She talked to him as if he were able to answer, although she left no awkward pauses. She told him what she did at university. She described the tutors, the large room lined with tiers of seats, where the medical students watched experiments, or scribbled in their notebooks, scribbles that they would have to spend time later in deciphering and recording legibly. She also gave him little descriptions of her fellow students, how they spoke, how they dressed, how they teased each other, and was rewarded, once or twice, by a hint of a smile at his lips. But every so often she had to wait until a fresh bout of heaving coughs subsided before she could carry on.

At last, stuck for something else to say, she told him about Archie Grassie. 'I met him at the Christmas Eve service,' she explained. 'He's Mrs Mathieson's young brother, and he's at the university, too, though he's a bit older than me. He's just got another year to go before he gets his divinity degree, and I don't know where he'll be going after that. I suppose he'll have to wait till he's called to a church.'

A faint pressure on her fingers let her know that the old man had understood why she was telling him this. 'I don't know if he's the one for me, Grandfather,' she murmured, 'but I wouldn't mind if he was. I like him, and I'm sure you'll like him too.' Her mouth dried up as she realized that the two would probably never meet.

As she fumbled for the handkerchief in the pocket of her cardigan, she was surprised by a rasping, 'Don't . . . cry . . . Dorrie.' There was a long pause, the silence shattered by the whistling of his lungs, and then he said, 'I'm . . . happy . . . to go.'

She jumped up and kissed the wrinkly cheek, tears streaming down hers as she said, 'D'you remember taking me to see the whisky still? And telling me about my father and his brother getting drunk, and my mother having to take them home? D'you remember ·the time I fell in the burn when we were out walking the dogs? I could only have been about four, but I'll never forget how you waded in to pull me out. Your shoes and socks were soaking, remember?'

Another squeeze, scarcely noticeable now, made her swallow convulsively. 'You always took my side, didn't you? You always stuck up for me. Who'll I have if you leave me?'

At that moment, Marianne returned, hurrying over to assess her husband's condition. 'Go downstairs and tell your father and mother to come up,' she ordered the weeping girl.

Marianne went all to pieces when her husband was pronounced dead, and Ruairidh, at a loss as to how to deal with her, did the only thing he could think of – he telephoned Andrew Rennie, who dropped all commitments and rushed to be with Marianne at this dreadful time. He was a pillar of strength to her, enabling her to voice her feelings, as she could not do to her family.

'Oh, Andrew,' she wept, when her son and daughter-in-law left them alone, 'how am I going to live without Hamish? I admit I didn't marry him for love, but love did blossom for us and he was the best husband a woman could ever have had.'

'I know, my dear,' Andrew murmured, gripping her hand as they sat by the fire.

'I feel awful, saying that to you when I know how you must feel . . .'

'I only feel great sadness for you, Marianne. I came to think very highly, and very fondly, of Hamish, and I can fully understand the depth of your sorrow. I wish that there was some way I could eradicate it, or alleviate it, but I feel helpless . . .'

'You *are* helping me, though, Andrew. I mean, nobody

can eradicate it, but you're making it easier for me to bear.'

They sat there for hours on end, neither saying much when Melda or Ruairidh came in, or when Ruby brought them a tray at lunchtime, only a perfunctory, 'Thank you', yet Marianne could actually feel the flow of affection and sympathy emanating from her old friend.

During the funeral service, unmindful of what other people would think, Andrew sat with one arm round her shoulders and his free hand grasping hers, giving her strength enough not to break down in front of the glen folk.

It was not until after the last of the visiting mourners departed – Hamish's business friends, men and women with whom he had come in contact during the latter years of his life – that Marianne said, horrified at the thought, 'You must have had to cancel an awful lot of appointments to be here for three whole days. Are you not afraid you'll lose your clients?'

Her concern touched him. 'Do not worry, my dear. The young assistant I took on some years ago has turned out so capable that when the senior partner retired last year and I stepped into his shoes, I gave Graham the chance to come in as the fourth member of the firm. He has a good manner with people, especially the old ladies – he would most likely make quite an impression on you.'

She managed to summon a smile. 'Yes, I'm an old lady now, of course.'

'I didn't mean it that way. You are not ... you never will be ... old to me.'

In the midst of the maelstrom that followed on the day of Hamish's death, Dorrie, with no one paying any heed to her, felt a desperate need to be alone, yet it seemed quite natural that she should meet Archie Grassie in the walk she took.

He held her hand in his as he said, 'I didn't like to

intrude, but I was hoping I might meet you.' He said nothing that might upset her, just tucking her arm through his and strolling along beside her, stopping every now and then when she began recalling times past with her beloved grandfather.

'I know what it is like to be the only young person in a bereaved house,' he told her when she stopped talking. 'Everybody is too busy to consider your feelings. It was the same when my mother died.'

Coming to a prickle-free mossy patch, he made her sit down with him, and put his arm round her shoulders. 'Let it out,' he advised, 'the anger that a loved one has been taken, the resentment at being left to mourn alone, the sadness of the memories of him that should be happy. But, Dorrie, I promise that they will be happy again, once you have accepted his death.'

'How do you know all these things?' she whispered, bewildered that he was describing her feelings so accurately. 'Was it the same for you?'

'It is the same for most people, my dear.'

After that first meeting, he arranged to see her every afternoon, neither of them saying very much, but his mere presence comforted the poor girl as nothing else would have done. He sat next to her through the ordeal of the kirk service, and stood at her side during the interment. They continued to meet every afternoon, sometimes also in the evening, getting to know each other in a way that they would never have done under different circumstances, and when it was time for them to return to Aberdeen, they travelled together.

Much closer now, they saw each other every weekend, sometimes in Glendarril but mostly in the city, and one night after a particularly tender leave-taking, she told her grandfather – she often spoke to him when she was alone – that Archie Grassie *was* the man for her. 'And I'm sure he feels the same about me,' she whispered into the dark-

ness of her room. 'He often knows exactly what I'm thinking, and not many men can do that with a girl.'

Something, however, kept her from telling her grandmother about Archie. She couldn't say what it was, just a
feeling that the old lady wouldn't approve, but there was
plenty of time to think about that when their studies were
over.

With war looming ever more certainly, Dorrie was planning for the actuality of it. It was all very well for her
father to say she should keep on with her studies, but, if
war did come, she wanted to be doing something to help,
not just taking screeds and screeds of notes that she might
never have occasion to use.

Her father had been horrified when she told him. 'What
do you propose to do?' he had asked, his eyes steely.

'I was thinking . . . well, I know I haven't got my degree
yet, but I could offer my services to one of the forces as a
first-aider, or something like that.'

His scowl told her what his answer would be, and she
was ready for it. 'Yes, I'm under age, and I know I'd need
parental –'

'Exactly, and I will not give my permission. You know
nothing of what a war entails, the horrors, the . . .
killings . . .' He stopped, clearly remembering his own
experience of armed conflict, then added, sadly, 'The dead
bodies didn't bother me so much as seeing the injured,
sometimes left to lie where they fell . . .'

She had been astonished at the change in him. She had
never heard him speak like that before, nor seen him so
distraught. 'But that was twenty years ago,' she pointed
out. 'Things are different now, modern equipment . . . there
wouldn't be any hand-to-hand fighting, I shouldn't think.
The seriously wounded would be transferred to hospitals,
and the slightly wounded would get first aid there and
then.'

'Dorothea,' his icy calmness and the use of her full name alarmed her, 'you are so childish you cannot, or will not, understand the meaning of war, and if you do not put this ridiculous idea out of your head, I shall be forced to remove you from university altogether, and have you home here where we can keep an eye on you.'

She thought better of arguing any more. What was the point? There might never be another war, and if it did come, she would take her own way whatever he said.

Over the next few months, Dorrie took more interest in the newspapers and the wireless news bulletins than she had ever done before, discussing with Archie the inroads that Hitler was making into other countries in Europe, agreeing with him that war was becoming more and more of a certainty. He told her that, if it did come, he intended offering his services as a chaplain to one of the armed forces, but she didn't tell him what she had planned. It was only right that she should do something, too, but she knew that he, like her father, would not be pleased about it.

Like the rest of Britain, the people of the glen heaved deeply relieved sighs when Neville Chamberlain returned from his talks with the Führer in Berlin in September with his assurance that there would be 'peace in our time', especially in the homes where a son, husband or lover was of the age to be called up or, worse still, volunteer.

'My Gordon was dyin' to get a excuse to get awa',' complained the wife of one of the younger of the Black family.

'Him and a lot more like him,' nodded Mima Rattray, who had been hearing the same from nearly all her customers that day. 'War always gives men itchy feet.'

'I suppose it's the thocht o' bein' free o' their wives that does it, the idea o' takin' up wi' the young lassies that hang aboot army camps.' Babsie Black shook her head at the perfidy of men and then added, with great satisfaction, 'But they'll ha'e to bide at hame noo.'

The men concerned – the young blood, the hotheads, the henpecked husbands and the youths whose mothers had a stranglehold on them – spent several nights in the Western or Royal or Crown Hotels in Laurencekirk – sometimes all three – drowning their disappointment. They had the sense to travel there by horse and cart, because Pat Black's Betsy knew her way blindfolded, and they'd get home safely, however drunk they were by closing time. Of course, this couldn't carry on for long; for, apart from heads and stomachs rebelling after several nights of it, money ran out, and the glen got back to normal.

But not for very long.

Chapter Twenty-eight

War was declared in September 1939, but it was into 1940 before its impact was felt in the glen. Many young hotheads had volunteered within the first six weeks, but soon conscription came for the twenty- to twenty-seven-year-olds. Ruairidh did not argue when Melda pressed Dorrie to give up her studies and learn how to work a loom; at least it kept her safe, and he was glad when even wives with young children came to offer their services. Melda organized a creche, but Ruairidh pessimistically said, 'I don't know why you're bothering. It probably won't be long before there's no work for anybody. There'll be no orders coming in.'

She had, however, thought of a way to safeguard the mill. Delegating Marianne to supervise the creche, and much against her husband's wishes, Melda took herself off to London in the early spring of 1941, bulldozing her way into an office in Whitehall with barely time to expound her plan before the Ministry of War was moved out of the capital. As it happened, by sheer good luck the officer who saw her had been at boarding school with Hector, Ruairidh's grandfather, and being a Scot himself, he promised to do everything he could to help.

Like the mills of God, the wheels of any ministry in war or peace work exceeding slow, so Ruairidh had doubts about Melda's version of her mission when the orders finally arrived. 'Ach!' he groaned. 'A dozen bolts of khaki, and the same of air-force blue. That'll not keep us going for long.'

'If they like what we send them, they'll double it, maybe

treble or more. It's just a pity we can't make up the uniforms, too.'

'If we can run full out making the cloth, I'll be happy,' sighed Ruairidh.

On the first Wednesday in June 1941, Archie Grassie telephoned Dorrie to say he would come to see her on the Sunday, because he was leaving Aberdeen on Monday.

Over the next few days, she was glad she was kept so busy. She had no time to brood during the day, and even when she went to bed, she was so tired that she fell asleep without even wondering where Archie might be sent.

They met in their usual place in the woods on Sunday afternoon, and as soon as she joined him, Archie said, 'I think I'm being sent to North Africa, and I'm glad to be going where I'm needed.'

Dorrie didn't feel at all glad. He would be in the heart of the fighting. What if he didn't come back? She couldn't voice her fear for him, she didn't want to instil fear in him, but she couldn't let him go without telling him how she felt. She waited until they came to the small glade where they had often tossed their thoughts and ideas to each other. Without a word, they stopped and sat down side by side and she turned to look at him. He wasn't what anyone would call truly handsome, but she loved the way his dark hair curled, and his fair skin made his brown eyes look almost black. His nose was inclined to be sharp, though, his mouth . . .

She gulped. She didn't want him to go to North Africa. She didn't want him to go anywhere, but was it safe to tell him that? 'I'll miss you,' she whispered.

His hand caught hers, and she looked up into his eyes, losing herself in the depth of them. 'Will you?' he murmured. 'Not as much as I'll miss you.'

They gazed at each other for several long moments, and then he sighed, 'Why did it take me this long to find out I love you?'

'I'm the same,' she burst out rapturously. 'I've just realized.'

With the realization came the need to kiss, to touch, to get to know each other in the fullest way, but not in haste. They made the most of every second of the time they had left, and somewhere in the midst of the passion, a proposal was made and accepted.

Some time later, they had to force themselves to break the spell and make their way back through the trees. 'I'd better come in with you, my darling,' Archie said, as they neared a side door. 'I expect your father would like me to ask him properly for your hand.'

'I suppose so,' she grinned, 'and we'd better not tell him I'm all yours already.'

'And every part of me is yours,' he assured her, giving her one last kiss.

Marianne was furious. If it wasn't bad enough that Dorrie's blood was one-quarter inherited from an insane minister, the headstrong girl was determined to marry the minister son of another minister, which meant that any children they had would be . . . what was a half plus a quarter? – three-quarters? That couldn't be right, could it? – whatever it was, there had better be no children of this marriage. It was unthinkable that the heir to the Glendarril title would be three-quarters a man of God . . . even more than that if you took Melda's real mother into account, for Grace had also been the daughter of a minister.

Marianne's obsession about Duncan Peat had deepened over the years into a phobia which included all ministers, a paranoia with neither reason nor rhyme behind it, which ridicule from her husband had forced her to keep hidden. No matter how hard she had tried to make Ruairidh understand that he shouldn't, he had given the two young people his blessing. No one paid any attention to her nowadays, she fumed. Gone were the days when everyone in the glen looked up to her and asked her advice when they were in any sort of trouble. Of course, with so many of the men called up or going off to fight of their own free will, most of the women were heads of their households and had learned to be strong.

What hurt her most, Marianne decided, was the way her own family treated her. She had been relegated to looking after the creche while Melda had taken complete charge of the mill, to let Ruairidh direct his full attention to the running of the estate . . . she said. It was true that the factor who had collected the rents from the tenant farmers and crofters, and the estate manager who used to arrange for any repairs necessary to the cottages, had both been called up, so Ruairidh did have everything to do himself, but they could let her have responsibility for something. She was capable of so much, and any elderly woman would manage to control a bunch of skirling under-school-age brats.

Her mind returned to the problem of Archie Grassie. He would have left Aberdeen by this time, and seemed to think he was bound for North Africa, where the war was not going too well for Britain, so maybe she was worrying for nothing. According to Lord Haw-Haw, the Germans and the Italians had the British in full retreat, so Archie might be killed – or would God not permit that to happen to a minister, a padre, as Archie called himself? There were rumours that some troops of the Highland Division were to be sent to Glendarril for mountain training. She hadn't liked the idea of hundreds of soldiers of all ranks milling around, but if one young officer managed to take Dorrie's fancy . . . she could send one of those 'Dear John' letters to Archie.

After all, he hadn't had time to buy her a ring, so they weren't really engaged. Not officially.

* * *

When it came, some three months later, the Invasion of Glendarril, as Ruairidh dubbed it, was not as big an upheaval as they had imagined, and his mother was quite pleased that only officers were billeted in the castle itself. This meant that Dorothea saw them every day, which would take her mind off Archie Grassie . . . hopefully. The lower ranks were distributed throughout the glen, in all houses large enough to sleep at least two, and with so many husbands and boyfriends away, everyone could foresee trouble – a proliferation of trouble. The school hall, which had formerly staged only concerts put on by the pupils at Christmas, was appropriated to provide weekly entertainment for the troops, and, because of the closeness of the original small community and the relatively small number of soldiers foisted upon them, no difference was made between officers and other ranks at the dances and various other amusements arranged by the Entertainments Officer.

The females in the glen soon adapted to the change. From fifteen to fifty, they welcomed the attention paid to them by these uniformed strangers, who did not remain strangers for long; who, in fact, soon got to know some of the women just as intimately as their absent husbands. Not to be outdone, the young girls, ignoring their mothers' warnings, relinquished their maidenhood at the first asking. It was all very exciting for both sexes – days spent working hard, and nights, to put it plainly, spent in every bit as physically demanding a manner, but so much more enjoyable.

As one young soldier sighed ecstatically to the boy who shared his room, 'If this is war, Lachie, I hope it goes on for ever.'

His friend, however, a tubby lad from the island of Islay, was finding the pace just a little too hectic. 'I chust hope I can keep going, Chamie,' he muttered. 'That Chanet would neffer let me stop if she got her way.'

Jamie gave a loud guffaw. 'And you're complaining?

Make the most of it, Lachie boy, and pray the powers that be have forgotten about us. If they haven't, we'll likely be posted to somewhere in the jungle or some other God-forsaken hole with no dames!'

The powers that be had their sights on all regiments, all battalions, of course, wherever they were, even in the most remote outpost, and with no prior notification – except a coded message to Lord Glendarril, telling him that the training had been completed – evacuation of the first batch of soldiers was speedily effected, and great was the consternation – the weeping and wailing and gnashing of teeth – of their hostesses when it was discovered that the men had virtually disappeared overnight. Five young girls, one barely fifteen, had been left pregnant, and fathers were vowing vengeance on the 'horny buggers' who had done the dirty deeds. The trouble was, they learned to their greater disgust, that their daughters didn't even know their names in most cases. Three mothers of girls who had been seduced, willingly or otherwise, were keeping their own secrets – two whose husbands had been overseas for more than a year, and one whose spouse thought he must have been drunk when he fathered the child his wife was carrying, because he couldn't remember a blessed thing about it.

Most of the pregnancies were kept hidden for as long as possible, only four anxious mothers booking the services of the 'howdie' as soon as they recognized the symptoms their teenage daughters were displaying and got the truth out of them.

Soon, as more soldiers came and went, even the most timid of the maids in the castle was telling lies in order to meet a soldier. 'Please, Cook,' little Evie pleaded on the day following her usual afternoon off, 'Ma wasna lookin' good yesterday an' I wanted to see what like she is the day.'

Mrs Burr's eyes held compassion that first time and the

girl was allowed an hour off, but on the request being repeated just two days later, she tumbled to what was going on. 'So your mother's no better, is she?' she asked sarcastically. 'That's funny, for Ruby saw her last night goin' to the Rural meetin'. But maybe you've got a different mother these days? Wi' a khaki uniform?'

Evie's face turned crimson, and remembering the girl's age, Mrs Burr said, 'You're only fourteen, lass, ower young to be goin' wi' lads. Wait till you're sixteen, that's time enough.'

The thought of the handsome youth she had met, the memory of his kiss, gave Evie the courage to protest indignantly. 'But he'll likely be sent awa' afore I'm sixteen, an' I promised to meet him. Please, Cook, even just half an hour?'

'Ach, I'm a right auld fool,' observed the woman, nodding her permission, 'but just this once, and you be careful, mind. Dinna let him tak' advantage o' you.'

Although this was exactly what the maid hoped he would do, she shook her head vigorously. 'Oh no, Cook! I'll no' let him touch me.'

At eight o'clock, therefore, Evie was hurrying through the rose garden to the side gate, her heart beating twenty to the dozen, her mind set on one thing. 'I've only got half an hour,' she told the young soldier when she reached their trysting place.

Bobby McIver needed no second telling and wasted no time in getting down to business, as Evie related to Jessie, her bed-mate, later that night. 'He started in kissin' right away, an' we didna even tak' a walk, for he had me doon on the grass in aboot twa seconds.'

'Ooh, Evie!' Jessie was not a great conversationalist, but the two words were enough to show how eager she was to hear more.

'So then he was kissin' me some mair, an' openin' my buttons at the same time, an' he says, "That's fine big tits

394

you've got, Evie," an' I was fine pleased aboot that, for I used to think they were ower big, made me top heavy, like.'

'Go on, then. Once he had your buttons open . . . ?'

'Oh, I canna tell you what it felt like, Jessie. He was kissin' me there, an' all, and I went a' shaky an' there was thrills goin' richt doon me, so when he put his hand up my skirt I didna stop him . . .' She stopped to look appealingly at her friend. 'He said he was showin' me how much he loves me, an' oh, it was good.'

'But you havena tell't me . . .'

Evie told her, in her own explicit words, because she didn't know the polite way to describe what she and the boy had done, but she would have been less than happy if she had heard what Bobby McIver was telling *his* friend.

'She's a walk-ower, Gibby. She only got a half-hour off, an' she was as desperate for it as me. A coupla minutes an' we was lying down, another coupla minutes an' I had her tits out, another coupla minutes an' she was letting me do the needful.'

'Lucky bugger!' muttered Gibby. 'You should've asked her if she'd a chum for me.'

'She's no' off again till Friday, but I'll see what I can do.'

Thus it came about that Jessie was enlisted, very willingly, into the deception that followed. In order to see the boys as often as they could, the two maids sneaked out every night after they were supposed to have gone to bed, splitting into pairs as soon as they met their lads. For Gibby, it was his first time with a girl, yet that didn't stop him from 'doing the needful' as Bobby had described it, and besides Jessie was an 'older woman' and soon showed him the ropes, and all four participants went to bed after their meetings thoroughly satisfied in every way.

This happy, carefree situation carried on for several weeks, until, one night on their way back to the cottage where they were billeted, Gibby asked about something that was puzzling him. 'I hardly like to say this, Bobby, but has Evie tell't you something?'

'Tell't me what?'

'Well, me an' Jessie was four nights withoot it 'cos she'd the curse, but you and Evie . . .'

Realization came with the impact of a punch in the face, and Bobby's eyes widened in apprehension. 'She hasna said onything, but, my God, Gibby, you're right enough. She hasna had the curse. Oh Christ, man, what'll I dae?'

His friend looked at him with deep pity. 'You should have used a French letter like me, but it's ower late now. There's no sense in shutting the stable door after the horse has bolted, as my granda used to say.'

'Never mind your bloody granda! What can I dae?'

'There's nothing you *can* dae, as far as I can see. She's just newly fifteen, so you canna wed her, an' I think it's against the law to . . .' He paused, then said, 'You say she hasna said onything yet? Maybe she doesna ken what it means? Maybe we'll be oot o' here afore it dawns on her?'

'You'd better no' say onything to Jessie. She surely doesna ken, either.'

'I'll no' say a word, but you'd better hope it's no' lang till we're posted.'

If Evie noticed a slight cooling off in her lover's ardour, she said nothing to him nor to Jessie, putting it down to the rumour that was going round that the boys' unit would soon be leaving the glen, and it was not until they had actually gone, without either boy promising to keep in touch, that it came to her that she and Jessie had just been used. What did not occur to her, however, was that she was carrying Bobby McIver's child, at least not until Ruby happened to pass a comment on how fat she was getting, and even then, it was Jessie who put two and two together.

'Hey, Evie, you're no' . . . that Bobby didna land you in the family way, did he?'

'What?' Evie's face blanched, then the colour flooded back. 'I dinna ken. How dae you . . . ?'

'Has your monthlies stopped?'

'I havena had them for a few month noo, but that suited me fine. Bobby wouldna have been . . .'

'Oh, God, Evie, you're expectin'! Did you no' ken the signs?'

Mrs Burr was not at all pleased, and cursed herself for being so stupid. Evie was easy meat for the likes of them soldiers; one kiss and she'd likely have been opening her legs. But however sorry she felt for the maid, she could do little to help, except promise to go with her when she confessed her sin to Lady Marianne. 'We can wait another month maybe, but her Ladyship's aye been real understanding to other lassies in the same predicament.'

As it happened, she did not have to carry out this task. Two mornings later, an agitated Jessie came running into the kitchen. 'Evie's no' in her bed, an' I never heard her goin' oot.'

The poor girl was found floating in the pond in the rose garden, but Jessie, good friend that she was, only said when questioned by the laird and the doctor, that Evie had been upset because the lad she'd been in love with had been sent away. Mrs Burr drew her own conclusion, also Robert Mowatt, and probably half the women in the glen, but her death had come as such a shock that not one person passed any comments on it.

As the months passed, Robert Mowatt became angrily aware that the population of the glen was to be greatly increased thanks to the activities of the young soldiers, and likely of the officers, too, who should have set a good example. In fact, the doctor reflected one day when he saw Meggie Park waddling along to the shop – her stomach grossly fat although her husband had been a prisoner of war in Germany for almost two years – he wouldn't be surprised if one or two of the married men in the glen who had not been called up had jumped on the bandwagon. If they happened to fill a belly or two in the process, the women concerned could always blame the army.

A compassionate man, Robert could sympathize with the poor souls who'd had little or no loving since their men went off to war, so he let it be known that he would attend such confinements free of any charge, be they the result of a liaison with a soldier or with a neighbour's husband.

'How can we expect people to behave decently?' he asked Ruairidh when the laird went round for a chat one night. 'The whole world's been turned upside down by war, and peace-time ethics and rules have gone out through the window.'

'You know,' Ruairidh observed, his eyes twinkling, 'I sometimes wish I'd been a lot younger so I could have had a fling, too.'

'You're not that old.'

'I'm over forty, and what would my mother have said if I'd put some girl in the family way?'

Robert grinned roguishly. 'She'd have been delighted if it had been a boy.'

'Aye,' Ruairidh sighed, 'she's still going on about there not being an heir to follow me.' He paused, considering the wisdom of saying more, then decided to get it off his chest. 'And she's still got that old obsession about ministers. She even let slip the other day that she's pleased Melda never had a son to inherit Duncan Peat's insanity.'

It was the doctor's turn to hesitate. 'I wish she could see sense. I've told her over and over again that Duncan Peat was not mad, just temporarily off balance, and I can vouch for Melda being as sane as any of us – saner maybe, for she has a good sensible head on her shoulders, which is more than I can say for Marianne, at times.'

Ruairidh sighed again. 'It's just that one thing she has a blockage about. She even worries about Dorrie being tainted and passing the madness on to any son she has – not that there's any chance of that till the war's over.' He straightened his back and concentrated on this new topic. 'Things are looking a bit brighter for us at the moment.'

'Yes, but Monty was the man for the job. I don't know why Ike was made over-all commander.'

'Um . . . I shouldn't be telling you this, but I know you won't let it go any further. I've heard on the grapevine that we're gearing up for the big push.'

Robert gave a derisive snort. 'That rumour's been going round for ages now.'

'We'll just have to wait and see, then, but it can't come soon enough for me. I haven't anyone close in the forces, but the past four years have seemed like four centuries.'

'It's the parents and sweethearts of the boys who are away fighting . . . it must be hell for them.'

'I can vouch for that,' the laird said morosely. I had a brother in the last war, remember, and he didn't come back.'

'Oh Lord, I'm sorry, Ruairidh! I didn't meant to upset –'

'I know you didn't, but it's the kind of grief that never leaves you. Mother has never been the same since that telegram was delivered, although losing Ranald brought her and Father closer together.'

Seeing the pain in his friend's eyes, Robert wished fervently that he had not opened his big mouth.

Melda felt compelled to talk about her daughter, although her mother-in-law would not have been her first choice as confidante. 'I don't know what to say to Dorrie. She hasn't heard from Archie for weeks now, and neither has his sister. Phyllis keeps saying he can't have been killed otherwise she'd have heard, but Dorrie never speaks about him. It's not good for her to keep it bottled up, is it?'

Marianne clicked her tongue. 'No, she'd be better if she

got it out.' She hesitated for a second, then said, 'I don't think he was the right one for her, anyway.'

Melda was outraged. 'Yes, I know you've had an ill will against him all along, just because he's a minister, but poor Dorrie really loves him.' She turned away before she told the old woman what she thought of her and her obsession. There was nothing for Dorrie to do but wait, and Phyllis Mathieson had promised to let them know the minute she heard anything.

Only two days later, when the minister's wife came to the castle, Melda knew it was bad news before Phyllis even opened her mouth. 'Archie hasn't been killed, has he?' she asked anxiously.

The woman nodded tearfully. 'I promised to let Dorrie know if . . . I heard anything. I won't stop . . . You'll understand I can't talk . . .' She whipped round and walked away.

Melda was left feeling completely at a loss. She hadn't had a chance to say how sorry she was, to try to give comfort . . . and how could she break it to Dorrie? What should she say? She could remember how she had felt when she'd learned about Rannie, and she hadn't really known whether she loved him or not. She looked up as Marianne came into the room, and in her despair, let fly at her. 'Well, you'll be pleased to know Archie Grassie's been killed!'

'Oh!' Marianne's hand flew to her heart. 'That's a cruel thing to say. I admit I didn't care for the idea of Dorrie marrying him, but I would never have wished him dead. Poor girl!'

'I don't know how to tell her.'

'Do you want me to . . . ?'

Melda shook her head. 'It's up to me, but I am not relishing the thought of it.'

The girl took it better than any of them had thought, weeping for only a very short time and then saying she wanted to be on her own and going up to her room. None of them was surprised, however, that she did not appear the following day, and it was the day after that before she came down for something to eat. Her eyes were red-rimmed, her face was puffed, her movements were slow and unsteady, but her voice was firm. 'I'm going to London.'

'What?' her mother, father and grandmother exclaimed almost in unison.

'I'm going to London,' she repeated. 'You'll manage fine without me at the mill, and I want to make use of what I learned at University, so I'm going to volunteer for the ambulance service.'

'You don't need to go to London for that,' Ruairidh pointed out. 'You could be somewhere much nearer home.'

'I want to be in the thick of it,' she said, looking round at them defiantly, although tears were glistening in her eyes. 'I have to do something to . . . keep my mind off . . .' Her voice broke.

Her father would have argued, but her mother laid a restraining hand on his arm. 'Are you sure that is what you want to do?'

'Positive!' She looked directly at Ruairidh. 'I'm old enough now not to need your permission.'

He nodded sadly. 'Yes, of course you are, and I will not stand in your way. I shall have the house in Piccadilly made ready for you to use any time you need it.'

'Thanks, Dad.'

Only two days later, Dorothea Bruce-Lyall was in London, volunteering as an ambulance driver, and Melda's life revolved around her daughter's letters.

The Allies had eventually gained a proper toehold in Normandy when the last of the 'war-babes' was delivered. As Campbell Scott, the dominie, remarked, 'This school is going to burst at the seams in five years.'

Contrary to what Marianne had feared, there had been very little scandal, because almost every girl had been involved in some way with the ever-changing series of lusty fresh-faced youths who had invaded the glen. In some cases, the boys had done the initiating, but in just as many, the girls had made the running. The women – except those who were too old and withered to be interested – had gone for the more mature men, the NCOs and officers, who were every bit as avid for sex as the rank and file. So it would have been the pot calling the kettle black if any snide remarks had been passed. They were all in the same boat – with the exception of the wives of the dominie, the doctor, the minister and the laird, who, although they may have been tempted, had foregone the pleasure – and many of them were dreading the day when their husbands or boyfriends would come home.

'The end of the war's going to be the telling time,' Marianne remarked to Flora Mowatt.

'The telling time?'

'The day of reckoning. Quite a few men will be coming home to find their wives have had children by somebody else. There'll be hell to pay.'

'So there should be,' Flora said grimly. 'When a woman marries, she pledges herself to her husband for life.'

'And he pledges himself to her,' Marianne retorted drily, 'and I bet most of them have been having a high old time with the *mademoiselles* and *Fräuleins*, yet they'll hit the roof about their wives being unfaithful to them.'

'What would you have done if you thought Hamish had been unfaithful to you?'

Marianne shrugged. 'I wouldn't have been too happy, but if he'd made another son, I'd have forgiven him.'

The doctor's wife shook her head. 'I couldn't be like that. If I thought Robert had made love to another woman, I'd want to kill him . . . then I'd kill myself.'

'To be honest,' Marianne admitted, 'I'd have been pleased in one way and angry in another. It must be terrible to know you've been betrayed. Still, there's not much fear of Ruairidh going off the straight and narrow. Nor Robert,' she added hastily.

Melda's fears were to be realized more quickly than she had imagined. Only seven short weeks and five short letters after Dorrie's departure, they received the official notification of her death. The officer in charge, the man who must have written a number of similar communications, praised her sterling work, her bravery and dedication in even the most horrendous of air raids, but there really was no easy way for him to tell them. Dorrie had apparently been helping to rescue some children in a building next door to one which had received a direct hit, when a wall caved in on top of her. It had taken several hours for them to get her out, but mercifully, the letter went on, she had not suffered. She had died instantly.

Melda did not believe this, but, as she pointed out to her husband, it was kind of the man to try to shield them from the truth. Once again, as at the time of Ranald's death, they clung to each other for comfort, and although their inevitable coupling was perhaps not so ardent as it had been then, it still afforded them some solace.

Feeling somewhat excluded, Marianne went to talk to Flora Mowatt. 'They've no time for me,' she complained. 'I miss Dorrie just as much as they do.'

Flora patted her hand. 'Of course you do, Marianne, dear, but she *was* their daughter.'

After a moment's thought, Marianne said, 'Yes, I can see the point you're making. When we lost Ranald, Hamish and I were like young lovers again. I wouldn't have come through that if it hadn't been for him ... and now I've nobody.'

'Don't get maudlin, my dear, it doesn't suit you.' Flora knew how to treat her old friend. 'You have Robert and me, and all the people in Glendarril know how you are feeling and sympathize.'

'Yes, I suppose so. You're right. I shouldn't feel sorry for myself, when so many of the people in the glen have lost somebody, too.'

'I know it's little comfort, but time does heal, and until it does, we must carry on as usual.'

Time did eventually not heal, exactly, but blunt the edge of the Bruce-Lyalls' grief, and life went on, though not quite the same as before.

The people of Glendarril did not bring 1945 in with their usual vigour. All reports from the war fronts grew more encouraging by the day, and what Marianne had called the 'telling time' – the day of reckoning – was looming ever closer for those women who had taken their pleasure where they could, which is how she thought of them, although Robert Mowatt regarded them as poor unfortunates. But, whichever way they judged themselves, the women understood that Nemesis was about to catch up with them, and the doctor was kept busy prescribing pills and powders for ailments brought on by nerves.

At precisely six o'clock on 8 May, the day on which Churchill had announced the end of hostilities, Robert took an unprecedented step. Having heard the steady tramp of feet going round to the side door, he thought dismally that he'd be lucky if he finished consulting by bedtime, and when he entered the waiting room to summon his first patient, he could have screamed. The place was filled to capacity! A second glance, however, told him that there was not one man there, and a marvellous idea struck him. They were all suffering from the same guilt and anxiety because their sins would soon be laid bare, so why shouldn't he attempt mass treatment?

'Good evening, ladies!' he boomed, smiling to hide his nervousness. 'We all know why so many of you are here tonight, and it seems to me that, rather than see each of you individually, it would be much quicker if I just talked to you here to let you see how futile it is to worry about something which nothing can change.'

A sign of unrest, accompanied by a low murmur, made him hasten on. 'Yes, I do realize that your men will be back shortly, and some of you have good reason to fear your husband's reaction to what you did, but I am practically sure that every man will be so glad to be home that he'll . . . if not exactly excuse you, at least accept the child he knew nothing about. Of course, he is bound to be angry at first, and it's up to you to make it up to him, to show him such love as you have never shown him before. Tell him how sorry you are, and that it happened because you missed him so much, and if he is still angry and threatens to leave you, assure him, through your tears, that you can not live without him any longer. Turning on the waterworks usually works – I know.'

He was relieved to see them looking hopefully at each other. 'You are wondering if my advice will work, and it may not in all cases, but surely you must be willing to try anything to keep your man? You must think calmly over what to say, no counteraccusations no matter what you suspect, and I feel certain the situation will ease. One word of warning, however. Do not, whatever the provocation, hint that he is not as good a lover as the child's father was. That would be fatal! Now, I'll leave you to talk about it, but I will be in the surgery for another half-hour if any of you want to see me privately. My advice would still be the same, and for those who say they can't sleep for worrying, a couple of aspirins is all you need.'

He had almost left the room when he hesitated and turned. 'They won't be demobilized straight away, you know, and it will be time enough to worry when you hear when your man will be home. Good night, ladies. I hope everything works out for you, but if it gets sticky, remind him that you weren't the only one to make a mistake. There must be hundreds, even thousands all over the world.'

The homecomings were spread over some months, and it was almost 1947 before the last stragglers arrived home, those who had been prisoners of war, those who had been in the fight against the Japanese. Oddly, they were the least upset about their womenfolk's infidelity. They were so glad to be home in one piece, to sit at their own firesides again, that nothing else mattered. Only a small minority of the rest went as far as breaking an engagement or ending a marriage, possibly, human nature being what it is, those who had also misbehaved, and who, for all they knew, may have left living souvenirs behind them.

As the doctor had hoped, most married life soon returned to normal and there followed a spate of legitimate pregnancies to keep him and the midwife busier than ever – the postwar baby boom, the bulge!

For the family at the castle, though, there was no homecoming to celebrate, and it very much looked as if there would be no more Bruce-Lyall babies ever again.

PART THREE
1955

Chapter Twenty-nine

It had been a long day, and Ruth Laverton was glad to sit down by the bed. Her mother was dozing at the moment, but likely not for very long. She had a knack of sleeping off and on in the afternoons and evenings and being awake all night, which wouldn't be so bad, Ruth mused, if she could also have a rest during the day. It was the lack of sleep that got her down.

She looked wryly at the pillow cases on her lap. She had noticed when she was ironing that the housewife openings were burst at the seams and she had meant to sew them, but, oh God, not right now! She would have to close her eyes for a wee while; they were stinging with tiredness.

The coals in the grate were glowing comfortably, but she'd have to be careful not to fall asleep and let the fire go out. The doctor had warned that she mustn't let her patient get cold. Her patient, she thought sadly. This was the woman who had borne her, who had struggled to bring her and her young sister up decently after their father died. She had worked her fingers to the bone for them, going out cleaning to keep them fed properly, doing without things herself in order to buy clothes for them. She deserved to be nursed with all the love she could get . . . for as long as she needed it.

No resentment, no bitterness. Her elder daughter mustn't think of it as a duty she was forced to carry out. She must look on it as a privilege and be glad to be given the chance to show her gratitude for all that her mother had done for her. It would help, though, if Gladys did a bit more to help, even if she just popped in for an hour every day. Of course, she always had an excuse why she couldn't – she had to wait in for the man to read her gas meter, or the electric meter; or she had to take up a hem on the new dress she had bought for Bob's firm's dinner dance, as well as pressing his suit and ironing a white shirt for him. They were always going out to enjoy themselves and she had a bottomless pit of excuses, but give her her due, she did sit with Mum for an hour every Saturday afternoon to let her sister do some shopping ... but only because Bob was a football fan who went to Pittodrie every week whether it was the first team who were playing a home match, or the reserves or the schoolboys. But she shouldn't criticize, Ruth told herself. Gladys had a husband to look after, whereas she ...

She heaved a long-drawn-out sigh. If she'd still had Mark, it would have been different. She should have known he wouldn't settle down to a dull job after the war, but she had loved him so much she didn't let him see how much she missed him when he became a long-distance lorry driver. She had Colin to look after, their beautiful son who was still only a toddler when his father was killed in a road accident on a French road in 1947. They had been married for just six years, a wartime wedding, and had been in their council house for less than eighteen months.

She had been so shocked that it seemed a good idea to move back in with her mother, who looked after Colin while she went out to work ... until the poor woman was diagnosed as having multiple sclerosis. The illness progressed slowly at first, still leaving her able to care for the small boy, but then it speeded up until she was completely bedridden and needed constant attention. She'd had to give up her own job to look after her, and there had just been the two widows' pensions coming in; there was no family allowance for an only child. Now there was this second illness, the most dreaded of all.

Becoming conscious that her fingernails were digging

into her palms, Ruth inhaled deeply and tried to relax as she let the breath edge out, then rising quietly, she lifted the poker and stirred the fire. When she straightened and caught sight of herself in the overmantel mirror, her hand went to her heart in dismay. She was only thirty-six, but her reflection was that of a woman well into her fifties. Her auburn hair was lank, her cheeks were wan and hollow. There were dark circles under her eyes, the eyes Mark used to call 'cerulean blue' but were now faded and almost blank. What did it matter, she thought. Nobody saw her except her mother and sister; her brother-in-law didn't bother to come in any more – Gladys had even stopped apologizing for him dropping her off on his way to somewhere else. Sitting down again, she couldn't help thinking that Bob Mennie was selfish to the very core.

'Ruthie.'

The weak voice shattered her reverie. 'What is it, Mum?' she asked anxiously, jumping up at once and bending over the bed. 'Is the pain getting worse?'

'That's not what –' Georgina Brown, Ina to her friends, broke off and looked earnestly at the younger woman. 'Something's preying on my mind, Ruthie. I should have told you a long time ago . . . but I kept putting it off.'

Ruth took the wasted hand in hers. 'I can see it's upsetting you, Mum, so don't bother telling me just now. Do it another time . . .'

'There won't be another time.'

'Don't be silly! Of course there will.'

'I know in myself I haven't long to go now, and –'

Her heart cramping, Ruth cried desperately, 'Don't say that! You maybe feel a bit low just now, but you'll feel better soon.'

Ina shook her head. 'I know I've got cancer, and I know you know, so you needn't pretend. I can feel my strength slipping away tonight and I can't go to meet my Maker with this on my mind. Sit down, Ruthie, lass.'

Her entire body apprehensive, Ruth sat down, leaning forward so that she could keep holding her mother's hand. 'All right, but don't overdo it. If I think it's too much for you, I'll stop listening.'

With her free hand, Ina pulled her handkerchief from the sleeve of the bedjacket Ruth had knitted for her last winter, and held it ready to wipe the tears she knew would come. 'I want you to listen to it all ... and say nothing. I've had to screw up my courage ... to speak about it, and I don't want you stopping me ... before I'm done.'

Her voice was gaining a little strength, but there were many pauses between sentences, even between phrases. 'I'm going back ... to when me and Jack was wed and ... planning on having a big family. We wanted three girls ... and three boys ... because we loved bairns ... but the years went by ... and we'd no luck.'

Stopping to take a few deep breaths, Ina flapped the hankie to prevent any interruption, and waited a few seconds before going on.

'We'd been wed for three years with still no sign ... there was none of that testing in them days to see if it was the wife's fault or the man's ... and I'd given up hope when I met a woman that had been at the school with me. She asked how many bairns me and Jack had ... and when I told her ... she persuaded me to ...'

The handkerchief was put to use here, but her look of appeal kept Ruth from saying or doing anything, and she waited for what she prayed was not what she had begun to suspect. Her faith in God, however, was to be severely shaken.

'I'm not your real mother, Ruthie!' Ina burst out, dabbing at her eyes. 'Me and Jack fostered you ... when you was eight weeks old.'

Her lips scarcely able to form the words, Ruth asked, 'And Gladys?'

Ina shook her head. 'The doctor said it was looking

on you as mine . . . that had stopped me worrying about conceiving . . . and that's how Gladys happened.'

'So you're *her* real mother?'

'Look, lass . . . I'm her natural mother . . . but I love you as much as I love her . . . more, maybe. She's not half the woman you are . . . more's the pity. If you hadn't been here to look after me . . . she'd have likely put me in a home.'

'No, she'd never have done that! She'd have shifted you to her house!' Feeling obligated to stick up for Gladys, Ruth secretly agreed with her mother. But Georgina Brown was not her mother – any more than Gladys was her sister! She was overwhelmed by a wave of something she had never known before, not quite self-pity, nor bitterness, nor anger . . . more a sense of insecurity.

'Oh, Ruthie,' Ina groaned, 'Don't look so lost. Maybe I shouldn't have told you.'

Ruth attempted to pull herself together, but there was one thing she had to know. 'You said fostered. Why didn't you adopt me?'

'At first, we thought we might . . . have to give you back . . . if your real mother claimed you . . . but when we didn't hear anything . . . we hoped they'd forgot we had you. Me and Jack spoke about adopting you . . . but we were scared to rock the boat, and once Gladys was born . . . well, we couldn't afford it. You see, we got so much a week for fostering you, but them that adopted got nothing. And I got the money . . . for your keep right up . . . till you started working.'

'But after Dad died, you were really hard up,' Ruth reminded her, 'and you had your own child to think about, so why didn't you send me back to where you got me?'

'It never crossed my mind, lass. As far as I was concerned . . . you were mine and . . . it was up to me to . . . provide for you.' There was a long pause, the effort of the sustained speech obviously too much, then Ina whispered, 'I'm awful tired, Ruthie . . . I need . . . to sleep.'

Ruth jumped up, alarmed by her mother's extra pallor. 'I'll make some Ovaltine for –'

'I don't want . . . just settle me . . . there's a . . . good lass.'

Barely five minutes later, Ina was breathing steadily, if a little shallowly, and Ruth went into the scullery to make herself a cup of tea. Her legs were shaking as she waited for the kettle to boil, which was not surprising in view of what she had just been told. It was a great shock to learn that the woman she had always thought was her mother wasn't her mother at all, and she hadn't found out where she had come from or got any clue as to who her real mother might be. Oh well, she'd have to contain her curiosity until morning.

Making herself as comfortable as she could in the wide easy chair at Ina's bedside, Ruth shut her eyes. She had learned over the past few months to make the most of every minute's peace she got.

Not being called upon even once to lift Ina to the commode, or to turn her to her other side, or to give her a sip of water, as she usually had to do several times a night, Ruth had slipped into a deeper sleep than she'd had for many weeks, and woke to the sound of the milkman rattling bottles outside. Before her body was fully mobile, her brain told her that her 'patient' had passed away, so she was not surprised that there was no pulse when she felt for one.

She flopped back into the depths of her chair, uncertain of what to do, unsure of how she felt. She was glad that her mother was free of pain at last but wished that she'd had the chance to ask her more about the fostering. Where had she, an infant at the time, been living for the first eight weeks of her life? Who had looked after her? Had her biological mother died, or had she been a poor young girl who couldn't afford to keep her? A girl who had been abandoned by the father of her child? Abandoned by her own father as well, likely. Thrown out of her home, she may well have taken her baby to an orphanage, or left her somewhere for someone to find. Dear God, there was no end of places she might have gone to after that, so how on earth was Ruth Laverton to find her?

But she must stop this agonizing, she reprimanded herself, getting slowly to her feet again. She had things to do to show her gratitude for being enfolded in this woman's family . . . and Gladys had better do her share, too. Ruth's stomach lurched. She could foresee trouble – there was always trouble when Gladys was asked to do anything.

Bob Mennie took in hand to arrange the funeral – 'It's a man's job,' he said – and his wife, Gladys, still unaware of her mother's dying revelation, left Ruth to do the catering while she went round the house earmarking all items she was laying claim to.

Ruth let her carry on. She couldn't very well have an argument while Ina's body was still in the house, and she had no claim on Ina's things. Strangely, it was Bob who told his wife on the morning of the funeral what he thought of her callousness.

'This is still Ruthie's home,' he pointed out, 'and you're not taking anything out of here without her say-so.'

Glaring fiercely at him, Gladys nevertheless stopped her ghoulish inspection.

Ruth had been in two minds about admitting that she had been a foster child, but she was so sickened by the way Gladys had behaved that she decided to wait until after the funeral. As soon as the last of the mourners had left the house, therefore, she made her announcement, her spirits lifting with the relief of getting if off her chest, and smiling at the expressions on the other two faces.

When it had sunk in, Gladys turned triumphantly to her

husband. 'She's not my mother's daughter, so she's not entitled to stay in this house.'

The bewildered man frowned. 'You can't throw her and Colin out on the street!'

'I'll give her time to find somewhere else, but everything here belongs to me.'

Bob glanced round disparagingly. 'There's nothing worth much, in any case.'

'We can sell what we don't want.' Gladys looked at Ruth defiantly. 'I'll be back tomorrow, so don't you dare take anything, and if you want something for a keepsake, you'd better ask me first.'

Their departure left Ruth sitting forlornly alone. She didn't need anything to remind her of Ina, who would always remain a part of her, as the mother she had more than succeeded in being. 'Oh, Mum,' she moaned, 'why did you have to tell me?'

After a while, she began to wonder why Ina had been so desperate to let her know. Were there letters about her fostering amongst the receipts and other important papers kept in the old handbag in the sideboard? Had Ina, in a roundabout way, given her a chance to find her birth mother, who would surely be in better circumstances now and might be pleased to be reunited with the child she had given up all those years before?

The old handbag, with its cracked leather and torn lining, nevertheless yielded more information than Ruth had ever hoped for. All preserved together in one thick brown envelope were three letters from a home for unmarried mothers in Yorkshire, recording an application for, the acceptance of, and the actual fostering of Ruth Bruce, date of birth 20.4.19, by John and Georgina Brown. Unfortunately, there was no birth certificate, and Ruth's disappointment was so great that she abandoned all hope of ever learning who her real mother had been, and stuffed the envelope back in its original place among the other papers.

Thankfully, Bob Mennie – the brother-in-law she had never cared for much – had succeeded in persuading Gladys not to turn her out of the house. 'Mind you,' he confided when he called to give Ruth the good news, 'I don't think she'd really have done it, not when it came to the point.'

Ruth wasn't so sure. They had never been close, Gladys always jealous of her older sister, always quick to take her spite out on her. But she couldn't run down Bob's wife to his face. 'No, I don't suppose she would.'

'Have you found out anything yet?' he enquired. 'About your mother . . . real mother, I mean?'

'Not a thing. I did find out where I was born, though – in a home for unmarried mothers in Yorkshire.'

'Well, that's something, isn't it?'

'It's a start, but they're not allowed to give out any information in case the woman concerned doesn't want to be found.'

'No? Well, don't give up hope. You'll maybe come across something else, if you keep looking. Now, are you not going to offer a starving man something to eat and drink?'

'The kettle's on,' she smiled, feeling much better for his encouraging remarks, 'and I was going to have a cheese sandwich if that'll do you?'

'That sister of yours . . .' He halted, looking somewhat confused, then grinned. 'She's not your real sister, of course . . .'

'I'll always look on her as my sister,' Ruth said truthfully.

'I could never get over the difference between you,' Bob observed now, 'but I aye thought it was not having any kids that made Glad a bit sour, if you see what I mean. Anyway, I was going to say she doesn't feed me properly, not like a hard-working man should be fed.'

'There's nothing coming over you that I can see,' Ruth laughed.

When her brother-in-law left, she washed up the dirty dishes and then took the old handbag out again. He was quite right – there could easily be something else in it, though she couldn't think what. She searched amongst the papers again, even emptying the brown envelope to see if she had missed something, but there were only the three letters she had already seen. Something urged her on, however, and she decided to clear out the whole bag; most of what was there wasn't worth keeping.

She spent a good hour opening folded sheets of paper, reading receipts, letters from Ina's old friends – possibly some who had long since lost contact with her but should be told of her passing, just the same – and ended up with three separate piles in front of her on the table: receipts for things like gas and electricity, coal, odds and ends of no importance, which could all be destroyed; receipts for larger items which were still in the house and which had better be kept; and a small bundle of letters from the women Ina kept in touch with.

Never one to procrastinate, Ruth got out the writing pad and wrote short, but friendly notes to Ina's friends. Maybe some of them had died, too, but at least those who were still alive would be glad she had let them know. The envelopes addressed and stamped, she felt like having another cup of tea and consigned the old everyday receipts to the fire while she waited for the kettle to boil.

Before she returned the other items to the handbag, she thought that it would be better for a good clean out, and pulled the lining away from the bottom to give it a shake, and as the dust and fragments of yellowed paper floated out, the lining tore a bit further and displayed the corner of another brown envelope which must have slipped down right out of sight . . . or perhaps it had been hidden there, she thought, in excitement.

Extracting this envelope, she found that Ina had written 'Andrew Rennie' on it. Who was Andrew Rennie? There was only one way to find out, so she carefully pulled out the wad of papers which she had thought to be a padded base to the bag and smoothed them out. Her mother, Ina, had said she was paid an allowance, and here was proof of it. Andrew Rennie had been the solicitor who had seen to the payments which had carried on until Ruth left school and started work. Fourteen years! A young girl, as she'd believed her real mother had been, would not have had been able to do that, so it must have been her father, who had obviously been a man of some means and most likely married. Well, she didn't want to know about him. She wasn't out for any financial gain. She just wanted to discover who her mother was.

Ruth went over and over the official notifications of ten pounds paid into the North of Scotland Bank every month. It was two pounds ten shillings a week, she realized, more than a working man could have earned at that time. But she had now come across the one person who would be able to give her the information she sought. Andrew Rennie would have known her mother, and he was under no obligation to keep her name and address secret, not like the home for unmarried mothers – unless he was a great friend of one or other of her parents. Should she go and see him? He could only turn her away. She'd be doing nothing legally wrong, so he couldn't report her to the police. Oh God, she'd have to go! She would always regret it if she didn't. Whatever happened, it was worth a try.

She rose early the following day, but knowing that solicitors' offices wouldn't be open at eight o'clock in the morning, she thought she would take a walk to clear her head. She hadn't slept well, with the turmoil her brain had been in. It was a lovely day, and she enjoyed ambling along the pavements, planning what to say. She would prefer to see Andrew Rennie himself – he must be a very old man by this time – but his files would have been kept and his successor in the practice would be able to lay his hands on the information she so desperately needed. There might be the matter of confidentiality to consider, but surely not after so many years.

She thought it might be best not to go there before half-past nine, and because it was hardly nine when she came on to Union Street, she passed time by window-shopping at Esslemont and Macintosh's store, then crossed the street when the clock on the Town House struck the quarter-past to have a look in Falconer's . . . she seldom shopped there, either; their prices were too high for her meagre income. At half-past, she headed for Bon Accord Square, her stomach churning, her heart beating twenty to the dozen as she climbed the steps to the office of Rennie and Dalgarno.

'Can I see Mr Rennie?' she asked the young receptionist.

The girl gaped. 'There's no Mr Rennie nowadays; there hasn't been for years and years. Would somebody else not do?'

'It must be Mr Rennie,' Ruth persisted. 'He's not dead, is he?'

'I don't know. I'm not long started here, but I'll ask.' The girl picked up the telephone receiver and turned a handle on the small box switchboard at the side of the counter. In just a second, she said, 'Miss Leslie, there's a lady here asking to see Mr Rennie . . . no, she says it must be him, nobody else.'

Replacing the handset, she looked at Ruth rather accusingly. 'Miss Leslie'll be through in a minute.'

A bespectacled, middle-aged, rake-thin woman in black came out of a door at Ruth's left. 'I believe you are asking to see Mr Rennie, Mrs . . . ?'

'Laverton, and it's very important.'

'Mr Rennie retired some time ago, Mrs Laverton, but I can give you an appointment with Mr Dalgarno. He is the senior partner now, and he would probably be able to help you.'

Thinking this highly improbable in view of the secrecy surrounding her birth, Ruth stuck to her guns. 'It's personal, something only Mr Rennie would know.'

Recognizing that this was a woman who would not be fobbed off, Miss Leslie tutted in vexation. 'In that case, Mrs Laverton, if you leave your address and telephone number, I will contact Mr Rennie at home and let you know if he agrees to see you.'

Ruth gave her address and, although she felt at a disadvantage when she admitted that she had no telephone, she added loftily, 'Perhaps you'd be good enough to write and tell me.'

While she walked home, unable to face sitting on a tramcar with other people, Ruth recalled Gladys's reaction two days ago to being told that her 'sister' wanted to find her real mother. 'All I can say is I think you're potty! A woman who gave up her baby all that time ago won't want to be reminded of it now. She's likely married with other children and doesn't want her man to know about you.'

'I'm only trying to find out who she is,' Ruth had protested, 'and even if I do, I'll maybe never pluck up courage to go and tell her who I am.'

'What's the point of finding out, then?' Gladys had sneered. 'Are you hoping she married into money so you can claim a share of it when she pops off?'

That, Ruth mused, had stuck in her craw. Money had nothing to do with it. Suppose her mother had married the richest man in Scotland – in Britain – she wasn't looking for any hand-outs. All she wanted was to see the woman who had borne her and keep a picture of her in her mind's eye, not to make herself known. She didn't blame her mother for abandoning a young infant – the poor thing had probably been forced into it by a pitiless mother whose only thought was to avoid scandal.

The following morning, Ruth received a letter.

Dear Mrs Laverton,

Mr Rennie sends his compliments and begs your forbearance for a few days, because he is not at liberty to divulge anything without first consulting the other parties concerned. He will, however, contact you as soon as possible to arrange a meeting.

Yours sincerely,
Margaret Leslie

Ruth returned the headed notepaper to the envelope with trembling fingers. The old solicitor must have got a shock when he learned that she was looking for her mother. Ruth's stomach gave a sudden lurch. But how could he have known who she was? She had given only her married name to Miss Leslie, no Christian name, so how could he have connected her with Ruth Bruce, which had been her name at the time she was born? He couldn't even have known of her as Ruth Brown, let alone Mrs Laverton.

There was something most peculiar about this . . . unless Mr Rennie was senile. If Miss Leslie had spoken to him on the telephone and was quoting his exact words, they could have been phrases he'd recalled using years ago, meaningless now, in which case there would be little point in keeping any meeting he arranged. Yet there was something still niggling at her about the wording of the letter. '. . . *not at liberty to divulge anything without first consulting the other parties concerned.*' It fitted too well to be accidental. The other parties would be her mother and . . . her father – whose permission would be essential before he could give out any information.

After turning it over and over in her mind, Ruth concluded that Mr Rennie must still have all his faculties. He had let her know in a roundabout way that he was aware of who she was – though heaven knew how he knew – and had given her a modicum of hope that he would tell her everything in a few days.

With the second post, however, another letter arrived, addressed in the angular and somewhat shaky hand of an older person. On opening it, Ruth was surprised to read that Mr Rennie himself had written to say that he would come to see her that very afternoon at three o'clock. Wondering why he had changed his mind, she set about vacuuming and dusting her already spotless living room.

The tall stranger doffed his homburg as she opened the door. 'Good afternoon, Mrs Laverton,' he said, 'I am Andrew Rennie.'

His smile lit up his whole face, she thought, also finding herself smiling light-heartedly, although she was as tense as a wound spring. 'I guessed you must be. Come in, please.'

He sat down at the table and laid his hat down in front of him. 'I am sorry about the change of plan,' he began, 'but I decided that I should meet you in person before I –'

'You wanted to find out if I really was who I claimed to be,' she interrupted. 'Or maybe if I was the kind of person my mother would want me to be?'

His grey eyes twinkled at her. 'I plead guilty on both counts.'

'Tell me, Mr Rennie, how did you know who I was?'

'Shall we leave that for the moment? Suffice it to say that as soon as Miss Leslie told me that you had asked for me specifically and said that no one else could help you, I knew who you were. Well, I was *almost* sure who you were, but one look at you has cleared any doubt from my mind. You are so like your grandmother.'

Ruth did not know what to say to this, but her heart beat all the faster at the thought of the grandmother she had never known, and in all likelihood would never know, since she must be dead by this time.

As if reading her thoughts, the old solicitor went on, 'She is still alive, you know . . .' He paused for a moment, with a faraway look in his eyes, then continued, more briskly than before. 'But enough of that. Tell me, how did you find out that you were . . . ?'

'My mother – the woman I always believed was my mother told me on her deathbed that I'd been fostered, and when I looked in the old handbag she kept all her important papers in, I found letters from a home for unmarried mothers about my fostering.'

Andrew Rennie nodded. 'Ah, yes. Brightfield.'

'I did think of going there to see if they would tell me who my mother was, but I guessed it would have been useless. It was thirty-six years ago and –'

'The present matron would have had no difficulty in tracing the details of your birth, but she would not have been at liberty to reveal them to you – not as the law stands – so you were quite right not to go there.' His long, tapering fingers raked through the thick silver hair. 'And is that all you know? That you were born in Brightfield?'

'That's all.' Her palms were sweating now, with the certainty that she was in for another huge disappointment. This old man wouldn't tell her anything more. He, too, would be bound by the law, and had probably just wanted to see how much she had found out herself.

But Ruth was off the mark, and when the solicitor started to speak again, it was as if his mind had gone back over the years. 'I always felt that Marianne was wrong in what she did.' He looked mournfully at her. 'She was your father's mother, and what she asked me to do was purely to save scandal. Even today, people ostracize unmarried girls who have children, and it was far worse then. Not only had she Melda's good name to protect, she also had her own family name to save. And no one ever knew. She left it to me to attend to everything, registering the births . . .'

Ruth's body jerked up. 'The births? More than one, you mean? At the same time, or . . .'

A flicker of wry amusement crossed the man's serious

face. 'At the same time. You were one of twins. As I was saying, I had to register the births, and I found a good man and woman to adopt – but, sadly, they only took the boy.'

Ruth watched him as his mind went back to a time when he'd had to put his ingenuity to such a use as never before, nor since. His eyes were fixed on a point behind her head, perhaps on the Dinah bank her father had bought her when she was very small – the metal bust of a black 'mammy' with a hand out in front waiting for someone to put a penny into it then press the lever on her shoulder to lift it to her mouth. But Mr Rennie wasn't consciously looking at Dinah, he was remembering, and he could probably recall the events of long ago more clearly than what had happened yesterday. Even at his age – and he must be nearly eighty – he was a nice-looking man, and he must have been quite handsome when he was young. Engrossed in her own thoughts, Ruth jumped at the sound of his soft voice.

'Marianne was desperate to stop the Bruce-Lyall name from being tarnished. Her family meant everything to her, and I had hoped that she would never know what I did ... that it would not come out until after we had both passed on.'

He raised his eyes and gave a start as they met Ruth's. 'Dear me, I am talking to myself again, am I? That is what comes of living alone for so long.'

She heaved a sigh of agreement to this. 'I've been a widow for eight years, and I sometimes speak to myself, as well.'

'You will have gathered that I do not want your grandmother to meet you and your brother, who was studying for the ministry the last I heard. It is this last, more than anything else, that I pray she never finds out, although I cannot explain my reason for that. I can only beseech you not to muddy the calm waters of the life she has left to her. Once she has gone, I will tell you all you want to know, your real name, the address of the castle, so that you may contact your mother, who, I am positive, will be extremely glad to make your acquaintance. Now, I feel rather tired, so I will take my leave of you, Mrs Laverton.'

Ruth had passed a restless night and she felt no better the following morning. Her mind was spinning like a top with what she had learned the previous day. Despite Mr Rennie's determination not to tell her anything, he had inadvertently revealed that her mother's name was Melda and that she came of a family called Bruce-Lyall, who lived in a castle somewhere, but he had asked her not to try to find them and she would have to wait until her grandmother died before she could do anything.

Having existed for hours on cups of tea, she scrambled some eggs at half-past five, and had made some toast and filled the teapot when someone knocked on her door. Dragging herself through to answer the summons, she was astonished to see Bob Mennie, her brother-in-law.

'Is something wrong with Gladys?' she asked in alarm.

'Not a thing.' He gave her a teasing smile. 'I just came to see how you were, Ruthie. You said you were trying to find out about your mother, and I wondered . . .'

'I've learned quite a lot,' she smiled, pleased to be able to tell somebody.

He accepted the tea she poured for him and listened gravely until she mentioned that the Bruce-Lyalls had a castle. 'My God, Ruthie!' he exclaimed. 'That's Lord Glendarril's place . . . I'd to make a delivery there once.' He leaned back in his chair and regarded her with interest. 'Don't tell me you're related to them? The Bruce-Lyalls are aristocracy, and if one of them's your mother, you haven't half landed on your feet. Gladys'll be jealous as hell.'

'Don't tell her,' Ruth pleaded. 'I'm not going near them yet. The solicitor asked me not to try to find them.'

'Did you promise him you wouldn't?'

'He didn't ask me to promise.'

'There you are, then. My God, I don't know how you can sit there so calmly when you could be living the life of Riley in a castle.'

'Oh, Bob, they won't want a working-class widow turning up on their doorstep. They'll think I'm begging for money.'

He leaned across and patted her hand. 'If what Mr Rennie said's true, and I can't see anybody making up a story like that, you're entitled to some of their money. Look, Ruthie, I'll tell you what. Tomorrow's Saturday, my half-day, so I'll drive you there. I finish work at twelve, so I'll have a quick wash and a bite to eat and I'll come for you about half-past one – it's not much more than thirty miles, so it won't take us long.'

'What'll Gladys say?' Ruth asked apprehensively.

'What she doesn't know won't hurt her,' he grinned. 'I'll say there's a schoolboy match at Pittodrie. I'd normally get home from the football round about quarter to six, so we've plenty of time.' He pushed back his chair and got to his feet. 'I'd better be going, before she starts wondering why I'm so late home from work. I don't want her to begin suspecting anything. Half-past one, remember.'

She made fresh tea when he went out. She had always thought of Bob Mennie as a selfish brute, but since her mother died, he couldn't have been nicer to her. And there was nothing nasty behind it; he'd never tried anything or said anything out of place. He was more than likely making up to her for the way Gladys was treating her.

Looking at the clock as she took the dirty dishes to the sink, she thought that this time tomorrow . . . she would either be jumping for joy at being accepted into the Bruce-Lyall fold, or more likely, weeping the bitter tears of rejection.

Chapter Thirty

❧

It was unforgiveable of Andrew, Marianne fumed. If he hadn't let the cat out of the bag, she could have carried the secret with her to the grave, and would never have had to meet ... Confronting the woman who had turned up yesterday had been like coming face to face with a part of the past she'd believed to be buried beyond recall, most upsetting. Thankfully, she'd succeeded in fooling the creature, though no doubt she'd be back demanding to be told the truth, and Ruairidh and his wife might not be so conveniently away next time.

Wait, though! Ruth Laverton, as she had called herself, could only have been wanting to get her hands on some of the Bruce-Lyall money, though she hadn't mentioned blackmail, so it might be a good idea to offer her some, to pay her to keep her mouth shut. It would have to be enough to do the trick, Marianne decided, which would be a bit of a problem since there was no cash in the coffers. The end of the war had been a blow for the mill. It was the end of the Ministry of Defence orders, and Fair Isle garments had gone out of fashion, so the mill was struggling and Ruairidh had ploughed all his resources into trying to get it back on its feet. The family, once so wealthy, was now in debt.

'With Dorothea gone,' he had said sadly, 'I have nobody to leave my money to, anyway.'

Marianne could feel the old tightness in her throat, the heaviness in her heart. Losing her dear Hamish had been almost unbearable, and Dorothea's death so soon after she'd gone to London had almost finished her. In a truly vulnerable state now, she toyed with the idea of publicly acknowledging Ruth Laverton as her granddaughter, and it took several minutes for her to discard it. She could not resurrect her son's illegitimate child and be the cause of endless scandal for him. Nor could she submit to blackmail, not that the woman had mentioned such a thing.

From the very start, when she'd first learned that Ruairidh and Melda had done something they shouldn't, her only thought had been to save the fact coming out. She had lied about the infant dying soon after birth, but only to save the family name from being besmirched. The family name, and all it encompassed, meant everything to her, more than it did to Ruairidh, more than it had to Hamish really, and she hadn't even been born into it.

Her daughter-in-law, of course, didn't care tuppence that they'd soon have to open the castle as an ancient monument and allow members of the public to roam through the place . . . except for the west wing, because Ruairidh had put his foot down about that. The family had to have some privacy, after all. But Melda would happily live in poverty as long as Ruairidh was with her. She had been devastated by Dorothea's death, and it had made her hard, fortifying her against any other tragedies that may befall her, but how would she react when, if, she learned that at least one of her first two children was still alive? She might erupt with the force of a long-dormant volcano . . . with the fire directed at the person who had tricked her into believing there had been only one child – which had died.

And yet, Marianne mused, her luck had held good so far. When that female had turned up like a nasty insect crawling out of the woodwork to disrupt her tranquillity, she had been alone in the house except for a recently engaged maid, who didn't count – it was difficult to get staff since the war; nobody wanted to go into service – and her bluff had worked. Ruth Laverton had gone away, perhaps not convinced that she was on the wrong track but surely a bit doubtful that Melda was her mother. She hadn't mentioned her sister, and she, Marianne, had not let on that she knew there was a twin, but Andrew knew and he'd likely insist on tying things up so that they'd be sure of getting their fair share of any money when their father passed on.

Sitting down at the old desk – her mind so occupied that it did not occur to her that this antique item alone would fetch a fortune if it were sold – Marianne left a message on the telephone with Andrew's housekeeper, asking him to come to see her the next afternoon – more of an order than an invitation, really. Ruairidh and Melda would not be back from the exhibition they'd gone to see in London until Monday, and Bessie always took all day Sunday off. She had to get Andrew on his own. He was older than she was, and had been very frail the last time she saw him, so it shouldn't be difficult to browbeat him into telling the woman, and the other twin, if she turned up, they were not who they thought they were. She could quite easily convince the fortune-hunters that some mistake had been made, that they were not Melda's children, that she, Lady Glendarril, had actually been there when those two doomed infants died.

Having told her solicitor which train to take, Marianne sent Gilchrist to meet him in the Bentley, and was delighted to see how doddery Andrew was when her chauffeur helped him out of the car and up the steps.

She kissed her old friend on the cheek, and was inwardly amused to see the roguish twinkle in his rheumy eyes when he slid his arm round her waist. Silly old fool! Surely he didn't still think she wanted him to . . . no, that was absurd. He hardly had the strength to put one foot past the other, never mind anything else. 'It's so good to see you, Andrew,' she murmured, squeezing his hand.

Completely under her spell already, he followed her into

the large drawing room. 'D'you know, Marianne,' he said, taking a seat by the window, 'I can remember sitting here so many times over the years, talking to Hamish and wishing that I had never brought the two of you together. He took the only girl I ever loved.'

She decided to spread the jam on thickly. 'I wish that, too. I was beginning to love you, Andrew, but he was so charming . . . and I was so young . . .'

Andrew was not quite so gullible as she had thought. 'But not so naïve as you are trying to make out. You knew what you were doing when you married him.'

'He told me he just wanted me so he could have sons, but I was blinded by the prospect of the wealth he would fall heir to, the idea of being a titled lady in a castle. I admit that, but I did discover that there is more to life than wordly possessions.'

He nodded gravely. 'Yes, there is, Marianne. There is compassion for your fellow men or women, and honesty, and abiding by the rules, all of which you have totally disregarded throughout your life.'

Stung by criticism from a man she had believed loved her without question, she snapped, 'And where was your compassion for me when you spun that vile story to that awful Ruth Laverton?'

'It *was* a vile story,' he agreed, 'yet true, nevertheless. At the time, I carried out your instructions and excused your heartlessness by telling myself that you were desperately covering up the results of Ruairidh's irresponsibility. When Ruth contacted me, and I realized that she was one of Melda's twins, I was pleased that your daughter-in-law would be reunited with one, at least, even after such a long time. Poor girl, she must often have wondered what had become of them.'

He paused and turned his eyes on Marianne accusingly. 'I found it extremely hard to believe that she had agreed to their being adopted, but loving you as I did, I could not contemplate the alternative – that you had forced her into it. It strikes me now, however, that there must have been a reason why she did not search for them after Ruairidh married her. How did you arrange that? Did you tell her they had died?'

Bowing to a Fate that seemed to be determined to catch her out, even after so many years, Marianne came to the conclusion that she had better confess. 'I'm afraid I did – to one anyway, and Melda was never told about the other one.' Feeling that the atmosphere inside had suddenly become oppressive, she said, 'Why don't we have a walk in the garden? We can talk just as well there, and we can take a seat if we get tired.'

Even in the warmth of the June day, both old people felt the need of a jacket before venturing outside, and so it was another few minutes before Marianne put her arm through Andrew's and guided his tottery feet along the path from the heavy studded door of the west wing to the vast rose garden. 'My father-in-law had this laid out to mark Edward's accession to the throne,' she informed him as they turned into the walled-in rectangle, adding quickly, 'Edward the Seventh, I mean. He and Hector were great friends, and he had often come here for the shooting when he was Prince of Wales. I wish I'd been around then, for I've heard so many stories about him with young girls, and I wouldn't have minded being his Princess ... but I'm speaking rubbish. I had my dear Hamish, hadn't I?' She stole a sideways glance at her companion and was confused to find him regarding her sadly.

'How little I knew you,' he sighed. 'I always hoped that you regretted marrying Hamish.'

'I never regretted marrying him, and I loved what the marriage brought me,' she declared, honest up to a point.

'So you ... never thought of leaving him ... for me?'

Marianne felt a rush of pity for him. For sixty years she

had flirted with him at every opportunity, led him to believe that he meant something to her other than her man of business, and he didn't deserve such scurrilous treatment – he was truly a decent man. She changed the subject abruptly. 'I said I'd tell you about Melda and the two babies. She was just a young thing, and not the kind of girl I wanted as a daughter-in-law, and she took everything on trust. She wouldn't hear of the child being adopted or put in an orphanage, so I threatened her that if she didn't do what I wanted, I would tell Ruairidh she'd been carrying on with one of the soldiers at the camp, and it was *his* baby. Then I started thinking she might wonder how the child was and so, not long after the births – she wasn't told she'd had two and with a difficult labour she wasn't in a fit state to know – I said the baby had died and she believed me. I made her promise never to breathe a word to anybody, especially Ruairidh.'

'Poor Melda,' muttered Andrew.

'Not so poor! She was besotted with the idea of marrying into the nobility, and she talked him into it not long after he came home –'

'Melda's not like you!' Andrew broke in harshly. 'She had always loved Ruairidh; she wouldn't have cared if he was destitute, and he had always loved her. I can't believe you were so cruel to her, Marianne . . .'

'She was just a doctor's daughter, after all. Middle class.'

'And what were you before my aunts took pity on you? What work did your father do?'

She had the grace to look slightly abashed. 'He just worked in a sawmill in Tipperton.'

'Yes, so you were from working stock, and none the worse for it. Your blood instilled new life into the Bruce-Lyalls. Your sons were much sturdier and healthier than their father and their grandfather. But tell me, were you ever sorry for leaving your home?'

'I had to leave. I told you, remember, I stole some

money.' And now, so long afterwards, Marianne felt the shame she had not felt at the time.

'Yes, I do remember. Five sovereigns, wasn't it, a lot in those days, more than a year's wages in many cases? Um, did you ever take anything from my aunts?'

'No, never!' She could sense a new coldness in his manner towards her which, after the long years of his constant devotion, pained her more than she could have thought possible. But she could not blame her old friend for despising her, not after all he had done for her in the past.

He had never been just a friend; he had always been a part of her that she could not do without, not a lover in the physical sense, but in a far more lasting capacity.

'Oh, Andrew, I must have a rest,' she gasped, plumping down on the wooden bench they were passing, one of several at the side of the walkway round the large pond.

She had hoped for at least a slight show of concern, but he sat down beside her without saying a word and it was some time before she ventured, in a small voice, 'I suppose you're shocked by the things I did, but will you do one last thing for me?'

'If it lies within my power,' he replied stiffly.

'Tell Melda's . . . tell Ruth and her twin, there must have been some mistake and they're not hers at all. Say I was there when both her babies died, and –'

He rose slowly but angrily to his feet, glaring venomously at her as he spat out, 'Good God, Marianne! I just do not know how you have the effrontery to ask me that!'

Turning, he took a step away from her, and she sprang to her feet to try to pacify him. The abrupt movement made a dizziness come over her, and trying to find something to steady her, she stretched out her arms. Tragically, she knocked Andrew off his feet and, feeling himself falling, he caught hold of her sleeve. Fingers clawing at empty air, it dawned on Marianne that there was nothing she could do to prevent the inevitable.

Falling heavily on top of him, her body ground the fluted tiles edging the path further into his temple, while she splashed face down into the water.

Chapter Thirty-one

❧

The front pages of the Scottish newspapers next day carried some mention of the 'catastrophic accident', mainly along the lines that it had almost been a double tragedy and speculating as to how it had happened.

The unusual occurrence even warranted articles in the national dailies, the more sensational proclaiming in large headlines:

'SUICIDE PACT GONE WRONG?'
'ONLY DEATH COULD PART MARIANNE AND ANDREW!'
'DEATH UNVEILS SECRET PASSION!'
'THE LADY AND HER LAWYER LOVER!'

The ages of the 'lovers' were not revealed until the end of the articles, within parenthesis and in tiny print which most of the readers passed over as not worth straining their eyes for. Those who did take the trouble were left feeling cheated. A man and woman both in their seventies? They wouldn't remember what passion was, if they'd ever experienced it, which was doubtful.

In less than a week after the funeral, the public's interest had moved on to other scandals, but in an airy office in Aberdeen's Bon Accord Square, Graham Dalgarno was having problems. He had intended executing Andrew Rennie's last will and testament before turning his mind to anything else, but it was not nearly as straightforward as he had imagined. No relatives remaining alive, the old man had left his entire estate to Lady Glendarril's *first two* grandchildren. The peculiar underlining of the words 'first two' when, as far as Graham knew, there was only one, who had died since the will had been drawn up, combined with the pencilled note at the side which read 'Ruth and Samuel', made him realize that he would have to go through the Bruce-Lyall papers to find answers to the suspicions which had jumped to his mind.

Andrew Rennie had jealously guarded his right as senior partner to deal with Lady Glendarril's affairs, and on his retiral, he had given orders that any future correspondence relating thereto should be laid aside for his attention. Hence, for the past ten years, he had come in once a month to bring her files up to date, and it was only after his death that Graham had got his hands on the key to the roll-top desk and the power to handle this prestigious account. But having access to what was more or less Lady Glendarril's life history was the beginning of his nightmare!

The first document he had come across was the dowager's will, which Andrew had no doubt helped her to draw up. It was a complicated document, changed several times over the years, first stating that everything she left was to go to her granddaughter, Dorothea Bruce-Lyall, and then a codicil which noted that because of Dorothea's death, Marianne's son, the present Viscount Glendarril, would inherit his mother's entire estate. Graham had thought it strange that no mention was made of the present Lady Glendarril, but this was something he would have to come to terms with when the dowager died.

He had discovered that the Ruth and Samuel, to whom the old man had left all his wordly goods, were not included in their grandmother's will, which, although it did seem very strange, was not something he should worry about meantime. His worry would lie in tracing them, finding out who was their father . . .

The thought which struck Graham then almost knocked him sideways. Was it possible? If so, it had been the best-kept secret ever, but then people with plenty of money could always find ways and means to cover up any indiscretions.

Graham's suspicions gathered momentum. Andrew was a crafty old beggar! He must have fathered two children on Marianne Bruce-Lyall when they were young and whisked them away somewhere out of sight! Graham had sensed that their relationship went much deeper than solicitor/client, but he had never dreamed . . .

Wait a minute! If Ruth and Samuel were Marianne's illegitimate *grand*children, she definitely wasn't their mother, and it meant that they had also been the late Hamish's grandchildren, unless . . . had he impregnated the present Lady Glendarril – the younger one – at some time? The idea of this was quite repugnant to Graham. Esmerelda – he had always thought it a beautiful name for the elegant woman, although he believed she was usually referred to as Melda – was not the kind to have a sordid affair with a man old enough to be her father. There must be another explanation, but he was blowed if he could think of one. He had better put all his other commitments aside to give him the time and the freedom to search the desk for birth certificates or other documents which would enable him to wind up Andrew Rennie's estate as he had wished.

Graham searched the top left drawer slowly and methodically, inwardly thanking his late partner for writing notes to remind himself of things he might otherwise have forgotten, but nothing he came across shed any light on the matter in hand. Disgruntled, he started on the drawer underneath, but found almost at once that it held only correspondence from various tradespeople in answer to complaints Marianne Glendarril had raised, and dating back as far as when she had first become a titled lady.

At four thirty, depressed and tired, and hungry because he had gone without lunch, Graham decided against taking the contents of the bottom drawer home in his briefcase.

He would leave it until the morning, when his mind would be fresher and more able to spot anything relevant.

Next day, he gave his secretary instructions that he was not to be disturbed and settled into the swivel chair again. After unlocking the bottom drawer, he saw that it contained a large tin box, black japanned like all the old deed boxes. His pulse quickened when he discovered that it, too, was locked. It seemed promising – a locked box in a locked drawer must conceal something of great importance. His fingers trembling, he took some time to find the correct key, but at last the latch snapped back. The papers he took out led him into a maze of legality – or illegality? – which would need to be sorted out before he could go any further.

His most astounding discovery in the first hour was that from 1919 to 1933, Andrew Rennie had been transferring money every six months from an account in his name with the Clydesdale Bank, but marked in his secret journal as belonging to 'Marianne'. As if this were not mystery enough, the money had been divided equally – one half going to an account with the Royal Bank of Scotland and the other to an account with the North of Scotland Bank – for the maintenance of two children. The question was – whose children?

If Andrew had used his own money, the answer would have been that they were his, but the fact that it was Marianne Glendarril who had actually paid would suggest otherwise. And in 1919, she herself would have been around forty, past child-bearing age? Would they have been spawned by one of her sons? The elder, Ranald, had been killed about nine months before the payments began, so he could have been the father, but that was pure conjecture.

Graham sifted through all the papers again in the hope of finding something more definite, trying to decipher all the pencilled notes which cropped up in the strangest places in Andrew's rather cramped scribbles – along the tops of pages, across corners, up or down the margins.

Nearing the end of another hour, when Graham was on the verge of giving up, something caught his eye. His dejected spirits soared as he studied the statement of interest in his hand. It was from a firm of brokers concerning a block of shares Lady Glendarril held in a tea plantation in Assam, and halfway down, between two lines of figures, was a faint insertion – so faint that it was a wonder he had noticed it: 'Ruth married Mark Laverton 21/7/41.'

Sitting back, Graham held the sheet of paper up to the window, turning it this way and that to make sure there was nothing else written on it. There wasn't, and this had no connection with the paper on which it was written. Andrew had obviously learned of the girl's marriage while he had been working with the statement, and had jotted it down to remind him. But this information gave Graham the incentive to carry on.

He set to with renewed vigour, and when, twenty minutes later, his secretary knocked on his door, he called, 'I told you I do not wish to be disturbed today.'

Jane McDonald opened the door a little and said, 'I'll get the lady to make an appointment then, shall I? When would be best?'

'You had better make it next week. Do I know her?'

'I don't think so. She said she spoke to Mr Rennie about ten days ago, and then she saw his death in the papers.'

Graham's head snapped up. 'Andrew never mentioned taking on a new client. Did she give her name?'

'Mrs Laverton.'

'Laverton?' He bounded up off his chair and practically shoved Miss McDonald out of his way in his haste to make sure that it was the correct Mrs Laverton.

His noisy entry to the waiting room startled the woman, who said, nervously, 'Mr Rennie was dealing . . . but when I saw his death in the papers, I wondered who . . .'

Feeling equally nervous, Graham cleared his throat. 'He retired from the firm ten years ago, Mrs Laverton, and since then, his only client has been –'

'My grandmother?'

He was pleased to have at least one of his suspicions confirmed.

'Um . . . can you tell me . . . what was your mother's name?'

'All I know is her first name is Melda.'

'Melda?' he gasped. 'But Esmeralda is the present Lady Glendarril and in that case, Ruairidh . . . Lord Glendarril . . . cannot be your father. They were married in – I think 1920, and you were born in 1919?'

She gave a smiling nod. 'If he *is* my father, I can't understand why they didn't claim me when they became husband and wife. I was fostered out, apparently, though I always thought the Browns were my real parents. My mother only told me she wasn't my birth mother when she was on her deathbed.'

When Graham learned that Samuel had been adopted, but had later been taken to Edinburgh by his adoptive parents, he burst out, 'Did Andrew Rennie tell you all this?'

She explained that the old solicitor had inadvertently let slip the Bruce-Lyall name and where they lived, and she told him about her visit to the castle itself. 'My grandmother was the only one I saw, and she swore there was some mistake, and she had no idea who I was. She was so convincing I started doubting what Mr Rennie had told me, then I read about his death, and I thought, why shouldn't I go and see if someone in his office knew anything?'

Graham was shocked by the dowager's behaviour. 'She did know who you were! She had authorized Rennie to deposit money in your foster parents' bank every month for your keep. Her son must have refused to marry your mother . . .' He stopped, looking more bemused than ever. 'But he did marry her after the war . . . I wonder, now? Is it possible that he hadn't known about his twins? I wouldn't put it past the old vixen to have covered up all traces of her son's indiscretions ... and threatened your mother with some dire calamity if she let the cat out of the bag.'

Ruth brightened. 'It must have been something like that! I can't see any mother, however young and inexperienced, not telling the man she loved about their babies ... and he must have loved her, too, or else he wouldn't have married her when he came home from the war.'

Graham hit his right fist into his left palm. 'One payment stopped in 1933, that would have been when you started earning for yourself, but the other went on until 1938. Although Samuel was legally adopted, Marianne, or Andrew on his own initiative, must have paid for a better education for him, because he was a boy. Her name had been kept out of it, so that no one would ever know that she had any connection ...' He stopped again, frowning. 'Ruairidh would have been in either France or Belgium at the time of the births, and I wouldn't put it past his mother to have sent Melda away during the latter months of her pregnancy.'

'That old besom has a lot to answer for,' Ruth said bitterly.

His heart went out to this woman who had clearly had a hard life right from the time of her birth, and who was dressed in well-worn clothes which told of ongoing financial struggles. She had not let herself go, however. Her chestnut hair, bobbed quite short, was gleaming with cleanliness, her face had been lightly powdered or whatever women did to take the shine off their skin, and her lips were not nearly as garish as some he had seen, just a little touch of lipstick. Her face was a perfect oval, but there was a sadness in her dark eyes.

Graham became aware that she was waiting for him to say something else, and said the first thing that came into his head. 'Why did you want to get in touch with your mother, Mrs Laverton? Were you planning to ask her for –'

'I want nothing from any of them!' she burst out. 'I just want to know the truth about myself, Mr Dalgarno, to see what my parents look like and what kind of people they are, and why they allowed other people to bring me up. I'm not out for revenge for being abandoned, don't think that, but I *would* like to make them feel a wee bit guilty. Can you understand that?'

'Indeed I can.' Graham seemed to make up his mind about something now. 'I hope you are not in a hurry, because I have some good news for you, something that will prevent the dowager from thinking you are after *her* money.' Noticing her bemusement, he smiled benignly. 'You are in for a wonderful surprise, Mrs Laverton, but perhaps you would prefer me to wait until your brother can be with you?'

'You've made me curious, so you might as well tell me now.'

It did not take him long to tell her of the legacy from Andrew Rennie, but it took some time for her to take in the extent of the wealth she and her as yet unknown brother had inherited. And he could see that he would have to make her understand Andrew Rennie's motive; that would be the only way she would feel free to accept such a large windfall.

'But why would he leave anything to Samuel and me?' she asked for the third time. 'Maybe he'd been given the job of making sure we had decent food and clothes, but his obligation was over when we started working.'

'Andrew was a very kind-hearted man,' Graham said patiently, 'and I think he wanted to make up to you for . . . and I'm nearly sure he had loved Marianne Glendarril since he was a young man, which was why he did everything she asked of him, but what she did to you when you went to Castle Lyall must have made him see her as she really was – a wicked schemer. I can't pretend to fathom out what happened ten days ago. I do not like to think that she was responsible for his death, Mrs Laverton, yet I have the nastiest feeling that she was.'

'Oh, surely not, Mr Dalgarno! It was an accident! But I'd like to know why Mr Rennie left his money to my brother and me. He had never met us when he drew up his will.'

'He knew you would get nothing from your grandmother, and I expect he felt sorry for you, Mrs Laverton.'

'Call me Ruth, please,' she begged. 'I don't know who I am or what's happening to me, but whatever my last name was, is, or will be, I'll always be Ruth.'

'And you must call me Graham; this Mr and Mrs business is far too formal. Well, Ruth, I advise you to go home now and I will do what I can to make Lady Glendarril agree to see you. I shall also go through Andrew's papers again with a fine-tooth comb, and pray that I find the answer to your brother's whereabouts.'

After she had left, Graham leaned back with a satisfied sigh. He hadn't solved all the mystery, but he knew now how fairy godmothers felt. It wasn't the first time he had sprung an inheritance on an unsuspecting beneficiary, but it was usually a distant relative or someone who had worked for the deceased, and never on this scale. Andrew Rennie had been a bachelor all his life, had lived frugally and invested his savings wisely, and Graham had already learned, from some tentative enquiries he had made, that the sum involved would be well into six figures. Ruth and Samuel would receive an amount far in excess of anything their grandmother could have left them.

His next task was to plan the meeting. He admired Ruth Laverton. However poor she was, however much in need, she would never grovel for help to her new-found family. His opinion of Esmerelda Glendarril, on the other hand, had been badly dented. He had met her only occasionally

444

over the years and did not know her well, but on the day of Andrew's funeral she had given the impression of being a gentle, caring person – very similar to Ruth, in fact.

It would be interesting to arrange for all parties concerned to meet, he mused, and to watch their reactions, but it would not be ethical. For one thing, Esmerelda may not have told her husband about the twins, and had she the guts to tell him after all this time? If she did, would Ruairidh believe her - would he even want to believe her? It would be upsetting for him, galling, to learn that the girl he loved had concealed the existence of their love children from him for so many years. He would doubt that they were his, and imagine that she'd had other lovers while he had been away fighting for his country, which would turn him against Ruth and Samuel.

Recognizing that a large confrontation was out of the question, Graham decided to stick to his original plan and talk to Lady Glendarril alone first. The outcome of that would decide what his next move should be.

Chapter Thirty-two

Melda couldn't think why Graham Dalgarno wanted to see her, or why he had insisted that she came to him. He could say all he wanted to say in front of her husband, surely?

Joe Gilchrist, the chauffeur/handyman who had often taken Marianne to see her solicitor, drew the Bentley to a smooth halt at the steps up to his office. 'When do you want to be picked up, your Ladyship?' he asked. 'When old Lady Glendarril used to come here, she always told me to come back for her in an hour, but if you want longer . . . ?'

Despite her misgivings, Melda managed a smile. 'No, an hour's long enough – maybe too long,' she grimaced wryly 'Should I just wait outside, then?'

The tightness in her chest eased a little. She had a feeling that the coming meeting was to be somewhat uncomfortable and it was good to know she could make her escape at any time. 'That might be best.'

Waiting until he came round to open the car door for her – he would be insulted if she didn't – she glanced around in admiration at the raised garden laid out between the two rows of tall granite buildings, because Bon Accord Square belied its name, and was, in fact, a long rectangle. The grass looked as well kept as the lawns at Castle Lyall, and whoever had been given the job of laying out the flowering shrubs had a good eye for colour. Reading her thoughts, Gilchrist grinned as he helped her on to the pavement. 'Me and Lady Marianne always said this was one of the bonniest streets in the town. Will you manage now, or will I . . . ?'

'I'll manage, thanks.' Taking a deep breath, she went slowly up the outside steps without holding on to the handrail.

With her usual abhorrence of being late for any appointments, she took a quick look at her watch, and her heart sank. Not quite ten to twelve. Her mother-in-law would have said it was just as bad mannered to catch people on the hop by being early as it was to keep them waiting. When she reached the top step, however, she was glad that she wasn't late, because Graham Dalgarno himself opened the glass door for her. He must have been watching for her.

'Good morning, Lady Glendarril,' he smiled, taking her hand in a tight grip and shaking it vigorously.

'Good morning, Mr Dalgarno,' she replied, trying to discover from his expression whether he had good or bad news to impart.

Shepherding her up a carpeted flight of stairs, he ushered her into his private office and gestured to the high-backed armchair he had drawn in for her. 'You'll be wondering why I asked you here?'

'I've been a bit curious,' she admitted, his obvious unease making her more apprehensive than ever.

'This is very difficult . . . perhaps we should have coffee . . . No, I think something stronger is called for.'

She watched him crossing to a tall filing cabinet and taking out a gill of whisky. Back at his desk, he produced two glasses big enough to hold a generous dram, not the little tot she had expected. 'Oh, just a mouthful for me,' she protested, as the amber liquid gurgled out of the small bottle. 'I'm not a drinker.'

'You're going to need it,' he warned.

Deciding to leave the whisky until she did need it, if at all, she looked at him searchingly. 'Why did you bring me here? What is so secret that you can't tell me in front of Ruairidh?'

Graham fortified himself before saying, 'I wasn't sure if he knew.'

Her brows came down, yet her eyes remained clear. 'Knew what?'

'I may be wrong in doing this, but I thought he should know about your two children.'

Her whole face closed now. 'I am afraid you have made a mistake, Mr Dalgarno. My only daughter died some years ago.'

Seeking the nerve to carry on, he took another sip. 'It was not ... er ... it was Ruth and Samuel I meant.'

If he had hoped to see signs of shame or guilt, he would have been disappointed. Her eyes showed only perplexity. 'Ruth and Samuel? I don't understand.'

Bracing himself, Graham said, as calmly as he could, 'I have in my desk, Lady Glendarril, two birth certificates which name you as the mother.'

Her cheeks blanched but she did not look away. 'Oh, my God. How did you find out about that?' Before he could answer, she burst out, 'But I only had one baby, a boy who died hours after he was born!' The grief she had thought she had mastered for ever surfaced without warning, and she bent her head to hide her distress.

'I knew it!' Graham erupted, making her raise her streaming eyes. 'I knew your mother-in-law had told you that your babies were dead. It *was* her, wasn't it, and you never saw the bodies?'

She shook her head and lifted the glass of spirits to her lips. Its fiery content burned its way down her gullet and enabled her to accept what she realized he was telling her. 'They gave me something to knock me out, and when I came round, she said the baby had died and it was best all round. She pretended to be sorry, but before the birth, she'd forced me to agree to having it adopted ... and I never got to see him. Nobody told me I'd had twins. What did she do with them?'

'As far as I can make out,' Graham said gently, 'she asked Andrew Rennie to do the dirty work for her. I do not know the full story, but it seems your son was adopted, but your daughter was just fostered. When I first learned of the money which had been paid out over a period of years for maintenance, I gave Lady Marianne full credit for providing for them, but it had likely been Andrew's idea, not hers.'

Draining her glass, Melda said, her voice low and quivering, 'I can't believe there were twins and they're still alive, and you talk as if you know what had happened to them . . .'

He lifted the whisky bottle again and poured what was left into her glass. 'Drink it!' he ordered, as she gripped her lips to show she didn't want it. 'I do know what happened to them, in fact . . .' He hesitated, then said softly, 'I kept searching through all Andrew's papers looking for information about Samuel, and I could find nothing until I took out the newspaper which I thought was lining the bottom drawer. It was an *Edinburgh Evening Citizen* dated October 1943, and I was about to dispose of it when it dawned on me that it must have some significance for Andrew to have kept it. It had! A small announcement inside stated that Samuel Fernie, only son of John and Margaret Fernie of Clermiston, had been posted as missing.'

Her gasp of dismay made him shake his head ruefully. 'I'm sorry, your Ladyship, I should not have come out with it like that.'

'It's quite all right. It's better that I know –'

'No, no, he is still alive! I looked up the Edinburgh telephone directory to see if there were any Fernies listed in Clermiston – on the outskirts of the city – and struck lucky with my second call. Samuel, or Sam as they call him, had been taken prisoner at Salerno, was transferred to Stalag 77 in Germany when the Italians gave up, and repatriated after the war ended.'

'Oh, thank God he wasn't killed,' Melda said, in a small voice. 'I don't think I could have borne to hear of his death a second time. Does he still live in Edinburgh, or does he work somewhere else?'

'With the money provided for his further education, Sam had gone to university in order to get a degree in medicine, but the war started before he graduated. Being a red-blooded Bruce-Lyall, although he was not aware of it, he gave up his studies and joined the Army Medical Corps. After the war, what he had seen in the prison camps – the helplessness and hopelessness of the captured Allied servicemen – made him vow to become a preacher if God spared him, so when he came home he went back to university and eventually gained his MD. He is now touring the Army of Occupation in Berlin, but Mrs Fernie, his adoptive mother, promised to write to him straight away, so it should not be long until we hear from him.'

It crossed Melda's mind that, in view of the calling of her real and adoptive fathers, it was strange that her son should have been drawn towards both medicine and the ministry, but it would probably send her mother-in-law over the edge into the madness she had wrongly attributed to all men of the cloth. But that was a bridge to be crossed later . . .

'And now, Mr Dalgarno, what about . . . Ruth?'

'She has only recently learned that she was fostered, your Ladyship.'

'If she's angry at me for giving her up, you'll have to –'

'Andrew had told her what happened, and she's a very understanding person. I think . . . I know that you won't be disappointed in how she has turned out . . . and she is desperate to meet you.'

'As I am to meet her.'

'Good! Shall I take her to Castle Lyall tomorrow?'

The alarm which flooded her face made him say, 'No, I shall have to give you time to adjust, and I can see you are

450

still suffering from the shock I gave you. Get that Scotch down, it should help.' While she obeyed, grimacing at each sip, he wondered why she had suddenly changed her mind about an early meeting.

'It's not that I don't want to see Ruth,' Melda muttered, as if she knew what he was thinking, 'but I have to prepare someone first.'

'Does Lord Glendarril not know . . . ?'

'No, I'm sorry to say, he doesn't. His mother threatened to tell him I'd been going with soldiers from the camp if I ever said anything to him.'

'But surely, if he loved you, he'd have known they were his?'

'I was frightened to risk it. I was very young, and I couldn't stand up to her. To tell the truth, I was grateful to her at first for whisking me off before anybody in the glen noticed I'd been a bad girl. I wouldn't have been allowed to marry Ruairidh if it had come out we'd had . . .'

'Didn't you ever feel like telling him after the war, the second war, that is? It's not such a crime nowadays.'

'It's still a disgrace, even yet, but it's not telling Ruairidh I'm worried about, it's my father. He knows nothing about this, and he'll be very hurt that I didn't tell him.'

'And your mother?' Graham prompted.

'My mother died about three years ago – she didn't know, either – and Ruairidh managed to get Dad to give up the house they moved to when he retired and come to live with us. I wouldn't be surprised if my mother-in-law had told him the whole thing any of the times Ruairidh and I were in London. She has always liked to make trouble, and she was acting really strangely for days before we left.'

She took out her handkerchief and dabbed her eyes. 'I'm sorry to get upset like this, Mr Dalgarno. I loved Uncle Andrew as much as my husband did, but – you'll find this hard to believe – it's Marianne I feel sorry for. In spite of all she did to me, all the nasty things she said over the years, I couldn't help but admire her, because she stuck to her guns, no matter what. If she got something into her head, nothing would shift it.'

Melda decided not to tell the solicitor about Marianne's obsession about ministers, not yet. She would, one day, if only to help him to understand why her mother-in-law had not let her keep her first two children.

Gathering up her gloves and handbag, she said, 'I'd better go home now, but I'll let you know when to bring . . . Ruth to the castle.'

After shaking her hand, the solicitor saw her down to her car, and stood until it went round the corner into Bon Accord Street and out of sight.

Contrary to her usual habit of sitting in front with Gilchrist when they were going home, Melda sat in the back, unable to make any small talk, unable to think of anything other than the momentous news which Graham Dalgarno had sprung on her. If it hadn't been for her father, she would have been overjoyed at finding another daughter to replace Dorrie. Her death had sent Melda into the lowest trough of her entire life, when she had sobbed for days, and kept thinking that it was terrible that she'd given birth to two children and not one was left alive – she hadn't known then that she had actually given birth to three. She'd been too distraught to speak to her mother-in-law, in case she attacked the woman in her misery. Marianne, of course, had also been at a low ebb, with Hamish having died so recently.

And now? Was she to be the cause of *her* father's death? He was quite frail these days – he hadn't been properly well since her mother's fatal heart attack, and she suspected that he would never get over the most recent shock he'd had. Apparently he had been away for the weekend visiting a friend in Montrose, and had returned on the Sunday evening about seven. Not finding Marianne anywhere in the west wing, he had gone to the rose garden, where she often took a stroll on a Sunday afternoon or early evening, and had been appalled, when he rounded the wall, to see two bodies lying half on the path and half in the pond. That would have been enough to give him a heart attack without him hurrying to see if he could do anything. Fortunately, Marianne had been able to raise her head out of the water before she lost consciousness – so she told them later – and, apart from being unable to get up off the ground, had suffered only superficial injuries, and shock.

First making sure that there was nothing he could do for Andrew, Robert had managed to lift Marianne to a sitting position and then rushed to telephone Dr Addison, the man who had taken over when he himself retired. And when, Melda recalled, she and Ruairidh arrived back on the Monday morning, both old people were in bed. It was strange that, despite Marianne's usual indomitable spirit and Robert's extra years, he had been up and about again days before she even stopped weeping. She had obviously cared very deeply for Andrew Rennie and seemed to blame herself for his death.

On arriving at the castle now, Melda hurried up to her mother-in-law's bedroom, her heart turning over at the sight of her father sitting by the bedside with one of Marianne's hands clasped between both of his. How pale and drawn they both looked, she thought, their silver heads only inches apart, their sunken eyes gazing fondly at each other. It was so unusual – they were inclined to be rather hostile as a rule – that Melda took a quick step forward in the belief that the old woman was dying.

Both turned slowly towards her now. 'Marianne's been telling me about your twins,' her father said, his voice trembling. 'It's taken her some time to get me to believe what she did to you, and I still can't understand why you didn't come and tell me at the time.'

Feeling like the young girl she had been then, Melda stuttered, 'I was s-scared to t-tell you.'

'But your mother and I would have stood by you.'

A shaking hand crept out from under the counterpane now, coming to rest on top of the other three. 'Too late to discuss the rights and wrongs of it now,' Marianne muttered. 'Everything that happened at that time was down to me. It was all my fault, and you shouldn't blame Melda or Andrew or anybody else, Robert. Just be glad that the two poor infants were taken care of. Ruth, the one who came to see me, is quite pretty, a bit like Ruairidh but with auburn hair more like I used to have, and she said nothing about her sister.'

Melda opened her mouth to correct the error, then closed it without saying anything. She couldn't help the shaft of perverse pleasure that shot through her at the idea of the surprise Marianne would get when she found out that the other twin had been male . . . a male who would be heir to the title since his parents' marriage had made him legitimate.

A grandson of Duncan Peat, whose very name her mother-in-law still hated with the same intensity as of old! And above all, a minister himself!

But her satisfaction was short-lived. She had a momentous task ahead of her – to confess to Ruairidh what she had never had the courage to tell him before, just because she had been too afraid of what his mother might do. Well, it wasn't Marianne she was afraid of now – what had she to fear from a frail woman in her seventies? – it was Ruairidh's reaction. Waiting in the drawing room for his return from the mill, she felt so chilled that she switched on the small electric fire which was kept handy for those days when it wasn't cold enough for a coal fire. What would he say? Would he despise her for being such a coward? Could he possibly forgive her? Or would he be so angry at the deception that he would turn her out?

When she heard the low purr of the Bentley – Gilchrist

always drove him to and from the mill – her heart thudded, her whole body stiffened in preparation for the battle she believed would come. He entered the room, smiling as he always did.

'What have you been doing with yourself today?' he asked brightly. Her silence made his expression change. 'Is anything wrong, Melda? Has Mother been more difficult than normal, or have she and your father had another difference of opinion?'

How patient he is, she thought. Most men would have felt irritated when she didn't answer straight away, but how would he take what she was about to tell him?

'Come on, darling,' he urged, 'I can see something's upset you.'

'I was talking to Graham Dalgarno today.'

'Ah, I didn't know he was coming, otherwise I'd have been here. What did he want?'

She conveniently postponed answering the question. 'He didn't come here, he asked me to go to Bon Accord Square.'

'Something about Andrew's will?'

'In a way.' She could detect little signs of exasperation in his eyes now, and deemed it wise not to procrastinate any longer. 'Sit down, Ruairidh, I've something to tell you.'

'Has dear old Uncle Andrew left us a fortune?'

She knew the light-hearted remark was forced. She knew him inside out. 'It's nothing to do with Andrew ... well, it has in a way, but ...' She stopped, wringing her hands in her confusion. 'Oh, I'm making heavy weather of this. Please, I beg you, just listen, and don't interrupt.'

She told him everything, from the day they learned of Ranald's death to the day she left the Brightfield Maternity Home for Unmarried Mothers, and he interrupted only once, to ask, 'Was Rannie the father?' At her response, 'No, Ruairidh, I swear he wasn't!' he said quietly, 'I just wanted to be sure,' and leaned back in his seat again, his face inscrutable.

When she stopped, shivering a little, she muttered, 'If you want to say something, do it now and get it over with.'

'I need time to think.' He had been sitting for several minutes, head down, hands at his temples, when he gave an abrupt exclamation and stood up. 'I'm going to have this out with Mother . . . No, she's no mother of mine, is she?'

His voice was so harsh that Melda put out her hand to stop him. 'Please don't, Ruairidh dear. What's the point now, after all this time?'

'I feel like killing her! I wish she had died along with Andrew! And he was as bad as she was! How could they? Keeping something like that from me? It was cruel! Wicked!'

'I kept it from you, too,' she reminded him softly.

He drew a deep breath to calm his rattled nerves, then thumped down on his chair again. 'It was different with you, Melda. You were so young – newly sixteen weren't you? – and I don't blame you for knuckling under with her, but . . .' He stopped, shaking his head. 'What I do find difficult to forgive is you not telling me, not even after we were married . . . not in all these years.'

Melda had been hoping, praying that he had put all the blame on his mother, but it appeared that he hadn't. 'I told you what she said she'd do if I breathed a word of it.' Her voice was strained.

'But surely you knew I wouldn't have believed her? I loved you so much I'd have trusted you, whatever lies she spun about you.'

'Like you said, I was still very young . . . I didn't know what to do. And she kept her side of the bargain, so I couldn't break my promise.'

'She manipulated you, Melda! Can't you see that? You owed it to me to tell me!'

Having been on a knife edge since her talk with Graham Dalgarno, this accusation that she was as much to blame

456

as the other two participants in the deception was too much for her. Bursting into tears, she jumped to her feet and ran out, pounding up the stairs and flinging herself on their large bed. She had half expected him to follow her, to apologize, but when it became clear that she was being left severely alone, she told herself that he had nothing to apologize for. After all, she *was* in the wrong; she should have told him as soon as he came home from the war. If he'd known about the child, he might have wanted to find out if it really had died. It wouldn't have mattered if they'd had to run away to be married, for Ruairidh to give up all claim to the title and the mill.

Her laboured thoughts came to a halt. It certainly wouldn't have mattered to *her*, but she couldn't have allowed him to give up his birthright. She had done the only thing possible under the circumstances ... but no matter how strongly she assured herself of this, it did not ease the pain in her heart, nor take the edge off her anger at ... herself as much as his mother.

It was almost an hour later, when she had exhausted all her tears and was drifting off into a troubled sleep, that her husband came in and, thankfully, she got no time to try to make further excuses, because he swept her up in his arms and she could feel his own salt tears on her lips as he kissed her.

'I'm so sorry, my dearest darling.'

The murmured words were all she needed. She knew that she was forgiven. Perhaps they could discuss it more fully in the morning, when they were both calmer, but perhaps not. It might be best to let the matter rest until Graham Dalgarno brought Ruth to the castle. Ruth! Their daughter. And they would meet their son, Samuel, as soon as Graham could arrange it.

It was probably all for the best that they would be introduced to only one at a time.

Chapter Thirty-three

❧❀❧

As the Ford Zephyr Zodiac sped down the main road south from Aberdeen, Graham Dalgarno could sense that an element of reluctance had crept in to Ruth's eagerness, probably a fear of rejection despite his assurances that Melda Glendarril was just as anxious to meet her as Ruth was to meet her mother.

His own mind, however, was not on the business in hand at all. It had been on Ruth Laverton since she had walked into his office three weeks ago, though it felt like a lifetime, and with her sitting so close to him, his blood was pounding, his mouth was dry. There was no denying his feelings for her, but how could he ask her to marry him? Her share of Andrew Rennie's estate would make her a wealthy woman, and she was bound to suspect him of being a fortune-hunter. After all, what had he to offer her?

His thoughts were thrust aside as he swung round a blind corner under a railway bridge and only just missed a Post Office van coming from the opposite direction. Afraid to take his attention off the road again, he didn't look at Ruth as he murmured, 'Sorry about that. I'm a bit preoccupied.'

'Me, too,' she smiled. 'I'd have felt better if my brother could have been here to support me.'

A third party was the last thing he'd have wanted, but he could understand how she felt. 'Maybe I should have put the visit off until he managed to get here, but I got such a shock when I learned who was on the phone that it never crossed my mind to postpone it. In any case, one long-lost relative at a time may be enough for your new family to cope with.'

'I'm so nervous, though. What if the old lady told them not to . . . ? What if they don't like me?'

'How could anyone not like you?' The astonished exclamation was out before he could stop it. 'I mean . . . well, you know what I mean.'

'Flatterer,' she grinned.

He was glad that she felt easy enough with him to say that. He had asked her to his office several times to discuss various points – mostly those needing no further discussion – and he had taken her out to lunch once, so they did know each other a little better now, but he'd have to be very careful. One false move and he might ruin any chance he had of courting her.

Marianne nodded knowingly at the faint click of a door closing. 'That's them going down now, Robert. We'd better start moving. They're to be here about three.'

What he had been trying to tell her for days was preying on his mind like a canker eating at him, and he could put it off no longer. She had to be told before going downstairs. 'Marianne,' he began tentatively, 'I have something to say.'

'Oh, for any sake, man! Not now!'

'It's crucially important. I should have told you long ago, but –'

'It can wait another hour or two, then! I don't want to miss anything.'

Giving up, Robert got to his feet and helped her to hers. 'Will you need your walking stick?'

'Not today. It would put me at a disadvantage.'

He could see her point, but hoped that she wouldn't fall or trip on a loose rug. She had been relying on Hamish's silver-topped cane since Andrew Rennie's death, which had had a quite drastic effect on her, so now he placed his hand under her elbow. 'I hope you are not planning anything,

Marianne,' he observed, closing the door. 'Remember, we two will be there purely as spectators.' He would have liked to issue a sterner warning, but it would have made her angry, and an angry Marianne was something to be avoided at all costs.

He couldn't help but admire her as she walked stiffly at his side. Her carriage was as erect as ever although her knees were affected by arthritis, and with his spine curving with osteoporosis, she was taller now than he. Both their heads were thatched with silver – his was natural, as he'd only been about forty when the black had started disappearing – whereas her once-coppery hair had faded to a horrible yellowish-grey and needed the enhancement of a colour rinse to make it silver with a hint of blue. She was still a good-looking woman, though. Her unblemished skin was practically free of wrinkles, while his was like corrugated cardboard.

Their descent of the stairs was slow, almost majestic, but he thought he had better put her in a good humour. 'You're going like a two-year-old,' he teased.

His little ploy did not work. 'This is no time to be joking,' she reprimanded him. 'God alone knows what Melda and Ruairidh will promise her. When I saw her, she struck me as being after something – and I must be there to stop it getting out of hand.'

With something of a jolt, it dawned on him that she had not been told of the boy twin, and he bitterly regretted not forcing her to listen to him before they came down. His face, therefore, as he steered her into the drawing room, was enough to warn his daughter of possible ructions.

Nothing was said for the next five minutes, each person in the room dreading the meeting which was almost upon them, and none more so than Robert Mowatt, his old secret lying heavily on his conscience. To take his mind off it, he studied Melda, who, at fifty-three could have passed for forty even under the closest scrutiny. Her dark hair needed no artificial colouring nor permanent waving. Then she turned her head towards him, and her brown eyes were so apprehensive that he gave her what he hoped was a reassuring smile and transferred his attention to her husband.

Though he was only two years older than Melda, Ruairidh's blond hair had appeared to turn white almost overnight. Whatever, it didn't detract from his appearance. In fact, the slicked-back wavy hair and the neat moustache, combined with his normally upright stance, would suggest to a stranger that he was a military man. It would have amused him to be told this, of course, because it was many a long year since he had come out of the Fusiliers.

The sound of a car drawing up outside made Melda jump up and make for the door. 'That's them!' she exclaimed unnecessarily, as Ruairidh followed her out.

Marianne looked at Robert in appeal, obviously not wanting to ask for help, but he shook his head. 'No, my dear, as I said before, we are spectators today. We will sit and watch, and we will not interfere!' He had to suppress a smile at her offended expression as she cast her eyes to heaven and snapped her mouth shut.

'Are you sure I look OK?' Ruth asked as the car glided to a standstill. 'I couldn't afford anything new to wear.'

Graham groaned at that. 'Oh, Ruth, I never thought! Why didn't you say something? I could have given you an advance on your inheritance.'

'I don't want any of Mr Rennie's money, nor any of the Bruce-Lyall money, either.'

'That's exactly what your brother said, too. How strange.'

'What's strange is that I *have* a brother, and these people will have to take me as I am.'

Longing to tell her that he would love to take her as she was, he had to be content with saying, 'They won't care what you're wearing.' He got out and came round to open

461

the door at her side. 'Well, Ruth, this is it! Good luck!'

The heavy door was opened before they reached it, and Melda ran down the steps, her colour heightened in the same way as Ruth's. 'Marianne was right!' she exclaimed, throwing her arms round her daughter. 'You *are* like your father.' Pulling Ruth inside she gave her a tight squeeze before passing her on to Ruairidh, who, after a moment's hesitation, also embraced her and then shook hands with Graham.

'Is Samuel not with you?' Melda asked Ruth, as she linked arms with her.

'He told Graham on the phone it'd be over a week before they could get a replacement for him.'

'Oh well, it's probably better that he's not here today. I haven't told your grandmother about him yet, so this gives me a bit more time to prepare her.'

Ruth felt a slight chill wash over her. The old lady was apparently even more of a dragon than she had seemed, but she made no comment on it.

'Come and meet my father, your grandfather,' Melda said, pulling her on. 'You met Ruairidh's mother before, of course. I hope you excused her rudeness to you then, but she hadn't long lost her dearest friend. Andrew Rennie's death hit her very hard. She shouldn't have been left on her own that day, but . . . there, it happened, and that's that. Here we are, and my father's dying to meet you.' Melda opened the drawing-room door and ushered her inside.

Ruth was taken by surprise at the bear hug Robert Mowatt gave her, and he made her sit next to him when the maid-of-all-work pushed in a trolley laid out for after-noon tea. 'This is some day!' he enthused, laying two thin slices of fruit loaf on his plate, then caught Marianne's reproving eye and said, apologetically, 'You met your grandmother before, of course.'

Marianne's smile was clearly forced, and the apology,

such as it was, just as evidently made because it was expected of her. 'I treated you rather badly last time you were here.'

'It's all right. I understand how you must have felt.'

'Your twin sister is not with you?'

Quite taken aback by such an unexpected question, Ruth stammered, 'My . . . my twi-twin's name is Samuel.' Then, remembering that the old lady hadn't been told about him, she said timidly, 'I don't have a sister . . . well, I thought I had, but now I've found out Gladys isn't really my sister.'

'I was right all along, you see, Mother-in-law.' Melda couldn't resist saying it. 'I did have a boy. He was the first of the two babies, though I didn't know I'd had two.' Her face darkened suddenly. 'But *you* knew there were two, and you must have known they were still alive.'

Marianne did not appear in the least abashed. 'I knew there were two, but I thought they were both girls, and I'd no idea what happened to them. I left all that to Andrew.'

In an effort to curb her arrogance, Ruairidh said, 'The less you say the better, Mother. I have only recently learned what you did, and if it wasn't that you're over seventy, I'd have thrown you out when Melda told me your actions, and the pain you caused her.'

Every vestige of colour left her face, and Robert stood up in alarm. 'Shall I take you upstairs, Marianne?'

'Leave her there,' Ruairidh ordered harshly. 'I want her to hear everything that's said. Maybe then she'll realize the extent of the damage she caused, to Ruth as well as Melda, and possibly also to . . . Samuel.'

Uncertain of what to do, Robert latched on to the last word, and gave Ruairidh a playful slap on the back. 'Just think, though. You have a son and heir at last, Ruairidh. Isn't that good news?'

'No! No!' Marianne's sharp cry startled them. 'Duncan Peat's grandson can *never* be Lord Glendarril! For one thing, he is not legitimate!'

Robert cleared his throat nervously. 'I thought you would realize, Marianne. He was born illegitimate, certainly, but —'

Graham Dalgarno broke his long silence now. 'By law, the parents' subsequent marriage legitimates any previous issue.'

There was a long, brooding pause before Marianne muttered, 'I can't remember Andrew ever telling me that, but maybe he did. Anyway, I take it that there is nothing I can do about it?'

Ignoring this, Robert addressed his next remark to Ruth. 'As a matter of interest, my dear, what type of work is your brother engaged in? Has he a trade, or a profession?'

She related what the solicitor had told her about Samuel's early career, then dropped her innocent bombshell. 'He took up the ministry after the war, and he's in Germany now.'

There was shock on all three Bruce-Lyall faces, but Marianne's was greatest. She opened and closed her mouth as if gasping for air, then let out a sudden screech of desperation, which went on and on until Robert leaped across and gave her a stinging slap on the cheek. The noise stopped instantly, and Graham and Ruth looked at each other in astonishment, while Melda and Ruairidh exchanged apprehensive glances, none of them knowing what to say or do.

They were thankful when Robert turned round and began to speak. 'I had better tell you something, all of you. I originally intended to make my confession only to Marianne, but she wouldn't listen, and present circumstances demand that I make a clean breast of it here and now.'

All eyes were on him as he returned purposefully to his seat, looked at Marianne and said, quite calmly, 'I hope you can forgive me, my dear. I should have told you this long ago, but I could not say anything as long as Flora was alive. I couldn't bear to hurt her in any way. Yes, I am well aware that it is three years since she died, but I mistakenly thought that you had forgotten your silly nonsense about Duncan Peat and all ministers, and I didn't want to stir it up again.'

She held her hand up weakly. 'Nothing you can say will make me change my mind about him.'

'I'm not even going to try. Just cast your mind back fifty-odd years and listen ... and don't say another word until I've finished.'

He spoke now as if he were telling a story, a story about a young wife who was longing for a child but whose doctor husband could not prevent her losing the three she managed to conceive; of another young woman married to a dour minister whose quick temper made him ill-treat her at the slightest provocation, and who made her douche every time he used her because he did not want children. Furthermore, he had become impotent over several months as a result of prostate trouble, which was why he knew that he was not the father of his wife's child.

'Grace came to me so often for treatment for bruises and cuts that I felt deeply sorry for her,' he went on. 'Unfortunately, as you are no doubt aware, pity is but a small step from love, and I began to call on her when I knew Duncan was out. I despised myself for being unfaithful to my dear Flora and tried to be extra loving to her, so I was mortified when ... well, I'm sure you can guess – I impregnated both of them.'

Gasping, Marianne burst out, 'Oh, Robert! I never dreamed! You should have told me!'

'I was deeply ashamed, and for Flora's sake, I couldn't admit it, not even to you,'

'But good God, Robert, it was me you should have told. You know what happened because I got hold of the wrong end of the stick. It's because of you Melda had to give up her twins.'

'You covered that up too well. I didn't know she was

465

pregnant. If I had, I'd have told you everything, I swear!'

'But you didn't even tell *her*! Not even after she was married.'

He bowed his head in abasement, then, deciding that he had to explain further, he went on, 'She looked on me as her father, and she got far more love from me than she would ever have got from Peat. I didn't want to turn her against me . . .'

The others in the room had listened to his story unfolding like a stage drama, but now Melda said, a little sadly, 'I wouldn't have turned against you; I haven't, not even now. In fact, I admire you for shielding . . . your wife. I loved her, but I didn't realize what a wonderful woman she was, taking in her husband's child by another woman and treating her like her own.'

'She *was* a wonderful woman, Melda.'

Marianne tutted loudly. 'Haven't you forgotten something, Robert? You knew how I felt all those years, yet you let me go on believing that man was her father.'

'I *did* try to give you a clue that he wasn't,' the old doctor defended himself.

'You did?' She looked puzzled for a moment, then said, 'Ah, yes, I remember. You tried to make me think it was that tinker.'

'Duncan thought it was him.'

'*I* never thought it was. I couldn't imagine Grace having anything to do with a tinker. But I *can* see her taking up with a doctor.'

The sneer on her face infuriated him. 'It wasn't like that, Marianne! You make it sound so sordid, when we truly loved each other. She, too, was a wonderful woman, putting up with that man for so long, and you have no idea how much I despised myself for what happened.'

Ruairidh had been far too astonished at his father-in-law's confession to take any part in what transpired, but he suddenly realized that he had to stop it. 'Robert,' he began quietly, 'I think we should let the matter rest there. I am glad you've told us, because it will save Mother making any scenes when Samuel comes, but I must make it quite clear that I consider you equally to blame for the heartache that was caused. And now, the subject is dead and buried and will not be resurrected again by anyone.'

He smiled at Ruth now. 'I don't know what you must think of us, my dear, but I would very much like to hear a little about your life.'

She told them that she had started work as an office girl at fourteen, rising to bookkeeper typist before being called up to the ATS when she was twenty-one. It was while serving as a clerk that she had met Mark Laverton, a young corporal in the RAOC, who later became her husband.

'We married in 1941 and we only had six years together,' she said, her eyes misting, 'though I did have his son. After Mark was killed in a road accident in France, my mother . . .' She paused in confusion. '. . . the woman who fostered me . . .'

'Please keep thinking of her as your mother,' Melda said quickly. 'She brought you up and cared for you . . . and I'm very grateful to her.'

'Well, she suggested I give up my house and move in with her – Dad had died a year before. It was a good arrangement, because I was able to take a job, and the extra money helped us to live quite comfortably. Then Mum fell ill, multiple sclerosis, and it developed so quickly that I'd to stop work to look after her. That was when things got tough. We only had two widows' pensions coming in, ten shillings each, and that had to cover everything, and for about four months before she died, she needed attention twenty-four hours a day . . . and it was very tiring. I don't know if I could have gone on like that for much longer.'

Graham Dalgarno had been marvelling at how well Ruth had stood up to the hardship of being left a widow with a small son, so he was pleased when Ruairidh murmured sympathetically, 'So you've had quite a hard life?'

'Not as bad as some, I suppose. It was a funny thing though, when I think about it. Mum fostered me because she hadn't had a child of her own, and she had Gladys thirteen months later.'

'That happens,' Robert said. 'If a woman has been trying unsuccessfully for a child, it is often her anxiety about it that prevents conception. When that anxiety is removed, as in your mother's case when she decided to foster you, nature takes its course.'

Something made Melda ask, 'What's your son's name, Ruth?'

'Colin. He's nearly ten.'

Ruairidh clapped his hands in glee. 'We have a grandson, Melda!'

Marianne, who had been sitting rather chastened since her son's homily, cut through his delight. 'I hope you do not expect any money from us? Tell her, Ruairidh.'

He looked embarrassed. 'What Mother means, Ruth, is that the mill was doing extremely well until the war ended. We'd been supplying uniforms to the army and air force, you see, and then . . . phutt! Nothing! And things kept on going downhill.'

'There wasn't the money going about,' Melda reminded him. 'People couldn't afford to buy clothes even after they stopped needing coupons for them, and, to be honest, after our daughter was killed, we both let things slide for a while. We're in pretty bad straits at the moment.'

It had taken Ruth several moments to get over Marianne's attack, but now she looked at the solicitor with her eyebrows raised. 'Graham, could I possibly . . . ?'

He grasped her meaning at once. 'It's entirely up to you, Ruth.'

She spoke now directly to Ruairidh. 'Apparently, Mr Rennie left most of his fortune to my brother and me –'

Marianne heard only one word. 'Fortune?' she muttered feebly.

It was Graham who leaped to his feet and scooped her frail body up in his arms. 'Show me the way to her room,' he said briskly, standing aside to let Robert go first.

Once Marianne was laid on her bed, the old doctor took a bottle of smelling salts from her dressing table and wafted it under her nose until she came round, then he ordered his daughter, who had followed them upstairs, and the solicitor to go. 'You know, Marianne,' he chided, when they were alone, 'you are the most stubborn woman I have ever come across. If you'd just sat quietly and listened like I told you, instead of interfering...' He wagged a reproachful finger at her. 'It's not your business who Andrew Rennie left his money to.'

'You don't understand, Robert,' she whispered. 'It's the irony of it. He always loved me, you know, and I didn't marry him because I thought he would never be rich. I wanted a husband with lots of money. I wanted a standing in society ... but ...' She shrugged woefully.

'It was your own fault you got nowhere in society. I remember Flora saying you told her you weren't going to mix with such a bunch of snobs.'

'Yes,' she agreed wistfully, 'that was my own fault, but I'd never have felt easy with them.'

'Still, you had years and years of being Queen of the Glen. Every man, woman and child looked up to you, and you enjoyed every minute of their adulation, didn't you?'

'Of course I enjoyed it, but that was years ago. I'm speaking about now. What have I got? Nothing! No money, a son and a daughter-in-law who'll probably never forgive me for keeping their children from them –'

'Marianne! They don't hold anything against you ... not now.'

'Ruth said Andrew left them a fortune. If I'd married him, I'd have been rich for a lot longer than I was. Of

469

course, if Melda hadn't let the mill run down ... Oh, I shouldn't blame her, should I? I know what it was like to lose a grown-up child.' She stopped, looking stricken as a new thought occurred to her. 'I took advantage of Andrew. I realize that now. I played on his love and expected him to do all sorts of things for me, be there when I needed comforting, and ... at the end ... I killed him.'

'You mustn't blame yourself for that. It was an accident!'

'It felt like I was to blame.' She looked up into his concerned face, her eyes pleading for understanding. 'Fate has played a dirty trick on me, Robert. After all my dreams of wealth and power, I've finished up a penniless, lonely old woman.'

'Stop feeling sorry for yourself! How can you be lonely with so many people around you?'

They were interrupted by a soft tap on the door, and Ruairidh held it open to allow Melda, Ruth and Graham to go in. 'We came to see how you were, Mother, and I'd say, by the look of you, you've recovered enough to hear what we have to tell you. First of all, in spite of all I could do to persuade her against it, Ruth is determined to sign her entire inheritance over to us as soon as it can be arranged. And that's not all, but I'll let Graham tell you the rest.'

The solicitor stepped closer to the bed. 'When I talked to Samuel on the telephone, Lady Glendarril, he asked if the money had originally been left to anyone else, and when I told him that before he and Ruth were born, it had been left to you, and that your close relationship with Andrew had continued until the day he died, Samuel asked me to draw up documents for the transfer of his share to you personally.'

'But I don't need his money,' she muttered. 'Not at my age.'

Robert, worried by the deep red spots which had appeared in her ashen cheeks, took hold of her trembling hand, ostensibly to steady her but actually to feel her pulse, which he was relieved to find, was only fractionally fast. 'You had better accept it,' he advised. 'You'll have the money you always wanted and the power to save the Castle Lyall from falling into other hands.'

'The power,' she repeated faintly. 'The power and the glory, for ever and ever, Amen.'

Looking wryly at Ruairidh, Robert said quietly, 'You had better go, all of you. This has been too much for her – she was a bit overwrought to begin with. I'll stay with her for a while, to make sure she's all right.'

Marianne looked at him pathetically when the door closed behind them. 'I was a very wicked woman at one time, Robert, but I was punished for it. First of all, I lost my darling Ranald, then my beloved Hamish, then dear Dorrie. Could it be that God is relenting now? Is He giving me a chance to redeem myself?'

'It seems that way,' he murmured cautiously.

'I'm going to plough it all into the estate. I'll make sure all the debts are paid. I'm going to get back on my feet again, and take a proper interest in what's going on.'

'That's the spirit! And don't forget, there *is* a Bruce-Lyall heir, after all.'

'And Ruth's Colin is a spare,' she smiled, 'like Hector insisted on. "An heir and a spare", that's what he used to say.' She fell silent for a moment, then said, 'I just hope Andrew's clerk doesn't talk them out of what they want to do with the money.'

Robert's drawn-out sigh told of exasperation. 'Graham Dalgarno isn't a clerk, he's the senior partner now, and he wouldn't have told you if he wasn't happy about it. For goodness' sake, woman, stop wallowing in self-pity and give a man a chance to be happy for you.'

'I'm sorry, Robert. I know I'm up and down and I'm being unreasonable. I don't know how you've managed to put up with me for so long.'

471

'Neither do I.' But his eyes were twinkling.

Downstairs, Melda was weeping softly but joyfully in her husband's arms. 'I can't believe it. It's like a fairy tale. We've got two children, the mill will soon be back on its feet, and –'

'God's in His heaven and all's right with the world,' he quoted, grinning. 'Like all fairy tales, it has a happy ending.'

'A truly happy ending,' she agreed. 'Ruth's nice, isn't she? I wish she would keep something for herself, though, to buy some new clothes. Did you notice the darns on the elbows of her cardigan? And her shoes were all down at the heels.'

Ruairidh burst out laughing. 'Trust you to see that. With all that went on here today, it amazes me that you had time to notice.'

'Yes, it's been quite an afternoon. I feel absolutely drained.'

'I do, too, so we should leave the analysing, the guessing and the planning until tomorrow, and take it easy for the rest of today. Not another word!' He laid his finger on her mouth to stop what she was about to say. 'I told Bessie we wouldn't need her after we'd had afternoon tea, so what about just going to bed? We can come down later for something to eat if we feel hungry.'

'Ruairidh Bruce-Lyall! What would Mother and Father say?' Melda gave a little snigger. 'That sounds as if they were a married couple, but you know what I mean. She'd be shocked.'

'So let her be shocked.'

'Are you all right, Ruth?'

'Yes, Graham, I'm fine. It's just that there's been so much to take in, I don't know how I feel about it yet. Do you think I'm daft to give up my inheritance?'

His heart almost stopped at the opportunity she was presenting to him. Could he? Should he? Taking a deep breath, he said, 'How can I when it has given me the courage to ... This is probably the worst place I could have chosen to ... Oh God, Ruth, I'm trying to ask you to marry me.'

He hadn't dared to look at her, and held his breath waiting for an answer which didn't come. 'I'm sorry,' he said flatly, after a few seconds, 'I shouldn't have placed you in such an awkward position. I quite understand –'

'No, you don't,' she replied gently. 'You took me by surprise, but I think I'm trying to say yes.'

'You are? I can't believe it!' Coming to an open gate into a field, he drew off the road and took her in his arms. 'You'll only be a Bruce-Lyall for a very short time in that case; just till I arrange the wedding. Won't you be sorry about that?'

Ruth cocked her head to one side to consider, then laughed, 'Ruth Bruce-Lyall's a bit of a tongue-twister, isn't it? Ruth Dalgarno's much easier, wouldn't you say?'

But nothing more was said, or needed to be said, for some considerable time.

ALWYN HAMILTON

was born in Toronto and spent her early years bouncing between Europe and Canada until her parents settled in France. After attending school in France, Alwyn went to Cambridge University to study History of Art at King's College. On graduating she returned to France and worked in a bookshop, where she rediscovered YA. She then moved to London where she now lives and put her degree to use working for an auction house. She is now a full-time writer and *Rebel of the Sands* was her first novel.

TRAITOR
TO THE
THRONE

✦ ALWYN ✦
HAMILTON

FABER & FABER

First published by Viking Penguin USA in 2017
First published in the UK in 2017
by Faber and Faber Limited
Bloomsbury House, 74–77 Great Russell Street,
London WC1B 3DA

Typeset in Plantin by M Rules
Printed and bound by CPI Group (UK) Ltd, Croydon, CR0 4YY

The right of Alwyn Hamilton to be identified as author
of this work has been asserted in accordance with Section 77
of the Copyright, Designs and Patents Act 1988

A CIP record for this book
is available from the British Library

ISBN 978-0-571-32541-2

For Rachel Rose Smith,
who's always got my back.

Character List

The Rebellion

Amani – Sharpshooter, Demdji marked by blue eyes, able to control desert sand, also goes by the moniker of the Blue Eyed Bandit.

Prince Ahmed Al-Oman Bin Izman – The Rebel Prince, leader of the Rebellion.

Jin – Prince of Miraji, brother of Ahmed, full name Ajinahd Al-Oman Bin Izman.

Shazad Al-Hamad – Daughter of a Mirajin general, among the original members of the rebellion, well trained fighter, strategist.

Delila – Demdji marked by purple hair, able to cast illusions out of light in the air. Ahmed's sister by blood, Jin's sister by adoption.

Hala – Demdji marked by golden skin, able to twist people's minds into hallucinations. Imin's sibling.

Imin – Demdji marked by golden eyes, able to shapeshift into any human form. Hala's sibling.

Izz and Maz – Twin Demdji, marked by blue skin and blue hair respectively, able to shapeshift into any animal form.

Bahi [Deceased] – Childhood friend of Shazad, disgraced Holy Man, killed by Noorsham.

Izman

Sultan Oman – Ruler of Miraji, Ahmed and Jin's father.

Prince Kadir – The Sultan's eldest son, Sultim, heir to the throne of Miraji.

Prince Naguib [Deceased] – One of the Sultan's sons, army commander, killed by the rebels in the battle of Fahali.

Lien [Deceased] – Xichian woman, wife of the Sultan. Jin's mother by blood, Ahmed and Delila's mother by adoption. Died of an illness.

Nadira [Deceased] – Ahmed and Delila's mother by blood. Killed by the Sultan for bearing a child to a Djinni.

The Last County

Tamid – Amani's best friend, Holy Father in training, walks with a limp due to a deformity at birth. Presumed dead.

Farrah – Amani's aunt, eldest sister to her mother.

Asid – Farrah's husband, a horse trader in Dustwalk.

Sayyida – Amani's aunt, middle sister, left Dustwalk before Amani was born to find her fortune in Izman.

Zahia [Deceased] – Amani's mother, hanged for the murder of her husband.

Hiza [Deceased] – Amani's mother's husband. Not Amani's father by blood. Killed by his wife.

Shira – Amani's cousin, Farrah's only daughter. Whereabouts unknown.

Fazim – Shira's lover.

Noorsham – Demdji marked by blue eyes, able to produce Djinni fire that can annihilate a whole city. Born in the mining town of Sazi. Whereabouts unknown.

Myths & Legends

First Beings – Immortal beings made by God, including Djinn, Buraqi and Rocs.

The Destroyer of Worlds – A being from the centre of the earth who came to the surface of the world to bring death and darkness. Defeated by humanity.

Ghouls – The Servants of the Destroyer of Worlds, includes Nightmares, Skinwalkers, and others.

The First Hero – The first mortal created by the Djinn to face the Destroyer of Worlds. Made out of sand and water and air and brought to life with Djinni fire. Also known as the First Mortal.

Princess Hawa – Legendary princess who sang the sun into the sky.

The Hero Attallah – Lover of Princess Hawa.

Chapter 1

The Foreign Prince

Once, in the desert kingdom of Miraji, there was a young prince who wanted his father's throne. He had no claim to it but the belief that his father was a weak ruler and that he would be stronger. And so he took the throne by force. In a single night of bloodshed the Sultan and the prince's brothers fell to the young prince's sword and the foreign army he led. When dawn came he was no longer a prince. He was the Sultan.

The young Sultan was known to take wives into his harem the same way he had his country: by force.

In the first year of his rule, two such wives gave birth to sons under the same stars. One wife was a girl born in the sands. Her son belonged to the desert. The other wife was a girl born across the water, in a kingdom called Xicha, and raised on the deck of a ship. Her son did not belong.

But the sons grew as brothers nonetheless, their mothers shielding them from the things the palace walls could not. And for a time, in the Sultan's harem, things were well.

Until the first wife gave birth again, but this time to a child that was not her husband's – a Djinni's daughter, with unnatural hair and unnatural fire in her blood. For her crime in betraying him, the Sultan turned his anger on his wife. She died under the force of his blows.

Such was his rage, the Sultan never noticed the second wife, who fled with their two sons and the Djinni's daughter, escaping back across the sea to the kingdom of Xicha, where she had been stolen from. There, her son, the Foreign Prince, could pretend that he belonged. The Desert Prince could not pretend; he was as foreign in this land as his brother had been in their father's. But neither prince was destined to stay long. Soon, both left Xicha for the open seas instead.

And for a time, on ships going anywhere and coming from nowhere, things were well for the brothers. They drifted from one foreign shore to another, belonging in each place equally.

Until one day, across the bow of the ship, Miraji appeared again.

The Desert Prince saw his country and remembered where he really belonged. On that familiar shore he left the ship and his brother. Though the Desert Prince asked his brother to join him, the Foreign Prince would not. His father's lands looked empty and barren to him and he could not understand what hold they had over his brother. And so they parted ways. The Foreign Prince stayed on the sea for a time, raging silently that his brother had chosen the desert over the sea.

Finally the day came when the Foreign Prince could no longer be separated from his brother. When he returned to the desert of Miraji, he found that his brother had set it on fire with rebellion. The Desert Prince talked of great things, of great ideas, of equality and of prosperity. He was surrounded by new brothers and sisters who loved the desert as he did. He was now known as the Rebel Prince. But still he welcomed the man who had been his brother his whole life with open arms.

And for a time things were well in the Rebellion.

Until there was a girl. A girl called the Blue-Eyed Bandit, who had been made in the sands and sharpened by the desert and who burned with all of its fire. And for the first time the Foreign Prince understood what it was that his brother loved in this desert.

The Foreign Prince and the Blue-Eyed Bandit

crossed the sands together, all the way to a great battle in the city of Fahali, where the Sultan's foreign allies had rooted themselves.

In that battle of Fahali the rebels won their first great victory. They defended the desert against the Sultan who would have burned it alive. They freed the Demdji, another Djinni's child, whom the Sultan would have turned into a weapon against his will. They killed the young commander, their brother who would have shed blood until he could win praise from his father, the Sultan. They ruptured the Sultan's alliance with the foreigners who had been punishing the desert for decades. And the rebels claimed part of the desert for themselves.

The story of the battle of Fahali spread quickly. And with it spread news that the desert might be a prize for the taking again. For the desert of Miraji was the only place where the old magic and the new machines were able to exist together. The only country that could spit out guns quickly enough to arm men to fight in the great war raging between the nations of the north.

New eyes from foreign shores turned to Miraji, hungry ones. More foreign armies descended on the desert, coming from all sides, each trying to claim a new alliance, or the country itself. And while enemies from outside gnawed at the Sultan's borders and kept his army occupied, the rebels seized city after city from the inside, knocking them out of the Sultan's hands and rallying the people to their side.

And for a time things were well for the Rebellion, for the Blue-Eyed Bandit, and for the Foreign Prince.

Until the balance started to shift against the Rebel Prince. Two dozen rebels were lost in a trap set for them in the sands, where they were surrounded and outgunned. A city rose up against the Sultan, crying out the Rebel Prince's name in the night. But those who had saw the next dawn with the blank eyes of the dead. And the Blue-Eyed Bandit fell to a bullet in a battle in the mountains, gravely wounded and only just clinging to life. There, for the first time since the threads of their stories had become tangled, the Blue-Eyed Bandit's and the Foreign Prince's paths split.

While the Blue-Eyed Bandit clung to her life, the Foreign Prince was sent to the eastern border of the desert. There, an army from Xicha was camped. The Foreign Prince stole a uniform and walked into the Xichian camp as if he belonged. It was easy there, where he did not look foreign any more. He stood with them as they battled the Sultan's forces, spying in secret for the Rebel Prince.

And for a time things were well, hiding among the foreign army.

Until the missive came from the enemy camp, its bearer wearing the Sultan's gold and white and holding up a flag of peace.

The Foreign Prince would have killed for news of what came in that missive for his own side, but there was no need. It was known that he spoke the desert language. He was summoned into the Xichian general's tent to translate between the Sultan's envoy and the Xichian, neither of them knowing he was an enemy of them both. As he translated he learned that the Sultan was calling for a ceasefire. He was tired of bloodshed, the message said. He was ready to negotiate. The Foreign Prince learned that the ruler of Miraji was summoning all the foreign rulers to him to talk of a new alliance. The Sultan asked for any king or queen or emperor or prince who would lay claim to his desert to come to his palace to make their case.

The missive went to the Xichian emperor the next morning. And the guns stopped. The ceasefire had started. Next would come negotiations. Then peace between the Sultan and the invaders. And without the need to mind his shores, the desert ruler's eyes would turn inward again.

The Foreign Prince understood it was time to return to his brother. Their rebellion was about to turn into a war.

Chapter 2

I'd always liked this shirt. It was a shame about all
the blood.

Most of it wasn't mine, at least. The shirt wasn't
mine, either, for that matter – I'd borrowed it from
Shazad and never bothered to give it back. Well, she
probably wouldn't want it now.

'Stop!'

I was jerked to a halt. My hands were tied, and the
rope chafed painfully along the raw skin of my wrists. I
hissed a curse under my breath as I tilted my head back,
finally looking up from my dusty boots to lock eyes with
the glare of the desert sun.

The walls of Saramotai cast a mighty long shadow
in the last of the light.

These walls were legendary. They had stood
indifferent to one of the greatest battles of the First
War, between the hero Attallah and the Destroyer of

Worlds. They were so ancient they looked like they'd been built out of the bones of the desert itself. But the words slapped in sloppy white paint above the gates . . . those were new.

Welcome to the Free City.

I could see where the paint had dripped between the cracks in the ancient stones before drying in the heat.

I had a few things to say about being dragged to a so-called Free City tied up like a goat on a spit, but even I knew I was better off not running my mouth just now.

'Declare yourself or I'll shoot!' someone called from the city wall. The words were a whole lot more impressive than the voice that came with them. I could hear the crack of youth on that last word. I squinted up through my sheema at the kid pointing a rifle at me from the top of the walls. He couldn't have been any older than thirteen. He was all limbs and joints. He didn't look like he could've held that gun right if his life depended on it. Which it probably did. This being Miraji and all.

'It's us, Ikar, you little idiot,' the man holding me bellowed in my ear. I winced. Shouting really didn't seem necessary. 'Now, open the gates right now or, God help me, I'm going to have your father beat you harder than one of his horseshoes until some brains go in.'

'Hossam?' Ikar didn't lower the gun right away. He

was twitchy as all get-out. Which wasn't the best thing when he had one finger on the trigger of a rifle. 'Who's that with you?' He waved his gun in my direction. I turned my body on instinct as the barrel swung wildly. He didn't look like he could hit the broad side of a barn if he was trying, but I wasn't ruling out that he might hit me by accident. If he did, better to get shot in the shoulder than the chest.

'This' – a hint of pride crept into Hossam's voice as he jerked my face up to the sunlight like I was a hunted carcass – 'is the Blue-Eyed Bandit.'

That name landed with more weight than it used to, drawing silence down behind it. On top of the wall Ikar stared. Even this far away I saw his jaw open, going slack for a moment, then close.

'Open the gates!' Ikar squawked finally, scrambling down. 'Open the gates!'

The huge iron doors swung open painfully slow, fighting against the sand that had built up over the day. Hossam and the other men with us jostled me forward in a hurry as the ancient hinges groaned.

The gates didn't open all the way, only enough for one man to get through at a time. Even after thousands of years those gates looked as strong as they had at the dawn of humanity. They were iron through and through, as thick as the span of a man's arms, and operated by some system of weights and gears that no other city had been able to duplicate. There'd be no breaking these gates down. And everyone knew there was no climbing the walls of Saramotai.

Seemed like the only way into the city these days was by being dragged through the gates as a prisoner with a hand around your neck. Lucky me.

Saramotai was west of the middle mountains. Which meant it was ours. Or at least, it was supposed to be. After the battle at Fahali, Ahmed had declared this territory his. Most cities had sworn their allegiance quickly enough, as the Gallan occupiers who'd held this half of the desert for so long emptied out of the streets. Or we'd claimed their allegiance away from the Sultan.

Saramotai was another story.

Welcome to the Free City.

Saramotai had declared its own laws, taking rebellion one step further.

Ahmed talked a whole lot about equality and wealth for the poor. The people of Saramotai had decided the only way to create equality was to strike down those who were above them. That the only way to become rich was to take their wealth. So they'd turned against the rich under the guise of accepting Ahmed's rule.

But Ahmed knew a grab for power when he saw one. We didn't know all that much about Malik Al-Kizzam, the man who'd taken over Saramotai, except that he'd been a servant to the emir and now the emir was dead and Malik lived in his grand estate.

So we sent a few folk to find out more. And do something about it if we didn't like it.

They didn't come back.

That was a problem. Another problem was getting in after them.

And so here I was, my hands tied so tight behind my back I was losing feeling in them and a fresh wound on my collarbone where a knife had just barely missed my neck. Funny how being successful felt exactly the same as getting captured.

Hossam shoved me ahead of him through the narrow gap in the gates. I stumbled and went sprawling in the sand face-first, my elbow bashing into the iron gate painfully as I went down.

Son of a bitch, that hurt more than I thought it would.

A hiss of pain escaped through my teeth as I rolled over. Sand stuck to my hands where sweat had pooled under the ropes, clinging to my skin. Then Hossam grabbed me, yanking me to my feet. He hustled me inside, the gate clanging quickly shut behind us. It was almost like they were afraid of something.

A small crowd had already gathered inside the gate

to gawk. Half were clutching guns. More than a few of those were pointed at me.

So my reputation really did precede me.

'Hossam.' Someone pushed to the front. He was older than my captors, with serious eyes that took in my sorry state. He looked at me more levelly than the others. He wouldn't be blinded by the same eagerness. 'What happened?'

'We caught her in the mountains,' Hossam crowed. 'She tried to ambush us when we were on our way back from trading for the guns.' Two of the other men with us dropped bags that were heavy with weapons on the ground proudly, as if to show off that I hadn't gotten in their way. The guns weren't of Mirajin make. Amonpourian. Stupid-looking things. Ornate and carved, made by hand instead of machine, and charged at twice what they were worth because someone had gone to the trouble of making them pretty. It didn't matter how pretty something was, it'd kill you just as dead. That, I'd learned from Shazad.

'Just her?' the man with the serious eyes asked. 'On her own?' His gaze flicked to me. Like he might be able to suss out the truth just from looking at me. Whether a girl of seventeen would really think she could take on a half dozen grown men with nothing but a handful of bullets and think she could win. Whether the famous

Blue-Eyed Bandit could really be *that* stupid.

I preferred 'reckless'.

But I kept my mouth shut. The more I talked, the more likely I was to say something that'd backfire on me. *Stay silent, look sullen, try not to get yourself killed.*

If all else fails, just stick with that last one.

'Are you really the Blue-Eyed Bandit?' Ikar blurted out, making everyone's head turn. He'd scrambled down from his watchpost on the wall to come gawk at me with the rest. He leaned forward eagerly across the barrel of his gun. If it went off now it'd take both his hands and part of his face with it. 'Is it true what they say about you?'

Stay silent. Look sullen. Try not to get yourself killed. 'Depends what they're saying, I suppose.' Damn it. That didn't last so long. 'And you shouldn't hold your gun like that.'

Ikar shifted his grip absently, never taking his eyes off me. 'They say that you can shoot a man's eye out fifty feet away in the pitch dark. That you walked through a hail of bullets in Iliaz, and walked out with the Sultan's secret war plans.' I remembered Iliaz going a little differently. It ended with a bullet in me, for one. 'That you seduced one of the Emir of Jalaz's wives while they were visiting Izman.' Now, that was a new one. I'd heard the one about seducing the emir himself. But maybe the emir's wife liked women, too. Or maybe the story had twisted in the telling, since half the tales of the Blue-Eyed Bandit seemed to make out I was a man these days. I'd stopped wearing wraps to pretend I was a boy, but apparently I'd need to fill out a little more to convince some people that the bandit was a girl.

'You killed a hundred Gallan soldiers at Fahali,' he pushed on, his words tripping over each other, undeterred by my silence. 'And I heard you escaped from Malal on the back of a giant blue Roc, and flooded the prayer house behind you.'

'You shouldn't believe everything you hear,' I interjected as Ikar finally paused for breath, his eyes the size of two louzi pieces with excitement.

He sagged, disappointed. He was just a kid, as eager to believe all the stories as I had been when I was his age. Though he looked younger than I ever remembered being. He shouldn't be here holding a gun like this. But then, this was what the desert did to us. It made us dreamers with weapons. I ran my tongue along my teeth. 'And the prayer house in Malal was an accident . . . mostly.'

A whisper went through the crowd. I'd be lying if I said it didn't send a little thrill down my spine. And lying was a sin.

14

It'd been close to half a year since I'd stood in Fahali with Ahmed, Jin, Shazad, Hala, and the twins, Izz and Maz. Us against two armies and Noorsham, a Demdji turned into a weapon by the Sultan; a Demdji who also happened to be my brother.

Us against impossible odds and a devastatingly powerful Demdji. But we'd survived. And from there the story of the battle of Fahali had travelled across the desert faster even than the story of the Sultim trials had. I'd heard it told a dozen times by folk who didn't know the Rebellion was listening. Our exploits got greater and less plausible with every telling but the tale always ended the same way, with a sense that, while the storyteller might be done, the story wasn't. One way or another, the desert wasn't going to be the same after the battle of Fahali.

The legend of the Blue-Eyed Bandit had grown along with the tale of Fahali, until I was a story that I didn't wholly recognise. It claimed that the Blue-Eyed Bandit was a thief instead of a rebel. That I tricked my way into people's beds to get information for my Prince. That I'd killed my own brother on the battlefield. I hated that one the most. Maybe because there'd been a moment, finger on the trigger, where it was almost true. And I had let him escape. Which was almost as bad. He was out there somewhere with all of that power. And, unlike me, he didn't have any other Demdji to help him.

Sometimes, late at night, after the rest of the camp had gone to sleep, I'd say out loud that he was alive. Just to know whether it was true or not. So far I could say it without hesitation. But I was scared that there would come a day when I wouldn't be able to any more. That would mean it was a lie, and my brother had died, alone and scared, somewhere in this merciless, war-torn desert.

'If she's as dangerous as they say, we ought to kill her,' someone called from the crowd. It was a man with a bright yellow military sash across his chest that looked like it'd been stitched back together from scraps. I noticed a few were wearing those. These must be the newly appointed guard of Saramotai, since they'd gone and killed the real guard. He was holding a gun. It was pointed at my stomach. Stomach wounds were no good. They killed you slowly.

'But if she's the Blue-Eyed Bandit, she's with the Rebel Prince.' Someone else spoke up. 'Doesn't that mean she's on our side?' Now, that was the million-fouza question.

'Funny way to treat someone on your side.' I shifted my bound hands pointedly. A murmur went through the crowd. That was good; it meant they weren't as united as they looked from the outside of their impenetrable wall. 'So if we're all friends here, how about you untie me and we can talk?'

'Nice try, Bandit.' Hossam gripped me tighter. 'We're not giving you a chance to get your hands on a gun. I've heard the stories of how you killed a dozen men with a single bullet.' I was pretty sure that wasn't possible. Besides, I didn't need a gun to take down a dozen men.

It was almost funny. They'd used rope to tie me. Not iron. If ever there was iron touching my skin, I was as human as they were. So long as there wasn't, I could raise the desert against them. Which meant I could do more damage with my hands tied than I ever could with a gun in them. But damage wasn't the plan.

'Malik should decide what we do with the Bandit anyway.' The serious-eyed man rubbed his hand over his chin nervously as he mentioned their self-appointed leader.

'I do have a name, you know,' I offered.

'Malik isn't back yet,' the same one who'd been pointing the gun at me snapped. He seemed like the tense sort. 'She could do anything before he gets back.'

'It's Amani. My name, that is.' No one was listening. 'In case you were wondering.' This arguing might go on for a while. Ruling by committee never went quick. It barely ever worked at all.

'Then lock her away until Malik gets here,' a voice from somewhere in the back of the crowd called.

'He's right,' another voice called from the other side, another face I couldn't see. 'Throw her in jail where she can't make any trouble.'

A ripple of agreement spread through the crowd. Finally the man with sad eyes jerked his head in a sharp nod.

The crowd parted hastily as Hossam started to pull me through. Only they didn't move very far. Everyone wanted to get a look at the Blue-Eyed Bandit. They stared and jostled for space as I was pulled past them. I knew exactly what they were seeing. A girl younger than some of their daughters, with a split lip and dark hair stuck to her face by blood and sweat. Legends were never what you expected when you saw them up close. I was no exception. The only thing that made me any different from every other skinny, dark-skinned desert girl was eyes that burned a brighter blue than the midday sky. Like the hottest part of a fire.

'Are you one of *them*?' It was a new voice, rising shrill above the din of the crowd. A woman with a yellow sheema shoved to the front. The cloth was stitched with flowers that almost matched my eyes. There was a desperate urgency in her face that made me nervous.

There was something about the way she said *them*. Like she might mean *Demdji*.

Even folk who knew about Demdji couldn't usually pick me out as one. We children of Djinn and mortal women looked more human than most folk reckoned. Hell, I'd even fooled myself for near seventeen years. Mostly I didn't look unnatural, just half-foreign.

My eyes were what gave me away, but only if you knew what you were looking for. And it seemed like this woman did.

'Hossam.' The woman staggered to keep up as he dragged me through the streets. 'If she's one of them, she's worth just as much as my Ranaa. We could trade her instead. We could—'

But Hossam shoved her aside, letting her be swallowed back into the crowd as he dragged me deeper into the city.

The streets of Saramotai were as narrow as they were ancient, forcing the crowd to thin and then dissipate as we moved. Walls pressed close around us in the lengthening shadows, tight enough in some places that my shoulders touched on both sides. We passed between two brightly painted houses with their doors blown in. Gunpowder marks on walls. Boarded-up entryways and windows. There were more and more marks of war the further we walked. A city where the

19

fighting had come from inside, instead of beyond the walls. I supposed that was called a rebellion.

The smell of rotting flesh came before I saw the bodies.

We passed under a narrow arch half covered by a carpet drying in the sun. The tassels brushed my neck as I ducked under. When I looked back up, I saw two dozen bodies swinging by their necks. They were strung together across the great exterior wall like lanterns.

Lanterns who'd had their eyes picked out by vultures.

It was hard to tell if they'd been old or young or pretty or scarred. But they'd all been wealthy. The birds hadn't gotten to the kurtas stitched with richly dyed thread or the delicate muslin sleeves of their khalats. I almost gagged at the smell. Death and desert heat made quick work of bodies.

The sun was setting behind me. Which meant that when sunrise came the bodies would blaze with light.

A new dawn. A new desert.

Chapter 3

The prison almost smelled worse than the corpses.

Hossam shoved me down the steps that led underground into the jail cells. I had time to glimpse a long line of iron-barred cells facing each other across a narrow hallway before Hossam pushed me inside one. My shoulder hit the ground hard. Damn, that was going to bruise.

I didn't try to get back up. I lay with my head against the cool stone floor as Hossam locked the jail cell behind me. The clang of iron on iron set my teeth on edge. I still didn't move as the footsteps faded up the stairs. I waited three full breaths before struggling to my feet using my bound hands and elbows.

There was one small window at the top of my cell that gave just enough light that I wasn't fumbling around in the dark. Through the iron bars I could see into the cell across from mine. A girl no older than ten was curled up in the corner, shivering in a pale green khalat that had gone grubby, watching me with huge eyes.

I leaned my face into the bars of the cell. The cold iron bit deep into the Demdji part of me.

'Imin?' I called down the prison. 'Mahdi?' I waited with bated breath as only silence answered. Then all the way at the other end of the prison I saw the edge of a face appear, pressed against the bars, fingers curling around the iron desperately.

'Amani?' a voice called back. It sounded cracked with thirst, but an annoyingly nasal, imperious note remained. The one I'd gotten to know over the last few months since Mahdi and a few others from the intellectual set in Izman had made the trek out of the city and to our camp. 'Is that you? What are you doing here?'

'It's me.' My shoulders sagged in relief. They were still alive. I wasn't too late. 'I'm here to rescue you.'

'Shame about you getting captured, too, then, isn't it?'

I bit my tongue. It figured I could count on Mahdi to still be rude to me even from the inside of a jail cell. I didn't think a whole lot of Mahdi or any of the rest of the weedy city boys who'd come to the heart of the Rebellion so late. After we'd already spilled so much blood to claim half the desert. But still, these were the men who'd supported Ahmed when he first came to Izman. The ones he'd traded philosophies with, and first started to fan the spark of rebellion with. Besides, if I let everyone I found annoying die, we'd be mighty thin on allies.

'Well' – I put on my sweetest voice – 'how else was I meant to get through the gates after you bungled your mission so badly that they put the entire city on lockdown?'

I was met with a satisfyingly sullen silence from the other end of the prison. It would be hard for even Mahdi to argue that he hadn't failed from the wrong side of a prison door. Still, I could gloat later. Now the last of the daylight was starting to retreat, I was going to have to move quickly. I stepped away from the iron bars. Rubbing my fingers together, I tried to work some blood back into my hands.

The sand that had stuck between them when I'd pretended to trip at the gates shifted in anticipation. It was in the folds of my clothes, too – in my hair, against the sweat of my skin. That was the beauty of the desert. It got into everything, right down to your soul.

Jin said that to me once.

I brushed aside that memory as I closed my eyes. I took a deep breath and pulled the sand away from my skin – every grain, every particle answering my call and tugging away from me until it hung in careful suspension in the air.

When I opened my eyes I was surrounded by a haze of sand that glowed golden in the last of the late afternoon sun streaming into the cell.

In the cell across from mine, the little girl in the green khalat straightened a little, leaning out of the gloom to get a closer look.

I sucked in a breath and the sand gathered together into a shape like a whip. I moved my tied hands away from my body as far as I could, shifting the sand with the motion. None of the other Demdji seemed to understand why I needed to move when I used my power. Hala said it made me look like some Izmani market charlatan of the lowest order. But she'd been born with her power at her fingertips. Where I came from, a weapon needed a hand to use it.

The sand slashed between my wrists like a blade, severing the rope. My arms snapped free.

Now I could do some real damage.

I grabbed hold of the sand and slashed my arm downwards in one clean arc, like the blow of a sword. The sand went with it, smashing into the lock of the cell with all the power of a whole desert storm gathered into one blow.

The lock shattered with a satisfying crack. And just like that, I was free.

The little girl in green stared as I kicked the door open, careful not to touch the iron as I gathered the sand back into my fist.

'So.' I sauntered down the length of the hallway, tugging away at what was left of the severed rope on my wrists. The rope came away from my right hand easily, leaving a red welt behind. I worked at the knot on my left hand as I came to a stop outside the cell that held Mahdi. 'How're those diplomatic negotiations going for you?' The last of the rope on my hands slithered away to the floor.

Mahdi looked sour. 'Are you here to mock us or to rescue us?'

'I don't see any reason I can't do both.' I leaned my elbows into the cell door and propped my chin on my fist. 'Remind me again how you told Shazad you didn't need us to come with you, because women just couldn't be taken seriously in political negotiations?'

'Actually' – a voice piped up from the back of the cell – 'I think what he said was that you and Shazad would be "unnecessary distractions".'

Imin moved to the door so I could see him clearly. I didn't recognise his face but I'd know those sardonic yellow eyes anywhere. Our Demdji shape-shifter. Last

25

time I'd seen Imin, leaving camp, she'd been wearing a petite female shape in oversized men's clothes – to lighten the load for the horse. It was a familiar body I'd seen her wear more than once now. Though it was just one in an infinite deck of human shapes Imin could wear: boy, girl, man, or woman. I was used to Imin's ever-changing face by now. It meant that some days she was a small girl with big eyes being dwarfed by the horse she was riding, or a fighter with the strength to lift someone off the ground with one hand. Other days he was a skinny scholar, looking annoyed but harmless in the back of a cell in Saramotai. But boy or girl, man or woman, those startling gold eyes never changed.

'*That's* right.' I turned back to Mahdi. 'Maybe I'd forgotten, on account of how amazed I was that she didn't knock all your teeth in then and there.'

'Are you done?' Mahdi looked like he'd bitten into a pickled lemon. 'Or are you going to waste more time that we could be using to escape?'

'Yeah, yeah, all right.' I stepped back, reaching out a hand. The sand answered, gathering itself into my fist. I pulled back my hand, feeling the power build in my chest, holding it for a moment before I smashed the sand down. The lock exploded.

'Finally.' Mahdi sounded exasperated, like I was a servant who'd just taken an unreasonably long time to bring him his food. He tried to shove past me, but I stuck my arm out, stopping him.

'What—' he started, outrage already rising. I clapped my hand over his mouth, shutting him up, as I listened. I saw the change in his face the moment he heard it, too. Footsteps on the staircase. The guards had heard us.

'You had to be so loud?' he whispered as I removed my hand.

'You know, next time I may not bother saving you.' I shoved him back into his cell, my mind already rushing ahead to how I was going to get us out of there alive. Imin pushed past Mahdi, stepping out of the cell. I didn't stop him. I couldn't have if I'd wanted to. He was already shifting as he went, shedding the harmless scholar's body until he was two heads taller than me and twice as wide. I wouldn't want to meet this shape of Imin's in a dark alley. He rolled his shoulders uncomfortably inside his shirt, now tight across his body. A seam split at the shoulder.

Full dark had almost fallen by now. The cells were lit only by a dim gloom. I could see the swing of lamplight on the staircase. Good, that'd be an advantage. I flattened myself to the blind spot at the bottom of the stairs. Imin followed my lead, doing the same on the other side.

We waited, listening to the steps on the stairs getting louder. I counted four sets of boots, at least. Maybe five. We were outnumbered and they were armed, but they'd have to come single file, which meant numbers counted for nothing. Lamplight played across the walls as they descended. I had the element of surprise on my side. And, like Shazad always said, when you were fighting someone twice your size you had to make the first blow count. The blow they were never expecting in the first place. All the better if you could make it your last one, too.

Across from me the little girl in green had shifted so she was right up against the bars, watching us, fascinated. I pressed my finger to my lips, trying to make her understand. The girl nodded. Good. She was young but she was a desert girl all the same. She knew how to survive.

I moved the moment the first guard's head came into view.

One violent burst of sand knocked straight into his temple, sending him careening into the bars on the little girl's cell. She staggered back as his skull cracked against the iron. Imin grabbed the soldier behind, hoisting him off the ground and slamming him to the wall. His startled face was the last thing I saw as his lamp hit the ground, shattering. Extinguishing. And I was as good as blind.

A gunshot sounded, setting off a chorus of screams, inside the cells and out. Underneath I heard one voice shouting a prayer. I whispered a curse instead as I flattened myself to the wall. I was least likely to get hit by a stray bullet if I wasn't out in the open. I had to think. They were as blind as we were. But they were armed and I had to figure they wouldn't mind killing a prisoner with a stray bullet as much as I would. Another gunshot went off, and this time there was a cry that sounded more like pain than fear. My mind struggled to think through the sudden rising panic, as I strained to follow the sounds. It'd been a long time since I was alone in a fight. If Shazad were here she'd know a way out of this. I could fight back in the dark, but I was as likely to hit Imin or the little girl in green as an enemy. I needed light. Badly.

And then, as if in answer to a prayer, the sun rose in the prison.

Starbursts filled my eyes. I was still blinded, but this time by the sudden glare of light. I blinked wildly, trying to see through the sunspots.

My vision cleared dangerously slowly, my panicked heartbeat reminding me that I was useless and blind and surrounded by armed enemies. My surroundings came into focus one little piece at a time. Two guards on the ground. Not moving. Three more rubbing their eyes, guns loose in their fingers. Imin pressed against the wall, bleeding from his shoulder. And inside the cell, the little girl in green, with a tiny sun, no bigger than a fist, cupped in her hands. Her face glowed in the pale light, casting strange shadows over her face from below that made her look a whole lot older. And I could see now that those huge eyes she'd been watching me with were as unnatural as mine or Imin's. The colour of a dying ember.

She was a Demdji.

Chapter 4

There'd be time to worry about my new Demdji ally later. For now I had to use the gift she was giving us. The guards' guns were already rising towards me – a burst of sand knocked them out of their hands. One guard staggered back into Imin. Imin grabbed him, and with one sharp twist I heard a neck crack.

A guard sprung at me, knife drawn. I split the sand in two, using half to knock his hand aside before he could get near, even as I turned the rest solid in my hand, forming it into a curved blade of sand. It cut clean across his throat, drawing blood. Imin grabbed a fallen gun. He might not be as good a shot as I was, but in a space this closely confined it'd be hard to miss. I ducked as Imin fired. More screams came from inside the cells, the sound of gunshots bouncing off the stone walls drowning them out.

And then silence. I straightened. It was over. Imin and I were still alive. The guards weren't.

Mahdi stepped out of the cell, his lip curling up in faint judgment at the bodies as he took in the carnage. That was the thing about the intellectual types. They wanted to remake the world, but they seemed to think they could do it without any blood. I ignored him as I turned towards the cell holding the little Demdji girl in a green khalat. She was still cradling the tiny sun, staring at me with sombre red eyes. They were unsettlingly bright.

I splintered her lock with a burst of sand. 'You're—' I started as I dragged the door open, but the little girl was already on her feet, shoving past me out of her cell towards the other end of the prison.

'Samira!' she called. She got close to the bars, but didn't touch them. She knew enough to stay away from iron. More than I had when I was her age. I leaned against the stone wall. I was starting to feel the exhaustion creeping in on me now that the fighting was done.

'Ranaa!' Another girl pushed her way to the front of the cell, kneeling on the floor so she was eye level with the young Demdji. She looked like she'd been beautiful before prison got to her. Now she just looked tired. Dark eyes sunk into a drawn face. I checked her over quickly for any sign of a Demdji mark but she looked as human as they came. She was probably of an age with me. Not old enough to be the girl's mother. A sister maybe? She reached through the bars, resting a hand against the little girl's face. 'Are you all right?'

The young Demdji, Ranaa, turned to me, her mouth already twisting into an angry pout. 'Let her out.' It was an order, not a request. And from someone who was used to giving them, too.

'No one ever taught you to say please, kid?' It slipped out, even though this wasn't the place to start teaching manners. And I probably wasn't the person to, either.

Ranaa stared me down. That probably worked on most folk. I was used to Demdji and even I found those red eyes unsettling. I remembered some stories saying that Adil the conqueror was so evil his eyes burned red. She was used to getting what she wanted with those eyes. But I wasn't all that used to doing what I was told. I twirled the sand around my fingers, waiting.

'Let her out, *please*,' she tried, before stomping one bare foot. 'Now.'

I pushed away from the wall with a sigh. At least I'd tried. 'Move back.' I could give orders, too.

The second the lock shattered, Ranaa fell forward, flinging her small arms around the older girl's neck, still carefully holding the ball of light in one hand as the other one clutched the dirty fabric of her khalat. I could see into the rest of the cell from the glow of the tiny sun in her hand. The cramped space was stuffed with prisoners, so close together they didn't have room to lie down, a dozen women piled on top of each other. They were already scrambling to their feet, collapsing out of the cell with relief, gasping for freedom, leaving Imin and Mahdi to try to get them in some sort of order.

They were all girls or women. The remaining cells were no different, I realised, glancing around at the cautious, anxious faces pressing out of the gloom against the bars, wary of us but tentatively hoping for rescue. Mahdi and Imin had found a set of keys on one of the dead men and were busying themselves freeing the rest of the captives. I supposed that was easier than shattering the locks. Prisoners spilled from one cell after another, sometimes rushing to embrace someone else, sometimes just staggering out, looking like skittish animals.

'The men?' I asked Samira as she disentangled herself from Ranaa, figuring I already knew the answer.

'They were more dangerous.' Samira said, 'At least that's what Malik said when he—' She cut herself off, shutting her eyes like she could stop herself from seeing them die at the hand of the man who'd usurped power in her city. 'And they were less valuable.'

It took me a moment to understand the significant

gaze she gave me over Ranaa's head. Then it sunk in. The women who were staggering out of the cells were young. There were a lot of rumours lately about slavers taking advantage of the war. Kidnapping girls from our half of the desert and selling them to soldiers stationed far from their wives, or to rich men in Izman. And then there was the matter of a Demdji's value . . .

'Ranaa.' I riffled through my mind. I'd heard that name once already today. The woman wearing the sheema stitched with blue flowers, I realised. The one who'd wanted to know if I was a Demdji. Now I understood why she recognised me. 'Your mother is worried about you.'

The little girl gave me a disdainful once-over, her face still pressed into Samira's chest. 'Then why didn't she come and get me out?'

'Ranaa,' Samira hissed reproachfully. I guessed I wasn't the only one who'd tried to teach the little Demdji manners. Samira had steadied herself against the door of the cell. I reached down a hand for her, helping her to her feet from where she was kneeling. Ranaa still clung to the edge of her dirty khalat, making it that much harder for Samira to move, weak as she was. 'Forgive her,' Samira said to me. She had a finely cut accent that reminded me of Shazad's, though it was a whole lot gentler. 'She doesn't often have cause to speak to strangers.' The last was followed with a pointed look at the little girl.

'Your sister?' I asked.

'After a sort.' Samira rested one hand on the younger girl's head. 'My father is' – she hesitated – '*was* the Emir of Saramotai. He's dead now.' Her voice was flat and matter of fact, hiding the hurt underneath. I knew what it was like to watch a parent die. 'Her mother was a servant in my father's household. When Ranaa was born looking ... different, her mother begged my father to hide her from the Gallan.' Samira searched my face. Usually I could pass for human, even with my blue eyes. But there were a few people who were more than a little familiar with Demdji who could spot me, like Jin had. 'You would understand why, I expect.'

I'd been lucky. I'd survived the Gallan for sixteen years without being recognised for what I was because I could pass for human. Ranaa would never be able to. And to the Gallan anything that wasn't human was a monster. A Demdji was no different from a Skinwalker or a Nightmare to them. Ranaa with her red eyes would be dead as soon as they caught sight of her.

Samira ran her fingers gently through the little girl's hair, a soothing motion that spoke of too many nights coaxing a scared little girl to sleep. 'We took her in and hid her. After she started doing ... this' – Samira's fingers danced over the light in Ranaa's hands – 'my father said she must be Princess Hawa resurrected.'

The story of Princess Hawa was one of my favorites growing up. It was from the very early days of humanity, back when the Destroyer of Worlds was still walking the earth. Hawa was the daughter of the first Sultan of Izman. Princess Hawa's voice was so beautiful that it brought anyone who heard it to their knees. It was her singing that brought a Skinwalker to her, disguised in the shape of one of her servants. He stole her eyes straight from her head. Princess Hawa screamed and the hero Attallah came to save her before the Skinwalker could take her tongue, too. He tricked the ghoul and won her eyes back for her. And when Hawa's sight was restored to her and she saw Attallah for the first time her heart stopped in her breast. What Hawa felt was so new and strange that she thought she was dying. Hawa sent Attallah away because of how much it pained her to look upon him. But after he was gone, her heart only hurt more. They were the first mortals to ever fall in love, the stories said.

One day, news reached Hawa in Izman that a great city across the desert was besieged by ghouls and that Attallah was fighting there. The city tried to build new defences each day, but every night the ghouls came along and tore them down, forcing the city to start again at dawn, when the ghouls retreated. On hearing that Attallah was almost certainly doomed, Hawa walked out into the desert beyond Izman and cried such agonised tears that a Buraqi, the immortal horses made of sand and wind, took pity on her and came to her aid. She rode the Buraqi across the sand, singing so brightly that the sun came into the sky as she rushed to Attallah's side. When she reached Saramotai she held the sun in the sky, and the ghouls at bay, for a hundred days, long enough for the people of Saramotai to build their great, impenetrable walls, working day and night until they were safe. When the work was finally done, she released the sun and, safe behind the walls of the great city, she married her love, Attallah.

Hawa stood watch on those walls as Attallah rode back out into battle each night and returned to her at dawn. For a hundred more nights Attallah went beyond the gates to defend the city. He was untouchable in battle. No ghoul's claw could so much as scratch him. She stood vigil every night until, on the hundred and first night of her watch, a stray arrow from the battle reached the walls and struck Princess Hawa down.

When Attallah saw her fall from the walls, his heart stopped from grief. The defences that had guarded him so well for a hundred nights fell away and the ghouls overwhelmed him, tearing his heart from his chest. But in the moment that they both died, the sun bloomed in the dead of night one last time. The ghouls could not fight in the sun. Instead they burned, and the city was saved with Hawa's and Attallah's last breath. The people of the city named it in her honour: Saramotai. It meant 'the princess's death' in the first language.

I wondered if it was a Djinni's idea of a joke to give his daughter, born in Hawa's city, the same gift that she had.

But Hawa was human. Or at least that was what the story said. I'd never wondered about it before. Folks in old stories sometimes just had powers that came from nowhere. Or maybe Hawa was one of us, and centuries of retellings had buried the fact that Hawa was a Demdji and not a true princess. After all, retellings of the Sultim trials made gentle, pretty Delila out to be a hideous beast with horns growing out of her head. And some stories of the Blue-Eyed Bandit left out the small matter that I was a girl.

'After Fahali we thought it would be safe for her.' Samira pulled Ranaa closer to her. 'Turns out even if they don't want to destroy her, some folk want her for other things.' It was stupid superstition that a piece of a Demdji could cure all ills. Hala, our golden-skinned Demdji, Imin's sister, carried a reminder of that every day: two of her fingers had been cut off and sold.

Probably to cure some rich man's troubled stomach. 'The rumour is even the Sultan is after a Demdji.'

'We know about that,' I cut her off, sharper than I meant to. I'd been more worried about the Sultan tracking Noorsham down than anything else after we'd heard that rumour. I'd figured the chances there was another Demdji out there who could match my brother's pure destructive power seemed mighty slim. Even I couldn't raze a city the way Noorsham had. Still, we'd been careful the last few months not to let word spread that the Blue-Eyed Bandit and the Demdji who summoned desert storms were one and the same. Not that it mattered. I wasn't ever going to let the Sultan take me alive. But now I considered the tiny sun in Ranaa's hands. It was harmless enough, cupped in her palms like that. It might not be so harmless multiplied a hundredfold. The Sultan's chances were looking better now.

'Your rebellion has kept him out of this side of the desert so far,' Samira said. 'How long do you think you can keep him out?'

As long as it took. I'd be damned before I'd let the Sultan do to any other Demdji what he'd done to Noorsham. Ranaa might be a cloistered brat who'd developed a big head from being told her whole life she was the reincarnation of a legendary princess. But she was a Demdji. And we took care of our own.

'I can get her to safety.' I couldn't leave her here. Not when there was a chance they might find her and I might find myself staring over the barrel of a gun at her next. 'Out of the city.'

'I don't want to go anywhere with you,' Ranaa argued. We both ignored her.

'Prince Ahmed wants to make this country safe for Demdji, but until then, I know where she can be protected.'

Samira hesitated a moment. 'Can I come with her?'

My shoulders eased in relief. 'That depends. Can you walk?'

Imin helped Samira, keeping her standing upright as she limped towards the stairs, Ranaa still clinging to her. I was about to turn away when Ranaa's light grazed the far wall. The cell wasn't quite empty. A woman in a pale yellow khalat was still curled in the corner, not moving.

For a second I thought she was dead, weakened by days in the dark cramped prison. Then her back rose and fell, just slightly. She was still breathing. I crouched down and laid a hand on the bare skin of her arm. It was hotter than it ought to be down here away from the sun. She was sick with fever. My touch started her awake, and wide wild eyes flew open. She gaped at me through a dirty curtain of hair, in panic. Blood and muck caked it against her cheek, and her lips were cracked with thirst. 'Can you stand?' I asked. She didn't answer, just stared at me with huge dark eyes. She looked worse than anyone else I'd seen stumble out of these cells. She could barely stay awake, let alone make a run for it.

'Imin!' I called. 'I need some help here. Can you—'

'Zahia?' The name was whispered almost as a prayer, rasping out of a throat that sounded bone-dry, a second before her head lolled backwards and she lapsed back into feverish sleep.

I stilled. Every part of me. I wondered if this was what Hawa felt when her heart stopped in her chest.

Suddenly I wasn't the Blue-Eyed Bandit. I wasn't a rebel giving orders. I wasn't even a Demdji. I was a girl from Dustwalk again. Because that was the last place I had heard anyone say my mother's name.

Chapter 5

'What is it?' Imin appeared at my elbow.

'I—' I stumbled over my words, trying to pull my mind out of the past. There were other women in the desert named Zahia. It was a common enough name. But she'd looked at me like she *knew* me and said my mother's name. And that wasn't all that common.

No. I wasn't a restless, reckless girl at the end of the desert any more. I was the Blue-Eyed Bandit, and this was a rescue. I nodded towards the unconscious figure on the ground. 'Can you carry her?' My voice was steadier than I felt.

Imin, still wearing the shape he'd fought in, lifted the unconscious woman off the ground as easy as a rag doll.

'This is ridiculous, Amani,' Mahdi hissed, pushing through the crowd of freed women as I followed Imin out of the cell. They didn't look so good, but they were alive and standing on two feet. 'Freeing people is one thing, but you want us to escape while *carrying* someone out?'

'We are not leaving her behind.' I'd made the mistake of leaving someone in need behind to save myself before – my friend Tamid, the night I'd fled Dustwalk with Jin. I'd been scared and desperate and frantic. I'd taken Jin's hand without thinking, and I'd left Tamid to bleed out in the sand. I'd left him to die. I couldn't undo what had happened that night. But I wasn't the girl from Dustwalk any more. I could make sure nobody got left behind again.

'Who knows how to use a gun?' I asked the group of women. No one moved. 'Oh, come on, it's not that hard. You point and shoot.' Samira's hand went up first. A few more followed her lead nervously. 'Take them off the bodies,' I ordered, swiping one for myself. I flicked the chamber of the gun open; the slightest touch of iron instantly made my power slip away. But there was a full round. I flicked it shut again and tucked it against my hip, careful not to let any part of it touch my skin. I didn't strictly need a gun. I had the entire desert. But it was always nice to have options. 'Let's move.'

It was after dark and the streets of Saramotai were empty. A whole lot emptier than they ought to be this soon after nightfall.

'Curfew,' Mahdi explained in a low whisper as we moved. 'The peasant usurper's way of keeping the population under control.' He didn't need to say *peasant* with quite that much disdain, but I wasn't about to come to the defence of Malik after he'd taken Saramotai by force and corrupted Ahmed's name.

Curfew was going to make things a whole lot easier or a whole lot harder. Right in front of the prison the road split. I hesitated. I couldn't remember where I'd come from.

'Which way to the gates?' I asked in a low voice. The women following us stared at me with huge, terrified eyes. Finally, Samira loosed her arm from Ranaa's grip and pointed silently to the right. She almost managed to hide the fact that she was shaking. I kept my finger on the trigger as we pressed forward.

I hated to admit that Mahdi was right, but we weren't exactly inconspicuous sneaking out of the prison trailing dozens of wealthy-looking women in torn khalats. And I wasn't counting on the women I'd given guns to – they held them like baskets to market instead of weapons. I had my suspicions that Mahdi could talk someone to death, but otherwise he was useless. And carrying the unconscious woman who'd called me by my mother's name made it more than a little difficult for Imin to fight if we ran into trouble.

I supposed I'd just have to keep us out of trouble, then. That wasn't exactly my strong suit.

Still, we didn't meet with any resistance as we passed quietly through the deserted streets of Saramotai, retracing my steps from earlier in the day. I was just starting to think we were going to make it, when we rounded the last corner and two dozen men with rifles looked up at us.

Damn.

They were clustered around the city gates in gleaming white-and-gold uniforms. Mirajin uniforms. And not the makeshift ones of the guards who'd blundered into the prison and to their deaths. Real ones. Which meant they were the Sultan's men. On our side of the desert for the first time since Fahali.

I let out the most colourful Xichian curse Jin had taught me as my gun leapt into my hand on instinct. I knew it was too late, though – we were caught. One of the women behind me panicked, and before I could stop her she was gone, darting towards the maze of city streets like a frightened rabbit looking for cover.

I'd watched birds of prey hunt. The rabbit never made it.

A shot went off. Another chorus of screams behind me. And a cry of pain, cut off by a second bullet.

The woman was sprawled on the street, blood

mixing with dirt. The bullet had torn straight through her heart. No one else moved.

I kept my finger steady on the trigger. Two dozen guns were up and pointing at us. I just had the one. No matter what anybody had heard about the Blue-Eyed Bandit, it wasn't actually possible to take out two dozen men with one bullet. Or even with my Demdji gift. Not without someone else getting shot.

'So this is the legendary Blue-Eyed Bandit.' The man who spoke wasn't wearing a uniform. Instead he was dressed in a gaudy blue kurta that he'd paired with a badly matched purple sheema. He was the only one who didn't have a rifle pointed at my head.

So Malik, the usurper of Saramotai, had returned.

I was dimly aware of Ikar, perched at his watchpost above the gate, legs dangling as he craned over the scene. 'I'd just been informed you were gracing our city with your illustrious presence.'

He used awfully big words that didn't seem all that comfortable in his mouth. His hollow face was skeletal in the buttery glow of the lamp. I'd grown up in a desperate place; I knew the look of someone who'd been ravaged by life. Only instead of lying down and taking his fate, he'd decided to take someone else's fate from them instead. I could guess that the kurta on his back was the emir's. He had the shape of someone who'd

47

worked and scraped and wanted and suffered, dressed in the clothes of someone who'd never known true want. My finger twitched on the trigger. I was itching to shoot something, but that wouldn't get us out alive.

The small contingent of Sultan's men shifted nervously, looking at me, like they were trying to decide whether I really was the Blue-Eyed Bandit. It looked like stories about me had made it all the way to Izman.

'And you're Malik,' I said. 'You know, I'd heard when you hanged that lot of people, you did it in the name of my prince. But it looks to me like your loyalty lies elsewhere.' I gave the soldiers a mock salute with my free hand. 'Not so much a revolutionary as an opportunist, by the look of things.'

'Oh, I believe wholeheartedly in the cause of your Rebel Prince.' When Malik smiled in the light of the lamps held by the nearby soldiers, he looked like he was baring his teeth. 'Your prince calls for freedom and equality in our desert. I've spent my whole life bowing to men who thought they were greater than me. Equality means I should never have to bow again. Not to the Sultan, not to the prince, and not' – he turned and spat towards Samira, making her flinch under his sudden attention – 'to your father, either.' The movement dashed light and shadow across the walls of Saramotai. Two huge figures hewn into the stone flanked the gates on this side: Hawa and Attallah, joining hands across the curve of the arch.

I hadn't seen them on my way in, not with my back to them. I wondered what they would think if they knew that the city they'd fought so long to save from the outside had rotted from the inside.

Paint had long since faded off the stone, though I thought I could make out the red of Attallah's sheema. And I'd swear Hawa's eyes were still flaked with blue.

'I'm making my own equality,' Malik said, pulling my attention back to him. 'What does it matter if I'm raising up the low or bringing the folk up on high to their knees, so long as everyone winds up with their feet in the same dust? And she' – he pointed at Ranaa – 'is going to buy our freedom.'

'Your feet aren't in the dust.' Samira pushed Ranaa behind herself protectively. She was doing a mighty fine job of hiding her fear. There was nothing but hate in her as she stood between the man who'd already killed most of her family and the one tiny piece of it left. 'You're standing on the backs of the dead.'

'The Rebel Prince will lose this war.' One of the Sultan's soldiers stepped forward. 'Malik is a wise man to see it.' The words sounded forced and false, like it pained him to pander to Malik. 'The Sultan has agreed to give Saramotai to Lord Malik when he reclaims this half of the desert. In exchange for the Demdji girl.' The Sultan might want another Demdji to replace Noorsham, but I wouldn't stake a single louzi that he was willing to give up part of the desert for her. Malik was just stupid enough to think that the Sultan would keep his promise.

'You're outnumbered.' That had never mattered much to me before. 'Drop the gun, Bandit.' Malik sneered.

'There's only one man who gets to call me that,' I said. 'And you're not near as good-looking as him.'

Malik's temper snapped faster than I expected. The gun that had stayed so arrogantly by his side was out and in his hand in the space of a breath, pressing to my forehead in the next. Behind me I felt Imin shift forward, like he might try to do something. I held up a hand, palm flat, hoping he would take the hint and not get us both killed. From the corner of my eye I saw him go still. The women from the prison were watching the scene unfold with huge terrified eyes. One of them had started crying silently.

It would've been nice if the bite of an iron barrel next to my skin was unfamiliar. But this was far from the first time I'd been threatened like this. 'You've got a smart mouth on you, anyone ever tell you that?' That wasn't a first, either. But telling him that didn't seem all that smart.

'Malik.' The soldier who'd spoken stepped forward, looking like his patience was wearing thin. 'The Sultan will want her alive.'

'The Sultan is *not* my master.' Malik's face had turned savage. He pushed the gun harder against my skull. I could feel the barrel of the pistol pressing between my eyes. My heart quickened instinctively, but I fought down that fear. I wasn't going to die today.

'You just cost me twenty fouza,' I sighed. 'I made a bet I could make it out of this city without anybody threatening to kill me, and thanks to you, I've just lost.'

Malik wasn't smart enough to be worried that someone with a pistol between her eyes was talking back instead of crying and cowering. 'Well' – he pulled back the hammer on the pistol – 'lucky for you, you're not going to be alive long enough to pay up.'

'Malik!' The soldier stepped forward again, his irritation falling away now. Seemed they had only just figured out they were dealing with an unstable man. By some unseen signal from their captain the weapons were shifting, away from the women behind me, towards Malik.

'Any last words, Bandit? Maybe you'd like to beg for your life?'

'Or ...' A voice seemed to float out of midair by Malik's ear. 'Maybe *you* would?'

Malik tensed visibly, in that way men did when they were in danger. It was a stance I'd become intimately familiar with in the past half a year. A thin bead of blood ran down his throat, even though it seemed like there was nothing around him but air.

The tension in my shoulders finally eased. The trouble with having invisible backup was that you never knew exactly where she was.

The air shimmered as the illusion cast by Delila dropped, leaving Shazad standing where there'd been nothing a moment before. Her dark hair was tightly braided to her head like a crown, a white sheema hung loose around her neck, and her simple desert clothes looked expensive. She was everything that Malik hated and she had him helpless. She looked dangerous, and not just because one of her blades was pressed to Malik's throat, but because she looked like her deepest wish was to get to use it.

Finally, and far too late, fear dawned slowly across his face.

'If I were you,' I said, 'now'd be the time I'd drop that gun and start reaching for the sky.'

Chapter 6

I was so close to Malik, I could see his face vacillating between despair and desparate action. He chose the second one. But I was faster than his stupid brain could work. I dropped to my knees a second before the gun went off, the bullet burying itself harmlessly in the wall behind me. Malik hit the ground next to me a second later, a new red necklace from Shazad's sword gracing his throat.

But we weren't done yet.

'That took you long enough,' I said to Shazad, rising to my feet as I whipped my hands up. On the other side of the walls of Saramotai, the desert surged in answer. After using nothing but a handful of sand down in the prison, the power of having the whole desert at my fingertips was almost intoxicating.

'I see you managed not to get yourself shot this time.' Shazad whirled to face the remaining soldiers as I did the same. 'You still owe me those twenty fouza, though.'

'Double or nothing?' I offered over my shoulder as we met back to back.

The captain was already giving orders to the confused soldiers, recovering awfully quick considering a new enemy had just appeared out of thin air.

'Delila!' Shazad called an order of her own. 'Drop our cover.'

The illusion lifted like a curtain before a show. Suddenly half the Sultan's men who'd been standing a moment earlier were crumpled on the ground, and our rebels were in their place, weapons drawn. Behind them was Delila, face still round with innocence, her purple hair that came from not being wholly human falling into wide, frightened-looking eyes. She dropped her hands, shaking with effort and nerves. She was scared but that wasn't stopping her.

'Navid!' From behind me, Imin spotted him instantly among the crowd of rebels.

A tall, desert-built man, Navid was one of our recruits from Fahali. We hadn't been trying to recruit people there, but after the battle it was hard to stop them joining up. Navid was one of the best. He was tough as anybody would need to be to survive this war we were fighting. And as earnest as you needed to be to think we stood a chance. He was hard not to like. But it still surprised me that Imin loved him.

Navid's eyes went wide with relief as he spotted Imin, recognising his beloved no matter the shape. It was a moment of distraction, his defence lowering in his relief that Imin was alive. I saw it, and so did the soldier on his right.

The desert poured over the edge of the walls of Saramotai, cascading around the carving of Princess Hawa, knocking soldiers off their feet. I wrenched my arm up, flinging a burst of sand towards the soldier who would've killed Navid, knocking him down, and startling Navid's attention back away from Imin.

'Watch your back, Navid!'

I was already turning away. The sand turned into a hurricane around me. I swung one arm down, crashing sand across a soldier's face as he lunged for Delila, pushing him away from her. A shout came from behind me. I spun in time to see a soldier lunging for me, sword up. I started to gather the sand into a blade in my hand but I was too slow. And I didn't need to. Steel screamed against steel. Shazad's blade landed a breath away from my throat, kissing the soldier's weapon. The blood that would've been all over his sword pulsed noisily through my ears. In one move that was too quick for me to see, he was on the ground.

'You ought to take your own advice.' Shazad tossed me a spare gun.

'Why would I need to watch my back when you've got it?' I caught the pistol a moment too late to shoot. Instead I slammed the handle straight into the face of the nearest soldier, the blow cracking up my arm, blood from his nose spurting across my hand.

The fight would be short and bloody. There were already more soldiers on the ground than standing. I fired. And now there was one more. I turned, already looking for my next target.

I didn't see exactly what happened next. Only splintered moments.

Another gun at the edge of my vision as I raised my own weapon. Exhaustion making me sluggish. Making my mind slow to understand what I was seeing.

That the gun wasn't pointed at me.

It was pointed at Samira. And the soldier already had a finger on the trigger.

Everything happened then in the same second.

Ranaa moved, swinging herself in front of Samira.

His gun went off. So did mine.

His bullet tore through green khalat and skin mercilessly.

One split second and it was over. The fighting was done as quick as it had started. In the silence all I

heard was Samira screaming Ranaa's name as the little
Demdji's heart pumped out her blood onto the street,
the tiny sun in her hand dying with her.

Chapter 7

Ahmed was waiting for us at the entrance to camp.

That wasn't a good sign.

Our Rebel Prince might not have the pretences of most royalty, but he didn't usually wait for us like a wife whose husband had stayed at the bar one drink too long, either.

'Delila.' He took a step out towards his sister, leaving the cover of the archway. Shazad checked the canyon walls for danger on instinct. The location of the camp was still safe as far as we knew, but if our enemies ever found out where we were, the top of the canyons surrounding us gave any attackers a clean shot with a rifle. At least one person had to care for Ahmed's safety, even if he wasn't going to do it himself. He didn't even seem to notice Shazad's concern; all his attention was on his sister. 'Are you all right?'

A part of me wanted to tell Ahmed that he ought to

58

have enough faith in us to bring his sister back in one piece. But then again, my shirt was now more red than white, which didn't exactly scream *Everything's fine!* Probably better to not draw attention to myself just now.

It was my blood. My attacker's blood. Ranaa's blood.

We'd tried to save her. But everyone could tell it was too late. She died quickly in Samira's arms.

People die. I tried to remember that. It was what happened on missions. She wasn't the first, and unless we managed to kill the Sultan tomorrow and put Ahmed on the throne, she wasn't going to be the last. *This is the cost of starting a war,* said a nasty voice in my head that sounded too much like Malik.

Only she was a Demdji. We'd never lost a Demdji in the fighting before. Or a child.

This was the Sultan's fault. Not ours. He'd let the Gallan across our borders and let them kill Demdji in the first place. And he was the one hunting our kind down to use as weapons now. It was his fault she was dead. But we were still alive – me, Imin, Delila – and we weren't going to become another Noorsham. We were going to topple him before he could find another Demdji. I'd make sure of that.

'I'm fine.' Delila squirmed as her brother checked her over for injury. 'Really, Ahmed, I'm fine.'

Shazad gave me a significant look that she hid

behind the guise of scratching her nose. After half a year I could read Shazad like an open book. This one meant we were about to be in trouble.

So we hadn't exactly had permission to take Delila with us. But we'd known we'd need help if we were going to get past Saramotai's impenetrable walls. We'd also known that if we asked Ahmed if we could take Delila on a mission he'd say no. So we just hadn't asked him. It wasn't technically disobedience if we'd never been forbidden from doing it. Even though we both knew that excuse would fly just about as well as either of us could.

Personally I'd been hoping Ahmed might not notice that Delila was gone at all. He was busy running a whole rebellion, and we were gone only a handful of days. But then, unlike me, most people seemed to be able to keep track of their siblings.

'She did good, Ahmed,' I offered. 'A lot of folk would be dead if it weren't for her.' *A lot more folk.* But I didn't say that aloud. I knew Shazad heard it in my silence all the same. Delila just beamed at her feet as Ahmed finally tore his eyes off his sister to survey the state we were in and the rabble behind us. Some were riding, others were on foot if they were strong enough. Mahdi was among those who had declared he needed a horse after his ordeal. Imin had shifted to a girl's shape, riding double with Navid, whose arms were wrapped around her protectively.

'I see you managed to bring back Imin and Mahdi, and then some.' There was a wry hint under his indulgent smile.

Some of the ex-prisoners had stayed in Saramotai, but plenty of others had decided to leave with us. Women who had nothing to stay for. Whose husbands and sons had been among the bodies hanging from the walls. The woman who'd called me Zahia was one of them. The Holy Father in Saramotai had seen to her as best he could. Enough to tell me that she wouldn't die on the journey to camp. Mahdi argued about bringing her, but Shazad didn't question me when I said it seemed wrong to leave her helpless in the city that had tried to kill her. I could tell Shazad knew there was something I wasn't telling her. The woman had been weaving in and out of consciousness since we'd left the city, riding mostly tied with a sheema to another woman in front of her so she didn't slip off.

It wasn't exactly uncommon for strays to come back from missions. I ought to know – half a year ago, I was one. Jin had been meant to come back with news of the Sultan's so-called weapon. Instead he came back with me. And in the six months that'd passed since then, I'd long stopped being the rebel camp's newest arrival.

We'd been joined by rebel sympathisers like Navid, ignited to action after the battle at Fahali. Orphans picked up in Malal, clinging to the hem of Jin's shirt the whole way back to camp. A defecting soldier who'd been guided our way by Shazad's father, General Hamad. Sometimes Shazad would slip and refer to them as troops. Ahmed called them refugees. After a few weeks everyone was just a rebel.

'We need to debrief.' The words came with a significant look directed specifically at me and Shazad. Ahmed wasn't about to dig into us in front of everyone. But that didn't mean we were off the hook.

Shazad was already talking as we pushed through the gateway that led to camp, telling Ahmed what hasdhappened in Saramotai. She danced around arranging to get me captured and skipped to how she and Delila, invisible under Delila's illusion, had slipped in behind me the moment I'd pretended to trip in the doorway, waiting for nightfall to let the others in behind us. The less she could remind Ahmed we'd put his sister in danger, the better. The way she told it, you'd barely know there'd been a fight. We'd left Samira in charge of the city, Shazad told him.

'We need to send her reinforcements,' she said as we felt our way through the inside of the cliff towards camp. 'We left everyone we could to help.' 'Everyone we could' meant the half a dozen other men who had come with us to Saramotai. Navid would've made seven whole people but he wouldn't be separated from Imin again. It wasn't exactly an army that could hold a stronghold but it was what we had. 'It's not enough to hold the peace. We should send fifty well-trained soldiers, before somebody else develops any ambition and steps into Malik's shoes. And we need to reinforce the city against the Sultan. Ahmed' – Shazad lowered her voice, casting her eyes behind us to where the newly recruited rabble was feeling their way nervously through the dark tunnel – 'your father's troops were in our half of the desert.'

Ahmed didn't answer her right away, but as we neared the end of the tunnel I could see he understood the significance even better than I did. A whole lot of the power we held relied on appearances. Truth be told, we wouldn't be able to match the Sultan's army on a battlefield if they tried to take the desert back from us by force. Keeping our half of the desert relied on the Sultan believing our numbers were greater than they were. And that deception relied on his men never straying into our half of the desert to find out the truth.

As we stepped through the other side of the cliff face, I blinked against the sudden brightness. The summer light made the rebel camp look like one of

Delila's illusions – too beautiful and alive in this desert full of dust and death. A world apart.

The camp was twice the size it had been when I'd first seen it. I couldn't keep myself from glancing over my shoulder at the women of Saramotai following us. I'd gotten into the habit of watching the new refugees' faces when they first set eyes on the camp. I wasn't disappointed this time. One by one, they stepped out of the tunnel and got their first look at my home. For just a moment, grief and fear and exhaustion parted, giving way to wonder as they took in the oasis rolled out below them. Watching them, it felt for a second like I was seeing it with fresh eyes, too.

Except in the past six months I'd gotten used to coming home. I knew everything about the camp. I knew the faces that waited here and the scars they wore. Both the ones that brought them to our war, and the ones they'd gotten fighting for us. I knew which tents were slightly lopsided, and what the birds sounded like in late afternoon from the bathing pools, and that the smell of fresh-baked bread meant Lubna was on cooking duty for the day.

I half expected to see Jin sauntering toward me, like he had the last time I'd gotten back from a mission I'd been sent on without him. A smile on his face, his collar loose so I could see the edge of his tattoo, sleeves rolled up to his elbows so when he pulled me to him, making my own shirt ride up, the bare cool skin of his arms pressed against the desert-flushed heat of mine.

But it looked like he still hadn't come home.

Shazad was arguing with Ahmed over the details of who to send to Saramotai and how many, leaving me to take charge of our new refugees. I gave Imin and Navid instructions to get them settled. Take the sick and wounded to the Holy Father. Get everyone else working. Navid didn't need instruction; he'd been on the other side of it himself. But he still smiled genially as I gave it. When I was done, Imin started to help him guide the women to the other side of camp.

I caught Ahmed's gaze over Shazad's shoulder as she kept talking, with Mahdi interjecting every so often. Ahmed's eyes flicked pointedly to Delila. I understood. He didn't want her any more involved than she already was in this. 'Delila,' I said, catching her attention, 'would you go with Navid and Imin and make sure they can keep their hands off each other long enough to settle everyone?'

Delila might be naive, but she wasn't stupid. She knew what I was doing. I thought she might make one last stab at standing up for me and Shazad. But she ducked her head, pushing her purple hair behind her ears with false brightness, before following Imin and Navid and their gaggle of women from Saramotai.

Ahmed waited until she was out of earshot before he started. 'What were you two thinking?' He hadn't taken his eyes from his sister's back. 'Delila's a child and she is not trained to fight.'

'Not to mention that your plan almost wound up getting you shot in the head,' Mahdi butted in.

'Your total *lack* of a plan got you locked up in a jail cell, so I wouldn't point fingers if I were you. You know what they say: those who point fingers wind up with them broken so badly they point straight back at them.' Shazad had even less patience for Mahdi than I did. She'd known him longer. From the days before the Sultim trials in Izman.

'I'm pretty sure that's not a saying,' I said.

'You almost *died*,' Mahdi said again, like we might be too stupid to understand.

'You say that like it's the first time I've ever had a gun pointed at me,' I retorted as Shazad rolled her eyes. 'It's not even the first time this *month*.'

'My sister is not as accustomed to near death as you two.' Ahmed started walking, an unspoken signal that we should fall into step.

'We wouldn't have let anything happen to her, Ahmed,' Shazad said as she and I dropped into pace easily on either side of him, leaving Mahdi trying to elbow his way in.

'Besides, Delila's as Demdji as I am.' We passed out of the glaring sun at the edge of camp and into the shade of the oasis trees. We were headed towards Ahmed's pavilion. I was trying to remember just when I'd gotten quite so comfortable talking back to royalty. 'She wants to help, same as everyone else here.'

'That's not why you took her, though, is it?' Ahmed didn't look at me as we walked. 'You took her to prove a point.'

He was talking about Jin.

It'd been two months back that I'd gotten shot and nearly died while Jin and I were on a mission in Iliaz. I'd been lucky to survive. When I woke up, back at camp, stitched and bandaged, Jin was gone. Ahmed had sent him to the border while I was unconscious. To infiltrate the Xichian army, which had been gnawing at Miraji from the eastern border, trying to get a foothold in our desert ever since the Sultan's alliance with the Gallan had shattered.

I wasn't so petty as to drag his sister into danger just because he'd sent his brother into it when I might've been dying.

But then, I wasn't sure I could say that out loud, either.

'We can need her and prove a point at the same time.' Shazad stepped in, taking the bullet for me. We'd nearly reached Ahmed's pavilion as he halted, turning to face us. I staggered to a stop and for a moment, all I could see was the Rebel Prince facing me, outlined by the gold sun on his pavilion, standing half a pace above us like he could bring justice down on our heads at any second. Like he was our ruler instead of our friend.

It was then that I noticed the entrance to the pavilion was closed. That was why I could see the sun stitched into the tent flaps radiating from Ahmed like he was stepping straight out of the sun. I'd only ever see those closed when Ahmed was holding a war council. Something was wrong. Shazad realised it the same second I did.

'Hala's back,' Ahmed said. Something had to be wrong to get him to drop the subject of his sister so quickly. 'She got back from Izman just before you. Maz spied you on the horizon from the air, so we thought we'd wait, to ... talk.' His eyes danced to Mahdi, and then away so quickly I wouldn't have noticed if I hadn't been watching him so closely.

'What happened?' Shazad asked. 'Why didn't you tell Imin that Hala was back?' Imin and Hala were siblings. They shared a Djinni father. If Hala hadn't already been in Izman when Imin was captured, then there was no question we would have taken her instead of Delila. She would've torn through the mind of every inhabitant of Saramotai to get Imin out.

'Is Sayyida with her?' Mahdi butted in.

Sayyida. The reason Hala had been sent to Izman in the first place.

I'd never met Sayyida, but I'd heard plenty about her. She was the same age as me. She'd been married at fifteen to one of Shazad's father's soldiers. Shazad was the one who'd noticed she had more broken bones than her soldier husband. She was the one who had contrived to move Sayyida out of her husband's home to the Hidden House, a Rebellion safe house in Izman. From there she had gotten tangled up with the Rebellion. And with Mahdi, from the sound of things.

In the early days, right after the Sultim trials, Sayyida had managed to manoeuvre herself into a position in the Sultan's palace as a spy for the Rebellion. A month back, she'd missed sending her regular report. Ahmed waited a week. It was possible something else had gone wrong. And the last thing anyone wanted was to blow her cover if it was just a delay. A week of Mahdi nagging Ahmed every day to send someone for her before Hala finally went to find out what was happening.

'Is Sayyida all right?' Mahdi pressed. He sounded hopeful, though I could see the apprehension in his eyes as he looked over his prince's shoulder at the shut pavilion.

Ahmed's silence was answer enough.

Inside the pavilion Hala was kneeling on the ground, slumped over a pretty Mirajin girl, her golden hands resting on the girl's head. Hala didn't look up as we came in, and her eyes stayed screwed shut. She looked tired. Tired enough that she wasn't using an illusion to hide her missing fingers like she usually did. Her Demdji skin moved like molten gold, as every shuddering breath she took shifted the lamplight across it. A thin sheen of sweat clung to her. Not from heat, I realised, but from effort. She *was* using her Demdji powers, just not on her own vanity. She was using them on the girl on the ground. Sayyida, I guessed.

Sayyida's eyes were wide and unseeing, fixed on something far away that none of the rest of us could make out. Hala was inside her mind.

Mahdi dropped to his knees on her other side, across from Hala. 'Sayyida!' He gathered her up in his arms. 'Sayyida, can you hear me?'

'I'd appreciate it if you didn't do that.' Hala's familiar clipped voice sounded strained. She still didn't open her eyes. 'It's a little insulting to try to shake me out of her head like I'm a bad dream, seeing as I've been holding an illusion for the better part of a week to try to *help.*' A week? That would explain why Hala looked like she was cracking. It was hard for any of us but the shape-shifters to use our powers for more than a few hours at a time. Let alone a week.

'She was easy enough to find, waiting for me in a cell.' Hala slumped on the ground. She was shaking visibly. Barely hanging on. 'Getting in her head was the only way I could carry her all the way here quietly.' She looked desperately at Ahmed. 'Did you bring something to knock her out?'

Ahmed nodded, pulling a small bottle of something clear from his pocket.

'What happened to her?' Mahdi shifted so he was cradling Sayyida. I'd always figured Mahdi for a coward, but I realised now I'd never actually seen him look scared before. Not even on the wrong side of a prison door. And this fear wasn't for himself. It was possible he did belong in this rebellion after all.

Hala glanced to Ahmed for permission. He hesitated for a second before nodding. The only sign Hala gave that she was letting go of her power was the small sigh that slid out between her lips before she sat back on her heels. But the change in Sayyida was like watching night fall at high noon. Her blank peace turned to screaming, her head arching back as she writhed out of Mahdi's grip. She was thrashing blindly, like a trapped animal, clawing at Mahdi's clothes, at the ground, at anything.

Shazad took the bottle from Ahmed's hand and the sheema from her neck and poured the contents of the bottle into the cloth. Just the smell of it made my head spin a little. She latched one arm around Sayyida's body, trapping the screaming girl's arms against her sides, and pressed the soaked cloth against Sayyida's nose and mouth. Shazad pushed slightly on the girl's middle, forcing her to take a gasping, panicked breath, inhaling the full force of the fumes.

Mahdi hadn't moved. He just stared with hollow eyes as Sayyida's struggling got weaker until unconsciousness claimed her, making her go limp in Shazad's grip.

'Mahdi.' Ahmed broke the silence finally. 'Take Sayyida to the Holy Father's tent. She can rest there.'

Mahdi nodded, grateful for the escape. He wasn't a strong man; a scholar, not a fighter. His arms shook with the effort as he gathered her up. But none of us was about to insult him by offering him help.

'Rest isn't going to help her,' I said as the tent flap closed behind him. 'She's dying.' The truth came easily. Us Demdji couldn't tell a lie. Whatever they had done to her, it was killing her.

'I know,' Ahmed said. 'But trust me, it does very little good to tell someone that the one they love is dying.' He looked straight at me when he said that. I wondered what had passed between him and Jin when I was at death's door.

'What did they do to her?' Shazad's voice was tight. 'Did she tell them anything about us?' Of everyone in this camp, Shazad had more at stake than any of us. She belonged to a family at the heart of Izman, and if it ever got out that Shazad was on the Rebel Prince's side, there were a lot of people close to her the Sultan could easily reach for.

'Oh, forgive me, I didn't ask after the particulars of her torture while I was rescuing her all by myself, while also trying not to hand my Demdji self straight over to the Sultan,' Hala sniped. 'Maybe you'd like me to go back and trade myself in for some useless information?' Hala was normally short-tempered, just not with Shazad. Folk didn't exactly do well when they got smart with Shazad. Hala must be worse off than I'd realised.

'If the Sultan knew about you, we'd already have heard,' Ahmed said.

'We need a new spy in the palace.' Shazad drummed her fingers across the hilt of the sword at her side. 'Maybe it's time for me to return from my holy pilgrimage.' As far as anyone in Izman knew, Shazad Al-Hamad, General Hamad's devastatingly beautiful daughter, had come down with a bad bout of holiness.

She'd retreated to the sacred site of Azhar, where the First Mortal was said to have been made, to pray in silence and meditate. 'It's nearly Auranzeb. It would be a good reason to go back.'

'You get invited to Auranzeb?' My ears perked up. Auranzeb was held every year on the anniversary of the Sultan's coup for the Mirajin throne. A commemoration of the bloody night when he struck a bargain with the Gallan army and slaughtered his own father and half his brothers.

Even down in Dustwalk, we'd heard stories about the celebrations. Of fountains full of water flecked with gold, dancers who leapt through fire as entertainment, and food made of sugar that was sculpted so fine the folk who made it went blind.

'General's daughter privileges.' Shazad sounded bored already.

'No.' Ahmed cut across us quickly. 'I can't spare you. I might not be as good a strategist as you, but even I know you don't send your best general into the fray as a spy if you can help it.'

'And I'm so very dispensable?' Hala asked from where she was still slumped on the ground, a tinge of sarcasm in her voice. Ahmed ignored her. It was impossible to respond to every sarcastic thing Hala said and still have time to do anything else with your day. I reached out a hand, offering to help her up. She ignored me, stretching to steal a half-peeled orange from the table instead.

'We have to do something.' Shazad smoothed her hands compulsively over the map that was rolled out on the table. It used to be a single clean, crisp sheet of paper showing Miraji. Now it was a dozen different pieces showing far corners of the country. Cities with the names of rebels stationed there scrawled and crossed out; other pieces of paper overlapping one another as the desert shifted in our hands. There was a fresh note next to Saramotai. 'We can't just hide out in this desert forever, Ahmed.' I recognised the beginning of the same argument that Shazad and Ahmed had been having for months now. Shazad kept saying we needed to take the Rebellion to the capital if we wanted a shot at winning. Ahmed would say it was too risky, and Shazad would say nobody ever won a war on the defensive.

Ahmed rubbed two fingers across a spot at his hairline as he started his reply. There was a small scar there, almost invisible now. I'd noticed he rubbed it like it still hurt, though, every time he sent one of us off to do something that might be our death. Like that scar was where he kept his conscience. I didn't know how he'd gotten it. It was from the life Jin and Ahmed had before they came to Miraji.

Jin had told me the stories behind some of his scars once. On one of those dark nights in the desert between camp and a mission. Right after he'd earned a wound that would make a new scar right below the tattoo of the sun on his chest. We were a long way from any Holy Father to patch us up. Which left me. In the dark of his tent my hand had travelled across his bare skin, finding new bumps and marks while he told me where they'd come from. A drunk sailor's knife in a bar brawl in an Albish port. A broken bone on deck in a storm. Until my fingers found the one on his left shoulder, near the tattoo of the compass that was on the other side of his heart from the sun.

'That one,' he'd said, so close to me that his breath stirred the hair that had escaped from the hasty knot on my head, 'was from this bullet I caught in the shoulder when a pain-in-the-ass girl who was pretending to be a boy ditched me in the middle of a riot.'

'Well, it's a good thing that pain-in-the-ass girl stitched you up, too,' I'd joked, tracing his tattoo with my thumb.

Out of the corner of my eye I saw Jin's mouth pull up in the smallest edge of a smile. 'God, I knew I was in trouble even then. I was running for my life, bleeding on your floor, and all I could think about was kissing you and damn if we got caught.'

I'd told him that would've been idiotic. And then he'd kissed me until we were both stupid from it.

'What about Jin?' It slipped out without my meaning it to, interrupting the argument that had been going through its usual steps while my head was in a tent in the middle of the sands.

Ahmed shook his head, knuckles still resting against his forehead. 'No word.'

'And you don't think it's worth sending someone after him like we did for Sayyida?' It was out before I could check the anger in my words.

'So, you *are* angry about Jin.' Ahmed sounded tired.

'We're in the middle of a war.' It would be petty of me to be mad about Ahmed sending Jin away while my life hung in the balance. I supposed I was petty, then.

'We are.' Somehow his calm made it that much worse. From the corner of my eye I caught one of Shazad's looks. Only this one was traded with Hala instead of me, too quick for me to read. Hala shoved the last piece of the orange into her mouth, finally getting to her feet, stepping away so she was clear of me.

'That wasn't an answer,' Ahmed said to me. 'You think I was wrong for sending Jin to spy on the Xichian? When foreigners warring with my father are the only thing keeping him at bay?'

'Well it doesn't seem like it matters any more.' I snapped. 'The Sultan is back on our territory anyway, judging by all those dead soldiers we left in Saramotai.' Damn, I hadn't meant to say that. I tried a different track. 'I just think there might've been another way.' That didn't come out right, either. Even if I had been thinking it for months.

Ahmed linked his hands on top of his head. The gesture was so much like Jin it made me even angrier. 'You don't think I should've sent my brother out for the good of the country for *your* sake?'

'I think you could've waited to send him away.' My temper broke, and suddenly I was shouting. Shazad drew forward like she was going to stop me from saying something I might regret. 'At least until I woke up from being shot for *your* rebellion.'

I'd never seen Ahmed's temper flare before. But I knew I'd pushed too far even before his voice rose. 'He *asked* to go, Amani.'

The words were simple enough, but it took me a heartbeat to understand them all the same. Shazad and Hala had both gone still, watching the exchange.

'I didn't send him away.' Ahmed's voice wasn't raised any more but it hadn't lost any of its strength. 'He *asked* me for something that would take him away from here and from you. I tried to talk him out of it, but I love my brother enough that I didn't want him to have to watch you die, either. And I have spent the last two months lying to protect you, but I don't have *time* to keep you from acting out some misguided defiance against me because you think it's my fault he's gone.'

Hurt and anger warred inside me and I didn't know which one I wanted to pay attention to first. I wanted to call him a liar but I knew I wouldn't be able to. Everything he was saying sounded true. Truer than Ahmed sending Jin away with no care for either of us. Truer than Jin going against his will. I had almost died and Jin was going to let me do it alone.

'Amani—' Ahmed knew me as well as anyone. He knew my instinct was to run. And I knew it, too. I could feel the itch building in my legs. He went from ruler to friend again, reaching for me. Trying to stop me. But I was already out of his reach, pushing out of the stifling dark of the pavilion and into the mockingly bright sun of the oasis.

Chapter 8

Last time I'd seen Jin had been a few heartbeats before I was shot in the stomach.

We were in Iliaz, the key to the middle mountains. So long as Iliaz was in the Sultan's hands, there was no easy way into eastern Miraji. Meaning there was no way to take Izman, and with it the throne.

It was supposed to be a simple reconnaissance mission.

But it turned out we weren't the only enemies of the Sultan to figure out that winning Iliaz could mean winning Miraji. Iliaz was under siege from both the Albish and the Gamanix armies. I didn't know where either of those countries were, but Jin pointed out the flags on their tents as we lay flat on the mountaintop looking over their camps. And it turned out the young prince who was leading the army in Iliaz was a damn sight better as a commander than his brother Naguib had been.

He was holding his own in the mountain fortress against two armies at once, with minimal losses. Even Shazad was impressed. But she thought she could find a way through the siege all the same.

That was, give or take, how we wound up in the middle of a skirmish between the Emir of Iliaz's first command and two foreign armies. And the Iliaz first command was a whole lot bigger than any of us had expected.

I didn't remember much from that fight. Blasts of gunpowder sparking the night air from both sides, cries in tongues I didn't know, and blood dashing across the dusty rocks. Shazad a whirlwind of steel cutting our way out of the fight, me with the desert at my fingertips, Jin levelling his gun at Mirajin and foreigner alike. A scrape of bullet grazing my arm, untethering my power with just one iron kiss. Seeing the knife that was about to go through Jin's back a heartbeat before he saw it. A heartbeat that mattered in keeping him alive. Grabbing the pistol off my belt.

I stepped out of my cover and straight into the line of fire. The man with the knife went down with one pull of my trigger. Only there was another gun behind him, aimed at me by a dark-haired Mirajin soldier with a steady hand. His bullet tore straight through me. Like I wasn't Djinni fire and desert sand at all. Just flesh and blood.

Everything I knew about what happened next were things I was told after I woke up. Jin had grabbed me as I'd fallen, cutting three men down between us as he went.

I was bleeding so badly it looked like half my life was already on my clothes by the time he got to me. Shazad carved a path out of the last of the fray with a few swings of her swords and they got me onto Izz's back; he was shaped as a giant Roc, come to rescue us. Only there was no time to get me all the way back to our camp. I would have died first. They stopped at the first town they saw with a prayer house. It was on the Sultan's side of the country. Enemy ground. Izz, back in his human shape, made the Holy Father swear he would heal me, not harm me, then repeated it to make sure it was true before they handed me over. Shazad dragged Jin away when he tried to make the Holy Father work with a gun to his head.

The Holy Father didn't try to kill me, though I heard I came pretty close to dying once or twice all on my own. The bullet had just missed about three different ways of killing me. I'd only barely stopped bleeding by the time they had to move me again. The Holy Father warned them against it but Izz had been spotted. They got me back to camp as quickly as they could and handed me over to our Holy Father.

It turned out it was being a Demdji that'd saved me.

I'd burned away any chance of infection, quick and hot, all on my own. So the only thing the Holy Father had to worry about was the bleeding.

Near a week had passed the next time I opened my eyes, fighting my way out of a haze of drugs that'd been forced down me along with water. Shazad was asleep next to me. That was how I knew I must've been close to death. The sick tent had been Bahi's territory. She hadn't set foot in it since he'd died. Not even when she'd gotten hurt herself, the one time I'd ever seen a sword get past her guard. I'd stitched the thin slice across her arm instead.

She woke instantly as soon as I shifted, her eyes flying open, going for a weapon that wasn't there before focusing on me. 'Well, look who's back from the dead.'

Shazad found me in one of the pools of water that had been designated for washing. Dark cloths hung between the trees on all sides to shield it from view of the camp. It was shallow enough that I could sit in it and be covered up to my shoulders, and clear enough that I could see my toes at the bottom. The bottom of the pool was scattered with white and black pebbles smoothed by the water. I pushed them around the bottom with my toes. I'd been in here long enough that I'd scrubbed the dust out of my hair, and it had already dried in strange wild waves, curling around the edges of my scalp, like it had a habit of doing.

I was carefully using sand to scrub away the flecks of blood that were still clinging to the wound at my collarbone from Saramotai. I'd thought about going to the Holy Father for stitches but I figured he had enough on his hands with the refugee women. Including the one who had called me by my mother's name. I didn't know if she'd have woken up yet, but if she had, that was another reason to steer clear of the sick tent.

Shazad had stripped the desert off herself, too. She was wearing a white-and-yellow khalat that reminded me of the uniform of Miraji. It made her desert skin look all that much darker against the paleness of the linen. She had a bundle tucked under one arm.

'Jin has as much flight in him as he has fight, you know,' Shazad said. 'That's how Ahmed wound up alone in Izman in the first place.' I knew the story. When Ahmed had chosen to stay in the country where he was born, Jin had decided to move on, staying on the ship they'd been working on. He'd come back a few months later with Delila, after his mother died. 'He did it at the Sultim trials, too.' She shucked off her shoes. 'Vanished the night before and came back with a black eye and cracked rib he never explained to any of us.'

'He got in a brawl in a bar with a soldier about a girl.'

'Huh.' Shazad considered that, rolling up her shalvar. She sat at the edge of the pool, dipping her feet in to cool off. The sounds of the camp drifted around us on the slight breeze. Birdsong mingling with indistinct voices. 'All right, we're low on time. So I'm going to hurry this up. You're going to ask me if I knew he'd asked to leave. And I'm going to tell you that I didn't. And you're going to believe me because I've never lied to you before. Which is half the reason you like me so much.'

Well, she wasn't wrong about that. 'What's the other half, if you're so clever?'

'That you'd be *constantly* undressed if it wasn't for me.' The bundle under her arm unfurled into a khalat I'd seen at the bottom of her trunk of clothes before. It was the colour of the sky in the last moments before it turned to full desert night and dotted with what looked like tiny stars. I realised as it clinked in Shazad's hands that it wasn't stitching. They were gold beads. I hadn't exactly arrived at the Rebellion with enough clothing to fight a war, but Shazad had enough for the two of us. Even if nothing of hers ever fit me exactly right. But this was by far the most beautiful thing I'd ever seen her pull out of that chest of clothes.

'What's the occasion?' I asked, dragging myself through the water to lean on the edge of the pool next to her.

'Navid has somehow convinced Imin to marry him.'

I sucked in a breath so fast I inhaled some of the water and started coughing. Shazad slapped me on the back a few times.

Navid had been totally taken with Imin from the moment he arrived at the camp. It didn't seem to matter what shape Imin wore; Navid could spy the object of his affections across the camp without hesitating. He had very drunkenly declared his love on equinox a few months back, in front of the entire camp. I remembered grabbing Shazad's arm, bracing myself for the inevitable mockery and rejection from Imin. For some baffling reason it never came. Baffling, because Imin treated everyone but Hala with the sort of disdain that came only from true hurt. The kind the Rebellion had saved the Demdji from in the first place.

Imin had glanced around at all the staring faces with sardonic yellow eyes before asking us why we didn't have anything more interesting to stare at. Then Imin slipped a hand into Navid's, pulling him away from the firelight and our stunned silence.

'You have to attend,' Shazad said as I recovered from my attempt to breathe in water, 'and you have to be dressed to do it. Imin has already stolen three khalats from me for the occasion, because, and I quote, "none of my own clothes fit at the moment."'

I raised my eyebrows at her. 'Did you point out that Imin's a shape-shifter and can make anything fit?'

'You know I did.' Shazad pulled an annoyed face. 'It went down about as well as you would expect and now I'm down three more khalats.'

'You're going to run out of clothes at this rate.'

'And when that day comes I will lead a mission to Imin's tent to reclaim the spoils. But for now I managed to save this.' She gestured at the white linen clinging to her perfectly. 'And this. And I know where to reclaim this one from because you sleep four feet away from me.'

I ran my finger and thumb along the hem of the khalat she held out to me, my hand already dry in the unforgiving sun. I remembered something she'd told me once, on one of those dark nights when neither of us could sleep, and we stayed awake talking until we ran out of words or out of night. When she'd told her parents she was throwing her lot in with Ahmed, her father gave her those swords to fight the Rebellion with. Her mother gave her that khalat.

'That's the khalat you're supposed to wear into Izman. When we win this war.' *If we win.*

'We're still a long way from Izman,' Shazad said as if she'd heard the *if* I didn't voice. 'Might as well not let it rot at the bottom of my trunk. You can wear it if you swear to me you won't get blood on it.'

'It's dangerous to ask a Demdji to make a promise,' I said. Promises were like truth-telling. They would come true. Just not in the way you might expect.

'It's a wedding, Amani.' Shazad reached a hand down to help me out of the water. 'Even you aren't that good at getting into trouble.'

In Dustwalk, marriages happened fast. Most girls just dug out their best khalats, worn thin from years of sisters and mothers handing them down, and draped their sheemas over their heads to hide their faces in that uncertain time between engagement and marriage, lest a ghoul or Djinni notice a woman who belonged to no one, no longer a daughter but not yet a wife, either, and try to claim her for his own.

We didn't have a prayer house in camp, but we'd always made do. The Holy Father had prepared the ceremony in a clear space at the edge of the sand where the ground sloped up just enough to give a good view of the whole camp below in the last of the light. The wedding began at dusk, the sun setting over the canyon. Like they always did. A time of change in the day for a moment of change in two lives.

Imin wasn't wearing a repurposed sheema. It was a true wedding covering, made of fine cloth stitched with bright thread, and when the sun hit it, I could just see the outline of the face she had chosen through the thin yellow muslin. It wasn't one I'd seen on her before. Imin was our best spy, staying alive by looking unremarkable. But the face she'd chosen today was stunning, and she was beaming like I'd never seen Imin smile.

Hala caught my gaze as the two of them knelt in the sand side by side. It'd been an unspoken pact between us Demdji to keep one eye on Imin after that night Navid declared his love for her. None of us had ever seen Imin's walls drop for anyone in camp before Navid.

Imin and Hala might share a Djinni father, but by the sound of things they couldn't have had more different mothers. Rumour had it Hala had torn her mother's mind apart, driving her crazy on purpose because she hated the woman so much. The Rebellion had found Imin in a prison waiting for execution at the hands of the Gallan. Imin had spent sixteen years hidden in the house of grandparents who shielded their daughter's Demdji child. Alone and lonely, but safe. Until the day Imin's grandmother collapsed from the heat on their doorstep. Imin was otherwise alone in the house. The sixteen-year-old waited, hoping a neighbour would notice. But finally, desperate, Imin ran out to help wearing the same slender girl's form she'd donned to fight the heat that morning. The body was too weak to drag a grown woman, though. Imin shifted into a man's shape out in the open.

Word reached the Gallan. They killed Imin's whole family on the same doorstep, as they tried to block the soldiers' path.

Until Navid, Imin had treated anyone who wasn't a Demdji with distrust. Even me, on account of how I'd thought I was human for sixteen years.

It would take the slightest misstep from Navid to send Imin back behind walls. But even Hala hadn't been able to find anything wrong with him, and she'd been trying real hard. Anyone could see the way Navid looked at Imin. And it didn't change no matter what body our shape-shifter wore, woman or man, Mirajin or foreign.

The Holy Father stood between Navid and Imin as they faced us, sitting in the sand, legs crossed. He recited the usual blessings for a wedding as he filled two large clay bowls with fire. He handed one to Imin and one to Navid. He spoke of how humanity was made by the First Beings out of water and earth, carved by wind, and lit with a spark of Djinni fire. He reminded us that when Princess Hawa and Attallah became the first mortals ever to wed, their fires were twinned and burned so much brighter for it. All these centuries later we still uttered the same words they had.

As he spoke we came up, one by one, the women of the camp to Imin, the men to Navid. Each of us dropped something of ours into their fire to bless the union. In Dustwalk I'd always given an empty bullet casing or a lock of hair. I didn't have anything else to give.

For the first time in my life I had more, and I'd had to think about what I ought to give, as Shazad and I got ready. For just a second my fingers had drifted over the red sheema. The one Jin had given me in the burned-out mountain mining town of Sazi. As I closed my eyes for Shazad to press dark kohl into my lids, I could picture myself tossing it into the fire, watching the red cloth catch. It would go up in seconds. I was angry but I didn't hate him. I'd fastened it around my waist like a sash instead, the way I always did with Shazad's clothes.

I stood behind Hala, who held her hand above the fire, pricking each of the remaining three fingers on her left hand with a needle in quick succession. Blood was the traditional offering from family members, even if the father Imin and Hala shared didn't bleed. Bright red dots welled at the tips of her golden fingers, then sizzled noisily as the blood hit the fire. As Hala moved out of the way I held up my gift above the fire and a handful of desert sand slipped out between my fingers, scattering into the flames. I caught the slightest hint of a smile from Imin as I stepped aside, leaving room for

Shazad to drop a small comb of hers into the fire. Next to her, Ahmed dropped a Xichian coin into Navid's bowl. He wore a clean black kurta edged with red that made him look more like he belonged in a palace than in a rebellion. He and Shazad made a well-matched pair, standing side by side in front of the twinned wedding fires.

Behind Ahmed, the twins, Izz and Maz, were holding a blue feather, alternately snatching it out of each other's hands and shoving each other in a silent war over which one would get to drop it into the fire. The warning look Shazad gave them as she turned around was loud enough to get them both to behave. When they spotted me standing on Imin's side of the fire they waved frantically. I hadn't seen the twins since I'd been injured. They must've gotten back while we were in Saramotai.

When the whole camp was done, finally Imin and Navid turned to face each other to speak their vows.

'I give myself to you.' Imin carefully tipped her fire into the third bowl that the Holy Father held between them, the ashes of our gifts mingling with bright coal embers and sending up sparks as they spilled from one bowl to another. 'All that I am I give to you, and all that I have is yours. My life is yours to share. Until the day we die.'

Navid repeated the same as he tilted the contents of his bowl in after hers until a single fire, larger and brighter than the ones they had held alone, burned between them. The Holy Father waved his tattooed hands over it in blessing.

There was a moment of silence as the sun disappeared entirely behind the canyon wall, casting the camp into a gloom broken only by the fire. And then Navid sprang to his feet, unabashedly picking Imin up, arms around her waist, before pulling her into a kiss. The whole of the camp cheered. The ceremony was over. It was time for the celebrations to begin.

'Amani!' I didn't have a chance to turn around to see who'd called my name. A pair of bright blue arms grabbed me around the waist, spinning me around gleefully. I laughed, shoving Izz off as my feet found the ground again, staggering. Maz was wearing clothes, but Izz had already stripped down to nothing but his trousers. The twins had a real aversion to clothes. Their animal shapes didn't need them and it seemed to confuse them that their human shapes did.

Izz gestured at the bare blue skin of his chest and my khalat. 'We match.' He beamed stupidly at me.

'And luckily only one of us had to take off our shirt. I see you both survived Amonpour.' The Albish had made an alliance with our western neighbours of Amonpour after losing Miraji to the Gallan twnety years ago. According to Shazad it had been nothing more than some men's signatures on paper. Until the Albish suddenly got the news of the Gallan being turned out of the desert. And then suddenly they were using that piece of paper to convince Amonpour to let them camp on their borders, waiting for an opportune moment to try to claim Miraji as a prize again. They were getting a little too close to us for comfort so the twins had been sent to spy on the Albish troops camped along our western border. In case they got itchy feet and decided to march through our half of the desert. The last thing we needed was a fight on two fronts.

'Elephants!' Izz flung up his arms so excitedly I staggered back, nearly stumbling into the fire at the strange, foreign word. 'Amonpour has elephants. Did you know about elephants?'

'Were you holding out on us?' Maz slung an arm around his brother's bare shoulders, pointing at me accusingly. It was easy to forget one of them was blue and the other one just had blue hair when they were like this, moving and talking like one person. Maz's dark-skinned arm almost seemed like an extension of his brother's body.

Izz winked. 'Fess up, Demdji.'

I rolled my eyes at them. 'If I did I probably would

have kept it from you anyway, judging by the slightly crazy look in your eyes.'

'Do you want to see one?' Maz was already kicking off his shoes.

'We might need more space.' Izz started to gesture around himself, as if trying to get people out of the way.

There was no way this could end well. 'Is this going to be like the time you learned what a rhinoceros was all over again?'

The twins froze, swapping a sheepish expression. 'I mean—'

'Elephants are—'

'Slightly bigger, so—'

'Then how about you show me sometime when there aren't quite so many people, who aren't quite so full of liquor, around?' I suggested.

The twins traded a look as they seemed to silently debate the wisdom of that versus how badly they wanted to show me their new trick. Finally they nodded and contented themselves with giving me a very detailed explanation of what elephants looked like, and telling me nothing else about how Amonpour had gone. Well, I supposed we weren't invaded yet.

Torches were lit. Music had started and with it, dancing and eating and drinking. I was grateful to know that for a few hours we wouldn't be fighting a war. It was on nights like this in the rebel camp that I believed more than anything in what we could do. Nights when everyone stopped fighting long enough to live like we were promising the rest of Miraji it could.

It was a few hours after dark when I spotted him through the crowd.

I'd had enough to drink that I didn't trust my eyes at first. He was a flash of an impression as I spun. Head tilted back, laughing, at ease, like I'd seen him a thousand times. I lost my step, staggering too close to the fire. Someone grabbed me, pulling me back before I could set Shazad's clothes aflame. I tore myself out of the dancing and looked back, searching for him through the hazy mess of faces in the dark. But he was gone, as quick as if I'd imagined him. No, there, the crowd split.

Jin.

He was back.

He was standing on the other side of the fire, still wearing his travelling clothes, dust clinging to his dark hair. He looked like he hadn't shaved lately, either. I had a sudden flash of the last time he'd kissed me when he'd been a few days without a razor. My heart stumbled towards him, but I caught it, fighting to right it.

I turned away quickly, before he could spot me. I wasn't in any kind of state to face him now. My head was fuzzy with alcohol and exhaustion. I looked for Shazad. She was a few paces away, deep in conversation with Ahmed, hands moving as quick as the dance of insects around a fire as she argued something passionately. And a little tipsily. Shazad wasn't much for unnecessary motions when she was sober. But when she caught my eye she read me like an open book all the same. I gave a small nod behind myself. Her gaze steadied. Like it did when she was trying to track down an enemy in a fight. I saw the shock register on her face the moment she spied him. Good. That meant it was really him, not some conjuring by Hala designed to torture me.

I had hoped that by the time I saw him again I'd be ready to face him head on. But now I felt split open. Like if I faced him it was all going to come spilling out in words. I wiped away the sweat on my neck. My hand came away red.

For one stupid moment, I thought seeing Jin really had split me open. No – the wound across my collarbone had reopened. The rushed patch-up job in Saramotai hadn't fared all that well against the dancing and drinking. Shazad had called it a scratch, but right now it looked a lot like an escape to me.

Jin had run away. Fine. I could do the same.

*

The warmth and noise of the camp faded behind me as I picked my way toward the Holy Father's tent, set far to one side of the camp. It had changed some since it'd been Bahi's domain, the place I'd first woken up in camp, under a canopy of cloth stars. But that didn't make it any easier when I had to step inside. Half a year since Bahi had died at my brother's hands and I still thought I could smell burning flesh sometimes when I got too close to where he'd worked. It was no wonder Shazad steered clear. I'd known him a handful of weeks. She'd known him half her life. The new Holy Father had kept his patchwork of stars. It was the first thing I saw as I pushed my way into the tent.

A woman's head darted up from one of the beds. I hadn't been expecting anyone to be here. Leastways not anyone awake. In the bed nearest to the entrance Sayyida was sleeping still as the dead. Across from her was a young rebel whose name escaped me, bandaged from elbow to wrist, where there used to be a hand. He'd been dosed with something that would keep him dreaming he still had ten fingers, by the look of things. And in the third bed ... I'd almost forgotten about the woman we'd brought unconscious from Saramotai. The one who'd called me by my mother's name.

Seemed she wasn't unconscious any more.

'I – sorry.' I hovered, holding one tent flap back, looking for an excuse. Only I didn't need one. I belonged here. More than she did. So why was I shuffling my feet like I was a kid back in Dustwalk again? 'I didn't mean to wake you. I'm just bleeding.' I held up my hand. Like I needed to prove it to this stranger.

'The Holy Father isn't here.' The woman pushed herself to her elbows. Her eyes darted around frantically in the dim lamplight, like she was looking for some escape of her own.

'He's still at the celebrations.' I finally stepped over the threshold and let the tent flap fall shut. I tried not to look at Sayyida as I pressed forward. 'I just came for supplies.'

I'd been stuck in this tent for a good long while after I woke up from nearly dying. I could've drawn every corner of it from memory. Down to the iron-and-wood chest emblazoned with holy words, where the Holy Father kept his supplies.

'It's locked,' the woman said as I dropped down next to the chest.

'I know.' I reached up for the small blue glass oil lamp that the Holy Father always kept burning when there was someone in the sick tent overnight. Nobody ought to be left to suffer and die in the dark. I felt around the base until my fingers closed around the tiny iron key that he kept lodged there. The trunk lock gave way with a satisfying click.

Inside were rows and rows of bottles and needles and powders and tiny knives all neatly lined up. It was so unlike Bahi's mess of tools and supplies scattered out across the ground that it almost hurt a little. Like there was less of him left in camp every day since he died.

'Believe it or not, this isn't my first visit,' I said over my shoulder, as I picked out a bottle of something clear I'd seen the Holy Father clean wounds with before and put it to one side. I held the set of needles up to the light, squinting. I'd never noticed how big they looked until now, but I had to figure one of them was smaller than the others.

'You're going to sew yourself up?' she asked from behind me, like she didn't know whether she ought to be appalled or impressed.

'Not the first time for that, either.' I picked a needle at random before turning around to face her head on. She looked a whole lot better than she had when we'd found her in that cell in Saramotai and she'd barely been able to focus on me. Her fever seemed to have broken and she was alert now, her face almost a normal colour.

'I—' she started and then hesitated, running her tongue along cracked lips. 'I've got some talent with healing. If you'd rather not.'

I didn't need her help. I could take the supplies and leave. I could forget I'd ever been the girl from Dustwalk who had a mother named Zahia. But if I left now I'd have to face Jin. And I was having trouble thinking of a single time running away from my problems had actually worked. Besides, it wasn't like I was all that excited about shoving a sharp object into my own skin.

I sat across from her, handing over the bottle, thread, and needle. She seemed skittish as she pulled away the collar of the khalat. Her fingers drifted over the wound, dabbing the liquid over where the blood had caked, making a hundred tiny pinpricks of pain sing behind it. But I wasn't paying it much mind. I was watching her face in the dim glow of the lamplight. Trying to recognise something there I might know.

'You've been drinking,' she said finally. 'I can smell it on you. That'll be why it started again. Thins the blood. You don't need stitches, just a bandage and to learn how to hold your drink.'

It was the way she said *drink* that made me sure. Her accent had been worn smooth by years in other places, places that didn't swallow that word like they were always thirsty, but there was no mistaking it. Not with the way the rest of the words dropped and rose. I could've picked out that accent in the cacophony of a bazaar. It was my accent.

'You called me Zahia,' I said, biting the bullet so fast I didn't have time to lose my nerve. 'That was my mother's name. Zahia Al-Hiza.' I watched her close for a reaction. 'But she was born Zahia Al-Fadi.'

The woman's face folded like a bad hand of cards. She pulled away from me, dropping the collar of my khalat, and pressed the back of her hands to her lips, stifling what sounded like a sob.

I stared at her, unsure of what to do. I ought to give her some privacy or some comfort. But I couldn't tear my gaze away from her.

'That would make you Amani, then.' Her voice sounded choked when she finally spoke again. She shook her head angrily, as if to dispel the tears. Desert girls didn't cry. 'You look exactly like Zahia at your age.' I'd heard that before. She reached out a hand like she was going to touch me. There were tears in her eyes. 'It's like seeing my sister the day I left Dustwalk all over again.'

'Your sister?' I pulled away before her fingers could so much as graze my cheek. 'You're Safiyah Al-Fadi?' I saw it as soon as she said it. I might be the spitting image of my mother but I saw her in this woman, too. She was the middle sister of the three Al-Fadi girls. My mother and Aunt Farrah's mythical third sister. The one who had famously vanished out of Dustwalk to make her own life. Who my mother always talked about running away to find. Who I'd been headed for when I first left Dustwalk. Before I'd chosen Jin and the Rebellion. 'You're supposed to be in Izman.'

'I *was* in Izman.' She suddenly busied herself, pulling bottles out of the Holy Father's trunk, checking them over with a quick, practised eye. 'I went there to find my fortune. I was there for nearly seventeen years.' She uncorked one without a label to sniff the contents, carefully avoiding meeting my eye.

I didn't like that she was here. It didn't seem right that in this whole huge sprawling desert we would find each other somewhere neither of us was ever meant to be. It seemed like the world had bent itself over backwards trying to push us together. Had I done this? I raked my mind for the things I'd said in the days Jin and I had walked across the desert, when I'd still thought I was going to wind up in Izman. Had I told some truth by accident? Before I'd known I was Demdji and that I couldn't lie – before I'd understood how dangerous it was to speak truths about the future, that it would twist the universe to make them true? All I'd have to have done was tell Jin I was going to find my aunt and the universe would rearrange the stars to make it so. And give me some kind of poisoned version of the truth.

Or was this just dumb luck?

Her nervous fingers finally settled on a bottle. She tipped out something thick and foul-smelling onto her fingertips and dabbed it across my wound.

'So how come you left Izman?'

'Because fortune is a funny thing.' I waited, but it seemed that was all the explanation I was going to get for how she'd wound up in Saramotai. 'Though I must admit I didn't think it was going to lead me to being imprisoned by a revolutionary who wanted to overturn the world order.'

'Malik wasn't ours,' I argued, wincing against the pressure of her fingers on my collarbone.

'Do you hand pick all your followers?' She pressed a little harder on my wound than she needed to. 'He did things in your prince's name; that's enough for me. He nearly killed me doing it, too. You know, some of this desert didn't ask for a rebellion that might get us killed.' She pulled away from me, wiping her fingers on a cloth. 'But I suppose, as the Holy Father in Dustwalk would have said, Fortune and Fate.'

Three words and I was standing back in the prayer house in Dustwalk all over again, being preached to. That was an old expression the Holy Father used when times were hard. *Fortune and Fate.* It meant that fortune and fate weren't always the same.

I understood that better than anyone.

'Here.' My aunt Safiyah dusted her hands off quickly, pulling out another of the bottles from the Holy Father's chest. 'Take this for the pain. It'll help you sleep.'

It was her accent, mingled with those words, talk of sleep and medicines, that drew the memory out of the corner of my mind.

Tamid.

It hit me like a blow to the chest.

I'd pushed down all thoughts of him for months now. But it was as if she'd summoned him here, with her Dustwalk accent, the tiny bottle of medicine in the dim light, the sick longing for people I used to know. He was the only friend I had before this place and the Rebellion. Who used to stitch me up and sneak me things until the pain went away.

Who I left to die in the sand.

Was this how truth-telling myself to my aunt would twist around on me? Reminding me of who I was before Ahmed's rebellion? Of the people who'd suffered and died because of things I did?

All of a sudden, taking something that would send me to sleep and away from that memory seemed awful tempting.

But before I could take the bottle, the entrance to the tent flapped open violently. My head snapped around. My first thought was that Jin had followed me here. But through the lingering haze of drink I saw two figures silhouetted in the light of the lamp, against the backdrop of the dark outside. Jin would have come after me alone. And they were tangled together like two drunk wedding revellers looking for some privacy, stumbling into the wrong tent.

Then they shifted, and the light caught the knife.

I was on my feet in a heartbeat even as I heard a voice I knew well choke out my name.

It was Delila.

Chapter 9

The figures staggered backwards out from the tent. But it was too late to run. I was already on my feet.

'Stay here,' I ordered Safiyah, swiping up a knife as I went.

'Stop!' The order came at me as I burst out of the sick tent after them. Before I could see clearly. Before I even recognised the second figure holding Delila hostage. Dark hair flopping over his proud brow, his eyes panicked in a way I'd never seen before. Surprise staggered the strength in my voice. 'Mahdi?'

He was holding Delila around her waist. A knife was pressed across her throat so hard he'd already drawn blood. I could see it running in a fresh trickle down her skin and under her khalat, staining it.

'Don't come any further!' He was shaking hard.

'Mahdi.' I kept my voice level, even though my mind

was making a mad dash for an explanation. 'What the hell are you doing?'

'I'm saving her.' Mahdi's voice rose frantically. I checked how far we were from the wedding. Too far for anyone to hear him, no matter how loud he got. 'I'm saving Sayyida. Raise your hands where I can see them!'

I kept eye contact with Delila as I did what he said, desperately trying to tell her it was going to be all right. I was not going to let her die here.

'What's in your hand?' he called out, urgently.

The knife.

'I'm letting it go,' I said, keeping my voice level. I unclenched my fist and let it drop. It planted blade-down in the sand. 'I'm unarmed now.'

'No, you're not.' Mahdi pulled at Delila, and she whimpered. He was frantic, manic – and that knife was awfully close to her throat. 'You've got an entire desert around you.'

He wasn't wrong. I could have him down in a handful of seconds if I wanted. But I couldn't make sure that knife didn't go through Delila as he fell.

'Mahdi.' I spoke carefully, the same voice I'd use to soothe a skittish horse. 'How exactly do you think sticking a knife to Delila's throat is going to help Sayyida?'

'She's a Demdji!' He spat out the words like it was

obvious. 'Some people think that it's having *part* of a Demdji that cures ills. But they're wrong. That's just peasant superstition. A few pieces of purple hair aren't going to bring my Sayyida back.' He was unbalanced. He was desperate. He had a knife to Delila's throat. I'd never wished more that I could move the desert without needing to move my body. I tried anyway, tugging at the edge of the sand with just my mind. It crept along reluctantly before sagging back down. I needed help. 'I've read books. *Whosoever takes the life of a Demdji shall have their life in equal measure.*' He recited like it was holy text even though I knew it wasn't anything I'd ever heard preached.

'What's that supposed to mean?' I had to buy some time. Enough to think of a distraction.

'It means Sayyida can survive if she kills Delila. I'd trade any Demdji's life for Sayyida's. In a heartbeat.'

There. Something behind him. A flash of movement in the moonlight. It darted silently from one shadow to the next. In a moment, as he passed from one tree to another, I got a clear view of him.

Jin.

I caught myself just quickly enough to flick my eyes back to Mahdi before he could notice where I was looking. He'd followed me after all. And he had a shot at getting us all out of here without bloodshed if I could just hold Mahdi's attention long enough. I didn't need a distraction. I was the distraction.

'And then what?' I had to give Jin a chance to get close to him. 'What's your plan? Ahmed would never forgive you for killing his sister – you must know that.'

'I don't *care* about Ahmed.' Mahdi's accent was becoming more grating the more frantic he got. 'This whole rebellion is going to hell on a fast horse, anyway.'

'I'm pretty sure we're not the ones going to hell in this situation,' I said. Jin was only ten paces behind him now. Close enough so I saw the corner of his mouth pull up at my barb, even though his eyes never left his sister.

'Even you can see it, surely.' Mahdi didn't seem to hear me. He was leaning forward, desperately, like he could convince me, too. Like I might step aside and let him past. 'Ahmed has bitten off more than he can chew. Saramotai is just the beginning – there will be other uprisings, and the war with the foreigners will end and the Sultan will destroy us. Ahmed is too weak to hold this whole country. We can't save everyone. So I'm saving someone I can.'

Jin was close now. Too close. The moonlight hit him as he left the cover of the trees, sending a spike of shadow across Mahdi's path. Mahdi's eyes went wide as he spun to face this new threat. His blade bit into the soft skin of Delila's throat with the sudden motion, drawing blood.

Delila screamed.

The time for distraction was done. I flung my arm in an arc, exploding a burst of sand right into Mahdi's face, blinding him as Jin darted forward. His hand latched over Mahdi's, twisting the knife away from Delila's neck. It changed course, plunging toward Jin's chest instead. I whipped my palm flat, and the sand shifted below Mahdi's feet, throwing him off balance, the knife sailing harmlessly by Jin's shoulder.

Mahdi went down, his fingers snapping like dry kindling in Jin's grip, the knife falling from his hand. He hit the sand with an agonised cry, even as Jin caught Delila.

And then it was over. Delila collapsed into Jin, sobbing, a smear of blood from her neck darkening his desert-white shirt. His eyes met mine over his sister's head.

So much for avoiding him.

Chapter 10

The stitched sun in the crown of the pavilion glowed dimly in the lamplight. It wasn't enough to fill the whole of the pavilion, and the dark seemed to press in around the five of us.

Me, Shazad, Hala, Jin, and Ahmed.

There should have been more of us. If Bahi was alive. If Delila wasn't being patched up by my aunt. If Mahdi wasn't a traitor now locked up and under guard. If we hadn't all agreed Imin should be given *one* night away from the Rebellion for the wedding.

'You should have killed him outright, if you ask me.' Hala's eyes were far away, but I knew she was talking to me.

'No one did ask you,' I retorted. All I could think of was the fear in Mahdi's eyes as he held Delila, shaking. Reasoning with me for Sayyida's life because he was too proud to beg. 'You trying to tell me you wouldn't have done the same if Imin was the one dying in that tent?'

'No.' Hala's voice was low, in that threatening way she got sometimes when it came to her sibling. 'I'm trying to tell you that it just as easily *could* have been Imin. Or you, or me, or the twins. Every single one of us risks our life every day for selfish people like him and *this* is how they repay us.' Selfish was what this desert did best. I knew that better than anyone.

'Love makes people selfish,' Jin said, so softly I almost believed I wasn't meant to have heard it. A sudden hot, angry rush rose up in me. But before I could snap anything back, Hala spoke up again.

'I don't believe half of what's been done to me was for love. Unless you want to count love of money.' Hala raised her left hand into the light pointedly, with its missing two fingers. 'Why should the rest of us suffer just because Amani seems to get to pick and choose who gets to live based on how she feels that day?'

'Hala, that's enough,' Shazad warned.

But Hala ignored her. 'You seem exceptionally good at putting the rest of us in danger. Today it's Mahdi. Last time you seemed to think your brother's life was worth more than everyone else's in this desert. How long before another burned-out crater appears where a city used to be? Or he finds us and turns another one of us to dust like Bahi? Or maybe someone will manage to hunt him down like they did Imin and they'll take his eyes and he can die slowly when you could have given him mercy.'

I went at her like a bullet from a gun.

Shazad was between us in a second. Before I could get to Hala, before Hala could conjure some horror in my mind in retaliation.

'I said, *that's enough.*' She held me back, arms on my shoulders, bracing me as Hala sneered at me over her shoulder. I strained against her, but familiar hands grabbed me, dragging me back away from the fight. Jin. I didn't bother to fight as he pulled me against him easily. The familiar heat of his body as my back met his chest.

'Stop. You know you don't really want to fight her, Amani.' He spoke in my ear, low enough so that I was the only one who heard him. So that his breath stirred the hair at the nape of my neck. Everything in me wanted to lean back into him, feel his heartbeat against my spine, and relax back into his presence. But I stilled before I could, forcing myself to pull away from him. To put air between us.

'Let me go.' His grip loosened as he felt my body lock up below his touch. I shook him off and his hands dropped away. I could still feel the heat of his palms lingering on my upper arms. Like burn marks. Except Demdji weren't supposed to burn so easily.

'Everyone in this tent has people we'd turn the world inside out to protect.' Shazad turned to Hala. 'This is not about blood or love. This is about treason. Mahdi has committed a crime against us, and there is judgment to be passed.'

Ahmed hadn't said a word yet. But now we were all looking at him.

Finally, he spoke. 'My father would choose execution.'

'It's what your brother would choose, too,' Jin said from behind me. He'd retreated a safe distance from me. Even without looking at him I was keenly aware of him.

'You're advocating revenge?' Ahmed said. 'An eye for an eye?'

'It's not an eye for an eye,' Jin said. 'Delila is still alive. Thanks to Amani. So I'm only advocating for one eye.'

Ahmed's fingers drummed along the map. 'It doesn't seem to me that a Sultan should hand out rulings out of spite.'

Mahdi's words whispered into my mind. *Too weak to hold this whole country.*

Jin took a step towards Ahmed. 'Our sister—'

'She's *not* your sister.' His hand slammed against the table, bringing silence instantly. None of us had ever heard Ahmed lash out at Jin like that. Even Shazad drew back, her eyes flicking between the two brothers. Like she might have to hold one of them back, too. Jin and Delila might not share any blood – not like she did with Ahmed through their mother, or like Jin and Ahmed did through their father – but they'd been raised together. Jin had never called Delila anything but his sister and Delila considered both princes her brothers. But Ahmed was the one who tied them together. 'And it's not your decision. It's mine.'

Jin tightened his jaw. 'Fine. While you make *your* decision, I'll go watch over *your* sister. Like I watched over her after my mother died. My mother who saved your life, lest we forget. And who died while you were here playing saviour to the country that enslaved her and tried to kill your sister.'

'Everyone get out.' Ahmed never took his eyes from his brother as he gave the command. 'This conversation is between me and my brother.'

'Don't bother.' Jin pushed open the tent flap in one violent movement. 'We're done here.' The night air spilled into the pavilion behind him, pouring the light from Ahmed's tent across the sand like a beacon.

That was when the gunshot came.

The whole world seemed to slow around us as we stood frozen, our minds struggling to catch up. A bullet was buried in the middle of the table, embedded a hair's breadth to the left of Ahmed's hand. Straight above it was a hole in the canopy, right through the yellow of the fabric sun.

Shazad reacted first. Grabbing Ahmed by the front of his shirt, she wrenched him to the ground and under the table a second before the next gunshot sounded. Then another one.

Jin grabbed me at the same moment, sending me sprawling, knocking the air from my lungs. I hit the ground hard, and a stab of violent pain tore through my right shoulder. I cried out. Not a bullet, though. I knew what that felt like. Jin shielded me with his body as bullets tore through the flimsy canvas of the tent.

Sayyida.

The idea hit as hard and sudden as a bullet to the brain. The timing was too perfect. She hadn't 'escaped' with Hala. She'd been bait. A trap. They'd followed her straight back to us.

Screaming started outside, followed by more gunfire. Another bullet struck near us, sending up a spray of sand dangerously close to where Jin and I were. The soldiers were shooting blind, but that didn't mean they weren't going to hit us.

I reached for my power, but it danced tauntingly out of my grasp. I felt something cold against my hip. I twisted to get a better look. My shirt had ridden up, and the iron of Jin's belt buckle was pressing into my bare skin, stripping me of my Djinni half. We both winced as another bullet slammed into the table above Ahmed's and Shazad's heads.

'Jin.' The fall had knocked the air out of my lungs, and there was a shooting pain in my right arm, like it might be broken. It was hard to talk with Jin's solid weight on top of me. 'Belt buckle,' I finally gasped, my chest burning.

Jin understood. He shifted quickly away from me. I felt the iron leave my skin. And suddenly the panic wasn't a roaring sensation trapped in my chest any more. It was pouring out of me. Into the desert. Into the sand.

I called the desert into a storm.

I felt it rise in the sands outside, picking up strength as it went. I pushed it as far from us as I could, to the edges of camp, but sand whipped at the torn walls of the tent all the same. I closed my eyes and let the desert work itself into a frenzy. The gunfire stopped, faltering under the force of the whirlwind even as it crashed into the side of the pavilion, lifting it from the ground, carrying it away like it was nothing.

Outside, the sandstorm had whipped the camp's fear into chaos. Rebels were rushing to tie sheemas around their faces as others gathered supplies or tried to calm horses. Everybody knew what our evacuation plan was. But it was one thing knowing it, another trying to execute it in the dead of night with bullets tearing through the air.

I fought for better control. I tried to breathe as I rose onto my knees. The gunfire had come from above. That meant they were on the walls of the canyon. I shifted, pushing my hands outward, pushing my power towards them, creating a shield from the gunfire as best I could.

As the sand moved, I saw the first rebel's body. Fresh red blood was spilling out of the bullet wound in his chest. I felt my control slip and grabbed at it again.

Shazad was on her feet, already giving orders as I kept the air raging around us, pulling the chaos into order.

'Amani! We have to go!' Shazad screamed over the roaring of sand, reaching for me.

'I can cover your escape!' I called back. 'Get everyone else out!'

'Not without you.' Shazad shook her head. Her dark hair was already coming free from its braid, whipping into her face frantically. Behind her I could see people desperately saddling horses, some clambering onto the backs of the twins in the forms of giant Rocs.

'Yes, without me!' I screamed back. I wanted to tell her that I'd be fine. But Demdji promises weren't safe to make. 'Get everyone else to safety. Get Ahmed to safety. They need you with them, and you need me here.'

Shazad hesitated a moment. My friend was fighting it. But our general knew I was right. Half the camp would die without some kind of cover. And right now I was the only cover we had.

Shazad half turned. She glanced over her shoulder to where Ahmed was trying to calm the panic enough to get people away, then back to me. 'If you don't follow behind' – she dropped down in front of me, clasping my shoulder for just a moment – 'you'd better believe I'll come after you.'

And then she was gone. I turned everything I had in me outwards. I emptied myself into the desert, a perfect cyclone shielding the edges of the camp, cutting our people's escape off from the soldiers' sight.

I didn't know how long I held it. As long as I could, before my arms started to shake. I was distantly aware of the chaos around me. Of supplies being loaded, of horses being led to the entrance of the camp, of Izz and Maz shooting into the air under a hail of gunfire. Of shouting, far away.

But all I really knew was the desert. I was wholly part of the sandstorm until I thought I might scatter to dust and whip away with it. I was losing control. It wasn't just my arms. My whole body was trembling with the effort. The sand was whipping through my hair instead of towards the enemy. I needed to let go. And if I had any shot of getting out, I needed to do it now.

I pushed myself to my feet. My legs buckled hard below me. Arms around my waist caught me before I could hit the ground.

'I've got you,' Jin said in my ear. 'Let go; I've got you.'

A horse was rearing and kicking, panicking as the storm started to close in around us as my control wavered. 'Why . . . are you . . . still here?' I gasped out. 'Shazad—'

My head was swimming with the effort of keeping a grip on the sand. If I let go, the sand would race in and bury this place, drowning anyone who hadn't made it out yet. 'She's got most everyone else out.' The solidness of Jin's body was the only thing propping me up now.

'Not you.'

'Like hell I'd leave you behind to get yourself killed.' His voice was low and sure in my ear as his body curled around mine. Protecting me as he urged the horse forward. He pushed me into the saddle, swinging himself up behind me. A gun went off nearby, too close for comfort. 'Amani. Let go. I've got you, I promise. Trust me.'

So I let go.

Chapter 11

We rode like we were trying to beat the sunset to the horizon. The army was behind us. We had to get far enough into the mountains to outstrip them.

I slipped out of consciousness somewhere around leaving camp and slept away the few hours of darkness we had left. When I woke up, leaning against Jin, a new dawn was on us and we had an army in pursuit. The last of my power went into raising the desert behind us, creating as much of a shield as I could between the soldiers and our little party.

Jin and I weren't alone. About a dozen stragglers from camp who hadn't managed to get out with the twins or Shazad's first wave of riders were with us. Some of them were riding double on the last of our horses. I couldn't make out their faces as we raced across the burning sands. And I didn't know who had gotten away with Ahmed and Shazad or if whoever was with us could ride well enough to keep up. They didn't really have a choice right now.

My arm was a constant shooting pain up my side that got worse every time I checked behind. It took everything in me to keep it up and keep the pain from shattering my focus.

Finally I couldn't hold on any longer, and neither could the horses. If we hadn't outrun them by now, we would have to stand and fight. I dropped the shield behind us. Jin seemed to feel the tension flee my body. He wheeled the panting beast around, gun drawn, checking behind us for pursuers. My vision blurred from the sheer relief of not using my power any more. I shielded my eyes against the last of the desert sun. We were all perfectly still as we scanned the horizon for any sign of movement. But there was nothing behind us but open sand. We'd lost them.

'We can pitch camp here,' Jin commanded, his voice reverberating through his chest, into my back. He was hoarse with thirst.

'We're not safe,' I started to argue.

'We're never safe,' Jin said, so only I heard.

'We've got no cover, and the horses—'

'The horses aren't going to make it any farther without a rest and we can't outrun them on foot,' Jin said in my ear. 'And we can't outrun them without you, either. We'll post a watch, move again if there's even a cloud of dust on the horizon.'

He slipped off our horse and started giving orders to pitch tents and go through the supplies people had grabbed as we evacuated. He uncapped something at his side and took a swig before passing it to me.

I brought the water skin to my mouth and with shaking hands sipped slowly, cradling my injured shoulder close to my body. There were a dozen of us, give or take. That meant a whole lot of missing faces who were now just bodies in the sand if they hadn't gotten away with Ahmed and Shazad. I was the only Demdji among us. Hopefully that meant Hala and Delila were together, and between them, they could hide even a big group of moving rebels. And Shazad would get them all to safety. I had to trust they'd be waiting for us.

My aunt, Safiyah, was among those who'd escaped with us, as were two of the other women from Saramotai. I supposed it was hard to follow an escape plan when you didn't know it. Safiyah was helping dole out food. A few other familiar faces were dotted around. Relief eased my heart a little.

There'd be no fire tonight. It left us vulnerable to Nightmares or Skinwalkers but we were a lot more vulnerable if we lit a beacon to the Sultan's army. We'd just have to ring the camp in whatever iron we had and hope for the best.

Everyone was ravaged from the escape. Some were already stuffing bread into their mouths and simply collapsing as the sun sank low. We'd need to set a watch, and divvy up the supplies among the horses and pitch the tents. And there were a thousand and one other things to think of. But my head was spinning and I couldn't think of them.

I downed the water until my head steadied. We wouldn't have to make it last that long anyhow. By now I knew our part of the desert. We were a three-day ride from the port city of Ghasab, but at the pace we'd set, riding all night and through the day, we'd be there by sunset tomorrow. From there we could resupply and rejoin with everyone at the meeting point in the mountains. Well, everyone who'd gotten away.

I stowed the water away and gingerly tried to slide off the horse, testing my weight on my tender right arm as I braced myself against the saddle. It surrendered instantly, buckling me towards the sand in a messy heap.

'You're hurt.' Jin reached down toward where I was sprawled. I ignored his hand and pulled myself up with my good arm, using the stirrup. The horse was so tired it barely protested.

'I'll survive.' I tried to hold my arm as normal as I could as I turned away from him. 'I always have.'

'Amani!' He raised his voice as I walked away, loud enough so a few of the rebels glanced our way, before quickly getting back to work. Everyone knew enough to stay out of it. 'I watched you walk across an entire desert. I've memorised the way you move. And right now you're moving like you've dislocated your shoulder. You need to let me take a look at it.'

'I can give you something for the pain,' Safiyah interrupted, brushing sand off her fingers. *Almost* everyone knew enough to stay out of it.

'She doesn't need something for the pain,' Jin said evenly. He was talking to Safiyah, but his eyes never left me. 'She needs someone to pop her arm back in its socket before we have to saw it off.'

That made me stop.

I turned back to face him. He had unwrapped his sheema and wound it around his neck and I could see his face clearly. Jin had always been good at bluffing. A faint smile reappeared, like he could read what I was thinking more easily than I could. That smile always meant trouble. 'Willing to chance it, Bandit?'

I was almost sure he was lying. But I wasn't more sure than I was fond of having two working arms.

'Fine.' I extended my arm to him as far as I could,

like a kid holding out a wounded animal she'd found in the desert. Jin didn't take it. Instead he put a hand on my back. The familiar thrill rushed up my spine. My body didn't seem to know I was angry at him. He led me into the small blue tent I claimed when we were on the move. Someone had pitched it for me. He let the tent flap fall shut behind us, sealing us in privacy.

The tent was too low to stand in. I stooped stubbornly until Jin pulled me to the ground to sit across from him. Night was descending fast around us, but there was still just enough light to see by. Outside I could hear the shuffle of the camp as it got ready for a night in the desert.

'I need to see it.' His voice was gentle now that we were alone. It took me a second to understand what he meant.

'Fine,' I said again, avoiding his gaze.

Very carefully, he put one hand on my upper arm and slid the other one under my khalat at the collar. His fingers were warm and familiar. Once he would've made a joke about getting his hands under my clothes. But now a silent tension hung between us – until I couldn't stand it any more. 'You sure you know what you're doing?'

'Trust me.' Jin wasn't looking me in the face, though he was so close to me it was almost the only place he could look. 'I had to learn on the *Black Seagull*, before this all started.' *This*. I knew he meant the Rebellion. I almost laughed. It was such a small word to mean all of us and everything we'd done and everything we still had left to do. 'A lot of sailors got hurt getting tangled up in ropes.'

He did something that sent a stab of pain through my side. I hissed through my teeth.

'Sorry.'

'You goddamn should be.' Pain sharpened my tongue. 'This happened when you shoved me, you know.'

'You're right,' Jin deadpanned, fingers still prodding gently at me. 'I should've let you get shot; that's so much easier to recover from.'

'And what would you know about that?' We were running for our lives. This wasn't the right time to be picking a fight, not in the middle of a war. But I hadn't been the one to bring it up. 'You weren't around when I did.'

'You'd rather I'd stayed to watch you die?' Jin's jaw was tight.

'I didn't die.'

'But you might have.'

'And you might've died off spying on the Xichian!' Silence dropped between us. But we didn't move.

Neither of us pulled away or forward. Jin's fingers still explored my tender shoulder.

He finally spoke again. 'It's dislocated. But not broken.' He was just above me now, so all I could see was his mouth and the shadow of stubble along his jaw. My shoulder braced between his two hands. 'This part is going to hurt like hell. You ready?'

'Well, when you put it that way, how could I say no?' That slight curve to his mouth that always made me feel like we were in this together appeared. 'I'm ready.'

'All right.' He shifted so we were face-to-face. 'I'm going to pop your shoulder back in on three.' I gritted my teeth and prepared myself. 'One ...'

I took a deep breath.

'Two ...'

Before I could tense in anticipation of 'three', Jin wrenched my arm out and up.

Pain stabbed from my elbow to my shoulder and tumbled out of my mouth violently. 'Son of a bitch!' Another curse ripped out after it in Xichian, then one in Jarpoorian that Jin had taught me while we crossed the desert, the pain drawing out every insult in every language that I knew. I was halfway through a colourful curse in Gallan when Jin kissed me.

Any more words I might have had died

cataclysmically the second his mouth found mine. My thoughts fell to ruins right behind.

I'd almost forgotten what being kissed by Jin was like.

God, did he ever know how to kiss me.

He kissed me like it was the first time and the last time. Like we were both going to burn alive from it. And I folded into him like I didn't care. The Rebellion might be falling apart around us, the whole desert even, but for now we were both still alive and we were together, and the anger between us had turned into a different fire that drew us both into the middle of it until I wasn't sure which one of us was consuming the other one.

He pulled away with sudden, gut-wrenching speed, breaking us apart as quickly as we'd come together. My own ragged breathing filled the silence that followed. It was full dark now. All I could make out was the rise and fall of his shoulders and the paleness of his white shirt.

'Why did you do that?' It came out in a low breath. I was close enough that I saw the rise and fall of his throat when he swallowed. I had the sudden urge to rest my mouth there and taste whether his breath was as unsteady and as uncertain as mine.

But when Jin spoke, his voice was as steady as a rock. 'To distract you. How's the pain?'

I realised that the screaming pain in my arm had

gone silent as the rest of my body came alive in answer to Jin's kiss. He was right; it didn't hurt half as bad as it had when he'd twisted it back into place.

He picked something up off the ground – my red sheema, I realised. It must've slipped off. Jin touched my arm again, but this time his hand was just flesh and blood on my elbow, not fire invading my skin. He tied the sheema around my arm and looped it over my neck like a sling, tying it behind my neck in one firm knot before pushing himself to his feet. 'Besides . . .' His voice was light, like it was all a joke and we were just two strangers flirting with each other before parting ways again. Not two people who were as tangled as we were. Who had crossed the desert together. Who had faced death together over and over. 'Who could resist a mouth like that?'

He stole another kiss from me so whip quick that he was gone before I even fully felt it.

I sat in the dark long after he went, not rising even when I heard the sounds of a hastily thrown together meal being eaten outside. I wasn't that hungry anyway. I felt raw. Burned out. Scorched earth. I distantly remembered that phrase – Shazad had taught it to me. It was something to do with war strategy. I wasn't sure if Jin and I were at war or not.

I listened to the camp settle around me as everything

ran through my head. Everything we had gone through. Everything left ahead of us. Everything that he wouldn't say. The more silence fell over the camp, the more noise my anger made.

We were both as stubborn as hell, but one of us was going to have to crack eventually.

I was on my feet before I could think about it, tearing away the tent flap. The camp had gone completely silent now, everyone settled into their tents except whoever had been set to keep watch. I strode across the camp. I knew Jin's tent on sight, red and patched on one side and set up straight across from mine. I wasn't sure what I was going to do – shout at him or kiss him or something else entirely.

I'd decide when I saw him.

I was almost there – two paces from his tent – when something clamped over my mouth, hard. Panic spiked in my chest as a cloth covered my face like a gag, smelling sickly sweet, like spilled liquor.

Instinct took over. I drove my elbow backwards. A scream of pain tore through my injured shoulder. A mistake. My mouth opened in a gasp. I inhaled and the smell invaded my mouth, clinging to my tongue, my throat, all the way down to my lungs.

I was being poisoned.

The effects were instant. My legs buckled and the world tilted sideways.

The Sultan's army had found us.

Why hadn't we had warning? I could've done something. I could've raised the desert. I could've stopped them. Now I could barely fight. I thrashed helplessly, my fingers clawing at the hand on my mouth. I twisted to the side, struggling to throw my weight downwards. Mostly knowing it was already too late. As I fell I saw two bodies slumped in the sand, not moving.

The watch, already dead.

I needed to warn the others. The world was fading. I was slipping away. I was going to die. Jin. I needed to give him a chance to escape. To save the others.

I opened my mouth to scream a warning. The darkness swallowed it with me.

Chapter 12

I woke up being violently sick. Vomit splattered next to me across the wooden floor, by a bucket. I grabbed it before the second heave came.

Everything left in my stomach came up.

I squeezed my eyes shut and tightened my arms around the metal bucket. I ignored the cloying smell of vomit climbing up from the bottom. My head was still spinning, my stomach still churning. I didn't move straight away, even after I was sure there was nothing left to choke up but my own liver.

I seemed to still be alive. Which was unexpected. I'd feel good about it when I stopped retching my insides up. And which meant I'd been drugged, not poisoned. The army ought to have killed me. They ought to have killed all of us.

Maybe they'd kept me alive because I was a Demdji, and I was valuable. Or because I was a girl and I looked helpless. But they didn't have any reason to take the rest of the camp alive. They'd have no reason not to take one look at Jin, who always looked like he could be trouble, asleep, and put a bullet through him to keep him out of the way.

There was one way I could know for sure. I couldn't speak anything that wasn't the truth. If I couldn't say it out loud, then he was gone.

I swallowed the bile in my throat.

'Jin is alive.'

The truth slipped out like a prayer into the dark, so huge and so certain I felt like I finally understood how Princess Hawa had been able to call the dawn. The words felt as important as the rising sun, easing the panic in my chest.

Jin was alive. Probably a captive in this place like I was.

I started listing names quickly. Shazad, Ahmed, Delila, Hala, Imin – they were alive, one after the other. Not once did my tongue stumble. They were all fine. Well, trying to say they were fine out loud might be pushing my luck, seeing as we'd all just lost our home. But alive. And so was I. And I wasn't about to let that change.

I was going to live long enough to get back to them.

The room was moving, I realised then. Was I on a train? The floor shifted below me and my stomach heaved again. No, this was different. There was no steady, juddering feeling. This was more like being rocked in a cradle by a drunken giant.

As my head cleared I took stock of things. I gingerly set the bucket down again and eased myself up. I could sit up. That wasn't nothing to start with. And thanks to the light coming through a small window above me, I could see.

I was on a bed in a cramped room with damp wooden walls and a damp floor. The light had the feel of late afternoon. Burned sky after a long day in the desert. It'd been night when I was taken, so that meant I'd been asleep nearly a whole day. At least a whole day.

I shifted, trying to stand up, but my right hand pulled me up short. I was tied to the frame of the bed.

No. Not tied. Chained.

Iron was biting into my skin. I could feel it the moment I reached for my power. I shoved up the sleeve on my arm to get a look at it. The iron was clamped like an angry hand on a child's wrist. Only not completely. A sliver of light leaked between my skin and the iron.

I could work with that.

Without thinking, I reached for my sheema. My fingers scraped across bare neck instead. It felt like being punched in the stomach.

It was gone. I remembered now. Jin had tied it like a sling. I'd been struggling as the drug filled my nose and mouth, and the sheema slipped off me. Gone in the sand.

It was stupid. It was just a thing. Just a stupid strip of red cloth against the desert sun. Except it was a stupid thing Jin had given me. Snatched off a clothesline in Sazi, the day we'd escaped Dustwalk. I'd never stopped wearing it since then. Even when I was angry at him. It was mine. And now it was gone.

But there were other ways out of this.

I worried at the stitching on my shirt until the side of it gave way. Tearing off a strip of cloth, I started to stuff it between my skin and the iron manacle. It wasn't exactly easy work – the manacle was tight and the cloth was awkward and thick. But I kept going all the same, working the piece of cloth in one bit at a time.

There. I felt it the moment the iron stopped touching my skin. My power rushed back in.

I was tired and thirsty, and my mouth tasted of vomit and some unknown drug that was still lingering in my lungs, but I could do this. I reached for the desert outside with everything I had. I felt it surge in answer, only to have it slip away. I pulled again, but nothing came. It felt like reaching for something just a little too far away.

I fought down the panic. There were still other ways. Like there'd been in Saramotai. I took a deep breath and closed my eyes. I could feel it now as I calmed myself. Even against the strange lurching of the room and my dizzy head. The sand that clung to my skin.

I raised my free hand in one quick violent motion, tearing the sand from every part of me that I could find, scraping skin off with it. I slashed the sand down towards my arm in one sharp motion.

The chain on the manacle splintered like wood under an axe. And I was free.

I bolted for the door, fighting the haze that was clinging to my mind like a lingering desert exhaustion. The floor tilted below me, pitching me out into a long dark hallway. At one end light leaked through from whatever was above. The floor heaved again below me.

Something connected in my mind, pieces from stories. Some I'd heard around campfires, and some Jin had told me.

This wasn't a train.

I was on a ship.

Wooden steps rose to meet me in the spot of sunshine, and I bashed my shin into a step as I scrambled upwards, the ground tilting yet again. And then I was up in the sunlight and fresh air.

I was momentarily blinded by the sudden glare after the dark. But I'd never been the sort to stop running just because I couldn't see where I was going. As my vision cleared I bolted forward, focusing on the place where the ship seemed to end.

Shouts followed me, but I didn't stop. I pushed my legs forward into one last violent whip of speed. I crashed full force into the rail at the edge of the ship. My escape.

Only there was no escape.

I'd once asked Jin if the sand sea was like the real sea. He'd given me that knowing smile he used to use when he knew something I didn't. Before I stripped all his secrets away and that smile became mine.

But now I knew.

There was water as far as the eye could see. More water than I'd seen in my whole life, more water than I'd known even existed in the world. I'd seen rivers and I'd seen pools, and I'd even seen some desert cities that had the luxury of fountains. I'd never seen anything like this.

It was as vast as the desert. And it kept me as trapped as I ever had been in Dustwalk by the miles and miles of burning sand.

Hands grabbed me from behind, yanking me away from the railing like someone thought I might throw myself off and into the mouth of the sea.

The haze of the world was starting to fade, and I was becoming aware of other things around me now. The strange smell that I could only guess was the drowned, endless stretch of sea around me. Shouts and cries, someone asking how the hell I'd gotten out.

It was a rabble of men who surrounded me. Mirajin, and no mistaking it – their skin was desert dark, and darker still for some of them. Bright sheemas covered their faces, and their hands were hard from work and raw with welts. I held on to my handful of sand, even though I knew I couldn't take down half their number before someone would shoot me. Not when there were already three pistols aimed at me.

And then there, standing among the crowd of men in a white khalat so brilliant it hurt my eyes, was the reason Jin was still alive. It wasn't the Sultan's army who'd taken me after all.

It was my aunt Safiyah.

'You drugged me.' My voice sounded scratchy. My aunt whose hands danced with practised ease through the medicines in the Holy Father's supply chest. She'd made the food. She could have slipped anything into it to knock out the rebels so she could escape. How easy would it have been for her to grab me as I stormed to Jin's tent, and knock me out with something stolen when I'd left her alone with his supplies unlocked. Twice she'd tried to push bottles that would put me to sleep. *For the pain*.

Shazad always said I was bad at watching my back. That was why she did it for me. Shazad would've also said this was one of those times to keep my mouth shut. But Shazad wasn't here. Because this woman had kidnapped me. 'You know, last time *I* drugged someone who trusted me,' I said, 'I had the decency to leave him where he was.'

'God, I wish you didn't sound so much like her, too.' She spoke low enough so I was sure I was the only one who heard. Safiyah circled around me, to where the sailor was still holding my arms. I felt her touch the strip of torn shirt still stuffed between my skin and the manacle. 'Clever.' She almost sounded proud of me. 'So you can use your Demdji tricks.'

I tried to pull away but the sailor held me fast. 'You know what I am.' It wasn't a question, but that didn't mean I didn't want answers.

'I've been trading medicines in Izman since before you were even born.' She pulled the cloth free from my wrist almost gently. 'Do you really think you're the first Demdji I've ever come across? Your kind are a rare breed. And worth a small fortune each. People in my trade learn to recognise the signs. I guessed because of your eyes, but I knew when that sandstorm saved us out in the desert. And your mother was always so secretive about you in her letters.'

She was in Saramotai for no good reason. No good reason except that the Emir of Saramotai had just started bragging to the world he had a child with eyes

141

like dying embers who wielded the sun in her hands. Ranaa had been worth something. But my aunt had missed her chance to take the little Demdji girl. So she'd taken me instead.

'It's not true, you know.' I remembered what Mahdi had told me, his knife held to Delila's throat. 'What they say about carving us up like meat to cure your ills.'

'The thing is,' she said, not quite looking at me as she twisted the piece of cloth back around her own hand, 'what really matters is that they're saying it at all.' She was right. Stories and belief meant more than truth. I knew that as the Blue-Eyed Bandit. But I wouldn't be the Blue-Eyed Bandit any more after she took my eyes.

Then to the man holding me, she said, 'Put her with the other girls for safekeeping.'

We went deeper into the ship than I'd come from. Far deeper. Back down into the deepest dark of its heaving wooden stomach and then down further still. I didn't know where we were going, but I knew we were getting close. I could hear the crying long before I could see them.

The room where the other girls were being kept made the tiny cell I'd woken up in look like the lap of luxury. They were chained to the wooden walls by both arms, and a shallow swamp of water sloshed around where they were sitting, lapping in the dark at their shivering bodies.

There were about a dozen of them. I caught glimpses of their faces in the swinging lamplight as I was led through. A pale girl with ivory blonde curls, in the rags of a foreign blue dress that looked like it had once been shaped like a bell; a dark-skinned girl whose eyes were closed, her head tipped back – the only sign she was still alive was her lips moving in prayer; a Xichian girl with a curtain of jet hair and pure murder in her eyes as she tracked the man holding me; a single other Mirajin girl in a plain khalat shivering against the cold. They looked as different from each other as day and night and sky and sand, but they were all beautiful. And that was what frightened me the most.

I'd heard the stories from Delila of how Jin's mother had been brought to the harem. A Xichian merchant's daughter who lived her life on the deck of a ship – a deck that turned slick with the blood of her family on the day they were boarded by pirates. Lien, sixteen and beautiful, was the only survivor, taken in chains and silk rags to the new Sultan of Miraji, who'd just killed his father and brothers to take the throne for himself. Who was building a harem to assure his succession.

She was sold for a hundred louzi into those walls, where she would bear a son to a man she loathed.

Where only the death of a friend she loved like a sister would give her the chance to escape back to the sea, clutching a newborn, with two young princes clinging to her hem.

Sometimes I doubted if Jin even knew those stories of his mother. They weren't the sorts of things women told their sons. They were the sorts of things women told other women. *Beware*, they told their daughters. *People will hurt you because you're beautiful.*

I wasn't beautiful. I wasn't here because of that. I was here because I was powerful.

This time the iron manacles bit hard into my skin. Safiyah and the man turned to go, taking the light with them. I couldn't just let them leave me here in chains. It was too much like surrendering.

'You know what they say – that betraying your own blood means you'll be forever cursed in the eyes of God,' I called after Safiyah. The water was already lapping at my clothes. I was still wearing Shazad's khalat, I realised. The water was soaking through it to my skin. 'The Holy Father preached that a whole lot in Dustwalk, too.'

I didn't expect Safiyah to stop. But she did. She stood in the doorway a long moment, her back to me, as the man vanished ahead of her.

'That he did.' She turned back to face me. And for

the first time, she scared me. It was the calm in her face. It told me she hadn't hesitated in doing this to me. Not even for a minute. 'Your mother and I always used to go to prayers. Every single day. Not just holy days, not just prayer days. Every day. We'd take up prayer mats next to each other and squeeze our eyes shut and pray like we were told to. We prayed for our lives. To get out of Dustwalk.' I hadn't noticed it before, this coldness in Safiyah. But it was clear as daybreak now as she crouched across from me. 'I loved my sister like the sun loves the sky. I would have done anything for her. And then she died, and left you. And you look so like her. It's like seeing a Skinwalker wearing my sister's face. Do you have any notion of what that's like? Looking at the thing that killed someone you loved, a thing that isn't even wholly human but seems to think she is?'

I watched the lamplight swing threateningly across her face, casting her into startling light and then darkness as it went. 'Dustwalk killed my mother.'

'Because she was protecting *you*. She was protecting you from the man who called himself your father. Would you like to know what her last letter to me said?'

I wanted to say no. But that would be a lie.

'She told me you weren't really her husband's. That he knew. He'd always known. That she feared for you now that you were older. That it was time to run. That she would die to protect you if she had to, but if she did, she would take him with her.'

I was back in the desert, that day. The day the gunshots had come. They said my mother had gone crazy. She hadn't. She had killed her husband knowing full well that she might die. And she'd done it for me.

'She was going to come and join me, you know. Before you. I hated you from the moment she told me that she would have to delay leaving because she couldn't cross the desert while she was with child. Or when you were too small. And yet still, I built my life thinking one day I would be able to share it with my little sister. I did terrible things to make a life for both of us. Dustwalk killed my sister. But she died because she was your mother. And now I'm going to take the life I should have always had. And you are going to buy it for me.'

'If you hate me so much, why not take my eyes out here and now?' I spat out at her. Let her show if she really hated me as much as she thought she did. 'Just get it over with.'

'Believe me, if I could have saved myself from carrying you across the desert I would have.' My aunt tossed a smile back at me lazily. 'But you're worth your weight in gold, you know.'

I'd heard that before. In Saramotai, about Ranaa. And again from Hala, after rescuing Sayyida from Izman.

She wasn't just going to take my eyes to sell on to some rich Izmani whose heart was going to give out on him. She was taking me to the Sultan.

Chapter 13

I was blind. Everything I saw was inside my mind, and outside that was just a darkness that went on forever and ever, sometimes punctured by noises.

In my better moments I knew it was the drugs. I was trapped in nightmares of fire and sand. Of sand on fire. A desert full of people burning. People I knew but whose names didn't exist in this dream. And a pair of blue eyes like mine watching it all. Because I still had eyes. I just couldn't figure out how to open them.

At some point I became aware that something had changed. I was being moved. And I could hear voices. Like I was listening from the bottom of a well.

'You know the Sultim likes Mirajin girls.'

The Sultim. I knew that name. Far away, I knew what it meant.

'This one isn't for the harem.' Another voice. A woman's. One I knew. It made me want to reach for my power. I stretched out my mind for it. The darkness started to creep in again. I lost my grip on the sand and the voices. The last thing I heard before it swallowed me again was '—dangerous.'

A spark of consciousness woke at the very back of my mind.

Dangerous.

They'd better believe I was.

I came to all at once, a dozen bits of awareness competing for my attention. The cold of the table under me, the sharp pain riddling my body. The crystal-white glare of sunlight on my eyelids, a cacophony of birds, and something else, something that tasted unnatural. More drugs, I realised.

But I finally managed to open my eyes. The room was bright and airy and flooded with light reflecting brightly off a marble ceiling above me. The stone was the colour of every sky I'd ever seen all at once. It was the pink and red of the wounded dawn, the dark violet of a calm dusk, and as brilliantly unsettling as the clear blue glare of high noon.

I'd never been anywhere this rich before. Not even the emir's house in Saramotai.

The palace. I was in the Sultan's palace.

We'd spent long hours trying to figure out ways to get

more spies into the Sultan's palace. Months easing people from our side in through the kitchens. And I'd just been carried unconscious over the threshold like it was nothing.

And now I needed to get out.

I might've laughed at the irony of it if I didn't think it'd hurt so much.

The world was starting to put itself back together as I took stock of the situation. I was weaker than I ought to be. And I could already feel my eyelids getting heavy again, wanting to return to sleep. I had to sit up. I pressed my elbows into the cold marble slab and tried to push myself up. Pain stabbed across my entire body at the movement. I hissed air through my teeth and the sheet that'd been covering me slithered away.

I grabbed at it, and pinpricks of pain screamed back at me across my arms. Then I caught sight of myself for the first time. Under the soft white sheet I was wrapped in bandages. They covered almost every part of my body. Wrists to shoulders. Around my chest and all the way down my back. Tentatively I reached down and grazed my fingers over my legs. My hand met cloth instead of skin. I looked like a doll sewn out of linen. Only dolls didn't usually spot fresh blood like I was.

And here I'd been figuring nothing would be worse than waking up shackled on a ship.

I didn't exactly like being proven wrong.

And as the pain of whatever was under the bandages subsided, I realised I was alone. That was a nice surprise. I spied a familiar blue khalat flung over a nearby chair. The one Shazad had given me before Imin's wedding. I didn't even know how many days it'd been since then.

Moving awkwardly with my sore muscles and bandaged limbs, I retrieved the stained fabric and pulled it on, fumbling with the tiny buttons that ran up the front. At least my hands seemed undamaged. Now I just wished I had a fistful of sand or a pistol to fill them. Hell, at this point I'd even take a knife. But I couldn't see any weapons among the clutter of the room.

Gauzy pink curtains fluttered from a huge archway. I moved gingerly toward them. Wind that tasted of familiar desert heat rippled them as I passed out onto the balcony.

Izman sprawled out below me.

It was like nothing I'd ever seen. A flat, blue-tiled roof with a gushing fountain on it leaned close enough to its neighbour to whisper city secrets. Beyond that, yellow flowers tumbled down sun-baked walls that were competing for space in the shade of their neighbours. Purple canopies crowned another house, and a golden dome pressed against minarets that jutted up like spears challenging the sky.

Jin said once that I couldn't understand how big Izman really was. If I ever saw him alive again, I might even be glad enough to admit that he'd been right.

It looked like a jumble of rooftops that went all the way to the end of the world. Only I knew that wasn't right. Somewhere out there was the desert I'd come from. I reached for it with my mind. For the sand and grit. But I couldn't feel anything. The desert had been ruthlessly polished out of here. I'd have to reach beyond the palace walls for that.

I gauged the distance between the top of the wall and the balcony.

I could probably make that jump on a good day. The throbbing pain in my body reminded me today was not a good day. But all it would take was one leap of faith, and I could be in the city. If I made it. If not, I would be a broken body in the garden below. Which still might be better than getting stuck here.

No. I was going to live to see Shazad again, like she'd asked me to promise. I was going to live to see Ahmed on the throne. And I was going to live to make Jin explain just why he thought he could kiss me after leaving me.

I'd have to go through the door. Only I wasn't about to try to walk through it like I was a guest instead of a prisoner. There would be a guard outside, no doubt about it.

There were no weapons in the room, but there was a glass jar filled with dried flowers. I picked it up off its shelf and positioned myself with my back flat against the door. And then let it go. It shattered on the colourful tiles.

That ought to get someone's attention.

I dropped to my knees, ignoring the screaming pain in my body, as I searched through the glass for the biggest shard. It had worked; I could hear footsteps through the door, someone coming to investigate. My hand closed around a piece of glass the size of my thumb, shattered to a sharp point. I curled my hand around it just tight enough not to draw blood, staying in my crouch, back flat to the wall by the door – ready for whoever came through. It had worked in Saramotai and I didn't believe the Sultan's guards were any brighter than Malik's.

The door swung open. I stayed low, heart pounding. All I saw was a flash of pale grey fabric before I moved. I slashed towards the back of the knees. It sliced through thin linen, gouging straight for the soft flesh underneath.

Instead, the glass scraped noisily off something hard.

A wound gaped in the fabric of the trousers where my makeshift weapon had struck, revealing gleaming bronze joints underneath.

For a second all I could think of was Noorsham in the bronze armour designed to control him. Heavy words in his Last County accent echoing around inside a hollow shell. But the voice that came now was a different one.

'Careful!' It sounded familiar, although it wasn't talking to me. I tipped my head back slowly, looking up at the man staring down at me dispassionately. 'She's armed.'

I thought I was ready for whatever I was facing here. I was dead wrong. Because in the doorway, with a new slice in his clothes, carefully parted hair stuck to his forehead, was Tamid.

The world tilted out from under me even as a guard in uniform stepped around him, weapon drawn. He grabbed me, ripping my meagre glass weapon out of my hand. It was already stained red from where I had opened my palm with it, gripping it in shock.

I didn't even feel it. I didn't even fight as the guard wrenched me back to the middle of the room, forcing me against the cold marble slab where I'd woken up.

I twisted in his grasp. Not to escape. But because I couldn't stand to lose sight of Tamid.

Tamid who I'd grown up with. Tamid who, after my mother died, had been the only person in all of Dustwalk I'd cared about. Tamid who'd been my only friend for years. Who I'd last seen bleeding out in the sand while I rode away on the back of a Buraqi with Jin.

You're dead. The words shot from my brain to my mouth and stopped short. The untruth couldn't get any farther. Because he wasn't dead. He was alive and stubbornly collecting the broken glass from the floor. Like he didn't even know me. Only the slight furrow between his brows betrayed that he was focusing far too hard for such a simple task. Avoiding looking at me at all costs.

He wasn't using a crutch, I realised. Last time I'd seen Tamid, Prince Naguib had put a bullet straight through his twisted knee when I wouldn't give him the answers he wanted. I'd seen Tamid fall to his side, screaming. My fault. I'd seen men take lesser injuries than that and lose a leg, but here he was standing on two. I heard a small click as he moved, metal on metal, like the repeating system in a revolver. Through his torn trouser leg I saw what looked like a joint made out of brass. My heart lurched. One flesh-and-blood leg and one metallic leg.

'What should I do with her?' the soldier asked.

'Tie it down to the table.' Tamid picked up the last piece of glass. He'd called me *it*. Like I was less than a friend he'd chosen to turn into an enemy. Like I was less than human.

The soldier's hands pressed painfully into my bandaged skin as he tried to hold me. I cried out without meaning to. The noise startled Tamid into looking at me.

'Don't—' he started, drawing the guard's attention. I saw my opening.

Make the first hit count.

I slammed my head forward. My skull connected with his, sending a crack of pain through my head. 'Son of a bitch!' I cursed, as the soldier stumbled back, clutching his forehead. I rolled off the table and made for the door. But I was too slow – the soldier was already grabbing the front of my khalat, raising his fist, angling for my face. I turned away like Shazad had taught me, aiming to catch the fist with my shoulder.

The blow never came.

Weighty silence fell over the room.

I looked up. A man was holding back the soldier's fist. For a sliver of a second I thought it was Ahmed. Sunlight still danced blearily across my vision after days in darkness, edging his profile with gold. Dark hair with the hint of a curl in it fell over a proud desert-dark brow. Sharp, determined dark eyes smudged with a sleepless night. Only his mouth was different. Set in a steady, sure line, it didn't wear the soft uncertain question that sometimes hovered on Ahmed's.

But he was cast from the same mould. Or rather, Ahmed was cast from the mould of this man. I shouldn't have been surprised. Sons tended to take after their fathers.

'You should know when you have been bested, soldier,' the Sultan said, keeping hold of his fist.

The soldier's hand unwound itself from the front of my shirt quickly. I pulled back, out of reach. And just like that, all of the Sultan's attention turned on me.

I'd never figured the Sultan would look so much like my prince. I'd imagined him like every faded colour drawing in the storybooks about cruel rulers who were overturned by clever heroes. Fat and old and greedy, and dressed in clothes that cost enough coin to feed a family for a year. I ought to have known better. If I'd learned anything from being the Blue-Eyed Bandit, it was that stories and the truth were rarely the same thing.

The Sultan had been the same age Ahmed was now when he took the throne. Ahmed and Jin were both born barely a year into his rule. I was decent enough at arithmetic to know that meant the man in front of me now hadn't seen four decades yet.

'You've brought me a fighter.' He wasn't speaking to me. I noticed a fourth figure, hovering in the door. My aunt. Anger flooded out all my common sense. I moved again, lunging at her on instinct. I knew I wouldn't make it far, but the Sultan caught me before I'd gotten a step, hands on my shoulders. 'Stop,' he ordered. 'You'll do yourself more harm than you will to her.' He was right. The sudden motion had made my head light. My strength was draining out of me, even if the will to fight wasn't. I sagged in his grip.

'Good,' the Sultan praised me gently, like I was an animal who'd done a trick. 'Now let's take a look at you.' He reached for my face. I recoiled on instinct, but I had nowhere to go. I'd been here before – on a dark night in Dustwalk and with Commander Naguib, another son of the Sultan's. I'd had the bruises he gave me across my cheek for weeks.

But the Sultan cupped my chin gently. He'd been a fighter when he'd taken the throne. They said he'd killed half his brothers that day himself. Two decades didn't seem to have made him any weaker. His fingers were calloused from use. For hunting. For war. For killing Ahmed and Delila's mother. But they were terribly gentle peeling my matted hair away from my face so he could see me clearer.

'Blue eyes,' he said, without taking his hands away. 'Unusual for a Mirajin girl.'

My heart caught in my chest. What had my aunt and Tamid told him? That I'd come from the Rebellion? Would he believe them? Had the stories of the Blue-Eyed Bandit reached as high as the Sultan? 'Your aunt has told me all about you, Amani.'

'She's a liar.' It spilled out, fast and angry. 'Whatever she's told you, she can't be trusted.'

'So you're saying you're not a Demdji, as she claims? Or are you just accusing her of being faithless to her own flesh and blood?'

'Don't bother, Amani,' my aunt interjected. 'You might have everyone else in Dustwalk fooled, but your mother confided in me.' I understood the heavy look she was giving me over the Sultan's shoulder. She'd told him we'd come straight from Dustwalk. She *was* a liar. Not on my account, but she'd lied all the same. She hadn't told him about the Rebellion. And she was warning me with those veiled words. It would be bad for both of us if the Sultan found out where I'd really come from. He'd have questions for her, no doubt. Besides, I was valuable as a Demdji, not as a rebel.

'She wouldn't be the first, you know,' the Sultan said to me. 'To bring me a false Demdji. I've already had plenty of fathers and mothers travel from little towns at the end of my country just like yours, bringing me daughters with their hair dipped in saffron to make it look yellow, or their skin painted blue, thinking I would not know the difference.'

He ran his hand across my cheekbone. There was a wound there; I could feel the dull throb of it under his thumb. I couldn't remember how I'd gotten it. His eyes travelled between me and my aunt. 'You despise this woman. And I don't blame you. Do you go to prayers?' I kept my eyes on him, although I could feel Tamid watching me, tucked against the wall, like he could become part of it. Last time I'd truly attended prayers had been in Dustwalk and he'd been beside me, trying to make me be quiet as I shifted restlessly. 'The Holy Books tell us worse than traitors are those who betray their own flesh and blood. Aunts who sell their nieces. Sons who rebel against their fathers.' I tensed. 'So, I will strike a deal with you. The same one I have struck with all the false Demdji who've come before you. If you can tell me that you are not the daughter of a Djinni, I will release you, with as much gold as you can carry, and your aunt will be punished in a way of your choosing. If you need any inspiration, the girl whose father dyed her skin chose to have him strung up by his toes until all his blood rushed into his brain and killed him.' He tapped my cheek, like we were sharing a joke. 'All you have to do is say six little words: *I am not a Djinni's daughter*, and you can have your freedom. Or stay silent and your aunt will walk away with all that gold.'

It was a damn good offer. Freedom and revenge. Only I'd have to lie for it.

'Go ahead,' he said. I focused on his mouth as the

words formed, that one part of him that didn't look like Ahmed.

I couldn't lie, but I could be deceitful. I'd done it before. I'd dodged my way out of plenty of things without speaking a single word that wasn't true.

'I didn't know my father.' *Tamid will vouch for me.* But I didn't want to bring him into this just now if I didn't have to. The Sultan gave no sign that he knew that anything connected me and Tamid. Tamid could've told the Sultan that he knew me as more than a Demdji. He knew me as the girl who'd gotten a bullet put through his knee and ridden off with the Rebellion. But if he hadn't already, I wasn't about to be the one to sell us out. 'My mother never said a word about him to me, and the whole of Dustwalk figured he was a Gallan soldier—'

The Sultan pressed his fingers to my lips, cutting me off sharply. He was leaning in so close now he filled my whole world. There was something unsettlingly familiar about him – more than just the face he shared with Ahmed. I just couldn't quite put my finger on what it was.

'I don't want to hear tricks or half-truths.' He spoke so low only I could hear. 'My father was a fool and he died at my hands, with a surprised look on his face. I am clearly not a fool, or else my rebel son would have done the same to me already. Now' – he carefully peeled one last strand of hair away from my face – 'all I want is six simple words from you.'

The Blue-Eyed Bandit might be the stuff of campfire stories, but Demdji, we were the stuff of legends. Half of Miraji wasn't even sure we were real. But the Sultan seemed well informed.

I had to lie. I couldn't lie, but I had to. Everything depended on it. Not just me getting out of here, and not just my life. Everyone's. If I couldn't lie now, he might pull truth after truth from my lips – maybe even about the Rebellion. He'd pull knowledge out of my silences. And he'd turn me into a weapon like he had with Noorsham. Into a slave.

I reached desperately for the lie that would get me out of there. Get me away from this enemy wearing the face of my prince.

I fought with everything in me. But everything in me was Demdji.

And Demdji couldn't tell lies.

The Sultan laughed. It was an unexpectedly honest sound. 'No need to strain yourself. I knew what you were from the moment I saw you, little Demdji.' He'd been toying with me.

'Reward this good woman.' He gestured to my aunt lazily. The soldier snapped to attention and gestured for my aunt to follow him. His shoulders seemed to sag in relief as he left the room. She looked so damn pleased with herself as she turned, disappearing from the room. And I hated her. God, I hated her.

From the corner of my eye I noticed Tamid shifting in the corner, like he was expecting a dismissal, too. Like he'd rather leave than watch whatever the Sultan was about to do to me.

'Sit down, Amani,' the Sultan ordered.

I didn't want to sit. I wanted to stand and face our enemy. But suddenly, and against my will, my body moved on its own, folding my legs under myself until I was sitting back on the marble slab where I'd woken up.

Panic rose up, almost choking me. I'd never been betrayed by my own body like that before. 'What did you do to me?'

The Sultan didn't answer right away. 'Your eyes betrayed you from the start.' *Traitor eyes.* 'There was another Demdji before you. He had blue eyes, too.' Noorsham. He was talking about Noorsham. 'It's one of the great justices of our world that your kind, for all your power, are yet so vulnerable to words.' They'd had Noorsham's true name. That was how they'd controlled him. Noorsham had worn a mask, made of bronze, engraved with his name. The Sultan knew Noorsham's true name. 'What do you think the chances are there are two Demdji in the desert with blue eyes who *don't*

163

share the same father? I would say they were small.' Which meant the Sultan knew our father's name. And my true name. My eyes shot around the room, looking for a bronze suit like the one they'd encased Noorsham in. But the room looked like nothing more than a Holy Father's chambers. Tamid had always wanted to be a Holy Man.

'We lost our last Demdji, unfortunately,' the Sultan was saying. 'It was our young Tamid's idea to make things a little more secure this time.' He nodded to my one-time friend. Tamid was still looking anywhere but at me.

And finally I understood what was below the bandages.

'You put metal beneath my skin.' It would be bronze. Bronze with my name on it. My true name. Including the name of my real father. Like they'd used to control Noorsham. I looked for a bronze ring on his hand like the one Naguib had used to control Noorsham. Something I could wrench off his fingers, breaking his control over me and letting me make a run for it. Instead I spied a small bandage across the Sultan's forearm. Like mine. He was taking precautions.

'Bronze.' The Sultan touched one of the scars. 'And iron.'

Iron.

My stomach lurched at that. They had cut my skin open, put iron underneath it, and stitched me back up.

I was powerless.

Only ... the Sultan had wanted Noorsham so he could use his power as a weapon. If that wasn't why he wanted me, then what had he just paid my aunt so highly for?

'You're wondering why,' the Sultan said. I wished I wasn't so easy to read. 'I made the mistake last time of thinking I could control a Demdji. But there are so many loopholes. So many small gaps in my orders you could squeeze through. As a girl you are largely harmless if you do wriggle through those loopholes. As a Demdji ... well, the chance of harnessing your power is not worth the price if you disobeyed and turned it against me. It would be like letting you loose in my palace with a gun.' He mentioned guns in a cast-off comment, but it still made me nervous. He couldn't know I was the Blue-Eyed Bandit. If he did, he'd know I was part of the Rebellion and I doubted we'd be having such a pleasant conversation. 'The iron was Tamid's idea again. He has been *very* useful since coming to the palace. He is from the Last County, too, you know – where was it, my boy?'

'Sazi,' Tamid said. It was a bare-faced lie. Sazi was near enough Dustwalk, but far enough away that I'd never been there until I went with Jin. It was where Noorsham was from. Where Naguib had been encamped before coming to Dustwalk. Tamid was hiding from the Sultan that we were from the same place. He hated me enough to stick iron under my skin but not to put a noose around my neck, it seemed.

I willed Tamid to look at me. But he kept his eyes firmly on the ground. I was so stupid. I'd seen him and for just a second I'd felt like nothing had changed. But I was wrong. I should've known that. Last time I was with Tamid I was a girl who left people behind. And he was a boy who'd never have betrayed me.

'Your part of the desert remembers things that most of the rest of us have forgotten,' the Sultan was saying.

'So what good am I to you as a Demdji with no power?' I carefully turned my attention back to the Sultan.

The Sultan smiled enigmatically. 'Follow me and find out.'

And against my will, I felt my feet move. I just had time to glance over my shoulder to see Tamid finally look up at me, his face marked with something that looked a lot like worry, before the door closed between us.

Chapter 14

I had to follow him, but I didn't have to shut up about it. 'Where are we going?' Smooth marble echoed my own words mockingly back at me as we wove our way through the palace. 'Where are you taking me?'

The Sultan didn't answer any of the questions I shouted at his back as I trailed him. Finally he stopped in the middle of a hallway. I halted a few paces from him. Behind us an archway twice my height opened into a small garden filled with roaming peacocks. Across from it, so as to be framed in the line of sight from the door, was a mosaic of Princess Hawa. She stood on what I guessed were the walls of Saramotai, hands spread wide as the sun rose behind her. Her eyes stared straight ahead. They were blue in this picture, too. Just like they'd been in Saramotai.

The Sultan pressed a hand to Hawa's. I heard a click, and then the section of the wall that extended from one of Hawa's hands to the other shifted, swinging out like a door. Behind it a long staircase plunged downward sinto darkness.

We'd passed the last guard a way back now. And there were none here. Whatever was at the bottom of those stairs was truly meant to stay secret. 'What's down there?' My voice bounced eerily down the stone steps.

'There are some things that are better to do in places where God is blind.' The Destroyer of Worlds came from the place where God was blind, they said. Deep inside the earth. 'After you.'

Pressing a hand to the wall for balance, I counted the steps as we descended. Thirty-three was a holy number. It was the number of Djinn who gathered together to forge the First Mortal in their war against the Destroyer of Worlds.

I stumbled in the dark at the bottom. The Sultan was close behind me. He steadied me with a hand on my waist. For a moment I was back in the camp, Jin's hand on me. *I've got you.* I pulled away quickly.

This wasn't like the rest of the palace. Instead of smooth marble, the walls were rough-hewn stone. A low ceiling was supported by squat pillars that went on line after line into the shadows, like ancient soldiers standing to attention. The only light came from a hole in the ceiling, casting a bright circle in the dark vaults. As we got closer to the light, I could see the pillars were carved with patterns that had been worn down, like centuries had run them smooth. Maybe longer than centuries. I wasn't sure how old the world was. But this seemed like a place that was here at the beginning of it. The years had buried this place, but it had survived.

Standing under the light was like being at the bottom of a well. The circle of light was about as wide as my arms stretched out. But the sky above was only the size of a half-louzi piece. My bare toes brushed something cold. Looking down in the lamplight, I realised that there was iron set into the ground in a perfect circle, patterns woven through it. An identical circle glinted off to my left. And another, just beyond that, covered in dust and dirt.

'What are these?' I pulled away from the iron instinctively.

'You're from the edge of the desert,' the Sultan said. 'You are a descendant of the nomads who carried stories across the sands. You must know all the ones of the old days, in the times that the Djinn walked among us openly. When they still loved mortals. Well.' He gave me a sly glance. 'You are walking proof that they do still, occasionally. But there was also a time when *my* ancestors ruled with the help of the Djinn. That was what the Sultim trials were, thousands of years ago.

Tasks set by the Djinn to choose the worthiest among the Sultan's sons. Not a series of foolish tests designed to turn men on each other.' A series of foolish tests which Ahmed had won outright. 'In those days, princes would climb mountains and ride Rocs to bring back a single one of their feathers. They drank water under the sleepless eye of the Wanderer. True feats. But though we cling to those traditions, the days of worthy princes are long gone. As are the days when the Djinn used to come here and surrender their power inside these circles in good faith, while the Sultan surrendered his weapons, and they traded counsel.'

I ran my toe along the edge of the circle. I'd heard of these in stories. Places where the Sultan summoned a Djinni by his true name and then released him again. It was a sign of trust. If I counted the circles, would there be thirty-three of those, too?

'You are going to summon a Djinni here, Amani,' the Sultan said.

My head shot up. I'd seen plenty of things that were created before mortals. Buraqi. Nightmares. Skinwalkers. But the Djinn were different. They weren't just the stuff legends were made of. They were our creators. Nobody saw Djinn any more, though a few folk in Dustwalk claimed to have found one at the bottom of a strong bottle. And, I supposed, my mother had. 'So desperate for greater counsel in these troubled times, Your Exalted Highness?' He didn't take the bait.

'The stories make it sound easy – you can simply call a First Being so long as you have their true name.' Like princesses and paupers alike in the stories, calling for help at their hour of need with a true name earned through some virtuous deed at the start of the tale. 'But you need so much more than that. You also need to be able to call them in the first language.' The Sultan pulled a folded piece of paper from his pocket. 'And you need one more thing. Care to venture a guess?'

I didn't take the paper. 'If I were taking a stab in the dark' – I heard the bile on my own tongue – 'I'd say it was a Demdji.'

So this was why he was willing to pay a Demdji's weight in gold. This was why he'd shoved iron under my skin. He didn't need my powers. He was going to order me to summon a Djinni.

I knew the stories of the wars that the Djinn had fought alongside humanity. Adil the Conqueror who leashed a Djinni in iron and brought cities to their knees before he came face-to-face with the Grey Prince. The Djinni who built the walls of Izman in a single night as a gift to his beloved. A Demdji's power was nothing compared to what I knew a Djinni could do.

I thought he'd order me to take the paper. But the

Sultan just smiled indulgently. 'A true language.' A language without lies. 'A true tongue.' A Demdji who couldn't lie. Who could say *You will come to me* in the first language and make it so. 'And a true name. In this case, the same one buried under your skin. Part of your true name.' My eyes shot to the paper without meaning to. 'Your father's name.'

My father's. My real father. The Sultan hadn't ordered me to take the paper. But still my hand twitched towards it against my judgement. My father was in my reach.

'Take it,' the Sultan ordered finally. 'If you want to.'

My fingers closing around the paper at the order betrayed me. I wanted to let go of the paper. I wanted to fight it. But I wanted to know, too. I raised the paper so I could see it in the light from the well.

And there it was.

Black ink scrawled onto white paper. My father's name.

Bahadur.

For the first time in my seventeen years I knew my real name. The same one that was etched into bronze and slipped beneath my skin.

I was Amani Al-Bahadur.

'Read it aloud.' It was an order. And I couldn't disobey.

My mouth moved against my will, reciting the ancient language written on the paper. The words almost fell out, so easily for a language I didn't speak, like they belonged there. Like the Djinni half of me recognised this language better than any other.

I got to the end too quickly, and my father's name slid across my tongue as easily as fat over a fire. And then I was done. I fell silent.

Nothing happened for a moment.

Then the iron circle burst into flames.

Chapter 15

I staggered back as a huge column of blue fire rose up from the circle in front of me. It was higher than the low-vaulted ceiling, filling the well all the way up to the sky. It burned hot and quick and brighter than any flame I'd ever seen. It fought for a few moments at the edges of the iron circle, at some invisible barrier, before, just as suddenly as it had appeared, pulling itself into the centre of the circle, taking a shape.

I blinked against the light floating in my eyes, like I'd just stared straight at the sun and gone blind for a moment.

Then my vision cleared and I saw my father for the first time.

Bahadur looked like a man who had been made out of fire.

No. That wasn't right. I might not be so devout as some, but I knew my holy stories. Djinn weren't humans made out of fire. We were Djinn made out of dirt and water with just a hint of their flame to give us life. A spark from a bonfire. We were a far duller version of them.

Bahadur's skin shifted and moved with dark blue flames. Flames the same colour as my eyes.

I didn't feel heat pouring off him. But I could feel something else, something that I couldn't name but that went past my skin and struck me in the soul. He stood as tall as one of the huge pillars down here in this ancient palace vault. Only he wasn't just holding up a palace. He was holding up the world. One of God's First Beings who had made the First Mortal. Who had made all of mankind.

Who'd made me.

I realised that what I was feeling was power. True, raw power, the kind that didn't come from a title or a crown but from the soul of the world itself.

He kept shifting as I stared at him. And I realised he was shrinking and shifting at the same time, changing his appearance. It reminded me of the way Imin shifted when changing shape. Until he wasn't blue fire and light any more. He was dark skin and dark hair, as much flesh and blood as any desert dweller. Still, even blunted to look like us, there was no mistaking that he was different. He was too handsome, too carefully carved, too perfect to look like a mortal man. And he hadn't made his eyes look human. They were made of the same changing fire as the rest of him, except they burned more steadily. They burned white-hot around the edges, and bright blue around a perfect black pupil. And they seemed to scrape me inside out.

'You called me.' Three such mundane words that carried so much weight. His attention shifted slowly to the Sultan. 'Though not, I see, for yourself.'

The Sultan was a powerful man. But he was a man just the same, and standing next to a Djinni he looked like nothing more than a spark hovering around a bonfire.

'Now.' Bahadur sounded almost bored as he spoke to the Sultan. 'What would you ask of me? Is it gold? Power? Love? Eternal life? All four, perhaps?'

'I'm not foolish enough to ask anything from you.'

Bahadur considered him without blinking. I realised I was watching him closely, searching his features for something familiar, something I might share with him other than our eyes. 'I have seen more days and met more mortals than there are grains of sand in your desert. I have met paupers and kings and everything in between. I have never met a man who didn't want something. It does not matter if you are a dirty-kneed child on the street or a man who already has more power and gold than you know what to do with. You always want something.'

'And you always use our wants against us,' the Sultan said. 'You take our needs and our desires and you twist them until our only wish is that we hadn't asked for your help at all.' He wasn't wrong. I'd read those stories, too. The ones of Massil, and of the Djinni who destroyed an entire sea in revenge on one merchant. The tinker who died in the desert looking for gold he was promised by a captured Djinni. 'And in the end' – the Sultan swept his foot over the edge of the circle tauntingly – 'we never get what we want.'

'So you do want something.'

'Of course,' the Sultan said. 'Everyone wants *something*. But I am not foolish enough to ask you for it. You are going to give it to me, with no strings attached.'

When Bahadur laughed it echoed all the way down the vaults. 'And why would I do that?'

'She is one of yours, you know.' He meant me, though his eyes never strayed from his Djinni prize.

'Of course I know.' Bahadur didn't take his eyes off the Sultan. *Look at me*, a part of me wanted to shout at him. Another wanted to shout at myself for wanting him to. I'd done just fine my whole life without a father. I didn't need one now. 'Why do you think we mark them?'

The Sultan pulled a knife out of his belt. 'Little

Demdji. Take this and drive it through your stomach.'
My body went cold. It was an order.

'No.' I said it out loud, like refusing could make it real. But it was no good – my hands had already started to move.

'Do it slowly,' the Sultan ordered, 'so that it hurts.'

There was nothing I could do. My hand was moving, reaching out for the knife, curling around the handle, turning the blade so it pointed at my centre. I fought it. My arms trembled with effort. But there was no helping it. The knife was slowly driving itself towards my stomach.

'Your daughter will die here.' The Sultan addressed Bahadur. 'Unless I stop that knife.' Stomach wounds killed you slowly. 'Give me the names of your fellow Djinn, and I will order her to drop the knife.'

Bahadur still didn't even glance my way. He watched the Sultan with flat blue eyes as the blade inched towards my body. He was an immortal First Being. Second only to God himself. To him even the Sultan, the ruler of the whole desert, was nothing. I was nothing, and I was his daughter. He sank down in the circle, crossing his legs gracefully as he went.

'All of you die eventually.' He smiled in that indulgent way parents do at children. Except it wasn't at me. 'It's what mortals do best.'

The knife was still inching towards my stomach and he didn't care. He was going to let me die. The knife pressed against the cloth of Shazad's khalat. I was always getting blood on the clothes she lent me. This time she probably wouldn't forgive me. She'd never forgive me for dying on her in the middle of the war.

'Yes,' the Sultan agreed. 'Everything dies eventually.' He turned away from the Djinni, like *he* was the one who was nothing. If he was disappointed in Bahadur's refusal, it barely showed. 'Drop the knife.' The order was thrown at me.

I wrenched the knife away from my stomach, letting it clatter to the ground. My body was my own again. It had been a bluff. A stupid failed bluff against an immortal being. I was shaking. Hard. But anger chased out fear fast. Anger at my own body. At the Sultan. But most of all, that Bahadur would look on, so indifferent to me, as I died.

He had made me drop the knife. But he hadn't told me not to pick it back up.

My fingers curled back around the hilt, and I moved, plunging the knife toward the Sultan's throat. One final gesture to end everything.

'Stop.' The order came a second too soon. Seizing my muscles with the knife a hair's breadth from his skin. I'd been a second from killing him.

For the first time Bahadur was watching me with interest.

The Sultan's gaze flicked from the knife to me. I expected rage. I expected retribution. But none came. His lip just twitched up. 'You're a dangerous little Demdji, aren't you?' And then I knew why his mouth looked familiar.

His face was Ahmed's, but that smile – that smile was all Jin.

Chapter 16

I was valuable.

That was why I was still alive.

That was why he'd stopped the knife.

I was going to be kept in the harem. That was
what the Sultan said. Kept. Not like a prisoner. More
like an especially nicely crafted gun. Stored until I was
needed again.

Other orders came with it as I was handed over to
a servant woman in a khalat the colour of pale sand,
her dark hair bound up in a sheema. Like she might
have to worry about the desert sun in the shaded halls
of the palace.

'You will stay in the palace,' he instructed calmly. I
wanted to fight. But while my mind might be able to rebel
against it, my body wouldn't be able to. 'You won't set
foot beyond the walls of the harem without permission
from a member of the palace.' He understood Demdji

too well. He chose his words carefully. *Don't leave the harem.* Not, *Don't try to escape.* Trying and succeeding were two different things to a Demdji.

I spared a glance down the steps as the Sultan ordered me back up. Towards Bahadur. My father – though the word felt unnatural. He watched us go from where he sat inside the small circle. Darkness folded around him as our lamp retreated but I could still see him long after I ought to have been able to. Like he still burned with his own fire, even in human form. He was a thousandfold more powerful than I was. He had lived countless lives before I was even born. But he was as trapped as I was here. What hope did I have of getting out if he couldn't?

'And you will not harm any person here. Or yourself.' He worried that I'd kill myself. That I'd try to slip through his grip into nothingness. I didn't want to know what he had planned for me that was so bad that killing myself might be better. 'But if any harm comes to me – if I die – you will walk up to the highest tower in this palace and throw yourself off it.' If he died, I died.

A dozen other orders took root inside my bones as I was led through more polished marble hallways by the woman dressed in the colour of false sand. My legs obeyed the Sultan's last orders. 'Go with her. Do what she says.'

We passed under a low stone archway. I could just make out figures of dancing women twined together carved into the stone. I felt steam in the air before we'd gone much further, the cloying scent of flowers and spices already winding their way to my body. As easy to get drunk on as liquor when you'd been in the dried-out desert for too long.

We emerged into the most immense baths I'd ever seen. The room was tiled in iridescent blues and pinks and yellows in wild, hypnotic mosaic patterns from floor to ceiling. The steam climbing from the heated pools gave everything a slick sheen, from the walls to the girls.

And there were a lot of girls.

I'd heard stories about the Sultan's harem, where women were kept for the pleasure of the Sultan and the Sultim. And to breed future princes to fight for the throne, and princesses to be sold for political alliances. Here they were, running soap in long languid circles across their bare shoulders or floating at the edge of the water, eyes closed as attendants ran oils through their hair. A few lay on the nearby beds, long limbs being kneaded by clever hands as they dozed.

The attendant started to undress me without speaking, undoing the tiny clasps at the front of Shazad's khalat as I stared. I let her.

And then I spied the man. He looked like a fox in the henhouse. And a hungry one, too. He lounged on a bed, propped up by a stack of pillows, stripped to the waist. Probably a year or two my senior, he looked like something hewn out of stone, with heavy square features without a single graceful subtlety to offset them. He ought to have been handsome, but there was a nastiness to the tilt of his mouth that meant he'd never be.

Three impossibly pretty Mirajin girls were draped around him, wrapped in nothing but long linen sheets, long dark hair hanging in thick wet waves around their bare shoulders. One of them sat at his feet, trailing her legs lazily in the steaming water, leaning into the knee of a slighter girl who was folded into his side. The last one lay with her head in his lap, eyes shut as he trailed his fingers through her hair absently, pouty lips pressed into a contented smile.

His attention wasn't on any of them, though – it was fixed on two girls standing across from him, both bare as the day they were born, being inspected inch by inch by an attendant. Like the servants were looking for any flaw that might keep these girls from being admitted into this world of perfect, beautiful women. I recognised them, I realised as the attendant peeled away my khalat and wrapped me in a plain linen sheet, though it took my tired mind a moment to place them. They'd been on the ship with me, brought by the slavers to be offered to the harem.

What had happened to the girls not chosen for the harem? Had they been sold to other men in less prestigious houses? Or were the rumours true – that slavers drowned any girl rejected by the Sultan's harem?

As if she sensed me staring, the small girl pressed into his side looked my way. Something passed over her face as she leaned in to whisper to the girl lounging across the man's lap. The girl with the pretty pout. Her eyes snapped open, focusing on me so quickly it was plain as day she'd only been pretending to sleep. She pursed her full mouth pensively as she twisted so that she could whisper something to the other two. The laugh that followed bounced off the tiles around me.

It drew the man's attention my way.

'You're new,' he addressed me as the girls pretended to try to hide their smiles. I hated his voice instantly. It stuck to his words like it was tasting them, and in turn they seemed to cling to my skin.

'You should bow to the Sultim.' The pout-lipped girl yawned, stretching conspicuously across his body like a cat in the sun. So this was the Sultim – the firstborn of the Sultan's sons. Prince Kadir. Heir to the throne we were fighting for. The son who had faced Ahmed in the last challenge of the Sultim trials.

I'd long since passed the time when I might've been impressed by a prince. In the last handful of days alone I'd kissed one and yelled at another. But this one was my enemy.

So I didn't bow as the attendants carefully unwound my bandages, conscious of this man's eyes on me, as more of my skin was bared to the air.

There were ugly red welts where the iron had been shoved under my skin. The girls let out a bark of laughter as they appeared. 'Maybe the tailor Abdul made her, my love,' the pout-lipped one said, considering me. The other two girls tittered.

That stung.

'The Tailor Abdul' was a story about a man who was too picky with his wives. He married his first wife because her face was so lovely. He married his second because her body was desirable; and the third because she had such a good heart. But he bemoaned that his first wife was cruel, that his second wife had an unsightly face, and that his third wife had an ugly body.

And so he hired the tailor Abdul to make him the perfect wife. The skilled tailor did as he was told without objection. He sewed the first wife's head onto the body of the second wife, and then he sewed the good heart of the third wife into the body so neatly that he didn't even scar her perfect chest. What was left of the women was tossed out into the desert. In the end the wives got their revenge, as the husband was eaten alive by a Skinwalker who wore all the discarded pieces of his wives.

I stopped my hand from drifting to the marks on my arms. I was a Demdji, a soldier of the Rebellion, the Blue-Eyed Bandit. I'd faced a whole lot worse than bratty harem girls.

But Kadir only smiled. 'In that case, she was tailored for me.'

'It looks more like he made her for the menagerie,' another girl started, failing to read her Sultim's mood. 'Or he mixed her arms up with a monkey's.' The girls' titters burst into laughter. But they had lost the Sultim's attention. He pushed himself to his feet, almost spilling the girl in his lap off him.

'You look Mirajin.' The spark of interest in his voice was dangerous as he closed the short distance between us. 'It's so rare they're able to bring me Mirajin girls. Your kind are my favourites, though. You're western Mirajin, I suppose.' I didn't answer. He didn't seem to need me to. He grabbed my chin, tilting my face to catch the light and looking me over like a merchant might look at a horse. I would've hit him but the Sultan's orders kept my hands at my sides. 'At least my brother's rebellion is good for something. Wars mean more prisoners.'

It had long been known that the harem was a dangerous place to be. I'd heard in the days of Sultan Oman's father some women did come to him by choice. But more were prisoners of war. Slaves bought from foreign shores. Women captured off ships like Jin's mother. Now we had a war in Miraji. That would mean more slavers taking advantage of the chaos to take Mirajin women.

'Has the blessed Sultima even seen you yet?' the girl who'd been displaced from her Sultim's lap called out, trying to regain his attention.

'All the new girls for the Sultim are meant to be seen by the Sultima,' the petite cohort agreed, like she was parroting something someone else had said.

'Yes, she needs to deem you worthy.' The girl who'd been at his feet butted in, too, eager to please.

'Or not worthy.' The pout-lipped girl smirked.

'Be quiet, Ayet, there's no need to disturb the Sultima.' The Sultim's hand left my face, travelling down my neck, across my collarbone, making my skin crawl.

'She is off-limits.' The servant with me spoke up just as Kadir's hand reached the border of the white linen sheet that covered me. She had the clipped, matronly tone of a mother without much patience. The Sultim opened his mouth with a dismissal that never came as she cut across him. 'Your father's orders.'

Mention of the Sultan drew Kadir's hand up short. For a second he seemed to blaze with defiance. And then it was gone, covered as he dropped his arm and shrugged, brushing past me instead, like that was what he'd intended to do all along. His wives gathered themselves up, following him. Ayet's eyes dropped to Shazad's discarded khalat as she passed. So fine a few days ago at the wedding. Before we were attacked. Before I was kissed and kidnapped and cut into. But still beautiful. Her left foot caught the fabric, flicking it and sending it flying into one of the pools, soaking the fabric through.

'Oops.' Ayet flashed me her teeth. 'Sorry.' She flicked one last droplet off her hair at me as she left, followed by a burst of giggles and whispers that bounced off the walls of the baths.

I felt the back of my neck go hot.

When Ahmed took this palace, I was going to burn the harem to the ground.

189

Chapter 17

The harem stripped me of the desert.

The attendants dumped water over my head and scrubbed at my skin until it was screaming and raw. Until they'd robbed me of the skin that'd been caked with sand and blood and sweat and gunpowder and fire and Jin's hands.

They pulled me out of the steaming water. I let one of the girls wrap me in a big, dry linen sheet and lay me down gently next to the bath. Something warm dripped across my skin, like oil. It smelled of flowers I didn't know. The other girl ran a comb through my hair, scraping gently at my scalp.

I'd spent my whole life fighting. Fighting to stay alive in Dustwalk as the girl with the gun. Fighting to escape death in that dead-end desert town. Fighting to get across the desert. The Blue-Eyed Bandit. Fighting for Ahmed. For the Rebellion. *A new dawn. A new desert*.

But as the comb scraped through my hair over and over again, I wasn't sure I had any fight left in me.

I let sleep claim me.

Tomorrow. I'd fight tomorrow.

It didn't take a whole lot of time for me to figure out that the harem was full of invisible chains and walls meant to look like they weren't there.

It felt like a maze, designed to turn me around, over and over, until I wasn't sure how I'd come in or if there was a way out any more. There were dozens of gardens, which fit together like honeycombs. Some of them were plain stretches of grass, with a single fountain gushing endless water and pillows scattered throughout. Others were so thick with flowers and vines and sculptures I couldn't even see the walls any more. But the walls were always there.

I couldn't count how many folk lived in the harem. Dozens of wives belonging to the Sultan and Sultim alike. And children, too – the princes and princesses born to the Sultan's wives. All of them younger than sixteen. The age they were finally released from the harem. To pass from their father's hands to their husbands'. Or to die for him on the battlefield like Naguib had. All of them Ahmed and Jin's brothers and sisters.

Finally I found one of the borders: a gate crafted out of iron and gold that stood ajar. My legs stumbled to a stop as I tried to pass through. I fought against the feeling holding me back, but it was no good – my body seized like I'd been grabbed by some invisible hand. My blood turned to stone and a fist twisted in my gut, pulling me back.

I'd been ordered not to leave.

I couldn't go any further.

I needed to get word back to the Rebellion. Even if I didn't know exactly where the Rebellion was. Shazad's family was in Izman, though. And Izman was on the other side of these walls. A few feet away. It might as well have been a whole desert between us.

There had to be a crack, some way out of the harem. Even if I couldn't get out, there had to be some way to get out a warning, at least, that the Sultan had a Djinni.

That he had my father.

I pushed that thought away. He wasn't my father any more than my mother's husband had been.

If he were my father he would've cared if I'd died or not.

My mother had raised me on a thousand stories of girls who were saved by the Djinn, princesses rescued from towers, peasant girls rescued from poverty.

Turned out, stories were just stories.

I was on my own.

It ought to be a familiar feeling. I used to think I was on my own in Dustwalk, too. But that had never been true. I'd had Tamid back then. Now there were dozens of tiny incisions healing all over my body reminding me why I couldn't trust my oldest friend. My fingers found one of the tiny pieces of metal under the skin of my arm. It hurt when I pressed my thumb against it. I pushed harder.

For the first time in my life I really was alone.

It was on my third day in the harem that I stumbled into the menagerie.

The noise was the first thing I noticed – a riot of different screams coming from iron cages crowned in intricate latticework domes. There were hundreds of birds perched among the iron bars, dressed in colours to make a Djinni jealous. The yellow of fresh lemons. Green like the grass in the Dev's Valley before we fled. Red like the sheema I'd lost. Blue like my eyes. Only not quite. Nothing was really the same blue as my eyes. Except for Noorsham's. And Bahadur's. The ones that had watched, burning low with indifference, as the knife inched towards my skin. The ones that hadn't even blinked or deigned to turn away. Like watching me wouldn't cause him any pain.

I turned away from the birds.

Huge peacocks fanned their tails as I passed another cage. In another, a pair of tigers lounged in a patch of sunlight, sprawled across each other, yawning wide enough so I could see teeth the length of my fingers. There had been some painted on the walls of the secret door leading into the rebel camp, too. But those were pictures, a thousand years old, the size of my hand. These were far from that.

I stumbled to a stop at the furthest cage.

The thing inside was nearly as big as a Roc. A solid behemoth of grey skin and thick limbs and unnaturally large ears. I caught my body pressing up against the bars. Like I might be able to squeeze through and touch it.

On the opposite side of the cage was a girl, sitting with her knees drawn up to her chin. She couldn't be more than fifteen. Too young to be one of the Sultim's wives. She had to be the Sultan's daughter, then. One of his brood of princesses, who were never spoken about half so much as the princes. Something about her reminded me of Delila, even though, I realised, she'd share blood with Jin, which Delila didn't. But still, there was a softness in the curve of her cheeks, like she hadn't fully finished unsticking herself from childhood yet, either. And she was handling something that looked like a toy she was modelling out of red clay around a metal skeleton, making a tiny model of the beast. She nudged one of the legs as I watched; it bent naturally, guided by small metallic joints inside.

'What is it?' I asked. She looked up, startled out of her work, staring at me through the bars of the cage. The words had slipped out without meaning to.

'An elephant,' she said quietly.

My heart twisted painfully as I thought of Izz and Maz excitedly explaining elephants to me.

This was what they had seen across our borders. A real live elephant.

'Come to visit your family?' The sneering voice behind me was far from welcome. I turned to meet it all the same. It was Ayet, the wife who'd kicked my khalat into the pool my first day in the harem. With her were the two other girls who always seemed to flank her like some sort of personal guard. I'd learned from overheard conversations they were called Mouhna and Uzma.

'And your families are in the Sultan's kennels, I suppose.' I watched the insult dawn across all three of their faces at once. Ayet recovered fast.

'You seem to think that we are your enemies,' Ayet said. 'But we can help you. Do you know where we are?' She didn't wait for me to answer. 'This is the very menagerie where the Sultan's wife Nadira met

195

the Djinni who gave her a demon child.' Nadira was Ahmed and Delila's mother. Everyone knew that story. One day the Sultan's wife was wandering the gardens of the palace, when she stumbled upon a frog that had accidentally leapt into one of the Sultan's birdcages and could not find his way out again.

I glanced at the birds in the cage.

The birds kept pecking at him. Nadira took pity on the creature and, opening the cage, reached in with no care for the way the birds pecked at her own hands, turning them bloody and scratched. As soon as she set the frog back down, he transformed into his true form, that of a Djinni.

'See, here's the thing.' Ayet and her girls circled me like a pack of roving animals. 'Girls who don't find their right place in the harem don't tend to last long. The Sultim likes Mirajin girls.' Ayet's hand slammed into my chest, surprisingly hard, knocking me back towards the nearest cage. One of the tigers glanced up, curious. 'But he's only ever got room for three of us on display. So when someone new comes in, another one has to go. And none of us wants to disappear. Which means *you* don't have a purpose here.'

'I've got no interest in your idiot husband.' I wanted to shove her hand away. But I couldn't. The Sultan had given me orders. I couldn't fight back.

Ayet wasn't convinced. 'Do you know what else happened here? This is where the Sultan killed Nadira after she gave birth to an abomination.' She took a step towards me. 'Because here, nobody can hear screams over the birds.' Sure enough, the birds in the cages were in chaos now, their voices drowning out the rest of the harem just spitting distance away. 'Go ahead. Call out for help.'

'You should leave her alone.' The voice wasn't strong. It was barely a squeak among the chorus of wild-feathered birds. But it was loud enough to be heard. It was the girl with the toy elephant. She was watching this all play out from the opposite side of the cage. Her eyes were wide with fear. But she'd spoken up all the same.

Ayet sneered, but a sharp-tongued insult never came. 'This is our business, Leyla. The Sultan hasn't taken a new wife in a decade, which means she's clearly here for our blessed husband the Sultim, not your father.'

'If you're so sure of that' – Leyla got to her feet uncertainly, clutching the clay elephant like a child a dozen years younger – 'I can just go ask *my father.*'

Invoking the Sultan was like uttering a magic word. The kind that summoned powerful spirits and opened doors in cliff faces. All Leyla had to do was mention him and it was as if he were here.

Ayet caved first. She rolled her eyes, like she wanted me to think I wasn't worth her time, and turned away.

'Consider this a warning.' She tossed the words over her shoulder as she swanned out. I watched her go, hating her. Hating that I couldn't break her nose like I wanted to.

Across the menagerie Leyla was winding the mechanism in her hands absently. 'You'll get used to them.' I didn't plan on having to get used to them. I was getting out of there before I had time to.

Since arriving in the harem, I'd stayed in my rooms when I wasn't looking for a way out. The attendants brought me fresh clothes and a basin to wash in and meals, seeming to anticipate what I needed without me ever needing to speak a word. But that night, no food came.

I couldn't help but think Ayet might have something to do with that. Just because she couldn't tear me apart like a wild animal didn't mean she was done trying to make me suffer for some imagined designs I had on her Sultim. The last thing I needed was another prince in my life. I had a hard enough time with the two I'd already acquired.

I waited until it was dark outside before finally giving in to my growling stomach. Even I wasn't stubborn enough to starve to death.

Women were dotted all over the garden where

the meal was served, sitting in tightly knotted clusters around dishes of food that they shared between them. So tightly knotted that it'd be impossible to untie one long enough to get to the food. I was suddenly back in my first night in the rebel camp, before I'd known everyone's name. When I'd been an intruder. Except I'd been an intruder with Shazad and Bahi to guide me then.

I spied Leyla then, the only person I could see sitting by herself. She was almost done making the toy elephant, by the looks of things, and the modelled clay was taking shape around the articulated metal joints. As I watched her, she wound up a small key in the back of the toy. It marched with jolting, violent steps towards one of the small children sitting with the huddle of women nearest her. The little boy reached for it excitedly, but his mother snatched him away, pulling him onto her lap, knocking the thing over in the process.

The moment of joy that had bloomed on Leyla's face at operating the tiny thing disappeared, as she ducked her head. A girl like that would be eaten alive in the desert. Then again, a girl from the desert could get eaten alive in the palace.

I picked up the toy from where it was now lying uselessly on the ground, legs still jerking forward. I held it out to her. She looked up at me with eyes that seemed to take up her whole face.

'You helped me today, in the menagerie.' She just stared at me. I wanted to say that I could've handled myself. And that would've been true if I weren't trapped by a hundred tiny pieces of metal under my skin. 'Thank you.'

She nodded and took the toy. I sat down next to her without invitation. I didn't really have anywhere else to go. I was being nice to her because I was going to need allies in the harem. That was what I told myself. Not because she had big lost eyes that made me think of Delila's.

Ayet and her two parasites were in a tight knot a little way off. Waves of disdain were rolling off them even from this far away. When they caught me looking back Ayet whispered something to Mouhna. They descended into fits of giggles like crowing birds.

'They're afraid of you,' Leyla volunteered. 'They think you'll take their place with Kadir.'

I snorted. 'Believe me, I have no interest in your brother.'

An attendant appeared, handing me a plate heavy with savoury-smelling meats. My stomach growled in grateful answer.

'He's not my brother.' Leyla's jaw set firmly. 'I mean, yes, I suppose. We're both children of my most exalted father the Sultan. But in the harem the only people we call brother or sister are those who share the same mother. I only have one brother, Rahim. He's gone from the harem now.' She sounded far away.

'And your mother?' I asked.

'She was a Gamanix engineer's daughter.' She turned the small toy over in her hands. Jin had told me about that country. It was where the twinned compasses he and Ahmed each always kept had been made. A country that had learned to meld magic and machines. This explained how she'd learned to make little mechanised toys. 'She vanished when I was eight years old.' Leyla said it so calm and straightforward it caught me off guard.

'What do you mean, vanished?' I asked.

'Oh, it happens in the harem,' Leyla said. 'Women disappear when they lose their use. That's why Ayet is so afraid of you. She hasn't been able to conceive a child for the Sultim. If you replace her, she could vanish just like the others. It happens every day.'

I took a bite of my food absently, listening to Leyla talk. It hit my tongue like an ember, igniting my mouth. Tears sprang to my eyes as I spat the food in the grass, coughing violently.

'Can't handle our fine food?' Mouhna called from across the garden. Next to her Ayet and Uzma were doubled over in fits of giggles as Mouhna popped a piece of bread in her mouth, puckering her lips at me deliberately as she savoured it. 'A present from the blessed Sultima.'

Leyla picked up something red from my plate. Her nose wrinkled. 'Suicide pepper,' she said, tossing it into the nearest fire grate.

'What in hell is a suicide pepper?' I was still coughing. Leyla pressed a glass into my hands. I downed it, cooling the burning on my tongue.

'It's a foreign spice. My father tries to keep it out of the harem, but it's—' She ran her tongue over her lips nervously. 'Sometimes girls here use it . . . to escape.' It took me a heartbeat to realise what she meant by 'escape'.

Suicide pepper.

So some folk had found a way out. It wasn't the sort of escape I had planned. But if those peppers were coming in from the outside, there had to be a way to get things out, too. Some way for the whispers to make it through these walls.

'Who is the blessed Sultima?' I'd heard her mentioned already. When I first arrived. In the baths.

'The Sultim's first wife.' Leyla looked up, surprised. 'Well, not the first that he took. He took Ayet as a wife the day after he won the Sultim trials. But the blessed Sultima is the only one of Kadir's wives who has been able to conceive a child.'

They must hate her. My aunt Farrah had hated Nida, my uncle's youngest wife. But Farrah's place as first wife had been secured by three sons. It was Nida who had to kiss her feet to get anything. They might be talking about the Sultim instead of a desert horse trader, but they were still just jealous wives. And I understood how these things worked. The first wife was the most powerful woman in the household – in this case, in the harem.

'Where would one find the Sultima?'

Chapter 18

The Sultima was a legend in the harem.

Chosen by God to be the mother of the next heir of Miraji. The only woman worthy of conceiving a child by the Sultim. She kept herself locked in her rooms most of the time. Women in the harem whispered that it was because she was praying. But I remembered something Shazad had told me once: if you could stay out of your enemy's line of sight, they'd always count your forces stronger than they were.

And from the whispers I'd heard, the harem was full of the Sultima's enemies.

But if there was one thing I knew about legends, it was that we were still flesh and blood. And flesh and blood had to come out of her rooms eventually.

Two days after Mouhna fed me the suicide pepper, Leyla woke me up with news. The blessed Sultima had finally emerged to bathe.

I spotted the Sultima before I'd even fully emerged from the hallway into the baths. She was sitting with her back to the entrance, dangling one leg in the water, with the other braced under her, twisted just enough towards me so that I could see the swell of her stomach. Her age singled her out. I'd seen other pregnant women in the harem, but they belonged to the Sultan. He'd stopped taking wives nearly ten years back; his wives were nearer in age to him now – most had seen at least three decades or close to it. Even from afar I could tell the Sultima hadn't seen eighteen years yet. She was running her hands over her middle over and over in soothing motions, head tilted forward in thought.

From here, the blessed Sultima looked just like any other heavily pregnant desert girl. It wasn't so much that I'd expected her to go to the baths draped in pearls and rubies, but after all the rumours and whispers, I figured I'd get something more than a girl in a thin white khalat.

She wasn't alone. At the other side of the water, Kadir was sprawled, wearing a loose shalvar and nothing else. He was bare from the waist up. I hadn't thought Jin shared anything with this brother, but the aversion to shirts seemed to be a family trait.

There were about a half dozen other girls I recognised from the harem in the water, too. A collection of Kadir's wives, splashing around in the water, giggling, long white khalats sticking to them.

I'd been here long enough to realise that most of the women in the harem weren't Mirajin. They were pale northern women stolen off ships, foreign-featured eastern girls sold as slaves, dark-skinned Amonpourian girls taken in border skirmishes. But there was no mistaking this girl for anything but desert born, even from behind. The linen stuck against her body from the steam that curled up from the baths; damp dark hair clung to her face. She didn't exactly look like the all-powerful Sultima, the chosen vessel of the future Sultan of Miraji.

And then she looked up, startled by the sound of my footsteps, eyes darting over her shoulder towards me, and my heart leapt into my mouth.

Oh, damn every power in heaven and hell, what did I do to deserve this?

I was face-to-face with the Sultima I'd heard so much about. The only woman pure enough to conceive a child by the Sultim Kadir. The girl sent by God to assure the future of Miraji.

Only I knew her as my cousin Shira. And the only thing God had ever sent her to do was make my life a living hell.

Jin told me once fate had a cruel sense of humour.

I was starting to believe him. First Tamid and now Shira. I'd crossed an entire desert but it was like I'd been dragged back home to face everything I'd left in my dust when I ran.

Shira looked as surprised as I was. Her mouth formed a small O before pressing tightly into a hard line. We stared at each other across the narrow stretch of tiles left between us. Our wills locked, the same way they'd done a hundred times across the tiny bedroom in my aunt's house.

'Well,' Shira said. She'd lost her accent. I could hear it even in that one word. Or maybe not lost – smothered under something that passed for a northern accent. 'Paint me purple and call me a Djinni if it isn't my least favourite cousin.'

There was a retort on the tip of my tongue. I caught it from slipping out by the skin of my teeth. *The Sultan has a Djinni*, I reminded myself. *He has a First Being trapped at his will and nothing is stopping him from using it against the rebels at any second. And then it could be over. For me. For Ahmed, Jin, Shazad, and the whole Rebellion.*

I didn't know much about other families, but I reckoned most of the time when you had to pretend to be nice to them, there weren't this many lives at stake.

'I thought you were dead,' I said. *You and Tamid both.* Last time I'd seen Shira she'd been on a train racing towards Izman with Prince Naguib, taken captive because they figured there was a chance she'd know where I was going. And if they found me, they found Jin, and if they found Jin, they found the Rebellion.

After Jin and I had gotten off the train, she'd lost her use. Noorsham had told me she'd been left in the palace to die. Only she wasn't just still alive. She was thriving. I wondered if she knew Tamid had survived being abandoned to fend for himself in this palace, too. If she knew what he was doing for the Sultan. If she even cared. She never had.

I shoved away thoughts of Tamid angrily. Shira was easier to face. It'd never been that complicated between us. We hated each other. Old hate was easier to face than Tamid's new disdain.

'You ought to know better than that.' My cousin smiled that seductive smile at me. 'Us desert girls are survivors. Although I'm curious about how you plan on surviving long here.' I stepped under the iridescent stones of the archway and into the harem baths proper. I ignored the tendrils of steam curling around my body like clinging fingers. 'Last time I saw you, weren't you riding off with some rebel traitor? Traitors don't survive long here.' Her eyes darted across the baths pointedly towards where Kadir was lounging. The bathing hall was as wide across as the whole of Dustwalk, far enough that Kadir hadn't noticed me yet. He picked something up from a pile at his elbow and tossed it in a high arc into the middle of the pool. As it caught the light I realised it was a ruby as big as my thumb.

It hit the water with a careless splash. A chaos of screeches and giggles followed as the six girls in the water dove towards where the ruby had disappeared under the surface, splashing and piling over each other as Kadir watched them hungrily. The shrieking and the splashing covered our voices.

'Now, what do you think my prince would make of your allegiance to his traitor brother if I told him?'

My sudden fear must've been scrawled all over my face because Shira smiled like a cat who'd eaten a canary.

God damn her. I'd come here for help, not to get sold out by her. 'Shira.' I closed the last few steps between us from the entrance to the edge of the water, dropping down in a crouch next to her, lowering my voice. 'If you tell Kadir I'm part of—' I caught the words back before I said them out loud. '—what you know,' I said carefully, eyes darting towards a girl who'd just surfaced near us in the water. 'I swear to God, Shira, if you breathe a word, I'll—' I scrambled for something to threaten her with, just like the bargaining games we used to play in Dustwalk. She wouldn't tell her mother

I'd been out all night with Tamid and I wouldn't tell her father she'd been in the stables letting Fazim get his hands under her clothes. Only this wasn't Dustwalk any more, and if she told on me, I'd get more than a switch to the back – I'd get myself, and probably a few hundred other people, killed. And then it slipped out: 'I'll just have to go ahead and tell him that kid of yours isn't his.'

Shira's whole face went still.

'Oh, God.' The truth of my own words hit me. 'The baby isn't the Sultim's.'

'Keep your voice down,' Shira hissed. Across the baths, one of the girls surged out of the water with a scream of triumph, her fist fastened around the ruby, tight as a noose. She kicked her way to the edge of the pool, showing the red stone proudly to Kadir, who leaned down to steal a kiss from her. She dropped the ruby into a small pile of colourful jewels on the side of the baths, keeping it separate from the piles of the other girls. When they were done, the Sultim would set their prizes into a necklace and gift it to them. It was like watching children play a game. Only the games in this harem could end with losing your head. The Sultim pulled another small yellow diamond from his dwindling pile.

'What the hell were you thinking?' Infidelity meant death in the harem – even I knew that. It had happened to Ahmed's mother when she gave birth to Delila. And it had happened to other women, too; there were countless stories, too many to ignore. Men who slipped into the harem without permission. Servants, princes who were not heirs . . . in every single tale it cost everyone involved their lives. Shira was a lot of things, but stupid wasn't one of them.

'I wanted to survive.' Shira's fingernails clicked dully against the tiles at the edge of the bath. I realised they'd been filed down low. She always used to keep them longer in Dustwalk. 'You left me and Tamid to die in Dustwalk so you could stay alive.'

She said Tamid's name different from how she used to back in Dustwalk. It didn't stick to the roof of her mouth with disdain. I supposed whatever they'd gone through together was the sort of thing that was bound to turn you into allies.

'Is Tamid the one who—' I started, already dreading the answer.

'Don't be ridiculous,' Shira snapped. 'I wouldn't risk giving the Sultan a cripple for a son.'

'And you really wonder why I think you're awful?' I clenched my fists, fighting the old urge to defend Tamid. He wouldn't fight for me. I wondered if she was why he loathed me now. Had she infected him with her hatred of me on the journey? Or had I made him hate me all on my own?

'Is what I did to survive any worse than what you did?' She moved her foot in slow circles through the water, sending out ripples. 'Naguib abandoned me here after I was no good to him any more. I would have died if I hadn't proved myself more interesting than the other girls in the harem.' A new chorus of shrieking emerged from the gaggle of girls, as another jewel sailed into the water. 'But even being the Sultim's favourite will only keep you alive here so long. So I've done the only thing I could that really ensured my survival.' She ran her hands along her swollen stomach, her jaw working. 'And you can tell whoever you want. No one will believe *you*.'

Good God, she was not making this easy. It'd been a long time since we'd last bickered in Dustwalk. I'd faced a whole lot of folk worse than her. But she was making me feel like we were right back under her mother's roof and there was nothing I wanted more than to best her just once.

'Yes, they will, Shira.' If she wasn't going to flinch, neither was I. Because if I knew one thing for sure, it was that if anyone found out Shira was carrying some other man's child and pretending it was the Sultim's, she'd lose her head. I held her life in my hands just the same as she did mine. 'And I reckon you know that.'

Shira stared me down. Being Sultima suited her; even I had to admit it. There was weight in those eyes that'd make most folk want to drop their gaze first. But I'd grown up shooting; I could outlast her.

'Fine, it's a deal.' Sure enough, Shira blinked first. 'I won't tell on you if you won't tell on me.'

'You're going to have to do me one better than that, cousin.'

'You want something else?' She scoffed, still running her hands across her stomach over and over. She had a whole lot of power here. But she didn't have any over me. Finally she pursed her lips, as if the words she was about to spit out tasted bitter. 'Of course you do. Fine.' Then Shira tossed her head back and laughed like I'd just said the funniest thing in the world. For a second I thought she'd lost her mind. Her voice echoed around the tiled walls, carrying over the commotion in the water and making Kadir look up. And he saw me. Damn it. Shira gave me a satisfied smirk. 'Better talk fast, cousin. I'm guessing you're the new toy Kadir keeps talking about. The one he's not allowed to have. So you have until he gets here to play with you to spit out what you want.'

I really wanted to push her into the water. 'Rumour has it you've got a way to pass contraband in and out of the harem.'

'Who says that?'

'People,' I evaded. 'Do you or don't you?' I kept one eye on Kadir as he got to his feet, sauntering lazily around the iridescent blue tiles of the pool towards us. It was like being tracked by a hungry Skinwalker. I wanted to get out before he got to me.

'I might,' she said, hedging. Wasting time. 'What is it you're so desperate to get in that you'd threaten my life for it? A bottle of liquor? New clothes? That certainly seems worth the price of my head.' It wasn't a half-bad attempt to make me feel sorry about blackmailing her. Anyone else and I might've actually *been* sorry.

'I don't want anything brought in.' I kept an eye on Kadir, getting closer now. 'I need to get a message out. Can you do that?'

'I suppose so.' Shira ran her tongue over her teeth, deliberately slowly. She was trying to keep me here. 'I'd need some time.'

'I don't have a whole lot of that. Can you help me or do I tell your husband that you climbed into another man's bed and get you hanged?' He was halfway across to us now.

'I can help.' Shira set her jaw angrily, resting her hand on her middle. 'If you—'

'Come to join the game?' Kadir called, interrupting whatever Shira had been about to say next. He was close enough to be heard. His eyes travelled up and down my body. 'You're a little overdressed.'

I pushed myself to my feet. Shazad had taught me enough to know that you didn't stand against an enemy from lower ground. 'I'm dressed just fine for leaving, Your Exalted Highness.'

Kadir made a noise at the back of his throat, like a hum of agreement. Except it sounded an awful lot like a laugh. 'You are free to leave, of course.' He was rolling a perfect white pearl between his thumb and forefinger. He circled around in front of me, standing between me and the way out. Then he tossed the pearl carelessly aside, letting it land in the water. The girls, who'd been watching the exchange, didn't scramble for it. 'As soon as you bring me back that pearl.'

'I can't swim,' I said. Anywhere else I'd be able to stand up for myself. I'd be able to fight him. But I was helpless. I tried to hold myself like I wasn't.

'Then you can't leave.' He smirked. 'That pearl is very precious to me.'

I couldn't fight him. Just the thought of raising my fist and putting it in his too-pleased-with-himself-looking face made the tug of the Sultan's orders twinge in my stomach. And I wasn't sure what he'd try to do if I walked out. What he could do. Or whether the Sultan had warned him against hurting me.

If the Sultan cared whether his Demdji prize got hurt. I didn't even know why I was still alive. He had his Djinni.

The silence was broken by a splash as one of the other girls dove under the water and sprang back up a moment later, the pearl between her fingers. 'I got bored waiting,' she said, pouting prettily, her pale hair sticking to her forehead as she brandished the pearl. But there was a tightness to her smile. And I understood what she'd done. For me. The risk.

The tension broke as Kadir lounged over to her. Shira was on her feet, grabbing me by the elbow, pushing me out of the baths. 'Tonight.' She shoved me back towards the safety of the gardens. 'Meet me by the Weeping Wall after dark.'

Chapter 19

The Weeping Wall was the easternmost wall of the harem, a small, closed-off part of the garden dominated by the biggest tree I'd ever seen in my life. It would've taken three of me to get my arms all the way around it, and the branches stretched so far they touched the top of the walls on either side.

According to the women of the harem, it was the place where Sultima Sabriya had waited for Sultim Aziz a thousand years ago. He had gone to war on the distant eastern border and left his love in the harem. The Weeping Wall was the closest she had been able to get to him while he was away in battle. She stood there every day, waiting for him, her tears watering the tree so that it grew higher and higher every day. Until one day it was finally high enough for her to climb to see over the walls of the harem to where her husband's army was. That day, the other women found her on the ground, screaming and wailing and clawing at the wall. She couldn't be consoled and she cried until her voice left her; and the tree grew greater still.

Three days later the news came that Aziz had been killed in battle. That was what Sabriya had seen from the top of the tree, across the walls, across deserts and cities and seas.

The wall looked just like every other in the harem in the dim light of my oil lamp. Ivy blooming with flowers all the colour of the setting sun climbed from the earth up the stone wall, trying to hide the fact that we were in a prison. I pushed the ivy aside, setting my hands against the solid stone. My fingers met an uneven surface. When I held the lamp up I realised it looked like a gouge – several of them. The kind fingernails might leave.

'And her wailing carried on for seven nights and seven days.' I jumped at Shira's voice behind me. She was draped in a dark blue khalat that made her melt in with the shadows. 'Until the Sultan could listen to her grief no more, and he strung her up where only the stars could hear her wail.'

I dropped my hand. 'Who knew such love could exist in the harem.'

Shira didn't miss the sarcasm in my voice. 'Anyone less self-centred than you.' I was about to retort that she didn't love Kadir, no more than she'd loved Naguib. But then I realised that her hands had drifted to her pregnant stomach as she spoke. Folk did terrifying things for the ones they loved. That, I'd learned from stories. I even had a bullet wound scar across my hip from Iliaz to prove it.

'So what now?' I raised an eyebrow at her expectantly, a trick I'd learned from Jin.

'Oh, now we wait, cousin.' Shira leaned against the huge tree, tilting her head back.

I was going to have to play along with Shira's game. I flopped against the tree next to her. 'How long?'

Shira tipped her head back further. 'It could be a while. I can't tell. It's hard to see the sky properly from the city.'

I leaned my head back against the trunk, my hair snagging in the rough bark. She wasn't wrong. Through the crisscrossing branches of the huge tree I could see the dark sky, but with the lights from the palace and the city, I couldn't make out the stars.

'So.' Shira broke the silence after a moment. 'Are you really with the Rebel Prince?' She was fiddling with something, and I realised it was a rope that ran the length of the tree, like a pulley. She was tugging it absently, up and down. At the top, above the line of the harem walls, a piece of cloth stirred in the wind.

'I really am.' She was signalling someone. It could be a trap for all I knew. I couldn't do much about it if it was except face it when it came.

'Who would've thought it?' Shira smiled. 'Two girls from Dustwalk, with royalty. What was it the Holy Father used to say?' Her accent was slipping. I wondered if she noticed. 'Men who worship at the feet of power either rise with it—'

'—or get trampled,' I said, filling in the saying. 'Good thing we aren't men, then.' I didn't know why I was buying into her game. But I was real low on people I could talk to in this place. Leyla was sweet enough, but she was still the Sultan's daughter. And Tamid wasn't worth thinking about. He might be alive, but my friend had still died in the sand in Dustwalk. Shira's dark eyes met my pale ones. A moment of recognition passed between us. We'd both hitched our wagons to powerful folk, just on different sides. If that was the choice, to rise or be flattened, chances were one of us was going to wind up rising and the other one dead.

'Shira—' I started. I wasn't sure how I was going to finish.

I never did. Because a man stepped out of the Weeping Wall.

I'd seen a whole lot of Demdji do impossible things, but I'd be lying if I said I'd been expecting that.

The man was flesh and blood, and though at first glance he was dressed in desert clothes, he was distinctly un-Mirajin. He had hair the colour of sand, held back by a sheema that looked like it had been tied by someone with no hands, and pale skin that glowed in the lamplight. And his eyes were nearly as blue as mine. For a second I thought he was a Demdji.

'Blessed Sultima,' he said, his voice low and tinged with an accent. Not a Demdji, then, just a foreigner.

He pulled himself to his full height, giving me a better view of him. Dark polished boots different from anything I'd ever seen in the desert rose to his knees, his loose desert trouser legs stuffed inside, and he wore a white shirt open at the collar. I got the strangest impression he was pausing for effect. After a beat, he stepped forward dramatically.

That was when his arm got stuck in one of the vines that hung from the wall.

It sort of ruined the effect.

He recovered as well as he could, untangling his arm. Then he plucked one of the flowers from the vine and offered it to Shira with an extravagant bow. 'Your beauty grows with every passing day.'

His badly tied sheema flopped open, falling off his face so I could see him clearly. He wasn't a whole lot older than we were, and a light constellation of freckles over his pale nose made him look even younger. He was northern but not Gallan; his words sounded wrong, and I'd seen enough of the Gallan to know he wasn't one of them. He straightened and flung the sheema over his shoulder like the sweep of a cloak. Shira took the flower and pressed it to her nose.

So this was how Shira smuggled things into the harem. And, judging by the look he was giving her, this was how she'd managed to get herself pregnant, too.

Finally the foreign man seemed to notice me.

'This is—' Shira started, but he didn't let her finish.

'Allow me to introduce myself.' He snatched up my right hand without asking. I resisted the urge to yank it out of his grip. Shazad would call that undiplomatic. 'Especially to such a beautiful young woman.' He raised my hand to his lips, in some strange foreign gesture, and kissed it. 'I,' he declared, straightening dramatically, 'am the Blue-Eyed Bandit.'

I choked on a snort that got stuck in my throat and turned into an uncontrollable cough. Shira patted me awkwardly on the back as I doubled over, bracing my free hand against my knees.

'Yes, I know, my reputation precedes me.' My *reputation precedes you*. But I still couldn't talk through my coughing. 'Don't let it intimidate you. I didn't really defeat a thousand soldiers in Fahali.'

He leaned forward conspiratorially, still clutching my hand, now twining his fingers through mine. 'It was merely hundreds.'

'Is that right?' I'd finally managed to catch my breath. I remembered Fahali like a blur. Gunpowder and blood and sand, and myself in the middle of it. 'So tell me, how did you flood the prayer house at Malal?'

'Well.' There was a glint in his eyes. He talked from the top of his mouth, unlike the Gallan, who talked from the back. 'I could tell you, but I'd rather not give you any dangerous ideas.'

I probably ought to stop enjoying this. But I couldn't remember the last time I'd had something to laugh about in this damn rebellion. Definitely not since we'd fled the Dev's Valley. 'And how about the fight at Iliaz? Is it true what they say? That the Blue-Eyed Bandit was outgunned and outnumbered and surrounded by enemies on all sides?'

He didn't miss a beat, his chest swelling as he drew me towards him. 'Oh, well, you know, what others call outnumbered, I call a challenge.'

'I heard the Blue-Eyed Bandit got shot in the hip.' I'd let him pull me close enough that we were almost chest to chest now. 'Can I see the scar?'

'My lady is very forward.' He grinned widely at me. 'Where I come from, you have to know a girl more than a few minutes before she'll try to get your clothes off.' He tilted his head forward, winking at me.

'Well, how about I take my clothes off, then.' Before I could think better of it, I stepped back and tugged up the side of my shirt. The huge ugly scar was hard to miss, even in the dark. 'Because I heard the scar looked something like this.' I was pretty sure nothing he'd ever brought into the harem for Shira was as priceless as the look on his face just then. It was almost worth the risk of giving him my identity. It might not have been a smart thing to do, now I thought about it, but it sure was satisfying. He dropped my hand as I let my shirt fall back, pulling away from him. 'And, see, I was in Fahali, and I don't remember you being there.'

He scratched the back of his head sheepishly as I went on. 'I remember fighting the Gallan soldiers in the sand and I remember men burning alive on both sides, but I don't remember you.' The act was gone now – he was watching me with real interest. 'But I gather you're the reason everyone thinks I can be in two different places at once. And why I keep hearing rumours about the Blue-Eyed Bandit seducing so many women.' That part made sense now. He was as handsome as anything, even when he looked ridiculous at the same time. And he knew it, too.

'What can I say, I walk into their homes to take

their jewels and they give me their hearts.' He winked at Shira, who smiled enigmatically into the flower he'd given her. No, Shira was too clever to give anything away to a man she couldn't truly have. She'd taken from him. She'd used him for her child and she was still using him.

'So this is your way to the outside world?' I asked my cousin.

Shira was twirling the flower he'd given her between her fingers, looking pleased with herself. 'Sam was sneaking in and ... wooing one of the Sultan's more gullible daughters, Miassa. I noticed she kept disappearing and coming back with her hair and clothes all mussed. It didn't take long to catch her – very silly of her to start running around with other men when she was already engaged to be married to the Emir of Bashib. I promised not to turn them both in to her father if Sam helped me.'

'It all worked out for the best.' The foreigner, Sam, shrugged again, as if to say it wasn't her brains he was interested in anyway. 'The Emir of Bashib leaves his wife alone a great deal; it's not hard for the Blue-Eyed Bandit to visit her still now and again.'

There he went, using my name again. My temper flared. 'Believe me when I tell you, I know the Blue-Eyed Bandit, and you're not me. So who are you really?'

'Well.' He leaned his shoulder back against the wall.

'You can't blame a fellow for cashing in on a very good story. Nobody told me the real Blue-Eyed Bandit was so much more ...' He looked me up and down, eyes seeming to linger on the places I'd fleshed out recently. Half a year of decent meals with the Rebellion meant I wouldn't be able to pass for a boy any more. I raised an eyebrow at him in a challenge. He coughed. 'So much more. And I *am* a bandit. Well, more of a thief, I suppose. When all these stories started spreading, it was only sensible that I take advantage of my God-given looks.' He winked one of those mocking blue eyes at me. 'You wouldn't believe how much easier it is to strike a good deal when you're practically a living legend. They say you're very good. Though you're obviously not that good if you wound up locked in here.'

I wished I could punch him.

'How did you get in here?' I asked instead.

'I'm Albish.' He said it like it explained everything. When he was met with my blank expression, he continued. 'Our country is crawling with magic. My mother is a quarter Faye and my father half.' Faye. That was the northern word for their Djinn. Only they were creatures of water and soft earth. 'If it's stone, I can walk through it. See?' He'd allowed himself to sink back while he was talking to me and was now elbow deep in the stone wall of the palace.

It was as impressive as anything I could do; I'd give him that. 'What's an Albish thief doing in Izman?'

'My talents were wasted in Albis.' He righted himself and the stone shifted just a little bit back into place. 'Thought I'd bring them to your desert, where people wouldn't expect a man of my talents to come after their jewels. The habit of locking valuables in an iron box doesn't seem to have made it here yet.' He wasn't lying. I could tell that much. But he was hiding something I couldn't quite put my finger on. There were easier places to go than Izman if it was just money he was after. Countries that weren't in the middle of a war, for one. But he was what I'd been waiting for, someone who could get in and out of the palace at will. And I'd been raised in Dustwalk, where we didn't look gift horses in the mouth.

I grabbed my cousin's arm and pulled her away from the wall, out of earshot of Sam, the Blue-Eyed Bandit impostor. She shook me off with a roll of her eyes that needled at me, but this wasn't the time to get annoyed at her. 'Can I trust him? Truthfully, Shira – can I trust him with something important? A whole lot of lives?'

'I've had him send letters for me to Dustwalk,' she said after a moment. 'To my family.' I wondered if I was imagining the hardness in the way she said *my*.

Even now she couldn't help but remind me that, though we shared blood and had lived under the same roof, I'd never truly be part of her family. 'Well, letters and some money.' I'd barely given any thought to Dustwalk in months, except to thank God that I was out of there. But I cast my mind back now. Dustwalk without a factory, with nothing, destroyed. It would be a miracle if the whole town hadn't decamped or starved to death by now.

Shira trusted this man with her family. I could trust him with mine. I turned back to Sam, who was incompetently trying to tie his sheema back up. 'Could you carry a message out for me?'

'Of course.' I winced as he tucked the edge of his sheema in all wrong. It was painful to watch. A toddler could do better than that. 'How much?'

'How much what?'

'How much will you pay me to carry this message?' He repeated it carefully, like it might be his Mirajin that was at fault.

I glanced at Shira, who splayed empty hands at me pointedly. 'The Sultim thinks I'm too modest to wear any of the jewellery he gives me.' Now that I thought about it, I realised she was surprisingly unadorned for the harem. Ayet wore gold bangles from wrist to elbow some days. She clacked with metal with every gesture.

'Truth is, I just put them to very good use. Everything that happens within the walls of the harem is a trade. The sooner you figure that out, the more likely you are to survive.'

'I don't have any jewels,' I said to Sam. 'You've already taken my reputation. Isn't that enough?'

'Well, you weren't making very good use of it. I think I've done you a favour. Besides, stories belong to the people,' he said. 'And considering you are very much trapped, it's going to take more than that.'

I ran my tongue across my teeth, thinking. I could probably get something to trade with if I had a few days. Some of the girls in the harem weren't all that careful. It wouldn't be that hard to take a bangle off them when they slept. But I wasn't sure I had that much time to waste. And there might be another way. 'The message I need you to carry, it's for Shazad Al-Hamad, General Hamad's daughter, he's—'

'I know who General Hamad is,' Sam said, and for a moment the cocky, smiling man was gone.

'Then you ought to know he's got money. A lot of it. And so does his daughter.' I paused, then added, 'His breathtakingly gorgeous daughter.' Shazad would have my head if she could hear me describe her like this to some foreign thief. I wasn't even sure she was in Izman, but she was still my best shot.

'I like her already,' Sam said. But there was a note of sarcasm under there. He rubbed a spot on the base of one of the fingers of his left hand. It was a distracted gesture, far away. I got the feeling he didn't even wholly know what he was doing. 'Why should she believe me? The general's rich, spoiled daughter.' Shazad would definitely have Sam's head for calling her spoiled. Here was hoping he had the good sense not to do it to her face.

'Just tell her the Blue-Eyed Bandit is in the palace.' I didn't dare give him anything else to pass on to her. Not about the Sultan having a Djinni or anything else. Not yet, anyway. I'd risked enough by giving him my identity. 'The real one. And that she needs someone to watch her back.'

Chapter 20

The Nameless Boy

In a kingdom across the sea, a farmer and his wife lived in a hovel with their six children. They were so poor, they had nothing to give their children but love. And quickly they learned that love was not enough to keep their children fed or warm. Three of their children died in their first winter, too weak to survive the cold. So when their seventh child was born, a son, on the darkest, coldest day of the bleak winter, they did not give him a name, so prepared were they for him to die.

But their nameless son survived that darkest day. And the one that followed. He lived through his first winter and into the spring. And he lived through his second winter. And, in his second spring, he finally earned a name.

The once-nameless boy was quick and clever and had a talent for going places he was not meant to be, so long as the walls were made of stone. And he saw that his family was poor while others were rich and he did not think this was fair. So when his mother became sick, in the boy's seventh winter, he took food from kitchens with more shelves than his to feed her and he took silver from other houses to buy her medicine. That was how he walked into the castle on the hill that belonged to the lord of that county, and into the life of the lord's young daughter.

The lord's young daughter was lonely in the great castle, but she was rich, too, and she had learned she could have anything by asking for it. So when she asked for the boy's friendship, he gave it to her gladly. He taught her games and she taught him to read. She learned she was gifted at skipping stones across a pond on a bright summer day and he learned he was gifted at languages spoken in distant corners of the world.

As they grew older, he became healthy and strong and handsome. So handsome that the lord's daughter noticed. She was still rich and there had never been anything in the world that she could not get simply by asking. So when she asked for the boy's heart, he gave that to her gladly, too.

The two met secretly in all the hidden places they had found together as children.

The once-nameless boy's brothers warned him against the lord's daughter. They had all married poor girls who lived in the shadow of the great castle and though they were poor, they were all happy enough. But the once-nameless boy had read too many stories of worthy farmers' sons who married princesses, and highwaymen who stole rich ladies' hearts, to heed his brothers' warnings. He believed that he had stolen the girl's heart as well as gifted her his.

So the boy was greatly surprised when it was announced to the whole county that the lord's daughter was to be married to the second son of the lord from a neighbouring county.

The once-nameless boy left word for the lord's daughter asking her to meet him in their secret place by the water. He waited there all night, but she did not come. He waited the next night and still she did not come; and the next night after that, too. Finally, the night before the lord's daughter was to be wed, the once-nameless boy walked through the walls of the castle and, there, he found the lord's daughter, pale hair spread across a white silk pillow, beautiful and fair in the moonlight. He knelt by her bed and woke her from her slumber and asked her to come away with him, to run away and marry him. He was on his knees, but he did not beg because he never thought he would need to.

He never imagined she would refuse him. But the lord's daughter did not take his hand. Instead she laughed at him and called her guards, handing him back his heart on the way out of the castle.

And so he learned then that girls with titles did not marry once-nameless boys.

The boy became determined to no longer be nameless. So he signed his life to his queen and donned a uniform, pledging to earn his name by fighting for his sovereign and his land. He travelled to a kingdom across the sea, the land without winter.

There, instead of a name for himself, he found blood and guns and sand. He knew that nobody lost their names as quickly as the dead, so he fled once more. He hid himself in the sprawling city of Izman, a kaleidoscope of sights and sounds like he'd never known. When he first grew hungry he remembered what he had once been good at: going places he didn't belong. He stole a loaf of bread his first night in the city, which he ate sitting atop a prayer house, looking out over the rooftops. On the second night he stole a fistful of foreign coins that he traded for a bed. On his third he took a necklace which could have easily fed all his parents' children for a year. As he learned to slip in and out with ease among the streets, he heard a name being whispered. One that didn't truly seem to belong to anyone. A legend. So he took it for himself. He used the name to take other things. Rich people's jewels and careless men's wives. He even stole a princess's heart, like the thieves in the stories he knew. But this time he was not foolish enough to give his in return. He had learned not to give things away to anyone who asked.

And so he had a name. And it fit him so well that he almost started to believe it was truly his. Until he met the girl who it belonged to. The girl in the harem with eyes that could light the world on fire. She was asking for his help.

He was to carry a message to a general's daughter. He found her home easily. It was a large house with a red door in the wealthiest part of the city. He waited on a corner, watching the door, servants coming and going, watching people wearing a small fortune's worth of jewels on their hands wave at each other, as he waited for the girl.

Finally he saw the general's daughter.

He knew her before she even placed her hand on the red door. She was beautiful enough that it was as difficult to look at her as it was to stare at the sun. She was like something crafted her whole life with the purpose only to be seen and coveted. And she moved with the easy certainty of someone who knew that her place in the world was above most.

As soon as he saw her he recognised her, though they had never met.

Her hair and skin and eyes were dark, where the lord's daughter had been as pale as milk. Her clothes were colours stolen from the Djinn, where the lord's daughter's had been the colours of the rainy skies and the rivers and the fresh grass. But they were the same. She was the kind of girl who thought she deserved everything just by asking for it.

And he knew that if he knocked on the red door he would be turned away with a scoff and a wave. Because nameless bandits were not invited in to talk to generals' daughters.

So he waited for nightfall in the city. Windows in the street lit up one by one and then went dark as silence drew down across the city. Except for the window that belonged to the general's daughter. He watched that window into the dark hours of the night until finally that light went out, too. And the once-nameless boy did what he did best and walked into somewhere he wasn't supposed to go, straight through the wall and up the stairs to where she slept.

She was sprawled across colourful pillows, dark hair covering her face. He knelt down next to her bed, to wake her from her slumber. But before he could say a word he found a knife to his throat.

It had happened so quickly he hadn't seen the general's daughter move.

'Who are you?' she asked. She didn't look afraid. He saw then that he'd been entirely wrong. She was not like the lord's daughter at all. She had not been crafted to be seen and coveted. She had crafted herself to fool the world. And the easy certainty of her step was the knowledge that she was being underestimated. And she got what she asked for because she asked for it from the right end of a blade. 'Answer me quickly and correctly or you'll never speak another lie again.' She pressed the blade towards his throat.

And suddenly, the once-nameless boy knew he didn't want a stolen name, tarnished with use. What he wanted desperately was a name good enough to give to this girl. But until he had that, he would have to use another.

'I've come in the name of the Blue-Eyed Bandit.'

Chapter 21

I knew something was different when I was woken up by three servants instead of by the sun. I was being propped up to a sitting position and my kurti pulled over my head before I was even fully awake.

'What's happening?' I made a grab for the hem, but something new was being draped around me already.

'The Sultim has ordered that you will attend him in court today.' The servant who answered was the same one who'd brought me into the harem. I'd never gotten her name out of her.

And here I thought I was off-limits. But I supposed that was only to being treated as a wife, not as a thing to be polished up and put on display. I yanked my arm back towards myself as a woman scraped something rough along my fingernails. She grabbed my hand back and started again, making me wince at the noise.

'It's a great honour.' The servant gathered my

long hair up, fastening a clasp behind my neck. Not a necklace, I realised; this was meant to pass for a khalat. It was fine blue cloth stitched with black that matched my hair. Except it left half of me bare. My arms, my shoulder, and half my back were exposed. I almost laughed. This would never pass for desert clothes, not in a place where the sun beat down on every bit of skin it could find. This was the luxury of a city. And the decadence of a harem. She pulled me to my feet so that the clothes fell over my loose shalvar. At least I seemed to be allowed to keep that on.

I could make this real difficult for them if I wanted to. I could resist and make the Sultan dictate my every movement. But the last thing I wanted was more orders.

And I got the feeling that, as hard as I could make things for them, the Sultim could probably make them a whole lot harder for me.

Besides, I was being permitted to leave the harem, even if it wasn't out of the palace. It'd been seven days since I'd sent Sam to Shazad. Seven days of the same lazy indifference that marked every day in the harem. It wasn't like waking up in the rebel camp. The tension in my bones wasn't matched by anyone else's. The restlessness of an impending battle, the fear of not knowing – they were mine alone. I'd even gone to the Weeping Wall once or twice and strung up the white cloth into the huge tree, hoping the signal would bring him back. Nothing.

Everything depended on a stupid boy who couldn't even tie a sheema right and there was nothing else I could do except wait for news. Wait like Sabriya for Prince Aziz. Helpless and blind to see who would die in battle. I felt like I might lose my mind.

I'd be damn stupid to turn down a shot at getting a look outside.

The parts of the palace that they led me through now weren't near so empty as those I had followed the Sultan through. Servants scurried past us, heads bowed, carrying platters heavy with colourful fruit or crisp clean linens. A small gaggle of Xichian men in what looked like travelling clothes sat in a garden that we passed. My neck craned their way instinctively as Jin dashed across my thoughts. A man dressed finely enough to be an emir and trailing three identically dressed women swept down the hallway ahead of us, disappearing up a staircase. A pair of foreign-looking men in strange uniforms stepped aside as we passed. My heart jumped at the sight of them. They looked Gallan. But no, their uniform was wrong. Albish, maybe?

We rounded another corner. I knew the Gallan on sight. Two soldiers flanked an unremarkable-looking man in plain clothes. Their uniforms were glaringly familiar, sending a twist of fear through me. But the soldiers weren't the most unsettling ones. There was something about the plain-clothed Gallan man; his eyes cut right through me. I could feel them in my back as we continued on.

Two dozen curious faces turned my way the second the doors to the Sultan's receiving garden opened. All of them belonged to men, seated haphazardly around the garden on cushions. The Sultan's councillors. They were all soft-looking intellectual types. Like Mahdi. Pale from lack of sunlight, too many hours spent inside studying the world and not enough living in it. Servants hovered around them like a swarm, wielding fans and pitchers of sweet fruit juices.

There was only one man who stood apart from the circus. He was about of an age with Ahmed and Jin and wearing a spotless white-and-gold army uniform. He didn't sit. Instead he stood, straight as a statue, arms clasped behind his back, eyes straight ahead like he was awaiting orders. There was a pang of familiarity as I looked at him that I couldn't quite place.

At the head of the garden, raised above his court, was the Sultan. He lifted his eyebrows a tiny bit as he saw me. So he hadn't known that his son had given me permission to leave the harem. Kadir sat at his right hand. Ayet was draped around her husband's shoulders, wearing the same khalat I was, but in a glaring red with silver threads. She was there to be shown off and she knew it, too, twisting her bare back to the court, showing off the complicated henna designs that decorated her spine. At Kadir's feet was Uzma, wearing the same garment in green across her tiny frame. I glanced around for Mouhna. She wasn't anywhere to be seen.

Kadir pointedly rested his hand on the cushion to the opposite side of Ayet. I would've given just about anything to not have to sit there. But I didn't have that choice.

An attendant busied herself arranging the long hem of my khalat around me so I was entirely covered. Kadir dismissed her with a wave of the hand. As soon as she was gone I stuck my bare foot out from under the hem. It wasn't much, but it was the best I could manage, as small acts of defiance went. I caught the eye of the the man in military clothes as I looked up. He was watching me, hiding a smile behind his hand, pretending to scratch his eyebrow.

'Kadir.' The Sultan spoke across me, low enough that the rest of the court couldn't hear. 'Do you not have enough of your own women to keep you entertained?'

'I would have, Father.' Something silent passed

between Kadir and the Sultan that I didn't understand. 'But I seem to have misplaced one of them.' He must mean Mouhna. I remembered what Leyla had said about women disappearing from the harem all the time. Like her mother had. 'I needed one more to complete my Mirajin set.' Kadir reached out and ran a hand lazily along one of the scars on my back. My body shuddered angrily in response.

The way the Sultan smiled would've fooled the rest of the court into thinking he was having the most genial conversation with his son. 'Lay that hand on her again and you will lose it.' I felt an unexpected surge of gratitude towards the Sultan for coming to my defence. I quashed it. It was his fault I was here, unable to defend myself.

The Sultan straightened. 'Bring in the first petitioner.' He raised his voice, coming to stand at the gate that led into the court.

'Commander Abbas Al-Abbas,' a servant announced. 'Of the Eleventh Command.'

The soldier who came in bowed low before speaking. 'Your Exalted Honour. I have come to plead for a release from my command.'

'This is a serious request, in a time of war.' The Sultan considered him. 'It's clearly not for lack of bravery that you wish to be relieved, or else you wouldn't be here facing me.' The soldier seemed to swell with pride for a moment at being called brave.

'News has come from my father's home. My brother, his heir, has been called by God to the Holy Order. My father has no other sons. If I don't return, my sisters' husbands will squabble for his land. I wish to go home to take my place as his heir.'

The Sultan considered him. 'What do you think, Rahim?' He was talking to the young soldier, the one who'd seemed familiar. Rahim. I knew his name. Leyla's brother, I realised. The only one among the army of the Sultan's sons that she truly considered her family. Sure enough, he had Leyla's same clever, watchful eyes. Though Leyla's years in the harem meant that I could see some of the paleness of their Gamanix mother in her. Years spent outside the palace walls had made Rahim look Mirajin through and through. It looked like he even shared some of his father's stronger features with Ahmed.

'I very much doubt my opinion could add anything you don't already know, exalted Father.' Rahim's words were respectful, but there was something else there. I got the feeling the two were playing a game I didn't quite understand.

'Modesty has never suited you, Rahim.' The Sultan went on, waving his hand. 'I'm sure you have insights, having been a soldier for so long now. Share them.'

'I think the eastern border is exposed and that the Eleventh Command needs a soldier leading them who wishes to lead,' Rahim said. The Sultan didn't speak again straight away. He was waiting for something else. A silent battle of wills crossed the court.

'And' – Rahim broke first – 'the Holy Books teach us a man's first duty is to his father.'

The Sultan smiled, like he'd won some victory. 'Commander Abbas Al-Abbas. Your request is granted.' The soldier's shoulders sagged in relief. 'You will be relieved of your command. Name your replacement and we will raise him up in your place.'

I forgot the next petitioner's endless name and title almost before the man was done announcing it. Just like I forgot what he was asking for as soon as he started talking. One after another, the petitioners followed each other in front of the Sultan.

One man wanted money. The next wanted land. The next wanted more guards in his quarter of the city. Rebels, he reported, were multiplying among the dockworkers. The next wanted the Blue-Eyed Bandit brought to justice. He'd stolen his wife's jewels and seduced his daughter, he reported.

Well, if Sam was still alive to be muddying my name, I supposed that meant at least Shazad hadn't skewered him on sight. Or he hadn't bothered to deliver my message yet.

The Sultan listened patiently before asking the man what more he thought the throne could do about the Blue-Eyed Bandit. I watched him carefully as he spread his hands in sympathy. There was already a price on the Bandit's head for his collaboration with the Rebel Prince, he explained, but no one had been able to find him. The man might as well be a spirit in the desert. Or a fiction.

I resented being called a fiction. But then, I'd resent being found out and tortured out of my mind like Sayyida a whole lot more. I was suddenly stupidly grateful to Sam, even if he did decide it wasn't worth his time getting my message to Shazad.

My foot was falling asleep and I had to shift positions restlessly over and over to keep it from going dead altogether as one boring request followed the other.

I finally gave up all pretence and pulled my knees up to my chin, wrapping my arms around them to keep myself steady.

I was half-asleep by the time the man in chains appeared. Everybody who'd been wilting in the afternoon sun came alive again. 'Aziz Al-Asif.' The man in fine clothes who was leading the chained man took a bow as the servant announced him. 'And his brother, Lord Huda Al-Asif.'

'Your Exalted Highness.' Aziz Al-Asif stooped low. 'It is my deepest regret that I have come to ask that you condemn my brother to death. He has been conspiring to rebellion.'

'Is that so.' There was an amused edge to the Sultan's voice. 'Because that is not what my spies have reported to me. What they *have* reported to me is that you are power hungry and that you are the one conspiring to ally with my son's rebellion. Which can only lead me to believe that you are lying to me in order for your brother to be executed. When he is gone, you can take sole ownership of the seat of your father's lands.' A rustle went around the garden. 'Release Lord Huda.' The Sultan gestured towards the two guards by the door. 'And take young Aziz prisoner.'

'Your Majesty,' Aziz exclaimed loudly, 'I have committed no crime!'

'You have.' The Sultan cut across him, and there was no mistaking the authority in his voice. 'Attempting to kill your brother is a crime. Lying to your Sultan is a crime. Thinking that you can leverage my son's rebellion to your own uses is not a crime but it is not something I will tolerate. Your execution will be at sunset, unless your brother sees fit to save you.' The Sultan looked at Lord Huda, who was rubbing his wrists. He didn't object. 'Spread the word in the city, then,' the Sultan said. 'I want the men and women of Izman to see what it costs to try to betray their ruler.'

Suddenly I was standing back with Ahmed in his tent as he couldn't make up his mind about Mahdi. As he refused to order an execution. As he failed to give a straight order. All I'd wanted was for him to make a goddamn decision. To be a ruler. A good one. A great one. A strong one.

The Sultan hadn't even hesitated.

Aziz's protests were still fading as the next person was called.

The day was heavy, and as the sun shifted, it turned its full glare onto us. I could feel sweat beading on my neck, running below my clothes. I could feel my eyes drifting shut as the midday heat started to prey on me. The only person who didn't show he felt it was the Sultan.

'Announcing Shazad Al-Hamad.'

I came awake as fast as if I'd been shot in the back. For a second I thought I'd dreamed it. That I'd really dozed off and imagined Shazad come to rescue me. But there, standing at the entrance to the garden, wearing a khalat the colour of a breaking dawn and that faint smile that meant she knew she was outsmarting someone, was Shazad.

Chapter 22

Shazad was here. Some of the fear that had been crouched in my chest since I'd woken up on a ship escaped. I could kiss Sam's idiot face for getting my message to her.

'Well,' the Sultan said, 'this is an unexpected honour.'

'The honour is all mine, Your Exalted Highness.' Her voice was so achingly familiar here in this strange place. It was the voice of a hundred nights in the camp and under desert skies, of conspiracy and treason and rebellion. 'I have returned from my pilgrimage.' She dropped to her knees. 'I come to pay tribute to my most exalted Sultan and Sultim.' She dropped into a low bow from her knees until her nose almost touched the ground. She was damn good at that. I supposed she had had sixteen years of practice before the Rebellion.

The Sultan considered her. 'I thought perhaps you had come to enquire after the return of your father from the war front.' If he meant to throw her off balance with a mention of General Hamad, he'd picked the wrong girl. Shazad started to answer, but I never heard what she said. A screech, like a knife across iron, split the sky, cutting her off.

The entire courtyard stilled. But something inside me woke up.

I knew that sound.

'That's a Roc.' Prince Rahim said out loud what I was thinking. His eyes were on the sky and he was on his feet. 'And nearby, too.'

'In the city?' Kadir scoffed, but he wasn't leaning back so idly any more. 'That's ridiculous.'

'Of course, brother.' Rahim held himself like a soldier, his hand resting, out of some old habit, on a weapon that wasn't there. 'What would I possibly know – I've only been stationed in the mountains of Iliaz for half a decade. I only heard Rocs screaming every night while you were still sleeping in the harem by your mother. But you know better, I'm sure.'

Kadir took a step towards Rahim. Rahim held his ground. Kadir was broader than his brother by a good bit. But as Rahim flexed his fists, I saw the scar across his hand. It reminded me of the scars on Jin's knuckles.

Kadir's hands were smooth. Rahim's hands showed the signs of a fight.

The scream of the Roc came again, closer this time, pulling them apart. The gathered crowd, frozen a moment earlier, turned into chaos. Men started to run for cover, and the Sultan shouted orders to his soldiers, sending them towards the walls, unslinging guns as they went.

I didn't move. I just stayed, craning my head backwards. Because I knew that scream. And then the shadow passed. Low enough to be seen clearly but high enough that it was out of the range of guns. As it soared overhead two huge blue wings obscured the sun, plunging the courtyard into shadow.

That wasn't a Roc. It was Izz.

A bolt of excitement shot through me, taking me to my feet. Izz was here. In the city.

Something was trailing out behind Izz, scattering in his wake. For a second I thought they were white cloths. But as they flittered down in the wind, I saw they were paper; a rain of paper from the sky.

I reached up as soon as the first sheet came close enough and snatched it before it hit the ground.

Ahmed's sun was printed at the top. I traced the lines of it the way I'd traced the ink on Jin's chest so many times. Printed below it, in sloppy black ink, it said:

A NEW DAWN. A NEW DESERT.

*We call for Sultan Oman Al-Hasim Bin
Izman of Miraji to step down from his throne
and stand trial for treason.*

*Sultan Oman is accused of these crimes
against Miraji and its people:*

- *Subjecting his country to unfit foreign rule
  in the form of the Gallan army*
- *Untried execution of parties accused of
  violating Gallan law*
- *Persecution of his own people without
  just cause*
- *Persecution of Mirajin citizens for unproven
  Djinni magic in their bloodline*
- *Oppression of working citizens through
  unfair wages*
- *Enslavement of women across Miraji*

The list went on.

*We demand the traitorous Sultan Oman be
separated from his throne for his crimes and
that his rightful heir, Prince Ahmed Al-Oman*

Bin Izman, true victor of the Sultim trials, be allowed to ascend in his place and return this desert to its rightful glory.

If he does not comply and surrender the throne, we will seize it on behalf of the people of Miraji.

A NEW DAWN. A NEW DESERT.

The Rebellion had come to Izman.

I read it over again. I was so absorbed I didn't notice anyone near me until I felt the hand on the back of my neck. I started to spin, but Uzma had already darted up behind me, quiet as a shadow, unclasping the khalat where it was fastened at the nape of my neck.

The fabric came undone, slithering off me towards the ground. I grabbed at it, letting Ahmed's sun slip to the ground, but too late to keep my body totally hidden.

Uzma's nasty little eyes took in my body, judging it, finding it wanting in every possible way with one glance.

'Now, *that* is a nasty scar. Did the tailor Abdul not stitch you together right?' She meant the one on my right hip, where the bullet had gone through in Iliaz. My fingers were still fumbling with the clasp at my neck to tie the khalat back up. I could feel my skin burning under her mocking gaze. 'It all makes sense now. Let me guess: you're a whore who got pregnant, and they had to try to cut the thing out of you.'

I gave up on the clasp without the servants to help me and reached up to knot the loose ends of fabric together. Uzma took a smirking step toward me as I struggled. One of the pamphlets crumpled under her bare foot, Ahmed's sun wrinkling.

'How about you step away from her.' The voice was iron and silk and wholly familiar. 'Before I knock you back.'

Shazad wasn't armed. But she looked as dangerous as she would've been with both her blades drawn as she stepped between me and Uzma. I tugged the knot tighter at the base of my neck. When I looked up, the smirk on Uzma's face flickered.

Shazad leaned forward, forcing Uzma to stagger backwards. 'My apologies,' Shazad said in a tone that didn't sound sorry at all. 'That may have sounded like a suggestion. It wasn't. Go.'

Uzma took two steps back, heading straight for Ayet, who was watching from the shadow of one of the pillars. Then Izz screamed again and both of them disappeared, fleeing for cover. Leaving me facing my best friend amid the chaos of the rapidly emptying courtyard.

'I told you about watching your back.' Shazad said.

'I told you I knew I could count on you to do it for me.' I longed to embrace her, but there were too many people around still. I could explain it away if we were caught talking but embracing might be harder. I had to be satisfied with plucking at the ornate sleeves of her khalat. 'I reckon you're the only person I know who can look that intimidating while wearing something with quite so many flowers on it.'

Shazad flashed me a messy smile. 'All the better to be underestimated in. Come on.' Shazad grabbed my hand, glancing around quickly. 'We're getting out of here. Now.' She started pulling me towards the gates. Nobody was looking at us as Izz screamed, passing over the palace again. The Sultan had vanished and everyone else was running for cover. It was a good chance to get out. 'This is supposed to be a distraction?' I gestured at the pamphlets littering the ground underfoot.

'Things can be a distraction and serve the cause at the same time.' Shazad was still pulling me towards the gate. 'Can you walk any faster than this?'

My mind caught up too slow. I pulled Shazad to a stop. 'It wouldn't matter if I could outrun a Buraqi. I'm trapped.' I filled her in as quickly as I could, as chaos reigned around us still. The iron under my skin, and one piece of bronze, allowing the Sultan to control me.

Shazad's face darkened as she listened. She took it

in with the same sharpened focus she always had when things were serious. 'So we cut it out of you.'

'I know I'm not as clever as you but that did cross my mind,' I deadpanned to her. 'It could be anywhere and I'm as likely to bleed out as anything if you start sticking knives into me.'

'I'm not leaving you here,' Shazad argued.

'You don't have a choice right now,' I said. 'Shazad—' I was long on things I wanted to say to her and short on time. Soon enough, the chaos Izz had created was going to die down and someone was going to notice us. There was only one thing that mattered. One last piece I hadn't told her. 'The Sultan has a Djinni.'

Shazad opened her mouth. Then closed it. 'Say that again.'

There wasn't a whole lot Shazad couldn't do. She could command armies; she could form strategies that she could see play out eight steps ahead of anyone else. She could fight and maybe even win a war that we were outnumbered and outgunned in. But there was outgunned and then there was fighting a gun with a stick. If the Sultan had even one Djinni, that wasn't anything an army of mortals could stand against.

'So we need to get both you and this Djinni—'

'Bahadur,' I filled in, even though I wasn't sure why it mattered. He was just another Djinni. He was a Djinni who had fathered me and whose name was half of mine. But he wasn't my father. Izz screamed and dove low. Guns went off. We both ducked on instinct.

'—both you and Bahadur out of the palace.' She made it sound simple.

'Freeing a Djinni isn't like breaking Sayyida out of prison.' Not that that had exactly ended well anyway. 'He's trapped here, just like I am.'

'I'll get some people to look into it.' Shazad pushed her hair impatiently off her face. Somehow, even dressed up to look as harmless as a flower, there was no mistaking what she was capable of. 'God knows, half of the Rebellion isn't doing anything useful right now. Izman is its own kind of prison. And it's swarming with soldiers since the ceasefire.'

'Ceasefire?' I interrupted.

Shazad looked at me, startled, like for a moment she'd forgotten I'd been absent. Her mouth pressed into a grim line as she broke the news. 'The Sultan has called for a ceasefire. An end to the fighting with the invaders until their foreign rulers can come to Izman to negotiate a new alliance. That's the news Jin was bringing us back from the Xichian camp before—' she hesitated, '—everything."

The mention of Jin made my heart clench. Something about the way she said his name was off.

But I had more pride in myself than to ask about him when we were at war.

'That's why the palace is swarming with foreigners,' I said instead, thinking of the crowd of uniforms and strange men we'd passed on our way here. 'You think the foreigner rulers will come?'

'Rumor has it one of the Princes of Xicha has already set sail. And the Gallan Emperor and Albish Queen have both sent their ambassadors ahead of them.' I thought of the plain-clothed man whose eyes had chilled me. 'They'll come. If they don't, there's too great a chance the Sultan will make an alliance with one of their enemies. Meanwhile, soldiers from all sorts of places are flooding into the city from every border to pave the way.' Shazad tapped her fingers to her thumb one after the other in quick sequence. It was a nervous gesture. It meant there was more. Problems she wasn't telling me. Complications with the Rebellion that I wasn't privy to.

'What does that mean for us?' I recognized this feeling of being helpless when there was so much to be done. I used to feel like this in Dustwalk.

'Nothing good.' She caught the nervous tic and stopped, balling her hand into a fist. 'Especially now. But the Sultan can only ally with one country. As soon as an alliance is struck, war will spark again. The rumors say he's planning to announce his new ally at Auranzeb. But until then . . .' she trailed off. I knew what she meant. Until then we had trouble. And it could only get worse with the Sultan having an immortal being at his command.

My mind turned over. There might be another way to figure out how to free a Djinni. I'd just have to get out of the harem long enough to find out. But something kept me from mentioning that to Shazad. We were running out of time. Izz's distraction could work only so long, and we couldn't be caught conspiring.

But I couldn't let her leave without asking: 'Shazad, is everyone all right?' I didn't ask what I wanted to ask. It was stupid and selfish. But his name hammered against my teeth. *Is Jin all right?*

'Not everyone.' For not being a Demdji, Shazad had always been the honest sort. 'Mahdi died in the escape from the camp and we couldn't save Sayyida. A few others. But the death toll is as low as can be expected. Ahmed is alive, Delila, Hala, Imin, the twins. They're all here in the city.'

'And Jin?' I couldn't stop myself any more. She hadn't mentioned him, which couldn't mean anything good. Neither could the hesitation that followed my question.

'No one is exactly sure where Jin is right now,'

Shazad said finally. 'He ...' She shoved her loose hair up off the nape of her neck. 'After you disappeared in the dead of night, he rode a horse half to death to get to the meeting point. When you weren't there, he broke Ahmed's nose and turned back around in the desert. To find you. Thank you for proving me right in my scepticism about the lack of detail in *that* plan, at least.' I knew she was trying to lighten the mood, but worry had taken root in my chest. It hadn't ever crossed my mind that Jin wasn't with the rest of the rebels.

'He's still alive.' I tested the words out loud. And then I realised what she'd said. 'He broke Ahmed's nose?'

Shazad scratched her ear, looking as sheepish as I'd ever seen her. 'Ahmed might've implied that if Jin stopped treating you as casually as some girl he'd just met in a dockside bar, maybe you'd stop running away.' A surge of indignation that Ahmed thought I'd leave the Rebellion over a lovers' spat struck in my chest. 'Jin hit Ahmed so fast even I couldn't get between them. It was impressive, actually.'

Izz screamed again. Further away. The chaos was settling down.

'I have to go,' Shazad said. We were out of time. 'I'm going to figure out a way to get you out of here. Until then, stay out of trouble.' It came out halfway between an order from my general and a plea from my friend.

'You know better than to ask a Demdji to make a promise.' This might be the last I ever saw of her. That was true every time we parted. But this time more than ever. Now I was on enemy ground. 'And you know better than to believe I'm going to stay out of trouble.'

Chapter 23

I had a plan. Well, *plan* might be a strong word. Shazad was the plan maker between the two of us. This was more like the beginnings of an idea that I was hoping wouldn't get me killed. Which was more my style.

I could figure out the rest of it later. For now, I didn't need to get free of the palace. I just had to get out of the harem. And there was only one man who could make it happen.

'Why do you want to leave?' Leyla was making another toy for the harem's children, though I wasn't sure why. Most of their mothers wouldn't let them play with the toys she'd already made. Was this just her way of keeping herself sane in this place where she fit so badly? This one looked like a tiny person. He lay forgotten in her hands, clay limbs splayed, as she looked at me with her huge, earnest eyes. 'The harem is nicer than a lot of other places you could wind up.'

I liked Leyla. A part of me wanted to blurt out the honest truth, make her a real ally here in this place. But she was still the Sultan's daughter. And big innocent eyes weren't a good enough reason to gamble with the lives of everyone I loved. Jin's face flashed across my mind. The way I'd last seen him, half-shadowed in the tent, on the run, uncertainty hanging between us as the kiss ended. His face was quickly chased away by others'. Shazad. Ahmed. Delila. The twins. Even Hala.

'It'd be nice to be able to get out of the path of your brother,' I said finally. 'I mean Kadir,' I corrected, remembering what she'd told me about her only real brother being the one who shared her mother. Prince Rahim, the soldier among scholars in the Sultan's circles. I'd mentioned seeing him in court the day before to Leyla, but she'd shifted the subject quickly. 'Not to mention Ayet and Uzma, who have it in for me.' Watching Shazad frighten Uzma might've been satisfying, but the humiliation still burned hot and fierce. 'If I could convince your father to give me the run of the palace, we could stay out of each other's ways.'

Leyla's eyes dashed back to the ground, and she chewed at her lip anxiously. I knew her well enough by now to recognise when she was thinking something over. I also knew better than to interrupt someone smarter than me when they were thinking. Something else I'd learned from Shazad.

'Bassam turns thirteen the day after tomorrow.' Leyla spilled the words out in a rush. Whatever I'd been expecting her to come out with, that wasn't it. 'Bassam is one of my father's sons by his wife Thana. My father has a tradition – for every one of his sons on their thirteenth birthday, he teaches them to shoot a bow. As my grandfather did for his sons. And his father before him. They are not to eat again until they eat something they have killed themselves. He has done it with every one of his sons.'

Not every single one. How had Ahmed and Jin spent their thirteenth birthdays? They hadn't been hunting with their father. Had they been on a ship, or some foreign shore? Had they even known what day it was to be able to mark it?

I had an image of a scene that never was. The two of them standing side by side with their father's hands on their shoulders, bowstrings drawn back, competing to impress him.

'He'll come to the harem for Bassam.' Leyla returned her eyes to her work, the small clay man. She was sculpting a face for him. 'If you wanted to ask him for something.'

*

The largest of the harem gardens was twice the size of the rebel camp – a huge swathe of green crowned with a blue lake that rolled down from the walls of the palace, across the cliff that overlooked the sea, before slamming hard into another wall. Another border, the edge of the palace. The water was dotted with fat birds, flapping their glaringly pale feathers lazily, sending water droplets sprawling in a bright arc through the sun.

From my position sitting by the iron gate that led back into the heart of the harem, it looked like a picture printed in a storybook. The Sultan was standing on the shore with a boy I guessed was Bassam. This son was thin and wiry and trying hard to look older than he really was. He held a longbow drawn back across his body, arms shaking just a little bit from the effort, clearly trying to hide it from his father.

I'd watched him miss a dozen shots already, the arrows splashing uselessly into the water. After each shot came an exercise in patience as Bassam tossed a handful of bread into the lake and then withdrew to wait for the birds to come back and settle. Until they felt safe enough again for him to try to kill them. Now his father reached out, resting one reassuring hand on his shoulder. The way the boy swelled happily under his touch, I half wondered if he'd been missing on purpose, to steal a bit more time with his father.

I imagined a younger Jin standing there in Bassam's place. I'd never seen a person need anyone else less than Jin did. It was hard to picture how he would react to his father's hand on his shoulder, if he would have held himself straighter, too, eager for his father's pride.

Bassam loosed the bowstring with one easy gesture. I knew with the practised eye of a girl from Dustwalk that this shot was different from the others.

The arrow flew true, passing straight through the neck of the nearest duck. The bird let out a pained squawk that sent the rest of the flock darting up in the air in a panic. A servant scrambled forward, pulling the bird out of the water by its long neck.

The Sultan laughed, throwing his head back as he clapped his son on the shoulder proudly. There was no mistaking the look of pure joy that passed over the young prince's face. For just a moment, in the late afternoon sun, they might've been any father and son sharing a moment of happiness.

And then the Sultan's eyes fell on me, hovering on the edge of the garden. He patted his son on the shoulder again, squeezing it tightly with pride before sending the boy on his way, carrying the dead bird slung over his shoulder.

When his son had vanished, he gestured me over.

'Hardly anybody uses bows any more, you know,'

I said when I was close enough to be heard. 'Guns are cleaner.'

'But not so quiet when you are trying to hunt,' the Sultan said. 'They scare your prey off. Besides, this is a tradition. My father did it for me, and his father did it for him.' And the Sultan had killed his father and now a handful of his sons were counting on following that tradition, too. 'What do you want, little Demdji?'

I ran my tongue along my teeth nervously. Chances were, he'd see right through me. But Shazad had said it herself the day Sayyida was brought back: we needed eyes in the palace. The *whole* palace. I could be those eyes. 'I want to be able to leave the harem.'

I couldn't leave the palace, but information could. Shazad had put Sam on the Rebellion's payroll. The past three nights, since the day Izz had dropped paper from the sky, I'd had a standing meeting with Sam at dusk by the Weeping Wall. Shazad would figure out what to do about him later, but for now, his only task was to slip into the harem every night to meet with me and make sure I hadn't sold out the whole Rebellion on a royal order. It was an awfully boring task. Or as Sam put it, it was the easiest money he'd ever made, being paid to come look at a pretty girl every night. If I succeeded here, I could make his job a little more interesting.

The Sultan played with the string of his bow. 'And you want to leave because . . .?'

'Because I can't stand it there much longer.' It was a truth. A half-truth. And it wasn't going to be enough. 'And I can't stand your son.'

The Sultan leaned on the bow. 'Which one?' he asked wryly. There it was again: that faint prickle down my skin, like we were both in on a secret, like we were both playing some game. No, that was ridiculous. If he knew I was allied with Ahmed, all he had to do was command me to tell him where he was. He could use me to lead him to Shazad and from there the rest of the Rebellion.

'Kadir.' I shook off the feeling. 'He looks at me like I'm a flower in that garden for him to pluck.'

The Sultan twanged the string of the bow again, like he was playing a musical instrument. 'You know that you are my prisoner, little Demdji. If I wanted to, I could order you to lie in one spot, completely still, until I needed you for something. I could make you grow roots and stay there waiting for an order. Or' – the Sultan paused, twanging the bowstring pointedly – 'to be plucked.' My skin crawled. 'But . . . I admire you coming to find me here. Tell me, little Demdji: can you shoot?'

'Yes,' I said, because, as much as I didn't care for him to know just how good I was with a gun, I couldn't lie. Shazad always said our greatest strength was being underestimated. But the Sultan always saw through me when I tried to dodge around a truth with a half-truth. 'I can shoot.'

He extended the bow towards me. I didn't take it immediately. 'You want something,' he said. 'People who want things have to earn them.'

'I know how to earn things. I didn't grow up in a palace.'

'Good,' the Sultan said, that hint of Jin's smile lingering. 'Then you should understand this. Take the bow.'

I did as I was told because I didn't have a choice, though I didn't know if he'd meant to give me an order.

'If you can bring down a duck, I will give you free range of the palace – at least, as much as anyone else has. If you don't . . . well, then I hope your bed is comfortable, because you will lie there a very long time.'

I ran my fingers down the taut string of the bow. It was an old weapon. Something from the storybooks. Before guns. I remembered some legend about the archer who took out a Roc's eye with an arrow.

I stood in a shooting stance and tried to pull the string back.

'Not like that.' The Sultan's hands were on my shoulders. I tensed automatically. But there was nothing lingering in the way he touched me. He gripped my shoulders like he had the young prince's. Like I'd seen fathers in Dustwalk do when they were teaching their sons to shoot a gun. No one had ever done that for me. I'd taught myself to shoot while my father was drunk. And not really my father anyway. Though he cared about whether I lived or died just as much as my real father did, as it turned out. 'Widen your stance,' he ordered, lightly kicking my ankles apart with his instep. 'And draw the bow across your body.'

I was keenly aware of him watching me as I drew the bowstring back. I took aim at the nearest duck the same way I would with a gun. I lined up my sight carefully. If I had a gun, my bullet would go straight through the bird.

I'd gotten good at killing birds in the past few months. When you were camping in the mountains, it was helpful to be able to hunt.

I loosed the bowstring. It scraped painfully along my arm. The arrow flew and missed the bird by a foot, plunging into the water. The flock of birds panicked at the noise, spiralling upwards into the sky in a flapping mess of feathers and squawking.

I swore, dropping the bow, clutching my scraped arm.

'Let me see.' The Sultan took hold of my wrist, another order I couldn't disobey. My forearm was already welting.

'You should have an arm guard,' he commanded. 'Here.' He pulled his sheema off from around his neck. It was the colour of the fresh saffron in dishes in the harem. He wrapped it neatly around my arm.

The sight of it brought on a pang of longing as I remembered my old red sheema. Jin.

The Sultan finished tying off the sheema with a final yank, fastening the knot around my wrist. 'When the birds return, try again. And this time, draw the bowstring higher – closer to your cheek.' I had to obey, though I half thought he had forgotten who he was speaking to. That he meant them as instructions more than orders.

We waited in silence until the birds returned and settled again. I wanted to call them stupid for coming back to something that might get them killed so readily. But then, I was standing next to the Sultan of my own will.

I missed again with my second shot. And my third. I could feel my neck prickling with shame, keenly aware of the Sultan watching me miss over and over. I needed to win. I needed to be able to leave the harem. I needed to save my family from my father.

'Your Exalted Highness.' A servant's voice made us both turn. He was bent low. 'You are awaited for negotiations by the Gallan ambassador.' My ears perked up. It was starting. The negotiations for this country. To turn us back over to them. Why I needed to be able to report back.

'Wait,' I called out as the Sultan turned to go. 'I can do this.'

The Sultan considered for a moment. And then he nodded. 'Then find me when you have.'

The sun crept across the sky as I tried. I could feel the sweat running down my neck and I was half-tempted to unwrap the sheema from my arm and tie it around my head. But the throbbing welt there told me not to. There was nothing to be done about the blistering in my fingers, though. Or the creeping ache in my arm as my muscles protested being pulled back the same way one more painful time. Shaking to release the bowstring.

Some servants came and placed a jug of water and a bowl of dates next to me when the sun got high. I ignored them both. I could do this.

I pulled back. Another arrow dove into the water. The birds scattered.

I cursed under my breath.

Damn this.

I had done harder things.

Before the birds could fully escape I reached down and plucked out another arrow. I nocked it quickly and aimed for the still-flapping squawking mess of birds. I found the duck I wanted to hit. And I didn't hesitate. I didn't waste time trying to line up my shot. I aimed with certainty, the way I always had with a gun.

And I loosed the arrow.

The duck separated itself from the flock, plummeted, and hit the grass even as my heart took off.

I barged through the palace, dripping a trail of blood behind me as I held the dead bird by the neck.

The Sultan had told me to come find him when I'd succeeded, and the tug of an order on my gut kept me moving. I didn't think about what I was doing until I'd pushed past the guard, who didn't try to stop me, and burst through the doors.

Dozens of heads turned to look at me as I crashed in. A thought flitted through my mind that I shouldn't be doing this. But it was a little late for that. I strode up to the table, my eyes on the Sultan, and slammed my prize down on the table in front of him, making his cup shake.

The Sultan looked at the dead duck.

It was only then that I took stock of my surroundings. The council room was full to bursting. With men in uniforms. Uniforms of all sorts. Golden Mirajin uniforms and the blue of the Gallan empire.

And they were all staring at me: a wild-eyed girl who had just slammed a dead duck with an arrow through its neck down on the table in front of her Sultan. Prince Rahim was hiding a smile under the pretence of scratching his nose, but nobody else seemed amused.

I had just interrupted one of the Sultan's councils to decide the outcome of the ceasefire and the fate of our whole country, with a dead duck.

I wondered if this was what would cost me my head.

'Well, it seems you are a half-decent shot after all,' the Sultan said, too low for anyone else to hear. 'You will leave the harem at any time you please.' There was a short pause in which a moment of hope bloomed, that he might really leave that loophole for me, one that would allow me slip out of his grip and back to the Rebellion . . . 'But you will do so with a guard. And you will not leave the palace.' My hope died. I was stupid to even entertain it to start with. The Sultan wasn't an incautious man. And then, raising his voice: 'Someone take this duck to the kitchens and my Demdji to somewhere she belongs.' I saw the Gallan delegation's heads lift at the word *Demdji*. They'd call me a demon but they knew what that word meant all the same. I wondered if the Sultan was rubbing me in their faces. That didn't seem much of a political tactic.

A servant lifted the duck by the neck gingerly. The

papers spread across the desk shifted as he did. I caught sight of a map of Miraji, drawn in faded black ink. Marked with newer blue lines. On our half of the desert. It was barely a glimpse of a corner but it was enough. I saw it. Circled in fresh blue ink was a tiny black dot, labelled in careful print: Saramotai.

My mind dashed to Samira. To the rebels Shazad was going to send to hold the city. To Ikar on the walls. And the women who'd chosen to stay behind. All of them sitting like a bull's-eye inside the blue ink circle.

A servant was already taking my arm, urging me out of the room. Trying to move me on. But I couldn't go. Not without knowing what was happening to the city we'd already given so much to free. My mind started running, trying to find a way to stay. To get those papers.

The Gallan ambassador was talking to the Sultan now. 'We have a command a thousand men strong coming from the homeland with His Majesty for Auranzeb. They will need to be armed if they are to hold Saramotai. Furthermore—'

'He's lying.' The words slipped out. The servant holding my arm hissed a warning through his teeth, tugging me towards the door harder now. But the Sultan held up his hand, stopping him.

'What was that, little Demdji?'

'He's lying,' I said again, louder this time. I tried the next words on my tongue, looking for the untruth. 'The Gallan troops coming with their king aren't as many as he says.' There it was.

The Sultan ran one calloused finger in a ring around the rim of his glass. His mind was as quick as Ahmed's. I was a Demdji. If I said someone was lying, then that was God's honest truth.

'Where did you learn Gallan?' the Sultan asked me.

Now, that was a dangerous question. Some of the truth of it was Jin and a long desert crossing and sleepless nights keeping watch.

'The Last County suffered under the Gallan alliance.' It was a half-truth folded up in deception, usually too obvious to get past the Sultan. But I was offering him a gift. It might be enough. 'And us Demdji, we pick things up fast.'

The Sultan's finger made another thoughtful loop of the rim of his glass. 'I am sorry that you suffered,' he said finally. 'Much of my desert did.' Finally he addressed the translator. 'Tell the Gallan ambassador that I know there aren't a thousand Gallan soldiers arriving with his king. And that I want the real number.'

The translator's eyes darted nervously between the Sultan and me as he spoke. The Gallan ambassador looked surprised as the words reached him. His eyes flicked to me, seeming to understand that I had something to do with this. But he didn't miss a beat as he started speaking again in that guttural language of the west. I didn't catch every word, but I did catch the number. 'He's still lying,' I said again quickly. 'There aren't five hundred.'

The Sultan considered me as he spoke to his translator. 'Tell the ambassador that perhaps lying is more tolerated in Gallandie, but in Miraji, it is a sin. Tell him that this is not the first time since our alliance ruptured that one of his countrymen has tried to deceive me into providing weapons for their troops overseas in order to continue their war in the north, under the guise of arming only those allies coming to our desert. Tell him that he has one more chance to tell me the real number or I will halt negotiations altogether until his king arrives.'

'Two hundred.' The translator spoke finally, after a tense moment. The Sultan's eyes flicked to me along with the rest of the room.

'It's the truth.' It rolled easily off my tongue.

'Well.' The Sultan tapped the edge of his glass. 'That's a fairly substantial difference, isn't it, Ambassador? No, there's no need to translate that.' He waved as the translator started to lean in to speak. 'The ambassador understands my meaning. And I think he, and everyone else here, understands that they are better off not lying to me. Sit down, Amani.'

He gestured to a seat behind himself. It was an order. I couldn't disobey it. And I wanted to stay. This was what I had asked for. But my legs still shook a little as I folded down onto the cushion behind the Sultan.

It wasn't until I was settled that I realised he had called me by my name. Not little Demdji.

I had his attention now. I just prayed I didn't have enough for him to start calling me the Blue-Eyed Bandit.

Chapter 24

The duck I'd killed was served dressed in candied oranges and pomegranates, on a platter the colour of Hala's skin, my arrow still through its neck. I wondered if that was part of the lesson. When a bullet disappeared inside flesh, you could almost forget it. The arrow wasn't that kind.

The council had gone on well past the sunset, as translators worked frantically, translating Gallan and Albish and Xichian and Gamanix. My head was churning with everything I'd heard in that room, turning it over and over like a prayer until I knew it by heart. I was going to try my damned hardest not to forget a word of it before I could get the news out to Shazad. One wrong detail, one point misremembered, and I could cost thousands of lives. I tried to sift out anything useless with every rotation through my head, leaving only what I could use.

The Sultan was going to march troops to take back Saramotai. If negotiations were successful, the city would go back to the Gallans' hands. A direct access point back into the desert and into Amonpour. Amonpour was allied with the Albish. There was an Albish camp on the border that would be in their path. They would march in three days. The Sultan was going to march troops to take back Saramotai . . .

'You seem distracted.' The Sultan interrupted my thoughts as he settled across from me.

'Your rooms are just about the same size as the whole town where I grew up.' It was a quick jab, meant to distract him, lest he think to order me to tell him what I was thinking about. *I'm considering everything I'm going to tell the Rebellion about your plans.*

Truth be told, his rooms were the size you'd expect for the ruler of the whole desert. I was brought in only as far as the antechamber, but I could see more doors leading off to a bedchamber with a thick red carpet, and into private baths on another side. The walls in the receiving chamber were gold and white mosaics that reflected the light of the oil lamps around us so well I almost thought it was still day. Except that above us a huge glass dome gave a clear view of the sky. And to one side a balcony overlooked the sheer drop down the cliffs to the sea.

'Dustwalk.' He seemed to pull the name from the far reaches of his mind. 'Tell me about it.' It was an order. Whether he meant it to be or not.

'It's a small town at the end of the desert. I grew up there.' It was the truth and it was obedience to his order. Even if it wasn't what he was after. One wrong word about Dustwalk and I might give away everything. 'I'd rather not talk about it.'

For all the size of the room, the table we were seated at was small enough that, if he'd wanted to, he could've reached across it and slit my throat with the long knife he was toying with.

I didn't like being around the Sultan any longer than I had to. Not when he had so much power over me. Not when all it would take was one false word for him to find out who I was. Besides, it was after dark. Which meant I was already late to meet Sam by the Weeping Wall. I hadn't told him about my plan to get out of the harem, seeing as I had no way of being sure I'd succeed or not. I sure hadn't been expecting the plan to succeed so well that it would end with me sitting across from the Sultan. For once I had a whole lot more to tell Sam than he had to tell me. I just had to get back in time to meet him. And before I accidentally revealed the whole Rebellion to the Sultan.

He was watching me now. As if wondering whether

to push the point of my hometown or release me from the order. But I was beginning to understand how the Sultan worked. If I gave him some truth, some weakness, on my own, he'd stop circling me. 'I hated that godforsaken dead-end town.' I gave him that admission. 'Please don't make me talk about it.'

He considered me slowly. 'You hated everything about it?'

I was about to tell him yes, but it wouldn't get past my tongue. *Tamid*, I realised. That was holding me back. I worried at one of the scars healing on my arm, feeling the little piece of metal shift underneath. I ought to hate him now. But I didn't know if I could hate him back then. 'No,' I said finally. 'Not everything.'

I thought he would press me. But he just nodded. 'Help yourself to the food.' Another order I couldn't disobey. I had to make him order me to leave. I couldn't last a whole dinner with the Sultan pulling little truths out of me one by one.

'Why am I here?' I started to spear the oranges off the duck one by one, putting them onto my plate. 'You've got a whole garden full of wives and daughters – you could *pluck* one of them out to eat with you if you're lonely.'

I knew I was crossing into dangerous territory now. But if I was going to get expelled back to the relative safety of the harem in time to meet Sam, I couldn't mince my words. But the Sultan just sighed in resignation as he knocked my fork aside and started to carve a knife through the brown crackling flesh. 'Perhaps I just enjoy your company.'

'I don't believe you.' I watched the knife work its way through the skin, cutting a perfect round circle off the bone.

'You're right, perhaps *enjoy* is a strong word.' He placed the meat carefully onto my plate for me. 'I find you interesting. Now' – the Sultan drew back – 'eat something.'

I ignored the meat and leaned across the table to spear another candied orange straight off the skin of the duck instead. It hit my tongue in a burst of sweet and bitter like nothing I'd ever had. I leaned across again to take another one while I was still chewing the first. I caught sight of a faint smile on the Sultan's face. 'What?' I asked, mouth full.

'Nothing.' The Sultan was still toying with the knife in his hand. 'I just wish you could see the look on your face. If it could be bottled, it would be the elixir the alchemist Midhat was hunting for.' In the stories, Midhat was an alchemist of great talent and great misery who lost his mind trying to make and bottle joy since he could not find it in the world. 'Then again' – the Sultan switched his grip on the knife, sawing at the meat of the duck I'd killed – 'if I could've bottled the look on our foreign friends' faces when you dropped this onto the council table, that would also give me a great deal of joy.' He carved a leg of the duck and placed it on his own plate. Last time I'd eaten a duck, it'd been one Izz had caught in Iliaz. It still had the marks of a crocodile's teeth through it, and the fat spat off it into the fire, making Jin curse when a bit sizzled and hit his wrist. Now I was taking food from the same hands that had held his mother down and claimed her by force when the Sultan was the same age as Jin. Probably in these same rooms.

'Your Exalted Highness.' The servant had appeared at the door so silently that I started. He was dropped into a deep bow at the door. 'The Gallan ambassador has asked to see you. I advised him you were otherwise occupied, but he has been very insistent.'

'The Gallan ambassador summons me to him in my own palace.' The Sultan sounded more resigned than anything as he pushed away from the table. 'Excuse me.' My eyes followed him all the way to the door.

I was on my feet as soon as he'd disappeared.

I flung open two wrong doors until I found the one that led to his office.

Facing me, instead of a wall, was a huge glass window overlooking Izman. From all the way up here, in the night, the city looked like a second sky, windows dancing with lights like stars across an otherwise dark sea. The Sultan's kingdom spread out below him. It was the closest I'd come to Izman since the day I woke up in Tamid's workroom. I resisted the impulse to press my hands against the glass like a child.

The other three walls seemed designed to match the window by night. Blue plaster, inset with what looked like yellow glass stars that would catch the sun in the day.

It reminded me of Ahmed's pavilion. Back in a home that was gone now.

I tried to imagine my prince here, when we took the city, keeping the peace.

But right now we were still in the middle of a war and I wasn't going to pass up an opportunity to find something that might win it.

The room was dominated by a huge desk that was covered in papers and books and maps and pens. I doubted he'd miss some of it if it went missing. It was just a question of what to take.

The Sultan is coming back. I tried to say the words out loud, but they wouldn't cross my tongue. I was safe for now, as I started to carefully lift papers off the desk, holding them up to the glow of light from the city through the window. I tried over and over again to repeat the words as I worked. An early warning system. I found a sheet of paper scribbled with figures and numbers I didn't understand. Another one was a map of Miraji. It detailed troop movements, but those I'd heard about already in the meeting earlier. My fingers faltered over a familiar-looking drawing of armour. It was the suit of metal they'd put on Noorsham. There were words scribbled along the edges. The ones used to control him.

There were more schematics like it underneath. And others for what looked like machine parts. One of the pieces of paper was held down by a tiny piece of metal the size of a coin. My name was carved into it along with a jumble of other words in the first language. So this was what I had under my skin. I fought my urge to fling it through the window and watch the glass shatter.

I took one of the sketches and kept exploring. I pulled out a few interesting-looking pieces of paper. One looked like supply routes. Shazad would be able to decipher that easier than I could. There was another one that looked like a map of Izman. There were dots of red ink interspersed across the paper. I held it up to the light, trying to figure out what they might be marking. But I didn't know Izman.

'The Sultan is coming back.' The words slipped

out into the silence of the room, setting off a jump of panic in my chest. I didn't have any pockets. I shoved the papers into the waist of my shalvar as I hurried out of the study, tugging my kurti back down over it.

I was back at the table picking at my food when the Sultan reappeared, taking his seat across from me. 'What did he want?' I asked as he picked the knife back up. I prayed he couldn't hear the raggedness of my breathing.

'You.' He said it in such a matter-of-fact way that it took me aback. 'You know, in the Gallans' so-called religion they believe First Beings are creatures of evil. And their children are monsters.'

'I know what they believe.' My mouth had suddenly gone dry. I reached for the pitcher of sweet wine. The sudden movement made the paper stuffed inside my clothes crackle and I stilled.

'They want me to hand you over.' If the Sultan had noticed the noise, then he was doing a mighty fine job of hiding it. 'To be brought to justice, they say. Which is a pretext, of course. They are hiding behind religious righteousness because they don't want to admit that you are a serious threat to their being able to lie to my face and sway an alliance back in their favour.'

'One of them called me a barbarian.' I heard the bile on my own tongue. As far as I was concerned, killing off First Beings and Demdji was more barbaric than killing a duck.

'Good,' the Sultan said. 'It would serve all of them well to remember that the people of Miraji can hold their own. Even if it is just against a duck.' I wasn't sure where the swell of pride came from. 'You want to know why you're here, Amani, dining in my chambers? It sends a message. When we were allied with the Gallan I would have had to hand you over to hang. Now' – he picked up the pitcher I'd been too frightened to reach any further for – 'you are free to be my guest.'

'You hate them.' I couldn't keep it in any longer. 'They hate us. They're using us. Why make another alliance?' My voice had risen without my meaning it to.

The Sultan turned his dark gaze on me. It struck me again how Ahmed had his eyes. Then he grinned, like he was surprised by a child doing something particularly clever. 'You sound a lot like the folk who follow my rebel son.'

'You asked me about Dustwalk.' I diverted his attention away from Ahmed. 'I'm from the deepest, darkest parts of your desert. I've seen first-hand what your alliances have done to folk. Cities under Gallan rule where it was the law to shoot a Demdji in the head. Everybody in Dustwalk working for as close to nothing as you can get without starving to make weapons for foreigners. It made for a poor, starving, frightened desert.'

'How old are you, Amani?'

'Seventeen.' I pulled myself up to my full height. Trying to look it. Careful of the stolen papers sticking to my skin as I moved.

The bone of the duck leg on his plate cracked under his knife. 'You weren't even alive when I took my father's throne. Even those who were have forgotten how things were back then. We were at war. And it wasn't one that we should have been fighting – the war between the Gallan and the Albish. We were a prize in the race between all of our foreign friends. Half the countries in the world wanted to claim our land. But in the end it came down to those two ancient enemies and their never-ending war of false beliefs.'

The leg of the duck finally came free in a snap of cartilage and sinews ripping free under the sawing of the Sultan's knife. There was something about the noise of cracking bone echoing around the polished marble halls and glass dome that set my teeth on edge. The Sultan calmly spooned orange sauce across the flesh as he spoke.

'And my father let it happen. He was foolish and cowardly. He thought we could fight the same way our country had in my grandfather's day. He thought we could stand against two armies and somehow not get annihilated. Even General Hamad advised my father he couldn't win a war on two fronts. Well, Captain Hamad then. I made him a general after his advice proved to be so sound.'

He was talking about Shazad's father. General Hamad had no loyalty to this Sultan. Shazad had always known her father despised his ruler. But he had backed the Sultan's ideas twenty years ago all the same. There was a time when even a man on our side had thought our enemy was in the right.

'The only way to win was to form an alliance, grant them access to what they wanted from us on our terms. My father wouldn't do it. Neither would my brother who had won the Sultim trials. Just because he was able to best eleven of our brothers in an arena somehow that made him fit to decide the fate of this country?'

Not any more fit than Kadir was. But I didn't interrupt. Getting myself turned out of the Sultan's presence didn't seem so important now. I'd learned history in school. But it was different to hear it from the Sultan's own tongue. It would be like hearing the tale of the First Mortal from Bahadur, who would have stood with the other Djinn at the birth of mortality and watched him face down death.

The Sultan seemed to sense my attention on him

all at once. He looked up from where he was sawing at his meat. Glancing between my empty hands and my still-full plate.

'I did what needed to be done, Amani,' he said calmly.

He had chosen a side to keep us from being torn apart between two of them. In one bloody night Prince Oman, a nobody among the Sultan's sons, too young even to be allowed to compete for Sultim, had led the Gallan armies into the palace, killed his own father, and slain the brothers he knew would stand between him and the throne: the Sultim and the others who had fought in the trials. By morning he sat in his father's place and the Gallan were our allies. Or our occupiers.

'What I did twenty years ago was the only way to keep this country from falling completely into their hands. The Gallan have annexed enough countries. I couldn't allow us to be next.' He sawed at his food carefully as he spoke. 'The world is a lot more complicated than it seems when you are seventeen, Amani.'

'And how old were you when you turned our country over to the Gallan?' I knew he hadn't been all that much older than I was now. The same age as Ahmed, give or take.

The Sultan smiled around the piece of duck he was chewing. 'Young enough that I spent the next nineteen years trying to find a way to drive them out. And I was very close to succeeding, you know.' Noorsham. He'd been trying to use my brother, a Demdji, as a weapon to kill the Gallan, and never mind his own people who wound up caught in the crossfire. 'A little more time and I could've rid this country of them forever.' He picked up his wine, drinking deep from the cup.

A little more time. If we hadn't interfered. If we hadn't saved Fahali. Saved our people. Saved my brother. And he reckoned he could've saved the whole country. They would have been a sacrifice for the greater good.

'You're not eating.'

I wasn't hungry. But I speared a piece of cold meat all the same. The orange had congealed into a sticky paste around it. It was too sweet when it hit my tongue now. *You're wrong.* The words, too, were sticky on my tongue. I couldn't spit them out. I wished Shazad were here. She knew more than I did. She'd read up on history and philosophy and had better schooling with her father's tutors than I'd had in a busted-down schoolhouse at the end of the desert. She was better at debating things than I was. But we'd both been in Saramotai. A power play disguised in a just cause. 'Awfully convenient how saving this country meant you becoming Sultan without the Sultim trials.'

'The Sultim trials are another antiquated tradition.'

The Sultan placed his wine back on the table, carefully steadying it by the stem. 'Hand-to-hand combat between brothers and riddles to prove a man had half a brain might've been the best way to pick a leader when we were just a collection of tents in the desert fighting the Destroyer of Worlds' monsters, but wars are different now. Wit and wisdom are not the same. Neither are skill and knowledge. And Sultans don't go out on the battlefield with a sword any more. There are better ways to lead.'

'You held a Sultim trial anyway.' I reached for another orange off the duck, moving slowly so as not to rustle the stolen supply route map hidden in my waistband.

'Yes, and look how well that served me. I acquired a rebel son out for my throne as a result of it.' He laughed to himself, as he pushed the gold platter closer towards me. A low, self-deprecating chuckle that reminded me of Jin. 'I had to hold the trials, to show the people that though I had taken my throne by ... other means, I was still upholding the traditions of our country. As antiquated as it is, it can still serve a purpose.' He settled back in his seat again, watching me eat. 'In some countries, the people love their royals best when they are celebrating weddings or new royal children. If only that were the case with my people, I would never run out of their love. But the Mirajin people are not so easily bought. They never love my family more than when we are fighting to the death for the right to rule them. They never love me so much as they do on Auranzeb when I remind them that I killed twelve of my brothers with my own hands in one night.' He said it so calmly that whatever warmth his laugh had brought into the room drained out of it instantly. 'I try not to remind them that it was the same night I handed them over to the enemy they hate so much. But really, this is a violent country, Amani. You're proof of that. Our dinner is proof of that.' He tapped the arrow through the duck's neck. 'I put a knife in your hand and your first instinct was to stab me.'

'You tried to stab me first,' I objected without thinking. That time he really did laugh, in earnest.

'This is a hard desert. It needs a hard man to rule it.' *A harder man than Ahmed.* The thought shot across my mind again. I shoved it away as forcefully as I could. The Sultan had said it himself, rulers were different these days. And what Ahmed lacked in strength he made up for by being good. A better man than most of us. He was so good, in fact, that Shazad and I hadn't even hesitated when it came to taking Delila to Saramotai. We'd disobeyed our ruler without a second thought. Without any fear of consequences.

Shazad would say it was a poor ruler who needed

to rely on fear to make his people obey. I might not be so well versed in philosophy, but it seemed to me like without obedience a man was no ruler at all.

Was Ahmed really going to run this whole country if he couldn't even get me and Shazad and his sister to fall in line?

'There is nothing I wouldn't do for this country, Amani. Still.' He smiled indulgently. 'I will grant you that Kadir would perhaps have not been my first choice to succeed me were it not for the trials.' He played with the stem of his glass, seeming to drift far away.

'Who would you have picked?' I wasn't sure if I meant it as an earnest question or a challenge of whether he actually knew any of his sons well enough to pick one. But the Sultan seemed to sincerely consider my question.

'Rahim is a great deal stronger than I gave him credit for as a boy.' Leyla's brother. The prince who held himself like a military man and who had challenged Kadir in court and sat on the war council with him. 'He might have made a good ruler, if I had kept him closer. And if he weren't so ruled by his emotions.' The light through the glass dome caught the rim of his glass as he spun it. 'But truthfully, had he only been raised in my palace, Ahmed might be the best choice.' That caught me off guard.

'You mean the Rebel Prince,' I said carefully, all too aware I was treading on dangerous ground now.

'My son believes he is helping this country; I know he truly does.' He called Ahmed his son. Ahmed always called the Sultan his father, too. Jin never did. To Jin he was always 'the Sultan'. Like he was trying to sever any strings between himself and his father. But it seemed like Ahmed and the Sultan had less interest in severing those ties. 'The trouble with belief is that it's not the same as truth.'

The memory rose from the quiet part of my mind where most of my memories of Jin lived. A night in the desert. Jin telling me belief was a foreign language to logic. But what else did we have?

The Sultan let go of the stem of his glass. He wiped his fingers clean of grease and orange pulp before pulling a familiar piece of yellow paper from his pocket. It was folded into smaller squares, and it looked worn out from folding over and over again. From across the table, I looked at Ahmed's sun on it upside down. *A new dawn. A new desert.*

'These are all very fine ideas he has,' the Sultan said. 'But you sat in that council today, Amani. Do you think my son knows how many guns we can promise the Gallan without overtaxing our own resources? Do you think he knows that the Albish queen, the latest in a long line of sorceresses, is rumoured to have hardly any magic left to defend her country with? That the Xichian emperor has not picked an heir yet and their whole country is on the brink of civil war?' He really seemed to expect me to answer.

'I don't know.' It was the truth. I wasn't privy to everything Ahmed knew. But if I were being more than truthful, if I were being honest, I'd give him a real answer. *No. He doesn't know.*

'If the world were simple,' the Sultan said as he smoothed the tract out across the table, 'we could be free of foreign powers, an independent nation. But we are a country with borders, with friends and enemies at all of them. And unlike my son I am not interested in conscripting this entire country to defend it. How many untrained men and women do you think have died fighting for his beliefs?'

Ranaa's face invaded my mind. The little Demdji from Saramotai. The stray bullet. Watching the light in her hands extinguish as her power went, then her life.

The Sultan's army had wanted her. But if it weren't for us trying to save her, she'd be here instead of me. She might be sitting on soft pillows, hair clean and scented with lavender, mouth sticky with candied oranges. Instead of turned to ashes on a funeral pyre and scattered into the desert sand.

'If the throne changes hands, we will be invaded. My son is an idealist. Idealists make great leaders, but they never make good rulers. So I'll tell you what I believe, Amani. I believe that if my son's rebellion were ever to succeed, or even to gain enough of a foothold to cast doubt upon my rule, we would be torn to shreds by foreign powers. It would destroy Miraji, just like my father would have destroyed it before us.'

Chapter 25

It was closer to dawn than dusk when I returned to the harem. I hated the quiet. I could hear my fears that much louder for it.

Back in the rebel camp there was no such thing as silence, even in the darkest hours of night. There was the clink of weapons on those keeping watch. Conversations whispered in the night. The riffling of paper from Ahmed's tent as he worried long after the rest of us had stopped. Here, any night sound was covered by the gentle running of water or the patter of birds.

My fingers were slick with fat from the skin of the duck and sticky with the sweetness of the orange. I wiped my hands across the hem of my kurti as I stepped into my rooms, starting to pull the clothes over my head.

'What kind of time do you call this, young lady?' The voice made me jump violently. Dropping the hem of my shirt, I reached for a weapon I didn't have.

Exhaustion and confusion blurred my vision for a moment. There was a figure sitting on my bed in a khalat. A khalat I recognised ... because it belonged to Shazad, I realised after a moment. Only the person wearing it was a head taller than Shazad, at least, and had wider shoulders that pulled at the fabric enough to make some of the stitching pop. The face was hidden by a sheema, one blond curl escaping underneath to drop lazily over pale blue eyes.

Sam.

'What the hell are you doing here?' I hissed, glancing around nervously as I dropped down on the mat across from him. 'Someone might see you.'

'Oh, plenty of folk have.' Sam lowered his voice to a whisper to match me. He loosened the sheema around his face. It was tied correctly this time; I could only guess his way of knotting it haphazardly like an infant had bugged Shazad as much as it did me. 'But who's going to notice another woman in here?' He had a point. Women seemed to appear and disappear in the harem without anyone batting an eye. 'Shazad's idea. She didn't think it was a good idea for you to get caught with a man in your bed. Although I don't know if I have the figure to pull off this khalat.' He cinched it around his waist with his hands, like he was trying to make it fit him properly.

'Don't worry, none of us can fill out a khalat the way Shazad can,' I said. But there was something nagging at me. 'Jin's not back yet.' It wasn't a question. I didn't even have to test the truth out on my tongue before saying it. Because if Jin were back, Sam wouldn't be here alone.

Sam kicked back, lacing his hands behind his head. 'This is the Rebel Prince's missing brother I keep hearing about? He's the one you wish was waiting for you in your bed right now, I gather.' He winked at me.

I dodged the comment. 'He wouldn't make nearly so convincing a girl as you do,' I said. 'Are you wearing make-up?'

'Oh, yes, just a little. Shazad did it for me.' He preened a little.

'She must like you. I'm usually the only person she does that for.'

'She was worried about you after you missed meeting me by the Weeping Wall tonight.' I'd missed my meeting time with Sam by a long way after I'd given up trying to escape the dinner. 'In particular she was concerned you might – and these are her words – "do something typically Amani-ish" and get yourself caught. She's got the entire camp packed up and ready to move again if I didn't find you by dawn.'

Somewhere in the midst of dining with the Sultan

I'd stopped feeling afraid of him finding out who I was. Sam's words were a sharp reminder that I wasn't risking only my own life. We'd been found once already.

'I've been waiting for so long I was beginning to think she was right and that I'd have to take up the mantle of the Blue-Eyed Bandit permanently. And after being filled in on what "something typically Amani-ish" means, I'm not sure I'm up to the task. Did you really throw yourself under the hooves of a Buraqi? I'd lose a rib doing that.'

I rolled my eyes, letting the joke in his voice burn away some of the guilt. 'If there was ever motivation to stay alive ...' I trailed off. I couldn't exactly tell him that Shazad had been wrong to worry. I had, after all, nearly been trampled by a Buraqi, twice. And I *had* sat across from our enemy and discussed Ahmed over dinner that night. 'You can tell Shazad I'm still alive. And I have free rein in the palace now. You should lead with that.' I dropped down next to him. 'Before you tell her that I missed our meeting because I was dining with the Sultan.'

Sam burst out laughing so loud I was worried he might wake someone. The harem had thin walls. 'So what does a rebel talk to the Sultan about these days? Though my mother always said to keep politics away from the dinner table – so perhaps you just discussed the weather? Though, best I can tell, you only have one type of weather here.'

I could still taste the orange on my lips when I ran my tongue across them. I considered what the Sultan had said about the fact that he was trying to stop a war. A war Ahmed was helping to instigate. That giving over this information would help the Rebellion but might hurt Miraji.

'The Sultan is going after Saramotai.' I reached into my shirt and pulled out the map of the supply route. The drawing of Noorsham's armour was wrapped around my upper arm. 'Five hundred men are to leave Izman in three days, marching on the city through Iliaz.' Sam stayed quiet as I pulled confidential information out of my clothes. Which was commendable, really. 'There are too many to stop. Izz or Maz can get there ahead of the Sultan's troops with a warning easily and evacuate everyone.'

'Evacuate them where?' Sam said.

'I don't know.' I finally pulled the map of Izman out from the waistband of my trousers and leaned back, sprawling my aching legs across the bed of pillows so that they tangled with the hem of his borrowed khalat. 'But it's either get them out or someone talks Ahmed into letting Delila try to make a whole city disappear long enough to baffle the Sultan's troops. Tell Shazad. She'll know what to do.'

'Seems like you already know what to do.'

I shrugged. I'd spent the last half a year listening to Shazad and Ahmed strategise. I'd picked up a few things. 'There's more.' I laid out the movements of other soldiers for Sam, struggling to remember all the details from the war council. There were more travelling south into the territory that Ahmed had claimed. Sensing a weakness. But it was a diversion; Saramotai was the only city they were going to take back for now.

'When the troops start to leave the city, it won't be so swarming with soldiers any more,' I pointed out. 'Shazad said half the Rebellion was short on things to do; well, this is a good chance to change that. Supply routes to the army, and I don't know what this one is marking' – I pointed out the red dots – 'but seems worth looking into.' I handed him the stack of papers and gave him as much as I could remember from the war council, each a precarious building block towards peace in Miraji that we could dismantle, that we could seize and use as a weapon in the Rebellion. And I tried to shake the feeling that I was a traitor to my whole country with every word I spoke.

Chapter 26

Now that I could leave the harem, I spent as little time as I could there. The palace could've been a barren wasteland to rival the Last County and I wouldn't have cared, so long as it was free of Kadir and Ayet and the rest of the gaggle of wives.

I was required a few hours every day at the Sultan's meetings. He met with each of the foreign delegations separately. The Albish ambassador was an ancient man with pale age-spotted hands that shook so hard he couldn't hold a pen. I overheard him tell his scribe that I reminded him of his granddaughter. He didn't lie as viciously as the Gallan but he didn't come ready to hand over the truth, either. He might wear a kinder face but he wanted something from us, same as the Gallan did. The Xichian didn't have an ambassador. They sent a general who eyed me with distrust with every word I spoke.

I sat behind the Sultan in each meeting, to his right,

where he could catch my eye when someone was talking and know the truth of it. I kept the men negotiating the terms of the ceasefire honest. And I learned as much as I could while I was at it. I learned where the foreign troops were stationed along our borders. I learned who the Sultan trusted and what he knew about the Rebellion. His son Rahim, Leyla's brother, attended every single meeting. He scarcely spoke unless his father asked him something directly. A few times I caught him watching me.

After a few meetings I learned that I couldn't avoid Kadir entirely outside of the harem. Every so often, he would turn up at negotiations, too, forcing a place for himself at the table. Unlike his brother, he offered opinions his father didn't ask for. Once I caught one of the ministers rolling his eyes as Kadir spoke.

Kadir was the only person who seemed to be able to get a word out of Prince Rahim unsolicited. The two princes sparked off each other like angry flint. I remembered what the Sultan had said, that Rahim would make a good choice for Sultim if he weren't so ruled by his emotions. So far I hadn't seen any emotion from him except hatred for Kadir.

I returned to the harem every night to meet with Sam at dusk and hand over what I'd gathered.

What was left of the days belonged to me to spend

however I wanted outside the walls of the harem. I explored as freely as I could, while carefully avoiding the foreigners who were gradually invading the palace. There were a hundred more gardens that bloomed so thick with flowers I could barely get the doors open, or where music seemed to drift through the walls along with a breeze that smelled of salt and bright air. It wasn't until I climbed a tower that looked out over the water, and the same air picked up my clothes and hair in a rush, that I realised it was the sea. I'd spent my short time on the sea drugged and bound. But that wasn't the memory the sea air stirred up. It was sitting on a dusty shop floor, as far from the water as I could be, with my fingers dancing along the tattoos on Jin's skin.

Once, I rounded a corner to see a figure ahead walking with a limp that was so familiar I was ready to turn and run. I stopped walking so abruptly when I saw him that the guard accompanying me that day walked straight into me. The shame on his face was the most expression I ever got out of one of them. It was nice to know they were human somewhere under that uniform, at least. It turned out it was only an Albish soldier, wounded by a Mirajin bullet before the ceasefire. Besides, Tamid didn't walk with a limp any more, I remembered.

I was putting on a good show of wandering aimlessly. But the Sultan wasn't stupid enough to give me complete freedom in the palace, either; a soldier waited for me outside the gates of the harem every morning and latched on to me like a silent shadow. The soldier changed every day, and none spoke except to tell me when I was wanted at a meeting. If I tried to take a turn I wasn't supposed to, my guard just became a new wall between me and whatever door or passageway I was heading for. A heavily armed wall that just stared straight ahead until I took the hint.

But I wasn't about to give up. I needed to get back to Bahadur. The Djinni. My father. The Sultan's new hidden weapon. I had to find a way to free him before the Sultan could use him to annihilate us.

I wished I wasn't so familiar with the feeling of waking up in trouble. But the harem was softening me. Used to be, an intruder's presence would've woken me well before getting close enough to put a blade against my neck.

I wrenched myself to sitting, heart racing in panic, ready to face whatever threat the night was bringing. Soldiers. Ghouls.

Worse. Ayet.

The light of the mostly full moon shivered along

the blade in her hand as she drew away from me. Not a knife, I realised: scissors. More dangerous was the smile on her face. In her other hand, her fist was curled around a long dark braid.

My hand flew to my scalp. The last person who'd bothered to cut my hair was my mother before she died. In the years since, it had reached close to halfway down my spine, though it spent most of its time twisted under my shcema. Now it ended bluntly, just above my shoulders.

'Let's see how much he wants you now that you look like a boy.' Ayet wound a piece of my slaughtered hair around her finger with a sneer.

Anger rushed through me, fiercer than anything so stupid and vain warranted. But I didn't care if it was stupid and vain. I moved as fast as I knew how, lunging for her. Before she could so much as flinch, the scissors were in my hand. I might not be able to hurt her, but she didn't know that. I pressed the blade against her throat and had the satisfaction of watching her eyes widen.

'Listen to me.' I had a grip on the front of her khalat before she could make a run for it. 'I have bigger things to deal with than your jealousy about your husband's wandering eyes. So why don't you go take this out on someone who actually *wants* to steal him from you.'

Ayet laughed bitterly, throat moving against the

blunt scissors pressed to her neck. 'You really think this is jealousy? You think I *want* Kadir? What I *want* is to survive the harem. This place is a battlefield. And I think you must know that. Or else what did you do with Mouhna and Uzma?'

'What are you talking about?' Trying as hard as I could to stay out of the way of Kadir and his wives, I hadn't been in the harem enough to notice anything about Uzma since she'd tried to humiliate me in court.

'Uzma has disappeared.' Ayet sneered, but I could see the fear behind those eyes now. Girls like her were dropping like flies and all she had to protect herself was a pair of scissors. 'Just like Mouhna. People vanish out of the harem all the time. But Kadir only has three Mirajin wives. And then *you* arrive and two of them disappear. Do you think that's a coincidence?'

'No.' Coincidence didn't have so cruel a sense of humour. Jin said that to me once. 'But I know this wasn't me.'

It took me until midmorning the next day to find Shira. She was sprawled across a throne of cushions in the shade of a huge tree, attended by a half dozen servants. Two women stood guard, while one laid cool cloths on her skin, another fanned her, and another massaged her feet. The last one was immobile but ready, sweat beading down from the lip of the pitcher over her hands. She looked flushed and uncomfortable standing just outside of the shade.

It looked like the future Sultan of Miraji already had his own court, even if he was really the son of a fake Blue-Eyed Bandit. And Shira was taking advantage of it for the few weeks left before she gave birth to him. She was a long way from Dustwalk now.

As I got closer, one of the servants standing guard blocked my path. 'The blessed Sultima has no desire for company today.' *Sure, the blessed Sultima looks as solitary as a hermit today.* It was on the tip of my tongue, but my Demdji side didn't recognise the difference between sarcasm and a lie. I had to satisfy myself with raising my eyebrow at the small crowd surrounding her. The woman didn't seem to appreciate the irony.

'Shira,' I called out, over the servant's shoulder. She lifted her head enough to squint at me, sucking on a date pit between her fingers. She pulled an annoyed face but waved her hand.

'Let her through.' The servant moved aside reluctantly. I gave Shira a pointed look. With another dramatic sigh she dismissed them. Everything from the wave of her fingers to the sprawl of her body looked lazy, but her sharp eyes never left me. 'So that's what Ayet wanted scissors for,' she said by way of greeting, as her court dissipated. 'I *was* wondering. You know, I thought about cutting it all off back in Dustwalk when you slept a few feet away from me, but I actually worried short hair might suit you.' She tilted her head. 'I guess I was wrong.'

'You got Sam to smuggle you in a pair of scissors?' I caught myself tugging on the ends where they didn't quite reach my shoulders and dropped my hand. But not before Shira caught the gesture.

'You're surprised?' She ran her hands along her swollen middle.

I supposed I shouldn't be. Shira and Sam might not be anything more than a means to an end for each other, but she was carrying a child that meant something to both of them. Still, I'd figured Sam was with us now. The notion that he might still be getting into other trouble we didn't know about while smuggling information for us made me uneasy. And I'd be lying if I said I wasn't just a little bit angry he could be so cummy with me, all while handing over tools to humiliate me with when I wasn't looking.

'Just be grateful I refused to procure her a knife. A slit throat would suit you even less than' – she waved a hand vaguely – 'that.'

I swallowed back a retort. I couldn't get into a war of words with my cousin just now. 'What kind of game are you playing, Shira?'

'It's called survival.' Shira extended a hand towards me, opening and closing her fingers like a demanding child. I took her hand, helping her sit up so she could look at me straight on instead of from the ground. She moved slowly, one hand splayed protectively over her middle. 'I would do anything for the survival of my son.'

'And what are you going to do if your son is born looking like Sam?' I challenged. 'Blue eyes look awfully suspicious on desert folks, I can tell you that much.'

'He won't be.' She said it with such determination I could almost believe she could truth-tell it into existence even though I was the Demdji here. 'I haven't done all this just to fail at the end. Do you know how *hard* I have worked to never be alone here in the harem since it became known that I was pregnant? I traded those scissors for a secret from Ayet that I can hold on to like a shield against her. Because I need to keep her away from me more than I need to keep her away from *you*. Don't get me wrong, you're an excellent distraction, but when I give birth it is *over* for his other wives unless they can give him a son, too. And they can't. And they all *know* that. So do you honestly think Ayet is above doing away with a pregnant girl to keep herself alive? I've seen what you'd do for survival, Amani. I know you understand.'

Tamid bleeding out onto the sand. I pushed the image away. 'Is that why Mouhna and Uzma have disappeared? Your survival?'

'Interesting.' Shira sucked on the date pit between her teeth. 'Here I'd been thinking Mouhna and Uzma were your doing. Seeing how you're rubbing elbows with the Sultan now. They weren't all that nice to you. And it looks to me like you've got the power to make them disappear if you wanted . . .'

If I was going to get rid of them, I'd start with Ayet. I shoved that thought away. 'So if it wasn't my doing or your doing . . . Girls don't just vanish into thin air.'

'Not outside of stories, at least.' Shira ran her tongue along her teeth, a hint of worry creasing her eyebrows as she looked far away. Then her attention snapped back to me. 'Let's say I wanted your help for something.' Shira peeled one of the cloths from her forehead. 'What would you want in trade?'

'Why should I help you?' I crossed my arms. 'I've got your life to trade you if I need anything. What else have I got to gain from you?'

'You're a lot worse at this survival game than I thought you'd be.' Shira sounded really and truly exasperated. Like we were kids again and I was too stupid to understand the rules to some game she'd made up in the schoolyard.

'Then why don't you tell me how you want to play?'

'I want information,' Shira said. 'I've seen you with Leyla. The scrawny princess with no charm.'

'What about her?' I sounded defensive even to my own ears. Whatever time I did spend in the harem was usually spent with Leyla. We took our meals together. Usually I ate while her food went cold as her whole attention spilled into whatever little mechanical toy she was constructing.

'She's up to something,' Shira said simply.

'Leyla?' I failed to keep the scepticism out of my voice this time. 'Is it all the toys she builds for children that makes you suspicious, or the fact that she's still almost a child herself?'

'She sneaks around.' Shira reached for a fresh cooling cloth. 'She leaves the harem and I don't know where she's going. I can't follow her. But you can.'

'You want to know where she's going?' It was hard to take her seriously when she was making accusations against someone two years younger than us. 'You're worried about *Leyla*?'

'Of course not.' Shira rolled her eyes. 'I'm worried about her brother.' Prince Rahim. Ah. Now, that didn't sound so stupid. 'Rumour has it he's in a great deal of favour with his father the Sultan.' That much was true. I remembered what the Sultan had said about Rahim over duck that night.

'You think he might have designs on the throne.'
I suddenly saw where her train of thought was going.
There was no love lost between Rahim and Kadir. I just
didn't know if he hated him enough to snatch away his
wives. But if he did, Shira had to be a target.

'Oh, look at that, you're not as dumb as you act.'
Shira draped the new damp cloth over her brow; it sent
rivulets of water across her eyebrows and down her
cheeks. 'The rumour was that before Kadir proved he
was able to conceive an heir' – she ran her hand along
her swollen middle – 'the Sultan was close to taking the
throne from him. Rahim was said to be the favourite.
Why else is he back in court when he's a commander in
Iliaz?' That name sparked a pain in my side where the
bullet scar was. Iliaz was a sore reminder of being shot.
'If he does have designs on the throne and he's using
his sister's knowledge of the harem to get to it, I want to
know. And there *must* be something you want in return
for information on Leyla and her brother.'

Leyla had helped me when I needed to get free
of the harem. She'd guided me in my first days in the
harem. She'd saved me from Kadir's wives. She was as
close to a friend as I was going to get inside these walls.

And I wasn't the girl who betrayed friends any
more. Only Shira didn't know that. She knew me as the
girl from Dustwalk who left Tamid bleeding in the sand.

Who would do what she needed to get what she wanted.

But the beginnings of an idea were sparking in my mind. I'd been looking for a way to shed my guard. This might be one.

'What if I needed a distraction? For the guards.'

'A distraction like a pregnant Sultima pretending to go into childbirth weeks early?' She caught on quick.

'And folk in Dustwalk used to say you were as dumb as you were pretty.' I couldn't keep it in, petty as it was. I was still angry with her about my hair.

'I made it through sixteen years in that town with a whole lot less trouble than you did,' Shira pointed out. 'Why do you need a distraction anyway? Are you trying to slip off to see a certain cripple of yours hiding in the palace? Because you ought to know, you might not get as warm a welcome as you're hoping for.'

'Tamid is none of your business.' My thumb jabbed at the metal under my arm painfully. It was almost a tic now. She'd found my sore spot. And the smile playing over her mouth said she knew it.

'Oh, so you do know he's here.' She saw the answer written all over my face. 'They took both of us. Because you left us.'

'You wanted to go, because Fazim was done with you.' That blow landed so hard that I almost regretted it the second the stricken look bloomed over her face.

But she'd hit first. It was a bad idea to play chicken with someone who'd known you your whole life. Nobody came out a winner.

Shira pulled the mask of Sultima back on. 'Say you'll bring me information about Leyla and I'll be your distraction.' She stuck out one hand, heavy with new gold bangles. One of them no doubt already traded to Sam for the scissors that had cut my hair. They clattered impatiently together. 'Do we have a deal?'

I took her hand and pulled her to her feet. 'Let's go.'

I had to admit Shira wasn't a half-bad actress. Her screams were so convincing I worried a few times that fate really was cruel enough to send her into labour the same moment she'd been faking it. She sure slumped on me heavily enough as we staggered through the gates of the harem. Her cries and sobs covered my words to the guard waiting for me. He was young and his eyes went wide with panic as his Sultima collapsed into his arms.

And just like that, Shira had shifted from my shoulder to his, grabbing all his attention and weighing him down as I staggered back, out of his view. For a second his head turned to follow me, remembering his duty. But a new scream from Shira quickly drew him back.

And then I was gone, running as fast as I could. Shira's screams faded behind me as I bolted across the courtyard and into the halls of the palace toward the mosaic of Hawa.

I'd been told that my eyes were the colour of the sea on a bright day. That they were the shade of the desert sky. Foreigner's eyes. Traitor eyes.

But the truth was I'd never seen anything exactly the same colour as my eyes until I met Noorsham. We had our father's eyes.

It was a foreign feeling for those same blue eyes to watch me from where Bahadur sat in the iron circle as I descended the steps into the palace vaults. He didn't speak when I reached the edge of the circle. Neither did I.

'You're not meant to be here, are you?' Bahadur finally spoke.

I'd only briefly wondered about my father in the years since I'd figured out that my mother's husband wasn't really my father. With my blue eyes, I'd always figured he was some foreign soldier, and I didn't want to be half-foreign. So I didn't think about it.

I'd been a bit more curious since finding out I was a Demdji. Since I'd learned my eyes were a mark my father left me along with my power. I'd wondered what

I would feel when I finally came face-to-face with him, just the two of us.

I hadn't expected that I'd feel so much anger.

'I'm here because I need to know how to free you.' I crossed my arms over my body, locking my anger inside my gut. There was no room for it here, no time. 'Not because I especially care whether or not you ever get to go back to making me some more Demdji siblings who might destroy the world. But I might care if the Sultan uses you to burn all his enemies alive or bury their cities in sand.'

'I only buried a city in sand once.' He meant Massil, I realised. I'd been there, with Jin. Before I even knew what I was. Before we crossed the sand sea.

'You didn't think that might've been an overreaction?' I asked.

Bahadur watched me carefully, never blinking those blue eyes. 'I don't need you to free me, Amani. I have existed since time began. This is not the first time I have been summoned and held by a mortal with more greed than caution. Eventually, I always find myself free, one way or another. When it happens doesn't matter.'

'Well, it matters to me.' The words came out more violently than I'd meant them to. 'You might live forever. But our kind is known for running out of time. This is all the time I have. This is all the time any of us has. And we've got a war to win before it's over and lives that'll get lost earlier if we don't. So tell me, if you've been captured so many times before, are there words to free you?'

'There are, though I do not know them. But there is another way. One you already know. Because you know the story of Akim and his wife.'

My mother had told me that story when I was young. I hadn't thought of it in years. Akim was a scholar. A wise man, but a poor one. Knowledge did not often bring wealth, no matter what the holy texts said. And in his studies he stumbled across the true name of a Djinni.

He used this to summon the Djinni to him and trap him in a circle of iron coins.

One day while descending to get more sugar from the basement, Akim's wife found the Djinni. She was much neglected by her husband in favour of his books. And so she was easily tempted by the Djinni. He told her that if she only freed him, he could give her the child she so desired.

So Akim's wife broke the circle of coins that held the Djinni and freed him.

At this point in the story, my mother would usually pause dramatically before throwing a handful of gunpowder in the fireplace and letting it explode. Releasing the Djinni without banishing him with the right words was like releasing a dam of fire.

The Djinni burned Akim's wife alive, and with her, the rest of the house.

'You killed Akim and his wife.' It wasn't a question. It was a truth.

'Yes.' There wasn't a hint of remorse there. 'That might have been an overreaction,' he admitted.

We would have to break the circle. Only this circle wasn't made of coins. It was set into the ground. We'd need something powerful. Something like gunpowder.

Bahadur was my father. I didn't think he'd burn me inside out. But there was no telling.

'There were other ways for you to learn how to free me. There are others with this knowledge.' Bahadur watched me from inside the circle. He was inhumanly still. He didn't shift with restlessness or fiddle with his clothing as a human would. 'Why did you really take such pains to come see me, Amani?'

'Do you remember my mother?' I hated myself for asking. For caring if he remembered one woman out of what I was sure were many in thousands of years. 'Zahia Al-Fadi. From Dustwalk. Do you remember her?'

'I remember everyone.' Did I imagine the change in my father's voice, the slight shift from the flat empty tone he'd addressed me with so far? 'Your mother was very beautiful. You look like her. She was running away from her home. Through the mountains. She wouldn't have made it very far. She had enough supplies for a few days, not a real escape. She would have been forced to turn back or die eventually. I had sprung one of your people's ancient traps. The ones you set for the Buraqi. Crude, but, being iron, it did what it should have. Zahia found me in it. She released me.'

'So why didn't you save her?' There it was. The question I'd really wanted to ask. Not whether my mother had made any kind of lasting mark on this immortal, powerful being, but why it hadn't been enough for him to save her life. How he could leave her with me, a child who she'd eventually die protecting, and not have the decency to step in. 'You could have, couldn't you? You could have saved her.'

'Yes. I could have appeared on the day your people chose to hang her and I could have cut her down and carried her away. Like in all those stories she told you as a child. But to what end? To keep her in a tower for a handful more years as my wife? She was mortal. Even you, who have a little bit of my fire, you will die, too, one day. Dying is what you do. It is the only thing that you all do without fault or fail. If I had saved her then, she would have died another way later.'

'But she would have had longer.' I could hear the tears in my own voice. 'We could have escaped.' *Her death wouldn't have been my fault.*

'You did escape,' he said.

My temper snapped. 'Don't you find it tiring not caring about anything, ever, for all eternity?' I didn't want to cry in front of him. I hated how much I cared if I cried in front of him. But it was too late. Through the tears, I could hear footsteps now, distantly. Soldiers were coming for me. 'You let my mother hang. You let me and Noorsham face each other in war – both of us your children.' The footsteps were behind me now. I was screaming. 'You stood there while I held that knife against my stomach! You made us. Why don't you care about us?' And then it was too late. The soldiers were grabbing me, yanking me away from my father, dragging me up the stairs as I fought against them, still shouting.

Something pricked the side of my neck. A needle, I realised, in the hands of the guard. There was something on the metal. I knew instantly. Something to make me sleep.

Suddenly everything rushed to my head. I felt the floor tip out from under me. I would've hit the ground except someone caught me. Strong arms.

'Amani.' My name punctured the storm of feelings. 'I've got you.'

Jin.

No. When my vision cleared, the Sultan was the one propping me up. He was strong. I tried to struggle, but with one swift gesture, his hands went under my knees and he lifted me into his arms like I was a child. He started to walk, each step shaking me closer to his heartbeat.

'I wanted—' I struggled for some half-truth to cover what I had been doing. My mouth felt fuzzy as the drugs kicked in, the motion making me sick.

'You wanted to see your father.'

I waited for the punishment. For the anger. We passed out of the cool shade of the courtyard, through another set of doors. Tree canopies spread out high above me, the sunlight dancing through their branches.

'Yes,' I admitted. And that was the simplest truth. I had wanted to face him. I'd wanted an explanation. I was swimming in and out of dreams now. I was starting to shake, too. Every part of me wanted to curl into the warmth of another body holding me. Like I was a small child being carried by my father.

But he wasn't my father. He was Ahmed's and Jin's and Naguib's and Kadir's and Rahim's and Leyla's and he was a murderer.

I was dimly aware that we were in the harem. I felt the Sultan kneel down and then I was being laid down in a bed thick with scattered pillows that crowded around me.

'Fathers often disappoint us, Amani.'

Chapter 27

There was a gift next to me when I woke up. It had been left while I slept, a conspicuously perfect tidy package of paper and ribbon amid the haphazard mess of pillows flung around my room. It swam into focus slowly as I emerged from the haze of drugs.

I pressed myself up onto my elbows, ignoring the pitcher of water next to me. No matter how dry my mouth was I wasn't about to risk something that might send me back to sleep. I poked at the gift with my foot cautiously, half expecting some trick from Ayet. When nothing exploded, I finally picked it up.

Blue fabric appeared below the paper. It was a khalat. The fabric was the colour that the sea had been, the brief glimpse of it I'd had from the deck of the ship. And the hem and the sleeves were trimmed in gold stitching. When I looked at the embroidery closely, I realised it was the story of Princess Hawa, in tiny golden detail. On my right sleeve, where she rode the Buraqi across the desert, there were even tiny gold beads showing the dust kicked up under its hooves. It was the most beautiful thing I'd ever seen.

I'd hated wearing blue most of my life. It just made my eyes more obvious than they already were. It was one of a thousand reasons I'd loved the red sheema Jin stole for me. Only I didn't hate this khalat.

I slipped it on, revelling in the feeling of the fabric against my skin. It occurred to me that I'd never worn a piece of clothing that had never been worn by anyone else before. My clothes in Dustwalk were all cast-offs from cousins. I'd bought second-hand clothes in Juniper City when I fled there. Even my clothes in the rebel camp were Shazad's. This was the first thing I'd ever worn that truly fit me. It had been made for me. And I knew what it meant.

It was forgiveness for going to see Bahadur.

In spite of the Sultan's gift I didn't know what I might've lost by tricking my way out of the harem. The Sultan's trust, definitely. My freedom, too, probably. There was nothing stopping him from stripping away the freedom he'd given me with just a few words. He wouldn't be wrong not to trust me to leave the harem. I ran my thumb over the raised golden thread of the sleeve as

I headed for the edge of the harem. I was working to destroy him, after all.

But even though my step slowed the closer I got to the gates I didn't meet any invisible barriers there. I passed through the archway that led towards the palace the same way I had yesterday, when Shira and I had been tricking our way out. Still, I didn't quite dare drop my guard just yet. But there was no battalion of soldiers waiting for me at the gates, either. Just one man, same as always. Only it wasn't a soldier. Or rather, it wasn't just any soldier.

Prince Rahim, Leyla's brother, wearing his commander's uniform, was waiting for me outside the gates, hands clasped behind his back. The one who'd spoken that day in court as if he was born on a battlefield. The one who'd watched me with dark eyes that made me nervous so often during negotiations. He didn't speak a whole lot, but when he did, it was always something worth hearing.

'Well, at least I know you won't be able to outrun me in that,' Rahim said, taking in my khalat. He offered me his right arm.

'Isn't being my escort a bit below the station of a prince?' I asked, pushing past him and heading towards the now-familiar path to the council chamber. He fell into step behind me.

'I managed to convince my father that you might need someone with a little more experience to watch you. Possibly someone bright enough to know that the Sultima isn't due to give birth for weeks. Not a bad trick, though.'

'Am I supposed to be flattered,' I asked as we passed under a blue-and-white mosaic archway, 'that I get a commander watching me?'

Rahim's lip twitched up. 'You don't remember me.' It wasn't a question.

We've never met before. It was on the tip of my tongue. But it wouldn't go any further. I looked at him curiously out of the corner of my eye as we walked, my mind racing to place him. I thought he looked familiar when I first met him but I'd chalked that up to his resemblance to Leyla. And to their father. 'Then again' – he tapped the place my scar was, by my hip – 'you did go down awfully fast with that bullet.'

A blast. The smell of gunpowder. A shooting pain in my side. Then darkness. In Iliaz. A soldier behind Jin raising a gun, finger already on the trigger. I knew him all at once.

I stopped short. 'You shot me in Iliaz.'

'I did.' Rahim kept walking, apparently satisfied now that we were such old friends with a history of gunpowder and near death between us. 'Although, luckily for us, it looks like I didn't do an especially good job of it. So here's hoping you can forgive me and we can start over.'

He knew. He'd seen me in Iliaz, which meant he knew who I was. He knew I wasn't just a Demdji from the Last County.

Rahim realised I wasn't following him any more. He stopped, too, turning back to face me. 'I had my suspicions as soon as I saw you at court that day. But I wasn't sure until my brother's charming wife decided to . . . expose you a little.' He looked embarrassed saying it, at least. But I still felt the heat of the old humiliation prickle across my skin. 'I knew as soon as I saw the scar on your hip.'

'So why am I walking to a council meeting with you instead of hanging by my ankles in a cell telling your father all the secrets of the Rebellion?'

'We hang people by the wrists now instead of the ankles,' Rahim said. 'Keeps prisoners more lucid if all the blood doesn't rush to their head.' I couldn't tell if he was joking.

'You don't have much of a way with words, anyone ever tell you that?'

'That's why I'm a soldier, not a politician. Or I used to be.' Rahim drummed his fingers across the sword on his belt. 'My father and I aren't on the best of terms.'

'And selling out the Blue-Eyed Bandit to him wouldn't put you back in his good graces?' I asked.

'My father doesn't have any good graces. He's just very good at pretending he does when it suits him. Which puts you and me on the interesting same side of hating my father.'

I watched him carefully. This had to be a trick. Some ploy of the Sultan's. Only I was at his mercy. He didn't need to send me a fake traitor; he could just order me to tell him everything I knew about the Rebellion. *You're lying to me.* I tried it out, but it wouldn't get past my tongue. He wasn't lying. But he wasn't telling the whole truth, either.

'What is it you want? From us being on the same side, that is.'

'A new dawn.' Rahim flicked one of the tracts that had fallen from the sky out at me between his fingers. It was creased from the pocket of his uniform. 'A new desert.'

'Are you saying you want to put Ahmed on the throne?' It seemed Shira was dead wrong about him having designs on being the new Sultan.

'I'm saying I want my father off the throne and I can help you. On one condition. I want you and your rebellion to get my sister out of the palace.'

'Leyla?' Little round-faced Leyla who made toys for

the children in the harem and who reminded me of my littlest cousins even though she had a decade on them. 'Why? She's as safe here as anywhere else and she told me herself it could be a lot worse.'

'If I'm right, she's in danger.'

I thought of Shira, asking me for Leyla's secrets, watching her out of the corner of her eye, ready to take down any threats to her child before they could do the same to her. But somehow I didn't think that was what Rahim meant. Men weren't usually aware of the politics of women.

'What kind of danger?'

He didn't answer the question. 'You're a Demdji. I've seen you do your little trick every day in my father's war meetings. So, am I telling the truth?'

'Yes.' It came out easily.

'Am I trying to trick you?'

I tried yes again, but it wouldn't come out. 'No.'

'Can you trust me?'

I don't trust anybody in here. 'Yes.' But I wasn't giving up that easily. 'But I want to know why. A lot of folk don't get along with their fathers.' I'd learned that first-hand the day before in the vaults. 'Doesn't mean most want them dead.'

'Fathers don't usually send their children away to die when they're twelve years old, either.' Rahim said it so matter-of-factly it surprised me. 'Or at least, that's what I've heard. I don't have much of a point of comparison.' Rahim started walking again and this time I moved with him.

'How'd you get sent away?' I kept pace with him. 'Seems like half the harem would kill for a chance at escape.' Me included.

Rahim didn't answer right away and when he did he picked his words carefully, deciding what to tell me and what to keep from me. 'I tried to crack Kadir's skull open with my bare hands.' I hadn't been expecting that answer.

'And how'd that work out for you?' I asked.

Rahim caught my eye out of the corner of his. 'That's what you ask me? Not why?'

'I've met Kadir, I can guess why.'

'I wanted to take something from my father the same way he did from me. Women vanish out of the harem every day. Most children just have to accept when their mothers vanish without a word. I wasn't prepared to be one of them.' I remembered how calm Leyla had seemed when she told me that her mother had been taken away from her. She shared a mother with Rahim. I had to imagine he hadn't been quite as placid as his sister. 'It took three soldiers to pull me off Kadir. His nose is still crooked, you'll notice.'

He scratched the bridge of his own perfectly straight nose, hiding a laugh. It was the Sultan's nose, I realised. That was what made him look like Ahmed.

'So how come you're not dead?' I asked.

'It looks bad for the Sultan to kill his own sons. Especially after he already had so much of his family's blood on his hands. So my father decided to send me away to war to die quietly, or at least somewhere he wouldn't hear. My father underestimated me.'

'You became the commander instead.'

'The youngest ever. And the best.' He wasn't bragging, I realised. He sounded like Shazad. Easily certain that he was right. 'Now, will you get my sister out?'

I shouldn't be doing this. It ought to be Ahmed or Shazad or even Jin here negotiating with Rahim. This wasn't a job for the Blue-Eyed Bandit. But right now I was the only one here. 'That depends what you've got.'

'How about an army?' That wasn't a bad opening offer. 'The Emir of Iliaz is due to arrive for Auranzeb. He has as little love for the Sultan as I do and the fighting force of Iliaz nearly matches the rest of Miraji's combined. A word from me and that army can be your Rebel Prince's.' We'd arrived.

The Sultan looked up as we entered. 'Ah, Rahim, I see you managed to get Amani all the way here without her running off.' It was a gentle barb. 'Congratulations. No mean feat, it would seem.'

It would take one word. Just one to his father now, telling him that I was the Blue-Eyed Bandit. And just like that, everything would be over. He could betray me before we'd even made an alliance.

But he didn't. Rahim stepped aside, letting me in the room ahead of him, like a gentleman. As I passed he said in a low voice, 'I can get your rebellion an army. Tell me I'm lying.'

I didn't say anything as I took my place behind the Sultan. I could only speak the truth.

Chapter 28

'You know, where I come from, there's an ancient expression, passed down from parents to children.' Sam spread his hands like he was seeing it written out in big letters floating in front of him. '"Don't ally with people who have tried to kill you."'

'You just made that up.' Shazad leaned back against the wall that she and Sam had just walked through. She was the only person I knew who wouldn't be even a tiny bit ruffled by being pulled through a wall by a man we only barely trusted.

'I did.' Sam winked at her. 'But you can't deny it's a good policy.'

'Shazad nearly slit your throat when you first met,' I pointed out. 'And you're here.' I was keeping one eye on the gate into the garden, in case anyone wandered our way. It was morning and the sunlight glaring down on our meeting, with the rest of the harem awake, made me nervous. But dawn had beaten Sam back to the rebel camp with Rahim's offer. And Shazad wasn't willing to wait another day.

'Well, that's just because Shazad's charm trumps all wisdom.' Sam winked at Shazad, who ignored him. 'Besides, I'm just the messenger. That's how I'm going to avoid getting shot.'

'What?' He was doing that thing where he talked nonsense again.

'It's an Albish expression, it means – never mind.' He shook his head, fighting a laugh. It was one of those rare smiles on him that looked real, not calculated or designed to charm me. The ones that actually made me like him.

But Shazad's eyes had a faraway look. Like she was working through a problem quickly in her mind. I already knew where she would get to. She'd been telling Ahmed for ages we needed a real fighting force. And now I was offering her one. She was taking it seriously enough to come here herself. She hadn't even made a comment about my missing hair, even though I knew she'd noticed.

'We can trust him?'

'He's hiding something,' I said. 'He won't tell me why he's frightened for Leyla, for one. But he hasn't lied to me. He hates his father, and he has no designs on the throne.' No matter what Shira suspected, that truth fell easily off my tongue.

'What do you think?' Shazad turned to Sam. He looked taken aback for a moment by the full force of her attention.

'I think it's not my place to make decisions about whom you should trust,' Sam said, recovering. 'I mean, you obviously have excellent taste.' He gestured to himself.

'She meant about being able to get Leyla out of the palace.'

'Oh, well.' He cleared his throat. 'I can walk her out of here. As easily as I walked you in.' Sam's smile looked pasted on again. 'Only, in my experience, someone usually notices when princesses go missing from palaces.'

'You've got a lot of experience kidnapping princesses, do you?' Shazad said.

'I'll have you know that princesses find me irresistible.' He leaned in conspiratorially. 'I'm still working on bandits and generals.'

'He's right,' I interrupted before they could descend into arguing again. 'Wives seem to disappear from the harem all too often, but the daughters seem to be a little bit more closely watched. She can't just vanish; she'd be missed.'

'And then you'll be questioned. Rahim will get found out along with the rest of us and we'll lose any shot of getting both you and that Djinni out of the Sultan's hands.' Shazad was steps ahead as usual. I'd told them about my encounter with my father. Or at least as much of it as mattered. That the only way we were going to get him free was if we broke the circle. We'd need some kind of explosive. And even I knew you couldn't exactly blow something up in this palace without people noticing.

'So we've got to strike a single blow,' Shazad was working it through out loud. 'We get everyone out at once or no one at all.' She was right. If we got my father out, we lost any chance of helping Leyla and Rahim escape. If we walked the two of them out of the palace, my father was left in the Sultan's hands. So we'd have to get all three of them out at the same time. One shot was all we were going to get. One shot for three targets.

'Auranzeb,' I said, drawing Shazad's and Sam's eyes my way. 'We can use Auranzeb as our cover. This isn't the sort of thing that you and I and a handful of good luck can pull off on our own. We'll need backup, and from what I've heard, there's enough strangers coming in at Auranzeb that we ought to be able to get a few more in.'

Shazad considered it for a long moment. Neither Sam nor I spoke as she ran through past celebrations at the palace in her mind. 'Auranzeb could work. We could get Imin in easily. Hala, too, if she gets back from Saramotai in time. Maybe two or three more, without pushing our luck too much.' She could see the celebration laid out in front of her like a battlefield, and I could tell she was looking for openings and escape routes. A smile started to dawn slowly across her face. It died suddenly as she looked up. 'What about you?'

She was right. It wasn't three people who needed to be freed from the palace. It was four. I couldn't stay here. No matter what blow we struck at Auranzeb, everything could be undone if I didn't leave with them.

We could break the circle. But so long as the Sultan had me in his control he could just summon my father back. They could abduct Leyla and Rahim to safety and win a whole army. But the Sultan could make me give away every name in the Rebellion before they could strike.

'Let's cross that bridge when we come to it.' I tried to sound easy about it. 'For now, I'll tell Rahim that we'll take his deal. We've got a while before Auranzeb yet.'

Sam started talking again, laying out the plan. But Shazad wasn't fooled. We were both thinking the same thing.

I couldn't be left behind at Auranzeb. At least not alive.

Chapter 29

War was building. Everybody could feel it. Even those of us who hadn't been alive for the last war, when the Sultan took his throne.

And nobody seemed to know exactly what side they were on yet.

Inside the palace, I saw it in the rising tension in the council room. I saw it in the way the Xichian general's hand slammed down, knocking over a pitcher of wine that drenched the papers sprawled across the table. I saw it in the number of guns and swords that surrounded the Albish queen when she arrived at the palace, taking the place of her elderly ambassador in negotiations.

Having Rahim as my guard made getting around a whole lot easier. After a few days I understood why the Sultan had allowed Rahim to talk his way into the role of my protector. He and Kadir despised each other. And the Sultan had made clear he didn't approve of

Kadir's eyes on me by putting another one of his sons as my shield.

Rahim fed me more information that made it back to Sam as fast as anything. I was able to warn him when the Sultan's city guard thought they were closing in on the new location of the rebel camp in the city. They never found anything. And two days later they had brand-new intelligence that would lead them in circles at the opposite end of Izman.

The news that the Sultan was negotiating with foreigners slipped out somehow, too. Nobody had forgotten how much they hated Gallan rule. New tracts circulated in the streets reminding the Mirajin people what they had already suffered at the hands of our occupiers and our Sultan. But when the soldiers tried to trace where they might have come from, they wound up chasing their own tails.

The Rebellion was rising up like bursts of gunpowder all over Izman. Most exploded in neighbourhoods that had suffered under Gallan rule. A NEW DAWN was burned onto walls in the night. Bombs made in kitchens were flung at soldiers in the streets. Folk had started painting Ahmed's sun on hulls of ships. The Rebellion was spreading, further than it ever had before. The Sultan's army came after the culprits. But the names of those they planned to arrest were in the Rebellion's hands before the army's. By the time men in uniform got to their doors, their homes were empty.

I brought Sam a report of thirty Izmani citizens languishing in prison, due to be hanged as examples of what happened when you supported the Rebellion. Last time, it'd been a whole tavern arrested when a bit too much alcohol had them standing on the table chanting Ahmed's name. The Rebellion had managed to get half of them free of the noose before the trap opened below their feet. The rest had choked to death slowly. The Sultan's hangman had made the rope too short, deliberately. So they'd suffer.

So Ahmed would watch them suffer.

We'd get there first this time. Or we hoped we would.

We had the people. We had the city. But there was no taking the palace. Not without the army Rahim had promised us. And there were a whole lot of fires to keep burning until then. Fires we'd started, for the most part. Sam told me it felt like we were trying to plug holes in a wicker basket. I couldn't remember when Sam had started saying *we* instead of *you*.

'There's a plan to rebuild the factory in the Last County,' I told Sam when we were a few short weeks away from Auranzeb. 'The one outside Dustwalk. Once they've reclaimed our half of the desert.' As a gesture of goodwill to the Gallan, of future willingness to continue to provide them with weapons in their war against any other country that didn't share their beliefs. 'They're sending a small party down there, soldiers and engineers, to assess the feasibility of it.'

'What am I missing?' Sam might be a posturer most days, but he wasn't stupid, either, even though he behaved like he was half the time.

'Dustwalk is where I'm from,' I said, leaning back against the tree. I was tired. Cool air ran its fingers through my hair, lulling me. 'I was born there. It might not be that nice a place, but it still deserves better than this.'

Sam nodded. 'So we make sure their party never makes it back.'

He listened to me rattle off the rest of what I'd gathered since I last saw him. But when I was done, he didn't leave straightaway. 'You know,' he said, still leaning on the wall across from me, 'I heard a lot of stories about the Blue-Eyed Bandit. Granted, some of them were about me. I particularly like the one about how the Blue-Eyed Bandit stole the necklace right off a woman's neck, got caught, and still managed to seduce her.'

'Is there a point to this, or are you just trying to remind me that the longer I'm in here, the more sullied my reputation becomes?'

'My point,' Sam said, 'is that none of those stories said the Blue-Eyed Bandit was a coward.' That got my attention.

'Oh, so is your point actually that you'd like to get punched in the face?'

'If I'd known the famous Bandit, who fought at Fahali and struck fear into the Sultan's soldiers, was this lily-livered, I probably wouldn't have taken her reputation. It's bad for business to be known as a cowardly bandit. And you should take my stealing your reputation as high praise. I could easily have chosen to be the Blond Bandit or the Dashingly Handsome Bandit or—'

'I swear to God, Sam.'

'No, really, go ahead and tell me I couldn't rightfully call myself the Dashingly Handsome Bandit – eh, truth-teller? Tell me I'm not handsome, I challenge you. See? You can't.'

'You really seem to think I'm not going to break your nose.'

'See' – Sam wavered back on track – 'cowardice is the only reason I can possibly think of that makes any sense of why you *still* haven't gone to speak to the person who might be able to get that little piece of bronze under your skin out so that you can leave the palace with us.'

I sobered. 'Shazad told you about Tamid.' I felt a little bit betrayed by that. 'It's not that easy.'

'It's certainly harder if you don't try. And for all my many feats of bravery, I'm deeply afraid of your general, so I sincerely don't want to bring back the news that you haven't even tried yet. Because guess which of us will get blamed? It's not the one she actually likes.'

'Shazad likes you fine,' I said offhandedly. 'Why do you even care?'

'She depends on you. You don't see it, but she does.' For just a moment he actually seemed serious. 'And I don't think you're selfish enough to die on her just to avoid an uncomfortable conversation. Besides, if you die, I can't be in two places at once any more.'

I ignored that last part. Sam annoyed me even more than usual when he was right.

I dragged my feet as we left the negotiations the next day, forcing Rahim to drop back with me.

The Sultan caught his eye, a question mark there. A spark of suspicion neither of us could afford. Rahim saw it, too. He leaned in towards his father, whispering low in his ear. 'The Gallan ambassador has the look in his eye of a man about to do something very foolish.' He wasn't wrong about that. I'd torn down three of the Gallan ambassador's lies in the meeting, as he got angrier and angrier. 'If he were one of my soldiers, I would have him run drills until he cooled off. As he isn't, I think it's best to let him go ahead.'

The Sultan considered me before nodding, letting me and Rahim drag back behind the rest.

'There's a—' *Prisoner* wouldn't get past my tongue. 'A boy. From the Last County. He only has one leg.'

'I know him.'

'Can you get me to him?' I pressed.

'Do you want to tell me what you need with him badly enough to risk going places my father doesn't want you?'

'Do you want to tell me why your sister so desperately needs to be saved from the harem?'

Rahim scratched the edge of his mouth, hiding a smile. 'This way.'

I started to recognize this part of the palace as we came to the foot of a long winding staircase. My first day in the palace, I'd clambered down this, body aching with fresh wounds, fighting legs that couldn't help but obey the Sultan's order to follow him.

I heard voices as we got closer to the top. I recognized Tamid's instantly. It was a voice that went with laughing ourselves stupid after we'd been sent out of the schoolroom for misbehaving. With nights falling asleep while he read me the Holy Books after my mother died. The other was soft and female. A part of me wanted to turn back. To avoid sticking my fingers in this wound. But Sam had been talking sense for once. I had no right to be a coward in this rebellion.

I pushed the door open.

Two startled heads looked up at me. Tamid was sitting on the edge of the same table I'd woken up on. The sight of him was so heartbreakingly familiar that for a moment I wanted to rush to him and pour everything out. His left trouser leg was rolled up to his knee. Or where there ought to have been a knee.

Instead there was a bronze disc hiding the place where his leg ended. It was secured to the scarred skin with a leather strap. There was nothing attached to it. The rest of Tamid's leg – the hollow, polished bronze – was in Leyla's hands, as she sat across from him. She gaped at me and Rahim with wide eyes, mouth moving open and shut in silent panic.

Well. I hadn't been expecting *that*. I didn't think Rahim had, either.

'Don't tell Father!' she blurted out finally. It was exactly the wrong thing to say. Though the fact that she was suddenly flushed from neck to chin wasn't doing her any favours, either. 'I was just here to make sure it wasn't . . .' She trailed off.

'Squeaking,' Tamid filled in even as Leyla made a noise that sounded an awful lot like a squeak herself.

'The joints were squeaking. Leyla came to tune my leg up. Seeing as she built it and all.'

'I bet she did.' Rahim eyed Tamid in that way that fathers and brothers eyed boys who looked at their daughters and sisters wrong. So this was the secret Leyla was keeping, which Shira wanted so bad. Shira thought she was sneaking off to plot against her with her brother, but she was just an infatuated girl leaving the harem to see a boy.

It might've been funny if I wasn't certain that Shira could use this, too. More than once I'd gotten a beating for sneaking off to see Tamid. And I wasn't a princess. And I hadn't been in love with him. Was this why Rahim was so desperate to get Leyla out of the palace? Would she get punished for this as much as Tamid would? But there was something else passing between the siblings, skipping straight over Tamid. 'You designed that, Leyla?' Rahim gestured at the articulated bronze limb in her hands.

She nodded nervously. 'I thought – it might be useful.' So she didn't just make toys for children in the harem. That was impressive, I had to admit.

But Rahim was angry in a way I didn't wholly understand. 'Come on, Leyla, I'll walk you back to the harem. There are some things we need to discuss anyway.' Good, it was long past time to tell Leyla about the plan for Auranzeb. The holiday was only a handful of days away now and she needed to know we were getting her out of there.

What followed was the longest, most awkward minute of my life as Leyla reattached Tamid's leg. Everybody was trying their hardest not to look at anyone else. The sound of mechanisms clicking together punctuated the silence as Leyla worked. When she was finally, mercifully, done, Rahim practically dragged her out of the room, remembering me at the last second. 'Amani, I'll come back and get you.'

Tamid and I didn't speak as Leyla followed her brother out. The awkwardness stretched between us long after their footsteps had faded.

'I'd love to be able to storm away, but, you know.' Tamid tapped on his leg, below the knee. A hollow sound reverberated back. I winced. 'It seems like you ought to be the one to leave. Out of respect.'

'Tamid—'

'Do you want to know how I lost my leg, Amani?' Tamid cut me off.

'I know how.' I remembered that last dark night in Dustwalk clearer than any of the hazy days that came before.

'No.' Tamid slammed his hand down against the table underneath him. I might've flinched if I wasn't so used to the sound of gunfire aimed at me. 'You don't. You saw Naguib shoot me and then you left. You weren't there while I lay screaming in the sand. You weren't there when Shira started striking bargains, saying she could help find you. That she knew you better than almost anyone, that she knew where you'd go. Better than *almost* anyone.' His hands shook as he clenched them into fists. 'You didn't see them tear me away from my mother to take me with them, too, on the off chance I might be useful. You weren't with me on that train that rattled its way to Izman.' I had been on that train. I'd seen Shira on that train. I'd kissed Jin on that train. Not ever imagining Tamid might be on board, too.

'Naguib said he'd left you to bleed out in Dustwalk. I thought you were dead, Tamid.' The words I'd comforted myself with for months since that day sounded like a poor excuse now he was standing in front of me in the flesh.

'So did I.' His right hand was a fist against his thigh now. 'I thought I was dead while I writhed in agony and when I got here and the Holy Father said it was infected. That it would have to come off. You weren't here when they sawed off my leg, Amani. But now you are. Let me guess: you want my help. You want me to tell you which little metal bump under your skin is the one you need to cut out to escape.' My fingers pressed so hard against the metal on my arm I wondered if it

351

would bruise. Tamid knew me well enough to read my silence.

He pushed himself off the edge of the table. I pretended not to notice the slight wince as his freshly oiled leg hit the ground, or the way he steadied himself for a fraction of a heartbeat before he started to work his way around the small space, tidying up even though it was already spotless. Straightening bottles so the labels all faced out in a perfect line, making them clink with every twist. He slammed a door shut that led towards a small side chamber, where I could see a bed. 'You're predictable as anything. You know, back in Dustwalk, you always figured I didn't sleep all that well. But that wasn't true. It was just that, if I knew you'd gotten a beating, I'd lie awake waiting for you to crawl through my window asking for something.'

I hadn't known that. I swallowed the tears that were welling up in my throat. 'I don't believe you hate me as much as you want me to think you do.'

'How do you figure?' Leyla had left her tools behind, and he started lining those up. He sounded disinterested.

'Because if you really hated me, you'd have turned me over to the Sultan as a rebel by now.' I saw the truth of it as soon as I said it. 'Instead, you pretended not to know me the day I got here. You've been helping the Sultan a whole lot of other ways.' This truth came out like an accusation. It was easier to accuse him as a rebel against an enemy than as a girl against an old friend. 'You gave him the knowledge he needed to control Noorsham and to control me. And enough first language to capture a Djinni. But you didn't give me up.' I saw him wince at the mention of the Djinni. I seized on it. He might not care enough about me any more to help, but I knew Tamid. If you cut him he'd bleed holy words. 'He's going to be able to kill a whole lot more people with a Djinni on his side, you know.'

'I know.'

'And that's all right with you, is it?'

'Do you mean because it's unholy, or because of how I feel—' Just for a second his fingers slipped, sending a small circular instrument skidding off the table and to the ground. 'Because of how I felt, about you?'

How did you feel about me? But that wasn't a fair question when I already knew the answer. I saw it now, written all over him.

'He's our Sultan, Amani. Our job is to obey, not to question.'

'You don't believe that.' A simple truth slipping out. I retrieved the metal tube off the floor and handed it back to him. 'Not you who went to prayers every single day. You don't believe keeping a Djinni prisoner is the right thing.'

'It doesn't matter what I think. I've scoured the books in the Sultan's library and I couldn't find the words to release a Djinni, only to bind one—' He caught himself, looking at me straight on now. He ignored the metal tube I still had in my hand, refusing even that peace offering.

'You only know the words to bind them, not to release them?' I imagined my father trapped under the palace forever as we mortals did what we did best: died, and then forgot about him, trapping him there for all eternity.

'What do you care?' Tamid asked.

'Turns out I'm in the business of saving lives now.'

'Well, it's a shame that wasn't your line of employment ten months ago when you left me to die.'

'They did this to you, Tamid.' I held my ground. 'Not me.'

'Yes, they did,' he said. 'But it was you who left me behind.'

I didn't have anything I could say to that.

Tamid tilted his head further away from me. On most men I knew, the dark hair would've fallen in front of his eyes, hiding them from me. But Tamid's hair was always perfectly combed against his head. 'What do I have to say to make you leave, Amani?'

That was all he needed to say.

Chapter 30

I leaned against a pillar in the courtyard at the bottom of the steps. Back on steady ground, pressing my hands back into the marble hard. I forced my tears to dry. I forced myself to remember I was a desert girl. I didn't have water to spare. And this wasn't any kind of place to show weakness. The palace was as dangerous as the desert at night.

Rahim had told me to wait for him. I wasn't meant to be without a guard. I didn't know how long his talk with Leyla would take. But, while it was awful tempting to go snooping around, I couldn't risk getting caught unaccompanied. It would blow Rahim's cover, too. And I doubted the Sultan would forgive me a second time after I'd gone to see Bahadur. As soon as that thought shot across my mind I wondered what it was doing there. It shouldn't matter; I'd never minded getting into trouble before. It was because my head might wind up on the chopping block, I told myself. It was because losing his trust would mean losing access to the information we needed.

So I waited, trying to ignore the itch below my skin to move, to do something, listening to the sounds of the fountain and the birds who populated this part of the palace, trapped here by clipped wings, just like the ducks in the pond. The sudden rattle of a door was as loud as a gunshot.

I reacted on instinct, plastering myself behind the pillar into the shadows. It didn't matter who was coming; I couldn't get caught alone. A fraction of a heartbeat later a door on the other side of the courtyard slammed open. The crack of the handle hitting the stone was so loud it almost covered the woman's cry. I couldn't ignore the itch any more. I peered around the pillar.

Two figures in Mirajin soldiers' uniforms were dragging a girl between them through the door. She thrashed violently against their grip, screaming so loudly I was sure someone was going to come running. The birds, I realised, remembering that day in the menagerie, what Ayet had said – no one would be able to hear her screaming over the birds. My fingers twitched for a weapon. For a gun. For something to help. But my hands were empty and bound by the Sultan's orders to do no harm. And even I knew I couldn't take on two soldiers with no weapon.

Then they emerged into the sunlight and I saw the thrashing captive's face.

Uzma.

Kadir's wife. Who had made it her duty to humiliate me that day in court and had vanished into thin air afterwards. Uzma's eyes were as blank as polished glass, like any spark that had ever lived behind them had been snuffed out. I knew exactly where I'd seen that same look before. Back at camp, on Sayyida after Hala rescued her from the palace. Only Sayyida had been a spy. What had Uzma possibly done to be tortured out of her mind?

They vanished around the corner, the screams fading quickly.

I didn't move right away. I could feel myself torn between following them and staying out of trouble, just once in my life. Trailing two guards and a screaming woman was a surefire way to get myself caught. Besides, it might not be the best way to figure out what was going on. I glanced at the door where they had come from. It was almost definitely locked. But it might not be. It would be stupid and reckless to dart out into the open and risk getting seen regardless.

Well, it looked like I was stupid and reckless, then.

My feet carried me in one short burst across the

courtyard. The dying sunlight bounced off the door strangely. As I got closer, I realised why. The door was made of metal. Only someone had painted it to look like wood.

And it was humming.

I stretched my fingers tentatively towards the door. I could feel the hum building like a pull underneath my skin as I inched closer. My fingertips grazed the door. It was like touching fire without getting burned: all of the power of it, none of the heat. Tiny needles started at my fingertips and travelled up, making my breath hitch and my heart race even though I was standing still.

Suddenly, a pair of hands grabbed me and slammed me into the metal hard, sending pain shooting up my body, an explosion of feeling across every bit of skin that I had.

And then I was staring up into the cruel face of the Gallan ambassador. Behind him was Kadir. Before I could speak a word, the man drove a hand into my middle, pinning me still, knocking the air out of my lungs.

'In my country,' the Gallan ambassador said in his thick accent, 'we hang demons' children by the throat.' His hand tightened on my windpipe, forcing me up straight. 'But I don't have any rope with me.'

God, the metal door at my back was starting to hurt now. I could feel my thoughts blurring and my vision going black as his hand tightened around my throat. My hands scrabbled uselessly against the back of the hand gripping my windpipe. There were a dozen things I should've been able to do to fight back against him. I could've clawed the soft spots inside his wrists, jabbed at his eyes, driven my leg into his groin. Except the Sultan had ordered me not to harm anyone. I was going to die. The panic started in earnest now. I was going to really and truly die.

And then suddenly I could breathe again. Air flooded back in a gasp as the hand released my throat. I wrenched myself away from the wall, falling to all fours. I knelt there for three long breaths, waiting to remember how to breathe. A crack like breaking bone sounded, and a cry of pain. I looked up in time to see Kadir reel back, clutching his nose.

Over him, blazing with the setting sun at his back, stood Rahim, his brother's blood on his fist. The light blurred his features so I almost couldn't recognise him. He looked like every hero I'd ever imagined from the old stories: the First Mortal facing death instead of running from it; Attallah outside the walls of Saramotai, outnumbered; the Grey Prince against the Conqueror. He didn't look real.

And then he dropped to his knees across from me and he was human again. 'Amani.' He tipped my head back, checking me with the sure hands of someone who knew a battlefield injury. 'Are you all right?' I could see behind him now that there were two soldiers with him and they were holding the Gallan ambassador away from me. 'Amani,' Rahim pressed. 'Talk to me or I'm taking you to the Holy Father.'

'I'm fine.' My voice came out scratchy but still mine. 'I'm sure I have something to wear that'll go well with the bruising.' Rahim helped me to my feet. I touched my throat, sensitive where the ambassador's fingers had tried to crush my windpipe.

'Soldiers.' Kadir had recovered enough from his broken nose to speak. He pulled his hands away from his face though blood was still gushing across his mouth. 'Release the ambassador. Take my brother away instead.'

The soldiers didn't move. Instead they both looked at Rahim for instructions. I noticed their uniforms then. They were Mirajin, but instead of the standard white and gold of the palace they were emblazoned on the chest with the same blue stripe as Rahim's. They were from his command in Iliaz. The emir must've arrived. This was why he'd been late coming back for me. He'd found his men.

'Stay where you are.' Rahim gave the order with a controlled ease I'd never seen in him before. I realised this was where he truly belonged, among soldiers, not among politicians in a palace. He was a soldier through and through. No, not a soldier. A commander.

Kadir's gaze flicked frantically between the soldiers and Rahim. 'I said let him go. I order you as your Sultim!' His voice, thick with the blood of a broken nose, rose with anger.

They might as well have been deaf. Rahim calmly took his time pulling off the jacket of his uniform and placing it around my shoulders before addressing his brother. 'These are my men, brother. They follow their commander, not their Sultim.

'Escort him back to his chambers,' Rahim ordered the soldiers holding the Gallan ambassador. 'Before we start an international incident. Amani, let's go.'

Rahim had already turned away when Kadir pulled the pistol from his belt. I cried a warning, but too slow. The gun went off, hitting one of the soldiers. It was a sloppy shot, the shoulder instead of the chest, but it was enough to make his grip slacken.

The Gallan ambassador wrenched himself free of the soldier's grip. The foreigner grabbed the blade on his belt, diving for the wounded soldier. Rahim moved quickly, his own weapon already drawn, meeting the ambassador's blade in the air in one easy gesture before it could run his soldier through.

Kadir was still raging. He raised his gun again, pointing it straight at Rahim's back. I moved as fast as Shazad had taught me.

He had a loose grip on the gun – I couldn't tell if it was anger or just bad training. I might not be able to hurt him, but I didn't have to let him kill Rahim, either. I slammed my palm flat against the place where the grip of the gun was sticking out from his fist. The gun went off, the bullet hitting the wall, as his fingers flew open. The gun jolted upwards, out of his hand. I caught it easily before it hit the ground, flipping it around in my fingers with familiar ease.

I aimed the pistol at Kadir. He went still, staring at me over the barrel of the gun, like he couldn't quite understand what had happened. 'You're not going to shoot me.'

That was true enough. I couldn't. I had orders against it. But he didn't know that. I pulled back the hammer on the pistol all the same. 'Want to bet your life on that?' My fingers were shaking from trying to pull the trigger. And I was that ten-year-old girl again, holding on to a too-big rifle for dear life. Knowing that if I dropped it, I'd be helpless.

'Drop the gun, Amani.'

Even if I hadn't known the voice, the tug in my gut at the order would've given him away.

No. I fought against it.

But my arms were already moving without wanting to. I fought it until my arms screamed. The gun clattered to the ground.

When I turned around, the two soldiers were standing at sharp attention, the injured one clutching his shoulder. At their feet the ambassador's body was slumped in the grass. His hands, which had been wrapped around my throat a few moments earlier, were limp now. The bloodstained sword was in Rahim's hand.

And, surveying the whole scene, from my discarded gun to the blood spreading out from under the ambassador's body, his expression unreadable, was the Sultan.

The Sultan's fingers drummed out a pattern on the ivory and wood chessboard inlay of his desk as his eyes traced the line of my throat. It was going to bloom into an impressive bruise shaped like the Gallan ambassador's hand in a few hours, but for now, it still felt raw and red. We were in the Sultan's study. The same one I'd stolen those papers from a few weeks back. There was a weight to the room with the Sultan in it that hadn't been there without him. Like all the maps on the walls and spread across the desk were extensions of him. Jin had once told me I was this desert. I wondered if he'd change his mind if he saw in here.

I'd been allowed to sit. Ordered, more like. But his sons stood at attention behind me. The Sultan ordered me to tell him what had happened. He wanted the truth, he said. And that was what I gave him. I left out Leyla, but I couldn't avoid Tamid. The Sultan would question why I'd been alone in the palace when I wasn't supposed to be. I tiptoed around that part of the story as carefully as I could, my heart in my mouth. One wrong word and it could all be over. *I asked Rahim to take me to the Holy Father. He left to give us privacy.* I tried not to let relief leak into my words as I slipped on to the next part of the story without any questions from the Sultan.

When I finished speaking, no one said anything for a good few moments. I had a strange feeling like I was back in school, in trouble along with Tamid for something stupid I'd done, facing the anger of a teacher. The three of us lined up in front of the Sultan like we were quarrelling children, not soldiers and spies fighting for a country. The Sultan was silent as the last of the sunlight outside faded. Through the huge window I could see the lights of Izman start to flicker to life.

My mind kept running back to the same thought: the gun. The Sultan had seen me holding a gun to his heir's head. Holding it like I knew what I was doing. Holding it like the Blue-Eyed Bandit would hold a gun. He had to know I was more than just a desert girl now.

But I didn't try to explain it. The guilty always talked first. Rahim and I were both smart enough not to interrupt the Sultan's silence.

'Father—' Which made us both smarter than Kadir.

'I didn't give you permission to speak.' The Sultan sounded calm. Unnervingly calm. Deceptively calm. 'You are a thief, Kadir.' Kadir bristled, but the Sultan was already talking again. 'Don't disagree with me. You tried to take something of mine.' He gestured to me. I hated being referred to as belonging to the Sultan. But I couldn't help the surge of satisfaction over being worth more to him than Kadir right now. 'And trade it for the support of the Gallan.'

'She's not human, Father!' Kadir's voice rose. He sounded close to stomping his foot in rage like a child.

'Everyone knew that, brother,' Rahim interjected. His calm just made Kadir angrier. 'If you only just figured that out, I have some concerns about the intelligence of our future ruler.'

The Sultan held up his hand. 'If you think now is the time for bickering, with a foreign diplomat dead in my palace, then I have questions about *your* intelligence, Rahim.' He nodded at Kadir to continue.

'The negotiations were lasting forever. And the Gallan were never going to make a new alliance with us so long as you were so blatantly flaunting a half-human thing in violation of their beliefs. They came to me' – his chest swelled with pride – 'and demanded her death before they would negotiate any further.'

The Sultan didn't raise his voice, but even I shrank under the look he gave Kadir. And it wasn't even directed at me. 'They demanded her death because she is making lying to me about their resources and their intentions more difficult, and revealing that the Gallan empire is stretched thinner than they would like us to think.' He spoke slowly, carefully, like he was explaining something to a child. 'And they came to you because you have *clearly* been itching to get your hands on her in some way for weeks now.'

Kadir sneered, flopping into the other chair petulantly as his father spoke.

The silence that followed was worse than the glare. 'I didn't give you permission to sit.'

Kadir started a laugh, like he thought his father might be joking.

'Stand up,' the Sultan ordered calmly. 'Take an example from your brother for once. Perhaps I should have sent you to Iliaz instead of him.'

I remembered what Rahim had told me – that the

Sultan had sent him to Iliaz to die. I understood the threat implied in his words. But it was lost on Kadir.

'All that military training didn't help him beat me in the Sultim trials.' Kadir stood, shoving the chair so it clattered angrily against his father's desk, shifting some of the papers from the edge onto the floor. 'So, what, are you going to put him on the throne instead of me now?'

'The Sultim trials are sacred.' The Sultan kept all his attention on his son, ignoring the disrupted papers on the ground. 'Overturning them would turn the people more against us than they already are. You'd have to die before we held another Sultim trial, Kadir.'

'So unless you're going to do everyone a favour . . .' Rahim muttered.

I snorted under my breath, drawing the Sultan's gaze. I stifled it too late. The Sultan had already noticed the connection between me and Rahim. But his gaze shifted away again without comment.

'The Gallan king is due to arrive tomorrow, in advance of Auranzeb.' The Sultan's fingers returned to drumming out the same pattern. 'You will come with me to meet him, Kadir. And you will tell him the same story I will. That the ambassador went into the city without a guard and was killed by rebels on the street. Do you understand?'

Kadir's jaw worked angrily for a moment. But if

he thought his father was going to give in first, he was badly mistaken. 'Yes.'

'Good. You are dismissed.'

Kadir slammed the door behind him on his way out, like an angry child.

'That lie may not be wise, Father,' Rahim said. 'If it looks to the Gallan like you can't control your own people—'

'Then we may look weak. I had considered that and I don't in fact need a lesson in political strategy from my *son*.' The Sultan cut him off impatiently. 'If we are *lucky*, it may give the Gallan soldiers who come with him some incentive to help keep the peace in Izman leading up to Auranzeb. The only alternative is to turn *you* over to Gallan justice. Perhaps you'd prefer that.'

Rahim's jaw screwed itself shut.

'Rahim saved my life.' I couldn't keep quiet any longer. The Sultan's attention swung to me and immediately I regretted talking. But I was already going now. 'He ought to be rewarded, not *threatened*.' The Sultan didn't speak and I didn't back down. I couldn't afford to now. 'I figured I was here to tell the truth.'

Finally he seemed to check his temper. 'She's right. Your soldiers did well today, Rahim.' Somehow it still didn't sound like praise. 'At your orders, no less.' More like veiled suspicion.

'Yes, they did.' Rahim was as smart as his father. He didn't offer excuses for his men obeying his orders over Kadir's. He kept his answers short. Like a good soldier would. Or a traitor. Waiting to be dismissed.

'The rebels raided an incoming shipment of weapons at the south gate yesterday.' The Sultan spoke again. 'How do you think they knew where those were, Rahim?'

I was sure the Sultan could hear my heart speed up. I knew exactly which shipment he meant. They knew because Rahim had told me and I'd told Sam. Did he suspect us? Was it an accusation? Or was he asking his son's military advice as a peace offering? I prayed wildly that he wouldn't turn the question on me, that it wouldn't be in this moment that we lost everything.

'There is a war going on.' Rahim kept his eyes straight ahead, over his father's head, like a soldier at attention. 'Your soldiers are unhappy. Unhappy soldiers drink and they talk.' He chose his words so carefully that they were true. That I could have repeated them without hesitation. Though not carefully enough not to insult his father's rule.

'We killed two rebels in the raid,' the Sultan said. My stomach clenched. A list of possible rebels I knew cascaded through my head. Imagining them all dead. Suddenly I desperately wanted to run to the Weeping

Wall and Sam and find out who. Find out if I'd never be seeing Shazad again. Or Hala. Or one of the twins. But the Sultan wasn't watching me. His gaze was on Rahim. Waiting for a reaction? 'Next time I want one alive for questioning. Your soldiers from Iliaz seem well trained. Have Lord Bilal designate half of them to join the city guards on patrol.' My shoulders eased in relief.

'As you wish, Father.' Rahim didn't wait to be dismissed. He just offered his father a quick bow before turning on his heel.

And then it was just me and him. A long moment passed in silence. I half thought the Sultan had forgotten me. I was about to point out that I hadn't been dismissed when the Sultan spoke again.

'You're from the end of the desert.' It wasn't what I'd been expecting.

'The very end,' I agreed. There was nothing after Dustwalk but uninhabitable mountains.

'They say your people's blood runs thicker with the old stories than elsewhere.' That much was true. That was how Tamid had known how to control Noorsham. How to trap a Djinni. All the things that the north had forgotten. 'Do you know the stories of the Abdals?'

I did.

In the days before humans the Djinn made servants out of dirt. Simple creatures made from clay and animated only when they were given orders by a Djinni. Good for nothing except to follow orders from their immortal masters.

'The Abdals were as much their creation as we are, and yet the holy texts refer to humans as the first children of the Djinn. I understand why now.' He riffled his hands through his hair as he leaned back in his chair. It was an exasperated gesture that looked so much like Ahmed it made me homesick. 'The Abdals didn't have it in them to be nearly so difficult as children.'

'Abdals would be a fair bit harder to leave a country to, though.' It slipped out before I could bite my tongue. I was too comfortable with him. He might look like him, but he wasn't Ahmed. But the Sultan surprised me by laughing.

'True enough. Though it would be easier to govern over a country full of Abdals. I wouldn't have to constantly try to convince them I am doing what is best for them.' One of the maps pinned up on the wall showed the whole world. Miraji was in the middle. Amonpour crowding our borders on one side. Gallandie looming over the north, swallowing countries as it went towards Jarpoor and the Ionian Peninsula and Xicha, the country that had sheltered Ahmed, Jin, and Delila for years. Albis a fortress holding against Gallandie's expansion in the sea and Gamanix on land. It was a big world. 'The people of Miraji are rising up in protest of the Gallan, of the Albish, of the Xichian, of all our foreign friends and enemies.'

I swallowed and felt the pain in my throat from where I'd almost just been choked to death by one such foreigner. 'So don't renew an alliance with them.'

I knew I'd overstepped. I knew as soon as the words left my mouth. But the Sultan didn't rage at me the way he had at his sons. He didn't sneer at me. He didn't try to explain to me like he had when we sat across from each other over dinner in the next room.

'You're dismissed, Amani.' And somehow that was worse than anything else he could've said.

Chapter 31

'I think they're fading.' Leyla inspected the marks along my throat. They'd bloomed into a glorious necklace of purple fingerprints by the next day. 'They ought to be gone by Auranzeb.' That seemed to be everyone in the harem's biggest worry on my behalf. That my near death would clash with my khalat. Across the garden I could see two women whispering behind their hands, casting me looks. Good God, I hated this place. Leyla's gentle hands dropped away. 'I really think you ought to go see Tamid, though; he might be able to give you something for that.'

'I'll survive.'

Her big eyes were wide with something unspoken. 'What?' I asked.

'Rahim told me, about Auranzeb. About getting out. And just . . . I wouldn't want to leave Tamid behind.'

I started. Had Tamid told her about me? That I'd done exactly that? Was that a jab meant to hit me in that old wound? But there didn't seem to be any kind of malice behind her words.

Leyla bowed her head, brushing her hair nervously behind her ear, avoiding my gaze. She was in love with Tamid. Or at least she thought she was. She was still shy of sixteen. And she'd spent her whole life trapped in a palace. Tamid had to be one of the first men our age she'd ever encountered who wasn't a brother to her. No wonder she'd think she was in love with him.

And he was clever and he was kind. No wonder she'd really fall in love with him.

And she was right. I couldn't leave him behind a second time.

When Sam walked through the wall that night he had a split lip and he was walking like he might've bruised his ribs. It was the one sign he brought with him that things were getting close to boiling point on the outside. He only ever gave me good news from the Rebellion. That Saramotai was safe. That an ambush had been successful. That the delegation meant to inspect the remains of the factory in Dustwalk had never made it that far.

'You want me to break out four people from this palace now, and I only have two hands.' Sam scratched at the scab on his lip. I slapped his hand away. He was going to make it scar.

'Three people.'

'Four,' Sam said. 'I'm counting you. How long have you known me now? Do you really still underestimate the prowess of the Blue-Eyed Bandit?' He flung his sheema over his shoulder. It snagged on one of the branches of the Weeping Wall tree.

'Is it just me, or have you gotten more ridiculous?' It was so like Sam to try to dodge anything even a little bit serious. Like the real possibility I might not be able to escape at Auranzeb with them.

'Ridiculously smitten with you.' He'd managed to extract the sheema with some dignity. I realised he was trying to make me laugh. And it was working.

'You're not smitten with me, you're—' *In love with someone else*. It almost slipped out, but I stopped myself in time. Sam spent a lot of time bragging about conquests. I was more than sure half of them were invented. But I'd never heard him talk about anyone in particular that he actually cared about. I searched his face now, looking for a hint of something truthful under there. But I was the one with traitor eyes, not him.

'You sound awfully sure of yourself, my beautiful friend.' He was all swagger as he planted his hands on either side of me against the tree. 'Want to bet on that?'

He was going to kiss me, I realised. Or he wanted me to think he was. To prove some stupid point.

'Your lip is bleeding.' I reached out to where the split was, but Sam caught my hand playfully as he leaned in a little closer. I didn't feel anything. Not the way I did when Jin looked at me the way Sam was. Or was pretending to. No rush of heat invading my whole body. The world around him was still as sharp as it had been before he touched me. He wasn't Jin. But he was here when Jin wasn't.

The laugh was unmistakable. Our heads snapped around, pulling us apart before his mouth could find mine.

Ayet was in the gateway to the Weeping Wall garden, head thrown back to the sky in a laugh, like she was thanking the heavens for the gift that'd been sent to her. Seventeen years of desert instincts reared in my chest. Only I wasn't in the desert now. And this was a different kind of danger.

'You know, in all this time looking for a way to keep you out of my husband's bed,' Ayet said, 'I never thought it would be as incredibly *obvious* as this. You're just one of the hundreds of women in the harem *stupid* enough to take a lover.'

'Ayet—' I took a step forward and she took one back. I stopped, keenly aware that she could bolt like a startled animal any second and run to sell me out. 'Don't do this. It's not—'

'Oh, it's very much too late to negotiate, Amani.' And

then she whipped around, racing back into the harem.

'Well,' Sam said. 'This seems like it might be a problem.'

It was a matter of hours until the Sultan and Kadir were back from greeting the Gallan king. From lying to him and saying it was the Rebellion who had killed his ambassador. A handful of hours to stop Ayet before she got the chance to spill the news to her husband. Stop her or get everyone out.

Sam was making a run for it back to the rebel camp for help. I still didn't know where it was and I was grateful for that. If the Sultan ordered me to tell him, my ignorance would buy them some time at least. But they still had to be prepared to run.

In the meantime, I was going to try to stop Ayet.

If there was one person who was a bigger threat to Ayet than I was, it was Shira. And she was still standing. I needed to know how. Shira bartered in information. She had something that kept Ayet off her back. And I needed it.

I burst back towards the core of the harem, breathing hard. Something was different. I felt it immediately. I spotted Leyla, dark hair gathered up off her neck, staring across the garden, worrying her thumbnail. 'Leyla.' I dashed across to her. 'Listen to me. Ayet just found out – it's complicated. If she speaks to your father or to Kadir, we're not going to be able to get you out of the palace at Auranzeb like we planned. So you need to be prepared to leave tonight if I tell you to. And I need to find Shira,' I summarised quickly. 'Do you know where she is?'

Leyla looked startled as I spilled the information out at her. But she grasped on to the last question. 'The Sultima? Her baby's coming. Someone has sent word to Kadir.'

That was it, I realised. That was the restless wildness filling the harem. Damn. Bad timing. 'Leyla, where is she?'

Shira's screams got louder as I burst down the hallway. There were a handful more harem women, sprawled in prayer outside the door. A servant woman rushed out, carrying a blood-soaked cloth. Shira's screams followed her out. Then the door slammed shut again, muffling them.

And then, suddenly, silence dropped like a stone in Shira's rooms.

I held my breath. Trying to count out heartbeats as the silence stretched. Waiting. Waiting for it to be broken by something. A shout. An accusation. A midwife stepping out to let us know that Shira hadn't survived.

It was a baby's wail that ended it.

I let a sigh of relief escape. It wasn't even all the way out of my lungs before there was another scream.

Not Shira's this time.

I moved like a shot for the door, tearing it open. Shira was collapsed in a heap of sweaty hair and bloodied cloth, clutching a small swaddled bundle to her chest, her knees pulled up around the baby, like she could protect it. The three women around her were staring like they'd been turned to stone. A fourth was slumped against the wall, hands clasped over her mouth, shaking.

I took another step forward, until I could clearly see the small bundle Shira was holding. The baby didn't have Sam's blue eyes. He had blue hair. Like Maz's hair. A bright violent blue. Like the hottest part of a flame.

This wasn't Sam's son. It was a Djinni's. Shira had given birth to a Demdji.

Suddenly Leyla and Rahim weren't the most important people to get out of here. 'Shira.' I dropped by her side. 'Can you walk?'

Shira finally lifted her eyes from the baby. 'I can run if I've got to.' Whatever polish the city'd given to her accent, it was gone now. She sounded Dustwalk through and through. She pushed herself off the bed slowly, but without so much as shaking. I'd never seen Shira look so impressive before. She'd had an air about her when she stood as the Sultima, in her fine clothes and unearned arrogance. But that was different from the fierceness she wore now, wrapped in a ruined khalat and sheets, holding her son.

'Let's go, then.'

The lack of guards in the harem had made Shira scared for her life since she conceived, but it might be what saved her life now. There was no one to stop us as we pushed our way out of her rooms. Mothers, sisters, wives, sons, servants – they all gaped mutely, unsure of what to do. Though I was sure somebody'd had the sense to run for help.

We didn't have much time. But we had some. My heart was racing.

'Shira.' I glanced around a corner. It was a quiet garden thick with flowers, and empty now. We were close to the Weeping Wall. I just prayed that Sam would be there to help us when we got there. 'I need to know. What did you hold over Ayet all these months? What did you have that kept her away from you?'

Shira stumbled, and I caught her. 'I'll tell you if you get me out of here alive,' she joked. Even now, with death on her heels, Shira was still the bargainer of the harem.

'Shira, please.'

'A husband,' Shira said finally. 'Another husband, outside the walls of the harem. She put poison in his food after he broke two of her ribs. She bribed her way though her . . . inspection.' She tried to put it delicately. 'A few words of truth in the Sultim's ear and I could've made her disappear. Silk rope around the throat in her sleep and disposed of in the sea. That's how they go when the Sultim wants to make them disappear quietly.' I clung to the words. I had to get to Ayet before she got to Kadir. I had to let her know I could ruin her in return if she tried to blow my cover.

We were almost at the Weeping Wall. So close to freedom.

I heard the familiar click of pistol holsters against belts. The sound of boots hammering into the ground.

It was moments before we were surrounded by men in uniform with the Sultan and Sultim with them.

Kadir shoved his way through the ranks. He surged towards Shira. I started to move between the Sultim and my cousin. But two soldiers grabbed him first. Kadir started to fight them. 'Stand *down*. She's my wife. And a liar and a whore.' He was struggling. 'It is my right to do with her as I see fit. And I am going to make her bleed for her treason.'

Shira shifted her child against her chest, staring down Kadir, as fearless as I had ever seen her. 'I did this to stay alive. Because you are a vicious, stupid, impotent man.'

Kadir lunged for her. The Sultan gave a flick of his wrist and Kadir was pulled back by the soldiers again. 'Take my son somewhere he can regain a level head.'

'My *wife*—' Kadir started, but the Sultan cut across him.

'This is business for rulers. Not petty husbands.'

I could hear Kadir's protests as he was dragged across the garden.

'You know what the penalty is for violating your marriage vows, Shira.' The Sultan's voice was calm as they disappeared. I had an image of a moment like this, fifteen years ago: Delila being carried away as the Sultan wrapped his hands around Ahmed's mother's throat.

'Kadir will *never* father a child. He can't. And I reckon you know that, too, Your Exalted Highness.' Shira pulled herself up straight. 'I did what I had to do for our country.'

'I believe that some part of you thinks that you did,' the Sultan said. 'I always liked you, Shira; this is a shame. You were cleverer than most. I've heard that you like to strike bargains. I have one last one for you. Your son's life, in exchange for the name of the Djinni who fathered him.'

'Shira—' I warned. But it was too late.

'Fereshteh.' She raised her chin in defiance, oblivious

that she had just given the Sultan another Djinni's true name. 'He told me he would make me the mother of a ruler. A true prince. A great Sultan. A greater Sultan than Kadir could ever hope to be.'

I had never seen uncertainty on the Sultan's face before. But I thought I saw it there for just a moment. And I couldn't blame him. A truth out of a Djinni's mouth was a powerful thing. If Shira wasn't lying, she might be holding a future ruler.

'Fereshteh,' the Sultan repeated. 'Good. Take the child, Amani.' It was an order and I was already fighting my arms' urge to obey.

'What will happen to Shira?' My arms were moving without my meaning them to. The Sultan had never looked so much like Ahmed as he did in that moment. It was the same face Ahmed wore when he told me something he knew I didn't want to hear but that had to be done anyway. 'Please,' I said. Shira was whispering to her son, making him promises she wasn't going to be able to keep. Clutching at the only moments she was going to have with her child. My mind was racing, trying to find something. An escape, anything. But we were trapped. Some things there was just no way out of. Her child was in my arms. 'Please don't kill her.'

My cousin's eyes met mine. Her lips parted. The Sultan's words came back to me. Shira was good at making bargains. And she had one last thing to trade. One last coin she could try to buy her life with. Me. She could offer the Sultan the Blue-Eyed Bandit and the whole Rebellion in exchange for her life.

She could destroy me now. I didn't have anything.

'His name is Fadi,' she said. Fadi was our grandfather's name. The name our mothers had before they were married.

'Lock her away,' the Sultan ordered dispassionately, already turning. Already forgetting her now that she was just another useless girl in the harem. 'Amani, come with me. Bring the child.'

Fadi wailed louder in my arms the further away we got from his mother.

Chapter 32

The Traitor Djinni

In the days that only immortals remembered, the world was changeless. The sun did not rise or set. The sea had no tides. The Djinn had no fear, nor joy, nor grief, nor pain. Nothing lived or died. Everything just was.

Then the First War came.

It brought with it dawn and dusk. It brought with it high seas and new mountains and valleys. And more than anything, it brought mortality.

The humans were made with a spark of Djinni fire, but they were not endless. And that seemed to make all the difference in the world. That changed everything. They didn't just exist. They were born and they died. And in between they felt so much that it drew the immortals to them, though they were only sparks to the Djinn's greater fires.

As the war ended, the Djinn of the great desert gathered and gazed across a changed world. The land that had been theirs. The war had ended. The mortals had served their purpose. They had fought. They had died.

Then they multiplied.

The Djinn looked on incredulously as the humans built walls and cities and found a life outside of war. They found new wars to fight. The Djinn wondered if they should let the humans carry on. The Djinn had made the mortals; now the war was over, they could unmake them if they so chose.

Some of the Djinn argued that humanity had served its purpose. Humans would only cause trouble. Better to burn them now, all at once. Return them to the earth from which they had been made before they overran it.

The Djinni Fereshteh agreed with this. The world was simpler before mortals. He had watched his own son, born to a human woman, survive a dozen battles with the Destroyer of Worlds's creatures, only to die in a brawl with another mortal. And though the Djinn had quickly forgotten to be afraid of death when the Destroyer of Worlds was defeated, they were slower to forget this new thing the humans called grief. It seemed like a feeling too great to contain for a Djinni who was eternal.

But the Djinni Darayavahush argued against destroying them. He said humans should be allowed to live. They had earned their right to share the earth by defeating the Destroyer of Worlds. They were remarkable; they had fallen in waves on hundreds of battlefields but had somehow continued to stand in the way of the Destroyer of Worlds's armies. Such will to survive should not be ignored.

The Djinn argued as years passed and a generation of humans passed into another. They argued as cities rose where there had been none before and new rulers succeeded old ones for the throne. As the mortals slowly forgot the time of the Destroyer of Worlds.

Finally, when the last of the mortals who had lived to see the First War passed into death, the Djinn gathered at the home of one among them who had claimed an old battlefield as his domain, a place where the earth had been ripped into a great valley where no other Djinn wished to live. They decided on a vote. They would cast a black stone into the water if they believed it was best to end mortality, and a white stone to let the mortals live.

The stones piled up, black, then white, one after another, until the two sides were exactly equally matched and only the Djinni Bahadur was left to cast a vote that would decide the fate of all of humanity.

Fereshteh felt sure that Bahadur would cast for his side. Bahadur, too, had watched a mortal child of his die. A daughter with blue eyes and the sun in her hands who the humans called a princess, one of their foolish words to pretend any one of them was more powerful than another. Surely Bahadur had felt the same pain Fereshteh had. He would want to end it just as much.

And yet when Bahadur finally cast his stone, it was as white as bone. Fereshteh's side lost. And thus all the Djinn made an oath – that none among them would annihilate mortality. And because they were Djinn that oath was the truth.

Centuries passed.

Fereshteh didn't know how many, for only those whose days were numbered counted them. He tried to stay away from the humans at first. But they were constantly changing. It was hard not to watch them. Every time Fereshteh thought he had grown bored of them they did something new. They made something new, sometimes out of nothing. Palaces rose higher than before. Train tracks carried them across the desert. Music sprang seemingly from their minds to their fingers. And every so often Fereshteh could not resist temptation any more. But time taught him ways to avoid the grief. He never looked over the children he gave mortal women. He had no interest in watching little pieces of himself be destroyed by the world his fellow Djinn had allowed to continue.

Then there came a day when Fereshteh heard his name being called with an order he could not disobey. And so it was that he came to stand prisoner in front of a Sultan and a Demdji. A Demdji holding a child that Fereshteh had marked as his own, though he had already forgotten the child's mother. It was easier that way.

But he remembered all his children. And he remembered the pain he had felt when each of them died. So when the Sultan held a knife above this child, and asked for the names of his fellow Djinn, he surrendered easily. He could not watch this spark of himself die.

He gave Darayavahush's name first. He gave the Sultan only the names of the Djinn who had been stupid enough to think that humanity was harmless and worth saving. The ones who had cast a vote to let them live. Half the Djinn in the desert.

And he laughed as, one by one, they became trapped by the creatures they had chosen to let live.

Chapter 33

The Sultan had been dangerous enough with one Djinni. Now he had an army of them. They might've created humanity to fight their wars, but there were stories of what happened when immortals entered the wars of men, too. Cruel conquerors who leashed them in iron and turned their powers against helpless nations. The heroes who won Djinn over to their side by sheer virtue and flattened their enemies. No matter what the circumstances, immortals were unstoppable.

My thoughts were in a storm as the Sultan led me back to the harem, one firm hand on my spine. There was too much to do and not enough time.

I had to get news of the other Djinn to Sam. And I had to make sure Fadi, who was screaming in my arms, was safe in the palace. I had to find a way to save Shira. And I had to do it before Ayet betrayed me to the Sultan. Shira giving birth had distracted everyone, but it was only a matter of time now before Ayet got Kadir or someone else to listen to her and the Sultan found out I was the Blue-Eyed Bandit. And then it would be over. I had to do everything I could to help before it all ended.

'Father.' My thoughts were interrupted by Rahim. He was striding down the hallway toward us, his collar unfastened, hair dishevelled, trailed by two servants. Dawn was just breaking but he looked like he hadn't had any sleep all night. He would be in trouble too when Ayet sold me out. What was he still doing here? 'A word.'

He drew his father to one side, out of earshot from me, leaning in close to say something rapid-fire under his breath. I was suddenly nervous. He was still here, and there was no way Rahim would let Leyla's life be put in danger. He'd choose her over me in a second. I had no doubt about that. Same as I'd do for any of the Rebellion over the two of them. I didn't begrudge him that. But it hadn't ever crossed my mind that he might save his own skin by selling mine out instead of waiting until Ayet could do it for us.

'Forgive me.' The two servants with Rahim stepped in front of me, blocking my view of my so-called ally. One was reaching for Fadi in my arms expectantly, her head bowed.

'No.' I pulled Fadi closer to my pounding heart. I wasn't going to hand him over. I might not be able to do anything else before I got found out, but I wasn't about to let another Demdji get swallowed up in the harem and disappear.

'He needs to be fed.' The second servant spoke up, a note of exasperation in her voice. 'Now's not the time to be difficult.' It was the closest I'd ever seen to insolence in one of the harem servants. It made me look twice at her, but in spite of her voice, her head was bowed low in respect. She'd said it loud enough for the Sultan's eyes to dart over.

'Hand it over, Amani.' The Sultan gave me a distracted order as he continued his conversation with Rahim. I tried to catch his eye over his father's shoulder, but Rahim might as well never have known me for all the attention he was giving me.

'It's all right.' The first servant, too, sounded familiar somehow, although I was sure I'd never seen her in the harem before. 'We'll take good care of him.'

In that moment, as the Sultan turned his back entirely on us, the first servant dared to lift her head fully and I was face-to-face with Hala.

She was hiding her golden skin from sight with an illusion but it was still umistakably her. It was unsettling; she was both wholly familiar and completely strange. Her high, arrogant cheekbones and long nose were unmistakable, but she looked younger and more vulnerable without her golden veneer.

And the other servant. I looked closer now. Her eyes were wrong. They weren't the desert dark they ought to have been. Instead they were the colour of liquid gold.

Imin.

My heart sped up. Something was in motion. But I wasn't sure what.

Imin winked at me. It was so quick that even if the Sultan had noticed, it would've been mistaken for a blink. I loosened my grip on the baby in my arms as I passed him over to Hala. I'd been given an order, yes, but there weren't many people in the world I'd trust with Fadi more than Hala. She might not scream maternal instinct, but Demdji took care of their own.

I didn't have time to watch them disappear into the harem before Imin grabbed my arm. 'Walk quickly. And don't look back.'

'What's happening?' I asked under my breath as we moved fast down the hallway. Too quickly, I realised. If the Sultan took his eyes off Rahim for even a second, he'd realise I was all but running.

'Something that passes for a plan at short notice, that's what. Take a right here.' We turned the corner and then we were out of the Sultan's view. Rahim wasn't betraying us, I realised; he was a distraction. I felt suddenly ashamed for believing he'd turn on us so easily.

By the time he was done talking to his father, the Sultan would think I was back in the harem. If he wondered at all.

'Fadi, the baby,' I started. 'The Sultan will look for him, you need to—' Imin's eyes rolled to the sky, cutting me off.

'Believe it or not, we *can* make a stab at executing a plan without you.' Imin slowed down as we left the cool of the marble palace walls and passed into one of the huge, sprawling gardens. It was only early morning, so the unrelenting heat of the day hadn't set in yet, but I still squinted against the sun after the dark of the vaults.

We stopped, ducking behind a tree, out of sight of anyone who might walk by. Imin yanked the servant's clothes off in one quick gesture. Underneath was a palace guard's uniform that had been made for someone a whole lot taller and broader. Imin started unrolling the sleeves and loosening the belt buckle, making room for a new body. 'We can't just walk a baby out of the harem. Someone would notice he was gone. Unless the Sultan thinks he's dead, that is. If, say, half of the harem were to see Kadir drown the baby in a fit of rage, for instance.'

Hala could do that. That's why they'd risk bringing her into the palace. All she'd have to do was take Fadi back to the harem and then play the scene out in the heads of whoever happened to be nearby. She could even put it into Kadir's head if she wanted to. She could make him believe he'd really killed him. And even if she didn't get to Kadir, who would the Sultan believe, a dozen wives and daughters in the harem who saw it happen, or a son with a violent temper? Especially when the child was nowhere to be found. 'Then my dear sister can just walk him out the palace door to safety under the cover of an illusion.' Imin shook out the long sleeves so they fell over the dainty hands of her female form. 'It's almost easy.'

Imin was right. This could work. We could save Fadi. 'And his mother?' I asked, anticipation building in my chest. 'My cousin Shira – how do we get her out?'

'We're not going to—' Imin started, then quickly stopped herself before she could truth-tell the future. But I knew what she had been about to say. *We're not going to save Shira.* It didn't matter whether she said it or not; it seemed like it was already decided.

'Why?' I asked. 'If we can get Fadi out, why not Shira? Sam has clearly just walked you and Hala through the walls, he could—'

'The prison is iron bars all the way through; there's no way for Sam to walk in there and walk her back out.' Imin didn't meet my eyes. 'But I can walk *you* in there to see her before she's executed.' So that was what the guard's uniform was for. 'She's asking for you.'

'That's not a good reason not to save her.' Imin was holding the truth back. I just didn't know why. 'If Hala wanted to, she could get a soldier to unlock Shira's cell and walk her out under the Sultan's nose. Which means there's some other reason saving Shira's not part of the plan.' It wasn't a question. 'Why?'

Imin straightened. She was drowning in the guard's uniform. She looked liked a child playing dress-up in grown-up's garb. But her face was wise beyond her eighteen years. 'Because we haven't given up on saving *you* yet.' Understanding hit me all at once. Because if Shira disappeared, I might as well turn myself in. An infant could disappear believably, but Shira's death couldn't be faked near so easy. If she was gone, she'd be counted as escaped. And sooner or later the Sultan's eyes would turn to me, the girl who had already tried to help her once. And he would ask questions and I would sell out the whole Rebellion with a word.

It was Shira or everyone else.

'But Ayet—' I started to tell her that I was already done for. That I'd been stupid and careless and gotten myself caught. That it was over for me anyway.

'You don't need to worry about Ayet.' Imin started to shape-shift, to fill out the uniform. He was a head taller than I was in a few seconds.

'What do you mean?'

He didn't answer, scratching at his chin angrily as it filled out with a beard. 'I hate these things.' Whichever soldier's shape he was stealing had a voice for giving orders, deep and ponderous. 'Navid has been growing a beard since we fled camp so now kissing him is like rubbing my face against burlap. You're lucky Jin's always been clean-shaven, you know.'

'At least Navid doesn't occasionally vanish to parts unknown on you,' I offered back. I pressed my palms against my eyes, pushing back against the exhaustion. 'So we're supposed to just let Shira die?'

'The way it seems to me, one of you has to,' Imin said. 'If you really wanted me to, I could save her. But I'd have to kill you here and now so that you couldn't betray us.' He drummed his fingers along the knife at his belt. I knew Imin meant it. He'd do anything for this rebellion, just like any of us. And that'd include killing me. 'You can do a lot more for the Rebellion alive. And she—' Imin hesitated, like he didn't want to say it. But he was a Demdji. He had to be truthful. 'She can do a lot more by dying.'

Even in summer it wasn't warm in the palace prison. I felt the chill sink into my bones as Imin and I descended the worn stone steps. The guard at the door hadn't even tried to stop us after one glance at Imin in uniform. We would be left alone down here.

Shira was shivering in a corner, wearing the same clothes she'd given birth in, her back turned to the door. I took a step toward her, but Imin stopped me, one hand on my shoulder. He pointed toward the cell neighbouring Shira's.

It took only a few steps closer to the cell to realise that what I'd thought was a pile of discarded clothing was moving. Just barely. Only the faint rise and fall of breathing. It was a woman, collapsed on her side, dark hair spilling across her face. But I knew the khalat she was wearing, the colour of roses with stitching the same shade as overripe cherries. It was the same one she'd worn that day in the menagerie.

'Ayet?'

'It's no good.' Shira still had her back to us. 'She doesn't talk any more. She might as well be dead except she's still breathing.' Like Sayyida and Uzma. Driven mad. This was what Imin meant by saying that I didn't need to worry about Ayet betraying me. Slowly Shira turned over, working her way to sitting with the help of the wall. 'You wanted to know where girls disappear to.' She waved one hand in a gesture so grand she might've been showing off a golden-domed palace. 'This is where we go. I told you I had nothing to do with it.' She dropped her arm; it fell limp to her side. 'Good news is, only one of us has to die today.'

'Shira—'

'Don't try to comfort me.' Her tone was the same

one she'd used when we shared a floor in Dustwalk, dripping with disdain. But she didn't fool me that easy any more. She was a desperate girl. 'And *you*,' she shot at Imin, who was hovering behind me on the stairs, 'you don't have to watch us like that, you know. I'm already condemned to die. What else am I *possibly* going to get up to between now and sundown?'

Well, being condemned to death sure hadn't made her any more polite. I thought about telling her that Imin was on our side. But that wasn't what really mattered to Shira. I gave Imin the tiniest nod and he retreated back up the steps, out of earshot.

'So.' I slid down the wall next to the cell so we were sitting side by side. Seventeen years, I couldn't think of a single time we'd sat together. Not in Dustwalk. Not in the harem. It'd been us facing off against each other every single time. Now we were sitting side by side with a row of steadfast iron bars between us. 'You asked for me.'

'Funny, isn't it? The last person I ever want to see is the last person I get to see alive.'

'You don't have to explain, Shira.' Half a year and I'd started realising every conversation I had with someone in the Rebellion might be our last. Sometimes it was. But it was harder to push that out of my head when I knew for sure that Shira was a dead woman. 'Nobody wants to die alone.'

'Oh, good God, don't be so pathetic; it's depressing.' Shira rolled her eyes so far back I thought she might lose them inside her head. 'There's only one thing I want from you. Your rebel friends were here. They said—' She swallowed hard, like she was trying to hide from me that she'd hoped, even just for a second, that this might not be the end. 'They said they couldn't get me out.' A stab of guilt went through my heart. They could. But they were saving me over her. I was choosing my new family over my old. 'But they said they would help Fadi.' She opened her eyes, her fingers curling around the bars. 'I didn't become Sultima by trusting anyone and everyone. I want to hear it from you. You might not be much, but you're still the only blood I've got here. Tell me my son is safe.'

'Hala's gotten him out of the palace.' As the words spilled off my tongue I knew they were true. 'We can protect him.'

A tension I hadn't even realised was there fled her body as I spoke, a fear she'd been holding deep in her bones since the first time I'd seen her in the baths. Had she looked at me that day, my Demdji eyes, and understood that she was going to be done for on the day she gave birth? Before I knew the harem, I might've asked why she'd taken the risk of lying with anyone other than her husband. If she was really stupid and arrogant enough to think that she wouldn't suffer the same fate as Ahmed and Delila's mother. Of every other harem woman who had ever strayed into another man's arms. But I'd seen enough since entering the harem to know there were other ways to die here. Ayet was proof of that.

'Why didn't you try to sell me out to the Sultan in exchange for your own life?' It slipped out. I never believed anyone ever did anything that wasn't for themselves before the Rebellion. And there were parts of me I couldn't shake from before the Rebellion. The parts that kept me alive. 'You know who I am. You knew your life was all but forfeit. If survival in the harem is one big game, why not play your last piece?'

I knew the look she gave me from days together in the Dustwalk schoolhouse. The one she saved if you said something particularly stupid in class. The one that made sure that you knew not just that you were stupid but that she was a whole lot smarter than you. 'The Sultan doesn't make trades. Everyone knows that. He hasn't traded anything since he traded Miraji's freedom for a throne. That's a mistake you only make once. He *takes* instead. And he would've taken the knowledge of your treachery from me and then we would've both been dead. And I want *one* of us alive. I'd rather it be me, of course, but you'll have to do.' A slight smile appeared on her face at her own joke at death's doors. But it was gone quickly. 'When I'm gone I want you still around with your idiotic idealist rebellion to gut the Sultan and Kadir.' The more she talked, the more her accent leaked out through the cracks. Our accent from the Last County. 'I hate *them* and I hate what they did. And I almost succeeded in taking their throne, too.'

'Wait.' I cut her off before she could chase her own thoughts too far away from me. 'What do you mean you almost took their throne?'

'Fereshteh promised.' She said it with the certainty of a child repeating something she truly believed. Who didn't understand that promises were just words. But Fereshteh was a Djinni. If it was dangerous for Demdji to make promises, how bad was one from a real live Djinni? A thousand stories of Djinni promises granted in horrifying torturous ways tumbled towards the front of my mind.

'I figured out that the harem was an unwinnable game, early on. The only *real* way to win is by becoming the mother not just to a prince but a Sultim. Only Kadir can't sire any princes. And Fereshteh was just there, in the harem gardens one day. Like he'd stepped out of a story and into my life to save me. And he said that he could give me a son. And just like that I had a way to win the unwinnable game. To survive past Kadir losing interest in me in his bed and become the Sultima.' Her eyes were far away. 'And when I touched him he turned from fire to flesh. And he asked what I would wish for our child.'

'What do you mean, what you wished?' My mouth had gone dry.

Shira's bloodshot eyes snapped open, like she'd been startled from the edge of drifting to sleep. 'He said he could grant me a single wish for his child. Every Djinni can.'

'Shira.' I chose my words carefully. 'You've heard the stories as well as I have. A wish from a Djinni—'

'In the stories men *steal* wishes. They trick and lie and cheat for an easy way to change their fortunes. That's why the Djinn twist them. Thieves don't prosper from wishes. But if the wish is given freely ...' Then there was no need to twist it. They could really give someone their heart's desire.

'You wished for more than a prince.' But my mind wasn't wholly with Shira any more. It was racing across the sands back to Dustwalk. To my own mother. If she'd been given the chance to wish for anything, what had she wished for me? What great boon had my father granted to me? 'You wished for your son to be Sultan.'

'The only way to win the game.' Shira tipped her head back against the cold stone wall, a small sigh slipping through her lips. That was when the tears started to come. 'I wished to be the mother of a ruler. I wouldn't have to scrape to survive any more. I could have everything I ever wanted.' A Djinni's word was truth. If Fereshteh had promised Shira that Fadi would be Sultan one day, what did that mean for Ahmed? 'But I lost.' Tears rolled down her face. I'd never seen Shira cry before. It looked unnatural on her somehow.

'Shira, do you want me to go?'

'No.' She didn't open her eyes. 'You're right. Nobody wants to die alone.'

I expected to feel grief. But all I found inside was anger. And suddenly I was furious. And I didn't know who I was angry at. At myself for not getting her out quickly enough. At her for being stupid enough to get caught. At the Sultan for doing this to both of us.

'I should have wished for something else,' she said finally as the tears stopped. When she opened her eyes again there was a fire there I'd never seen in her. One I suddenly realised had been there all along. Back in Dustwalk when I thought I'd been the only one who wanted to get out as badly as I did. In the harem when I thought I was the only one hiding something. She'd just veiled it a whole lot better than I had. 'Tell me that you're going to win, Amani. That you're going to kill them all. That you're going to take our country away from them and that my son will be safe in a world that doesn't want to destroy him. That's my real wish. Tell me that.'

I opened my mouth and then closed it again, fighting for the words. Truth-telling was a dangerous game. There were so many words I wanted to say. *No harm will come to your son. I'm not going to let it. Your son will live free and grow strong and clever. He will live to watch this rotten rule crumble. He will live to see tyrants fall and heroes rise in their place. He will have the childhood we never could. He will run until his legs are tired if he wants to, just chasing the horizon, or he will grow roots here if he'd rather. He will be a son any mother would be proud of and no harm will ever come to him in the world that we are going to make after you are gone.*

It was too dangerous to promise any of that. I wasn't an all-powerful Djinni; I couldn't make promises. All I could manage was, 'I don't know what will happen, Shira. But I do know what I'm fighting for.'

'You'd better.' Shira leaned her head against the cool metal. 'Because I'm going to die for it. That's what I traded your rebellion for.' Her tears had dried now. 'I promised them that if they got my son out, I would show this city how a desert girl dies.'

The crowd in the square outside the palace was restless and roaring with noise. I could hear it before I even reached the balcony at the front of the palace. It was nearly dusk and they'd taken Shira away. They had offered her fresh clothes, but she'd turned them down. She hadn't been dragged; she hadn't fought or wailed. She'd stood up when they came for her, like a Sultima going to greet her subjects instead of a girl going to die.

She'd made me promise I would stay with her until the end. I might not be able to follow her onto the execution platform, but I wasn't about to break a promise to a dying girl. Nobody tried to stop me as I strode through the palace halls, Imin trailing me like a shadow.

I stepped through the curtains and got my first good look at Izman since the day I'd arrived. The balcony was half-shielded by a finely carved wooden latticework screen so that we could see the city without the people of the city seeing us. It overlooked a huge square, twice the size the rebel camp had taken up in the canyon. And it was filled to bursting. News of the execution of the Sultima had spread quickly. People were crowding to see a harem woman die for giving birth to a monster. It was like something out of the stories, but they were going to witness it.

The crowds jostled for a view around a stone platform that sat directly below the balcony. Looking down on it from this angle, I could see the stone wasn't as smooth as it would look from below. It was carved with scenes from the darkness of hell. Men being eaten by Skinwalkers, Nightmares feeding off a child, a woman whose head was being held aloft by a ghoul with horns. That would be the last thing anyone led to the executioner's block would see.

That was the last thing Shira was going to see.

I almost missed Tamid. He stood in the shadows of the corner looking miserable. Shira and Tamid had barely ever traded a word at home, no matter how small Dustwalk was. I got the feeling they would've hated each other if they had. But it occurred to me that Shira and Tamid had made it out of Dustwalk together. They had survived. They had survived what I'd done to them. They'd been together when I'd left them behind. That had to mean something.

'It was a mistake to arrange this execution without consulting me, Kadir.' I caught the edge of the Sultan's conversation as I brushed by. He was furious. 'The city is already restless. You should dispose of her in private. Like you did her child.' Hala had succeeded in convincing the Sultan that the harem had watched Kadir murder Fadi. Good. He was safe.

'She is my wife.' Kadir sounded violent, even in the face of his father's calmer anger. 'She is mine to do with what I please.'

Kadir spotted me as he spun away on his heel from his father. A nasty smile spread over his face. 'You' – he shot the order to Imin – 'you're dismissed. Go find somewhere else to be.'

I sensed the other Demdji tense behind me. But he couldn't refuse. He sketched a quick bow before ducking out.

'I'm glad you're here.' Kadir sidled across the balcony towards me. My eyes darted for the Sultan, inadvertently, looking for help. But his attention was elsewhere. Rahim was nowhere in sight, either. Tamid was watching us. But there'd be no help from him. Even if he didn't hate me, he was no match for a prince.

Kadir's hand found the small of my back like he thought I was some puppet and he could pull all my strings. He shoved me past two of his wives, who were watching from behind the lattice screen, hiding from the crowd, out into the open at the edge of the balcony, where I was exposed. A few eyes from the crowd drew up towards us as we appeared.

'You tried to help her get away.' Kadir leaned into me, the pressure of his body forcing me against the railing, trapping me between him and open air and the sight of my cousin below. I could feel every inch of my body that he was touching fighting back against the feeling of him pressed to me. I hated more than anything that I couldn't fight back. His breath was hot on my neck as he spoke. 'And now I want you to watch her die.'

I didn't need him to make me watch her die. No matter what happened, I would give her that. I wouldn't do it for Kadir. I'd do it for Shira. Because whatever else she was, she was my flesh and blood and she deserved that much from me. She deserved a whole lot more, in fact. But this was all I had to give.

A roar came with Shira's appearance onstage. Some of it was jeers, but those were drowned out quickly.

She had been right not to change, I realised now.

Shira in her silks and muslins and jewels and fine make-up looked like nobility. But as she was now, dressed in a plain white khalat, she looked like a desert girl. She looked like one of the crowd she was facing, not something out of the palace. Folk were cheering *for* her, I realised, not for her head.

When she stepped up onto the stone, she was still shaking, her naked feet barely holding her up.

The restless crowd settled enough to listen as the executioner started to announce her so-called crimes. Shira stood with her head held high, back as straight as an iron bar. A light breeze picked up her hair. It was long and loose around her shoulders and it moved enough to expose her neck. The wind seemed to draw her eyes up.

She tilted her head back, spotting me and Kadir on the balcony easily. She ignored her husband, locking gazes with me instead. There was a slight curve to her mouth. That was the only warning I had.

The executioner was still reading. 'For treason against the Sultim—'

'I am loyal to the *true* Sultim!' The words burst out of Shira's lips, startling the executioner into silence. 'The true Sultim, Prince Ahmed!' Her words stirred an answer in the crowd. 'He was chosen by fate at the trials! Not by the hands of his father! A father who himself defied our traditions! I know the will of the Djinn, and they are punishing these false rulers. Kadir will never be able to give our country an heir!'

A rush of pride swelled in my chest. The Sultan had been right. It was a mistake to execute her in public. Kadir had given his legendary Sultima the biggest stage in Miraji to spill all their secrets on. She was one girl, seconds away from death, and she was using her last breath to do more than a rain of pamphlets from a Roc could. Even if they silenced her now, this story would spread all over Miraji and get grander with every retelling.

'If Kadir ever sits on the throne, he will be the last Sultan of Miraji!'

Kadir shoved away from me as his Sultima spoke,

pushing back inside, shouting orders. But he was far too late. The damage was done, and silencing her now looked like they were trying to stifle the truth. I didn't move, though I caught the Sultan's gaze for just a moment. He looked resigned. As if he knew this would come out of his son's stupidity.

'He will die without an heir to take his place and our country will fall back into foreign hands.' Shira was still talking, her voice carrying over the beginnings of restlessness in the crowd. 'The same foreign hands that the false Sultan makes deals with behind closed doors. Prince Ahmed is Miraji's only hope! He is the true heir—'

She was still shouting as the guards wrestled her forward, forcing her head down onto the block. 'A new dawn!' she screamed as a guard forced her head down so hard that her chin connected with the block, opening a huge gash.

The din of the crowd was drowning out anything more she would have said, but she held my gaze as the executioner stepped up. I leaned forward, closing the distance between us as much as I could, my hips pressed against the railing, my body craning over the balcony.

I held her eyes until the axe came down.

Chapter 34

I couldn't tell where the first stone came from. It sailed out of the crowd, smacking into the wall next to the balcony.

'A new dawn!' someone screamed from the crowd. 'A new desert!' The Rebellion's cry picked up all around the square. The crowd below turned into a mob with frightening speed. Another rock flew, smacking into the screen around the balcony. The closest guard flinched back. Those out in the open with me were already retreating.

I saw the bomb as it prepared to sail. A flash of fire in the crowd. A bottle stuck with a burning cloth, aimed towards the balcony. I dove for cover inside. Even as I prepared to hit the ground, I spotted Tamid, staring through the screen, eyes pressed to the openings, fingers laced through the carved wood. I grabbed him and pulled him to the ground sprawling, even as the bottle struck the screen, exploding in a burst of flames and glass against the wood.

When I looked up, coughing, some of the screen was missing; the rest was catching fire. There was another soldier who'd been standing too close sprawled near us, crying out in agony as blood bloomed across one ruined side of his face. Tamid stared at the man, eyes wide. I supposed he wasn't quite so used to dodging death as I was.

'Bottle bombs, just like we used to make back home,' I offered, pushing myself off him. I checked around quickly, making sure no one had noticed. The chaos was a distraction. The Sultan had already vanished. Gone to safety or to give orders to fortify the palace, I figured. To quell the crowds. I just hoped the Rebellion was ready to protect them. 'We need to find cover.' I offered my former friend a hand up. 'Come on.'

Tamid got us back to his rooms safely, through hallways choked with soldiers, headed into the streets to keep the peace. Hundreds of men passing us, their boots pounding into the marble floor. He slammed the door behind us and bolted it shut. He leaned on the door for a moment, out of breath, as I slumped into the chair at his desk while he took another by the balcony.

We lapsed into uncomfortable silence. I could hear the rioting outside over our ragged breathing. Shouts of rebellion; gunfire. Once, something that sounded like an explosion. I thought I might've seen the flash of light it gave off across Tamid's face as he peered out over the city. And I was stuck in here. Helpless.

Gradually my breathing slowed as night fell outside. The rioting faded to the back of my consciousness. I was left listening to the roar of grief in my head instead. I'd been helpless to save Shira, too. I'd watched her die. I might not have always liked her. But I'd never wanted her dead. And now she was gone. Another casualty of the cause.

I could've gone back to the harem. But I wanted to be there even less than I wanted to be here. When it got too dark to see, Tamid started to work his way around the room, his metal leg clicking with every step, lighting oil lamps as he went.

There was a book open on the table. I noticed it as the lamp above it came alive. A picture fiercer than any of the faded drawings I'd ever seen in the books that found their way down to Dustwalk glared out of the pages. It was a Djinni made of blue fire standing next to a girl with blue eyes with the sun in her hands.

Princess Hawa.

'Do you have anything to drink in here?' I asked finally when the last lamp was lit and I couldn't take it any more. 'Remember in Dustwalk, when anybody died, everybody got together for a drink to honour the dead.

Or are you too holy to drink now?'

'Did you drink to me, after you left me for dead?' Tamid asked, shaking out the match.

After leaving Dustwalk I remembered drinking with Jin in a bar in Sazi. I didn't even know why I was drinking then. I wanted to say I was sorry again. But my silence spoke for me.

Tamid pulled open a cupboard. It was lined with jars and bottles of stuff that looked more like poison than booze. But he reached towards the back and pulled out a half-empty bottle with the label scratched off. There was no mistaking the amber liquid inside. 'I only drank because you were a bad influence, anyway.' He pulled the cork from the bottle.

'I only have one glass.' He poured a measure into a glass and another into an empty jar. 'I don't get that many guests around here.' He handed me the jar.

That wasn't what it had looked like with Leyla, but maybe they had better things to do than drink together. 'The jar is clean, I promise. If I wanted you dead, you're right, I could've already done it.'

'To the dead,' I said. I took a sip, burning away the smart retort on the tip of my tongue before I could say something I'd regret. 'Who weren't so lucky as me.'

Tamid rolled his glass between his palms. 'I didn't think you'd care about Shira.'

I wished I had it in me to be angry about that. But he wasn't wrong. The girl I was when I'd left Tamid bleeding in the sand wouldn't have cared. But the world was bigger than Dustwalk, it turned out. 'Well, I guess you were wrong.'

We fell silent again as I sipped at my liquor, letting it burn on the way down. Tamid just stared at his own glass. Finally he seemed to decide something. 'Leyla says you're planning to abduct me.'

'*Abduct* is an awfully strong word.' I'd accused Jin of abducting me once. But we'd both known that was a lie. I'd wanted to go. Even if it had meant leaving Tamid. 'But yeah, more or less.'

'Why? Is it just that you don't want me helping the Sultan any more?' He didn't look at me. 'Or did Leyla just ask you too sweetly to refuse? Or is it that – what was it you said? You're in the business of saving lives now?' There was scorn on his tongue but he was giving me a chance to be honest with him. I couldn't waste it.

'Because I wouldn't leave you behind if I got the chance again.' It slipped out as easily as only the truth could. My gaze was fixed on his fake leg. 'You never wanted to run away with me.'

'And that was a reason to leave me to die, was it?' It had been the wrong thing to say. He leaned away from me, taking away whatever small distance I'd closed

416

between us by saving him on the balcony. By sharing a drink with him here.

'That's not what I meant and you know it.' I didn't want to fight with him. I didn't want to fight any more at all today. I just wanted my friend back when I'd already lost one to the executioner. 'I'm just saying, you wouldn't even run away from somewhere you hated with your oldest friend. I'm having trouble imagining that you've now become the sort to run off with a princess. Are you really going to leave with Leyla? You're not going to try to snitch on us to her father?' I tried to sound disinterested. But a lot of folk would die if Tamid decided he was loyal to the Sultan. 'You can't blame me for having my doubts. Between the two of us, there's only one who's in a habit of running away with royalty.'

Tamid looked up at me over his glass so fast I knew he'd been faking disinterest in me. 'That foreigner who stole the Buraqi was royalty?'

I realised I'd said it without meaning to. Slipped out as natural as if I could still trust Tamid.

'His name is Jin,' I said. 'And yes.'

'Where is he now?'

I'd managed not to ask myself that question since Ayet had caught me with Sam in the garden. But in that moment, when I was sure she was going to turn us in and it was all going to end, one stupid thought had flitted through my head.

I wasn't ever going to see Jin again.

I might die and he was off doing God knew what, God knew where, with God knew who.

The thought that had chased it was selfish: If he were here, Jin wouldn't let me die. He would leave the captured Djinn in the Sultan's hands, risk everything, before he'd let me die.

'Your guess is as good as mine.' I drank.

'Not all that great being left behind by someone you're in love with, is it?' Tamid raised his glass in a salute before taking a sip.

You only ever thought you were in love with me. But I couldn't say it out loud. That caught me off guard. 'No,' I admitted into my drink. 'It's not.' We were silent. 'What about you and Leyla?' I asked finally. 'Where will you two go if we do get you out?'

'Maybe home.' Tamid shrugged. 'Back to Dustwalk.'

I scoffed without meaning to. Tamid looked up, offended. 'Oh, come on,' I defended. 'Maybe you didn't want to leave like you did, but don't tell me after seeing everything else that's out here, you just want to go back to that hellhole. Or do you have fonder memories of all the names that town called you than I do?'

'I'm not like you, Amani. All I ever wanted was a

418

simple life as a Holy Man with a wife. I always figured you'd change your mind and see it my way eventually.' Dark eyes darted to me before sliding away again. The memory of him proposing marriage was heavy between us.

There was a part of him that still didn't understand. I could see that now, more clearly than I'd ever been able to back in Dustwalk. I'd move the whole world to make up for what I'd done to Tamid. But I wouldn't ever give it up for him. Not for anyone. The difference was, Jin had never asked me to. He'd taken my hand to show it to me instead. 'This life – Djinn, princes – it's too much for me. I haven't changed my mind about what I want in this life, Amani. And neither have you.'

A thought struck me and I couldn't hold back the laugh that bubbled up. I pressed the back of my hand to my mouth as I nearly choked on my drink. Tamid looked at me askance. 'I'm not laughing at you.' I waved a hand at him, my nose burning from the liquor. 'I was just – I was trying to picture your father if you brought a princess home for a wife.'

I saw it dawn on Tamid's face, too. He rolled his eyes skyward. 'God save me.' Tamid's father was a hard man. He'd tried to drown Tamid as a baby when he was born with a crooked leg. He was also patriotic to the very core. He invoked the Sultan's name at every occasion. *What would the Sultan think of my weakling of a son, Tamid? What would the Sultan think that a boy in his country can be bested by a girl, Tamid?*

'What would the Sultan think of you taking his daughter to wife, Tamid?' I did my best imitation of Tamid's father, like I had when we lived in Dustwalk. Tamid dropped his head into his hands, but he was smiling as I laughed, the alcohol making me feel lighter.

'What about *you*?' Tamid rolled his glass between his hands, the faint smile lingering. 'You can't leave. In this grand escape plan, what happens to you?'

I'd been wondering that, too. The thought was suddenly sobering. Shazad had always been willing to give up her own life for the Rebellion. But I didn't know whether she'd be willing to give up mine or if I'd have to do it myself. Imin had already volunteered if she couldn't. 'I don't leave this palace so long as the Sultan's got control over me.' I tried to shrug casually. But Tamid had known me far too long. He could read me better than anyone.

Almost anyone. Jin had understood who I was better than Tamid ever had. And Shazad had seen who I could be. Tamid had always seen who he wanted to. But he still knew when I was hiding something. *Traitor eyes.*

'I'd die for this, Tamid. I don't want to have to. I'd do just about anything to not have to.' I listened to the roar of the crowds outside. 'But it's a whole lot bigger than my life or anyone else's.'

Tamid set his glass down. 'I want you to know I don't believe in your rebellion.'

'I figured.' I downed the rest of my drink.

'And your prince is as likely to destroy this country as anything else.' I figured that, too. But I didn't say that. 'But you were right: I don't hate you enough to want to watch you die. Take your shirt off.' That wasn't what I'd been expecting him to say.

'Do you say that to all the girls?' It slipped out. It was a stupid thing to say to someone who wasn't my friend any more. Who'd been in love with me once. It was stupid to make a joke when Shira's blood was still cooling in the square and the riot in the streets was still raging. But against all odds, Tamid laughed. He laughed exactly like he used to, with a slight roll of his eyes, like he wanted me to think he was humouring me by laughing. But I knew him better than that.

'No,' Tamid picked up a tiny knife with a blade no longer than one of my fingernails. 'Just the ones I'm about to cut a piece of bronze out of.'

He was serious, I realised. He was going to help me. He knew where the pieces of metal in my skin were. He could take out the one controlling me. That forced me to stay here.

He was going to save my life.

Chapter 35

I could hear Auranzeb already starting on the other side of the wall. The sound of laughter drifted through, high and clear like a bell, a riot of voices, Mirajin and foreign alike, and music running like a soft current underneath.

We stood in the shadow of the harem walls outside the gate, whispering knots of perfectly made-up girls all around me. They kept their distance from me. Nobody in the harem seemed to know exactly what I'd had to do with the events around the blessed Sultima, but that hadn't stopped the rumours from spreading. Some were even saying they'd seen me help Kadir drown Fadi. I knew they were lying because Hala wasn't stupid or spiteful enough to plant that image in their heads. I cast around for Leyla, an ally, but I couldn't find her in the dim light leaking through from the other garden. The shuffle of cloth and breathing and the occasional excited whisper were the only sounds to be heard on our side. We were like penned creatures, waiting. I forced out a long breath, trying to calm my racing heart.

This was it. Tonight we freed the Djinn and Leyla. And one way or another it was my last night in the harem.

My left hand strayed to my side, a nervous habit I'd been trying to break the last few days. The last thing I needed was anyone noticing the tiny healing cut under my arm where Tamid had sliced the piece of bronze out of my skin. The iron was still there. He told me without meeting my gaze that he hadn't exactly planned on getting the shards of metal out, that I might bleed out if he tried. But I understood the truth of it. He was willing to help me escape, but he wasn't going to help the Rebellion by giving me back my power. He wasn't a Traitor like me.

The riots had lasted all night after Shira died. They were being called the Blessed Sultima's Uprising, for now. But stories were written by the winners. If we lost this war, chances were the name would change to the Disgraced Sultima's Uprising. They'd left a tension in the air that put a frantic damper on the preparations for Auranzeb. I could feel it even inside the safety of the palace walls.

When daybreak had come after the night of rioting, the Rebellion had claimed part of the city. Sam told me our side had used the riots to erect barricades all the way, hemming off most of the slums and some other parts of the city to claim them in the name of the Rebellion.

In one night we'd taken rebel ground in the capital itself. If that didn't send a message, I didn't know what would. There were suns painted on buildings across the city and, most unsettlingly, there was one in bright red paint smeared on a wall at the heart of the palace. Nobody could account for that, except for Imin, that is. But she was now a tiny, doe-eyed servant in the kitchen, and no one would suspect someone so small to be able to reach that high.

The dawn had also found the streets littered with bodies. A whole lot of them were wearing uniforms. According to Sam, Shazad had run a flawless strategy even if it was in city streets instead of a battlefield. And even if some of her troops thought they were just looting and burning, she'd managed to nudge them carefully one way or another, leading them like soldiers even if they didn't know it.

Still, even though we'd won more than we'd lost, there was a nervous edge among the rebels. If there was ever a time for the Sultan to turn his new Djinni army out against us, it was now.

But it'd been three days and no immortals walked the streets yet. This was still a war among humans. And Demdji. And tonight I was about to get back to the side I belonged on.

The servants of the harem had dressed me in Mirajin colours. White and gold. Like the army. Only I looked like a different kind of soldier. The white glowed pale and rich next to my desert-dark skin. The cloth clung to my skin like a lover's fingers, ending in a hem heavy with golden stitching that climbed upwards, scattered with pearls. I imagined walking past Kadir's wives, and them grabbing at my khalat like they did at the pearls underwater. My arms were bare from the elbows down, except where golden bracelets rattled heavily at my wrists. In the burnished light, the gold powder that had been dusted over my whole body made it seem like the sun lived under my skin.

They had clucked over my shorn hair before finally resigning themselves to running sweet-smelling oils through it so that it stayed straight. They wove my hair through with strands of pure gold, threads of it that mixed in with the black and caught the light. I found it hard to care about my shorn hair any more. Whatever anger I'd ever had at Ayet left me when I saw her curled up on the floor of the prison, dead-eyed. She'd fought and she'd lost and I felt sorry for her.

When they were done they crowned me with a tiny circlet made of miniature gold leaves with pearls as berries. My mouth had been stained darker gold.

Every woman from the harem who was being allowed into the party was dressed in the same colours I was, Mirajin gold and white. But I was blinding. Like some untouchable gold sculpture that had been crafted to place in a palace and be admired. There was nothing of the desert girl left. I looked more beautiful than I'd ever seen myself, but unnatural, like a stranger.

But I knew who I was. I was still a rebel.

And tonight we were going to strike a real blow.

'Announcing' – the call came from the other side of the door – 'the flowers of the harem.' A hush fell over the crowd, expectant. The doors swung open. The girls around me rushed forward like children towards a new gift. I was jostled as I followed at a slower pace. I imagined for the guests it was like watching birds burst free from their cages, a surge of white and gold as we were released among the people.

The gardens were seductive in the late afternoon light. Fountains bubbled happily among guests in their finest clothes, music twisting its spell with the smells of jasmine and sweet food. High above us the sky was strung with golden ropes from one side of the garden to the other; small glass decorations hung from them, catching the light. When I craned my head back I saw they were crystal birds hanging from the golden wires. A servant passed me with a tray of soft cakes dusted in white powder. I took one and shoved it into my mouth, tasting the sugar exploding on my tongue as it melted there. I tried to savour it, but it dissolved quickly, until only the memory was left between the tip of my tongue and the top of my mouth.

I heard whispers go up in the crowd as we passed. The Albish queen's eyes swept over one of the girls, who was wearing a sheer muslin dress that showed a whole lot more of her than you'd expect, and glanced away in disgust, smoothing her hands over her own full, heavy skirts.

I ignored her, my eyes darting around for faces I knew, for Shazad or Rahim. I caught the Sultan's gaze through the crowd. Some of the revellers looked like they'd already started celebrating like the next dawn would never come. But not our exalted ruler. He was as sharp as anything. He raised a still-full glass to me in greeting before his attention was pulled elsewhere. I let out a long breath. I couldn't look suspicious. I took a slow route around the gardens instead. Like I wasn't looking for anyone at all.

Rahim found me before I could make it very far. 'I've been assigned to keep an eye on you tonight by my exalted father.' He was wearing a crisp white dress uniform and a sword at his side that didn't look decorative to me. 'There are a fair few foreigners around and apparently even after nearly getting you killed once I can still be trusted.'

'Once I lost someone a hand during an ambush.' It'd been early days in the Rebellion. After Fahali, before getting a bullet to the stomach. 'It was my fault. When Ahmed sent me out again in a similar raid, I asked if he was really going to trust me. He said I was a lot less likely to make the mistake a second time than someone else was to make it the first.'

'Well, let's hope that's the only thing my brother and my exalted father have in common. On that note, let's go find your rebellion.' He extended an arm to me. I held up my gold-dusted hands apologetically. 'Ah,' he dropped his arm. 'Of course: look but don't touch.'

We walked side by side through the glow of the garden. On a night like this, it would be easy to forget we were celebrating the Sultan's coup. Two decades ago to the day, he had allied with the Gallan and taken our country by force. The sun had gone down with Sultan Oman's father on the throne. Dawn had found him dead in his bed, and the palace packed with Gallan uniforms. The Sultim was found face down in a garden, like he had tried to run. Many of the Sultan's other brothers met the same fate. He couldn't afford any challenges to the throne. He'd left only the women and the brothers who were younger than him alive ... Twenty years ago tonight the palace had been full of death and blood; now soft lights and music drifted through the walls and the buzz of conversation seemed to lull us all away from any memories of that night.

Except there were the statues. Among the guests and the musicians and the servants passing around wine and food, the garden was dotted with statues made of what looked like clay and bronze. They were frozen in agonisingly twisted shapes, buckled to their knees, arms up like they were protecting themselves.

'I knew Prince Hakim when he was a boy, you know.' The speaker was some Mirajin lord or other, talking to a young, pretty girl. He was gesturing at a statue.

They were the princes. Bronze sculptures of the twelve princes the Sultan had killed when he took his throne.

Someone had rested a glass in one of their upturned palms, leaving the dead prince's agonised face to stare up at a half-finished wineglass smudged with oily fingerprints.

'Well, those are in bad taste,' a voice said in my ear, making me jump. A server was standing by my elbow with a tray piled with basbousa. I had an odd feeling of recognising him, only I didn't. Until he rolled his eyes skywards.

'Imin.' I cast around carefully in case we were overheard.

'Those colours don't suit you at all, by the way.' His eyes swept me appraisingly. If I'd had any doubt left in my mind that it was him, it evaporated at the disdain in those bright yellow eyes that betrayed him as a Demdji.

'He's one of yours?' Rahim guessed. 'How did he get in?' He didn't know the half of it and now wasn't the time to explain that Imin was the same tiny female servant Rahim had helped abduct Shira's baby a few days earlier.

'I've got my ways.' Imin took a piece of the sweet cake off his own tray and put it in his mouth. 'Shazad is looking for you two.' He licked his fingers clean and pointed. Shazad was a little way off, hair wrapped in tight braids around her head, like a crown. 'She says it's high time you kept up your side of the bargain and introduced us to whoever's got this so-called army of yours.'

'*She's* with your rebellion?' Rahim inspected Shazad sceptically across the garden. 'General Hamad's daughter? I always thought she was just a pretty face.'

'So does everyone else,' I said. 'That's how we

figured she wouldn't get searched too closely on the way in. Shazad's the one who carried in enough explosives to free every Djinni down in the vaults.'

'Explosives,' Rahim repeated. He sounded nervous.

'You didn't tell him the plan?' Imin asked, shoving more food into his mouth.

'We didn't even *have* a plan until a few days ago,' I said defensively. 'I've been busy since then.' My hand drifted again to the tiny cut in my side.

Imin turned to Rahim. 'According to Shazad, every Auranzeb, when the sun sets, the Sultan gives a speech, which means that all eyes will be on him. Using that as cover, Sam will sneak Amani and Shazad through the walls and out of the party.' Imin jerked his head sideways, indicating our impostor Blue-Eyed Bandit. My eyes skated straight over him before I spied him. He was dressed in an Albish army uniform. So that was how he was getting around inconspicuously.

'Isn't it a crime to impersonate a soldier?' My heart was starting to beat painfully in my chest now. There was so much that could go wrong tonight. Not being wholly sure I could count on Sam was just one of them.

'I hear it's a crime to desert the Albish army, too.' Imin sucked on his teeth, moving around a seed caught there. He made a terrible servant. It was amazing that he'd gotten this far without getting caught. But he was right:

the uniform fit Sam too well to have been stolen. Too well to be anything but tailored for him. My eyes went to the congregation of Albish soldiers, accompanying their queen here. It was a huge risk he was taking, as a deserter in their midst. And he was taking it for us.

Even as I watched him, his eyes dashed across the garden, landing on Shazad, who had started to cross the garden toward us. Sam's eyes never left her. No, I realized, not exactly for *us*. Damn. I'd seen men fall for Shazad before but I'd never seen her fall back. This couldn't end well.

'Hala will meet you on the other side of the wall,' Imin went on. 'She'll make you disappear long enough that you can get to the Djinn and set the explosives.'

'And my sister?' Rahim asked. He was casting around the garden for her. Come to think of it, I still hadn't seen her, either.

'You're not a very patient man.' Imin took his time, deliberately chewing. 'If everything goes according to plan, Sam will get Shazad and Amani out of the palace straight from the vaults, and then double back through *that* wall for you and your sister.' He nodded again, the other way this time.

'You get Leyla, and wait for Sam in the southeast corner of the garden, away from the chaos that's bound to come when something blows up in the palace,' I said, shifting carefully as someone brushed past us, dangerously close to overhearing our conversation.

'Then we figured Hala will get Tamid out under cover of an illusion, and I will get out in the chaos, just looking like another servant running from an explosion. What could possibly go wrong?'

'A lot could go wrong,' Rahim pointed out.

'It's still far from being the worst plan we've ever come up with.' I tried to comfort him.

'No, the worst we've ever come up with ended with you flooding a prayer house,' Imin offered, which was true but far from helpful right now. 'So that's not really saying much.'

'Everybody survived that,' I said defensively. Rahim was looking at me, an uneasy look on his face.

'Welcome to the Rebellion.' Shazad had reached us; she greeted Rahim with a devastating smile. 'We make do with what we can get. Now, are you going to give us an army or not?'

We found Lord Bilal, Emir of Iliaz, leaning against one of the grotesque sculptures, eyes hooded. He was young, but he looked like he was already exhausted by life, or maybe by his own importance. It didn't seem smart to tell him that out loud when we were trying to form an alliance. I probably ought to let Shazad talk.

'So.' Lord Bilal looked me over. 'You're the blue-eyed rebel everyone is talking about.' He glanced at Shazad. 'And you must be the face of the operation. You're too pretty to be anything else.' I watched my friend bite down on her annoyance.

'And you're the emir looking to turn rebel.' She wore a bright smile the whole time and flapped her hands airily. Looking at her you'd think she was just a beautiful girl flirting with a man. Not a rebel planning a full-scale war. I realised why he'd chosen to wait for us here, in this corner of the garden. The music that drifted through the walls covered any conversation around us. I could only guess it covered our words, too. Still, Shazad spoke quietly.

'I'm my father's son.' Lord Bilal shrugged one elaborately tasselled shoulder lazily. I thought I caught what looked like a sceptical eyeroll from Rahim. But when I looked at him head on, he was ever the soldier. Rahim had served under Lord Bilal's father first. He'd know better than anyone if the son lived up to the father. 'My father had no loyalty to the throne. He never forgave Sultan Oman for turning Miraji over to foreign hands. He used to go on and on about how Iliaz is the most powerful county in Miraji, how the rest of the country depended on us. He'd tell you until your ears bled how Iliaz didn't need the rest of Miraji. It could survive as an independent nation.'

'Are you saying you want your own country in exchange for your army?' That sure wasn't asking for much.

'Are you in a position to negotiate that with me?'

Abducting Delila without permission was one thing. Giving away part of Ahmed's country without his permission, that wasn't something even Shazad and I could do. 'No,' Shazad said finally. 'Even I'm not *pretty* enough for that.' I snorted under my breath. She went to elbow me in the side, almost forgetting where we were, but she caught herself before she did, turning it into a gesture rearranging her sleeve. 'But we can get you to Ahmed.' Shazad paused pointedly. 'Provided you can give me some numbers that will impress me.'

Lord Bilal raised an eyebrow at Rahim. His commander stepped in easily. 'There are three thousand men garrisoned at Iliaz. Twice that number retired in the province who can be called upon.'

'And you have enough weapons to arm them all?' Shazad disguised the tactical question with a careful laugh, touching Rahim's arm as if he'd just said something hilariously funny.

'Amani.' Imin, in the guise of a servant, appeared again at our side with an elaborate bow. 'The Sultan is headed this way.'

I traded a glance with Shazad. 'Go,' she said. 'I've got this.'

My stomach was too tied in knots to eat or drink as I left them. I made a show of inspecting the horrible statues that surrounded the garden to keep from glancing over my shoulder every few moments at Shazad and Lord Bilal in negotiations, Rahim in between them. The statues' bronze faces reminded me of Noorsham. Only his bronze mask had been smooth and featureless. These were wretched reminders of what the Sultan could do to us if he caught us in our treason before we could escape.

'Announcing' – the voice rang out through the courtyard again – 'Prince Bao of the Glorious Empire of Xicha.'

I felt that tug of something that reminded me of Jin.

A small crowd of Xichian men stood at the top of the stairs. They were dressed in bright clothes that looked as foreign as anything I'd ever seen the Gallan wear, but entirely different at the same time. I'd seen the occasional Xichian dress on Delila, but there wasn't a single woman among them.

A green-and-blue robe was draped over the narrow frame of the man at the head of the party. The six men around him were of similar builds. They reminded me of Mahdi and the rest of Ahmed's scholarly set.

Except for one figure at the back. He wasn't taller, but his shoulders were broader than those of the scholarly-looking men that surrounded him, and he held himself like he was ready for a fight.

My mouth went dry.

Instead of snapping, the string tugged harder. I took a step forward without meaning to, trying to get a closer look. Through the crowd, among the mass of people, his face swung straight towards me. Like we were tied together by some invisible bond. Like we were the needles of the paired compasses.

Jin's eyes found mine. I was wrong. He didn't have his father's smile. Because that troublemaker curve to his mouth was all ours.

Chapter 36

There was an entire garden between us and we were on enemy ground. One mistake, one false move could cost the whole Rebellion. And still it took everything in me to keep my feet grounded. Not to obey that tug.

It was more painful than any order the Sultan had ever given me.

Jin leaned in and whispered something to the Xichian man next to him as they descended the steps into the garden. The man nodded, turning to say something back. The crowd shifted, and he vanished. I battled my instinct to move towards him. To fight my way through the crowd and damn the Sultan watching me.

I started to move slowly towards where I'd seen him disappear. Or as slowly as I could with my heart beating out the rhythm of gunfire. I dodged around foreigners in strange clothes, Mirajin folksin fine colours, dangerous men in uniforms. Only I couldn't see him. I'd lost him. Again.

'Amani.' His voice by my ear sounded exactly the same way it had the last time I'd seen him. In the desert. On the run. Breathless from kissing me in the tent.

When I turned around he was so close I could've reached out and touched him. Only if there was one surefire way for us to both die as gruesome a death as the bronze men around us, that would be it.

His eyes travelled the length of me, from the top of my perfectly combed head all the way to my bare feet. I was suddenly more keenly aware of my appearance than I'd been all night. That I was a golden-glowing girl, not wearing a whole lot, who'd been polished like the other harem girls for the express purpose of being looked at by other men but not touched. The other Xichian man with Jin was doing exactly that, his gaze snaking across every piece of uncovered skin I had. But Jin didn't seem to notice that I was painted gold and on display as if to taunt him.

'You cut your hair,' he said finally. It was such a thing for him to notice, among everything else. The clearest wound I wore in the open of everything that had happened in the walls of the harem.

'Not deliberately.' It was too much to explain to him now everything that had happened. But Jin could read some of it on my face. In the two-word answer.

'Amani, did they—' He stopped himself. *Did they hurt you?* stalled there. I knew why. If someone had hurt me and he hadn't been able to stop it, I didn't know what the chances were that he'd forgive himself. 'Are you all right?'

Now, that was a heavy question. 'I'll live.'

His face changed, hand curling into a fist at his side. And when he spoke again his voice was low and urgent. 'I swear to God, if he's hurt you, Amani, I will make him suffer for it.' I didn't have to guess who *he* was. The Sultan.

'You don't believe in God.' It was all I could think to say.

His hand twitched forward, like he wanted to pull me to him, away from everything else happening around us. 'Then I swear to you.'

I had to ball my hands together to not reach for him. I remembered being little, my arms shaking from the effort of holding up a rifle too heavy for a ten-year-old. All I wanted in the entire world was to let the gun drop. To release my hands and let it fall. The effort of holding it up was too much. It was tearing into my muscle.

But staying alive depended on me holding that rifle up. Learning to shoot.

I kept my arms where they were. Shaking with effort.

'Jin,' I said as low as I could in Mirajin. 'It's not safe for us to talk.'

'I really don't give a damn about safe or not.' His voice was low and sure. And for a moment I thought he really might grab me. Just take my hand and run us both out of there. Then he remembered himself; the gesture turned into a bow as he stepped out of the way of the man behind him. It was one of the Xichian men, trailing him like a shadow. 'I'm the translator for Prince Bao tonight, of the Xichian Empire. So long as we talk through him, we'll be fine.' The man inclined his head, oblivious, saying something in Xichian.

'What happened to his other translator?' I asked through what I hoped was a deceptively polite smile.

'He came down with a bad case of broken ribs this afternoon.' Jin winked at me over the prince's head, which was still bowed in front of me. 'The prince has a weakness for beautiful women so it wasn't all that hard to steer him over to you. Say something back, as if I've been translating to you.'

I hadn't seen Jin in two months. And last time we'd been fighting and his hands had been inside my clothes, and his mouth over mine. There were months of unspilled words between us. Not to mention I probably ought to let him know that as soon as the last of the light that was currently stretching our shadows faded, there

441

was the small matter of freeing a whole lot of Djinn. There was too much to say and too little time, and it was too hard to spill it all through a polite smile. 'Where the hell have you been?' I asked finally, through a forced smile at Prince Bao, as if I was talking to him and not demanding an explanation through my teeth.

I didn't catch Jin's expression as he turned away from me and said something quick in Xichian. I recognised it as some sort of polite platitude. The man said something back, nodding and smiling, handing it to Jin to translate. And finally Jin could turn back to me.

'I was looking for you.' His right hand was still curled into a fist, bouncing tensely against his leg.

'Well, that was stupid,' I said, and Jin stifled a laugh as I pressed my lips together and tried to radiate politeness at the foreign man who seemed to think I didn't know he was staring at my chest. 'I was right here.'

'Yes, Shazad has already gone into great detail about my choices.'

'Shazad knows you're here?'

It was starting to get dark. It wouldn't be long before need tore us apart again. 'In Izman, yes. Here in the palace ... less so.' Then there it was. That smile that pulled me into trouble straight after him. I fought the impulse to return it. 'You'd better say something back to your prince.'

Jin said something quick in Xichian; I only caught the edges of it, but it sounded like he was telling him that Mirajin wasn't so economic a language as Xichian. He barely waited for Prince Bao's answer before turning back to face me. 'I came to make sure you leave this place tonight. Even if we don't manage to get anyone else out, you're coming with us. Do you understand?'

A smile pulled at my mouth in spite of myself. I ignored the grin Prince Bao gave me back, clearly thinking I was smiling for him. 'Are you saying you're here to rescue me?'

Jin raised a shoulder. 'Well, when you put it that way . . .'

I wanted to reach out to him. More than anything. I wanted to fold into him. I wanted to remind him that this was a war. That we could fight and run and stay together all we wanted, but we weren't always going to be able to keep each other safe. 'Jin—'

'A Demdji *and* a budding diplomat, I see.' The new voice sent pinpricks down my spine before I could answer. We'd been so wrapped up in our covert conversation that I hadn't noticed the Sultan approach. The Sultan placed a hand on my back.

Needles climbed the length of my spine. I felt Jin's tension, and he turned it quickly into a bow. Prince Bao followed suit. And then he rose, and I watched Jin stand face-to-face with his father for the first time since he'd been a child in the harem.

I knew exactly what he saw because it was what I had seen: Ahmed aged by another two decades. His brother, our prince, and our enemy becoming muddled into one. But I couldn't even begin to imagine what he felt, having to stand toe to toe with the man who had bought his mother and enslaved her in his harem. Who had killed his brother's mother with his bare hands. Who had taken me. And having to smile politely.

Don't lose your head, I willed silently under my breath. *Not now. Don't get us both killed.*

And then he bowed his head in front of his father and, keeping the smile fixed on his face, he made the introduction, presenting the Xichian prince to the Sultan with a long string of titles as Prince Bao nodded along deliberately.

'You speak Mirajin very well,' the Sultan said in compliment to Jin when he was done, barely sparing a glance at the foreign prince. I held my breath. The stories spoke of Ahmed and Delila disappearing into the night as if by magic. But the stories were only a sliver of the truth, twisted after passing across so many tongues.

The Sultan was a smart man. I'd learned that much here. Surely he must've known how the two of them really escaped. He must have figured out that the Xichian woman who'd disappeared the same night as his son and the Demdji baby had been responsible. Surely he remembered that, while the stories had forgotten him, there had been another son who had vanished that night, too.

But if he did, none of it showed on his face.

And nothing showed on Jin's. 'Thank you,' he said in his perfect Mirajin. 'Your Majesty does me a great honour.'

But the Sultan wasn't done with him yet. 'Your mother was Mirajin, perhaps?'

Don't lie. I'm standing right here. Don't lie. If he asks me I can't lie for you.

'My father, Your Exalted Highness.'

The Sultan nodded. 'If you will excuse me,' he said to Jin, extending an arm for me. 'I need to steal Amani. If your prince doesn't mind, of course.'

I knew Jin well enough to see what the idea of letting me go did to him. That he'd rather square off against his father right here in the middle of the garden than let me walk away with our enemy. With the man who'd already taken me from him the first time.

Jin inclined his head slightly. 'Of course, Your Exalted Highness. I will make your apologies to Prince Bao.' The Xichian prince's head bobbed along cheerfully, oblivious to the tension around him.

And then the Sultan was clasping my arm in his, ignoring the gold dust from my arm rubbing off onto his sleeve, and I had no choice but to follow him away from Jin, and not look back.

'You shouldn't be on your own,' he said as he led me away. 'There are a great many enemies of your kind here tonight. I had asked Rahim to watch you.'

'He found an old friend of his from Iliaz.' It was as good as I could give him.

'He found more than that, by the looks of things.' He gave a pointed look to where Lord Bilal, Rahim, and Shazad were still deep in conversation. That he'd noticed that at all made me nervous as anything. 'He found a pretty face.' My chest eased a little. So long as he didn't suspect Shazad and Rahim of doing any more than flirting, then we didn't have to worry. 'Though I suspect that one could be a match for him in wits as well.'

I'd watched Shazad get underestimated time and time again. Even Rahim had doubted her value tonight, in spite of my word. It frightened me that the Sultan had sized her up so easily.

'Why am I here?' I asked, trying to draw his attention away from my wayward guardian and my friend. 'If it's so dangerous.'

'Because . . .' The Sultan stopped walking. We'd

come to an alcove in a wall of the garden, shielded from the crowd. 'You asked me why we must renew our alliances with foreign powers who place their own countries over Miraji. I want you to have the answer to that question, Amani.' He released my arm. 'Stay here.' The order didn't come with the old pull. But the Sultan didn't know that. As far as he knew, I'd grow roots.

The Sultan stepped up onto the raised platform in the garden. The tension that had been rising in my chest since dawn was nearly bursting me. Night was falling around us and nobody had lit any lamps around the garden to ward against it. The only light came from the lamps strung above the platform, plunging the crowd into darkness.

It was almost too perfect a cover to slip out under.

'Esteemed guests! Welcome. I am honoured by your presence,' the Sultan called through the gardens, summoning all attention onto him. Conversations went out like snuffed matches all around us as clusters of people turned into a crowd around the raised platform.

I started to push my way through against the bodies pushing towards the platform. I was headed towards the edge of the garden. To rejoin the Rebellion and get the hell out of here. Assuming I didn't wind up burned alive like Akim's wife for releasing the Djinn.

The Sultan's voice carried on from the stage. He was talking about peace and about power. Meaningless platitudes. Around me snatches of translation drifted out of the crowd. Shazad appeared next to me as I dodged around a Mirajin woman who rattled with rubies. Neither of us spoke or broke our pace as we came together, like two currents merging into a river.

As we got further, Sam dropped into place between us, splitting off from the other soldiers in the same uniform as him, but with different loyalties. We broke free of the crowd finally. Sam pulled ahead of us as we approached the wall, and he grabbed our hands, the gold dust from my palm staining his as we pressed between two of the clay-and-bronze sculptures. 'Hold your breath,' he instructed as I fought my instinct to flinch away from walking straight into a wall.

We should've met hard stone. Instead it was like stepping into sand. Like the wall had changed its form for us, from solid to soft. Only it was reluctant to. Even as we pushed through I felt it trying to trap us there. The stone was pressing against my skin, fighting back to the shape it had been for thousands of years. I squeezed my eyes shut. After surviving the harem and the Sultan I was going to die here anyway. I was going to be entombed in the walls of the palace forever.

And then air hit my skin again and I was through,

stumbling out the other side. Away from the Auranzeb celebrations. Into the quiet of the polished palace halls.

'Took you long enough.' Hala greeted us on the other side. She looked like herself, golden skin and all, dressed in simple desert clothes, as she waited. Sam had gotten her in a few hours before. Waiting seemed to have put her in an even better mood than she was usually in. Her eyes swept me. 'That colour doesn't suit you.'

'Yes, I've already been over this with Imin. Thank you for your input.' I decided to ignore Hala, turning to Shazad instead. 'You knew Jin was back and nobody thought to mention it to me?'

She paused, unwrapping the sash around her waist, revealing rolls and rolls of gunpowder hidden inside. Sam and Shazad traded a sort of conspiratorial look. The kind Shazad and I used to share. I was reminded with a pang of how long I'd been gone.

'Don't lie to me, Shazad. Of all people, don't you lie to me.'

'Yes, he got back yesterday,' Shazad admitted. 'Izz found him. When we went down to Dustwalk after your tip about the factory. He was looking for you down there. He seemed to think you might have changed your mind and headed home with that aunt of yours. Idiot.'

'For what it's worth' – Sam piped up – 'I did vote to tell you.'

'For what it's worth,' Shazad said, 'you're a thief, not a rebel, so you don't get a vote—'

'I really don't think you've got the moral high ground here,' Sam returned, leaning against the wall looking all too pleased with himself. He was enjoying Shazad's attention, whatever form it came in. 'And another thing—'

Hala groaned, cutting him off. 'While *someone* might be fascinated by this, they are not people currently trying to get you across a palace unseen. Do you mind?'

I led the way.

We stayed close to Hala, moving as slowly as we could. It made it easier for her to fool the minds of the soldiers we passed standing guard inside the palace. They were few and far between. Resources were spread thin tonight. But not a single one of them blinked as we walked straight in front of them; their minds were twisted firmly by Hala's power so all they saw was empty hallway. We moved quietly down now-familiar hallways and around corners until finally we came face-to-face with Princess Hawa's mosaic. Sam didn't wait for me to speak, grabbing our hands again, pulling us through the wall.

We came out, half stumbling, at the top of the old stone stairs that I'd walked down the first time

I'd woken in the palace, the Sultan holding a lamp in front of us, so I could see only one step in front of me at a time.

Only I could see the bottom of the steps now. We weren't alone in the palace vaults. My arm shot out, stopping Shazad from going any further. She understood the signal instantly, pausing where she was.

We moved carefully, lowering ourselves on the stairs like ghouls in the night, crouching until we were at the edge of the shadows, until we could see clearly into the crypt.

The vaults flickered with the movement of the captured Djinn. There were eighteen of them now. Eighteen names that I had called one by one to be trapped. And though they'd all taken the form of men there was still something unnatural about them. They stood like pillars of immortal power around the vaults, sometimes catching light that couldn't come from anywhere. The sheer force of their presence felt like a physical blow.

A half dozen men in uniform carrying torches were huddled around Fereshteh. He was exactly where I had left him after calling him, trapped inside the iron circle. Only somebody had placed what looked like a cage over him. It was made of brass and iron and gold and glass all interlocking in complicated patterns, jointed in a thousand places, arches of metal curving into each other.

The other captured Djinn looked on curiously from within their own circles, like parents watching something their child had made and they didn't wholly understand. For a fraction of a second Bahadur's eyes darted up our way before going back to the other immortals.

Something shifted in the circle of soldiers and the figure who had been working at the machine came into view. I knew Leyla instantly, even from this far away.

So this was why I hadn't been able to find her in the gardens. She was moving anxiously, hands dancing across complicated-looking pieces of machinery as easily as they ever did with the little toys she made in the harem.

She twisted something, stepping back suddenly. The whole circle of soldiers took a step back with her.

For two heartbeats nothing happened.

And then the machine came alive.

The bars of the cage started to move, slowly at first. Then faster.

Inside the machine, Fereshteh watched curiously as the blades moved. He didn't look afraid, but panic was starting to rise in my chest. The machine whirred faster and faster, huge blades swinging in evenly paced circles, like each one was a moving horizon across a huge globe. The bronze blades rising like dawn, the dark iron blades cutting across bringing the sunset. Faster and faster. Until it was a blur of machine around the Djinni.

A sense of dread filled my chest. We had to free him. We had to free him now before it was too late. I started to move forward, blind to the danger. And then one of the pieces of the machine, an iron blade, snapped into place. It swung suddenly, arching upwards towards the sky. It froze there for a moment. I saw what was going to happen a second before it did.

It drove straight through Fereshteh's chest.

Inside, the immortal Djinni, one of God's First Beings, who was made at the same time as the world, who had seen the birth of humanity, who had watched the first immortals fall and seen the first stars born, who had faced the Destroyer of Worlds, died.

Chapter 37

The Djinn were made from a fire that never went out. An ever-burning smokeless fire that came from God. And in the early days of the world the First Beings lived in an endless day.

Then the Destroyer of Worlds came. And with her she brought the darkness. She brought night. And she brought fear.

And then she brought death.

Wielding iron, she killed the first immortal Djinni. And when he died, he burst into a star. One after another, the Djinn fell that way, filling our sky.

Watching Fereshteh die was like beholding a star on earth. White burned across my eyes, and I was blinded. I heard someone scream. I heard Shazad shout something I couldn't make out.

Slowly the light retreated from under my eyelids, leaving me blinking but able to see again. Inside the machine, Fereshteh's body was gone. What was left was burning bright as a star, and the metal of the machine around him was blazing incandescent. I felt the hairs on the back of my neck stand up painfully. I knew where I'd felt this before. The metal door, before the Gallan tried to kill me. Even as we watched, the light whipped up a wire I hadn't seen before, igniting, racing along the ceiling, darting above us.

There was a shout from below as the flash of light above our heads illuminated us too sharply to miss. The time for subterfuge was over. Sam grabbed us both by the hand, wrenching us up the steps and back through the door so fast I barely had time to take a breath before we plunged through.

Hala staggered back as we stumbled through.

'Hala.' I tore my hand out of Sam's for a moment. He stumbled to a stop, but Shazad didn't. She was a few paces ahead of us, already running back towards the garden. 'Leyla – she's down there. Get her out.'

She didn't even argue with me. I didn't give her time. I was running, chasing on Shazad's heels back towards the gardens. I glanced over my shoulder before we rounded a corner, just in time to see the door in the mosaic open, unsuspecting soldiers spilling out towards a waiting Hala, who grabbed hold of their minds before they'd taken a step. And then Shazad wrenched me around the corner. Hala and Leyla were on their own.

Sam grabbed hold of me as we approached the wall, dragging me towards it.

We burst through the wall, gasping, just as the Sultan's speech ended. Applause burst around us and for a moment I felt destabilised, plunging away from what we'd just seen, chasing the starlight, back to the normality of the palace.

And then, all around the darkened garden, lights started to come on. Not oil light. Not fire and flickering torchlight. Just light. Fire without heat. And it was coursing out from the machine that had just killed the Djinni, and then getting trapped in the crystal birds that I'd seen earlier, hanging from strings and staying there, flaring to life.

Bottled starlight.

Awed sounds filled the garden as the lights illuminated the amazed faces of the Auranzeb guests.

And then, in the corner of the garden, something moved. I snapped around in time to see one of the statues shift. One of the figures of the Sultan's dead brothers straightened his head. And then the one next to him. And the one next to him.

The metal men straightened up and took a step. And another. The crowd started to turn around, expecting another party trick. But this wasn't a trick.

'What are they doing?' I heard the fear in Shazad's voice. It was rare to hear her afraid. But I knew she was remembering the same thing I was. A train. A boy in a metal suit. Burning hands. Bahi's screams.

A foreign man in the crowd was forced to stagger back as a statue advanced on him.

I was sitting across from the Sultan in his study when he spoke about the servants of clay the Djinn made before humanity. The Abdals. Creatures of clay who obeyed any order. I was listening when he talked about the first time he had made a mistake thinking he could control a Demdji. That our power wasn't worth the risk of disobedience.

It didn't mean he'd given up on having that power.

It meant he'd given up on disobedience.

The metal things were stepping past the Mirajin, towards the foreign guests. Penning them in.

I heard the Sultan telling me Mirajin forces alone couldn't stand against the threats on our borders.

It was a trap. Auranzeb. The ceasefire. Everything. It was a trap to lure them here.

I knew what was going to happen the second before it did. One of the Albish soldiers lunged between the metal man and his queen. The statue raised one hand.

I was watching his face when he burned. He burned like Bahi had burned in Noorsham's hands. He burned like something lit with Djinni fire.

Chapter 38

The screams started, some of them snuffing out before they could start, as the Abdals turned their stolen Djinni magic on them. Mirajin soldiers were pouring into the gardens now, too, cutting off anyone who tried to run. The smell of blood mingled with the smell of burning.

I realised that I was waiting for an order from Shazad that hadn't come yet. That she was frozen next to me. Pressed against the wall, watching men and women burn the same way she'd watched Bahi burn. If she wasn't going to take charge, someone else would have to. My eyes darted around the garden for Jin. I couldn't see him.

'Sam,' I ordered, 'you need to start getting people out from our side. As many as you can, and then you get out. Shazad—' She jolted as I grabbed her arm. I did my best imitation of her. We needed someone to be Shazad and she wasn't herself just now. 'I need you to pull yourself together.' She was pale, but she nodded. 'How do you feel about using that gunpowder to blow the gates?'

The gates were on the other side of the garden, chaos and death blooming in between us. I saw her mind working. The Abdals were attacking only the foreigners. They wouldn't cause her any trouble, seeing as she was Mirajin. But there were too many soldiers. There was no crossing that. 'I need a weapon,' Shazad said, finally sounding close to normal. She was wrapping a sheema around her face, hiding her identity.

'I might be able to help with that.' Rahim appeared by my elbow. There was already blood on his uniform. He held out a foreign-looking sword to Shazad. 'Are you as good as Amani says you are?'

'No, I'm even better.' Shazad grabbed the blade out of his hand. 'Together?'

The Sultan had been right. They were a well-matched pair. They burst into movement as easily as if they had been trained as one person their whole lives. Soldiers' bodies fell around them as they moved, fighting their way across the chaos. At the same time, Sam turned, plunging into the crowd, discarding his Albish uniform jacket as he went.

Tamid.

He darted across my mind all of a sudden. Hala was supposed to get him out. But the plan had changed. She was getting Leyla now. I had to get to him. I couldn't leave him behind again.

I was running before the thought had even finished, dodging around the chaos in the garden. I plunged into the hallways, headed for Tamid's rooms, the noise from the garden fading into the distance.

The sound of clattering feet in pursuit replaced it. I glanced over my shoulder as I ran. My escape from the gardens hadn't gone unnoticed. A handful of soldiers were behind me. A gunshot sounded just as I flung myself around a corner. The bullet hit where my head would've been. Plaster sprayed like blood, peppering my skin. Orders must not be to capture me, then.

I careened around the next corner, my bare feet skidding on smooth marble.

And then, like a Djinni blossoming from the sand, Jin was there at the other end of the hallway, firing at something I couldn't see. My heart took off and I felt myself speed up.

He turned, gun up, raised toward me as I bolted down the hall. The soldiers were close behind me, but he wouldn't have a clear shot at them, not with me in the way. I pumped my legs harder; I had to get to him before they got a shot off at me.

I could almost hear the hammers pulling back on the guards' rifles.

I crashed into Jin full speed. His arm curled around me. He turned me sharply just as the guards lined up their shots, until there was nothing but his body between me and the bullets.

I could feel the pistol pressing into my back. I curled one hand around it and Jin's grip yielded.

It was like being home.

I aimed in the space around Jin's body that was still shielding me. Three quick shots. And then there weren't any more. Not from me. Not from them.

Because I didn't miss.

I pulled away from Jin. There were three bodies slumped on the ground, dead, and then there was nothing but Jin filling my vision.

'You're bleeding.' Jin's hands were frantically searching my body.

I was shaking hard. The sensation of being back in his hands. Of us being together again. Of pure relief.

'Not mine.' I shook my head. I had no idea where the blood had come from. 'We have to move. We need to get people out—'

'We are.' Jin grabbed my hand. 'They're getting as many people out as possible. Shazad is taking care of the gates and and Imin escaped with your friend Tamid in the confusion. We need to—' We burst around a corner. Kadir stood in our way, flanked by two of the Abdals, their twisted bronze faces staring at us blankly. Like Noorsham. But without any eyes. Without any flesh or blood inside. Or any doubt.

This was what the Sultan had wanted. Soldiers who couldn't turn traitor. Demdji who didn't have a conscience. Who wouldn't fight his control.

I fired on instinct. My last bullet. It plunged straight through the clay where its heart should have been. It didn't even stagger.

'Well, little Demdji bitch.' Kadir raised his gun towards us. 'No traitor brother of mine around to save you now.'

'Want to bet?' Jin stepped in front of me, shielding me from Kadir, ready to fight him. But Kadir wasn't interested in a fair fight; his finger was already pressing down on the trigger.

That was when the gates exploded.

The Sultim staggered, his shot going wide. It was enough. I grabbed Jin's hand. We bolted for the stairs, a spiral leading up and up and up. Our feet pounded against stone as we climbed, Kadir close behind. We burst out onto a hallway. And I realised suddenly that I knew where we were.

I spun towards the room at the end of the hallway. It was Tamid's workroom. The one where I'd been able to see the roofs of Miraji. When I'd thought about jumping.

I slammed the door behind us, shoving the bolt into place a second before Kadir crashed into it, making the wood shake. In the corner of the room, one of the glass bottles fell from the shelf and shattered across the ground.

There. A coil of rope among the bottles and the bandages.

I grabbed it with one hand and ran to the balcony, Jin close on my heels. It was a narrow jump between the edge of the balcony and the wall. And from there it'd be an easy climb down.

'I think we can make that.' I was breathing hard. I was trying to be sure. I thought it was about the same distance as it was between Tamid's roof and the one next to it at his house back in Dustwalk. I'd made that jump before. But that was so long ago it was hard to remember. And the drop here was a whole lot farther.

'I wish I shared your confidence, Bandit.' Jin's breathing suddenly sounded shallow. I looked over and saw him clutching his side.

I grabbed his hand and pulled it away. It was a long cut. A stray bullet, maybe. 'Damn it.' I looked around desperately. Kadir was hammering on the door behind us.

We were trapped. No way back. Only forward. 'If I can make it' – I tied the rope to the banister of the balcony – 'can you crawl?'

That smile pulled at the edge of Jin's mouth. 'Have I told you that you're exceptional lately?'

'No.' I looped the rope around the edge of the balcony again. 'You disappeared on me for a few months without explanation instead.'

Jin spun me around to face him. 'You' – he kissed me quickly, on the left corner of my mouth, sending a rush through me – 'are' – the right corner of my mouth this time – 'exceptional.'

I didn't wait for it. I pulled him to me, kissing him fiercely before pushing him away. 'We don't really have time for this now.'

'I know. I'm distracting you.' He tugged on the piece of rope and the loop I'd made came untied. 'As exceptional as you may be, you're also exceptionally bad at knots.' He started doing something complicated, his fingers working deftly. And then he turned to me. In a few quick motions he'd looped the other end of the rope around my middle. 'If you're going to risk your life, might as well do it safely.'

'You're sure that will hold?' I looked at the tangle around the railing uncertainly.

'You can trust a sailor with knots,' Jin said. 'And you can trust me with you.'

He steadied me with one hand as I climbed up. No matter how far down the drop looked from the balcony, it looked a lot worse standing on the balcony's railing. The jump might not be all that far, but it was a long way to fall and a narrow landing.

I could probably make that.

The door rattled behind us. Kadir pounding his way in.

I was half-sure I could make that.

I took a deep breath.

I was about to find out.

I jumped.

Open air yawned below me. For a second I wondered if this was how Izz and Maz felt, when they shifted into animals.

When they flew.

My bare feet hit the wall, stumbling. I grabbed on to one of the crenellations for balance. I teetered there for a second before I found my footing. I pulled the knot around my middle and wrapped it around the crenellation. The rest of the rope hung down the other side of the wall, almost to the bottom. At least close enough to get us out of the palace.

It looked solid enough and, God, it had better be.

On the other side of the balcony, Jin swung himself over the edge. He locked his hands and legs around the rope. The knot next to me tugged as Jin leaned his weight onto the rope.

It held.

And still held as Jin tugged his way across. One inch at a time, leaving a trail of blood behind.

All I could do from the wall was watch, heart in my throat, as every tug brought him closer to me. He was nearly halfway across when the lock to the door broke.

Kadir burst through in a storm of rage.

I had my gun up and pointed before he had made it to the balcony. I didn't have any bullets. Just a bluff. 'Touch that rope and I can make you sorry that you were ever born, Kadir.'

'You're lying.' But he didn't come any closer, rooted, chest heaving with rage.

'I'm a Demdji.' I pulled the hammer back on the empty gun. 'I can't lie.'

Neither of us moved. We were in a stand-off now. I stood on the wall, gun up, pointing it straight at Kadir as Jin dragged himself the rest of the way across the rope. One inch at a time. Slowly. Slowly. He didn't have to be fast; he just had to be faster than Kadir's brain worked. Faster than the Sultim would take to realise I had nothing but an empty gun.

'Kadir.' The voice at the door made me jump so hard that I had to steady myself on the wall.

The Sultan was alone, stepping through the door. There were no guards with him. No Abdals.

'Father.' Kadir held out one hand. 'Careful, she has a gun.'

His gaze darted from me to Kadir, to the gun, back to Kadir. His mind wouldn't work nearly so slow as his eldest son's. I urged Jin silently to hurry. He was a handbreadth away now.

The Sultan dropped a hand on his firstborn's shoulder. 'Oh, my son. You are a fool.'

Then the Sultan pulled out a knife.

I started to shout, started an empty threat that I couldn't finish with no bullets left in the gun. A promise to stay in the palace if he let Jin leave. Anything that might buy Jin the last few moments he needed to get across before the Sultan cut through the rope and killed him.

He didn't slash towards the rope. Instead the blade in his hand went straight through Kadir's throat.

It was a clean kill, like with a hunting prize. So clean that when Kadir dropped to the ground, the annoyed protest was still written all over his face. So fast that I didn't have time to cry out before he was on the ground.

The shock rippled through me, freezing my tongue, my whole body.

The Sultan looked up at me calmly, wiping his firstborn's blood onto the dead prince's shirt. And suddenly I was sitting across the table from him again.

Listening to him tell me that his sons would drive this country into dust under foreign heels. That Kadir wasn't any more fit to rule than Ahmed.

There is nothing I wouldn't do for this country, Amani. The Sultan turned to face me. He wasn't stupid. He was going to figure out I was out of bullets pretty fast. I had to keep him busy, just a few moments. Until Jin made it across.

'You know, it's been a while since I went to prayers.' There was a weight crushing my chest as I spoke. I had hated Kadir. But, God, seeing him like that, with his eyes staring glassily up at the night sky, blood still gushing from his throat ... 'But I'm pretty sure God frowns on killing your own son.'

'Ah, yes.' The Sultan smiled placatingly. 'Cursed is the one who kills his own blood. Remember what we are celebrating, Amani: my ascent to this throne. I think I am past being able to escape that curse. Besides, Kadir would not have made a good ruler. It's my own fault, really. He was born too early in my reign. I was scarcely older than he is – was.' He spared a glance down at the body bleeding out on the balcony. 'I'd planned that the throne would pass him by, go straight to my grandchild, but of course, that wasn't to be. I hadn't counted on that power-hungry little wife of Kadir's to be so resourceful.' Shira. She had been dead a few days and already her name was being erased. When they told the stories of what happened in this war, was that all she would be, the power-hungry Sultima? He looked back at me. 'And I have to admit, I had not anticipated you managing to get yourself free.' He almost looked impressed. 'How did you do it?'

'You've overestimated the loyalty of your own people.' I wasn't going to give him Tamid's name. 'Do you really think this is going to save them? Make them rally to you again? Slaughtering anyone who stands in your way?'

'It's not about the dead foreigners downstairs, Amani. It's about all the ones left alive overseas.' The Sultan looked at me over the barrel of the gun. 'Do you know what happens in a country when the throne changes hands, Amani? Turmoil. Civil war. Too much war for them to turn their minds to invading us again anytime soon. And by the time they do, I will have an army of Abdals ready to defend our borders.'

An army of clay men with Demdji powers. Put that at our borders and he was right, we'd never be invaded again.

'The Demdji before you . . .' He meant Noorsham. He never used his name, like he never had mine until the day I'd killed that duck. Like we were things to him. 'He burned so bright. But I lost the protection he would've given this country.' Because I set him free. 'I wondered if I could re-create his fire. If I could create a bomb out of metal with the power of a Djinni. And instead I found the right fire to create life. Because that's what the Djinni fire is. It's life. It's energy. It gave us life. And I have just harnessed it. Not to destroy. To power this country. The Gallan claim the time of magic is over and turn to machinery. The Albish cling to their old ways. We will be among the countries that unite the two.'

'All at the cost of slaughtering our immortals.'

'The First Beings made us to fight their wars. But where have they been in our wars? While our borders are harried by foreigners with their greater numbers? While my people make it easier for them by turning against each other at the urging of my son?' He spoke patiently. Like he might do for his own children. Explaining a difficult lesson. Only he wasn't my father. My father was a Djinni. My father was a Djinni trapped inside the palace at his mercy. And for the first time since the Destroyer of Worlds was defeated, at very real risk of dying. My father hadn't cared when I had been about to die. Why should I care about him? But I did.

'The time of the immortal things is long over. We have taken this world from them. There is a reason that Demdji like you are rarities now. This world belongs to us. And this country belongs to us. It is the role of children to replace their parents. We are the Djinn's children.' The Sultan smiled a slow, lazy smile. 'And I think you're out of bullets.'

And then Jin was across. He grabbed the edge of the wall and pulled himself up with a grunt of pain, and then his arms were around my waist. He half leapt, half dropped, his hand looping around the rope as he went. And we were falling. On the other side of the palace walls.

And I was free.

Chapter 39

Izman was blazing still with Auranzeb celebrations, even in the ruins of the Blessed Sultima's Uprising. News hadn't reached the city yet of what was going on in the palace. That we were free of foreign rule. That the Sultim was dead.

I trusted Jin to lead us through the unfamiliar streets. The journey was painstakingly slow as we laced our way under the shadows of windows spilling out light and noise, through the winding side alleys of the unfamiliar city. Avoiding the big streets flooded with drunks and celebrations.

'Here.' Jin pulled me to a stop finally, by a small door in a white stucco wall in an alley so narrow the wall before us almost touched the one behind us. A gutter ran from the door through the narrow paved streets.

I wasn't sure what I was expecting on the other side.

For it to lead to another world maybe, like our old door. Or that it would spill down into a secret passage that would lead to wherever the rest of the Rebellion had set up since we'd lost the Dev's Valley.

Instead we stepped into a large kitchen warmly lit by the embers of a dying fire. It was about the most normal kitchen I'd ever been in. Just like my aunt's back in Dustwalk. Except this one didn't seem to be in low supply of food. Gleaming pots and pans hung from the ceiling between drying herbs and spices. Tinned supplies lined the shelves.

I slammed the door shut on the night behind us. I didn't have time to consider where we were, except safe. Jin and I collapsed next to the fireplace, his back against the wall. I was on my knees facing him.

'You're covered in blood.' I eased him down off my shoulder. 'I need to see.'

'I'm fine.' But he let me tug the hem of his shirt over his head all the same, wincing as his arms went up over his head. His bloodstained shirt hit the floor in a ball even as he rested his arms on top of his head, stretching his chest out and giving me unhindered access. He wasn't lying to me, at least; the better part of the blood didn't seem to be his. Some stained his skin, but aside from the wound in his side that had kept him from jumping to the wall and a huge bruise blooming like a cloud under the tattoo of the bird over his ribs, he didn't seem too badly hurt.

I noticed it then. A bright red cloth wrapped around the top of his left arm like an armband. I might've thought it was a bandage, but I'd know my sheema anywhere.

I reached out without thinking, fingers skimming the edge of where the fabric met his skin. His eyes snapped open at the touch, and he looked down, like he'd forgotten he was wearing it. 'This is yours.' His fingers started to fumble with the knot on the inside of his arm.

I sat back on my heels. 'I thought I'd lost it.' It was stupid. It was nothing but a piece of cloth. It wasn't the Rebellion; it wasn't Jin. It was just a thing. A thing I didn't think I'd ever get back.

'I thought you'd left it.' He didn't look at me. He was still fiddling with the knot. It was fastened tightly. Like he'd been desperate not to lose it.

'Left it?' Finally the knot came apart in his fingers.

'The morning after you vanished.' His shoulders were taut as he unwound the red sheema from his arm. 'You were gone, and this was outside my tent.' I must've lost it in the scuffle with Safiyah. When I'd been standing outside his tent. Deciding whether to go in. 'It seemed like a message.'

The skin under where it had been tied was paler. Like it hadn't seen the sun in a while. He handed me the sheema. I took one end. Our history hung between us, a dozen tiny reminders of the first days we'd known each other. When things had been simpler. He'd been the Eastern Snake and I'd been the Blue-Eyed Bandit and it'd been just the two of us, not the two of us and a whole revolution. A whole country.

I started to say something about how stupid it was to think I'd leave and tell him with a discarded sheema. But then, we hadn't been all that good at telling each other things.

'You left first.' I pulled at the edge of the sheema. 'When I was hurt, you left me.'

'You walked into the path of a bullet, Amani.' He smoothed back a piece of hair from my face gently, his fingers running down it to where it ended bluntly from the wound inflicted by Ayet's scissors. He looked at me like he was relearning my face. I didn't need to memorise him again. He looked exactly the same as when I'd left him. Did I look different from my time in the harem? 'You walked into it without a care for your own life.'

'That's what I do,' I said. 'That's what you do, too.'

'I know.' Jin's hands fell away from my hair, settling on my shoulders instead, lacing at the nape of my neck. 'But that doesn't mean I had to like it.'

'You were mad at me for almost dying?' I was so close to him that all I had to do was breathe for us to be touching. I felt like he was holding me together between his hands, but the heat of them made me feel like I might vibrate out of my skin.

'At you, at Ahmed, at myself, at everyone.' He was finally looking at me square on. The dying embers cast his face in a warm glow as his thumb ran circles over the back of my neck. 'I'm not good at losing people, Amani, and you know I don't give a damn about this country.' The rest of him was still now, something solid to hang on to. But his fingers were sliding into my hair, making me shiver. 'Not the way Ahmed does and not the way Shazad does. I came here because I give a damn about him, and I give a damn about Delila, and they both love this place. I give a damn about you and you are this place. I thought I had to do without you if you were so determined to leave the world. But then you were gone and I would have torn the desert apart looking for you.'

I wanted to say something that would help. I wanted to say that he didn't have to be scared of me dying. But that would be a lie. We were in a war. No lives were safe. I couldn't promise him a future where I didn't take another bullet and he couldn't promise me one, either. The same reckless hope that had us fighting at all was as likely to kill us.

So I didn't say anything as I closed the last of the distance between us.

He said he would have torn the desert apart looking for me. And I felt in that kiss his desperation as his mouth found mine.

It wasn't enough with Jin; it was never enough. His hands were in the mess of my torn palace clothes, trying to find me under the too-heavy stitching and the weight of the gaudy khalat. One hand tangled into my hair, pulling away the delicate gold circlet that still clung there. He freed it from my hair, casting it aside, pulling pieces of the palace away from me, trying to return me to him.

It was like being caught in a wildfire, desperate for breath, like if we stopped we would extinguish. Without thinking, I pulled my hands away from his chest. It took one quick movement for my torn khalat to come off and join his shirt in the heap on the ground, until I was wearing nothing but the thin linen chemise underneath.

His fingers found the hem, pushing it up, and then they were against my stomach, grazing the scar on my hip. I suddenly realised I was shaking. I pressed against him, skin to skin, looking for some kind of warmth. His hands found the small of my back, stilling me against him.

I felt us slow. My heartbeat slow. The wildfire turned to embers as Jin held me flush against him. I realised how close we were to the edge of doing something more. His skin against mine, his hands climbing my body, sinking me into him.

The door to the kitchen clattered open, wrenching us violently apart. Sam stumbled into the kitchen carrying an unconscious Leyla.

'What happened?' I was on my feet in a second. Jin was easing himself up the wall carefully behind me.

'She made the crucial error of resisting.' Hala followed through the door, dropping the illusion of looking human as she did, her skin going back to its normal golden hue. 'She was fighting us, saying she couldn't leave her brother behind. Turns out she could.' She took my still-glittering skin in with one sweeping glance, though half the gold dust had faded in the escape. 'Well, this is a sorry sight,' she said by way of greeting. Her eyes danced to Jin.

Some of the dust from my skin had rubbed off on Jin, a smear of gold from his left ear to his mouth. Jin wiped a hand absentmindedly across his jaw. It was no good; the gold from my skin was all over his hands, too. I might've been embarrassed if it wasn't for the unconscious princesses and old friends in this tiny kitchen pulling my mind in other directions.

'The others?' Jin asked, giving up.

His question was answered before Hala could.

Imin stumbled in, servant's garb badly torn. Shazad pushed her way into the kitchen behind Imin. She had Tamid by the arm. He tried to shake her off angrily as she pushed him ahead of her. Shazad let him go slowly, making it clear she didn't have to before she did. And then she saw me and that sloppy smile broke over her face as she closed the distance with a hug. I felt my own arms, like they were finally untethered, fling themselves around her.

'Rahim?' I asked.

'Alive.' She released me. 'Captured. He's a soldier through and through. We needed someone to cover our escape. And he wouldn't run.' She looked at me. 'We're going to fix this.' And I believed her. Because I was back. I wasn't a prisoner any more and we could do anything. Her hand tightened on my back. And then Imin was demanding her attention and she split away from me. And I was facing Tamid, who was staring at the ground intently, leaning wrong on his fake leg.

And then my arms were around him. Relief wracked through my body. 'Thank you.' I pulled him close.

But Tamid didn't return the gesture. He pulled away. 'I'm not a traitor, Amani. I didn't do it' – his eyes went to Jin – 'for your rebellion.' The only time Tamid had met Jin he'd been pulling me up onto a Buraqi while I left Tamid bleeding in the sand. My guess was that wouldn't particularly endear him to my childhood friend.

'Well, then.' Shazad clapped a hand on his shoulder, as I swallowed the lump in my throat. 'I guess we'll be keeping both you and the princess under lock and key for a while. Come on.'

'Where are we?' I asked finally, glad my voice sounded normal as we started towards the door leading out of the kitchen and into the house.

'My house,' Shazad said. I tripped on the bottom step of the kitchen. Jin steadied me. 'My father is away and I sent my mother and my brother to our house on the coast. I didn't want to put them in danger.'

'We're camping out in General Hamad's house?' I asked.

'No.' Jin's hand was at the base of my back. 'That would be like asking to get caught. We are using it, but most of the camp—' He winced as he reached for the door, grasping his side. I opened it for him. A fine dining room, dark now, waited on the other side. 'There's a garden, not far from here,' Jin explained as we crossed slowly. 'It's linked to this house by a tunnel.'

Jin led me through another door, his hand looping tighter on my waist. I realised he'd scarcely let me go since we'd left the palace. We were propping each other up.

The tunnel started in the cellar, behind two huge

boxes that were labelled as being flour but that sounded a lot like guns when I disturbed one of them as we pushed by. Shazad struck an oil lamp to life and led the way.

I wasn't sure how far we walked. It was more than twice the length of Dustwalk, though. I counted my paces for that long before giving up. And then a pinprick of light appeared ahead of us. Another door, I realised.

I hesitated. Dozens of memories of coming home to the Dev's peace flooded in. Of standing outside the door in the cliff face, and waiting for it to let me leave the desert dust and come home. That was gone now. That home wouldn't be waiting for me on the other side of this door. It wouldn't spill open onto an oasis that had been built out of magic and turned into the Rebellion's refuge. The people who had died in our escape wouldn't be on the other side waiting for me. I didn't know what to expect. But I wanted to come home all the same.

I stepped through.

It was quieter than the old camp. That was the first thing I noticed. And I realised why in an instant. The huge walls that stretched up around the property might block everything from sight except the sky, but we were still in the middle of a city. There were ears all around.

But the place was still blazing with light and with movement.

It wasn't the desert, but the memory of the desert was still there. Tents were scattered among the campfires and a makeshift armoury had been set up against one of the walls. Lanterns and laundry crisscrossed patterns over the sky. It almost looked like hope.

'Amani!' Delila was the first person to see me. She was sprinting across the garden and flung her arms around me, pulling me from Jin's grip. 'You're alive! They got you out! What happened to your hair? I like it, though! You look older. I wanted to come and help, too, but no one would let me.'

I realised as she pushed her hair behind her ears that it looked darker. And not just by some trick of the light or because of an illusion she was casting. It had been dyed black with henna, hiding the telltale Demdji purple. A safety measure in the big city. Ahmed was taking no risks with his little sister.

'We've been over this,' Shazad said. 'We need to keep one of you two in the camp at all times just in case we need to hide it.' She gestured between Delila and Hala, who smiled tightly.

'And somehow I'm always the expendable one.'

'Nice to see you, too, little sister,' Jin joked as she pulled away from me. With a foolish grin Delila flung herself at Jin. I was sure the greeting I was getting was a pale shadow in comparison to what Jin had had when he finally returned.

Navid was on us, grabbing Imin, still in the bloody servant's garb, in a tight embrace. All those days with Imin roaming the palace and no news couldn't have been easy on Navid. But Imin had been right – the beard didn't suit him.

And then I was being passed from hand to hand, friends and rebels I barely knew alike patting me on the back, hugging me, congratulating me on staying alive. On escaping. Thanking me for my sacrifice when I'd stayed so long in the harem. The twins turned into two cats and twined themselves around my legs, almost tripping me with every step I took. I felt like a piece of myself was being returned to me with every person, pulling me out of the harem, pulling away the grief over Shira, the anger over my aunt, everything that had happened in the last few months, as I slipped from one hand to another.

And then like the parting of a curtain I was standing face-to-face with Ahmed. I was sure that every moment of doubt I'd had in the past months, all of it, was scrawled across my traitor eyes. Every time I'd seen his father decide more quickly. Every time I'd feared that the Sultan was right and Ahmed wasn't ready. Every time I'd been stupid enough to listen to a murderer and a tyrant.

'Ahmed—'

'Amani.' He grabbed me roughly by the shoulder, jolting me forward into a hug. I collapsed gratefully. Ahmed was a lot easier to believe in when he was flesh and blood in front of me. 'Welcome home.'

Chapter 40

The ripples of the night before hit us one by one.

The events of Auranzeb were twisted by the palace before being spread among the people of Izman. The Sultan announced Miraji's independence from foreign rule. Any country that threatened our borders would burn for it.

The announcement went on to say that in the fighting of the night Prince Kadir had been killed. He had died bravely in combat, killed by his own brothers, the Rebel Prince and Prince Rahim, who had turned on his family unexpectedly, along with Lord Bilal, who had escaped. Prince Rahim had been apprehended trying to flee like a coward. He would be cursed forever for killing his own blood. The Sultan was grieving his son. There was no news about an execution for Rahim. After what had happened at Shira's execution I could see why the Sultan might not want to risk another public beheading.

There were going to be new Sultim trials. To choose a new heir to Miraji. The Sultan had told me the people never loved the throne so much as when princes were killing each other for it. He'd murdered his own son and now he was using his death to win the people back over from the Rebellion to the throne.

But we could use it, too. We would remind the city that the Sultim trials had already chosen an heir. Prince Ahmed.

In light of the recent events, the palace announced there would be a new curfew. The Sultan's army of Abdals would patrol the streets. They could not be reasoned with or argued against. Anyone found on the streets between sundown and sunrise would be executed. It was for safety, the palace said. After all, only dark intentions belonged to the dark hours of the night. They didn't say it was to hobble the Rebellion, but we all heard the meaning behind the words.

And we were hobbled.

It was strange, hearing it from the outside, after being on the inside for so long. We were operating blind again just when we couldn't afford to. It was agreed that Imin would go back to the palace, to be our eyes.

'Isn't there another way?' I knuckled my eyes tiredly as I went over it with the others. We were in Shazad's father's office. It had been set up as a war room of sorts. Not that much had needed to change for that. There was something comforting about it even though we could scarcely have been further from Ahmed's pavilion back in the rebel camp. The walls were pinned with maps and notes. The map of Izman I'd stolen from the Sultan's desk the night we'd eaten together was right in the middle. I recognised a lot of the rest as information I'd passed on from inside the palace.

Some of it Rahim had given me.

I'd escaped, but he was still inside. And we needed to know what was happening to him. So I felt a stab of guilt as I voiced my objection. 'I'm not sure it's smart to put another Demdji in the Sultan's hands.' Rahim had been my ally, but no one knew better than I did the risks of Imin getting found out.

Navid looked hopeful at my objection. He was sitting in a huge armchair in the corner, arms circled around Imin. She was wearing a petite feminine shape, small enough that she fit into her husband's arms like she was a missing piece who'd belonged there all along. Her legs were tucked under her as she leaned against his chest comfortably, eyes closed. She was exhausted but awake. The night before had taken its toll on everyone. Hala was truly asleep in a corner. Jin was sitting on Shazad's father's desk, shirt flung over his back, as Shazad inspected the wound on his side.

'You need to get this seen to properly,' Shazad said to Jin. 'Somewhere you won't bleed all over my father's study. Go find Hadjara.' We'd lost our Holy Father in the escape from the Dev's Valley. Until we had someone new, Hadjara was a decent seamstress.

'If you don't need me—' Jin said, easing himself to his feet.

'We've done fine without you so far, brother,' Ahmed commented. It was a low blow. Shazad and I shared a look. This new tension that hung between Ahmed and Jin wasn't good for anyone.

But Jin didn't say anything as he brushed past me on his way to the door, fingers dancing across the back of my hand like he wanted to take it. 'Don't volunteer for anything stupid while I'm gone.'

'We don't have that many other choices that I can see,' Imin said as the door closed behind Jin. 'Unless someone else would like to reveal now that they've been sitting on a secret shape-shifting skill so I can take a break. Anyone? No? I didn't think so.'

'I'd offer, but I don't think foreigners are all that welcome in the palace at the moment,' Sam offered. He was watching Shazad. 'And I don't make a beautiful enough woman to pass in the harem very long. Amani can vouch for that.'

'It's true,' I admitted. 'He doesn't have the cleavage to pull off a khalat.' Shazad snorted.

'Someone has to go,' Imin said, uncurling herself from her husband's grip, shifting easily from wife to rebel. 'If I get caught I can always take poison before he gets his claws into me like he did Amani.' I wasn't entirely sure she was joking.

We stole a few hours of sleep after daybreak, when we were sure the palace was done feeding lies to the people and the rush of the night before had worn off. We were in Shazad's home, which meant she had her own rooms inside the house. That was the moment it hit me in earnest that our old home was gone. Our tent was gone. The small space that we had shared for half a year and that had become as familiar as my bed in Dustwalk had ever been.

I figured I could've found my own tent. If I'd wanted to. Start getting settled into this new camp. Instead, I found Jin. He was dozing in the shade of an orange tree with huge, sprawling branches. His shirt was riding up and I could see the place Hadjara had patched him up. He startled awake as I stretched out next to him, stilling as he realised it was me. I knew he was watching me. In the scarce few months we'd had between Fahali and the bullet that caught me in the side, we'd stolen plenty of moments together in the desert but never slept side by side. He shifted slightly so he was on his side facing me as I settled down, pillowing my head with my arm. The grass was still cool from the night. I might be sleeping on the ground again, but I had the feeling I would rest easier here than I had on a hundred cushions in the harem. 'I haven't gotten around to setting up a new tent yet.' His arm found the small of my back. 'Seeing as I only just got back from chasing down this girl I know.'

'Next time you should try to keep better track of her,' I said as I closed my eyes, leaning my head into him.

'I'm counting on it.' He settled me against him. That was the last thing I heard before I dozed off.

Shazad woke us both sometime in the afternoon; her hair was wet from a bath and twisted up into a knot at the back of her head. I wondered if she'd had any real rest since Auranzeb. Leyla had finally come to, she told us.

Shazad had made good on her promise of chains. Tamid and Leyla had been confined to two of the many empty rooms in the house, chained and locked until we could count on them not making a run for it. I'd tried to go see Tamid in the room adjoining Leyla's, but he'd pretended to be sleeping, which was a clear enough message for me.

Leyla looked like a trapped animal, her knees pulled up to her chin, eyes darting between me, Jin, Ahmed, and Shazad, like she was trying to watch us all at once.

No. Not a trapped animal. She was looking at us like we might be the animals. About to tear her apart at any second. I remembered the day I met her, in the menagerie. When she'd been building a small mechanical elephant and I'd been the one being circled by Kadir's wives. But this was different. At least I figured it was.

'So,' Ahmed said conversationally, sitting down at the end of the bed. She drew her legs in a bit further. 'You built an army of machine and magic for my father.'

'I didn't—' Leyla had always sounded young, but her small voice was almost gone now. 'Please, don't hurt me. I didn't have a choice in helping him.'

'Nobody's going to hurt you,' Ahmed said gently at the same time that Shazad made a disbelieving noise at the back of her throat.

'Everyone has a choice,' Shazad said when Leyla looked at her with wide, startled eyes. I kicked her ankle. Hard. The last thing we needed was to scare Leyla too badly to talk. She looked at me sharply.

'My choice was to help my father or watch my brother die.' Leyla buried her face in her chained-up hands miserably. 'What would you have done?' And then she started to cry. Out of nowhere, big ugly sobs that shook her whole body violently.

'Your father threatened Rahim?' I asked, instead of letting Shazad answer that question. 'He told you he would hurt him if you didn't help him?' Rahim had been worried about Leyla being in danger in the harem, but it looked like he was the one being threatened.

'Rahim has no idea. He never knew what happened to our mother.' Leyla wiped at her running nose with her sleeve as best she could with tied hands. 'All those years back. She told my father she could make him a machine that could power all of Miraji. That could change the world.' Her mother had been the daughter of a Gamanix engineer. The country that melded magic and machines. 'And she did it. Except that it needed to take its energy from somewhere. It took it from her.' Leyla wiped angrily at the tears welling in her eyes. 'Just like it did for all the other people who came after her.'

'Like Sayyida,' I realised. 'And Ayet.' And Mouhna and Uzma. Girls who had disappeared out of the harem without a trace. A place where girls disappeared all the time without causing any ripples.

'They were tests. You can take—' Leyla squeezed her eyes shut. 'The Holy Books say that mortals are made with a spark of Djinni fire. The machine takes that spark and can give life to something else. Not true life, but – what they have. My father figured if he could do that with a mortal life, what could be done with an immortal one?' Leyla looked pained.

'You can power an army that doesn't fall when faced with bullets,' Shazad filled in, understanding what it was we'd all seen the night before. The gravity of what we were facing moved between the four of us. 'That doesn't tire or eat. That can stand against Miraji's enemies.'

'Including us,' I said, grimly. 'How do they work?'

Leyla shrugged, looking miserable. 'The same way all magic does. Words, words, words.'

'So how do we stop them?' Shazad interrupted before Leyla could tumble down some rabbit hole of self-pity.

'It's almost impossible.' Leyla shook her head, tears squeezing out of her eyes. 'You'd have to destroy the power source and—'

'The machine,' Jin said. He took a step forward and Leyla flinched away from him. I put a hand on his arm, stopping him. He might technically share the same blood as Leyla, but he was a dangerous-looking tattooed stranger to her, not a brother.

'How do we do that?' Shazad asked. 'We've got enough gunpowder to blow the whole thing if we can—'

'No,' Leyla said hurriedly, her eyes wide and panicked. 'You'd destroy the whole city!' Like in the story of Akim and his wife. Djinni fire out of control. 'The Djinni has to be released, not unleashed. The energy released with the right words. Same as he was captured with.' Then Leyla looked straight at me. 'Amani bound him. She's the only one who can unbind him.'

And just like that, everyone was looking at me. If I'd known I was doomed to get this much attention I might've brushed my hair.

Chapter 41

'I'm not going to lie to you all.' Ahmed looked around the kitchen crowded with rebels. 'This is going to be a challenge.' It was a good thing for morale that Ahmed wasn't a Demdji. If he couldn't lie, I was pretty sure he would've struggled to use the word *challenge* instead of, say, *disaster*.

We were two dozen or so packed to the rafters around Shazad's kitchen, leaning against the colourful tiles that swirled around the walls like steam off a fine dish, our heads bumping pans that hung from the ceiling. Shazad stood next to Ahmed, at his right hand like she always did. Jin was leaning on the fireplace; if you didn't know he was injured, you might not even guess he was using it for support. Sam had retreated to the back, letting his hand pass in and out of the wall absentmindedly.

I cradled the cup of strong coffee in my hands. I'd

slept a few more restless hours, but not enough. There were faces that should have been here that weren't, people who had died in the escape from the valley. There were new faces I didn't know. Still, even in the strange setting, it felt just like it used to in Ahmed's pavilion in the camp. We'd lost that home, but we were still fighting to make a new one.

The curtains in the kitchen were red, drawn against peeping eyes on the street. They turned the room bloody as the dawn.

A new dawn. A new desert.

'We're outnumbered,' Ahmed said, 'outmanoeuvred and outgunned.'

Jin caught my eye across the room, an eyebrow going up as if to say, *Not much of an inspirational speech.* I snorted.

'And out-Demdjied, judging by those things at Auranzeb,' someone muttered from the back. A ripple of assent went through the room. The rumours of the Abdals and their strange powers had spread frighteningly fast. Shazad said there were already signs of it snuffing what sparks of dissent we'd been able to ignite in the streets.

'Yes, thank you, Yasir. And that's where we start.' Shazad took control easily as she stepped up to the table. Ahmed ceded the room to her. I had an image of Shazad next to Ahmed on the throne. As his Sultana as well as his general, her head dipped over some problem with a golden crown slipping down her brow. It would suit her. 'We have three problems of pressing urgency right now, and thanks to our real Blue-Eyed Bandit, now returned to us – no offence,' she tossed over her shoulder at Sam, 'we might have solutions for them.'

'Even if she did create one of those problems in the first place,' Hala muttered.

I ignored her. As I stepped forward, eyes followed me. I might not have been back long but I'd already noticed the change. I wasn't just the Blue-Eyed Bandit any more; I was the girl who had made it out of the palace alive, who had stood toe to toe with the Sultan and escaped. 'The first problem is that we need an army, a true army that can go up against the Sultan's. If we can forge an alliance with Lord Bilal, then we have a fighting force. We've arranged a meeting with Lord Bilal a few hours from now. Before dark. By the end of it, here's hoping we'll have an army.'

'Assuming he hasn't already fled the city,' Hala added.

'Did you get more pessimistic since I left,' I asked, 'or did I just forget what a pain in the ass you are?'

'Well, you know what they say about absence making the heart grow fonder.' Hala shot a fake smile my way. 'Isn't optimism what got you captured in the first place?'

'Please keep in mind how many ways I know to kill you both if you don't shut up,' Shazad interrupted before we could descend into an all-out brawl. A laugh went around the room, lightening the weight of the mood.

'Our second problem,' Ahmed said, trying to get the room back on track, 'is that even if we do get an army, we can only stand against another army of flesh and blood. Not one made out of mechanical parts and magic. Which is why we need to get Amani to that machine.'

'And right now it'll be too well defended. There's no way we can get anywhere near it,' Shazad said. 'Not unless we draw the Sultan and his whole army away from guarding it. Which, as it turns out, wars are very useful tools for.'

Everyone stared at Shazad. 'Are you suggesting we start a war just to get Amani into the palace?' someone said from the back of the room.

'No,' Shazad said. 'We need to start a war anyway. I'm suggesting we use the war to make our odds of winning a little better by giving Amani the opportunity to sneak into the palace.'

Even if I could get inside I wouldn't be able to deactivate the machine without the right words to free the Djinn in the first language. Words not even Tamid knew.

'Bringing us to our final problem,' Ahmed pressed on. 'Which is that Amani is currently . . . incapacitated.'

That settled the room soon enough. I self-consciously rubbed the spot on my arm where I could feel one of the pieces of iron sewed into my flesh. It was like prodding at a loose tooth. An instinct, a tic, feeling that little shoot of pain when I pressed it in, reminding myself this wasn't truly part of me. Reminding me I was useless with my body riddled with iron scars.

'Where are we on finding a Holy Man we can trust?' Shazad asked, leaning her knuckles on the table. 'Someone to cut the iron out of Amani?' I knew what the words cost her. In the months since Bahi had died, I didn't know if I'd truly heard Shazad talk so plainly about Holy Fathers. Not even when I'd been shot through the stomach. But then again, I had been unconscious for most of that.

'More or less exactly where we were the last three times you asked me that,' said Sam. He was on edge. 'Holy Men are largely in the pockets of your Sultan. They'd all sell you out in a heartbeat sooner than they'd help you.'

And Tamid couldn't be trusted not to stick a blade in me either, given how he felt about the Rebellion.

'Can't we take a chance?' I rubbed my finger along my forearm, worrying at the piece of metal below there. I wanted to claw it out of my skin myself.

'No,' Jin said without hesitation, speaking for the first time. Everyone's head swivelled towards him. Jin didn't tend to speak up at war meetings, unless he had something that needed saying. Which meant folk tended to listen. Only there was an uneasiness among the rebels now. He hadn't disappeared on just me. He'd abandoned the whole Rebellion. 'We're not taking chances with you.'

'So either we find someone,' I concluded, 'or I've got to walk into the palace more or less defenceless.'

'Welcome back to being human,' Shazad said. 'I'll get you some guns.'

'Sam.' I caught him as the kitchen emptied He was peeling an orange stolen out of one of the baskets hanging from the ceiling. 'I need your help.' I stopped speaking as Shazad brushed past me, calling out to someone quickly about the weapons supply. That earned me a raised eyebrow from Sam.

'Something your general can't help you with?'

I lowered my voice as I pulled him into an out-of-the-way corner. 'I think I know somebody who might be able to help get the iron out of my skin. Not a Holy Man. A woman. My aunt.'

Sam paused, orange wedge halfway to his mouth. 'The woman who drugged you and kidnapped you and sold you to the harem? Yes, she seems very trustworthy.'

'Please, Sam, I need help. You walked in and out of the harem at will for months. You have no idea what it's like to be in there and feel powerless to leave or defend yourself.' I tugged up my shirt, showing the scar on my hip, the same one I'd shown him the first time we met. 'This happened even when I had my power. If I have to, I'll walk into the palace again without it, but I'm twice as likely to get killed doing that and you know it. But I'd take just about any risk not to. Now, will you help me?'

Sam considered, peeling off another piece of the orange. 'How much?'

'How much what?'

'How much are you going to pay me to find your oh-so-very-trustworthy aunt?'

My shoulders sagged. 'Really? After all this, you want to keep pretending you're doing it for the money?'

'Why else would I be doing it?' he asked. 'I'm a bandit, remember?'

'Because you want to be something more than that,' I said finally. It had been a gamble. A guess. But the way it fell off my tongue so easily I was sure I was right. I'd watched Sam walk through walls with injuries for this rebellion. Walk into Auranzeb as a traitor to his own people for this rebellion. He wasn't doing this for money any more. 'That's why you're still here.'

'That'd be an awfully stupid reason.' Sam scratched his eyebrow. I stayed silent. 'I'll see what I can do.'

Chapter 42

As it turned out, the Hidden House wasn't all that hidden. It was a bathhouse at the intersection of two twisting streets lined with colourful awnings in the middle of Izman. To me, they looked exactly like every other street we'd passed through on the way there. The city was an immense maze, and if it wasn't for Ahmed gently nudging me around twists and turns, I'd have gotten lost sooner than I'd ever been in the desert.

As we got closer, steam heavy with the smells of flowers and spices curled out of lattice windows, sliding its fingers into my hair, taunting me with memories of the harem. Ahmed gave me a small nudge, indicating I should look up. As I did, the name finally made sense. All the buildings in this corner of Izman seemed to stand an even three storeys tall. The Hidden House stretched up two storeys higher than any of the others around it. And the roof was shielded by canopies of vines and desert flowers that tumbled down the walls, hiding it from prying eyes.

Shazad had picked this place for the meeting with Lord Bilal. Except she'd told him to meet her elsewhere first. With no guards and no weapons. It was up to Shazad to meet him there and bring him here. We were taking our precautions. We were asking him to put an awful lot of faith in us.

Jin had gone first, out in the open, to see if he drew any attack and to sweep the place for traps. Ahmed and I followed, looking like an ordinary couple walking the streets of Izman instead of a prince and a bodyguard with a gun secreted in the folds of her khalat. But we made it as far as the house without incident.

Ahmed pushed open the door and let himself in. At a desk a girl's head darted up. 'Well, if it isn't our Rebel Prince.' She flicked a book shut and shot me a look. 'You can take your finger off that trigger – you're safe here.' I hadn't even realised I'd been gripping my gun. I eased my finger off. But I didn't reholster it. 'Your brother is on the roof,' the girl said to Ahmed.

'What is this place?' I asked, as we started up the stairs.

'It's a safe haven.' Ahmed stepped aside, letting me go first. I wasn't sure if he was being polite or if that was what I was supposed to do as his guard. 'Not ours. Sara's.' He tilted his head backwards at the girl at the desk. 'She was married at sixteen. Widowed at seventeen. Nobody but Sara knows what her husband died of, since no one could prove that it was poison, but he left her with broken bones and a great deal of money.' My mind darted to Ayet without meaning to. If she'd wound up here instead of in the palace she might not have been my enemy. She might have been one of us. She might still be all right. Or she might have taken a bullet for the Rebellion and died outright. 'She took the money and made this. It's a place for women who might not want to be with their husbands. For whatever reason. A place that keeps women safe from them. Sayyida came from here. And we found Hala here, too.'

'Hala's married?' I almost tripped on the step.

'Who do you think took her fingers?' Ahmed steadied me. 'You all right?'

'Fine.' I waved him off. 'So how come it looks gaudier than a whorehouse at Shihabian?' I asked.

Ahmed laughed, catching me off guard. Ahmed had a good laugh; I'd forgotten that. It'd been a damn long time since I'd heard it. 'Sara's theory is that if folk think they know what you're up to, they don't dig much deeper and risk finding the truth. And everybody thinks they know what we're up to, with a house full of women, with men coming in and out every day, and the occasional child appearing.' Sara. Now I remembered why that name rang a bell. Standing on a mountain in a desert, the day before Bahi died, Shazad teasing him about a child with a woman named Sara. 'She likes to say she just added some pillows. We sent Fadi here. He'll be safe.'

We climbed four flights of stairs until we reached the roof. Jin was there, waiting, shadowed under a canopy of greenery. His shoulders eased visibly when he saw us. 'No trouble on the way?'

'We're fine,' I said. 'No trouble here?' He shook his head.

We lapsed into tense silence as we waited for Shazad. It was meant to be a half hour before she arrived. It was closer to a full hour and panic had my guts wrapped in a knot wondering what had happened to her when she emerged at the top of the stairs with Bilal, hooded and blindfolded.

We'd told him to meet Shazad unarmed and alone. We'd set almost all of the terms of our meeting and we'd set them high, expecting a negotiation. But Shazad said he hadn't even flinched. He'd agreed to come to us, defenceless. That was the sort of thing that made you suspect a trap. Shazad kept scanning the skies around us warily as she pulled the hood from his head and uncovered his eyes.

'Don't worry,' Bilal said lazily, 'I don't have anything up my sleeves. You can ask any one of your Demdji if you don't believe me.'

Everyone looked at me. So he knew what I was. 'He's telling the truth,' I said. I could tell what Shazad was thinking. There was something wrong with a man who had so little regard for his own life.

'Good.' Bilal stuck his hands in his pockets. He was wearing an ugly purple-and-gold kurta that was too loose on him and billowed around his arms. He fit right in with the gaudiness of the Hidden House. 'So you're the famous Rebel Prince.' Bilal looked Ahmed over. 'I thought you'd be taller.'

'You shouldn't believe everything you hear,' Ahmed said.

'I hear you might actually be able to topple your father,' Bilal offered. 'With some help from my army.'

'That,' Ahmed said, 'you should believe.'

'Good,' Bilal said. 'I want to end this parade of invaders. It's tiresome. If my army can topple your father, it is yours to command. I never had much interest in commanding anyway. That was always Rahim's strength. He was like a second son to my father. But I will want something in return.'

'When I am Sultan' – Ahmed was prepared – 'I will declare Iliaz independent. You can be the ruler of your own kingdom, as long as you are prepared to swear allegiance to the throne of Miraji.'

'Oh, I don't care about that.' Bilal shook his head. 'That was just a pretext to feed your pretty general something big enough to get me face-to-face with you. If I'd told her what I was truly after outright, I had the feeling she'd turn me down on the spot on your behalf. Women – they can be so unreasonable.'

'And what is it that you're after?' Ahmed asked. He was careful with his wording. He didn't say, *Name it*. Even though we all knew how desperate we were.

'You can keep your kingdom, every last piece of it.' Bilal said. 'In exchange for my army, all I want is one of your Demdji as a wife.'

The silence that filled the moment that followed was tangible. It was the silence of shock from all of us on the roof. It was the silence in which Ahmed didn't immediately refuse him.

'The Demdji are not mine to offer,' Ahmed said finally, picking his words carefully. 'Iliaz, on the other hand—'

'I have no interest in being the king of my own country.' Bilal waved a languid hand. 'An independent Iliaz was my father's dream. He was an ambitious man. A great man. I'm a dying man. The Holy Men say it's

507

in my blood. I have a handful of years left to live. If I'm lucky.'

I saw it now, in the loose-fitting clothing, the pallor of his skin, the way he held himself like he was always tired. It wasn't arrogance. It was illness. 'Even if you did win the war and grant me my own kingdom, I would rule over it for how long? One year, two?'

'So where do we come in?' I couldn't keep my mouth shut any longer. Not when he was negotiating for one of us. 'If you just want a wife to give you a son before you die, I'm sure you can find someone who's not a Demdji.'

Bilal smiled wanly. 'Everyone has this notion that the Demdji have powers to heal. That is why on the black market you can buy scraps of hair or strange skin. Or floating blue eyeballs to heal you.' His eyes travelled across us. 'But that is a watered-down story. Some will say that the true healing power lies in taking a Demdji's life.' I remembered Mahdi holding his knife to Delila's throat, trying to drag her to Sayyida, to save her life. Saying Delila would die so she could live. 'It's a mistranslation from Old Mirajin, you see.' Bilal looked at us. 'The true phrase is not whoever takes a Demdji life, but whoever owns a Demdji life. Whoever is *given* a Demdji's life. Surely you know the story of Hawa and Attallah.'

Hawa and Attallah had made oaths to each other.

The stories said that theirs was a love so great that it shielded Attallah in battle. But if she was a Demdji . . .

Wedding vows. It hit me like a punch in the gut.

I give myself to you. All that I am I give to you. And all that I have is yours. My life is yours to share.

Until the day we die.

They were nothing but ritual for most. But in the mouth of a Demdji, they were truth-telling. That was how the legend had been born – Hawa had kept Attallah alive with her words. So long as she watched him on the walls, her life tied to his, he lived. When she fell, he fell, too. He didn't die from grief. He died from a Demdji truth.

Dead silence had fallen around us as that understanding sank in.

'Give me one of your Demdji,' Bilal said, and his eyes scraped across me. 'She will be treated well. I will not harm her. Though I will expect her to perform all her wifely duties.' I saw Jin's hand tighten. 'I will ask only one son of her. And in return, I will honour her by taking no other wife. I want to live to see my hair turn grey and meet my grandchildren. And I will give you an army and a country. One girl, in exchange for a throne.'

He let the weight of his words settle over us. 'I see you need to consider this. I ride for Iliaz in the morning.

If you want an army, come find me there with a wife. If you don't—' He shrugged. 'I will watch you and your rebels burn under your father's new weapons from my fortress and die in my own bed long before the war is over and the Sultan comes for me. And if you hate me for it, we can settle that after death.'

Chapter 43

I missed the desert nights like an ache. Shira had been right, you couldn't see the stars from Izman. The city was too flooded with noise and light, too bright to make out the constellations of the dead.

But I knew it wasn't really the stars I missed. Everything had changed. We weren't an upstart rebellion in the desert any more. I missed the simplicity of being sure that what we were doing was right. That it was worth it.

We were starting a war. And a war demanded sacrifice. I could feel the uneasy restlessness in the camp.

'There's an easy way out of this, you know.' When Jin talked, with my head leaning against his chest, I felt it in my bones before I truly heard him. It was long past dark and we were both already half-asleep.

It'd been a long, quiet walk back after Bilal's proposal. Even Shazad hadn't had anything to say.

Ahmed and Jin had fallen into step ahead of me, deep in an angry conversation. They were working it out at the same time as everyone else was. Hala and Imin were both already married. Which left me and Delila. The two of us were the only ones who were able to offer ourselves up to Bilal in sacrifice if we wanted that army. If we wanted to make this a real fight, not a slow massacre.

I knew what Jin meant. If he and I got married, I was off the table, too.

'I know,' I said. I didn't say anything else. I didn't say that I knew Jin would never forgive himself if he saved me over Delila. That if Ahmed tried to force my hand he wasn't the kind of ruler I'd want leading an army anyway. I didn't say that I'd walked across the entire desert to *not* wind up having marriage chosen for me, even if it was to Jin.

But my silence spoke for me.

He wrapped his arms around me and pulled me against his chest. He was warm and solid. I tucked my head low, my mouth resting against his heartbeat, over the sun tattoo.

He fell asleep eventually. I didn't.

After a few restless hours I pulled myself out of his arms. We were mostly sleeping without tents in the warm summer air. I picked my way through the bodies that were strewn across the grass. Like dead on a battlefield. The house was quiet as I made my way back to the kitchen.

It looked a lot bigger without half of the Rebellion stuffed into it. I started rifling through the tins on Shazad's shelf. Looking for coffee.

The door to the kitchen crashed open, making me jump so violently I knocked a glass bottle to the ground with an ear-splitting shatter. An unfamiliar man staggered into the kitchen. I was about to go on the attack when he got close enough to the fire that I saw yellow eyes. 'Imin?' I relaxed, even as he collapsed into a chair by the fire, breathing hard. 'Are you all right?'

'I had to run all the way here,' he panted. He was wearing a young man's face and his beardless cheeks looked flushed. 'The city is swarming with those Abdal things. One nearly saw me a few streets back. But I couldn't get out of the palace all day and I had to tell someone. Rahim . . .'

That name got my attention. 'Is he all right?'

'No,' Imin deadpanned. 'He's a prisoner. He's obviously *not* all right. But he's not dead, either. And judging by all the talk in the kitchens, he's not going to be. Rahim is respected in the Sultan's army. Executing him would be bad for morale, they're saying. And bad for the Sultan among the people. So he's being sent away, transported to some work camp where he can die quietly.'

That sounded like good news, the first in a long while, but I didn't get my hopes up yet. 'When are they moving him?'

Imin treated me to another eye roll. 'Do you think I ran through Abdal-infested streets for my health? Tomorrow night.'

I found Ahmed in the general's study. There was one flickering lamp that leaked its light under the bottom of the door. It made me think of the story of the jealous Djinni who flickered a tempting light in the night, luring children out of their parents' homes, making them chase the fire far enough into the night that he could snatch them up and keep them as pets.

I could hear voices from halfway down the hallway.

'Delila . . .' Ahmed sounded tired. 'You can't—'

'Yes, I can!' Delila raised her voice. I paused, just shy of the threshold. 'You're the one who can't, Ahmed. There wouldn't even be a war if it wasn't for me. This whole thing started because I was born. That's why Mother – I mean Lien – had to run. That's why you two had to start working when you were younger than I am now to feed us. I'm the reason you and Jin grew up in Xicha and that's why this whole revolution started in the first place. That's why Bahi is dead, and Mahdi and Sayyida and everyone else. I started this war and you will not even let me fight it. So I'm going to help finish it.'

I stepped back just as Delila stormed out of the study, the door hitting the wall loudly enough to wake half the house. She didn't even see me as she pushed her way down the hallway. I waited until she was out of sight before I stepped into the light on the threshold.

Ahmed's head shot up as my shadow crossed into the study. It had been resting on his palms, his elbows propped on the desk. His gaze struggled to focus on me. There was an empty bottle next to him. I wondered how full it'd been when he started.

'Amani.' He stretched up, and the candlelight travelled across his face, flicking one side into light then the other, so he looked like two people. I'd never seen Ahmed drunk before, I realised. 'If you're here to do the selfless thing and offer yourself up to Lord Bilal for an army, I'm afraid my sister just beat you to it.'

'Doing the selfless thing doesn't sound a whole lot like me.' I sank down into the chair across from him without being invited.

'Jin would never forgive me if I were to let you go.' Ahmed shook his head. 'If I let Delila go, he won't, either, but I'll probably never forgive myself, so at least we'll both hate me equally then.' *Let you go*, he said. Not *make you go*. Ahmed was my ruler; he could order me to do the selfless thing. To surrender myself instead of his sister. But that hadn't even crossed his mind.

Because he wasn't his father.

There had been moments in the palace when that had frightened me. That he might not be strong enough, knowledgeable enough, that he might be too idealistic. But that was what Miraji needed. Miraji needed a ruler like Ahmed. I was just afraid that a ruler like Ahmed could never seize the country from a ruler like the Sultan.

'It should be easy, shouldn't it? One person for an entire country. My sister or an army.'

'No,' I said. I thought of the ease with which the Sultan had ordered an execution. 'I don't think ruling is ever supposed to be easy. But, what if there was another way?'

'To win the Rebellion without an army?' He cast me a wan smile. 'With more riots and lost lives? More cities falling out of my hands like Saramotai? With a death count rising as my father creates machines to make slaughter easy?'

'No. What if there was another way to gain control over the army from Iliaz?'

Ahmed looked up at me, a flicker of hope on his face.

'Rahim,' I said. 'He was commander of Iliaz's army before Bilal was ever the emir. They know him. They respect him.' I thought of how easily his soldiers had fallen into line when Rahim had ordered them against Kadir the day the Gallan ambassador almost strangled me. 'I think they would follow him. With or without Bilal's consent.'

'Are you suggesting we send Imin—'

'No.' I shook my head. 'Imin might be able to take his shape, but wouldn't be able to take Rahim's place.'

'Imin's done it before,' Ahmed said. 'Impersonated someone for us.'

'Not for so long. You don't think that if Imin walked into camp with your face and started giving us orders, everyone would notice it wasn't you quicker than anything? We need the real Rahim. No more tricks, just a good old-fashioned rescue.'

Ahmed leaned back in his chair. 'Is that the only reason you want to save him?'

'I don't like leaving people behind.' Especially not people whom I owed my life to.

'Amani, with the whole city looking over their shoulders and Abdals patrolling the streets every night ... this sounds like a suicide mission.' Ahmed rubbed his eyes. 'And we're going to need the others here if we're planning one of those.'

Chapter 44

It was dawn before we had a plan that wouldn't end with us all dying by Abdal fire.

We started looking for the most likely place to intercept the transport taking Rahim out of the city. We needed to get to it before it left Izman. Fighting in the confined space of the city streets was to our advantage; if it got out into open ground, we didn't stand a chance. Sam stepped through the wall as we all stood craned over a map of Izman. There was an ugly bruise on his cheek that hadn't been there last time I saw him.

'Where'd you get that?' Shazad asked, distracted for a moment.

'A friend,' Sam said cagily before joining us around the table. He shot me a meaningful glance I couldn't quite read. And then it was gone. 'What are we doing?' he asked. 'Picking out summer homes?'

'Picking a good place for an ambush,' I said. The

Sultan was sending Rahim's transport across the city with human guards and Abdals alike. We weren't worried about the mortal soldiers. Hala could take care of them. And if she couldn't, bullets could.

The Abdals were a different story.

We needed Leyla.

She was messy with sleep when she was brought before us in chains. But her eyes were wide and awake and frightened. Even though she wasn't so much younger than us, she looked like a child standing across from Shazad.

'Leyla.' My friend leaned on the desk. 'Think very hard about the answer you are going to give me before you speak. Is there a way to stop the Abdals? Any way you can think of?'

Leyla's eyes darted around the room nervously, between me and Imin, and the men who were her flesh and blood without being her true brothers. 'I'm not sure—' she whispered. 'I don't want anyone else to get hurt if I'm wrong.' Her voice was thick with unshed tears. I resisted the urge to comfort her. There'd be someone to feel sorry for her if we rescued Rahim. Until then she was going to have to grow up.

'This is your brother's life at stake, Leyla,' I said. 'He would've done anything to save you. The least you can do is try to save him.'

She chewed nervously on her lower lip. I couldn't tell if she was looking for an answer or if she already knew it and was deciding whether to tell us. 'You could try destroying the word.'

'The word?' Ahmed asked.

'The one that gives them life. It channels the Djinn's fire into their spark. I put it inside their feet.' Leyla shifted nervously. 'It was the hardest place for anyone to do them damage,' she said. 'They look like people so folk will naturally aim for their heads or their hearts. Who would think to aim for a foot?'

'That's smart,' Shazad admitted. 'And very inconvenient for us.'

'Do you think they could be fooled by an illusion?' I asked. 'Not like Hala climbing into their heads; like a veil.' Like one of Delila's illusions. But I didn't mention her by name. It would be an argument to take Delila with us if the answer was yes and that was not an argument we'd be having in front of Leyla.

'They might,' she admitted. 'Do you have someone here who can cast illusions like that?'

'Thank you, Leyla.' Ahmed's voice carried dismissal. 'You've been very helpful.'

Ahmed looked at me as Leyla was led back away, steeling himself.

I was ready for a fight. 'You can't protect her forever,

Ahmed; we need Delila—'

'I know.' He held up a hand to stop me. 'I know I can't protect her forever. So I will count on you two to do it.' Ahmed rubbed his hand tiredly across his face. 'Get some rest before you go save my brother.'

Sam hung back with me as the others made their way to their beds even as the sun made its way into the sky. Jin cast a look back for me, but I waved him on.

'I found your aunt,' Sam said when we were out of earshot of the others. 'She is in a very fine set of rooms above a gold merchant's, living beyond the means of a simple medicine trader, by all accounts. It made her easy to find.' She was living off the gold she'd traded me for. It was a sort of poetic justice that it had allowed Sam to find her.

'Fine.' I shook my head. It was heavy with sleep and too many plans, too many things that could go wrong in rescuing Rahim. 'We can go in a few days and—'

'If you do that, you'll be finding an empty house,' Sam said, interrupting me. 'She's packing up her life and leaving the city tomorrow. A lot of people are. Too much unrest in the city. And now the curfew. Cities are never a good place to be in times of war.'

Of course. It'd sounded too much like good luck to be true.

'So we'd have to go tonight to have a stab at getting her to cut the iron out of me.'

I would need more than Sam's help for that.

'And you're coming to *me*.' The circles of exhaustion under Hala's eyes made the skin there look a deeper shade of gold. 'Me, instead of your darling Shazad or your beloved Jin?'

They don't know how to crawl inside someone's head like you do. It was on the tip of my tongue. But she wasn't wrong. Shazad or Jin and a few well-placed threats could probably get me the same thing. That wasn't the real reason I was here. We were both Demdji, and we owed each other the truth.

'They're human,' I said. They would fight beside me. We would die for each other. But no matter what, they would never understand this the same way Hala did. To have a part of myself trapped away. That someone had hurt me because of what I was. That I wanted to hurt her back. 'The story around camp is that your mother sold you in marriage to the man who took your fingers.'

Hala's face changed at once. 'Do you know what our mothers get,' she replied as I watched the motion of her golden fingers through her inky hair, 'along with us, from our fathers?'

'A wish,' I said, remembering my conversation with Shira in the prison.

'Do you know what your mother wished for?'

'No,' I admitted. I supposed I ought to ask my father, if we ever succeeded at getting me back into the palace.

'Mine wished for gold,' Hala said. It was such a stupid simple wish. The one that every peasant and tinker and beggar made in stories. I didn't press her. I just waited. She had this look like she wanted to tell me, her golden lips parted slightly. If I didn't push, she would.

'My mother had grown up poor and she wished to be rich,' she said finally. 'And maybe she meant it well. Maybe she found out she was going to have a child and wished for wealth to be able to raise me in comfort instead of in the gutter where she'd grown up. That's the lie I used to tell myself when I was little. But I could never say it out loud.' Her smile was bitter. 'And then the money ran out, and what she had left was me, her golden daughter.'

She leaned back, and the light in the opening of the tent made her skin flash. She was one of the only people bothering with a tent. It occurred to me she might be hiding. The golden daughter of a woman who loved gold too much. We'd both been traded in for gold in our own way.

'I'll help you.'

*

I found Jin shaving inside the house, in a small room set off from the study. For the long nights when the general didn't get to his bed, I guessed. A beaten brass basin was half-filled with water underneath a cracked mirror. It was just a little bit too low for him, so that he had to stoop over. His shirt was flung over the door handle. From behind him I could see the way the muscles on his bare shoulders bunched, moving the compass tattooed on the other side of his heart. There was a new tattoo on the opposite shoulder. A series of small black dots across his skin. Like a burst of sand. As he straightened he spotted me in the reflection, leaning in the doorway watching him.

'That one's new.' The room was small enough that I only had to take one step to be close enough to touch it.

'I got it done while I was with the Xichian army.' His skin was hot under my hand as my fingers danced across the dots, one at a time. 'I was thinking about this girl I knew.' He turned around quickly, catching my hand. He smelled of mint mostly, but there was an undercurrent of desert dust and gunpowder when he kissed me that made me desperately homesick. That made it harder to speak what I had to say next.

'Jin, I'm going to tell you something,' I said, pulling away, 'and I don't want you to ask me any questions about it. I just want you to trust me. Tonight, there's something I've got to do before we rescue Rahim. And

I need Sam and Hala for it, and I don't want to tell you what it is in case it doesn't work.'

'I hate everything about this already.' Jin wiped a stray streak of water off his jaw with the back of his hand.

'I had a feeling you might. But I've got to tell someone, and Shazad is more likely to try to stop me. And she needs to get to the ambush point. You both do. We can't chance this falling apart on my account.'

'One way to be sure of that is for you to just come with us.' Jin toyed with the ends of my shortened hair, considering me carefully, trying to read me. But for this I was determined not to let anything show.

'Get to the intersection.' I stood my ground. 'Wait for us there. If everything goes right we can still get there in time to intercept Rahim.'

'Is that a promise?' I knew when Jin was saying yes without really saying it. I had him on my side.

'Djinn's daughters shouldn't make promises.' I pushed myself up, reaching for a shadow near his ear where the razor had missed, close enough to him to feel his heartbeat. 'It usually doesn't end well.'

Jin turned his head instead, catching me off guard with a kiss, fast and sure. He broke it off quickly, but he didn't pull away. He just smiled against my mouth. 'Then this had better not be the end, Bandit.'

Chapter 45

The rooms my aunt kept above the gold merchant's were cluttered with chests, half-packed, some of them stuffed to overflowing. When Sam walked us through the wall I smacked my shin into one of them, and barely kept in the string of curses that sprang to my tongue.

We picked our way through the mess carefully; silks and muslins spilling out of a trunk brushed against my leg like clinging cloth fingers. A rope of pearls was wound carelessly on top of another chest. So this was what selling someone out to the Sultan bought you.

And in the middle of it all, sprawled across a bed, slept my aunt.

'Ready?' Hala whispered. I nodded because I wasn't sure I'd be able to answer truthfully. Hala didn't deign to wave her hands over my aunt's body like the street performers did. There was no sign that she was doing anything at all except a slight crease of concentration on her forehead.

My aunt came awake with a violent gasp as Hala seized control of her mind.

For a second, she looked around, wild-eyed. Then she saw me and her gaze focused in recognition.

'Zahia,' she gasped out. I watched her fight it for a moment, the line between reality and dream. Between the knowledge that her sister was dead and what she was seeing standing in front of her. It took only a few blinks before the illusion won.

'Safiyah.' I sat on the edge of her bed. 'I need your help.' I rested my hand next to hers on the cover. I couldn't quite bring myself to clasp it in pleading.

But Safiyah did it for me. She laced her fingers with mine and pulled my hand to her lips. 'Of course.' There were tears in her eyes now. 'For you, I would flood the desert.' She paused expectantly, looking at me. And I realised it was one half of a saying. Something that'd passed between Safiyah and my mother. Some secret bond between sisters.

Only it wasn't secret. I knew it. My mother had said it to me before. But there was no way I could say it to Safiyah.

I thought of Shazad. My sister in arms. We had

recognised something in each other the first time we met and we were tied. By more than blood.

I would probably want to destroy anyone who stole her life, too. The way I had my mother's.

'For my sister . . .' I willed the words off my tongue. 'I would set the sea on fire.'

The rest was like walking my aunt through a dream world. She led me into her kitchen. It was a small room crowded with hanging spices as well as jars and jars of things that belonged in an apothecary. She cleared the kitchen table, talking the whole while, snippets of conversations meant for my mother which I barely understood. It was eighteen years of all the pent-up things she'd wanted to talk to her sister about while there'd been a desert between them. All the secret private jokes between sisters in a life before this one. The language of two women I'd never really known.

'You need to strip,' she told me. As one, Hala and I turned to look at Sam meaningfully.

He held up his hands like we had him at gunpoint. 'I'll, um . . . keep watch,' he said, backing through the wall.

I stripped and lay down on my aunt's table. She plucked a tiny knife out of the pile and started cleaning it. I'd been stabbed and shot and beaten and plenty of other things in my life. But I still didn't love the look of this knife. With a roll of her eyes Hala slipped her hand into mine as my aunt stepped forward, swiping a piece of fabric, wet with something that made my skin tingle, across the spot where the first shard of metal was embedded.

The tiny knife pressed into my arm. I felt the needle of pain shoot through me. I tensed instinctively, squeezing my eyes shut. But the feeling of my skin breaking never came. And then the hard table below me was gone. I moved my fingers and found soft sand beneath my skin.

I opened my eyes. I was staring up at stars. Desert stars, the way they blazed in the open nothingness against the dark, the last burning light of the desert.

This was an illusion. I knew that because I knew Hala. And I knew I was lying on a kitchen table with a knife cutting metal out of my arm and being stitched back up by my aunt.

But knowing the stars above me weren't real didn't matter – same as realising you were in dream didn't help you wake up. I didn't fight it, this unexpected kindness of Hala stealing away the pain from my mind. Instead I stretched my fingers out across the sand, revelling in the feeling of it against my skin, even if it was all in my head.

The illusion Hala had woven in my mind shattered. The desert and the stars were gone and the kitchen was back. Pain across my body woke up. I hissed and quickly Hala grabbed my mind again and the pain faded as she pulled it out of my head.

I must've been under the illusion for a good long while beacuse there were twelve tiny pieces of iron lying in a glass dish next to the table. There was a tiny symbol printed into each of them. The Sultan's seal. I got angry all over again. That was so like him. He could've just shoved iron under my skin from a scrap pile, but these pieces had been specially made.

'The last one . . .' I felt my aunt's fingers exploring my skin; I felt the slight pressure on my stomach, just above my hip, a hand's breadth away from my navel. Her dreamlike expression looked worried now. 'It was so near your stomach, Zahia,' she said to me. 'There were scars here already, like an old healed wound.' She frowned, like she was struggling to remember what had hurt her sister. But I knew what it was. That was where Rahim had shot me. Where the wound had healed over a long, torturous month. 'The scar tissue makes it almost impossible to remove it all without making it worse,' Safiyah was saying now. 'I'm worried I've made it worse.'

I pushed myself up, ignoring the returning pain of the smattering of twelve tiny wounds across my skin. This might be the city. But it was still desert land. There was desert dust everywhere. I pulled on it. A stabbing pain tore through my side as I did, right where my old scar was, blinding for a moment. But sure enough, I felt the ground shift, a thousand tiny grains of sand rushing towards my fingers.

I felt the rush of using my power through the pain. It would have to do. I released the sand and the pain receded.

'We need to go.'

'Hold on.' Hala stopped me as I started to get dressed. 'What do you want to do with her?' She meant my aunt. 'Do you want me to tear her mind apart?' Like Hala had done to her mother who had sold her. Who had used her daughter so selfishly.

I wanted her to hurt.

Ahmed would tell me that an eye for an eye would make the whole world blind. Shazad would tell me that was why you had to stab people through both eyes the first time around.

'Did it make you feel better?' I asked. It wasn't an accusation. It was a real question. I wanted to know. I wanted to know if hurting my aunt like she'd hurt me would take away this anger rotting in my chest. 'When you tore your mother's mind apart? Did it help?'

Hala turned away from my aunt first. 'We need to go.'

Chapter 46

Moving through the streets of Izman after dark wasn't exactly easy – not with the Abdals and not with my skin rebelling with pain in every step. Without Hala in my mind, the kingdom of cuts on my body screamed in pain.

But speed was essential.

We rounded a corner, and moonlight bounced off metal and clay. Hala grabbed my arm, shoving me between two houses, into the shadows. We didn't dare move. The Abdal passed by the mouth of the alley, close enough that I could've reached out and touched it. And then the sound of steps again, closer, coming from the other end of the street, working their way towards us. Penning us in. Sam didn't hesitate, grabbing my hand and Hala's. 'Hold your breath or get dead very fast.'

I just had time to suck in a lungful of air before he dragged us both backwards through the wall. We stumbled into a small kitchen. I could hear the rushing of my own heartbeat in time with the steps outside, slowing as they passed. We waited a solid few breaths until Sam dragged us back out.

We reached the intersection where we were due to meet, with seconds to spare.

A rope ladder dangled from the rooftop as promised. I started to climb as Hala and Sam slipped into a side alley. Jin reached a hand down for me, clasping my arm as he pulled me up the last few feet on top of the roof. A hiss of pain escaped through my teeth as his thumb hit one of my wounds.

'Is there a reason you keep coming back injured when I leave you for five seconds, or is it—' His voice carried too loud, and I clapped a hand over his mouth, shutting him up.

'Don't flatter yourself,' I said quietly. 'I'm always getting injured when you're around, too.' I was raw inside and out. I didn't feel like explaining my encounter with my aunt just then. I pressed a finger to my lips. When he nodded, I slowly peeled my hand away.

We flattened ourselves on the edge of the roof. Jin handed me the rifle a second before the Abdal appeared around the corner.

Its steps echoed around the empty streets, accompanied by the rattle of the wheels of the prison wagon that followed behind and a dozen more boots, on human feet this time.

A word carved into metal, powering the Abdal like a heart, in the right heel. Somewhere no one would ever have the instinct to hit. We didn't need instinct; we had insider information.

Another step.

Two more.

I took a deep breath.

I squinted against the dark, trying to track the glint of metal in the moonlight. Somewhere high above, a curtain twitched, then fell shut, casting the street back into shadows almost as quickly as it had illuminated it.

But it was enough.

I pulled the trigger.

It was a perfect shot. It clipped the edge of the bronze heel guard, bending it at an angle. I almost laughed. Thank God for soft metal.

The men surrounding the carriage were pulling out weapons already, looking for the threat. But that wasn't my problem.

Jin's gun went off next to me even as Shazad stepped through Delila's veil of illusion, appearing like an avenging spirit below, blades drawn.

I took a second shot. It went through soft clay flesh.

And a third. And I saw it. The shine of metal under the clay skin. Somewhere inside there was a word. Giving the thing life. A soldier turned a gun toward me and fell.

And for a moment it was like old times. Like the days before Iliaz. The three of us against the world. The simplicity of rebellion, where every little victory could win a war.

My next bullet hit hard.

When mortal things died, they fell. They fell like the soldiers littering the streets under our gunfire. But the Abdal didn't. It stopped. Just stopped as abruptly as I would have when the Sultan gave me an order.

And the streets were still again.

I clambered down after Jin.

The Abdal stood unnervingly frozen. I'd seen enough of Leyla's little inventions close up to know this one was different. It was as much a creation of a Djinni as I was.

The lock at the back of the carriage splintered under another gunshot, taking my focus with it. I joined Shazad and Jin at the back of the wagon, as the door swung open. Rahim was bound and gagged, a sack pulled over his head. I held up a hand, stopping Jin and Shazad. Rahim had rescued me once; I owed him the same.

The wagon rocked gently under my weight as I entered.

I pulled the bag off Rahim's head. He jerked, like he was ready to fight, arms bound and all. He stopped when he saw me, holding still long enough to let me pull the gag from his mouth. 'What's happening?' he rasped.

'This is a rescue,' Shazad said from behind me, framed in the doorway, one arm braced against the roof of the carriage. 'Obviously.'

'You got us an army,' Jin added as I sliced the ropes around his arms free. 'Now how do you feel about leading it?'

Rahim glanced over his shoulder uncertainly between us. The impossibly beautiful general, a half-Xichian prince he didn't yet know was his brother, an impostor Blue-Eyed Bandit, a Demdji with purple hair dyed black toying nervously with an illusion of a flower, another doing nothing to hide the gold of her skin. I didn't have to imagine what he was thinking. I'd been in his place eight months ago. His gaze finally landed back on me.

'Welcome to the Rebellion,' I said. 'You get used to it.'

We moved as quickly as we could back through the darkened and deserted streets of Izman. The Abdals patrolling the streets in a steady chequerboard rhythm might not be called by the commotion, but that didn't mean we were going to make ourselves a moving target. We caught Rahim up in interrupted whispers as we worked our way back towards Shazad's home.

We told him that Leyla was safe.

That we were going to take the army from Lord Bilal by force.

That he was going to help us do it.

Rahim didn't even blink. Maybe rebellion ran in the blood of the Sultan's sons. Maybe it ought to be called treason. Whatever it was, we were going to use it to take the throne.

Shazad's house was quiet when we pushed through the kitchen door. It was late, I supposed. But still, something about the quiet needled at me. The tension of returning from a mission was missing.

Ahmed waiting to make sure we were all coming home alive. Waiting for his sister.

Imin waiting for Hala.

My senses had reached a fever pitch by the time we were climbing the stairs at the end of the tunnel into the garden. I was on the last step when my boot hit something that rolled away with a familiar ping. A bullet. It skittered into the silent garden and then vanished.

A feeling of wrongness hit me a fraction of a second too late. I heard the click of two machine cogs slotting together. The whirr of metal pieces working, spinning faster and faster, and then snicking into place. That was the only warning I had before the illusion disappeared.

Chaos bloomed as the serene front dropped away. Bodies littered the ground, rebels mostly, only one or two men in uniform, weapons still in hand. The corpses sprawled across shattered tents, staining the ground red. Survivors were shoved back against the walls, bound by their hands. They were on their knees with soldiers gathered around them. Ahmed. Imin. Izz and Maz. Navid. Tamid. All still alive, at least.

And facing us was a whole host of Abdals.

They had created the illusion, I realised. They didn't just have Noorsham's power to destroy. They were as powerful as Demdji. And leading them . . .

'Yes, Amani.' The Sultan smiled Jin's smile at me. The one that meant trouble. Like he could read my mind. Out of the chaos around him, our bound and dead rebels, one figure emerged. Leyla unbound. And unafraid. She was wearing a jacket that looked like it belonged to the Sultan over the same clothes she'd been wearing since Auranzeb. That trapped-animal look in her eyes was gone. She wore a satisfied smirk instead as her father spoke.

'It was a trap.'

Chapter 47

I pulled out my gun, already knowing it was too late. Two dozen guns clattered to attention, ready to shoot us if they had to. Shazad and Jin had weapons drawn, spoiling for a fight.

They would die; they both would. I could see it now. We were all trapped. Me, Jin, Shazad, Rahim, Delila, Hala, and – I looked around for Sam. He was gone. Nowhere to be seen. We were surrounded. We were outnumbered. But that wasn't going to stop them from going down fighting.

'Stand down!' Ahmed ordered from where he was kneeling. 'Everyone stand down, weapons down.'

I could see Shazad struggling with every fibre of her being against the order as Jin's hand opened and closed on the gun in the corner of my vision. But my attention belonged to the Sultan. His eyes were locked on me. I could almost hear him. That weighted, reasonable voice that made me feel like we were all just children acting out. *You know how this ends if you fight, Amani.*

'Do as he says,' I said. 'Weapons down.' I tossed my gun to the ground. The iron left my skin with a sigh of relief.

Finally Shazad's swords clattered to the ground noisily. Jin's gun followed. I was unarmed. But I wasn't helpless. The Sultan might have choreographed this, but there was something he wasn't expecting.

Somewhere at the edge of my awareness, beyond the city walls, I reached for the desert.

'Very wise.' The Sultan nodded to Ahmed, tied and trapped. 'You know, it never ceases to amaze me how ironic the world can be. That the son who is most like me is the only one who wants to denounce me.'

'Well, that's just not true.' Rahim stepped between me and his father. I used the shield of his body to shift my hands a tiny bit. I tried to pull without my arms, without any sweeping movements. I pulled from deep down in my gut, the part of me that had kept me alive against all odds until now. It came with a shooting pain in my old wound.

'I'd denounce you in a second, Father.'

Far away, the desert surged up in answer.

'That's why you're on that side of Father's guns and I'm on this one.' Leyla finally spoke. Her shy, lilting voice, which had always sounded sweet, took on a different tone now as it bounced around the walls of the garden. Gone were the wide, tear-filled eyes. 'I'm the one who didn't betray my family.'

Her brother met her gaze across the courtyard. 'You were my family,' he said softly. 'I was trying to save you. After I found you were as talented as Mother with machines, I knew our father would try to use you the same way he did her. That *destroyed* her, Leyla.'

'I didn't need saving.' She tugged the jacket closer around herself against the night air. 'I took care of myself from the day you left me among those women and their plots. I learned to survive. To make myself useful.' She had said that to me once in the harem, as Mouhna and Uzma and Ayet disappeared, one after the other. If you weren't useful, you were liable to vanish, invisible. And who was more invisible than a princess alone in the harem?

So invisible, I hadn't even considered that Ayet had disappeared after I'd told Leyla that she'd caught me and Sam in the Weeping Wall garden. That Uzma and Mouhna had gone missing after the incident with the suicide pepper and humiliating me in court. So invisible it hadn't crossed anyone's mind that she'd witnessed their nastiness, too. That it had been her idea to select them to put into the machine, not the

Sultan's. 'You were gone and I was here, finishing what Mother started.' Leyla's smile was as sweet as ever, and she aimed it at Rahim like a weapon. 'She would have wanted that. It was the Gallan she hated. Not our father.'

'You lied to me,' I said. And I hadn't spotted it because she was a big-eyed, shy girl with a sweet face.

'Demdji are *always* the easiest to lie to. Your kind never expects it,' the Sultan said. 'What good daughter wouldn't obey the word of her father?' He made a motion, like he was pulling back a bowstring and loosing it. I was holding an entire sandstorm in my mind on the edge of the city, dragging it forward over walls and rooftops. I felt it stagger as something punched through my heart. The horrible, humiliating memory of wanting to impress him, of wanting to please him. Of doubting Ahmed for him.

'Little Blue-Eyed Bandit, so very trusting, over and over.' I flinched at the nickname as he started towards me. Jin shifted angrily at the edge of my vision, but he knew better than to try anything as his father drew closer. 'Oh, yes, Amani, I knew from the moment I saw your little blue eyes.'

All those desperate attempts to hide it from the Sultan, to keep Ahmed from coming up so that the truth wouldn't slip past my traitorous tongue. And he'd been letting me get away with it, letting me dance around the subject. Because he already knew I was allied with Ahmed.

The Sultan chucked me under the chin gently as he reached me. 'I could've made you tell me what you knew, but that wouldn't have gotten me to Ahmed. It was a great deal easier to use you to feed fake information to your prince. Once Leyla told me Rahim was a traitor, I could use him to pass information to you.'

I caught a flash of movement behind the Sultan. A figure in the shadows. I looked back at the Sultan, quick as I could. Trying not to betray what I'd seen. I tightened my fist, keeping my grip on the desert.

He turned away. 'I have to say I rather enjoyed watching you scramble around putting out fires, never noticing the others I wanted you to look away from. While you were looking at Saramotai, I was taking back Fahali. While you were saving traitors from the gallows, I had men arresting dissenters in their own homes. And while you were running around trying to save my traitor son, I was emptying your traitor camp and arresting my other traitor son.' He dropped one hand on Leyla's shoulder. 'She's done a great deal of good work. How did you think we found you in your little valley hideaway?' He held something up. It was a compass. Just like the ones Jin and Ahmed had, only smaller. They'd told me once, I remembered, that those were of Gamanix make. Leyla's mother was a Gamanix engineer. 'We hid one of these on your spy before we released her to be . . . rescued.' Sayyida. She was a trap, too.

'And when I found out from Rahim you were planning to escape . . .' Leyla bounced, excited. 'Do you want to see?' It was that same light in her face that I'd seen when she was showing some new toy to the children in the harem. She turned, gesturing to the soldiers. Two of them dragged Tamid away from the wall. He struggled to keep up with them on his fake leg.

I took a step forward and this time, it was Jin who caught me, pulling me back. They forced Tamid to the ground, sitting with his bronze leg splayed out in front of him. Leyla unfastened it with practised ease. She had made it, after all. Proudly she turned the detached leg toward me. Perfectly fitted in the hollow bronze of Tamid's calf was a compass.

'I fitted it after I convinced you Tamid should come with us, and he was none the wiser that I was using him to help bring my father to your camp.'

This was my fault. I had led them to us. I had saved Tamid. I hadn't left him behind and I was still being punished.

I pulled, one last violent yank on my Demdji powers.

And then the sky darkened. The sandstorm was on us.

The Sultan's head shot up as the shadow fell across us. The raging cloud of sand had rushed in to crown the garden. I raised my hands, taking full grip of it – there was no point pretending now.

I poured everything I had into the sand. All my anger. All my defiance. All my desperation. I whipped the storm into a frenzy before slamming my arms down, pulling the full force of the desert around us.

I looked for the Sultan. He was watching me. The last thing I saw was him smiling at me the same way he had that first day in the war room over the dead duck. Like he was proud.

Then the sandstorm swallowed us.

'Amani!' Shazad's voice shouted some order to me that was swallowed in the chaos. I turned to face her just in time to see an Abdal rising up behind her, raised hand glowing red. I swung my arm. I felt something tear in my side where my wound had been as the sand turned into a blade and crashed through the Abdal's leg, cutting into clay flesh and metal bone and severing it, sending the thing toppling to the ground.

'Watch your back!' I shouted at her. I didn't need orders for once. I knew what I was fighting for. I knew who I was fighting. I knew what I needed to do.

We needed the rest of the Demdji. And we needed them out. I couldn't leave any Demdji in the Sultan's hands. I couldn't let him do the same thing to them that he'd done to me.

I slammed my arms down, severing the iron around Izz, then Maz. The twins burst into motion, flesh turning to feathers, fingers to talons as they plunged into the air, then back down. Delila was running for Ahmed as I freed him. And then Imin, who staggered forward, towards Navid.

A bullet caught Hala in the leg. She screamed, staggering forward. She would've hit the ground except Sam was there. He grabbed her, arms under her legs, and the two of them vanished through a wall. I turned my attention elsewhere. I'd lost Ahmed in the chaos.

We weren't winning, but we didn't have to. We just had to get as many people out as we could. I grabbed a fistful of sand and twisted hard. A stab of violent pain answered in my stomach. And then it was gone. The sand staggered, then dropped. And just like that our cover was gone.

The pain in my side doubled as I tried to grab hold of the sand again. And suddenly, it was blinding. My body was made of pain where it ought to have been flesh and blood. I staggered to my knees, gasping.

'Amani.' When I could see again I realised Shazad

was kneeling in front of me. The way she said my name made me think it wasn't the first time. She looked scared. Two other rebels were standing over us, covering her back while she had mine. 'What's happening?'

I didn't know. I couldn't even talk for the agony. Something my aunt had cut open so carefully inside me felt like it'd ripped in my side.

'That's it, you're getting out of here.'

'No!'

But Shazad was already helping me to my feet. I tried to pull away, to stand on my own. But she kept her grip.

'Don't argue. Last time you got left behind, *this* happened.' She meant the Djinn and the Abdals and everything else. 'Demdji get out first, and that's an order from your general and your friend. Jin!' She caught his attention across the chaos of the garden. He was with us in a second. 'Get her out of here.'

He didn't need to be told twice and I was in no state to fight an order. His arms were under my knees and shoulders, lifting me off the ground. I remembered the night of Auranzeb.

Are you saying you're here to rescue me?

This was how to rescue a girl. I might've laughed if everything didn't hurt so much. Shazad covered us as he lifted me towards Izz, who was wearing the shape of a giant Roc, carrying people to safety as fast as he could.

Jin and I were on his back and off the ground with one powerful wingbeat, carrying us high over the rooftops of Izman. Shots punctured the night behind us. They had a clear aim without the cover of the sandstorm. But Izz dodged expertly, moving too quickly to be a target. As we rose I could see Izman spreading out below us like a map, houses dotted with tiny pinpricks of light at the windows among dark streets. And just beyond the rambling walls and roofs was the sea, looking pink with the dawn. We were almost out of range. Even through the blinding pain I could tell. Almost. Just a little higher, just a little further, and we'd be out and gone and Izz could drop me and Jin somewhere safe and go back for the others.

I didn't hear the gunshot that hit us. But I felt it. In the sudden jerking motion of Izz's body as iron punctured his skin. In the scream that erupted from him. In a blur of pain, I realised they'd hit his wing. Jin's arms tightened around me.

For a moment I was back in the harem, looking out over the water with the Sultan at my side, bow drawn as I took aim for the birds. The moment my arrow went through my kill. Watching it plummet to the ground and we were falling, too.

Izz was fighting not to plunge us back into the camp. To carry us further away. To get us out. The Sultan couldn't capture another Demdji. I could feel the iron biting into him, and the pain hobbling his injured wing.

A last few frantic wingbeats carried us forward, the wind grabbing at us. And then we burst free of the city, of the roofs and streets and the walls that would shatter us when we crashed. We were out over the sea, a sheer drop of a cliff face from the city into the water.

We were falling. Izz's body flipped, spilling us out as he screamed in agony, frantically beating his wings. Jin's grip left my waist.

I had just a moment to catch sight of the water below as I slipped from his back, plunging towards it.

I didn't even feel it when the water swallowed me whole.

Chapter 48

I'd never understood drowning.

I was a desert girl. The sea was made of sand where I was from. And that obeyed me. This. This was an attack.

Water invaded every part of me. Rushing to swallow my body hungrily. Rushing into my nose and my mouth. I was suffocating and the world was narrowed to black. Turned out I was good at drowning for a desert girl.

And then I was surging out of the depths of the water; air hit my face. Something slammed into my lungs. Light burst across my vision. It bloomed then faded to black. And then again. Pain and light wracking through me. Battling for my body.

And then stars. Stars above me. And a mouth was on mine.

I wasn't dying. This was one of Hala's illusions. Except it wasn't. Jin hovered above me. I saw the lines of his face, etched in the predawn light as the pain slammed into my lungs again. Burning. Burning.

I was a Djinni's daughter. Burning was what I did.

And then the stars vanished and I was staring at the ground and the sight of bile and water spilling out across sand. Expelled from my lungs as I vomited half the sea out. Even after it was all gone I was on my hands and knees retching violently.

I felt a gentle hand on my back. 'Remind me to teach you how to swim sometime.' The joke sounded strained. But I laughed anyway. It turned into more coughing as I knelt doubled over, shaking, trying to put myself back together.

The shadow of Izman, set high on the cliff above, loomed over us. It was an awfully long fall. I saw the pain written across Jin's face, his hair sticking to his brow. I pushed a piece away. My heart was slowing. The chaos of the fight. Of surviving. Some of the pain in my side had subsided.

It was quiet and calm here on the shore as the sun rose. Just for a moment. But the stars were glaring down accusation at me. And I had to let the rest of the world back in eventually.

'Izz?' I asked. I didn't see a giant blue Roc anywhere. He'd been hit by a bullet. He wouldn't be able to shift again with that in him.

'I'm not sure.' Jin shook his head. 'We got lucky; we fell and hit the water. Izz didn't fall with us. By the time I'd surfaced with you, I'd lost sight of him.' The water lapped innocently at our bodies, but out there it was a churning mass that'd swallow you whole.

'And the others?'

Jin shook his head. 'I don't know. Sam got some out. I saw others fall. I lost track of Ahmed and my sister in the fighting and then you dropped.' He sat back. He was shaking. 'So this is what you didn't want me to know about.'

I reached for the sand in my mind, but I could feel the stabbing sensation where my old wound was and I stopped. I might have the iron out of my skin, but it wasn't so easy to shift back. I sank my fingers into the waterlogged sand under myself and forced my heartbeat to slow. 'Ahmed is alive.' It fell off my tongue easily. The truth. 'Shazad is alive.' The names tumbled off my tongue one after the other. Delila, Imin, Hala, Izz, Maz, Sam, Rahim. Our people were still alive.

'Anyone who made it out will head for the Hidden House.' Jin pushed his soaked hair back off his face as he stood up, reaching down for me. 'We need to get back there; it'll be safe—'

'Maybe not for long.' I took Jin's hand, letting him help me to my feet. I was still unsteady from how I'd stopped breathing for a bit. 'It just takes one person to talk.'

It was painfully slow going to get back up the cliffs to the city. As the sun worked across the sky, we waded where the water was shallow enough. Jin swam some of it with me hanging on to his shoulders until finally we found a place where the ground up to the city sloped enough to climb. The sun was high over us by then and still we did not move quickly. Jin caught me when I stumbled, but a few times we still had to stop to rest. For me to catch my breath as the pain in my side throbbed. We finally found flat ground just outside the city walls. We were far from alone. A crush of people were fighting their way in through the gates.

Someone shoved by me, jostling me back into Jin, who steadied me.

'Hey.' Jin caught a man by the shoulder. The man turned, clearly spoiling for a fight. He backed down when he caught sight of Jin, who had the look of knowing how to kill a man and being half-desperate, too. 'What's going on?'

'The Rebel Prince,' the man said. My heart jumped at the mention of Ahmed. 'The Rebel Prince has been captured. He's going to be executed on the palace steps.'

'When?' I shoved forward; I couldn't keep it in any more. The man's eyes swept me disdainfully, from my dishevelled hair to my clothes dried stiff with seawater against my body. He might not want to mouth off to Jin, but I wasn't half so intimidating as my foreign prince.

'Answer her,' Jin pressed.

'Sundown,' the man said, shaking Jin's hand off, already pushing towards the crowd. 'He's lifting the curfew for one night for it. And if you don't let me go I'm going to miss it.'

Jin and I traded a glance before our gazes went to the horizon, across the sea.

The sky was already darkening.

Chapter 49

The Rebel Prince

When men and women on long desert roads sat around
campfires, where only the stars could see them, they
told the tale of the Rebel Prince as best they knew it.
And they told the truth as best they could. But not all
of it. Never all of it.

When they told of his days in the harem, they never
told of his brother the Foreign Prince, born under the
same stars. They told of the night his half-Djinni sister
was born, but they never knew of the young woman who
risked her own life to take three children away to safety
as the Rebel Prince's mother died. And when they told
of the Sultim trials, they left out the general's beautiful
daughter who trained him and fought beside him until
he was ready to face the challenge.

In years to come in the desert, when the caravans warded against the fear of the night with stories of great men, they would tell of the day that the people of Izman gathered at dusk in the thousands to get their first glimpse of the Rebel Prince since the Sultim trials, as he stood on an executioner's stage. Waiting for the axe to fall.

The stories would never tell that the Rebel Prince was not the only captive of the Sultan on that day. They would never know that he could have escaped capture had he not made so many of his people escape before him. They would never tell that he had laid down his weapons and surrendered himself to his father in order to save those others who were left behind.

The storytellers never knew that the man who stood on that stage did it by his own choice. That he could have escaped his fate if he were a less good man. A less brave man.

On that day, a hundred thousand men and women would come to watch and each would tell the story of what they saw there. The tales would cross the sands in the months that followed, repeated across the desert and on foreign shores. The same stories would be told again among caravans in the centuries that followed, when the time came to teach their children of all the great heroes who had come before them in the desert.

But there would only ever be six people who would know the story of what truly happened that day. The people of the caravans would never know what came to pass in the prison cells below the palace between dawn and dusk. Before the moment that all of Izman saw on the stage.

Six people, who had all fought side by side and were imprisoned side by side for it. They sat in the dark, awaiting their fates like thousands who had sat there before them. They passed whispers inside their cell, swearing that the Rebellion would not die there with them. Though by dawn, two of them would be dead.

Six people who would never tell the story of what took place on the day that would be known forever as the day the Rebel Prince died.

Chapter 50

When the legendary Princess Hawa died at Saramotai time lost all sense. The sun rose to watch her fall. It stopped in the sky in the dead of night. And the stars stared down alongside to witness the birth of grief in a new world. The entire world held its breath as Attallah dropped dead because his heart was torn in two.

Time didn't stop now. It was already running out. There was no time to plan. No time to race for reinforcements or even a gun. I didn't know what to do. Or even what I was running towards. I just knew that I was running, pressing through the mob in the streets, racing towards the palace.

No time to get help. No time to plan a rescue. That was what the Sultan was counting on.

He was going to execute Ahmed and we barely even had time to get there, let alone plan how to get him out.

We were going to have to make a plan on the fly. Like we always did.

We were good at that.

I saw a man with a gun as we shoved by. 'Jin.' I grabbed his arm. He stopped, looking where I was pointing. I didn't need to say anything further. Jin grabbed the man, wrenching his arms behind his back, holding him as I grabbed the gun. And then we were moving again, rushing away from the man's shouted accusations.

The crowd started to get too thick before we were even within sight of the palace. I pushed. The streets were choked with people and I couldn't move any more.

I couldn't even see the square. I shoved forward, but soon I was trapped in the mass of bodies. I squirmed through until I was shoved up against a wall. I looked up.

I couldn't climb that. Not alone. But I could get up there with help. Jin knew what I was thinking before I'd even finished thinking it.

'You'll be alone,' he said. Someone jostled him, pressing us closer together, until we were flush against the wall. Alone, with a gun, powerless and bleeding from a half dozen places.

'I know.' I ran my tongue along my lips. They were caked with salt.

Jin lifted me up. I grabbed the ledge above, dragging myself up painfully. And painfully slow, fighting through the stabbing in my side.

My feet hit the ledge and I started to run, ignoring the shooting pain in my body. A jump carried me easily over the narrow gap onto the next roof. I landed hard, scraping my knee. I was back up, leaving a streak of new blood behind. I jumped to the next roof, startling some birds into flight. I kept going. Shoving forward, onwards and onwards, until there was nowhere to go. And I was standing on a roof overlooking the square in front of the palace.

Ahmed stood alone, chained by his wrists to the stage set above the heaving mass of people. His eyes were cast down. I knew what he was seeing. The images of pain and death. The writhing monsters.

The last thing Shira had seen.

The last thing Ahmed would see.

Unless I saved him.

A man was reading out what I could only guess was a list of my Rebel Prince's supposed crimes. I couldn't hear him over the din of the crowd. Above him I spotted the balcony from which I'd watched Shira die. They had shielded it with iron instead of carved wood after the riots. Through the gaps in the lattice I thought I could just make out the Sultan, surveying the scene, come to watch another son die.

As the list reached its end, Ahmed finally looked up, out over the sea of Mirajin citizens. Facing his people.

'The Sultan,' the man cried, 'in his great wisdom and mercy, has agreed to grant leniency to any other rebels. They will keep their heads but be condemned to a life of penance serving this country, which they betrayed.' Leniency my ass. The Sultan had told me himself he needed to win back the love of his people. I remembered him chastising Kadir for Shira's execution. The people didn't love you for killing an innocent. 'But, for his crimes against his own blood, Prince Ahmed has been condemned to die.' But Ahmed, he'd told the people, had killed Kadir, his own brother. They had to see Ahmed die.

I aimed my gun at the balcony, squinting. That was a small target from this far. Even for me. And I didn't know if I had a shot to waste.

Over the roofs of Miraji behind me, the sun was setting.

I flattened myself on my stomach and aimed the gun. God, I hoped it was a good gun. I didn't have a plan beyond shooting the executioner. But that had to be enough, for now at least. I had to save Ahmed and then I could worry about whatever came next.

The executioner stepped onto the stage and my heart stuttered. They hadn't sent a man to kill Ahmed. The Sultan had sent an Abdal.

Even I couldn't make that shot.

I had the executioner in my crosshairs and I was helpless. I aimed the gun all the same. I fired. One clean shot, through the knee. A scream went up from the crowd at the sound of gunfire. But the executioner didn't so much as stagger. I fired again and again and again, aiming desperately for the tiny target of its foot. Until the gun in my hand was empty.

Until the Abdal had reached Ahmed.

It forced him to his knees in front of the wooden block they'd laid there. Ahmed didn't fight. He knelt down with dignity, his eyes going down to the gruesome scenes below as he laid his head on the executioner's block.

I reached out for the desert. I could feel it scattered through the streets, sand invading the city. I started to gather it to me but the pain stabbed through my side, sending me down with a cry, scattering the sand back to street dust.

The mechanical man took one step backwards. Swinging the axe upwards. And I was helpless. I was helpless without my Demdji powers, without any bullets. Unable to stop it. Unable to do anything.

'Ahmed!' His name ripped out of me. Through the crowd. Over the din of people calling out, pressing forward, calling for his head, for his freedom.

I was too far away for him to hear me. Too far away to reach him. But somehow from the block his head tilted up just as the axe swung high. He looked straight at me. His eyes met mine.

The low rays of the sun struck the iron of the axe, turning it into a blazing light as it reached its pinnacle.

But the sun didn't stop. Time didn't stop. The world didn't show any sympathy for my grief.

The axe fell. It turned from sunlight to iron. To blood.

Chapter 51

I didn't cry until I was safe.

I wasn't even sure how we got back to the Hidden House. All I knew was a hand leading me through streets that had turned to chaos as soon as the axe fell. Through a world that had stopped making sense. Jin. He could've been leading me to the executioner's block and I wouldn't have known until I was looking up at the crowd with the axe hanging above me.

But then we were through the doors, into the safe haven of the Hidden House, where we'd all been together only two nights before. Sara was waiting inside the doors, a screaming baby on her hip. Her lips were moving, but I didn't hear anything she said. Jin pulled me past her. And it came on like a punch to the gut. My knees gave out below me on the stairs.

I sobbed. For all the dead. For all the losses. For the

things that had been taken away. It was seared into my mind forever. The blade. The blood. The eyes.

The look in his eyes as they met mine across the crowd.

A second before he died.

And it was my fault. Mine and someone I trusted. Someone I thought was innocent.

The scream came on so sudden and violent that I had to stuff my sheema into my mouth to keep it from being heard through the walls of the house. It tasted of sweat and sand and of Jin's skin somehow.

I could hear the sounds from the next room. Voices dropped low, tentative with uncertainty and thick with grief. What was left of the Rebellion. The folk who'd escaped the attack at Shazad's.

The murmur was soothing. I closed my eyes and leaned my head against the wall.

Too many people had traded their lives for someone else's now.

Bahi had burned to save Shazad.

Shira had walked to the executioner's block for her son.

Rahim had thrown himself on the mercy of his merciless father for Leyla.

My mother had bowed her head to a noose for me.

I thought about revenge and about love and about

sacrifice and the great and terrible things I'd seen people do. I thought about how many people I'd seen lay their lives down for the Rebellion, over and over.

I thought about the moment the axe fell. The eyes locking with mine a second before the light left them.

The stairs creaked with a new weight next to me. I knew it was Jin without opening my eyes. I knew before he leaned his weight into my side. Before he laced his hand with mine, running his thumb across my palm in a slow circle.

'We're not done yet.' My voice scraped out. Almost gone but still there. I finally opened my eyes.

'I know.'

The low murmur of voices died with our entrance, leaving nothing but the chanting in the streets below. A constant thrum like a heartbeat. Good. Silence was death. And the Rebellion wasn't dead yet.

And every eye in the room was on me. Rebels I knew well and rebels I didn't.

Hala's golden hands were wrapped around a steaming cup someone had given her, dark hair all over her face. Sara sat in a corner, her son asleep in her arms, staring through the shutters into the street below and blinking back tears. Sam was running his finger around the rim of an empty glass, over and over. Maz was wrapped in a blanket, shaking violently, blue hair sticking up at all angles. Tamid was stitching the wound in Izz's arm from where the bullet had torn through his wing, obviously grateful for something to do.

There was only one spot left free, at the head of the table. Half of the people in the room were sitting on the floor rather than take that place. I felt Jin tense behind me as he saw it.

I cleared my throat, but my voice came out steady. 'We need a plan.' I fought the instinct to look for Shazad to start making one with me. She'd been taken with Ahmed. Delila. Imin. Rahim. Navid. They'd all been captured, along with dozens of others.

'What is there left to plan?' Hala was looking into her coffee cup instead of at me. She squeezed her eyes shut. 'You don't think it's only a matter of time before that axe comes down again, and again and again—'

'Hala.' Maz cut her off with a hand on her arm. She pulled herself up short, opening her eyes, staring me down. I flinched at the gaze. Her eyes might be the dark brown of any desert girl's, but they still reminded me of Imin's golden eyes.

'—until everyone else is gone, too,' she finished.

'No.' I held my ground. The Sultan might've thought he was using me, those months in the palace. But I hadn't spent all that time there without learning a thing or two about the man who ruled over Miraji. The Sultan was smart. Too smart to risk more rioting in the streets. 'The Sultan is losing his grip on his people. He knows that. That's why Rahim wasn't executed. He needed Ahmed to die publicly.' Someone in a corner made a noise like a sob, quickly smothered in their sheema. 'But for the rest of them, he gains more by showing mercy than by showing force.'

'You're thinking he'll send them away,' Hala said.

'Instead of executing them,' Maz filled in. A spark of life flared back in the room briefly.

I had to tell them the rest, the thing I'd figured out. I was going to have to tell all of them. But my eyes kept drifting to Hala in her corner. Waiting was not going to make it easier.

'There's something else.' The room went quiet. 'We lost someone today.' I could see it all in my mind. A head lifting on the block. Meeting my eyes. Creatures of illusion and deceit. 'But it wasn't Ahmed.' My eyes the colour of the sky. His the same shade as molten gold. Staring straight at me. I knew those eyes. But they weren't Ahmed's.

My meaning dawned slowly through the room. Slowest across the golden-skinned Demdji's face.

Imin.

'Hala, I'm so sorry.'

Grief and rage warred across her face while the rest of us were silent for Imin. Her head dropped into her hands.

Ahmed wouldn't have let anyone go to the executioner's block for him. But he wasn't the only one being kept prisoner. Half the Rebellion would've sooner walked onto that stage than let Ahmed do it. Shazad would've worked out the plan, in all the confusion of the attack. Delila with her hair dyed dark, concealing her Demdji side; she might not be able to hide a whole rebellion but she was good enough to hide her brother, for a time, conceal his identity under an illusion of a different face. Whichever one Imin had been wearing when they were taken. And Imin was good enough to take Ahmed's place. Not just good enough. More than good.

Imin had walked into an execution for our prince.

'Ahmed is alive.'

I looked around the table, the small cramped room in this, our last refuge. 'The Sultan might've bested us today, but he *can't* plan for everything. He didn't plan on me slipping out of his grip.' I met Tamid's eyes. 'He didn't plan on us escaping. And he sure as hell didn't plan on Ahmed living. So he's not planning on us saving him, either.'

'Who is going to lead us?' Izz asked. His eyes turned to Jin.

'Don't look at me,' Jin said. He was leaning against the door frame. Like he might disappear on the Rebellion again any second.

'I can lead us.' That drew every eye in the room to me. I waited. But there wasn't a single word of protest. Not a word of argument.

I was a Demdji. I was the Blue-Eyed Bandit. I was their friend. I had learned strategy from Shazad. I had been among the enemy. I hadn't left them when Jin had. And they believed me when I said that I could lead.

We were going to rescue our people, our friends, our family. And when we had them all back we were going to march Rahim to Iliaz for an army. I pressed away from the wall. I was unsteady, but I was still standing. We were still here.

And this time, the Sultan had given us an advantage – the only thing that was truly invincible. Not an immortal creature. But an idea. A legend. A story.

The Blue-Eyed Bandit was always more powerful than I was. The Rebel Prince was always more powerful than Ahmed. And now, we could write a better story than the prodigal prince. One no one would ever forget. One the entirety of Miraji would stand behind.

The prince who returned from the dead to take his throne and save his people.

Acknowledgements

I owe a lot of thanks to a lot of people, both for all the support since the release of *Rebel of the Sands*, and all the support in writing this book. I haven't even started and I'm already worried about forgetting someone. So to everyone who was there for these books and for me: friends and family who offered anything from a kind word or a drink to help get the book from my brain to the laptop; publishing professionals who helped get this book from my laptop to the bookstore; booksellers and librarians who helped get it from the shelf into readers' hands – please know that I am grateful!

First, always, my parents, who somehow managed to raise me with both the absurd belief I could achieve anything I set my mind to, and the very pragmatic understanding that I would have to work hard for it. I wouldn't have aspired to or achieved one book, let alone two, if not for them. And I probably wouldn't have finished if they hadn't provided a steady supply of both encouragement and alcohol in the final weeks of drafting.

I'm still not sure who I sold my soul to in order to land an agent who is as smart, passionate about books, and supportive (and a million other things I don't have room to list here) as mine. I can probably do without a soul, but I know I can't do without Molly Ker Hawn in my corner.

Thank you also to the rest of the Bent Agency and the wonderful foreign rights agents they work with for all they have done for *Rebel*.

I think the trick to putting a good book on shelves is to work with people who are smarter than you are. So thank you to Kendra Levin, who I suspect of being psychic because she understands what I'm trying to achieve even before I do, as well as somehow always managing to time encouraging emails exactly when doubt is about to get the better of me. And to Naomi Colthurst who brought so much positivity and enthusiasm to this book that I'm pretty sure I syphoned some of it from her to be able to finish editing.

To use the old cliché it takes a village. So to my two transatlantic villages at Penguin Random House and Faber & Faber, thank you.

Ken Wright and Leah Thaxton for being so

wonderfully supportive of me and of *Rebel* throughout the whole process. As well as Stephen Page. And to Alice Swan who brought Amani and crew to their UK home in the first place.

My publicists on both sides of the pond. Elyse Marshall who I'm pretty sure could power a small country with her positivity, and who can organise a bookish jaunt around the US and make it look easy. And in the UK Hannah Love, who kept me (semi) sane in my jaunts around the UK and who sometimes goes as far as to dress as my creepy twin. Thank you for getting my books to readers!

To Maggie Rosenthal, Krista Ahlberg, Natasha Brown, Sarah Barlow, Mohammed Kasim and Naomi Burt, for all the hard work you do on this book day to day that I don't see, but also for the parts that I do see like seriously smart contributions and comments about this book. The kind that clearly come from a great deal of care. I'm so grateful to have had so many additional eyes and brains on these words.

To the people who make my books look good. Theresa Evangelista, Will Steele and Emma Eldridge for my covers. And to Kate Renner for designing the US insides, including the awesome map, and for having an endless amount of patience when dealing with my complete geographical incompetence.

To the whole of the marketing and social media teams. Emily Romero, Rachel Cone-Gorham, Anna Jarzab, Madison Killen, Erin Berger, Lisa Kelly, Mia Garcia, Christina Colangelo, Kara Brammer, Erin Toller, Briana Woods-Conklin, Lily Arango, Megan Stitt, Carmela Iaria, Venessa Carson, Kathryn Bhirud, Alexis Watts, Rachel Wease, Rachel Lodi, Susan Holmes and Niriksha Bharadia. And especially Amanda Mustafic and Kaitlin Kneafsey for all your support on the road. And Bri Lockhart and Leah Schiano for being early readers of this book and just in general endlessly awesome human beings when it comes to book love.

To the whole of the sales teams on both sides of the Atlantic, especially Biff Donovan, Sheila Hennessy, Colleen Conway and Doni Kay who were kind enough to guide me as I traversed the US and introduce me to some awesome booksellers. And to the Faber sales team, David Woodhouse, Miles Poyton, Clare Stern and Kim Lund.

And to all the incredible booksellers I met in Boston, Chicago, Seattle, and Raleigh who were kind enough to be readers of a very early draft of *Rebel*. In particular Kelly Morton, Allison Maurer, Lauren D'Alessio, Betsy Balyeat, Rosemary Publiese and Kathleen March who wrote such nice things about that early draft. And Gaby Salpeter for your enthusiasm about a later draft. And to every bookseller in the UK who has been such a wonderful champion of the book, in particular Aimee and Kate at Waterstones Piccadilly, Chloe at Foyles and Jamie-Lee at Waterstones Birmingham.

And though you are too many to name, thank you to all the awesome bloggers, vloggers and general YA supporters who have been so enthusiastic in spreading the word about a new author online.

This book is dedicated to my friend, Rachel Rose Smith, who is one of the smartest, kindest people I know and who has been there for me in the best and worst times both around writing and outside of the bookish world. She only begins a long list of people I have been lucky enough to accumulate in my life. And who I will wear out my fingers trying to name. But particular thanks go to Michella Domenici for being my first fangirl always. Amelia Hodgson who always has the time to help dig me out of plot hole. Justine Caillaud for being a creative support since I was able to pick up a pen. Meredith Sykes, for the early read and the necklace made of sand. Christie Coho, for keeping me sane. Cecilia Vinesse for coffee, food and puppies. And Roshani Chokshi for actual medical advice about scars and metal under the skin. And Juno Dawson for excellent advice about tackling pronoun use for a gender-fluid shapeshifting character.

For being kind enough to write nice blurb for *Rebel*: Rae Carson, Alison Goodman and Erin Lange.

And to everyone else who has been there through this, who has pushed this book into the hands of others or offered a kind word, advice or an ear in the good times and the less good times, personal and writerly alike . . . Jon Andrews, Kat Berry, Anne Caillaud, Emma Carroll, Lexi Casale, Sophie Cass, Traci Chee, Jess Cluess, Noirin Collins, Laure Eve, Max (Hamilton) Fitz-James, Maya (M.G Leonard) Gabrielle, Stephanie Garber, Jeff Giles, Meave Hamill, Janet Hamilton-Davies, Heidi Heilig, Bonnie-Sue Hitchcock, Mariam Khan, Rachel Marsh, Kiran Millwood-Hargrave, Anne Murphy, Elisa Peccerillo-Palliser, Marieke Peleman, Chelsey Pippin, Harriet Reuter-Hapgood, Marie Rutkoski, Melinda Salisbury, Samantha Shannon, Tara Sim, Evelyn Skye, Carlie Sorosiak, Solange Sykes, Emma Theriault, Annik Vrana, Katherine Webber, Anna Wessman and all of my fellow '16er authors for getting it. Also, the whole of my bookclub crew for being bookish with me, and the very nice people at Artisan coffee who basically fueled this book and have let me spend more hours in their establishment than in my own home. And so many more, thank you all!

And finally thank you to all the readers of *Rebel of the Sands* who have taken the time to share your enthusiasm for my first book, and your anticipation for this one. I think I'm supposed to write for myself first. But I've always wanted to write for others. And you make that possible.